Light

In

The

Basement

Book 1: Finality

A Novel By
Irene Egerton Perry

C.&.P ublishing
4140 Clemmons Road, Suite 358
Clemmons, North Carolina 27012

To Call: 336-998-2679
E-mail: info@cepublishing.net or CEPublishing@aol.com

If you're unable to order this book from your bookseller, you may order toll-free directly from the publisher. Call 1-888-289-3374

Grateful acknowledgement is made for permission to use the following copyrighted songs:
His Eye is on the Sparrow
Summertime
The Rose

ISBN: 0-9652655-0-1
Library of Congress Catalog Card Number: 00-110467

First Printing February 2001
Printing Number 10 9 8 7 6 5 4 3 2 1
Printed on acid free paper in the United States of America

Original Cover **Artwork by Marsha Hatcher**, Artist of Jacksonville, Florida
Author's **Photograph by Harden Richards** of Winston-Salem, North Carolina
Cover Design and layout by **Free To Soar** of Birmingham, Alabama
Web site: **www.FreeToSoar.com**

Other Releases to look for by Irene Egerton Perry:

Light In the Basement, Book 2 Transitions
Release Date: 2001

Light In the Basement, Book 3 Beginnings
Release Date: 2001

*D*edication

This book is dedicated to my mother, Pearl Sylvia Bostic. And, to my two children, Raymond Christopher Perry and Elizabethe Irene Perry.

Heartfelt Dedications...

To my Mother—Pearl Sylvia Bostic. My strongest supporter. My champion of counseling and teacher for life. The one who motivates me beyond words. Thank you for your help. Your inspiration. Your dedication. Your love. Your kindness. Your late night talks. For you just being a kind and sweet mother. Your concern and most of all your financial support during the almost six-year stint it took me to write this novel trilogy is absolutely appreciated. You're the best Mother in the entire world. I love you. I love you. I love you. As I've gotten older, I've come to marvel at your strength, your wisdom, and your determination.

To Carmen Irene Munroe—My grandmother who died from cancer on December 26, 1981. Providence had it so that I received your name. I thank you for the jewelry that was passed down to me upon your death. Your things, Ma. I named my daughter Elizabethe Irene so the legacy of this name will continue. But it was you, Ma. I know it was. It was you whispering to me. You wanted me to show and know the magnificence of the homeland. Now, I truly understand. I thank you, and I miss you desperately. I still can recall how you used to dance with Nanette and me around your living room during those early days in your home on Cambridge Place. We danced to many of the old Calypsonians who still are around and to the many others who have passed on. Thank you.

To my two children: Raymond Christopher and Elizabethe Irene, who for almost six years exercised the patience of Job as I told them, "No, we can't do that either because Mommy's writing. Yes, I know it's Christmas. I don't have enough money to buy you that, but we sure got a whole lot of love, though." (Smile) Remember those conversations?

Christopher: You are my strong prince who went off to military academy and now on to college. Enjoy your college years, and maintain good grades in the process. Live your dreams, son. Elizabethe, at twelve years old, you're my little writer in the making. Your mind is constantly twirling with new ideas that are unique, different, and thoroughly surprising. Keep it up. I love you, Christopher and Elizabethe.

To my five sisters: Rosalind Pettiford Cox, Mary Egerton Shepperd, Nanette Sharon Egerton, and Michelle Loren Egerton—our future Hollywood star. To Mary "Wis" Gilbert, a sister I met later in life. I thank you, and I love you all. Rossie, I thank you for suggesting *His Eye is on the Sparrow.* Thanks for all your words of encouragement. Nanette, thanks for being an angel and helping mother out with Elizabethe and Christopher—*and* also for your constant support, financially and mentally. Mary, when I couldn't come home for Christmas of 1997, I thank you for taking Elizabethe with you to pick out a Christmas tree.

Mary Egerton Shepperd: I thank you in another special way. You're my benefactor. That was a gift that was most extraordinary and utterly beautiful to receive from you, my sister. I thank you from the bottom of my heart, girl. I do.

To my three brothers: James "Jimmy" Bostic. Thanks for being the wise, street scholar that you are. Thomas W. Egerton. Thanks for being who you are, and you know who that is! D Mack "Marquis" Egerton. Thank you for knowing to never give up.

To the matriarchs of my family: My Auntie Cynthia Story and cousin Mercedes Mann, both of Brooklyn. To my cousin Elaine McCray of Atlanta.

To Edith Kaseen Williams. My friend and closest colleague these last few years. I adore you. I've known you since 1978. Thanks for being patient with me, guiding me, supporting me when you could have walked away, and most importantly, for making me laugh with your spicy views about life. You taught me a lot.

Shirley Marie Williams—I've known you since 1977. Thanks for being my North Carolina mother, for those scrumptious Sunday dinners prepared by you, Edith and/or Louis. Shirley, you're definitely a prayer warrior, and I thank you for being on my side. I love your family like my blood family.

To David Thompson, President of PNS Colorado of Denver. Thank you, David. You motivated me when I didn't have the strength to write. You believed in me when I no longer believed in myself. You encouraged me when I didn't think I had an ounce of strength left to tiptoe any further. You're a wonderful friend and confidante, and I love you dearly.

To Vanessa Davis Griggs. Trust me when I say this. Words can't even express what you mean to me. You walked right into my life and left an imprint on my heart. You're special, girl. You're a delightful friend and fellow author who became my dear sisterene, my strong shoulder for listening, and my confidante. I see us spending many more years together laughing and talking about the wonderfulness of life. *HALLELUJAHHHHH! THANK YOU! THANK YOU! THANK YOU!* (And you know what I mean.) Let the church say, amen!

To my totally fantastic, devoted, kind-hearted editor—Dr. Patricia Bonner. A heavy-duty sistah from Bainbridge, Georgia and an English professor at North Carolina Agricultural & Technical State University of Greensboro, NC. Your historical, literary, and writing knowledge is phenomenal, Dr. Bonner. You were wonderful, Pat. I'll never forget those beginning days. After talking with me via telephone for only two minutes, you said that you would love to do it...love to work on the project. You taught me sooooo much, and we developed such a bond. I love you, and I'll never forget you. *Never!* Kiss and thanks. Yes, I know the characters rambled in places, but as you told me on a number of occasions, it's my characters talking.

To my assistant editor, Tanya Walker from Georgetown, South Carolina, who became a friend in the process. Thank you, girl. Even though I was older than you, I had to constantly remind you to treat me like one of your college students. Thanks much for your youthful insight. Lynn Watts of Winston-Salem and Dr. John Crawford of Greensboro, your assistance was greatly appreciated.

To Marsha Hatcher, a wonderful artist. Thanks for your patience, your recommendations, and your vision.

For all the people that hung in there with me to keep the business going, I'm grateful. Thomas Moore—you're the best bartender out. Lillian Owens of Greensboro. Rubilina Durham of Winston-Salem, Allison Dockery of Lexington, NC. Allison, I thank you for stepping in when David stepped out. I appreciate your patience. Tonya Sheffield—my North Carolina little sister. Thank you.

Bessie Mae Singletary, it's been a rocky ride, girl. We've been friends since the early eighties. We weren't always successful in our endeavors, but we were always determined. There were times we were way up, but a lot of times we were down. But guess what, girl? We made it through with smiles on our faces. Peace and love to you. Regardless of what anyone says, live your life to the fullest.

Birtha Bynum—you have been Nannette and my friend since I was thirteen, Nanette was eleven, and you were eight. Birtha, you said that when you read the manuscript, you shed tears, you cracked up, and you got horny. You are a stone trip. To Rosa Perry and Rosalind Perry of DC—my ex-sister-in-laws that are still my sister-in-laws. I thank you for reading my pages and giving me your opinions.

Over the years, the following people played a significant part in my life—Tina Hagan—my neighbor for over twenty years. Hasn't it been interesting? Thanks, girl. You always made me know I could spend a night in your home for any reason—and no explanation was ever necessary. To Mrs. Rosa Perry, Mrs. Elizabeth Tinsley, and Rev. and Mrs. Charles Gray. Thanks for the memories.

Verbal Love Flowers goes to Margarette Perkins of Rocky Mount—the most antique collecting mama in the entire world! To LeGoria Payton of Detroit—the Queen Sisterene of the year. My friend for now and as we journey along the road to old age. After you stopped checking our foreheads to make sure we didn't have a fever, you kept smiles on our faces. You're such a delight to know. Cyntonia Williams and Marlene Suit—you two ladies gave to me when you had little to give. Thank you.

To Dr. J. Ray Butler, who never stopped believing in me when he possessed every right to do so. I thank you from the bottom of my heart, Dr. Butler. Your patience and kind spirit is unmatchable.

To Debra Verdell of Lexington. You're still my lioness at the gate. To Samuel Robert "Sammy" Lomax of DC. Thanks for the inspirational old school music. It inspired me to write pages upon pages. You're definitely the Keeper of the Funk Era.

Special thanks to Don and Jane Marsden. Yall are the best neighbors. To Verona Hatton and Martha Watson—thanks for being there during those early years. To Mark Lacey of Greensboro. To Neville Francis, attorney. To Sylviaette Simmons, the helper bee of the year. To Paul Fletcher—a great guy and greater friend. To Rhonda Murphy of Thomasville—thank you, Rhonda. To Geraldine Johnson—remember those days in the seventies? To Wanda McIntyre—for your knowing, comforting spirit.

To Celia Kilgour of Kilgour and Sweet. Thanks for sharing wonderful and fabulous Black designers with me. Mr. Shaka King, you were like a walking fashion encyclopaedia. Thanks for all the names. You network the old-fashioned way.

To the Literary Voices Book Club—Terrie Gentry, Tiffany Gentry-Jackson, Mayea Brown, Maria Connor, Michael Covington, Latisha Dixon, Eric Ellison, Robert LeMay, Christopher Martin, Bryant McIver, Joel McIver, Todd McIver, Melissa Moore, Kim Nesbitt, Tracy Staples, Jeannette Sellers, and Shawn Williams. Thanks for your early partial review, your criticism, and your support.

This list can go and on, but I'll finally end it. Along the journey to complete this work, there were many, many people that provided a helping hand, fervent prayers, encouraging words, financial aid, and quiet support. Writing is such a private, individual thing, but survival for a struggling writer involves the collaborative support of many people. If I've forgotten anyone, please charge it to my head and not to my heart.

My hope is that *Light in the Basement* educates you, enlightens you, provokes you, angers you, and causes you to have on-going dialogue. It is also my sincere wish that *Light in the Basement* entertains you, makes you laugh, and makes you cry. But most importantly, I hope *Light in the Basement* motivates you to flip the switch inside your mind...inside your innermost being so that you too can truly discover your ***Light in the Basement.***

*P*eace and love to all,

*I*rene *E*gerton *P*erry

If you have built castles in the air,
your work need not be lost;
that is where they should be.

Now put the foundations under them.

Henry David Thoreau

Light

In

The

Basement

Book 1: Finality

Chapter One

Sitting outside on Arman's bedroom deck, Symone Angela Poussaint sipped steaming hot cappuccino and gazed quietly into the horizons as she observed the North Carolina June sky turn a soft burnt orange. Last night, she slept for exactly four hours and right now she was in a rotten mood. While she reflected on life, mainly her own, she decided that watching the morning unfold would be significantly more memorable than lying in bed beside a sleeping Arman.

Symone slowly turned around, peered through the double French doors, and noticed Arman hadn't budged one bit from the lazy, snoring sleep. With both feet propped up on another outdoor chair, Symone held the hot cup with both hands and continued to consider her problems. She was thirty-nine years old, successful, miserable, and sexually deprived. All in that order. In seven months, she would be forty. The big Four-0.

Oh, well. Enough of that kind of thinking, Symone thought.

Symone gulped down the last of the lukewarm cappuccino, stood up, and stretched her hands toward the sky. Ninety minutes later, she was dressed in a Kilgour & Sweet fuchsia double-breasted power suit. She smoothed the skirt, took another reassuring glance in the full-length bedroom mirror, and quickly turned to finish packing.

Despite the twenty pounds, you look good—real good, girl, Symone thought to herself. *Hell, but you can't have everything.*

A former part-time model in college, Symone maintained the look but not the weight. She stood five-feet-ten inches tall and was covered with a Nestle Chocolate candy bar complexion with long, shapely legs. Her Trinidadian face was beautifully etched in the Caribbean tradition of jet black moon eyes, full sensuous lips, and a magnetic smile. She always wore her thick black hair in a fashionable sixties flip. An extremely intelligent woman with a sharp business mind, men often exclaimed she possessed the ultimate total package of beauty and brains.

Standing on Arman's front porch ten minutes later, Symone quickly kissed Arman good-bye. She noticed the sun rising above the trees and the morning dew on the car. A quiet Symone walked away from Arman and put the small Chanel overnight bag in the trunk. She eased into the bucket seat, making sure Arman received an excellent view of legs, stockings, garters, and pieces of thighs. Symone revved the engine and flipped on the wipers to remove the moisture from the front windows.

Damn! I should be able to do the same thing with men, Symone thought with a wicked grin. *Just simply turn a knob and zap them away with one clean swipe.*

While she glanced toward Arman's house once more, Symone watched him doofishly walk inside. Slowly, she rolled her eyes and sucked her teeth in disgust.

For the past three days, the weather had been unbearable and miserably warm. Just like the weekend with Arman. And it appeared that today was going to be another hot, humid one. Evidently, the heavens knew Symone's departure from the resort community was three days too late, and when the sun peeked though the clouds, it provided a pristine farewell reflection of Lake Norman, North Carolina.

Symone glanced at her watch. It was seven-thirty. Much too early for her, but she had to head to Winston-Salem. Due in the Akao Building office for a crucial Monday morning meeting with The Zawadi Corporation, Symone needed to arrive no later than nine-thirty. Quickly, she calculated the sixty-mile distance and realized for once, she had plenty enough time and would be prompt. Pecola Reynolds, her business partner, would be ecstatic.

Finally leaving Arman's house, Symone slowly backed the black Mercedes sports coupe down Arman's long winding driveway. Trying her utmost to be careful about backing out, she quickly glanced in the rearview mirror and side to side at the trees to avoid the beautiful flowers growing along Arman's perfectly manicured lawn. Symone considered intentionally rolling over the pink roses, yellow tulips, and white lilies that majestically lined the driveway, but she wisely realized such a mischievous action wouldn't be a nice gesture so early in the morning.

Symone slowly shook her head, smiled sadly to herself, and decided to concentrate on the task at hand. Since Symone surprised herself with the ultra-pricey car this past January for her thirty-ninth birthday, she had been involved in three minor accidents. Two of them were caused from running into something while she was backing up.

As Symone realized she was getting depressed, she stopped the car, rested her head against the steering wheel, and thought of encouraging words for several minutes. After wallowing in self-pity a moment, she tightly squeezed the black steering wheel to garner the ironclad confidence for which she was known and stared at the lush green oak trees dotting Arman's lawn. Then, she resumed backing up. The tree-lined, winding driveway must have been about two-thousand feet long, and Symone wondered why in the hell she didn't turn the car around in the front yard.

Suddenly, the rays of the early morning sun shined brighter than ever, and she decided to drive with the top down. She stopped the car again, placed the gear in park, and walked around to the trunk. When she opened the large floral square box and removed the Carlos of New York *baddd* scarf driving hat, she pulled it firmly down on her head. She tied the long, white sash in a quick knot under her chin, another one at the nape of her neck, and eased back into the car. Before backing onto the street, she glanced at herself in the rearview mirror and flashed a semi-confident smile revealing straight white teeth.

In an attempt to erase the memory of the weekend, she searched for the *Marvin Gaye Greatest Hits* CD. When she finally located it, she selected *Got to Give it Up* and placed the song on the repeat mode.

Just ten miles up the road and for possibly the twenty-fifth time since Symone left Arman's house, she told herself, "Symone girl, this ain't it. That man definitely isn't the one for you."

While driving down I-77 at sixty-nine miles per hour with music blasting and Christian Roth sunglasses in place, she mentally revisited the weekend to remind herself why Arman couldn't provide what she needed.

At the constant urgings of Pecola, Symone arrived at Arman's house early Friday afternoon. Six hours later, the weekend was just as boring as she thought. Yet, she persevered and wanted to see if Arman and she could make a go of this boyfriend/girlfriend relationship thing.

Friday evening was spent at the Excelsior Club in Charlotte. A lively club where lilting music, flowing drinks, and friendly Black folks were having the time of their lives dancing to old jam favorites by The Moments, Donna Summer, Sam & Dave, The Chi-lites, LTD, The Emotions, and The Commodores to name a few.

While Arman and Symone watched the crowd like an unhappy married couple out for a once a year evening date, the club was jumping as people enjoyed fantastic moments dancing the stroll, the twist, the jerk, and the boogaloo. Arman didn't speak to her, nor she to him. They simply listened to the sixties and seventies music and vicariously enjoyed the ambiance of long ago high school years as they watched the fortyish and over crowd relive younger days by conjuring up old timey dance moves.

Arman turned down Symone's eight requests to dance. She knew it was exactly eight because she counted each one. He said he was tired. So, she in turn resorted to tapping feet and having a serious dance contest with the chair. Jealousy was Arman's middle name, and if she even thought about accepting a twirl around the floor with another man, he would've turned the club out. Of course, several fine, Black brothers asked, and that made matters even worse. Since she about wiggled out the seat, it was obvious to every man in there she was itching to jump on the floor. So naturally all evening, they continued to beg.

I think this is totally ridiculous! Symone thought furiously as she observed the jubilant Excelsior crowd jam to the beat of *The Electric Slide.* Symone never understood Arman's narrow philosophy when they journeyed out on dates. He knew she came with him. The main thing is *she knew she* came with him, and she was going to leave with him. So what was the big deal? If he preferred to simply sit and listen to music, they could've done that at his house.

First of all, Symone wanted to dance. Dance hard, sweat dripping, clothes clinging to her skin kind of dancing. Secondly, if Arman knew his body wasn't up to par, he should have planned a birthday weekend in a physical therapist's whirlpool instead of with a woman who was thirty-nine, believed she acted twenty-nine, and possessed tremendous energy to release on the dance floor.

One thing for sure, Arman was in a cooking mood during Symone's visit. Saturday morning, he fixed country ham, grits, and eggs and served Symone in bed. Later that evening, he grilled a dinner of sumptuous lobster tails, shrimp, and baked corn, and served it out by the pool. After drinking three tulip-shaped champagne glasses of Courvoisier on the rocks, Symone was high as a kite. She felt horny as hell and suggested that they make wild, passionate love in the master bedroom Jacuzzi. However, in a very casual voice, Arman announced he suddenly developed severe leg cramps, and the possibility of having sex came to a screeching halt.

The more Symone thought about Arman, the more she realized that the brother should be in a rest home somewhere and not trying to date someone as vivacious as her. On a number of occasions, they openly discussed what needed to be done to meet halfway and make the relationship work for the both of them. However, so far, nothing had changed. At least not with him.

Arman March Guthrie, Jr. was forty-five years old, tall, about six-foot three, real dark-skinned, with a full beard and pepper gray hair. Definitely her type. He and his wife divorced three years ago, and it took him two years to get over it. But Symone admired the fact that he continued to support his ex-wife by paying all her bills so that she could retain the lifestyle to which she was accustomed when they were married. Arman also received full custody of his four children. With the help of a live-in housekeeper, he was raising his three boys and one girl alone. Well, almost. Anyway, for the birthday weekend, all four children were visiting their mother in Tega Cay.

President of a twenty-year old engineering firm in Charlotte, Symone had to admit that Arman owned a spectacular seven-thousand square feet contemporary house. And, without question, the home possessed one of the best views of Lake Norman and was furnished luxuriously. He categorically was Symone's standard as far as his upstanding reputation in the Charlotte business community, economic clout and status were concerned. But that was about as far as the attraction compass stretched as Arman had more aches and pains than a one-hundred-year-old retired football player. Plus, the major negative that kept Symone continually frustrated was his lovemaking abilities. Arman simply didn't have any.

How a man could go through almost fifty years of life and never learn to fuck or suck was beyond her. However, Symone decided she was through trying to teach men. This was it. The last one. The Symone Angela Poussaint University was closed. She wasn't taking any more students. Would not explain one more sexual move to another man. Classes were filled to capacity. No more training. No more scholarships. No more waivers. No more preparatory quizzes for the final lovemaking exam. If men wouldn't eat and couldn't beat the meat, then they certainly couldn't compete in the lovemaking game. All men needed to realize that and needed to learn and understand such crucial skills were a major requirement for performing fulfilling sex, especially for men nearing fifty.

Arman also failed other relationship tests with consistently low grades. There was no conversation, loving, affection, or spontaneity. Nothing! Zilch! Nada! The bad part about it was he continued to flop miserably. Symone was tired of it. She didn't need it. Didn't want it. And she was going to end it. Almost seven months was long enough. As soon as she reached the office, she would inform Pecola of her decision.

Symone glanced briefly in the rearview mirror and changed to the faster left lane of traffic. She smiled to herself as she realized that the relationship with Arman was her fault once again. Initially, she judged Arman regarding his business reputation and the materials displayed throughout the house and expected nothing less than a Don Juan romance plus continuous moaning and groaning sexual rendezvous. But the man's elaborate trappings were just that—elaborate trappings. Because as far as she was concerned, Arman's ability to look GQ and make passionate love stopped at his marbled front foyer.

Symone's right foot slightly pressed the accelerator, which increased the speed to eighty. She turned up *Got to Give it Up* a couple of decibels, and she thought about what happened yesterday evening with Arman.

Around five o'clock Sunday afternoon, Symone was sipping on her second glass of Dom Perignon and watching Arman administer the final touches for the grilled chicken breasts, shrimp, and potatoes. Since she finished mixing the Romaine salad just ten minutes earlier, she decided to relax outside on the patio with him.

The music stopped, and Arman glanced her way with an expression and a grunt sound that meant, ok play something else. She stood up slowly, stretched her legs, and walked inside to the stereo. Slowly, she flipped through the one-hundred CDs and decided to select the sultry sounds of Melva Houston—a Mount Airy jazz singer that Symone absolutely adored. After reviewing the different cuts, she inserted it in the player. Symone poured another glass of champagne. With the bottle hanging in her left hand and sipping a glass of bubbly from the other, she carefully danced back outside and plopped down on the chaise lounge.

Ninety minutes later, they finished eating. For an hour, they sat in silence side by side on separate chaise lounges. Listening to Cannonball Adderly, they watched the sun slide into the lake. No talking. No nothing. Thirty minutes earlier, Symone gently reached for Arman's hand. However, after letting her hold it for probably five minutes at the most, the birthday boy complained about sweat streaming through his fingers and quickly pried free from her affectionate grip.

Twenty minutes after that, Symone slowly walked outside to get Arman's gift. The decision to leave was really up to her. Since she didn't want to hurt his feelings, she allowed the decision to be up to him, too. Instead of strolling to the Mercedes to get Arman's present out of the back seat, Symone should be taking her overnight bag to the car to drive like a wild woman straight down I-77 to Winston-Salem.

However Symone didn't leave, and as she opened the car door, she realized the weekend wasn't going to improve. Symone grimaced as she thought about spending another boring night with Arman.

Wait until I speak to Pecola, she thought. If it wasn't for their last discussion three weeks ago at Pecola's surprise fortieth birthday party, right now Symone would be anywhere but with him.

"...Come on, chile. Give him another chance," Pecola coaxed in a motherly fashion that night.

While Arman snored loudly in the den, the two were sitting on the edge of Symone's backyard swimming pool with their feet rippling through the warm turquoise water as they sipped Bordeaux. It was midnight and the house and grounds were jumping to the sounds of Shelia E. As both women reflected on life, they drank silently for several minutes. The song faded as DJ Cool Breeze slid into Roger Troutman's *I Heard it Through the Grapevine.*

A group of six people standing beside the gazebo located not more than fifteen feet away boogied to the music and chuckled loudly. Symone began snapping her fingers, turned around, and grinned as she watched their smooth steps. Other guests' laughter and music floated throughout the hot May evening as they mingled around Symone's manicured lawn and wandered in and out her house dancing, laughing, and chitchatting on a variety of subjects.

Pecola brought Symone back to the reality of the Arman subject.

"Arman's a nice guy, honeychile. He's progressive and settled. That's the type of person you need in your life right now, Symone," Pecola insisted wisely. Pecola took a sip of wine and stared at her knowingly. Reluctantly, Symone turned to face her gaze.

"It's not clicking, Pecola. We sit around and look at each other as if we're married senior citizens or something. Why should I go through that?" she exclaimed through clenched teeth. Pecola quickly glanced at her and shrugged her shoulders with marginal understanding. "I'm not going through that with a new relationship. I've already been there, done that with Billy. And I was married to him."

While driving down the highway to Winston-Salem on Monday morning, a grinning Symone recalled that poolside conversation with Pecola as if it occurred two hours ago.

Pecola persevered with her approval of the union. "Arman's a nice guy, Symone. He's well-known in the business world," she continued as her voice trailed off.

"And—?"

While Pecola tried to think of other positives, her gaze was cemented to the star carpeted sky. "Plus, the brother got bucks, too. Hell, what else can I say?" she asked nonchalantly. She leaned back on both palms and kicked the water several times with her feet.

"What else can you say? Good question. Nothing. You're right about one thing. The man is settled all right, and I'm settling for someone less than who I want. This decision *is* up to me," Symone said flatly as she swallowed the last of her wine and glanced around to observe her massive, well-lit house.

"I know that."

"Good." Symone placed the empty glass on the brass tray.

"We got that settled." Pecola smiled.

"I got money, too," Symone added suddenly with a twinge of pride as she gazed at her perfectly polished ruby red nails, diamonds glittering on her fingers, and the Cartier Tank watch on her left wrist. "A helluva lot more than he does, too."

"I know that, girl," Pecola said quickly. "I'm just saying that Arman is a man of means, and he can definitely take care of you in the way you need to be."

"How's that, Pecola?"

"You know? What you're used to. That's all, chile. I know you probably got more money than him and everybody else combined here at my party," Pecola exclaimed with a crazy expression on her face.

Suddenly, several groups near the swimming pool jumped up and down yelling and began dancing with hands in the air screaming, "Heyyy! Ho! Heyyy! Ho! Shake what your Mama gave you cause your Daddy ain't gave you sheee-it!" as DJ Cool Breeze played the Godfather of Soul's *The Big Payback.*

Pecola and Symone laughed, bouncing and leaning to the left—then to the right repeatedly. Giving each other a high five and doing an elbow dance while screaming, "Aaahhh! Sookie, sookie, now!"

On the Monday two weeks after Symone's poolside discussion with Pecola, Arman called the office, pleading that he desperately wanted to see her again. He declared he missed her affectionate ways and yearned to hear her West Indian accent.

For six and half straight months, Symone dated him. Slowly but surely, she began to pull away. After Arman slept all through Pecola's birthday party, Symone refused to even phone him. Now, almost rolling into the seventh month, Arman made the telephone call because he wanted to know and had the nerve to ask, what was going on? He told her that he wanted to talk, and they did. Symone honestly explained her reasons why once more, and he said that he understood and would do better if she gave him another chance. She said that she would. Then, he invited Symone to spend the birthday weekend with him.

Prior to that weekend visit, Symone had experienced two stressful weeks. More than anything else, she was anxiously awaiting the opportunity to be near Lake Norman, to gaze at the tranquil water and to release wads of stress.

Chapter Two

While shaking her head, Symone kept her mind focused on the early Monday morning bumper to bumper traffic on I-77 North. She remembered what happened when she gave Arman his birthday gift.

Still trying to figure out if she should just leave, Symone slammed her car door closed and strolled back up to Arman's house with her gorgeously wrapped birthday boxes under her arms. A believer in selecting nice gifts for all her friends, she purchased a Black Cameo lapel pin and matching cuff links set. When she returned to the house, Arman had already finished cleaning off the patio and decided he was ready to go to bed. But with her limited singing skills, Symone serenaded him with the *Happy Birthday* song and gave him a deep, slow tongue kiss.

A surprised Arman opened the gifts, thanked her profusely, and proceeded to head toward the stairs. Halfway up the steps, he turned and said that he preferred to show thanks in a really special way—by making her serve hard time in his chamber of love.

Yeah right! If it's anything like the last time, Symone thought cynically, *you wouldn't recognize a love chamber if they locked you up in one.*

Thirty minutes later, Symone and Arman were frolicking below the mirrored ceiling in the king-sized brass bed. Symone expertly showered his body with a trail of kisses that began with the ears, traveled down to the chest, and to each toe. She returned to his middle where she lingered until he screamed repeatedly for her to stop because he couldn't take it any longer. He gently flipped Symone on her back which signaled to her that it was her turn to receive foreplay. Instead, Arman complimented Symone on the agility of her tongue. He quickly positioned himself on top and plunged into her.

Symone couldn't believe it. She silently screamed, *Hey! Whoa! Hold up! Wait a damn minute! Lord, I needed foreplay, too.* Hell, she desperately wanted to have an orgasm. This was exactly what they talked about the last time they were together and when he called her. She couldn't believe he was doing it again. Like he wasn't listening or something. He knew how she felt about it. He had told her that he'd definitely provide foreplay the next time.

All Symone asked was for Arman to spend a little time on her. The same way he expected it for himself. At this stage in her life, this is what she desired...some degree of reciprocity and a good old orgasm for a woman who nowadays rarely ever experienced one unless oral sex was performed.

A groaning Arman forcefully rammed in and out of her repeatedly. Even though Symone was pissed off as hell, she began to experience a small twinge of ecstasy.

"Oh, Symone. This feels so fantastic," Arman exclaimed out of breath. "Talk dirty to me, baby. Tell me it feels great for you too, baby," he coaxed while he held her hair, kissed, and sucked her neck. When they began, the General Electric digital clock's red numbers flashed 8:30. "Talk to me, Symone."

"It feels great for me, Arman," she calmly lied without breaking a sweat because she knew he wanted her to say it. "Ooooh! Ummm! Ummm!"

Symone added several other fake moans of satisfaction, knowing she certainly deserved the Oscar Award for best actress. With a sudden burst of spastic jerking, and at exactly 8:39, Arman hollered. He released himself and collapsed out of breath. Symone also screamed crazily, but hers was more from shock. Once again, their lovemaking ended in record time.

"Damn, woman! Your stuff is so tight and good. I can't stay up on it too long, Symone," he explained weakly, totally out of breath and rolled off to catch a few more gasps of air.

If it's that damn good, Symone thought angrily, *you should've stayed up there longer than that.*

Five minutes later, Arman was comatose and snoring loudly like an overweight pig. Symone reached over him and grabbed a Virginia Slims 100 cigarette and flipped on the brass lamp with the yellow bulb. She didn't even smoke anymore.

Oh! So you're smoking again? Symone thought as she lit the cigarette. In the moonlight of the room, the smoke traveled slowly above the bed. Symone watched it glide carefully up like the smoke in a chimney. With each rippled line, she continued to reflect some more.

"Arman? Are you up, Arman?" she asked, knowing that he wasn't. She took another deep puff and blew a big cloud of smoke in his face. "Say something."

No answer. She inhaled deeply each time, watched him out the corner of her eyes and waited. Symone suddenly thought about what Pecola's sister, Pauletta, told her during Pecola's birthday party poolside chat. While Pauletta gyrated slowly from left to right to the sounds of Linda Jones' *Hypnotized* she pontificated, which was the word Pauletta used to describe the spur-of-the-moment advice, about the forty and over relationship theory existing in America.

Pauletta spoke loudly for all to hear. "Sister gurl, let me tell you something this day," she said while looking toward Symone with semi-glazed eyes definitely caused by consuming too much celebratory liquor.

"Men are into what they're going to get rather than what they're going to give, gurlfriend." By then, several other women were sitting poolside with feet splashing in the water, discussing a range of subjects with the main theme being men, and nodding their heads vigorously. Symone had to admit Arman certainly fit that description.

While sipping a tall glass of Crown Royal on the rocks and smoking a Marlboro Lights through a gold holder, Pauletta appeared to be speaking from experience that night. However at the time, Pecola couldn't understand why her sister made such a startling comment.

A year older than Pecola, Pauletta was happily married to Hannibal Bing, her husband of sixteen years. Hannibal owned a Ford Lincoln Mercury dealership in Augusta, Georgia, and Pauletta was executive vice-president of commercial loans at National Bank. She was a major decision-maker at the bank in a position that was normally held by white boys. The Bings lived in a colossal six bedroom house and had five, clean, scrubbed-face children who attended private schools. Symone believed Pauletta sounded like she harbored a secret.

Just thinking of Pauletta's words made Symone shake her head slowly a very long time, and she glared angrily at a sleeping Arman again. If looks could kill, Arman would've been dead fifteen minutes ago.

"Wake up, baby," Symone demanded to Arman. "Puhleeze go get me a hot towel."

Symone nudged him a couple of times. Yet, the snoring continued.

"Damn, I'll get it my own self. I'm so sick of this," she grumbled disgustingly.

Symone strolled to the bathroom and opened her legs wide. She fished out the now sticky latex condom lodged in her and threw it in the toilet. She reached for the perfectly displayed AMG monogrammed blue towel and turned the hot water knob. While the water soaked through the towel, Symone gazed at her reflection in the mirror.

Look at you, girl. You're thirty-nine years old, and you're still the one who's always getting the towel, Symone thought. *Always fulfilling the man first and waiting for your turn. Something is definitely wrong with this picture. Is this what your life is all about now?*

Slowly, Symone twisted the steaming hot towel to squeeze out the excess water. She walked to the bed and soothingly sponged Arman down, being careful to wipe his face, chest, and between his legs. He opened his eyes for a brief moment and grunted. No "thank you, Symone baby." No nothing.

Deep in thought, Symone quietly returned to the bathroom and toweled herself off. As she gazed into the mirror, the sad reflection on her face loomed back at her. Suddenly, Symone broke down and cried for several minutes. She wiped her eyes with the back of her left hand. Then, she carefully scrubbed off the dry spots of lovemaking. She quietly returned to bed, turned off the lamp, and eased between the sheets.

The darkness of the room was a silent ally which, in a strange way, blocked out Arman's snoring. Symone lit another cigarette and watched the orange glow flare brighter when she inhaled. Seconds later, she squished it out in the ashtray as she reminded herself she wasn't a smoker and hadn't inhaled a cigarette in twelve years.

Now she realized Arman's cigarettes should've been a clue! *What man in his right mind smoked Virginia Slims cigarettes?* she questioned while cynically shaking her head. The certified wimp.

Symone listened to the romantic, natural medleys of the night and was glad Arman chose to sleep with the French doors open. The North Carolina summer evening permeated the room, and even the crickets sounded as if they were having a great party. One that Symone wished she could join. Instead, she flipped the brass lamp on again and walked to the bedroom stereo to search for an appropriate CD to play. She wasn't tired, and she certainly wasn't sexually satisfied.

Arman's music filing system was unusual. The top forty and jazz CDs were kept downstairs; however, old jam songs were neatly stored in a wooden cherry holder beside the bedroom stereo system. Interesting. Symone selected a Stylistics cassette. With a red golf umbrella dubbing as the ultimate dance partner, she quietly sashayed around the room to *Break Up to Make Up.* Afterwards, she eased back into the bed. As Symone thought about getting an early start in the morning so she would be at the Zawadi meeting on time, she listened to the remainder of the nostalgic songs until she eventually drifted off into a deep sleep.

A growling stomach jerked Symone's mind back to the present and off her daydreaming about what went wrong at Arman's house over the weekend. Since she was so focused on leaving Arman, she didn't want him to fix her any breakfast, even though he offered repeatedly. Plus, breakfast was being prepared for her at the office, and she didn't want to spoil her appetite. Still, she needed something.

With her head slowly bobbing to the soulful crooning of Marvin, thirty miles outside of Winston-Salem, Symone veered off the 150 Exit in Statesville. To coat her stomach, she wanted to get a steaming hot cup of coffee. At the red light, she turned right onto Main Street and headed for the Quik Market near downtown. Still thinking about the bad weekend with Arman, a slight headache was forming above her ears. Symone felt that she needed to also get a Goody's Headache Powder to knock out the soft thudding before it turned into a full-fledge migraine. Symone threw her leather pocketbook strap over her right shoulder and walked toward the store.

"Nice car, my young sistah," said an older Black man with a caramel leathery complexioned face. Leaning beside the store's front door, he was wearing a greasy, Lane College baseball cap. The man was close enough to be seen but not to the extent he blocked access to the store; he immediately shuffled from his position to open the door for her.

Startled and preoccupied, Symone quickly looked him over from head to toe. He wore a pair of filthy Air Jordans, soiled blue jeans, and a red plaid, short-sleeve shirt opened at the collar that revealed a gray, hairy chest. However, she noticed a regaled quietness about him.

"Mighty fine car, young lady."

"Uh. Thank you for the compliment and your politeness, sir," she mumbled softly as she walked through the door. The man noticed that a twinge of sadness traced the edge of the woman's weary, half-hearted smile.

"My pleasure, ma'am. I love to see my Black folks who've made it," he exclaimed sincerely in a soothing voice and tipped his hat toward her and the Mercedes sports convertible.

"Thank you." She smiled at him and slowly walked to the counter to purchase the headache powder and to find out the location of the coffee machine. It was in the rear of the store. Ten minutes later, Symone headed out. The same gentleman opened the door before she had a chance. Still somewhat depressed, she walked with her eyes glued to the ground.

"It's a beautiful day." It was a question, yet a statement at the same time. He didn't wait for an answer. "Have a great day, ma'am! Hold your head up and smile big! Remember things ain't as bad as they always seem," he proclaimed calmly with a huge grin.

Symone froze and lifted her head. A stunned Symone turned, stared at him, and studied his face for a moment. "Thank you. I needed that," she said genuinely surprised by his comments. He stuck out his hand, and they shook like old friends. After ten minutes of pleasant, motivating conversation, he became the immediate burst of energy she needed. Suddenly, she reached in her pocketbook and pulled out a business card. She gave it to him and told him if he ever needed anything to please give her a call. His name was Fernando Ball, III, and he made sure to pronounce The Third proudly.

Symone strolled to the car with a large smile on her face, and as she backed out she waved at him. Why she became friendly with a complete stranger, she would never know. She never ever did stuff like that and was surprised at the candor she exhibited with him. Maybe because it was Monday. Who the hell knows? However, she knew Alex, her compassionate best friend, would be proud. Alex always said that things happened for a reason, and sometimes people learn more from a stranger than they do from the people they speak to every day. Symone blew into the cup and took a sip of hot coffee. She waved good-bye to Fernando.

Fernando smiled, too, as he returned the wave. Always considered an extremely intuitive man, he was known for his odd, psychic sixth sense. He dug the already wrinkled card out his pants pockets. It was a light turquoise-colored linen one with the name *Symone Angela Poussaint, Trustee,* embossed in gold. He studied it for several minutes.

Although Fernando had no idea when or where he would meet her again, somehow he knew it was inevitable. Ten minutes after she drove off, the future events of their next meeting suddenly flashed before him. Fernando closed his eyes and slowly shook his head heavily as he realized it would be under much different and such tragic circumstances. While happily singing along with Marvin Gaye, Symone confidently turned left onto Main Street and headed toward I-40 East.

Ten miles from Winston-Salem, Symone's car phone rang. *Got to Give it Up* was still blasting strong, and Symone almost didn't hear the shrill ring. She lowered the volume just a tad.

"Hel-lo," she said brightly with a melodic ring. It was Pecola.

"Honeychile, where are you?" she asked slowly in her truly, deep and unique southern voice.

Symone told Pecola that every time she heard her say honeychile when they first met, she imagined her under a frilly white parasol, resting on the front porch of a South Carolina white pillared plantation mansion. Pecola was fanning herself and batting her eyes while a wonderfully buff, handsome and charcoal Black slave massaged her feet.

Even if Pecola owned fifty companies, it tickled Symone that Pecola always said honeychile like she knew a person from those red dirt, bare and ashy feet days when she was growing up on a huge farm near Greensboro, North Carolina. Although, there were occasions when Pecola was hurt when people appeared offended by the southern drawl and prima donna sweetness, they recognized that it was simply a part of who Pecola was once they got to know her. They realized she was an excellent, savvy businesswoman endowed with extraordinary intelligence and knew how to shift from Miss Scarlet O'Hara to Miss MBA when necessary. Symone glanced at her watch. It was 8:40 a.m.

"Tell me where you are, Sy."

"I'm in my car, girl," she replied with a throaty laugh.

"Chile, I know you're in the car. I mean where are you in respect to time?" she questioned slightly concerned. Pecola knew Symone always had a small problem with promptness.

"You'll be happy to know that I'm about eight miles from Winston, girl," she advised as she glanced in the rearview mirror. An Irish Green Lotus convertible was almost on her rear bumper. Symone slowly changed to the right lane and stared in disbelief when the fiftyish, tanned white driver winked and waved as he zoomed by.

You go, boy. My speedometer needle shows I'm doing eighty, Symone thought. *So you must be hitting eighty-five or ninety.*

"You're eight miles from Winston, Sy?"

"That's what I said."

"Hallelujah, honeychile! Hallelujah!" Pecola exclaimed with religious fervor. "Hurry up in here."

"What happened, Pecola?"

"After you left on Friday, I asked Tanya to prepare those serious muffins for our preliminary meeting at ninety-thirty," she said in an always-out-of-breath-way.

Mother of two difficult teen-aged boys who aspired to be rap artists and cursed every three words, Tanya Gray was the executive chef for both organizations. She prepared the gourmet meals for spa guests and also handled meeting luncheons held in MO's second floor executive dining room. Girlfriend could prepare anything from chitlins to an exquisite Beluga caviar dip.

"I want you to get here, so you can enjoy the muffins."

"I will."

"Are you listening to the Tom Joyner Morning Show?"

"Nope."

"You're kidding. That's not you atall. Something must be up."

"It is. You're right. It's rare for me to not listen to them in the morning, but I'm having my private party with Marvin Gaye."

"That's a shame. You would've enjoyed it, Sy. They were informative but funny as hell. I just cut if off, and they had me laughing all over the place."

"Good. Tell me about it when I get there. I'm minutes away," Symone added and explained the chance meeting with Fernando.

"Chile, you better be careful with stuff like that. A complete stranger. He might be the next Boston Strangler or something. Honeychile, *puhleeze,*" she blurted out and paused a moment to sip Irish Cream cappuccino. "Anyway, I'm glad to see you're close. This is great! Take care, chile. Love ya. I'll see you when your behind gets here."

"Love ya too, Pecola."

Chapter Three

Fifteen minutes later, Symone pulled into the Akao building parking lot and steered her car in the reserved slot. Quickly, she glanced behind the building and noticed that even with the employee vehicles, there were an additional twelve cars in adjacent spaces. Great. Business was already booming in the spa.

For the past thirteen years, Pecola Marva Reynolds and Symone owned two phenomenally successful and lucrative companies in Winston-Salem, North Carolina. One was Meetings Odyssey, a full service conference planning management company, and the second one was Akao Studios, a metropolitan day spa. This morning's meeting was a wonderful opportunity for them. The Zawadi Corporation was number forty-four on the Fortune 500 List. MO was in the throes of serious negotiations to handle the company's upcoming fiftieth anniversary celebration conference, which required organizing the entire conference for approximately twenty thousand attendees.

Symone grabbed her leather briefcase from the back seat, closed the car door, and walked inside. She spoke to the receptionist and took the time to chat with several clients waiting in the lobby. *Stay in my Corner* sounds piped through the air, and Symone smiled to herself as she realized it must be the Dells' day.

Now, Symone truly knew it was Monday. On the first business day, it was generally an unofficial mandatory requirement that old jam classic music played softly throughout the Akao building. Back in the day, Pecola was a sterling, award-winning singer in high school, and that was exactly how she jump-started each week. Listening to the sounds of the doo wop age. As Pecola described it, the Motown groove of the street corner groups belting out the love songs without synthesizers, electronics, no nothing.

Since Pecola wanted clients and employees to become familiar with the oldies but goldies tunes, it was Pecola's small way to pay homage to the singers who harmonized beautifully and used only the strength of their voices to serenade in a cappella. Symone reminded herself to definitely advise Missy Pecola that since she adored the old jam music so much, the next time she probably would have enjoyed the Excelsior Club with Arman more so than she did.

It was nine o'clock, and Symone pressed the security code to access the second floor where Meetings Odyssey's personnel were scurrying around like busy bees. As she walked to her office, she greeted everyone with a large smile and a perky good morning. A small crowd congregated around the coffee and cappuccino center in the kitchen, no doubt enjoying bran muffins prepared by Tanya. Knowing Pecola, if she requested muffins for their meeting, she requested extra for the other employees as well.

Each person graced Symone with respectful, good-natured smiles. They weren't fearful ones. In the beginning, Symone expected respectful smiles each and every day they gazed her way, but Alex always said that business owners might pay salaries and people needed to work, but employers only earned their respect by treating them with respect.

Alex was absolutely right. Even though their personal lives got screwed up every now and then, Pecola and Symone tried to keep their bad moods and sometimes nasty, arrogant behavior to themselves. It was their mood, and there was no need to aim the negative attitude at anyone else in the office. At least not until they saw Alex. Of course, they dumped it on her with the fervent hope she would coach them through it.

In a matter of five minutes, Symone flipped on her office light, dropped the briefcase on the couch, removed her driving hat and proceeded to pat her hair back into place. Symone walked into her private bathroom and steadily gazed at her reflection. She combed the loose strands of hair in place and washed her hands.

Since Symone took the long route to her office, she didn't notice if Pecola was in her office. While checking her daily calendar, Symone rocked back in her leather chair to reflect a moment. The huge corner window-lined office was luxuriously decorated. A custom made, plush couch adorned the wall directly in front of the mahogany executive desk which sat on a thick Persian rug. Original African art by Lois Mailou Jones, William Tolliver, and Phoebe Beasley were positioned on the Caribbean sea-colored walls, and other ethnic artifacts graced appropriate spots throughout. Baccarat silver crystal lamps and candy dishes were displayed on each table beside the couch. Right beside the window was a mahogany circular table with five chairs. Positioned right in the center of the table was a crystal bowl of fresh fruit that was replenished every day by the dining room staff. A computer terminal and photos of family and friends adorned the credenza behind Symone's desk.

Symone inhaled deeply, stood up, and decided to go search for Pecola. Before Symone turned the corner, she heard girlfriend's southern drawl float out the dining room as *The Love We Had* glided through the ceiling speakers. Just as Pecola glanced up from giving instructions to Tanya, Symone peeked inside. Pecola dropped everything, raced over to her, and the two women embraced and kissed, pecking each other on the cheek being sure to not transfer lipstick to the other's face. As she spoke, Pecola's green eyes sparkled. *She must be in a great damn mood for once,* thought Symone.

"Chile, how did it go? How did it go?" Pecola rattled from pure joy.

"I'll tell you. Not now, though."

"I know we don't have time to talk, but we can catch up on everything when we get-together with Alex at four," she said while patting Symone's arm. "In the meantime, all is going well for our noon meeting with Zawadi."

Tanya turned around and smiled at Pecola's non-stop talking. "Hi, Sy. Did ya have a great weekend?"

"It was ok, girl," Symone replied as she slowly stretched her neck from side to side.

"Just ok?" Tanya asked.

"Exactly, Tanya." While they spoke, Pecola quietly examined her newly manicured acrylic nails.

"That doesn't sound good," Tanya answered.

"It wasn't. How are the boys, Tanya?" Symone inquired in a concerned voice.

"They're doing fine, too. I just thanked Pecola again for the books yall gave my boys," she said sincerely.

Both Symone and Pecola were avid readers of African-American literature in any form— poetry, fiction, non-fiction, smap, pap, or dap. They didn't care what it was. If it was published and in bookstores, or posted on the Blackboard African-American Bestseller's list or the Quarterly Black Review Blacklist, then the Ujima Literary Society that Symone created years ago read it.

Ever since she was a young girl fresh from Trinidad, Symone's family was convinced that the keys to success in life were written in books. Both women believed that some Black people couldn't sometimes comprehend *what* was going on because they never picked up a book and refused to read and understand what was truly going down.

Even though Akao Spa earned tons of money from pampering services, the partners agreed that Black people, in many cases, spent too much time getting their nails and hair done, but they needed to devote just as much energy in developing their minds. In addition to having magazines in the lobby and to spark interest in reading, two wall-to-wall custom cherry wood bookshelves were installed which showcased current and older African-American book selections for Akao's clients' review while they waited to enter the spa.

For those reasons, Pecola and Symone gave Tanya three individually gift-wrapped boxes that included two books per box. One was *Think Big* to help her sons with their attitude. The other was a copy of *The Science of Rap*. Pecola and Symone believed this book would help Tanya's young boys understand that rap was a cultural phenomenon with roots all the way back to the African griot. It was the oral tradition of the slaves instead of just an opportunity to exhibit blatant disrespectful behavior to their elders. Both Pecola and Symone also promised the boys a bonus if they finished the books and turned in a thought-provoking, well-written book report.

As Symone walked to the table to get a muffin, she smiled softly and squeezed Tanya's arm. "We just hope the books will help them help you, Tanya. Like they say, 'It takes a whole village to raise a child.' Girrrlll, nowadays, maybe three villages," she said encouragingly with a grin.

"You're right," Tanya said as she took a deep breath and nodded her head slowly.

"I agree," Pecola mumbled.

"Well, let me let yall talk. I'll be back in fifteen minutes to check on things." Tanya's eyes moved to Pecola, and she spoke in a professional tone. "Do ya need anything else?"

Pecola's gaze traveled to the walnut sideboard and like a computer terminal, began clicking away approval ratings of one to ten. She carefully reviewed the bran muffins, the silver coffee service, the Lynn Chase fine bone china cups, saucers, sterling flatware, soft pink linen napkins, and other necessary items. Pecola gave it a nine and shook her head no.

"Tanya, everything is just great. Thanks a lot, girl," Pecola gushed as she gazed at Symone for verification who also slowly nodded her head in agreement.

Giving the setting another double check, Tanya quickly left the dining room. The walnut wood table accommodated twenty people, but only four place settings were displayed. Symone sat down and carefully observed Pecola who hadn't stopped talking to her since Tanya left the room.

"...Chile, I'm so proud of you and Arman working things out," Pecola was saying as she placed the linen napkin in her lap.

Pecola was astonished when Symone told her that she planned to break up with him, and Pecola continued to keep her fingers crossed for the relationship. Symone knew that paying Pecola a compliment would squelch that conversation. Pecola thrived on them because she believed that shopping and getting dressed was a religious experience deserving of non-stop praise and ultimate recognition.

"You look smashing, girl," Symone announced brightly admiring the outfit.

Pecola snatched the napkin with her left hand, jumped up, and pirouetted several times. She was dressed in a crinkled crepe, slightly fitted, chic black tank dress and matching bolero jacket with shoulder pads. Complementing Coreen Simpson bold gold jewelry graced Pecola's neck, ears, and wrists plus two black combs were neatly placed in the chestnut sandy hair which was pulled back in a neat bun.

A gorgeous woman with an hourglass figure, Pecola stood five-feet-seven inches tall. Her skin-tone was a yellow-brown color. More yellow than brown, she was considered what Black folks called high yellow. Pecola was blessed with a delicate round face, large green eyes, pouty lips, and a slightly pointy nose. She looked especially pretty today dressed in black. Like Symone, she was a good twenty pounds overweight.

"You go, girl," Symone urged quietly in a deep voice.

Pecola's green eyes narrowed with good-natured suspicion, and she cocked her head to one side. "You're sure you really like it, Symone?" Pecola didn't wait for an answer while she primped her perfect bun. "It's a Byron Lars original, chile. You know one of my favorite designers. I bought it this weekend."

"Very nice."

"And you're sure?" she asked, speaking very fast with both hands on her hips. Symone nodded yes vigorously, and Pecola sat down pleased with the compliment.

"It's you, girl. It's cutting edge. It's hot," Symone laughingly cajoled on with a half grin.

"Good. I'm glad you agree. Well, you know me, chile. My behind cleans up very well," Pecola said as she sipped coffee and batted her eyes in a facetious manner. Symone smiled and shook her head slowly as she thought about how crazy her partner acted most times.

"I know you wanted to change the subject, Symone. But, that's ok." She snapped her fingers twice in signature fashion.

"No, I didn't."

"I'll take positive words from you any way I can get them," she added giggling. Symone rolled her eyes long and slow and placed the cup in the saucer.

Pecola glanced at her new Ebel watch, a surprise birthday gift from her husband, Carlos. It was 9:28, and they were right on time. The door opened, and two senior staff members joined the conference. For the next hour, they discussed the upcoming meeting with Elisha, their executive assistant, and Theodore "Ted" Bridgeforth, the executive representative who worked with new accounts. Along with Pecola and Symone, Ted was the only other Certified Meeting Planner or CMP within the organization. Employed with MO for over four years, Symone discovered him when she briefly dated Besa Mongella Ampofo, a Nigerian physics professor at Shaw University.

Symone adored highly intelligent Black men who were all the way live super freaks. She believed that the smarter men were, the higher level position they held and the more money they made, the kinkier and freakier they acted. However, based upon sexual exploits of their other friends which covered the spectrum from street bums to chairmen of the boards, Pecola believed such ideology was totally unsubstantiated. And to prove them wrong, Symone persevered with the behind-closed-door research with a variety of intelligent Black men and declared the freak philosophy as law.

Nevertheless, Ampofo fit such a category and invited Symone to speak at Shaw University's career day. After the speech, Ted approached her. Intent on working with a progressively mobile African-American firm, she was impressed with his positive attitude, impeccable attire, and especially the grade point average of three point nine in marketing. Two months later, Symone broke off with Ampofo. For some reason, his huge penis wouldn't stay hard during their lovemaking. It drove Symone crazy—Ampofo, too. Symone finally told an understanding Ampofo good-bye. But when Ted graduated Summa Cum Laude from Shaw University, they hired him.

Ted was an attractive dark-skinned man, not fine. Standing about five feet eleven, he wore a closely cropped haircut and dressed liked he stepped right out of *Ebony Male* or was *EM*ish, according to Pecola. He lived in a lovely cluster home in the Sherwood Forest section of the city. But his employers never saw him with a woman or even a man for that matter and their opinion on whether he was gay or straight was still reserved in their mind. Ted was very quiet, efficient, and well respected by his co-workers. They just couldn't tell a thing about his personal life.

Ivenue Collins, a tall, unattractive Black female and Tanya's right hand person on the dining room staff, opened the conference door once. She noticed all was well and quietly closed it.

As Elisha helped herself to a warm muffin to go with the steaming, hot cup of coffee, she submitted fresh computerized information for their review. It described the Zawadi Corporation from A to Z. Executive assistant to both women, Elisha was an extremely competent woman and the dear friend of Carlos' mother who recommended her for the job. Elisha resigned from a mediocre paying, dead-end secretarial job in marketing at MUB Industries to work with Pecola and Symone. MUB was the number one employer in Winston-Salem, and her departure shocked all her co-workers. But Elisha felt it was time to move on, and the devoted Elisha had worked for MO since its creation.

Only a few years older than the partners, Elisha became a mother figure, confidante, and jack of all trades around the office. The forty-seven year old mother of two grown daughters and granny of one, Elisha was considered the real five-star general of the company. Quite fastidious when it came to details, she knew the responsibilities of each position within the company from top to bottom and inside out. A petite, pecan-tan complexioned woman who always wore her hair in a French bun, she was an impeccable dresser who continually managed to keep the two owners focused on the integrity of their businesses.

Pecola and Symone were proud of the fact that employee turnover was zero. Unless an individual relocated to another town or because of other unusual circumstances, no one resigned from either company. Openings were filled in an interesting, but effective way...by word of mouth in the community, in church, and as Pecola said jokingly one day, even from her husband's barber.

Meetings Odyssey consisted of a staff of twenty-three. The Akao Studios spa personnel numbered twenty-nine. Combined, there were fifty-two individuals working for both companies, and they were well taken care of. All employees, whether they were part or full-time, received medical benefits, tuition reimbursement, profit sharing, and three weeks paid vacation after the first year.

Alex, a former corporate attorney and dubbed a present day savior for all mankind by Pecola, assisted Symone and Pecola with developing the unique benefits for their employees. In addition, the employees of the year, who were selected by fellow co-workers of each company, received an all-expense paid one week vacation for two, compliments of Pecola and Symone.

An honors graduate of Hampton University with double majors in English and Business Administration, Symone completed graduate work at the University of Pennsylvania Wharton School of Business. She was recruited by MUB Industries' headhunters to work in the marketing department of the world renowned media conglomerate. The stint didn't last long. Totally disgusted by the cutthroat tactics and unfair promotions of the modern day lily white corporate plantation, Symone resigned two years later. The ruthlessness of MUB Industries toward its employees and the viciousness of fellow MBAers trying to climb the ladder to success couldn't even compare with the leveraged buy-outs, unfair mergers, and hostile takeover case studies reviewed on a daily basis at Wharton.

Pregnant and married to Carlos at the age of sixteen, Pecola's educational achievements were obtained much differently than Symone's. Yet, those early circumstances did nothing to squelch any collegiate goals. Between having four babies, one right behind the other and managing a family, Pecola attended classes at North Carolina Agricultural and Technical State University, known as A&T in Greensboro. There she received a Bachelor of Science degree in architectural engineering and a master's degree in business administration.

Because the schedule offered to her was conducive to attending college classes, Pecola initially accepted the opportunity to assist Carlos and his family with designing and decorating homes throughout North Carolina. As President of the CR Construction Group, the Reynolds' family general contracting firm, Carlos managed the Winston-Salem office.

Symone and William "Billy" Butler were both graduates of Wharton and were making high-powered salaries. When they asked around for the best Black building contractor in North Carolina, everyone unanimously referred them to Carlos Reynolds. Symone and Billy eventually contracted with Carlos to build their lavish home on four wooded acres they purchased in Clemmons, a suburban community ten miles west of Winston-Salem. That was when Pecola and Symone met for the first time. The two women became instant friends. Six months after those initial introductions, they jokingly agreed to become business partners on the side with Pecola's dear friend, Alex. Three months later, Pecola, Alex, and Symone selected the companies they desired to create. They performed the proper research. And bam, Akao Studios was born. After Symone resigned from MUB, they formed Meetings Odyssey.

As a result of the ridiculousness Symone experienced working at MUB, she and Pecola fervently desired from the very beginning to create a company that supported families and their children in a working environment where employees received a sense of equity and unity and exhibited tremendous corporate dedication. Based upon the allegiance of Akao Studios and Meetings Odyssey personnel, so far, and knock on wood as Pecola always said, they succeeded with those lofty goals.

Chapter Four

At exactly 11:45, three executives from The Zawadi Corporation walked into the downstairs lobby. Carrying briefcases and dressed in the typical dark suits, wing-tip shoes, white button-down collars, and calm silk ties, they looked like banker triplets. This was the third meeting with Meetings Odyssey. The first two were held in Greensboro, just twenty-five miles away. This meeting would give the three vice presidents an opportunity to observe the inner-workings of the organization believed to be front-runners for the project. Once checked in, the Zawadi officials were quickly whisked to the second floor executive reception area overlooking I-40 where they waited for not more than six minutes.

With its light colored maple parquet flooring and shelves neatly crammed with books on either side of the magnificent picture window that offered a panoramic view of billowing oak trees and highway, the oak paneled reception area provided a stunning library presence. An oriental rug anchored the eighteen century Chinese alter table topped in marble and covered with poetry books from world renowned African-American authors. It was strategically positioned between two stately leather sofas.

Randolph Grace shook his head slowly with surprise. As vice president of marketing, he was thoroughly impressed with the Chinese table. During a business trip to Washington, DC, he and his wife purchased a similar one from an antique shop in Georgetown a mere ten months ago. On the other side, Reuben Jakes, vice president of national sales, was the token Black man for the meeting. Jakes was studying the lamp lit abstract expressionistic work of Daniel Simmons as well as literal art by Tom Feelings and Cleveland Wright. He thought the three artists were a startling combination in the elegantly decorated area.

Newly divorced, this would be Reuben Jakes first meeting with MO. From what his colleagues told him, he was in for a pleasant experience with this particular minority vendor. Thus far, Jakes was thoroughly impressed with the office decor and tried to imagine what would be next.

For the past three years, Gloria Lapiduss, a pretty dark-skinned, full-figured young woman of twenty-five, worked as Elisha's assistant. However, she was nominated to handle other responsibilities. Nikki, the second floor receptionist, called in sick and Gloria was the one asked to man the second floor front desk. As usual, Gloria watched with amusement as first time visitors to the Akao Building gingerly handled the African figurines as they walked and gawked around the executive offices receptionist area with futile attempts at maintaining a somewhat control shocked expression.

There were several wonderful things Gloria could say about her bosses. One thing was that they could decorate their behinds off and often requested staff to search out unique and different accessories for their work areas. Gloria was glad to see the fine brother was watching the Simmons' piece. After reading about the artist in *Essence,* Gloria showed Pecola a picture. Gloria told Pecola what she knew about the artist, and girlfriend actually told Gloria to check it out. Once Gloria completed her investigation, Pecola and Symone agreed that it would fit perfectly somewhere and purchased brotherman's work just like that.

They also were truly interested in giving a person a chance. Gloria's crazy husband, from which she was now divorced, stormed onto her job at Kukumbuka Foods Corporation. Standing at the entrance to her office, he loudly threatened her life as well as everybody else's within the company. Eventually, Gloria was fired for unrelated reasons, according to Kukumbuka Management.

Alex sang in the same church soprano choir with Gloria's mother, Parthenia Maxwell. Parthenia told Alex what happened and how the arbitration officer denied her truly intelligent daughter unemployment insurance and was only paid four weeks' severance pay. Always a diligent individual, Gloria had worked since she was thirteen. Never in her wildest dreams did she expect an interview, let alone a job, with the Black women she heard about as almost legends in Winston-Salem. These were women she assumed were too stuck up to employ a sistah down on her luck.

Such wasn't the case, and Gloria was hired on ninety days probation. Since that time, Gloria found out they were the two nicest people to work for and extremely smart sistahs from which she learned a great deal about the corporate world. An even more staggering surprise was when she discovered Symone was just like her. A woman who was a serious militant to her heart, protector of Black culture, and a staunch supporter of the Black experience in any form. Symone remained disgusted with how she felt Black folk in the business community assumed it essential when they created companies to embrace the reverse plantation philosophy and believed they had to surround themselves with white people in order to be considered successful.

Recently, Symone had Gloria laughing when she told her that if necessary, she would look under a volcano rock in Hawaii to find the wonderfully qualified Black people she knew who walked the streets. She said, "Hell, the white boys have been hiring each other for hundreds of years, Gloria. We as Black people need to practice the same policy. Learn how to hire—qualified—Black people. Plus, we don't have to look that hard because the accountants, attorneys, dentists, doctors, plumbers and whoever else are out there, girl. Support our own. Instead of African-Americans looking in the freakin' *Yellow Pages* nowadays, we need to be educated to first turn to the *Black Pages* for necessary services. Who knows? If we're faithful in our search, we might even find a special diamond in the rough, exceptional people, that need an opportunity to prove themselves."

Gloria believed she was a classic diamond example. Because Pecola and Symone gave her such an excellent chance, she was determined to not disappoint them. Pecola, Symone and Elisha were her mentors, and it was Gloria's goal to also receive CMP certification as soon as she completed college.

Gloria picked up the flashing white button to check the time on line sixteen. The main receptionist's line, line sixteen, was the way that the receptionist's electronically signaled the minutes that lapsed from the initial call downstairs that announced when guests arrived.

Brewster English, IV, vice president of operations of Zawadi, had an envied direct link to the ear of the vice-chairman. English was the Zawadi executive who personally recommended MO be considered for this project.

Three seconds after Gloria picked up line sixteen, Brewster English asked Gloria the location of the men's room. Gloria stood up and courteously pointed fifteen feet down the hall to the second door on the right. She silently chuckled again at his probable reaction when he saw the gold-filled faucet fixtures and handsomely decorated bathroom.

According to the computer message on line sixteen, the Zawadi executives had been waiting exactly five minutes. MO had a reputation for punctuality and for not allowing their clients wait for long periods of time in the reception areas. Now it was five minutes and counting. And, like clockwork, in sixty more seconds Pecola or Symone would walk out to greet them, or Gloria would be asked to escort the guests back to the oak-paneled conference room or to their exquisitely furnished offices. She placed the telephone in the rest and busied herself with entering data into the computer.

At precisely six minutes and ten seconds after the Zawadi executives arrived, Pecola buzzed the intercom and asked Gloria to escort the guests to the conference room. Gloria quietly explained that Mr. English was in the restroom, and she would be happy to do so as soon as he returned. When Pecola questioned if Gloria shook their hands firmly and if they were served cappuccino or coffee, Gloria told her yes to question one and that they refused the earlier request to receive something hot. Right after she hung up the phone, Mr. English returned to the reception area and softly mumbled a couple of words to Mr. Grace.

Gloria rose to her feet and asked the gentlemen to please follow her. While she smiled professionally, she instantly decided to take them the long way around. She remembered Pecola's firm exhortations during staff meetings where she explained perception was everything, and people made a mental judgment call five seconds after they laid eyes on an individual or a company. And, in those few seconds, it was determined if they were going to do business or not.

Also squeezed into the split second assessment was a review of the company or an individual's lifestyle, economic standings, and intellectual abilities. Those early moments were crucial because it was where individuals first sold themselves as well as the reputation of the organization they represented. Pecola always laughingly said that women especially needed to stop being wimpy. They should absolutely always maintain eye contact. During handshakes, they should pump the other person's hand firmly, not limp like, at least three times with a strong grip. This was a sign of confidence. As if Gloria were repeating the letters of the alphabets in first grade rote fashion, Pecola's prior words resounded loudly and methodically through Gloria's mind as she sauntered slowly through Meetings Odyssey busy offices with the visiting group.

The Zawadi executives strolled past various workstations and the light, airy offices. They observed the pleasant expressions of the employees and noticed the finest electronic gadgetry and the state of the art computer equipment that graced their desks. At the entrance of the conference room door, Gloria stood to the side. She motioned with her right hand for the guests to go in where Pecola, Symone, Elisha, and Ted stood around the huge mahogany conference table and awaited their entrance. After each group exchanged the customary pleasantries, they all sat down. Pecola leaned back to quietly ask Gloria to tell Tanya to bring Irish Cream cappuccino for seven. Afterwards, everyone relaxed. Five minutes later, Tanya and Ivenue, both dressed very courtly in tuxedo uniforms, delivered the order.

Elisha passed out slickly prepared thick packets to each person, which briefly analyzed the questions Zawadi raised over the past three months of proposal negotiations. As Ted moved to the front of the room, the meeting began with all eyes on him. The three Zawadi officials sat on one side of the table, and MO officials were on the other. Symone tried her best to ignore the fine brother named Reuben Jakes. He wasn't present at their last two meetings, but Symone believed he was added to strike a bond with MO personnel and to subtly inform them that The Zawadi Corporation hired Black folk—and at a high level too.

Reuben, on the other hand, remained impressed with the beautifully architected building, the tastefully lavish decor, and the efficiency of the staff and management. It took all the ROTC inner strength training available to Reuben for him to remain focused on the subject manner and to not check out the lovely owners whom he believed were two tough sistahs worthy of further unofficial research. As Reuben took a swallow of cappuccino, he tried to appear enraptured with Ted. The brother was very prepared and was running down the numbers expertly. Later on that night, Reuben decided he would definitely check out the lowdown with a few Kappa brothers who lived in Winston.

After fifteen minutes of animated talking, Ted was saying, "...Even the most creative marketing plan is only as good as its implementation. That's why Meetings Odyssey pays close attention to the details of each contract..."

Randolph Grace posed a question and was impressed as Pecola and Elisha checked their notes and quickly delivered the answer. The gentlemen discussed other items. Once again, responses were fired out rapidly.

It was Symone's turn, and she handled the middle section of the presentation. She showed a video slide show of MO past mega conferences. Symone discussed how MO proposed to handle various aspects of The Zawadi Corporation's fiftieth anniversary celebration. The Zawadi Corporation requested that the participants of this celebration engage in dialogue that would foster the collaboration needed to maintain, improve, and expand the operations of Zawadi for another fifty years. And Symone assured their executives that it would be done. Ivenue served the third round of cappuccino, and Pecola wrapped up the meeting which lasted ninety minutes.

"...In closing, we realize corporations are demanding more from their conference experiences. When Meetings Odyssey is selected to coordinate your celebration, we'll strive to ensure that The Zawadi Corporation's fiftieth anniversary attendees' needs are met explicitly. Without a doubt, all twenty thousand individuals in attendance at this celebration will have participated fully, yet believe they were treated individually," Pecola ended in her finest southern MBA voice. She performed so royally, even Symone felt like kissing her naked behind.

There was the usual clearing of throats and shuffling of papers. The Zawadi executives asked the questions MO expected them to, and they were answered competently by the four. Eventually, the business discussion slowly died down, and they glided into personal stories that officially closed the meeting. They slowly walked to the dining area adjacent to the conference room. The males had their arms folded or hands in trouser pockets looking professionally serious. Symone's antennas suddenly zoomed up through the fog of the well-rehearsed college information previously shared by the two white boys when she heard the handsome brother say he graduated from Morgan State University.

In the next breath, Reuben Jakes casually announced that he received his MBA from the Sloan School of Management at MIT. *Ah sookie, sookie now,* Symone thought. *Here's a smart Black man who's probably a freak!* However, she realized that she couldn't pursue any relationship possibilities there. Symone practiced a rule to not play where it might affect MO pay. As Pecola often said, "Don't mix your honey with your money, honeychile."

The dining room was elegantly set for seven with crystal and china on the soft pink linen tablecloth. Randolph Grace was once more impressed with the spaciously appointed dining room's view of oak trees out back, its walnut wood furniture, and he especially noticed the large English silver coffee server on the sideboard. Once they all were seated, Gloria graciously handed each one a calligraphy designed menu prepared by Alex. While the visitors silently reviewed the planned meal, the door opened; Tanya and Ivenue entered with silver trays topped with Caesar salads.

Going in Circles by Friends of Distinction softly piped through the polite clatter of silver against china. Brewster English commented that he remembered the song, which immediately endeared him in Pecola's heart. Pecola even allowed a *honeychile* to slip out. With a broad smile on his face, Brewster exclaimed that Pecola sounded just like his wife who was an English Professor at Greensboro College. The entree of glazed chicken breast strips with mushroom sauce, wild rice pilaf, steamed broccoli with lemon butter, and sour dough buttered rolls was outstanding. Pecola and Symone provided Tanya and Ivenue with two "thumbs up" winks.

While they chatted about how fabulous everything tasted, Tanya and Ivenue were on the money as they came in at the perfect moment to clear the china for each course and refilled glasses of Chardonnay at appropriate times. Although the Zawadi executives declared they were stuffed, they still managed to enjoy French Silk Pie with freshly ground French roast decaffeinated coffee. The luncheon ended. Everyone laid his or her napkin by the china plates and followed Gloria as she gave a tour of Meetings Odyssey offices.

Introductions were made to all MO personnel, and the satisfied group returned to the conference room. A few more pleasantries were exchanged. Briefcases were slammed shut. The four walked the Zawadi officials to the downstairs lobby, shook hands, and said a round of hearty good-byes. As Pecola and Brewster gazed toward one another, *The Bells* by the Originals lullabied the lobby. The two shared a private joke and ended up laughing and shaking hands again for a very long time. By now, Brewster knew from the lunch discussion that classic old jam songs was the only kind of music Pecola listened to twenty-four seven.

As Elisha, Pecola, Symone, and Ted climbed the steps to the second floor, they chatted calmly. But once in the privacy of Pecola's closed door office, they high-fived each other to death. Elisha gently interrupted the positive celebration for a brief moment. As the religious mother figure in the office as well, she wanted them to join hands. She whispered a short prayer of thanks to God for all their excellent blessings and to faithfully thank the Creator in advance for the Zawadi account she knew MO eventually would receive. Two seconds after Elisha said amen, they began hugging and high fiving each other again.

Alexandria Phylicia Johnson-Devereaux, lovingly known as Alex to her friends, followed the black suited maitre d' to an eight seat table by the window. He stopped, quickly glanced at her, and asked if the location was acceptable. It was. The late afternoon crowd was limited. The few better tables throughout O'Charley's, a steak and ale restaurant, was full of people involved in their own serious, private discussions. However, this one faced the street traffic and allowed Alex to watch cars and passersby. She thanked him and sat down. He handed her a menu. She requested two more and told him she would like an Evian with a slice of lemon. Alex checked her watch. It was 3:45 p.m. Since it was much too early to expect Pecola and Symone, Alex calculated that she had at least a half-hour of relaxation.

Three minutes later, a perky Black girl with dreadlocks pulled back in a neat ponytail served the water. She said her name was Lenda, and she explained that she would be the waitress for the meal. Alex thanked her and was proud to see both Lenda's starched apron and button down shirt was dazzling white and cleaned to the one-hundredth degree. And if she were honest, Alex was glad they would have a sistah serving their meal.

Symone certainly would love it too. She constantly discussed why African-Americans needed to receive an acute paradigm shift regarding culture, pride, opportunity, economic development, and whatever else she believed necessary for the cause and the advancement of Black folks. Not only would Symone be ecstatic about Lenda, she'd also politely question Lenda to find out if she attended a predominantly Black college and to see if she knew if any African-Americans had a financial interest in the restaurant. All of Symone's friends labeled her Malcolm X, Jr. Just thinking about Symone's fervency for the cause made Alex laugh quietly to herself.

While Alex waited for Pecola and Symone, she sipped water and reviewed her Cambridge weekly calendar. Since she resigned almost five years ago from D. Britt & Cox, North Carolina's number one law firm, she advised both family and friends that she wanted a free schedule but a full one. To date, Alex received exactly what she desired and enjoyed every moment of it.

A woman who drew peace about life from a steel-lined inner serenity, Alex possessed the amazing, personal resolve of a mini Green Beret platoon. She volunteered at her children's pre-school, at Baptist Hospital, and at her church. She served on boards, worked in the trenches with Winston-Salem's low-income youth, planned wonderful celebrations for friends, and basked in the freedom of simply marinating in the fresh, daily splendors of life.

Finally, at 4:15, Symone and Pecola entered the restaurant, and she waved to get their attention. Alex stood. The huge smile that always graced her pretty face welcomed them as they strutted over, avoiding waiters scurrying around the restaurant which was receiving more patrons by the minute. They hugged and kissed one another fiercely, and Alex presented each with a bouquet of fresh yellow roses wrapped in green lacy paper and ribbons gathered from her private greenhouse earlier that day.

Once they were all seated, Alex complimented Pecola on her gorgeous outfit. Pecola smiled broadly and exclaimed that Symone had complimented her earlier on the exact same thing. While they chatted amongst themselves, Lenda stood by patiently to receive the orders. Pecola selected a glass of champagne. Symone advised she wanted a Bailey's on the rocks, and Alex ordered another Evian with two slices of lemons.

The three ladies became engrossed in an animated, dainty high-five conversation. A woman at a nearby table intently observed the trio over an *USA Today* newspaper and assumed that they were long lost sisters. That wasn't the case. The friends just saw one another for breakfast on Friday morning. However, no matter if one or two days passed, Alex acted like she hadn't seen her two friends in years.

Alex was extremely pretty with thick, long, coarse flowing black hair that hung below her shoulder blades. Symone always joked that there were African-American women with gorgeous hair, and then there was Alex. Most times, she wore it down with a perfectly matching signature headband. But today, her magnificent mane was corralled by a large white bow into a tamed ponytail. Slightly bow-legged with a graceful walk, she stood five feet seven inches tall. Since Alex and Pecola were the same height, Pecola often kidded to other people that Alex was her long, lost fraternal twin sister.

A dark complexioned woman with silky smooth cocoa skin and thick dark eyebrows, long curly lashes, a pointy ethnic nose, full lips, and warm gentle eyes, Alex appeared as if she had been immersed in a vat full of Hershey's Kisses chocolate. The first thing that immediately captivated everyone's attention was the beautiful dimpled smile and the loud, throaty laugh. An unusually unique, deeply spiritual individual ever since she was a child, her personality matched the prettiness, and she never had a cross word to say about anyone.

Both women knew Alex was a best friend when it counted. There were numerous occasions when Alex actually caressed them as a mother would a child. During those sad moments, Pecola and Symone cried like small children with their faces in her lap or on her shoulders—anywhere she could comfort them. Alex's husband, Madison, was concerned people who didn't know her would take her kindness for weakness. But he also said that he always felt better when he realized that Alex's two barracuda, female running buddies were nearby and wouldn't allow such a thing to happen when he wasn't around.

Alex was such an astonishingly meek and humble woman with a wise heart. It was almost as though the gods bestowed her with a spirit that was something of an innocent, delicate and rare flower. She always first thought of everyone else.

Symone and Pecola were extremely protective of her. And Madison was accurate with the barracuda description of them because they would fight people like twenty viciously trained pit bulls if they even thought someone attempted to hurt Alex's feelings. She didn't demand such adoration from them. It grew to such a level throughout the years. However, she cherished them in the same manner, and even though both women could afford anything they desired to buy, she still pampered and loved them like a fairy godmother.

Pecola said that she heard someone explain that the better people a person has as a friend, the better those people became as friends. The statement was absolutely true. Alex set the tone for their long-time relationship, which from the very beginning was based upon love, camaraderie, and the investment of sharing. Symone always told folks that Alex was a consummate genius for enjoying life. To just have Alex around and to just know her as a soul friend was truly one of her unexpected yet greatest gifts about moving to North Carolina.

A believer in exercise, Alex jogged two miles a day to maintain the svelte size eight figure. She remained a constant, quiet reminder to the others that they needed to watch their weight and lose the extra twenty pounds. A corporate attorney for a decade, she resigned the junior partnership when God blessed her with a miracle. It was when she was five months pregnant with son, Madison Nehemiah Devereaux, III, called Trey for short. Alex had been pregnant four prior times with them all ending in miscarriages in the first trimester. So determined to have this child, she kissed the corporate world good-bye at a time she earned a six-figure income, plus bonuses. Now, Alex was also the mother of a three-year old daughter named Purity Phylicia.

Alex and Madison, a pediatric neurosurgeon in Winston-Salem, raised their family in the small town of Advance, a quaint farming community sixteen miles from the big city of Winston-Salem. There the Devereauxs lived in a twenty-seven room country home, excluding bathrooms, with three Cocker Spaniels and a menagerie of other critters.

Even as a child, it was always Alex's ambition to build a home in Advance. When she was a young girl, Alex's father often drove his family out to Advance after church on Sundays to visit the owners of the McIntyre Plantation. The McIntyres was a white family entrenched in old money and for whom Alex's parents had worked for years. Alex grew up roaming the rolling hills and huge, grand, old rooms. After Alex's parents died, she and Madison discovered the most exquisite three-hundred-fifty acres with a spring fed lake in Advance. They knew that this was where they would build their home and raise a family.

Within a week of walking the land and researching architectural prototypes, Alex and Madison made the decision about the type of house they wanted built. Along with the help of Pecola, Symone, and Billy, as well as everyone else they knew those early years, Alex and Madison designed a spacious, lovely home for the six children the Devereauxs planned to have. With the towering oaks dotting the landscape, Alex and Madison believed the property would be an excellent place for their kids and even their adult friends to climb trees. They were right.

Thirteen years ago and after several minor design changes, Carlos' firm began construction. Today, the red brick Georgian mansion remained a country showplace. Anyone that knew the Devereauxs enjoyed attending the many affairs held there. Scott, a commercial pilot and friend who was like a brother to the three women, often joked that the only thing missing from the estate was an airstrip for him to land an airplane.

Alex, Pecola, and Symone had been such true, devoted and ferociously close friends for so many years. Alex first met Pecola in the senior Dr. Devereaux pediatrician's office in downtown Winston-Salem. It was on a Friday afternoon in November almost twenty years ago. Madison had just arrived home from Duke University where he was a second-year medical student. He needed to visit with his father and asked Alex to wait in the reception area.

In August of the same year, CR Construction Group opened its Winston-Salem headquarters with Carlos at the helm. At the same time, the twenty-one year old Pecola who was newly moved to the city, had three small children in tow with another one on the way.

While Pecola waited for the pediatric nurse to call their names for the two o'clock appointment with Dr. Devereaux, she struggled to keep the toddlers occupied. Alex observed the young mother's valiant attempts. Alex desperately loved children and wanted to provide the youthful woman a moment to breathe. So Alex began playing with the two oldest boys, Carlos, III, called CJ, and Haneef, who was the knee baby. With thumb in mouth, Elizabethe, Pecola's youngest child at the time, clutched her mother's widening waist.

After chitchatting with Pecola for several minutes, Alex was thoroughly amazed that the frail, skinny young woman with sparkling green eyes was the same age as she and managed to simultaneously raise a family and attend college at A&T. Alex was a senior with a double major in English and political science at Winston-Salem State University. It took all the strength she could muster with no children to just maintain a perfect 4.0 grade point average. Alex became fascinated with Pecola's determination and spunk and volunteered to baby-sit whenever she was available.

In a short time, the relationship blossomed into a unique alliance that spread to Carlos and Madison. When Pecola met Symone a few years later, she was introduced to Alex. Along with Symone and Billy, an architect and founder of a three-month old architectural firm at the time, the young couples developed the common, close attachments.

However, the three women's bond was much different, and they experienced such a rich friendship. Not in a monetary sense. But with camaraderie, spirit, and unconditional love for one another. Without a doubt, they got on each other nerves, yet they adored each other tremendously. But it also went deeper than that. Neither Pecola nor Symone realized it back then, but Alex knew. She always believed their friendship was a miracle and would last a lifetime. Alex understood how simple, everyday chance meetings were just divine avenues necessary for three women to come together and embark upon the road of sharing an extraordinary and inseparable relationship.

The years flew by. The friends attended the usual bevy of college homecomings, football games, sorority, fraternity, and social events. They even traveled the world together. But as was natural with the passage of much time and the advancement of empowering maturity, they suffered profound heartache, pain, break-ups and sorrow. While traveling through the many years together, the friends experienced the unanticipated brutal bumps, bruises, and detours along the way. During those acutely heart-wrenching periods, Alex poignantly explained with tears in her eyes that it was the typical price each person paid to walk the unique journey called life. And it was called pain and suffering—especially during moments of extraordinary tragedy.

Alex laughed loudly several times as she listened to Symone blankly discuss the miserable weekend with Arman. While she and Pecola enjoyed browsing for antique furniture and clothes, they constantly wondered how the weekend was going with Symone.

Lenda stopped by for the third time, and they finally placed their orders for the entree. Alex ordered baked flounder, rice pilaf, and a salad. Since Pecola and Symone enjoyed the light lunch with The Zawadi Corporation officials, they opted to share a house salad and another round of drinks. Alex raised an eyebrow over the menu, but the two jokingly told her to mind her own business about their drinking habits.

Halfway through the entree and since Symone was thoroughly exhausted from sharing the Arman saga, the discussion moved to The Zawadi Corporation. Alex was proud to hear that all went well. She said that she put the meeting in the Imani Box and would continue to pray MO received the coveted account. Alex also told Pecola how pretty the eighteen-carat gold diamond watch looked with her black dress and that Carlos certainly had excellent taste. Pecola smiled all over the place as she basked in hearing another compliment. Lenda arrived with hot rolls and additional blue cheese for Pecola, and both women watched amused as she placed fat laden clumps on the already drenched salad.

"...Pecola, I stopped by your parents' house on my way back from Burlington today. They asked me to tell you hey," Alex said while sipping Evian. Pecola acted as if she didn't hear the comment. As usual, the silence spoke volumes.

"You heard me, girl," persisted a smiling Alex. "They gave me six jars of canned string beans, two dozen eggs, and a half shoulder of sugar cured country ham."

"Hmmm. I could use some of that," Symone mumbled. She chewed a cucumber and watched Pecola's reaction. Alex placed the fork on the plate and stared in Pecola's face.

"Girl, I'm serious. Madison's going to have a fit. I'm talking about sugar cured country ham."

"That's good, chile. I'll call them tonight," Pecola lied brightly as she nibbled Iceberg lettuce.

Pecola's parents lived on a fifteen-acre farm on the other side of Greensboro. Whenever someone visited, they ended up receiving a country care package of fresh food.

"That country ham is artery clogging food at its finest," Symone noted and gave Alex a high five. "But it's the best."

"You're right, Sy," Alex agreed softly.

"Remind me to go visit them this weekend," Symone exclaimed eyeing Alex through bites of broccoli soaked in thousand island dressing.

Symone's ex-husband was from Tarboro, a place known to be one of the smallest towns in North Carolina. Since Symone's in-laws were entrenched in the southern tradition of providing home-grown care packages to visitors, she knew how wonderful it was to still receive boxes of preserves and various other goodies from Pecola's parents.

Pecola listened intently. She watched the passing traffic and noticed a sleek, red Ferrari zoom by and assumed it was Alex's brother-in-law. At the mention of her parents, Pecola felt a slight nervous pain in her chest. However, no one would ever know that from Pecola's facial expression. She was a sphinx when it came to any discussions about her parents, so she smiled and gave the impression all was fine. Symone and Alex were enjoying the good-natured questioning and realized it was time for Pecola to change the subject. She did. They winked at one another knowingly.

With a big little girl pout, Pecola suddenly asked why they hadn't inquired about her well-being since the death of her dogs. Pecola's two Schnauzers, Jed and Clampett, turned fifteen this year. A habitual watcher of three television shows, *Lifestyles of the Rich and Famous, The Andy Griffith Show*, and *The Beverly Hillbillies*, Pecola named the dogs after the rags to oil riches patriarch, Jed Clampett.

Because of severe arthritis, Clampett was put to sleep three months ago. The other one, Jed, died of natural causes two weeks before Pecola's fortieth birthday party in May. The dogs' deaths were traumatic for Pecola. She missed them desperately and was constantly in depression about it. While speaking to Alex and Symone during their evening three-way telephone chats, Pecola often broke down in tears. During those moments, she cried about how quiet the house was since her two dogs were gone.

"...Yall know what I'm going through," Pecola added. "The least yall could do was ask me about my depression."

"Ok, girl. Please forgive me," Alex said in a sincerely apologetic voice while slicing a square of flounder. She wasn't teasing and truly prayed for the Reynolds' family loss. Her three dogs were like her children, and she wouldn't know what to do if they died. Until a person experienced the death of a pet, it was difficult to even imagine the grief surrounding such a loss. "Do you forgive me for not asking?"

"I do," Pecola groaned. "Yall know it's been rough. If it continues, I might have to take a vacation."

"That's an interesting way to handle grief," Symone mumbled.

"How are you doing since you lost your canine babies?" Alex asked for the one-hundredth time with genuine concern. She squeezed lemon on a small section of her flounder, stuck it in her mouth and waited for a reply from Pecola. In the meantime, Symone mumbled that she was sorry her two canine, godchildren died unexpectedly. Before Pecola answered, she made sure her mouth was clear of food.

"Honeychile, I'm doing just fine," she quickly informed the two. She dabbed each corner of her mouth with the linen napkin and swallowed several gulps of champagne. Pecola thought rapidly for her benefit and theirs. She refused to ever allow her friends to figure out the secret regarding her distant feelings toward her parents.

"So what are you going to do about it?" Symone asked. "Carlos mentioned to me that he's thinking about getting you another dog."

"We're only talking about it. I'm just going to get two more dogs again. That's all. This time," she continued and hesitated ever so slightly with a mischievous smile on her face. "I plan to name them Robin and Leach."

Alex and Symone vigorously shook their heads, lifted their glasses in a toast, and burst out laughing. Pecola chuckled loudly too as she carefully eyed her friends.

Good, Pecola thought as she took another sip of champagne while gazing at them over the glass rim. *I'm glad those two still can't figure out why I don't want to see my parents.*

Chapter Five

At about the same time Lenda walked up with the dessert menu and while the women studied it, Scottfeld Broadus Alexander slammed the Porsche door shut and jogged to the Akao Building. He glanced at his watch. It was six o'clock. He wanted to catch Pecola and Symone before they left the office. MO's hours were nine to five. Pecola and Symone normally didn't leave the office until seven or so on Mondays. Their spa was opened nightly until eight, and sometimes they scheduled a late evening massage for themselves.

Scott would have arrived earlier, but Madison insisted that he needed to have one of Scott's old Jerry Butler tapes dubbed for his listening enjoyment. Since Madison wouldn't take no for an answer, one thing led to another. The men talked, played several CDs, munched on potato chips, and gulped down beer. The six men hanging with Scott ended up smoking Cuban cigars and playing a game of pool at Scott's house. They talked, and played several more classic soul CDs while drinking more beer and munching on pretzels.

Today, Scott and forty-nine other Black men from different parts of the United States just returned home from a five-day fishing trip on the banks of Hilton Head, South Carolina. Brothers from all the Black fraternities and colleges hung out, talked, bragged, lied about women, the daily grind, dreams, and back to women again.

The fishing trip all started twelve years ago when Isaiah Ribbs came up with the idea for him and just six friends. A graduate of Tuskegee University, a Kappa brother, and now an appellate judge down in Charlotte, North Carolina, Isaiah thought it would be an excellent way for him to stay in touch with his six friends who lived all over the United States. From that initial first trip, this brother told that brother and so on and so on. And over the years, the fishing trip mushroomed into a truly phenomenal event for the men.

This was the seventh year Scott attended the getaway, and the fun-filled days were absolutely great. The fishing trip simply was a casual meeting of the minds of sort. It gave the Black, fortyish and over men, the majority of whom were high level professionals, time for themselves and an opportunity to bond with one another. In the summer, it was a fishing and golf trip thing for males only. But in the winter, the men journeyed with wives and lady friends in tow to wherever the National Brotherhood of Skiers hosted their summit and mini-summit trips.

Scott opened the tinted door of the Akao Building. The cool, air-conditioned building hit him smack dead in the face, and the chill felt wonderful. Before he made it to the receptionist, he quickly glanced at the four Black women and two men in the lobby. One male he recognized was his sometime golfing buddy and fellow Que brother, Gloster Gantt. Gloster was a retired, professional football player for Tennessee. Several years ago, Gloster moved back home. A very successful businessman, Gloster was a NEWAYS Diamond and was involved in commercial real estate development in the city.

As president of the local alumni association for South Carolina State, Gloster always made sure to remind everyone that SCSU possessed the baddest teams in these whole United States of America. Scott and Gloster laughingly spoke about football and gave each other the Black power handshake. All through their laughter, both men declared they owned bragging rights for their respective colleges. Finally done taking jabs at each other's school, Gloster told Scott that he was at Akao Studios for his weekly manicure and facial appointment.

Gloster and Scott talked for several more minutes, and Gloster explained again to an amused Scott why his wife refused to let him go to Hilton Head this year. Scott teased him repeatedly about the heavy ball and chain around his neck. Gloster jokingly told Scott that he would see what it was like again one day. Gloster returned to his seat with a smile on his face and delved back into the *Harvard Business Review*. Scott noticed the longing stares of the women, took the time to briefly acknowledge each one, and kept on booking toward the mission at hand.

Scottfeld Broadus Alexander was a handsome man with a quiet voice and piercing eyes who always appeared relaxed and cordial. He was six feet five inches tall and possessed a chiseled, mahogany dark cocoa complexion. With a cleft in his chin, a thick mustache, and jet-black curly hair he wore in a closely cropped cut, hair was also his fourth name. The black, wiry chest mass of hair pushed out Scott's shirt collars and ran all the way down to his fingers. Pecola declared that this was an awesome, tempting attraction to even a cock-eyed and blind woman.

Each day Scott needed to shave, or he would look like Moses with a bushy beard. There were moments when he believed that the hair was both a blessing and an onus, and he suffered through the normal Black man shaving routine with the occasional in grown hair and razor bump problems. When Scott was heavily into the man meets woman circuit, the blessing was ladies by the hundreds freaked out about his chest hairs. As a result, he thus received tons of dates. A believer in exercise, Scott's taut muscles softly showed through the creme linen shirt and drawstring baggy pants he casually wore with leather brown sandals.

The female clients in the Akao Studios' reception area subtly eyed Scott several times. They all were wondering who in the hell stuff was he? Damn! Is the brotha single? Engaged? Married? And did he run around just a little bit even if he was somebody else's huzzband?

Another lady exited the spa's massive oak doors and gasped loudly when she saw Scott speaking with the young receptionist behind the cubicle. Scott had just finished hugging the receptionist when he felt three swift taps on his back. Quickly, he turned around. A light-skinned woman who acted like she knew him extremely well was blushing and grinning widely.

"Hey, Scott. How are you doing?" she asked loudly, basking in the fact that it was obvious he should know her, too.

"Hello there," he responded as his mind raced to figure out who in the hell she was. She grabbed his left arm for the benefit of the other women in the lobby and for her own to feel his buff biceps.

Dressed in a tight Ralph Lauren white polo shirt, navy micro-mini tennis skirt, white sneakers, socks, and sun-visor, she looked forty-five or so. But the snug-fitting attire made her appear as an overgrown teenager. Scott noticed faint dimples of cellulite on each thigh. He realized that the outfit must be a uniform. With thighs like that, the woman sho-nuff wasn't playing the tennis game. The woman squeezed Scott's arm even tighter, and her broad smile revealed clean teeth.

Whew! I'm glad to see they sparkle, Scott thought as he grinned back.

The other women's legs were crossed; they were sitting stoically on the leather couches. They were intently watching to see how the interesting scene between Scott and the woman would unfold.

Shapely Gordonetta Miles glanced at the show over the pages of *Black Child* magazine. She thought, *That man don't know your behind, sistergirl. Sit your Black behind down. Plus, you're talking too loud.* Gordonetta rolled her eyes miserably at whatever she didn't know; she just felt like doing it. She flipped several pages and tried to read.

"Ms. Miles, will you follow me, please?" the receptionist announced. Now Gordonetta was an attractive woman. Dressed in a form fitting black knit dress with white dots, she stood up and swished her way through the oak doors leading to the spa. The extra twisting of her waist was done for the benefit of the handsome Scott, and especially now for Gloster, since she heard he was a Que, and a former professional athlete.

"I'm Desiree Coleman, Scott," the woman said looking up into Scott's face.

"Oh, ok. Ok," Scott mumbled.

"You know me. I'm Pecola's friend. We're AKAs together. Remember? You danced with me at Pecola's surprise birthday party back in May. Remember?" she convinced him and herself too. "I was the one who rescued the sistah in the pool? Remember me now?"

The remaining three women sitting in the reception area gazed steadily in Scott's direction and were awaiting his response. One Black woman seething with anger about life went so far as to place a small one-hundred dollar wager in her mind that he would crack Desiree's face as she believed he had no idea who she was. There was a moment of silence. The three women were mentally on the edges of their seats.

As if it would help, Scott removed his black Oakley sunglasses. No, hell he *still* didn't remember who she was. He danced with a lot of women at Pecola's fortieth birthday party that night. But the ones he recalled were his closest friends. The others were merely blank faces in the crowd. Why pop her bubble? Once again, Scott laughed inwardly. He realized that what Symone and Pecola often teased him about was indeed quite accurate. He was truly a bona fide Alex convert through and through and refused to hurt anyone's feeling unless it was absolutely necessary.

"Remember me now, Scott?" Desiree continued when she noticed a small smile creep onto his face.

"Yeah I do. How ya doing, Desiree?" He extended a hand. She pulled it over her shoulders and hugged his waist tighter than she held his arm just moments earlier.

"I knew you knew. After I rescued the sistah out of the pool, everyone remembered me," Desiree bragged. "I was a hero that night."

Scott decided to ignore the rescue comment right now. When he heard about the pool incident, he was playing a game of eight ball in the basement playroom with Madison, as Carlos and a few other brothers looked on.

"That was a great party wasn't it?" Scott continued.

"Yes it was," she said while glaring victoriously at the other women out the corner of her eyes as if she knew what they were thinking. She turned to face Scott again and smiled up at him. "You know my huzzband said that he was on a Northworld flight to Los Angeles, and he saw you in the cockpit, Scott. "

A pretty, single, and very eligible woman dressed in a banker's uniform, navy suit with white blouse, eyes shot up from the pages of *Black Enterprise* magazine. Her interest level for Scott zoomed up when she heard that the tall walking perfection of a Black man was a commercial pilot. *Girlfriend, you say that brotha is a what?* she thought. The woman subtly dug into her burgundy Aigner pocketbook. Without removing her compact from inside her pocketbook, she checked for any facial flaws or cracks in the caked on Iman liquid foundation and to see if there was lipstick on her teeth.

She realized it was too late to do anything about the brown make-up smeared on the edges of her white collar. According to the clock on the wall, it was 6:10. Her appointment was scheduled for 6:30. She rose and strolled to ask the receptionist a question she already knew the answer to. She just wanted to get a better view of that Scott man from the front. On the way back to her seat, she gave Scott an inviting smile and a hungry expression. Scott returned the grin but ignored the look.

To regain Scott's attention, Desiree gently squeezed his arm with her newly polished, long red fingernails.

"...I'm sorry," Scott mumbled. "What did you just say, Desiree?"

"My huzzband, baby. He saw you. He was on a flight out of Greensboro going to the West Coast."

"I see."

"My huzzband says that you're the tallest pilot he's ever seen."

"He's right. I'm much taller than most," Scott said, still smiling. "In fact, I've been told I am the tallest one Northworld has."

"Is that right?"

"Yep."

"Then you *do* know my husband."

"Well, er..."

"Surely you know *my* huzzband, Wesley? He's a Kappa and a Barber Scotia College man. You know the one?" she added in a slow, gravelly southern voice no doubt brought on by sipping too many vodka and orange juices.

The other smartly dressed woman sitting in the reception area once again mentally wagered one-hundred dollars that Scott wouldn't recognize Desiree's husband. A transplanted

Bostonian convicted of unprovoked assault and battery charges a mere two years ago, the woman began nervously chewing on her right thumb. She wondered why southern Black folk always expected people to know whom in the hell they were talking about just because they mentioned some stupid fraternity, sorority, or college name. She definitely would discuss this reception room charade with Emma Belle. Emma Belle was the chic, blonde haired, white lady who styled her hair every two weeks and whom she assumed was the *real* owner of Akao Studios.

If that Desiree woman spoke another two minutes and continued to disturb the lobby guests with the trivial bull jive conversation, the woman from Boston had already decided she was going to scratch Desiree's eyes out. Only on behalf of Emma Belle, of course.

"Wesley certainly knows you," Desiree went on. "He always points you out to me."

"Wesley—Wesley," Scott wondered, trying to place the name.

"My Wesley is the vice president at National Bank in Winston-Salem. He works at the Knollwood Road office," Desiree purred as she slowly swayed to the sounds of The Intruders' *Cowboys to Girls.*

Yep, this must be Monday, Scott thought with a grin. *Pecola dug into the archives and got the old jam music kickin' as usual. Ok, Desiree. Hell, enough was enough.*

No, Scott wasn't familiar with Wesley. He dealt with the Black bank, Mechanics and Farmers. He didn't know Desiree. He didn't know her husband either. Scott glanced at his watch. Maybe this would clue her that he was in a hurry. Pecola had so many damn casual friends. Every time he turned around, there was another party or affair at another soror's house.

Scott thought about the Wesley name for another moment. The lobby was deathly quiet. Everyone sitting around could hear themselves breathe. He kept a straight face and nodded his head slowly.

"...And Wesley was elected to the Black Chamber of Commerce in—" Desiree was still bragging on about her husband.

"Yeah, I *do* know Wesley. Tell him I said hey, too." He quickly hugged Desiree again and walked toward the gate leading to upstairs.

Whew! Two female clients breathed another envious mental sigh of relief for Desiree even though at this point she was getting on their nerves, too. The other angry woman from Boston checked her fake Rolex watch. Good. There was thirty seconds left on her watch. That Desiree woman was one lucky lady. If Desiree had run out of time, the Boston woman thought *that Desiree's behind would've been mine.* She glared at Desiree with eyes identical to narrow slits.

"Scott! Oh, Scott," Desiree yelled after him. "Will you be at Pecola's 4th of July barbecue?"

"Yeah," Scott said nodding and without turning around.

What a nice guy, thought another lady. *That Scott man didn't know that Desiree woman from Adam's house cat. He certainly didn't know who Wesley was, either. I can always tell when a man is lying. My huzzband does it all the damn time!* She glanced over the cover of *Today's Black Woman* magazine. After smiling sweetly at the cute receptionist, the woman angrily flipped the page as she viciously thought about her philandering spouse.

Just as Scott turned left to take a jog up the stairs to the second floor, Elisha was stepping out of the elevator. They embraced one another fondly.

"...So they're not here?" Scott finally asked after speaking briefly with Elisha.

"No. Pecola and Symone scheduled a 4:00 date with Alex at O'Charley's," Elisha said to Scott while glancing down at her wristwatch. It was 6:15. "They're probably gone by now."

"Thanks for the 411, baby. You look good today, girl. Real good." Elisha blushed profusely. It was all internally because Scott couldn't tell one millimeter degree of change in Elisha's professional looking countenance. "See you, Elisha. I'm outta here."

Scott jogged backed out to his car and eased in. He told his best buddy, Rozelle, that they were heading over to O'Charley's.

Chapter Six

You can always tell a Morehouse Man, but you can't tell him much—especially when there are goals to be achieved! Those were the words, plus a few more, Scott added, that he heard on a daily basis as a student at the prestigious African-American all male college. And, he lived such a philosophy even before he reached Atlanta from his hometown of New Orleans, Louisiana.

Scott grew up in a traditional, old-fashioned Negro family of tall men, with the shortest one being six one. Simply put, the father was the head of the household, and the mother followed his instructions. Deacon Lindsay Anthony Alexander's words were not only law but also a refuge of glorious knowledge. Since he wanted his four sons to grow up in a home atmosphere that bred nothing but success, he was their consummate educator—their living example of character, integrity, and sensitivity.

When Scott was three years old, his mother enrolled him and twin brother, Granville, in kindergarten. They were tall enough and were quick learners. Since Thony Mae Alexander taught them all she could, she realized that it was time to get them in school. Older brothers Romallus and Lindsay, Jr. were placed in classes at the same tender age. So Thony Mae decided to do likewise with the two smarter baby boys even though their father preferred they wait until the official age of five.

Their parents' heated discussion about Scott and Granville attending the McDonogh Number Six Elementary School was the first and only argument Scott recalled in the Alexander home. It just wasn't done. But many years later, a girlfriend was pissed off as hell at Scott over trivial bull she imagined to be true and wanted to actually have a knock down drag out fist fight with him. She asked Scott if he ever argued, raised his voice or ever slapped a woman out of anger; he calmly told her no.

More than anything, Scott remembered the laughter that flowed freely from his parents. The Alexander boys basked in the knowledge that not only did their parents worship their children, but they also worshipped each other. Many nights, Scott listened to the happy chuckles that floated from his parents' bedroom. He didn't know what they were talking about or even what they were doing in there. But he knew that whatever it was, his mother enjoyed it immensely and chortled loudly and long. Scott enjoyed laughing too and knew he developed easy laughter from his mother.

A child practiced what he or she learned from his or her parents. And when Scott thought back on his life, he was taught love, the pursuit of education, to be fair, to talk things out, and to read, read, read. Books and magazines were everywhere. Whenever his father came home from work, he brought a new book for each son. His parents believed that having books around the Alexander household wasn't a luxury but an absolute, paramount necessity. Or as

Scott's Mama would say all the time as she read to her sons, "Baby boys, dem books are the best vitamins dere is for the mind."

Since Lindsay, Sr. worked as a sleeping car porter with the N&W Railroad and was out of town often, the four boys were wonderfully nurtured by their mother. Thony Mae was the pianist for Second Baptist Church Sixth District, a deaconess, a solid as a rock friend to all, and a dependable neighbor. A very tough disciplinarian, the brothers declared that as they got older, she was essentially responsible for their successes and also laid the foundation for their passion for knowledge. Plus, she always, always told her sons that the Alexander boys could go anywhere, do anything, and be anybody. And they believed her.

Back then, they were known in the uptown, clannish New Orleans community of the Thirteenth Ward for their affectionate ways and manners. Even now when they go back to New Orleans, older people in the neighborhood along Pierrier Street where the Alexander home still swings with an open door hospitality philosophy always ask, "Look a-here, look a-here, aren't you Thony Mae and Lindsay Anthony's boy...?"

Their father, on the other hand, taught them to be leaders in the world, to always look people in the eye, especially the white man, and to strive for excellence in any endeavor pursued. It was a wonderful combination. Even today, Scott wistfully reflected on those days as a child. His Pop would always hold the two eldest boys tightly on his lap. His Mama embraced him and Granville as they read to them voraciously. Each and every chance they got, Scott's parents read a wide variety of books to their children. Afterwards, his mother always laughed loudly and played the piano while they sang popular tunes. The four young boys, with their mouths raised to the ceiling, cracked on every other note. His parents were both avid blues singers and belted out songs like professionals. Even though his mother performed the reading and singing ritual when his father wasn't around, Scott enjoyed the affinity of the tender moments more so when his Pop was home. It was such a warm, loving home. When a child grew up in such a way, it was expected by the children and hoped that their parents would live forever. And if and when they should die, their children couldn't even fathom a life without them.

Since Scott started school at three, he enrolled at Morehouse when he just turned sixteen and graduated when he was almost twenty. Ever since he was eight years old, he knew which career path he wanted to take. With a major in aeronautical engineering, he mapped out the necessary steps to become the most successful commercial pilot in the entire world. A cadet of ROTC in college, he served in the Air Force for six years, again astutely focused on the road that would lead to achieving the ultimate goal.

Those aspirations occurred at an excellent time for Scott. As a result of affirmative action and the sudden urgency by Northworld Airlines to recruit women and highly qualified Black men to become pilots, Scott was hired by the company whose headquarters were located in North Carolina. For the first time in his life, he stepped foot in the southern, sleepy town of Winston-Salem to participate in the company's orientation and training program. That was over sixteen years ago.

The airline was a tightly run organization operated by Sanford born millionaire, Harris Alvin Greater, IV. A former pilot and marketing expert, who got tired of working for Pan American Airlines, Greater decided to use his daddy's money. As a result of blue-blood family ties, his iron-clad control of management, and his fastidious concern for the bottom line on financial reports, today the thirty-five year old airline remained number one in the world and stayed profitable in a volatile industry.

Fortunately for Scott's ambitions, the number of employees tripled since he joined the company. With the rapid expansion of Northworld into a variety of worldwide markets, he rose through the ranks and quickly achieved every goal he set. Now, at the age of forty-two, Scott piloted the 757 jets. It was a coveted assignment he received just this year, two weeks before his birthday in May. He had finally made it and was promoted from first officer to captain. Once again, he realized that he was dead on target as he had planned to fly the jumbo planes with the title of captain beside his name by the time he turned forty-five.

As was customary when career was the number one priority, there were the typical, relationship losses attributed to the quest. And unfortunately, Scott's marriage became a casualty. He married Rose Bobbie Stewart, his long-time girlfriend and the Black homecoming queen their senior year at Booker T. Washington High School in New Orleans. Two queens were nominated that year, one Black and the other white. The pretty Rose Bobbie received the unanimous support of both racial groups. She and Scott declared eternal puppy love for one another and from the ninth to the twelfth grades, the two were inseparable.

However, while Scott selected Morehouse College, Rose Bobbie chose to stay in Louisiana and attended Southern University at New Orleans. Scott believed the rift between the two began to surface even then. But both resolved to remain true to the high school sweetheart commitments of the white picket fence fantasy and the two point five children. In July of the same year of their college graduations, they married.

Rose Bobbie worked as a registered nurse. They bought a house. She became pregnant the first and the second year of the marriage. Eight years and two sons later, they were divorced. Yet, to this day, both Rose Bobbie and Scott remained cordial friends and still spend the holidays together.

During his marriage and on the days he was in town, Scott attempted to raise his boys in the same fashion he and his brothers were. He read to them constantly. Since Scott inherited his mother's musical and singing genes, he was an excellent pianist and possessed the natural ability to play either classical or down home blues proficiently.

At every opportunity, Scott always played the living room Wurlitzer upright piano and sang to Rose Bobbie while one boy sat on his left and the other one on his right. And just like his father, he schooled his sons to be leaders and constantly showed fatherly affection. Today, Scottfeld Broadus "BJ" Jr., the oldest one, and Granville "GJ" Jr., the baby boy, both stood almost as tall as their father at six feet four. They too were graduates of Morehouse, aspired to be superstar rap artists, and lived in Los Angeles.

Before Scott and Rose Bobbie broke up, they had several lengthy discussions about which parent should raise the boys. Eventually, Rose Bobbie received legal custody of the children. Initially, Scott recalled his childhood days, the nurturing of the strong father image and tried to fight it. Slowly but surely, he realized it wouldn't be fair to the boys, especially with him being out of town so frequently, and ultimately issued a no contest plea to the claim. To be near her family, Rose Bobbie returned to Louisiana and obtained a nursing job at Charity Hospital in New Orleans.

Since Scott felt the same responsibility toward his marriage as his father, he truly wanted to make the union work. Although when it didn't, he remained committed to the family. Throughout the years, Scott never shrugged off his paternal loyalty and made it a point to fly home to be with his sons, sometimes as often as once a week, if even just for a day.

Now as Scott looked back, it certainly was an excellent move to give Rose Bobbie custody of their sons. She was extremely settled, quiet, and worked the same eight to four nursing schedule year after year. The boys needed the stability. Scott was similar to a few of his buddies who married right out of Morehouse, then a few years later, they were divorced for various reasons. The House brothers discovered the word "pussy" was synonymous with damn great feelings and realized there was a whole lot of catching up to do.

After the divorce, Scott briefly transferred to several different cities with Northworld Airlines. His last move was from Newark to Houston, a city alive with excitement and bustling with women. Once there and because he could, he tried to screw everything that wasn't tied down since AIDS wasn't an issue back then, and wild, freaky sex was thought safe. Even the women who were tied down, Scott released them from whatever bondage they were under and screwed them, too. Married, single, engaged, judges, lawyers, and flight attendants, it didn't matter. It could be orgies or whatever. Name the place. Hell, name the state was Scott's motto. Scott would fly there to knock her boots, and any friends too, through the roof.

A few years later, Scott received a coveted opportunity to relocate to corporate headquarters in Winston-Salem and once again, the women were his to choose. And he did. However, a little more carefully as AIDS began to surface on the scene. Nevertheless, he still raved to close friends about the quaint southern city, the women, and the great times.

One such college buddy took Scott's conversations about Winston-Salem to heart. It was the crazy but smart Rozelle Gary Bellisarion. He was a fellow Que and Morehouse graduate who doubled majored in math and physics in undergrad and who decided to move his family eastward. A graduate of Harvard Business School, Rozelle was an unwilling participant of one too many earthquake jolts plus aftershocks on the West Coast. Rozelle, who was two years older than Scott, put out opportunity feelers in North Carolina.

Seven and half years ago, the headhunter agencies began their work. The already successful Rozelle received several plum opportunities. But the best one offered to him was with the M. Karenga Chemical Corporation. It was a Fortune 500 pharmaceutical empire located right in High Point, North Carolina, also known as the furniture capital of the world. Pleased with the lucrative deal, Rozelle and his wife, Jodria, moved their family to Winston-Salem.

Both native Tennesseans, Jodria and Rozelle said that it was high time for them and their four children to experience the seasons. Now, the parents of six children ages three to twelve,

Rozelle declared fertility vitamins must have been in the Winston-Salem water because the last two Bellisarion children were born after they moved to North Carolina.

Jodria Anne was a plump, pecan-tan complexioned woman. Standing about five four with bright eyes and a magnetic smile, she possessed a somewhat naive but understanding attitude about Rozelle. Nominated as the diet of the week most faithful member by Pecola, Jodria constantly discussed how she needed to lose the extra thirty pounds glued on her small frame. Nicknamed JAB by her closest friends, Jodria received an undergraduate degree from Spelman College and earned a graduate degree in child psychology from Dillard University. As was with all her friends, Jodria was entrenched in the sorority scene and was a devoted sister of Sigma Gamma Rho.

After Rozelle and Jodria moved to Winston-Salem, Jodria realized that she was tired of working and decided to stay home. And like she told Scott, Rozelle earned enough money for six well-paid people. So why should she kill herself, too? Since Rozelle and Jodria both were employed when they lived in California, an older Mexican woman lived with the family. But a housekeeper wasn't necessary once the move was made south. Jodria handled Rozelle and the children like an octopus statistician and only needed cleaning services twice a week.

Since there was a tremendous difference between the cost of living in San Francisco and Winston-Salem, the Bellisarions' were able to sell their home on the West Coast and coup an astounding profit. With the extra money earned, six months after they arrived in North Carolina, they built a beautifully spacious seven bedroom French Provincial home near the Black community of Castleshire Woods located in Winston-Salem.

With his signature gold, wire rimmed glasses, Rozelle was another story. He was a very clean shaven, attractive, distinguished looking dark-skinned man, with a pug nose and thick lips minus a mustache. A Black man without the signature hair above the lips was a rarity but understandable when one knew Rozelle's position in the company. As senior executive vice president of chemical development, Rozelle was the highest ranking Black official in the M. Karenga Chemical Corporation. Rozelle often said that not having a mustache was the only characteristic he patterned from his white boy colleagues at Karenga.

During the day, Rozelle wore custom tailored dark suits, winged tip shoes, and magnificently white starched, button down shirts with silk striped ties. This super intelligent Black man was deeply ensconced in white corporate America. However by night, the brilliant man with the lean hard body was the Rozelle Roving Ranger. People were definitely impressed with Rozelle's Harvard Degree credentials and expected to meet a stuck-up Black man who wanted to be white. That wasn't the case with Rozelle. He moved among the smartest minds in the world, but Rozelle remained a soul brother to his heart.

Rozelle boogied down with the best of them and knew every nightclub and strip club's address, telephone number, and hours of operations within a seventy-five mile radius of his house. Rozelle told everyone he was six feet, but they were convinced he was five eleven, if that tall. The crazy acting Rozelle often proclaimed himself the self-professed ladies' man of the century. It was nothing for Rozelle to shock everyone and break out in a Karl Kani hip hop uniform of an oversized shirt, baggy pants, a baseball cap, and sneakers just to play golf with the fellows on Saturday morning.

Both Rozelle's parents were math professors at Fisk University, and he followed in their footsteps by pulling a double major in college. All of his friends, including his wife who tried to rationalize why he had a wild hair up his butt, were thoroughly convinced that Rozelle's radical behavior was the result of the other Bellisarions' siblings ability to solve complex trigonometric problems by the age of ten.

Mathematics was the Bellarions' life. Naturally it was a shock to all when Rozelle discovered that there was more to living than algorithmic calculus quotients. This discovery occurred a little late in life. It was after he was married. Nevertheless, Rozelle went berserk chasing the skirts, and he became resident comedian along the way when he realized his other new mission in life was to amuse everyone.

Oftentimes, Rozelle's friends suggested he should give his laughter to the people in comedy clubs because Rozelle was often the center of attention. The always funny Rozelle moved people to either laugh hysterically or punch him unmercifully. He performed crazy antics just like Eddie Murphy. On a number of occasions, Jodria threatened to write a pleading letter inviting Mr. Murphy to visit Winston-Salem for a meeting with his protégé.

About four years ago, Rozelle discovered somehow or another that Symone was attracted to extremely intelligent and freaky men. According to rumor, she probably discussed this fact with him during one of those evenings when Symone got high as a kite on too many Courvoisier VSOP filled champagne glasses. Whatever happened, rumor has it that Symone told Rozelle of her very specific, explicit sexual requirements. Since Symone's drunken confession, Rozelle constantly propositioned Symone. He reminded her that he was one to be reckoned with. However, since Symone and Jodria vowed to be great friends, Symone ignored the potential research opportunity with Rozelle.

Although Rozelle's heart was permanently sealed to his college sweetheart, alias devoted wife and to their six children to whom he was a wonderful father, Rozelle was thoroughly captivated with Alex. He declared confidentially to Scott a million times that she had the most beautiful, gentle face he had ever seen.

Rozelle, often said, "Wooo, man! Alex has all the glamour and the realness in the world. And that's the epitome for any damn man. The best of both worlds is an ultimate fantasy."

As always, Scott told Rozelle to not even attempt to go over there with Alex, not with that kind of hunger for her. However, Rozelle ignored him. But, it was Rozelle's dream for his mind and his mind alone because Alex refused to allow her thoughts to travel to anyone other than Madison. Even though they had known each other almost seven years now, Rozelle's fantasy didn't wane. Still, whenever Rozelle saw Alex's lovely shaped bowed legs walk in a room, he shook his head, licked his lips slowly several times, and silently hollered, "Umph, Umph, Umph, Umph Umph."

Scott backed his car out of the Akao parking lot just as Rozelle inserted the other CD he purchased in Hilton Head. The two men listened quietly to the angelic voice of Deborah Cox and resumed the earlier discussion they were having during the drive over to the Akao Building from Scott's house.

"You're crazy, Rozelle," Scott said as he stopped for a red light. He turned to stare in his face. "One of these days, Jodria Anne is gonna kick your Black ass all over Winston-Salem. You know you deserve it, man."

While watching traffic out the window, Rozelle was dressed in an oversized Negro League baseball white cotton shirt, cut-off dungarees, sandals, and Morehouse baseball cap and was nodding his head. Slowly, he turned to face Scott's piercing gaze.

"You're right, man. I'm really doing better. Really, I am." He wore a huge grin, still bobbing his head to the music.

"Tell me what *actually* happened?"

"I done told you, man." Rozelle spoke with little patience. "Louise Duncan told her. She's Jodria Anne's soror, so you know what she told her was law, man. Louise should've been minding her own damn business anyway."

"True."

"The nosy witch told my wife that I was screwing Lulu Mae Urich who lives in our neighborhood. Lulu lives three road down from my house."

"Was it true?"

"Of course it was true, man. But I denied everything to Jodria Anne."

"That's understandable." Scott tried not to laugh.

"Check this out," Rozelle said, totally exasperated and hesitated.

"I'm listening."

"Out of curiosity, Jodria Anne drove her mini-van by Lulu's house two weeks ago. She noticed that she was having yard work done, and there was red dirt everywhere." Rozelle was silent for a moment. "A week ago Saturday, I rolled home around one o'clock in the morning."

"Where had you been?"

"At Lulu's house, man. Where do you think? Wooo! That woman is the wildest freak I've run into in years."

"What happened?"

"Sheee-it." Rozelle shook his head from side to side. "I drove my Grand Cherokee into our garage, and you'll never guess what happened?" He didn't wait for Scott to answer. "My jeep had red mud all over the tires."

"Aw no, RB."

"I know, Scott." He paused for a second. "When Jodria Anne saw the red dirt, I said 'Baby, Louise is dead wrong.' Then Jodria Anne walked to the garage door, flung it open, and pointed to the dirt on my tires, man."

"You didn't know she knew mud was on the tire?"

"Hell, until she pointed it out to me, *I* didn't *even* know it was there. It was wild, man. Woooo!" he said in a low voice remembering the obvious incriminating evidence. As Scott watched the traffic in front of him, he shook his head heavily.

"Aw, man. You know that ain't right. How in the hell you get out of that, Rozelle?"

"It was hard." Rozelle clapped his hand and gave Scott a sideways glance. "Man, I almost peed in my pants. Then Jodria Anne came back inside the house and sweetly asked, 'Where did that red dirt come from, Rozelle?' I walked to the door and looked at it, too—like I hadn't seen it before."

"Wooo."

"I told her, 'I don't know. Humph. It wasn't me, baby. I'm not the one seeing that Lulu woman who lives around the corner,'" he said and took a long pause. "Scott, that's my damn story, and I'm sticking to it. I can't get up off it. Ain't no way I'm gonna break weak and tell the truth either."

"Hell, man. It's a big country. Why mess with a woman in your own backyard? That doesn't make any sense, Rozelle. I'm not an angel or anything, but it ain't right. As much as your ass travels, you can have a woman anywhere in the world."

Rozelle slumped deeper in the passenger seat. He continued to stare straight ahead, raised his baseball cap slightly, and scratched his closely cropped hair with his left hand. Scott quickly turned and noticed the reflection of the plain gold wedding band always present on Rozelle's third finger.

What Scott said was true, and Rozelle agreed with him wholeheartedly. He could have a woman anywhere. A woman right around the corner was low-down dog disrespectful. Rozelle traveled to Chicago and New York a lot. Maybe next time, he'd have a frat brother hook him up with someone in the Big Apple.

"What about your other girlfriend? Amalya? The Delta. She's a good-looking redbone. What's her name? The one that has the condo all the way over in Lewisville."

"Shooot! I hate to bestow the title of girlfriend on anyone nowadays," Rozelle said, suddenly perking up as he thought about Amalya's shapely body. "These women out here nowadays are demanding and possessive. All of sudden Amalya is mad as hell because I'm married."

"Whaaat!"

"Man, you know I didn't try to hide sheee-it either," he explained to Scott as he had done so many times before. Scott nodded he understood.

"I'm sure you didn't."

"I laid the cards on the table from the very beginning. I told her I was married and in love with Jodria. But I was just a little mischievous," Rozelle added as he laughed for a moment.

"That's an interesting approach."

"And Amalya knows I love my six children. Now all of a sudden, she acts like I never told her any of this shit. I love my family, man. I ain't leaving my wife for no damn woman." As an afterthought, Rozelle added, "A jealous mistress? Wooo! That's a nightmare I don't need to have."

They reached another red light. For a moment, both men turned to gaze through their respective windows. The light turned green. While driving through three streets of the crawling six o'clock off-from-work traffic, Scott thought about Rozelle's explanation.

"Hell, you might not leave Jodria Anne, but she might leave you, man," Scott announced matter of factly. "Then what ya gonna do?"

While Scott maneuvered the car through Hanes Mall, Rozelle glanced at him a couple of times with a great deal of confusion on his face. It was as if the question had never been posed to him before even though it had. Maybe the ocean salt water that continually splashed on his face while at Hilton Head knocked him into thinking rationally about his adulterous lifestyle. Whatever the reasons, Rozelle's expression changed to one of concern.

Scott pulled into O'Charley's. He parked his sleek, shiny black Porsche straddling the white line of two spaces and cut off the ignition. He reached for the door handle and quickly turned toward Rozelle, who hadn't budged and was fixed with a strange stare. The two men watched one another for a moment.

"So have you figured out what you'll do if Jodria Anne leaves you?"

"I don't know what I'd do if Jodria Anne left me, man," Rozelle replied finally after much thought and as if speaking to himself.

"It figures."

"I really don't know," he added quietly shaking his head still gazing at Scott.

"That's what I thought. Ok? So just remember that shit the next time, man," Scott ended with a laugh and quickly jabbed him on the shoulder. It was rare to see Rozelle look so serious. "Come on, man. Let's go inside."

They touched fists, pointed an index finger at one another, and smiled quickly.

Chapter Seven

O'Charley's was a popular restaurant known for steak and yeast rolls and owned the title of Excellent Restaurant Award in Winston. There was always a long line of would-be-diners all outside O'Charley's front door. On the maitre d' podium rested a white legal size pad, which held the keys for the kingdom or the privilege to pay to eat. At least thirty black lines scratched over names of patrons already dining and the handwritten names of the ones anxiously waiting to enter to eat.

Scott and Rozelle sauntered pass the people milling around laughing and talking. They explained to the unattractive male waiter that they weren't the Ridenhour party of five just announced over the microphone. As the waiter batted his eyes which made Scott think there was a little sugar in his blood, he asked them to puhleeze step aside. Then he waved expansively to the five white people waiting patiently behind them.

Rozelle told Scott that he wanted to make a quick stop to the bathroom. He needed to pee. Plus he was excited about seeing Alex again and wanted to make sure his gold-rimmed glasses were spit shiny clean. From the time Rozelle slammed the car door to the few minutes it took to walk through O'Charley's front ones, just like that, he almost magically forgot the positive words he mentally whispered at least fifty times. "I'm gonna change. I'm gonna change. I'm gonna do better. I don't need to look at another woman."

Scott walked through the entryway and stood by the wooden and glass chest high partition surrounded by plastic benches to see if he saw them. No one was sitting in front of him, and he rested his knee on the end of the bench. He scanned the bar. They weren't there. He stood up quickly, surveyed the tables over the spacious, noisy dining room floor, and spotted them in a corner by the window.

Pecola's back was to him, but it was obvious they were deep in conversation. Symone and Alex's faces were clustered toward her, chins almost on the table, spellbound and listening intently to Pecola's every word. While waiting on Rozelle, Scott leaned on the partition, smiled to himself, and thought about the first time they met years ago.

Scott was lucky to have made life-long friends, and Rozelle was one of them. When Rozelle moved to Winston-Salem, different fraternity brothers told him about the monthly meetings of the Minority Association of Winston-Salem. Known as MAWS, these meetings were held at the Holiday Inn Express on University Parkway. Although Scott was aware of the group, he felt it wasn't a huge priority that he joined. On the other hand, Rozelle thought it would be a fantastic way to quickly meet a bunch of Black folks. To meet successful Blacks and to learn the real deal about the city of Winston, Rozelle became a member shortly after he arrived from the West Coast.

After Rozelle signed up for MAWS, he realized he enjoyed the sessions immensely. For twelve straight months, he invited Scott to attend a meeting. And for an entire year, Scott offered all kinds of ingenious excuses to keep from going. Finally, in January and after the thirteenth month of invites by Rozelle, Scott decided to attend.

The meeting started at 1:00 in the afternoon; however, MAWS officials requested everyone to arrive by 12:00 noon so the serious networking attendees would have an opportunity to socialize and exchange business cards for an hour. At 1:00 promptly, the session began. A review of official business was next. That session normally lasted thirty minutes and ended exactly at 1:30. Each month, different companies paid to sponsor the meeting activities and also to provide a presentation to the over two-hundred and fifty guests. On the day Scott attended, Meetings Odyssey and Akao Studios were the sponsors. Pecola, Symone, and Elisha were up front preparing the ballroom stage for their presentation.

Scott and Rozelle arrived around 1:35. Of course, Rozelle told Scott not to worry because a frat brother called just before he left the office to inform him that he would hold two seats at a great table down by the front. Trying to look professionally inconspicuous with his hands dug deep into his pants pocket, Rozelle walked slowly along the far wall closest to the entrance doors. Searching through the sea of faces, Rozelle was looking for their frat brother, Payton Griffey. After searching five minutes for Griffey, Rozelle and Griffey spotted each other right at the same time. Griffey frantically began waving an index finger at Rozelle.

Rozelle and Scott were in place at the front table no more than five minutes tops when Symone walked up to the podium. She introduced herself, then Pecola, who was standing to her left, and their smiling staff sitting at the front table. As each employee stood up, Pecola and Symone smiled widely and clapped vigorously. Then, the show began. Throughout the sales pitch, the two women took turns speaking, and it was obvious to everybody that they were friends as well as business partners. As if this were general every day information typically shared to packed audiences, they spoke without any degree of pretentiousness. The presentation was efficient, informative, and masterfully done. Simply impressive.

Toward the end, they showed a video that highlighted the Akao Building, the day spa, the MO's client roster, and the goals for each company. It was a stellar performance. Both Pecola and Symone described each company, the services provided there, and their educational backgrounds. Thirty minutes later, it was over. The crowd was spellbound. So were Rozelle and Scott. The intelligence equally displayed by both women was phenomenal, and all of the Black and white male executives were enraptured with the delivery. So were a few women. But the majority of them let envy blind them to the women's talent.

While the crowd clapped for at least two minutes, an extremely pretty woman with flowing black hair walked to the podium. She handed a huge bouquet of pink roses sprinkled with baby breaths to each presenter. Then she embraced and kissed them warmly. While hugging their waists, she strolled with them to their seats.

At the time Scott thought, *Who in the hell are these women? What are your names, baby? And where do you live?*

Scott's fantasy turned into a decision. He was going to first screw the one with the thick, long hair. Then the high-yellow one with the green eyes. Then he would round it off with the tall dark one. All in that order. As the waiter poured tea, Scott continued to observe the women's professional demeanor and noticed that they were the center of attention. The other guys at Griffey's table were oogling and dreaming too, but Scott continued to mentally work out his plan.

Since Griffey was a well-known pharmacist and a long-time native of Winston-Salem, Scott felt sure his frat brother should know the most minute details about the women. But as Griffey reminded him, he was married. His wife kept him chained to her side ever since they returned to Winston after they both graduated from Alcorn State University. Nevertheless, Griffey attempted to give the other brothers sitting around the table his sketchy 411 about each lady. Huddled over their entree of tasteless rubber chicken, silly putty string beans, lifeless salad, and cardboard rolls, the men listened intently to Griffey's skimpy information. As waiters poured tea and delivered plates, the banquet hall hummed with the busy conversation and clatter of silverware of the over two hundred guests.

After the lunch plates were removed, the dessert and coffee were served. The other eight powerful looking Black men at Griffey's table crossed their legs and tried to look cool. Now, they believed they knew just enough about the three attractive Black women and mentally developed the necessary rap to woo at least one. In the meantime, Rozelle kept hunching Scott. Under his breath, Rozelle raved about the one with the thick, long, black hair who also was slightly bowlegged. He went on to explain how he knew from experience that such wonderfully shaped limbs meant she could neatly wrap them around a Black man's ass with ease. Unbeknownst to the three African beauties, while they freely chatted away in their own little world, some serious projections were being made for their future sexual life.

Shortly after, the MAWS meeting ended. A preacher from the Black First Baptist Church on Highland Avenue in Winston delivered a dead prayer. In other words, he told everyone to stand up, shut up, do right, and go back to work. Out the corner of their eyes, the brothers at the table who were bold with plans merely eyed the women from a distance. Then they eased into their black or navy full-length cashmere coats, pushed their chairs in place, and went back to their offices.

Scott and Rozelle decided to hover around. The two were lurking silently like tigers in the African jungle aimed and ready to attack the gazelle. They both knew their outfits screamed EM style and appeared very Ebony Maleish. Normally this impressed the women like Hartz strips of flypaper. Scott was dressed to a T in a Shaka King black three-button wool pinstriped suit, a white linen cuffed shirt, a silk striped tie, black Italian shoes, an alpaca coat, scarf, and snap-brim Fedora. He exhibited a powerful and magnetic presence. Rozelle was basically dressed in a similar fashion with a sleek wool Miguel Navarro suit and appeared as Scott's twin brother. Dressed in navy, he too looked, as older southern Black folk would say, "cleaner than a mosquito's peter."

Since the women gave the presentation, they were the last ones to leave. Slowly, the crowd thinned down to fifty people, and the two men continued to eye the group. They glanced at their watches. Ten minutes passed. By now, there were about twenty-five attendees left. Three large, uniformed Black men with Holiday Inn Express nametags waited patiently to be told what to do with the women's cardboard boxes and two huge, black leather square valises.

Scott took a deep breath, walked up to the group, and politely introduced himself to each person. He made sure to hold the three women's hands longer than usual. By now, each lady was sliding into her full-length mink coat. In his best Ossie Davis voice and swagger, Scott told them that he was impressed with their presentation. He also told them that he was a Morehouse Man and a Northworld airline pilot. He was surprised when none of the women appeared impressed. Quite frankly, he was doubly floored as the two presenters immediately glared distastefully at Rozelle. Trying to impress them too, Rozelle shared his name, his profession, and the fact he graduated from Morehouse and Harvard Business School in five seconds.

Chapter Eight

At this point, Alex, Pecola, and Symone were heading toward the door. Their fur coats were billowing as they walked, and Rozelle and Scott fell in step with the group as if they were old friends. Once outside, Scott and Rozelle realized that the super stretched black Towncar was waiting for the entourage. They were even more impressed. While the three Holiday Inn Express employees helped the chauffeur load the women's items into the trunk, Scott and Rozelle attempted to chitchat with the three women again. Earlier, when they entered the building, both men noticed the limousine and wondered who reserved it for the day. Now they knew and told each other they liked the women's style even more. The limo driver slammed the trunk shut, checked his watch, and glanced the ladies' way.

The three women and Meetings Odyssey's five employees entered the limousine. The pretty black one with the flowing hair and slightly bowed legs said that it was a pleasure for her to meet Rozelle and Scott. Then she smiled widely and handed both a business card. She eased in the limo, too. The driver shut the door, jogged around to the other side, and they glided off. Just like that. So ended the first time Scottfeld Broadus Alexander laid eyes on Pecola, Alex, and Symone. And ever since that moment, somehow he knew that his life would forever be changed.

Scott waited two weeks before he called Alexandria Johnson-Devereaux, Junior Partner at D. Britt & Cox. When he spoke to her on a Monday, she gently asked that he call her Alex. After several minutes of interesting small talk, she invited him to lunch on the following Thursday. Scott knew he was in. *One down, and two women to go,* he thought. On vacation for three weeks, Scott planned to visit New Orleans. But to add an additional notch to his conqueror belt was more important right now, and the time off gave him plenty of free moments to work the seductive moves on Alex.

The first lunch was wonderful. So was the second brunch date the next Monday. On the Thursday of the same week, he enjoyed the third luncheon with Alex and realized it was time to give Alex the honor of being with him. It was obvious that Alex appeared anxious too. From the many years of dealing with women, Scott became a master of the game and felt he read the ladies like a tell all book. Scott cleared his throat. While they enjoyed banana cheesecake, he told Alex that he wanted to have an affair. In the same breath and with a huge knowing grin on his face, Scott added that he believed she desired the same.

For as long as Scott lives, he would never, ever forget how she gazed at him with those hurt but still tender and intense eyes. She bit her lip as if she were about to cry. However, in a soft voice etched with pain, she explained that she was offended and was surprised that he'd mistaken her kindness as an opportunity or a sign she wanted to have an affair. Alex added that she profoundly misjudged him as she assumed that he was a man of honor and character.

She went on to say that she was desperately in love with Madison and only him, and thought it was absolutely abominable for anyone to run around when an individual was married.

After the soft-spoken, verbal beating, Scott felt like a whipped dog. He wanted to run off and jump in a molten hot volcano, anything to escape the sad gaze she quietly directed his way for at least ten minutes. For the first time in his life, Scott felt like a first-class imbecile. However, he apologized to Alex and then some. With his face cemented to his Italian shoes, they quietly walked out the restaurant a short while later. She shook his hand firmly and relinquished a beautiful smile in the parking lot. For a brief moment he thought he noticed, but he wasn't sure, that tears glistened in her eyes.

While Scott watched intently, Alex slowly walked away. She eased into her burgundy Jaguar and glided off. He felt stupid. Greedy for the wrong thing when it was her classiness that pulled him to her. He drove home preoccupied. When he got there, he attacked the piano and got drunk off an entire bottle of Chivas Regal. Since his hangover was monstrous Friday morning, that afternoon Scott called Alex twice and apologized repeatedly. She laughed and said that all was forgiven—really it was. He fudged around empty shit for a few more minutes. Then he finally invited her to lunch on Monday. And Alex accepted.

Slowly but surely, Scott learned that his bloated ego developed from needlessly screwing plenty women for too many wrong reasons blew up in his face. It didn't work with Alex. Here he was having an animated and interesting conversation with a unique lady who possessed no desire to screw him. It was truly a different experience, and he was amazed that he enjoyed the moments. Moments where he wasn't chasing her but just having friendship. Refreshing.

Generally, when Scott took a woman out for dinner, he was her lover after the second date. On the third date, he was ready to sweep everything off the dinner table with his right hand and pump the woman from behind with two hundred and twenty-five pounds of rock hard flesh. Scott was spoiled. Ladies were easy to get, and he did what he wanted to them. The women had always been captivated by his rugged, handsome good looks, his Morehouse image, and his Northworld pilot position. And so was he. He achieved what he strived for all his life and expected the adulation.

Scott loved it. He was proud when women stared at him as he sauntered through airports in his pilot uniform. Not only that, he also knew the ladies were impressed with his intelligence, affectionate ways, and sexual prowess. They could perform whatever trick he wanted them to do, whenever, however he said it needed to be done. Up until the time he met Alex, he had accommodating women by the dozens. They dribbled just to be around Captain Scottfeld Broadus Alexander, to hang on his arm and to latch on to his identity.

But, not Alex. She wanted none of that. She had her own identity. She merely wanted to be friends. No more. No less. Gradually, Scott began to talk to Alex about his family. His mother, father, brothers, sons, and even his ex-wife, Rose Bobbie. He shared unusually private, intimate information...stuff he held close for years. Scott talked about his upbringing and the goals he had since he was eight. And, in a short time, he fell in love with Alex...not in the romantic sense. He began to cherish her as a friend and as a big brother. She explained to him, in a way that reminded him of his mother, that God loved humbleness. He enjoyed His people to fulfill dreams, but He also relished when they shared their blessings and treated their fellow human beings with respect and kindness. That was Alex's way. Sweet and gentle.

Scott had no sisters. But through Alex's genuine conversation, he finally understood why fathers acted a certain way toward daughters and why brothers learned to protect sisters. They embarked upon a sincere, platonic acquaintance, and he was honored to know her. For three straight months, they continued to meet, and Alex often told him that she enjoyed his company immensely.

By now, Scott learned about Alex's family. Both of her parents were dead. It was just Alex and a sister named Nanette, who was ten years younger than Alex. Nanette was married to Marlon Asa Dinzelle. An avid follower of professional basketball, Scott couldn't believe it. Marlon Dinzelle was one of the National Basketball League's most popular superstars who played for New York. He also was the winner of the Most Valuable Player award the same year Alex and Scott met.

In spite of staggering family tragedies, Scott observed that Alex spoke with pure excitement and possessed the most passionate view on life. She frankly shared the mental anguish of her miscarriages. The hunger to attain her dreams. And she spoke endlessly about her husband, Madison. Scott even had a chance to meet him during one of their outings. Scott came to know that the attractive, pleasant man was obviously just as in love with her as she was with him.

Three weeks into the fourth month, Alex explained to Scott that she told her two closest friends about the times they spent together. She wanted them to be friends with him, too. She arranged a luncheon with Pecola and Symone. But before the scheduled date, Alex told him about her friends.

"Don't try to impress them because you can't, Scott," Alex said. "They have the money to buy what they want. They're completely turned off by people when they attempt to needlessly flaunt positions, proclaim accolades, and brandish college degrees in their faces."

While Alex spoke, he grinned silently. He understood why he and Rozelle were sterling failures during their initial introductions at the MAWS monthly meeting. With love in her voice for her two friends, Alex also honestly explained that Symone was fragile right now. She was trying to recover from a bitter separation and an impending divorce battle with her husband. Dating a man right now was utterly out of the question for her. Pecola was married to Carlos, and Scott knew how Alex felt about men chasing what had already been claimed. Well, Pecola believed the same. Also, she was still recovering from two family catastrophes.

After the brief dos and don'ts, the four met two days later. They talked. Scott wore the most debonair face, his nicest Everett Hall black suit, and dapper accessories. The outing was an overwhelming success for him. As usual, Alex was graciously tenderhearted. Although Pecola and Symone were slightly impressed by the handsome man with the charming smile, they still were somewhat suspicious of his intentions. Throughout the afternoon, they watched him out the corner of their eyes.

For the next six months, Alex scheduled other luncheons regularly and the group discussed a variety of subjects. Scott was extremely easy to talk to. Pecola, Alex, and Symone enjoyed speaking with him for hours and began to openly share their dreams for their families and what they honestly expected from life. They also realized it was important to have a male perspective, and they relied on his honest advice.

Now when Scott often thought about images of the past, he recognized that they truly listened to his advice. But most importantly, those three ladies shared what they believed women desired to receive from him. An easy rapport. Comfortable friends. Slowly but surely, Scott began to experience an inexplicable desire to be around them more often, to even protect Symone and Pecola in the same small way he experienced with Alex. He became a closer friend with their husbands, children, and family. He desperately wanted to be an intricate part of their lives. To sing, to read, to be a shoulder for them—to be their friend and brother, too.

As a result of knowing them, Scott changed. So did his flagrant attitude toward females. He still had plenty of ladies around, but he noticed a difference. It didn't occur overnight. Slowly but surely, it was a deliberate process that he purposed to happen.

Time passed as time would. A year of knowing each other seemed short to him. Scott wanted to celebrate. They were having lunch at Ryan's, a steak and seafood restaurant on Coliseum Drive not too very far from the Akao Building. The waiter just refilled their glasses of unsweetened ice tea when Scott posed the question. Scott turned to Alex. He recalled what Alex said that she asked Pecola when they first met many years ago, and he opted to do the same.

"I remember you told me how you asked Pecola to be your friend years ago." To collect his thoughts, he paused a moment. "I'm going to do the same thing."

"Ok, Scott," Alex said surprised.

"I want to ask you a very important question," Scott said as he turned back to Alex after glancing Pecola's and Symone's way. He held Alex's right hand; he was truly willing to kneel on bended knees. "Would you allow me to be your friend and brother for the rest of my life, Alex?"

"Yes," Alex whispered, without hesitating a second.

Then Scott turned to Pecola and asked her the same question. Finally, he faced Symone with the exact same request. They both said yes, too. Because Alex said that she always wanted to have a big brother, soft, silent tears slid down her face, all the way past her smile. It was an emotional moment driven with sincerity, hope, and lifelong dedication for the friends. After Symone finished wiping Alex's tears, Scott smiled. Once again, he was reminded of the unabashed, tender affection the three women openly displayed for one another.

To cement the friendship, they decided to seal it with a right hand vow. They wanted Alex, who represented the root of the unusual relationship, to first place her right hand on the white linen tablecloth. Scott positioned his on top of hers. Symone rested hers on his. To seal the vow, Pecola placed her right hand on top. While dining in the quaint restaurant on that beautiful, crisp December day, they promised to love and cherish one another. Not as typical friends but as blood sisters and brother. They solemnly vowed the relationship would remain platonic. And Alex declared happily, "Our friendship will last a lifetime."

Chapter Nine

"...And this weekend," Symone was saying disgustingly to Alex and Pecola, "Arman had the nerve to tell me again that the reason he has a mirror over his bed is that he wants to wake up, open his eyes, and look at the first person that loves him." She paused and rolled her eyes toward the ceiling fan that was spinning silently above their heads. "Can yall believe that garbage? That man has three conversations. They're me, myself, and I. That's all he talks about."

Alex, Pecola, and Symone returned to the Arman subject again. No matter what they discussed over dinner this afternoon, Symone continued to revisit the weekend with Arman. Lenda walked up with the Crown Royal Fudge cake that oozed with chocolate syrup and was covered with whipped cream, cherries, and nuts. Since the three friends decided to share it, Lenda focused on slicing three equal pieces while their conversation rattled on. She handed the first plate to Alex who grimaced playfully when it was placed in front of her.

"I don't know how I allowed yall to convince me to eat this today, girlfriends. This is definitely going straight to my hips," Alex exclaimed as she cut a small piece with the fork and delicately stuck it in her mouth.

"Mine too," Pecola mumbled. "Quite frankly, it never left mine from the last time I was here."

"Mmmm. This is absolutely delicious, though," Alex cooed on and decided to jog an extra half mile in the morning.

"But isn't it good. Just enjoy it, puhleeze," Pecola insisted jokingly by scooping up a big hunk. She was glad that Lenda gave her the largest slice. "I know you'll run your behind off tomorrow trying to remove the one gram of carbohydrates you probably got from eating it."

"You know she will," Symone inserted.

"Plus, life ain't no fun living on salads and water. Misery loves company. Why should your behind wear size eight?" Pecola chuckled loudly and gave Symone a high five.

Symone continued her story about Arman. "Sistah girls, sistah girls, listen up. Remember how Arman acted when we all went with Scott to the New Orleans Jazzfest back in May? Yall remember how boring he was then, don't you?" Symone asked in an amusing voice as she stared steadily in their faces.

"Yes." Both Pecola and Alex vigorously nodded their heads. Alex recalled how she teasingly told Pecola, Rozelle, Jodria, and Madison that she even thought about sticking a straight pin in Arman to shake him up, to make him scream, or do something.

"How come yall aren't answering me?"

"We both mumbled yes, Sy," Alex said as she bit into more cake.

"Well, Arman was the exact same way this weekend. He was slow as molasses but not as tasty or as sweet," Symone drawled in a long drawn out southern voice to which Pecola and Alex laughed loudly. "He would make a slug look ambitious. I'm telling you."

"That's why I was surprised you went back to Lake Norman," Alex said, smiling.

"Pecola made me do it," Symone replied.

"I can't make you do dittly, girl," Pecola shot back. "You know I can't, Alex. No one can for that matter."

"Let me finish my story," Symone requested. "Guess what your sister told me about Arman, Pecola? It was the same night of your birthday party."

"God only knows," Pecola groaned as she considered her feisty, older sister, Pauletta.

"Pauletta said, 'That Arman should be dust to you right about now, gurl. Shake his behind and move your ass on. As pretty as you are, you don't need no extra junk like that clanging around you. Even though we ain't blood related, you're a nice chocolate sistah who looks just like me.' Then Pauletta said—"

"Oh, gawd," Pecola interrupted. "She said more?"

"Sho did. Pauletta stopped talking for a moment and said, 'Of course, we look darn good. Don't we, Symone.' Then, Pauletta winked at me. She had me laughing the whole time, but she was telling the truth," Symone laughed as she munched on cake. Alex and Pecola chuckled loudly at Pauletta's funny words "It was the same advice Pauletta gave me in New Orleans when she noticed how dead Arman was."

That really wasn't exactly how Pauletta phrased it. Girlfriend's advice was given with the help of profanity in all the right places. Symone knew that if she said it the exact same way as Pauletta, Alex would feel uneasy about all the curse words.

"Reverend Pauletta further said, 'It won't be no problem to get another bus, Symone! I know that to be true. Simply stand on the corner of life and wait for a nice, strong Mandingo warrior, air-conditioned one to roll by,'" Symone added. "'I'm telling you, Symone. Get off the freaking bus if it ain't taking you nowhere.'"

"Pecola, your sister is sooo crazy," Alex said with a huge smile.

"I know," Pecola agreed. "Don't remind me."

"Wait! I'm not finished, yall," Symone said. "Pauletta started screaming out into the night. 'Next. Next. Next.' Then she snapped her fingers to the left and then to the right all over the place. She was something else that night."

Symone glanced quickly at Pecola who suddenly stopped laughing and began staring at her in an odd way.

"She was," Alex said.

"Yall, Pauletta told me this in my ears—" Symone left out the part that Pauletta really sprayed her left ear with alcohol coated spit, and she needed two cocktail napkins to wipe her face. "She said, 'If that man ain't taking care of you, you do it.' Pauletta said, 'If you're going to take care of anything, you might as well take care of your own self, gurl.'" Symone ended her mimic of Pauletta by clapping her hands several times.

"Let's move on," Pecola said with concern covering her face.

"What's wrong with you, Pecola?" Symone wondered. "I'm letting yall know that I'm through with Arman."

"If he's not making you happy, it's about time, Sy," Alex said.

"Stop staring at me like that, girl," Symone demanded to Pecola as she raised her glass to sip more Bailey's.

"I'm not staring. I'm listening and paying attention to what you said that Pauletta told you. My sister is losing her mind. I'm shocked really," Pecola said with a look of disbelief.

"Why?" Symone asked. "You know how your sister is."

"I *told* Pauletta over and over again that night that her Black as—, I mean her behind, drank too many Remys," Pecola explained with a confused voice. Her thoughts wandered back to her sister, and Pecola hoped that nothing was brewing at the Hannibal and Pauletta Bing household in Augusta, Georgia. When Pecola got home tonight, she'd definitely call her sister to find out what was going on.

Nibbling more cake, Alex smiled. She recalled how Pauletta floated around the entire evening. Each time they talked, Alex was glad to see Pauletta was enjoying herself simply dancing to the oldies but goldies music. One time when DJ Cool Breeze played the Delfonics' *Break Your Promise,* Pauletta actually asked Alex to slow dance with her. That scene had the poolside women group slapping their thighs with amusement.

Alex recalled that it was at least two hours later; she wasn't positive about the specific time. But it was about that time the nosy Desiree Coleman raced into Symone's kitchen and told Pecola that her sister just jumped in the deep end of the swimming pool with all her clothes on. And with the way she was scratching and gasping in the water, Desiree wasn't sure if Pauletta could swim.

Symone shrugged and spoke to Alex and Pecola in a dejected voice. "Look, the deal is this. You can ask for what you want in a man and ask what you want from one, but there's no guarantee you'll get it."

"That's what my single friends say all the time," Pecola said.

"I'm telling you." Symone took a deep breath and leaned forward with her elbows on the table. "That Arman has a hamster brain when it comes to knowing what to do in a relationship. If I go out with him again, yall make sure you kick my behind for me."

Alex laughed loudly and almost choked on the cake. She sipped a little water to recover.

"At least you tried and were honest with Arman, Symone," Alex said in a comforting, raspy tone. "My sister told me that her friends say all the time they wished there was some way to get a resume from a man to determine exactly how he was with his former women."

"Tell Nanette that would be a great idea. Look this discussion is riveting, really it is. But can we puhleeze move on to something else?" Pecola asked. Symone rolled her eyes slowly, and Alex simply nodded yes.

It was Pecola's turn again. She told them all kinds of things about her weekend shopping spree, Carlos, and the AKA Sunday meeting to settle a few disputes. Of course, Pecola was proud to declare to them that if it weren't for her expertise and knowledge of various etiquette requirements, certain AKA social functions wouldn't be properly organized. With their mouths wide open, Alex and Symone listened in disbelief to her self-righteous attitude. A couple of times, Symone pantomimed and acted as if she were slowly playing a violin.

"Don't say it, Sy," Alex said to Symone when she saw her mouth open.

"I can't hold it any longer," Symone mumbled with a small grin.

"Hold what?" Pecola asked.

"You know what? The older you get, the more stuck-up you are, Pecola," Symone said. "You better get that nose of yours out of the air before you drown."

Pecola ignored her words. Once again, Pecola needed to tell another secret to Alex and Symone. The three women's heads were inches apart. Pecola placed both hands over her mouth and looked around to see if anyone else was listening. She whispered a few absolutely crazy words about the five hypochondriacs in her other women's group. Alex and Symone leaned back, laughed real loudly, and noticed Scott and Rozelle striding across the restaurant floor. As Scott strolled over, he put his finger over his lips. He mouthed a *Shhhhh* and shook his head quickly.

"...I told them, look—" Pecola was still talking non-stop. "I don't claim no sickness. I'm old timey in that regard. When people say, 'I believe I'm catching the flu,' I say to them, 'Don't say shi— I mean, stuff like that. I might have a few coughs, but that's the extent of it. I could never understand—"

Just then, Scott placed both hands over Pecola's face. So she wouldn't figure out who it was, Symone and Alex held her hands. One feel of Scott's hairy arms, and the game would end abruptly with an easy guess.

"I know who that is. That's my huzzband!" Pecola exclaimed in a lilting voice, bouncing up and down. "He's back from Hilton Head."

"Guess again, girl," Alex urged, laughing.

"If it ain't my huzzband...," Pecola said slowly, trying to think. This morning, Pecola spoke to her brother, Ezunial. He was in San Francisco at the time. If it wasn't Ezunial, it must be— She loved surprises especially games and shopping. Pecola got it. She knew.

"This is sooo boring," Symone said. "Somebody tell her who it is."

"It must be Madison," Pecola squealed.

"Gurl, puhleeze," Symone said ready to tell. "If it was Madison, don't you think he would've covered Alex's eyes?"

The lady who watched them earlier was now sitting with two other older women. The whole table glared distastefully in their direction.

Another flash came to Pecola. "Oh, honeychile. Honeychile! I got it now. It's my other brother, Scott," she exclaimed loud enough so that people several tables over stopped eating and gazed their way.

Scott removed his hands from her face. Pecola jerked hers away too and jumped out of her seat. Since she was especially close to Scott, she was definitely happy to see him.

"Hey, girl. Give it up," Scott requested smiling as he tightly squeezed her shoulders with a big hug and kissed her squarely on the lips. He did the same to Alex and Symone.

"Today's your lucky day, ladies. I'm back. Show me some love," Rozelle exclaimed and he held his arms out to hug everyone.

"Oh, gawd," Symone mumbled under her breath.

"Yall look gorgeous as usual." Rozelle quickly scanned their stylish attire.

"Thanks, baby," Pecola piped in.

"Just like an Easter morning," he added with a boisterous laugh, and Symone rolled her eyes at him. Rozelle attempted to plant a big kiss on their mouths too, but they quickly offered their cheeks instead.

Long time ago, they allowed Rozelle to kiss them the exact same way as Scott. But Alex said that she noticed a couple of times Rozelle stuck his tongue in her mouth. When it occurred a third and fourth time, Alex was positive she wasn't imagining things. Eventually, Pecola and Symone experienced the same promiscuous behavior. The affectionate peck for Rozelle came to a screeching halt and was delegated to their cheeks, forehead, or hands. There were occasions that Symone said she should have given him her feet to kiss. Then knowing his crazy ass, he would get a great kick out of that too.

Since Rozelle quickly moved to sit beside Alex, Symone shuffled over to the next chair. Scott sat between her and Pecola. Lenda stopped by to check on them, and Scott and Rozelle ordered Corona Extras. They also decided to share two dozen barbecued buffalo wings. By then, the women had finished their cake and pushed their plates away.

Now that Alex knew that Madison was back home, she repeatedly glanced at her wristwatch. She pulled out her cell phone and placed a call home. Cleopatra, her cleaning woman, answered. She told Alex that Madison was either in the garden or in the greenhouse. Alex said good-bye, folded the phone, and placed it back in her pocketbook.

Lenda delivered the two Coronas along with a basket of steaming hot yeast rolls and honey margarine. Scott grabbed a roll, sliced it open, and dumped the entire plastic container of the cholesterol inside. Seeing the butter ooze out, Symone decided she'd eat another roll since they smelled so good. After eating the Zawadi lunch, the O'Charley's house salad, and the fudge cake, Symone certainly wasn't hungry.

Scott pushed the lime in the Corona bottle and took a swallow. He proceeded to tell the women about the Hilton Head trip, the fun, and the golfing. A couple of times, Rozelle interrupted the discussion because he wanted to gaze into Alex's eyes for the umpteenth time since he sat down. Rozelle told Alex how pretty she looked today, and he wondered if anyone else had mentioned the same to her. She thanked him graciously and told him once again that after Madison, he was the craziest man she'd ever met.

As always, Alex was dressed elegantly. Normally, she preferred to wear an African ethnic look and often wore the regal African flowing outfits of one of her favorite designers, Therez Fleetwood. However, today, she wore a simple, white sleeveless dress and carried a matching white patent leather Chanel pocketbook. With his right arm wrapped around Alex's chair, Rozelle peered into her eyes again, grinned stupidly, and told her that was the most beautiful dress he had ever seen. While Alex gently patted his arm as if she were comforting a blubbering baby, the entire table burst out in raucous laughter.

A Black banker looking guy sat one booth across from them and gazed at the rowdy table over reading glasses perched on the tips of his nostrils. When he stopped minding their business and turned to face his companion, Rozelle perfectly mimicked the persnickety expression. After everyone finished laughing once more, Alex half jokingly told him that wasn't a nice thing to do.

Chapter Ten

Lenda delivered the blazing hot wings with ranch dressing, and the men tempted the ladies with one. They all refused. Both men chomped on the delicious looking drumettes, and Pecola ended up grabbing two anyway. The friendly good-natured ribbing continued for another hour or so. At eight o'clock, Alex finally announced that it was time for her to go. By then, Rozelle and Scott finished their third Coronas and nodded in agreement.

Scott stood up and reached for his wallet. Alex grabbed her purse. Rozelle dug in his pockets, and all five friends began arguing amicably about whom would pay the tab. After ten minutes of discussion, Symone concluded that it was her turn and proceeded to give Lenda, who waited patiently for the verdict, her platinum American Express. As Lenda processed the bill, Pecola excused herself to visit the bathroom.

Before Rozelle allowed Alex to get up again, he placed one hand on the back of her chair and the other one palm down on the table. "Lady, you're positively, simply gorgeous," Rozelle told her.

"Thank you." Alex laughed. "Make sure to tell Jodria Anne the exact same thing when you see her later."

"Some creeps never give up," Symone mumbled to Scott. When Rozelle heard her words, he abruptly threw her a cock-eyed stare.

"You're just jealous cause I didn't say the same thing to you," Rozelle said to Symone. To the consternation of the people eating nearby, their laughter erupted loudly.

When Lenda returned with the bill, Symone signed it with a flourish and a huge tip.

"I'm leaving this big ass tip to help Lenda with tuition at Livingston College in the fall. This is also on behalf of all the Black folks in Winston-Salem who don't tip when they ought to." They all laughed again.

An uppity woman at the table directly behind theirs sucked her teeth. Speaking under her breath to her male companion, she told him that all the laughing was getting on her nerves. And nobody could be that happy about nothing.

When Lenda noticed the tip, she couldn't believe it. She poured thanks over the group and asked them to pretty, pretty puhleeze sit in her section the next time they returned to O'Charley's. They all started for the door. By then, Pecola was heading toward the front as well. Alex grabbed toothpicks at the front counter for everyone and reprimanded that she'd better not catch nere person using them as they walked out the restaurant. There was another burst of loud laughter. Since folk didn't know what was going on, they assumed the rowdy bunch was high on liquor. But this was their customary behavior. The larger the group, the louder the noise. The other curious patrons were lucky. There were only five out for the evening this time.

Scott clutched Pecola and Alex's hands, and they walked toward the parking lot. Rozelle snatched Alex's hand. Symone, who was struggling to hold both bouquet of roses, grabbed Rozelle's other hand. The friends developed a human follow-the-leader with Pecola in the front. While sauntering along as if they were on a Conga line in Trinidad, they all giggled like high school teenagers and eventually stopped in front of Alex's red on white Jaguar.

When Alex turned forty in April, Madison surprised her with the car. She was a Delta and a Winston-Salem State University Ram to her heart. Every chance she got, Alex was determined to pay homage to her alma mater and her sorority's colors of red and white. If she wasn't driving in the colors, then more than likely she wore them. Although Alex kept glancing at her wristwatch, the friends ignored her anxiety and began another conversation. With his hands in his pocket and a smile on his face, Scott peered down at Alex.

"I tried to get Madison to follow us over here. The brother wanted to race home to see something. I believe he said something about some babies," Scott said with a half smirk and eyed the others.

"Whoop there it is!" shrieked Pecola, laughing.

For some strange reason, Rozelle now held Alex's hand as if he owned it. She looked down at the tight clasp and turned to stare at him. After he mouthed an air kiss, he smiled broadly. Alex stared at Pecola a moment and grinned, too.

"Why do you think Madison was in such a hurry, baby?" Scott asked Alex.

"He must be racing home to see his small babies because my huzzband knew his big baby wouldn't be home until about eight-thirty," Alex advised sweetly. "I asked Cleopatra to give him a perfume scented note for me." She winked at Pecola who was now struggling to pry her hand free from Rozelle's strong grip.

"Helll-lo. Whoop there it is," echoed Symone. They burst out laughing once more.

Alex quickly checked her watch again. "On that note, I'm leaving," she said as she stood on her tiptoes to give Scott a kiss. Scott was amusingly relentless.

"All I know is my man Madison pretty pleased me to death about that Jerry Butler song. I sure hope it was worth it," he said before leaning forward to return her peck.

"Whoop there it is! Work it, baby," Rozelle hollered as he stuck his right index finger on his tongue. He waved it in the air and proceeded to do a crazy version of the Cabbage Patch dance, his trademark.

"Spare me," Pecola smiled, watching Rozelle. "Lawd, don't get him started this evening."

"C'mon, ladies. Give me a big bootie slap," Rozelle exclaimed loudly as he twisted around the parking lot trying to bounce his behind into the women. Everyone laughed *a-gain.*

Suddenly, they all heard the repeated beeping of a car horn. When they turned around, Scott's girlfriend waved frantically out the window of a late model black Volvo. Charmaine pulled into the restaurant lot looking for a spot, but O'Charley's parking area brimmed with cars. After Charmaine drove through once, she finally parked toward the front in a space clearly marked *Handicap Only.* Alex groaned under her breath that it wasn't nice to do that.

Charmaine walked over to the group. As she approached them, the hum of their discussion died down.

"Ok. I bet your behind will be ready to leave now," Pecola teased Scott in a low voice as she watched him stalk Charmaine's progress with a penetrating stare.

Scott opened his arms, Charmaine snuggled into them, and he quickly kissed her. As Charmaine squeezed his neck, she smelled his always sweet breath and the Dion Scott Cologne. While the others whistled and clapped with big grins on their faces, Scott twirled Charmaine around. Once he put her down, she made sure to hug and kiss the others with just as much fervor.

"What you doing over here, baby?" Scott asked, surprised, his hands resting comfortably in his pants pocket which they all determined long ago was his favorite stance.

"I was heading to LeMenu at Hanes Mall," Charmaine said as she pointed across the street. Everyone turned to look. "Just as I was gettin' ready to turn right, I happened to glance to my left. There yall stood laughing about something as usual."

The friends quietly watched while the two spoke and observed how they looked dreamingly into one another's eyes.

"Did I interrupt anything?" Charmaine asked with a puzzled expression toward the others as she possessively held Scott's arm.

"Girl, no," Symone said firmly and paused a moment. She gazed toward the handicap parking space and felt the same as Alex about the illegal, thoughtless move. "We're heading home right now."

"Me too," Alex said. "Finally."

Symone was a lover of Volvos for as long as she could remember. In December, she traded the family's green Volvo for a Lincoln Towncar. After Pauletta raved about the merits of owning the American tradition, she decided that she would try an American car. Symone drove all the way to Augusta, Georgia to buy it. Nowadays, Symone's housekeeper drove the burgundy mini-van. Symone drove her Mercedes convertible. Whenever the family traveled as a group, they glided around with Symone at the wheel of the sky blue Towncar—or hear Pauletta say it, the living room on wheels.

"I like your new car, Charmaine," Symone added. The others also mumbled it was very pretty.

"Thanks, Sy. I picked it up on Saturday. It was time to trade in my old ancient Datsun, girl," she announced victoriously with pride.

Unable to pretend as if Charmaine didn't park in the handicap spot, Symone had to say something to her about it. "Girl, you need to move that car before you get a ticket."

Charmaine gazed at her sharply, then looked at the car, and back to the group again. The others nodded their head in agreement with Symone. Charmaine quickly laughed and said that she planned to park at the most for only five minutes. Scott moved behind her and encircled his arms around her waist, kissing her hair several times.

"Well, I see what's on your mind. So it's time for me to leave," Pecola coolly exclaimed as she watched Scott affectionately manhandle his woman. He was so openly romantic and caring with her, with everyone for that matter.

I'm still not sure if I like her. I just don't know. I don't think she's the right person for our Scott! It's something phony about her, Pecola thought and laughed to herself. *And I sho nuff knows about fake people like that. Just like Alex says, if Scott loves her, that was the main thing.*

Pecola quickly glanced around to see if she noticed obvious disapproval on anyone else' face. No. They were sphinxes too. As usual, they appeared extremely approving of whomever Scott dated. Especially Symone. Now, if that sistah didn't like Charmaine, she would've been in her car driving straight home to Clemmons by the time Charmaine blew the horn the second time. Of course, Alex loved everybody. So there wasn't any need for Pecola to even gaze her way.

"My dear friends. Yall take care. I'm really leaving this time," Alex said with determination. She knew how easy it was to slide into another conversation.

"I'm saddened that this afternoon went by too quickly once again," Rozelle joked as he wiped his eyes.

"Oh, look at the big baby," Symone purred. "He's wiping away those fake crocodile tears."

"It simply is way too soon for us to be heading our own separate ways," Rozelle added.

"Would someone puhleeze nozzle him?" Pecola urged Symone.

In spite of the brevity of Rozelle's feigned grief regarding the evening coming to a close, he reminded Alex to tell Madison that tee time would be 8:00 a.m. on Saturday morning at Winston Lake Golf Course.

Alex hugged and kissed Scott on the lips again. All the women did. They even lost their mind for a moment. They did the same thing to Rozelle who was exhilarated and restrained himself from sticking his tongue in Alex's mouth. He decided right there he would probably poke it in Alex's mouth the next time she dropped her guard again.

It took every ounce of inner strength Charmaine possessed to keep smiling at the display of emotions the friends showed toward one another. They strolled her way, and she grinned and kissed kissed everyone as if she were truly excited to be in the midst of their holier than thou farewells. When Pecola volunteered to take Rozelle home since they lived near each other, Charmaine was glad for the suggestion. But Scott reminded Rozelle that he had parked his car at the house.

Shooot! thought Rozelle. He was hoping to get a chance to gaze at Pecola's legs as she changed gears in the BMW. They all displayed two mile long gorgeous ones, but Pecola's reminded him of Tina Turner. And if she would let him, he would work an Ike on her. Just to be in her presence while she changed to first, second, third, and pressed the brake would be very sexy for Rozelle. It would give him a few wonderful free thrills. Not that he ever paid for them anyway.

"Look, Charmaine, I'm gonna drop Rozelle by his house. Then I'll come by the condo to pick you up." Charmaine wore a pretty pout as Scott continued. "Baby, I'm not flying out until Wednesday morning. So I'll have the pleasure of driving your fine behind to and from work tomorrow."

"It's just that I spend so little time with you, honey. I can't get enough of you." Charmaine swallowed the last part of the sentence in a big, wet kiss. Scott tasted her tongue and pulled away.

"Let's roll, everybody," Scott said. "I got to get back to my baby."

On that note, everyone started for his or her respective vehicles. Just before they entered their cars, another discussion erupted. It was between Symone, Pecola, Scott, and Rozelle about whether they were going to attend the National Black Arts Festival of Atlanta in a few weeks. Once again, Symone reminded them that she had everyone's tickets for the Hampton Jazz Festival and had blocked out a floor of rooms at the hotel. Alex remembered something else and jumped out the car with the important information even though she had mentioned the news earlier. She just wanted to yell another quick reminder.

"Remember to make a note to watch my brother-in-law on BET on July sixth," Alex hollered. "That's the Monday after July Fourth. Ok? They're going to celebrate Marlon's years in the National Basketball League. Don't forget, yall. I told Nanette I would remind yall again."

"You did just that, chile," Pecola yelled back. "Nanette will be proud of you."

The four friends nodded their heads "yes" vigorously since that was the fifth reminder for the day. Knowing Alex, she would probably remind them many more times before Marlon actually appeared on the show.

By then, Charmaine was in her Volvo listening to a Janet Jackson CD and hadn't heard a word Alex said. Charmaine was rummaging in the glove compartment for tissue to blow her nose when Alex tapped on the glass. Charmaine pressed the button, and the semi-black tinted window glided down.

"Charmaine, Nanette wanted me to remind everyone to watch Marlon. He'll be on the Woolfgang Youngblood Show on July 6th," Alex said happily in an excited voice.

"That's great, girl. I'll make sure my television is turned on that night."

"Thanks, Charmaine. My sister is sooo excited about it. I don't know why though," Alex added lightly with a huge smile. "As a professional basketball player, Marlon has been on television a thousand times."

Charmaine nodded her head with understanding. "But it still ain't nothing like seeing your man on national television. No matter how many times he has done it before. Tell Nanette I'll definitely be watching him."

"Great. Have a good evening," Alex ended in a jolly voice and headed toward her car.

Out the corner of Charmaine's eyes and behind the safety of the black Dakota Smith sunglasses, she stared Alex down as she daintily stepped in her car and drove off.

She's probably screwing Scott, too. Her Miss Goody Too Shoes Attitude does not fool me, Charmaine thought disgustingly as she checked the rearview mirror to back out the parking lot.

Charmaine noticed that the others were still chitchatting beside Symone's car. Scott rested a hand on Pecola's left shoulder as he laughed about the funny comments Rozelle made about the Virginia State University brother who got sick on the Hilton Head trip.

I know their behinds are probably laughing and talking about me, Charmaine said to herself. *I bet those three women are screwing the hell out of Scott and Rozelle. I'm sure they have orgies all the damn time. They're crazy if they think they can fool me.*

Chapter Eleven

Charmaine Violette Gumbel returned to the Winston-Salem scene six years ago. However, it took another year and a half for her to get her life together and venture outdoors with confidence. An award winning, renowned performer and choreographer skilled in ballet and interpretative modern dance, she traveled the world extensively jeteing across the great stages of Europe and North America. She received thunderous, standing ovations as often as people used the bathroom. Yet, it was the brutal divorce from Richard, a white man and prominent record company producer for Coast Coast Records in Chicago, who eventually crushed her spirit, stole her laughter, and destroyed her trust for people.

Originally a native of Lexington, a small town sixteen miles south of Winston, Charmaine always dreamed of opening a dance school in the larger sister city of Winston-Salem, known for its upwardly mobile Black folk. During a terribly miserable time with Richard eight years ago, she did some research. She discovered once again that Winston still didn't have an African-American dance school that catered specifically to Black children, one that provided ethnic classes and an understanding of how American dance was, in large part, a gift from Black America.

Now that Charmaine was discovering who she was, in hindsight, she realized the messy divorce six years ago was a dark and terrible storm that had magically brought sunshine into her life. It was the close of that abusive chapter in Charmaine's life that pushed her to take action about dancing in North Carolina again. After eighteen months of tremendous soul-searching and extensive therapy from a serious psychologist sistah in Greensboro by the name of Dr. Latifah Lett, she stepped out on a limb, rather delicately, and fulfilled the life long dream of opening the Charmaine Kuumba Academy of Winston-Salem.

Symone, a proponent of Black entrepreneurism in any form, discovered the unusual academy four years ago. Even though Symone had never personally met Charmaine, she told every Black person she knew with children and even those who were thinking about having some about the new downtown dance school that was opened just for Black people. When her twin daughters turned two, the eligible ages to begin classes, they both were quickly enrolled in Kuumba Academy.

Eighteen months ago, the friends attended the children's spring recital with such fanfare. They came along with a huge entourage of family and friends who came from as far away as California, Tennessee, and New York to see the adorable performances. Charmaine remembered her dance assistants advised that between Jodria and Symone, they purchased seventy-five tickets.

At the time, Scott was dating a beautiful North Carolina Central University law school professor named Georgiana Valentina River. He never noticed Charmaine even though

Symone whispered incessantly during the entire performance to anyone who listened about the choreographer's renowned global adventures. Ten months later, however, he and Georgiana's romance fizzled. During the parents' reception honoring Charmaine, which followed the spring recital for the next year, Symone introduced the then available Scott to Charmaine. Many more months went by. Scott just wasn't interested. After much urging by Symone and Alex, Scott eventually invited her out on a date.

A strikingly attractive woman of thirty-nine who stood about five feet six, Charmaine walked with the dancer's gait and absolutely straight posture. She was blessed with the face that made everyone assume she was ten years younger. The color of dark brown almond, she had large black eyes. She was endowed with a slender body, shapely legs, and dark curly hair that was coifed in a short shag fashion.

After Charmaine graduated from Howard University with a major in dance, she briefly toured with Alvin Ailey's dance company. Eventually, Charmaine moved to Europe for a short stint. From there, she headed to Chicago where she met Richard. He was an abusive but influential man, with whom she endured a miserable marriage. When she got the strength to finally walk out with children in tow, he scratched the palm of a few judge friends and finagled custody of their sons now ages twelve and eleven.

Since the boys lived with their father, their attitude changed radically. They eventually told her that she was an unfit mother and refused to see her. Initially, she was hurt. After ongoing counseling with Dr. Lett, however, she realized it wasn't her fault. Charmaine recognized that she shouldn't worry about it as much because she needed to understand her sons' negative thinking was influenced by Richard's insane need to hurt or punish her. In spite of her sons' iciness, she wrote to them weekly. She hoped that when they were older, they would understand what she suffered through, for their sakes alone, to stay in the marriage as long as she did.

When Charmaine left Hanes Mall thirty minutes later, she glanced across to O'Charley's and noticed that Scott and the others were now leaning on a light pole in the parking lot, still talking. She slowly rolled her eyes at the group and picked up the cellular phone to contact her friend, Bahati. Charmaine wanted to let her know that she wouldn't make the scheduled nine-thirty conference call with the other Zeta Phi Beta sisters to discuss the June 30th scholarship luncheon for upcoming high school seniors.

"...Yeah, yeah, that's right, Bahati. Something extremely important came up that was totally unexpected," Charmaine said with a sultry smile. "I thought I could take care of it tomorrow. Right—right. I'm glad you understand. Bye-bye."

Hell right it's important, Charmaine said to herself as she hung up the telephone. *Once again, I'm going to get screwed royally tonight. Aaah sookie, sookie now.*

Once in the silent comfort of her car, Alex took a deep breath and inserted the Leontyne Price CD. She turned right onto I-40 West and again briefly thought about her husband, Madison. Two seconds later, she dialed the seven digits to her home. This time, her husband answered the telephone.

"Hello," said the most beautiful bass voice in all America.

Pecola once told her that Madison knew exactly what he was doing when he went to medical school. With a voice like Barry White, it was much safer for him to be a pediatrician than an obstetrician. Sistah girl was too crazy.

"Hell-o." Madison spoke tentatively.

"Hey, baby," Alex said brightly. "I'm on my way home."

"I know, baby. I felt it," he added with a huge grin on his face. Madison talked with his eyes closed as he visualized her in the car looking very pretty, heading straight into his open arms. "I can't wait to see you."

"I missed you so much," she gushed and paused a moment. "I love you, Madison." Alex was so full of love for her husband. It seemed as if she couldn't contain her rapture.

"No, *I* love you." He thought a moment. "What are you wearing, Alex?"

"I'm wearing the most sexiest, loveliest black lacy panties and bra set," Alex said, laughing like a teen-ager. "Just like your nice firm hands, Madison, the set feels like silky satin against my skin."

"Umph, umph, umph."

"And, baby—" Alex licked her lips. "I have on a simple but classic white dress. There's a white hair bow in my hair."

"Mmmm. Sounds real good to me. Hurry up, baby. I'll see you when you get here," he said tenderly and kissed into the phone.

Alex laughed loudly and blew him a kiss back. The line clicked dead.

When Madison finally made love to his wife almost three years after he first saw her, it was on the night of their wedding. He was honored and moved to know she was still a virgin at the age of twenty-two. Alex never allowed their intimate tongue kissing to progress past the usual heavy petting stage. But in the back of his mind, he assumed she was quietly being taken care of by another collegian, which was exactly how he handled any sexual needs. Even then, he couldn't comprehend the jewel of a woman he was blessed to have as a lifetime companion.

On a hundred other occasions after he met her, he asked Alex to give him some of her loving. She was adamant, always refusing. She wanted to save herself for the night of their wedding. She often told him that her mother always said that the best gift a woman could give her husband was an unopened one.

At that time, Madison hadn't asked Alex to marry him. Yet, he instinctively knew from the time he saw the chocolate, sophomore beauty stepping on the Delta pledge line his senior year at Winston-Salem State University that he wanted her for life. Madison just knew it. He couldn't explain it, but he instantly knew three things. One day she would be his wife. She would change his life. And, she would be the mother of Devereaux children.

Madison first met Alex when he attended the step show with his steady girlfriend of four years. Her name was Destiny Densonlo. She was another cocoa dipped lovely whose father knew Madison's father and who was a gynecologist practicing in Greensboro. Also a senior, Destiny was the president of the Deltas. Madison was the Que Basileu, and the Deltas were their sisters. So dating Destiny projected the epitome of an ultimate sorority/fraternity love relationship at the Black college. He attended the step show for that reason and to be with the other Que brothers to observe their new male pledges strut their stuff as well.

WSSU campus was a small one. But it was large enough to miss people, and that was the only reason he gave for having never seen Alex before. As Destiny described each pledgee to him, she explained that Alex transferred from A&T and majored in pre-law. With the mass of thick, black hair flowing everywhere, he watched Alex step, grind, clap, shake, and move with her hands on her hips. He realized he needed to know more about this Alexandria Phylicia Johnson, who Destiny also offhandedly said transferred to WSSU to be near family.

Madison eventually approached Alex on the steps of O'Kelly Library, but she promptly dismissed him. With right hand on hip and her pretty eyes flashing, she asked him wasn't he the guy dating her soror, Destiny. She then explained that a relationship between the two was absolutely forbidden because he would be two-timing Destiny, and Alex could never betray her sister. She also added that such behavior by a Que gentleman would be quite abominable.

Well to say the least, Madison fixed that little problem. Four months into his senior year, he broke up with Destiny. Just—like—that. One day while sharing a ham and cheese sandwich in the Hauser Student Union Building, Madison frankly explained that the relationship couldn't possibly work. While Destiny hackingly choked on a piece of bread as she cried, Madison could barely stare into her face. For a brief moment there and because she was choking sooo much, Madison thought he was going to have to perform the Heimlich maneuver on her.

"…You're breaking my heart, Madison," Destiny told him. "What happened to you? What happened to *our* plans. *You* told *me* you were going to marry *me*. We could practice medicine together, and *we* would have a wonderful life with one another. Uh, I just don't understand what you're telling me today."

"Well, uh, Destiny," Madison said, trying not to notice the constant flow of tears from her eyes. "I got medical school in front of me. That's a long road, baby."

"Still, Madison—er—"

After listening to Madison talk softly for at least an hour or more, Destiny however eventually decided to accept his decision.

"…I thoroughly release you from all of the many promises you made to me, Madison," Destiny said in a very southern, strong, and dignified voice.

Although the tears continued to stream down her face, she managed to hold her head high. She wanted to leave the relationship with some degree of honor. Even though Madison walked away free and unscathed, he knew that Destiny hadn't. And for that he was sorry. But Alex. The prospect of having Alex turned his regret into joy.

From that point on, Madison became an ardent Alex fan as he observed her from a distance. He knew where her classes were held. Who she studied with. Discovered she lived in the Atkins Hall dormitory on campus. Learned everything about her. After he graduated, he really pursued her vigorously. Eventually in December of her junior year, Alex succumbed to his aggressive pursuits. It was almost fourteen months after he first met her. She told him that she would date him only once just to see. After that, the two became an item all through Alex's junior and senior year. When Alex graduated in May, they married three weeks later.

During those early years, Madison often likened Alex to a beautiful rose which perpetually bloomed in uniquely different ways. Subsequently, the flower became one of her favorites, and she gave friends overflowing bouquets of roses for the smallest occasion or reason. Madison was her lover and teacher. He taught her all he knew about sexual fulfillment, making sure during those frequent lessons that he was tender, skillful, and uninhibited.

Madison was Alex's first and only boyfriend, and she honestly wasn't knowledgeable about how to sexually please a man. But Alex was an avid student. Once she discovered the joyful pleasures of making love, even Madison's strong sexual energy couldn't keep up with the unbridled, wild passion she brought to each lovemaking rendezvous. Although Alex remained a consummate lady in public, she joyously transformed into an absolutely fabulous sex-crazed tigress in the bedroom.

Chapter Twelve

Eight years after they married, Madison received a phone call from Destiny who cleverly tracked him down through a frat brother. A gynecologist practicing in Knoxville, she announced that she would be in Winston-Salem for homecoming. She wanted to know if she could just see him for old time sakes on the Thursday evening before the Saturday game. Madison agreed, and the meeting place was arranged.

After a friendly dinner with Destiny, Madison decided to return with her to the Marriott Hotel bar. From there, he ended up going to the sixth floor presidential suite Destiny reserved for the weekend. Since she remembered that he was fond of old jam music, she inserted a Peaches & Herbs' cassette into the stereo. While *Close Your Eyes* played softly, he relaxed on the couch. He mentally questioned why he, a married man of eight years, was in another woman's hotel room.

In the meantime, Destiny quietly changed into a more comfortable outfit and returned to stand in front of the couch wearing only an open shoulder creme lace body suit. She clasped her hands behind her head, began grinding dreamily to *Let's Fall in Love,* and slowly leaned forward to loosen his tie. To this day, Madison attributed what happened next between him and Destiny to the fact that he and Alex lost a baby two months ago and the pressures of the surgeon profession were choking him.

Around 1:30 in the morning, Madison returned home to Advance with his feet heavy as one ton cement blocks. He kissed his wife long and hard. They embraced each other with unparalleled fierceness. Alex, dressed in a soft pink t-strap satin nightgown and relaxing upright in bed, watched Madison intently between the pages of *Black Fire.* He avoided her eyes. He couldn't bear to stare toward the full-size oil portrait of the two of them located strategically above the bed. Alex said that this portrait represented the purity of their marriage.

While Madison bathed in the Jacuzzi, Alex dimmed the lights and placed cinnamon L'Occitane candles throughout. Then, as she had so often done in the past, Alex lovingly soaped his toes, neck, and mid section. When she reached his eyes, she suddenly stared at him. She saw his pain and betrayal in his eyes. She dropped the bar of soap in the water and raced out the bathroom. Just as quickly, she returned and stood in the doorway, the silhouette of her body framed in the soft candlelight. By now, a concerned Madison was vigorously toweling off.

"I'm going for a walk, Madison."

"Hear me out, baby."

"Not right now. I need to be alone. Don't follow me," Alex said as she slipped into her mink jacket and tennis shoes. The walk lasted thirty minutes, and Madison was worried. He was wondering what she was going to do or even say when she came back.

"Don't do it again, Madison," Alex pleaded with hurt eyes when she returned to their bedroom. She inhaled deeply and looked straight at him for a moment. "Please don't ever do that to us, baby. You're all that I dreamed about and prayed for as a husband. My life is you."

"You're mine too, baby."

"I can't. I can't even imagine you with another woman," she added very quietly.

"But, Alex—"

Alex sadly leaned her head against the door. Her hand balled into a fist, she pounded firmly against the silk covered walls and shook her head as she cried softly. Madison remained speechless. Minutes later, she took another deep breath and smiled weakly.

"But I forgive you, Madison. I do," she said in a voice brimming with innocence, compassion, and paramount uncompromising love for him.

Madison was stunned from her reactions and felt a heaviness in his heart. Alex never balled a fist at anything. How could she know what happened? He shook his head slowly with utter guilt and quickly crossed the huge bedroom to be near her. Before he told her the truth, he studied her face a long time.

"Look, baby. I didn't do anything," he whispered tenderly in a voice trembling with emotions. "When I saw her, you were very present in my face all evening. I couldn't, Alex. I just couldn't do anything." He shook his head heavily; his gaze fixed on Alex.

Even though Madison secretly made love to Destiny the same time he dated and was engaged to Alex, he couldn't bring himself to make love to Destiny now that he was married. Alex said nothing. Her teary gaze was plastered to the mosaic tile floor. She continued to cry quietly, wiping her eyes with the back of her hands.

Madison lowered his voice another decibel. "Alex, don't cry, baby. I thought about the baby we just lost. Our love. I understood that what we have doesn't fall out of the sky every day. It just doesn't happen, baby. It's rare and it's special." He paused briefly. "I love you too much to allow anyone to have that part of me for a few hours. An evening. A week. Even a year, however long a man runs around." There was another pause. "I realized that, baby. I sat Destiny down on the couch in the suite and told her the same thing."

With her eyes still downcast, she hung onto his every word. Especially "the couch in the suite" and decided to not ask questions until he was done speaking.

"You're all that I could ever imagine, and I could never ever hurt you." Madison began to cry. He pushed the hair from her face and cupped her cheeks with his hands. "Look at me baby, please."

"Yes, Madison." Slowly, she raised her eyes and returned the stare.

"I knew in order for our marriage to be what we dreamed and talked about, we—you and me—" He hesitated and pointed an index finger at her heart and at his own. "We have to work at taking good care of it and at nourishing it, baby love."

"I know."

"We got to be committed to it because we're the stewards for this union. Not Destiny. Not anyone. Not whomever we might be tempted by," he said quietly as he kissed her forehead, nose, and lips.

"Oh, Madison."

"And I promise you with my life. I'll never ever make love to another woman. I just can't. I—want—you—to—understand—that. I honor and cherish you too much for that. You have my word, baby." He gently held her hands and kissed them. As an afterthought and to make the pledge very real within him, he softly said it again. "You have my solemn word, Alex."

Madison pulled Alex to him, and he tenderly kissed her twice on the lips. That was the promise Madison spoke to his wife that night. And since that promise was branded in Madison's soul, that was the closest Madison ever came to making love to another woman other than his wife.

After eighteen years of marriage, Madison still took her breath away when she gazed at him. Alex's heart still fluttered with excitement to know her husband was home from a trip. True, it was his time to be with the boys, but she missed him and knew the reunion would be sweet. The two were inseparable, and all their friends knew they were genuinely in love and couldn't even keep their hands off one another. Alex chuckled softly. If it were up to her and if he allowed her to, she would enjoy making love to him every minute of every day. She ballooned with endless love for Madison and didn't mind sharing the same news with anyone who would listen. But she didn't have to; most people could see the love that flowed between them.

Madison had such flawless features. He was the color of light brown sugar with wavy hair and a thick mustache. When he turned thirty-eight three years ago, he started graying at the temples and now projected an even more distinguished appearance. He was known for his piercing dark brown button eyes. Pauletta often said that his eyes were either indicative of a surgeon or were the freaky deaky eyes that made women either run away or run to lay—anywhere.

"Plus," Pauletta said in her usual crazy way, "Ain't doctors supposed to be ugly?"

So penetrating was Madison's gaze that sometimes people, especially women, glanced away from it. He stood tall and slender at six feet one. Now that Scott motivated them to exercise three times a week, Madison's lean body was in shape. Alex loved playing with the small patch of hair on his chest and often joked that it must be a good twenty strands there, so he needed to transplant the ones from his legs and arms.

Everyone that met Madison said that he was the most kindest, supportive, and honorable man they ever knew. Since there was nothing more attractive to women than a happily married man committed to remaining faithful to his wife, Madison was considered an excellent catch and remained the focus of much female attention. It was even rumored in certain ladies' circles in Winston-Salem that wagers were placed confidentially, and a challenge list developed to see who could woo Madison from his wife, if just for a night. Madison would have none of it. He was in love with Alex. Period.

When women propositioned Madison with marital indiscretion and it occurred very often, they always lost the bet and walked away both shocked by his honesty and embarrassed by their attempts. Also known as Mr. and Mrs. Social Butterfly, Dr. and Mrs. Devereaux frequently attended the popular social functions in Winston. Yet their attention either remained focused on each other or was directed toward their friends. Like his wife, Madison was very spiritual. But both Devereauxs knew how to throw a great old-fashioned party and have fantastic fun.

Madison was an overly affectionate man with everybody and was known as the resident male crybaby regarding emotional issues. He was the one who convinced the other Black guys in the group to become comfortable with hugging, kissing, and saying, "I love ya, man" to each other. Simply put, it was the friends' overwhelming consensus that he and Alex were the perfect combination as both consistently shared love with everyone that crossed their path. So their friends ferociously valued the Devereauxs' acquaintanceship. Their loyalty even more. Symone often teased that whatever omniscient power was responsible for hooking up perfect couples obviously skipped right on by her when it was time to dole out an appropriate husband such as the one Alex received.

Chapter Thirteen

Alex drove down Highway 801 in Advance and turned onto the private Rose Garden Lane. She stopped the car halfway down the triple lane two-mile stretch of paved road. Wanting to check her lipstick and eyeliner, she wanted to get a good look first with the rearview mirror and then with her compact case. When her eyes met her husband's, she always wanted to appear as perfect as possible.

As Alex passed the horses stable and bird boxes which edged the fence that bordered the road, she reminded herself to refill them with seeds tomorrow. She smiled as she gazed upon the large bronze angels with outstretched arms on both sides of the road that welcomed all visitors to the Devereauxs' home. Alex knew she was entering the peacefulness and tranquillity of her home then. The leaves of the oak, magnolia, and dogwood trees, which majestically lined the way, rustled softly from the summer evening breeze. Since the azaleas were also in full bloom, Alex believed the scene was such a perfect definition of southern, warm weather tranquillity. At the top of a slight woody hill, the Devereauxs' home, a huge two-story mansion, was visible. In between, she glided past the roads that lead to the secluded guest cottages as well as the pool and play area that stretched behind the garage side of the house.

When Alex pulled up, she noticed that the fluorescent lights remained on down in her glass greenhouse. Located on the other side of the lake near the formal gardens, she wondered if the greenhouse automatic light timer was clicked for eleven. For some reason, Alex decided to not park the car in the garage. She instead pulled around to the circular brick driveway and courtyard that was straddled by a lovely carpet of green grass. The front foyer chandelier was lit, and Alex noticed Madison's silhouette in the doorway. He was waiting for her. As Alex turned off the car's ignition, he opened the door and walked toward the car. The three black Cocker Spaniels raced out with their tails wagging, continuous barking, and panting while tracing circles among themselves around the car.

Since Alex wanted to have a baby so much, being pregnant was the most important thing in Alex's life, and she tried to become pregnant with just as much passion as she possessed for living life. However, after her fourth miscarriage over five years ago, Madison spent the last night in her hospital bed. And probably for the fifth time in her life, Alex was inconsolable. She cried pitifully about how they were living in such a wonderful, gigantic house built for babies, and now they would never have the six Devereaux children they planned and prayed for.

The next day when the Devereauxs drove up in their garage, Pecola and Symone jumped out from behind a closet door with the canine surprises, and five bouquets of long stemmed yellow roses. Pecola and Symone held the three precious little puppies that Madison brought for his wife the day after she miscarried. He named the dogs, *King, Queen,* and *Dreams.*

After Pecola and Symone left, he carried her up the winding staircase to the bedroom and tenderly explained his philosophy about her four miscarriages.

"...I want you to know that if we're never blessed with children, you'll always be my *Queen.* I'll be your *King,* and we'll live the life of our *Dreams* together," Madison said to a sad Alex. "If we can never have natural children, we'll adopt the six babies we said we wanted to have and love them supernaturally. Ok?"

"Ok," was all Alex could say in a raspy voice. She was overcome with emotions.

Once Madison and Alex thoroughly discussed the subject for the evening, Madison read passages from Maya Angelou's poem, *And Still I Rise.* They listened to the classic jazzy sounds of Errol Garner. Afterwards, they both fell asleep holding one another tightly.

It was a traumatic time for Alex, and she took a ninety-day leave of absence from D. Britt & Cox to deal with the loss of her fourth baby. During the time off, those three Cocker Spaniels became Alex and Madison's children. They remained particularly spoiled rotten and were treated the same by everyone else, especially by their christened Godparents, Pecola, Scott, Symone, and even Uncle Rozelle.

Even though they lived in a dark world of hope due to her infertility, Alex never gave up with having children. But it wasn't until Alex became pregnant the fifth time that she was finally able to carry this baby to term. To the joy of Alex, Madison, their family, and all their friends, she delivered a healthy baby boy. They named him Madison Devereaux, III and called him, Trey, for short. However, it was the dangerous sixth, high-risk pregnancy Alex experienced with having her daughter, Purity Phylicia, that bought Alex's childbearing to a close. Alex's gynecologist told her that she wouldn't be able to bear any other children. On hearing the sad news, she constantly cried in the presence of friends and family about her inability to have more children. With profound understanding and sensitivity, Madison came to the rescue. He once again explained to Alex the lovely philosophy of King, Queen, and Dreams.

When Alex got out of the car, Madison closed the car door. He wrapped his arms around her waist, and they tongue kissed long and hard. Since she'd just given the three dogs a quick head hug, they appeared satisfied, at least temporarily with the attention. As usual, she laughed again when she noticed the cubic zirconium studded red dog collars shimmering in the night. A gift from their Godmother Symone who said that they weren't common canine, visitors always laughed when they saw the dogs' jeweled necks.

Hugging each other's waists, Madison and Alex walked into the huge two-storied marbled foyer. Racing right behind them was Queen, King and Dreams with wet panting tongues and scurrying paws scratching frantic sounds on the marble floor. Alex quickly glanced straight ahead. The elegant entrance hall was sixty feet in depth, down to the decorative white columns that set off the family room. The hall had archways but no doors. This allowed friends immediate visual and physical access to the formal rooms, including the dining room. The Devereauxs designed it in such a way to provide perfect traffic flow for children and their constant entertaining.

Alex wondered why everything seemed so unusually still. Almost immediately, she realized that Trey and Purity weren't running around yelling and screaming behind the dogs. That was it. Holding hands, Alex and Madison walked up the sweeping *Gone With the Wind* looking double staircase that led to the second floor bedrooms. They tiptoed into each child's room. Alex tenderly kissed her two sleeping children on the forehead, cheeks, lips, and kneeled beside each one's bed to say a short prayer.

Although Alex and Madison had separate bathrooms adjacent to private closets, they never used them that way. Invariably, they ended up in Alex's bathroom, the frillier and prettier one of the two. When Alex telephoned Madison to let him know she was heading home, Madison prepared the luxurious Jacuzzi for bathing. Now the hot water bubbled with fragrant oils, and Alex sank her body into the warm water. While basking in the soothing pleasure of Madison's soft sponge scrubbing down her breasts, Alex gazed through the skylight, enjoying the beauty of the night sky. Afterwards, he toweled off the water and powdered her down in rose scented English talc.

To watch the heavens, the two strolled out to the bedroom balcony, which overlooked the lake, garden and swimming pool. This evening, the peacefulness of the starry sky rippled in the water's reflection. Although it was a huge home and was sophisticated enough for elegant dinner parties, it also exuded a welcoming, homey feeling. It was their ultimate, private refuge, a Shangri-La of sorts. When the front door closed, both often escaped from the realities of problems, sickness, and the stress of Madison's position as director of pediatric neurosurgery at Baptist Hospital in Winston-Salem. Virtually every room was filled with their collection of African art, and the finest names in the artistic African-American world graced their walls and shelves.

The Devereauxs desired a spacious house that melded comfort and grand style in a secluded country setting. They wanted their friends to enjoy the luxury but feel the warmth of the ambiance. The house made people want to come back for a visit.

Since she became a stay-at-home mother, Alex performed most of the housework along with her housekeeper, Cleopatra. However, Symone often told her that she needed full time help. Alex truly enjoyed tending the rooms by herself until Pecola convinced her to bend just a tad four years ago. She persuaded her to allow the local African-American firm of Edith Williams Maintenance and Services to come in. Once a month, a four-person team from the Williams company worked three days to give the mansion rooms a complete overhaul, which is exactly what Pecola did for her home. Therefore, as Pecola explained, it wouldn't be such hard work on her or Cleopatra to maintain the neat, spotless decor.

Finally, after listening to their arguments to hire extra help from Madison, Symone, and of course Pecola, Alex relented and agreed to the monthly cleaning service. Other than that, Alex only hired additional personnel when they were having large dinners, grand throw-down parties, or huge pajama nights for the over thirty crowd.

Chapter Fourteen

Once on the balcony, Madison stood behind Alex. He encircled his arms around her waist and snuggled his face into her neck and hair. Alex gazed into the sky and was awed by the hypnotic power of the night. Madison stepped back inside their bedroom and flipped on the switch to light the lake. At the same time, he decided to play *Baby Come to Me,* the Patti Austin and James Ingram song. He placed the song on the repeat mode.

Before going back outside to be with Alex, Madison silently watched the silhouette of her nude body as it leaned against the balcony pillar. As always, he noticed her bowlegs and wonderfully curved hips below the tiny firm waist. Madison remained mesmerized by her. Sometimes he joked to his brother, Marguis, that if he believed there was such a thing as roots or voodoo, then Alex bewitched him.

Madison returned to the balcony. They danced for a moment and gazed into the crystal clear night graced only with the full moon and stars. Alex became very quiet and took several deep breaths. He saw that her mind had quickly drifted away.

"What are you thinking, Alex?" he whispered as he kissed her neck again.

"You know what?" She stretched her right hand behind her and rubbed his hair as she spoke. "It's amazing, baby."

"I'm listening."

"I gaze at the perfectly pearl white moon, and I'm reminded that we live on a ball that merely hangs in the sky," she said quietly in an awed voice. "Can you believe that?"

For a few seconds Madison said nothing. Then he slowly turned her around and kissed her on the mouth.

"No, baby. I can't believe that." Madison moved back behind her, and he began slowly gliding his hands over the front of her body in erotic touches and peered out into the seductive darkness.

"To understand that fact about our planet is the most fascinating thing in the universe," Alex went on. "If we were living on the moon, we would watch the earth the same way."

Madison smiled down at her as he thought about what she said and considered the years they shared. They had been through a lot together. There were many days of so many tears and sorrow. But moments of joy and happiness were squeezed in along the way as well. Through it all, they remained blessed. Now, not only were they solid as husband and wife, but they were confidant, friend, and advisor to the other. And they still shared the magic of sex-crazed lovers.

For years now, Madison believed he and Alex were eternal soul mates. She however said that she knew it from the beginning. He felt his penis rising again, and it bounced along her back. Slowly, she turned around with hunger shining in her eyes. She smiled and bent to kiss his penis several times. The telephone rang. Alex grudgingly pulled away and said she would get it. It was Symone.

"Hey, Sy," Alex said, rubbing her neck.

"Are you busy, Alex?" Immediately, Alex recognized the sadness in Symone's voice.

"Not too busy for a friend. What's wrong, girl?"

"The usual," Symone said as she sipped champagne. "What were you doing when I called?"

"Madison and I were watching the sky. It's unusually pretty tonight, Symone."

"Well, don't let me keep you. No. You just take care. Tell Madison I said hello."

"Symone, I'll talk as long as you want me to, as long as you need. You know that. So tell me why you've called." She paused a moment and glanced at a hard and nude Madison walk to the bedroom bar to get a bottle of water.

"Alex?"

"Huh. Uh, yes, I'm sorry. Do you want to come over here and spend the night with us?"

Symone lived only eight miles away and could probably be at their door in about ten minutes. Madison smiled at the invitation and decided he'd call Symone tomorrow morning to check on her. He quickly swallowed a half glass of water and strolled to his spot outdoors.

"No, go back to Madison. I'll speak to you in the morning. Love ya, Alex."

"And, I love you, Symone. Have a good evening. Ok?"

"I'll try." Symone hung up.

Alex returned to the balcony, resumed her position in front of her husband, and his arms encircled her waist. She told Madison that Symone said hello. Still wanting to enjoy the magic of the night, more soft touches sent electrifying tingles through their bodies. Out of the blackness of the sky, a shooting star flashed by.

"Did you wish for anything, baby?" The lilt in his voice seemed to caress Alex.

Alex turned to face him and clung to his shoulders with her face buried in his chest.

"My life is like a fairy tale already, Madison," she whispered. "I'm living that dream. Those little girl dreams my Mama gave me when my dreams weren't big enough. Why should I wish for anything? I've everything I ever dreamed about right here on earth. Right now with you."

"You're sweet, baby."

Alex smiled up at him happily with love-colored eyes. "I missed you, Madison. The longing for you never dies down and never goes away."

"I surrendered, baby. Gave up. Couldn't fight my need for you—then—or—now."

"I can't either."

They kissed, first softly, then with hunger. Madison pulled back to stare into her eyes.

"Now tell me, Alex. Are you sure you didn't wish for even the smallest thing?" His caresses turned into tickling, and Alex burst into giggles.

"I don't want anything else in life. Just that our love stay this strong until there is no more breath in our bodies." Alex was silent. "I did pray for Symone. That she meets someone and be happy. I'm concerned for her, Madison. As soon as I got home, I stuck that prayer in my prayer box, in Imani."

Because he heard it so much, Madison smiled a little at that prayer. He also grinned about the box Alex constantly filled with different written prayer concerns and requests from her friends. She was sincerely committed to the power of prayer and named the box Imani, the seventh Kwanzaa principle that stood for faith. Like it was a naturally instinctive need, she prayed over those Imani needs each morning and every night. Madison pulled her closer and spoke nearly in a whisper.

"Sy will be fine, but let her go for tonight. I'm into you. My wife. My lover. My friend. Can I ever forget how lucky I am to have you, Alex?"

"No. Not lately." She smiled a little smile despite her preoccupation with the problems of her friend.

"Well, I'll scream it to the world if I have to. I want everyone to know just how much my life, my happiness depends on you." He laughed happily. "The next time we have a party, I'll announce it on the mike." He cupped both hands around his mouth and yelled out into the dark. "Contrary to popular belief in the media world, I'm a Black man living in America who truly loves and only adores his wife, Alex!"

They laughed. He pulled her closer to him again and kissed her gently on the mouth.

"Oh, Madison," she said.

"Come on, let's go inside, baby," he said as he grabbed her hand. "I have a Jerry Butler song I want to play just for you."

Madison guided her inside, pulled the screen door shut, and locked the latch. Then, he sat her down on the dual king, custom-made NiKolina bed he asked Cleopatra to cover in creme satin for tonight. He raced to insert the cassette tape he earlier threatened Scott with his life. Outside the bedroom door, Alex heard the dogs pacing along the parquet floor whimpering and wanting to come in. They were so spoiled, but she didn't want Dreams, King, and Queen in the room when they made love. Her special and private time with her husband was reserved only for them alone.

Madison came back into the bedroom and cleared his throat. He bowed stiffly at the waist and asked Alex for a dance. Of course, she accepted. And, now Alex truly understood why her sweet baby love asked Scott to dub the song. This was the first time she had ever heard *Simply Beautiful* and was hypnotized by the lyrics that rode the sweet-sounding melody. Immediately, she decided she'd select the song for their weekly Friday evening celebration of each other. The words were truly magnificent, absolutely marvelous. She pressed her face against Madison's chest and slow dragged the down home, fraternity basement party, red light, old-fashioned way. The song played four times. Smiling broadly, Madison swooped Alex up. He carried Alex to their bed and laid down beside her. Madison kissed her hard for a long time. He surprised her with a bouquet of Mme. Hardy white roses. On the note he slipped inside, it read, "Baby, nothing says love better than a rose. Your soul mate, Madison."

Madison told her that he picked the roses from their rose garden just today, especially for tonight. Then he gave her a rose emblem wrapped gift box.

When Alex opened it, she discovered a white stretch lace chemise, snap crotchless panties, and garters from Lise Charmel. She gasped from surprise and delight. Then she laughed and thanked him for courting her the old-fashioned way, with romance, gifts, and more romance. Whenever Madison traveled out of town, he brought a gift home for his wife.

While they sipped Fiji water and munched green, seedless grapes, Madison shared every detail about the trip. How crazy Rozelle, Carlos, Scott, and the other men acted. What they did in Hilton Head. The fish. The card games. The frat jokes. Alex was glad to hear that he golfed in the seventies, and she was proud to know that the foursome of Scott, Carlos, Madison, and DC, a crazy college buddy of Scott and Rozelle, came in third place in the mini-golf tournament.

Madison's face now possessed that hungry sexy look. He cupped her breasts and tenderly sucked both nipples continuously for long minutes. That was it for Alex, and the sex compass inside of her tingled with expectation.

"Lay back, baby. Allow me to take care of you tonight. As your King, I want to be your most wonderful fantasy, Alex." He licked her neck and face.

"Ohhh, Madison."

While Madison whispered to her, his hands glided over her firm breasts. With his index finger, he gently twirled her curly, thick pubic hairs in a circular motion.

"I love you more than life itself, baby," he breathed in her ears. "I thought about you the whole weekend. There are no words to tell you how much I missed you, Alex." His words were punctuated with kisses that left erotic imprints all over her. The sensations were ecstasy. With the moonlight filtering in, she smiled and pulled his face to hers. When they made love, Madison enjoyed gazing into Alex's eyes. When she moaned like she was in pain, it was an aphrodisiac for him. Her wanting him. Her body needing only what he could do for her made him excited as well.

To see their bodies twisting during lovemaking, a well-lit room was always required. This evening, a pair of antique lamps provided the additional soft glow. Madison adored his wife's body. Oftentimes, he gazed at it longingly even before he touched her as he received just as much stimulation by peering at her chocolatey nudeness against the creamy colored satin sheet. He believed her body was even more beautiful after she had the babies, and he always first lovingly kissed the delicate stretch mark lines around her navel.

"I was with you the whole time you were in Hilton Head, Madison. I was there, baby," she whispered as she held his head.

"You're always with me, Alex," he said fiercely as he had so often done in the past, especially after he returned from a trip. "Wherever I am, you're always there, baby. Whatever happens to you, happens to me. I feel your thoughts. Everything there is about you flows right through me, Alex." He had stopped to stare into the shiny sable eyes brimming with love for him. The Jerry Butler music stopped for the fourth time, and they didn't bother to put it on repeat.

"I love you so much, Madison."

"I love you. And I want to show that I know that you know that I know that," he replied with a soft laugh. For several minutes, he kissed the palm of each hand lightly with the brush of his tongue. Then he laid them gently at her side and slowly pried her legs apart at the knees. Waves of good feelings flowed between them.

As soon as Scott and Charmaine reached his house, they began groping and frantically undressing each other at the front door. Scott had only been gone for five days, but it felt more like a ten-year solitary confinement. Both were unashamedly horny. They took a thirty-second shower and walked hand in hand to the bed. Scott cupped Charmaine's breasts and tongued both nipples in circular motions until they became firm. Just as he moved toward her navel, the telephone rang. Scott thought it was his brother, Romallus, and that was the only reason he even answered it on the third ring. When they left Hilton Head earlier, Romallus who hated to travel via plane, told Scott he'd call as soon as he arrived in New Orleans.

"Hello, Scott. It's Symone," she said quietly in a questioning way.

"Hey, baby," he said totally preoccupied. He stuck his middle and index fingers in Charmaine, and she grinded her body in quick up and down motions.

"Is everything cool with you, Scottie?"

"Yes. The question is are you ok?" He was truly concerned. As he watched Charmaine gyrate, he silently prayed to God right now that Symone was doing fine. Charmaine moaned quietly as he continued to jab his fingers in and out. "Well, are you?"

"Yeah, I'm fine." The gleam in her voice was a lie.

"You're sure? I'll come get you, if necessary."

No, hell no! Your ass ain't leaving here this night for no damn body, thought Charmaine while she groaned and smiled from the delightful feelings his fingers brought.

"Sure you're ok, baby?"

"Believe me, Scott. Yes I am."

"Well, good then. Let me get back with you tomorrow morning. Love ya, baby."

"Love ya too, Scott," she said sadly and hung up.

Scott eased out of bed and twirled the dim switch to ultra low. To enhance the romantic mood, he walked around the room and placed ten lighted French vanilla candles in strategic locations in the bedroom. He strolled back to the bed and kissed Charmaine on the nose, neck, and lips. Scott sauntered to the stereo system and inserted several CDs by the Queen of Blues, Ms. Dinah Washington. He returned to the bed, nibbled and licked each of Charmaine's ears, then watched her eyes glare sexily at him.

Hungrily, he gazed at Charmaine's naked body stretched out with her arms above her head in the middle of the bed, just waiting for him. Just waiting for the deep-digging sex that snagged him from the first time he entered her. The vee shaped pubic hair was cut exactly the way he asked. It looked so pretty that he felt like kissing each strand. She appeared as a Black queen goddess expecting the appointed worshipper to provide any sexual requests. He had missed her while he was away. He was back. He was ready, and so was she. Charmaine smiled as if to challenge him to make her his all over again. He smiled back.

Scott realized the bed was absolutely perfect for moments such as these and reminded himself to again thank Alex, Pecola, and Symone with helping him design it. They told him that such a piece of furniture would mentally transfer a woman back to the days of African royalty—especially if she possessed a skilled, kingly Black man who turned into a beast when he made love upon it. The unusual four poster bed with pillars that almost reached to the ceiling was carved from dark, sleek teak and topped with scallop ornaments that were connected by a metal canopy. Scott draped the canopy in a sheer cream lace to make the aura of the room enchanting. The patio's double doors were opened. The summer breeze, only separated by the screen petition, ruffled the lace in a billowy fashion.

Scott switched on the answering machine and watched Charmaine seductively for a moment. Then he held each foot and licked and tenderly sucked all ten toes. He opened Charmaine's legs to form the letter vee. He watched her pussy intently for two minutes and told her that only she could satisfy his hunger. Now, the worshipper was back to please his queen. There would be no more interruptions. Scott grinned to himself.

I'm just as crazy as all of them, Scott thought. *They even got me believing this crazy King and Queen romance shit.* Charmaine knew what was coming next. She sighed deeply as Scott straddled first her left leg then her right one over his shoulders. To drown himself in her sweetness, he buried his face between them.

Pecola closed her eyes and sank against the BMW sedan leather seats. She thought about her friends. She laughed so much this evening until it gave her a headache. It was mandatory that she called Pauletta. After that call, Pecola would definitely call Jodria. She wanted to tell Jodria that if she hadn't found Eddie Murphy's address, Pecola would get it because Rozelle was one crazy brother. Mr. Eddie Murphy needed to meet his protégé, go on the road with Rozelle's act, or help him try out for Def Comedy Jam. Rozelle needed to do something.

Just as Pecola was in motion to plunge through the intersection, the light turned yellow then red at the corner of Vest Mill Road. Good. It gave Pecola a few moments to search for her favorite Junior Walker & the All-stars CD. The light quickly turned green, and an impatient driver behind her pressed long and hard on the horn twice. Pecola glanced disgustingly in the car's rearview mirror. She started to give the impatient driver the middle finger out the window but decided against it since it was dark and late. Instead, she turned right and pulled over to the shoulder of the road until she found the Junior Walker CD she needed to hear. She inserted the CD into the player and pulled back onto the highway. Acting carefree, Pecola began singing *Shotgun* extremely loud at full volume while snapping her fingers to the beat of Junior Walker.

Since Pecola hadn't heard from her husband, she decided to call home after driving two miles or so. Carlos answered on the third ring.

"Where have you been, Carlos honey?" she asked teasingly in a slow drawn out way.

"The question is, where have you been, Pecola? I called the office and paged your butt. I called you in your car twice not more than five minutes ago. No one answered, baby."

"I'm listening to Junior Walker and his All-stars, so you ought to understand why the music was blasting," she said laughing loudly as she still tried to hear the words even though the music was turned low.

"I do."

"I've been jamming and shotgunning down the highway by my damn self!" She continued to snap her fingers repeatedly. "I'm sure the other drivers drove by and thought I was crazy, baybee. Did you have a good time in Hilton Head, Carlos?" she asked as she blinked headlights twice for the slowpoke driver in front of her to move over.

"It was great, but I missed you, baby. How long will it be before you get here?"

"A least ten more minutes," she sang liltingly.

"Ok, baby. Great! Oh, by the way, I spoke to your parents today."

"Good," she fibbed again.

Why the hell does everyone want to tell me about my parents today? Pecola thought to herself.

"I called them before I left the office, too," she told her husband. Another untruth.

I tell you when you lie frequently, it becomes real easy to do it over and over again. That's another award my friends can give me, Ms. Lie Queen, Pecola thought. *I'm so good at lying about my parents, I can teach classes.*

"We had a bad mama jamma time in Hilton Head, baby," Carlos was sitting back sipping champagne and smoking a fat cigar. "But I'll tell you all about it when you get here. DC said hello. This was after he got over being seasick and remembered who he was."

"I know. Scott told us the same thing." They laughed again.

"Baby, I saw so many damn alligators on the golf course that I started to hit one in the head with a golf ball so I could make you shoes and pocketbooks."

"I can imagine. If they were like the ones we saw last summer, they were probably big as hell."

"Some of them were fourteen feet long, baby. I was cool about it. So cool that wherever I stood on the greens, there was a chilly draft floating around," he joked while laughing

"Were you a good ole little boy, Carlos?" she asked sweetly.

"I was as good as I can be."

"That's good, baby. So you men really didn't have any women around? Symone said that whenever Billy went on those trips, he *said* he *was* going with the boys. But he was really with the girls, fishing between their legs."

"Baby, no. That wasn't even me. It was totally a male thing. You know, bonding and shit," he assured her while laughing loudly at Pecola's crazy sense of humor.

"Good old fun."

"Exactly, baby. I tell you. I was sooo good, I feel like kissing my own behind," he added in a solemn voice, and they both laughed raucously.

"You're so funny, Carlos."

"I know. Anyway, hurry up, Sweet Pea. I got a fire going in the bedroom. And, I thought it would be nice to give you a nice 'hot baby' oil rubdown. A therapeutic and toe massage. If you know what I mean."

"Aaah, sookie, sookie now. I'm on my way, Lollipop!" Pecola shouted lovingly as she smiled and pressed the end button. She believed it was a little warm for a fire. But for the sake of romance, she was willing to go right along with any of her husband's plans.

If my man wants to kick in the fireplace in the dead of summer, well so be it, Pecola thought with a great, big wide grin. *After twenty-four years of marriage, a woman gots to go with the flow whenever her man says so.*

Pecola burst out laughing. She turned up the music and continued to enjoy the private saxophone party with Junior and the Boys.

Carlos walked to the bar and poured another glass of Cristal champagne; then he strolled to the bathroom to fill the Jacuzzi full of water. Pecola sounded like she experienced one of her long days, and she probably would love to wallow in a hot bath. He checked the water and made it as blazing as possible. Knowing Pecola, ten minutes would be more like forty minutes, so the water would be just right by the time she arrived. Carlos searched the linen closet and dropped in a couple of lavender bath cubes.

I'll have it perfect when she gets here, Carlos said to himself.

Carlos sauntered back into the bedroom, looked around for a moment, and placed two oak logs in the fireplace. A whole lot of shit rumbled through his mind, but he was determined not to worry but to stay focused on his wife and the late night time they would spend together. He opened the French doors and stepped out onto the terrace. Carlos took another sip from his glass and reflected on how great the bright, full moon and starry night sky looked. Almost like a watercolor painting. The nagging thoughts surfaced again. But he shook his head quickly and pushed his thoughts back to Pecola, and the evening he had planned. Not a whole lot. Just a hot oil massage. A little talk. Play with her hair. Drink a few glasses of champagne. Listen to music. And then make wonderful love to his wife. All in that order.

Being around a bunch of men for five days, talking about women and every other thing under the sun, Carlos was horny as a navy man commissioned to sea for six months and who hadn't see hide nor tail of pussy. Carlos strolled back inside and stuck in a Brownstone CD. He punched in the numbers for the last three tracks and started toward the bathroom. When he was done using the toilet, he gazed at his reflection. Carlos tightened the white terry cloth towel around his waist and silently thought, *Not too bad, Carlos. Man, not too bad for forty-two.*

Always considered a pretty man by the ladies, Carlos was just as light-skinned as Pecola. Some friends joked he was even two shades shinier. A standout Aggie basketball player at A&T back in the day, he stood six-foot-three. Carlos was proud of the fact he was a mere twenty pounds over his collegiate perfect weight of one ninety. But like he told his brother, "It was all muscle, baby."

Lean and trim with natural curly jet black hair, thick lips, a pointy nose, dreamy sky blue eyes, and a left cheek dimple, Carlos' rippled body was perfect. He continually thanked Scott for being the unrelenting conscience for convincing all their asses to get back in shape four years ago. Endowed with a small waist and broad shoulders, Carlos always wore a neatly shaven mustache and goatee. His goatee came in handy when he worried about things since it was quite comforting to rub his chin and think. And he did a lot of that lately, especially now that—

Dismiss it, man, Carlos' mind yelled at him. *Dismiss the shit.*

Although Carlos was a prominent player in college, he naturally wanted to play in the National Basketball League. But he knew if those hoop dreams fell through, there was a spot reserved for him in the family business his father started thirty-nine years ago. Today, CR Construction was the largest African-American owned general contracting firm in the southeast. The multi-million dollar company laid claim to building some of the most unique properties in various states.

At the age of twelve, Carlos began working with his father looking at blueprints. When he was thirteen, Carlos worked odd jobs in the field. But once he and his other siblings reached their sophomore year in high school, they were required to learn different assignments in the CR Construction Group executive offices. It was understood that none of the Reynolds children absorbed managerial responsibilities until they graduated from college. Those were the ground rules established by their father, and they were law.

So Carlos graduated with a BS in architectural engineering and a MBA from North Carolina A&T. Acting rebellious and in an effort to get as far away from his mother's color-struck dream world, his brother Rico journeyed to Fayetteville State University. It was an almost three hour drive from their home in Greensboro. There Rico met his wife, Darilyn, a Washington, DC native. Rico finished collegiate studies with the same two degrees as Carlos. Now Rico managed the Greensboro office. So like Alex said all the time, "Things happened for a reason."

Carlos and his brother were extremely close. Rico, who was often mistaken as Carlos' identical twin, normally followed the recommendations of his older brother in most areas of his life. However, although Carlos pledged Alpha Phi Alpha, Rico took another turn and decided to become a devoted Kappa Alpha Psi man. As a result of the brothers' different fraternities but loyal affection as siblings, it was the basis for sidesplitting jokes. During Reynolds' family gatherings, Carlos and Rico ribbed one another about the fact that each one believed they were involved in the best fraternity in the world.

Once Carlos assumed the helm of CR Construction, the company achieved phenomenal success, and their sales almost tripled. Carlos attributed his success to the fact that he was surrounded with nothing but his father's dedication to success ever since he could remember. Privileged to grow up in a solid, old-fashioned southern Black family that believed in hard work, business was discussed during their evening dinners, family reunions, parties, and every other chance they got.

During those moments, Carlos received an excellent understanding of the market and politics of the construction business. He realized that one person couldn't do it all. His father taught them that presidents of major organizations succeed because they must surround themselves with dedicated and excellently qualified people to monitor everything else. In other words, they were taught to learn how to delegate responsibility.

Carlos nodded his head with fondness when he thought about his mother and father. In April, they celebrated their golden anniversary, and he recalled them laughing, talking, and dancing at their anniversary party. They had come a long way. They married when his mother Mercedes was sixteen and Carlos Sr. was eighteen. Just like Carlos and Pecola. Carlos often heard that history repeated itself. At the rate he and Pecola were going, in another twenty-six years they would celebrate the same monumental event his parents had just celebrated.

Since the music stopped, Carlos slowly nodded his head with a smile, drained the glass, and stepped back inside the bedroom. He rummaged through the mahogany CD compartment, found a Terry Callier one and stuck it in, glanced at his watch, and figured his pretty Pecola should arrive in about five minutes. He checked the water, strolled back outside on the bedroom terrace, and continued to gaze at the black sky.

Whew! Carlos thought to himself with a quick jerk of his head. He was glad to see that the older his mother got, the less she was on her Puerto Rican kick. Carlos couldn't say the same about his mother when he was growing up. That was all he heard as a young boy growing up in Greensboro. And that was that the Reynolds family was not actually Black people. They were descendants of first-generation Puerto Ricans who relocated to North Carolina over sixty years ago. This was probably how Carlos' mother mentally dealt with her heritage.

With wavy Black hair down her back, Mercedes Reynolds brainwashed everyone to believe she wasn't the half-white woman they thought she was. She eventually persuaded her husband, Charles, a man who was just as light-skinned as she was, to legally change his name to Carlos two years after they married.

When Carlos and Mercedes' three children came along, they were named with appropriate Puerto Rican names and indoctrinated into their mother's thinking. Carlos was the oldest. Ricardo, also known as Rico, was next. There was Carlos' sister, Magdalia, who really wasn't sure what or who she was. As a result of Magdalia's confusion regarding her heritage, she refused to visit North Carolina, especially after she decided many years ago to embrace her mother's lie that she was a Puerto Rican. So she moved to Puerto Rico and began living as one.

Carlos swallowed the fiction as well and believed the descriptive hype about his mother's family. That was until he was eleven and went to the now infamous family reunion that was attended by his Aunt Coretta. That was his mother's very light-skinned only sister who everyone said was crazy as hell because she drank moonshine by the barrel.

Since Carlos was the oldest, that was the reason why his Aunt Coretta said that she pulled him aside to give him a good talking to. Carlos never forgot what she shared with him. On that day, his Aunt Coretta told him, "Let me tell you something, boy. The closest your Mammy's high yellow ass ever came to having Puerto Rican red blood near her body was if she looked at shittin' Puerto Rico on the map while she wore gotdamn red sunglasses."

Aunt Coretta went on to tell him that, "Your Mammy's ass was born in Graham, North Carolina. And the reason why we look this way was cause our Mammy was continually raped by Mr. Amos Colgate. He was the white man who owned the Colgate Cotton Mill there in Graham and lived in the big house where our Mammy worked as the maid. And, Carlos—Hell that's another thing. Your name is Charles. That's what your real name should be! Yessirree bob. That's right. Your Mammy made your father change his name from Charles to Carlos. And it twas bout damn time somebody told your ass the damn truth about who you are."

Those were Aunt Coretta's words exactly. Aunt Coretta eventually told Rico and Magdalia the same story, but Carlos never heard a word from his mother. He never discussed it with her. She was ashamed of who she was. Mercedes hated the white and the Black blood in her so much that she wanted to identify with another culture. The Puerto Ricans. That's what the rape of her mother did to her mind. Carlos realized that Mercedes never came to grips with her heritage the way his Aunt Coretta did. To be Black was below her. She didn't want to claim it. Refused to. She felt that if she ignored what happened to her mother, the truth of her heritage couldn't and wouldn't suffocate her from achieving the dreams of being accepted.

Carlos laughed out in the darkness just remembering his Aunt Coretta's awfully funny wit. Suddenly, he thought he heard Pecola come in. He stepped back inside the bedroom and loudly called her name; however, no one answered. He strolled over to the bar to refill his glass and stepped into the bathroom to turn off the water. Slowly, Carlos danced back outside and sat down on the Sonoma lounge chair with the flowery cushion. Since Pecola was heading home, he deactivated the alarm system.

That's why I told Pecola this house is too damn big for just the two of us. All our children are finally on their own. Jed and Clampett are dead, Carlos thought sadly. *Go ahead and say it, man. Say it! Your little girl is dead, too. It took you a long time to say that. Didn't it? It sure did. Damn, man! Life's a trip.*

But this was the house his Pecola baby wanted. After the family tragedy nine years ago, Carlos would've moved heaven and earth to please her, to just see her green eyes sparkle again. She said that she wanted her new home built just like the home on *The Beverly Hillbillies* Show with the winding staircase, high ceilings, and spacious rooms.

With the help of Rico, Carlos found one-hundred and fifty acres on the outskirts of Winston-Salem. Carlos kept ten acres for him and Pecola. They decided to reserve the same sized tracts for each Reynolds child. He then sold ten-acre tracts to nine other Black families, and Carlos designed a home for Pecola as close to the Clampetts as he could. Back then, Pecola didn't even have the strength to help the architect. Carlos' blue eyes watered as he remembered the tragic past, and he shook his head sadly. At the time, Carlos complied with whatever he could if he thought it would dry the river of tears that never seemed to stop falling from Pecola's eyes.

Well, enough of those thoughts, man, Carlos thought as he tried to smile. *Your woman is gonna be walking in any minute. You should be wearing a happy face for her, man.*

With its high ceiling and lots of natural light from the many magnificent windows she added to the plans the one day she ventured out of seclusion, the stately house was decorated beautifully. Carlos congratulated his wife. She was great at selecting perfect antiques, pieces of furniture, or complementing accessories to show off their home's elegant features.

Carlos gulped more champagne, stood up, and checked his wristwatch. Now he was worried. His Sweet Pea should have arrived by now. As Carlos started for the bedroom door leading to the hallway, he heard the jingling of bracelets and Pecola's one of a kind southern voice.

"Carlos?"

He was hiding behind the six panel oriental screen beside the bar.

"Carlos!" Pecola screamed and hurried outdoors, glancing to her left and her right on the terrace. She whirled around when she heard a slight rustle behind her.

"Hey, baby," he said smiling wide and held his arms out. Pecola flew into them and hugged his neck. Carlos raised her slightly off the floor, kissing her long and tenderly. Pecola tasted the sweetness of champagne on his tongue.

"Don't you look sexy and smell damn good, too," she said taking off her jacket and walking toward the closet.

While holding his stomach, Carlos performed a slinky wine-ing dance he learned from their many trips to Trinidad where they played mas with Symone. Pecola noticed that the thick black hair on his chest glistened in the firelight, and she wondered if Carlos dripped champagne on it when he heard her come up the stairs. When he did that two weeks ago, he asked Pecola to slowly lick it off.

"Pour me some champagne please, baby?" she muffled from inside her cavernous clothing closet. Since Carlos couldn't hear what she said, he strolled to the closet's doorway and leaned on it.

"What did you say, my queen?" he asked in a dignified voice as he rubbed his chin.

"Honey pumpkin—" She smiled broadly. "I said, my King. Pour me some champagne, puhleeze." There was a slight pause as she sat on the cloth-covered bench and removed her shoes.

"Pour champagne? I'll be happy to, queenie."

"I can always tell when you men-sus have been around Madison. That's all Scott and Rozelle talked about. The King and Queen romance converts Madison recruited the five days at Hilton Head." She stepped out of the dress and searched for an empty hanger.

"It was a lot of them, baby."

"I bet when they go home, their wives are gonna wonder what in the hell happened to their huzzbands. Symone said that Madison should give lessons, do the lecture circuit, and just take the romance show on the road, honey." She laughed and winked at him. "Shooot! That's great, baby. I ain't complaining. I'll take romance any way I can get it."

"My queen, then you know I'll be happy to retrieve the royal li-quer for you, Sweet Pea," he said over his shoulder with a thick British accent.

Pecola loved for him to call her Sweet Pea, too. Six years after they married, she was concerned about having four babies one right behind the other and assumed her pussy was now as wide as a triple lane highway. Carlos came to the rescue and set her mind at ease with praise. He said that her pussy was still as tight as one green pea skin and sweet as the purest brown sugar. Once Pecola heard the longing in his voice, she believed him and was fine forever more. After that, she tried to figure out a name to top Sweet Pea. A few years later, she told him that when she sucked his hard Johnson, it was like sucking a lollipop since it was so goooddddd. Hence, *Sweet Pea* and *Lollipop*.

An hour later, the bath and hot oil massage was completed. After studying the gorgeous night, Pecola and Carlos returned to their bedroom and relaxed on separate sofas and seductively eyed each other over the chess table. On one of Pecola and Alex's shopping sprees, they found a Clarence House jacquard covered sofa for a Devereaux guestroom. Pecola adored the sofa choice so much, she purchased two for the master suite, and the combo provided a quaint sitting area in front of the bedroom fireplace.

"Well, I'm glad to see it went ok today, Sweet Pea," Carlos said as he gave the naked and very relaxed Pecola another glass of champagne and went to sit back down.

"Honey dumplings, it went great. Like I told you earlier, I don't really want to talk about business tonight."

Pecola swallowed the bubbly and batted her eyes at him. Carlos moved from the other couch again and came to stand in front of her. The lights were dimmed, and fire reflections shimmered on his body. Pecola stared upward. Carlos reached for her hand and placed it on the towel knot. He stepped back. The terry cloth towel moved along with him, fell to the floor, and he stood nude before her.

"Umph! Umph! Umph!" she moaned seductively and licked her lips. Pecola could only stare at his penis. It was firm, hard, and bulging veiny with a nice circumcised head. She felt like licking him but decided she would start to spread soft kisses on his knees first. Carlos placed his hands in her hair. By the time she nibbled and sucked and nibbled up to the genital hairs, the telephone rang.

"Damn! Damn!" Carlos yelled. Pecola reluctantly rose to answer it. Since their three children knew their father was out of town, she assumed it might be one of them calling him to say hello. It was Symone.

"Are you busy, Pecola?" she asked and sighed deeply.

"Honeychile, just talking to Carlos. Are you ok, Symone?" she queried concerned.

"I'm fine. I just wanted to talk."

"Hey, Symone. My beautiful Trini girl," Carlos yelled loud enough to be heard by Symone as well as the neighbors who lived acres away.

Years ago when all the friends first traveled to Trinidad to play mas with Symone, a cousin laughingly said that Symone no longer sounded like a Trini. Since that time, Carlos often teased her with the pet name.

"Oh, my. Carlos is there?" she inquired in a very surprised voice.

"Of course, he's here. He lives here, chile. Remember?" replied Pecola laughing, too.

"Well, you know exactly what I mean, girl. Anyway, tell him I said hello."

"Carlos, Symone said hello," echoed Pecola. He glanced toward her and acknowledged the greeting with a stiff salute. Still, his eyes lingered around Pecola's breast area. Carlos pointed an index finger toward his mid-section and blew a kiss. Pecola smiled quietly.

"Whatever you need, I can help, chile," Pecola assured Symone as Carlos continued to drool. "Want to come spend the night?"

"Hell no! I don't want to come spend the night at your damn house, Pecola girl! Damn! Damn! Damn!" she screamed bitterly at the top of her voice.

Pecola refused to go over there and comment either way. It sounded like there was some other problems underlying Symone's yelling, and she had no clue why Symone was so upset. Maybe tomorrow. A few seconds passed.

"You feel better now, getting that out, honeychile?" Pecola asked sweetly and made an understanding smile in Carlos' direction, who by now was looking at her curiously. "Screaming helps."

Symone laughed cynically. "Yeah, I'm fine," she said slowly with a deep sigh as she frowned into the phone.

"You're sure, Symone?"

"Yep. Positive. I love you, Pecola. I'll talk to you at the office in the morning," she said dejectedly and hung up before she heard Pecola say, "I love your Black butt too, chile!"

As soon as Pecola hung up the telephone, Carlos recognized Pecola's sad expression. That signaled Symone was upset about something again. Carlos sat there and stared at Pecola a short eternity and hoped she wouldn't get depressed like she so often did when either one of her friends was distraught. Finally, Carlos held his arms out to her, and she plopped herself on his lap. As Carlos kissed Pecola's lips and stroked her breasts, he told her not to worry about Symone because she was a strong Black woman and would be fine.

Carlos escorted Pecola to the bedroom terrace where they peered at the loveliness of the pretty night once more. A shooting star zoomed by and both of them whispered silent pleas for family and friends. After Pecola calmed down, they tongue kissed long and tender. Then he carried her to the huge mahogany poster bed where they made soft and hard love to the sounds of Peabo Bryson.

Still pumping strong an hour and three orgasms later for Pecola, once again she was thankful that Carlos was long-winded and controlled. He expected her to be ultimately exhausted by the time he busted two or three nutts his own self. As they bumped and grinded with their bodies hanging halfway off the bed, she felt herself coming again. Suddenly, she realized she hadn't called Jodria or Paulettaaaaaaaaa!

Symone noticed the beauty of the evening as well. Emotionally exhausted, she planned to retire early around eight o'clock. However, that remained a fantasy, especially since she, Pecola, Rozelle, and Scott didn't leave O'Charley's parking lot until way after eight. By the time she reached home, she crawled upstairs to her bedroom. With her clothes quickly strewn all over the seventeenth century armchair she discovered a month ago in a High Point antique store, she drank two glasses of Brut Imperial Champagne in rapid succession and prayed out loud that she wasn't becoming an alcoholic like him.

Quietly, she strolled to the mirrored armoire and searched for something satiny. She found a charmeuse short night slip and wriggled into it. While she lay in bed, she quickly flipped through the pages of *Free To Soar Motivation* magazine. But her mind began to wander, and she couldn't concentrate. As she stared at the lavish canopy fabric of her bed for thirty minutes, she changed her mind about reading. Symone got up and decided it would be better to meditate with soothing background music.

Feeling a tad lonely, Symone decided to call her friends. Three phone calls later, she softly hung the phone up. As she sat on the edge of the bed, she watched the receiver for several minutes. Even though Alex, Scott, and Pecola tried to act as if they wanted to talk, all of them were really too busy to speak with her.

Everybody but me got a special person to be with on a night like this! Symone thought as she sipped more of her drink. *Still Symone girl, there was no need for you to curse at Pecola like that. Dammit! This is one of those nights that I truly hope I'm not an alcoholic. But I damn sure know I need some drinks to just even go to sleep.*

Symone was a number one fan of calypso and jazz. But tonight, she decided to play the Terry Ellis CD Alex gave to her guests who attended the Devereauxs' toga anniversary party last Saturday evening. Since Alex was an avid worshipper of opera, classical, and gospel music, she wasn't sure what to put in each guest's overflowing surprise basket. Alex told everyone that Scott was the one who recommended Ellis.

When the guests, adorned in an array of sheets, danced to the cuts last Saturday night, the beautiful singing of Ellis reminded them of their high school days. Symone chuckled abruptly. She recalled how Jodria laughed and said that it was amazing how over twenty years ago, every last one of them were anxious as hell to graduate from high school. Nowadays, they searched for music and all kinds of memorabilia to remind them of the wonderful time they spent there.

The natural moonlight reflection continued to filter through Symone's dark bedroom. Symone walked to the double French doors and flung them open. She wanted to simply inhale the air and enjoy the clear, beautiful summer night. Plus, she was a little high, and she really wanted to cry.

For the past year, it appeared that Symone wept all the time. She was turning into a first-class closet crybaby and realized that her schizophrenic behavior was a major concern for her friends. This evening was no different. Crying last night at Arman's and now. That was two days in a row. Alex declared crying cleansed the soul. Symone laughed crazily. *Yeah right!* Because right now she believed the cleansing was past the soul and lodged somewhere in her gut.

Symone turned away from the window and slowly strolled back to the bedroom wet bar to pour another big drink. She took her glass of champagne to the balcony, leaned on the railing, and gazed down at the lighted swimming pool turquoise water. The quiet night was disturbing her. The full moon hung majestically in the sky, and she thought it would be nice if she had a real man to share the moment and her bed with. This was such an evening to be enjoyed—for love, for romance, for some downright screwing.

Maybe I need to get two dogs like Pecola. I know the children want one. Maybe I will. Maybe I'll name my two Beverly and Hills.

Since the divorce from Billy three years ago, Symone officially shared her sprawling six bedroom, brick two-story colonial with three-year old twin daughters, Kyle and Sylvia, and eight-year old son, Jared, III. Before then, she and Billy were legally separated for three years. However, from desperate attempts to save their marriage, Symone practiced the revolving door policy with her ex-husband and ultimately became pregnant with the girls during divorce proceedings.

When Symone's son was born, she suggested that instead of calling the child, Billy Jr., to simply use his father's middle name, Jared. Now that she and Billy were divorced and continually arguing, she was glad that they agreed on it. Right now, with all the negative emotional heavy crap she constantly experienced with Billy, she'd probably go berserk if she had to say his name each time she spoke to her son.

There were four blessings Symone could twist her lips to praise Billy about. They were her three children and Miss Jessica. She was the super glue, real lady of the Poussaint home for the past ten years. Jessica Estherlene Harper was a fifty-one year old, plump, never been married, churchgoing saint of a mother figure, housekeeper, and resident conscience compass. Always dressed in a dazzling white, crisp, starched maid uniform, shoes, and frilly apron, Symone pleaded a number of times for Miss Jessica to wear casual clothes around the house. However, the older woman, who everyone said exhibited the epitome of southern Black culture, told Symone point blank she felt more professional and business-like in the customary housekeeper's attire.

Although Miss Jessica was recommended by Billy's mother as an excellent caregiver for future Butler grandchildren, Miss Jessica decided to stay on when Symone decided it was time for Billy's adulterous Black ass to leave. Symone's three children and Miss Jessica were all away on vacation. Symone felt desperately abandoned. Even so, the evening's loneliness was still much better than the desolation experienced with Arman. Symone took another sip of champagne and noticed a shooting star flashed through the black, starry sky. She prayed silently.

Each year, Symone's children spent their entire summer vacation with Symone's mother in Santa Cruz, Trinidad. The children's vacation also gave Miss Jessica ample time to visit her family and friends in Wilmington, North Carolina. However, if Symone continued to feel depressed, she seriously considered shocking everybody by taking a private flight home to Trinidad and dragging her three rambunctious children kicking and screaming back to Clemmons, North Carolina.

You really are crazy messed up if you're thinking about bringing your children home two and half months before time, girl, she thought.

Symone drained the last of her champagne. She walked inside, locked the door, and set the nightstand clock for eight a.m. Now, there was complete silence. Since that was also driving her crazy, she strolled over to the stereo and inserted an Abbey Lincoln CD. Symone pulled back the heavy curtains and quilting along the mammoth, trestle four poster walnut bed. Once again, she tried to go to sleep, dissatisfied. Her mind was full of jumbled thoughts, and she considered a number of problems without being able to focus on anything specific. It was time to go to the psychologist again.

When Symone and Billy legally separated for the last time, she visited Dr. Sega religiously each and every week for a year. And with each appointment, Dr. Sega told Symone what she already knew. She was depressed because she didn't want to end her marriage. Although it felt great to have another person explain and walk her through the obvious back then, Symone preferred to avoid that route this time.

Maybe I'll call my sister, Hazele. Hell! How can she help me? Symone thought wearily. *She has enough freakin' problems with that silly ass husband, Brutus. Still, it's times like these that you need to have a conversation with your sister.*

Symone quickly realized this wasn't a great idea either. Her two sisters, Hazele and Ameenah, as well as her brother Quentin, were in Trinidad with their mother. If Symone called Hazele, her mother would want to know what all the whispering was about and would assume the worst regarding both daughters. No, Symone would wait and have a conversation about her various problems with Hazele when she returned home to New York in two weeks.

There are moody times like this that I wished I still smoked, she mumbled to herself.

In the semi-darkness of the moonlit room, Symone was still overwhelmed with an inexplicable sense of loneliness, bitterness, and other emotions she couldn't describe. Five minutes later, Symone cried. After she wiped her eyes with the clean white Pratesi sheets Miss Jessica put on her bed before she left on Friday, Symone prayed out loud:

*Lord, when I was with Billy before, I felt like my breasts were
literally sliced opened, and my heart was being ripped and
pulled out of my chest. I prayed then he would change and our
marriage would work. Then I got divorced. And I said
ok. And I know I'm still trying to deal with our break-up.
That hurt me so deep. Lord, you know it did. He was
the second man to walk on my heart. Lord, you know
all about the first one. Now when I meet a new man, I
pray that it works, too. It hasn't worked with men and me.
Lord, it's not working with Arman. You see what's going
on down here in my life.*

*Lord, I now delete all the other prayer requests.
Just throw those away. I still pray for my family's health and
well-being. And I sincerely thank you for the way you have
blessed both of my companies. But now this is what I truly want.
I'm praying that you allow me to simply have pure
happiness...puhleeze. I'll know what happiness is because I
sure know what happiness isn't. I'm living it, Lord. So surely
it must be the opposite of what I'm experiencing now. Alex
says being happy is real easy to do once you know who you are.
I ask you, Who am I lord? Who—am—I? I know I'm here for a
reason. Alex has got it, Lord. Give me the key to the happiness
door. Help me to understand. Let happiness rain down on me
like a beautiful storm, Lord. Amen.*

Chapter Fifteen

"Hurry up, chile," Pecola screamed into the telephone like someone told her she had won the Virginia lottery. "Hurry up and turn on BET. Marlon is on the Woolfgang Youngblood's show."

"I know, girl. How many times have I told you that we don't get BET out here in Advance, Pecola? Nanette's taping it for me," Alex said while laughing calmly. "Girl, puhleeze. I was the one to tell you that he'd be on television tonight anyway. Remember at O'Charley's last month? Plus, I asked Elisha to remind you and Symone about it today."

"That's right, chile. I can tell I'm getting older. You sure did mention it to me. I was thinking Carlos was the one who told me." Pecola paused a moment to take a sip of lemonade. "How you doing otherwise?"

"I'm fine."

"You're fine? Who's been telling your butt that big lie again," she exclaimed and burst out laughing at her own humor and almost choked on the sweeter than sugar lemonade. Alex joined in and told Pecola she was absolutely crazy.

"I'm seriously thinking about getting a digital satellite system," Alex said as she nonchalantly flipped a magazine page. "That's one of the things I dislike about the cable company we subscribe to."

"What they do now?"

"It's what they haven't done. They have about three, probably four country music stations but no BET. As a matter of fact, I wrote a letter to the president of the company asking him why BET wasn't offered. He told me that enough people hadn't requested it. I wrote back and asked if enough people actually requested to have four blame country music stations put on? Probably not and—"

"Doesn't Woolfgang look good?" Symone blurted out which cut Alex off. "Umph, umph, umph. Check out Woolfgang's muscles? When you look up the word *fine* in the dictionary, you can believe brotherman will be there sitting right beside the F."

"Symone, you're on the line, too?" Alex asked, surprised. "I'm sooo glad I didn't say anything mean about your behind."

"Hey, that's ok. Talk about me all you want to. If people aren't talking about me, I get worried and wonder what's wrong with my public relations." Symone laughed loudly. "I needed to pee. Since I didn't want yall to hear the sound effects of pee hitting toilet water, I just picked up the phone again."

"Oh yeah, Alex. I was talking to Sy when *The Woolfgang Show* came on. Sorry, I forgot to tell you," Pecola explained as she crunched ice cubes in their ears.

"Girl, puhleeze." Alex began to laugh. "It's no big deal that Ms. Symone is on the phone."

"Tank yuh, tank yuh," Symone said, sounding like a West Indian.

"And you can't pick up BET? How boring. Hmmm," Pecola moaned. "You might as well get a digital system out there in Devereaux Land. I love ours. You got everything else out there on your ole country estate."

"You're right. Madison has been talking about it for ages, but we simply don't watch enough television to go digital." Alex began to laugh. "Symone, I'm definitely glad we're finally talking, especially since I haven't heard from you in a few days."

"Huh? What you just say, Alex? Anyway—" Pecola lowered her voice and spoke as if she was sharing a major secret. "Did yall know that Woolfgang is married to a white girl?"

"Whaaat! Get out of here. I didn't know he was married at all and to a white woman! I tell you, I can't believe these damn Hollywood types," Symone said sounding surprised and more angry as she spoke each word. "What is it with these trophy wives?"

"No, I'm serious, chile. I read about him in *Ebony Male.* Hell, you know I was very shocked too," Pecola informed hesitantly, knowing how excited Symone got about interracial marriages.

"I don't know why I'm shocked," Symone continued.

"I guess he got tired of shoveling black coal and decided he would deal with white snow. Plus, you know how that is. Coal is solid as a rock, but that snow melts on you each and every damn time, girlfriends," Pecola added with a crazy laugh.

"You've got to be kidding," Symone grumbled. "What are our Black men who marry white women thinking?"

"Thinking about what they want to do with their life," Pecola said.

"And BET lets him have a show? This is ridiculous. I should've known that would've been the case with a name like Woolfgang Youngblood! He probably wouldn't know what Black is if it knocked him in the face," Symone said through clenched teeth, ready to pour another drink. She arrived home only an hour ago. Since that time, she drank two tall glasses of Martell on the rocks.

"How do you know, girl?" Alex asked quietly.

"Trust me. I just know," Symone mumbled. "I tell you. It makes me so mad, and he's a fine brother, too. What a waste."

"True," Pecola said.

"It makes me want to jump through the television and choke his baldheaded butt. Never cared for cue ball men in the first place," Symone added disgustingly while trying not to curse too much with Alex on the line. "I'll never watch his show again. You can believe that sh—, I mean stuff!"

"I second that emotion, or I should say motion. His show is history in my book, I'll never watch it again, either," Pecola echoed sternly in total agreement, her eyes still glued to the screen.

"What has who he's married to got to do with him having a show? You two are something else. You know that?" Alex finally chirped in with a soothing voice.

"Well, it's the truth. That's how I feel, too," Pecola said smugly, refusing to budge from her viewpoint. "Hey. Sssh. Sssh. Marlon looks damn distinguished looking, too." Pecola stopped breathing. "Oh, damn! I didn't hear the question that Woolfgang just asked Marlon, but Marlon seems real upset about it."

"You're sure, Pecola?" Alex asked, concerned.

"No I'm not, chile. Look, this isn't working. Well, it's time for me to go." She took another sip of lemonade. "I'm not taping the show, and it's hard for me to talk and listen to what's going on here. One ear is with the TV, and the other ear is trying to listen to you two."

"Just give us the other ear. That'll settle everything," Alex replied with a laugh. "Plus, I distinctly thought I heard you just say you weren't going to watch his show anymore."

"Girl, puhleeze," Pecola moaned.

"You know what." Symone still was seething with anger at the news. "That's why I truly admire a successful Black man who has a Black woman at his side. Totally unbelievable."

"Our country—this world is changing, Symone," Alex said.

"Oooh! I hate that reason, Alex. *Changing?* Give me a break. If anything, our country is getting worse with hypocrisy with its supposed propaganda about racial equality," Symone hissed. "I bet when Woolfgang was growing up poor, he never had white women running him down then."

"But I bet white girls certainly starred up all in his wet dreams," Pecola exclaimed.

"That's for damn sure, Pecola," Symone agreed. "I'm against it. Very much so."

"You know Black folks are going to do what they want, Sy. If they don't think about stuff like that when they don't have money, you can believe everything goes when they become rich and more cosmopolitan," Alex explained in a comforting tone. She could always tell when they were at the first stages of anger. The curse words began to zoom out. "Remember what Marlon's uncle always said—"

Both Pecola and Symone ignored the calming advice.

"I ain't watching him no more," Pecola added. "I agree with Symone. Let's boycott the damn show, yall."

This sure will be my last time, Symone thought, still appalled by the information. *And, if Marlon weren't on, I'd cut my TV off right now. These movie star niggers make me sick. Why can't they share the spotlight and the wealth with a sistah? Why can't they give a sister the opportunity to enjoy the wealth? The fame? Let her enjoy luxury and world travel. They're still making Cinderellas out of white girls. Pecola and I can have a real discussion about this later.*

"Ooooh. It makes me quite angry," Symone grumbled.

"Don't be angry, girl," Alex said. "The only—"

"Don't be angry? Oh, I got a right to be angry. To be jealous and to be pissed off. Cause still, Black women believe in fairy tales despite all the bull that we got to witness. Those Black men are traitors. Nothing but rich-assed, famous traitors. You don't see those country music men prancing around with Black women on their arms."

"They do it," Pecola said. "But it's done behind closed doors."

"They know better. Black men need to learn from their example." Symone took a deep breath and spoke firmly. "No seriously. I'm hanging up. Yall take care."

"Oh yeah, I just remembered. Pecola and Symone, I've an appointment at the spa on Wednesday morning. So if I don't see yall tomorrow, I'll talk to yall then." To check a date, Alex reached for her appointment book. "All the children will be here on Friday, and I need to make sure you two are going to do what you did last year. Ok?"

"That'll be fine, chile," Pecola piped in hurriedly. She was still a little preoccupied with the show. "I got your pretty little calligraphy note asking me the same thing, sweet girl. Like I told you last week, I'll make a speech the same way I did for last year's opening ceremony for the children."

"Will you be there, Symone?" Alex asked.

"Of course. I've already started working on my speech, too. I'll be in the same spot in the corner." A whole lot of stuff about the stupidity of Black men and women flowed through her mind. "Lemme go, my sistahs. Pecola, I'll talk to you later. Cleopatra fixed fried chicken, macaroni and cheese, collard greens, and a coconut cake for me. I'm gonna go downstairs and have a second helping. I'll buzz you back after that. Ok?"

"Huh—uh, what did yall say?" Pecola asked, still preoccupied.

"You know it's too late to eat." Alex was always the weight conscious one.

"Uh huh. Uh, what the heck are yall talking about now?" Pecola questioned, her eyes glued to the TV screen.

"Pecola, let me interpret for you," Alex said with a throaty laugh. "Symone said that she'll call you later because she wants to do some serious talking with you. For some strange reason, she'd rather I not hear all the curse words that I know will be flying out my girl's body. That's what she meant."

"I see," Pecola mumbled. "Thanks for the interpretation, girl."

"Yall must be going through that phase again where yall are worrying about my so-called gentle ears," Alex teased. "But, hey. That's ok. It's not necessary, but it's ok. We still need to talk, Sy."

"Just let me know when, Alex," Symone said. "I'll be waiting."

There was a succession of, *I love yous* and *bye-byes* until all three lines went dead.

When Pecola called Alex, she was sitting on the sofa in the music room reading *American Visions* magazine while a Fontella Bass CD spread soft music all through the room. It was eight o'clock at night. Trey and Purity were in bed. Madison was out on an emergency call. Troubling thoughts clouded her mind, and Alex closed her eyes for several moments. She put the magazine down on the table. She rose to her feet and walked slowly toward the window to watch the lighted lake below. With a slight frown on her face, she thought about her brother-in-law, Marlon Asa Dinzelle, a kind, gentle man who at one time was one of the greatest athletes the world of professional basketball had ever seen.

King, Queen, and Dreams, who were resting peacefully underneath the grand piano, jumped up, followed Alex, and waited for her to make the next move. When they noticed she wasn't leaving the music room, they returned to another favorite spot beside a wing chair, curled up, and resumed napping.

Chapter Sixteen

Marlon and his college buddies, Steve Cannon, Lawrence Jamison, and Alonzo Blackwell, were extremely close from the time Marlon arrived his freshman year to North Carolina University at Franklinton. Up until the sixth grade, Marlon attended Catholic schools. When Marlon's father died suddenly of a heart attack during the summer Marlon was supposed to enter seventh grade, he convinced his mother to let him attend Kiser Middle School in Greensboro, North Carolina. That was where Marlon met Steve Cannon.

Their friendship lasted from the time Marlon was twelve, and Steve was thirteen. It lasted throughout all of their years at Grimsley High School in Greensboro. All through pick up games and basketball camps during the summer, Marlon and Steve played on the same team. They even made a pact to play basketball at the same college where they fantasized of winning the National Basketball College Championship together.

North Carolina University at Franklinton's basketball team achieved the impossible dream and won the National College Basketball Championship two years in a row. The success and prestige associated with those honors were magnificent for the friends. Seniors Cannon, Jamison, and Blackwell were drafted in the first round. They were selected one, five, and twentieth by Los Angeles, Chicago, and Charlotte, respectively. Marlon, then a junior, was New York's fifth pick in the second round.

Cannon, Jamison, Blackwell, and Marlon became celebrities of the National Basketball League. All four vowed to remain friends for life. It didn't matter that Marlon's initial contract wasn't as lucrative as the others. The bond that they developed was stronger than money and anything else that could be thrown at them. Since they were on different teams back then, Marlon said people believed that their friendship would eventually become enemy mines. That wasn't the case. When the buzzer sounded, they were competitive and played like warriors from rival tribes. At the end of the game, they fell comfortably into the warmth of their friendship. In the off season, they were inseparable. For one month during the summer, the guys took turns and spent a week in the city where each one lived.

It was Steve, Lawrence, and Alfonso's turn to visit Marlon. They had been in Winston-Salem for six days. It was a glorious sunny, Sunday afternoon in August, just like all the other days during their summer visit. They were scheduled to fly out on Tuesday morning to spend a week with Steve Cannon in Los Angeles. The four had just finished playing about seven pick up games on the outside courts at the East Winston YMCA. They thought about playing an eighth one, but it began to rain heavily.

Joking all the way, the four jumped into Marlon's custom-designed Jaguar convertible to take the ride out to his house in Advance. Nanette and Brenda, Cannon's wife, told them earlier that morning they'd have hickory smoked barbecue ribs cooked to perfection, baked beans with onions, potato salad, frosty chilled Michelob Lights, and Cristal champagne ready to pop when they arrived.

Marlon drove three miles to the Fastpak Convenience Store on Martin Luther King, Jr. Drive where they picked up eight, twenty-four ounce bottles of Gatorade. It stopped raining. The sun peeked through the puffy white clouds again. Lawrence suggested they ride with the convertible top down so that they could smell the wet North Carolina red dirt. A happy and contented Marlon called Nanette.

"...We're on our way to the crib, baby," Marlon told Nanette with a laugh as he wheeled the Jaguar onto I-40 West.

"Tell the lil' ladies that they better have my grub ready and my beer chilling," Steve Cannon yelled to Marlon. Flipping through Marlon's collection of CD's, Steve won the guys' unanimous approval to play Jodeci. "I want my towels cleaned, and my warm bed waiting for me. My woman best be in there, too."

"Ohhhh! Ohhhh! I heard him!" Nanette repeated to Brenda Cannon what her husband just said.

"You're in biggg trouble, man," Marlon joked to Steve.

"Me and Brenda want you to put Steve on the phone, baby," the feisty Nanette demanded of Marlon. "Let me tell him exactly what will be waiting for him when he gets here."

"Aw, baby—" Marlon smiled. "Can't it wait until we reach the crib?"

"What you think, Brend? Should we wait and jump Steve when he gets here?" Nanette asked her friend, and the cute Brenda nodded her head yes. "Tell Steve he's lucky. He got a reprieve from Brend *and* from me."

"That's great, baby. Look! We should be there in about fifteen minutes. Love you, Nae."

"I love you too, baby," Nanette said and hung up the phone just as she heard Steve mimic Marlon's closing words.

"Mad Dog is pussy whipped," Steve joked and glanced around at a smiling Alfonso and Lawrence who were nodding their heads in agreement. Steve turned the Jodeci's CD volume up to a staggering level. "Yall see how he talks to Nanette. My man is whipped!"

"I ain't the only one," Marlon shot back. "Your wives got all you niggers pussy whipped, too. I know the deal."

"Aw, man. Look at Mad Dog. He's trying to change the subject." Steve stopped speaking for a moment and rested his left hand on the driver's seat headrest. "Yall hear that fat beat by Jodeci? Don't yall know I knew those boys long before they made it big. Before they moved away from Charlotte and Munroe?"

"There he goes bragging again," Lawrence piped in, bobbing his head to the music.

"Straight up, man. Tell them, Mad Dog," Steve said to Marlon. "And we party together out in Cal-lee twenty-four seven with all the other West Coast rap groups, man."

"That's the problem with Steve," Alfonso said with a laugh. "Since he's in L.A., he acts like he knows everybody, and we don't know no damn body."

"Damn straight," Marlon agreed.

"Dog, I know key people in the game," Alfonso announced. "I'm a star, too."

"Uh oh," Marlon moaned. "His publicist been lying to him a-gain."

"Oh no. Oh no. Let's jump back on the subject we were on before you called Nae," Steve said to Marlon as he winked at the two guys in the back seat. "I think he changed the subject so we wouldn't bother his ass."

"Why you jump on that punk ass deal, Mad Dog?" Alfonso asked Marlon, who had just recently signed a new contract with New York that made him the highest paid player in basketball. A proud Alfonso patted Marlon on the back.

"It's a good one, man." Marlon glanced at Alfonso in the rearview window. "You know BJ locked the front office into a sweet one. Tell him, Cannon."

"BJ ain't shit," Lawrence said and nudged Alfonso with his elbow.

"Look, dog. Watch your mouth. Don't talk about our agent like that, man," Steve said, turning around pointing a straight finger at his two friends sitting in the back seat. "The brother is baddddd."

"New York earns billions every time yall win a championship, man," Lawrence said. "You could have gotten some serious bank."

"Well, if I were you, Marlon," Alfonso went on, now nudging Lawrence, "I wouldn't have taken less than five-hundred mill, baby. Especially after the way you kicked ass this year in the finals."

"Nigger, puhleeze," Steve interrupted. "The only reason why New York won—beat us in the finals is because I was out with my knee. That's the only way Marlon walked away with the championship ring this year."

"What about last year, dog?" Lawrence said to Steve as he leaned up to stare him straight in the face. "Last year you were healthy as a horse, and L.A. was still in loserville. Yall didn't even make it into the play-offs, man."

"Wooo! Thanks. You took the words right out of my mouth, man," Marlon laughed and saluted a grinning Steve.

Since New York was the world champions, Marlon's three friends continued to tease him about his past contract negotiations with the team's management. They constantly ribbed him about what monetary offer he could have gotten from the front office if only he had just listened to their wonderful advice and held out a little longer.

As a laughing Marlon drove down I-40 West, they joked about their past seasons in the National Basketball League. The music was loud. They were happy. They were living their dream life. Bobbing their heads from side to side, they continued to listen to the sultry jams of Jodeci. Young, black, and talented, the four men ate the North Carolina air with joy. Friends bound together and bound for success. But on that particular day, tragedy was hiding inside their joy. While gliding along the highway, the Jaguar hydroplaned, flipped over, slammed into a tree, and rested straight up in an embankment.

Steve, Lawrence, and Alfonso were killed instantly when they were thrown from the vehicle. Marlon, the only one who wore a seat belt, was in a coma for three days. His knees were crushed, and so was the opportunity for him to play professional basketball ever again. He had such a promising future. They all did. Within seconds, God's brown children and their careers came to a crushing end on that rain slick road three years ago.

Of course, the media blamed alcohol and drugs. Their autopsy report revealed neither was in Steve, Lawrence, or Alfonso's systems, and Marlon's tests all were negative, too. A long time ago, they agreed that drugs and abuse of alcohol were the destroyers of an athlete's body. The four vowed to never be a part of the drug scene that was easily accessible to professional athletes. Each one was totally involved in his respective city to fight the rampant spread of drug abuse and Black on Black youth violence. They were an example and role model to the young boys and girls from the old neighborhood and across the country that aspired to be like them.

Throughout their eight seasons in the NBL, they prided themselves on never having negative press. They donated huge sums of money to the Boys Club, and to other small non-profit organizations that benefited youths. All moneys were donated on behalf of the SLAM Group, a non-profit foundation they developed on a whim. The corporate title was created one night during a poker game where the first letters of Steve, Lawrence, Alfonso, and Marlon's names were combined.

They were serious about their efforts to make a difference in the urban communities. And before a check was written to an altruistic cause, SLAM did the necessary research. Sometimes one of the guys appeared as a representative, or they all visited the organization to see actual examples of how young people's lives were positively impacted by the program that requested the funds. As a result of the mega publicity highlighting their philanthropic deeds, eventually the guys in the NBL nicknamed the friends the SLAM Dunk Crew. They were scoring points with the underprivileged children and with the community.

Woolfgang Youngblood was also a former superstar guard for New York, and now hosted the weekly Monday evening show, *Where are they Now?* A fan of Marlon since he entered the NBL after his sterling career at North Carolina University, he was curious about Marlon's activities after basketball as well as many of his devoted viewers who wrote in asking about Marlon. So Woolfgang wanted to have this special interview with the six feet six inch tall, thirty-two year old, Marlon Asa Dinzelle.

Alex stepped away from the glass window and leaned on the music room's grand piano. She thought about calling her sister but decided against it. Nanette and Marlon were probably enjoying the interview with friends. Alex sure hoped so. She worried about Marlon all the time. Alex knew that Marlon never mentally or physically recovered from the tragic, freak accident. He even now walked with a very, slight limp. He continued to blame himself for the crash and often told her that he believed wherever he traveled, people recognized Mad Dog as the man who drove the car that killed his three friends. A part of Marlon seemed to be always sad. A part of his heart never felt the warmth of the sun.

Even though all of the guys possessed hefty insurance policies, a bitter lawsuit was settled which ensured their families were taken care of for life. But past that, Marlon continued to send money and gifts, and he would often visit their widows throughout the year.

Alex was ecstatic Marlon decided to create a marketing arm to his company a year ago. He and Nanette moved from Advance and bought another lovely home on Lake Norman. Everything seemed fine again with their marriage. The SLAM Foundation continued to make even larger, worthwhile donations, and Marlon was more determined to adhere to the mission of his dead friends. Marlon could now use the fame he grew to hate after the accident in a quiet, useful way. Although he traveled extensively, Alex believed his new marketing business helped him to recapture his spirit and to save his life. Still, the fiery brilliance never returned to Marlon's eyes, and he became a loner. When he returned home from trips now, he only wanted to be around family and an inner-circle of special friends.

Always particularly close to Alex, she often embraced him with an abundance of love and affection because she saw the sadness, which lurked in his demeanor. Even when he smiled, he acted as if he were merely going through the motions of living life. Two weeks ago, when Marlon spoke to Alex in her rose garden, he let Alex see his pain. He broke down, and his eyes sparkled with tears.

"...If I could relive that day all over again, I would've wished on the heads of my newborn twins boys that I was killed in the accident instead of my three friends," Marlon said to Alex. "I would rather have died too than to live with the memory."

"But God saved you," Alex told him. "He'll show you how to live with the grief, Marlon."

Alex's words seemed to briefly coat his sorrow and self-pity.

"I can't go past it. It's the center of my life." Marlon crushed his face into his hands and cried. "We were just out kickin' it, Alex."

"Hold on, Marlon," she pleaded with him. "You can outlast the weight of this. You got to fight it, baby. You must."

Alex was fearful for Marlon's life and spirit when he talked like that. Just thinking about that conversation caused Alex to tightly wrap her hands around her waist and walked away from the music room's window. She never knew what to say to him when he was living inside the memory of the accident.

On a continuous basis, all Alex could do was tell Marlon that he should, "Be thankful for where you are now and always know that your life was spared for a magnificent reason. Just remember to always thank God for every good thing that happened in your life, Marlon. To just thank Him for allowing you to have the ability to do all the things that you could do."

Oftentimes, Marlon peered right through her with such a cold stare and wouldn't respond either way. But Alex could *always* tell that his eyes hid internal torment. No one, no one at all, could ever imagine the depths of his remorse.

A quiet Alex sauntered back over to the tufted turquoise velvet sofa. She sat down and reached for the telephone to call Marlon. With her hand frozen in midair, she immediately remembered. How could she forget? Marlon wasn't at home enjoying the taped interview with Woolfgang. Earlier, Nanette told her that Marlon was once again in Grand Cayman until Friday afternoon. Suddenly, the dogs began yipping and yapping. They raced out the music room and turned left at the entryway. Their activity pierced Alex's daydreaming, and she checked the mantle clock. It was eleven-thirty. She quickly realized how very exhausted she was after the long day with Trey and Purity.

Alex smiled when she heard the faraway hum of Madison's heavy voice as he spoke to their dogs. Madison and Alex walked toward one another. Halfway up the hall, Madison noticed the worried expression on her face. As he embraced her, she told him she was concerned about Marlon, and he immediately knew why.

"...Alex, baby, you can't be everything to everybody," a weary Madison said. "Marlon will be fine."

"You're right." Alex wanted to sound convincing.

"It's time for us to go to bed, baby." Madison was exhausted from the two-hour emergency surgery that he had to perform on an eight-year old child, and he knew her day was just as long.

Chapter Seventeen

Alex finished praying over the Imani Box in the master bedroom and glanced at her watch. It was six-thirty Wednesday morning. She scheduled an appointment in Pecola and Symone's day spa for eleven. Before she headed to Winston-Salem, she wanted to work in her rose garden for at least an hour. She decided to rise a little earlier, bake some cookies, and pick fresh roses and Cala Lilies for the desks of Elisha, Ted, Symone, and Pecola. Alex wanted to surprise them with the fresh bouquet of flowers as a Wednesday treat.

As Alex prepared the bouquets, she smiled when she thought how her mother would adore her formal gardens. When Alex's mother was alive, she loved fresh flowers. Her mother always brought them home to brighten the dining room table, and she would place them throughout various rooms. Alex was just like her.

Alex really didn't discover gardening until she graduated from Winston-Salem State University. Afterwards, she started working on joint degrees, a MBA and a Juris Doctorate, at Wake Forest University. Those two degrees' course of study lasted four years. She and Madison were married for only two years when they decided that Alex should be closer to Wake Forest. So they rented a lovely condo in the historic Reynolda Village section of Winston-Salem. It was there that Alex unexpectedly fell in love with a neighbor's garden. Not long after, she was tending her own little section on the hillside behind the condo between classes, studying, and running back and forth to visit Madison in Durham.

Gardening was a wonderful discovery that changed Alex's life. Most times in the wee hours of the morning and evening, she was in the garden weeding, watering, and planting. Gardening for her was calming and profoundly therapeutic. Whenever there was a crisis in her life, she released herself to experience nothing but pleasant thoughts as she pruned, weeded, and mulched in her rose garden. Alex was extremely careful to select flowers that depicted her frilliness and femininity. Pretty flowers. Dainty roses and lilies. Alex spent many hours in the garden, especially in the fall because it was then that she planted the wonderful flowers for the spring.

When the spring blooms passed, Alex planted annuals for the summer. Therefore, their guests could savor the luscious array of colorful flowers during the Devereauxs' numerous summer activities. Oftentimes, when friends came by and if she wasn't inside the house pittling around, Madison and the children guided her friends to the garden.

Almost ten years ago, Madison contracted with Carlos to build the huge, glass greenhouse as a surprise thirtieth birthday gift for his wife. Alex would now have roses, orchids, lilies, and her other favorite flowers year round.

During the spring and summer months, Alex enjoyed gathering her two children and their guests in the garden. There she'd read beautiful sagas about the pre-slavery queens and kings in Africa, love stories, fantastical tales, or dreams she created as she went along. Before they left to go to Trinidad, Symone's little twins excitedly told their mother that they loved for their Tante Alex to read to them in the garden. Alex said that they probably felt like little princesses in a fairy tale book surrounded by such fragrant beauty.

As a romantic ending to the stories, Alex and the children often laughingly chased butterflies. This was done in the summer, and it was Alex's way to make the fairy tales seem real to the children. In the winter, she scattered pecans and other goodies for the squirrels and birds. Then she and the children scurried inside and watched from the quiet of the kitchen sunroom while the squirrels nibbled away at the treats.

Wellington Starks Hagan helped Alex to keep her garden perfectly manicured. He was a fifty-five year old cocoa complexioned Black man and church member. After Wellington signed up for MUB Industries' early retirement plan eight years ago, Alex talked him into opening a landscaping design business. With his expertise, Alex's garden and grounds remained a showplace with golf course green grass surrounding all the flowery handiwork. As a result of Wellington's excellent design reputation, he and Starks-Hagan Landscaping Services and Etceteras' staff of six maintained the perfectly manicured lawns and performed various odds jobs for Alex's other friends as well.

To enter the garden, brick cobblestone wide paths led from the first floor rooms' large glass doors located at the back of the house. Charming hand cast bonded marble figurines rested beside beautiful tulip clusters arrayed along the brick path, which stretched toward the garden's central point. Although Alex frequently used yellow, pink, and red for her design in her garden, white was the dominant one used. The white flowers created a dramatic backdrop at night when she and Madison looked at the garden from their bedroom balcony.

Without a doubt, everyone's favorite spot for pleasant conversations and quiet meditation was located majestically in the middle of the garden. The huge, old brick patio was surrounded by a rock aquatic garden with several large, colorful Japanese Koi. To the left of pink wrought iron furniture benches and ornate chairs were the side rose garden with a gazebo, and a fountain surrounded by hibiscus. A neoclassical urn and topiary trees were adjacent to them.

To enjoy the garden in inclement weather, years ago Madison designed a twelve-foot tall wooden trellis shelter which was now completely covered with flowery green vines. The covering added a touch of shade, but it also gave a sense of privacy to visitors who often desired to sit and chat with Alex while they savored cappuccino and toast. And, right beside it was the trademark wishing well that everyone swore by. Just as many adults threw pennies into the well as the children did. But before anyone tossed coins into the well, Madison and Alex always reminded them to *first make a wish and make it well.*

Alex laughed as she remembered the first time Scott came to visit. It was in the summer, and of course, she was out in the garden. Scott was surprised Alex tendered the garden in pretty Paperwhite or floral dresses and huge straw hats. Not in work clothes. To Alex, her garden was the Devereauxs' museum. It was an extension of their warm and spacious country home, and nothing but the finest flowery artwork was on display. She couldn't even imagine visiting a museum or an art show in overalls, so why would she work in her garden looking like that?

Alex loaded her car with the pretty bouquets and the baskets of warm cookies. She was finally ready for her 11:00 a.m. pampering that only Akao Studios could give her. At the suggestion of Pecola almost seven years ago, Alex scheduled her first Ultra Akao Package. It was a full day of pampering plus stress management and consisted of a European facial, body waxing, a relaxing mineral bath, a Swedish massage, skin care consultation, a pedicure, a therapeutic foot bath, a manicure, hairstyle, gourmet lunch, and a basket of spa goodies. She especially enjoyed receiving the bag of goodies. It was Pecola and Symone who asked Alex to select the various delicate soaps and cream given in each Ultra Package signature basket.

That was the first time Alex had ever pampered herself in such a way, and she loved how enormously wonderful her body felt afterwards. From that day on, Alex promised herself that she would treat herself to the luxury of the Ultra Akao package at least once a month. She lived for those visits. Each time Alex offered to pay for the pampering package, Pecola and Symone refused to allow Alex to pay for the treat because it was their monthly gift of love to her.

Driving about a half a mile up on Stratford Road, Alex noticed the Akao Building looming in the distance. Pecola and Symone christened their building Akao, which stood for "first born" in African. Since there were no other African-American owned full service meeting management companies or an exclusive day spa and salon in Winston-Salem, both ladies thought the name would be perfect. It was a beautiful, colossal brick building with white stately, tall, and circular columns. The glass front of the building reminded visitors of a South Carolina colonial mansion. Yet, the building resembled a contemporary home plopped right in the middle of the business district. Many of Akao clients often said that the distinctive building reminded them of a modern day White House.

Located on Stratford Road near Hanes Mall Boulevard, it was built over eleven years ago by CR Construction Group. The double front wooden oak doors opened into a marbled floor entry. With a waterfall just below the staircase and to the right of the elevators, the monster oak reception cubicle was strategically centered in the middle of the floor. Greenery hung from the ceiling. Huge, potted plants and palm trees adorned the first floor lobby.

As patrons of the arts, both Pecola and Symone used their building to promote rich African-American heritage by showcasing art in various styles throughout the two floors. The spacious first floor entrance was decorated as lavishly as the second floor executive reception area. However, the lobby was bright and airy. There were creme oversized leather couches, framed prints by renowned Black artists as John Scott, Denise Ward Brown, Synthia Saint James, Betye Saar, and Trinidadian artist, John Jardine-Otway. African sculptures also dotted the wall shelves and tables. To the left and right of the reception area against the far wall were the infamous cherrywood bookshelves. A favorite local artist of Pecola, Haywood L. Oubre, designed wire sculptures that were perched atop each bookshelf. As clients walked in, to their right and left were the massive double oak doors that opened to both sides of the spa.

The building was totally electronic. The only way to gain access to either the spa, the stairs' wrought iron gate, the handicap ramp leading upstairs to Meetings Odyssey, or the executive offices was the receptionist beeped a client in or a guest knew the entry code. Every quarter, the password was changed, but Pecola always made sure Alex was given a card with the new numbers.

When Alex arrived at Akao, she didn't notice Pecola, Ted, or even Elisha's car in the parking lot. She assumed that maybe they parked them in the enclosed, executive lot located under the building. Alex opened the lobby door and noticed four impeccably dressed African-American female clients relaxing on the long, leather sofas reading magazines. They all were sipping cappuccino and Victoria Tea. Victoria Tea was the only kind of tea that Akao served after Alex discovered the company on a visit to The Cameroon.

The sounds of Luther Vandross' *Power of Love* floated through the lobby ceiling speakers. When Alex stepped into the lobby and saw the women relaxing there, she had no idea who they were. But she spoke and waved to them anyway. Only two women waved back as the other two ladies, even though they heard her, acted as if they didn't even hear the pleasant greeting she showered their way.

"Good morning, Mrs. Devereaux," greeted Tierra, the receptionist, with her usual cheerfulness. She checked the book, glanced at the clock, and realized Alex's appointment wasn't until eleven.

"Good morning to you, Tierra. Please call me, Alex."

No matter how many times Alex asked Tierra to do so, she continued to recognize Alex by her last name. Tierra was always wonderfully pleasant, charming, and very efficient. According to Symone and Pecola, she was a jewel of an employee they found through Pecola's sorority connections.

Tierra was five-feet-four and looked as if she weighed about one-hundred ten pounds dripping wet. A petite young woman with lovely hazel eyes and a pecan complexion, she was a sharp dresser and constantly wore dark double-breasted power suits with gold buttons. Every time Alex saw Tierra, it seemed as if her hair was braided in a different style.

The young lady was an efficient receptionist, and no one walked passed her. An excellent lioness at the gate, she made sure the staff wasn't disturbed for any reason, unless of course it was for a planned appointment. Tierra was endowed with an uncanny memory. If clients visited the building once, she remembered and addressed them by their names the next time they walked through the oak doors.

"May I get you a cup of tea, cappuccino, or some fruit while you wait for your appointment, Mrs. Devereaux?" Tierra asked in a professional tone. She knew Mrs. Devereaux was extraordinarily special to her bosses and wanted to make sure she was comfortable and satisfied with the service.

"No, girl. But thanks for asking anyway. I'm going up to see Pecola and Symone. I brought roses and Cala Lilies for upstairs and baked a batch of my famous white chocolate macadamia nut cookies." She rested the flowery shopping bag on the oak cubicle and pulled out the baked goodies. "Here, have one."

Tierra glanced at the basket of cookies delicately wrapped in burgundy cellophane paper and tied with satin ribbons. She smiled and shook her head no.

"No thank you, Mrs. Devereaux. I'm trying to get this off," she explained and patted her flat stomach.

Alex smiled knowingly. "I understand how that might be for my stomach, but I don't see anything wrong with yours, Tierra."

Alex honestly couldn't see what Tierra was talking about, yet she realized young girls were always concerned about their midriff bulge even though it was almost invisible to everyone else. Alex strolled to the gate, entered the access code, and walked upstairs.

Chapter Eighteen

"Hey, girl," Alex said softly as she peeped her head in Symone's office. Symone was so busy writing, she never noticed her standing there. Alex's soft voice broke through Symone's thoughts, and she finally glanced up. Ten minutes earlier she was holding her head in her hands and rubbing her temples. She slept for only four hours last night, eased out of bed, and wrote furiously in her journal until five in the morning. "You're doing ok, Sy?"

"Yep. How are things going, girl?" she asked with a pasted on smile. "Come in and sit down for a moment." She pointed to the couch with a pen.

"Are you busy?"

"Yeah, kinda. I was just doing some paperwork. But hey, that's ok. I've been here since seven-thirty. You know that's rare for me, girl. What brings you this way?"

"You."

"Okayyy." Although depressed, Symone really was pleased as always to see her friend. She noticed the roses and lilies. "The flowers are beautiful!"

"Thank you." Alex grinned happily. "They're for you, Symone."

Alex walked slowly around the desk. She placed the arrangement on the credenza and gave Symone a rose emblem envelop with a card, a big kiss, and a tight hug. Symone was deeply moved by the gesture. No matter how many times Alex surprised her with special presents, it always caught her off guard.

July 8,
To my dear soul friend, Symone.
Girl, here is a beautiful thought I want to give to you.
Always remember the words of Oliver Wendell Holmes:
"Fame is the scentless sunflower, with gaudy crown of gold;
But friendship is the breathing rose with sweets in every fold."
Love to you, your soul friend, Alex.

Symone read the card, glanced at Alex with tenderness, and held her arms out for another hug.

"Thanks so much, Alex. The words are beautiful. And, uh, your calligraphy is getting better, girl. It really it is." Of course, she was joking. Alex's flowery handwriting was perfect as usual.

"I brought bouquets for Pecola, Elisha, and Ted. They weren't in their offices, so I left it on their desks."

"Uh huh." Symone shrugged nonchalantly as if she had no idea where they were either and acted as if she could frankly care less.

"I gave Pecola the same card. Last night, when Scott and Charmaine stopped over for dinner, I gave him one, too. Plus, I baked the staff white chocolate macadamia cookies. They're up in the kitchen by the cappuccino center. It's a happy Wednesday treat. You can have some, too. But, I made the cookies especially for them. Yall received the flowers."

"Girl, you made the Cadillac of cookies?" Symone asked. Pecola had given Alex's delicious cookies the Cadillac rating. "Only you would think of a happy Wednesday treat. Whoever heard of that, Alex?"

"I did."

"Thanks for the wonderful gesture, though."

"You're welcome."

"Did you have a good Sunday?" Symone asked, already knowing the answer and feeling a twinge of jealousy.

"It was wonderful, Symone. After church on Sunday evening, we had a picnic on the playroom floor."

"You're a mess. I'm going to be like you one day, girl."

"Don't be like me. Just choose to be who you are. That's all. Since we spoke the night Marlon was on TV, how come you haven't called me back? I phoned you Sunday morning and Monday afternoon."

"I know."

"I tried contacting you before you and Pecola called me and then again last night. Why won't you return my calls?" she questioned with a worried expression. "I've been talking to your answering machine for days, and I know you're there, Symone."

Symone felt badly. Alex's concern was sincere, and she didn't have an excuse for her behavior. For several weeks now, being friendly to others had not come easily. Being alone kept her from going over the edge. Nowadays, once Symone arrived home, she drank champagne, Bailey's, or whatever alcohol she could find. She listened to music and watched the answering machine as message after message was recorded from her friends.

Alex thought a moment before she continued talking. She walked over to the couch to sit down and breathe a long sigh as she helped herself to a banana from the crystal fruit bowl. Symone watched and waited because it was obvious Alex wanted and needed to say other things too, including the messy incident at Pecola's annual July Fourth barbecue. Desiree Coleman and Symone argued. Alex knew Symone was aggravated by the commotion it caused. She wanted to see how Symone was dealing with it.

"How are you handling what happened Saturday night, Sy?"

"I'm done with it. I said what I had to say. Some people can't handle that, so be it. That's life," Symone replied automatically. Her voice was liltingly quiet. "They want to say whatever they want to you; throw vicious comments in your face, then they expect you to sit there and take it. I don't hardly think it works that way with me."

Sensing a major discussion was around the corner, Symone looked at the open door and Alex got up and closed it.

"Symone, I think your reaction compass is off course just a tad. I wouldn't do the things you do or say the things you say. I just couldn't. Don't you know that?" Alex asked and sat back down on the couch.

"No, I don't know that," Symone snapped as she shuffled manila folders and furiously wrote notes on a white legal pad. She wasn't in the mood for small talk or a lecture and stopped briefly to gaze coldly at Alex. Slowly, Alex peeled the banana skin, took a bite, and swallowed before she continued.

"Ok. Since I've known you, do you think I would do anything to offend someone—just do whatever is considered morally wrong? All kinds of stuff. Do it just for spite?"

Symone considered the words and stared at her friend a moment before answering. Since she was so exhausted, she rubbed her burning, tired eyes. Alex's question echoed in her head. Only Alex could ask Symone such questions, and it not come off in a self-righteous way. If anybody talked to her like Alex, she would have gladly given that person a tongue-lashing. To her knowledge, Alex had never done anything out of the way to provoke anyone. However, one never could ever tell these days. Symone opened her eyes and answered the question slowly and quietly.

"You're right, Alex. I've never seen you do anything, as you say, *morally wrong*. By the way, I always believed that was so boring," she said dismissively with a shrug and short laugh. "But, who knows what goes on behind closed doors. Hell, I'm surprised at what I do behind them and in places where no one knows who I am. Don't you know that being moral is what we do in public—not what we do when no one is watching?"

Alex bit another piece of banana. "That's one way of looking at morality. It's not my way. What I'm saying is— Symone, you hurt people's feelings, sometimes for no reason. It's like you're a walking time bomb. You're just waiting for somebody to strike a match, so you can explode all over them and feel good about telling them off. I don't understand why you react that way." Alex's irritation was tempered with patient caring for her friend. She realized that as each day passed, Symone was becoming quite bitter about everything.

"I see."

"Now, I do agree that Black people need to become more economically educated. Have a sense of pride in our culture. You know when we have those discussions, heated or not, nine times out of ten, I'm on your side. The right side."

"Ok. I got it, Alex. I know why we're having this discussion. I've already told you that Saturday night isn't even a bad memory. I thought you said you were through with it, too." Symone grumbled as she swung around in her executive swivel chair to ignore Alex and pressed a battery of incorrect buttons on the computer keyboard.

"Symone, will you look at me, please?" Slowly, Symone turned around to face her with a penetrating stare of despair. Looking annoyed, Symone checked her watch to signal her impatience and shifted uncomfortably in her seat.

Alex studied Symone as she slumped in the big leather executive chair before her. Symone's eyes were bright and dry with anger. The friend who knew her like a sister. The person she cried with, sweated with, and shared secrets with. Now the friend Alex had known all these years was often so very unhappy. She watched Symone's smile disappear, and Alex felt helpless to do anything about it. As Alex watched her, a rush of love washed over her for

Symone, and she wanted to help her friend. Longed to see the happiness Symone used to carry with her like sunshine. In the past, most times Symone listened to her advice. Symone's other friends were futile in their attempts to reach her and pleaded with Alex to see what she could do.

"In other words, you're really not finished with rehashing the Saturday night fiasco?"

Alex took a deep breath. "Yes, I'm finished with it. But I told you I wanted to talk more about it when I saw you again. We're having this discussion because I believe you're who you are. And—I—love—you, Symone. Regardless of what you say or do."

"Thank you."

"You're my friend, and I take that very seriously. But when I disagree with you, I would be amiss if I didn't say something—"

"*And—?*" Symone continued to direct a hard gaze at her; however Alex persevered with the discussion.

"*And,* I disagreed with the way you handled Desiree last Saturday. It wasn't worth it. You should've just walked away from her. Some things you don't even dignify with an answer—or even with a look." Alex took several more bites, and the banana was finished.

Symone thought about what happened this weekend at Pecola's barbecue. As usual, she was minding her own business under the dimmed red lighting by the patio door. While she sipped a double Tanqueray Gin on the rocks, she thought about how her life was going a-gain, and the argument between her and Arman earlier that day. She had just returned from the wild bunch that was dancing under the tented dance floor outside on the Reynolds' spacious backyard lawn. To relax, she decided to mingle with the laid-back guests who were grooving to slow music in the downstairs playroom.

While Symone moved side to side to the music and watched several couples slow drag to the Special Delivery's *I Destroyed Your Love*, she thought about Arman. Unfortunately, he was her last resort for the barbecue. At the last minute, he had the nerve to concoct some ridiculously flimsy excuse about why he couldn't drive to Winston-Salem. She was really pissed off that she had to come to this barbecue without a date. It seemed that all of the guests were coupled off. They acted as if they knew everyone else from college days and from their sorority and fraternity monthly meetings. Plus, they all were dressed as if they were going to the Miss Black America Pageant instead of a backyard July Fourth picnic.

Naturally, when Desiree Coleman walked up to her to just say hello, she wondered why Desiree even took the time to speak to her. Symone didn't like Desiree, and it was quite obvious. Desiree was Pecola's friend. Not hers. And she tried to avoid her whenever they ended up at the same social function.

After Desiree said hello to Symone, Desiree's face held a taunting expression. In the next sneering breath, Desiree told Symone that her younger sister, Paula, had dated Symone's ex-husband, Billy, several times. And Desiree added that Billy was quite romantic and bought her little sister an expensive silk nightgown, slinky underwear, and pricey pieces of jewelry. Desiree went on and on about how the two had gone here and there.

"...And Billy is such an absolutely charming man," Desiree continued. "I can't understand where you went wrong as a wife, Symone."

In Symone's mind, those words translated to, "I've come over here to mess with you, bitch." Well, girlfriend got exactly what she deserved.

"Oh darling, Desiree. My sweet happily married, Desiree. Thank you for that bit of information," Symone ended up telling her. "The way you feel about me is sooo very important to my happiness and well-being. Since you know where I went wrong, pray tell, where did you go wrong?"

"What are you talking about?" Desiree asked with half-opened eyes. "What do you mean?"

"Your husband is quite charming. He can still charm the women, especially one fine, young sister in Walnut Cove. She's a Delta, too. Why don't you know about your husband's other woman?"

"You don't know what you're talking about. That's a damn lie."

"No it's not," Symone hissed to her. "Humph. You know so much about everybody else's business, but you don't know what your husband seems to be doing. It's amazing that everybody else in Winston-Salem sure does. You walked your evil ass up in my face and asked for this." Symone's hatred of Desiree was heard in her voice. "Now deal with it." Symone stared at her for a cold moment, downed her drink, and tried to walk away until Desiree reached for her arm.

"Let me tell you this, Symone—" Desiree's eyes were bulging with anger.

"You better get the away from me, Desiree! Before I—," Symone said, her voice rising higher, "before I'll kick your phony ass right on out of here!"

Pecola, who was speaking to other guests, was in earshot of Symone and Desiree's angry conversation. When she heard their voices getting heated and noticed Symone's rapid hand gestures as if she were going to punch Desiree in the face, Pecola intruded upon the situation. Pecola escorted Symone upstairs and outside to the front porch. She wanted to help her get calmed down.

Symone now shook her head sadly as she mentally reviewed the scene for the one-hundredth time since Saturday night.

"You're right, girl," Symone said nodding her head regrettably. "I guess I could've handled that one differently. At the time, I had enough of Desiree's nasty jabs. Self-righteous people get on my nerves. And Desiree, alias Miss Forty-five Year Old AKA Sister of the Year, is the Emmy winner for that category." She glanced toward the picture window and smiled faintly. Alex saw right through the weak grin and realized it was done to mask emotions from other hurt and sadness.

"I know."

Symone turned to face her again. "Alex, I may be a lot of things, but self-righteous I'm not. She just pushed some wrong buttons, and I went off! She didn't have to say those things to me about Billy. I was minding my own damn business," she snapped while waving both hands in the air. "You know that."

"I do."

"There are so many people in my life who just seem to want to mess me. Like Desiree, for instance. I can only take so much." Symone was silent, appeared defiant, and propped her chin on one hand.

"I understand, Symone," Alex sympathized quickly and quietly. "I really do. Don't get me wrong. Some people are just downright mean. They've been that way to me, too. I just believe that it's better to be nice to people when they're being vicious to you. The *Bible* says it's 'like heaping hot coals of fire on their forehead.' It tortures the heck out of them. Just try that the next time?"

"Quite frankly, I felt like slapping the ugly off her. I—came—that—close," Symone said in a deliberate monotone dripping with spite. She paused and made a sign with her thumb and index finger.

"I heard."

"What was I supposed to do, Alex? Tell me," she muttered again rebelliously. She noticed Alex's expression and inhaled deeply. "But since you insist, I'll do my best. If I think I'm going to cut someone up with my words, I'll count to ten before I speak. Hell, I'm not perfect."

"No one's perfect, Sy. I'm certainly not perfect either. Just try it, please. Words can be used like weapons. How we phrase them can do so much. They can kill a person or give life. Words have so much power, Symone." She paused briefly and rubbed her eye. "And another thing—"

"Since you're on a roll, don't let me stop you."

Alex smiled. "The way you've been speaking to all your friends lately isn't right either, girl. Words can encourage people when they're down, or words can send people into an abyss of despair, especially if they can't handle what's been said to them." Alex hesitated for a moment and took a deep breath again as she watched Symone listen with a blank expression.

Symone really wanted to start screaming at the top of her voice for everyone to leave her alone. Then Alex, Pecola, and the staff would agree that she had truly lost her mind. Since she knew that wasn't possible, since she wasn't able to say anything appropriate, and out of respect for their friendship, she refused to be stone-faced any longer and would try listening to what Alex believed she needed to say.

"Go ahead." Symone took a deep, controlling breath.

Alex managed a tight smile, something rare for her. "But I do pray each day that my life is a witness for the words I speak. I am my word, Symone. People need to realize that about themselves. Only I can determine if what I say is law in my life," she said earnestly and gave Symone another small smile. "This is who I am. Just like you're who you are. Alex is who she is. I wake up every day knowing that, thanking God for the day, for my family, for you, and all my friends. I can't explain it. My life isn't a dress rehearsal for those who see me outside my house. Then I'm another person at home. What you see is what you get."

According to Alex, each morning dawned a day for God's world of wonderful miracles to be experienced. She believed that when a person jumped out of bed, it was a chance for new beginnings. A new day for people to start afresh. A gift. Sunset didn't rise, and a morning wasn't complete without Alex singing,

I sing each day because I'm happy
I sing because I'm free
His eyes are on the sparrow,
And,...I...know...He...watches...me!

"That's why I say, what you see is what you get from me," Alex went on.

Symone apologized with a laugh. "I know that, Alex. Please forgive me for being hard on you about how you are. Ok?"

Alex was smiling now. "Oh, no. Don't do that, girl. There's no need to apologize to me. You've always voiced your opinions to me about any subject. Some I want to hear, and other stuff I would simply like to shut my ears to." She chuckled. "I'm ok with that. You're my best friend. Just stop being mean to your friends. Ok?"

Symone nodded slowly. "Alex, I'm always waiting for the big surprise. Sometimes, I get it in the form of a Desiree. Many times not. Just the same, the negative stuff causes you to keep your guard up. When people are nice to me, I think something is going on here. I say ok. I wonder why do they want to be my friends? Why?" The anger had disappeared from Symone's voice.

"I understand."

"I don't need or want no new friends. For what? They want to get close to me and get to know who my friends are now. Therefore, they can swim in my pool, get a free massage at Akao, or get some of the money that they think I have. Maybe it's even because somebody told them I'm like a daughter to the Eisner family." Symone clasped her hands behind her head, gazed at the recessed ceiling speaker in the left right corner, and rocked back in the chair.

"When you consider all those reasons, it would be difficult to accept new friends."

"Alex, I can see why celebrities are afraid to make new friends. I don't have public notoriety or the day-to-day recognition stuff that famous people have to go through. I have what I have, and there's a wall there. I know it's because of my childhood, and that's why I don't make friends easily," Symone said with another look of despair.

"I know that, Sy."

Carefully, Symone went on. "There are always people that'll betray you, and I'd rather not deal with them or their trips. You don't know that until it happens. Whatever the hell their game plan is, I don't know. I don't know how they are, but I know how I am. I see how people operate. They can be extremely vicious." Symone played with the pewter figurine letter opener as she spoke and made quick glances in Alex's direction. "The few friends I know now have already passed the resiliency test with me. I know them. They know me. They're completely truthful with me—whether I want them to be or not."

"Amen to that, girl." Symone tried to grin at Alex's comment. Instead, she nodded her head slowly.

"I'm not like you, Alex. I wasn't born with the sixth sense called trusting people. For me, it comes with a lot of time and a lot of talking. Of course, that's where I am with certain people. With my family. With you. Pecola. Scott. Madison. Carlos. Rozelle. Yall accept me for me. Yet, yall know I can be a stone damn bitch at times. A super bitch really. Scuse my French." She tried to smile, showing the pretty, perfect white teeth for which she was known. Upon hearing Symone curse, Alex smiled too and didn't flinch one muscle.

"Your French is quite appropriate."

Symone carefully considered her next words. "Alex, I've been betrayed at the lowest level. You know that. By my father—" she whispered the last three words, almost to herself, and shook her head heavily.

"Ohhh, Symone. I know." Alex didn't know what else to say.

"It's hard. Hard to trust, girl," she explained in a low voice as she lapsed into a thoughtful silence.

Just as suddenly, Symone rose from her chair and went to stand by the window and gazed blankly outdoors. As they both considered Symone's early years in Trinidad, quiet enveloped the room for long minutes. The faint siren sounds of a police car careening down Stratford Road caught Symone's attention, and she watched it until it swerved onto I-40.

Alex cleared her throat and quickly wiped the corner of each eye with an index finger because just thinking about Symone's childhood made her sad. There was another long pause as Alex thought of something appropriate to say. Symone walked slowly back to her chair and sat down. She reached over and took a paper clip off three sheets of paper and began twisting it out of shape. In reality, Symone really felt like crying, too.

"So Alex, you're a burst of fresh air in my life. That's for sure. My family says the same thing, and they're glad I have someone like you down here. Quite frankly, I'm protective of you. To be honest, I'm kind of jealous."

"Puhleeze."

"Cause your heart is so good, sometimes I think I don't want anyone else to have you as a friend. I want to keep you all to myself. It's ok sharing you with Pecola, Scott, and even your sister. But sometimes, that's as far as I want it to go."

"You're something else, Sy."

"As your friend, I don't want anyone to do or say anything to hurt you. Then they need to deal with me. In the beginning years ago, I used to— I would find myself trying to not do or say things you wouldn't like. I thought you were sooo special. I still do." Symone's voice trailed off, and she took a sip of the hazelnut cappuccino that Elisha placed on her desk at eight-thirty. It was ice cold, and she grimaced.

"You're special too, Sy."

"But with you, it's different. Having you as a friend is like having a famous person or let's say an influential person as a friend. You want to make sure all your tees are crossed and all your eyes are dotted, so that you wouldn't be cut off from the friendship," she explained in a firm voice as she considered the Eisners again.

"Symone, puhleeze."

"I'm serious. Of course, I was taught differently. Ever since I came to this country, I was taught to believe that we all are the same people but from distinctly different cultures and with just different opportunities. You know I was taught that by my uncles and the Eisners."

Alex was silent for a moment while she digested the very special words spoken by her friend. "Symone, I can't believe the things you say. Cut you off," Alex said, laughing. "I would *never* do that."

"Can never tell."

"You don't realize or even know how much I've learned from you. The list is endless about what you've taught me. You're so fervently sincere about friendship as well. I know you're protective of me as you are about the other people you love in your life. It's an honor and education just knowing you."

"Oh, puhleeze." Symone raised an eyebrow.

"That's right. More than you know you're like an egg. You're very hard all around but very delicate. Once you crack the shell, all the mushy stuff just falls out." Alex shared a wise, slow smile.

Symone laughed in disbelief at the egg analysis. She continued to stare at Alex with wide eyes and a small grin right at the same time her telephone rang. "Hold that thought, Alex."

Chapter Nineteen

"Tell Symone that I'm going home, but I'll be there for our luncheon meeting," Pecola instructed Elisha from her car. "Then Ted and I need to make one more stop before we head back to the office."

"I can't disturb her right now, Pecola," Elisha said. "Symone has been in a closed door meeting with Alex for about an hour."

"With Alex for an hour?" Pecola shrieked, and Ted glanced at her. "What's going on in there? They didn't tell me about no meeting."

"I don't think it's anything major, Pecola," Elisha said calmly. "It's probably about the opening ceremonies this weekend."

"Has anything changed?"

"I don't think so."

"I'm calling Symone right now. Take care, Elisha. See you in a few," Pecola said. At the same time, she was pushing the cell phone end button and trying to dial Symone's private line.

"...Is everything ok, Symone?" Pecola asked when Symone picked up her private line on the third ring.

"Of course it is, girl." Symone laughed.

"What are you doing in your office?"

"Nothing. Just working on paperwork."

"I thought Alex was there?"

"She is. So why ask me what I'm doing since you know?"

"Tell her that I said hello and ask her if Cleopatra is still coming to pick us up for the opening ceremonies?" Symone repeated to Alex what Pecola said.

"Look, Pecola. Let's hook up when you get in."

"Fine. I'll be there as soon as I can. Tell Alex to wait on me. Ok? And another thing, I need to talk to you when we're done with our meetings today."

"Join the club."

"What you mean by that?"

"Figure it out, Pecola. Look, I gots to go," Symone said, sounding impatient. "See you later."

"Humph. Later to you," Pecola said grudgingly and pressed the end button.

"Now what were you saying, Alex?" Symone asked as soon as she hung up the telephone.

"When I first met Pecola, then you, I said to myself. 'Boy do they curse a lot.' Most church people would tell me I should've run in the opposite direction."

"Good advice."

"It wasn't." Alex spoke solemnly with an intent gaze. "You know why? I looked beyond all of that, and I saw friends. Two powerful Black women. Not in worth and ownership but in personality and warmth. And I told myself that for some reason, they're the ones. They're the women God wants me to know closely."

"I remember."

"Girl, you know how I told Pecola I really didn't have friends other than my mother, my sister, and Madison. And I asked Pecola to be my friend, and she said that she would love it."

As Alex thought about Pecola back then, she chuckled softly. Symone grinned, too. They both recalled how Pecola often laughed as she told people that when Alex held her right hand in the proposal of friendship, she thought Alex was going to ask for permission to marry her butt.

"Pecola tells everybody that funny story."

"That might be funny now, but I wanted that, Symone. You were the second person I asked that question. I want friends," Alex said slowly and softly. " I need friends. All Black women deserve good friends. The kind our parents used to have. The kind that lasts for twenty and thirty years."

"I understand."

"My mama always said that if you don't give of yourself, you can't be a good friend. So that's why I try to share myself with you."

"You do a great job too, girl."

"I wanted friends so I could share with them, love them, buy them things, talk to them, treat them special, and love them as Black women should love each other. I wanted friends for those reason, Symone." She took a deep breath and peered thoughtfully in Symone's eyes with love and sincere commitment for their eternal friendship.

"I can't say that."

"I understand. Being friendly is key to success and peace of mind—you name it. It's the key in this world. You know when I walked in downstairs, I spoke and waved at four Black women sitting in the lobby. Only two of them waved back. I couldn't believe that. Black folks aren't like they used to be. They're cold or something. I know the other two women heard me speak. For whatever reason, they both decided to ignore my greeting. Long ago, Black folks waved at one another whether we knew each other or not. We did it in cars, outside, in stores, in church, and wherever we met other Black folks. We waved."

"Pauletta often says that this still goes on in the deep south or at least down her way in Augusta, Georgia."

"I'm sure it still does. Blacks always acknowledged each other. Things like that. With all the stuff going on during the Civil Rights Movement, we had to band together to try to get white folks to get up off of us. We never knew when we would need somebody to watch our backs from racist white folks. There was an unspoken communication of acknowledging one another."

"True. But nowadays, Black people barely speak to another Black person, especially the women." Alex shook her head from side to side. "Then when I drive through the streets of Winston-Salem, I wave at people. I'm still trying to share the beauty of just being friendly. Black folks cut their eyes at you because you're driving a Lexus or Mercedes. They wonder, 'Who are you? What do you do? Where are you from?' But, they still don't wave. I declare it's downright pitiful. I feel awfully sad when it happens. What's so hard about a wave?"

"Nothing at all."

Alex shifted her eyes to the window and spoke with a faraway expression. "When I was growing up on Cameron Avenue, everyone was so friendly and caring in my neighborhood. If I went outside and Mama was inside, you can believe that whoever was outside had their eyes on me. I always said, 'Yes ma'am' and 'No ma'am' to them in the same manner I did my parents. We all knew each other. We were in each other's house, and everyone knew each other's business. Sometimes they wanted it to be known. Other times, they didn't." Alex smiled and scratched her head quickly.

"You're right."

"I just don't know. I'm bout to agree with you, Symone. Mama used to say the same thing when she was alive. Black folks became cold and distant after integration. I guess we desperately so wanted to be accepted—that we adopted cold white ways or something." She turned aside, laughed a little, and wiped her fingers under her nose.

"We did."

"That's why I absolutely loved bell hook's book, *Sisters of the Yam.* It is a thrill for me to give that book as a gift to every woman and man I know."

"I know it is."

Symone smiled to herself remembering the prettily gift-wrapped box and lovely poem that accompanied *Sisters of the Yam* when she received the book from Alex. To lift their spirits about a life crisis or simply as a gesture of love, Alex freely gave friends and family book presents as frequently as other people ate Cheerios in the morning.

"Every woman, especially Black women, should read *Sisters of the Yam* and understand why we should be committed to one another as friends."

"I agree. It's an excellent book."

Alex nodded. "I believe God always intervenes and send the right people in your life, in my life. I want to be an encourager. A lover of sharing special moments with all my friends. Since my family was sooo small, friends to me are like sisters and brothers. I thoroughly cherish them."

"And we cherish you."

A wide smile lightened Alex's face. "Maybe it was because of my childhood. I don't know. Whatever. That's what friends are for. My Mama used to say friends are for a lifetime, and they come in all shapes, sizes, and philosophies."

"You got that right."

As Alex replayed her mother's words in her mind, she laughed a little, lifted the signature headband, and smoothed back her pretty, black hair.

"I truly believe those words. Some of Mama's best friends were the ones who never set foot in a church," Alex continued quietly and smiled just as quickly. "Isn't that something?

That's why I don't understand people who say they're friends, and yet go with a friend's husband and boyfriend. Then, they're always backbiting, talking about each other, ridiculing, and just killing each other with words. That's not a friend. That's an enemy. The worst kind of enemy. You can believe that whatever I have to say to you, I'll say it to your face and not behind your back. I know you're the same way."

Symone nodded and smiled. "You're right, Alex. Whatever I have to say about people, I'll tell them. They can deal with it because I am who I am." The memory of Desiree and Saturday night flashed quickly.

"You know I know that, honeychile. That's why when you curse or do whatever, I say to myself. 'Alex, this is life. Folks are a potpourri of bodies, traits, and words.'"

"Exactly."

"You know what Madison says all the time. He tells me that his friends are a pou pou platter of personalities." Alex giggled lightly. "But I accept it, you, and everything. I'm not going to say those curse words."

"I noticed," Symone said laughing.

"And I want to thank you because I do notice how you two try to be careful and not curse in front of me. Like I keep telling you and Pecola, it's not necessary. I accept yall the way you are."

"Girl, it gets rough sometimes. Alex, Alex—" Symone tried to speak and laugh at the same time. "It seems like lately the curse words will be right here." She pointed to the tip of her tongue. "Then my mind says, 'This is Alex. Don't say that.' So a damn becomes a darn. But like today, it sometimes just comes out the way it is."

"I know."

"What can I say? I'm a curse expert. I've acquired the talent over many, long years. It's amazing, though. I don't curse around the children or my mother, and I try not to do it around you. I control it when I want to. Isn't that interesting? But Pecola and I have had some real down right cursing times especially when we get angry with one another."

"Lord, I know that, too," Alex said. "I've been around yall a couple of times. You two could care less who's in the room when the discussion is an angry one and full of four letter words."

"Don't remind me."

"You know it's not that you can't control your cursing, Sy." Alex paused briefly.

"What do you mean?"

"Well, you wouldn't curse at a business meeting."

"True."

"Or at Miss Jessica."

"Definitely true."

"You do it with me because you feel very comfortable. With me, you can be yourself."

"I know that. Cursing is also how I choose to express myself, sometimes. You know me. I gots to be expressive, girl. When I curse, I'm merely expressing a depth of anger, happiness, or surprise."

Alex started clapping, and Symone laughed loudly. Symone began clapping, too.

"Spoken like a true politician, girl," Alex said brightly. "Still, I believe you can say whatever you want to me. Remember what I said. I look past your eggshell. I look at the mushy stuff. I look at your heart because I accept you for you. I'm not your mother or your conscience."

"Did Symone mentioned anything to you about us having a special meeting with Alex?" Pecola asked Ted. "She knew we had this meeting planned in Yanceyville."

"True. I'm not aware of any other meeting," Ted replied quickly, while bobbing his head to the CD sounds of Loose Ends singing *Hanging on a String*. He glanced at the bumper to bumper traffic on I-40 Westbound and was glad he wasn't driving back to Winston from Yanceyville this time

"I wonder what's going on?" Pecola said, almost to herself and began to dial Elisha's number. She refused to press the seventh number.

"What's going on where?"

"At the office, Ted. My gawd, are you following the conversation?"

"I'm trying to," he said with a short laugh as he pulled on his shirt cuffs and straightened his cuff links.

"What sooo funny?"

"You."

"Well, thanks a lot. That's one thing I can't stand about your behind. You're sooo damn honest."

"Look, if you want to find out what's going on, just call Sy and ask her."

"I will. No, I'll do better than that. I'll call Elisha." This time, Pecola dialed all seven numbers to Elisha's line. A calm speaking Elisha once again told her that Symone and Alex were still meeting behind closed doors, and she had no idea what they were talking about.

"Did that help?" Ted asked when she ended the call.

"Nope. Sure as hell didn't."

"I didn't think so." Ted chuckled lightly and gazed at Pecola who continued to shake her head from side to side. "Although it's a boring subject at the present time, but do you think we can finish our discussion about what we're going to say during our conference call with Carolina Pinnacle Studios officials?"

"Uh, yes. If you insist."

"I do insist, Mrs. Reynolds. It's a huge part of my job description."

Alex and Symone gazed into each other's eyes and exchanged silent smiles. "Symone, are you finally ready to tell me what's really wrong with you?" Alex pried gently with a little grin. "Are you sure you're not hiding out in your favorite little place? The dark basement of your mind?"

Symone thought about Alex's questions again. Her eyes were fixed somewhere past the windows as she considered problems, which included her family secrets and the Eisners. The world-renowned Jewish family that was just like blood relatives to the Poussaints. So many people were always there for her. In Trinidad, in New York, and even her friends in North Carolina. They couldn't even help her with this. She needed to walk herself through it and decided to remain mum on the subject. Alex was right about her once again. Alex always could read Symone like an open book. *It was* all there in her mental basement. But Symone also wasn't ready to open the door and share it with anyone. After several long, quiet minutes, Symone offered a feeble but typical explanation.

"There's nothing wrong. No more than the usual," Symone said and hoped her lie sounded like the truth. To convince Alex she was telling the truth, she turned to glance at her, made eye contact, and laughed quickly. "I'm just fine, really. Just sorting life stuff out, girl." The two friends eyed each other carefully. Finally, Alex took a deep breath.

"Sheese. I almost forgot the other thing. You know the children will be over on Friday evening for the opening dinner ceremonies?"

Each summer Alex invited children who lived in Winston-Salem's four public housing communities to spend seventeen days visiting the Devereauxs' estate. The children rode horses, swam in the pool, learned about African history, and simply reveled in the fresh air openness of Advance, North Carolina. Alex began the unique program last year. Since that time, she and Madison single-handedly worked with the children every month by having them over to their home. From the suggestions of Scott and Rozelle, Alex planned to change the procedure this year.

Alex decided that before each child returned home, they would be matched up with a family who was anxious to do their part for African-American youth in Winston-Salem. Each family was required to pick the child up at least once a month. However, Alex fervently hoped they would do as the Devereauxs did, and most times have the youngsters end up spending sometimes every weekend out of the month with them. Since the young boys and girls were divided by ages, Alex meticulously planned action-packed activities for the appropriate age groups.

The first seventeen-day session was for twenty-eight children who were eight to eleven years old. The second session was for twenty-eight children ages twelve through sixteen. Oftentimes, Pecola laughingly explained that the children probably believed they were in a fairy tale. Alex always prepared lavishly wrapped gifts, fun-filled games, amusement park rides, and garnered a wonderful array of speakers who were just as excited to do their part for all the children. Last year, Symone provided a powerful and motivating presentation where she explained the beauty, the regalness, and the gift of being a Black child in America.

"So *you* haven't forgotten that opening ceremonies are this week-end?"

"Sure haven't." Symone vigorously shook her head. "How can I forget, girl? Between Elisha jotting notes to me all over the place and with your leaving messages on my answering machine, it's totally impossible."

"You mean *all* my messages?" Alex asked teasingly.

"From the other twenty-five reminders Gloria gave me, there's no way I can overlook it. Did you pay Gloria, too?"

"Just in home-baked cookies."

"It figures." Her smile said she was joking. "When I opened my calendar this morning, guess what was highlighted in yellow as a reminder for me? The date for opening ceremonies. You know who did that? Pecola and Ted."

"Good." Alex broke out in her trademark laugh. "Anyway, let me get out of here."

"Don't rush."

"Do you think Pecola's back?" Alex asked as she glanced at her wristwatch, stood and stretched.

"I really don't know. You can check and see on the way out. Lemme check with Elisha on the intercom."

"No. That's not necessary. Girl, you're something else. As usual, it's an education speaking with you."

"Alex, puhleeze—"

Symone rose from behind her desk and walked around to stand beside her friend. She gave her a quick kiss. They hugged and rubbed one another's back longer and tighter than usual.

"I'll walk out with you, Alex," she said still holding her waist.

"No, that's ok. Like I told you, I've an eleven o'clock appointment downstairs for my Ultra Package. I'm fine. You just stay here and push those papers," Alex encouraged with a delighted expression as she motioned toward the folders stacked on top of Symone's desk.

"I plan to."

Alex truly believed that she had gotten through at least one of Symone's many walls. But she knew that she had not come close to going down in her dark basement. "I'll talk to you tonight." As an afterthought, Alex wanted to add something else. "Symone—"

"Lawd, what is it now, girl?"

"When you hear me asking for you on your answering machine, please pick up." Alex smiled as she opened the door.

"Yes, I will," Symone replied with a broad grin and sat back down. "I damn sure will, girl."

"Great."

"I promise you this. I'll be on my best behavior at our next get-together, my ace boon coon!" Symone yelled to Alex in a funny, high-pitched southern voice as Alex was heading out the door.

Alex simply shook her head, laughed to herself, and continued walking down the hallway to get to the spa.

Chapter Twenty

After the flurry of back-to-back Wednesday meetings, Symone looked up from her paper-covered desk and realized that it was five o'clock in the afternoon. She set aside her work, rose from her chair, and locked her office door. She briefly played with one of her favorite Remington bronze figurines on the credenza and walked over to stand by the window. Very methodically, she moved the African sculptures to the other side of the window and sat upright on the windowsill. It was her favorite place in the office. With her legs stretched out and crossed at the ankles, her mind whirled. Symone idly watched the rushed six-lane traffic on Stratford Road, and the mental video of her messed up life kept flashing in her face. Symone stared outside in disbelief as she revisited the whole events of her life leading up to where she was at this very moment. After the discussion with Alex earlier and during the two meetings with Pecola and Ted this afternoon, it took all the willpower Symone possessed to not break down and cry about those early days in Trinidad.

Only fifteen minutes later, Symone was still deep in thought. She brooded about her family secrets, Mummy, Uncle Willie, Uncle Cecil, and the wonderful Uncle Samuel Eisner. She heard Pecola knock several times, call out her name, and wait a few minutes for a response. Old painful memories had claimed Symone now, possessed her. No time for anyone, even a friend. Symone turned slightly to stare at the closed door, quickly turned back toward the window, and resumed her blank gazing. Eventually, Pecola stomped away.

All these years later, I've so much guilt about him, Symone thought. *Like I could have done something to help. How could I? I could barely help myself back then. Now is now, and that was then. I need to do better. Really I do. Like Pecola told me last Saturday night even though I tried to dismiss it with my usual nasty attitude, 'Chile, if you're missing something in life, you miss life. Shit, Symone,' Pecola said. 'Try to do what the rest of us do when we have a void. Try to fill it.' Pecola's right. Like she said, you can have a friend without being one. If I continued to act miserable, I certainly would fit in the "without being one" category for her, Alex, Scott, and everyone else that knew me. Pecola's words made sense. At the time, I felt like smacking her because it was the absolute truth.*

Symone sulked for a while longer. She peered through the glass at traffic for another thirty-five minutes; then she went around to Pecola's office.

"Where were you earlier?" Pecola asked, not looking at Symone, as she stacked papers in her briefcase. "Are you ok?"

"Yes, I am." Symone stopped speaking.

"Sure?"

"No I'm not, but I just wanted to apologize for not opening my door," Symone murmured. "I was stressed and had a lot on my mind. I'm sorry."

Before answering, Pecola stared directly into Symone's eyes and studied her troubled face. "Apologies accepted. I must admit I was hurt. Especially since I knew you were in there, I did think that was downright mean," Pecola added while shrugging her shoulders. "But in a way, I understand."

"Good," Symone said. Pecola stepped from around her desk, and the two hugged lovingly.

"Just snap the hell out of it, though, Sy."

"Trust me. I'm trying."

After Symone returned to her office, she decided to give her most favorite lover at the present time a call. But just as quickly, she realized that he told her he was going to a family reunion in Alabama and wouldn't be back until the week after the 4th of July. Symone considered choice number two. Right now, she needed an excellent, sexual head to toe lube job. She knew that if choice number two was available, he could handle the difficult assignment like an expert.

As Symone searched for his number, she brooded for a while once more. She cursed herself and cursed him for being so damn good in bed. Dammit. Why call him, though? Hire some damn body else, or wait until the other hunk returns from Alabama. *Be cool, Symone* she thought. *Girl, use your damn vibrator this time.* Once she found her pink telephone book stashed in the desk drawer back right corner, she quickly looked up number two's telephone number. Without any further hesitation, Symone dialed the seven digits to his private line.

"Hello," said the always-sexy baritone voice.

"Hel-lo to you, too."

"Symone?" he asked, astonished. Valentine's day was the last time she contacted him. And that was at least five months ago.

She took a deep breath. "Yeah, it's me."

"How can I help you, baby?"

"I want to fuck. I need a good lube job. Head to toe. The total package. Can you help me out?" She was nervous, trying to get the always-awkward request right.

"Sure, baby. I can help you, Ms. Freak. I'm glad you called me. You know your Mr. Freak will always give you exactly what you want, and—" he said laughing. "I'm more than capable of giving you what you need."

To get a visual picture of her naked Black, voluptuous body, he asked her to describe what she wore to work. Out of all the women he knew, and he dated plenty, she still remained the ultimate sex goddess dream combination of intelligence, beauty, and freakiness in the bedroom.

"Come on, baby. Talk to Big Papa."

"Well, uh, black patent leather sandals," she said, unwillingly obliging his request. Sheer black stockings. Of course, my stockings are held up by lacy garters."

"Wooo! I love garters, baby."

"My bra matches my garters. Well today, I didn't feel like wearing any panties. Let's see. A sleeveless black dress tops it off. So there."

"Hmmm. It's a Black thang with you today, huh?"

"Every day. Ok. Can you get away?" Symone tried to sound casual but hated herself more and more as she spoke to him.

"Of course, I can for you, baby. That's not a problem. What do you want me to do for you? Eat your—"

"Ohhh, yes. I certainly do," she said, cutting him off. "Among other things. My house at ten-thirty."

"I can only stay three hours, Symone. I'm heading to Boca Raton in the morning, and the plane leaves at nine-thirty sharp. Even though I'm fine as shit, it ain't waiting for me."

"Hey, that's all I need." Symone was glad to see that his confidence level was still at its all time high as usual. "Three hours is fine, baby. It's more than enough time." She knew he would make love to her for at least two and half non-stop hours. Then he would use the other thirty minutes to take a shower and screw again while the hot water massaged their bodies.

"You're sure there will be no arguments, Symone?"

"No arguments. Like I told you, I need to be fucked. I don't have time for trivial bullshit, pure and simple. I need to be turned every which way but loose. Can you handle that?"

"Sheee-it! Do you really need to ask me that question? You know me, and I know your sweet, Black behind. It's a done deal. I'll see you later. Chow, baby."

"Later to you, too."

"Hey, baby!" he yelled into the receiver before she hung up. "On second thought, I'll bring my clothes. That way, we can knock boots all night, long. Chow, baby." He hung up.

Angry at herself, Symone slammed the phone down. For a hot ten seconds after she placed the receiver in the cradle, Symone felt even worst than she thought possible about making the call. She was desperate. It was in the gutter time, and he was her last resort. But sex with him was intoxicating. She quickly dismissed canceling the evening when she thought about the good feelings he would give her, and his willingness to give and get some joy.

Hell, girl. Shit happens! Bro' man is good! Symone said to herself. *He can touch his nose with his tongue and treat me the same way. I done been there. Done that. Got the T-shirt to prove it. Hell no, girl. You got the tattoo he left on you to prove it! It definitely isn't the ten-second job like Arman. Why are you sweating it? If he didn't do it with me, it would be some other lonely sistah out there who would call his freaky deaky butt up.*

A hunger pain hit Symone. For a brief second, she thought about food. She realized she hadn't eaten since Tanya delivered Caesar Salads during their one o'clock meeting with Texas Southern University officials to handle a professors' conference. Just as quickly, Symone decided to call Pecola to tell her she loved her again. She needed to say it. She knew Pecola certainly would appreciate hearing it. She picked up the phone and punched the buttons to buzz through on Pecola's intercom.

"...I'm on my way out the door, girl," Pecola yelled into the speakerphone as she brushed her hair. "Scott's here."

"Hey, Scott." Symone chirped, smiling.

"Hey, baby," Scott replied. "I was heading over to your office, but Pecola said that you were busy."

"I was." Symone's voice was low, and she was frowning. 'But not anymore."

"Look, Sy—" Pecola cut in. "We're stopping by my house, and we're heading to an executive meeting."

"Is Carlos going with yall, too?" Symone wondered.

"No. He's out of town until 11:00 tonight," Pecola said, sliding into her suit jacket that Scott held up for her.

"Why don't yall go with me to eat a chitlins with hot sauce dinner at Cafe Bessie," Symone asked, praying for their company. There were a few moments of quiet, and Symone suddenly heard Pecola and Scott mumble words.

"Ok," Pecola said finally. "Meet us at the elevator in five minutes."

"Will be there," Symone exclaimed and raced to use the bathroom.

The three ended up going to Cafe Bessie, a soul food restaurant in East Winston. Since Pecola and Scott had to attend a MADD executive meeting, they enjoyed each other's company for only ninety minutes. Then, Symone slowly drove home to get ready for her lover.

Once in the safety of her bedroom, Symone took a hot bath. She listened to a Sarah Vaughn CD and waited patiently for the doorbell to chime. Stretched out on her bed, she was flipping through *Beloved*, the Ujima Literary Society choice for the month of July, and ignoring the TV when the doorbell sounded. Prompt as always, he rang it at exactly ten twenty-five. She pressed the speak button, and his heavy voice came through the bedroom intercom. Then, a sweet smelling Symone, dressed in a short, white satiny chemise with pretty stretched lace around her breasts, raced anxiously down the winding staircase to meet him.

Chapter Twenty-One

The woman exited the car and gazed at the front right fender. *A damn flat tire!* she thought. Because the woman wasn't sure how to change it, she told her sister that they needed to walk to the all night BP Foodmart & Gas Station located two miles down the road. As she turned to reach for her leather pocketbook out of the back seat, she noticed five burly white guys on the next corner to her right. She squeezed her eyes shut to make sure she wasn't seeing things, opened them, and saw that the men were still there.

Not knowing where to go, the woman turned to her left. Further up ahead, she noticed that there was the Luigi Italian restaurant with its strikingly bright red and white awnings visible, but it was closed. All of the businesses were. Ten seconds later, she glanced around again. There were fifteen men standing together. Some of the guys were unshaven. There were others with round hairy stomachs partially covered by dirty black T-shirts. As they started walking toward the woman and her sister, she screamed for her sister to get out the car. The passenger door latch jammed. She raced over and jerked it opened from the outside and dragged her sister out by the shoulders.

This time when they turned around, three Chinese and two Black men joined the group. *What in the hell was going on here?* the woman thought to herself. She took her sister's face in her hand, stared her in the eyes, and told her everything was going to be all right. Her sister began weeping silently, and they started running through the streets. By now the crowd swelled to thirty people, and all carried hatchets, machetes, and pitchforks. The woman held her sister's hand tightly. They raced up Main Street, ducked down Dockery Lane, and weaved through parked cars past the post office down below the Century Corner Drug Store. The delirious mob now yelled and screamed for them to stop running. Her sister cried and said she couldn't run anymore.

The two women hung a left onto Pickett Street and jumped a wire fence. The clearance wasn't high enough. Her sister slid on the pole, cut a deep gash in her right leg, and couldn't run another step. Frantically, the woman looked around. She found a large garbage can, shoved her sister in it, and told her she would return as soon as possible with the police. By the time she raced to the edge of the Human Office Building, she noticed a Chinese and Black man peering around the corner. The two strange-looking men yelled, "We've found her." Then, they charged at her. She whacked them repeatedly with a pine flat board full of rusty steel nails she discovered near the dumpster.

Quietly, the Chinese man stretched out his bloody hands to her for support. She ignored him and impulsively kicked them away and wailed a succession of deep piercing cries toward the sky. She desperately needed help and went running and screaming down DeLore Street past the junior high school, then turned left onto Hand Boulevard, which she remembered would have an excellent escape route across the railroad tracks to the police station.

However, unbeknownst to her, the road was boarded up six months ago, and a twenty-foot high cinder block dead end wall blocked access to the other part of town. Now, the angry crowd of forty people, all dressed in black capes and hoods, turned the corner and raced toward her. She thought she heard her sister plead and scream for her life to be spared. She wasn't sure. She knew this was it. She would be murdered; her worst nightmare came true. A split second later, an Indian man jerked her head back by her hair. Another Chinese guy held her shoulders in place. As the mob raised the hatchets, machetes, and pitchforks to kill her, she pressed her body against the brick wall. She closed her eyes and let out one blood curdling, terrifying scream.

"Are you ok, baby?" the man asked gently with both hands resting on her shoulders.

The woman jumped up whimpering, looked around frantically, and realized she was in the safety of her bedroom. Thank God her eyes were opened, and she was alive. Immediately, she began to cry and moan hysterically.

"You're still having those bad dreams, baby?"

"Yes, I, uh," she whispered in a hoarse voice.

He hugged her and noticed that she was soaking wet. Tenderly, he pulled off the pretty silk negligee she had on and figured out where to find another pretty one just like it. He located a blue satin nightshirt and helped his woman slide into it.

"Do you want some water, baby?"

"No. I'm fine. Thanks." She sat trembling with frightened eyes glaring around the bedroom. "What time is it?" Her voice was raspy.

He turned to check the digital clock. "It's five o'clock Thursday morning. Why?"

"It's the same time. The exact same time," she analyzed in a soft voice.

Speechless, the concerned man walked over to the bar and poured a glass of water for her anyway. He brought it back to her and made her drink most of it. She held the glass tightly with both hands. As she gulped the water, she nervously gazed at him over the rim.

"What did your sister say this time, baby?"

"She said—" The woman's tears began to fall again. "My sister said the same thing. She pleaded for my life, and she said please don't leave me. Pleaseee don't die on me," she moaned ever so softly. Once again, she explained the nightmare to him.

"Wow, baby." He shook his head slowly and rubbed his chin from concern.

"No matter how insignificant they are, I believe dreams have a meaning," the woman stammered with wide eyes and sipped more water. "What do you think it means, baby?"

"I don't know." He shifted his head to one side. "I really don't know."

"Something is happening inside of me. One thing for certain, it isn't going to go away. I'm so scared. Sooo scared!" she sobbed pitifully. "Why? Why would my sister scream every time, 'Pleaseee don't leave me. Pleaseee don't die on me.'"

"I don't know, baby. It's probably nothing." Since he never believed dreams meant anything and thought such thinking was quite superstitious, he considered what she said. "They're nothing."

"You're right," she replied and thought for a few moments. Her voice was suddenly stronger. "You're right," she repeated with a surge of optimism. "It's probably just a bad dream. Nothing more."

"Come on. We both have a busy schedule tomorrow. I got to be out of here by seven-thirty. Let's try to go back to sleep." To relieve the tension, he laughed quietly. "Since the sex was so great last night, my strength is gone." He checked the clock. It was five-thirty. He smiled at her. "I believe we both can get a couple more hours of sleep."

The man laid down, pulled her to him, and held her tightly. He at least could do that until seven-thirty.

Chapter Twenty-Two

When Symone's Uncles Willie and Cecil woke up that muggy, rainy Thursday morning in August almost forty-one years ago, the only thing on their minds was the plans to pick up the silver flatware set for Cecil's wife, Rosa. The brothers were on vacation from work and decided to treat their four small daughters to the three-foot tall, walking Black dolls. William "Willie" Turnball Poussaint also planned to buy lacy pink handkerchiefs for his wife, Odetta.

Nine months ago, the two families shopped for Christmas gifts, and Rosa admired the shimmering tableware setting in the Goldwynn Store on Delancy Street. From that day forward, Cecil Anderson Poussaint saved a small portion of his meager weekly salary to buy the flatware for her. Both Willie and Cecil were night factory workers at the Jack Frost Sugar Company on Long Island. During their evening meal breaks, the brothers meticulously mapped out a weekly budget to make the eight-place setting a reality. The way they'd buy it was this. If Cecil carefully saved a few cents a week, he would be able to buy Rosa the gift by the next Christmas.

Just six years earlier, Cecil, twenty-five, and brother, Willie, twenty-six, immigrated from Trinidad to the United States when they were sponsored by their mother's sister, Melissa Love Garib. Not long after they arrived and because of their aunt, whom they called Tante Love, they developed an alliance with St. Philips Episcopal Church in Harlem. According to Willie, they became members to receive a necessary weekly dose of spiritual vitamins. However, Cecil, the more free spirited and emotional one of the two, declared it was to meet Caribbean women whom they heard frequently worshipped at the church.

Tall men with cocoa, chiseled features, every Sunday the strikingly handsome brothers met eligible and anxious West Indian ladies. Since women found the brothers very attractive, finding that special person didn't take long. Ten months after they set foot on American soil, the two brothers quickly became engaged. One year later, they were married and had families on the way.

Both Willie and Cecil were hard workers since their childhood days in La Pastora, Santa Cruz, Trinidad where they toiled as low wage laborers on the cocoa and coffee estates there. Once in the United States however, they constantly tried to figure out different ways to earn extra money to support their growing families and to also work toward amassing the necessary deposit for their first real estate investment. Their ultimate dream was to purchase a Harlem apartment building similar to the one in which they lived. Early on, they listened to their landlord when he talked about the different buildings he owned throughout the city. From those brief conversations, the brothers realized that the acquisition of real estate was the key to paramount prosperity and believed such a purchase would certainly place them on the beginning road to success.

Since both men were excellent cooks, they continued to work nightly at the sugar factory. In January, however, Willie came up with the idea that on the weekends they should wear debonair, Trinidadian chef faces and serve a variety of spicy, West Indian food. From Friday to Saturday evenings, they cooked and sold covered plates to the other tenants who also lived in their apartment building on 117th Street in Harlem.

The brothers were consummate friends and were often seen laughing and talking together on the front stoop of the building. They were considered leaders and protectors of the other Trinidad and Tobago immigrants who rented apartments in the tenement building. If anyone was having financial or family problems, they talked to the Poussaint brothers whom they believed solved conflicts fairly, with understanding and motivating counsel. As a result of their stellar and friendly reputation in the neighborhood, the community residents patronized the makeshift apartment restaurant and made it an early, small success.

Within six months, the brothers' menu of stewed and curry chicken, beef, callaloo, fish cakes, bake, and rice and peas developed a small following in the Harlem community. So, four months before the planned December date, Cecil had saved up enough money. Now he was able to buy Rosa the silver flatware set.

As the Poussaint brothers walked toward the Silverstein Store, they chuckled merrily. Cecil held the coveted flatware set close to his heart, and he was proud of the accomplishment. Happy he was able to get it for Rosa sooner than planned. Both men talked about how surprised Rosa would be when Cecil gave her the surprise later that evening.

"Yuh know she not expecting dey gift ta Christmas, Cecil mon," Willie said with a huge grin on his face. Cecil nodded his head with understanding.

"Willie, dis will be a pleasant surprise far she tanight. She works so hard wit dey chillren and ting. Meh tought ta meyself. Why not, mon?" There was pride in Cecil's voice as he continued to tightly hold the gift to his chest.

Once inside the Silverstein Store, the brunette, female sales clerk told them they didn't have any of the walking dolls in stock. Since she heard the Eisner Variety Store received a shipment of dolls on Tuesday, she recommended that they try that shop which was located right next door. Before they left, Willie bought a dozen lacy, pink handkerchiefs for Odetta. They thanked the woman for the information and left the store to walk next door.

The Eisner Store was spacious and airy, with a shiny almond vanilla colored linoleum floor. It was packed from floor to ceiling with a wide variety of merchandise from household goods to clothes to a vast selection of toys. When Cecil and Willie walked into the air-conditioned shop, a pleasant looking, black-haired lady behind the counter greeted them with a cordial smile. Halfway down the main center aisle, a tall gentleman asked the brothers if he could help them. Cecil told him that they simply wanted to look around first. Three well-dressed white customers milled around the clothing area looking at the floral pedal pushers and Bermuda shorts neatly arranged on the circular clearance rack. As Willie and Cecil browsed along the expansive display of the stainless steel pots and pans, the woman rang up the purchases of two customers.

Cecil turned around and watched the salesman, who nodded to acknowledge his willingness to help and sauntered over to where the brothers were glancing through the *Reduced for Sale* racks of khaki pants.

"...What can I help you with today?" the male sales clerk asked with a wide grin which showed white even teeth.

The gentleman was just as tall as the Poussaint brothers were. Dressed in a starched white shirt, striped tie, and brown loafers, he appeared to be about twenty-five years old. He possessed piercing black eyes and a sensitive, strong, tanned face. After Willie explained they wanted to buy four Black walking dolls, he led them to the toy section in the back of the store.

"Are these the dolls you're interested in?" He still had a grin on his face while he pointed an index finger to the top shelf.

"Yes—Yes, tank yuh," replied Willie looking up too. Cecil nodded in agreement. "Dose are exactly dey ones weh need!" Willie exclaimed with a satisfied smile as he bobbed his head knowingly.

"Let me know if I can help you further," the gentleman added and turned to walk away.

Cecil and Willie glanced up at the dolls for about five minutes. Since there were about twenty dolls to choose from, they discussed which ones to buy and at what price. All of the dolls were packaged in blue boxes with see-through plastic fronts that allowed customers to clearly see the dolls' pretty, puffed up satin dresses. However, only two were adorned in pink outfits. Cecil decided that he definitely wanted those two since he believed pink was his two daughters' favorite colors. Willie, on the other hand, selected the ones with the blue and yellow dresses.

Once the decision was final, Willie motioned to the male sales clerk again that they had made their choices. As the young man glided back to where they were standing, the third remaining customer headed toward the door. The customer opened the front door and the gold bell, which announced customers exiting or entering the store, jingled repeatedly. Before heading out, she yelled a few parting words to the woman behind the counter and to the gentleman, who by now was quietly speaking with the Poussaint brothers. He glanced up, smiled warmly too, and waved good-bye to her.

Since Willie and Cecil wanted the four dolls that were all located on the top shelf, the three men haggled pleasantly over the doll prices for a few moments. When they all agreed on an acceptable amount, the salesman turned to walk toward the ladder. However, he never made it to the ladder. As he reached it, he suddenly collapsed into a heap and began jerking spastically while Willie and Cecil looked on in horror. Intending to place four flowery blue and yellow dresses back on the circular rack, the woman had just stepped from behind the counter. When she saw the man convulsing on the floor, fear went through her body and she let out a succession of piercing, shrill screams.

Willie and Cecil gazed frighteningly at each other. But they had the same thought to leave and immediately turned to head toward the front door. They didn't want any trouble. With the way things were for Colored people in New York, the two brothers believed they would be accused of harming the man, arrested for no apparent reason, and probably sentenced to twenty years in prison for a crime they didn't even commit. If they were lucky, maybe the

Americans would deport them back to Trinidad. In any event, they didn't want to stick around to see what would happen.

Cecil walked hurriedly toward the center of the store, glancing back over his shoulder as he made his way toward the front door. Halfway down, Willie stopped. He turned around, headed back to the man again, and gazed down into his face as he writhed on the floor.

"C'mon, Willie, mon. Leh weh go, mon!" Cecil shouted to his brother.

Willie turned to look at his brother momentarily and refused to leave the sick man. He continued to stare at the man jerking defenselessly on the floor. He walked closer toward him and peered down in his face again. It now appeared as if his eyes were rolling back into his head.

"Oh my God! My husband! Pleaseee! Help!" the woman yelled desperately and collapsed on the floor beside him. She squeezed her hands over her ears and let out another round of loud, deafening shrieks.

From the time the man fell to the floor to the moment the brothers decided to leave took a fast ten seconds, if that long. However, the seconds ticking away seemed like a lifetime of slow motion events. As several passersby walked along the street, they heard the shrieks of despair and assumed the worst. They peeped inside the store and saw the two tall, Colored men milling about. One white woman raced into Silverstein next door and crazily exclaimed there was a robbery going on in the Eisner Store.

"Oh Godddd! My husband! Help Me! Puhleeze! Puhleeze!" His wife wailed hysterically. She pleadingly stretched both her hands out to Willie for some type of assistance, and Willie noticed that her expression was etched with total horror. Willie wasn't sure what to do. But he believed he had seen several cases of such similar fits in Trinidad; he immediately thought he recognized that the man was indeed having the same kind of seizure he was familiar with.

"Cecil! Cecil! Oh god, nah, mon! Gimme a spoon, Cecil! Gimme a spoon, mon! Hurry! Hurry!"

Cecil hesitated and watched his brother as if he had truly lost his mind. He wanted to get the hell out of there. Cecil decided that he wasn't going to get no spoon and turned to head out of the store again. Next door, the Silverstein's daughter called the police and bellowed into the phone that five Colored people were robbing the Eisners.

"Cecil, mon! Dey spoon, mon! Gimme a spoon, Cecil! Oh God, mon. Hear meh, nah!"

Cecil breathed deeply, rolled his eyes toward the ceiling, and finally reached into the bag. He pulled a shiny silver spoon out, jogged the short distance to the back, and handed it to his brother. The woman watched Willie's swift movements, and she prayed loudly. It was an incoherent babbling of words in a language Willie didn't recognize. Willie promptly inserted the spoon in the man's mouth, and the convulsion ceased.

When the man's tense muscled body relaxed, the woman began to cry pitifully as she kissed his face several times. Very tenderly, she rubbed her husband's hair repeatedly. After a minute or so, she noticed that he was breathing evenly, yet his eyes remained closed and his skin was a palish gray color.

"Thank you. Thank you so much," she moaned softly as she glared up into Willie's eyes. She reached for Willie's hand. A little confused, Willie hesitated and retreated a step. After noticing the sincerity that covered her face, Willie extended his right hand anyway, and she held it tightly.

"Thank God you were here. Thank you so very much. I believe you saved him—my husband's life—" Her voice was filled with emotion. Willie slightly nodded his head and turned to saunter away.

By now, several other storekeepers were gathered along the front sidewalk. They were afraid to go in to confront the Colored vicious robbers but at the same time, they were afraid not to. Mr. Harvey Kleinfeld, the most courageous one of all, stormed through the front doors. His store was located on the other side of the Eisners, and he was the only shopkeeper who often openly admitted to owning a gun.

"Put your hands up right now!" Kleinfeld yelled at the top of his voice as he entered the building with a pistol drawn. His heart was pounding in his throat from fear.

Kleinfeld was ready to shoot the five Colored men that he was told were robbing the Eisner Store. Even though Kleinfeld realized he was outnumbered, he believed he could still pull the rescue attempt off. Willie and Cecil immediately threw their hands up in the air. The brown bag that held the flatware crashed to the floor with a consecutive string of loud clanging.

"Get on your stomach! Lay flat on your stomach I say!" The Poussaint brothers quickly followed his instructions.

"Harvey! They didn't do anything!" screamed Gerda Eisner while struggling to stand up at the same time. With an eagle eye scan, Kleinfeld glanced quickly around the store in search of where Gerda Eisner's voice was coming from.

"Whatya say!" He plowed forward carefully, still crouching and gripping the gun with both hands. "Gerda? Samuel? Are you ok? The police are on their way! Don't worry!"

"Harvey! They didn't do anything!" she repeated with panic. "Leave them be! They saved Samuel's life! Harvey, put the gun down! Everything is fine! Puhleeze put the gun down!"

Harvey Kleinfeld glared at the two Colored men on the floor, and he wondered where the other three were hiding. He continued to glare slowly around the store. Then he looked at the two men, thoroughly ignoring Gerda's demand. Suddenly, he cleared his throat. Then he glanced at Gerda again. Quite frankly, he was afraid to put the gun down, but since Gerda appeared fine, composed, and rational, he decided to obey her request. Gerda walked over to Willie and helped him up, and she did the same thing for Cecil. She smiled up at them and again thanked the two Poussaint brothers several times.

Five minutes later, the police and an ambulance arrived. By now the crowd outside was even larger. Several shopkeepers bragged about how Harvey Kleinfeld rescued the Eisners from five would be Colored robbers. While Gerda spoke to the officers, the ambulance attendants strapped Samuel onto the gurney. Willie and Cecil picked up the silverware set that was currently scattered all over the floor. Cecil now refused to leave until he loudly counted the forks, spoons and knives to make sure each piece was there. Of course, only the spoon was missing. Then the two brothers began to walk out of the store. Gerda noticed their feeble attempts to exit quietly and asked the policeman if he would excuse her for a moment. She stopped them.

"Please. Don't leave. May I have your names and telephone numbers first?" Her voice was full of concern, and she once again smiled warmly at the two brothers.

"Weh don't have a tellyphone," Willie explained hurriedly in a curt voice as he continued to walk toward the front door. He turned and flashed a weary smile at her. She was so sincere with the simple request, and he instantly felt guilty for being short with her.

"Give she Mrs. Jerusha Shannon's number, Willie. Weh accept calls dere," Cecil volunteered anxiously.

Mrs. Shannon was one of two tenants in the building who owned a telephone. The Poussaints lived in a seven-room apartment on the third floor of the six-story walk-up. Mrs. Shannon, a seamstress, lived on the fifth floor. For a small fee, she allowed certain neighbors to have access to her telephone.

"Give she Mrs. Shannon's number, mon," Cecil repeated. He was definitely ready to leave. Right now he could use a stiff rum drink and wanted his brother to answer any questions the woman asked so they could get the hell out the store and head as quickly as possible back to Harlem—a much friendlier territory for Colored people.

Willie wrote their names, address, and Mrs. Shannon's number on a piece of yellow paper. Finally, the brothers quickly left the Delancy Street store, and Gerda watched them leave. She smiled to herself, stuck the precious note in her pocketbook, and went back to be with her husband.

Three weeks later, the Poussaint families were getting ready to attend an afternoon service at St. Philips Episcopal. Odetta heard a knock at the apartment's door. When she opened it, Mrs. Shannon's chubby, eight-year old daughter, Teresa, stood before her with a bright smile on her face that matched her clothing.

Mrs. Shannon, who was from San Fernando, Trinidad, dressed her only child in pretty and frilly outfits each day of the week. On Sundays in the summer, Teresa was always dressed in bright citrus colors, which was a startling contrast against her coal colored, silky skin. Most times, she was adorned in a pretty yellow dress, and she often wore huge yellow hair satin ribbons that were almost as large as her head. Today wasn't any different.

A polite little girl, Teresa constantly acted as if she were speaking to the King or Queen of Africa when she addressed the adults who lived in the building. Before she spoke to Odetta, she pulled out the side of her frilly dress with each hand and curtsied slightly.

"Good afternoon, Mrs. Poussaint. Mummy sez dere is a tellyphone call far Mr. Willie." Her huge, brown eyes opened widely.

"Tank yuh, Teresa," Odetta answered with fondness. "Ah'll tell he. Yuh look beauteeful taday, Teresa."

She curtsied again. "Tank yuh, Mrs. Poussaint. Meh tole mey Mummy meh don' like dey big hair bows any longer, but she sez ah had'ta wear dem anyway," she added with child-like frustration and turned to skip away. A few minutes later, Willie walked upstairs to take the call.

"Hello. Good afternoon?"

"Hello. Is this William Turnball Poussaint?" asked a stately, unfamiliar voice.

"Yes it tis—?"

"Mr. Poussaint, this is Samuel Benjamin Eisner."

Willie racked his brain for a trace of familiarity. He didn't recognize the name.

"I'm the man whose life you saved three weeks ago. In my family's store down on Delancy Street. It was on a Thursday—"

Willie's expression changed from confusion to one of instant recognition. He smiled as he remembered the unusual chain of events that happened that Thursday afternoon. He and Cecil had their wives and other tenants of the building laughing in disbelief at the whole incident.

"Yes. Ah does remember now."

"Mr. Poussaint, I wanted to know if I could meet with you and your brother today." Samuel paused briefly and realized that this was an extremely short notice. "If that were possible?" he added with his voice trailing off.

Willie considered the request and also contemplated not meeting with the man. Why was it even necessary at all? True, he saved his life, but it was over. He didn't know when he would ever step his feet down on Delancy Street again. All he and Cecil wanted to do now was simply get on with their lives.

"Ah tank yuh, but weh on our way ta church. Ah need ta be goin'. Mey brudda and meh were just glad weh could do someting. Tank yuh far callin'."

Samuel Eisner pressed. "What about another day? Maybe next Sunday? Would that give you enough time to plan and arrange your schedule with your family, Mr. Poussaint?"

Willie thought for a moment and nodded his head slowly but said nothing. *Why not meet with him?*

"Sure, mon. Sure. No problem. Next Sunday will be fine." He rubbed the corner of his left eye.

"What time?"

Willie considered this question briefly. By the time they ate their Sunday meal, relaxed outside on the front stoop with their wives and the children, six o'clock would probably be a convenient time.

"Is six o'clock ok?"

"Six it is, Mr. Poussaint. I look forward to seeing you and your brother then. I'll send a car for you two. Let me make sure I have the correct address." Samuel Eisner read the address scribbled on the yellow notepaper. Willie confirmed it was correct, and they ended the call.

Willie walked slowly back downstairs. He told the rest of the family an Eisner car would be picking him and Cecil up on next Sunday at six o'clock.

When Samuel Eisner hung up the phone, he watched it for a few minutes. Finally, a huge smiled graced his face. Carefully, he rose to his feet and walked over to stand by the window. With both hands nestled in his pants pocket, he watched the green lush, trees of Central Park as he thought about the brief conversation with Willie Turnball Poussaint. Twenty minutes later, he asked the butler to have the chauffeur bring the limousine around for him and Gerda.

On the following Sunday at five-fifty in the evening, a white man dressed in a black chauffeur suit with gold buttons, white gloves, and black cap knocked on the Poussaint's third floor walk-up apartment door. When Cecil opened it, the uniformed gentleman politely explained that he was there on behalf of the Eisner family and he would be waiting for them downstairs.

Ten minutes later, the Poussaint brothers walked outside. Willie said later that evening that if he didn't know any better, he would have thought there was a parade taking place in front of their Harlem address. It appeared that the entire neighborhood on 117th Street was sitting on each building's front stoop. Others were hanging out the apartment windows, sitting on the fire escapes being nosy, and trying to figure out what was going on with the Poussaint brothers.

Even the small boys stopped playing a game of stickball and simply savored the moment of celebrityism for their Trinidadian neighbors. Before stepping into the shiny, sleek, long black limousine, Cecil turned to wave at Rosa and his daughters. When he did that, he noticed that every window in their apartment building was occupied with their friends resting comfortably on pillows or elbow seats as they watched the activity on the street below.

Mrs. Shannon, Odetta, and her three Poussaint children were relaxing on the stoop. As Odetta watched her husband get into the car, she began to cry. Mrs. Shannon and the other women neighbors tried to calm her. They realized it was useless, and Mrs. Shannon held the baby boy while Odetta wiped her eyes. Odetta was frightened for her husband and wondered why this Eisner man wanted to see him and Cecil.

Before the chauffeur shut the door, Teresa, dressed in a bright orange, frilly dress and huge hair bow, skipped to Mr. Willie. She curtsied and asked him if she could get in the big shiny car with him. Willie smiled at the precocious child and promised he would definitely ride her in a pretty car as soon as he got one. The chauffeur closed the door, jogged around to the front, and drove off.

Chapter Twenty-Three

Cecil and Willie were escorted to a lavish apartment building on New York's Fifth Avenue. They were led through an imported, black marble foyer with stately columns and shiny brass. Once they were seated in a beautifully decorated room with exquisite Georgian furniture, thick Persian rugs and silk curtains, they continued to stare at each other in disbelief at the rich trappings. Still trying to figure out the purpose of their visit, they whispered incessantly to each other while they waited for the Eisner man to make his entrance. Every thirty seconds or so, they continued to glance over their shoulders. The richly walnut paneled room was huge, and they didn't want anyone to sneak up on them while they frantically whispered repeatedly, "Oh God nah. Wat are weh doing here?"

After the brothers chatted quietly for no more than ten minutes, Samuel Eisner walked in. He greeted the brothers with a wide smile and a quick pat on the back. Samuel offered the two a drink. Once again Cecil fervently desired two stiff rum ones, but both he and Willie accepted a shot of bourbon instead. Robert Jick, whom Samuel Eisner introduced as being the family butler for over thirty years, promptly served the Poussaint brothers drinks on ornate, sterling silver trays.

The three men exchanged the usual pleasantries. They reintroduced themselves and even laughed freely about the unusual events that occurred in the Delancy Street store on that infamous Thursday. An hour into the engaging conversation, Samuel Eisner politely asked them to tell him about their experiences in the United States. They did. The Poussaint brothers began a graphic description of their lives from the time they were young boys in Santa Cruz, Trinidad. They described their families and discussed their jobs at the sugar factory. While they spoke, Samuel's eyes never wavered from their faces. He studied them intently. When they were done, Robert served another round of bourbon, and Samuel proceeded to tell them about his life as well.

"I'm my father's third son, and the youngest of four children. My mother bore me thirteen years after her third child. My father's namesake died when his fighter jet went down over Poland during the Second World War," he said slowly. "His name was Abraham Leon Eisner. Because he was my father's right hand man within the family business, my father refused to agree to permit my brother to enlist. He was old enough to go on his own, but out of respect for my father, he first asked for his permission. My father always responded vehemently with an 'absolutely not, my son.' However, for the first time in his life, Abraham disobeyed my father's request and eagerly signed up anyway. Two years after he enlisted, he was killed." He paused.

"My father's second son, my sister, and their families were killed at Auschwitz. It was only in their deaths that we discovered that my family's last stop was at one of the most infamous slaughterhouses of Nazi Germany. Survivors who saw them—knew them there, contacted us." Samuel stopped speaking briefly and rubbed his forehead nervously. "Before then, they were hidden by a gentile woman in her home for three years and two months. Eight months before the war ended, they were placed on a train and eventually gassed at Auschwitz." The weight of the past seemed to press on him. His tone was edged with tremendous, paramount sadness.

"When the war was over, we were contacted by the families who had protected them. They had risked their lives to hide them. Both my brother and sister had written letters to my parents, just in case they didn't live to see them again. My sister and brother never believed that brutal war would progress to the extent it did. They never fathomed that it was possible that they would be ripped from their homes, from their companies. They loved France. My sister especially. And they never believed the war skirmish would result in their deaths. Would spread as it did. Although many of our relatives fled the country, my sister and brother had insurmountable hope for France. And they wanted to stay with my grandfather at our chateau there. My grandmother had died twelve years earlier. She was buried on the estate, along with their stillborn child, and my grandfather refused to leave either one of them. When my sister and brother eventually decided it was time for them and their families to leave, of course by then it was too late for them to escape through Spain. To escape anywhere. They were all murdered. Killed. It was so brutal and unnecessary. So unnecessary. It is a tough lesson. Once again, you quickly realize that success and wealth don't make anyone immune to tragedy."

Willie and Cecil listened. Not sure what to say or do, they remained quiet. Cecil took a small sip of bourbon. As Samuel spoke, his face wasn't etched with bitterness, but it was merely wracked with utter despair as he recalled the faces of his relatives. Although Samuel watched the brothers carefully, his mind was transported to another world. Before continuing, Samuel waited again. His face was black with the memory of it all, and he could clearly see his sister's smiling face. Willie thought of his own mother and father's early brutal, death and intimately knew the sadness Samuel felt.

"...I know pain. I know hurt. I know about hope," Samuel continued with his piercing black eyes shining on the brothers. "I know about death. About sharing one's life in something you believe in. My brothers and my father taught me that. I learned that from my family—not by attending the most prominent schools in Europe and the United States."

Samuel's poignant conversation continued. Finally, he paused to take a break to enjoy a light meal with the brothers. Afterwards, he took them on a tour of the opulent twenty-six room Fifth Avenue apartment he shared with his wife. Samuel Eisner was twenty-seven. Gerda was twenty-five, and they had been married for only two years. Throughout the tour, Cecil and Willie's eyes were riveted to the elegant rooms that were lavishly furnished with the finest French antiques.

Obvious beauty was of the utmost importance to Gerda Eisner, who Samuel proudly bragged decorated each room by herself. Not only were the rooms lovely to look at, Samuel said that each room had to be heard to be appreciated. When the door opened into each room, classical music played softly in the background.

Once done with the tour, the three men settled in the library. It was a quaintly lit room paneled in a veneer of polished hardwood, with rich parquet floor, and silk damask curtains. They were served cognac. Samuel began to speak about his parents who lived in a much larger apartment one floor down. In addition, he told Cecil and Willie that Gerda and his parents were in Palm Beach, and he planned to join them as soon as he finished the meeting with them. Now, Willie was curious. He cleared his throat.

"Mr. Eisner—"

"Call me Samuel, please—"

"Uh, Samuel. Ah—don't—undertand," he stammered while he watched Cecil as if to say, "Help me out, nah." Cecil guzzled down a long shot of cognac. Robert quickly refilled his glass. "Why are yuh tellin' us dese tings? Uh, weh don't understand why yuh asked us here dis evening," he ended with a confused expression on his face. Cecil stared straight ahead, not looking at anything in particular. Samuel laughed freely for a few moments.

"That's right. I didn't say why I invited you, did I?" He seemed amused. Both Poussaint brothers vigorously shook their heads no and glared at each other. Samuel chuckled again and smiled warmly.

"Willie and Cecil—" He grinned again. "Do you know who I am?"

With a confused expression, the Poussaint brothers watched one another. Finally, Willie spoke.

"Yuh, Mr. Samuel Eisner."

"That's true I am. But do you *really* know who I am?"

"No, mon. Mey brudda and meh never saw yuh before dey day on Delancy Street. No. Weh don't know who yuh are," Willie explained as he shook his head heavily. Samuel gazed at them both with a serious expression.

"Are you familiar with the Empire State Building, my friends?"

"Yes. Yes. Of course, weh are, mon," both brothers answered almost simultaneously.

"Well, my family owns the Albany Building. It's even taller than that. It's the tallest building in the United States. The second tallest in the world."

As his eyes widened, Cecil quickly sipped more Cognac.

"Are you familiar with Manistein Wine and Foods Company, my friends?"

Willie and Cecil quickly glanced at each other again. They nodded their heads in unison.

"My family owns Eisner Industries. It's much larger than Manistein. Manistein is only number fifteen in the world. Eisner Industries is the third largest food conglomerate in the world. Have you heard of it?"

The Poussaint brothers shook their heads no. Cecil curled his hand around his chin then nodded his head slowly. It seemed he recalled something vaguely familiar about the name.

"Eisner Industries is an international conglomerate that also specializes in worldwide real estate development. The size of skyscraper office building proportions. Our other specialty is the foods and beverage industry." He paused briefly and grinned once more. "That's who I am, my friends."

Now, Willie took a lazy sip of cognac.

"Since I was ten years old, my father required that I work in the Delancy Street store. It was expected of my older brothers, too. Before my sister and brother moved to France, the same was expected of them. I guess it was done so that we might stay in touch with ourselves. And in a small way to remain connected to our customers whom they knew were everyday people all over the world. My grandfather required that my father work in their shops in France. My father was my grandfather's only surviving child. And *my* father followed suit with his four children." Samuel took another swallow of cognac.

"Ah see." Willie tried to answer intelligently.

"That day when I became ill, it was my day to work in the store. When Gerda and I became engaged three years ago, she often worked with me. That's why she was there, too. Six times a year, I worked in the store. It averaged out to about, oh let's see, every two months or so."

"Yuh only came in every two months?" Willie asked in disbelief. Cecil still couldn't talk. At this point, he was barely breathing.

"That's correct, Willie. I only worked six Thursdays a year in the store. Since we were considerably well known, of course the other storekeepers were quite protective of us, as you saw with Harvey Kleinfeld. You must forgive him. He's a dear old friend of my father." Samuel smiled again. "I'm from one of the most wealthiest families in the United States and France. As I said, my great, great, great grandfather was a Jewish aristocrat who eventually made his fortune from the Eisner Vineyards of France. Many generations ago, the Eisner family originally lived in Alsace Lorainne, France." Samuel took a long swallow of cognac and pondered a fleeting moment.

"Eventually, my family settled in the Loire Valley and accumulated vast land holdings there. To this day, we're a force in the wheat industry, too. After the war ended, we were able to reclaim much of our land. It took valiant efforts. My father has business and political ties all over the world. Those lifelong associations helped tremendously. But, we were still Jewish and the restitution of assets occurred slowly for my family. It was an extremely difficult and very arduous process, but finally it was done."

"But, uh, uh, Samuel. Why did yuh want ta see meh and mey brudda," Willie asked quietly. He pointed to Cecil who continued to stare straight ahead as if he were in a voodoo trance or an induced daze. Right now, Cecil wanted to avoid everyone's gaze. He simply wanted to concentrate on the unbelievable turn of events.

"I invited you here because you both saved my life. That's why, Willie. My physician told me that had you not stuck the spoon in my mouth, I would've choked on my tongue. I never suffered from such a fit before. I was involved in a minor rugby accident in college where I was knocked unconscious. My physician believe that the blow to my head at that time probably precipitated the epileptic seizure."

Willie quickly smiled. "Ah wasn't sure, but meh slowly recognized it as such. Wen ah was in Trinidad, our cousin suffered frum such fits. He died at fourteen. Ah wasn't wit he wen it happened. He had dey same fit and swallowed he tongue. He two friends panicked and didn't know ta search in he pocket far dey spoon he always walked wit." Sadness came with the memory. Cecil nodded, remembering the cousin who died suddenly from what he always called "the crazy fit."

"Then of course you understand the purpose of being prepared when such an attack happens. My wife. Gerda had no idea what was going on or even what to do." Samuel said his voice almost hoarse. His eyes were misty. "Nevertheless, I brought you here because you and Cecil saved my life. Before you came here today, I discussed this visit. I talked about you both with my father. I wanted to speak with you sooner, but I had to of course do a little research on the two of you."

"Research?" questioned Willie.

"Yes. Quite frankly, that's exactly what I did after it was decided what the Eisner family would do for you both. I wanted to know what type of men you were. Everywhere my people turned, they were told that you both were hardworking, honest, and fair men. Leaders of sort in Harlem. I was glad to hear such news," Samuel said with a grin. "And from your heroic behavior, I expected no less."

"Yuh talked ta weh naybors. Dey never tole us."

"It was nothing to tell, Willie. Don't worry about it. I hear you both are excellent cooks though," Samuel joked with a tiny smirk.

When the brothers heard the compliment, they straightened their shoulders and stuck their chests out just a tad.

"Tank yuh, Mr. Eis— Ah mean, Samuel," Willie said proudly. Cecil remained speechless.

"You both were described as what Jewish people know as Mensch."

"Mensch?" parroted Willie.

"Yes, Mensch. A person who's known as a gentleman and a scholar. A righteous man. A person whose word is his or her bond." He hesitated slightly. "That's what your neighbors said about you two."

Willie nodded his head with understanding. "Our naybors are wonderful people. Weh all work very hard ta earn our livings."

"I understand. I know," Samuel agreed with a short laugh. "I took the time because I wanted to have several talks with my father first and to share my feelings about that Thursday. I do nothing without my father's permission, and he agreed with my wishes."

"Yuh wishes—?" echoed Willie with a perplexed expression on his face.

Samuel grinned then chuckled quickly. He took a sip of Cognac and continued talking.

"Yes, my wishes. My father said, 'Samuel, had it not been for them, the continuation of the Eisner family, my last surviving son, the Eisner family heir, the Eisner family bloodline would have died with you. Would have perished on our Delancy Street store floor that day. I agree with your wishes, my son. I'm indebted to them, too.'"

"Yuh farther said dat?"

"Yes, he did. That's why I wanted to meet with you on last Sunday, but I realized it was such a short notice. You see my father wanted to meet you too. He was available then, but he's slightly ill and is in Palm Beach. That air is most conducive to his condition right now." Cecil cleared his throat and looked away, then down at his shiny, black tie-up shoes. He thought he was going to faint.

"I want nothing from you, Cecil and Willie. Understand that. I only want to give to you. That is all. Nothing more. My family has so much to give to you. That day you saved my life. Today, I want to give you life." He stared at both Willie and Cecil with sincerity. His voice was much lower than before, and he breathed in slowly before he spoke again.

"I want to give you life—," he whispered again, "a truly, exquisite life. Please understand that. It is nothing more that I want from you. You mentioned your dreams of owning real estate. I will help you both. For as long as you live, I will help you. Now, you are my brothers. Your pain will be my pain. Your family will be my family. I will forever be grateful to you both for your valiant actions, for taking a moment to care. If I had died on the floor that day, my father, my mother and my darling wife would have died, too. It would have devastated them. My parents would have been left with no living children. That would have been absolutely unbearable for them. And my wife. My wife would have been a young widow."

Suddenly, Cecil dropped his head into his hands and began to cry softly. Samuel was surprised and moved by the display of emotions, but he continued.

"My family. Their strength couldn't take another tragedy, my friends. My two brothers, sister, so many cousins, and their friends were taken from us in the war, and I know my death would have certainly caused the death of their spirit. It would have killed them all. Gerda, Mama, and Papa. I know this to be true. I know this within my soul. The two of you, Willie and Cecil, you both prevented that all from happening, and for this I will forever be grateful."

Samuel Eisner went on to say that they no longer needed to work at the sugar factory. He had already taken care of the arrangements. His father knew the owner, and on Friday evening, he was informed that the Poussaint brothers would no longer be employed there. When the meeting ended, the three men hugged one another and Cecil continued to cry again from pure, unspeakable joy.

Before they left, Samuel asked that they wait in the foyer while he went to get one last item. Two minutes later, he returned with a small wrapped package and handed it to Cecil.

"You forgot this one," he explained with a slight laugh. Cecil opened the tissue papered package. It was the spoon that saved Samuel's life. "Gerda said you loudly counted each piece before you left. Well, then you must know this last silver spoon was missing." Samuel was still laughing.

"Tank yuh, Mr. Eisner," Cecil finally spoke in a low, grateful voice. Samuel glared at him jokingly. "Ah mean Samuel, nah. Tank yuh. Ah believe meh will frame dey ting ta show ta everyone."

All three men laughed raucously again. Samuel shook Willie's hand firmly and stared into his eyes for several long minutes. While still holding his right hand, Samuel embraced Willie tightly as he patted his back. Then he did the same for Cecil.

"Samuel, dey generosity of yuh is overwhelming," Willie said quietly as they walked to the door.

"You saved my life. It's very simple, Willie. Very simple."

Shortly after, the Poussaint brothers were driven back to Harlem. During Cecil's talk with Willie in the quiet of the limousine, Cecil cried once more and again when he got home. He couldn't believe the Poussaint Brothers' good fortune. It wasn't until Willie and Cecil explained the conversation to their wives that Willie finally comprehended the enormity of how their lives would be forever changed. Only then. It was then that Willie broke down and wept too.

From that point on, Samuel Eisner personally worked with the Poussaint brothers and helped them to create the Poussaint Development Corporation. Along with the Eisners' monetary support, they became quite wealthy in the world of real estate development, which was a rarity for Black men during that time. Not only did the Eisner family give the brothers start-up capital for other business endeavors, they also set up blind trust funds for Cecil, Willie, their children, and even their unborn heirs. With the Eisner family backing each financial transaction, they quickly helped many tenants of their old building and the other friends who lived in the Harlem neighborhood to purchase homes. Both Cecil and Willie chose to remain in Harlem and purchased quaint, lovely mansions there on Stryver's Row between 138th and 139th Street.

Chapter Twenty-Four

One year after the Poussaint brothers saved Samuel's life, Gerda and Samuel were blessed with their first baby boy. The newborn son was the beginning era of another Eisner family generation. Now the debt the Eisner family believed they owed the Poussaints mushroomed a hundredfold.

As was expected, the Eisner family's generosity didn't go unnoticed. However, it was Gerda who became the resident diplomat of understanding and love to all who cared to listen. She felt it was her obligation and responsibility to explain to their well-heeled Jewish friends who couldn't understand the unique relationship between the affluent Eisner family and the two simple Trinidadian men.

A wealthy woman in her own right, Gerda repeatedly told the Delancy Street story with unabashed sincerity and awesome gratitude of the Poussaint brothers' deed. It was Gerda who made distant cousins, friends, and even the Eisner business associates alike to understand a magnificent fact. Had Samuel died that Thursday, their firstborn Jewish son and the Eisner heir never would have been created within her womb. For the ones who couldn't understand, Gerda felt it didn't matter. It was none of their business. The Eisner family, like other wealthy families everywhere, oftentimes made decisions many people considered ludicrous and therefore couldn't or wouldn't begin to understand the reasons behind such choices and logic. So be it. A year after their first son's birth, another boy was born. Eighteen months after that, a third Eisner son was heralded into the world.

Almost thirteen years after the three men met on Delancy Street, Samuel's father lay dying. With the birth of Samuel and Gerda's three sons, he at least lived to see the Eisner bloodline thrive. To give the Eisner patriarch an opportunity to share in his first grandson's coming of age ritual, the oldest grandson's Bar Mitzvah was scheduled before his thirteenth birthday.

Before Abraham Eisner became terminally ill, it was obvious that he worshipped and adored his three grandsons. He was the epitome of a grandfather to them, not only in the monetary sense, but also with affection, uncompromising love, and the cardinal dedication to pass on the knowledge of their crowning Jewish heritage. The three boys spent as much time in their grandfather's Fifth Avenue apartment as they did their own. They often traveled with him to France and spent many a day on their grandfather's knee while he meticulously shared the Eisner family tree with them.

Yet, on his deathbed, he also summoned Willie and Cecil to his side. The young and now successful hardworking men who Abraham grew to love as sons as well were absolutely devastated in grief by his illness. Once again, Abraham expressed his gratitude to them for saving his son's life. This was the typical ritual of the senior Eisner. It seemed that each and every time the families assembled for their monthly dinner together, Abraham thanked Willie and Cecil for saving Samuel's life. When the speech was over, family, friends, and the children smiled widely as Abraham lifted his crystal glass to the brothers in a traditional Hebrew L'Chaim toast, a time-honored Jewish toast to life, to health, and to happiness.

Now while Abraham spoke in a raspy voice, Cecil knelt down by his bed and tenderly embraced his feeble hand. Once more, Abraham recognized that Cecil was consistently the overly affectionate brother. Abraham smiled weakly and casually waved off the tears, but it did nothing to squelch the young man's sobs. While Abraham talked to the brothers, Willie couldn't handle the weight of his sadness. He walked to stand beside the bedroom window. With his hands dug deep into his pant's pockets, Willie listened to the older man's words and watched the Central Park busy street traffic below.

On that day, Abraham explained that his attorneys formulated other trust funds for the Poussaint brothers and their children. In addition, extensive trust funds were set up for their only sister, the lovely Keturah who remained in Trinidad and whom Abraham had met face to face only twice. Also, he formulated the same for Keturah's children. In a voice brimming with firmness and love, Abraham spoke quietly to the Poussaint brothers.

"...You must remember these things. Always remember the power of your bloodline, Willie and Cecil. Your future. Your children. Your children's children. Your unborn generations to come. That is paramount in this world, my sons. The strong continuation of your family. Your blood heirs. Teach your children the beauty and power of who they are, my sons. The power of their culture. There's wealth in knowledge. In education. It is the gift of wisdom and life. Protect the wealth of your family and share your trust secrets with no one. I say no one." He tried to raise himself up in bed on his elbows.

Abraham's feverish, glassy eyes traveled back and forth to each brother. He told them the same in the past. This time more than any other, he wanted them to comprehend the key to retaining wealth in families. Abraham realized that his days were short. He would die soon. He wanted the two Trinidadian brothers' ears to be sharply tuned into the private knowledge of many affluent families of the world.

"I say share it with no one that is not bloodline. Understand this private information about the wealthy and the well advised. That is your key to prosperity for generations to come. If you do share such secrets with outsiders, at such times when you are least expecting, those outsiders will change their loyalty. When your bloodlines marry, they must understand this. A non-bloodline person will come in and learn your ways. During messy divorces, it happens often. During such break-ups, those non-bloodline people will destroy, pilfer, and scatter your assets that should be reserved only for the Poussaint family, for future generations—for your unborn heirs. They will fight desperately in the court system to receive your assets as their own."

Abraham coughed ferociously several times and stopped speaking. Willie turned away from the window and went to briefly rub Abraham's shoulders. The female nurse who was sitting outside the closed bedroom door rushed in to help. However, Abraham quickly waved her out of the room. The nurse watched him with a worried expression, but she left quietly.

Willie helped him sip a small glass of water, rubbed his shoulders again, and held his hand briefly. When Abraham appeared as if he recovered from the bout of the hacking cough, Willie returned to his spot in front of the window, stayed a moment, and walked to the foot of the bed. Abraham lowered his tone a decibel, evidently concerned about being overheard by the nurse. In a raspy voice, he resumed speaking.

"You have a small family. It's just you two brothers and your sister. At the same time, your children and your sister's children—that is the start and the continuation of other Poussaint generations. The prosperous continuation of your family is sovereign. Such family practices—knowing the power of the trust—the power of the family—must be an important part of your life. Teach them that they must control everything they possess as trustees but own nothing as individuals. Management of the trust must be a part of those small Poussaint children's lives. They must know their roles as Poussaint Trustees. It should be as important to you, Willie and Cecil, and to them as the air they breath. You must gather them to your bosom, place them upon your knees, and you must share the story. Your children, your nieces, and your nephews must learn those family lessons now. It is absolutely necessary for your heirs to be aware of the crucialness of such trusts practices." Abraham's voice was strong despite his illness.

"My children—your children. Your nieces and nephews are the future for tomorrow. They all are. Your heirs—my son and grandchildren were the hope of past generations that gazed upon the same moon, stars, and sun in the heavenly distance. My ancestors hoped that when they were being tortured and murdered in Auschwitz—hoped that when they lived in France and gazed upon the heavens. Your ancestors hoped that when they lived in Trinidad. Our ancestors fervently hoped—I know they did. They hoped that when they looked into the heavens—I believed that they prayed that someone would remember—that no one would forget them. Their laughter. Their goodness. Their love. Their dedication to survive at all costs. I know they hoped that their human speck upon the world wouldn't go unnoticed. I am reminded of the words of Shakespeare. *The sun with one eye vieweth all the world....* No matter who we are. Where we live. Whether there is war in the land. Here in New York or in your land of Santa Cruz. In France. In Holland. Whether there is peace in the land or not—the sun and heavens never change their faces. As I lay here dying, I realize such understanding. It is quite amazing to me what men understand about life when they lay dying, my son."

Once more, Abraham paused to catch his breath and leaned forward. Then he fell backward and rested against the pillows again. For the first time that day, Willie began to cry softly, too. Cecil remained helpless with grief and continued to weep into his folded arms upon the bed.

"Yuh changed our lives, Mr. Eisner," Cecil sobbingly spoke as he held Abraham's hand. Throughout the years, they continued to recognize the patriarch by his last name out of respect, and refused to call him Abraham even though he encouraged them to do so. "Weh nevah in our wildest dreams believed weh would live such a life in America. Nevah. Ah love yuh far it. Ah love yuh too, too bad far it."

Abraham smiled wisely. "And I never thought I would live such a life in America either or have such dastardly deeds happen to my family in France. I never thought I would outlive so many of my friends and relatives. Never thought my son would be killed in a grisly, senseless war. To outlive three of my children—that is against the laws of nature. I know it occurs, but it must be against the laws of nature. It has to be. It is so unthinkable—the pain of such monumental, unexpected tragedies. But through it all, I realized I didn't want to outlive everyone else either. I didn't want to be alive all by myself with just butlers and maids caring for me. Now the Eisner bloodline continues to flourish. It's truly wonderful to die and know that my family will live on."

"But, uh—," Cecil tried to speak. So overcome with emotion, he couldn't and began weeping again. This time still, Willie too was without words and returned to the window. He continued to watch the trees of Central Park.

Abraham laughed quickly again. "You both changed my life, too. Always remember that Willie and Cecil. You think the moneys we gave—you think it came freely, don't you?"

Cecil idly nodded his head yes.

"Yes, I gave it to you freely, my son. But the money that I—the Eisner family have given you, it is nothing. Some people thought it was much. But it is nothing to me. I would have been nothing if Samuel had died, Cecil and Willie. Money without vibrant life is nothing. I know the appreciation you've shown for the spirit of my gift and for me as well. You two and your family members have always shown my family the utmost of gratitude. Yes, we gave the money freely. But you both worked hard and earned the Eisner family respect. That wasn't something that my wealth—that I could not do, create, buy, or even give to you both. The strength of respect. The beauty of respect. It is a most powerful characteristic—an awesome trait. You both earned it well." His smile was wide and weak. "You both earned it well." Abraham repeated the words and realized the growth that he knew was destined for them.

Abraham continued to speak quietly. "...I dealt with many businessmen, and of course, we have made several fortunes together. The looks upon their faces when we earned millions were those of stern, comfortable joy. But then my business associates expected no less. They expected to earn such vast amounts of money, and so did I."

"Yet, the looks upon your faces was something to behold. Initially, you two were always anxious, inquisitive bright seeds that were planted into the ground and blossomed into strong, oak trees. But the delightful joy in your faces never changed. I often told Samuel the same. You never lost the joy of appreciating your newly found wealth. You continued to help the people you knew in Harlem. You never forgot—never turned your backs and walked away from them. I noticed that. I treasured your compassionate actions. I know by now that you must have learned that it is quite difficult to have a sympathetic heart in the business world."

Willie interrupted him. "But yuh had a heart far us, Mr. Eisner."

"That is true. That is very true, Willie," Abraham agreed, nodding his head up and down.

"A huge heart," Cecil added.

"Thirteen years ago, God smiled upon us four that day on Delancy Street. He smiled upon you both to do something to save Samuel's life. He smiled so Samuel might live. He smiled so that I would open my heart and share," Abraham explained in a low voice. "To willingly share our wealth and to share our lives," he added with a sparkle in his eyes. "So yes. It does happen. But it is still difficult to have a heart in the world of business. For those reasons, I respected your generosity to your old neighbors. That is a characteristic money cannot buy. To have a knowing eye—the pupil of concern and compassion for others is a gift. Teach such powerful lessons to your bloodline. It is an honorable trait to do both—especially when you can—when you don't have to. Have them to know such too."

Abraham smiled swiftly. He looked toward the ceiling and spoke in a wistful voice that was full of love.

"So you say it was an honor for you two to know me. I too say it was my honor to know you as well, my sons. It certainly was. It certainly was."

Cecil tenderly kissed Abraham's wrinkled and veiny pale right hand several times. He began to cry, and the old man waved him off again. Willie turned from the window and walked to stand at the foot of the bed once more. Slowly, Abraham's weary eyes traveled to his handsome, cocoa face.

"Ah tank yuh wit mey life, Mr. Eisner," Willie said softly, wiping his eyes with his white handkerchief. "Ah too am like mey brudda, Cecil. Ah never knew weh would live such a life in America. On behalf of mey sister, ah tank yuh far providing far she children and far she. Dey Poussaints will always remain a family dat will never farget dey generosity of dey Eisner family. Nevah. How can weh? Yuh did more den give us money. More den repaid wat yuh considered a debt. Yuh gave us a golden opportunity. Yuh let us inta yuh world and inta yuh life."

"Enough," Abraham moaned.

"Weh never will farget," Willie whispered fervently. "Ah will teach mey chillren, mey nieces, and mey nephews all dat dere is ta know about dey closeness of familee. Dey will know who dey are. Dey too will know dere proud place as a Trustee in dis world. Dey will know dere places as Poussaints, Mr. Eisner."

To those words, Abraham slowly nodded his head, satisfied with their response. He smiled widely at Willie and closed his eyes. Abraham said a few more words to them and was too tired to continue. They knew he needed to rest.

Chapter Twenty-Five

Three months later, Abraham Eisner died. Not long after, his son officially took his rightful place at the helm of Eisner Industries. Six months to the day of Mr. Eisner's death, Willie received a desperate call from his sister, Keturah. Tragedy had struck.

"...Oh God nah. Mey baybee boy, Willie. Mey precious baybee. Lennious is dead, Willie. Oh God, Willie. Yuh must cum home. Yuh must cum ta Trinidad. Yuh must cum now, Willie. Go get Cecil, nah." She was sobbing uncontrollably. "Meh need mey bruddas here too too bad, Willie!"

The overseas call from Trinidad to Harlem was full of static, and Willie struggled to hear each word. Lennious dead? He and Cecil had just seen the ten-year old child when they journeyed to Trinidad only four months ago for Carnival.

"Keturah, gurl. Wat happened?"

"Willie, yuh must cum. Ohhhh Goddd, Willie," she pleaded desperately. "Mey other chillren are hurt too too bad, Willie. Tis such horror here, Willie."

"Where are dey other chillren, Keturah? Speak ta meh, nah."

The line became staticky again, and her voice faded out. It returned just as quickly.

"...Tis such horrors, Willie. Dey cryin'. Dey sadness. Ohhhh, mey Lawd. Dere is nothin' ta compare ta all of dey emotions of mey children's sadness. Mey horrors."

"Wat yuh say, Keturah? Oh God, gurl! Wat's goin' on?"

"Ohhh, Goddd, Willie. Yuh must see Lennious' twin sister. She carrying on too too bad far she twin. She miss he already, Willie. Lennious is lying out at dey house. He dead."

"Where's yuh husband, Keturah. Where's Honeyboy?" he asked in a voice dripping with panic. Her voice faded out again. "Hello! Keturah! Hello!"

"...Ah in town wit mey friend, Tutts, Willie. She took meh ta dey hotel house."

The static occurred even louder this time.

"Keturah, gurl!"

"...Willie, jus cum. Oh lawd. Mey life is gone. Mey life, Willie. Mey babies are hurtin' too too bad, Willie. Meh too. Willie, yuh mus jus cum!"

Suddenly, Willie faintly heard louder weeping noises in the background.

"Oh, Godddd. Yuh does hear dem, Willie. Dem dey— Dem mey four babies cryin' far dey dead brudda," Keturah was still weeping loudly through the line.

With wet, blurry eyes, Keturah sadly watched the twin sister of the dead child crush her body up against the kitchen corner and frantically place her palms over her ears. With eyes tightly closed, the overgrown but young child was whimpering and weeping pitifully in the corner, too. Keturah hugged the other three remaining children to her waist and bosom. While she spoke to her brother, the other children were shedding loud, heartbreaking tears as well.

Ten minutes later, Willie ended the call. First, he phoned Cecil who became frantic and hurled questions at Willie about his sister. Then Willie called Samuel Eisner and told him about the desperate conversation. As soon as Samuel hung up the phone, he rattled an urgent demand to his executive secretary. One minute later, she contacted corporate travel and told them to immediately prepare the jet for a trip to Trinidad, West Indies.

Years ago, while Willie and Cecil immigrated to the United States, Keturah chose to remain in Trinidad. She married Quentin Antoine "Honeyboy" Melenieux, a gentleman who owned a three hundred and fifty-acre cocoa and coffee estate in La Porta, Upper Santa Cruz, Trinidad. Keturah bore him five children. Their names were Quentin, fraternal twins Symone and Lennious, Hazele, and Ameenah.

Quentin Antoine "Honeyboy" Melenieux first noticed the sixteen year old Keturah Ciesta Poussaint when she began working on the Melenieux plantation. Along with her brothers Willie and Cecil, they lived on the estate with the other laborers. Although Honeyboy was interested in Keturah from the first time he saw her, he knew that she was below his class. Her family was from the poor section of Santa Cruz and had nothing to offer if he married her. However, his interest in her didn't wane, and he pursued her in spite of his father's displeasure with the relationship.

Honeyboy's father's dissatisfaction with his son was nothing new. He had been thoroughly disgusted with anything Honeyboy did, and he constantly reminded him of that fact. Since Honeyboy's mother died while bringing him into the world, every day Honeyboy was continually reminded verbally that he was a murderer. Honeyboy was brutally beaten by his father who blamed his only son for the early, tragic death of his young, beautiful wife.

Ten years older than Keturah, the Poussaint brothers thought Honeyboy was an excellent beau for Keturah. Both Willie and Cecil were pleased for their sister and knew that if she married Honeyboy, she would live a life that didn't include performing tedious labor in the cocoa, coffee and banana field plantation of the soil rich, fertile countryside valley of Santa Cruz, Trinidad.

A muscular built tall man, Honeyboy stood six foot four. With a flawless creamy, chocolate complexion, baldhead, bushy eyebrows, and a mustache, he always wore billowy white or creme shirts to accent his mahogany dark features. On a visit to England when he was twenty-two years old, he saw a famous, baldheaded Black actor appear in a Biblical movie. From that point on, the star immediately became Honeyboy's idol. When Honeyboy returned to Santa Cruz, he shaved his hair and had worn a baldhead ever since. Now, he walked around with the shiny, black baldhead and a thick gold rope chain around his neck. On it dangled a huge gold cross pendant encircled in a gold heart. People assumed the cross symbolized the words "Santa Cruz" which stood for holy cross in Spanish; however, Honeyboy often told them it went deeper than that. In addition, nestled in his pants belt, he carried a long, black, limber whip.

Honeyboy's great-great-great-grandfather first came to Santa Cruz from France with the enticement of producing an abundance of cocoa and coffee beans for Caribbean distribution.

With the promise of land made to the French planters, the other part of the deal was they had to be of the Catholic faith, too. Not having a problem with these requirements, a large number of Frenchmen journeyed to Santa Cruz to take advantage of the plantation opportunities there.

A fertile valley of varying cultures, Santa Cruz was known for its mixture of people from the Spanish, French, and African ancestry, and the vast production of the Melenieux crop was done successfully for several generations by those hard-working laborers of such diverse heritages. When the economy took a drastic turn for the worst, Honeyboy's married white great-grandfather decided to return to France. But, before he left for home, he prepared the proper legal papers and promptly signed over the three-hundred and fifty-acre plantation to his coal black-complexioned African mistress and their two mulatto children. The estate was then passed down from family to family. Then, it was left to Honeyboy when his father died.

Unbeknown to the outside world of Santa Cruz, Honeyboy had been barbarically abused by his father. As Honeyboy got older, he believed that he was made of different stock than his father and vowed to never pass such brutal customs on to his next generation. Honeyboy fervently declared to Willie and Cecil that he wanted to provide Keturah with a different life—a life of bliss and well-being on the lovely Santa Cruz estate that he owned. Honeyboy swore to himself that he would never punch or hit his new wife in the same way his father had beaten him. His fists and hands would only touch her in loving ways. He remembered the way his father's fists pounded his body.

With such grand expectations, Honeyboy married Keturah when she was twenty and he was thirty. Although his intentions regarding his young wife were valiant, they were short-lived. For the first three years of their marriage, he loved and cherished Keturah. Then, two months into the fourth year, their relationship turned vicious.

In Honeyboy's effort to keep the low wage laborers on the Poussaint Plantation and to prevent them from working on other estates throughout the countryside, he kept a large supply of rum and scotch available for the workers to drink. As a result of having the liquor around, not only did Honeyboy keep his workers drunk, but he also became an alcoholic along the way.

Many nights, Honeyboy drank and played cards with the estate laborers. When they were done, he stumbled up to the large, six-column landowner's house on the hill—the white Southern plantation-style home he shared with Keturah. Then, he would drag her out the bed and beat her unmercifully. A rage erupted and transformed him into raw, livid anger. The kind that's unfounded and has a life of its own. Sometimes, he even raped her—that was after he rammed his penis in her mouth for her to suck it.

Initially, Honeyboy pummeled Keturah because he told her that he didn't like the way she cleaned the house. He instructed her that she needed to reclean every room all over again. Next, it was because she cooked doubles a certain way. As more time progressed, Honeyboy decided that it wasn't necessary to give his wife a reason why he beat her. He continued to do it because he knew he could. Over and over again. After each drunken stupor, Honeyboy returned home, and Keturah became his human punching bag.

Keturah was a tall, big boned, caramel complexion woman who stood five eight and had licorice black hair that stretched to her shoulders. In the beginning, she fought her husband back. Her surprise, shock, and hatred of what he was doing to her gave her courage. She couldn't help but fight back—as best she could. But Keturah consistently lost each physical battle anyway. Honeyboy was stronger and grew angrier with her resistance. Brutal fists quickly battered her courage. So she would cower down to try to keep what she could from being bruised or busted or swollen or broken. She couldn't remember after which beating that she lost all will to strike back. To respond. To mount a defensive attack.

After several violent confrontations with his wife fighting back, Honeyboy told her, "...If yuh gonna act like a mon, meh gonna treat yuh like a mon. Ah'll lash yuh like ah does do dey men in dey field."

With those words, he promptly whipped her with three swift flicks of his infamous black whip. Then he proceeded to bury his fists into her and slapped her with the utmost, furious force. In a pitifully humbling manner, Keturah learned to quietly accept his abuse with the fervent hopes and prayer that one day her husband's fiery temper would change. She loved him still, despite his brutal nature.

As years passed, Keturah oftentimes considered telling someone—even confessing to her local Catholic priest about the beatings. Through it all, she was afraid and remained quiet. Honeyboy always seemed to know when those confessing thoughts flashed through her mind. It was then he always threatened to kill her, and the children if she spoke to anyone about what went on in the Melenieux household. Keturah continually asked herself, "Who could I tell?" She told no one. Not even her brothers. It was her hot, branding secret.

But then Keturah waged another battle. And that was for the sane survival of her children's minds. Because the children were born into such a miserable household and in an effort to protect their little resolve for life, it was Keturah's newfound mission to shield her babies from their father's rage. Initially, she became the armor between Honeyboy and the children; however, that changed, too. He began beating them with just as much savagery as he provided to their mother. Honeyboy began first with Quentin, the oldest son and his namesake. Then with twins Symone and Lennious. Finally, their younger sisters, Hazele and Ameenah.

That was what Symone recalled most about her early life in Trinidad. For as long as she could remember, Symone's family lived a secret life of abuse. Inside their home, the brutality of her father was frightening to witness. As the family traveled throughout Santa Cruz, they appeared to be the perfect plantation landowner's family. But it was the unmerciful beatings of her mother at the hands of her father that Symone's earliest recollection of when she understood the world wasn't a nice place for a small child to be. She was robbed of her innocence by violent love. Living with violence in her home erased the pleasantness of simply living life as a child on a sprawling estate.

Symone must have been three when she first saw the power of her father's fists. It occurred when she heard the repeated sounds of fist against flesh. The sounds of her father continually pounding his large fists into the soft, flesh of her mother. While she and her brothers and sisters watched on in horror, they cried softly. This was the memory that had been scorched in Symone's mind. Although she was so young, she never forgot it.

Chapter Twenty-Six

When Symone and her twin brother turned seven years old, her father invited her out to examine the cocoa plants. As they reached a secluded section of the field, Honeyboy asked her to stop walking and to look at him.

"Yes, Papa," she answered with wide-open eyes. Although she was only seven, Symone was about five feet tall and was considered extremely overgrown and big for her age.

"Meh didn't mean ta do it," she pleaded in a weak voice. She knew that even if she hadn't done anything, it was always a good idea to make up an excuse for Papa.

"Seamone, yuh have don' nutting atall dis time. Papa wants ta let yuh know how much ah luv yuh. Dat tis all. Do yuh luv yuh Papa?" There was a strange look in his eyes that she had never seen or noticed before.

"Yes, Papa. Ah do luv yuh." She tried to smile.

"Yuh luv Papa a lot, Seamone?"

"Yes, Papa. Meh luv yuh alot," she said quietly, mechanically.

Honeyboy suddenly pulled his eldest daughter to him, almost smothering her as he began to fondle her small, pointy breasts. As his large, greedy hands glided over Symone's front, he rammed his tongue in her mouth and breathed hotly into her ears. Poison touches that burned her skin. Symone was shocked, and she cried. Honeyboy ignored the childlike whimpering of his daughter, and he continued to roughly run his hands over her body. While he continued to move his hand up and down over her, Symone was paralyzed with fear and confusion. She stood there in his clutches, stunned, not knowing what to do or how to stop it.

After that first incident, Honeyboy continued to take his daughter out to the field on a weekly basis. During those times, he fondled Symone's shivering body, sucked her breasts, and performed oral sex on her. Honeyboy believed that his rape was love. And after eight months of trips to the field, he made her perform oral sex on him, too. After that rendezvous and as they rested peacefully in the privacy of the coffee fields, Honeyboy spoke to his daughter again.

"...Yuh mustn't tell yuh Mum about wat weh do, Seamone. It will make she cry. Because she doesn't understand dey luv weh share tagether. So yuh mustn't tell she. It will kill she, and yuh don't want dat ta happen wit yuh Mum. Yuh mustn't tell anyone. If yuh tell yuh Mum, yuh brothers, or yuh seesters, dey will be angry at yuh, Seamone. Yuh don't want dat. Meh know yuh don't."

Whenever her father spoke those words to her, Symone felt sad and lonely. That she was all by herself in the world with no one to tell and powerless to stop his assaults. And she certainly believed no one could love her or would continue to love her if they found out. She forgot where it all began. The times they were together became one big awful nightmare. Late at night, Symone often found herself shivering—not from the coldness she felt inside, but from the torturous memories of being with her Papa in such an unusual way.

Symone's father regularly performed such unthinkable sexual things with her. Oral sex. Masturbating in front of her, too. But when she turned nine, he began to have sexual intercourse with Symone. She remembered it distinctly because it occurred two days after her ninth birthday.

"...Did yuh like dey cake meh had Tutts make far yuh and Lennious on Friday, Seamone?" he asked, fingering her pubic area with his large fingers.

It was Sunday. Earlier that day, the family had gone to church, and Symone wore a pretty white dress her Mummy had gotten her for her birthday. On Friday, Symone and her twin brother had just celebrated their ninth birthday in spectacular fashion. Keturah hosted a party in the Melenieux's spacious yard where the surrounding neighbors, some of the laborers Honeyboy approved of to associate with his family, and their children attended the festivities. Since Keturah knew Lennious worshipped Calypso singers, she hired a local one to perform *Happy Birthday* and other favorite tunes for Lennious and Symone's pleasure. Since Symone didn't answer his question, Honeyboy asked her again.

"Did yuh like dey birthday cake, Seamone?"

"Yes, Papa. It was good." There was a small grin on her face as she relaxed comfortably on her father's stomach while his hands glided up and down the front of her blossoming, young body.

Now she felt guilty again. Sometimes, Symone was confused regarding her feelings about having her father touch her in such a way. There were days when what her father did to her felt good and comforting. Felt like he loved her. Yet, she knew deep down inside it was evil and bad. But on most days, it made her smile contently. Today, however, once more she realized it was wrong and repulsive to her to be with her father.

"...Papa wants ta show yuh another way weh can luv," he explained as he held her chin in his hand. Honeyboy smiled as he noticed his daughter's worried expression. He briefly became wistful. "Yuh know. Ah does always tink yuh look like mey pretty Mummy. Yuh really do, Seamone."

Symone smiled at her father. He always told her that she looked like his Mummy and Lennious looked like his Papa.

"Papa, yuh does tell mey dis same ting all dey time. And yuh does say Lennious looked jus like our Grandpapa."

Honeyboy's face became dark with pain as he recalled his father. He ignored those thoughts and again considered pleasant thoughts of his mother.

"But dis is true. Mey little Seamone is so pretty—so beauteeful. Just like mey Mummy. Yuh look just like her. She was so beauteeful." Honeyboy reminisced about the mother he never met and could only acknowledge through old, cracked photographs left by his father.

"It would have ben a nice ting ta know mey grandmum."

"You're so brown and beauteeful, Seamone." He looked at her dark, flawless complexion. It was amazing to him that Symone appeared to be so much like his mother whom he never saw and only dreamed about.

Suddenly, Honeyboy kissed Symone's forehead and lips tenderly. She kissed him back. The exact same way her Papa had taught her to kiss him. As he spoke, he laid her down on the ground. He opened her legs and performed oral sex on her. It felt pleasant to her, and the war inside her began again.

"Seamone, dis is dey new way Papa wants ta luv yuh. Dis is wat little gurls do far dere Papas ta make dem happy." He breathed quietly and proceeded to gently push his large penis in his daughter's nine-year old, shivering body. "Don't be scared, Seamone. Yuh Papa won't hurt yuh."

He lied. As Honeyboy's penis ripped into her, Symone began to whimper. Slowly, her sounds turned to hysterical screams. Honeyboy covered her mouth, and he continued to forcefully push his penis inside of her. Finally, it was over. Symone didn't understand what happened. She didn't know she had just lost her virginity at the hands of her father. There was blood all between her legs, and she cried hysterically again when she saw it. Honeyboy wiped her down with a blue wash rag he had in his pocket and told her not to worry because she would be fine. This happened to young girls when they were with their fathers.

Quietly, Symone pulled on her pink ruffled panties and tried to walk up to the main house. When she finally got to the front lawn, she saw her sisters and brothers playing. It was a struggle just for her to walk. Even though they wanted to play with her, she knew she couldn't play with them feeling the way she did. Once indoors, she calmly told her mother she wasn't feeling well, and she went straight to bed.

Later that evening, Symone was resting in the bedroom she shared with her younger sister, Hazele. Lennious came in and sat on the bed beside her. He desperately loved his twin sister—just as much or if not more than she loved him.

"...Yuh doing all right, Seamone?" His voice was tender as he moved her long hair back away from her face in small strands. Leaning down slowly, he softly kissed her cheek.

When Symone looked at him, it was as if she looked into a mirror. Lennious wore glasses. But, they were identical other than the fact that he was a boy and she was a girl. They were told this all of the time.

"Ah doing fine, Lennious. Just a little tired. Meh don't feel too good. Mey tummy hurt too too bad." The excruciating pain of her father pushing himself into her body flashed in her mind. She still felt something that felt like pee seeping out between her legs.

"Does yuh want sum hot tea far yuh belly, Seamone?"

"Mummy made sum far meh, Lennious. Meh don't need anymore right now. Tank yuh far asking, Lennious." Still, she thought about how she and her father "made luv" as he called it in the fields. Symone desperately wished that there were some way that she had the power to stop her Papa from touching her in the field or even being with her on the cocoa house cot. Now, her confusion and anger kept her frightened, and she hated to go outdoors in the yard. Everywhere she looked when she stepped outside, it reminded her of what she and her father continued to do together.

Every time Lennious looked at his sister, he believed he saw a frown behind her smile. Lennious wanted to cheer her up. A laughing Lennious stood up and began wine-ing around the room with both hands on his stomach as he rolled his belly in and out. With his dancing prowess, he never needed music. Very carefully, Lennious spread his legs. Slowly, he bent down and touched the floor and began wine-ing some more.

"Oiy. Aye. Oiy. Oiy. Aye. Seamone, ah know it's mey wine yuh does want ta see. Let's go and fete, dodo. Yuh mus know it's carneevale time." He continued to glide around the bedroom as he spoke and lifted his right leg. "Yuh know dis is how ah does wine, twin. C'mon, Seamone. Jump out dey bed, and cum wine wit meh."

"Ah can't." Slowly, she sadly shook her head no. She wanted to, but she didn't have the strength.

"Den throw yuh hands up in dey air, Seamone. Right dere in dey bed. Hands on yuh head, twin."

"Touch yuh toes far meh, twin," she said lovingly.

"Like dis?"

"Yuh lookin' nice, Lennious," Symone said, mustering a weak smile at his amusing antics.

"Watch mey bumcee, Seamone." He requested again and turned around. With his back toward her, he quickly twisted his behind from the left to the right. "Hands up in dey air, Seamone."

"Yuh gettin' on too too bad, Lennious. But ah not feelin' ta party right now, twin. Ah too sick."

Again Symone laughed feebly as she thought about how Lennious was entertaining her so well in his attempts to make her feel better. Between him and Hazele, they always tried to keep the family laughing at their comical ways. Breathing a little hard from all the dancing, Lennious finally came back and sat on the bed beside her.

"Yuh want meh ta sing ta yuh, Seamone?"

"Yuh know meh does want it, Lennious." Her smile grew larger.

"Yuh mus know meh luv yuh more den anyting in dey world. Mey dear sister. Mey twin." He hugged her neck tenderly. While they remained locked in the embrace, Symone's eyes watered with tears again.

"Ah does luv yuh, Lennious. Yuh must know yuh are mey world too. Mey sweet dodo darling. Dat's wat Mummy always does say about yuh, Lennious. Mey twin is sooo sweet. Yuh make meh happy, Lennious. Everyone in dey family does love he," Symone lullabied in a bad singing voice. Lennious chuckled happily as he listened to his sister make an attempt to sing. The entire family knew Symone couldn't sing one gracious note.

"Let meh sing far yuh, twin," Lennious volunteered in a delighted voice.

When Lennious was born, Keturah stood her ground against Honeyboy and named him Eric Eustus Lennious Melenieux. He was named after Dr. Eric Eustus Williams, the Prime Minister known also as the Father of Trinidad. Because of the Eric Eustus in his name, Lennious also believed he too would grow up to be prime minister one day and also thoroughly believed he was uniquely blessed to perform as well as any of the famous calypsonian kings. He loved going to the masquerade camps during the carnival season.

During Santa Cruz's celebrations for the carnival in Port of Spain, Lennious even won two singing contests. One when he was seven. Another when he was eight.

Quietly, Lennious began to sing to her *Second Spring*, the old Lord Melody tune. And Symone began to cry quiet tears. In a very mature manner, Lennious hugged his sister's neck and continued to sing the sweet calypso melody to her. He had such an unselfish love for his sister and would do anything to remove the sadness he often noticed on her face. However, the blissfulness the twins shared didn't last long. Honeyboy stormed into the house specifically looking for Lennious. It seemed that whenever Honeyboy lay with Symone, he took his guilt out on Lennious and often threw him into the cocoa houses for a couple of hours.

"...Lennious! Lennious! Come here, nah!" Honeyboy yelled angrily upstairs for him.

"Yes, Papa! Ah cumin'! Ah on mey way!" Lennious answered briskly as he stared in Symone's wet eyes. He pushed his glasses back up on his nose. Then he hugged and kissed his sister quickly and ran out the room.

Punishment all started for Keturah's five children in the cocoa houses when Symone and Lennious were five years old. Quentin was six. Hazele was four, and Ameenah was three. Honeyboy woke up with a savage look on his face and a new demented thought for punishing his children. He marched them down to the sprawling field's cocoa houses and placed a child in each one.

The cocoa houses were little, wooden sheds with no windows. With one entry doorway, the houses were four feet wide and ten feet long. One square sleeping cot was on the inside and on occasion the field laborers often rested inside the small cocoa houses at night. Ventilation came from the roofing part where slats of boards were placed side by side with one-inch of space between them. When the children were punished inside of it, the slight openings gave the youthful prisoners an opportunity to see shattering pieces of blue sky from their lonely spot on the inside of the locked cocoa house. Even in the daytime, the cocoa houses were pitched dark on the inside.

The cocoa houses were places where the huge bags of cocoa dried above their heads. Because of the boiling Trinidadian sun, the cocoa houses were real tormenting during the daytime. Keturah often pleaded with Honeyboy to please not punish the children in such a way. To not place them in the "sweat boxes" as she called them. She was afraid that one of the children would eventually suffocate if they were punished and locked inside the cocoa houses too long.

Whenever Lennious was placed in the cocoa house, he had to stay in his bed for two straight days to regain his strength. Even though he was sickly and considered an overly timid child by Honeyboy, Lennious always had a smile on his face. This smile always warmed the heart of his twin sister and his other siblings. Symone also felt guilty about him. She was his twin and a girl. Yet, she was the one who was the bigger, taller, and stronger twin.

At night when Symone watched the black, starry Trinidadian sky from her bedroom window, oftentimes, she prayed to God that He would take all her strength away and give it to her twin brother. Lennious was her life. Her world. She loved him more than anyone, that is except her Mummy. Because Papa was quite mean to Symone and her brothers and sisters, she oftentimes also prayed that God would take her Papa away, too. That God would stop the lashings and the screams that traveled throughout the house like a foul smell. Especially during those vicious moments when she heard the cries of her Mummy while her Papa beat her during the night. Symone was desperate, and she prayed to God for help. She prayed in the same manner when her Papa mistreated her twin, too.

Symone noticed how her Papa always treated Lennious much more cruelly than the other four children, and he often placed Lennious in the cocoa house all by himself. Without fail, Keturah weepingly broke down and would let him out. Even though she knew she would be brutally beaten by Honeyboy, she continually unlocked the door and let her child out anyway. A beating was a price she was willing to pay.

Chapter Twenty-Seven

A year after Honeyboy first had sexual intercourse with Symone, he returned home from the cocoa and coffee fields totally drunk. His family never saw him sober anymore, and they were convinced that he was permanently drunk. Because of his drunkenness, savage beatings were a weekly ritual for Keturah and the children. As she fed the children a dinner of rice and peas, stew chicken and bake, Keturah was liltingly humming to them the Mighty Sparrow tune, *Jean and Dinah*. Her children loved to hear her hum. Loved to hear their mother sing the calypso tunes too. Honeyboy stumbled in cursing at Keturah and screaming about his dead parents.

With frantic, spastic movements, Honeyboy crazily shoved the children's plates off the table. He began to throw pots around the kitchen and threw two chairs against the cabinets. Shivering with fear, all five children jumped up and stood against the wall by the sink. It was a powerful, silent moment as Keturah and the children watched on in horror—afraid of what might happen next. However drunk Honeyboy was determined the level of violence he inflicted upon his family.

"Honeyboy, puhleeze nah," Keturah pleaded as she gazed him in his glassy eyes. "Dey chillren mus eat dere food nah."

Very calmly, he walked over to Keturah and wrapped his large dark, brown hands around her neck. He began choking her, and the children cried out for their mother. Because of his five children's loud wails of despair, he removed his hands from her neck. While holding Keturah's hair in one hand, he slapped her, and she fell to the floor. The children raced to her. Honeyboy pushed and shoved each one of them away.

"Honeyboy, puleeze, nah," Keturah requested with wet eyes as she weakly pulled herself up from the floor.

When the children were younger, he used to beat her up in the privacy of the bedroom. Behind closed doors so the children wouldn't hear. But in the last three years, he would beat her up all over the house. In front of the children or not. It no longer mattered.

"Oh God nah. Puhleeze don't do dis ting in front of dey chillren. Don't—" Her eyes were hopeless.

Before Keturah could finish the sentence, his fist knocked her in the left cheek. She fell to the floor again and began to bleed from the mouth. The children, all huddled together, now began to cry and scream pitifully.

Glaring down at his wife, Honeyboy yelled crazily. "Dat's where yuh belong. On dey floor. Dat's yuh place in dis house. Ah want yuh ta feel less den dey dog dat yuh are." He kicked Keturah with his left foot. As usual, Honeyboy wore his black, hard leather farming boots. Keturah yelled out in woeful pain again as he dug his boots into her body. Quentin threw himself on his father. While Honeyboy repeatedly punched his son in the chest, he shoved him to the floor.

"Ah hate yuh too too bad!" Quentin screamed as he stared up at his father's angry, tortured face. "Yuh mus leave mey Mummy alone. Yuh mus. Ah pray yuh gon die! Ah pray dat at night. Yuh nutting but evil bacchanal in dey house. Yuh meanness cause nutting but serious horrors here." Quentin was brave enough to look his father in the eye. Honeyboy walked over to him and slapped him hard in the face to make him quiet.

"Oh God nah, Honeyboy. Leave dey boy be!" Keturah screamed and Honeyboy now unleashed his temper on his wife again.

Slowly, Honeyboy sauntered back over to where Keturah was crumpled in the corner and punched her in the stomach.

"Woman, let meh tell yuh dis! Don't say a ting ta meh. Don't say nutting. Who gave yuh permission ta speak? Wen ah tell yuh ta sit down, yuh sit down. Wen ah tell yuh ta stand, yuh stand up. Wen ah tell yuh ta grovel, yuh grovel, gurl. Yuh were nutting but a poor laborer until ah married yuh," He exploded wildly. Her humiliation was keener as he berated her in front of the children. "Yuh do wat ah tell yuh. If ah tell yuh ta pick dey coffee, yuh pick each bean one at dey time. Ah dey master of dis estate. Ah in control here. If meh need ta lash it in ta yuh, yuh will know dat dese tings ah tell yuh is tru. Yuh do wat ah tell yuh!"

Honeyboy watched Keturah long and hard as she laid on the floor whimpering. Then he kicked her twice to make sure she believed his words were true and turned to leave. When he stormed out of the kitchen, he threw two table chairs against the wall as he walked toward the front door. The five children rushed to their mother's side. Honeyboy quickly came back inside, and the children frighteningly scattered once more. He yelled for Symone.

"Seamone! Cum and help meh check on dey cocoa, gurl. Quentin help meh yesterday. Taday it's yuh turn."

Slowly, Symone pulled herself away from the other children; however, Lennious held her hand and wouldn't let her go. Symone's eyes traveled around, and she glanced solemnly at the scene in the kitchen. Hazele and Ameenah were huddled in the corner crying miserably. Quentin was comforting Mummy, and Lennious was trying to comfort her. Symone realized that they all were living in a prison. A prison controlled by her maniacal Papa. Her eyes welled with tears, and she quickly wiped them away. She realized there was no escape from the horrors. No escape atall.

"Don't yuh go, Seamone," Lennious whispered with a tear-streaked face. "Ah will help yuh wit dey cocoa. Papa is too too mad far yuh ta go alone, Seamone. He might lash yuh far no reason."

"Ah fine, Lennious. Ah just fine. Go be wit Mummy. Ah be back soon." There was weariness in her voice.

After Honeyboy and Symone were in the appropriate place down in the coffee field, Symone turned to speak to her father.

"Papa is dere someting wrong wit meh dat yuh want meh ta do dis wit yuh? Yuh tole meh yuh wouldn't hurt Mummy if ah did dis luv ting wit yuh, Papa. Weh be doing dis a long time, but yuh still hurt Mummy too too bad." The memory of her mother's crumpled body squished in the corner was branded in her mind.

Honeyboy raised his hand to hit her. Symone cowered down frighteningly and turned her face away to ward off the blow.

"Please don't, Papa. Don't, Papa. No need ta get vexed, Papa. In dey beginning, yuh jus promised meh yuh wouldn't hurt mey Mummy, mey seesters, and mey bruddas if weh luv each other in such a way. But yuh haven't stopped lashing mey Mummy, Papa. Did yuh tell a lie?" Honeyboy simply stared at her.

"Long time yuh always told meh ta hate liars and ta always be truthful, Papa. Meh is so confused." Her voice was now weakening. "Ah sooo confused, Papa. Sometimes wat yuh tell meh weh do is right, yet ah believe sometimes it tis wrong, Papa. Ah confused. Ah feelin' ta tell someone dey truth about all of dis, Papa. Ah yuh daughter. Yuh eldest daughter, Papa. It doesn't seem right. Ah yuh flesh and blood. Ah just ten years old. Mey can't take much more. And yuh tell meh dis wat Papas does do ta show dere daughters luv? Meh don't undertand it. Ah feelin' ta tell someone dey truth." Her tone had grown desperate.

Honeyboy threw his daughter a threatening stare. Symone persevered with the conversation. She was simply tired, broken in spirit, and didn't care what happened next or what he did to her. As usual, she believed she was the only one who made sense in her family. She acted one way to please her mother. She acted a certain way to be a strong sister to her brothers and younger sisters. She appeared as an older woman and lover for her Papa. Initially, she believed if she did what her father wanted, then she could keep peace in the house. However, she realized that didn't work with him either.

"...But meh haven't told our secret, Papa. Ah keep it all in mey head. Right here," she explained, pointing to her right temple several times. "But it does gettin crowded up in mey head, Papa. It's so dark sometimes far meh in mey head, Papa. It's hard far meh. If mey face lookin' like it fret, it tis, Papa. Yuh does know how difficult it tis far meh ta keep dey secrets dat Hazele ask meh ta keep frum Ameenah. So yuh know it hard far meh ta keep dis secret inside. It hurt meh so bad, Papa. It hurt so bad—not tellin' anyone. Ah feel like ah want ta bust wit dey truth, but meh can't. Den everyone will be angry wit meh." She fought the tears that threatened to fall. She took a deep breath and continued.

"Mummy concerned about meh and mey school work. Ah can't do mey school lessons dey Catholic seesters does give meh. Ah so confused, Papa. Yuh said yuh wouldn't hurt mey Mummy no longer, but yuh did it again taday. Yuh do it all dey time, Papa. Am ah not makin' yuh happy? Am ah not doin' it right far yuh? Am ah not luvin' yuh right? Dey way yuh taught meh ta do it?"

Honeyboy listened to the words of his daughter. In a sobering moment, he saw the sadness in her eyes and asked himself why he continued to ravage her in such a way. Why he felt it necessary to beat Keturah, and the other children. For a brief moment, Honeyboy felt guilt, but it was quickly squelched in fiery thoughts of calm rationalization that he was the lord and master of his family and he could do anything he wanted. His father treated him in the same manner and nobody in Santa Cruz acted like they noticed or cared to even stop it.

Suddenly, Honeyboy easily laced his thoughts about his life with his father's brutality toward him. He felt a nothingness feeling again. No remorse. No shame. Just vast emptiness while he did what he needed to do to Symone.

To remove the sounds of Symone's pleading voice from his mind, Honeyboy shook his head quickly from side to side and abruptly instructed Symone to lay down on the ground. Very humbly, she did as she was told and sadly removed her clean, lacy, white panties. When Honeyboy unzipped his pants, his large hard penis quickly popped out, and Symone turned her face away. As usual, she went blank. That's how she was able to deal with what her father continued to do to her, and what she did to him. She pretended she wasn't there and convinced herself that she was someone else. As Honeyboy inserted his penis into his daughter's body, she watched the blue, perfect Trinidadian sky. Symone prayed she would die, or that he would die, too.

Honeyboy's penis moved slowly in and out of his daughter's body. Then his pace became faster, and he began breathing harder. Symone knew her father's pumping and sweating would be over soon. Through all of Honeyboy's grunting, neither he nor Symone heard the crunching dry leaves upon the earth that announced someone was walking toward them. For a few shocked moments, the curious young child watched his father and sister having sex. He began to cry softly.

"...Papa, don't hurt mey sister. Mey twin," Lennious said quietly as he watched his father continue to quickly move his black, large organ in and out of Symone's body. Suddenly, Symone heard Lennious' gentle voice. The quiet speaking of her twin brother pierced the mental walls of her self-induced trance. From shock, she blinked her eyes quickly. Honeyboy still hadn't heard a thing and continued to swiftly gyrate away.

"Papa, don't hurt mey twin!" Lennious screamed hysterically. "Leave she! Yuh must leave she alone! Yuh mus!" He rushed over to the two bodies twisting on the ground.

With all the strength Lennious could muster, he struggled to pull his father off his sister. When Honeyboy turned around and realized Lennious had discovered them, his face became even blacker with rage. Naked from the waist down, Honeyboy jumped off Symone. He knocked Lennious to the ground with one clean punch to the boy's forehead, which caused his glasses to fall to another place in the field.

"Be gone from meh, nah," Honeyboy yelled as he crouched over his son. He slugged him on the arm and chest several times.

"Papa, leave he! Oh, Goddd. Don't! Puhleeze, don't!" Symone screamed as she scrambled on her knees along the ground to help her brother.

Lennious remained motionless as Honeyboy viciously kicked him several times in the stomach. To protect Lennious from her father's further brutal blows, she threw herself over her brother. Symone glared up in her father's face with desperate, angry eyes.

"Papa—! Oh God, nah! Papa, puhleeze don't kick he again! Puhleeze kick meh instead! Ah'll take dey kickin', Papa. Ah dey stronger twin. Ah'll take dey blows far Lennious, Papa. Just don't hurt he. Ah love he so, Papa. He mey dear, dear friend. Mey brudda is mey world. Ah'll do wat yuh want mey ta do ta keep dey peace."

"Dis is madness," Honeyboy grumbled, ignoring Symone's words and staring at Lennious.

"Leh meh take Lennious up ta dey house. Den ah'll cum back and do it right far yuh, Papa. Dey way yuh taught meh. Just don't hurt he. Don't hurt mey, Mummy. Don't hurt Quentin, Hazele, and Ameenah anymore. Ah'll do it right, Papa. Ah'll make luv right wit yuh Papa as soon as meh take Lennious up ta dey house. Wait far meh, and ah'll cum back and luv yuh right." She pleaded in between tears. "Puhleeze, Papa. Puhleeze!"

While Symone spoke, she hugged her brother who still hadn't moved. With tightly balled fists, Honeyboy continued to stare angrily at Symone as he shook his head slowly from side to side. He breathed in deeply. Finally, he walked away and pulled his clothes on. While cursing loudly, he stomped off toward the main house.

Later on that night in the privacy of their bedroom, Honeyboy apologized to his wife again. In a soft, sobering tone, he seemed genuinely sorry. Keturah heard the words; however, she didn't believe them. She didn't think she or the children could take much more. Lennious was sick too too bad, and she couldn't understand what made Honeyboy lash him in such a way today. Her husband knew the child was weak and even the smallest Trinidadian wind would blow him down.

Maybe. Just maybe she should tell Willie or Cecil. But why worry them in New York? Keturah thought about her own childhood horror and remained mum. However, she finally broke down and told her good friend, Tutts. Tutts told Keturah that she should tell her brothers. But Keturah was afraid about what Honeyboy would do to them once they arrived in Trinidad. No. She would remain quiet. Keturah considered the frightened words of Tutts when she saw Keturah's black and blue marks this afternoon. When Tutts noticed the swollen lip and black eye again, she wept softly as she spoke.

"...Keturah, yuh got ta tell somebodee other den meh. Yuh need ta tell yuh bruddas dey truth. Dey can save yuh life, gurl. Honeyboy is not goin' ta change. He will continue ta choose ta move he hands through dey air ta hit yuh. Every time he does do dis, ah scared far yuh. Ah scared far yuh and yuh chillren, Keturah. Ah know yuh does feel terrified and feel like yuh can't do anyting because yuh too too scared yuhself, but ah beseech yuh. Yuh must tell yuh bruddas, gurl."

"Ah don't know wat ta do, Tutts. Surely ah know weh does hate one another. Weh must hate each other ta live in such horrors so. But meh is afraid ta leave he, and ah afraid ta stay. Wat about mey chillren? Honeyboy does threatened if meh leave, he will kill mey chillren. Mey five babies. Den he would kill mey two living bruddas."

"Aye. Aye. How can Honeyboy kill yuh bruddas? Let meh tell yuh dis, Keturah, gurl. Cecil and Willie are famous in New York now. Dey can kill he, gurl. Somebody will kill he. Dey mon mean too bad, gurl. Mey blood runs cold each time ah does see yuh like dis." Her voice was laced with hate for the vicious Honeyboy. She sadly watched Keturah's swollen face and shook her head slowly. "Yuh must tell Cecil and Willie before Honeyboy kills yuh, or worse, yuh chillren. Keturah, yuh must."

Keturah began to cry. "It will be fine in dey morning, Tutts."

"It will not be fine in dey morning, Keturah. Yuh can't cover up dey bruises. Well yuh might, but yuh chillren does still hear dey screams in dey night and does know dey lashings does follow dem. It's such wicked horrors wat Honeyboy does do ta yuh."

Keturah now wept loudly as she talked to her friend in the kitchen.

"Ah does ask meyself, Tutts. Why does meh allow such? Why does meh let he lash meh up so bad, Tutts? Why? Wat makes meh tink ah does deserve such treatment? Wat type of person am meh dat ah does take it?" She shook her head miserably. "Tis not in mey spirit ta accept such. But meh do it. Ah accept it each and every time he does lash meh so badly. It tis not in mey spirit ta live such a way, Tutts. It tis not. It tis not."

"Ah know it tis not, gurl. Long time ah tell yuh, yuh mus tell yuh famous bruddas of dis horrible treatment. Yuh mus, Keturah. Oh God nah! Look at yuh! It mus stop!"

Keturah realized Tutts was right. *But wat could she do? Lord knows—wat could she do?* she thought while Honeyboy was making his regular apology. Immediately, Honeyboy's words punctured her quiet, tornado driven thoughts again. From disgust, she mentally sucked her teeth when she heard him speak his forgiving speech nonsense to her.

"...Meh sorry, Keturah. Ah didn't mean ta hurt yuh taday. Meh luv yuh too too bad, gurl. Yuh mus know dat. Meh became drunk and blacked out. Meh didn't mean ta mash up dey house. Dat's why ah was vexed so. Dey rum too too strong far mey system. Meh sorry." He spoke softly as he gazed into his wife's slender back.

Honeyboy gently rubbed her neck with affection. She still was a lovely woman to him despite the pounding her body took from his fists. He wanted to have sex with her now too. He even loved her. Keturah pretended she was asleep even though she never knew how he would react to her rejecting his sexual advances. She prayed that he would leave her alone and not viciously rape her once more as he so often did when she told him no.

Suddenly, Honeyboy had a violent urge to shove his penis in Keturah's mouth again. He knew she didn't like that. But he decided against it. For the first time in a long time, he was able to place a clamp on his uncontrollable anger and violent, twisted impulses. Since Honeyboy was still reeling from the fact that Lennious stumbled upon him and Symone in the field, he calmly decided to not force Keturah into having uninhibited sex with him tonight.

The next, day Lennious died suddenly. Keturah made the frantic call to New York to her brothers. Later on that evening, Honeyboy was a little concerned when Keturah told everyone that Willie and Cecil planned to leave New York immediately. She weepingly informed her husband that her brothers were going to come home to Santa Cruz to assist in the burial of Lennious.

Honeyboy became slightly nervous. In the past, when Keturah's now successful brothers came to Trinidad, they always wrote letters to Keturah, and she was aware of their visits at least two months in advance. Honeyboy never laid a hand on her if he knew Willie or Cecil would be visiting. However, since Lennious died so unexpectedly, Keturah's fresh bruises from the day-old beating would be obvious to Willie and Cecil. For once in his life, Honeyboy realized he would be facing some serious consequences when the Poussaint brothers saw their sister's battered body, swollen black eye, and busted lips. There would be no way he could explain it away either. There simply was no way.

Chapter Twenty-Eight

When Willie and Cecil arrived home to Santa Cruz, they were appalled at the appearance of Keturah. Very quickly, she laughed and told them it was nothing. But both brothers also noticed the dead, lifeless eyes of Keturah's four children. Later that night and in the privacy of his guestroom, Cecil even cried about the despairing countenance of his sister, his nieces, and nephew.

Three days after Cecil and Willie arrived, Lennious was buried in the estate's family cemetery. The dead boy's sisters and brother couldn't stop crying about the tragic death of their brother. In the past, Keturah's children always loved seeing their Uncle Cecil and Uncle Willie when they came home. They were men like their Papa, yet they were different from him. They were kind and loving to them—so unlike their Papa.

Before, when Cecil and Willie arrived home for carnival with their families, they always brought beautiful gifts and clothes for their sister's five children. Keturah's children also noticed how their uncles' children—their first cousins—laughed freely, had bright dancing eyes, genuine fast smiles, and wore such pretty clothes. In Santa Cruz, the uncles treated Keturah's children like their own and took them for walks around the estate and carried them on their shoulders, too. Many times, they even hugged and kissed them the same way their Mummy did.

Normally, Keturah's children adored seeing their uncles' faces and jumped all over them with excitement before they stepped in the front door. This time, however, Willie and Cecil noticed that when they arrived, the children's reception was unusually quiet with inconsolable eyes. Unbeknownst to the brothers, the children had been threatened by their father. He told them that no one, absolutely no one, was to share any information about Lennious' death. That was nothing new. Keturah and her children never discussed any of the horrible things that went on in their house. They never talked about why Honeyboy placed the children in the cocoa houses or why he was so brutal with them or their mother. It was a veneer of lies and deceit for their neighbors in Santa Cruz as well as for the uncles when they arrived.

Willie and Cecil ended up staying for three weeks. During that time, Keturah admitted nothing to them.

"...Yuh face is battered badly, Keturah," Cecil said, looking at Willie with concern. "Wat happened ta yuh, gurl? Just tell us, and we'll take care of it."

"Yuh does remember our mudda, our papa, and Angel?" Keturah asked them sadly after being silent for a few, long seconds. "Leave everyting be. Puhleeze don't say nutting ta Honeyboy. Ah begging yuh, mey brudda. Leave mey husband be."

On the day Cecil and Willie were leaving, Keturah allowed the children to stay home from school. As Cecil and Willie prepared their suitcases for the car waiting to pick them up, the children clung to their uncles and pleaded that they stay in Trinidad. An hour later, Willie and Cecil walked out into the yard. They knew it was time for Honeyboy to come up to the house for dinner, and they wanted to speak with him first.

Dressed in a sparkling, cream-colored sleeveless shirt, wide brim straw hat, black knickers, and knee work boots, Willie noticed how Honeyboy stood out in the crowd of the four men walking toward the front yard. Honeyboy's muscles rippled through his clothing as they walked. The obvious strength of Keturah's husband projected a powerful presence to his brother-in-laws as they watched Honeyboy speak briefly to the other three men who eventually wandered off in another direction. As Honeyboy saw Cecil and Willie walking toward him, he smiled broadly.

"Yuh does be leaving already?" Honeyboy asked congenially as he quickly glanced at the expensive gray tapered double-breasted traveling suits, the white shirts and Panama-styled hats worn by Cecil and Willie.

Honeyboy thought the brothers wore the fine business attire with a proud flair. It gave him the impression that Willie and Cecil now thought they were better than he was. Quite frankly, Honeyboy was glad to see them be gone from his house. Every time he turned around, he felt their eyes burn upon his back. For the past three weeks, he believed the Poussaint brothers watched his every step.

"Yuh does be leaving already?" Honeyboy inquired again when Cecil and Willie didn't answer his question. "Ah enjoyed lime-ing wit yuh. Yuh mus cum back home ta Trinidad soon."

Cecil slowly nodded his head and curled his hand around his chin. Before the brothers departed the house, Keturah cried as she tightly hugged their necks. Once again, she tried to convince both of them that she was fine and to puhleeze just quietly leave Santa Cruz. Cecil abruptly glanced over his shoulders to see if his sister was still standing on the porch watching them.

Keturah wasn't. She had just stepped inside the house to take care of Ameenah who had just wet her orange shorts from the excitement of her uncles' departure. With sad expressions on their dark, round moon faces, Quentin, Symone, and Hazele were leaning against the tall white columns and staring at their uncles as they walked toward their father.

Honeyboy removed his straw hat, and the sun glistened on his shiny, black, bald head. He nonchalantly wiped his face and head with a huge, red bandanna and continued to offer the Poussaint brothers his good-bye smile. Suddenly, Cecil walked to stand directly in front of Honeyboy and spoke between clenched teeth. As soon as Cecil began to speak, Honeyboy's smile faded.

"...Oh God, nah, mon. Wat could Keturah have done far yuh ta hurt she so, Honeyboy?" Cecil asked in an angry voice. "Wat could she have done, mon? Ah don't even recognize mey sister's eyes. Her spirit has ben mashed all over dey place," Cecil continued in a shaking speech.

Cecil stared his brother-in-law in the eyes. The tears of anger began to fall slowly down his cheeks. Honeyboy blinked quickly from the shock of seeing Cecil's tears. He immediately thought such was a weak display of emotions for a grown man. Especially a man of Santa Cruz heritage.

"Cecil, mon. Keturah and ah had a serious bacchanal. But it tis nutting. It doesn't happen other den dey one time a few weeks ago. Dey day befar Lennious died. Dat tis all," Honeyboy lied and tried to laugh it off.

"Yuh lie," Cecil snarled.

"It tis nutting, mon," Honeyboy said in a deceitfully, pleasant voice. Known as the master of manipulation by his laborers, Honeyboy believed he could sweet talk his way out of everything, including this conversation as well.

"Honeyboy, only a raving lunatic could do such tings to a wooman. Yuh mus be mad at dey world, mon." Cecil wiped the water off his face.

Instantly, Cecil felt like stabbing Honeyboy through the heart with the pocketknife he had in his pants pocket. However, he inhaled deeply, and thought about how Keturah reminded him of the tragic deaths of their parents and other brother. Instead, he turned and sauntered away to calm his anger.

"C'mon, Cecil. Ah does not normally do such a ting. Dat not meh atall, mon—," Honeyboy lied again, talking to Cecil's back.

Willie observed Honeyboy's nervous behavior, and Willie was becoming angrier as Honeyboy spoke. When Cecil walked away, Willie watched Honeyboy at least two minutes before he said a word to him. Now Willie moved to stand directly in front of Honeyboy, too. He spoke no more than twelve inches from Honeyboy's face.

"Ah am like mey brudda, Honeyboy. Ah emotional too. Ah crying too—on dey outside and on dey inside of mey body. But dis ting ah does tell yuh taday," he explained as he took a deep breath and briefly watched the flawless sheet of blue Trinidadian sky. The tears in his eyes would not fall. "Ah noticed dey spirit in mey sister's eyes are gone too, mon. Cecil is right. Keturah has no more spirit in she body. No more life in she eyes. She was always a strong wooman. Ah never saw she in such a way befar."

"Dis talk not necessary atall," Honeyboy said with a wide smile.

"Ah tought yuh would give she a good life," Willie went on. "Dat's wat yuh promised ta Cecil and meh many years ago. But it looks like all yuh have done is stole she life, Honeyboy. But dis ah does promise yuh, mon. Ah does promise dis on dey heads of mey dead Mudda and Farther. If meh ever hear or see yuh does lash mey sister again in such a way, ah does promise yuh ah will kill yuh where yuh stand, Honeyboy. She does not have ta tell on yuh either. If ah does tink yuh beat on her, ah will kill yuh. Ah does mean it. Let meh tell yuh dis again. Ah will kill yuh where yuh stand."

"Willie, mon," Honeyboy groaned. "Does yuh tink ah does do it all dey time? It merely was an isolated—"

"Mey nieces, and mey nephew," Willie interrupted Honeyboy's obvious lying. "Dose chillren are dey Poussaints' future, mon."

"Yuh crazee, mon! Dey are Melenieux, Willie," Honeyboy shouted. "Dey are mey chillren. Dey have mey name, and dey wear it proudly. Yuh can't tell meh nutting, mon. Mey family has been in dis fertile valley far generations. Meh—"

"Touch she agin," Willie challenged.

Honeyboy sucked his teeth several times and flippantly waved his hands in the air. "Mon, puleeze. Wat yuh sayin' ain't botherin' meh atall."

As Willie stared icily at Honeyboy, he continued speaking patiently and quietly.

"Dose four chillren remaining alive inside dey place," Willie explained and pointed to the huge white house in the distance where the three children were still standing quietly on the porch looking at the scene between the men.

"Honeyboy—dose small chillren. Yuh chillren. Keturah's chillren. Quentin, Symone, Hazele and Ameenah are left living. Dey are dey Poussaint family's future. Ah will not let yuh destroy dere spirit—dere lust far life wit yuh strupidness. Ah will not, Honeyboy. Understand meh. Dey are mey bloodline, and ah will not allow it. Dat is a well-known proven fact. Ah will not let yuh do it. Ah will not," he declared again in a firm voice that was now obviously breaking from supreme melancholy thoughts about his sister and her children.

"Honeyboy, if ah mus buy all dey land frum here ta Port of Spain, den pay ta have a road built directly ta mey sister's house—dis house, ah will do it. If ah must buy a car and den find someone ta teach she ta drive it ta get away frum yuh, or hire a chauffeur ta drive it far she, ah will do it. If ah mus pay ta have dey tellyphone wires stretched ta yuh house, ah will do it. Ah will do wat ah mus so dat Keturah can just pick up dey tellyphone and call meh and Cecil ta let us know wenever yuh does even tink about lashing she again. And ah promise yuh, mon. Ah will come back ta Santa Cruz, and ah will kill yuh where yuh stand." Willie's face was covered with a black, ruthless expression. His eyes were cold and piercing. Since both men were the same height, Honeyboy saw an ugliness in Willie's eyes that he had never seen before, and he was somewhat frightened by it. Yet, he rebounded nicely.

Honeyboy sucked his teeth several times. "Willie, ah don't want ta hear nutting else yuh saying, mon. Yuh tink since yuh does gone ta America, yuh can come back ta mey house and tell meh such tings. Yuh tink yuh better den meh, nah. Yuh were nutting but laborers wen yuh left. Workin' on mey estate. Workin' for dey Melenieuxs. And yuh nutting but rich laborers since yuh cum back. Yuh don't own no land in La Porta, Santa Cruz. All dat yuh does see here around yuh is all mine. Melenieux land. Ah am dey estate owner here!" Honeyboy exclaimed with a huge smile that revealed perfect white teeth.

It took all the strength Willie had to hold his tightly coiled fists at his side. If it weren't for Keturah's daily pleadings to her brothers to puhleeze leave Honeyboy alone, Willie and Cecil would have ambushed him and killed him dead the same day they arrived home to Santa Cruz. For a few moments, Willie and Honeyboy fiercely stared one another in the eyes.

"...Honeyboy, lash she again, mon. And wen ah does find it out, ah promise yuh. Ah going ta show yuh how it is ta feel such pain. Ah going ta show yuh how it does feel ta be lashed mightily in dey same way as yuh have beaten Keturah. Ah promise, Honeyboy. Ah does promise yuh wit mey life. Yuh arse will be dead, mon. Wen it does happen again, ah cuming at yuh and ah cuming far yuh. Remember dis dat ah tell yuh. If yuh ever does touch mey seester again, yuh gon be a dead mon," Willie said angrily and turned to calmly walk away as Cecil followed him.

On a Thursday two weeks after Willie and Cecil left, Honeyboy savagely beat Keturah one last time. He waited two weeks to make sure the brothers were gone from Trinidad. He didn't want them to double back and get him. Convinced sufficient time had passed, he came home on Wednesday night in his usual drunken stupor and beat Keturah worse than ever before.

The next day, Tutts came by the house. Before she went down to the coffee fields, she wanted to simply say good morning to Keturah. Tutts couldn't believe what she saw. As Keturah lay motionless in her bed, the four children were crying grievously in Symone's bedroom. Honeyboy beat Keturah so unmercifully that both her eyes were swollen shut and the children were afraid to look at her. Keturah couldn't even see to help the children get dressed for school. The older children were too weak with fear and hurt for their mother to consider dressing themselves, let alone even with helping the two younger ones get into their uniforms either.

Tutts packed salve ointment and healing leaves upon her friend's eyes. After Tutts did that, she realized she needed medicinal power a little stronger than what she could provide. Tutts raced to the voodoo woman who lived in the woods not far from the Melenieux estate. There the woman gave her an old-fashioned Trinidadian cure to open Keturah's eyes. Through it all, Keturah refused to call Willie and Cecil when she considered her life as a child and the deaths of her mother, brother, and father. She weepingly told Tutts that Honeyboy had believed she had told her brothers the truth about him; however, Keturah said that she had told them nothing. She refused to breathe an impolite word to her brothers about her husband.

With the same frenzy he whipped his wife, Honeyboy performed sexual actions with Symone that were just as savage as the beatings he inflicted upon Keturah. Although Symone realized that her father acted wilder than usual, she accepted the horrendous treatment and continued to remain silent about the assaults. During the particularly tense time, Honeyboy lashed the other children equally so. After Honeyboy's brother-in-laws left, sometimes his mean actions toward his family even scared him. Often he talked to himself to make himself stop. He was afraid that if he didn't, he would end up severely injuring one of them. Still, he remained undaunted with his need to lay with Symone. Now he began taking Symone to the cocoa houses to molest her and sometimes raped his oldest daughter two and three times a week.

Chapter Twenty-Nine

On the Friday morning four months after Honeyboy savagely beat his wife, Keturah was up at the house cooking dinner. The children were in school. During a short break, Honeyboy was in the sprawling coffee field joking with his closest laborer friends beside the trunk of the tree. Thirty minutes earlier, he performed an amazing whip trick. Since Honeyboy wanted to again show the workers his whip flicking abilities, he laughed loudly as he removed the whip from his belt. Once more, Honeyboy demonstrated how he could wrap the black whip around a slender empty rum bottle. As Honeyboy raised his arm to show his whip prowess, a sharp stomach and chest pain seemed to rip his body apart, and he fell suddenly to the ground.

Slowly, Honeyboy's eyes glided around the crystal blue Trinidadian sky, and the billowing clouds in the distance. Immediately he knew. It was a different level of mental awareness. One he had never experienced before. He absolutely knew he would never see the splendor and beauty of his homeland ever again in this natural life. Never glimpse the nightfall over the horizon. Never ever gaze upon the red orange sunset.

Not knowing what to do to help Honeyboy to his feet, two laborers tried to raise him up. However, it was useless. He was a massive man, and with life's vitality removed from his body, he was even heavier. Through it all, Honeyboy intimately inhaled the exquisite, fertile valley Caribbean air. The smell of the coffee bean plants. A scent that was with Honeyboy all his life—was all that he knew suddenly floated through his nostrils. Honeyboy realized that this was the last time he would ever again smell such a blissful aroma. Those pungent smells of which he was quite familiar. The perfumed fragrance of the cocoa, the coffee, and the bananas growing upon the lands of his estate. Suddenly, the faces of Keturah and his children loomed in Honeyboy's eyes. Even the sad yet smiling face of Lennious was remarkably present, too.

With his back flat against the moist, grassy ground and with all his powerful strength gone from his body, for the first time in Honeyboy's life, he felt total, unspeakable remorse for the life he had lived. While lying with his eyes directed upward, he heard the frantic footsteps of the men around his head. Another laborer wiped Honeyboy's forehead and propped his limp head onto a makeshift pillow that was made with the sweaty, dirty shirts of the men.

"Go get Tutts far meh, nah—" Honeyboy requested in a sad raspy voice to Stephen who glared at Honeyboy with a terrified expression on his face. Stephen was his foreman and right hand man. His buddy. His lime-ing partner. Stephen froze and couldn't move.

"Stephen, yuh must go get she far mey nah. Run quick!"

Sobbing all the way, Stephen went for her. Today, Tutts was working in the coffee fields, too. Since Honeyboy knew he was too far away from the main house—five miles down into the field, Tutts could pass his last words onto his wife. Honeyboy really wanted to look upon his faithful and lovely Keturah's face one last moment, but he knew he didn't have enough time to do it.

Minutes later, Tutts was by his side. When she saw Honeyboy stretched out on the ground, she screamed. One of the laborers was fanning his face with a piece of cardboard. Honeyboy's grayish countenance convinced Tutts he was gazing death in the face. Just as quickly, all the hate she harbored for the man slowly melted away to sadness. Tutts fell to the ground and propped his head upon her lap, and she gently wiped his face with the apron of her dress. With glassy, weak eyes, Honeyboy soaked her face in his consciousness for a brief instant.

"Tank yuh far cuming, Tutts," he said humbly and tried to smile. "Tank yuh far cuming ta be wit meh as ah lay dying, Tutts." His voice was soft, and he read the scared look in her eyes.

"Oh God, nah, Honeyboy. Let weh go get Keturah." She turned and glared at Stephen. "Run, Stephen. Run far she, mon. Run far he wife."

Honeyboy shook his head idly from side to side and mouthed a silent no.

"Tis no time far she ta cum, Tutts. Tis no time, gurl. Ah wanted ta see she, but it's no time, Tutts." Honeyboy felt himself slipping toward death, and Tutts saw tears glide down the side of his face.

"Tutts, as a Catholic ah must tell yuh dis. Ah must tell yuh. Tell Keturah far mey. Ah must tell yuh tings befar meh die. Let she know far meh, Tutts. Ah mus confess." He swallowed agonizingly. Tutts turned around and noticed the crowd of laborers forming a large group directly behind her.

"Be gone nah!" Tutts shouted with wet eyes. She crazily waved her hands at her fellow workers. "Be gone, nah. He confessin'. Go give he peace, nah." She desperately embraced Honeyboy's heavy head to her bosom.

The group scattered and gave Honeyboy and Tutts privacy. As Honeyboy spoke, Tutts heard the whimpering sounds of grief from the people now standing in the distance behind her. After Honeyboy prayed for forgiveness, he continued to speak softly.

"...Ah sorry now, Tutts. Ah sorry far mey life. Oh, Goddd. So sorry, Tutts. Tell Keturah far mey. She mus know dis ting is frum mey heart, Tutts. She mus know. Tell her far mey, nah. And dey chillren, Tutts. Tell dem too. Such serious bacchanal ah encountered as a child, Tutts." Honeyboy swallowed with difficulty.

"Ah listenin'."

"It was mey father, Tutts. He beat dey meanness and evilness inta meh. He lashed mey every day. All dey days of mey life—he does do it ta meh, Tutts. Mey life was ruled by rage, Tutts. Dey rage mey had about dey meanness done ta meh by he. Mey father does give mey such fierce blows and ah does do dey same ta mey wife and mey chillren. Ask dem far fargiveness Tutts too. And, Tutts—dis dey other ting ah mus say." He paused everso swiftly and his eyes closed momentarily.

"Wat is it?"

"Tell, Seamone. Tell she far meh," he whispered crazily. Suddenly, Honeyboy felt frightened, and he paused swiftly.

"Tell she wat, Honeyboy?"

"Where's mey heart, Tutts?" he asked in a weak voice. "Place mey hands upon mey heart. Ah does want ta feel it on mey flesh. Yuh know mey mudda does always wear a similar gold chain around she neck wit dey cross upon she heart, Tutts. Let meh touch it, Tutts." Very carefully, Tutts wrapped Honeyboy's right hand around his gold cross heart pendant.

"Tutts, yuh mus speak wit Seamone far meh, too. Yuh mus tell she—," he spoke in a humble voice as his eyes suddenly glistened with a wave of tears. "Yuh mus tell mey oldest daughter, Tutts. Seamone was sooo beauteeful ta meh. She was so much like mey mudda. Every time ah does look at Seamone, ah saw mey mudda staring back at meh."

"Ah don't understand wat yuh saying."

"Oh God, nah, Tutts! Ah see mey Mummy now far sure. Dere she is! Oh, Lawd! Look, Tutts! Ah does see she, Tutts!"

More tears fell from Honeyboy's eyes, and Tutts gripped his left hand tightly as she cried softly as well.

"...Oh God, Tutts. Ah does see her. Mey Mummy, nah. She be waving at meh. Ah does see her clearly far dey first time in all mey whole life. Mey Mummy is waiting far meh. Oh God, Tutts! Dere be mey Lennious, too. He has a smile upon he face. He finally happy far meh. Mey son happy too too bad, Tutts," he exclaimed as more tears fell. "Tell Keturah, nah. Tell Seamone nah, Tutts. Tell Quentin, Hazele, and Ameenah dat ah going ta be wit mey Mummy and mey sweet baby boy, Lennious, whose never meant no harm ta no one atall. But tell Seamone dis last ting far meh. Tell she dat ah sorry and was mad with rage dey times..."

For the next couple of minutes, Honeyboy talked to Tutts, and she cried. She was shocked at the words he shared. And since she still didn't know what to do, she continued to listen and gently squeezed his hand.

Honeyboy heard Tutts' frantic voice getting dim, faint, and far away as she pleaded with him to wait for Keturah.

"...Tell Keturah far meh. Make sure yuh does tell mey, beauteeful, beauteeful Seamone all dat ah does tell yuh, Tutts. All dat ah does tell yuh—," he whispered heavily.

With those last words went the last of Honeyboy's strength. Still holding the pendant in his hand, Honeyboy had said all he felt he needed to say. He took another deep, last breath. Finally, his miserably tortured life was over. With his eyes opened and focused on his beloved La Porta, Upper Santa Cruz's cobalt blue sky, he died in Tutts' arms. For several minutes, Tutts moaned and rocked backwards and forth at the sadness of the last dying moments with him. Carefully, she closed Honeyboy's eyes, and she began to weep quietly about what he had just told her.

The laborers gently laid Honeyboy's body into the cart, and Tutts and the others slowly rode to the house. Stephen had to calm the two horses pulling the wagon. Both animals raised their heads as the cart was being dragged along. By now, the thirty laborers who were working throughout the coffee fields heard what was going on, and they congregated along the roadside as the cart glided down the dirt path. The men took off their straw hats, and the women merely stared. Although Honeyboy wasn't the best estate owner in the valley, he always paid them in a timely manner and he joked with them. Then too he always had good rum to drink. Now the laborers were saddened by his death. But they were also worried about their livelihood. Their families' survival.

Once the cart arrived at the house, Tutts told Stephen she would go inside and speak with Keturah. Five minutes after Tutts walked inside the back door, the three men who rode up with Honeyboy's body heard nothing. Then there was a succession of agonized, piercing screams from within the house.

"...Oh God, nah, Tutts. Honeyboy dead! He just left meh dis mornin so full of heself," she wept with sad eyes and fell to the floor.

"Ah sorry, Keturah. Ah does know, but it tis true. He dead, gurl. He told meh ta tell yuh he does be sorry far all dey wrong," Tutts whispered in a tired voice.

"Oh, God! Why do ah have such horrors in mey life. Frum dey time ah was a child, nutting but bad fate rule mey life. Why?"

"He told meh ta tell yuh," Tutts continued. Her voice was measured, and she decided to keep the other puzzling words he shared with her tucked away in her heart for another time.

Keturah continued to cry quietly on the floor, and she glared up into Tutts' face.

"Ah hated he so, Tutts. Ah loved he, too. Ah was scared of he, but ah loved he. Ah hated he too too bad. Ah loved he, too. He was mey chillren's father still. Mey emotions were always so confusing about he," she explained as she wrung her hands.

"Ah does know, gurl. Meh could tell yuh loved he. In spite of everyting he does do ta yuh, yuh still loved he. But, Keturah, he said dat he was sorry too too bad. He said dat he luv yuh, gurl. Dat's wat he does say ta meh over and over again. Tis was a sad sight ta see," Tutts said dully as she still considered the other confusing things Honeyboy said to her about Symone.

After their talk, Tutts and Keturah went outside to the cart where Keturah calmly instructed the men to carry Honeyboy inside and to lay him on the bed in the second spare room. The arduously sad task done, the men promptly left to go down in the field to pick up the other workers. Keturah walked into the room where Honeyboy laid, and she watched him for a silent moment. Suddenly, she went to get the pail and filled it with water. As she cried, she washed Honeyboy down and struggled to put clean clothes on his lifeless body. Tutts offered to help, but Keturah meekly said that she would privately prepare her husband's body herself.

Chapter Thirty

When the children came home from school, they were told their father was dead. All four children cried pathetically from a combination of relief, sorrow, and love. Hazele and Ameenah especially wept the loudest of all. Honeyboy often allowed his two youngest girls to play games with him upon his knees. During those rare times, he was just as tender with them as he was angry with them. The two young girls clung to those refreshing memories and wept continuously for their father. Keturah and Tutts explained to the children that their father, with his last dying breath, told them he loved them very, very much and that he was sorry for the way he had treated them.

As the two women spoke quietly to the children, Symone crushed her hands to her head and began to scream crazily.

"...Ah glad he dead! Ah glad he dead!" Symone yelled with a tear-streaked face. "He never does tell us such tings wen he does live. All he does do wen he live was hurt mey Mummy. He hurt meh too too bad."

When Tutts heard Symone's touching words, she began to weep vigorously too as she once more remembered parts of Honeyboy's puzzling confession.

"Mummy, yuh know dis tis true wat ah sayin'. Yuh know dis is so, Mummy. Papa does hurt Quentin, Hazele, and Ameenah. He does hurt mey dead twin. Mey sweet brudda Lennious who ah does adore more den anyting in dey whole wide world. Ah does glad he dead!" Her screams now turned into agonizing sobbing as she poured tears into her Catholic school skirt uniform. The other three children were weeping just as loudly around her.

"Don't bawl on so, Seamone," Keturah said softly.

"Ah will so. Ah does glad he dead, Mummy! Yuh know ah right about wat meh say. He does hurt meh bad, Mummy. Wit all dey lashing and tings he does do ta meh, he does break mey spirit, Mummy." She fiercely gazed into both her mother's and Tutts' wet eyes. "He does hurt meh too too bad, and ah does glad he dead."

Symone realized that buried within her hate of her father was love. She was confused. With the pernicious thoughts of when her father touched her and made her body respond, she wanted to hate him. Yet, somehow or another she also was compelled to hold onto the instinctive daughterly love she had in her heart for him in spite of his treatment of her. Keturah carefully watched Tutts' face. With a quick shake of the head, Keturah motioned to Tutts to remain silent and to not tell Symone the other words from her father—not right now. All the children appeared too distraught to hear anything else for the moment. Suddenly, Quentin's face became hard with anger, too.

"Ah glad he dead, too! Ah like Seamone! At night while he does lash mey Mummy, ah prayed he does die quick quick!" Quentin hollered. The young boy looked just like Honeyboy. He stormed from the room. Keturah didn't follow him; she wanted to give her son time alone to deal with the loss of his father.

Still pouting and with tears of confusion in his eyes, Quentin walked down the hall to the doorway of the room where his father laid still on the bed. With blurry vision, Quentin wistfully watched his dead Papa for a few moments and began crying bitterly again. Suddenly, he was sad and felt guilt because God had actually answered his many prayer requests. Then just as quickly, Quentin ceased weeping and raced out into the yard to the fresh air and the Trinidadian violent blue sunset.

While Tutts remained with the children, Keturah journeyed to town where she placed a call to Willie and Cecil in Harlem. In a grief stricken voice, she explained that the death angel had visited the Melenieux house once again.

Samuel Eisner met the Poussaint Family at Kennedy Airport with a huge smile upon his face. As the chauffeurs helped with the luggage, Willie quickly told Keturah's children that the white man with the wide smile was their uncle, too. The children grinned slightly and clung desperately to their mother. That is except Hazele. She smiled and abruptly hugged Samuel Eisner's neck. Then she retreated just as quickly and protectively grabbed Ameenah's hand.

Since Symone, her brother, and her sisters had lived a life of fear for so long, they appeared timid and frightened when individuals approached them. The children only spoke when spoken to and even in those cases, no one was sure what they said because their voices were so low. Now as the mentally battered Melenieux family assembled in the private corporate hangar terminal of Kennedy International Airport, the children as well as Keturah continued to quietly gaze at one another. While they waited to be instructed on what to do next, they huddled together like battered and frightened refugees.

Two weeks after Honeyboy was buried, Keturah finally broke down and shared her entire story of abuse with her brothers. Willie and Cecil in turn shared the horrors of their sister's life with Samuel Eisner. The day after Keturah's confession, the brothers convinced their sister to come back to New York with them. Then Samuel made the necessary telephone calls and the sponsorship of Keturah and her children to come to America was handled in a few days. Once in New York and after Willie and Cecil shared all the other additional gory details of Keturah's life, Samuel Eisner told the brothers he would hire the best psychologists in the world to immediately begin counseling the five members of the Melenieux family.

Because he was from a family familiar with paramount, paralyzing grief, Samuel Eisner knew that Keturah and her children's haggard expressions only told half the story. They needed to talk it out with trained professionals skilled in the area of such unusual violence and sustained mental abuse. Samuel wanted to do whatever he could to help the Melenieux family members deal with the horrendous sufferings they experienced in Trinidad so they could walk the path to a normal and wonderful life in the United States. A second life. A second chance. Each could blossom into their own flower.

Even though Keturah's brothers lived in Harlem and even though they tried to convince her to live there as well, eleven months after Keturah arrived in New York, she decided to move to Brooklyn. There she purchased a home in the Bedford-Stuyvesant section of the city where she discovered a small gathering of other Trinidadian immigrants. After living with Cecil and Willie for almost a year, it was obvious they were quite overprotective of her. Keturah thought the move to another New York location would give her an opportunity to blossom and grow without being under the watchful eyes of her brothers.

Once in New York, Symone then grew up in a life brimming with love and wealth. She was very much indulged by Samuel Eisner and his family. House of Dior. Wonderful jewelry. Lavish toys. Exotic travels. Since Samuel Eisner didn't have any daughters, Keturah's girls enjoyed expensive shopping and elegant luncheon trips with him. Symone's every whim was taken care of; it was a lifestyle that gave her optimism. After the ghastly days with her Papa, it was quite difficult for her to separate this new type of love and affection from her three uncles with what she had experienced in Trinidad. She remained haunted by her past. For thirty-seven straight months after she arrived in the United States, she suffered with severe, gruesome nightmares about Lennious and her father's large invasive hands.

One noted psychologist Uncle Samuel hired often told Keturah, Cecil, and Willie that the years in Trinidad were a painful, horrible chapter in Symone's life, as well as for her sisters and brother. It would take time—months—even years for all the children to heal and knock down the cement lined mental walls of fear and pain. Along with the incestuous relationship with her father that Symone never discussed with anyone, Lennious' death left a permanent ache in her heart.

Symone and her family grew up around the genteel, yet wealthy community of New York's Fifth Avenue. As a result of this prominent lifestyle, they counted and called well-known and internationally famous people aunts, uncles, and friends of the family. However, Symone continued to be quiet and somewhat reclusive even as a teen-ager. This made Keturah worry. Keturah's other children adjusted to the drastic change in moving to the United States. But not Symone. Keturah was deeply concerned for her oldest daughter and told her brothers the same.

In an effort to forget all of her private and public suffering, Symone constantly tried to escape from the past by reading books. She had a deep fascination with books by such Black authors as Frances Harper, Richard Wright, Wole Soyinka, Dr. John Henrik Clarke, and Zora Neale Hurston. There were many other books her uncles required her to read from the time she was thirteen. But she loved reading fairy tales. Once the uncles realized such literary gifts brought a smile to their niece's grief-stricken face, they continually provided her with a steady selection of mystical, youthful novels that allowed Symone to walk into the dreams and worlds of others' imagination.

True, her life was converted into a lovely contrast to her life in Santa Cruz. Before moving to America and into the love of her family, she never believed in the creative ramblings of fairy tales. She didn't think they were achievable—not even remotely possible. But every day, as she gazed out her prettily decorated Brooklyn bedroom window, Symone quietly prayed that if fairy tales were indeed possible, then she hoped and prayed she would never wake up from the one she was currently living in America. Never awaken from the blissful dream of knowing her three uncles, living in New York. Or most importantly ever waking up and meeting another man as vicious as her Papa. Each time she finished reading a fairy tale, the truth of the past loomed before her. It refused to leave her alone. There were times it totally conquered her thinking, and she would ball up in a corner in her room. Her family noticed the ritual as well.

With explicit instructions from Uncle Willie to drag Symone out of her reclusive shell, Teresa Shannon decided that Symone would be her play-play daughter. Because of their close relationship, Symone really liked and trusted Teresa, who through the years had become like a goddaughter to Uncle Willie. Almost eleven years older than Symone, Teresa often babysat Keturah's children. Even though Teresa despised wearing the brightly colored dresses when she was a young girl living in Harlem, the brilliant attire became her signature trademark as she got older. Because of Teresa's influences, Symone too also enjoyed wearing bright citrus colors of orange, lemon, raspberry, and lime.

Up until the time Symone entered Hampton Institute, family members only bought vividly colored clothes for her. They did whatever was necessary to make her happy. The high brow psychologists said that Symone wore the bright clothes to get attention. But that wasn't true. Symone wore them because even though she continually cried quiet tears and was scared on the inside, no one could tell. The clothes protected her. They were her masks. From the time she was seven, she hid her grief and pain of being with her father like an expertly trained sphinx. Even though Honeyboy was dead, her soul still crawled with the filth of his cruel invasion of her body. Many times, she took baths three and four times a day.

Three years after Symone met Teresa; however, Symone slowly began to change. Just knowing the flashy, adventurous Teresa saved her life, and Symone no longer thought about suicide to free herself of the ongoing guilt. Although Symone remained a reclusive young girl, she began to dress flashily in bright clothes, too. Discovering the joy of wearing the bright clothing made her feel fresh, sparkling clean and alive, just like a newly sprouted yellow tulip on a sunny spring day.

Chapter Thirty-One

Jerking her mind back to the present, Symone breathed deeply and rubbed her forehead. She was at home—in Clemmons, North Carolina. She gazed out the French doors of her master bedroom suite. There was a bittersweet smile on her face as she silently reviewed the speech about her family. Traveling down the crooked road of those past years of her life made her suddenly laugh loudly. Although many years had passed, Symone distinctly remembered all the bright outfits Teresa recommended that she wear on a daily basis.

Symone laughed again. When she enrolled at Hampton, something snapped inside of her, and she stopped being a walking psychedelic fashion show. She simply believed it was time. That it wasn't necessary to dress in such a flashy manner any longer in order to make a statement that she did not now need. Symone nodded her head slowly. She had definitely come a long way since those early days.

Immediately, Symone became pensive when she thought about Teresa. She was the older sister Symone never had, and she never forgot how Teresa helped her make it through those early years. Kept her spirit alive. During Symone's junior year at Hampton, Teresa died of a heroin overdose. Three homeless people discovered her slightly decomposed body in an abandoned Brooklyn tenement building.

Mrs. Shannon never knew why her daughter slowly resorted to drugs. Teresa was a registered nurse. She was a gorgeous woman. She had money saved and owned her own home. Mrs. Shannon thought that was enough to keep anyone satisfied. Obviously to Teresa, it wasn't. She evidently felt she needed something more.

Once again, Symone shook her head heavily. All families have stories they tell over and over again. Either those stories were utterly somber or they were joyously triumphant. The Poussaint family was no different. Since Symone first came to the United States, she was continually reminded by her uncles of the almost unbelievable tale about how the Poussaint received their millions. She smiled to herself once more, took a deep breath, and shook her head sadly. It was time to take a nap.

Symone reviewed the speech she planned to give for the opening ceremony at Alex's house on Saturday afternoon. She made another notation beside the last paragraph of the presentation. She scanned the pages once more. Satisfied she had done her best by sharing tidbits of information about the Eisner and the Poussaint families in her speech, she placed the white legal pad pages back on the French mahogany desk and inhaled deeply. She got up and stood in front of the wall bookshelf. Slowly, she fingered the sterling silver frame that held the old black and white photo of Lennious. Many decades ago and so many emotions ago. She thought about how her twin always loved to dance and sing for her.

Symone would always be grateful to Uncle Cecil and Uncle Willie. Whenever they came home to Trinidad, they took tons of pictures of Keturah and her children, and now Symone embraced those poignant memories frozen in time. Now, Symone could often look at Lennious' face and remember him and how he lived and erase the memory of the way he died. Symone's eyes traveled to her nightstand where she stared at the other photo of her and Lennious hugging each other's neck on the porch of their Santa Cruz home. They were all pictures of her twin brother taken over thirty years ago. But the love and grief Symone experienced as she watched them was both powerfully new and fresh. Slowly, she stepped idly to her bed, sat down and watched Lennious' smiling, dark face from there. *And my dear dead twin brother. He continues to be more a part of my life than even I understand,* Symone thought.

Now with her head bowed in her hands, Symone thought about the speech she was to make. Just as she did back in July, she decided to leave certain events of her life out of the speech she was scheduled to deliver tomorrow afternoon. For this two-week period, the children who visited the Devereauxs' home were ages twelve to sixteen. Three weeks ago, Alex and Madison welcomed twenty-eight children ages eight to eleven. Even though the youthful audience would be a little older this time, still just hearing about Symone's gory days in Trinidad would probably make the children think they were all right in the midst of a horror movie.

Each time Symone thought about the past, she became depressed. More than ever before, she noticed these emotions since Alex had the children visit in July of last year. Last summer when Symone was asked to give a speech about her life, the overwhelming bouts of depression began to resurface then. It was amazing. That was the only reason she believed she had been unusually despondent and bitter for the past thirteen months. What else could it be? Just recalling. Just simply remembering all the finite details of her life with Papa. The ones that she had neatly packed away in the special, dark basement of her mind resurfaced with just as much tenacity. Each time she recalled the pain of her father's brutality, she was weighted down with tremendous sadness and guilt. Today wasn't any different.

Symone rose to her feet and went to stand out on the bedroom terrace. After watching the startling, blue sky for several minutes, she went to the bar and quickly drank several glasses of mineral water. So many memories to deal with. She took another sip of water. So many damn descriptive memories. Symone would never forget the time Quentin locked her up in the basement of their new Brooklyn brownstone when she had just turned twelve years old.

Keturah and her four children had just moved in a week earlier from Harlem, and the children were playing hide-and-seek throughout their large five-story home in Brooklyn. When Symone ran down the basement steps, Quentin saw her. Then he playfully cut off the lights and locked the door. Immediately groping along the wall, Symone struggled to find her bearing and the steps that led up to the main floor. Blinded by the dark and frightened beyond all reason, she ran back up the stairs, stumbling, and started pounding on the bolted door. She became hysterical and began screaming wildly.

"...Quentin! Quentin! Yuh mus open dey door! Quentin! Oh, God. Quentin!" she pleaded to her grinning brother who stood right beside the locked door. "Oh God, Quentin! Turn on dey light in dey basement, Quentin! Yuh must let meh out! Oh, God. Where is mey dear brudda? Oh God, nah. Lennious, oh God. Ah believe meh will die here in dey dark."

When Quentin heard the frightened words of his sister and realized she wasn't enjoying the game any longer, he quickly released the lock and flipped up the basement's light switch located on the inside wall. Symone fell into his arms, exhausted, still crying.

"Oh God, gurl. Wat is it? Ah jus playin' wit yuh. Yuh know ah does mean yuh no harm, Seamone." He tightly hugged his sister's shoulders. "But dey light switch was right dere, gurl. Look and see where it tis so dat yuh will know where it tis dey next time yuh does go down dere and yuh can flip it on wenever yuh does get ready ta," he explained in a concerned, soothing voice as he pointed to the inside wall.

When Symone refused to glance in the direction of her brother's pointing finger, he shut the heavy, wooden door. Still holding her brother's hands, she fell to the floor and watched his face.

"Quentin, it was sooo awful. Meh tought ah was back in Santa Cruz in dey cocoa houses. Ah didn't know dey light switch was inside wit meh. If ah does know it was dere, ah would've quickly cut it on." Symone was still trying to recover from the shocking experience. To keep the frenzied thoughts from zooming out of control, she shook her head quickly.

"Ah does know yuh would, Seamone."

"Quentin, all dat ah does see was darkness in mey mind down dere. It was horrible, Quentin. It was so dark. So dark in dey basement. Meh saw Papa and Lennious, Quentin. Yuh mus promise yuh will never ever do such a ting. Never ever do it ta meh again. Never ever do it ta Hazele or ta Ameenah either," she whispered in a tired voice.

"Ah promise yuh, Seamone. Ah won't." He never would intentionally do anything to make her or any of his sisters think about the cocoa houses again. He wouldn't do anything to make himself think about them either.

"Promise meh again," Symone asked her brother in a forceful voice.

"Ah does promise, Seamone. Yuh know ah does mean it." His voice was tender as he gazed affectionately into her eyes.

Just then Ameenah and Hazele walked up.

"Wat wrong wit yuh, Seamone?" Ameenah inquired with scared eyes as she looked down at her sister sitting sprawled out on the floor. Ameenah cried the most out of all Keturah's children and would start weeping if someone even appeared slightly unhappy.

"Nutting atall. Quentin locked meh down in dere," Symone said softly and pointed to the closed door.

Hazele viciously punched Quentin on the left arm for causing her older sister to be scared. Quentin didn't hit her back and patiently watched Hazele's mischievous smiling face for a moment. Although his Papa was a fighter, Quentin wasn't. He simply preferred to solve problems by discussing them first. Keturah often said that her son could probably be an excellent divorce attorney.

Symone quickly shook her head. "Hazele! Don't do such ta yuh big brudda. Ah fine," Symone said in a strong voice.

"Well meh and Ameenah be hiding far long time, and weh decided ta cum and look far yuh since no one does cum ta try ta find our private hiding place," Hazele explained as she sucked her teeth with hands on her now chubby hips.

Very calmly, Quentin explained to his two younger sisters what happened with Symone, and the words she told him when she realized the basement door was locked. Ameenah immediately became sad. Quentin tickled her stomach, and she was fine again. After the four children tried to laugh about the dark basement and the hot cocoa houses, they continued to play games. But it was the chubby Hazele who suggested they play another game outside in the backyard—in the light of the day.

As Symone recalled that day, she smiled again and went back inside the bedroom to refill her glass with more mineral water. She never forgot that incident in the basement. It haunted her each and every time she walked by the large, wooden door of the basement in her childhood home. Symone even refused to go down there unless she had someone with her. Since the basement reminded her of the cocoa houses, she was controlled by the mere existence of such a place even being in her new house.

Enough of those thoughts about the past, Symone thought to herself. *Get off of it, girl. This is the present, Symone. The past is gone. Enjoy the hot weather, girl.*

It was an ultra hot day for the beginning of August. The temperature was at the one-hundred degree mark for three days in the row, and Symone hoped the weatherman was right when he announced it would be a little cooler tomorrow. Immediately, the lure of the cool pool convinced Symone it would be a wonderful idea to swim several laps in the pool. Then she would take a relaxing Jacuzzi soak outdoors to help raise her spirits.

While changing into her turquoise halter-style spandex bathing suit, Symone decided to call home to Trinidad. Symone spoke to her three children on Wednesday but felt a need to hear their voices—in addition to her mother's. As Symone dialed the number to her Santa Cruz home, morose thoughts immediately leaped to the front of her brain. While the phone rang, she cried softly.

"Good day," answered Tutts Poyer in her heavily accented voice.

Since the tears were tumbling down quite rapidly, Symone hung up the phone. She began sobbing loudly and nervously paced up and down the master bedroom suite. *Tante Tutts sounded happy as usual,* Symone thought with a bittersweet smile. With coffee smooth skin and soft, white cotton hair, Tutts was the woman who kept everything running smoothly on the estate while the Poussaints were in the United States. Born in St. James, a suburb of Port-of Spain, Trinidad, Tutts was always there for Keturah ever since she moved to Santa Cruz when she was a young girl.

In the beginning, Tutts and Keturah worked side by side on the Melenieux plantation over fifty years ago. And today they still were together. Yet when Keturah married Honeyboy, Tutts continued to work as a laborer on the estate. Both women remained close in spite of the fact Honeyboy initially despised the friendship. Even though Keturah tried to convince her to move to the United States when she did after Honeyboy died, Tutts remained in Trinidad and chose instead to live in the main house.

Over the years, Keturah modernized the spacious main home with a large, fancy gourmet kitchen, air conditioning and lovely furnishings. Both Uncles Willie and Cecil eventually built beautiful plantation style homes on the estate as well. That still wasn't enough room for guests visiting from all over the world. Therefore, Keturah and Uncle Cecil had ten additional miniature style plantation homes built around the spacious property, and they were nestled amongst the towering palm and fruit trees. This was especially necessary since many friends and family often journeyed to the West Indies with the Poussaints every February to enjoy the internationally renowned carnival held in Port of Spain, Trinidad.

Each year, the excited friends masqueraded around in colorful costumes within a section of a huge band of other revelers from all over the world. Known as playing mas, the revelers are dressed in brilliantly colored costumes festooned with feathers and glitter. With flags held high and waving as they go, the high spirited masqueraders in the band anxiously dance down on the Savannah as they await the moment when they can cross the stage and be judged.

Symone never missed carnival in Trinidad. It was a ritual. If anyone knew her, they knew it was an unspoken fact that by the second week in January or no later than the first of February, and that was only in rare business meeting cases, Symone would be heading to Trinidad. With her children, sisters, brother, cousins, friends and whoever else in tow, this was their vacation. For at least three weeks to a month, Symone was at home in the West Indies freely sashaying around the streets and acting wild as a pepper induced bull.

During carnival, the Poussaints' home overflowed with friends and relatives. They came and stayed from a week to sometimes a month. Since the guesthouses provided the same modern features as the main home, Uncle Willie laughingly said that he had to drag friends to the airport each year. Once guests experienced the hospitality of the Poussaint home, they told everyone they knew that they wanted to drop everything in the United States and move to Upper La Porta, Santa Cruz, Trinidad for a quiet life in the Caribbean country. It was quite relaxing for Symone to visit there. When the children were off from school for the summer, Symone especially loved her three children going to Trinidad for the entire summer. Of course, not only did it give her and Miss Jessica a much needed break, but also it especially gave the children a sense of their West Indian culture.

On the outside of the main home, several hammocks swung freely between the palm and fruit trees that dotted the yard. Most times that was where most guests relaxed peacefully while they ate juicy mangoes, sipped a cool glass of sweet water, or enjoyed a wonderful Trinidadian snack specialty of shark and bake. Fifteen years ago, Uncle Willie spared no expenses and installed a huge swimming pool with a bath house. The many grandchildren especially enjoyed the refreshing cool water now in the hot Trinidadian summers. Especially if their grandparents didn't feel like taking them to the golden sands of Maracas Beach, an almost hour ride from Santa Cruz.

If Tutts knew exactly when guests were coming in from the United States, she made sure the accommodations would be perfectly welcoming. She, as well as Myrtle Steptoe, the woman who was hired by Keturah to cook and clean the large main house, made sure all the rooms were airy and filled with fresh flowers when guests visited. Tutts loved the smell of things stewing and baking in the ample kitchen, and the house always smelled like a Trinidadian restaurant. Keturah jokingly said that Tutts cooked more than Myrtle. Since Keturah treated Tutts like a sister, her children recognized her as their aunt. The Poussaint children also acknowledged Tutts' only son, Nati, as their cousin. Keturah's children always referred to Tutts as Tante, the West Indian title for aunt.

Symone never forgot the first time she journeyed home for carnival after moving to New York. She was twelve years old and it was quite a scary experience for her. Even though she knew her Papa was dead, somehow or another, she believed he would jump out of one of the cocoa houses and roughly grab her to him again. To this day, whenever she went home, she never went down to the cocoa houses. Quite frankly, if it were really up to her, she would burn them all to the ground.

As Symone glared at the telephone, she wiped the tears from her eyes. *This crying is ridiculous. You got to get a grip, girl* she told herself. However, she stretched herself out on the bed. She watched the intricate patterns of fabric on her trestle bed. After thinking about Trinidad for a few minutes, she sat straight up and stared at the phone. Symone finally dialed the number again, and Tante Tutts spoke the greeting once more.

"Good day," Tutts answered again in her heavily accented voice.

"Tante Tutts, how are you doing? It's Symone."

"Oh God, Seamone, gurl. How ya doin' nah? Did yuh jus call dey house?"

"Yes I did. Somehow or another, the call was disconnected."

"Tis everyting ok wit yuh? Yuh Mum and meh jus spoke wit yuh on Wednesday, gurl. Ameenah and Hazele called dis mornin'. Dey seemply wanted ta check on dere chillren. Hazele asked about yuh. While weh sipped chick punch on dey front porch, yuh Mummy spoke about yuh and Quentin. Tis everyting ok wit yuh, Seamone?" she asked again.

"Everyting is fine, Tante. Is Mummy there?"

"She in dey yard gathering flowers far dey keetchen table. Let meh get she far yuh."

"How are my children, Tante?"

"Gurl, yuh know dey are jus fine. Playin' and ting in dey yard wit dey cousins."

"I bet they've gotten black as can be," Symone said as she considered the harshness of the Trinidadian sun on her three children's skin. They always returned to North Carolina at least four shades darker than their normal cocoa complexions.

"Yuh know it tis true." Tutts chuckled for a few seconds as she considered how dark the children had gotten. "Yuh truly know so. Dey are browner den yuh wen yuh were a baybee playin' so around dey house. Do yuh want ta speak wit dem, Seamone?" she asked in her musical, flowing voice.

"Yes, but I need to speak with Mummy first."

"Let meh go get she far yuh."

As Symone waited a few minutes for her mother to pick up the phone, Symone thoughtfully watched the swimming pool's turquoise water through the beveled-mirror panes on the French doors. Once again, Symone noticed it was such a lovely, hot, summer day.

"Seamone? Seamone, is everyting well?" Keturah asked in a concerned voice, still holding freshly cut flowers in her hand.

"Everything is fine, Mummy. I won't keep you. I just wanted to call and say hello. I was tinking about you. My sisters and my brothers." She refused to say *and Papa, too*. "I was tinking about Lennious real heavy today too, Mummy."

Immediately, Keturah became wistful as she considered her son who died almost thirty years ago. It was such a long time ago. Quick flashes of sad memories flashed in Keturah's mind. She often realized how so much had changed for her and her children since the days with Honeyboy.

"Ah know yuh does still miss he. Mey sweet Lennious was yuh twin, and yuh had a special bond wit he. Ah know dat, gurl. Like ah did wit mey brudda, Angel."

"Excuse me? Who?" Symone asked since she was confused. Keturah realized she said too much and was quiet for a few long seconds.

"Uh, ah does mean dat ah still miss Lennious, too." Keturah's voice was sad. She tried to quickly recover from her spiraling thoughts about the past with Honeyboy as well as with her own parents. "Don't trouble yuhself wit such horrors, Seamone. Jus don't, gurl."

"I know, Mummy. I know. I'm fine. Really I am. I just wanted to hear your voice. And to—to tell you that I love you, Mummy."

"Oh God nah, gurl," Keturah laughed lilting, freely, and loud. "Such a sweet ting ta say and do. Well, ah luv yuh too." She paused briefly. "Yuh sure everyting is lovely wit yuh?" she asked, still a little worried as always for her oldest daughter as she was for all of her other three children's well-being.

"Everyting is fine, Mummy. I was just thinking about you. That's all."

Symone chatted with her mother for five minutes or so. Then told her mother she loved her again. Keturah went to get Jared and the girls.

"Hello, Mummy," Jared said out of breath.

"Hey, boy. How are things going, son? Are you having a good time?"

"Yeah, Mummy. It's hot, hot, hot, though. But we're having a great time," he said in his always businesslike voice. At eight and half years old, he acted just like his father. He looked like him, too. Symone heard the twins whining in the background for their brother to give them the phone.

"Stop pulling on me, Kyle. You better cut it out right—now," Jared instructed in an angry voice. "Mummy, please talk to them. They make me sick. They're always acting sooo stupid about everything."

"Please don't call your sisters stupid, boy."

"They *are* stupid," he said stubbornly.

"Jared—"

"Get your hands off of me, Sylvia," he said disgustingly and jerked his left arm away. "Mummy, I need to go back outside. I'm taking care of Tante Hazele's children for Grandmum. Bye-bye," he said hurriedly and dropped the phone, which didn't give Symone a chance to say she loved him.

"Mummy—" Sylvia said in her three and half year old, soft toddler voice which was followed by a lot of breathing and grunting.

"Hey—little—girl," Symone said excitedly in a long drawn out way. "How are you doing?"

"Fine, Mummy." There were several more moments of heavy breathing, more grunting and a bit of struggling.

"Sylvia, baby?"

"Top it, Kyle," Sylvia exclaimed to her aggressive twin sister. Sylvia tried to remove her sister's death lock chubby handgrip from the curly telephone cord. "Top now. Mummy. Ah'm talking fir—"

Symone heard the phone knock against a hard object. It sounded like the twins were actually fighting over the phone to determine who would speak first.

"Aye, aye. Wat's goin' on in here? Don't hit she. Don't hit yuh seester. Stop it," Tante Tutts scolded calmly and took the phone from Sylvia who still tightly held it with all her might.

"Seamone, did yuh speak ta both of dem?" Tante Tutts asked pleasantly with a smile on her face and hand on hip.

"Not yet. I think it will work now since you're nearby, Tante," Symone replied with a vigorous laugh. "How are their glasses holding up? Mummy didn't mention if they broke them yet."

Just before they left, Sylvia and Kyle were both diagnosed with twenty forty vision and were required to wear glasses. In a way, when Symone saw her bespectacled two daughters, she thought about her twin. Even though Lennious was required to wear glasses as a child, Symone always had twenty twenty vision.

"Dey glasses are holding up just fine, gurl. Ah does tell yuh Mudda dat dey gurls look cute wit dem on," Tutts assured with a small chuckle.

"I think they look cute too, Tante. But that's probably because I'm their mother. I know they'll change when they get older, and do what most people do. They'll probably wear contact lenses."

Symone heard her daughters' voices in the background pleading. *Let meh speak ta mey Mummy*, they whined over and over.

"Dey does be getting impatient again, Seamone. Let meh let yuh speak wit dem."

Tante Tutts monitored the girls, and Symone spoke with each one for a while. This time she spoke with Sylvia first. Then, she spoke with Kyle. She told them she would see them Labor Day weekend. Especially since they would be playing in the Kiddie Carnival the Saturday before Labor Day. Playing mas in the Brooklyn's New York West Indian-American Day Carnival Parade was a yearly, religious ritual for the Poussaint family too, and this year wasn't any different.

Symone finally ended the call. She reminded herself that the next time she called home, she needed to speak with Kyle first. Even though they were three and half years old, the girls always remembered who went first the last time they spoke with their mother. After she giggled quietly about the telephone conversation with her children, Symone decided to call Alex. She wanted to let Alex know that she wasn't feeling well. Symone wouldn't be able to make the Devereauxs' fish fry dinner scheduled for this evening, welcoming the twenty-eight children to their home. She just didn't think she was in the mood to be cordial with those twenty-eight excited children, let alone mingle with a bunch of happy adults.

Fifteen minutes later, Symone placed some mellow music, soothing sounds on this time. A little Keiko Matsui, Thelonious Monk, and Oscar Peterson Trio CDs. Symone placed the CD system on the random mode. She was relieved that Alex accepted her lame excuse and didn't pry for the real reasons why she wasn't coming to their home. Humming to the beautiful sounds of Keiko Matsui, Symone turned on the stereo backyard speakers. Armed with a large brim straw hat, SPF 30 sunscreen, a great book, a towel, and a fat juicy mango, she headed outdoors to the swimming pool.

Chapter Thirty-Two

"...That's why I want to know what time you'll get over here today," Madison said to Scott as he cradled the telephone receiver on his shoulder and reached into the refrigerator to get orange juice.

"Let's see."

Madison walked over to the cabinet to get a glass and poured himself some juice. Since he was having a hard time clearly hearing Scott's words, he turned down the Lakeside album, which was blasting over the kitchen stereo speakers. When Madison opened the refrigerator, the three dogs combed the floor to see what they could find to eat.

"Give me a time, man."

"I *told* you. It's hard to say. Why?"

"Well, I was asking cause I thought we could talk about job possibilities for your brother when you got here."

"I don't think that'll be a good time to discuss Romallus. He'll be with me."

"I agree with you, man. That's what I was getting ready to say. Alex told me that Romallus decided to come into Greensboro this afternoon instead of taking the early flight in the morning. Your brother thought that would push you too much," Madison explained in an understanding voice.

"He was right."

Madison handed each dog four milk bones that they crunched loudly and very quickly. When they were through, they all glanced up at their master with the hopes that he would give them something else to nibble on.

"So I wanted to be careful with our conversations at least in front of him."

"I appreciate that, man," Scott said. "You know how Romallus is. My brother needs help to get the type of job he's qualified to receive, especially with his past drug history. But he's acting like he wants me to step away from it. You know that's hard for me to do, man."

"Heck, don't worry about it. I got it covered. I won't mention anything to Romallus the whole time he's here," Madison said with a huge laugh. "You know my frat brother, Marshall Fudge, out of Baton Rouge?"

Scott's mind began to race to figure out who he was. "I'm thinking, man. I can't place him right now. Let me think—"

On the night of Pecola's fortieth birthday party, Scott asked Madison to check employment contacts for Romallus in the Louisiana, Mississippi and Alabama areas. Madison said he would work on it. Madison called Scott to share what job opportunities, if any, he had located. Since Scott was supposed to pick Romallus up from the airport, Scott thought it would be better to have a conversation with Madison before then. Scott's two sons were also coming in today from Los Angeles, and Romallus' change in his arrival day worked out well.

Since Madison and Alex were in contact with friends all over the world, Scott always jokingly likened the Devereauxs to an international corporate headhunter agency. Even Rozelle told them a number of times that he should have contacted them before he considered moving to North Carolina. Because he didn't meet the Devereauxs until after he relocated to North Carolina, of course that would have been impossible. That was typical Rozelle. From the United States to the Caribbean and even Europe too, the relationships the Devereauxs developed with college and graduate school friends throughout the years remained faithful and true. No matter which city in any country the friends visited, nine times out of ten, Madison and Alex knew influential people who lived there, who owned this company or that palatial home. Then the Devereauxs and whoever else traveled along with them on vacation were always invited over for a meal.

Scott remembered where their friend's hospitality was showcased three years ago when a group of eight couples journeyed to Bahia, Brazil. Alex phoned a friend. The entire entourage was invited to have brunch at one of their contacts' spectacular home, which had a drop-dead view of endless white, soft sand and the emerald ocean.

"C'mon, man. You know Fudge." Madison still edged on after a few silent moments. "Think about it. He's loud and always a jokester."

"That could be anybody."

"Ok. One time you said that he acted worst than Rozelle, and that smart people must suffer from the same sickness of letting go when they are amongst friends," Madison cackled into the line. "Remember, man?"

"Fudge. Fudge. The name sounds familiar," Scott replied slowly while he puffed on a cigar as he bobbed his head to the sounds of *I'm So In Love With You.*

Before Charmaine left this morning, she surprised him with an Al Green's Greatest Hits CD. Nestled on the red leather club chair in the library of his home office, Scott had been listening to the tracks all afternoon.

"Remember? You met him last year for the fortieth time at the CIAA tournament. He attends every year, man. Last year, he went with us to Hilton Head. This year he couldn't go. He was attending a special reunion in Atlanta with some of his old college buddies," Madison explained and paused a moment. "Remember, he's a graduate of Xavier University," he added in an effort to jar Scott's memory.

"Ok. Ok. He's a doctor too. Right, Madison? A heart surgeon."

"Yeah, man. That's the one. Boy, your butt is getting old. I didn't think you would ever figure out who I was talking about."

"Nigger, puhleeze. Yall got so many damn friends. I can't keep up with them all, Madison. You know that deal."

"Anyway, Marshall works with all kinds of urban youth programs in his spare time. He's involved with Black Cardiologists of Louisiana, One-Hundred Black Men of Baton Rouge, the Chamber of Commerce, Big Brothers Big Sisters, and Leadership Baton Rouge. You know. The whole Black man in America affiliation stuff," he outlined in an amusing voice.

Although Madison couldn't see him right now, Scott vigorously nodded his head with great understanding.

"More importantly," continued Madison sipping his orange juice, "he's the Basileus of the Que chapter there. All the boards and associations. You name it, and he's on it. The laundry list is endless. Since Romallus wants to stay in Louisiana, I thought Fudge would be our best shot for any employment opportunities."

"That sounds great," Scott said with a smile and took another puff.

Scott remembered the crazy antics of Marshall while he visited for the CIAA basketball tournament. He began to laugh. Madison was right. Scott was fascinated with the Louisiana brother's wit and the way he gulped Jack Daniel's straight from the bottle.

"Wooo. I know who you're talking about. I remember clearly now. That brother is definitely crazy," exclaimed Scott, laughing loudly.

"That he is. But he's good man. If there's an excellent opportunity involving young people, he'll know about it. It's a shame your brother isn't a Que. The Sigma affiliation may hurt him just a little bit," Madison said, chuckling loudly. "So you really believe he's doing ok, Scott?" he asked with concern and took a long drink of juice.

"Yeah, I know he is, Madison," Scott answered quickly. "What about you, man?"

Suddenly, Scott stopped bobbing his head to the music and sat up straight. He placed the cigar in the ashtray and watched the smoke climb and disappear in the air.

"Without question, I do. It's just that when I speak with you, you always talk about him with hesitation." Madison's voice was covered with anxiety.

"It's more worry than anything else. He's been through a lot. I just worry, and I shouldn't do that. I know it's wrong. Romallus has been clean now for six and half years. I want to help him grab a great opportunity. A chance," Scott replied, speaking slowly as he leaned back in the chair. "It's my way of thanking him for helping with Carlos Jr. If Romallus moved to Winston-Salem, Carlos would hire him as a project manager at CR Construction Group like yesterday. But that's not what he wants. He wants to be near Pop. He says he doesn't want my help. His helping CJ wasn't about that. You know how he is."

"I do, Scott."

"Since the two of you talk a lot now, I thought it could come from that angle."

"No problem, Scott. I'll call Marshall tonight."

"Where's Alex? Let me speak to her."

"She is in the garden reading *Long Journey Home* to all those children. You know the strict orders. Do not disturb. All twenty-eight children are here and are they excited, Scott. Carlos and I were outside working out the sleeping arrangements. We had a couple of changes with the senior citizens who decided to stay in the guesthouses."

"I don't blame them."

Madison laughed and continued speaking. "Carlos and I also tried to put up two tents. A couple of the older boys said they never slept in an outdoor tent and wanted to know if they could sleep there instead of sleeping in one of the guestrooms. We tried to make it happen for them, but it didn't work. It wasn't that we couldn't do it, Iceman," he said confidently, laughing. "It was hot as heck outside. I told Carlos, 'Man, your behind constructs multi-million dollar office buildings, and we're sweating like dogs and struggling to put together a simple tent?'"

"That was a good question," Scott said as he grinned into the phone. "What did he say, Madison?"

"Carlos just laughed and laughed. Then he said that tent blueprints were a little different from buildings. Wellington, the yardman, and his staff had to take over that assignment. You know those brothers live in the sun. I only like it for enjoyment." Madison laughed.

Scott continued to chuckle for a few moments too. "Ok. Tell Alex I said hello, and I'll be there to do my part as soon as I can. Thanks, Madison. I appreciate the help with Romallus."

"No problem. It's a done deal as far as I'm concerned. Man, let's try to get together within the next three weeks or so and go somewhere for a few days."

"You know the Iceman himself stays ready. Just say when, Madison."

"You bet. I'll get back to you about a time and place when we talk after my phone call to Marshall. Check your schedule before you leave home, Scott. What time do you plan to be here?"

Scott checked his watch. "Ummm. It's hard to say. I've already packed a few things for the weekend. I'll be leaving for the airport in an hour. I should be over there at least by four. Let's see." He checked his watch again. It was 1:00 p.m. "No later than five. Why?"

"Don't eat nothing before you get here. I'm telling you we got food all over the place. Cafe Bessie's soul food is covering every available space in the conservatory off the kitchen. Fried pork chops. Fried Chicken. Baked ham with pineapples and brown sugar all over it. String beans. Candied yams. All kinds of stuff, man. You name it. The older people who are helping us this time brought their special pies and cakes."

"My kind of food."

"It's a trip. The hamburgers, hot-dogs, and steaks will be ready to hit the grill around six or so. Cleopatra is picking up Marlon's favorite fish for frying later. You know how everyone swears Marlon is the quintessential fish fryer. His whole attitude changes during the summertime, man. Alex already has his special red and white Ram chef hat. Then she bought him a black and white cow apron." Madison laughed. "With all this food, I'll have to exercise at least five times a week for the next two weeks to get the extra pounds off, Scott."

"I'm with Marlon. You know I'm a hot fish and grilled food freak myself. So I'm ready, Madison. Are Pecola and Symone there yet?"

"Nah, man. You know those two. Cleopatra went to pick up Pecola and check on a few last things for Alex. Symone called and said she wasn't coming."

"She wasn't coming?"

"That's what she said, Iceman."

"What about her speech tomorrow?"

"Oh, don't worry about that. She just said she wasn't coming tonight. Wasn't feeling well. She told Alex that she would definitely be here for the opening ceremonies tomorrow afternoon at five." Madison stopped to catch his breath and sip more juice.

"I wonder what's wrong?" Scott asked. "I called her just before I called you, and she was swimming. Miss Jessica told me she didn't want to disturb her, but she didn't mention a thang about her being sick. Hmmm."

Chapter Thirty-Three

While washing dishes, Miss Jessica hummed to the gospel singing of Karen Clark-Sheard as she placed the last of the plates and silverware in the rack. Just as Miss Jessica glanced out of the kitchen window, she noticed that Symone finally stepped out of the swimming pool and was drying off. Miss Jessica smiled, wiped her wet hands with a dishtowel, and headed out to the backyard.

"Symone, baby!" Miss Jessica yelled as she walked down the cobblestone path.

"Yesss. What happened?" Symone asked, glancing around as she rubbed sunscreen on her shoulders.

"Nothing happened, baby. I just wanted to tell you that Scott called while you were swimming. He said for you to call him when you have a chance. It's important."

"How important?"

"He didn't say, baby," Miss Jessica said handing Symone the portable telephone. "Want me to dial his number for you?"

"No. I'll do it but not right now." Symone took a deep breath. "I *really* didn't want the phone out here during my private time with myself."

"Ok. I'll take it back in."

"Thank you, Miss Jessica."

"I should be heading home in about two hours or so. Do you need anything else to help you to relax your nerves, sugar?"

"Nope," Symone snapped. "Just some peace and quiet and for my friends to leave me alone for at least one hour."

"Ok, baby," Miss Jessica said, staring sideways at her. Symone threw the damp towel in the chaise lounge, took a quick sip of water, and headed toward the Jacuzzi.

"By the way, I told Alex that Charmaine said she won't be here until six tomorrow night," Madison was saying to Scott.

"What she say?"

"Alex simply moved things around, and Charmaine's speech about the influences of African-American dance is now set for seven p.m. Nothing is written in stone. Who knows how the opening ceremonies will turn out."

"That'll work out well for Charmaine. Before she left this morning, she told me that she spoke to you."

"Carlos is here. His parents are, too. They even plan to spend the night. That surprised me, Iceman. I guess they heard about last month's welcoming day from Carlos and wanted to see for themselves. Like last month, Carlos' brother, Rico, is here along with his wife, and their three children. Rozelle isn't here yet. He's working half a day, so he'll be here any minute. Jodria is already here with their six children. You better claim your bedroom, man."

"I told Alex that I wanted me and my family to camp out at either the pool house or one of the guesthouses. The guesthouse closest to the swimming pool this time. Too much activity in the main house. Last year during that first opening weekend, those young folks were sliding down the banisters around seven in the morning. Hell, I didn't go to bed until five."

"Well, you can forget the pool house. The two lifeguards Alex hired are camping out there. She told them that they were on twenty-four hour notice—like doctors just in case the children wanted to swim real, real early in the morning. If I'm not mistaken, seems like she did tell Cleopatra to keep the guesthouse closest to the pool available for you. That means there's a personal wooden nameplate on the door waiting for your behind," Madison declared in an excited voice as King jumped on his right thigh. Madison scratched the dog's head briefly.

"As usual, it sounds like a great big party is getting off the ground at your house, man." Scott enjoyed the thought that the Devereauxs had the most delightful get-togethers.

"I love it, man. I simply love it! Before the night's over with, it'll be just as crowded here as it would be during Winston-Salem State's homecoming," Madison continued with a loud laugh. "Hold on just a moment. I heard a boisterous voice. A crazy holler."

"Woof-woof! Woof-woof-woof! Woof! Woof!" the three dogs barked in succession with their high-pitched sounds.

Madison put the phone down. Two minutes later, he returned to the telephone call with Scott.

"I'm back, man. Delete what I said about Rozelle. He just blew through the door."

Scott heard Rozelle yelling in the background for him to get his ass over there.

"Tell him I'll be there as soon as possible," Scott told Madison, laughing.

"Give me the phone. Give me the damn phone," Rozelle shouted in Madison's ear.

"Madison, don't give that nut the phone. I got to go and get ready to meet my family."

"Just a minute, Iceman." Madison smiled. "Hold on again."

Scott heard the mumbling of several voices. It now sounded like Carlos and Rico walked into the kitchen. The two Reynolds brothers were talking to Madison and Rozelle.

According to Madison, the Devereauxs' stainless steel state of the art kitchen with dark oak cabinets was the popular, most special, cozy room in the house. Today was no different. Alex preferred their bedroom and the music room. However, Madison swore their friends always seemed to end up in the kitchen because it had an aura of "everyone pitch in and cook a throw down pot of whatever philosophy." Madison believed that when folks pitched in during those gourmet adventures, it was a culinary salute of such intimate measures to everyone involved in the process.

During those "cooking jam sessions," as Madison affectionately titled them, some guests hung out along the kitchen's long, bi-level center island. Others chitchatted around the huge oak dining table with the lazy Susan or congregated in the seating area in the glass to ceiling conservatory. In the warm months, the friends enjoyed great, casual moments while they relaxed on the Devereauxs' colonnade porch which was right off the kitchen and overlooked the lake. While sidestepping the dogs, Madison picked up the phone.

"I'm back, Scott," Madison said. "Carlos said that he was thinking about us going away for a few days, too. We got two weeks with the children. I was off today, and I'll be off from the hospital until Tuesday. After that, I'm going to take Alex on a mini-vacation when this two-week period is over. Just a minute, Scott."

"C'mon and give your Uncle Rozzie a hug," Rozelle lovingly said to his canine godchildren. All three dogs jumped all over Rozelle's legs, and he roughly hugged their necks. "My godchildren get cuter and cuter every day, Madison. I might have to break down and buy a Cocker Spaniel to go along with the Bellisarion's family pretty black Chihuahua, my Delilah."

"He's crazy." Carlos simply shook his head and smiled.

"I still can't believe Jodria Anne didn't mind you naming that dog Delilah," Rico joked as he chewed on a kiwi fruit.

"Believe it, man. I got it like that. Three years ago, Jodria Anne said if I finally agreed to our having a dog, she and the children would let me name it. After I saw the other Chihuahuas prancing around the breeder's backyard, I said that such a cute ole dog was all right with me, baby. Even as a little puppy when I watched Delilah step highly, I knew I had chosen the best name. I figured she should be recognized as something prissy and awesomely tempting to the other common dawgs in our neighborhood," Rozelle ended with a thunderous laugh. "If you guys know what I mean? But Jodria doesn't let Delilah out without supervision anyway."

"Woof-woof-woof! Woof-woof! Woof! Woof-woof!" the dogs barked merrily again at the other guests coming in.

Scott heard the faint hum of voices in the background again. Now, he wished that he were at Madison's instead of trying to deal with the partying over the telephone.

"Ok. I'm back, Scott. Marlon and three of his boys just walked in. Rico and Carlos are in here, too. It's getting wild, man. Just a minute, Scott," exclaimed Madison once more.

There was a succession of *Hey, man. What's up.* The men greeted one another with a tight grab of the right hand. While still holding hands tightly, they bumped chests together with their hands between them and quickly patted each other on the back.

"Shooot. Woooo. Damn! Yall still some big ass men. Like the big red oak trees of California. What the hell yall eat since I saw yall last month?" Rozelle yelled as he stared at the three professional basketball players.

"The same soulfood," Marlon answered for his friends.

"Every time I see yall's behind, yall get taller and taller. Yall are just some tall ass niggers," Rozelle said loudly and quickly looked at Madison. "Man, I'm sorry about cursing in your home. Sorry about that."

Madison shook his head, casually waved his hand and laughed. "Don't worry about it, man."

"Yo, baby. What yall bring me this time?" Rozelle asked jokingly as he glared up in the basketball players' faces again. "An autographed basketball. A jersey. Where's my stuff? You know what I want. The only Black cheerleader on the squad. The time clock. Any little old

NBL momento." The three pro players just watched him and began laughing at how crazy Rozelle was. Scott held on for another five minutes. He smiled, too, as he heard the banter between the men.

"Scott, I'm back," Madison said. "Sorry to keep you holding so long."

"Marlon's there already?"

"Yep!"

"Well, I know those twenty-eight children are going to be happy to see those professional basketball players. Who he get to come this time?" Scott asked.

"He has Oscar Oakley, Kemper Dennis, and Christopher Perry. The same ones he had with him last month." Madison answered.

"Get out of here, man. Let me throw my sneakers in my bag right now. I thought Kemper and Oakley said they couldn't come this month."

"Maybe they enjoyed it so much last month, they thought they couldn't miss this one either," Madison explained as he swallowed more juice.

"Madison, I kicked Christopher's ass on the basketball court just last week down at my crib on Lake Norman. I guess he and Marlon wanted to come back for more punishment," Scott said, trying to mask his sarcasm. "Tell them what I said."

Madison repeated the message. Of course, he added some extra jabs.

"Nigger, puleeze," hollered Marlon, gagging on his laugh.

"C'mon, Carlos. Help me out here, man. You were the one who was the North Carolina A&T man. The Aggie standout. You going to let them dog me, man?" Scott teased. Madison repeated Scott's words to everyone.

"I got your back, Iceman. If they try to take you on, you know they got to deal with me," Carlos yelled, so Scott could hear him.

"Man, puleeze," Marlon declared again. "I got seriously bad knees, but I can still kick Scott's ass. Yours too, Carlos. The only way you guys can beat my three homies here. The only way you two can humanly possibly do that is if they allowed yall to play on Trey's basketball goal. Hell, I know Alex and Madison bought the goal for their son, but we can take yall out on it any day. That's tall enough for yall to deal with, especially if Rozelle is playing."

"See. See. See what you done did. Man, put his ass on speaker," Rozelle demanded, and Madison promptly pushed the speaker button in. With arms folded at his chest, Madison leaned against the center island to listen.

"Go ahead and talk, Scott," Madison instructed as he gulped juice. "Everyone can hear now."

With big grins on their faces, the other pro players nodded their heads in agreement with Marlon's comment about the basketball goal. Just then, Trey walked into the kitchen from outdoors. He was looking for his father, but when he saw Marlon, he reached for his uncle's hand.

"Hey, lil man," Marlon exclaimed with a huge smile as he reached his arms out to pick his nephew up. Trey hugged his uncle's neck tightly. "I was just talking about you, Trey. How ya doing, lil guy?"

"Fine, Uncle Marlon," he answered politely and glanced at his father who smiled proudly.

"Have you been playing basketball the way I taught you, Trey? On your new goal your Mommy and Daddy bought for you?"

Trey vigorously nodded his head yes.

"Open your mouth and speak, son," Madison encouraged Trey softly.

"Yes I have, Uncle Marlon." He was shy as he noticed that all the men were staring at him. "I'm gonna be good like you one day," Trey then exclaimed in a boasting voice.

Slowly, Trey's eyes traveled around to all the men in the kitchen again, and he grinned widely at each one. Marlon passed the four and half year old boy to Carlos who hugged him as well. Before it was over, the young boy was passed into the arms of all the men where he was kissed and fondly embraced. As Trey was being hoisted around like a rag doll, he giggled loudly as the men tickled him on his stomach and kissed him on his forehead. Since Oscar Oakley's father had taught him that a man wasn't supposed to kiss boys but only shake their hands, Oscar merely tickled Trey on his stomach. Finally, Trey made it into his father's arms. Madison kissed him on the lips and tenderly gazed in his eyes for a brief moment.

"What do you need, son?" Madison asked lightly, basking in pride for his namesake.

"Nothing, Daddy. I needed to use the bathroom. Then I'm going back out to the garden. Mommy's reading to us."

Madison put his son down, and Trey turned to walk away.

"First, tell your Uncle Scottie hello," Madison instructed his son. "He's the only one that wasn't here to give you a big kiss, too."

Since he didn't see his Uncle Scottie in the room, Trey looked around to see what his father was talking about. Madison pointed to the phone.

"Hello, Uncle Scottie," Trey said in his soft voice with his head raised in the air.

"Hey, lil buddy. I'll see you when I get there. Ok? You been a good boy?"

Before Trey answered, he paused and gazed at the mosaic-tiled floor. He eyed his father carefully and hesitated before speaking.

"Answer the question. Tell him the truth, Trey," Madison urged him on in a firm voice.

"No. Not too good, Uncle Scottie." Trey fidgeted and watched his father again. "Mommy had me to sit in time-out today. I wouldn't listen to her," he explained quietly as the other men listened and attempted to maintain serious faces. Rico and Marlon snickered quietly.

"That doesn't even sound like you Trey. It must've been a rough morning for you to get in trouble?"

Trey simply smiled and didn't respond. He walked to stand beside Madison. He stood on his tiptoes to tightly hug his father's waist and ran out of the kitchen.

"Ok, Scott. I guess he decided to avoid that line of questioning. It's Alex's lawyer side of him coming out," Madison said laughing.

"What happened, man? That's not like Trey to get in trouble. Everyone knows he acts like you. Looks like you, too," Scott continued knowing how Madison loved the comparison. "Now that little Purity. I bet she was behind most of it, man."

"You're right, man. Alex caught him punching the living daylights out of his sister in the playroom this morning. But Alex probably missed how Miss Purity was acting like her usual grown self which resulted in Trey beating her up the way he did. My babygirl is only three and half, but she's a mess, man."

"You gots that right." Marlon nodded.

"Since Alex caught Trey in the act, she told me that she had to chastise him. When Alex told him not to punch his sister anymore, Trey punched her one last time for good measure. So Alex made him sit in time-out while she and Cleopatra fixed breakfast." Madison remembered Trey's sad face when he walked into the kitchen and noticed his son sitting quietly in the chair by the refrigerator.

"Must've been a bummer," Marlon moaned.

"That's why I tell Marlon all the time, Purity is feisty just like his wife. Alex agrees that her daughter acts more like her sister too," Madison explained as he watched the amused face of his brother-in-law. Marlon nodded that he understood.

All of the men laughed in agreement. Even though Alex and Nanette looked like twins, the sisters' personality differences were staggering. Alex was the sweet, demure one. Nanette was feisty, aggressive, and would tell a person off with little provocation. As the laughter faded down, Carlos asked a question through the joking.

"Hold on, Scott," Madison asked since he heard the phone beep, signaling another call was coming through.

Chapter Thirty-Four

While Pecola waited for Cleopatra in the downstairs' library of her home, she cuddled up on the peach leather sofa there and finished reading the last five pages of the inspirational novel, *Destiny Unlimited*. It already seemed like the summer was almost over for her even though Labor Day was at least a month away. Since she turned forty in May, it seemed like all she did lately was read, eat, read, and read some more.

Pecola had already completed Nikki Giovanni's *My Soul is a Witness,* Ujima's selection for August. She read two other large books in record time, and this time she decided she wanted to delve into words of motivation and inspiration. Cleopatra recommended the Vanessa Davis Griggs' novel, and the book certainly provided such an escape. This was the first book Pecola had ever read by Griggs. For the past couple of days, she couldn't put it down. Pecola felt like writing a letter to the editor to find out when the author's next book, *The Rose of Jericho*, would be released. As Pecola flipped to the next to the last page, the telephone rang. She sucked her teeth, rolled her eyes, and grudgingly rose to answer it.

"Hello." Pecola's voice was dry.

"Peakee-cola, chile! How yer doing, baybee!" her mother exclaimed loudly.

"Hey, Mama. Mama, puhleeze. It's *Pecola,* Mama. You're the one who named me, and I don't know why you insist on calling my name like that."

"Oh, honeychile. Now yer knows what Ise means!" Oseola Dudley exclaimed as she placed one hand on her full hips. "Ise jus gots through speakin' with Paulietta, and her wants me and yer daddy to comes to Augusta for two weeks. So weese goin go on down thataway. Yer and Carlos wants to comes with us, Peakee-cola?"

It's Pauletta, Mama. You named her, too, Pecola thought with an aggravated expression.

"Paulietta toles me to ax yer if yer wanted to come at least for the weekend. She be callin yer at Alex to checks on it."

While her mother spoke, Pecola impatiently rolled her eyes toward the ceiling and shook her head slowly.

"No, ma'am. I can't make it."

"But honeychile, Ise never sez when it were. How yer knows yer can't make it, chile?" Oseola was cheerful despite Pecola's callous impatience.

"Well uh, ma'am. What I was saying is I can't say if I'll be in town or not, Mama."

"Mama understand, Honeychile. Yer jus sooo busy, baby. Do yer have time to goes over to Alex and Madison tonight since yer so busy and tall?"

"Yes ma'am. Cleopatra is going to pick me up any moment, now. That's why I need to be getting ready to go. I need to hang up, Mama."

"Ise understand, baby," Oseola replied quickly. However, she plowed forward into another conversation anyway. "Ise declare Ise enjoyed Alex, Madison, and those chilluns last night."

"Alex told me, Mama."

"They gots two precious, purdy babies. They came by to picks up some fresh country ham and all them fresh eggs we gathered for all them chilluns coming to visit. Yer know what, babychile?" Her mother wasn't expecting an answer. "They ended up and stays for dinner. Yer knows Ise always has a big dinner. Ise cooked country style steak with brown gravy, buttery mash potatoes, string beans, and stewed apples. Yer knows my yeast rolls was nice and hot. We ate up one of my good ole sweet potato pies for dessert. Ise gives them one to take home. Dem chilluns enjoys each bit of everything and wipes their plates clean with the rolls likes big chilluns," she ended laughing as she rested a hand on her full hips again.

"Alex told me, Mama."

"The chilluns chased a few chickens afterwards. They never caught nere one. Yer Daddy let them touch the dirty hog noses a spell," she cackled into the phone wire. "Yer knows Alex only got dem clean pigs at her house. Never understood how Black folks have pigs as clean as Madison and Alex." She laughed again. "Couldn't get the cows to come up. Yer Daddy heehawed and heehawed for them to come around. They didn't come, honeychile." Her mother laughed some more. "Whooo, chile. But Ise tell yer that lil boy of Alex and Madison looks just like his daddy, honeychile. Like he spits him out or something. That little Tre-day."

Pecola rolled her eyes toward the ceiling and interrupted her. "Mama, puhleeze. His name is Trey."

"Yer knows what Ise means, honeychile. Anyways, the baby girl looks like Alex. Cute as can be. That Puree baby—"

"Mama, her name is *Purity*," she immediately corrected again.

Not only does Mama hack up folks' names, but she butchers the English language, too, thought Pecola disgustingly.

"Them some special chilluns. Puree and Tre-day gaves yer daddy a big ole sweet wet sugar. Then Madison sez to them babies, 'Give Granddaddy Rufus a big hug.' Them purdy babies hugged yer daddy's neck sooo tight, honeychile. Then Madison sez, 'Give Grandma Oseola a big ole hug, too.' Them purdy babies hugged my neck, honeychile. It was a sight to see."

"Ummm-hmmm."

"Weese just loves them. They comes and visits all dey time. Cute as can be. Them little colored, chubby hands hugging my neck, Peakee-cola. Bout made me cry, chile. They're just so, so precious, honeychile. So precious. They just reminds me of my three chilluns—youse, Paulietta, and Ezoonial Jr.'s babies. Ise just loves them to death. Such a sweet, sweet little family."

It's Ezunial, Mama. Pecola rolled her eyes again and absentmindedly looked at her perfectly, manicured pink nails.

"Mama, Alex *told* me," Pecola said without much feeling. She inhaled deeply, quietly. "Mama, I need to be going."

"Honeychile, Ise understands. Member next week Ise gonna cook a good ole fashion meal for them chilluns on all day Thursday. That be the day Ise tole Alex Ise would help her. Same day Ise helped when the younger ones came last month. Alex sez them chilluns went on so about my golden fried chicken, and my fat biscuits, honeychile," she explained loudly. "Hold on jes a minute, babygirl. Yer daddy wants me to say something to yer." There was a few moments of silence on the line.

"Mama—"

"Say what it tis now, Rufus. Peakee-cola ain't got all day," she rushed him in her always boisterous voice. Oseola patiently listened to her husband.

"Umph, Peakee-cola. Yer Daddy sez Rico and Carlos picked up some fresh eggs this morning. Carlos gots jes a dozen since it's jes yer and him in that big ole house. Well lawd have mercy, Rufus. What time did they come?" Now Oseola was frustrated that she missed seeing Carlos and Rico.

Pecola heard her soft-spoken father mumble a few words. Oseola nodded her head slowly with understanding.

"Lawd, Ise didn't even know they were here. Must've comes when Ise went to my missionary board visit at the hospital this morning. Hold on jes a moment, Peakee-cola."

Rufus quietly explained to Oseola that was exactly when they came.

"Umph, umph, umph, honeychile. I sho hate I didn't sees my sweet ole Carlos, and that purdy boy, Rico. Lawd have mercy. Ain't that a shame," she bellowed into the phone as she shook her head sadly.

"Mama, I really need to be getting ready to go to Madison and Alex."

"Yes, Ise understands Peakee-cola. Now like Ise was saying. Last month, when Ise made my big ole country biscuits, country ham, buttery grits, and spotted gravy for them young chilluns, Alex saids dem chilluns talked about that country breakfast all them remaining days they was up there. Yer Mama gonna do the same thing for this group, honeychile. Yer be in town that day, Peakee-cola?"

"No, Mama. I don't think I'll be there," she lied easily. "I believe I'm either out of town that night, or I've a MADD meeting to go to. But if I don't have to do either one, I'll certainly be there helping out the Devereauxs as much as possible. I'm sorry if I'll miss you, Mama," she said, feigning disappointment.

"Honeychile, Ise understands," Oseola said just as Pecola heard the doorbell chime.

"Mama, I got to go! That's Cleopatra coming to pick me up. Take care, Mama."

"Yer takes cares, Peakee-cola. Ise loves yer, baby. Tell ole Cleopatra Ise sez hello. Kiss her two purdy little boys for me, honeychile. Ok, Peakee-cola. Think about going with me and yer Daddy to Paulietta. I loves yer, baby."

"Ummm-hmmm. Bye, Mama," she said quickly as she hung up the phone. As Pecola considered the conversation with her mother, she shook her head impatiently. Pecola walked down the hall and opened the door. It wasn't Cleopatra. It was the newspaperman stopping by to collect the monthly newspaper bill. Aggravated that Cleopatra hadn't come yet, an irritated Pecola called Alex to find out what happened.

Chapter Thirty-five

"...Madison," Carlos was asking. "Did you talk with Scott about our going away soon?"

"What took you so long, man?" Scott wondered.

"Pecola beeped in. Cleopatra hadn't picked her up. She was worried and wondered if she was on her way."

"I gotta get dressed, man," Scott said, ready to hang up.

"Hold up, Scott! As I was saying—," Madison said loudly since he could barely hear over the talk in the kitchen.

"Talk to me, man. I thought you said that you and Carlos talked about going away," Scott said as he took several puffs of the cigar.

"Madison talked about taking Alex away after all this is over with, Iceman. I merely suggested that we go to the mountains," Carlos answered as he sipped a chilled Corona.

"The mountains?" Rozelle asked as he gulped orange juice and loosened his tie.

"Yeah. You and Scott haven't been with us to this place. But it's up in the mountains. It's absolutely beautiful there. The last time we went up there, we went to the Great Smoky Mountain Resort," Carlos said as he motioned to Madison, Rico, and Marlon. "Remember? We were there about three years ago."

"Yeah, I remember that now," Scott said. "Yall scheduled it around the time my Pop got sick all of a sudden, and I had to go to New Orleans."

"That's right, man. It's located right on the edge of North Carolina and Tennessee. Right across from Dolly Parton's place. As a matter of fact, you can walk right into Tennessee from the North Carolina line," Carlos said knowingly. "Blowing Rock, North Carolina and the Smoky Mountain Resorts is the best one up there. Don't yall agree?" Carlos looked in Rico, Madison, and Marlon's direction. All three vigorously nodded their heads.

"Scott, you know I like to fish. The whole summertime thang," Marlon said excitedly. "It's a great place. Of course, you can catch the fish right there and eat it on the spot, too. Smoked trout, man. It's the best."

"Yep, the fishing is great. Really, any time you go up there it's good, man," Madison added. "Especially when your nerves are bad, and people are sticking the needles in you all over the place. The last time I went, I had had two back-to-back, difficult, and tedious surgeries. Mentally, I was drained. Totally exhausted. The trip to the mountains helped me keep livin' with a smile. You need to go up there for the rest and relaxation. By the time I got halfway there, the stress of the hospital fell away. I could feel it happening, man. It was wild."

"I'm ready to go. Say no more, man. Sign me up," Rozelle yelled. "I'm bout due for a three-day getaway. So is Jodria Anne. Just let me know when."

"Rozelle, you'll love it, too. We can do a little bit of white water rafting. Now that's something that will give you a new lease on life once you do it," Carlos continued. "I'm telling you. It's one of the most beautiful places God made on earth. Even the eggs are so good. It's like they are hatched before they get to the hens. You know how delicious Pecola's parents' eggs are." Carlos laughed quickly as all the men nodded yes.

"That's the truth," Rozelle agreed.

"By the way, I got a dozen for you Scott, Rozelle, and Marlon. If I knew for sure you guys were coming," Carlos explained as he watched Marlon's friends, "I would've bought yall some fresh eggs."

"Yeah, right," Christopher Perry mumbled.

"My in-laws got an egg producing plant over there on that farm in Greensboro. Rico and I went over there early this morning, and my father-in-law loaded us up with all kinds of vittles," Carlos added with a huge smile.

"I'm like Rozelle. Just give me the dates for the mountains, and I'll check my calendar. I'm sold," Scott declared as he took another puff of cigar.

Marlon breathed deeply and remembered the three days they had white water rafting and fishing. Of the four seasons, he absolutely adored the summertime more than any other. This pleasant memory was tinged with sadness. The trip to the mountains occurred a month before the freak accident with the SLAM Dunk Crew.

"When we went up the last time, we stayed in the old timey cabins and got up around six or seven in the morning. Oh, man. I felt a little bit like Daniel Boone's son. We ate a country breakfast of homemade gravy, sausages, eggs, and biscuits," Marlon recalled with a smile. He tried to sound pleasant in an effort to shake the depressed mood he felt rising within him. "Carlos is right. When you're up there, it's like the doctor gave you a shot and cleaned up any sinus problems you might have. We got up anywhere between six and seven-thirty and ate breakfast."

"C'mon, Slim. I thought you said you got up at six or seven," Rozelle hollered as he glared up into Marlon's face. "Make up your mind, man."

"Let me finish the story," Marlon insisted through his laughter. "Then we waited about two hours to allow the food to settle. After that, we went white water rafting, man. That was a trip. Truly spectacular. Wasn't it?" Marlon said, glancing at Rico, Carlos, and Madison. They all nodded their heads yes. "We went up on a Friday and came back on Monday," Marlon said wistfully. He smiled and jokingly jabbed Christopher Perry on the shoulder several times.

Christopher Perry was a twenty-six year old, six-seven guard for Seattle. He and Marlon had been friends for five years. The friendship was developed two years before Marlon's car accident and ever since Christopher had been recruited into the NBL at twenty-one years of age. The same age Marlon went into the big leagues. A native of Beaufort, North Carolina, Christopher attended North Carolina University as well and had always been a worshipping fan of Marlon since he was a young boy playing ball in Beaufort.

Like Marlon, Christopher's father died when he was in the sixth grade, and his common sensical grandmother, whom he lovingly called Granny, raised him. After Marlon received his National Basketball League pro contract, he still often visited North Carolina University Campus to give the up and coming basketball team inspirational words of encouragement.

When Marlon came back for those talks, Christopher was so awed to be in the same room with his idol, that he was always unusually quiet around him.

When Christopher was drafted number twenty-eight in the first round by Seattle, he thought he had developed the nerve to tell Marlon how he had been his role model and how Marlon influenced his style of play. Yet, Christopher still couldn't fix his mouth to say the words he dreamed about sharing with Marlon and remained silent. So awed by his talented Black mentor, his thoughts lost their voice. His Granny finally told him, "...Just go on and tell that ole Marlon Dinzelle what's on your mind, honey. Just go on and do it, baby."

Christopher did exactly that, and the two had been friends ever since. After Steve, Alfonso, and Lawrence were killed, he and Marlon became even closer. When Marlon moved to Lake Norman two years ago, Christopher bought a home there, too. A honey complexioned, good-looking guy with a black hairy chest and a thin, black mustache that matched his goatee, Pecola always went crazy when she saw Christopher. She declared he reminded her of a younger Carlos.

Christopher, however, had a slight, inexplicable secret crush on Cleopatra. She reminded him of a younger version of his grandmother. Although his wife of three years was just as tall and light-skinned as Cleopatra, there was such a marked contrast in their personalities. Cleopatra projected a warm elegance, and Christopher melted whenever he gazed into her eyes. On the other hand, his wife, Janette, was an extremely selfish woman. A single child, Janette had been pampered all her life by her doting parents and even more so now during her successful career as a super model. Unfortunately, Christopher didn't discover the true person Janette was until after he married her.

Whenever Christopher came to Advance or Winston-Salem with Marlon, Cleopatra always fixed deliciously breathtaking coconut cakes and sweet potato pies. She even prepared full course meals of collard greens, pinto beans, fried chicken, juicy potato salad, and neck bones. That wasn't all. Cleopatra always had the most mouthwatering, the yellowest, butter filled, delicious cornbread. Not only was Cleopatra always laughing and quite anxious to make everyone feel quite comfortable in the Devereauxs' home as well as her own, she also cooked those same old-fashioned down home country meals like his Granny.

Marlon nudged Christopher's shoulder again, and Christopher laughed at him.

"...Wake up from your daydreaming, man. C'mon, man. Answer the question. Do you want to go to the mountains?" Marlon asked, still grinning as Christopher nudged his shoulder.

"MAD Dog, puleeze. I'm like Rozelle and Scott. I'm convinced. You don't even have to even ask the question. Other than the few basketball camps I'm working with this summer, I'm chillin' just like you," Christopher piped in. "Let me know the dates, and I'll be right there. I might even bring my wife along especially so I can drown her damn ass." The other men laughed loudly at his comment that they could relate to.

"Ah, man. Why you go over there and make a bad remark like that?" Rozelle teased as he gazed in Madison's face. "Your ass is in big trouble now. Ain't he, bro?"

"Hey, man. That ain't a nice thing to say about your other half," Madison admonished with a smile.

"Madison, I done told Christopher he needed to attend your impromptu King, Queen, and Dreams classes," Marlon shouted. He playfully jabbed Christopher on the left shoulder several times once more.

When King, Queen and Dreams heard their names, they quickly raised their heads and raced over to Marlon. Marlon vigorously massaged their backs for a few moments. After the quick display of attention, the animals went back to rest in front of the kitchen fireplace. Their favorite place in the room. Until they spotted crumbs falling to the floor again like they did earlier when those strange people placed all the good food on the counters or until someone gave them something extra to eat, the dogs merely planned to relax quietly in their favorite spot.

"Drown your wife?" Rico wondered, nudging Carlos. "Not a good move, man."

"It sho ain't," Madison nodded.

Christopher was a bit embarrassed at his comment. It sounded a tad too real to his ears, so he changed the subject.

"Yo, man. Yall chill. Don't take me serious. I was just joking," Christopher exclaimed as he winked at Madison who winked back with a broad smile. "Just joking. If I mistreated my wife in any shape, form, or fashion, my Granny would kick my butt in her extra pointy church shoes from Beaufort to Morehead City back to Beaufort again."

The men laughed once more. Rico walked over to the stereo speakers and turned up the music, which had been turned down since Madison began his conversation with Scott.

Rozelle broke out into a wide smile when he heard the words of *It's All the Way Live*. Rozelle loudly sang along with the music as he cabbage patched around the floor in his business attire. "Man, I was listening to Jodria's Lakeside tape just last night. This is great, Madison."

"I bet you were dancing to them. Remember that I was the one that gave Jodria the tape I dubbed from the album. That's why I told you people it ain't nothing like my old jam album collection. I don't look at those videos. I don't play the radio, except when it's the old school time. I only meditate, radiate, and luxuriate upon the melodies of the Motown sound, baby," Madison bragged as the other men also bobbed their heads to the music. "I like my CDs, but I love my album collection. It's vintage old school jamming. My views are the same as Pecola. The old timey music. That's when folk were truly singing back then."

"C'mon, man. They got some groups that kick it the same way nowadays," Oscar exclaimed as he swayed to the music.

At twenty-nine years old, Oscar was the six-eleven center who played for Charlotte and lived in Southern Pines, North Carolina. A place where he could play golf round the clock in the off season.

"I understand what you're saying, Oscar. But I still believe there ain't nothing like the singers from the fifties, sixties, and seventies," Madison said with stellar conviction. "There's a big difference in my opinion—from today and to even back then. Nowadays, I know a lot of the singers are trying to go there. They're trying to recapture the essence of the good old days with their songs and all the remakes. There ain't nothing like those old school singers. The

Four Tops. Sam Cooke. Sam & Dave. Bobby Womack. Wilson Pickett. The Dramatics. You know. Them boys."

"Don't try to tell him about those days. The reason they're copying stuff from way back when is because they can't think of a damn thing to write that's not been written," Carlos advised as he munched on an apple. "Plus, their asses were nothing but little baby boys back then—if they were even born. They need to be like me and have an appreciation of both styles."

"I'm with you, Oscar," Rozelle said trying to give the young guy moral support. "I'm up on today's new school groove. My frat brother likes the sad, old timey blues. Scott is hooked on that. You can forget about influencing my other frat brother, Madison. He's hopelessly deadlocked on that old stuff."

"That's right. I am. You gots to remember that I'm New Orleans born and bred, baby," Scott quickly reminded everyone.

"Everyone knows that, man. Look at this breakdown. Madison's wife loves that classical and gospel gig stuff. Madison checks out the oldies but goldies twenty-four seven. Give me a little bit of new soul stuff. I'm talking a little bit of Horace Brown. Don't forget D'Angelo, Eric Benet and Maxwell!" Rozelle hollered in a funny voice and clapped his hand several times.

"They might be a little close to old school," Marlon said.

"I try to expose Scott, Madison, and Pecola to the finer things of life. Reggae. A little bit of Bob Marley. Shabba. You know stuff like that. Now Carlos and me got the same taste with hip music. I dig musical stuff like TLC, SWV, 702, All For One, Usher, and a few other young people out there," Rozelle explained in a businesslike voice, and Carlos nodded in agreement.

"You're just trying to recapture your youth, man," Scott rattled in hurriedly over the wire.

"I ain't trying to recapture a damn thing," Rozelle shot back. "I done recaptured it a long time ago especially after tackling an MBA at Harvard. Hell, my ass had to. If anything, I had to recapture my sanity." The men laughed loudly at Rozelle's comments.

"I'm with you, Rozelle. We got some great singers now," Christopher inserted as he tried to perform a few fancy steps to the music.

"I like Lakeside, too." Kemper said. He sang softly while he danced waving his hands in the air.

When Rozelle walked in, his jacket was flung over his shoulders. Now it was sprawled across the kitchen chair. He removed the collar bar and loosened his tie at the neck. As he danced, he was rolling up his shirtsleeves.

"Aw, man. When you gonna learn another dance?" bellowed Carlos as he nudged Rico on his shoulder. His laughter floated through the room.

"Let me show him the Georgia Bounce," Oscar declared as he tried to demonstrate what he just learned on his last trip to Atlanta. He began bouncing around the kitchen. "Move your shoulders like you're riding a horse and you're bouncing along."

"Aaaah sookie, sookie, now. The weekend is still young. Don't get me started too early, man," Rozelle hollered as he continued to cabbage patch. "Help me out, Marlon."

"My knees, man. You know my knees. I can't hang with that old dance anyway."

"Yo, baby! That's it, Oscar. Do your Georgia Bounce, baby," Christopher yelled as he tried to do his own version of the dance.

Scott laughed into the line. "It's Rozelle, Scott. He's cabbage patching again," explained Madison. "Plus, the other brothers are trying to compete with him. You know how that is."

"I thought that's what it sounded like Rozelle was doing," Scott said as he imagined his buddy gliding around the Devereauxs' spacious country kitchen.

"I learned how to do this when we went to a club right outside of Atlanta in Decatur. Man, it was great. They swear that's where all the professional Black folks hang out. It's where the leaders and the money hang out. There was some other ball players there. They played the old school hits from the seventies and eighties. It's was all good, man," Oscar declared, still gliding around the floor.

"What's the name of the club?" Rico asked as he continued to sashay to the sounds.

"Cafe Unique. It was serious, man. Three to four hundred people. Huge bar. Elevated dance floor. It was really nice. Nobody bum rushing you for autographs or nothing like that."

"Was there a lot of white people there? Whenever I go to a club with them, their dancing totally throws me off," Christopher exclaimed in a funny voice. "Jerking all over the damn place. All out of tune."

"Wasn't no whites nowhere," Oscar replied with a wide grin.

"That must have been nice," Rozelle piped in. "I'll make sure I check it out the next time I head to Atlanta on business."

"Man, it was really nice. It was right. It truly was. Jesse Birth told me about the place. Oh snap, Marlon. Jesse told me to tell you that he would get here some time in the morning."

Marlon simply nodded his head.

"That big seven foot giant motha. Has Jesse learned how to rebound yet?" Rozelle asked in a funny voice as he stared into Oscar's chest.

Jesse Birth was the twenty-nine year old center for Atlanta. Another North Carolina native, he and Marlon had been friends for many years, and he often helped Marlon by speaking to youth for the SLAM Foundation.

"Damn seven foot tall. If he can't dunk, we can't use him. Then his ass can't even shoot a free throw. The easiest place where someone can make a shot is from the free throw line. Nobody's bothering your ass. Nothing, man. He can't even improve on the free throw line, I think he's overrated and overpaid," Rozelle continued still staring into Oscar's chest.

"Rozelle's on the money with that, bro," Carlos declared as he munched on crackers with hogshead cheese covered in hot sauce. For some reason, he had the munchies. He took another swallow of Corona. "Jesse looks likes he jumps two inches off the ground. At seven foot tall, he should be grabbing every damn thing off the boards, man. He's too big. I think he needs to lose a few pounds."

"When Jesse gets here tomorrow, I'm going to tell him exactly what yall said, man. Especially you, Rozelle. You brought it up. He's going to squish your short ass," Oscar said taking up for his friend.

"That'll be the only thing he'll squish because he sure can't squish the damn basketball, man," Rozelle added with a sly grin and a funny swagger since he began cabbage patching again. All the men in the kitchen burst out laughing.

"What you got to drink, man?" Marlon asked through the noise.

"I love this song, too," Rico said of *All The Way Live*. Singly loudly, he snapped his fingers and began dancing around the kitchen with his hands in the air.

"Right on, soul brother. You go, Rico. Get on down. Let's party tonight, man." Rozelle was yelling while the other men watched his deft signature cabbage patch movements. "I always said Rico was my kind of man, Carlos."

"Aaaah, man. *Soul brother?* Man, I done told yall. Yall are some old ass men," exclaimed Christopher. "Nobody says "soul brother" or "get on down" no more except you old ass men! I only hear it when I hang with you guys."

"What you got to drink, man?" Marlon asked again since he didn't think Madison heard him the first time.

Madison shrugged and placed his hands in the air. "I don't know. Alex loaded all refrigerators down for the weekend. Just check it out. You know the routine."

Although Madison and Alex didn't drink hard liquor other than champagne and wine, they often kept a well-stocked bar and refrigerator for their friends' enjoyment. It was especially so when the Devereauxs were having a get-together. The men chatted with Scott for another five minutes, and then they finally headed out to the colonnade porch. Madison watched them leave. While relaxing casually on the white wicker furniture, their discussion traveled again to pro basketball. Madison took a deep breath and pressed the button to take Scott off speaker.

"...All those men are stone trips. Yall done heard me say it before, but I'll say it again. You guys are a pou pou platter of personalities," Madison said with fondness. "Oh, yeah. Alex got Romallus' favorite. That New Orleans brew, Abita Beer, is chillin' for him downstairs in the basement playroom. She was afraid that if she put them up here or in the theater lounge, some of the other guys would drink it before he got here."

"She's amazing, man. I know my brother thanks her already. I thank *you* about Romallus," Scott reminded once more with affection lacing his voice.

"Hey, man. Don't worry. It's a done deal."

"What's a done deal?" Rozelle was being nosy as he stepped back inside the kitchen.

"None of your business, Rozelle," Madison answered with a huge laugh. "Go get your trumpet out the car. Iceman should be here around five. Cleopatra will be back with the fish and crabs long before then. I told Alex I would throw together a New Orleans fish fry since the Alexander boys are rolling into town."

"It's on, baby," Rozelle said.

"Since you love my wife so much, I know you want to fulfill her every wish, Rozelle. So do your part to make sure that tonight we have a New Orleans stomping-throw-down good party-by-poolside," Madison teased on with a sparkle in his eyes.

Rozelle grinned widely as he thought about Alex's smiling face. "You're just trying to get rid of me, man."

"No I'm not, RB. Talk to him, Scott."

Madison handed Rozelle the phone. "He's right, Rozelle. My piano fingers will be ready to rock when I get over there," Scott added. "So pull your trumpet out, man. Romallus is bringing his saxophone, and my boys will be rapping." Rozelle gave Madison the phone.

"Ok, I will. You know that, Madison. I'll do anything for my second wife. The second love of my life," Rozelle added with a smile and promptly left the kitchen to go upstairs to the designated guest bedroom to change his clothes.

"It's a done deal, Scott. All we need to do is tie it up and put a pretty bow on it. I'll take care of that part when I speak to Marshall tonight."

"Thanks, Madison."

"Hey, man. No problem. Just hurry up and get here."

"I will. You can believe that," Scott declared with emphasis. "Talk to you later."

Finally, the two friends ended the phone call.

Chapter Thirty-Six

It was a done deal, Scott thought. Madison, like his wife, was true to his word. If there was a job working with young people in Baton Rouge, New Orleans, or the state of Louisiana for that matter, Madison would pull in all markers to make it happen. This would be excellent for his brother who had been working dead end jobs a while. Romallus was talented. He was a fifth degree black belt martial arts expert and an excellent motivational speaker. Now that he truly had his life back on track, he'd be a wonderful inspiration for the kids he wanted to work with.

All of the Alexander boys were smart, and Romallus wasn't any different. He received a football scholarship to Grambling State University, majored in Math, and graduated magna cum laude. Since he didn't make it to the National Football Association as he had hoped, he decided to earn an MBA from Carnegie Mellon University. Once again, he graduated with honors and obtained a degree with high distinction. Recruited by Johnson Merrell, the nation's number one brokerage firm, Romallus had been a rising star on Wall Street for five years. However, his star rapidly faded in a world of drug abuse where cocaine was the initial culprit.

Scott couldn't believe six-and-a-half years had passed since the last time Romallus was hooked on crack cocaine, angel dust, alcohol, and whatever else he could get his hands on.

Time flies, Scott thought. When the frantic call came through almost seven years ago, Scott had just returned home from a four-day trip. Romallus was desperate.

"...Scott, I'm an addict. Oh shit, man. I need some help really bad, man." Romallus' voice was raspy.

Scott already knew that his brother's reason for living now was drugs, but Romallus needed to reach the point he recognized it, too. Before the phone call, Romallus had been in New Orleans for six months, and Scott was concerned for their father. Even though Scott provided personal home care round the clock for his Pop, his seventy-one year old father told him that several more items were discovered missing from the house each week. Scott's father believed Romallus stole them, pawned the goods, and used the money to buy drugs.

"Scotto—," Romallus weakly called his brother by the Alexander family pet name for him.

"Yes, Rommie."

"I'm an addict, man," he repeated and started to say something else, but Scott interrupted him.

"Where are you, Romallus?" Scott was thoroughly moved by his brother's confession, which he knew was the first step to recovery.

Scott realized that if he was going to help Romallus save his life, he had to allow him to die first. The kind of death that felt real. Suffering. The humiliating kind that only drugs can bring. Nothing else worked in the past. It sounded as if Romallus was buried deep this time. Always a smooth talker since drugs demanded that he become a trickster, Romallus had declared several times before that he was ready to stop. Scott could only hope and pray that this time he was serious.

"Tell me where you are, Rommie?"

"I'm at home in New Orleans. I'm with Pop, man." Scott heard the sobs of desperation come through the telephone wire. "I need help, man. I feel so bad. I believe the only thing left for me to do is die." Romallus blew his nose. He was doubled over, head between his knees, and was crying pitifully loud. He cleared his throat.

"How can I help you, Rommie?"

"I've been running and running. I'm trying to run toward Mama, Lindsay, Jr., and Granville. I can't reach them, Scotto. I see them, but I can't get to them, man. I'm tired of trying. I'm real tired, man. Please help me. I'm sooo damn tired. I'm serious, man." The pain covered his sobs.

"Talk to me, Rommie."

"Scotto, I'm serious. Very serious. Serious as fuck. Help me. Help me again. Just one more time? One—more—time, puhleeze. I'm so tired of living like this."

"You know I'll take care of you," Scott assured him. "I'm your brother, man. I'm on the next plane out. I'll be there. I'll take care of you, and do what needs to be done. Don't worry, Romallus. Don't worry about a thing, man." And, Scott saved his brother's life. Cause he never stopped loving him.

This was a momentous sixth and half birthday for Romallus. Romallus often said that this kindergarten age birthday was the real day he was born and given a chance at living without shooting up. Before Romallus walked out of the prestigious Kujichagulia Drug Center of New Orleans, he slid down the razor blade of life that involved drugs, homelessness, and poverty for seven long years. From New York to New Orleans, Romallus did whatever he needed to live on the streets, maintain his habit, and stay alive.

Romallus' life had now changed, and Scott was committed to helping him on his trek to success. Scott wanted to do all he could to ensure Romallus stayed on a natural high. Romallus knew that Scott was his shadow, his guardian angel.

Remembering the past, Scott's face was laced with a small smile. After Romallus left Kujichagulia Drug Center those many years ago, Scott recalled how Romallus went berserk chasing women. Just recently, Romallus told his brother that he had finally begun to calm down regarding women.

I guess to experience a nut and not be high was more than Romallus could take, and he wanted to experience those feelings over and over again, Scott thought with a smile. Thoughts about Romallus and his women made Scott think about Charmaine. He quickly walked over to the telephone and dialed her number.

"Good afternoon. Thank you for calling Charmaine Kuumba Academy of Winston-Salem," Tiffany Carter, Charmaine's assistant, answered brightly.

"Hey, Tif. How you doing, baby?"

"Hi, Scott. I'm doing just great," she gushed as she recognized his voice. Tiffany thought he was sooo fine. More importantly, he was quite friendly, and a first-class gentleman who always treated her with the utmost of respect.

"I'm glad to hear you're doing great. How's everything been since I spoke to you yesterday?" Sometimes, Scott believed he called Charmaine too much.

"Just fantastic, Scott." Tiffany giggled. "Let me get Charmaine for you. She just finished a class about ten minutes ago."

"Thanks, Tif." While Scott waited for Charmaine to pick up the phone, he hummed along with Al Green.

"Hey, baby," Charmaine said softly.

"Hey, baby to you. I just called to say I love you and to let you know I was thinking about you."

"Ohhhh, Scott. That's so sweet, baby. I love you, too."

"What are you wearing, baby?"

"I have on my black leotards, my ankle warmers, tights and ballet shoes. How does that sound, baby?"

"It would sound even better—look better if you were here standing over my face as you took each piece off."

Charmaine giggled. "What do *you* have on, Scott?"

"I'm wearing a red silk bathrobe. After you left and after I regained my strength from our lovemaking this morning, I cooked me some grits and another cheese omelet. I did all of that while I was buck naked, baby. I've been buck naked underneath my robe ever since." As she visualized his rugged body, she giggled again.

"Sounds like I need to be there sitting right on your lap." Her voice was liltingly seductive.

"You gots that right, baby. Although I've been tasting your lipstick all day, what I really want right now is—"

"I'm listening, Scottie."

"You need to be here sitting on my face."

"Oooh, baby, baby. That could work." They both laughed.

"Have you decided on an answer to my question?"

"Nooo. I, uh," she said slowly.

"Does that mean no is the answer, or does that mean no you don't know?"

"It means no I haven't decided yet. But I'll let you know tonight. Ok, baby?"

"That'll be fine. I look forward to seeing you later." Scott's voice oozed with sex, and he was satisfied.

"I hear Al Green in the background. Knowing you, you've probably been listening to those old songs since this morning."

"You got that right, baby. It's been AG and me since you left. According to Madison, it'll be non-stop, back in the day music for the entire weekend."

"That's typical Madison." Tiffany signaled that Charmaine's client had arrived for the meeting. "Scott, let me go, baby. I've an appointment with a sister from Oldtown. She wants to enroll her seven-year old son and nephew in my Saturday morning ballet and tap class."

"Fine, baby. Take care. I love you. Ride the wing of those words through the day."

"You know it will. It always does, Scott baby." She left a sweet taste in his mouth after she hung up.

Scott placed the receiver in the holder and listened to *Let's Stay Together* several times. His heart followed each one of Al Green's words. Finally, he got up and stood by the window for a few minutes. He realized he couldn't meditate on Al Green any longer even though he truly wanted to. Romallus and his sons would be waiting at the airport. Scott went upstairs to take a shower and headed off to the airport to pick up his family.

Pecola's front door rang again. It was Cleopatra this time. Still thinking about the aggravating conversation with her mother, Pecola shook her head impatiently. Pecola walked down her long, downstairs hallway. She picked up the Afrocentric weekender bag, her pocketbook, and quickly headed for the front door. She disarmed the alarm and opened the door. Standing on the front porch with a huge smile on her ugly face was Cleopatra. Pecola reached out to embrace her affectionately, and they both walked to the black super stretch limousine parked in the circular driveway.

"Pecola, how you doing?" Cleopatra asked in an excited voice. Cleopatra didn't give her a chance to answer. The Black, nice-looking chauffeur, whom Pecola didn't recognize, took the small bag out of Pecola's hand. He assisted them into the car, placed the bag inside as well, and shut the door. "Today has been a truly busy one. Let me tell you."

"I bet. I just hung up from talking with Madison. I was looking for you."

"I've been trying to get here. I needed to pick up Madison and the other boys' kente cloth. So how are you doing otherwise, girl?"

"Fine now, honeychile. I'm doing just fabulous." Pecola checked her watch. "You're fifteen minutes late. That isn't even like you, Miss Prompt," Pecola joked, somewhat surprised.

Cleopatra bobbed her head quickly. "I know. I dropped the last six children off at the Devereauxs about ten o'clock this morning. Then I helped Alex get a few things together before I came back out to get you and I had to make a few more other stops. I need to make another stop."

"Where to now?"

"Alex wanted me to pick up the fish. After the fish market, we'll head out to Advance."

"What about Clemmons? Aren't you're picking Symone up, too?

"No. Symone's not coming. She called Alex and said that she would be over early in the morning. Said she wasn't feeling well."

"What in the hell's wrong with her? I spoke to her this morning for a long time, and she said she was fine."

"I don't know, Pecola. That's what she told Alex. So that's the story."

Pecola considered calling Symone from the limo but decided to wait.

"I'll call Symone when I get to Alex's." Pecola was concerned. "How are the children doing? Are they excited, Cleopatra?"

"Girl, you know they are. Alex had four limousines reserved to pick everyone up. You know how she is about having everyone ride in limousines. Anyway—," Cleopatra said as she batted her long lashes. Pecola just looked at her out the corner of her eyes. While Cleopatra spoke, she made various check marks on the to-do list that she and Alex put together.

"Give me the run down, Cleopatra."

"Well, we told the parents and guardians that the children had to be ready at eight this morning, and I started picking them up then. With the last group I dropped off, the limo barely pulled up into the Devereauxs' driveway before they all were jumping out yelling and screaming like they didn't have any sense. They were so happy to see Alex and Madison. So happy to be in the country, girl. It was wonderful."

"I bet they were excited," Pecola agreed, laughing.

"And Madison is sooo crazy. He's playing some old album. He says it's his theme song for the next two weeks."

"Yep, that sounds like Madison. What's the theme song this time, Cleopatra? Last month it was The Brothers Johnson's *Stomp*. That certainly had the place rocking. No matter what the occasion, Madison always has a theme song. I think he just likes saying he has a theme. Alex told me that of course Madison was going to go with the old school. You know that's my cup of tea. So what's the theme song, girl?" Pecola repeated the question.

"I believe it's *Live all the Way*." Her voice was hesitant.

"*Live all the Way*," Pecola repeated slowly with a confused expression. She said the title again. "Honeychillle, you mean it's *All the Way Live?*" Pecola sang a few bars for her.

"Yeah that's it, girl. You go girl with that voice," Cleopatra said and giggled. "Well they have the outside speakers blaring. Even the senior citizens were trying to tap their feet to it."

"Honeychile! Honeychile! Aaaah sookie, sookie, now. My man, Madison, knows how to play the right kind of music. I've told Alex a thousand times that Madison should've been my husband." Pecola laughed. "We got the same damn taste for back-in-the-day music."

Cleopatra laughed freely. "Alex said that he picked out various old songs for the entire weekend. When DJ Cool Breeze arrives tomorrow, Madison has everything worked out. It's going to be a full house. That's for sure. You know Rico and Carlos have been around the place all morning helping Madison. Old crazy Rozelle came while I was there."

Cleopatra was pleased to know what was going on at the Devereauxs' house. Giving first hand information felt delicious. Cleopatra was determined to make sure everything runs smoothly. It was her job to make sure a lot of the stress was taken off of Alex's shoulders.

"Is Jodria there, Cleopatra?"

"Yeah, she's there. So is Darilyn, your nieces, nephews, and a few other people. When I was pulling out to come get you, Marlon and his friends drove up. He came with three of the same cutie-pie professional basketball players he always hangs with. Marlon told me that the others would be there tomorrow. They looked like they spilled out of a pearly cream tank or something. It was a pretty car though. The new chauffeur almost went crazy when he saw those guys. He said it was a customized Hummer or something."

"Well that's the same kind of car Gloster drives."

"Really. I couldn't tell. It appeared so huge, especially since the guys who were getting out of it were sooo tall. Marlon hugged me all over the place and told me that it was a little something he treated himself to. Anyway, the chauffeur recognized the players from television. When we pulled off, he asked me about them. But I acted like it was no big deal, girl," she rattled on excitedly.

"Good."

"He couldn't believe he was seeing those basketball players in living color. He was stargazing like crazy. I told him that we see them all the time and how Marlon knows everybody. He knows movie stars. All the professional athletes and singers. When Marlon comes to town, he has his basketball buddies around him. He knows everybody," she repeated again and took a brief pause to scribble a note.

"Uh huh," Pecola moaned.

"Of course, I never gave him any names or anything like that. Protect their privacy. That's what Alex says. They might not want to let people know that they often come to Winston-Salem or Advance. You know I believe in protecting their privacy, too," she explained with wide eyes and pointed to the driver while her Cambridge planner hid her fingers. "Now, he wants me to get him Marlon's autograph. He didn't even ask about the other guys. Isn't that amazing? Marlon doesn't even play ball anymore, but people are always asking him for his autograph. That's because he's such a nice guy."

Pecola glared at Cleopatra briefly and thought how she was certainly turning into a little Miss Perfect Events Organizer—just like Alex.

"By the way, where is Togo?" Pecola asked while making a few head movements toward the new driver. "That's who normally drives the main limo when Alex has something going on. Even when it's ladies night out."

"He's in Minnesota. This is the weekend of his wedding. Remember he's getting married to that girl from Minneapolis."

"I forgot. Sometimes, I think I got Alzheimer's or something."

"Whaaat!" Cleopatra glared at her sharply.

"I'm serious, girl. Half the time I can't find my keys, can't remember dates. The other day I couldn't find my car at Thruway Shopping Center."

"Girl, that's not Alzheimer's. That's just old age. If you told me you forgot you had a car, I would say you've Alzheimer's all right. You're just getting old, girl," Cleopatra said wisely with a jumbo grin.

"Thanks a lot, Cleopatra. Thanks for reminding me."

The two of them cackled loudly together. Cleopatra hummed to herself and swayed to the soothing sounds of the Toni Braxton CD she asked the chauffeur to play. Pecola moved to the music as well and reached over to remove cherry chapstick from her new overnight bag. She also wanted to check her eyeliner with the compact mirror.

"You like my bag, Cleopatra girl?"

Cleopatra nodded her head yes as she helped herself to a glass full of Pepsi. She handed a glass to Pecola who thanked her sweetly and waited patiently for the compliment.

"What you think, Cleopatra?"

"It's really pretty, Pecola girl."

"Thanks, chile. Symone got it for me when she went to New York last week. You know she had to go there for that emergency with Hazele and her husband?" Cleopatra nodded her head yes. "Hazele took her to some shop in the city, and she found it there. The designer's name is Duran. Supposedly, he only makes African-inspired stuff."

"I know. She told me the same thing. She bought a set for me, too." Cleopatra checked the to-do list again for good measure. "Not like yours, though. Mine has more black in it. It's absolutely beautiful. I kissed her all over the place. Of course, she told me to cut it out. It wasn't necessary. You know how she is about stuff like that."

"She did?" Pecola asked with a twinge of jealousy and surprise. "She didn't tell me that, chile."

Cleopatra shrugged her shoulders, smiled quickly, and continued to review the list.

Pecola rolled her eyes theatrically, sucked her teeth, and wondered why Symone didn't tell her about that. All she needed was to go out somewhere and have Cleopatra or any one of their other friends for that matter, carrying the same pocketbook and luggage as she was. Symone was just as bad as Alex was. Symone continually laughed about Alex surprising folks with a wide variety of gifts, but Pecola often told Symone that she definitely was in contention for Alex's first place honors for gift giving.

"Let me tell you, girl. Guess who's coming tonight, Pecola? Bump the pro b-ball players. I know you and Symone will enjoy looking at their bodies though as usual," she added with a glint in her eyes.

"Absolutely."

"But I don't even care about those fine basketball players being there. Guess who's coming, Pecola?" She sounded like an eager young kid.

"Who, chile?"

"Scott's two sons. GJ and SJ. That's who. They're going to talk about the rap music industry this week. Girl, I think they're the two finest Black men I've seen in a long time. If they weren't so young, I would ask Alex to help me date at least one of them. They look just like their father. Super tall. Six foot four. Handsome. Hairy chest and all, girl. Umph, umph, umph," she raved with a big smile. She glanced out the window and noticed that the limo was now gliding down Martin Luther King Drive.

I don't think Scott's sons would go out with you, girl. Even if you were young enough. Your ass is too ugly for them, Pecola thought with a pretentious attitude and sly grin.

Immediately, Pecola felt guilty for thinking such horrid thoughts about Cleopatra. But it was true. Sometimes she believed she was the only one who admitted it. Even though Symone told Pecola that it wasn't nice to say awful things about people you associate with on a frequent basis, Pecola didn't care. She constantly told Symone that Cleopatra was one of the ugliest women she had ever seen in her whole life.

Pecola wouldn't dare share this with Alex. It would upset her too bad. Plus, Pecola was sure Alex noticed it. There was no way Alex couldn't. There was no way the other friends didn't notice it either. There was no way they absolutely could not see what Pecola saw whenever she looked at Cleopatra. Pecola couldn't understand the secrecy. It was like all the others were sworn to a righteous silence. They had taken a blood oath against speaking about

Cleopatra's face. Like Symone, who thought Pecola was crazy whenever she mentioned anything about Cleopatra, Alex had to be totally blind to not see the obvious.

When Pecola opened her eyes again, she noticed that the limo had pulled up in front of Forsyth Seafood Market & Grill. The driver came around to open the door for Cleopatra.

"Pecola, I'll be right back," Cleopatra said with a flurry as Pecola gazed her in the eyes and grinned understandingly. "This is my last stop, girl. I need to go speak with Charles and Virginia Hardesty. I know Alex told me that there was an order placed for fresh croakers, spots, jumbo shrimp, and live crabs. But Alex said that she also spoke with Virginia, and she was going to throw some other stuff in that's not on my list. I'll be right back, girl." The chauffeur helped her out of the car, and she stepped daintily inside the fish store.

Pecola shook her head and giggled lightly. Cleopatra almost walked like Alex now. Without question, Cleopatra was totally devoted to Alex and deservedly so. Oftentimes, Pecola told Alex that she picked up stray people as often as normal folks adopted stray animals. That was exactly how Alex discovered Cleopatra on the streets of Winston-Salem.

After Alex's parents died, she and Nanette refused to sell the Cameron Avenue home they had lived in while growing up. They rented it out to a distant male cousin. However, ten years later, the cousin moved to Pensacola, Florida, and the house was available once more. Until they found someone else to rent it, Alex continually checked on the empty home or was down in Winston-Salem to show it to perspective tenants.

On one particular such Wednesday while Alex was driving to her parents' home to show it to her soror's brother, she saw a tall, light skinned woman with two small boys walking along Martin Luther King Drive. In the woman's hand, she held a long wiry and limber green, tree switch. Every three feet or so, the woman would sting the children's legs with it. The two boys cried, stumbled, fell, got up, and tried to walk again. When Alex saw this, of course her heart went out to the children, but it also went out to the woman.

Alex wondered why the woman continued to lash out at the children in such an angry way. The two boys were just babies. Pregnant with Trey at the time, Alex felt an even more kinship with the children. She thought about turning the car around to see if the woman needed a ride. However, she changed her mind when she considered how Madison constantly begged her to please be careful about running all over Winston-Salem trying to help people that she didn't know. Especially since she was now seven months pregnant.

Still thinking about the tragic scene, Alex stopped into the McDonald's on Martin Luther King Drive to get a cup of coffee before she went to her parents' house. While she sipped the hot coffee by the window, the woman and the two boys walked in. The abusive behavior continued and the pitiful crying of the children moved Alex to speak to the woman. Plus, she noticed the small whelps all over the boys' legs.

Alex introduced herself to the woman. Trying to get a conversation going, Alex chitchatted about what she was doing in Winston. The woman eventually mumbled that her name was Cleopatra Zee Crutchfield. After she saw Alex still wasn't budging and remained standing beside her table with a pleasant expression on her face, she also told her that her two boys were named Beckett and Grandison. Beckett was two, and Grandison was three. Finally, Alex sat down at the table and found out that she lived in Cleveland Avenue Homes. The public housing community just three blocks over. Two years ago, Cleopatra had moved to

Winston-Salem from Tupelo, Mississippi with her husband. Just eight months after they arrived, her husband walked out. She hadn't heard from him since. Once again, Alex felt sorry for someone less fortunate and tried to figure out how she could help.

"...Well, tell me what your gift is, Cleopatra?" Alex asked.

"My gift, ma'am?" Cleopatra's eyes were downcast.

Cleopatra refused to take her eyes off the table and appeared timid about raising her head to stare Alex in the face. Immediately, Alex thought about the slaves who were taught to not stare at anyone—especially a white man in the face. Being from Mississippi, Alex considered maybe Cleopatra's parents had been influenced by such old slave habits and had taught her the same practice for all people in general.

"Cleopatra, please look at me," Alex pleaded in a soft voice.

After a couple of long seconds, the younger woman slowly raised her eyes to meet Alex's. When she did that, Alex saw the biggest, prettiest brown eyes with long, curly lashes. Satisfied, Alex smiled.

"Thank you, Cleopatra. Ok. Now tell me what your gift is? What are you good at?"

Cleopatra looked down again. With eyes glued to the table, she spoke.

"Ma'am. Uh, I guess my gift is cleaning houses, ma'am. And, er, and cooking."

"Those are wonderful gifts, Cleopatra. Just wonderful, girl." Alex laughed in delight. It was a throaty one.

"Ma'am?"

"If I'm having a big party and my house needs to be cleaned, I need to find someone who has the gift of cleaning so that my house will look nice when the guests arrive. I wouldn't want anyone to come to a dirty house. Would I?" Cleopatra didn't answer her. "So everybody has a gift, and it sounds like yours is cleaning. Plus, I would still need to have a talented person help me to prepare a large meal so everyone could eat, too. I certainly couldn't cook all that food by myself. So, the same extraordinary gift would apply for cooking. That's a wonderful talent too, Cleopatra. Sounds like you got at least two glorious gifts, girl!"

Cleopatra refused to answer Alex, whom she perceived as almost mocking her. She was so generous with her comments. Quite frankly, she was ready to bolt out of McDonald's and grab her two boys up along the way to simply get away from her. Instead, Cleopatra watched her sons playing quietly on the floor. Alex smiled warmly. Her heart ballooned with a compassionate desire to assist the woman in any way she could.

"You know what? Last year my cleaning lady retired from cleaning houses. Mrs. Derrickson was sixty-five. Don't you think it was time for her to stop cleaning and rest a spell, Cleopatra?"

"Yes ma'am." Cleopatra mumbled and idly nodded her head.

"You know I haven't had anyone steady since then." Alex paused briefly. "Cleopatra, I would like to give you an opportunity to help me," Alex said gingerly as she considered what Madison would say about it first especially since he gave her specific orders to not try to save the world during this pregnancy. Cleopatra raised her head slightly.

"An opportunity, ma'am?" She looked down again.

"Yes. An opportunity, girl. An opportunity to enhance my life and change yours for the better."

"But ma'am, you don't know me."

"I know," Alex said lightly. "I can get to know you. We can learn about each other and become friends. Since you say you're real good at cleaning houses, I have a lot of friends Mrs. Derrickson cleaned for. If you do real well for me, then I know they'll use you. Just be good at what you do."

Cleopatra felt a rare, bare inkling of hope creep up, and she decided to explain her credentials to the overly kind woman.

"Ma'am, I've been cleaning houses right along side my Mama since I was six years old. Been cooking that long, too. I'm a good cleaner. I just hadn't had any luck finding anyone to let me in their house. I don't have a car. Don't have nothing, ma'am. No man, and no help. No relatives here. As I was walking to McDonald's, I was thinking that it's time for me to go back home to Tupelo. All I ever have knowed how to do is cook and clean." Her eyes were glued to the table.

"I understand, Cleopatra."

"Ma'am, you may not believe this. I mean you may can't tell it by the condition I'm in now, but I went to Mississippi Valley State College for two years. Majored in home economics. I was the first one in my family to do that—to go away to college, ma'am. I saved my money from cleaning houses all over Tupelo and started The Valley—college when I was twenty."

"That's wonderful."

"I listened to television and the radio. I taught myself how to speak proper like. I read a bunch of books, too. After I got through cleaning houses, it was a way out for me. Reading was a way for me to dream of other places to live other than Tupelo. I love Tupelo, ma'am. But there's more than Tupelo in this big wide world, and I wanted to see the world, too." Cleopatra's eyes filled with tears, and she wiped them away with the back of her hands. She stopped speaking for a moment to try to stop her tears that were intermingled with her words.

"I understand."

"Ma'am, I'm a real determined person. Real determined. I had to drop out of The Valley when I became pregnant with him." Cleopatra's voice was sad as she pointed to Grandison, the oldest boy, who was still playing quietly on the floor. "Then I got married real fast—so he would have his daddy with him. This last year, I just haven't had much luck lately, ma'am. I'm poor. Living inside of need. Need new clothes. Need food. Need. Need. Need. I realized that. I'm reminded of that every day I wake up and gaze out my window. But I've always read about so much more. It's been very hard, ma'am."

"I can imagine."

Cleopatra looked at the children again. Beckett's nose was runny with snot now, and Cleopatra swiftly wiped it with the square, white table napkins.

"I can't give them what they need with me being like this, ma'am. It's hard on me, and I make it hard on them. I just can't give them what they need. That's the hardest part of all of this."

"I understand, Cleopatra," Alex said. "I got friends who got pregnant when they weren't expecting to. It was hard for them in the beginning. Real hard. I know, girl." Alex now had tears in her eyes. She thought about Pecola, and two of her sorors who became pregnant at sixteen. She was simply moved by the young woman's confession. Cleopatra was quiet for several minutes before she spoke again.

"Ma'am. I know I can. If you just let me, I know I can do it. Give me a chance, puhleeze. I promise you that when I dust, you'll be able to see your face in your furniture. It'll be just like a mirror. I'll make your bathroom look brand new. Your toilet bowl will sparkle just like a pretty, shiny, diamond ring," she said confidently still looking down.

That day, Alex drove Cleopatra home, and she promised Cleopatra she would pick her up on Saturday at eleven. As Madison and Alex relaxed in their bed later that night, she spoke to him about Cleopatra. At the end of the conversation, Alex began to cry softly.

"...Madison, there are people who have no hope of getting out of bed. Who are sunk in despair, baby. She sounds that way to me, baby. The way she was whipping those children today was awful. She doesn't have much money. No hope for the future. That's why she's abusing those precious baby boys. It's twisted love. Suffering will make you do sick, violent things. They're such pretty little boys, Madison. She'll injure their precious little spirits if she continues to live life feeling hopeless like that."

"I know," Madison said and hugged her close to him.

"Madison, you should've seen her. That's what I heard in her voice today, baby. Total despair. That's why I want to help her. You know I need help with the house anyway."

"Alex, you can't save the world." He spoke quietly as he held her shoulders and stared into her eyes. "You just can't, baby. Think about your health and our baby, honey. You can't be driving someone back and forth to Winston-Salem two and three times a week. You should be in bed."

"I know I can't save the world, baby. I know that. But I believe if I can touch one person at a time, that could help. If I can light one candle, one life at a time, that could be a start, Madison. That could be a huge start, baby," she repeated ever so softly.

Not the type of husband for saying no about any request his wife asked him to consider, Madison told her it would be fine to have Cleopatra, a blame pure divine stranger, to clean their home on Saturday.

The next day when Alex told Pecola, Symone, and Nanette about Cleopatra, they all quickly told her to be careful with strangers. Nevertheless, Alex persevered with helping Cleopatra. Every week for about four months, Cleopatra faithfully cleaned Alex's house without incident. Even more, she cleaned it impeccably. Afterwards, she began cleaning for Nanette, Symone, Jodria, and a few other friends as well. Eventually, Pecola believed it was finally safe for Cleopatra to clean the Reynolds' home.

Chapter Thirty-Seven

On the Saturday Cleopatra was scheduled to come to Pecola's house, Pecola was upstairs polishing her toes as she watched the video of her Friday's taping of *Oprah*. When the bell rang, Pecola raced downstairs to answer the door and opened it with a huge smile on her face. From a quick glance at Cleopatra's appearance, Pecola automatically assumed the woman was lost.

"...I'm sorry, but you got the wrong house," Pecola said quickly and proceeded to slam the door in the woman's face.

"Ma'am, puhleeze. Don't close the door. Excuse me, ma'am. I'm here to see—" Cleopatra spoke quietly. She reached into her cheap, plastic pocketbook to retrieve the wrinkled piece of paper with the directions and name on it. "A Mrs. Pecola Reynolds. My name is Cleopatra. Alex said that you wanted me to be here today promptly at 10:00 a.m."

Pecola checked her watch. It was nine forty-five. *So this was Cleopatra? As ugly as she is, who in the hell named her Cleopatra?* Pecola thought smugly with wide eyes.

"Oh, I'm sorry. I'm sooo sorry, honeychile. Please forgive me," Pecola stammered along trying to cover up her shock. "Girl, I'm PMSing today. My period's on, and you know how that is. I've a lot on my mind. Yes, you're at the right house. Of course, I'm Pecola Reynolds," she said as she eyed her suspiciously.

After Pecola showed Cleopatra around and told her where the clean embroidered sheets and towels were, Pecola proceeded to explain what she wanted done.

"...Now, Cleopatra, I don't want to see any fingerprints on the stairway banisters, honeychile. I want it to shine—like sparkly, shimmering shining. Ok, chile? I'm very finicky about that. So make sure you dust that really good," Pecola requested in a superior sounding voice.

"Yes, ma'am. I'll clean anyway you want me to, Mrs. Reynolds," Cleopatra said looking down at the floor.

"Good, honeychile. When my banisters aren't done right, that's the only thing that drives me crazy," Pecola added as she batted her eyes, sucked her teeth, and quickly shook her head from side to side.

Cleopatra simply smiled and said that she understood. She went about dusting the furniture downstairs in the living room. Pecola raced upstairs to the master bedroom and locked the door. To squelch out the telephone conversation, she put on The Unifics album. She turned *Court of Love* volume up very high and immediately called Symone. Pecola knew better than to call Alex.

"...Symone chile, that girl is ugly. I mean *real* ugly, chile," she exclaimed into the phone in a quiet voice as she pressed the lobe of her other ear with an index finger. "How come you didn't tell me?"

"It wasn't nothing to tell, Pecola. All I was concerned about was if she could help Miss Jessica or not. She does a great job. Leave it alone, Pecola."

Pecola stopped speaking for a moment. She thought she heard suspicious movements outside the bedroom door.

"Hold on just a minute, girl," Pecola commanded in a high-pitched voice. She stopped talking just briefly to go check. No one was lurking in the hallway, and she raced back into the room and picked up the phone.

"Pecola! Pecola! What happened?"

"I'm back," she whispered feverishly. "Honeychile, she is ugly as sin. That's a shame she's sooo ugly. The ugly stick hit her real bad, and girlfriend got it going on with the ugly family. I mean to tell you. I ain't got no reason to lie about homegirl. Wooo! She's ugly as shit," Pecola rattled on in a crazy, hysterical voice.

"Pecola, girl. Enough."

"That woman is a wonder to behold. Didn't you notice that, Symone? I know I ain't that crazy, now. Am I the only one who has said anything about it? Surely you noticed something different, chile? I can't believe Jodria hasn't said anything to me either. She's sooo ugly, it makes my face hurt when I look at her. I mean gawd, Symone. Honeychile, I can't believe you never thought to warn me about this." She inhaled deeply and fanned her face with one hand. "Wait until I speak to Nanette, Jodria, and our other friends."

"Pecola, don't say anything to anyone else. Puhleeze, girl. Leave it alone. You know that's not nice. What has what you say she looks like have to do with her abilities, Pecola? Why is that sooo important to you? Nobody's perfect—especially me, girl." Symone laughed, paused quickly, and inhaled deeply.

"Just unbelievably ugly. Umph, umph, umph, umph."

"She's a truly incredible young lady. Superb personality. She's smart, quick and funny. Alex adores her. I do, too. Miss Jessica loves her to death. The main thing is she does absolutely fabulous cleaning."

Pecola ignored the praise Symone lavished upon the cleaning woman that she said was twenty-six years old.

"I mean really, Symone. Look at her. She got baked the hell out of nappy damn kinky, reddish hair. Real light complexioned. Lighter than me, chile. Freckles. Acne potted skin. Pink damn bubble lips. I haven't seen nothing like that face in years."

Symone remained silent as she listened to Pecola's shameless attitude and sadly shook her head.

"She has beautiful eyes, Pecola. Look at those."

"I hell damn would if I could get pass the face, honeychile. She's a consummate ugly woman. Let me tell you, chile."

Symone patiently scolded Pecola for the next several minutes. Pecola finally thought it best if she calmed herself down. All she needed was to get Symone all upset. Then, Symone would call and tell Alex. Alex would then call Pecola and would verbally crucify her about what Alex called Pecola's self-righteous attitude about people whom Pecola believed were different from her, and her so-called acceptable friends. And Pecola certainly didn't want to deal with Alex's quiet yet truthful wrath either right now.

It took several more months for Pecola to get past Cleopatra's physical appearance. But it finally happened. Pecola also discovered that Cleopatra was indeed an enjoyable person to know, an excellent housekeeper, and a marvelous cook. It took Pecola a whole nother year to stop talking about how ugly she was. Then Pecola went through another phase. She couldn't believe that anyone could name a child that ugly, Cleopatra. However, two years after she started working for the friends, Cleopatra showed Pecola her birth certificate.

Alex was taking Cleopatra on a seven-day Caribbean cruise, and Cleopatra needed to have her driver's license and birth certificate to prove her United States citizenship. Sure enough. There it was. Cleopatra Zee Barrow was clearly typed on the official document. It was authentic. Raised seal and all from the state of Mississippi. Pecola was finally convinced that Cleopatra was indeed Cleopatra's birth name and not some title Cleopatra made up along the way to make her self-esteem soar. Pecola again became even more flabbergasted when she met Cleopatra's only younger brother, Samson Barrow, Jr. for the first time. Cleopatra proudly said that he was nicknamed Prettyguy. Pecola thought that his nickname must have been the joke of Tupelo. Samson was just as ugly as his sister. The only difference was, Pecola secretly told Symone, was that he had a thick, black mustache.

Just twenty months ago, the soror's brother who lived in Alex's parents' home moved out. Alex and Nanette considered donating the house to the Deltas or to another charity. But Madison recommended they instead give or sell it to Cleopatra. In the end, Alex and Nanette allowed Cleopatra to buy the house for little of nothing because Cleopatra insisted that she wanted to pay a monthly mortgage. She had read in a book that's what people did when they purchased a home. Madison believed Cleopatra, more than anyone else, would love and appreciate the house in a magnificent way. He was right.

Cleopatra and her two adorable sons moved into the three-bedroom home, and she kept it absolutely spit shiny, spotless. Like Rozelle said all the time, "...Man, you could even eat a full course meal off Cleopatra's bathroom floor." Since Cleopatra was the first person in her family to own a home, she was thoroughly proud of the accomplishment. The house became a petite version of the Devereauxs' country showplace. She even tried to decorate the quaint brick home in such a manner as Alex and Madison's place in Advance.

Pecola chuckled to herself as she considered the men in the group. Although no one said anything to Pecola about it, it seemed that every last one of the men had made a silent vow to honor Cleopatra with flowery compliments. Madison, Carlos, Rozelle, Scott, Rico, Marlon, and anyone else they invited into their tight inner circle of men often kept Cleopatra smiling too. As fine as Christopher Perry was, he even constantly told Cleopatra she had such a lovely, elegant air about her. Pecola couldn't believe it when she heard him say that. Every time one of the guys saw Cleopatra, they embraced her shoulders tightly. They told her how gorgeously beautiful and pretty she was and they shared any other flattering comments they could think of. Pecola was now convinced that Cleopatra believed the flowery hype as well.

It had been almost five years since Cleopatra started working for Alex, and everyone understood why Cleopatra adored Alex immensely. By knowing Alex, Cleopatra blossomed from within and developed an air of confidence. Her posture changed, and she carried herself with a stately, efficient air. She even developed a cute, dainty walk. Alex told Cleopatra that with such powerfully beautiful eyes, she should always gaze people in their eyes when she spoke to them. "...You should always walk tall with your head held high, girl" is what she told her, too.

However, there was only one amusing complaint the friends consistently shared about Cleopatra's work. Cleopatra now believed she was a premier interior decorator as well. When she cleaned their houses, she often decided to move various furniture accessories to places throughout the homes where she thought they would be more appropriate. That happened to Pecola like six months after she started. Pecola didn't know about Cleopatra's decorating penchant and assumed the three items had been stolen.

"...Cleopatra? Where's the Spanish leather humidor? The crocodile embossed one that sits on our bedroom table. The one between the two couches? It has Carlos' initials on it!" Pecola was slightly hysterical.

"Girl, I put that in the library. I read in a book one time that men smoke cigars in the library. I thought Carlos would like it down there better, Pecola," she said in a calm light voice.

Pecola took a deep breath. "Honeychile, he has a huge oak humidor in the library over in the corner. It doesn't look like one until you open it up. Those cigars are kept up here in case he wants to take a smoke in the bedroom, chile." Pecola breathed deeply again. "Did you move my Louis XVI chair, and Ming Dynasty temple guard? I keep the guard in the foyer—to help protect my family's life and the afterlife of my other family members," Pecola explained in an exasperated voice.

"Your life and your family's afterlife? Girl, you know that's God's job to do that. Not an old statue," Cleopatra giggled pleasantly as she shook her head. "Yeah, I moved those things as well. I placed them *all* in the library, too. It made such a nice, unusual setting. Go look and see, Pecola. I bet you'll agree with me."

"Cleopatra, chile. Puhleeze don't move things around. Just clean, puhleeze," Pecola reminded in a kind voice. "Just clean, girl. Don't be creative. Ok?"

Pecola laughed to herself as she considered that first incident. If Pecola was honest, she was just simply glad to see that Cleopatra hadn't taken the three things home. However, Pecola's request that Cleopatra squelch her decorating ambitions went unheeded. And to this day, Cleopatra continually moved pieces of accessories around the houses she cleaned whenever she got good and ready.

Pecola glanced out of the tinted black windows of the limousine. With two men from the fish market carrying extremely large boxes behind her, Pecola noticed how Cleopatra daintily stepped out the fish store door. In typical Alex, ladylike fashion, Cleopatra slid back into the car and checked off the last item on the list.

"I'm sorry it took so long, Pecola," she apologized as she wrote a quick note on the white legal paper and closed the burgundy Cambridge planner. "Alex ordered so much fish and crabs that by the time I got through speaking with Charles and Virginia, I was thoroughly confused. I had to call Alex and double check on things. But we finally got it worked out."

"That's good."

Cleopatra took a deep breath and turned around to watch the men load the fish in the trunk.

"Are you ok, girl?" Cleopatra was smiling and talking to her like Alex would.

Pecola turned to stare into her face briefly and flashed a genuine smile. "Yes, I'm fine, chile. I was just thinking about the good time we'll have tonight frying fish and listening to the old school jams, Cleo." Pecola rested her head against the leather seat to take the twenty-minute ride to Advance.

Miss Jessica walked up and placed a large glass of sweetened ice tea on the gazebo table. Symone finished swimming over ninety minutes ago. After she relaxed in the Jacuzzi a while, that helped her weary spirit. A slightly rejuvenated Symone decided to read a few more pages of *The Prophet* before she went back inside.

"Sugar, this was the first glass I poured from the fresh new pitcher I made. I placed a few more lemons in it this time," Miss Jessica explained as she removed the other empty glass, the sparse mango remnants, and placed them on the wicker tray she held in her hands.

"Thanks so much, Miss Jessica." Symone laughed lightly. She was in a much better mood than when Miss Jessica came out to tell her that Scott called. "I'm sorry for snapping at you earlier."

"Don't worry about a thang, baby. You know your Miss Jessica don't think nothing of it. Don't you know that by now?"

"I do." Somewhat embarrassed, Symone glanced down at her hands.

"Would you like another mango, Symone?"

"No. That was the last one, Miss Jessica. I declare it was good though. Maybe I'm homesick or something. I don't know. There's nothing like mangoes from Trinidad, but that one was pretty close. You know how Ameenah is. My sister made sure I brought a bunch of them back here from my trip to New York on Monday."

"And you ate all of them, sugar?"

"No, Miss Jessica." Symone laughed quickly. "I took a few to Pecola, Alex, and Scott. Didn't you eat a couple of them, too?"

"Sugar, I sure did. They were good, too." She paused briefly to watch Symone. "Now sugar, do you think you should be sitting out here in this here hot sun especially since you said you weren't feeling well, baby?"

"I'm fine, Miss Jessica. It's not so bad under the gazebo. I'm just a little tired. There's a lot on my mind."

"Sugar, I done told you about stretching your brain sooo much. It'll cause wrinkles on that pretty face. That's what you took today off for. You haven't rested one bit. I saw you in your bedroom working on that computer and writing since seven o'clock this morning. You work too hard, baby."

"I was working on my presentation for tomorrow at Alex's house. That did take a lot out of me," she admitted with a bittersweet grin.

Symone sipped several swallows of tea, and the ice rattled in the glass. She smiled as she thought about the maternal warnings from her housekeeper.

"Mmmm. Oh, Miss Jessica. This tea is absolutely delicious."

Miss Jessica nodded proudly and smiled. "I know it is, sugar. I put just a wee bit more sugar in it this time. Just the way you like it. I started not to do that since it's so hot and all. Too much sugar in this heat will rush to your head, make you sick, and fall out."

Miss Jessica placed the tray down on the table. She pressed her left palm against Symone's forehead and shook her head heavily as if she believed that Symone had a temperature of one- hundred and ten.

"Sugar, you feel real, real hot. It's probably time for you to come on inside, baby."

Symone appreciated the motherly gesture and waved her hand in a casual manner.

"I'm fine. Really I am." She noticed that Miss Jessica had finally changed from her white uniform and apron.

Miss Jessica wore a rose-colored elastic waist knit dress, stockings, and open toed flat shoes. No matter if it were a hundred plus degrees outside, as long as Miss Jessica was going to take a trip, she wore taupe colored stockings that were too light for her caramel complexioned legs. They always made her legs look ashy.

"You look very nice," Symone complimented in a pleasant voice. She rattled her ice and took another sip of tea.

"Thanks, sugar. I guess I better be heading on home to Wilmington. I got to stop at Alex and Madison's first. I promised them they would have the banana puddings I made for tonight. I thought you could take them over there. Since you're not going to attend the opening dinner, I decided I would go ahead and take care of it." She offered Symone a wide smile. "You know how Maddy loves my banana pudding, sugar. I made six large casserole dishes for him, and all them children they're serving tonight."

Symone swallowed more tea and grinned slightly as she eyed Miss Jessica with an amused expression.

"Now you know I done took a section out for you. It's in the green covered bowl on the first shelf in the refrigerator. Since you said you weren't feeling good, I changed your bedding again. I put on the prettiest embroidered sheets and comforter, too. I wanted to brighten your spirits up a bit. You know the sea coral, floral one?"

Symone nodded her head yes.

"And, I sprinkled some of my good smelling talc all over it, too. You know the ones my little girls love for their Miss Jessica to put on their bed?" Symone nodded yes again. "Well, I put the same on yours, sugar. Might make you think you're a little girl again too in Trinidad."

Symone hastily shook her head. "I certainly don't need to think about being a small girl again."

"That's right, sugar. I plum forgot. You sure don't want to visit those days again." She spoke to Symone's sad eyes. "You want me to change that music, sugar? I done heard those same three albums so much myself, I believe I can drag your big old grand piano outside and play the songs now," she joked with a long throaty laugh as she checked her watch.

"No, they're fine." Symone grinned a little smile, too. "The jazz sounds relaxed my mind a whole lot. I'll turn them off when I go inside."

"I didn't cook anything for you cause I just knew you would be at Alex and Maddy's. So you're sure you'll be fine until Sunday when I get back?"

"Of course I will, Miss Jessica. You know that."

"I know. I know. I just worry 'bout you. That's all. Anyway Symone, give me a sugar. I'll see you on Sunday evening, baby. Ok?"

Symone kissed and tightly hugged the older woman. Miss Jessica picked the tray up off the table and turned to walk away.

"Miss Jessica—?"

She stopped walking and slowly whirled around to watch her.

"Yes, sugar."

"I love you," Symone said under her breath. "Thanks for everything."

"You welcome, baby."

"Don't forget Ora Mae's birthday gifts are in the front closet. I put the children's toys in the van for you. Alex said that those games were a hit with Purity and Trey. You know my two girls enjoy playing with them, too."

Miss Jessica smiled to herself while she considered the generosity of Symone to her entire family down in Wilmington. Symone was by far the kindest, most generous employer she had ever done domestic work for. Whenever Miss Jessica decided to visit with her family, Symone always surprised them with a van full of clothes, toys, money and whatever else she believed they needed to have.

"Remember to tell Leroy Lee that if the three suits don't fit him, all he needs to do is take them to the JC Penny's in Wilmington. Make sure you take the receipt, Miss Jessica."

"Everything is loaded in the van, sugar. I got everything you're sending. My sister and husband thank you already. I know they'll be callin' up here to let you know the same tonight," she added as she waved good-bye. After taking five more steps, she remembered something else. "Oh, baby—"

"Yes." Symone smiled and waited.

"I almost forgot to tell you this. Ameenah called. She said that she and her husband would be down at their place on Sag Harbor this weekend. Just in case you needed to call her, you would know where she was. Ok?"

"Thanks for telling me, Miss Jessica. I had planned to call my sisters and brother when I went inside. I would've gotten a little concerned if she weren't there. Thank you."

"Anytime, baby. You take care of yourself. Ok?" she said in a concerned voice again and turned to saunter inside the house. Symone watched the sweet, gentle woman walk away. She picked *The Prophet* off her lap and continued reading.

Chapter Thirty-Eight

Thirty minutes later, Symone decided it was time to go in. After she took a quick shower, she went downstairs and searched around in the kitchen for popcorn. There wasn't any, and Symone decided to go to the store and get some. She threw on a pair of royal blue shorts, a white sleeveless midriff top, sandals, and a Hampton University Pirates baseball cap. As she was leaving for the grocery store, the phone rang. She raced back from the garage door to answer it.

"Good afternoon." Her voice was flat.

"Hel-loo, Symone. My special, baby."

Symone recognized Orlando Kelly's voice immediately, and she took a long, deep quiet breath. She had run into guys who were ok lovers. Then, there was Orlando Buster Kelly, III. Simply put, he wanted to screw her brains out, and that was ok especially at a time like this. There certainly was a place for men like him, and once in a while "touch up" was all she needed. It was just a wonderful screw, but it was the type of sex that ruined a woman if she got it too often.

This brother kissed, licked, and ate pussy for a good forty-five minutes. Simply unbelievable. One time Orlando licked her so hard and soft, that four orgasms racked her body. It was so intense that Symone actually felt a drugged euphoria. It was like she floated out of her body. When she came back to reality, Orlando was on the side of the bed looking at her and asking her if she were satisfied. Orlando, big, tall, bronze "sex machine" was the consummate lover. Electrifying touches. Soulful lover. And, that even wasn't an accurate description. Orlando was a connoisseur at the art of sucking pussy. All of these thoughts zoomed through her mind when she heard his voice repeat her name.

"Are you there, baby?"

"Ummm-hmmm. I'm here, Orlando."

"Good. I'm so glad you're home. It's me again."

I know that, she thought. "I was just thinking about what I had to do when you called."

"Are you busy, baby?" he asked softly and prayed that she wasn't.

"I was heading out to the grocery store. Why you want to know?" she asked, but she knew the answer.

I thank you, Lord! I thank you, Lord! Symone thought and felt like dancing a jig. The shooting star prayer was finally answered. As she heard Chubby Checker's animated words float through her ears, she felt like dancing the twist.

"I want you to come to my condo tonight, baby. Maybe I can come to your house. Whatever works for you," he propositioned with his voice trailing off.

"Orlando, I don't know if I can do that this evening."

"Why not? Are your children at home?" He was disappointed, and she heard it in his voice. "You're too busy for me?"

"Why not? Because I said so. I'm busy." *Remember, Symone,* she told herself. *Please play hard to get with this man.* "I've a major speech to make tomorrow afternoon. And, *no* my children aren't here. It's the summertime, and you know they're in Trinidad."

"That's right. I forgot. If you'd allow me to see your beautiful Black ass more often, I'd remembered those minute details about your life." He hesitated a moment. "You say you got a presentation on Saturday afternoon?"

"That's right. I'm an entrepreneur. Remember? I work all the time. Just like preachers," she replied smugly.

"Symone, even preachers don't work everyday. They just act like they do, baby. Maybe I can give you the energy you need for your presentation. What you think about that?" He laughed.

Symone thought about that idea briefly. She had no other plans for this evening. Miss Jessica would be in Wilmington until Sunday. One thing about Orlando, brotherman was an excellent, pleasure freak. Feeling a little stressed, she toyed with the possibility of enjoying his exquisite, vagina tongue spanking and lovemaking this evening. She expected no less from him.

Orlando wasn't the type of man Symone would take out to a social function or take home to Mummy. People wouldn't understand. Symone didn't even understand sometimes. Orlando was young. Too young to appear in public with her. Symone wondered if people would assume he was her son. And Orlando's conversation was geared only toward spiritual matters. Although he was an exceptional partner for her, Symone realized a woman kept such relationships like that behind closed doors. Since Orlando was an exercise freak and worked out in the gym every day, one thing Orlando could do was show his body and make hard, hour-long lasting love. When Symone thought about it, that was exactly what she needed.

"Talk to me, baby. I'm waiting to hear a word. What do you think about me loving you this evening, Symone?" His voice was whispy, sexy, and urgent. He wanted her, and that turned him on even more.

"Ok. Ok. Give me a few hours and come to my house. What you got in mind for this evening?" she asked in a sexy voice.

"I want to be your one-hundred and fifty percent freak for the evening. I thought about freaking and thought about you, baby."

"Good."

Orlando thought for a second and checked his watch. "First, I've a pastor and deacon board meeting I must attend at six. I should be done by eight p.m. Is nine ok?"

"Nine is fine," Symone replied almost too quickly.

It was amazing how Orlando always figured out when to call her. Especially when she was in need of the raw loving only he could give. After Arman, he would be a breath of fresh air. Plus, she still had a lot of guilt about going to bed with that other male creep. Her last resort since Orlando was out of town at a family reunion. It definitely was past time for Symone to receive a sexual lube job from someone else—from someone she could enjoy freely.

Orlando smiled. "Tell me how to get to your house again, baby." She could hear the pleasure in his voice.

"You call me up to come screw me, and you can't remember how to get to my house? I can't believe this, Orlando. Just track it by my pussy radar."

"Damn straight. Your pussy is damn good enough to track by radar, baby. But I can't read radar signs. If you let me visit your ass more often, I would know how to get to your house. You know I don't have a sense of direction either," he laughed into the line.

"Uh huh."

"Still, I can't wait to see you, Symone. I'm backed up baby—real bad. Terribly bad. I need a good release like you. My tongue is ready for you too, baby. I mean real ready. When I get there, all I want you to do is open your legs, so that I can look at your pussy. Let my eyes get some loving, and I plan to suck you dry." He paused briefly, nodded his head, and licked his lips. "Yeah, that's exactly what I want to do with you tonight."

His words radiated erotic heat, and Symone could feel her crotch throbbing in anticipation of Orlando's visit. She gave him the directions to Clemmons again. By now, she was ready to meet him halfway. As far as Symone was concerned, they could do it in his car along I-40.

"Bring some condoms, Orlando," she reminded as always.

"*Condoms a damn gain?* You know I like to make love without them, baby."

"We go through this every time. I understand how you feel. I don't like them either. But, I haven't seen you in about what—three months. No glove, no love, baby."

Symone thought about contracting AIDS and tried to push that possibility to the back of her mind. It was a reality she wanted to avoid. Symone held her breath while he considered the demand for a moment.

"That's fine, Symone. If that's what you want, I'll do anything for you. You know that. So is that what you want, baby?"

Symone breathed easier and smiled into the phone. "Yeah, that's what I want." *Who knows where he has been? I know where I've been,* Symone thought. *AIDS is some scary shit. I don't want to go out—at least not like that—even though I know that eventually I'm going to die. Sure, Orlando's beef stick is extremely nice. With a condom on, you can still get the entire busto. Damn!* Symone was getting excited just thinking about it.

"Symone, baby?" he spoke huskily.

"Yes, Orlando?" She was getting hornier and hornier by the minute.

"I'll be there around nine. Make sure you have on my favorite creme-colored bikinis, garters, and sleek high heels, baby. No bra. Ok? I want to see your pretty, Black titties as soon as you open the door."

"Ok, Orlando. I'll see you then, and you'll see them then. I know this will be a great evening. I'll see you in a few hours." She hung up the phone, not giving him a chance to say anything else. Symone wanted the entire conversation to sound more like a business transaction rather than a rendezvous. That was how she was able to keep her emotional distance from him. Once again, she realized it didn't work.

During the week, Orlando Buster Kelly, III was employed as a medical salesman for Karamu Pharmaceutical Company of Greensboro, North Carolina. It was always Symone's fantasy to have a young, tenderoni boy toy stud, and he was the perfect one for such a dream. Orlando was twenty-four years old and had been working in Greensboro for three months when Symone stumbled upon him two years ago.

Orlando was fresh out of college then. A Virginia Union graduate where he pledged Alpha Phi Alpha, he was Mr. Black and Gold all the way. Orlando was a very tall, truly dark-skinned man with a neat haircut and a full jet black, curly beard. Except for his age, Orlando was absolutely her type. Of course, he was muscular and a truly impeccable dresser which made his blue chip stock ratings soar up in Symone's mind even more. To Symone, it was just something about a Black man who could dress well.

Since their Papa loved to dress fashionably, Symone's sister, Hazele, often declared that all three Poussaint girls got such male standards from him. Symone didn't know where it came from. All she knew was if there was a tall, dark-skinned, Black man on the loose, if he dressed nicely, if he was smart, and if he could speak intelligently on a wide variety of subjects, then he had po-ten-tial.

That was Orlando. Originally from Alabama, he and his family moved to Greensboro when he was eight. Orlando's father was a preacher. His grandfather was a preacher, and Orlando willingly followed in their footsteps and became one, too. He had been preaching since he was ten years old, and was now the pastor of a medium sized Pentecostal church in Greensboro. However, his call to the ministry and his responsibility to preach to his congregation of over three-hundred and fifty members each and every Sunday didn't prevent him from needing to be with a sexually uninhibited woman.

Symone assumed that she was the secret super freak Orlando needed, especially since he had to be discreet. She wasn't talking. He damn sure wasn't either. But it worked out for both of them. He was the private distraction for Symone. A spectacular, excellent freaky one at that.

Orlando definitely satisfied any sexual fantasies she considered. That's where it ended. They weren't in love, or at least she wasn't in love with him. She didn't want him to love her, either. She was petrified about getting too attached to him or his penis, so she tried to treat his wonderful lovemaking like a business meeting. The only difference was she wasn't making any money from the deal, and he wasn't a perspective Fortune 500 client for Meetings Odyssey. Symone merely enjoyed every minute she was with him. That was all. Yet, she remained afraid of him. The way he talked to her. The way he loved her body. Looked at her. His gentleness. His understanding of life which was way beyond his twenty-four years. It frightened her. How he made her body easily talk back to his superb sexing and made it reply to his sensual, inquisitive love questions. Symone told Hazele that he was the ultimate gentle giant. Not only in height but also within his heart.

So Symone kept her distance and only called Orlando when it was categorically, absolutely necessary for her to do so. Then Orlando and she would meet wherever she told him to, or he would come to Clemmons. Long lasting lovemaking would follow. The kind that left imprints all over her body. When it was over, she wanted it to be over. They had a lot of fun in their secret space. Laughed and talked together on a wide range of subjects, too. Danced naked in the moonlight. But she refused to release herself to him.

Hazele was right as usual. Hazele told Symone that she was afraid of Orlando. That Symone was. She was afraid of what would happen if she truly revamped her thinking and readily accepted him as a man, not just a much younger man to play with. Not just a man who was almost sixteen years younger than she was. Symone was afraid to accept him as a potential male candidate who could possibly change her life if she gave him and herself the proper opportunity. Even though Symone realized that Orlando diligently tried to pierce her hard shell each and every chance they were together, Symone steeled herself and refused to totally succumb to his charming ways. If he were a few years older, maybe she would.

Symone shared the sexual rendezvous moments with no one in North Carolina. Not even Pecola, Scott, and Alex were aware of these little escapades with this man. Only her sister Hazele knew, but she lived in New York. Orlando was Symone's little North Carolina secret discovery. Her Flintstones Vitamins for every quarter, and she certainly was going to keep it that way. The good thing about it was he wasn't required to take classes from Symone Angela Poussaint University. He was a professor at the same school. As a matter of fact, Orlando taught the doctoral thesis classes there.

Symone felt her body throb again with expectation. She rationalized why was she doing this. Was it for the orgasm? Probably. The only way she experienced an orgasm was through oral sex, and Orlando was the Grammy winner for that category. He didn't mind doing it. She certainly did not mind having it done. Why not let him come over? Sometimes, she believed she was similar to the Black woman in Spike Lee's movie, *She's Gotta Have It.* She realized and accepted the fact she needed a good lay every so often.

Everyone does. Both males and females. Whether folks want to acknowledge it or not, they get that urge. I must confess there ain't nothing like a down-right, get down dirty, walk the floor, do the dog, let's holler, and tie me up screwing session. I don't mind owning up to it. I gotta admit it to myself, Symone thought with a wonderfully loud laugh.

Until she found someone with those same sexual qualifications that she was willing to fall in love with—to release her mind and soul with, Orlando would continue to service her with pleasure. To pick up a few items, Symone raced to 5-Star Supermarket. She quickly returned home to take a vinegar douche and a hot, perfumed, Jacuzzi bubble bath.

Chapter Thirty-Nine

When Symone returned from Winston-Salem, she popped and ate two bowls of popcorn. Afterwards, she placed lighted candles all around the Jacuzzi and poured herself a glass of chilled Chardonnay. While Symone relaxed and meditated in the warmth of the hot Jacuzzi water, she listened to the sounds of the international folk singer, Odetta. Finally, it was time to scrub herself with African black soap. She soaked her body. The water made her skin feel soft, supple. Afterwards, she massaged her body with a mixture of fragrant oils and shea butter.

At eight-forty five p.m., Orlando rang the bell. Symone opened the door exactly the way he requested. Garters and all. She put on a pair of creme elbow length satin gloves to enhance the outfit. Before she closed the door and even had a chance to activate the alarm system, he began to flick his tongue along her back as he enjoyed the scrumptious taste and smell of her body.

"Just look at you, with your fine chocolate ass. You're just too fine for your own damn good, girl," Orlando exclaimed in a husky voice as he began sucking her breasts while she rubbed his hair.

"Oooh, Orlando."

"Your titties are perfect and overflowing all over the place." His voice was muffled. Orlando sucked her nipples like he was starving. He stopped to tenderly savor them with his hungry stare. Very serenely, he idly glided his hands around the full shape of each breast. To make them stick out even more and appear fuller, Symone straightened her shoulders.

"You like them?"

"As always, they're gorgeous, baby," he mumbled as he began to suck them again.

"Damn. Damn. That feels great, Orlando," Symone groaned.

"Your personal freak is back, baby. I'm back in full living color."

"I know, Orlando. Freak me anyway you want to, baby."

"I plan to, baby. Just like you like it. I plan to do just that," he breathed hotly on her nipples. "You know I'll do anything for you. I'll freak you the way you want to be freaked, how you say you want to be freaked, when you want to be freaked, and wherever you want to be freaked. You know that, baby. Your ass gots to know that by now."

Symone gave him a contented smile with a deep sigh. Gently, he laid her down on the sweeping staircase steps. Symone propped her elbows on one step, and her high-heeled feet on the bottom ones. As she smiled and licked her lips in anticipation, she watched him take off his clothes. Orlando hastily removed his tailored navy suit, suspenders, cuff links, white linen shirt, waving stripe imported silk twill tie, boxer shorts, socks, and shoes. Then he pounced upon her like a sleek Jaguar.

While Orlando moaned from the pleasurable taste of her skin, he tongued her entire body with little licks and tiny kisses. He helped her to straddle her legs over his shoulders, and she placed both her hands on his head. He kissed and sucked her pussy for what seemed like a blissful eternity. Symone felt on fire with ecstasy. She screamed his name over and over as she savored every excruciating wonderful sensation his tongue spanking provided.

Symone counted it. Three damn times. She climaxed three times, and he was still caressing, licking.

"Woooo, baby! Uh, baby," she breathed hard trying to talk intelligently. She was too weak to speak.

"Hmmm, Symone." He eyed her through her legs but didn't stop. "Delicious, baby."

"Uh, Orlando. Do you think we can go upstairs now and get—uh—on my bed?" Symone asked slowly. She was out of breath. Her eyes were half-open as she was still savoring the superb passionate packed feelings his tongue provided. Lying on the stairs in such a way could hurt her back. He was a young thing, but she was almost forty.

"What do you want to do?"

"Let's go upstairs, puhleeze."

"Sure, baby," he mumbled between nibbles. Delight was in his eyes as he enjoyed her chocolate body.

"Lawd, thanks."

Orlando left hand reached for the banister, and he rose to his feet. Kissing her toes several times, he reached for her right hand to pull her toward him.

"Let me carry you, baby."

"You're sure?"

"I asked you, didn't I?"

Orlando easily hoisted Symone in his arms. Even though she thought she was too heavy to be picked up, he wasn't even breathing hard. Carefully, he climbed the long winding staircase. With her arms wrapped around his neck, he walked slowly. It seemed that with each step he took, he lovingly kissed some part of her face.

"Symone, I love making love to you." He breathed into her hair. "I love your body, too."

"How the hell can that be, Orlando?" she asked, almost shyly. "You know I'm kind of overweight."

He shook his head quickly. "You're just fine, baby. Black women need to realize that they're not shaped like magazine models. Like those damn European white women they splash all over television and magazines that are sooo thin with no ass. They look like Q-tips. A round head with a stick underneath it."

"You're sooo funny, but you sound like my brother. He calls them lollipops."

"He's right. Black women aren't like that. My Black women have full bodies with big luscious asses."

"Ohhh, Orlando."

"I'm serious. That's beautiful to me. Makes me want to take a bite out of them." His voice was soulfully soothing. "I believe my Black women are wonderful, no matter if they're full-size, half-size, and big size. It doesn't matter, baby. You remember my lady I told you about? Ursula Gibbons? She was the one who wanted me to marry her? I dated her for three years at Virginia Union? Member?"

"Yes," she said laughingly. "Hell, after knowing you for just two years, I can see why she wanted you to marry her. Especially if you made love to her like this."

"I did it with her the exact same way. Total satisfaction for her and for me. Of course, I got a little more experience under my belt," he bragged in a pleasant voice.

With her arms wrapped around his neck, he continued to slowly saunter up the steps.

"Orlando, you probably blew her mind, baby."

"Well, I don't know about all of that. I done told you before how she was a tall, buxom mama. A thoroughly, voluptuously full-figured one, too. Much bigger than you, and I picked her up, too. Now that always blew her mind. As long as they have a good heart just like yours," he said as he nuzzled his face in her hair.

Symone again blushed at the compliment. He always told her that she had an enormous, tender heart. That she was a compassionate person with great sensitivity toward other people, and that was one of her most fiercely guarded secrets—especially since she desperately tried to keep it hidden from the world. But Orlando said that since God blessed him with the spiritual gift of discernment, he could tell those things about her.

"...That's the most important thing, baby. Their hearts," he added quickly. "And, just give me some meat to feel on. I don't want a flat-ass woman who is skinnier than six o'clock. Nah. That's not for me, baby. I want my woman to have some meat on her bones. My mother is a full-size, plump lady. Mama is just fine. So are my sisters. That's how they make Black women back in Leeds, Alabama. I'm a country boy at heart. Back in Alabama, women got that kind of stuff on their bodies, baby."

"You're a trip, Orlando." Symone rested her head against his left shoulder. They reached the upstairs hallway.

"No, I'm nothing but the truth. When I look at that magazine that feature the people voted the fifty most beautiful people in the world, I ask myself, according to whose standards? Who are they going by? Who the hell voted? When I open the damn magazine up and see two skinny ass Black women, a few white boys and forty bone thin white women, I know whose standards they are. White folks' standards. White folks' images, girl."

"You're right."

"It's certainly not mine. They didn't ask me for my vote," he said in such a matter of fact tone. "It's unbelievable, baby. Supposedly, those women are supposed to be the elite of the elite. Hell, where? What that says to me is that the people who voted have a very disturbing and distorted opinion about everyone else whose not shaped like that."

Symone giggled at his comments. He stopped walking and began to slowly twirl around in the wide hallway for a few moments. Symone held onto his neck even tighter. With each twirl, he kissed her forehead. Orlando had the uncanny ability to continually make her feel like such a small girl. A very protected small girl. He began walking again.

"Now somebody like the sistah you showed me in those two movies that time. She would definitely get my vote. You know the one you said that was born in Winston-Salem. She was a statuesque beauty. I'm trying to figure out if they have a current Black movie star that even looks like they might be in her league nowadays. What's her name again, baby?"

"Oh, I know, baby. You're talking about Pam Grier."

He stopped walking and thought for a moment. "Yeah, I believe you're right. That's the one. Now she was awesome to behold in those movies, baby."

"You mean *Coffy* and *Get Foxy Brown*. The ones I showed you the last time you were here.

"Yes," he breathed quickly. The twirling made him a little tired. "I thought she was a fine Black goddess. Not as fine as you, though. But the sistah was tough, Symone."

"I agree with you on that, Orlando. She did have a nice body. Very curvy."

"Well, my Ursula kinda looks like her, too. Same complexion. Is shaped the exact same way—just like her. Add a whole bunch of meat to the curves, baby. That was Ursula Gibbons, baby. Every bodacious bit of her."

"Orlando, you're too wild. You always talk about her. It seems like she meant a lot to you, baby. It's a shame yall broke up."

"No, it wasn't, but she did mean a lot to me. She needed to grow up some more and pick up a little more maturity that only life could give her. I don't hate we broke up. Cause if I was dating her, I never would've messed with you. Only date one woman at a time, baby."

"That's a damn good trait to have."

"I think it is, too. I learned that from my father and my granddaddy. Cause now that's what they told me. They both were a one-woman man before they got married. I can only go by what they told me." Orlando laughed happily. "Symone baby, what's the name of that song? I tell you I can't think of it. My memory is off tonight. Must be because I hear your body calling me," he joked lightly and paused a moment and thought about the song.

"Which song?" Symone giggled again.

"I believe it's titled *Baby Got Back*."

"Yeah, by Sir Mix-A-Lot."

"Uh huh. That's exactly what I want my baby to have. Back. She got to have plenty enough of it too. A juicy, chocolate back where I can set a damn dinner plate on it. Then I can sit down, eat some collards greens, potato salad, and pig feet off of it if I feel like it."

Symone burst out laughing once more. "You're too crazy, Orlando."

"I know, baby. In order to be a preacher, you got to be a little crazy. Cause hard-headed and hardhearted deacons along with other church folk are a stone trip to deal with, baby."

"I can imagine."

"Listen to me, baby. Along with the bodacious back, I want my woman to have a fat front, too. The biggest titties in all of God's creation. That's why I love your pretty black titties, babies. They're awesome. Beautiful. Like an exquisite, priceless sculpture. Lawd have mercy, help me somebody. I need some help here," he exclaimed in a preacher sounding voice.

They both laughed loudly as he walked through the bedroom door. Gracefully, he placed her in the middle of the bed. With his large hands clasped behind his head, he watched her. He kept his white sleeveless, undershirt on especially for her. She always told him that she loved looking at his chocolate muscular broad shoulders against the white Hanes 100% cotton shirt. He slowly removed it and tossed it over his head. He carefully removed her gloves, high heels, garters, and stockings, savoring each touch.

"Making love is emotional, Symone. It's an ultimate spiritual experience for me, baby," he touchingly explained as he always did before he made love to her.

"I know, Orlando."

"There's nothing more inviting than the wide opened legs of a woman. It's nothing more beautiful than the moaning and groaning of a Black man and a Black woman making love, baby." His sex hungry gazed locked onto her eyes. "God is wonderful. Isn't he, baby?"

"Yesss, Orlando."

"God made the body in a stupendous way. New climaxes are like treasures waiting to be discovered. When you came over and over and over again on the stairs, I know it felt like the climaxes were just as great as your first one, but more phenomenal than the last one. It's truly amazing for me to have your clit tremble in my mouth," he said the last five words even more softly as he walked over to the bar and got some ice.

"For me too, Orlando."

Slowly, he teased her body with ice cubes for a few minutes. Then he eased into bed and resumed the position he was in on the steps.

Orlando's absolutely right about this climax thing, Symone thought with a fulfilled smile. *I believe having him love me with his lips is the most wonderful, spectacular feeling I've ever experienced in my life. Damn! Damn! Damn! This feels sooo damn good.*

Still screaming his name, Symone stretched her arms above her head and glared at the elaborate fabric of the trestle bed. The ambiance of the huge and cozy bedroom reeked of fulfilling romance. Five minutes before he came to her house, Symone had placed Black Love scented candles on several surfaces of furniture throughout the bedroom, and their soft light still danced in the semi-darkened room. When the doorbell chimed to announce Orlando's arrival, she inserted several Grover Washington CDs, and Mr. Washington and his boys were blowing melodious jazz sounds throughout the room.

Finally, she wasn't sure how much later, Orlando began kissing her thigh and slowly crawled up to her mouth where they tongue kissed. Symone rolled him over on his back. She licked his body from his feet to his ears, nibbled, and munched on his ass. Then, she made sure to suck his toes, ankles, knees, neck, ears, nipples, every inch of his cocoa skin, and especially his hard penis for long luscious moments. Her petal soft tongue movements mesmerized him. Once again, he was overcome by her sexual expertise.

In spite of the fact Symone wouldn't let Orlando see her often, he knew he had it bad. It was a serious longing. An awesome Love Jones for her. But he knew she was always careful. Distant. He wished she would open up to him even though he realized it wasn't going to happen. At least not right now. She was too poised for that. Yet, Orlando knew that he had fallen in love with her anyway. As he repeatedly whispered Symone's name, she meticulously showered loving affection upon his body while he ran his fingers through her hair. Then it was time for him to enter her.

"Whoa, Orlando! Wait a minute, puhleeze!" She suddenly realized he didn't have on his condom. Orlando appeared puzzled and hurt.

"Uh, baby. What's wrong, Symone?" he asked, breathing hard.

"We forgot the condom, Orlando," she added out of breath, still trying to scoot out of the way of his nice size penis, which continued to bob against her upper thigh.

"Aw, baby. It's all the way downstairs in the foyer with my clothes. Do I have to go get it now? Damn! We're right in the thick of things, Symone. With all the kissing and sucking we did to each other, what difference does it make anyway? Our body love juices are flowing all over the damn place. The sheet is wet as hell."

"And—" She wouldn't budge.

"I got to go get it now?" he asked in an exasperated voice.

"Did I stutter?" she replied, squeezing her legs together at the knees. "I don't have any up here. You're not getting between my legs without a rubber, baby. That's final."

"Symone, baby? I don't make love with no one else but you," he admitted truthfully. "You know I can't be all over the place. My church reputation in Greensboro would be ruined. Honestly, baby."

"I'm honest and serious, too, Orlando. You're a good one, but I'm not that crazy. I like living better," she explained with a short laugh.

Good wasn't even the right word to describe him. The brother was stellar, exceptional, powerful, fabulous, and in a league of his own. Right stupendous, Symone thought to herself.

"Come on, Symone."

"No! You come on. I've already told you, Orlando. No condom. No pussy. Period."

Orlando mumbled a few curse words and went downstairs to retrieve the condoms. He returned to the bedroom with one on. When he entered her, she tightly wrapped her legs around his behind. Very gently, he moved around in her being sure to caress and kiss her breasts with each sensual movement. Together, they watched his penis pump in and out of her.

"...You like that? You like looking at it go in and out of you, baby? You like that, Symone baby?"

"Yesss, Orlando. Yes I do like that. I like all of that, baby. All of you, baby."

They especially enjoyed reveling in that sexual position. Then their bodies carefully began to rhythmically grind together, gently, slowly, and tenderly at first until it built to a wild pace.

Orlando would suddenly stop pumping, ease out of her, push her legs up, and suck her pussy some more. He did that repeatedly. The thoroughness of his lovemaking drove her crazy. She hollered and moaned continuously. While the two lovers frantically pounded their bodies into each other, their tongues danced furiously, and they talked dirty into the other's ears. By the time they were finished two hours later, Symone's bed sheets and comforter was on the floor. Although Symone never climaxed when she had intercourse, it was still an exceptionally excellent lovemaking session for her. Exactly what she needed from him.

Chapter Forty

Once Symone caught her breath, she wriggled out of Orlando's overwhelming, affectionate embrace. She jumped up and went into the bathroom. Slowly, she wiped herself down and stared at her reflection in the mirror. Just as quickly, she looked away from it. She ran the water extra hot and prepared a warm towel for Orlando. She wiped him off, too. He thanked her several times for her kind, gentle ways and kissed the back of each hand.

Symone walked back into the bathroom and rested the damp towel on the Jacuzzi. Then, she returned to the bed and slid into a bright lemon colored, silk paisley robe. She walked to the French doors and opened them. It was time for her to breathe in the clear, fresh summer night air. Carefully, she walked out on the terrace, leaned against the steel railing, and looked at the lighted swimming pool. The air was still humid and hot. As she listened to the cricket peals of sounds in the night, she wondered how the evening went at the Devereauxs' house.

"Come on back to bed, Symone. Come on, so we can cuddle up, baby."

Orlando inserted a Sonny Rollins CD and hummed along to the melodious saxophone sounds. A smiling Orlando took the time to fix the damp bedding back the exact way it looked when he got upstairs and saw the romantic bedroom. With his head in the palm of his hands, he rested comfortably in the middle of the bed with his legs crossed at the knees and let his eyes travel all over the gorgeous bedroom. Pale blue billowing, floor length silk draperies hung from ornate iron rods. Lovely French antique pieces of furniture were scattered throughout. Two mahogany bookshelves were jammed pack with Symone's stellar collection of African-American books. Orlando always noticed that books were everywhere—throughout the entire home. The books that weren't on the shelves in her bedroom were positioned like building blocks atop the mahogany and marble coffee table in front of the linen covered sofa.

Orlando stopped eyeing the magnificent room and drew a deep breath. He was also thinking about what she would fix for the two of them to eat this time. She always threw some Trinidadian snack together for him to taste.

"Symone, I was just thinking about the West Indian treat I know you're whipping up for me tonight. Do you want me to run the hot water for us in the Jacuzzi so we can really wash each other off better, baby?"

Symone turned to glare into the dimly lit bedroom and watched him. He seemed to be enjoying himself in her bed all right. Quickly, she turned back to stare out into the darkness. As her thoughts briskly traveled to Trinidad and to her Papa, she was brooding anger. Anger at all men. She rolled her eyes and sucked her teeth. It was time for Orlando to leave. She refused to answer him.

"Come on back to bed, baby. I want to cuddle," he repeated this time with more urgency. Orlando glanced through the French doors and saw her motionless shadow and the candlelight flickering reflections of the bright yellow robe in the black, dark night.

Orlando got out of bed and sauntered to the bar to get a small bottle of mineral water from the refrigerator. Very quickly, he gulped it down. He went out on the terrace and gazed below onto the lighted backyard, too. He flipped on the terrace lamp. The level, but slightly sloped lawn was perfectly manicured and appeared as an immaculate sheet of green glass. With an island of orange and yellow marigolds along with pink, red, and white begonias growing around the massive gazebo, the area reminded Orlando of a miniature botanical garden. In the back right corner of the yard, a large ritzy playhouse and a towering, intricate wooden swing set were positioned down to the far right of the pool. Large, umbrella looking oak and maple trees dotted the sides and far end of the property. To the far left section of the yard was a tennis court. Adjacent to that was a half court basketball area.

Enclosed by a tall, black wrought iron railing, the swimming pool's turquoise water mirrored gentle ripple spots of lights from the lamps that were placed in each corner of the pool area. Royal blue and white floral cushion chairs and chaise lounges were strategically sitting at poolside. *No doubt to signify Hampton's colors,* Orlando thought with a smile. To provide privacy in the back, a five-foot tall sculptured hedge of red top shrubbery was wrapped around the edges of the entire four-acre lot.

Orlando inhaled deeply. "It's truly beautiful out here, Symone. I know I say this every time I come. But you have a lovely, lovely home, baby," Orlando said as he moved to stand behind her.

Symone ignored his compliment. Gently, he hugged her waist and kissed each side of her shoulder. The gesture made her skin feel filthy and feel as if there were five convicted sex abusers with their dirty and invasive fifty fingers crawling on her skin. Symone viciously shrugged out of the affectionate embrace and stomped away to stand in another place on the terrace. Her hair was slightly disheveled around her face, and she held onto the wrought iron rail for a second.

"What's wrong, baby?" he asked in a confused voice as he looked into her wild-eyed expression. "Did I do something?"

"No, Orlando. You didn't do a damn ting. That's the sad part about all this shit," she mumbled under her breath.

"What you say, Symone?"

"Nutting. It's not that important."

"What is it, baby?"

"I'm tired. I'm just tinking about my speech for tomorrow afternoon. That's all."

"We've known each other for two years, Symone. Why won't you let me get any closer to you?"

"Because I don't want you to, that's why. Not right now," she said in a mean short voice. "Not right now," she repeated with a softer tone. She was determined not to look at the hurt she knew was in his eyes and continued to glare out into the distance.

"I'm in love with you, Symone."

"No you're not, Orlando."

"Yes I am, baby."

"Babyboy, don't be. You need to go find yourself a nice, young, church-going kind of girl."

"I don't want to find a nice, young church going kind of girl, Symone. I *said* I want you." He moved closer to her and spoke with a short grin. "I see your spirit. I see your beauty. I see the love deep inside of you that I know I can strangle out of you. I love you, Symone."

She started laughing hysterically for a few moments and briefly stretched her arms behind her head. "Hell, you can't be in love with me. I don't see you that much. It's just your age, baby," she explained in a patronizing voice.

"Shooot. Nah hell, my age hasn't got a thing to do with this. Age has nothing to do with my maturity, baby. I know what I feel. Age has never been a thing with me. It's nothing but a number. If I waited to deal with women my age that had some sense, I would never go out. Wouldn't do a damn thing. But I've found you, and I want you. Totally. I'm a preacher, and I counsel people ten and twenty years older than me. Some of them are double your age and triple my age, Symone. I mean it, baby. Understand what I'm saying. I'm in love with you."

"Well, you better cut if off because I'm not in love with you, Orlando. We're fucking partners, pure and simple. That's what we said we would be to each other in the beginning. Devoted, freaky, and lifetime members of the confidential *I Love To Fuck Club*. I got too much to deal with to get caught up in a lovey dovey relationship right now, especially with a young tenderoni preacher that's pussy whipped." She turned to face him. Her eyes were distant, cold and black with anger.

"Whaaat!"

"Sometimes love and sex don't go together, baby. You hope it does. A lot of times, you get the sex without the love. That's where I am right now. I don't want to be loved, Orlando." She inhaled deeply and gazed at all the sparkling stars in the sky.

"Just try it, baby."

"Many times, I stand on this terrace and look out into the horizon. I soak in the full moon and the wonders of the starry night. I admire the gorgeous sky, and I think that I do want love. I say to myself, 'Is this all there is to life, Symone? But, Symone you have everything else, girl. You got all this fucking money. Enough to run a major city. Great friends. Real estate. Girl, you even control your own business empire. You collect expensive antiques. Priceless artwork. Hell, girl now all you need to do now is lose the extra twenty pounds. Find a good damn man. Pick out a hellatious engagement ring. Take him as a husband and have two more children, so I can have five babies just like my Mummy did.' Those are the times I believe that having a man's love is my deepest wish, and it would be the perfect answer to my problems, Orlando. My solution for happiness. My acceptance of me and who I am. I believe that's what I urgently need in my life during those times."

"I understand, Symone. I know what you're saying. Everybody in the world is looking for something to grab on to. To love, to hold tightly, and to feel fulfilled, baby."

"I'm not everybody, Orlando. I'm me. I'm Symone Angela Poussaint. I was raised to be a force in this world and to be a leader," she snapped. "But I'm tired of it all, Orlando. So much of my life is about doing things and getting things done. Forgetting. Remembering. Helping with this charity and that worthwhile cause. Having people pulling at me and talking about me for all the wrong reasons. They're always wanting things from me. Throughout it all, I'm still trying to hold all this other shit together. My companies. Being there for everybody. My family. My sanity. Sometimes I simply want to just check out of society and figure out a way to find peace. To find that quiet, calm, and happy place in my mind. I want just pure, wondrous light in the basement of my mind. Just damn peace and happiness, baby," she said in an angry voice that was eerily soft. She tried to stop herself from losing it with him as she considered the Sunday after her ninth birthday when her father raped her the first time.

"I feel you, Symone. I know."

Symone stopped speaking briefly, Orlando noticed the stony expression on her dark-skinned face. Suddenly, she laughed out loudly and looked back up at the sky. She tightened her bathrobe sash and crossed her arms defensively at her breasts.

"There are more times than not where there are times and evenings like this. When I again gaze out into the starry night and remember days like today when I don't like myself. When I don't even want to live in this body or have my mind. Times that I hate who I am. That I despise who I had to be. Loathe what I had to do long ago. Then I realize that I really don't need a relationship. I don't want the bullshit that comes with it. I really don't want love," she said, her voice hostile. She jerked her eyes away from his and continued speaking out into the night.

"Yes, you do want love, baby. Everybody does."

"I can't be loved right now, Orlando. If you truly knew who I was, I know you wouldn't want to love me. I simply want to fuck, and that's it." Her back stiffened with internal misery.

"I guess I'm like a damn man in that respect. I'm like him. Like my—," she said and stopped abruptly while shaking her head from side to side with tightly closed eyes. She refused to say her father's name. To give him credit for the way she felt about love and men.

"I learned how to treat men the way they used to treat me. How they treat women nowadays and how they treated the women I've known in the past who were close to me. How they treat their children. Men are cold, calculating, brutal, abusive, and distant. They're that way with their wives, especially to their children and definitely to themselves. They're brutal to little girls, and they do things to them that make them suffer in horrible, torturous silence for years. Most men are damn mean. Just like me." Her words were abrupt, sharp, and bitter. Her words slapped Orlando in his face.

"Symone!" he whispered desperately. "What's wrong?"

"That's why I don't want you to hold me, cuddle me, or fall in love with me, Orlando. Because I'm mean, too. You got that, Orlando? I just want you to fuck me. Then get dressed and leave me the hell alone. Just fuck me good. I'll guarantee you; I'll fuck you good back. Sure will. With pleasure. Satisfaction guaranteed is my motto. I've been fucking for a long time, baby. A very damn long time," she repeated wistfully. "Then, when we're done, I can be on my merry way. That's all I need from men right now. A good fuck." She spit the last word out at him and made it sound more obscene than it really was—than Orlando thought was even humanly possible.

"Damn!" Orlando mumbled.

"Guess what happens when men don't know how to do it right, Orlando? Don't know how to make good loving to me? The way I know I deserve. I get downright angry and tell them, too. You know why, Orlando?" He didn't answer her. "I've been taught to fuck real well by a pro. By my—" She refused to say 'by her father'. "That's what I give to men, and that's exactly what I expect in return. A good fuck."

Orlando heard the words. He received them. He accepted them, but he was too shocked to respond to them.

"Symone, what the hell is wrong with you, baby?" he finally asked after several minutes. He peered quickly at the lighted swimming pool then turned rapidly to stare at her. She ignored his gaze. "I've never seen you act or talk like this before. I know we ain't Ozzie and Harriet by no means, but there's some other shit happening here that I can't figure out."

She sucked her teeth. "Just because you're a preacher, you're not supposed to be able to figure every damn thing out," she said sarcastically and took a deep breath. "Orlando, I simply want to fuck. You need to get it, babyboy. So your ass won't get hurt real bad by this older woman, you need to listen to me. You need to get it. Understand it. Chew on it. Swallow it. Digest it. Shit it back out in your toilet for you to comprehend it. Do what the hell ever. I'm not willing to release my mind or my soul to anyone, yet. If you feel you can't deal with me under those terms, you can walk away. You need to walk away from me. You did what you were supposed to do tonight. You performed spectacularly."

"Whaaat!"

"You deserve a round of applause." She clapped her hands six times and bowed at the waist. "I thank you. Now, I got my sexual vitamins for the next ninety days or so. So you can fucking leave the premises, now," she mumbled without looking at him.

Slowly, Orlando shook his head from side to side and let out a long agonized breath.

"I've never seen you this way before. Most times, we've a lot of fun when we're together. Dancing to your Trinidadian music. Laughing. Drinking. Talking. Soaking and frolicking in the Jacuzzi together. Hell, I've always known there was a cold spot in you. That you were distant. I was aware there were several layers. Hell, a damn shell so thick I couldn't penetrate. But you were never this mean to me, Symone," he said in sad voice. "This shit you're talking ain't necessary, and I certainly don't deserve it. Save that shit for niggers who do dog you. What's wrong, Symone, baby? Do you want me to pray for you?"

Orlando was thoroughly surprised to hear Symone speak with such hostility. She whirled around to stare at him again.

"Pray for me? Hell no! Hell no, I don't want you to pray for me. How in the hell can you pray for me when you and I just committed fornication?" she hissed at him with dark eyes. "Hell no, I don't want you to pray for me. I want you to understand me. Pray for your church members who don't see this side of you. Who don't know your ass like I do. Who don't know you're a freak when you're not in a pulpit? Who don't know you fuck like a stallion and preach like a saint. Who don't know you curse like a sailor, but on Wednesdays and Sundays you belt out gospel songs like a Mahalia Jackson prodigy. Pray for them who don't know you lick pussy like a starving cat lapping milk and pray like the *Bible's* King David sings. Pray for those people but not for me," she said with disgust. "I'll pray for my own damn self. I know your ass, Mr. Preacher Man."

"Symone, baby. What in the hell?" She cut him off.

"That's what I said. I don't want you to pray for me. I'll say it again. Nah hell, no don't pray for me! All you've shown me about religion is that God is easy to adore in general but difficult to obey in action. That's what you've showed my ass. That your faith is nothing more than a buffet line for you to pick and chose your secret entrees when you feel like it. Or do it on Wednesday and Sunday when your religious, sanctimonious attitude is necessary to show to your precious members. That's what you do, Orlando. That's probably what a lot of other preachers in this city and cities all around the world do. Yall drink, smoke, fuck, and cuss with the best of them. All yall lying asses do the same ting. How many are there like you lurking around in churches nowadays? That's why I don't believe in all that glory, reverence, down-right stupid, and blind devotion people have for preachers anyway. Yall are nothing but a bunch of hypocrites. Nothing but the epitome of hypocrisy with a religious sly smile on your face.

"Jesus, Symone!"

"You screw women in your churches. I done heard about what preachers like you do. The same female members you're supposed to minister to all the time. It's downright sickening. Jackleg—bootleg preachers is what I call them. Educated and religious wolves in sheep clothing. Preaching God's words and don't mean it from their hearts. They wouldn't recognize God if they tripped over Him. And you know what I'm talking about, too," she said looking at him but not expecting him to respond.

"Symone, wait a minute! Puhleeze!" he interrupted futilely.

"Let meee finish, Orlando! Because you preachers hide behind your so-called goodness, you're worse than the lowest adulterous male dogs you find on any street corner nowadays anyway. The only difference is that you just walk around in business suits. Believe it or not, people do expect some people to be decent and be the moral compass. Damn preachers are supposed to do that. But yall can't even carry that torch with any degree of honesty. No! Hell no, don't pray for me. Preachers are nothing but damn wicked, money scoundrels in my book, and ah don't need no one like that or you praying for me," Symone continued sharply.

Her angry tone now took on an edge of blind hysteria. Orlando exhaled deeply and gazed briefly at the dark, starry sky and braced himself for another onslaught of verbal abuse. At this point, he realized it was useless to try to interject a word of calmness. She was on a wild roll.

"That's another ting. Ah hate hypocrites, too," Symone said as her rage caused her to lapse into anger. "That's what preachers are. Telling people how to live and living every way but the right way their own damn selves. Ah know. Because I'm looking at the biggest daddy in the bunch! The very difference between you and me Orlando is that people know me. People know about Symone. Hell, even my friends know that I'm a first class bitch who got a doctorate in bitchology from Bastard University. They know who ah am. How many of your church members really know about you?"

"Whaaat?"

"Who knows about you other than your holier than thou attitude that is always on display for your members? Ah don't hide behind a velvet cloak on Sunday morning. What you see is what you get with me, Orlando. I'm not one for hooping and hollering in someone's church on Sunday morning then act like a pure damn devil Monday through Saturday. You're looking at the Symone whose the same Symone twenty-four seven. Bitchy ass damn, miserable Symone.

Ah truly believe that God at least respects me for that much. For being honest and not faking it. People who do that fake running and jumping on Sunday morning at church don't respect Him. They're just wearing religion like a Halloween night costume. They just take it off on Monday morning. So you ask me if I want you to pray for me? Hell no!" she yelled crazily.

Orlando nervously wiped his creased brow with his hand and tried to allow a small smile to grace his sad face. He was naked, but her savage words wrapped around his skin like a poisonous snake and sent cold chills through his body. Orlando looked away, his eyes narrowing pensively.

"Wooo, girl," he whispered to himself. "Wooo! My goodness. Who done messed with my baby while I was gone? How the hell did our ultra superb, romantic evening jump all the damn way over here? Wow, baby!"

"Hmph. You figure it out."

"Oh, man. I don't know what has happened to you since I saw you three months ago. But wooo! This is deep, baby. Very deep. Real deep. And I'm not sure about the other messages flowing throughout your words. I don't know who has hurt you like this. But if I knew his name, I would personally kick his ass up and down Winston-Salem for you, Symone. Free of charge. That's for damn sure too," he exclaimed with a bewildered expression. His countenance was wrapped with confusion, and he continued quickly before she could get a word in.

"Listen to me, Symone. There's a lot of hate, hurt, and anger in your voice, baby. I always tell my members that hate is misplaced fear, and anger is buried love. As human beings, we tend to substitute anger for any kind of squelched emotions. Being scared. For anything, baby. You need to release it, Symone. Release whatever you're harboring inside of your mind because it'll literally eat you alive with bitterness, baby," he said in a bruised voice. He was wounded, vastly so. Yet his young eyes gleamed with understanding and compassion.

"You know what, baby? You're right." He laughed cynically as he worriedly rubbed his chin. "I know exactly what you mean. I see why you don't want to love me. Why you don't want to return my love. I know why you're scared of what's bursting from me for you. Your ass can't handle it. You're scared of it. You can't love anyone else until you first love yourself, Symone. You hate your ownself too much for that. I tell people that day in and day out. Over and over again. That's what I believe should be the national anthem for the United damn States of America, anyway. Should be the therapy song for the whole wide world. Love your own damn self first. Then work on loving other people."

Symone thought about what he said for a few seconds. Orlando sounded just like Alex. He was absolutely right, and that made Symone mushroom with another high degree of furious anger.

"Why does something has to be wrong with me, Orlando?" she screamed wildly while waving her hands frantically which made her hair even more disheveled.

"Then tell me what is it?"

"Men have been doing this for years. Acting the way I act for years. Fucking women. Leaving them. Hurting them. Abusing them. Then the men have the nerve to expect the women to talk and lie and say that they love them after all the hell they put us through. Well,

I'm not that way!" Her voice was a high-pitched shriek. She placed her palms over her ears and closed her eyes.

"Symone, if you want me to listen, then that's what I'll do. I love you. If it takes all night, I'm going to hang in here and talk you through this, baby. If nothing else, we've always been friends and could talk about anything," he said with a hopeful, childish grin.

"Quite frankly, I want you to leave my house right now." Her voice was tired.

"Leave your house?" he asked in disbelief. "But we haven't danced your Calypso way yet. You know I love to see you dance like that." Orlando spoke with intense, pleading eyes.

"So."

"We haven't eaten smoked oysters with cheese. Sipped wine, enjoyed a little curry something by candlelight, and made love some more," he edged on in an amusing voice to stifle her melancholy mood. "You sure you want me to leave, baby?"

"That's what I said, and I didn't stutter either. Just leave," she snapped angrily.

"Is that what you really want me to do, Symone?" he asked quietly as he walked toward her and touched her right arm. Symone jerked it away.

"I need to be myself. Just go. Puhleeze."

Visibly shaken, Orlando frowned. "This has been an unbelievable roller coaster trip with you tonight. Totally." Orlando began shaking his head from side to side, back and forth with his eyes closed. "One minute we were loving the hell out of each other and bam!" he said as he clapped his hands loudly several times. He shook his head again. "Oh, man. It's like a Dr. Jekyl and Mr. Hyde program going on here tonight, baby. It's a real live trip."

Symone's face was set in a hard, vicious, unrecognizable mask. "Well, hell you wanted a confidential freak, and you got one. Don't worry. I'll never go to Greensboro's *Carolina Peacemaker* or the *National Enquirer* and spill my guts about your sexual activities with me, Reverend Orlando Buster Kelly the Third," she sneered his church title in a sarcastic manner. "You can believe that shit, but I never said I was that perfect. You got yourself a real live freak that loves to fuck in a woman's body, but I got the heart of a cold-blooded, ruthless man. It's pure and simple," she ended with tears in her eyes. "Just tuck your big ass, black, wrinkled looking dick in your boxer shorts and leave my house."

Symone quickly turned to gaze out into the distance and allowed the water to fall from her eyes onto her bathrobe. Rather than let him see her cry, she wanted to act tough and mean. Since she was hurting from the fresh memories of years ago, she wanted to make him suffer tonight, too. To injure his feelings, too. She realized he didn't deserve it. But right now, she didn't care. He was a man who happened to be in the line of fire.

Orlando took a deep breath and disappeared into the house. For a few moments, he walked listlessly to and fro in the huge bedroom, sat on the sofa, and stared off into the unlit marble and wood fireplace.

Realizing it was useless to utter one word to Symone, Orlando decided to take a long, hot shower. When he was done, he got dressed and sipped two bottles of mineral water. Symone never came in from the terrace. By now she was sitting on the chaise lounge chasing thoughts of Symone. He walked to the French doors and spoke out into the darkness.

"I'm ready to leave, baby," he said in a soft voice.

"Ok," Symone said weakly after a moment. Now she had a lot of regret about the brutal words she directed at him.

Quietly, she walked beside him as he walked down the hall and down the stairs. Symone felt physically weak. Talking to him in such a vile way took a lot of energy out of her. As she gingerly walked down the steps, she gripped the banister for support. When Orlando reached the front door, he stopped abruptly. He glared straight ahead and rested his forehead on the foyer glass window. With slow deliberate movements, he turned to face her and raised Symone's chin with his right hand. She didn't stop him, but her eyes were downcast.

"Symone, look at me," he insisted in a quiet voice.

She raised her eyes to meet his. By now she imagined they were swollen, red, and bloodshot. The whole time he got dressed to leave, the tears tumbled down unmercifully. Even though she realized she talked to him unusually mean, she still didn't feel like apologizing, and she certainly didn't want his company any longer. She simply wanted to be left alone.

"Symone, baby. Release it, girl. Whatever it is, release it. Stop denying your feelings about your pain, Symone. It's there, and it's hurting you, baby. It's destroying you, and you're showing it with bitter anger. You've been blessed too much to be so bitter. Look at this damn big ass house. Your house. Fifty people could probably live in here and never run into each other for at least a fucking month." He noticed the swollen eyes and despite her vicious attack, he wanted to make her laugh.

"Uh, Orlando—"

"You're a businesswoman. Beautiful. Smart. You got everything people would claw and fight for and would love to have. But if you don't have peace, serenity, and love in your heart, all this pretty stuff will become quite insignificant because you're dying inside. The true beauty. The true joy of life is loving yourself, Symone. Not having material things. Pretty things. Release it, Symone. Release yourself from that mental prison, baby." He inhaled deeply. "Believe it or not, I might be young, but I understand. I hear the words of hurt, pained, sad, and bitter people all the damn time. The pitiful pleadings from down in their souls don't change either. A lot of money. No damn money. It's no different, baby. The way they handle it might be." He spoke tenderly to her. He paused a moment to catch his breath and to ponder what to say next.

"Remember when you first met me how you said you thought that I acted more mature than my years?" That compliment she lavished on him six months after they met was certainly a source of pride. Still refusing to meet his gaze, she quickly nodded her head yes and struggled not to cry in front of him.

"Symone, as a preacher, I've been hearing all kinds of heartbreaking stories for years. Even when I was a teenager preaching, older people talked to me about their problems. Yours is no different. Everybody got his or her story. I don't know what your story is. Whatever happened to you is no different from other people. Faces change, but the game of life remains the same. Maybe the characters in your life story have different names. Are shaped differently.

They might be tall, skinny, fat, or live in different countries, states, or cities. Pain is pain, and hurt is hurt, Symone. Life's piranhas don't have no respect of person and no regard for color or race, baby. Until you figure out how you need to release it, it will destroy you, baby. From the inside out, it will literally and completely destroy you. You're running around from something that's inside of you, and you can't escape from that, baby. Believe me, I know," he ended in an almost whisper.

Orlando stared at the fancy grandfather clock in the exquisitely decorated marbled foyer. It was three o'clock in the morning.

"Symone?" His voice was much lower, and he breathed slowly.

"I'm listening, Orlando," she replied in a feeble voice.

"Just release it, baby. Do whatever you need to do. Go to a psychologist. For many years, Black people have been taught we can work things out ourselves or any problems can be prayed away. As long as we suffer through it the good old Christian way—in the end—the sweet by and by, we'll receive our reward in heaven. We believe that only through prayer and constant talking, that it will be done." He paused and ruefully shook his head.

"Yes."

"Baby, don't get me wrong. Prayer is powerful. I believe in it, Symone. I know that it works. Without a doubt, it has sustained Black folk throughout generations. But God also provided other forms of help, Symone. Sometimes Black folk don't go to psychologists because a lot of us didn't grow up or lived in a place where anybody we knew was getting therapy. Maybe it was too expensive. Maybe they think it won't matter. Hell, I don't know. Most Black folk had to work things out on their own. It's a legacy we got honestly through suffering in this country. Sometimes they went to a preacher. The church has always been a strong influence in the Black community," Orlando said, laughing lightly as he considered her remarks about preachers and churches.

Without question, Symone heard every word he said. Once more, she quietly realized he was quite mature for his years. He stood there talking with his car keys in one hands and Symone's chin in the other. She considered apologizing crazily to him, but instead her moist eyes were riveted to his pants pocket and she refused to glance up in his face.

"...Symone, baby. Maybe Black folks talked to their good friends. Somewhere. I don't know, baby," he whispered tenderly. "But I do believe in my heart that there's a place for therapy. Because I don't have all the answers, I tell my members the same thing. There are times Black folks need to see psychologists. So if you need to visit a counselor of some sort, release your pride and just do it, baby. Whatever works. Do whatever you need to do to free yourself from the bitterness prison you're living in. Only you have the key for that mental jail house door. That dark basement door you often told me about," he said softly with a bittersweet grin.

"Symone, I truly heard a lot in what you told me. I don't know what happened to you, baby. But only you can determine how and when you plan to really really deal with it, baby. You can't keep spewing unprovoked hate-filled words to people and not expect to feel their anger or disgust. I'm a preacher. And the way you talked to me left a sour, stinking, rotten taste in my mouth. And maybe that's how the awful, naked truth sounds about me being a preacher and needing to be with you, but there's a better way to talk to me."

"Yes. I understand." That's was all Symone could say.

"Everybody's got their story. It's how you deal with it that makes it a happy or sad one. Just let it go. Nobody's going to come and rescue you from it, Symone. Nobody's going to come and save you. It won't be no great escape. You got to rescue yourself sometimes. Give those awful memories a life TKO, baby. Allow that inner genius of light that you have come out so that it can match your outward genius, baby. The outward genius in you that everyone knows about and that is a legend in the business world," he said tenderly and kissed her on the nose. "The genius of light that matches what's truly in your heart, baby."

For the last time for the evening, his eyes soaked her in from her neatly polished cranberry toes to the top of her shiny, black disheveled hair.

"Symone, I'll call you. I don't know when, but I'll call you. In the meantime, you take care. If you need me, page me or call me. You know I'll be right there whenever you think it's time for you to see me again. You were brutal tonight, girl. Real baddd. Your words cut deep, baby. In spite of how you shot the shit at me the way you did, I don't believe you truly wanted to hurt me. I really don't." While he said a quick prayer, he was still for a few seconds. "You know my Granddaddy Buster once told me that the most brilliant and warm-hearted people he knew were oftentimes the ones affected with internal, reckless demons they couldn't sometimes explain or run away from, baby. I always remembered those words, Symone. I don't know why. But I always did. It's hard, baby. Damn hard to hold sooo much in after so many years of keeping it held in. Hell, I don't know."

Orlando's words were ripping at Symone's innermost being. She closed her eyes a moment. She knew why he was a minister. His heart was kind. Forgiving. Orlando breathed deeply and was silent for several minutes while he watched her face again. Slowly, she opened her eyes and glanced fleetingly into his eyes. Just as quickly, her eyes were downcast again. Orlando believed Symone was simply beautiful. A Black goddess. He was honored to know her. With her, he could be free and didn't have to act like a pastor of a church. Orlando could merely laugh like a circus clown with her about silly subjects. Quite often, he thanked God she was in his life. He fervently prayed she always would continue to allow herself to be the periodic, relaxing getaway he so desperately needed to have in his life, too.

"Baby, I don't believe you truly wanted to hurt me," he repeated sadly and laughed soberly. His voice trembled with the sincere effort of controlling his own waterfall of tears. "I just happened to be the one that was here, Symone. I was an innocent victim of your wrath, but it still hurts. You talked to me like a low down dirty, scrawny, ass damn dog you see running along the highway. The kind of skinny, raggedy dog that hadn't eaten in two weeks," he added with a slight smirk. "But as a preacher, people talk shit about me all the time. I know that. Most times it's just not in my face though," he said softly with a noble smile.

"Orlandoooo." By now, the tears that Symone struggled to keep from falling were running down her cheeks, and Orlando quickly wiped them away with a white handkerchief he snatched out of his suit pocket.

"Shooot. Look at you, Symone. Nah, baby. Nah. Nah. Ok. Ok. Now, I ain't going to have no crying. C'mon, babygirl. Not after the way you talked all that shit to me," he said lightly.

He embraced her tightly, briefly. She didn't resist, but her shoulders were shaking intensely as she sobbed pitifully. Orlando consolingly squeezed her shoulders even tighter.

She felt protected, safe in his arms while she pressed her face against his large, muscular chest. The sobs gradually subsided. He released Symone and looked at her tearstreaked face for a brief moment. Carefully, he wiped her eyes again.

"I knew you weren't that mean, baby. You couldn't be. I know the character of people, and I know you. I thought I knew your heart. Now I know I was right. Real down to the core mean ass women don't cry. Super duper mean women curse niggers out. Shoot and stab them, too. They keep on stepping without a care in the world. They got to splash water on their face to have tears."

"Uh, Orlando. I didn't mean. You don't under—"

"Don't, baby," he said, interrupting her. He held both hands up like he was surrendering with a white flag. "Don't worry about me. Just think about what *I* said. Call me, Symone. You know I'll come. I got it bad like that for you, baby. So when you call, I'll come running," he said with a slight grin. Orlando opened the door and walked out.

Symone watched his tall, young but strong body walk down the bluestone pathway. When he backed his avocado green Explorer out the driveway and turned onto the street, she stepped back inside and closed the door. Slowly, Symone climbed the stairs to her bedroom and stood in front of the CD player for a few minutes. She decided she wanted to still listen to jazz and inserted a Max Roach and a Chuck Mangione CD. Symone considered playing some calypso. The music of Trinidad & Tobago. The sultry sounds of her homeland. The music and lyrics she adored more than any other in the entire whole wide world.

But Symone couldn't handle the memories she knew such music would cause to sprout in her mind again. She knew that was the reasons she didn't play Calypso as much. She loved her home in Santa Cruz. Loved the culture and adored the people. But she also understood that was why most times she tried desperately to not even act or even talk like a Trinidadian. All of it. The music. The words. The language that was so intrinsic in her family in New York. The words in the calypso songs. It hurt her to listen to them. It took her too far back. It hurdled her to the days when Lennious happily danced for her in her bedroom. To those moments with her Papa. Instead of Calypso, she settled on the soothing, relaxing sounds of jazz once more.

With a tearful gaze directed at the bedroom ceiling, she wished there were some way that she could suffocate the thoughts of Papa. A way to choke it out of her. She wished there were some way. Why were they tormenting her with so much force? Why now? Why the memories of Lennious? It happened so many years ago. All her life she worked diligently to keep those memories tucked in a special, private place. She had buried that part of her past in Trinidad, but obviously it had not been buried completely. Why were they beginning to haunt her again? To resurface now so brilliantly? Why?

Symone realized that there was nothing she could do about burning them out of her mind. Since she didn't have any answers for herself, she decided to write in her journal for an hour. At four-twenty in the morning, a dreamless sleep finally overtook her.

Chapter Forty-One

Alex quietly arose from bed and said her prayers over the Imani Box. It was six o'clock Saturday morning. She went to use the bathroom, where she sat on the bidet for a few minutes. As she walked back into the room, she decided to go stare at Madison while he was sleeping. He was so handsome. Peaceful. Very gently, she kissed him on the lips and smiled. Since she was naked, she slipped into a green silk, flowing dashiki. She walked to the bookshelf, removed two books, and opened the glass doors, then walked outside. From the bedroom's balcony, the cobblestone brickwork in the garden resembled a swirling Byzantine mosaic design, and as always, Alex enjoyed the sweeping beauty of the formal gardens.

During the fish fry last evening, at least thirty-five children or more and even several of the crazy acting adults had a wonderful time climbing the large oak trees located throughout the backyard. With the trees twinkling with tiny, white lights, the evening's stage was a mystical, lovely setting, and everyone had a great time. Alex took a deep breath and inhaled the clear, intoxicatingly fresh Advance morning air. There was a slight mist handing over the oak trees and lake.

While she sat outdoors in the rocking chair, she read the appropriate message in *Acts of Faith*. Once done with that daily routine, she began to read the last sixty pages of *Five Negro Presidents* by J.A. Rogers. The book was the gift Symone had given out to everyone last Saturday at her house. All the friends enjoyed a semi-formal evening there while listening and dancing to the sounds of two live bands, Young Byrd and The JBs. Alex read for about forty-five minutes. She placed the book on the chair and stood up to gaze at the tranquillity and serenity of the backyard again. To simply listen to the tweet tweet, melodic musical sounds of the hummingbirds, crickets, and frogs. As always, she whispered her most favorite words of Socrates. *I pray thee, O God, that I may be beautiful within.*

Wrapped in total quiet, Alex leaned on the balcony's pillar and soaked in the greenery of the verdant, lush landscape for at least thirty minutes. With a unique sense for all of nature's beauty, she loved seeing things grow. She believed that nature and its beauty were meant to savor, enjoy, and was one of God's many wonderful gifts to humanity. And going out in the early, quiet morning to look around was one of the first things she did every day.

Very quietly, Madison walked up behind her. Before he came outdoors, he had watched her silently for about fifteen minutes. He always enjoyed gazing at her when she didn't know he was doing it. Alex was a rare beauty to him, and he fervently believed that he was truly blessed to have her. Without a doubt, Madison certainly cherished the eighteen extraordinary years they had shared together as husband and wife and only envisioned them sharing another eighteen years together. Thirty-six years as one. Alex would be fifty-eight and he would be fifty-nine.

Ever so gently, Madison wrapped his arms around her waist and kissed her on the neck. Alex turned around, and they kissed tenderly. Without brushing their teeth—nothing. Madison and Alex simply loved the taste of each other's mouth any time it was opened to receive their kisses of affection.

"Good morning, baby," he said when they stopped to catch their breath. He nuzzled her nose with his and continued to hold her waist.

"Good morning to you, Madison." She spoke softly as she shyly gazed into his eyes and kissed him on the lips again. He still made her feel like a frivolous, giddy-eyed teen-ager.

Madison began grabbing the silk dashiki together at Alex's thighs in order to pull it off over her head.

"Honey, you can't do that out here. You never know where all the children might be lurking." Alex laughed and glanced quickly around the backyard. Undaunted, Madison kissed her neck again and cupped her right breast.

"Ok." He breathed hot air into her thick, black hair. "Let me undress you inside our bedroom. I want to taste you, baby. You were supposed to give me some last night. More like this morning, but your behind fell asleep. I bet you don't even remember that I was the one who put you to bed."

"You're right. I didn't know what happened. I was sooo tired. I remembered someone laying me down and kissing me between my legs. In the deep recesses of my mind, it felt very, very, very good. Was that you, Madison?" she asked teasingly knowing that it was.

"I'm guilty, baby," he exclaimed and held up both hands defenselessly. "I tried to wake you like a man needing to love his woman, but you weren't budging atall. Finally, I said to myself, 'My baby is sooo knocked out. Maybe, she'll think she's having a great wet dream or something.' You certainly tasted sweet and delicious to me, whether you were awake or not." Madison licked his lips. Alex giggled freely and squinted her nose.

"Have you brushed your teeth yet, Madison?"

"No. Have you brushed yours?"

"No, baby," Alex said lightly. She kissed his fingertips, each side of his shoulders, and the palm of each hand.

"Good. We got that settled. I didn't think you did either," he answered quickly and squinted his nose, too. Alex giggled again. "Let's go inside."

"That's fine, baby."

"I'll brush your teeth, Alex. You can brush mine. We can take a hot shower and make wild love before our house gets crazy again. This time you can be awake and a willing participant, and you can enjoy the magic of your husband's tongue," Madison joked lightly as he softly rubbed his hand between Alex's legs to massage her bushy pubic hair. "How's that, baby?"

"That sounds fine to me, baby. *Real* fine to me," she repeated with pleasure all over her voice while he continued to softly touch her clitoris in twirling motions with his finger.

"Great, baby," he replied easily and picked her up. She wrapped her legs around his body, and he carried her into the bathroom to steal some good loving.

Symone glanced at her watch. It was seven fifteen in the morning, and she was already knocking on the Devereauxs twelve-foot front, double doors. When no one responded to her knocks, Symone decided to ring the bell. Cleopatra opened it with a wide smile on her face. After the Devereauxs, Symone, Nanette, Scott, and Jodria were Cleopatra's next four favorite people.

"Symone, girl. I can't believe you're here this early," Cleopatra blurted in a delightful voice as she checked her watch, and Cleopatra reached to hug Symone.

"I know, girl. My ass can't believe it either. I got an early call from my Uncle Samuel. He's in the Orient and woke me up. After that, I decided to get up and head out," Symone replied as they headed down the marble entryway toward the kitchen. Symone noticed that the colorful yellow and red roses, mixed with white lilies were placed in crystal clear vases around the granite counters and on the tables.

"Why did you ring the bell, Symone? You know the door was open—is always open around here."

"I know. I got a lot on my mind, girl. Didn't even think about it."

"The fresh flowers smell good as usual." Symone inhaled the sweet fragrance of a yellow tea rose.

"Well you know Alex. She wants flowers everywhere. Watch out for the thorns, girl."

"Too late," Symone declared as she examined her pricked thumb and glanced around the kitchen. "The house is flooded with a helluva lot of roses today. More than usual."

Symone's words brought a knowing smile to Cleopatra's face. "Alex believes that when fresh flowers are in every room, people can enjoy themselves and inhale the beauty. Makes them think they're right outdoors," Cleopatra recited perfectly. "With the children having their own little rose garden area, they were ready to cut the flowers from their gardens as soon as they got here yesterday. Want some hot toasted almond creme coffee, Symone? What about cappuccino?"

"Nah. I'll get some juice. That gourmet coffee does smell just like a fat Almond Joy candy bar, girl." Symone spoke softly as she searched in the refrigerator for orange juice. She found it on the top shelf and poured herself a large glass full. King, Queen, and Dreams suddenly rushed in the kitchen. Symone bent down to greet the dogs.

"How's Tante Symone's precious little doggies doing? Eeeky peeky poo. Eeeky peeky poo. Yall doing ok?" she asked her canine godchildren as she nestled all three furry necks for a few moments. They responded by wagging their tails and licking her legs.

"Aren't they spoiled, Symone?"

"You know they are. Pecola says that they're not really dogs, but real people who happen to be in dog bodies. She said she learned that from Jed and Clampett."

"That's what everyone says about those dogs. They do act just like people, but Alex treats them that way, too. Everyone does. Girl, let me tell you. You truly missed a sho nuff wonderful evening last night," Cleopatra declared in a pleasant voice as she pulled a carton of brown eggs out of the refrigerator.

"I'm sure I did, Cleopatra. I believe you. I was too tired and had a lot on my mind. That's all." Symone's tone was apologetic as she thought about the depressing Friday, and then the shitty evening with Orlando. "Anyway, let me take my things upstairs. I got over here early because I wanted to take a horse ride for a couple of hours. Alone. To give myself time to think."

"You ok?" Cleopatra was concerned. "Want me to take your bags upstairs and hang your clothes up in the closet for you, Sy?"

"No. Thanks, Missy Cleopatra." Symone smiled at Cleopatra's kindness. "I'll do it myself. Which guestroom is available? I don't want to stumble onto something I don't need to."

"There's two bedrooms left. Alex saved the pink rose one for you. At one time, she mentioned the doll room, too. So they both are still available. Just pick which one you want. Rozelle, Jodria, Carlos, Pecola, Nanette, her babies, Carlos' parents, Madison's college roommate, wife, and children plus a couple from Atlanta, are sprawled all over the place upstairs."

"Whew! There's a lot of people here."

"The typical. Half of the children decided they wanted to sleep downstairs in the playroom. Another six are sleeping outside in tents. The rest are sleeping in the guesthouses. Marlon and his friends are camping out there, as well as the four senior citizens. Scott, Romallus, GJ, and SJ are somewhere. Girl, I tell you. It was crazy last night trying to coordinate sleeping arrangements."

"Scott's sons are here? Hmmm. I thought they were on tour."

"Yeah, they're here. They were on tour with KRS-One, but they had a break and decided to come especially since their father asked them to. Aren't they fine, Symone? Tall, dark, hairy, and handsome. Just like their father, girl."

"Cleopatra, you're a mess, but you're right. They're two fine young Black men. Yes, they do look like Scott. They're just a little young for my blood," Symone admitted with a slight grin. *Not really though,* she thought just as quickly. Especially when she considered that Scott's sons were just a few years younger than Orlando was.

"Not too young for mine."

Symone smiled. "You've kept up with everyone as usual. That must be your other gift. Organizing shit."

Cleopatra laughed without restraint. "You're right, Sy. I went to bed at one o'clock this morning. My job is to make sure everything runs smoothly for Alex. In order to make that happen, I needed to get a little more rest than everyone else, girl. They tell me that the action didn't stop until after five this morning. If I'm not mistaken, I think some card playing activity is still going on at the guesthouses down by the small pond. Can you imagine that?"

"Knowing the group we're dealing with, five o'clock was early." Symone laughed. "Normally, the parties are two-day marathon trips."

"Anyway, I'm just getting ready to start breakfast for Alex and Madison. I wanted to surprise them and serve the lovebirds in bed. You want something, Sy? Eggs, bacon, and pancakes. I'll be happy to make it for you."

"No thanks. Let me go and stake out my room before some more folk show up and take my spot," Symone teased as she sipped more juice. She placed the glass on the granite counter, picked up her garment bag, and walked out the kitchen.

Symone walked up the stairs and into the spacious doll guestroom. On every available surface, Alex had at least two-hundred and forty-seven Black porcelain dolls wearing gorgeous dresses displayed throughout the room. Alex was especially fond of the twenty-five Adrienne McDonald Urban Faerie Black rag dolls sprawled throughout as well. Jodria often told Alex that this particular guestroom was really a museum and not a spare bedroom. A massive plantation style poster mahogany bed was adorned with pillows, frills, and other dolls were centered between the two tall windows of the blue and white delicately decorated room. Symone smiled as she eyed the handsome, elegant decor. She positioned her bag on the antique mahogany chest located at the foot of the bed and left the room. As Symone headed out of the door, she saw Purity roaming about in the hallway. Rubbing her face and crying softly, she was heading back to her bedroom. Purity began twisting her short pink, ruffle nylon nightgown around her fingers while walking barefoot with her Huggy Bean doll dragging along on the floor behind her.

"Hey, little girl," Symone said with a lot of life in her voice. Purity slowly turned around and smiled widely when she saw her Tante Symone. She raced into Symone's outstretched arms and gave her a sloppy, wet kiss on the lips.

"Hello, Tante Suhmone."

"What are you doing up so early, girl?"

"Uh, I needed to peepee," she explained softly as she rubbed both eyes with her fists and rested her head on Symone's shoulder. Symone carried Purity into her bedroom and discovered that her bathroom door was tightly shut. She opened it and helped her to use the toilet. When Purity was done, Symone carried the child back to bed.

"Are you still sleepy, little girl?"

"Uh huh." Purity nodded her head and moaned.

"Let Tante Symone get you back to sleep. Ok?" Purity nodded her head again. "If this is all the talking you're doing now, then Tante Symone knows you're very, very sleepy. You're normally talking twenty miles per hour, little girl. You didn't have anybody sleeping with you in your pretty room?" Symone inquired as she glanced at Purity's large brass embellished iron canopy bed.

"No. Uh, Tante Suhmone," she answered in a tired voice and yawned. Symone assumed Purity probably drove her little guests crazy with her controlling nature, and they decided that they would rather sleep elsewhere than be with her.

"Does Trey have his friends sleeping with him?"

"Ummm-hmmm. My brudda has sum babies in his room, too," she said with half-closed eyes. "I wuv you, Tante Symone."

"I wuv you too, little girl," Symone said with a smile and covered Purity with a flowery pink sheet. While Symone lightly hummed an African nursery song, she rubbed Purity's full head of black hair, and the small child quickly fell back to sleep. Everyone said that Purity looked just like Alex, and she did. Madison often joked that for a three and half year old girl, she had too much hair on that little head of hers, and he was surprised she didn't tumble over from the weight of it. It was obvious to everyone that she was another Alex in the making. As

Symone glanced around the bright room with its cheerful medley of colorful floral purple and white prints, she realized that Purity's bedroom was crammed with just as many Porcelain black dolls and Urban Faerie black rag dolls as the other guest room.

Symone watched Purity closely. Before she left, she wanted to make sure she was asleep. She was. Symone gently kissed Purity's forehead. She tiptoed out of the room toward the master bedroom and loudly knocked on the door. While she waited for someone to open it, she heard a lot of giggling and the music of The Penguin's *Earth Angel, Will You Be Mine* floating from inside their room. She knocked hard again. With her hair totally disheveled and holding a lacy raspberry-colored kimono together at her neck, Alex finally opened the door slightly.

"Symone?" she said in a shocked voice as she glanced around at the clock on the nightstand. "It's seven-forty in the morning. What the heck are you doing here so early?"

"Couldn't sleep and just decided I would get an early start. I really wanted to take an early morning horse ride. What was all that giggling in there about before you opened the door?" Symone asked and tried to gaze over Alex's shoulder toward the bed. "You sure your ass ain't got three men in there with you?"

"Girl, you're sooo crazy. You know I started to go horseback riding this morning, but I decided to read instead. I couldn't sleep either. You know how nervous I get when we plan a special day. Anyway, give me a hug." The two friends hugged each other tightly. "Just give me another thirty minutes, and I'll be downstairs. Ok?"

"I don't understand. I know you say you're nervous, but you're normally so calm and centered, girl. It'll be perfect, Alex. Just relax. Leave stress city to your friends. We tend to know those streets well."

"Hey, Symone baby!" Madison yelled out from bed.

"Hey, Madison. Yall sound too happy for me so early in the morning." Symone laughed as she spoke. "Girl, I ran into Purity. She was roaming the hall and probably knocked on your door. With all that freaky deaky sex going on in there, yall probably didn't even hear the pitiful knocks from your daughter."

"Get out of here. She slept in our bed most of the night. When we got to bed, it was sooo late. Well, really this morning. I was so tired, and I don't remember a thing. Madison said that he took her out of our bed and put her in her room at four this morning. It was around the same time we came in from the pool."

"Alex, baby—" Madison called softly for her. "I'm waiting, Pookie bear."

"I'm coming, baby." Alex winked at Symone as she answered Madison.

"Before you go, which bedroom is Pecola in?"

"She's in the African gold room, Symone. Love ya."

"Ok, Alex. Love ya, too."

Chapter Forty-Two

Symone walked down the hall and knocked hard several times on that door. With walls painted the color of butter, the African gold room was decorated with lovely, authentic African artifacts. The various pieces were collected from Alex and Madison's numerous trips to Africa, in addition to Out of Africa, a Dallas shop that Alex patronized via long distance ordering.

Two minutes later, Pecola stumbled out of bed and opened the door. She was dressed in one of the dozen A&T Aggie sexy, silk nightshirts Carlos had tailored made just for his wife's fortieth birthday. With her infamous black sleep mask atop her chestnut sandy hair, Pecola looked like she had a slight hangover. She gave Symone a brief, limp hug.

"Hey, honeychile. What in the hell are you doing up so early? What time is it?" Pecola asked in a hoarse voice and squinted around to see the clock on the bookshelf.

"It's early."

"It's not even eight o'clock yet. You know that isn't even you for a Saturday morning. Something must be up. What's wrong, girl? Come on inside," she invited drowsingly while she yawned. As Pecola rubbed her bleary eyes and scratched her behind, she headed slowly back to bed. She plopped herself on it and turned to face Symone as she fluffed then cuddled the pillow.

"As you can see, Carlos isn't here. Well he was, but left about an hour ago. He was only here for two minutes. I guess to make sure I was still breathing. He knew I had a slight hangover. He's over in the guesthouse with Scott and his family. Marlon and those fine ass basketball players are hanging out there, too. Do you know what I mean, chile?" she announced with a glint in her bloodshot eyes. Symone simply smiled with understanding.

"I know exactly what you mean, Pecola."

"If I'm not mistaken, they're still playing poker, bid whist, and spades. They're operating about four tables over there. Plus, they're listening to The J.B. Horns featuring PeeWee, Fred, and Maceo. Some wild CDs that Romallus brought for Scott from New Orleans. Believe you me, they're having a seriously funky good time, girl." Pecola laughed.

"I can imagine."

"They're drinking white liquor and beer like pure divine lushes. Before it's over with, I betcha they'll be drunk as skunks. Alex said that she didn't care what they did out there in the guesthouses as long as they kept all their drinking and partying away from the children's eyes and as long as they were alive and kicking at five o'clock today."

"Pecola, you look rough as hell. What truck ran into you?"

Pecola yawned and stretched her arms above her head. "Thanks for the flowery compliment. I know I don't look like my normal glamorous self, honeychile. My ass didn't go to bed until five this morning, and they were still swimming in the pool. We played volleyball under the lamps and could barely see the damn ball. Did all kinds of things last night. You name it. There was every bit fifty adults hanging out dancing like six crazy fools around the pool to the oldies till four-thirty this morning. The Front Page Band rocked the house marvelously, girl."

"That's an excellent band. Hmmm. Normally things don't stop until we see the sun rising over the lake. And we only do it then because Alex is totally mesmerized by the sunset and wants everyone around her to appreciate it, too. You know how she is? She wants folks to take delight in birds, flowers, the sunrise and sunset. What made yall stop at four-thirty?"

"Hell, I don't know. We just did. Before then, it was a serious house party that I hate you missed," she rattled on non-stop.

"Me too."

"The lifeguards Alex hired said that when they turned down the driveway, they checked the directions to make sure they were at the right place. They expected a bunch of bourgeois niggers. The real seditty acting ones. You know those seriously highfalutin kind of folk to be here. Can you believe that?" she asked in an incredulous manner with wide, green eyes. "I mean really. Nice people like us acting seditty and all."

"If they had met you first, their first assumption would've been right, girl," Symone said casually. Pecola sucked her teeth with mock anger. "Just kidding, Pecola."

"No you're not."

"Don't take it personal. You know how your head is in the self-righteous cloud sometimes? Let me get this clear? Those two guys said they expected a bunch of what? Bourgeois? Who said that?" Symone asked, shocked.

"The lifeguards, chile. Aren't you listening? Are you still sleep or what? That's who said it. I guess they thought we don't have fun. Hell, I don't know. That's what they said to Rozelle. Of course, he told me. You know how Rozelle is; he can't keep a thing to himself."

"Pecola, you can't either."

"You're right. You're right, chile. My buddy, Rozelle. I guess we got the same trait if you know what I mean?" She patted her opened mouth several times and sat up.

Symone rolled her eyes and grinned. "Hell, they ain't seen nothing, Pecola. If they could see how this place jumps during Winston-Salem State University and A&T's homecomings. It's the same way during the CIAA Tournament, too."

"You're right," Pecola agreed and gave Symone a limp high five. "Anyway, the two guys said that they never knew that Black folks who lived in a house like this knew anything about having a throw down serious pool party like that. The two lifeguards were jamming back. They had nice dark-skinned bodies, chile. You know. Your type," Pecola interjected with a sly expression as she gazed into Symone's tired eyes.

"Hell, your type. Any type is really your type especially since your behind been married since you were sixteen."

"I'll disregard that comment for right now." Pecola rolled her eyes dramatically and yawned once more. Her fifteenth one since Symone sat on the bed. "Thank God nobody needed to be rescued from the pool last night. If they had to depend on those two guys, they probably would have drowned like four-ton bricks."

"What happened?"

"They were too busy dancing with us. That's what. Can you believe they were still eating Cajun style crab and crawfish when I left to come to bed? Romallus brought a huge box of crawfish from New Orleans. Between the hot sauce, the liquor, the music, and the dancing all over the place, I thought I was going to collapse, girl. I'm telling you. My tongue has been deadened and soiled by all the hot sauce Romallus made me taste. Look at it," she said and stuck her tongue out for Symone to see.

"It does look a little tender with small bumps on it," Symone agreed to make Pecola feel better. Quite frankly, she didn't notice a thing.

Pecola nodded her head knowingly. "Umph hmmm. It figures. I knew you could tell once you looked at it. While Marlon was frying fish, we had a Karaoke contest by the pool and Madison won. He did a mean Otis Redding's *Sitting on the Dock of the Bay*. Chile, it was sooo funny. Rico swore he was the real winner, and that the whole thing was fixed since Madison lived here. We all told Rico to sit down. By then, it was too late. Carlos, Darilyn, and Jodria snuck up behind him and pushed him in the pool." Pecola was giggling now.

"Did he have on his bathing suit, too?"

"No. He had on his mink damn coat! Of course, he did. It was a pool party, fish fry, and barbecue combo pack, chile. Are you up or what? I'm the one you woke up. Listen, girl. Listen carefully. I made sure I soaked in everything so I could give you all the eeny meeny details." She inhaled deeply.

"Sheese. Don't get excited. I'm just asking a question."

"After that, Rozelle squirted everyone with that big green water gun he carries around." Symone began to laugh. "Guess who else had one?"

"I don't know. Who? I thought Jodria hid that toy gun from Rozelle."

"You think that makes any difference with that crazy nigger, chile? Rozelle went out and brought not only one this time, but he brought three. One was for Marlon and Christopher to use. Rozelle is just awful."

"I know. I'm convinced the men we know are nothing more than boys in adult bodies, girl."

Pecola nodded her head and giggled. She waved her hand for Symone to be quiet. "Then we hustled, chile. We did the Soul Train line, the bump, and electric slided most of the night. That electric slide line was kicking, girl. Folks were clapping, screaming, laughing and snapping their fingers. I was blowing my whistle. I couldn't even hear the O'Jays' *Love's Train* that was blasting all over the place. Ain't nothing like a bunch of crazy Black men and women electric sliding, honeychile. Our bodies were twisting all over the place."

"Yall only electric slided to one song?"

"Chile, no. We did it to the Spinners' *I'll Be Around, We are Family*, and some other songs with that slide beat. I'm telling you that Madison made sure the old school music was the deal," she answered as she massaged her temples. "By then I had my bathing suit cover off. I didn't care dittly about my extra twenty pounds. It was sooo hot, and I was sooo high on Nanette's knock out Pina Coladas. I said what the hell? I told myself, 'Shake your tailfeather, girl.' So I was shaking it like crazy with just my skimpy bikini on, chile."

"No you didn't wear a bikini, Pecola."

"Yes I did, too. Who says a forty-year old Black woman can't wear a bikini, honeychile? Black women got so much good stuff to show. You know it. Full titties. Lovely, round asses. It's just like my Coca-Cola shape, chile. Kinda small waist. Blossoming at the top and the bottom. It's time for us to kill those old one piece jobs and flaunt our voluptuous bodies, Sy," she added as she gave her another high five.

"Pecola, you're sooo crazy."

"I know, but I got a lot of compliments, too. That's why I could tell half the mensus were tipsy and couldn't see my little midriff bulge sticking out. Hell, everyone had on cute bathing suits, even the men. Christopher Perry and Jodria were taking pictures like crazy."

"They always do that."

"Now, I'm truly afraid to see myself once they get those rolls of film developed, but it's too late now. We're all friends. So whatever. Carlos was supposed to be the camcorder operator. After he tasted Rozelle's white liquor, that didn't last long, and Scott eventually took over that job. Go into the theater sometime today and look at the videotapes from last night. Whatever I left out, I'll guarantee you that'll give you an idea of how crazy it was, honeychile"

"I might do just that after I come in from the horse trail. You're sure it's in the theater already?"

"Hell, yeah. It is. Before he went to bed, Madison made sure it was in there. He was afraid somebody might try to see if their video cameras could swim." Pecola stretched her legs and yawned. "So he took everybody's cameras inside and placed them in the theater. Anyway, let me finish with the juicy details, chile. After we stopped doing the electric slide, Booker T played a little Jamaican music. You know Dennis Brown and Ken Boothe Cds."

"I love them."

"I know. We reggaed for a while. That's when Booker T yelled out, 'Where's that Trini girl tonight?' I believe that was after he had smoked about five joints. Blunts, probably. It must've suddenly hit him you were missing. He was high as ten damn kites. No lie. He kept yelling, 'Where's my Trini girl?'"

"Wow." Symone laughed freely at Booker T's pet name for her. "It does sounds like it was fun, girl."

"Of course, it was sho nuff fun. Fun ain't even the right word." Pecola's eyes were wide with the warm, fresh memory. "Everybody told him you were sick. But honnnneychile, I reggaed my ass off. I also threw in a little bit of those movements that I learned from going to Trinidad to play mas with you. So did Jodria, Nanette, and Darilyn. Even Alex had it going on like a big greasy pot of neck bones. DJ Cool Breeze played Bob Marley's *Jamming* and *Could You Be Loved*. It was all over but the shouting for me."

"Yah, mon. Reggae does have a sweet beat, mon," Symone said in a thick West Indian accent. They both laughed.

"Honeychillle, listen to me! We were premier Miss Bahama Mamas of the evening. Then Romallus convinced Madison to finally change the music to some ole Zydeco music that's supposedly synonymous with Louisiana. Let me think of the name of the guy that Romallus said was the most influential musician." Pecola paused and scratched her head for a moment. She wanted to make sure she gave Symone all of the details about the opening evening.

"Can't you remember?"

"I think he say it was Clifton Chenier." Pecola hesitated again. "The other two were Boozoo Chavis and Stanley "Buckwheat Zydeco" Dural. I'm not sure if I'm pronouncing their names right."

"I love those names. Romallus has an extensive collection of Zydeco music. He bring any other Cds?" When Pecola didn't answer, Symone nudged her. "Welllll—"

"I'm trying to remember. Dopsie was the name. That's it. It was a Rockin' Dopsie, Jr. CD. The other one was a Rockin' Sidney CD. Girl, everyone was a rockin' like fools, and it was crazy. Romallus grabbed my hand and tried to show me how to do what he said was the LaLa dance. It was some two step thing. He said, 'Pecola, just let yourself go.' Remember how he tried to show that to everyone last year at my Fourth of July barbecue and at Scott's birthday party this year?"

Symone bobbed her head yes and smiled at her friend. Symone knew if she wanted the exact details about last evening, Pecola was the perfect one to give it to her just like it happened. When it came to gossiping, her mind was like a video camera.

"Well, Romallus tried it again. I believe he thinks he's Mr. Ambassador for New Orleans himself. I thought Scott was bad, but his brother definitely got him beat in that area. Anyway, chile—" she said as she inhaled deeply again and batted her eyes in her typical way. "Romallus explained to me that long time ago, they used to perform the LaLa dance to snappy music made with a washboard, an accordion, a spoon, and anything else that made a musical sound. We did that dance the rest of the night. You know that crew. It was wild as usual. Now I can barely move these forty-year old bones," Pecola revealed with another lazy yawn and a quick chuckle.

"This is a trip. Where were the children when all this was going on?"

"Quite frankly, some of them were hanging out with us. Remember this is the older group this time around. Some of the other children were riding on the carousel, himalaya, and other amusement rides Alex had set up for them. It's like a damn state fair down there once again. Some of them were in bed, girl. They at least acted like they had some sense."

"Down where? The rides were in the front yard last month. I didn't see any rides."

"Chile, I know. Alex changed the spot. To find the rides, you got to walk past the small side of the garden toward the open, grassy field. Alex has the same four student mentors from Winston-Salem State University. You know the ones she had last month. They're still responsible for monitoring and talking to seven children each. You know. Be like a camp leader, especially when there are other activities going on. Specifically crazy adult activities. Last night was a classic example. Girlfriend thought of everything this summer, chile."

"I'm glad. It was too much on just her, Madison, and a few of her friends last summer, girl."

Pecola nodded in agreement and stretched again.

"Hell, it was rough on me last year. Guess what, honeychile?" She asked the question like a conspirator.

"At this point I don't know, Pecola. What, girl?" Symone braced herself and waited for what Pecola had to say.

"Welll—" She spoke slowly, gazed at her nails first, and glanced slyly at Symone. "As usual, Charmaine tried to watch Scott like a damn hawk. She's so afraid someone's gonna get her stuff. It was sooo funny, but I'm going to tell you the truth. Two of Nanette's nursing buddies from Houston-Tillotson College was checking him out like crazy. They were real pretty girls. Two single, heavy-duty corporate women from Texas who sho nuff had their eyes on Scott. On everybody for that matter."

"Get out of here!"

"Hmph. Trust me. I had to actually place a damn anchor around Carlos to let them know he was mine," she declared with wide eyes. "I couldn't believe it. Young girls nowadays don't play. It's open season as far as they're concerned. They are a new breed of men snatchers. It's yours, mine, and ours. They don't give a shit. Lord, things sure have changed these days. When these young girls want a man, they want him. And a wife doesn't mean anything to them. A wife is nothing more than a four letter word, honey."

"What am I going to do with you?"

"Humph. You know the deal." To let Symone know she was telling the truth about young girls, Pecola slowly nodded her head up and down, rolled her eyes, and waved her hands.

"Puhleeze."

"When Nanette's friends found out Scott wasn't married and was a Northworld pilot, it was watch out. They told Nanette he was fair game as far as they were concerned. Nanette said that both of them drooled over Scott's hairy chest and body all night long. Since he's sooo concerned about staying in shape, you know how good he looks in a bathing suit. How luscious he looks, period. Umph. Umph. Umph."

"Pecola, you're too much. They broke the mold with you," Symone said as she listened to Pecola rattle on and on.

"Let me finish, girl," Pecola said rapidly waving her left hand at her. "I believe when the two Texas ladies realized they couldn't get anywhere with Scott since he's sooo in love with Charmaine, they went after Scott's sons. Then, they latched onto Romallus, too. The whole Alexander family is fine as hell anyway. So naturally, I could understand those ladies' persistent pursuit, honeychile."

"Get out of here, Pecola."

"No. I'm serious. Romallus danced with them most of the night. Every time I turned around, they had him sandwiched on the dance floor. I don't think Charmaine saw them scoping Scott, though. She was sooo busy trying to show everyone how she could dance better than all of the other women at poolside. That got on my nerves. She really did. I hate a show-off."

"You got some nerve to say you hate a show-off especially as much as you like to show your ass. You're crazy, girl."

"I know. Still, I betcha that's why Charmaine tried to out dance everyone. She was kinda half naked wearing a tiger-print bikini which I know was definitely too tight for her body."

"Get out of here, girl."

"I'm telling you, Symone. The Black folks were half-naked last night. It must've been in the August air." She sucked her teeth again. "Charmaine is so damn jealous, girl. You know she is? It wouldn't have made a difference about Nanette's two college friends. It would've just given her something else to be uptight about. I'm telling you. She doesn't like you, Alex, or me either. I know about junk like that."

There was a long pause. "You know that's not true, Pecola. She's always very nice to all of us. Why do you keep saying that?" Symone shook her head and smiled at Pecola. "I recommend you stop talking about Scott's lady like that, girl. If I didn't know any better, I'd almost think you were jealous and wanted him for yourself."

"That definitely ain't it. If anything, I'm overly protective of him. Charmaine doesn't like us, Symone. I believe she only tolerates us because she knows Scott loves us like the sisters he never had."

"Well—" Before Symone spoke further, she thought for a few moments. "I just never get that from her, Pecola. I got my own damn problems to deal with, so I can certainly miss a lot of negative vibes floating around."

"Hell, I get that from her. I got problems, too. That's how come I know exactly how she is, and there isn't a damn thing she can do about it either. She has no alternative but to accept us. In reality, she's totally jealous of him being around us. I can't believe you can't tell it either."

"I can't."

"I expect that type of blindness from Alex. *But you?* You especially tend to be suspicious about people penetrating our circle of friends. You need to remove the fish scales from your eyes. Period. I know you and Alex always think I'm always imagining things about everybody. Yall constantly say I'm wrong about this person and that person, but watch my word. I feel it in my gut, girl."

"Don't let me remind you how you've been totally wrong in your gut many times before," Symone said fondly with a wide grin. "A number of times."

"I know, honeychile. This is different. She's very jealous, and there's a thin line between jealousy and possessiveness. That can be frightening." Pecola had a glint in her eyes. "She acts like she doesn't trust him, and the basic problem with that is this—"

"Oh, gawd." Symone glared at the ceiling and bobbed her head with a surprised expression on her face. "Since when have you taken Dr. Gwendolyn Goldsby Grant's place as resident psychologist of relationships, Pecola?"

"Listen to me! You know how I feel about things like that. If she can't trust Scott, then she can't be trusted either, honeychile. Scott is faithful as hell to her," Pecola added knowingly and with urgency. She didn't wait for Symone to respond to her comments. As if Pecola suddenly realized something else, she glanced at the clock again.

"Oh, Goddd," Symone moaned. "What's wrong now?"

"What in the hell are you doing over here so early, Symone? Are you feeling better?" she asked in a suspicious tone with a raised eyebrow. "How come you didn't tell me you brought Cleopatra a bag that looked just like mine but had a little more black on it, honeychile?"

"Damn, Pecola. What's this? A trial? It's amazing how you can jump from one subject to another. You've asked me a thousand questions since I sat on this bed. I simply wanted to take a horsey ride. That's all. That's why I'm here early." Symone ignored the question about Cleopatra's bag. "Anyway, let me go. All I want to do is go horseback riding, and I've already been delayed. Why don't you come with me?"

"Chile, I'm going back to bed," Pecola said emphatically and she slipped between the sheets. She pulled the black mask down over her eyes. "I'll talk to you when you get back. Ok? I got to air out my head from all that partying last night. It was rough, girl."

"Good. I'm glad you're not coming with me. I was just trying to be polite. I wanted to ride by myself anyway."

Pecola sucked her teeth and grabbed the sheet over her head. Symone chuckled and walked out the room.

Downstairs in the kitchen, Symone finished drinking another glass of orange juice and placed the glass in the dishwasher. While Cleopatra chitchatted along, Symone found several apples for the horses and placed them in a wiry wicker brown basket.

"I'm serious, Cleopatra. You better slow down on the breakfast, girl. I think the Devereauxs are kicking up a few bed bugs, if you know what I mean."

As Cleopatra placed three garden fresh white lilies in a crystal vase, she watched her with a puzzled expression.

"Bedbugs?"

Symone nodded her head in a knowing manner. The aroma of frying bacon permeated throughout the kitchen and made Symone realize she was kind of hungry.

"Trust me. You know. In other words, they're doing the wild thing, girl," Symone advised with a sly grin. "But I'll take a piece of watermelon myself."

Cleopatra glanced at the watermelon slices that were layered perfectly on the flowery, bone china plate. "Girl, help yourself," she declared and handed the plate to Symone who quickly grabbed two slices.

"Hmmm. This is sweet, Cleo."

"Aren't they? Carlos and Rico brought them over here from Pecola's parents' garden. There were ten of them here last night. This is the last one, girl. The way they were eating them at poolside was a trip. They were slinging watermelons seeds like crazy."

"I can imagine." Symone laughed and quickly ate the two slices as she headed toward the door. Cleopatra followed her. "You know there ain't nothing like Black folk, summertime, and watermelon in North Carolina. If nothing else, I learned that about moving down here."

"You're sooo crazy, Symone."

"I'm serious, girl. Heed my advice. If I were you, I would hold that breakfast for at least forty-five minutes to an hour."

"Are you ok, Symone? You sound hoarse, and you look a little tired."

"I'm fine. I feel better than I sound really. It's stress, girl. Plus, there was just a whole lot of talking last night. That's all." Symone spoke calmly and considered Orlando again. Maybe she should call him now and apologize about the things she told him. Maybe later.

"Stress will kill you. Think about relaxing your mind."

"What I really need is a vacation. My trip to New York for my sister totally stressed me out. Some of my other old baggage is springing up as well. I'm seriously thinking about— about lulling some strange man into submission. Then we're going to disappear to one of the

Eisner's chateaus in France. You know the peaceful one that's in a vineyard?" Cleopatra nodded, and Symone paused briefly and continued to fantasize about the perfect vacation.

"That does sound lovely and inviting, Symone."

"You know my brother and three of his college buddies went to Pamplona, Spain last month."

"Alex told me about Quentin going there! Did he actually run with the bulls?"

"No, girl. He said that they ran in front of the bulls. Can you believe that about Quentin? He swore that it was a big thrill. A rush. A way to get rid of stress."

"A stress reliever? I still can't believe that. Real stress is running for your life. When I heard he had done that, I asked Alex, 'Quentin who?' I assumed she was talking about a white lawyer friend of hers. I really did. I just couldn't imagine anybody Black doing something crazy like that, Symone."

"Believe it. He did it and is sending me pictures to prove it."

"I read about racing with the bulls in a book. *The Sun Also Rises*, Hemingway's book, made running with the bulls so popular and glamorous, but it's a Spanish tradition that dates back to 1591. I would never run with no crazy animals like that. Knowing my luck, I would be the one who would trip, fall, and get gorged to death. Not me and not my man. Girl, that's a stone trip."

Symone laughed loudly and nodded her head in agreement. "I know. You're like a walking encyclopedia. You know that. You need to go on *Jeopardy*."

"Really, Symone?"

"Yeah. I mean it, Cleo. It seems as if you always know background information about everything someone mentions, girl."

"You know me. I just read a lot. That's all. That's why I know about the bulls. I still can't believe Quentin did it."

"Join the club. My sisters were just as shocked he was going, too. My brother is unusually quiet about stuff. He went to Lincoln University to become an attorney, but he and his college buddies are pure thrill seekers. Shirt and tie daredevils. It must be in the Pennsylvania water they consumed while they were in college. Maybe it's a sense of adventure. Hell, I don't know. Remember how last year they swam with the sharks."

"I know, girl. Every time Alex brings Quentin's name up when she talks about those adventure vacations, I always assume she's talking about somebody else or at least somebody white. Black folks just don't do certain insane, suicidal pleasures. We just don't, girl," Cleopatra said laughing. "And Quentin, too? When you speak to him, he always acts so calm, so quiet, and nice."

"I know. That's what everyone says. Yet to look at my brothers and his buddies in their dapper business suits, you just wouldn't know they were wild like that. You know he refused to tell my mother he was going. Mummy probably would've had a heart attack."

"Well, I know you're not going there on vacation. Are you, Symone?"

"No, girl. It's too late for me to go because it's over with now. I'm thinking about going to France. Either that or I'm going to charter a sailboat in Mustique. After Trinidad and Tobago, that's one of my most favorite Caribbean islands. It's so beautiful and quiet. Maybe I'll go from island to island. Do a little bit of wind surfing on top of the crystal clear turquoise water. I need to do something crazy and wild myself before my children come back from summer vacation in a month. You and the boys want to come with me, Cleo?"

"That sounds good, Symone. Let me know when. If I'm not busy helping Alex, you know I'll go. But if it's in three weeks, I can't go. Madison said he wanted to take me and my boys to the mountains with him and Alex especially since I worked so hard, too," she exclaimed with a broad smile. "Just last week I told my Mama, Daddy, and Samson how yall always are wanting to take me on vacation."

"Because we love you, and you deserve it, girl. You work so hard keeping us straight. I told Alex that you're simply a younger version of Miss Jessica." Symone and Cleopatra laughed freely.

"Thanks, Symone. Alex told me you said that." Cleopatra gazed into Symone's sad eyes and reached to hug her tightly. Symone hugged her back with just as much affection.

"Hell, girl. Why you acting so sentimental with me so early this morning?"

"My mind told me to do it, Sy. You seemed to need a hug. That's why."

"Thank you." Symone slowly shook her head. "If I do decide to go away, I certainly will let you know."

"Great."

"Grandison and Beckett love jet skiing and parasailing. You know they'll get a kick out of floating from island to island in the Caribbean. They'll feel like pirates or something," Symone said as she imagined herself relaxing nude on a private sugary white sandy beach.

"Hell, I'll go! I got my bags packed already, baby," bellowed Rozelle as he walked down the winding mahogany staircase with a cup of coffee in his right hand.

They both turned around to watch him. Cleopatra burst out laughing. Symone mumbled *Oh Gawd.*

"Good morning, ladies. Check out the sexy cow lady. My Miss Buffalo girl," Rozelle said as he stepped off the last stair into the foyer. He noticed Symone's cowboy roper boots and had to tease her. Rozelle glanced at his wristwatch. "Where you headed this early in the morning, baby? The show doesn't start for almost another eight hours. Normally, you would be running to get to your seat five minutes before you were scheduled to speak."

"Good morning, Rozelle," Symone greeted in a pleasant voice.

"Good morning, baby. It's kinda early for you to be out, especially for a Saturday morning. Isn't it?" he asked as they reached to hug each other affectionately. He made sure to plant a long hard kiss on her cheek. When he finally released her, Symone slowly shook her head from side to side, and Cleopatra cackled loudly.

"All I want to do is go horseback riding this morning. I declare if another person asks me why I'm up so early, I believe I'm going to scream."

"Don't you look cute in your boots and thangs?" Rozelle idly watched her up and down. "Your Hampton Pirates baseball cap. That sexy white halter top and jeans shorts. Don't you think so, Cleopatra, baby?"

"Yes, Rozelle," Cleopatra said and simply nodded.

"Want me to go with you, Symone?" Rozelle asked. "Want some company on the horse trail?"

"Nope," Symone exclaimed.

"Cause I lost a few hands at cards, I decided to come give my wife a good morning kiss especially since she hadn't seen me since last night."

"That must've shocked the hell out of Jodria Anne," Symone said flippantly. "And no, I don't want company, Rozelle. Go on back and play cards with the fellas."

"The boys wanted me to pick up another bottle of Hennessy, but that can wait," Rozelle said. "I'd rather go with you."

"I'd rather you take your friends the liquor," Symone said.

"Give me ten minutes. I'll meet you down at the stables, baby." Rozelle totally disregarded her comments. He got on his knees and pretended he was praying as well as begging. "Puhleeze, Sy. Puhleeze!"

"If I had a good heart, I'd feel sorry for him and let him go with me," Symone said to Cleopatra.

"Come on. Puhleeze, baby," Rozelle continued to plead.

"All right already," Symone exclaimed with mock frustration.

"Good. I'll see you in a few," Rozelle said and struggled to stand up. He turned and gave Cleopatra a quick kiss on the cheek. He drank the rest of the coffee. "Cleopatra, baby. Just like you, this coffee was smokin', baby. This was exactly what I needed after dealing with those crazy ass men down at the Atlantic City guesthouses."

"That's a good name for that place. Especially if yall are drinking and playing cards the way Pecola told me you were. Which one are yall in, Rozelle?" Symone asked.

"Pecola's been talking again? I tell you that girl can't keep nothing to herself."

"You can't either, Rozelle. You're just like a refrigerator. An old-fashioned icebox, too. Instead of food, you allow private information to slide in your ear, and then you take it right back out again," Cleopatra declared and gave Symone a high five. Both women laughed for a few moments.

"Aren't we supposed to be real tight, Cleopatra?"

"I just believe in telling the truth, Rozelle," Cleopatra confessed, amused at his banter. "Especially when it concerns you."

"Anyway, cowgirl, Alex said that if we were going to be acting like we didn't have any sense, she told Marlon and his boys and Scott and his family to take the two guesthouses that are clustered together," Rozelle said, facing Symone. "Initially, Scott wanted the one beside the pool. After Alex heard their plans, she said 'Oh no—not this day.' You know the two guesthouses down by the pond?"

"I do." Symone nodded her head slowly.

"There's a lot of privacy there. Plus, they're far away from the other seven guesthouses and far away from this house, too. Shooot! I needed a damn golf cart to just get up here to visit my baby this morning. Guess who asked about you, Symone?"

"Who? Your younger brother? He's here?"

"No."

"I can never guess, then," Symone answered swiftly.

"Booker T asked about you and talked about you, baby. He couldn't believe you weren't here last night."

"I know. Pecola told me."

"Damn. Did she leave anything out?" Rozelle stopped speaking and gazed at the alabaster ceiling with a funny grin on his face. "Don't worry. Let me answer that. Hell no. Knowing her, probably not. Anyway, I told him you should be sliding in—probably around four fifty-nine today."

"You see. That's how much you know me. Shocked you didn't I? Marlon's uncle is too crazy. I can't wait to see him, though. Booker T just wanted to know where I was, so we could discuss political issues you wouldn't know much about, Rozelle. That's all."

"Baby, puhleeze. I can handle any subject. Hell, I can handle you, too. You know that, baby," he bragged and winked at her and Cleopatra.

"Here, let me take your cup, Rozelle. You go ahead and get ready so you won't have Symone waiting a long time," Cleopatra instructed in a motherly tone.

"You're right, Cleo. You got fifteen minutes, Rozelle. I'll get the horses ready. After then, I'm on my way with or without you," Symone said. Her voice was stern. Truly, she was ready to go out into the peace and quiet of the trail all by herself. "You got fifteen minutes, Rozelle. Fifteen minutes."

Chapter Forty-Three

Symone walked down the circular front driveway toward the pasture, but she turned around and decided to go by the wishing well for a few moments. Very carefully, she walked down the old gray stone path to enter the formal gardens. As she walked the brick cobblestones to the well, Symone noticed the loveliness of the Devereauxs' private Shangri-La retreat. With its sweeping oak trees, elm trees, and golf course green grass, the splendor of the land was absolutely magnificent. On the edge of the pleasure she got from the beauty around her were her own miserable thoughts about last night with Orlando. As Symone headed down the curving path, she felt like she wanted to cry. Needed to cry. But she stopped herself. Held back the tears cause she'd been crying too much.

The wishing well was housed in a graceful pavilion with Tuscan columns like those built onto the colonnade porch off the Devereauxs' country kitchen. Alex said that she wanted the wishing well to be set in a private place near the formal gardens. Such a location would give people an opportunity to not only peacefully consider their wishes but have the solitude to meditate as they considered their heart's desires among nature. A person could really feel close to God with all this natural beauty. In the quiet peacefulness of the gardens, Symone thought about her life for a few minutes. Just as quickly, she tossed five pennies into the well, turned around, and headed toward the pasture.

Once down at the fence near the stables, Symone stood on the bottom rail and pulled out the silver whistle. She blew it loudly with all her might several times and hoped the horses weren't too far down in the pasture to hear the piercing appeal for them to come up. The rolling green pasture was seventy-five acres enclosed by a three rail PVC white fence, and the sweeping land was home to fifteen geldings. Symone's most favorite one to ride was Starbright. He was a chestnut light brown horse with a flaxen mane and tail. With four socks and white bey with star stripe and snip, Alex subsequently named the horse, Starbright.

Since Starbright reminded Symone of the horses she used to ride when she was a little girl in Trinidad, this was the animal she consistently selected when she came to the Devereauxs to take a peaceful trip along the trail. Symone blew the whistle several times again and waited a little longer. Ten minutes later, she heard the distant sound of horses neighing as four of them galloped toward her. Symone also heard voices behind her. She turned around and was surprised to see Pecola grudgingly stumbling along down the hill with Rozelle.

"...Look who I convinced to come with us, Symone. The second member of the Blue Belles. The first member wouldn't open her bedroom door, baby. All I could hear floating through those doors were The Chantels' *Maybe*. I kept knocking, but nothing happened."

Symone sucked her teeth and said a few curse words under her breath.

"Then, baby," Rozelle continued happily, "I walked down the hall to my room. You know just to throw on something a little sturdier, and the door to Pecola's room was wide open. She said you did that to her on purpose. I woke her up again. After I told her I would wash her down myself and even between her legs, she couldn't do anything but get up to avoid my personal loving hygiene care. Do you know what I mean, Symone? Here she is, and here I am, baby."

Symone simply eyed the two of them. With her nose in the air and Alex's Chanel black sunglasses in place, Pecola was already swatting at imaginary bugs she believed were encircling her face.

"Well, there goes my quiet ride," Symone said with a bittersweet smile as she climbed the fence to get into the pasture. She patted the horses' backs and gave each one an apple. Finally, she haltered Starbright. She snapped a lead line to the halter and handed the line to Pecola who was now standing beside her and still didn't look like she was totally awake or convinced she wanted to go riding.

"Go get another halter and line from the stables, Rozelle," Symone instructed firmly. He could tell that she was aggravated. Rozelle was leaning with his elbows on the fence taking in the serene scene of the four horses swishing their tails from side to side. "I only picked up two."

"Ok, boss," Rozelle said. While he went to handle the task, Symone performed the same routine with the other horse.

"If you don't want me to come now, just let me know, honeychile," Pecola said with her hands on her hips. Still frustrated, she swiftly fanned other bugs.

"Girl, puhleeze. Hell, I didn't want Rozelle to go, but he pleaded with me on his knees. You know I'm a sucker for a man on his knees especially when they're looking up at my body. I don't mind. I was just simply looking for a quiet morning along the trail."

"I heard."

"Out of all my friends, I got the two most talkingest ones in the bunch going along with me. So I can certainly forget about tranquillity on this day." She squeezed Pecola's hand tightly. "You do look kinda of cute with Madison's cowboy hat on your head."

"Thank you, chile." Pecola smiled happily at the compliment. "I just pulled it out of the downstairs' closet. When I couldn't find my sunglasses, Cleopatra gave me Alex's. Who knows where I laid my shades down last night?"

"I'm sure," Symone mumbled.

"But I'm glad you noticed how cute it looked. That's what Rozelle told me," Pecola raved smugly, satisfied that Symone was ok with her riding horses along with her.

Fifteen minutes later, Symone, Pecola, and Rozelle had the saddles and bridles in place and were ready to go. From past horse trips, the three friends knew that if they took the entire trail from beginning to end, they would be out for at least four hours. Designed to go through the dense wooded area of the Devereauxs' land, the trail led through narrow streams, slight hills, and the natural settings where an occasional deer shot across their path. Without a doubt, such tranquillity and beauty gave riders moments to mediate.

To satisfy Symone's need for tranquillity, Rozelle and Pecola didn't say one word for a good thirty minutes. A record for both of them. Immersed in their own thoughts, they all rode and allowed the ambiance of the quiet, the green lush trees, and the birds singing their early morning lullaby songs to envelope them.

"Isn't this wonderful? Blue sky. Birds singing. So what happened to you yesterday, Symone? The brass band was out. I had my trumpet ready. Where were you, baby?" Rozelle asked quietly as he stared straight ahead at the trail.

"Hmmm," Symone mumbled since the question pierced her thoughts about Orlando and Trinidad. "I told you I wasn't feeling well. Plus, I was busy, Rozelle."

"Busy working or busy making love?" Rozelle joked and swiftly gazed at Pecola who smiled back in anticipation of the answer.

"A combination of both," Symone replied and hoped he would drop the subject.

"Was the nigger ok?" Rozelle pushed further.

"Yeah. He was ok."

"Whose this guy? Is he new?" Pecola asked, surprised since she believed she knew about all of Symone's men.

"Nobody yall know. Once again, I sabotaged an evening with a wonderfully nice guy. The evening and me fell flat on my face with a loud thud."

"Babycakes, it's not how many times you fall down. It's how many times you get up that counts," Rozelle said. "That works for relationships, too. Damn sure applies for marriages."

"What happened, Symone? Who was it?" Pecola inquired, still trying to figure out who it was.

"It's a secret, girl."

"Hmmm. A secret lover. Let me see who was missing last night. Can you think of anyone, Pecola?" Rozelle questioned, and Pecola shook her head no.

"Yall are such busy bodies. It's good to know that as usual my business is my business. Don't worry about who it was. He did his job, and I sent him on his way. Quite frankly, my mind was too out there yesterday to deal with anyone. I could barely deal with my own self. That's how miserable I was."

"Who was it, Symone? Arman came down from Charlotte?" Pecola asked nosily again and hoped it was Arman. The man she was pulling for as an appropriate companion for Symone.

"Hell no!" Symone exclaimed. "It wasn't that deadbeat man."

"If you sent him on his way, you're too cold. Cold as ice in Antarctica, baby," Rozelle interjected with a wide grin.

"No, I'm not. I needed to be by myself. I'm just honest."

"Cold-blooded, girl," Rozelle repeated. "Just cold."

"I'm sorry if I didn't attend all my etiquette classes. Even though my family wanted me to be a stellar debutante, I guess all those Fifth Avenue charm lessons didn't work out. Did they? As a strong Black woman, I simply realized that there are occasions I just want to make love sometimes. You know how men are. And I didn't have the patience to accommodate all the macho bravado yall go through when women don't say the words yall want to hear," Symone said still trying to sound tough about the evening with Orlando.

"Cold, girl. Just cold-blooded," Rozelle repeated, shaking his head and joking with her. "When you treat men badly, they'll get you back somehow or another, baby. Remember that James Brown's song, *This is a Man's World.* Pure and simple, baby. We got our ways to righting wrongs."

"That doesn't mean a thing to me, baby. I know it's a man's world. I just never paid any attention to that and continue to do what the hell I want in my sweet ole woman kind of way," Symone replied just as easily.

"Still trying to act tough and cold, girl." Rozelle winked at Pecola. "But I know you. It ain't nothing but a front."

"Humph. That's what you think. That's what you would like to think. Men need to realize that if they're gonna deal with me, they need to learn how to put on a strong suit of armor because who knows what's gonna be thrown at them. That's pure and simple," Symone continued defiantly.

"I know you," Rozelle said again, which was aggravating Symone. "Just cold, girl."

"No, I'm not cold! Women of my generation weren't trained to be confrontational. We've been taught to smile all the time and to be sooo congenial. When we're not that, everybody else believes we're troublemakers or bitches." For some reason, Symone felt a need to explain this to Rozelle.

"Cold, girl," Rozelle repeated quietly. "My buddy, Darius, told me how you got up in his face that night when we were at the Hampton Jazz Festival. He said you told him off big time, baybee." ·

"For a nigger like Darius, I sure did tell him off. He's a successful and top-of-his-game businessman who expects me to fall all over him because he got an MBA from Stanford. You're right I shot him to hell. I bet he didn't tell you the whole story, either. He was trying to play me like that by telling me about all his credentials."

"So boring," Pecola said.

"He bragged like crazy, and you know I hate a braggart, Rozelle. Then he fudged around to ask me about our having sex and asked me if we could kick it together. He doesn't even know me that well. Naturally, I turned around to see if he was speaking to another woman behind me. Now, I got to admit the brother is fine as all hell, but he certainly got the wrong sister."

"I was there when she got him, Rozelle," Pecola admitted as she recalled Darius' startled face. "If I only had my camcorder on, it would've been a serious Kodak moment, honeychile. The girl was in rare form. I hope to die. Symone tore him up from the floor up."

"Anyway, I don't have time for men like that, Rozelle. Be direct," Symone said and smiled at the memory of a pleasurable performance; one she was pleased with. "I don't play games about sex, baby. I'm not shy about that. If I decide I'm going to bed with you, you'll know it because I'll do just that. But I'm not going to stroke your ego in the process. If I want to screw you, I'll tell you to your face."

"She would," Pecola nodded.

"Or I'll call you up and say, 'It's time for me to do it, baby.' I want you. *You've* been selected to love me till I cry. Love me hard, long, and kinda soft for a good three hours. Make it sooo good that I scream your name all night. Then leave me be. Period."

Rozelle burst out laughing. "Damn, girl. You're too much. I don't know what you said to Darius, but you shocked him. He said it was cold. Since I told him you preferred to rap with tall, smart men all the time, he was surprised you ripped him. He's an intelligent brother, too. The kind you love, Symone. You're too cold, girl."

"How can you see his intelligence if all his stupid ass is doing is bragging?" Symone snapped. "That doesn't sound like an intelligent man to me."

"Cold, girl," Pecola piped in too as she laughed gaily. "I agree with my man, Rozelle. I done told Symone that one day she's going to be selected as the Hall of Fame honorary lifetime member for the one-hundred percent proverbial bitch attitude award."

"Ok. Ok, I'm a bitch, but I'm a nice bitch with a big heart." She laughed quickly. "Since I'm almost forty, I really don't mind the bitch title anymore. I've kinda grown into it. I declare I'm ready for a place. Some place where people—where single women especially can have meaningless sex with various partners. They don't have to worry about massaging male egos. Yall know what I'm saying? Isn't there a place like that?"

"You're damn right. Even though a lot of people are trying to bring it back, it's long gone. They called it the life of twenty years ago. Times have changed sho nuff," Pecola declared and took a deep breath.

"You got that right, baby. Back in college, all you had to worry about was having a banging good time with fifty girls if you wanted to. Hell, the worst disease you could get was VD, a few crabs, and a serious itch. You went to the infirmary, and they took care of it on campus. Nowadays, AIDS will kill you and having sex could cause your death. These other diseases will make your dick drop off if your woman doesn't cut it off first. Wooo!"

All three friends cracked up. They were quiet again. Once more they rode along the path hearing only the breathing of the horses and crunching of their hoofs against the dry leaves and twigs cracking on the ground.

"Why do you think she does it?" Pecola asked, not speaking to anyone in particular.

Once again it was a question that pierced Symone's private thoughts regarding Trinidad and last night with Orlando. She leaned forward on the horse to gaze at Pecola. In the middle of them, Rozelle was riding a dark brown gelding named Misty. With Madison's creme cowboy hat propped on his head and trying to look like a cowboy, Symone couldn't see Pecola. When no one responded, Pecola asked the question again.

"Seriously, yall. Why do yall think she does it?"

"Does what, Pecola?" Symone asked quietly, knowing what she meant.

"Why does Alex go all out of her way to work with children?" Pecola said. "To work with people in general the way she does? Why? That's all I'm asking. What makes a person act so goody-too-shoes about every damn thing?"

"Girl, you're crazy," Rozelle said, steering his horse. "One of Alex's favorite philosophies that she adopted from Rudyard Kipling is *Always prefer to believe the best of everybody—it saves so much trouble...*"

"I think people resent people who do things well, Pecola. It's just human nature. For some reason, they get mad at them," Symone advised swiftly.

"Hell, Symone," Pecola said. "I don't resent Alex. You know that. I'm just trying to ask questions about me, honeychile."

"I definitely don't think it's a goody-too-shoes issue, Pecola baby. Why did you say it like that?" Symone watched Rozelle as he spoke.

"Maybe it's not goody-too-shoes. Hell, I don't know what I'm trying to say. What determines if some people are real nice like Alex, are like other people, are like me, or are a bitch like, Symone?" Pecola questioned in an amusing voice.

"Whaaat, girl?" Symone groaned.

Pecola smiled at Symone's reaction and continued talking. "Or, is like Rozelle. Don't get me wrong, it ain't anything wrong with being like us. We're good people. Even though Alex acts like everyone else, she does act goody-too-shoes. She always has been that way, too. When we first met, I used to tell Alex that all the time. At the opening ceremonies just last month, I even told her the same thing. Well, you know her. She just laughed and told me I was crazy as usual. If nothing else, I know that much about me is right."

"Pecola, you're sooo funny. I don't think it's because she's a goody-too-shoes sort of person," Symone said laughing as she cleared her throat.

"Alex is a nice lady. That's her nature," Rozelle inserted. "Like some people are hot-headed, stubborn, and stingy, Alex happens to be a giving sister."

"I'm with you," Symone said. "I believe that at some point in time, you have to say 'Ok, what am I going to do to make a difference? I have the money. So what can I do?' That's why I believe Alex does it, Pecola. It's her mission to help and serve people. It's her lifeblood to care for someone who's not as fortunate as she is. I understand in a way. I really do. When you have money, it's kinda like a bittersweet privilege. At least it is for me because there's some degree of guilt within you as well."

"But why?" Pecola was puzzled.

"Your heart goes out to the ones who don't have as much money as you do. You believe you want to help everyone, but you know you can't. You simply can't save the world. So you figure out a way to make a difference in as many quiet little ways as you can. That's what Alex does. I understand because I try to do the same thing."

"Hell, I have big money, too," Pecola exclaimed. "I certainly thank God for that. Let me tell you one thing. I know what's it's like to have money, and I know what it's like to not have any. Believe you me, I prefer the days of having it. Sometimes I walk outside in my yard, and I'm speechless. When I see my Beverly Hillbillies house—"

"Have mercy," Rozelle said, and Symone's laughter cut Pecola off.

"I'm serious, yall. I love my house. Really. I'm speechless about what I have. I just never ever knew my life would turn into what it is. That I would have all that I have now. I always believed I would be a famous singer. Still, I marvel at everything I have," Pecola confessed softly as she considered her early, poor years in Greensboro. "You can believe I don't want to lose my money either. I'll work damn hard to keep it. Does that sound selfish?"

"No. I don't think that's selfish," Symone replied. "We both work hard to keep our businesses thriving, Pecola. That's our responsibility in the corporate world. That's human nature for us to handle our business affairs with integrity, so that we can continue to earn money honestly. That's why I enjoy our businesses so much. It's something that I had a hand in creating. I wanted to make it on my own. Yet, by the same token, I look at what the Eisners' have provided for me, and it's like whoa! I don't have to do a damn thing, and it just keeps growing right along. In those cases, I do feel guilt once more. Because I realize I've sooo, sooo much, and others have sooo little. Having money is a privilege. As a result of that privilege, it's my responsibility to help people. I prefer to not let people know what I'm doing for them or let them know where the help is coming from. I like being an anonymous giver. You ain't got to worry about people ringing your doorbell all the time."

"I'm with you, baby," Rozelle said, staring straight ahead, looking serious.

"In the past, you've told me how you feel guilty about your trust fund, Symone. I understand all of that you're saying, but I wouldn't feel guilty one bit. I would enjoy my money, girl. You're different than me. I probably wouldn't work nowhere," Pecola said, and Rozelle chuckled heartily. "No. I'm just kidding, honeychile."

"I wouldn't work either," Rozelle piped in.

"Join the lazy lima bean club," Symone said.

Pecola nodded that she understood. "All I'm saying is that Alex goes all out. Way out. But why? What is she trying to prove? Keep in mind I asked Alex the exact same thing I'm asking yall. So yall know I'm not saying anything behind my friend's back. I don't do that."

Rozelle noticed how two squirrels scooted out in front of them and scurried up a tall maple tree. He rode on in silence for several moments before he spoke.

"I don't know why she does it either, Pecola. After I met her years ago, she made me aware that I wasn't doing shit. That's for sure. All I was doing was talking a good game, Pecola," he replied in just as quiet a voice as Pecola. "It's a travesty to have children suffering in our own backyard. These communities aren't far away from our own pretty, spacious and expensive homes. Well—all of them aren't really suffering, but they're still suffering for attention. You know it must get hard sometimes for them. They're children of the working poor, single mothers and fathers on welfare. They got to struggle for every little bitty thing because they don't have access to money and to well-paying jobs. Plus, they're suffering for a glimpse of other things. A chance to see another life."

"That's true, Rozelle," Symone said.

"Some children need an opportunity to have another perspective of the world and even another perspective of Black people. To not do something to make it happen is just as bad. I guess it was absolutely intolerable for Alex to stand by and do nothing for those children—for any children that are in need. Whether it's little or big, we must do something. The small blessings in life aren't small blessings to people who have nothing. Like Alex says all the time, if people are given a chance to excel in life, you can believe they'll rise to the occasion and do just that."

"Here. Here. I certainly agree with that philosophy. That's what happened to me!" Pecola shouted out into the air, and all three friends burst out laughing.

"I agree, too. I understand wholeheartedly myself!" Symone screamed as she remembered her early days in America. "How do you build up a child's pride—children's pride? The pride of those who live in those poor communities? Their self-esteem. These are the same children who historically have been told their chances to make it and be successful in this world are slim to none. That's why I support any activity Alex does. I really, really do."

"Me, too." Rozelle said with a large grin on his face. "I sho do. You know Alex is always doing something anyway. After Scott and I spoke with her and Madison, I guess Alex felt that if she combined the efforts of her close friends as actively concerned people, that was one way we all could work together to see change. Alex isn't selfish, and she wants everyone to feel a sense of worth about his or her life, too. Before last year, she had always been working with children, senior citizens, doggies, cats, horses, and whoever else she would get to listen to her views about life."

"I guess you're right, Rozelle. Sometimes I look at my life and I say to myself, 'Pecola, don't be sooo damn selfish, girl. Don't be that way. Get off that ego trip. Don't act that way toward your…,'" Pecola said softly and couldn't finish the sentence about her parents.

"You say what? Let me hear that confession again," Symone joked lightly.

"I say to myself, 'Pecola don't be that way.' That's all. I know sometimes yall think I'm pretentious. Sometimes I am, and a lot of times I'm not. But I really want to work on me. It's time for me to make a difference in someone else's life, too. Alex tells me all the time that when I learn how to give freely of myself, it'll help make a difference in my life. It'll make me feel fulfilled."

"I understand, Pecola." Symone smiled.

"Do you really, Symone? I know we got Akao and Meetings Odyssey, and our people receive excellent salaries. But I'm talking about being sincere like Alex. Making a difference in a tremendous sort of way for people other than the ones who draw a paycheck from you. I want to look at people and see their hearts. How in the hell does someone do that? Nine times out of ten, I can't get pass their designer clothes," Pecola confessed with a lazy smile. "I can't get past the desire to know if they've had a face-lift or not. I'm trying to figure out where they live. Since I'm among my true friends, I'm just being honest with this situation, yall."

"I appreciate your honesty, Pecola," Rozelle said.

"Me too," Symone piped in. "Honesty heals old ways."

Now Pecola paused with melancholy as she considered all the lies and deceit that encircled her secret life.

"The other Pecola is so intrinsic in me. There's this woman that I've created in my mind. Quite honestly, I don't know sometimes," she ended with her voice trailing off again. "Then, I think what will people think of me if I decide to—?"

Symone swiftly shook her head and smiled quickly. "I love you dearly, but that's one of your major problems. Worrying about what people think, Pecola. The hell with them. If you continue to aggravate yourself with pleasing sorors and maintaining a certain status quo, you'll find out that you soon need to belong in a home for the terminally tense. It'll stress you out sooo damn much that you'll discover that enough isn't enough for some people. No matter what you do, you'll never please your snooty friends or those wannabee niggers you hang around with. Maybe those sorors and those highfalutin folk you run behind all the time weren't your friends in the first place."

"I know it's a hard job for you, but somebody's got to do it, Pecola. Hobnobbing with your outrageously politically correct and socially acceptable people," Rozelle interjected. "But Symone is right, baby. Be free like me."

"Well, not that free, Pecola," Symone said. "Carlos will kill your behind if you acted like Rozelle."

"One thing I learned a long time ago," Rozelle went on. "I find that the wannabes are the bigger snobs than the already-have-money bees." Both women broke out into friendly laughter.

"I've been exposed to both, Rozelle," Symone said with surety. "And folks with money can act just as stone-hearted and snobbish, too. Sometimes, you don't even have to have money. If you know the person that does have the bucks, you act ridiculous. It's all by association. Money can't change you. In some cases, it makes folks worse."

"Pecola baby, you can't live a fun and fulfilled life if you're worrying about pride all the time. Do what you feel like doing, baby," Rozelle said understandingly.

"I agree with you, Rozelle," Symone said. "Who knows what the answer to life is? Do you know?"

"You're asking me, honeychile?" Pecola wondered.

"I'm just asking the question, Pecola," Symone mumbled and paused. "Madison and Alex believe that a person has to look within themselves to find those answers. How am I supposed to know the answer to life? Damn! I can't see shit inside of me. It's so damn cloudy in my head cause I got a helluva lot of problems too, girl."

"Who knows how to make this thing called life work? We all are transitioning with our lives all the time. It's just something about the fortyish age bracket. You tend to question life a little more thoroughly," Rozelle said slowly. "I think Alex is special because she doesn't concern herself with stuff like that. She doesn't look up at you. She doesn't look down on you. No matter who you are, no matter where you live, she'll connect with you and with people from all walks of life."

"She certainly does that," Symone nodded.

"I liken her to our own local Mother Teresa," Rozelle said with a quick laugh. "She doesn't care about going into the trenches to help whoever lives in the ghetto, the projects, dirty houses, or into the homeless shelters. One time she told me that it was no big deal to her. She doesn't see the dirt, and she doesn't care about it. She only sees their spirit. Their desire to survive and to have something. Now that's a powerful place to be mentally. It's an awesome statement. Anytime you can go back, reach down, and get some of the people society has forgotten, that says a lot to me."

"Here. Here," Symone chimed in.

"Alex knows everybody can't do what she does," Rozelle went on. "I'm sure she knows a lot of people don't even want to think about what she's doing. But I believe her main message to her friends is to just do something. She never tells us what we should do. *Never.* But her actions speak loudly. That's what I hear loud and clear."

"Me too, Rozelle," Pecola nodded.

"Now take someone like Pecola here. She ain't never seen hide nor tail of the inside of a housing project complex. If Pecola stepped into one of those homes, her nose would be so high in the air she would drown."

"Wait a damn minute," Pecola inserted swiftly to defend her honor and really felt more like kicking the hell out of Rozelle for making such a statement. "That's not even true. I'm being totally honest today, yall. Hang with me. Like my children say all the time, don't dis me like that, RB."

"Rozelle, I'm with you on that," Symone agreed. "I love my girl. Right is right, and your ass is certainly on the money about Pecola's nose being in the air sometimes, Rozelle."

"That's enough, my friends," Pecola yelled with a twinge of amusement. "I done told, yall. Don't dog me. I'm trying to be real with this truthness kick. I declare it must be the clear, fresh air of the horse trail that has put me in a real live confessional mode."

"What I was saying about Alex is this, ladies." Rozelle smiled and then continued. "She's genuine. She doesn't try to change who she is or try to make you think she's any better than you because of all she has. She doesn't force herself to do what she does. It's innately, Pecola. She doesn't have to struggle to do it. Anything that's not in your heart, it's not going to work, baby."

"Absolutely," Symone said.

"I do know that much about life," Rozelle explained wistfully. "That tried and true learning came from my Grandma Zula. Anyway, people can tell when it's not real. I believe Alex does it because it's real. That's the big difference between people who are struggling about what to do—about pleasing folks. I believe that."

"Here. Here," Symone said in agreement.

"Alex is real. Pure and simple. I don't believe there's a fake bone in her body. There's nothing phony about her. She's a quiet leader," Rozelle went on. "To be a leader in any form and to be able to connect, you got to have a strong sense of self. She has that big time. In this world, there are only a few people who aren't afraid of taking risks with other people. They don't care what people think about them."

"I don't care," Symone murmured.

"Alex is that way about everyone," Rozelle said. "I think the three of us are too selective when it comes to dealing with certain people. We pick and choose carefully. Yall know we do that, but not Alex. She embraces everyone. Alex feels that if she can take a chance with a machine in Las Vegas and Atlantic City, then she knows she can sure as hell take a chance with human beings who can talk, breathe, and make a difference."

"Bravo!" Pecola yelled, and Rozelle laughed. "She gets my vote for president."

"Alex lovingly leads us around all the time on the faithful human dog leash," Rozelle joked with a big smile. "And you can believe there's nothing that you, me, or Symone wouldn't do for Alex."

Both women vigorously nodded their heads. "You're right about that," Symone and Pecola exclaimed simultaneously.

"As a matter of fact, I tell Scott all the time that she's probably the strongest one in our circle of friends," Rozelle said and hesitated momentarily. "I know people think she's all this prissy pooh pooh kind of person. Hell, she's definitely that, yet Alex got a lot of downright brash sassiness in her as well. Since she's so giving and sooo true blue, everyone is overly protective of her because we think that someone's going to take advantage of her since she's so nice. She's deep, but it's her spirituality, too. That's also her greatest strength, and that's how she reaches everyone. It's that casual, spiritual strength that allows her to weave threads of love throughout people's lives with her own."

"Damn, Rozelle! Are you Alex's campaign manager or what?" Pecola wondered.

"Hell, I know I sound like a sugar tit commercial. Yall sure there ain't no camera crews out here recording this conversation?" Rozelle asked jokingly. "But it's true, baby. I mean everything I'm saying. She's like our quiet leader with steel shoulders. Our moral conscience and it's not that she has intentionally placed herself in that moral position. She doesn't even try to stand there in such a manner."

"True," Symone said.

"It's like her attitude and reverence for human life—to help people see their gifts deem it so for us." Rozelle's voice was serious. "All jokes aside. All I can say is that she's a wonderful testimony for me. I know it is for Jodria Anne, too. Both she and Madison have such wonderful character. Hell, I can go on and on."

"Well—" Symone hesitated for a moment. She knew what she was going to say next was going to offend her two friends, so she decided to remain quiet—at least for now.

Chapter Forty-Four

"That was a wonderful breakfast, Cleo. Madison and I enjoyed every morsel of it," Alex crooned, stepping into the sunny kitchen where she saw Jodria and Cleopatra talking quietly to one another. "Is everything ok?"

"It's hunky dory," a smiling Cleopatra said and began taking the breakfast dishes off the bed tray that Alex placed on the marble and granite counter. "Want more coffee?"

"Nope," Alex answered and reached to give Jodria a good morning hug. "I'm full, girl. Yall ready to start fixing breakfast for the children?"

"Sure am," the chubby Jodria said. Still trying to wake up, she took a sip of hot cappuccino and gave Alex a sleepy smile. "That's why I'm sitting here, girl—barely."

"Alex, I was just telling Jodria that her sister-in-law should file bankruptcy. The same way you recommended my fourth cousin do in Tupelo," Cleopatra said and poured milk into the self-rising flour. "Isn't that right?"

"It depends, Cleo," Alex replied and turned to stare at Jodria who was now munching on her fourth piece of bacon. "What happened, JAB?"

"I *told* you about her. The one who has the high, five figure, credit card debt," Jodria mumbled with a mouth full of food. "You know Juliana?"

"The one who is a molecular biologist?" Alex asked, and Jodria nodded slowly.

"I can't see how a molecular biologist would be financially strapped," Cleopatra exclaimed. "They make too much money. Jodria was telling me that her husband is a biologist too. Umph."

"It happens, Cleo," Alex said. "Is the mortgage company still ready to foreclose on her home?"

"Yes," Jodria answered. "But Juliana refuses to give us any more details. She won't take a dime from Rozelle or her parents. Both she and her husband are very smart, but it's like they don't have any common sense about what's getting ready to happen to them."

"They're probably embarrassed, JAB," Alex said. "Upset at themselves. They're college graduates. They got master's degrees, and they can't believe the turn of events in their lives."

"I know what happened," Cleopatra said, glancing sharply around at Jodria and Alex. "They used their credit cards like cash. They didn't save, and they didn't plan properly."

"Absolutely," Jodria agreed. "I told Juliana the same thing."

"It depends on how you said it, too," Alex said, thinking for a moment.

"I was honest with my sister-in-law," Jodria explained. "That's exactly what they need right now. A relative to tell them the hard truth."

"When is the foreclosure sale?" Alex asked.

"It's in one week," Jodria replied. "What are they going to do? Rozelle's parents are worried sick about it. They're concerned that their three grandchildren will be out on the streets, but his sister and her husband are acting like martyrs or something. They're going down with the ship with their heads held high and for what?"

"Cleo is right," Alex said. "If they don't want help from family, they should file Chapter 13 bankruptcy."

"Why that one?" Jodria wondered. "I heard of another bankruptcy called Chapter 7."

"I don't recommend Chapter 7. If they filed Chapter 7, the Trustee could liquidate all their assets to satisfy the creditors. That means taking their house, selling it and using the money to pay the creditors. With Chapter 13, they would help them reorganize. If they got the income, they can probably handle the payments."

"Ok, I see," Jodria nodded, still not sure.

"If the foreclosure sale is in two weeks, they can file bankruptcy up until the time of the foreclosure sale." Alex thought some more. "If the foreclosure sale is at one o'clock on Thursday, they can file bankruptcy at nine o'clock on Thursday morning. They still will be protected."

"You're kidding," Jodria exclaimed with wide eyes. "I didn't know that."

"A lot of Black people don't, girl. They would rather lose their home than to file bankruptcy," Alex went on. "They're already on a financial slide, so what difference does it make by filing."

"But it takes ten years for bankruptcy to leave their credit report," Jodria said.

"What do they want, JAB? Do they want to be on the street?" Alex inquired abruptly. "If they're in foreclosure, they got bad credit now anyway. What do they expect?"

"Hell, I don't know. The American dream. Whatever the hell that is," Jodria mumbled. "I'll tell them what you said, though."

"You already told me that the mortgage company isn't working with them to work out payments," Alex continued.

"They're not," Jodria said, eating.

"Take it out of the mortgage company hands. File bankruptcy. Black folks would rather lose their home, go homeless and live in a shelter than to take this drastic an action. That's ridiculous. They gots to realize that bankruptcy laws weren't set up for Black people. They were created over one-hundred years ago. White people had more things then. Not us."

"Totally true," Cleopatra nodded. "I remember reading that."

"So we need to learn how to take advantage of laws that were set up to help in financial situations like that. Go into any bankruptcy court nowadays and look at whose there. The majority of the people sitting in there are white. When necessary, they've no problem filing the pertinent paperwork to go into bankruptcy," Alex went on.

"But their credit is still messed up," Jodria insisted. "And then they put your name in the newspapers."

"Sooo! At least they'll still have their house and their car," Alex said and shook her head from side to side. "That's true what you're saying, Jodria. Bankruptcy will be on their credit report, but they can work on having it removed. Credit repair does happen."

"Ok." Jodria inhaled deeply. "I'll tell Juliana."

"They can go right down to an office supply store and get the bankruptcy forms. If they have any questions, I'll be happy to help them in a legal capacity—pro bono." Alex paused.

"Or, they can also select an attorney to help them. The fee is one thousand dollars right now. It might be more in certain areas of the country. Those fees don't come out of the debtors' pockets up front."

"Debtors?" Jodria asked, and Cleopatra started laughing.

"Yes. When people go into bankruptcy, they're considered debtors. It's just a title to embarrass people even more." Alex sipped water before she continued. "But the debtors' fees will be taken out of their bankruptcy payments. For one year, it averages to about one-hundred per month."

Cleopatra whistled. "Wow! So if you know the ins and outs of bankruptcy, and you're an attorney," she figured slowly, "you can do real well. If you help one-hundred people a month file their petition papers, your earnings are ten thousand per month. That's not a bad job."

"Exactly," Alex answered.

"Law school here I come," Cleopatra joked. Both Alex and Jodria giggled.

"In addition," Alex said, "the debtors have to pay the trustee of the bankruptcy court a fee of five percent, give or take a percentage point. If I'm not mistaken, it's five percent of their total debt."

"You're kidding. That trustee is probably rolling in dough. Hmmm. I never knew that," Jodria moaned and swallowed some apple juice. "Why is that so?"

"That's the way it's set up. Bankruptcy is big business. There are major corporations that file bankruptcy on a continuous basis. Although they might be showing a profit on one subsidiary, the other division is losing money. So they file bankruptcy to reorganize and keep their creditors at bay. Black folks need to realize we should do the same thing for our homes, businesses, and whatever. It's not a stigma. Far as I'm concern, it's a conscientious business decision."

"My Cousin Minder is so happy he filed bankruptcy," Cleopatra said, checking on the frying bacon as she talked. "He's thanking the lord all over the place. He had filed bankruptcy two years ago and thought he couldn't file it for another ten years."

"That inaccurate too," Alex said. "A person can file bankruptcy every six months, if necessary."

"My Cousin Minder didn't know that. He got laid off at the cotton mill nine months ago. So, he called me on a Tuesday. I think my family believes I know everything. I don't know anything. I just work for people that do." Cleopatra stopped talking to catch her breath. "I told Alex about my Cousin Minder on that same Tuesday. She called Cousin Minder back on Tuesday afternoon. His foreclosure sale was on Thursday. He filed bankruptcy on Wednesday, and they couldn't touch his house, his car, his property, or nothing."

"Sounds like it works," Jodria said.

"It does," Alex said. "When he filed, I told him to write his case number down and reference that in a letter to all of his creditors. He only had two. His mortgage company and the finance company for his car."

"But that was enough for Cousin Minder," Cleopatra said.

"Bankruptcy is like a stay of execution. Just imagine if you were due to be electrocuted at midnight, Jodria. If the Supreme Court gave you a stay, they couldn't electrocute you. Well, it's the same way with bankruptcy. Once your petition is filed, all actions cease. Whether those creditors or sheriffs want them to go on, it's out of their hands. That's the federal law, baby!"

"Since then, I've read more about foreclosures," Cleopatra inserted quickly. "Alex is right. It *is* big business. They have two-hundred foreclosures a day in North Carolina alone. Lawyers, investors, clerks of courts, and all kinds of greedy people make money with foreclosed property. I think it's terrible."

"It is," Alex agreed.

"But when Alex told Cousin Minder what to do, I've been educating everybody I run into to do the same thing. Get ruthless like the mortgage companies and the investors, file bankruptcy. If you research mortgages, you'll see how illegal they are in the first place. Banks aren't lending *you* money. They're using *your* house to make money on money they *never* gave *you* to buy the house, but they say *you* owe them. They're passing paper around. If you ask me, it's very crooked."

"Whaaat," Jodria exclaimed "Your Cousin Minder and my sister-in-law didn't pay their mortgages."

"True," Cleopatra nodded. "Since they didn't plan right, they ran into hard times. There's no disputing that. I've been there, Jodria. Maybe people lost their jobs. Maybe a man got a divorce. I don't know what happens in people's lives. It's real hard these days. Just like your sister-in-law, Juliana, who knows what happened to them? But I do know there's a way to get out of it. You can believe if it ever happens to me, I'll do the same thing."

Jodria clapped for several seconds. "Woooo! You go, girl," she roared and looked at Alex. "You're creating a legal monster here."

"Madison told me the same thing the other day," Alex said, walking over to hug Cleopatra. "But that's not what it is. Cleo just soaks everything up since she reads a wide variety of books like crazy. That's how she really learns what she knows."

"You help me, too," Cleopatra said to Alex. "So do you, Jodria. Yall all do."

"Where's Pecola?" Alex asked, suddenly realizing she wasn't around. "I noticed she wasn't upstairs in her bedroom, either."

"She went horseback riding with Symone," Cleopatra informed.

"So did Rozelle," Jodria announced.

"Omigodddd," Alex moaned. "Symone insisted she wanted to take a quiet ride. All—by—her—self."

"Don't remind me," Cleopatra said, beating eggs and a little sugar into the huge bowl of pancake mix. "Next thing I know, Rozelle invited himself. But before he left, he convinced Pecola to go with him."

"Uh oh," Alex muttered with a jumbo grin. "Knowing those three the way I do, they're probably at each other's necks right about now."

"You gots that right," Jodria said and took another large bite of the warm hot cross bun Cleopatra just handed to her out of the oven. "Can you imagine a quiet trip along the horse trail with my crazy husband, the non-stop talking Pecola, and the depressed Symone? My, my, my, my. That's some interesting combination."

Chapter Forty-Five

"Go ahead and say what you're thinking, Sy," Rozelle finally edged on when she still hadn't said anything almost ten minutes later.

"Uh, you forced me," Symone moaned.

"Since when anyone has to twist your arm to say anything," Pecola said. "Get real."

"Ok. This is strictly my opinion. Alex would never say this about any organization that she diligently works with. I believe she doesn't think her sorority, the other organizations that she's involved in, and the boards she serves on do enough. They don't do things that are tangible. That she can at least see actual results from, and you know how she dumps plenty of money in those organizations, too."

"I definitely can't see that, Symone." Pecola was astonished by her comments. "I send hefty checks to A&T and to the alumni association all the damn time. I support every AKA activity. Carlos sends money to A&T as well. The same thing for the Alphas. We both do our part in more ways than one, chile."

"I'm sure glad Carlos writes checks to the damn Alphas. The Ques don't want him to write a check to us anyway, baby. We don't like rubber," Rozelle interjected amusingly in an attempt to lighten up the moment.

"*A bad check? Carlos?* Nigger, puhleeze," Pecola groaned as she rolled her eyes and sucked her teeth at him.

"C'mon, Rozelle. We're trying to be serious here. Listen to me, Pecola. I think that's great you and Carlos support your organizations with your money. That's wonderful, but what about your time outside of that? I know you're saying since I'm the only one who isn't involved in a sorority, that's why I'm talking like that. I realize that everyone—all my friends are deeply entrenched in sororities and fraternities. So naturally you think my viewpoint is biased. But when you really look at it, what the hell are yall doing, girl?" Symone asked, exasperated.

"I hate to hear people ask 'What are sororities and fraternities doing?' when they're not in one," Pecola said. "Oooh! That aggravates me."

"Symone," Rozelle said, after taking a deep breath. "The premise for fraternities and sororities is to of course promote education, help kids, and teach them to set and attain every last one of their goals."

"That sounds great, Rozelle," Symone nodded. "That's a wonderful premise, but is it practiced nationwide? Worldwide? That's all, I'm asking. The point is that once folks become a member of a sorority or a fraternity, some of those same folk forget the mission. They start profiling saying you aren't as good as I am because I'm an Alpha or a Sigma. I'm an AKA or a Delta, so I can't deal with you. That's being a member of a Greek organization for the wrong reasons. That's not what it should be about. Now the camaraderie is there, but—"

"Hell, Symone. That's not the only reason Greek groups meet, chile." Pecola wanted to stop Symone from making other negative comments about the traditional Greek Black organizations.

"Ok. Ok. Other than meeting on a continuous basis, Pecola. And believe you me I know that Black folks love to meet," Symone added. "It makes me so sick that we're known for having meetings all over the place. But the question is, what are we accomplishing by all these meetings? We meet to discuss meetings. It's sickening. That's why we don't have effective leaders nowadays. They're too busy meeting. Leaders are too scared to stick their necks out as leaders. You don't pick your battle. As a leader you should constantly be in the forefront. We don't have leaders like the Harriett Tubman or the Frederick Douglas types any more."

"Here. Here. That makes sense to me, baby," Rozelle exclaimed. "But we're talking about sororities and fraternities. Everybody isn't born a leader."

"Then in sororities, I notice how the various sisters try to outdress each other. Plus yall provide scholarships to children who don't need it. Children whose parents are doctors, lawyers, business owners and corporate folk—who make enough money to pay their children's way to go to school. Yall determine scholarships and awards based upon who raises the most money. That doesn't make sense to me. It would be hard for a poor child to raise a lot of money. Who are they going to collect the money from? Definitely not their project or poor neighbors who are struggling like they are. Hell, if they're going to raise a helluva lot of money, they might as well keep it for themselves and pay their own way to college. Don't give it to an organization that will simply piece meal it to them," Symone stated in an appalled voice.

"Symone, chile!" Pecola shouted. "You're wrong. My sorority for one sponsors poor familes all the time. It's done quietly and without a lot of fanfare."

"That's good. Then when I read in the newspapers that professional people and other sorrows and frat children get those scholarships, I can't believe it," Symone continued. "It's like it's planned. It's like certain people in the organization get together to help make sure that their chosen friend's child raises the most money."

"What is this nonsense you're saying?" Pecola asked.

"Once again, it boils down to who knows who," Symone went on. "Now, don't get me wrong, I believe in networking. Why give *those* children the scholarships? Go out into those urban areas, into the projects, and into the other poor sections of town where children *really* need help. Seek them out."

"That's done, Symone," Pecola said.

"But then, I'm even more shocked when I read the amount that frats and sorors give. Most organizations hand those scholarship recipients an envelope with a measly $500 check in it. It's no more than $1,000. What in the hell can that do? Black folks have been giving $500 scholarships for twenty years. It's ridiculous. It's time for organization to go for the whole ride. The full scholarship. Hell, they got enough people in those organizations who are professionals and can afford to drop at least a thousand dollars a piece to help a deserving kid."

"Who in the hell are you to talk, Symone? Money was set aside for you ever since you were ten-years old," Pecola said disgustingly as she considered her friend's misunderstanding of sororities. "Everyone doesn't have your kind of money, chile. They didn't have a trust fund at ten years old. Everybody doesn't call one of the richest white men in the whole wide world uncle, either."

"What has that got to do with anything, Pecola?" Symone muttered. "My Uncle Samuel isn't the richest man in the world. Hell, you should know that. You keep up with his wealth, position, and power more than I do. Remember, you're the one that always reminds me of my uncle's standing in *Forbes* magazine anyway."

"You're right, Sy. You know Pecola's nothing but an alias. Her real name is *Ms. Lifestyles of the Rich and Famous*. I know she keeps up with that information. No matter how many times I hear it, I can't comprehend that your uncle's estimated net worth is twenty-two billion dollars," Rozelle said with a short laugh as he performed some mathematical calculations.

"Hell, I don't have the billions." Symone spoke harshly.

"I know, but you got a helluva lot, baby. I see why you always try to keep that association confidential. My ass would too, girl," Rozelle teased and blew Symone a kiss, which she ignored.

"Whoopty doo," Pecola snapped back and rolled her eyes at Rozelle. "I'm not going to change what I said. Everybody don't have a damn trust fund set up by one of the richest families in the world, honeychile. They don't have *your* bucks."

"I know that, Pecola. Believe me I do." After taking deep breaths, Symone spoke calmly. "I'm aware of that every day I wake up each morning and hear Tom Joyner on the radio, read the newspapers, look at my tree lined street with huge homes, or walk around Winston-Salem. I realize I have more than a lot of people, girl."

"To say the least," Pecola mumbled under her breath.

"That's exactly what I said earlier," Symone said and stared directly into Pecola's eyes. "But what I have isn't going to make me stay quiet. I'm just saying that collectively, Black folks can do anything we put our minds to if we stop being so cheap with giving, or stop blaming our problems on our being Black. Just give, girl. Traditionally, we don't give. We'd rather buy a Benz, BMW, Lexus, Navigator, or a Grand Cherokee Jeep. A whole lot of disposable things that don't impact our future generations or society one iota."

"Don't talk about my Jeep, baby. That's cause for a serious knock down drag out fight with black grease smeared all over our bodies." Rozelle was serious and funny.

"May I puhleeze finish my point, Rozelle baby?" Symone asked impatiently. "We don't support our colleges the way we should, and that's a shame. Some Black folk would rather drop dead than write a ten thousand check to the United Negro College Fund. Traditionally, we're very stingy people. That's a shame."

"That's pure bullshit, and I don't agree with a thang you're saying, Symone," Pecola blurted. "Everyone can't write a ten thousand dollar check. For some people, ten dollars is worth ten thousand dollars to them."

"Good point, Pecola," Rozelle said.

"Each year, we should dig deep into our pockets. We should always support the Black colleges cause they gave Black people foundations for life. Instead of supporting organizations, we rather buy cars, clothes, and diamond baubles."

"Now baby, I believe the reason Black folks don't support their colleges as much is because when we graduate from college, we don't earn as much money on the jobs as our white counterparts," Rozelle explained. "You know how it is for a lot of us to struggle against the glass ceiling which is more like a brick ceiling in many cases. It's hard to penetrate sometimes, baby. And—"

"I understand what you're saying, Rozelle," Symone said, cutting him off.

"Let me finish, baby," Rozelle said. "Black men and women in the corporate world always got to bring something extra to the table, and the odds are statistically you won't make it up or even make it in. When I attend those high-level chemical meetings and conferences for my company, most times I rarely ever see other Black folks who have broken through the glass ceiling. I know for me, it gets lonely out there. So there are a lot of us who are struggling trying to make it. We gots to support our families. Do all that other stuff just to live and to be a Black person in America." Rozelle hoped his wisdom penetrated Symone's view, but it didn't.

"I think those are lousy excuses, Rozelle," Symone said.

"Whaaat, baby!" Rozelle asked, shocked.

"I'm serious. We just haven't gotten our priorities straight. They're all mixed up. We're struggling how?" Symone mumbled. "Sure there are many who still struggle. But many more have made it. We struggle to buy that house, that car, and those clothes. Black folks always talk about struggling when it comes to giving money to a worthwhile cause."

Aggravated, Pecola frowned and shook her head. "Well, you don't have to struggle, Symone. Never have. Why do you say *we* all the time," Pecola asked quietly and Symone ignored the question.

"Why not struggle and send money to our schools. That's why white schools have better facilities and more famous and published Ph.Ds. Their alumni give back," Rozelle said. "But they get a lot of government and corporate funding. So naturally, they have the high-tech computers, the beautiful buildings on the manicured ground, the best teachers, and those stellar programs to offer perspective students."

"True," Symone agreed. "If Black folks just give back, if corporations and other entities gave to Black schools the way they give to the white ones, our schools could have an even bigger impact. We would have the best, too. But Black people simply love to *show* their affluence. We rather buy those cars and wear white designers clothes that don't give a damn about us other than how we can flash their clothes on television or in the workplace. Then we can brag and say we're wearing a Frizty Fritzy."

"Fritzy Fritzy?" Rozelle spoke questioningly. "I never heard of them."

"I'm just saying whoever. Fritzy is a name I made up, Rozelle. I notice that about Seventh Avenue. Even when I go to the designer shows in New York with Uncle Samuel and Auntie Gerda, we always get front row seats to those white designers shows. The shows that are considered the most powerful and highly coveted ones in the world. But what I notice most and what I observed even when I was a child was that there weren't many Black models strutting down the runway."

"That hadn't change even today," Pecola said in a huff.

"When I attended my first fashion show with my uncle," Symone continued. "I was about fifteen years old. Since we were so grounded in our culture and history, I even asked Uncle Samuel where all the models were who looked like me. When I asked him that, he laughed casually about my question. But you can believe the next time we went to the same show, they didn't have just one Black model prancing down the runway, they had a whole lot of other ones. Maybe he said something to somebody about it. I don't know. He never told me."

"That's power," Rozelle mumbled quietly, and Pecola glared at him again.

"That's so typical with these white designers. Sure they have the two Black models they dote on. But as much as Black folks think it's ultimate to wear some of these designers' clothes, we need to hold such people accountable. You want my dollars? Let me see Black representation in your advertisements and on the runways. That's why I don't buy their things all the time because they don't have enough Black representation for me. I don't care how wealthy *I* am, I don't have to wear those designer clothes to validate *who* I am."

"Ladeeda," Pecola mumbled.

"And our media isn't any better," Symone raced on. "With a lot of the magazines that are geared toward Black folks, it's rare to see Black designers even featured in their pages. It's terrible. Really it is."

"What's the purpose of the Black magazine if we're not supporting each other within the pages," exclaimed Rozelle. "Girl, you got to be kidding."

"No, I'm not kidding," Symone replied. "Just check out the Black magazines that you subscribe to and see how many Black designers adorn their pages. It's a travesty and a disgrace. What trips me out is that during certain months, they got the nerve to highlight and do a special issue on Black designers one month out of the year. Big deal. If our magazines we read that espouse fashion and beauty don't allow Black designers to be featured in their fashion lay-outs on a regular basis, you can see why it's not practiced in those other European magazines."

"Oh, lordy. Must we go there today?" Pecola moaned, interrupting her since she knew what was coming next.

"Alex told me that last month she was so tired of it that she even called *Black Jewel* magazine and asked them if those were Black designers featured on their pages. I think she said four or five pages had this stellar lay-out featuring and promoting the *Black Jewel* Fashion Shows that were scheduled to go all across the country this year. Jodria's sorority is even hosting one."

"I know that, Symone," Pecola said. "You should, too. The flashiness and the dashiness is it. Folks love it. They host it every year."

"Hell, I know that too, Pecola. But I don't like it because I don't dress in that wild, unrealistic clothing."

"I don't dress that way either, honeychile," Pecola shot back. "But I enjoy looking at it."

Symone breathed deeply. "When you do that kind of show year after year, Black folks assume that dressing flashily is classic dressing. I don't care who endorses those outrageous fashion shows. They never excite me. Just give me timeless classic and elegance. Whether it's a Black fashion or a white fashion show, it doesn't matter to me. I'm into classics."

"Well, if you feel that way, just don't go no more, Symone," Pecola said.

"I wasn't talking about that in the first place, Pecola. Most times I don't go." Symone inhaled deeply. "You're taking this conversation way too seriously, girl."

"It ain't all of that, Pecola baby," Rozelle added quietly. "Nothing to make a big deal about."

"Thanks, brotherman. Anyway—" Symone said and looked at Rozelle. "Alex called the fashion editor at *Black Jewel* magazine. First, Alex was shocked that the editor wasn't even a sistah. She was from Singapore somewhere. Alex told the editor that she wears couture clothing and that she was Black. She went on to say that since *Black Jewel* was a Black magazine, Alex wanted to know why she wasn't familiar with the designers' names featured in the fine print of the magazine credits. She asked the fashion editor who these unfamiliar people were. Of course, the woman went through some empty reason and said that the designers were all French, Italian, Philippino, and everything else, but they weren't Black designers."

"That's unreal, but I'm sure it's true, baby." Rozelle inhaled quickly.

Symone laughed suddenly. "Alex told the editor that if she didn't see more Black representation in the future, she was going to cancel her subscription. Hell, that's why there are research teams working on a magazine staff. Do your research and find the Black folks who can deliver those goods for your magazine. Find the perfume companies, cosmetics folk, and furniture designers. Whatever. Find them and discover them, too. If you use them in your pages, and your readers are interested, that's how companies generate sales. I mean really. Gimme a break. Maybe I'm crazy or something. But in my heart, I know that there's a Black business out there that can supply me with whatever I need."

"That's what my Jodria always says," Rozelle nodded.

"I believe that, Rozelle. It might require my going all the way across town," Symone added. "Or when I'm in New York, I go around the corner to a little family owned store. When I bought my Benz, I did the same thing. I realize there aren't many Black folks who own Mercedes dealerships."

"Honeychillle," Pecola grumbled. "That's why I 'm surprised you bought the car."

"C'mon now, Pecola. You know just like I do that Black people don't own car companies. You know that. They might own dealerships, but it stops there." Symone took a deep breath, and her voice became patient. "I wanted a convertible Mercedes. I did my research on line to find the brother who *did* have a Mercedes dealership. I bought it from him, but my warranty is covered here. So it can be done."

"Whoopty doo," Pecola muttered.

"I did my research. It's not about doing anybody a big favor. It's about patronizing your own. It's about Black people collectively deciding to do the right thing with every dollar we spend. Some of us might not ever vote for a public official, but we're always spending money each and every day. To me, that's like voting. All I'm saying is our magazines that features us should *really* feature us."

"We shouldn't be surprised by anything nowadays. It's about economics, baby. The lean green. That's the color that moves folks. You know that better than anybody, Sy. The marketing plan might be to sell their products mainly to Black folks," Rozelle said with a little swagger of his head. "We all got MBAs out here even though it don't take a MBA to figure out the economics of that. Sell your products to Black people, but check this out. They receive their mega advertising big bucks from white-owned businesses. That's flagrant in every— well, in most publications I've seen. It's typical. If those publications change the complexion of their advertising dollars, other changes will follow with good fashion layouts that feature Black designers. Still, it must be rough for our Black fashion designers. Other Black business owners are trying to penetrate that glass ceiling put in place by our own people."

"It is," Symone agreed. "Hazele hears about it all the time. Black designers come into her restaurant in the Village and complain like you wouldn't believe. I'm sure they're always at odds with it. I know I am, and I'm not a designer. Having Black magazines that focus on Black people but promote white businesses is nothing more than false advertising."

"Without a doubt," Rozelle exclaimed.

"The problem is these magazines use all these Black faces to sell white products and white clothes," Symone said. "Then they always tell the Black designers that they don't have the things necessary to make it into their Black magazines. But the magazine *is* for Black people. The magazine owners act like white people. Just sell the product. As long as there is a Black face on it, you know Black people will buy it. Most times we do. We're hungry for print media and anything that features us positively. I betcha those white magazines don't use us in their layouts. They use white designers twenty-four seven. So when are our supposed magazines going to stop practices like that?"

"Aw, man," Rozelle said. "I'm telling you. That's a damn shame. It probably goes unnoticed because once again, Black people don't question it."

"I know, Rozelle. But I'm to the point now, I question everything. According to Hazele's friends, it's the fault of the fashion editors and the editors of the magazine. Those people in power positions aren't strong enough to take the stand they should take about what goes in the magazine. Hazele said that one designer told her that a Black publisher told her this. Now listen closely." Symone paused slightly. "The publisher actually told the brother that they didn't know if they should feature Black designs in their magazine. They didn't know if it would sell or if their Black readers would accept it. Can yall believe that?"

"Get out of here, Symone." Rozelle said, surprised. "*And the brother is publishing a magazine that is geared toward Black people?* That's what I'm saying. It's all economic, baby. Unbelievable."

"No, I'm serious. That's exactly who they're marketing their magazine to. Yet, they don't think it's gonna sell. But Hazele says the *mom* and *pop* magazines in New York that feature Black designs are selling off the newsstand rack like crazy. But those are the magazines that can't get national distribution to take their magazine across the country. It makes me down right sick to hear it. That's why I'm always asking Black business folks, and anybody else that I can, 'What are we doing?' Hell, it's not always white people all the time. It's that stupid ass Willie Lynch thinking that's so embedded in some of us that it's like the skin on our bodies. It's like what in the hell are *we* allowing?"

Rozelle slowly nodded his head. "That's a good question, baby. "When I was growing up, there was an old saying back in Memphis. 'White is right. If you're Black, stay back.' In certain circles, I understand that philosophy still holds true," he said as he gazed off into the distance. "When I think about it, it sounds like these Black male magazines are the same way. Check out who they feature all the time. The only way my partners and me find out about the brothers' we wear is that we learn about it from each other. That's how we found out about Anthony McIntosh's Duende Line. Marlon discovered him in New York and gave each one of us the brother's business card. I mean the brother has hooked us up with some seriously, immaculately tailored clothes, baby."

"Which one is he, Rozelle?" Pecola asked.

"Pecola, you should know," Rozelle replied. "Carlos had on an Anthony McIntosh suit when we were at Symone's house last weekend. You know the tapered, black single-breasted one he wore? He had a couple of ladies after him that night. The mood was right. Rich jazz music. A fly man. Remember?"

"Don't remind me, Rozelle. It's seems like lately my husband wears 'I'm available' deodorant or something." Pecola hesitated slightly. "I do remember the suit now, but I can't keep up with Carlos' wardrobe. His closet is as big as mine is. Half the time, I don't know where he gets his clothes. I think he is just as bad as I am. My man is a serious freak about looking good."

"Carlos can dress. No question about it." Rozelle laughed quickly. "So you're saying Alex called up the *Black Jewel* magazine? You go, Alex baby. I can see my Alex now. She was probably schooling those people with courteous, righteous anger. When it comes to certain issues, sometimes she's just as socially conscious as you are, Symone."

"She is, Rozelle," Pecola said. "Just in a more quiet way, honeychile. That's why people listen to her more. They appreciate her commonsensical advice. She doesn't try to shove shit down folk's throat like Symone does."

"Whaaaat!" Symone gasped. Pecola's reply caught Symone off guard. "Excuse me, Pecola?"

"You heard me right, chile," Pecola snapped "I said it plainly enough, Sy. I haven't got any speech impediments either. You heard exactly what I said."

Symone shook her head slowly and turned to look at Pecola. Pecola decided to gaze off into the distance.

"Based on what Alex told me," Symone said curtly, "and based on what I know from reading all kinds of magazines and from being an advocate for change in how we do business in this country, I believe that all Black people should hold our print media responsible. When fashion is featured in our Black publications and they expect us to subscribe to their magazines, every last Black person in America should call up those magazines and ask them who the hell are those designers featured? Read the fine print that describes what the Black models are wearing. Are they Black designers or what? Yall know how it is. Most people buy what they see others wear, whether it's the magazine or on television."

"You're right about that, baby," Rozelle agreed. "Other brothers and I talk about fashion all the time. That's why I know I look damn good when I step into the office every day."

"When I go to the designers' shows in New York and Europe with my family, I want to see someone who looks like me," Symone went on. "Somebody who has a little ass on their back. If the models don't have the ass, I want to see a model that looks like a Black woman, especially if those designers want me to buy their clothes. It's as if those Seventh Avenue designers cannot conceive that Black folks wear couture clothes or that Black designers can even design at that level. Mostly everything I buy is couture especially for those special occasions. In ninety-nine percent of the cases, all the designers I patronize are Black. I don't know. I get so aggravated. It's like those power people in the so-called-fashion-know don't think we can wear their expensive clothes or something."

"That's it, baby," Rozelle commented. "You remember when that one designer went so far as to say he didn't make his clothes for Black people? When I heard that, I must admit I thought about you. But guess what? Black folks obviously didn't hear it because we're the ones who wear a lot of his designs like clockwork. It's a sickening shame. I've seen cats being arrested on the six o'clock news with his shirts and pants on. Their wrists are manacled and shackled like a big dog, but they still got his clothes on. We live and breathe what the Hollywood stars on TV say and do. Every day we bust out and throw big dollars their way."

"I agree with you there. We believe in television so much, it dictates almost all the choices we make in our lives. Whatever we see stars wear on television is what we tend to buy." Pecola spoke soberly and inhaled. "Still, I believe Symone thinks that talking about things all the time is going to make people change. Folks are going to do what they want. Wear what they want. Buy what they want. Live with who they want to especially if that makes them feel good and especially if they see it on television, on a friend, or wherever."

Symone frowned at Pecola. "I know that, but I'm not going to *ever* shut-up talking about what I believe in. I'll continue to pour my energy in what I believe is right. I'll keep putting it out there. If nothing else, I'll enlighten those who wish to be. You got to be strong about what you believe in. Whether it's my fervency about who I am, my culture, about friendship, children, or whatever, you gots to be strong about it," she repeated with emphasis. "When a person stands on shifting sand, how can you be an advocate for anything. I'm not that way. I'll not be quiet. Why should I?"

"Why should you? Because—" Pecola was studying Symone before she answered her. "Because I'm sick of hearing you whine all the time about the wrongs of the world. You're always talking about white people this, and Black people should do that. I'm sure a few other people we know well are sick of it, too. That's why," Pecola said tartly. It came out more harshly than Pecola intended.

Symone gazed at Pecola in astonishment and rolled her eyes at her. "I'm not going to entertain that remark with a response."

"Let's keep it cool out here, ladies," Rozelle inserted. "Lawd, I should've stayed and played cards with the fellows."

"Yeah, you should have," Pecola agreed coolly.

Chapter Forty-Six

"It's hot as a motha in here. Who cut the air condition off? Where in the hell is Rozelle?" Carlos asked his brother, opening the front door and letting the fresh, country air glide into the spacious guesthouse. "He said that he was going to get us another bottle of Hennessy."

"Not that we need any more." Rico bobbed his head, smiling. "Keep in mind the man said that he was also going to check on his wife. They might be making love."

"You think so?" Scott said, wiping the remains of club soda from his mustache. "You got a dirty mind and a filthy mouth, Rico. That's all it is, man. You need to train your baby brother better than that, Carlos."

"It's useless." Carlos' voice was scratchy from drinking.

"I'm outta here, guys. I'm heading up to the big house for breakfast." As BJ spoke, he headed toward the door, but Carlos closed it and stood in front of it.

BJ stood up and pulled his Negro League baseball cap firmly down on his head. A medium built, caramel complexioned guy whose gold-rimmed glasses were always cemented to his serious face, BJ was Booker T's oldest son and Marlon Dinzelle's agent and closest advisor. His typical attire was a Fedora, matching tee shirt, a nice tailored Justice Felani suit, and custom made shoes. Since Alex wanted him to hang with the kids, he was dressed casually in a FUBU athletic top and shorts.

"Where you going, man?" Carlos asked.

"Alex just buzzed me and told me that breakfast would be served in about thirty minutes," BJ added.

"C'mon, BJ. Finish telling us about the wonderful world of sports, man. If you go up for breakfast now, you're gonna end up eating with all those kids," Scott warned, and Carlos went to sit back down. "Wait around for second or third seating. It'll be a lot more quieter, and Cleopatra will make sure your food will be hot when it reaches your plate, man."

BJ nodded and sat down. He picked up the rap magazine that was published by his good friend and began to study it. Rico handed Scott another Cuban cigar. BJ glanced at it and smiled. Even though the guys knew the cigars were from Cuba, Scott always insisted that the friends leave the bands on as a sign of prestige and as a reminder the illegal cigars were delivered specially to them all the way from Cuba. With the fat cigar hanging out his mouth, Scott walked over to the CD player and skipped to the Duke Ellington's tune, *Don't Get Around Much Anymore.*

"We're listening, BJ," Carlos said and leaned back against the couch with his head resting on the palm of his hands. He and Rico had just lost another round of spades to Scott and BJ. Carlos didn't know if he was too drunk or too tired to play any more cards. In any event, he decided he didn't want to stare at another joker, spade, heart, club, or diamond for at least another twenty-four hour period. "Go ahead, man. We're all ears."

BJ closed *Rap Sheet* magazine, breathed deeply, and wondered how in the hell he ended up hanging out with his father's close cronies listening to old jazz greats like Billy Taylor and Duke Ellington. And his father was rapping with his partners in the other guesthouse where they were probably vibing to the likes of Lauryn Hill, Nas, DMX, and Jay-Z. BJ glanced at Rico, Carlos, and Scott. Savoring their cigars, the threesome nodded back at him but said nothing. BJ's weary eyes scanned the four other, older men who were snoring loudly on the two paisley colored couches. It was time for him to head over to Marlon's guesthouse. These older guys were exhausted. But after dancing the evening away, then staying up all night playing cards while they drank white liquor mixed with Hennessy, who could blame them.

"...That's why whenever you see an NBL game," BJ was saying fifteen minutes later.

"I clare," Rico moaned, swaying from side to side to the beat of *Imagine My Frustration*. "Can't nobody sing that like Ella Fitzgerald, man. "

"You're right," Scott said in agreement. "Duke Ellington put that song together with another dude and, uh— Hell, I can't think of the cat's name right now, but the brother was damn good."

"Strayhorn. His name was Billy Strayhorn," BJ informed quickly and took a deep, impatient breath.

"How you know, Half-pint?" Rico joked. "You too young for deep information like that."

"I might be young, but my pop ain't," BJ said. "He's my encyclopedia for life."

"Your specialty is sports," Rico continued. "Like we asked you earlier, tell us about basketball."

"Keep in mind," BJ replied. "The National Basketball League is considered a non-profit organization."

"How in the hell can that be?" Carlos exploded. "They don't do nothing but make a huge profit."

"That's the way the white boy owners set it up. It's sweet now. Most professional leagues operate as a 501C6. That's the association," BJ explained with his typical business-like posture. "For pro basketball, the infrastructure—the support system is the 501C6. The association handles television rights. If you aren't a part of their club, you can't roll with them. All the owners pay a fee to be involved in the association. It's exclusive. That's why they have the ability to vote on which city they want another team or if a particular person will be an acceptable, potential owner."

"Yeah, right. They sell teams all the time," Carlos said. "But it looks like when a brother tries to buy a team, his money becomes counterfeit, baby."

"Man, you're crazy," BJ said with a laugh. "Counterfeit money? Hmmm. That's a headshaker. It's just that those motherfuckers got a lock on it, man. Team owners operate in a pretty tight and private fraternity."

"Alex wants to eventually set up a 5013C non-profit to work with the children." Rico looked directly into BJ's eyes. "What's the difference between a 501C3 and a 501C6?"

"It's a helluva difference," BJ continued, slowing moving his body to *Mood Indigo*. "If Alex does a 501C3, she answers to the state. A 501C6 answers to nobody. They make their own laws. They don't answer to the state or the federal government. In many cases, they don't pay taxes."

"No damn taxes?"

"Exactly, Carlos," BJ answered him. "The employees pay the taxes?"

"Who are the employees?" Scott asked, slowly turning the cigar in his mouth.

"The basketball players. The players pay the taxes because they're commerce for the association, or nothing more than high-priced slaves. They don't own anything but their natural born skills. When you see all those kids, grown folks, groupies, and sports nuts buying those uniforms and anything else they can get their hands on at the games, all that money belongs to the owners, baby. You think Marlon owned his jersey number when he retired from basketball as a result of his car accident. Do you think he can market it any way he wants to? Hell no!"

"So you mean to tell me that New York's owner has the rights to Mad Dog's jersey forever?" Scott asked.

"He damn sure does. His jersey and his number that Marlon made famous. *Every damn thing.* Plus, any other items that the NBL sells. All their athletic gear you seen worn or used by the NBL players are all property of the team owners and their association," BJ answered. Now he was getting impatient since he needed to go check on Marlon. BJ recognized that Marlon's knees were hurting him. Although Marlon didn't mention a thing to him, BJ could always tell when his first cousin was in pain. Another thing BJ realized, he was hungry as hell and wanted to eat breakfast.

"The owners have *total* control." BJ sighed. "That's why their title is owner, man." Several of the guys laughed.

"But they retired Marlon's number," Rico said, waving his cigar at BJ and bobbing his head to *Take the A Train.*

"Read my lips," BJ said and stared each one of them in the eyes. "The owners own it and control it, man."

"That's pretty good. I see why the players try to keep the owners in check," Carlos said. "So you're saying owners earn money from ticket sales, television rights, radio, etc. etc. etc."

"Exactly," BJ muttered. "But players can only keep so much in check. They don't own dittly. They're not in control of any other than being the majority in control on the basketball courts, man."

"That's for gotdamn sure," Scott said with a huge smile.

"Marlon said that the players in the league are talking about going on strike this entire season," Carlos added, taking a long drag on his cigar.

"Let there be a strike," BJ said. "Sure the owners will lose money, but I guarantee you this. The players will lose a lot more. Before it's over, they'll be quietly begging the union representatives to let them come back and play for a portion of the season. That's what you won't hear on the news. More than likely, they'll settle for a bad deal for the players in the league."

"All of this is wonderful information. But as for me, I'm getting ready to roll up to the big house," Rico announced, rising to his feet and gazing out the window. He squished his cigar out in the brass ashtray. "Where the hell is Rozelle?"

"That's the million dollar question. I don't know. He's probably goofing off, but I'm getting ready to find out," Scott said standing up and stretching his long arms toward the ceiling. With the half-smoked cigar dangling out the corner of his mouth, a smiling Scott slapped BJ on the back. "Yall come on. Let's go eat, then we can hit the boards. I'm ready to kick some young bucks' ass."

"In your dreams." BJ bobbed his head with confidence and checked the time on his 18-carat gold Parmigiani Fleurier wristwatch. "You know who got the best team out here in Devereaux Land?"

"We do," Rico piped in. "Age ain't nothing but a number, and we ball with the best on the block each and every week. Your crew ain't no big deal, BJ."

"Wooo! Is Rozelle on your team? Is that why you're looking so fucking hard for him?" BJ wondered. "That nigger talks so much bullshit, he can't even dribble straight."

"If we find him, he's on our team. Why? You got a problem with that?" Scott asked with a swagger, and a grinning BJ didn't say anything. "If we don't find RB, we're playing b-ball anyway. It's about time, you, Marlon, and especially his boys that are visiting be taught a damn good lesson, man."

Chapter Forty-Seven

"Your ass definitely should've stayed and played cards with the fellows, Rozelle." Pecola was pouting now. "We probably wouldn't be having this dreadful discussion."

"Shiiit! Don't blame me, Pecola," Rozelle said curtly. "My boys are probably searching for me as we speak. Ain't this a bitch? I decided to stop playing cards since that all night stress was wearing me out. They sent me for Hennessy and look where I ended up. The stress with you two ladies is wearing me the hell out."

"So you ended up with us. That's not going to change anything," Symone said. "I'm still going to get my point across."

"That's what I was afraid of," Rozelle mumbled.

"Me too," Pecola muttered and gazed up at a tall oak tree.

"Yall know what I'm saying is damn true." Symone's tone changed from being patient to that of chilled confidence. "You know Black people are always competing with each other. Then the next person who's trying to keep up with who they consider the top dog Black Jones' will race out and buy this white designer's clothes. They do it because he or she too thinks it's all of that because they see it on the Jones' they're trying to keep up with. Our Black rap stars and other musicians have made certain designers quite powerful. I'm convinced they don't even understand the economics of what they're doing."

"It's not that they don't understand," Rozelle said. "They just don't care. Rap stars and other musicians are constantly in front of the camera making videos and for publicity appearances. You would think they should create their own clothing line, then push their own label. The broadcast media is an excellent forum."

"We got to think collectively," Symone continued. "Employ the Ujamaa principles and practice collective economics. Stop being so pretentious and uppity about your accomplishments. Wear Black. Buy Black. Give Black. Think Black. And give back. Give to a worthwhile cause. Give back to your college. It just makes me sooo aggravated that Black people got the wrong priorities."

"I am not changing what I said, chile," Pecola said dryly. "Everybody ain't got a trust fund like you."

"Ummm-humm!" The trust fund issue hit Rozelle again. "Ever since you were ten years old, and you're almost forty now. Hmmm. I thought that's what you told me one time, baby. I'm convinced I'm stalking the wrong friend. I need to chase you and leave Alex alone. I'm ready to divorce Jodria right now. Grrrrrr," he joked, growling like a dog as he always did when he discussed money with Symone.

"That's what I get from sharing private information with a supposedly close friend like you, Rozelle. Let me finish the point I'm trying to make, puhleeze," Symone requested.

"Those are things I never liked about those pageants, debutante balls, sororities, fraternities, guilds, and those other little cliquish clubs. That's why I'll never join one. I get asked all the damn time. 'Symone, what did you pledge? Are you a member of a sorority?' When I say no, they ask me 'Why don't you pledge with our alumni chapter, girl?' I guess because I have an MBA from Wharton, own businesses in the city, and I still haven't been claimed by any sorority so they think I'm interested."

"It's all in your mind," Pecola said.

"It's not," Symone snapped. "Every time I'm asked, I simply say no thank you in a very polite voice. I really feel like screaming, 'Hell no. I ain't got the time for nonsense or for bullshit. Plus, yall are too stuck up and too snooty for your own good. I like my membership in the Me Phi Me Sorority better. Let me do my thing by my own self.' So I say hello, good-bye, and I'll see you later."

Pecola impatiently checked her watch. "Symone, as usual it's obvious that you can't be objective about sororities, fraternities, and the other organizations that *I'm* involved with. You don't even know all the things that my sorority and other clubs are doing because you're not involved, chile. We're constantly volunteering our time and donating moneys to many causes you don't even know about or can't even understand for that matter. We don't publicize every little good deed we perform. Most times, non-Greeks hear *all* about the social events we sponsor."

"True," Rozelle agreed.

"I hate when people jump to conclusions about worthwhile organizations when they're not participating in anything their own selves." Pecola's voice was mean as she defended her coveted position in her sorority and her various clubs.

"Untrue statement." Symone sounded like a defiant, little girl.

"My sorors do more than look pretty. We continue to formulate worthwhile projects in Winston-Salem and all over the world, girl. Even Alex's sorority has a fine arts center here. And in case you didn't know, that place was incorporated by the Alumnae Chapter of Delta Sigma Theta Sorority, Inc." Pecola sarcastically spoke the entire name in a long drawn out way specifically emphasizing each word for Symone's ears.

"I know about the place, and I think that's fantastic. Now explain to me what *else* your sorority is doing, Pecola? What are the other organizations you're involved with doing? Tell me so that I can know that I'm lying on sororities and those other clubs you so desperately love to be a part of, Pecola. Hell, tell me what your fraternity is doing, Rozelle? I would like to hear it."

"Hey, I didn't say anything either way," Rozelle said. "I'm listening to what the both of you are saying, Symone."

"Don't be a wimp," Pecola moaned and rolled her eyes at him. "You're supposed to be stronger than that."

"Don't get me wrong, Symone," Rozelle added. "I've established many wonderful ties as a Que, but I also believe some of the comments you made are accurate, baby."

"Say whaaat!" Pecola exclaimed as she batted her eyes heavenward in exasperation.

"Let me finish, Pecola. Sometimes fraternities and sororities have forgotten their main focus, our main mission. There *is* a lot of business to be done in helping Blacks and getting a grip on strengthening our communities. Like raising money for full ride scholarships or partial scholarships that can really make a difference in a young student's tuition balance."

"We do all of that," Pecola said. "It just doesn't make the headlines."

"Quite honestly," Rozelle continued. "I don't think we do enough of that or enough tutoring, or enough on educating our young people about our history. Our beginnings by passing on the richness of it. Nowadays, it's the Crypts and the Bloods. That's a fraternity that you hear more about than you do the Greek groups. It's a shame that a lot of Black folks in urban areas are only familiar with gang affiliations. We should do more to educate young children. Volunteer at schools even when we're not required to do so and even though our children don't attend those schools. Become those children's mentors and their local role models. Most Black kids have never heard of a Greek fraternity."

"Rozelle!" Pecola exclaimed totally frustrated with his little speech. "What is wrong with you?"

"Let me finish, Pecola." Her anger surprised him. "Instead of fraternities being separate in ideas and thinking that our fraternity or sorority is better than yours, we need to focus on developing our future. The children. Our families. We need to bond together. Aim toward helping our own Black kids to excel. The Que colors. The purple and gold are the best colors out. Hell, I know that better than anyone. I love how I feel when I'm around my brothers. The stepping. The privilege of being a Que. The fun. The tradition. But all that socializing should be secondary when each Greek fraternity can come together to help the other solve cultural and economic problems."

"I agree," Symone said.

"As a professional group with thousands and thousands of powerful men, we should be developing our own banking systems with a financial base from the Ques and the other Greek organizations throughout the country," Rozelle went on. "We all should be creating investments, restoring communities, and real estate development. Fraternities and sororities, that is if we work together as one, can formulate a helluva lot of other economic development avenues. We could still maintain our separate Greek identities, too."

Damn traitor. All Symone needed was someone to agree with her, Pecola thought as she sadly shook her head from side to side.

Symone glanced around Rozelle and noticed Pecola's disappointment. "Why are you shaking your head like that, Pecola?" Symone asked.

"I was thinking that Rozelle is a Greek traitor," Pecola admitted. "That's why I was shaking my head. That's all you needed was someone to agree with you."

"I'm not a traitor, Pecola."

"You see what I'm saying?" Symone asked. "Pecola, you're simply protecting your sorority and those clubs that don't do anything. Rozelle is simply telling the truth."

"I didn't say that," Rozelle blurted.

"It's nobody but us out here in the woods having an honest discussion about issues among friends," Symone added.

"He's still a traitor!" Pecola hissed.

"I know you got to protect your sisterhood," Symone said. "I know there are secrets yall can't divulge to me about your fraternity and your sorority. All that fierce sisterhood and brotherhood stuff yall hold dear."

"You sound *very* jealous about the closeness we have and about what we can't share with you, Sy," Pecola exclaimed. "That's exactly what it is."

"Hell, I don't want you to tell me nothing."

"We wouldn't do it anyway," Pecola said. "You can believe that."

"You're so entrenched in that sorority scene, you would rather call Rozelle a traitor than figure out what yall can do to change a behavior that has been practiced for years and years and years. Figure out what you can say at the next meeting to start a new way of being for your sisters," Symone continued in an all-knowing voice. "I'm not saying all sororities and fraternities aren't doing nothing. If they're doing great work, thank the Lord."

"They are," Pecola exclaimed. "But because you don't read it in the news, you don't believe it's true, Sy."

"I'll be the first to give them recognition and applause. In my time, I've just not seen a lot of that." Symone hesitated. "I know there's a lot of socializing involved, but I'm simply asking you to tell me *what* in the hell are *yall* doing?"

While Symone spoke, Pecola watched the trail and shook her head sadly.

"I thank God you don't say things like this at any of our parties and other social gatherings, chile. We wouldn't have no customers at Akao Studios," Pecola mumbled under her breath.

"Excuse me. Any customers?" Symone echoed almost hysterically. "Helllooo! Our business isn't based on sororities, fraternities, and clubs in Winston-Salem, girl. Sure, a lot of them do patronize us, but we got a lot of other customers that come to the spa for which I'm very, very grateful. Sororities, fraternities, and those cliquish clubs here cannot determine the success or failure of our business, Pecola"

"I didn't say that, Sy," Pecola exclaimed.

"I thank God we don't depend on only Black organizations to support us. That's another thing. If a certain block of Black folks think you're too prosperous, they would rather go somewhere else. Lawd, don't let them see you're driving a certain car. They think somewhere in the back of their little minds that their patronizing your business every two weeks, once every six months, or once a year is giving you all the money necessary to pay for your new car."

"Enough is enough, honeychile!" Pecola hollered in undisguised disgust with the conversation. "Give it a rest! Sheeish!"

Rozelle remained quiet. Once again, he wished he had gone to pick up the bottle of Hennessy like he was supposed to. All he could do now is say *uh oh* under his breath and brace himself. Things were getting a little testy in the air again.

"You know what I'm saying is true, Pecola," Symone rattled on. "They're always saying something about us. When I bought my Benz, what did people say to you?"

"They didn't say it to me. Believe it or not, they know we're friends," Pecola groaned. "But I'm sure you'll remind us what they said to others."

"*You* told *me* that several of *your* Guild friends asked somebody that knew you well all about *my* car," Symone said. "It was that second hand gossip that you always hear about, Rozelle. They didn't come to my face and ask me nothing. Because they think I'm crazy anyway, they knew better than that."

"That's not what it is," Pecola mumbled.

"Yet, they wanted to know 'Why is Symone driving a car like that? I declare that Benz is so flashy. They must be robbing people with their high prices over there in that big ole Akao Building. They're probably selling drugs or something on the side. Somebody done dropped a bag full of money in their lobby,'" Symone said, believing she mimicked the snobbish, nosey people of Winston-Salem. She exhaled quickly and shook her head heavily.

"Oh gawd," grumbled Pecola. "Don't tell me I'm going to hear that story again."

Symone suddenly looked puzzled and ignored her statement.

"You see what I'm saying, Rozelle. But they don't ask questions about stuff like that when they go shopping at Walmart, Steinmart, Kohl's, Neiman Marcus, Bloomingdales, Saks Fifth Avenue, or the Oriental hair care products store on the corner. Are they robbing people, too? Do they feel like they're responsible for their success because I'm sure the founders or board members of those businesses I just mentioned aren't driving Pintos. I drive what I want to drive, live where I want, and buy what I want. Hell, it's my money."

"Damn, honeychile." Pecola took a deep, impatient breath. "I should've brought my violin out here, so I could play while I listened to your typical sob story."

Symone stared in disbelief at Pecola. "But some Black Folks—not all of them because I don't do it, and yall don't do it either. I know there are plenty others who are just like the three of us who buy specifically from only Blacks as often as we can. There are some Black people who rather give it to the white businessman than give another sister or brother an opportunity to be successful in business. That's why I say the Greek groups aren't our only customers, Pecola. If you pull up our computer printout on Monday, what I'm saying will be verified in black and white. You'll see who our customers are. Maybe in your mind they're the *only* ones that patronize us."

Pecola and Symone exchanged a long, careful mean look between each other. By now, Pecola was getting quite angry.

"What you're saying might be partially true about our customer base, Symone," Pecola admitted. "I still don't believe these are comments you should make in public. That causes the ones who *are* involved in sororities, fraternities, and various other clubs around to not patronize us. So we *would* lose some of our customers, especially if they think you're talking about their particular Greek group," Pecola explained smugly and gazed at Rozelle to get an agreeing nod.

"Uh oh," Rozelle breathed lightly, and Pecola sucked her teeth at him. He knew Pecola's statement wasn't another appropriate one that would do a thing to calm Symone down. If anything, Pecola was adding more fuel to the fire. Rozelle continued to laugh under his breath and merely watched the white, billowing clouds in the sky.

Symone counted to five. "Girl, let me get this straight. You know I've always said things like this." Symone articulated each word carefully. "Pecola, you're saying they won't patronize us because I'm telling the truth?"

"The truth to who? By what standards, Sy?" Pecola quipped with her eyes flashing anger.

"The truth to the world, girl. You know it's the pure divine damn truth. Hell, if I hadn't learned nothing else, I should know by now folks don't like to hear the truth," Symone said and thought *including me sometimes* as she recalled Orlando's words last night.

"Then you better add yourself to that list, Symone."

"What list, Pecola?"

"Don't act dumb all of a sudden, honeychile. Add yourself to the not-wanting-to-hear-the-truth-list." Pecola sounded annoyed that Symone even asked the question. "You know the one? You should know it very well."

"C'mon, Pecola. Let's be serious."

"I am."

"Ask any Black business owner has that ever happened to them?"

"Ok."

"Hell, it has happened to us. Ask them if their Black brothers and sisters stopped patronizing them because they thought they were making too much money and shouldn't be driving a certain kind of foreign car? Hell, an expensive American car for that matter. If you don't know anything else about me, you sure as hell know that I'm not going to lick nobody's behind. I won't do it to fraternity men, sorority women, debutante ball organizers, the president of the United damn States of America, and who the hell ever. I'll give them excellent service just like any other entrepreneurial woman, but I'm not going to bite my tongue. My lips aren't going to be stuck to nobody's ass for no business in the first place, girl."

Pecola glared at the trees leaves swaying in the distance.

"I don't want to discuss it anymore," Pecola snapped now visibly upset. "I think you're getting too carried away over this conversation. You were the one who said you wanted a quiet horse ride. I mean it. I don't want to talk about this no more."

"Well, I do." Symone raced on despite Pecola's frustration with the subject. "I need to say one last word. Remember when we helped Corvina Happy? You know that young girl who attended Winston-Salem State two years ago. It was Corvina's third year, and she was a junior. Pecola, you remember? The one Cleopatra found out about who was walking around campus with holes in her shoes."

Pecola refused to answer Symone. *Hell, yeah I remember her. We paid the poor child's college fees. How can I forget her?*

"Anyway—" Since Pecola wouldn't answer her, Symone spoke to Rozelle. "Let me finish telling *you* about her, Rozelle. Corvina told us that the sisters in the sororities on campus used to laugh at her because she didn't have good shoes to wear. She only had one pair, and that pair had large holes in them. Just a very smart girl who was determined to go to school. She got a partial scholarship and worked part time at Food Lion to take care of the rest. I got mad when I heard her story, Rozelle. Pecola and I did something about it. We paid her way through school. Whatever the college didn't pick up, we gave her the money. That way she wouldn't have to work like a dog while she tried to study at the same time." Pecola was looking off into the distance to appear as if she wasn't interested in the conversation.

"I'm proud of you two girls. Damn proud and bout ready to cry, too." Rozelle wanted to lighten up the mood.

"Instead of the sororities helping her out, Corvina told Pecola and me some sad things," Symone said disgustedly. "Pecola knows this is true because she was right there and heard every word Corvina said to us in our conference room that day. She explained that those girls in the sorority talked about how Corvina didn't have this and how she didn't have that. They laughed about the holes, her old clothes, and they treated her horribly. If those sororities were sooo interested in making a difference, they would've taken up a collection and gotten the girl some damn shoes."

"That's what Corvina told us," Pecola moaned. "We never verified the information, Symone."

"Well, mighty funny that day you acted like you believed her, Pecola," Symone's eyes went back to Pecola. "Oh, c'mon, girl. We sure didn't verify it, but Cleopatra did. I trust her implicitly. Why should Cleo lie?"

"I'm not saying anyone's lying." Pecola knew she was getting worked up again, but she couldn't stop it. "I'm just saying we took their word for it."

"We sure did. I'll do it again especially if someone like Cleo—that I know is on the up and up tells us about it. If necessary, I'll do it twenty times over. I just say that while yall are pledging, stepping, or doing whatever, get involved on campus with sensitive issues. Take up a petty cash collection of money for needy students. Collect canned goods to give out to senior citizens and provide other services to community residents," Symone said firmly with a frown. While Rozelle listened intently to the heated discussion, he decided to remain quiet and take in the verdant scenery.

"We do all the things you mentioned on a national level and on the local level," Pecola said.

"Good," Symone replied.

"But there you go again," Pecola muttered with clench teeth. "Thinking that you got all the self-righteous answers."

"Just make your sorority an environment where people won't be ashamed to come and confess their needs. Where they won't fear they'll be ridiculed because they're poor," Symone raced on. "Then, everyone will know the group has a mission other than recruiting new women. Do something. Even at Hampton, I could never tell what the fraternities and sororities were doing. I knew they went on line. I knew they crossed over. I knew they stuck together, but I was waiting for something else to happen. I've always been taught to have concern for people, to help out when I could, to work together, and to help because I can. All I saw about sororities and fraternities when I was in college was that they were quite cliquish, they partied non-stop every weekend, and they were stuck up."

"Are you finished babbling on about shit you don't know nothing about, Symone? Because quite frankly, I don't want to talk about this anymore," Pecola muttered in a tired voice.

"If you want me to be done, I'll be finished, girl." Symone was quiet for a second. "Rozelle, what are you thinking about now?"

Rozelle breathed deeply. "While you were talking, I was thinking. I asked myself, 'Do I do enough within my fraternity? To hell with everyone else. I'm involved in a number of various organizations, too! As a Que, I asked myself, 'What do *you* do? Other than wearing a brand on both of my arms, what do *you* do, man? Other than being financial, what do *you* do, man? My voice said 'No. You're not doing as much as you can do either to make your fraternity excel, man. Just like what Alex does to us about worthwhile causes. In a quiet way, she has become our conscience. Maybe I need to be that conscience for my brothers, too."

"This is pure unadulterated bullshit," Pecola groaned hastily. "What's wrong with you, Rozelle?"

"Step up to the plate, Pecola," Rozelle said. "I agree with Symone on some of the things she said. Sure you gots to sift through the self-righteous, know-it-all attitude bullshit parts of her talk. If you do that, then ten percent of what she's saying will make great sense to you."

"Excuse me?" Symone asked.

"You heard me, Sy. I didn't stutter either," Rozelle went on. "A few of your points hit home with me. I agree that to be in a fraternity or sorority is more than just acknowledging the name of your group. We got to get involved somewhere on an individual basis. That's what I try to do. Change, baby. We got to make a change economically. Real estate is a perfect way to start. If each fraternity in each town in this country figures out a way to buy property, look at the economic impact of that. We can invest in apartment buildings, commercial property, hotels, and single family homes. Anything to take charge of economics for our group and for our people."

"That's what I'm saying, Rozelle," Symone nodded. "There are many ways for all of us to collectively work as a group. Without a doubt, many individuals can become affluent by dealing in real estate and by making wise investments. Prominent Black groups should work toward that same goal as well."

"It's time you take your lips out of Symone's butt, Rozelle." Pecola barely got her words out in a calm manner. "Honeychile, this talking is giving me a headache. I'm ready to go back to the stables."

Rozelle shook his head and stared at Pecola. He was stunned. "I know for a fact that some of the guys aren't financial and haven't paid their dues in years. But yet they run around town bragging about their frat is this and my frat is that. I know there are circumstances where people can't pay dues, but we pay for everything else when we want to. Symone is right *only* in that area. I got to side with her even though I hate to," he added with a smile.

"Then don't," Pecola announced.

"Look, Pecola. We're all trying to figure out the right thang to do. I'm being honest cause yall are like my sisters." Symone glanced at Pecola and Rozelle. "I wouldn't say this to just anybody outside our circle."

"Yeah right," Pecola said. "Symone is an outsider. She isn't Greek."

"I understand, baby. Listen to what I'm saying." Rozelle laughed quietly and continued. "Some of our Black folks *don't* believe in supporting our organization with dollars. You know that, Pecola. They only believe in doing it with lip service or with a show. In their minds, they believe it's good enough to support a Greek organization by having a sticker on the back window of their car. Maybe it's a square tag on the front of their car's license plate, which shows the Greek letters to scream to the world so they'll know who they are. In this day and time, I agree we need to do a helluva lot more than that, baby."

Pecola stared at Rozelle with open wide, shocked eyes. "Puhleeze, Rozelle. I can't believe you're talking about your frat brothers like that. What is wrong with you?" Pecola asked, glaring angrily in Rozelle's face. "I done told yall. This discussion is getting me too pissed off. It's time to end it. If you don't, I'm going to turn this horse around and go back to the stables. I mean it."

"Pecola, baby," Rozelle pleaded.

"That ain't even right, Pecola." Symone smiled indulgently. "All he's talking about is what needs to be done to work together as a group. I don't believe he's talking about his frat brothers in particular, Pecola."

"That's what you think, but I know better," Pecola grumbled in an even more aggravated tone. "Humph. Yall both are working my nerves. It's not even necessary. Why do you even have to go there, Sy? Why? You don't have to bash *our* organizations like you're God or something. Why do you do this?"

"Because I always think when people ask me what I think, I got to tell them. Sometimes people don't want to hear that. The truth," Symone replied huffingly.

"That's probably because nobody asked you what you thought this early in the morning any way, honeychile," Pecola snapped back.

"You bought it up, Pecola. The whole subject." Symone shook her head heavily. "You know what, Pecola?"

"What, honeychile? Pray tell me what?" Pecola demanded. "Especially since you know it all—"

"Your capacity for denial is awesome, girl," Symone said. "It's absolutely awesome."

Pecola paused a few long seconds as she tried to regain her composure. "Oh, lawdy. Have mercy on me. You got some nerve, Sy. Look, don't even get me to talking about you out here. If anybody has denial, it's you. You put the letter D in the word denial in the first place—especially as much as you try to deny half of what has gone on and gone wrong in your life from the time you were little up until now, honeychile."

"What do you mean by that, Pecola?" Symone asked with a frantic edge in her voice.

Rozelle whistled softly and cleared his throat. "Ladies, I know this is what friends are for. You know to enlighten, to delight, and to make each other feel uptight. As I was listening to what you sweet ladies are saying, that should be all for any serious talk today, folks. Time to change the conversation. Lawd have mercy on my soul! I do believe it's time to have a moment of silence again." Rozelle voice was sounding like an old-fashioned preacher since he sensed a serious, uncontrollable argument brewing between the two women. Symone grudgingly agreed and tried to laugh at his mimic of a preacher. However, Pecola was still mad and silent.

But Rozelle's instructions worked. For the next thirty minutes or so, the three friends rode along quietly. With each step the horses took through the lovely trail, Pecola was finally able to enjoy the squirrels scurrying away and the harmonious sounds of the crickets and birds singing their natural melodies throughout the air. Since the relaxed, peaceful atmosphere of the trail enveloped Pecola once again, her attitude with Symone and Rozelle slowly evaporated. Pecola noticed a flock of Canadian geese flying in natural precision above their heads, and she inhaled deeply.

Chapter Forty-Eight

"...You're sooo funny, Pauletta," Alex raved to Pecola's sister who was helping set the table for the third group of breakfast eaters. "I'm glad you decided to come to opening ceremonies."

"Me too," Pauletta piped in and winked at Jodria and Nanette who were placing juice glasses on the place mats. "Where's Madison?"

"Madison, Darilyn, several other adults, and some of the older children who helped with first and second seating breakfast are in the theater watching *The Inkwell*," Alex said. "Marlon got Madison the television version for the children. My baby loves that old movie. It motivates him on how to enjoy the summer and have wonderful fun with Black folks."

"I love it my own self," Pauletta said and noticed that the other ladies were vigorously nodding their heads, too. "But you and Madison don't need no motivation. Yall know how to throw the ultimate, summertime party."

Once the women were through with their chores in the dining room, they walked back into the kitchen where Pauletta made them laugh some more. Just as tall and gorgeous as Pecola, Pauletta's brown skin was the complete opposite to her sister's high yellow complexion. With the complexion of rich, smooth, dark chocolate, Pauletta also had green eyes, which was a genetic tradition in her family. An executive at National Bank in Augusta, Georgia, Pauletta still spoke with a deep, throaty southern accent and kept her hair styled in a neat bob that fell below her ears. A chain smoker for the last thirteen years, the only way Pauletta inhaled a cigarette was through a classy, silver cigarette holder. When her friends saw Pauletta smoke, they often commented that she gave them the impression she was a diva similar to the Black dancers who worked in the Moulin Rouge Club in Las Vegas.

"Cleopatra, I'm going to transport your southern-cooking-ass directly to Augusta, girl," Pauletta teased, when she noticed the grits, scrambled cheese eggs, bacon, Parks sausages, stewed apples, pear preserves, French toast sticks, and pancakes that Cleopatra was preparing for the third round of breakfast. "You throw down in the kitchen like them old-fashioned big house cooks from way back when. My mama is the same way, girl. Is that homemade preserves?"

"Uh huh. I got the pears from the trees down back," Cleopatra announced proudly and pointed out the kitchen window toward the orchard where Alex and Madison grew a wide variety of fruit trees. "That's what Mama Oseola tells me, too. It's an honor to have your mama praise me, Miss Pauletta."

"I done told you, baby. Letta is my name!" Pauletta loudly snapped her fingers several times. "And fine Black men with big, round, firm asses is my game!" she sang in her throaty voice, and Cleopatra blushed.

"Oh, Pauletta," Nanette squealed and grabbed her hand with affection. "I'm going upstairs to wake Rehema. She loves to hear you talk, so she needs to hear this."

"If my mama told you any-thing-at-all, believe it. My mama speaks nothing but the stone-to-the bone truth, Cleo." Pauletta reached for a slice of bacon and the perfectly round pancakes. "Girrrrl! These pancakes are marvelous. Yall know I'm too greedy. Just before I came over here, I ate one of my Mama's big breakfasts. Umph. Umph. Umph. Umph. Umph, honeychile."

"You can't have her," Jodria exclaimed while stirring the huge pot of grits, so they wouldn't lump up. "We wouldn't know what to do without Cleopatra keeping us straight."

"That's for sure." Alex spoke just when Purity raced into the kitchen looking for her mother.

"Mommy, Mommy," Purity squealed. "I want my Mommy!"

"You're ok, baby?" Purity nodded yes to her mother and stuck her right thumb in her mouth.

"Come on over here and give your Auntie Letta a big ole, sweet sugar," Pauletta said to Purity with outstretched arms. Purity clung tightly to her mother's thighs. The little girl shook her head no, closed her eyes, and buried her face in Alex's sarong pants. "I clare that baby got hair like Medusa. It's all over the place, Alex. You and Nanette's hair ain't bad, either." All the women that were congregated around the kitchen island laughed like someone told a hilarious joke.

"You're a mess, Pauletta," Alex said warmly, still gently massaging Purity on her back.

"I know," Pauletta agreed. "What's wrong, baby? Talk to Auntie Letta."

"When Purity acts that way, I don't think it's cute at all. I told Alex she shouldn't let her get away with that kind of disrespectful behavior. Our Mama never would allow it," Nanette said and threw her hands up. "Purity is spoiled rotten."

"And your twin boys ain't? Girl, you know the deal. Alex is an old assed mother. She doesn't know any better. But humph, all our children are spoiled. Where's my cosmopolitan, Nanette?" Pauletta asked, winking at her. "You know you make the best."

"Coming right up, girl," a smiling Nanette replied. No matter what Pauletta said to her, Nanette absolutely adored Pauletta and her strong, southern spirit. Pauletta wasn't stuck-up like Pecola. Nanette believed that Pauletta's spirit hadn't changed since the first day Alex introduced her to Pauletta when she was a little girl. She always treated her the same—as if she was a grown up—even when she was younger. Nanette went to the bar located on the other side of the kitchen in search of the Absolut, Cointreau, cranberry juice, and the other ingredients necessary for the martini recipe.

"It's too early to have a martini," Jodria said while she munched on the last of her fifth French toast stick. She reached for her sixth one and dipped it into some pear preserve.

"Too early for who?" Pauletta replied. "Speak for yourself, JAB."

"I thought you wanted to play tennis with me," Jodria went on.

"I did. I still do." Pauletta nodded. "My martini will be my energy pill. It's hot as hell out there, and I need something to control my underarm sweat glands from acting up."

"Enjoy," Nanette instructed several minutes later, handing the cosmopolitan to Pauletta.

"Hmmm," Paulette moaned luxuriously after she took several sips. "It's wonderfully smooth. You go with your bad self, girl."

"I can't believe Hannibal didn't come with you," Alex commented while she dumped the buttery grits into a big serving bowl.

"I can't believe my husband didn't come with me, either." Pauletta swallowed more cosmopolitan and thought about the vicious argument she and Hannibal had last night just before she left Augusta. "Well, he's just getting back home from the National Black Expo. I guess he was tired. Anyway, when will my sister be back?"

"They should've been back by now." Cleopatra glanced up at the kitchen wall clock. "I know Pecola and Rozelle didn't eat anything before they left, so they're both probably very hungry."

"And Symone went horseback riding with them?" Pauletta wondered. "Wooo, chile. How she doing these days?"

"The same," Nanette chirped in, and Alex threw her sister a motherly, stern stare. "How's Hannibal doing, Letta?"

"The same, Nanette. My husband is just wonderful," Pauletta mumbled and sipped more of her drink. But Alex noticed that Pauletta's intense green eyes turned cold and were signaling something else. Pauletta was visibly vulnerable for a fleeting moment. Just as quickly, Pauletta's wide smile returned, and she laughed suddenly. "Let's leave it at that. You're ready to go play tennis, Jodria?"

"...Truly, it's something absolutely special about the Devereauxs horse trail," Rozelle observed softly. Each and every time Rozelle rode through the trail, he became very philosophical to the core and had a wonderful communion with nature.

"Absolutely fabulous," Symone agreed.

"I see why you wanted to ride out by yourself, Symone." Rozelle was silent for a moment. "The beauty of the landscape is so powerful, it's unsettling. In another sense, it's quite refreshing. I'm glad I begged you to let me come."

"I'm glad you came too, Rozelle." Symone replied quickly. "Really I am."

"Me too," Pecola piped in.

Rozelle hesitated a moment. "Back to your question, Pecola."

"Back to what question?"

"The question about why Alex does this?"

"Ah hell, Rozelle. I thought we were finished with *that* heavy topic, babychile."

"I'm not going to talk about sororities or fraternities, Pecola. Don't worry, baby. I won't let Symone talk about them either. You asked why do we think Alex does this?" he asked as he steered Misty along the curve in the trail. "This is how I look at it. I'm a math-minded man. Naturally, I believe there are formulas to every situation, ladies. After knowing Alex and Madison, I'm convinced they do it because they want to. It's because they can. The Devereauxs enjoy giving. They know the children enjoy and appreciate what they do for them.

Hell, I do, too. I can come up here, visit with them, and feel ok. It's just serenity up here on their land and in their home."

"For me too, Rozelle." As Symone spoke, she inhaled the clean air.

"The whole three hundred and fifty acres is like heaven to me. I can ride the horses or come up here and practice a few golf swings on Madison's private course," Rozelle reminisced easily.

"I'm telling you. They got everything here. There's no need for them to leave the property. That is except for food," Pecola joked and burst out laughing.

"I know, baby. They do. Then there are those spring and summer afternoons where I sit around with Madison and Alex just sipping ice cold, sweet tea and shooting the breeze after a hard week with those crazy ass white folk I got to be nice to at the office every day all week long. I sit in the garden and watch a pack of butterflies fluttering all over the place. Along with Alex, Madison, their children, my children, and along with Jodria Anne, we enjoy that kind of thing. It's such a peace about them and about here.

"The reason Alex and Madison have peace is because they're in love." Symone was feeling quite philosophical, too. "I ain't never seen that kind of relationship before. I'm serious. They're simply two extraordinary people who have neither the inclination nor the necessary to pay much attention to what the rest of the world thinks about them or what they do. They're in their own little world, so they go around loving each other and everyone else. They don't worry about it because they're already there mentally."

"You go with your philosophical explanation, honeychile." Pecola nodded her head with agreement. "I'm convinced, and I'll vote for them."

The three friends rode along for about fifty yards in silence wondering which way the conversation was going to go.

"I know Alex and Madison got a few millions dollars worth of valuables in their home and guesthouses, but their front and back doors swing open all the time. It's the same way with their hearts. They don't even think about people taking anything." Rozelle spoke with a chuckle.

"Why should they?" Symone asked.

"But yall know Alex. Hell, ladies—," Rozelle said, still laughing loudly. "If this was my spread, I would require everybody invited out here take a lie detector test and submit to a metal detector scan when they stepped outside to go home. That way, I could check and see if they had any of my antiques stashed underneath their suit jackets."

Pecola and Symone laughed at him.

"Uh—" Symone earnestly pondered her next words. "I think Alex and Madison are lucky, though. They love hard. Yet they have all of this, and they appreciate it. That's the key, yall."

"The key?" Pecola asked.

"Yeah. Having it all and enjoying it, too," Symone said sadly as she recalled Orlando's honest words to her last night.

"What's having it all, Symone?" Rozelle wanted to know.

Once more, Symone thought for a long moment before she answered. "Well, you know. I'm not sure, RB. To me—I imagine it's just being happy. Alex says it's knowing who you really are. It goes along with having happiness, peace of mind, and that inner serenity with all the material stuff a person can possess," Symone explained just as tentatively.

"Hell, my ass certainly got a long, long way to go," Pecola said forlornly.

Rozelle merely nodded his head and smiled. "Symone, I need to think about your answer a little bit more. Put a mental paper clip on that, and I'll get back to you, baby. I swear. We've discussed some seriously heavy subjects today, and my mind needs a rest. It needs to chill. I just want to swallow the clean air and the beauty."

Rozelle was quiet again for several minutes. He cleared his throat and glanced tenderly at Pecola and Symone.

"You know what, ladies, I'm lucky. Damn lucky to have you three crazy women as friends. I'm glad Scott and I ran into yall. Well, we more or less stalked yall at the MAWS conference."

"I remember," Pecola said, and all three of them burst out laughing as they recalled their initial meeting at the minority luncheon.

"Not only did I think yall were three sexy women, but it's been nice for me and for Jodria Anne, too." While Rozelle talked, Pecola rolled her eyes. It's great for my children to know yall as Tante Pecola and Tante Symone. Back in Tennessee where we're from, we only call folks aunt and uncle. You know those typical southern titles. It's nothing formal atall."

"You're too crazy, Rozelle," Symone exclaimed freely. "I just like Tante better than Aunt. That's how I was raised in Trinidad. When Pecola and I first met, I simply asked her to let her children call me Tante rather than Aunt Symone. I'll never forget the first time Carlos, Jr. called me Aunt Symone. It just didn't sound right to me."

"Hell," Rozelle yelled. "I know the story about what you wanted crap, Miss Uppity."

"Please don't call me uppity, RB."

"Listen at that, Rozelle. She loves to call people stuck up, wannabes, and snooty, but she doesn't want to be called uppity," Pecola jibed swiftly.

"Honeychile, I ain't stuttin' you," Symone answered in a thick Southern accent.

"Well, let's not get another negative discussion started, ladies. It might get out of hand this time. Yall might be fighting out here all over the brown leaves, horse huffs, and dirt. I'm just saying that yall's friendship gives my children an opportunity to be around people who are just like our relatives in Tennessee."

"I understand," Symone said.

"That helps for children to have close cousins and friends they can grow up with and be around to bond with. It wasn't that way when we were in California. That's one of the reasons I moved near Castleshire Woods," Rozelle continued. "Sure, it was an older Black neighborhood, and I could've moved anywhere I wanted to in the city. But I was determined to not let my children grow up around no people of their own race like they did in California. Jodria and I made that mistake once."

"I believe I've made that same mistake by living out in Clemmons," Symone said. "Even though I got the house in my divorce settlement, I'm ready to move near you, Rozelle."

"Hey, I got it, baby. I know your concern," Rozelle added. "When me and my baby moved here, we talked about it and decided that 'Black neighborhood here we come.' When my children did have company out in California, I had to actually drive thirty to forty-five minutes across town to get their friends to spend the night with them."

"You're singing to the choir, baby," Symone nodded.

"I know that trip very well. Believe you me, I love the closeness of it all here in North Carolina," Rozelle said. "After dealing with white folks Monday through Friday, I need some soul brothers and sisters to call me up and say let's go party, man. That helps to rejuvenate my mind and to help keep me focused. It's easy to get caught up in that corporate world bravado madness and believe you need to only associate with white folks. Then you stand out like a fly in rice all the time. To hell with that trip."

"I know, Rozelle. Trust me. I've been there," Symone said. "That's why I left MUB Industries to open my own business. You can't be Black in Corporate America. They'll break you down. Corporate America without a doubt is a serious tightrope act, baby."

"You gots that right, Sy. As an entrepreneur, the tight rope is still there, but it's certainly is different," Pecola confirmed.

"I figured if I'm going to walk a tightrope, it might as well be with my own business," Symone added. "After business school, I didn't want to work with my uncles. That was too easy. Let me make my own way."

"I guess you could make your own way when you got money the way you got it. You can do that. That always trips me out. When I see rich people on television crying about how they wanted to make their own way, I laugh. With trust fund money, you can do more than make your own way. Hell, you can *have* your own way. All rich folks got to do is just think of an idea and pull the right people together to make it happen. Pull their money together to make it happen. It ain't like you gots to go down and apply for a loan at the Small Business Administration or at the local bank where they turn Black folks' ideas down by the barrel loads just for the hell of it. You think of something, and you do it," Rozelle said flippantly, and a happy Pecola erupted with laughter.

"Whoo, honeychile," Pecola raved. "You're see what I'm saying now, Rozelle baby."

"Don't start that again, Rozelle," Symone said. "Remember? You were the one who told Pecola and me to not speak negatively anymore."

Rozelle chuckled lightly too and stared at a possum as it waddled along in the woods. They rode along in silence for a few more minutes.

"Shooot! If it wasn't for me, Scott never would've attended the MAWS conference in the first place," Rozelle reminded as he so often did.

"Damn, Rozelle. If I hear that again, I promise you I'll scream," Pecola teased him.

"I mean it," Rozelle said. "I'm just glad that Jodria Anne knows yall. It certainly has changed her tremendously."

"That's another thing, Rozelle," Symone edged on. "Jodria Anne."

"What?" Rozelle asked with a quizzical expression. "What about her?"

"Well, Rozelle." Symone hesitated. "Uh, when all the women went out last week—"

"You mean jazz night at your house?"

"Hell no, Rozelle," Symone snapped. "Last Friday night when all the ladies went out to see the new Samuel Jackson movie. While we were having dinner at Cafe Trinidad later that evening—"

"Where?" Rozelle asked quickly.

"The Trinidad Cafe," Symone went on. "You know the piano bar that's located downtown right across the street from Unique Upstairs. Don't even try it. You're acting like you don't know what I'm talking about. Long story short; Jodria told us about the red dirt story, bro."

"She sho did," Pecola said. "And it was terrible."

"Maybe being out with the girls made her think about you and it," Symone confessed as she looked around to see Pecola's reaction. As Pecola guided her horse, Spirit, around a fallen pine branch, she kept her eyes on the path. Rozelle was quiet for several minutes, and Symone spoke again first.

"That's not right, Rozelle. Don't play with her emotions like that. Jodria loves you more than anything. In my opinion, she loves you too much. Why, I'll never know," Symone said with a small laugh.

"Here. Here." Pecola agreed. "I'm telling you. If Carlos had done some shit like that, I would've shown my Colored red ass all over Winston. For real, RB."

"Now wait a minute, ladies."

"That was wrong with you to deal with a woman who lived up the street from yall, Rozelle. You're married, my man. As much money as you make and as much as you travel nationally and internationally, you can find women anywhere," Symone continued to admonish in a sisterly way.

Rozelle quickly glanced at Pecola who slowly nodded her head that Symone was right. Then he turned to gaze at Symone.

"I know. I know, ladies. Come on," Rozelle pleaded. "Don't come down on your homeboy so hard, baby. I thought we came out here for tranquillity, serenity, peace, and quiet. Not a whole lot of serious lectures."

"Jodria loves you, Rozelle," Symone insisted. "She takes care of you and those children like a mother sergeant. You know that."

"You're on the money, baby. Yall are right," Rozelle acknowledged. "Scott told me the same thing."

Pecola shook her head and gazed up at the sky. "Jodria has a huge heart like Alex," she said with understanding. "I see why those two hit it off so well. For you to act up and openly run around on her, that's downright awful, RB. It's one thing to be a philanderer, but it's another thing to have it known."

"You're right, Pecola. Listen to us, RB. We wouldn't constantly talk to you about it if we didn't care for Jodria or care for you," Symone said as she wiped the sweat off her forehead with her right hand. "Your wife is a good woman. She loves you and only you, Rozelle. If I was your woman, I wouldn't take it."

"Listen to that big talk, Pecola," Rozelle said as he gripped the reins to step into a small stream. "Wait a minute, Symone. Evidently, you forgot you told me about you and Billy."

"I haven't forgotten," Symone said.

"Good. Cause I remember how you put up with a lot from him. Remember, Sy?" Rozelle asked, trying to jar her memory.

Symone suddenly nodded her head and quietly considered her turbulent marriage with Billy for a moment. Eventually, she offered Pecola and Rozelle a small smile.

"I guess you're right," Symone said finally. "I did take a lot from Billy. You do what you can do until something else makes you decide to change. That's no excuse for you. You're still married. I'm not, Rozelle. Anyway, I realize you got a wild hair up your butt, but tone it down in your neighborhood. Ok? Pecola, help me out here."

"You know it' so beautiful out here." Pecola was gazing at the huge maple trees in the distance. "The trees. The woods. The birds and their tweet tweet sounds. The whistling of the mockingbirds and the fluttering of the butterflies. All of it. Alex and Madison could probably bottle this and sell it to a whole lot of stressed out people."

"Hmmm," Rozelle hummed. "I need to write a business plan for them."

"They own everything they can see in every direction." She tightly sucked in her nose and inhaled the fresh air. "That's wonderful. During times like this, it makes me hate that Carlos split up our land to those ten other families. We would have one-hundred and fifty acres similar to this. Hindsight is twenty-twenty on a lot of things," Pecola declared wistfully as she considered her other secret life.

"Are you listening to *this* conversation, girl?" Symone asked after she patiently listen to Pecola babble on.

"Honeychile, of course I am," Pecola replied. "I'm with you. I'm merely taking in the scenery. Believe it or not, I can do two things at the same time."

Rozelle offered them both a sheepish grin, which they ignored.

"Somebody needs to simply kick Rozelle's ass. That's all. Oh, I know what we can do, Symone. Let's find a tall, lean, young ebony male stud for Jodria. One of those pro basketball players that Marlon hangs with. The ones with the hard, sho-nuff, hard bodies. Set her up for a night of fantasy and fun," Pecola said. Symone glanced around Rozelle's back, and Pecola winked an eye at her.

"No yall ain't," Rozelle yelled. "Not with my wife. Nobody touches my sweet baby's stuff but me." Rozelle stuck his tongue out at Symone and Pecola.

"If you want to keep your tongue, you better keep it in your mouth," Symone teased. "That's your problem now. Probably sticking it in places you shouldn't."

"So." Rozelle stuck his tongue out again.

"Oh, chile. I got it now. The double standard rules. As a man, you can dip your stick in another woman's clit, but no man can jam his stand in your wife's stuff. Unbelievable. Men are a stone trip," Pecola said as she shook her head from side to side.

"What's the verdict, Rozelle?" Symone asked insistently. Rozelle waffled mightily and took a deep breath.

"Ok. Enough," he finally said.

"You really got a nice wife," Symone reminded him. "No one deserves the embarrassment and shame you bring on her. The shame you bring on yourself. Nowadays, I wouldn't put up with that the same way I did with Billy."

"Sure you would, girl."

"No I wouldn't, Rozelle. I've been damaged."

"Damaged?"

"Yeah. That's right. Damaged by love, hurt, pain, and by men. I heard Pauletta say that one time. I thought to myself that sounds like me," Symone said as she leaned forward slightly and patted Starbright on the neck.

"Honeychile! Honeychile! Symone has always been outspoken, but I believe it was the Billy era, that very turbulent marriage chapter in her life, that pushed her straight over the edge, Rozelle. That's when she turned into a stone bitch," Pecola declared boisterously. "I noticed she moved to sho nuff Bitchdomville after Billy."

"That's not when it happened, but Billy did have a lot to do with it, girl," Symone admitted with a big smile and sighed. "I would've worked on my marriage until I was seventy-five, but I could only do so much. I'm only one half of the marriage union, baby. Billy's heart wasn't in it."

"I done told you. That's where you messed up," Pecola said. "A great marriage begins with two complete people, honeychile. Not a half of a person. You know that. You just can't have two halves trying to make a whole. It's not going to work."

Symone glared in disbelief at Pecola. "My prior comment stands. Since when have you taken Dr. Gwendolyn Goldsby's place on relationships, girl?"

"Humph. I know what I'm talking about."

"Then live it."

"Say what, chile?"

"If you ask me, the nigger was crazy, Symone," Rozelle said.

"I'm down with your opinion," Symone answered Rozelle. "But I must admit I learned a lot from Billy. What I learned from my ex-husband was worth more than my MBA from Wharton or my degree from Hampton."

"You go, honeychile," Pecola said.

"I'm serious," Symone continued. "While I was married to Billy, I did discover I was more worried about Billy's well-being than he was about mine. Just think about it like this. If I'm constantly thinking about and worrying if you're happy, then you're constantly thinking about and worrying if you're happy, too. Then who the hell is thinking and worrying about me? No damn body. So I finally figured I had to start thinking about myself."

Rozelle and Pecola broke out with laughter. "That makes sense," Rozelle eventually mumbled.

"Then years ago," Symone continued, "Hazele gave me a copy of "The Art of Being A Necessary Bitch." It was an article she found in *Essence*. Hell, I was truly on my way then. I realized I wasn't all alone in acting up and being a bonafide bitch every now and then."

"I know, honeychile," Pecola said. "It's something about getting older. You tend to say exactly how you feel more often. It's that fortyish age. Pauletta says you start fermenting."

"And your sister knows the deal," Symone exclaimed.

"I'm telling you," Pecola nodded. "At forty, you kick butts and take names later."

"You're right, Pecola. I'll be forty in January. More than ever, I realize I don't need anybody to validate what I want to say or do. Those days are gone where I needed to listen to praising words to massage my ego. Yall know what I'm talking about? That necessary outside validation a lot of us needs to help us make it through the day. I really needed to be stroked when I first came to this country." As Symone talked, she wistfully remembered her bruised and broken spirit as a ten-year-old girl. "Not anymore. Like Alex said, instead of sponging off of positive statements from other people, we need to learn how to give it to ourselves. Outside validation—kiss my Black ass."

"I heard that, girl," Pecola said.

"I know you're difficult to handle, but I bet I could take care of you, Sy. Take care of you too, Pecola," Rozelle joked, eyeing them both with a debonair shake of his head.

"Nigger, puhleeze. See. See. Look at your ass. Only a sho nuff maggot would make a statement like that," Pecola exclaimed.

"Oh, I didn't tell you," Rozelle said. "I joined *that* fraternity, too. We call it the Maggot Fraternity. It's MF for short. We got members throughout the whole world, but it's the MF distinction that confuses people. They think it's a curse word."

"Yeah right, Rozelle," Pecola agreed. "You're crazy but realize this, my brother. You can't handle this good ole Greensboro country stuff anyway."

"*And* you certainly can't handle my stuff, Rozelle. The ones who are lucky enough to get it barely know what to do with it." Symone's laughter traveled through her words.

"Why don't yall just give me a little chance?" Rozelle requested in a sly tone.

"No way, Jose. Nothing but a pure maggot," Pecola hissed jokingly.

"You see what I mean with your crazy ass. You know Jodria is our very, very close friend, and we like her," Symone explained as she reached over to punch him on his left shoulder. Rozelle leaned out of the way, and she missed him. Pecola punched him on the right one instead.

"Ouch! Damn, girl!" he yelled and blew Pecola a lingering air kiss.

"Honeychile—" Pecola groaned. "The last time you asked me a stupid ass question like that, I told Jodria on you."

"What my wife say?"

"She told me to ignore you since you were harmless. That's exactly what Jodria said," Pecola replied laughing. "And that's exactly what I'm doing. Ignoring your ass. But I'm still convinced a male whore is a whore until his dick won't rise any more, and he's old as the hills. Not only is he limping on one leg, but his dick is limp, too. That's the only reason why he'll stop chasing women."

"You're too crazy, baby," Rozelle said wiping the sweat from his mouth, and he whistled. For the next ten minutes, they rode on in silence once more.

Chapter Forty-Nine

"This is such beautiful land, Pecola," Rozelle marveled as he passed the lush green section of a huge gathering of oak and pine trees. The silence and serenity of the trail was intoxicating.

"Honeychile, I know." Pecola inhaled deeply and smiled.

"I'm going to be honest with you two. When yall initially said you were going to come with me, I was pissed off since I really wanted to be by myself," Symone confessed and hesitated ever so slightly. "Now, I'm glad yall came. We haven't had a chance to talk in a while with Rozelle—at least like this. This was great. Don't you think it was, Pecola?"

"It was exhausting and wonderful," Pecola mumbled.

"I'm glad I came, too," Rozelle piped in. "Are you really ok, Symone?" Rozelle pried in a brotherly way. "You know all of your friends are talking about the bad mood you've been in this last year, baby. Jumping into folk's stuff and cursing them out for simple reasons."

"Uh oh. You're stepping on dangerous territory, RB," Pecola said. "Believe me."

"I know, Rozelle. You're right. Hey, watch your mouth, Pecola." Symone chuckled quickly. "Alex spoke to me last month and straightened me out real good. It's a lot of past stuff that keeps flashing through my mind. That's all." Symone explained in a soft voice as she recalled yesterday's thoughts about her family and Orlando.

"I remembered what you told me about your life in Trinidad, Sy. Without question, that is some heavy problems to be messed up about. Don't dwell on it, babygirl." Rozelle's voice was tender. "Ok? You're too smart for that. All of us are too old. Carrying all that around will give you wrinkles on that gorgeous face, then nobody will want you. Plow forward, baby. Take my advice. It's real. Ain't I telling her right, Pecola?"

"Damn, Rozelle!" Pecola exclaimed. "That's the most intelligent thing you've said today. Isn't it, Symone?"

Symone nodded and smiled at Pecola's remarks. "Thanks a lot, Rozelle. I got to agree with Pecola on that one. That was thought-provoking."

Rozelle checked his watch. "It's almost twelve. We've been out here for almost three hours. Alex said that the trail is a four-hour ride. Since I never rode the full course, I wouldn't know that for sure."

Suddenly, two deers dashed across the path in the front of the horses. It spooked Pecola's horse more so than the other two horses. Pecola needed to tighten, work with the reins, and shout *whoa* several times to calm the nervous horse. Since everyone knew Pecola was raised on a large farm in Greensboro, Rozelle and Symone expected her to handle the startled horse in an expert fashion. She did exactly that.

"I could tell your ass was raised in the country, Miss Buffalo Girl. C'mon, let's go through here." Rozelle pointed to an opening in the trail, and he gazed heavenward. "Check out the sky."

The sun had gone behind the clouds, and the sky was streaked in a grayish blue. However, it was still balmy and warm.

"If it rains, my hair will get messed up," Pecola said, worried. "I just got it done yesterday, and last night's pool party didn't' help my doo."

"I believe a thunderstorm is a brewing, and I certainly don't want to be caught out here among all these trees, especially if there is any lightning going down. C'mon, ladies. Let's go through here," he said as he directed Misty up the slight hill toward the opening. "By the time we get back to the stables and hose the horses down, who knows. Wooo! They might come looking for us. They might even think we found a great place along the trail and decided to have a menage a trois like crazy ass jungle bunnies."

"Nigger, puhleeze. If nothing else, Jodria knows Symone and me are her soul friends. Knowing how efficient Cleopatra is, she probably handed her a monogrammed announcement and told Jodria that you were with us. My girl knows your wife knows you're safe. If anything, Jodria knows we'll try to knock some sense into your brain, baby," Pecola said. "That's for sure."

Once back at the stables, Rozelle, Symone, and Pecola hosed the horses down with lukewarm water, and the three friends headed back up to the house. Laughing as they walked, Rozelle was between the two women. As he told them crazy stories about his job, he gripped their hands tightly.

"…I'm serious. The other thing I want yall to let me know is when you two need me to take care of you. Yall know I'm a freak?" Rozelle asked with a glint in his eyes. "I'm an old assed freak who ain't got no damn limitations. Don't yall know that's what friends are for?"

"Yeah right, Rozelle," Pecola replied in a mock exasperation and punched him on the arm again. "Once a male whore, always a male whore. Isn't he hopeless, Sy?"

"That's right. One-hundred percent crazy." Symone spoke with an inward smile. "That's Rozelle. I believe everything we said to him went in one ear and flashed out the other. It's just that simple, girl. I really don't know why we even try to talk any sense into him or why we have him as a friend."

When Rozelle heard the Caribbean music floating down from the basketball court, he added a bouncy pep to his gait.

"…I'm telling you, babygirl. They rocked the place last night. You missed it, Symone. It seems like they're starting the day the same way," Rozelle said as he swayed to the reggae music blasting away.

Shaggy's *Boombastic* CD was playing. No doubt Booker T selected it. Listening to reggae music was the only way Booker T said anybody should play basketball in the summertime. When he was around, that was exactly how it was done. The reggae way. With its erotic beat, he said the sultry reggae sounds automatically took athletes' minds to the Caribbean where they could envision themselves playing on a court surrounded by palm trees, heavenly pink sand beaches, and cobalt blue water.

Booker T was initially leaning on a tree watching ten guys play a vigorous game of basketball. Earlier, he had played two full court games himself, and now he was rather tired. At the age of forty-seven, Booker T certainly was still in great shape, but he couldn't hang like he used to and easily admitted when enough was enough. Booker T took another sideways glance at Marlon. Immediately, he became concerned for his nephew. Today, Marlon's knees were bothering him unusually so—more than he let on. Yet, he never complained about the pain.

Earlier that morning, Marlon even needed to walk with the use of crutches. That was something he knew Marlon despised doing. Booker T noticed a sad expression graced Marlon's face. His nephew watched the energetic game of basketball from the sidelines in a chaise lounge that Madison placed for him under the huge maple tree. With one of his twin baby boys sleeping peacefully on his lap, Marlon had a distant look on his face. Booker T sadly shook his head and hoped that Marlon would snap out of the melancholy mood—at least before the afternoon ceremonies.

"Life would be terrible without women in the summertime," Booker T said when he heard Rozelle announcing he was coming up the hill and went to meet the three friends. "Wooo, baby. They definitely ain't teaching those kinds of moves on the basketball court," Booker T exclaimed as he saw Symone and Pecola twist their halter clad bodies as they walked up the hill. "Here comes my Trini girl. Uh oh. Tear up my damn world, baby."

"Hey, Booker T." Symone waved at him and smiled excitedly.

"Mess me right on up, baby. That happens whenever I look at you," he shouted to Symone with outstretched arms while walking toward them. "What's up, ladies? Talk to me, puhleeze," Booker T said anxiously and affectionately hugged and kissed Symone. He did the same to Pecola.

"It's good seeing you, Booker T," Symone gushed.

"Where were you last night?" Booker T questioned grinning from ear to ear.

Pecola believed he had a slight crush on Symone, but he could forget it. Pecola knew Booker T was too short for Symone's taste.

"Well, it's like this." Symone hesitated.

"Come on and talk to me. Give me the scoop on your evening away from here. I missed dancing reggae style with you last night, Sy."

"I know, Booker T. Pecola told me."

Booker T turned to face Pecola.

"And, how's your fine self doing this morning, Pecola? Let me show you how you were dancing last night, bikini and all, baby."

Moving as if he was a drum major doing a slow motion march in a Black College band, Booker T proceeded to mimic what Pecola thought was her sensual reggae dance routine. Pecola, Rozelle, and Symone burst out laughing.

"I didn't do it like that," Pecola squealed. While gazing into Rozelle and Symone's faces, he hugged Pecola again.

"Your girl here shimmied the night away like a motha in her pink and green bikini. She had that bootie thang going on. Just joking with you, baby," he laughed as he held Pecola tightly before releasing her.

"I told her all about it, Booker T." Pecola smiled.

"How the hell you doing this morning, Pecola?" he repeated again looking her up and down. "Does Carlos know you're out here dressed like that with those Daisy Duke shorts and cowboy hat. Damn, girl!"

"I'm just fine, Booker T," Pecola answered with a chuckle. *It's a shame I can't say the same about you*, she thought quickly.

"Just looking at you, my day just got damn brighter, baby," Booker T said. A delighted Pecola smiled sweetly and batted her eyes at the words of praise.

Although Booker T was charming, serious, positive, overly confident, and intelligent, Pecola thought he was an unattractive guy. In her opinion, he and Marlon were not that much to look at, and all Marlon's millions couldn't fix either one of their faces. Both Booker T and Marlon were caramel complexioned nicely built men. At six feet six inches tall, of course Marlon was the giant of the two. Only about five feet eleven inches tall, Booker T still had an icon reputation in the field of professional ball and was remembered as an awesome pro basketball player back in the day when he wooed folk with his movements on the recreation center courts of Greensboro, North Carolina.

As a result of a minor knee injury, Booker T believed he was forced to prematurely retire years ago from the American Basketball League's Carolina team. Even nowadays, he still was able to work some serious moves on the basketball court and always showed out spectacularly around Marlon's professional basketball buddies. Always adorned in his infamous skullcap, Booker T was a baldheaded, marijuana smoking man. His fascination with the green flower was a result of his dabbling in the aphrodisiac during his flower child and hippie era. Initially, he kept his marijuana smoking habit a secret. However, after he read up on the medicinal qualities of weed, years ago he broke out to announce his belief to others. In his opinion, weed was certainly not a drug and definitely nothing to be afraid of. Booker T said that smoking joints was like taking vitamins that assisted truly intelligent, brain sharp and gifted people, of which he was one. It gave a person an opportunity to meditate relaxingly on the more serious issues of life.

After Booker T's demise with the Carolina team, he was courted by colleges to coach. He eventually accepted the position of head basketball coach at Benedict College in Columbia, South Carolina, where he served in that capacity for many years. However, when Marlon had the car accident, it was initially diagnosed Marlon would never walk again. Marlon was like a son to him. Booker T immediately resigned from Benedict to assist with nursing the devastated Marlon back to health and to revive his morale to the positive thinking days of old.

A staunch supporter of the Black experience in any form, Booker T was an avid member of the Blank Panther Party years ago during its heyday in Greensboro. During that brief stint with the organization, Booker T was the assistant to the Minister of Information. Booker T said that the one of the many goals of Black Panther Party was to provide social programs for the poor communities of Greensboro and the entire United States. As a result of that Panther experience, Booker T continually talked about white folks, the importance of family, Black history, and economic development for Black people. Since those subjects were Symone's favorite topics as well, Pecola understood why Booker T and Symone got along so well.

As Booker T, Pecola, Rozelle, and Symone continued to watch the game from the sidelines, Booker T and Symone began speaking quietly about Marlon's July appearance on the *Woolfgang Youngblood Show.* They agreed it was an informative and delightful one-hour interview that gave the world a rare but truly intimate view of Marlon, especially since after the accident. Even though Marlon had been on numerous shows since the death of his three friends, he hadn't been that revealing about his life with anybody in the media. Both Booker T and Symone were definitely surprised Marlon opened up and was quite honest about his personal life after basketball.

During their discussion, Symone casually announced that she found out that Woolfgang was married to a white girl. Marlon had also told her that Woolfgang supported the woman's family and had even set the father and woman's family up in a variety of businesses. But according to Marlon's reliable sources, he hadn't done anything for his Black family who still lived in almost squalor conditions in Bennettsville, South Carolina. Rumor had it that his younger sister lived in the Chelsea Projects of Manhattan. Friends of Marlon confirmed that was true, too. Booker T couldn't believe the information.

"...Was he raised by his family in Bennettsville?"

"I'm telling you," Symone replied. "That's what Marlon told me."

"Baby, that stupid Willie Lynch thinking makes me sick. It's so typical, though. It would be fine if he helped support his blood the same way he takes care of that white woman. Blood is thicker than water, baby," Booker T said tightly. "A lot of times when certain niggers make it, those niggers get sooo brainwashed, they certainly forget who the hell they are as far as Black men are concerned. So you know they don't even know where they came from. I'm serious; it makes me sick to see it unfold, baby."

"No, it makes me sicker," Symone agreed as she rolled her eyes heavenward. "It should be against the law for a Black man to be so damn stupid."

"Yeah, right. But don't forget that they got Black women just as stupid, baby."

"You're right, Booker T," she said laughing. "I forget sometimes because I'm looking at it from a female perspective. Still, it should be against the law."

"That would be great, baby. The prison system would definitely be overcrowded with stupid ass niggers like Woolfgang, though. One day brothers and sisters will learn that when they marry outside the race, all they're doing is giving the economic power back into the hands of white folks who stole it from them in the first place, Symone."

"I know," she agreed easily. "I talk about it every day."

"…Man, my grandmother got better moves than that Oscar. I need to be in there to show you my badass spinning fade away jump shot," Rozelle hollered vigorously from the sidelines, but the players ignored the needling.

Symone and Booker T stopped talking. Their focus turned back to the basketball game. Booker T went off to talk with Rozelle while Symone and Pecola continued to fantasize about the sweaty hard bodies. The two women whispered about the glistening, wet pelts of water dripping down the pro players' skin, and they listened quietly to the squeak squeak sounds of the sneakers against the court.

"…It's an extraordinary thing to watch those bodies work. Isn't it, girl?" Symone asked Pecola in a low voice.

"Honeychile, I know. Umph, umph, umph. They're delicious to look at. Simply absolutely, positively delicious, chile. Aren't they buff as hell?" Pecola whispered as if she told Symone a precious secret.

"Yeah, girl. That's for sure. Look at those tight buns."

Shaggy's version of Mungo Jerry's track *In the Summertime* was blasting out the stereo speakers. Pecola and Symone slowly swayed from side to side to the music, enjoying the music mixed in with their laughter and their hungry eyes.

"It's going to be me and you, baby," Rico said as he tried to guard smooth moving Christopher Perry.

Christopher faked a move, twirled, and went straight to the basket. He was immediately fouled intentionally by Rico who realized it was a hopeless case to even try and stop him. Since the guys all good-naturedly agreed it was a flagrant one, they tried to go by the pick-up rules for the day and allowed Christopher to go to the line.

"…I ain't got to worry about you getting any of those free throws," Oscar Hextall said to his buddy.

Oscar was playing on the opposing team, and he was right. Christopher missed it, and Carlos rebounded. He threw it down court to Miles Valley, a sixteen-year-old who lived in Kimberly Park Projects. Miles was thoroughly excited to be playing with the pros and the other older guys.

"Nice pass, man!" Oscar shouted and pointed a straight finger at Carlos as Miles put the ball up for two easy points. He delightfully gave his older teammates a round of vigorous high fives.

When Scott, Romallus, Carlos, and the other players noticed Symone and Pecola under the tree gazing at the game, they waved back. Playing only in skimpy shorts, their bodies were dripping wet with sweat. Pecola remained mesmerized by the hairy chests of Christopher, Oscar, and Romallus. She was used to seeing Carlos and Scott. It was no big thing to see them running around half-naked playing ball. In Pecola's opinion, there was nothing like a muscularly built Black man with a hairy chest. Once more, she thanked God for sunglasses. Behind the black lens, no one could see how her married eyes were roaming freely up and down the sweaty, tight bodies.

"...What did I tell you, man?" Rozelle hollered, antagonizing his friends' opponents. "Your tall asses can't even make a free throw. Nobody's bothering you. Man, you need to practice this summer."

Christopher waved him off and continued to focus on guarding Rico, who every now and then threw in a swift move that surprised even Christopher.

"Yo, baby. Yo, baby," Oscar yelled for Carlos to pass the ball to him.

"Where's everybody?" Rozelle asked, looking at Booker T as he glanced around the yard.

"Man, everybody's inside having breakfast." Booker T checked his watch and saw that it was already twelve-thirty. "The last group went in around eleven-fifteen, and they should be out any minute."

Booker T's attention turned to the game again. "Jam him. Jam him up if he gets the ball." Booker T yelled instructions to Scott, Rico, and Carlos about Christopher who was dribbling expertly down the court. From the pressure, Christopher passed the ball to his teammate.

"...Push it, baby!" Christopher shouted to Kemper through the squeaking noises of the tennis shoes.

"Check him tight, baby! Check him! You can do it, man!" Oscar instructed the young Miles who was trying to keep up with Madison who received the fast, hard pass from Kemper.

"Uh, I got him covered, man," Miles hollered to his teammates just as Madison maneuvered through a slight opening down the middle and made an easy lay-up into the basket.

"That's all you got to do is show out on a young kid, man?" Scott teasingly yelled to Madison who waved him off. Teasing was part of their game. Booker T and Rozelle turned around to watch the game again.

"...Yo, baby. Yo, you, man! I'm talking to you! You're supposed to be on offense and don't you forget it!" Rozelle screamed to Scott who ignored the jibing from the sidelines. "I know it's time for my ass to get into this game. It's necessary to show some of my Oscar Robertson moves on their behind, man," he explained to Booker T as the two men soulfully pounded fists together.

"I'm with you," Booker T agreed.

"Ah, man. Look at that shit! Mr. McGoo wouldn't miss that shot, man," Rozelle hollered.

"Gimme a time out, man," Carlos yelled as he made the time out signal with his hands. Kemper had been taking him to the hoop all through the game and then some. He was tired. On the last play, Jesse Birth "no-looked-it" to Kemper who went in for the jam all over Carlos. Carlos realized it was helpless to even try and guard the young pro player.

"Look at you. That's what you get trying to be a weekend warrior. Shooting hoops part time. Man, you need to take more time than a time out with your old damn ass in the first place," Rozelle exclaimed as he noticed Carlos doubled over with his hands on knees, staring at the ground trying to catch his breath. "Stick to golfing, man. You got those bragging rights down pat. At your old age, the greens are your best domain."

Carlos gazed up at Rozelle and threw him a halfway evil stare. Still bending over, Carlos disgustingly waved his hand and shook his head at Rozelle.

"We're just too much for them, man," Christopher shouted for all to hear as he raised the chilled jar of Gatorade to his mouth. "They've been trying to play us tight on the defense, but they can't handle the heat. So they're hacking the hell out of us, man. You know it. You see the deal. Wild ass fouls—all kinds of shit," he continued, laughing as he looked toward Booker T and Rozelle. A smiling Christopher suddenly waved at Pecola and Symone, and they quickly waved back.

Chapter Fifty

Fifteen minutes later, Symone and Pecola decided to head toward the house. While walking down the path, they waved at Marlon who waved back. Symone decided to stop and talk with Marlon. Pecola said that was fine, but she was going to go take a brief nap before the afternoon ceremony.

"How you doing, Marlon?" Symone asked softly when she noticed his downcast expression. He quickly tried to turn his frown into a smile. She bent over and gave Marlon a light kiss on the right cheek. He embraced Symone affectionately, and she kissed the sleeping baby boy on the sole of its left foot.

"I'm fine, girl. You're looking good as usual. Damn sexy if you want to know the truth," he said, now beginning to laugh with his hand over his mouth.

"Thanks, Marlon. I knew you could brighten up my day." Symone sat on the grassy ground and wrapped both arms around her knees. "I was just telling Booker T that I thought your interview on the Woolfgang Youngblood Show was marvelous. It certainly was a naked look at your life. You were getting it all out, man. I said to myself, I know that's not the Marlon I know. You surprised me."

"I know. I felt, ah, how could I say it? I felt free that afternoon. So far I haven't regretted it. You know how the media is, Sy. You got to be sooo damn careful about what you say, or they'll take it and run with it," he explained as he rubbed his right knee. Marlon watched the hazy gray-blue sky and inhaled deeply. "I have days like that when I'm feeling freer than other days." He inhaled again.

"I've free feeling days too, Marlon. Lately, they're few and far between."

"I know, baby." He bobbed his head with understanding. "Today is certainly not one of those days I feel like sharing with folks. I guess what I try to do when it's not a free feeling day is to reach deep within myself."

"I need to learn how to reach deep, Marlon. Teach myself how to reach some damn where. There are times I believe my life is a masterpiece. Then, there are other times, I believe it's a pure divine mess."

"Talk to yourself, Symone. That's what life is. Man, living *is* a trip. It's a constant talking trip, though. All through my life, I've been able to reach deep down by talking to myself. I reach deep down into my inner being."

"I try."

"It works, baby. I go inside to my private place of peace. There I can kick shit around and discover what I need to keep holding on. It's what I've been taught from my parents and from Booker T. I've always been taught to never give up. Hell, I know the routine. Yet, you know how it is on days like today." He hesitated briefly.

"I'm listening."

"On days like today, I feel like chalking it all up, Sy. I really do. Just letting this shit go, baby," he said almost inaudibly, and there was a brief, heavy pause.

"Don't go there, Marlon. Chalking it up is pretty heavy, baby. There's a whole lot of ways of giving up on life, especially if you're talking about chalking things up the way I think you're talking about. Stay strong. You know how it is. What does Booker T always say? If your mind wanders crazily, then your body follows right behind."

"I guess I need to go to another level," Marlon interrupted her and spoke as if he were preoccupied. "Whichever level that is I don't know, Sy."

"Which twin is this?" Symone asked quickly trying to change the subject. She noticed Marlon's grimace as he slowly massaged both knees.

Out of the corner of her eyes, she quickly glanced at the surgical scars on Marlon's knees that looked like a road map, which was deeply embedded in his dark caramel skin. Just thinking of Marlon's injury caused sadness to envelop her body even more. She didn't feel qualified to talk to him about holding on to life with a smile.

"Talk to me, Marlon. Which twin is it?" Before Marlon answered, he smiled at her. He sensed she changed the subject intentionally.

"Well, I hate to say it, but I'm like you. I can't tell either, baby. Nanette swears I got Solomon, and she has Fletcher. In a few months, maybe I'll know. For right now, I'm just not sure. I hope we got it straight on their birth certificates." They both laughed.

"Having a twin is a wonderful phenomenon, Marlon. While my brother was alive, he was my whole wide world," she recalled wistfully as she considered Lennious. "When I was little, my twin and I were such remarkable companions to each other. It was like we had developed our own little way of communicating together. I watch Kyle and Sylvia together. They do the same things me and Lennious did."

"It's amazing you said that. Nanette tells me all the time that my boys cry at the same time and sleep in the same position. Since I'm out of town a lot, I don't notice it as much. It's kind of unique the way nature allows some women to have two to five babies all at once."

"It is unique. You know my brother and I were identical. We looked just alike. There were times we had the same thought at the same moment, Marlon. It was sooo special. Lennious was such a comfort to me. I'm almost forty years old, and I still remember how he was so calm and quite protective of me. He always used to refer to me as 'meh twin this, and meh twin that. Meh precious, precious twin sister,'" she recalled in a Trinidadian accent laced with a bitter-sweet laugh. "I only hope my girls and your sons can experience the beauty of having such a bond of enjoying each other as twins should." Her voice was nostalgically sad, as old memories became fresh once again.

"I'm sure they will. I'm hoping they become stand-out basketball players like the Grantee twins."

"I bet you do. Hell, as much money as they're making, I don't blame you."

"How are you doing, Sy?" Marlon asked with concern in his eyes. "I missed you last night. Nanette kept asking for you and started to call you. So did Alex. Around midnight, she got quiet for a little while. Then, Nanette got worried about her sister. You know how Alex is. She wants everyone to be happy. Man, she even talked about driving over to your house. It was three o'clock in the morning, but Pecola convinced her to leave you alone. She told her that if there were something really wrong, you would let them know. Your friends sho nuff missed you last night, girl."

"I know. I wanted to be here, but I had to deal with some serious shit. Real serious. You know how that is?"

"Damn right, I know exactly what you're saying," Marlon replied and took another swig of John Courage beer.

"Are you ready to give your speech this evening, Marlon?"

"As ready as I'm gonna be. I'm just chillin' and trying to give my legs a rest. I think I hung out too much on them yesterday. Dancing last night and trying to jam some boards yesterday afternoon with the fellas for a couple of minutes."

"You were on the court, too?" Symone asked, surprised since she knew he rarely stepped onto a basketball court for any reason.

"Just for a little while. I couldn't take more than that. Hell, that's the price you pay. I have good days and bad days with my legs. Today is one of my bad days, Sy. I hadn't had one like this in at least seven months. Hey, you know me. I'll make it, baby. Always have, and I always will."

"I know you will." She smiled quickly. "I saw you on ESPN during the National Basketball League draft. What the hell were you doing there?"

"You know BJ. He was representing who he thought would be the number one draft pick."

"Vance Staples?"

"Yep."

"He *was* the number one pick."

"I know. BJ's rolling, baby."

"That's very good."

"I love going to the drafts, Sy. I get invited all the time. It must be my maturity in the business, baby. I've reached senior citizen status now," he added lightly with his voice trailing off, then he stopped speaking. Marlon breathed deeply and tried to relax.

"You know what it is, Marlon. It isn't anybody like you now or then. You're royalty in the universe of basketball. Nanette says it about you all the time."

"Nae's supposed to. She's my wife."

"But so does everyone else I hear say your name. My brother told me that you're one of basketball's greatest champions. A damn legend." There was merriness in her voice, but she still noticed his anxiety. "Just think I know your scrawny ass. Your popularity is confirmed all the time in the newspapers and whatever. That's why people are always after you, Marlon. I'm sure it's an honor."

Marlon's grin was wider. Before he responded, both he and Symone sang a couple of lines to the sounds of Bob Marley's *Three Little Birds.*

"If you're trying to perk me up today, it's working, baby. It damn sho nuff is, girl."

"I'm glad."

"Yes, being famous is an honor, but the NBL draft is just an exciting time, Sy. That's all. That's why I go. I want to just see those young guys turn into millionaires overnight."

"Well, I hope they know what to do with the money. I know they're in shock that they're getting paid to do what they love."

"You're right. Some of them *do know* what to do with it and helluva lots of them don't. If it wasn't for BJ and Booker T's guidance, I just don't know."

"You had wonderful support."

"True. You can have advisors, but my mama said you still got to have common sense."

"Absolutely. Larryetta is right."

"I was a trip like those other new jocks getting in the league. After my head started swelling from all the attention, I couldn't believe it was happening. That *I* actually was in the NBL."

"That must've been a thrill for you."

"That's how I felt, Sy. I used to think, 'Damn, man! They're paying me millions to do this? To dribble and shoot a ball? To play the sport I get complete joy out of grooving on the court with my buddies in the summertime for free? Hey, this ain't a bad gig.'" Symone and Marlon burst out laughing.

"I don't know who's crazier. You or Booker T."

"We're probably tied for first place," he exclaimed as he gulped beer. "When I signed my first contract, Booker T told me to take my newfound fame one day at a time. One day I woke up and I said, 'Damn! Gotdamn! Whoa, man! Look-a-here. Look-a-here. You mean all those thousands of people are here to get my autograph. They're laughing, cheering, clapping, and screaming *my* name. So this is celebrity status. It's wild, baby.'"

"I'm sure it is."

Still laughing, Marlon tried to speak. "Even now, Booker T reminds me how he used to tell me that if my head got too big to fit through the door, it was time for me to stay outside. That's when I got my crib down at Hilton Head."

"I guess he was trying to tell you that fame ain't nothing to play with or take lightly. That's wild, Marlon."

"Everything about the game is, baby."

"If what you told me about the business side of basketball is true, that part sounds even crazy."

"It's wicked what goes on behind the scene, Sy. It's very rough."

"In that case, I should've been at the drafts with you screaming at all those doting rookies. I'd be telling them 'Don't trust the owners as far as you can see them, baby. All those rich white owners got serious egos beyond belief. While your freshly drafted ass is hugging your mother and father, they're already making deals behind your back. Marlon, my buddy back in North Carolina, done told me the deal about unscrupulous agents and all kinds of predators in professional sports,'" Symone screamed out into the air.

"Girl, you're too crazy. I bet your Uncle Samuel shakes his head and wonders where he went wrong when you discuss your philosophies with him."

"I know I can be a little different from the normal crowd. That's what I've been told in the last couple of days, so we both are on the same track." Symone spoke easily as she sipped a little of Marlon's beer he offered to her. She swallowed several more gulps and handed the bottle back to him.

"That's why we vibe so well together, baby."

"Thanks." Symone smiled, and patted his hand. "My Uncle Samuel just listens to me and shakes his head. He tells me all the time that he needs a few more people like me working for him. Someone who disagrees regardless of the consequences. Somebody who isn't a yes man. Other than that, my Uncles Samuel, Willie, and Cecil have always taught me, my sisters and my brother to be fierce, independent thinking individuals."

"Is that so?" Marlon grinned quickly. "I hadn't noticed that."

"I don't know how else to be. After we came to New York, I was brought up in a family where you respect people. You have your own mind, and you don't ever lose your dedication to what you believe in." Symone sighed and weighed her words carefully. She was silent and still for at least a couple of minutes.

"I'm listening, baby."

"I really don't know why I listen to my own drum, Marlon. Whatever I feel passionate about, it's my mission to speak out about it. I guess I just took this philosophy to another level regarding my ferocity about economic development and racial issues for my people. I fervently believe in that. How I speak to yall is exactly how I speak to my three uncles."

"Get out of here!"

"Absolutely. I've told you this before. Don't act surprised. Now the way I speak on it or the controversial things I say, that's what surprises my family in New York more than anything else."

"I bet it does, girl," he said and glanced at the plane that appeared as a tiny dot in the blue sky. The sun was peeking through the clouds again.

"Tell me more about the draft."

"Well, the draft is amazing. I still get into it. Just looking at the brothers' happy faces when they hear their names called is wonderful. Talk about joy. Poor folks' joy that travels all through your body. With all my health problems, the last two years were the only time I've missed the draft. This time, me, Christopher, Booker T, and Oscar went along with BJ."

"I know. I saw yall on TV. I said to myself, 'Look at those guys trying to act all cool and shit,'" she said with a quick laugh. "According to the newspaper, they said that you and an entourage of seven were in attendance."

"I done told your ass, don't trust the media. They were wrong as usual, Sy. It was an entourage of ten at the table." He laughed but couldn't hide his irritation. "The media gets on my gotdamn nerves. They never report on shit right in my life. I hate them."

"If I didn't know you, I could never tell. You're doing a good job, especially when they interview you. You cover up how you feel about the media very well."

"I gots to because of endorsements, and shit like that. But I'm telling you. They're fucking crazy. They try to dictate the type of person you are, how you should live, what you should say, and are always trying to make you out to be the bad guy. Those fuckers are nothing but manipulators of the truth."

"I agree with you on that, Marlon." Symone remembered how after Marlon's accident the media tried to destroy his reputation by feeding negative, unsubstantiated information to the public. Symone often heard Marlon say that since he was negatively bombarded by the press during the accident, they robbed him of his privacy to grieve. He never forgave them for that either and grew to hate them.

"How did you know I was going to be on television? I hadn't told anyone I was going to the NBL draft. I wanted to slide in there real quiet like."

Symone simply smiled at him. "I ain't saying, and when can *you* slide anywhere quietly."

"I know. Nanette called you. My wife is something else. I tell BJ that all the time. He needs to give her an extra fee for handling all my publicity. I tell her that she's in the wrong field. Instead of her being a nurse, she needs to go into public relations. My baby is a trip."

"No. She just loves you, Marlon. It's good to be loved, though. Very good." Symone mumbled the last two words as she scratched the grassy ground with a small stick.

"It is, and I love her. There's no question about it. Not one," he said solemnly as the turbulent moments that they had been through since the car accident flashed in his thoughts.

"Are you going to the draft next year?"

"Probably."

"I would like to go with you, Marlon."

"Really?"

"Yes, *really*, Marlon."

"By the way, I met a guy there I hadn't seen in a couple of years. He said that he lives in Winston-Salem since he and his family just relocated from Chicago. He was tall and dark-skinned. I say about six-four Super dresser. I recognized the Perry White suit immediately. I know my Cal-lee designers. The brother was stepping right, Sy."

"Hmmm. That certainly does sound like my type."

"He was, Sy. When I saw him, I thought about you. It was especially so since my wife told me to be on the look out for you a nice, super tall, intelligent, and dark-skinned, man." Symone laughed at the description.

"Remind me to thank Nanette again." Symone laughed. "The description is perfect. Just add a hard-body to the resume. Even though my own body isn't hard right now, that's exactly what I prefer. It sounds like you've been on the job searching for me."

Marlon laughed. "Your body is fine, girl. My buddies think you got it going on."

"Really?"

"Yeah, really. That's what they say about all of yall. You, Pecola, Darilyn, Pauletta, and Alex. Yall are older women holding up real well," Marlon joked as he gulped more beer.

"Older women holding up well? Thanks a lot, Marlon."

"Just wanted to let you know the real deal, baby. I'm still on the job looking for a man for you. This guy I met at the draft is baldheaded, and I know you can't stand cue ball men, baby."

"Whoa! That's right. I'm glad you remember. Don't like them atall." Symone thought for a moment. "Yet, I'm still curious. What's his name?"

"You know I can't think of it. Mickey or Michael something or nother. Wow! I'm tired. I later found out he's married. The buzz is the brother is a top notched, tough-ass sports attorney. He hustled me a little while when I was at North Carolina University, but you know where I was heading."

"So this wasn't your first time meeting him?"

"Shit no. I've met him before, but I don't deal with him. Very rarely do I see him. Can you believe that? I'm telling you, Sy. It gets crowded at the draft and all the other social events that surround it—that surround pro ball period. So it's real easy for people to pass right through the cracks. I talked to him for about fifteen minutes. If it wasn't for BJ and my brother handling my legal shit, I would've jumped ship and tried to hook up with him. The brotha got it going on, too, just like you, girl. He talks like he really knows the ins and outs of the pro ball business."

"He should."

"Exactly. He represents some heavyweights in the business."

"I'm just glad to see he's a Black man penetrating that industry. I know white boys probably got the corner on that market."

"That they do and a whole lot of other markets in the world of professional sports."

"I'm just curious. Why won't more Black athletes use Blacks agents and attorneys more often, Marlon?"

"The vibe is that the Black agents don't know how to market and promote their clients."

"And the white agents do?"

"Well, not really. White agents *did* have a head start in the industry."

"So did white players."

"True." Marlon paused briefly. "I can only tell you the reason *I* chose my agent. Sure BJ is my cousin, but he's smart. He's all business, and he's tough as all hell. When he goes in to negotiate with the GMs, BJ don't take no mess."

"The GMs?"

"GM stands for general managers."

"Ok, Marlon. I'm with you."

"Booker T knew I was going pro. Sometimes, I think more so than me," Marlon added with a smile. "Even though BJ was there, Booker T still wanted me to research other agents. When we won that second championship at NCU, I got serious as a motha trying to figure out the best person to deal for me. Booker T laid some names on me. I knew about a few. Plus, I knew I wanted to get paid. Coach had a direct line to a bunch—"

"A bunch of white boys."

"Exactly."

"You see what I'm saying?" she said with her eyebrows arched in such a way to indicate how serious she was. "That networking is real in their lives. When I was young and working in the Eisners' stores, I noticed that. It was an absolutely phenomenal lesson for me. If another Jewish person came in and wanted to know about who did this or who did that, there always was a Rolodex available."

"Good system."

"It is. Whatever was needed or whoever had it, they flipped to the Rolodex. Made a call. Spoke to a friend. They made it happen. From the Eisners, I learned so much about helping your *own* people out first. That was drummed into me. I got a Ph.D. in helping out, business wise and personally. If you don't do it for your own, who will?"

Marlon nodded slowly but said nothing. He glanced at his watch, and his eyes gently drifted to the vigorous activity of the men on the basketball court. Finally, after a few preoccupied minutes, he spoke.

"You're right. Absolutely right," he replied carefully in a low voice. A vision of him frantically steering the Jaguar again lurched to the front of his brain. That had been happening all day, and it was fucking with him. Symone was now watching his expression, and Marlon noticed her worried brow. With closed eyes, he quickly shook his head. When he opened them, he grinned broadly at Symone.

"Are you ok, Marlon?"

"Yeah, baby. I'm fine. I got a little headache," he lied easily. "That's all."

Suddenly, Solomon started crying and Marlon propped the baby up on his left shoulder. He very gently began patting his son's back to settle the whimpering. Symone and Marlon became silent, and they merely listened to the blasting reggae sounds of Maxi Priest and Shabba. Slowly, Marlon's eyes began to follow the basketball game again, and he inhaled softly several times. Watching the way his family and friends moved easily on the court palming each other with excitement for making a great shot, Marlon didn't want to talk anymore. Symone honored his silence and thought about going to sleep.

Chapter Fifty-One

When Symone woke up thirty minutes later, she gave Marlon a sideways glance. Since he was still watching the game, Symone remained quiet and began making designs in the grassy ground. Looking toward the big house, Symone suddenly saw Alex walking toward them. Alex had a large smile on her face, and three of the Devereauxs' clean pigs were following her. Dressed in paisley print sarong pants and little white cotton sleeveless sweater, which revealed her flat stomach, Alex looked adorable with her ponytail hair bobbing behind her.

"Hey, girl," Alex greeted happily.

"Hi, Alex. You and Madison decided to finally get unstuck?" Symone asked.

"Yeah, girl. It happened hours ago. You know we never get bored with each other around here," she said casually as she leaned over to kiss Symone on the forehead and to embrace her shoulders. Symone hugged her neck affectionately and also attempted to pet the three pigs on their backs. But they each squealed loudly and quickly scurried away toward the direction of the lake.

"Alex and her man are into each other, Sy. The last time Nanette and I were here for dinner, we thought we were going to have to turn a high-powered hose on Alex and Madison—just to get them unstuck, too."

"Stop exaggerating, Marlon." Alex waved her hand at him.

"I know what you mean because I see it all the time, Marlon."

While the basketball players were taking a brief time out, Madison suddenly noticed his wife talking to Symone and Marlon.

"...Hey there, baby. You sweet, fine chocolate thing!" Madison shouted to Alex and whistled. His teammates slapped him on the back.

"Hey, baby!" Alex yelled back just as graciously and waved at him.

Marlon and Symone laughed at their obvious need to connect. Pleasure. Their love was showing in the clear day. Alex directed her attention back to Symone and Marlon.

"That Madison is something else. Umph. Umph. Umph. Isn't he? My baby is in all his glory right about now. As long as he can host a good old-fashioned North Carolina barbecue and fish fry for our friends, then shoot some hoops with the boys, you know my baby is on cloud nine all the way live."

"That's the only way to live, baby," Marlon said in a soulful rhythm. "Be full of passion, and keep it physical."

"Hmmm. Physical passion. That sounds just good to me. What about you, Alex girl?" Symone winked at Marlon, and Alex pinched Symone's arm. "Marlon, you're right about Madison, but Alex is the same way. Without question, I tell her all the time that Barbara Smith ain't got nothing on her."

"I second that emotion," Marlon said.

"Your talent is as big as your heart," Symone added. "Alex, you're the ultimate hostess, and you've really turned it into an art form. You love it too, girl. All the people. The music. The fanfare. Getting off on making everybody else happy is your joy. Eat this joy up."

Marlon smiled. "It's all good, baby."

"Five people have already told me how yall had the place rocking here last night, girl."

"It was, Symone," Alex said. "We had a wild and wonderful time. It was total wild enjoyment, but you know the crew we move with. They expect nothing less, girl."

"How's Trey today?" Symone asked. "I haven't seen my sweet little boy yet, Alex."

"Trey, Purity, Rozelle's little ones, and a few other children are in the sandbox making castles."

"So Purity is being sociable this morning?"

"So far she's doing fine, Sy. We haven't had any of the children running into the house complaining about her yet." Alex broke out with her throaty laugh. "My babygirl is so much. Sometimes I look at her and wonder where she got that personality from."

"I do believe a little bit of it came from Nanette, but a lot of it came from you. You know how controlling you can get when you want everyone to do their part around here."

"*Alex is controlling*? Baby, puhleeze," Marlon interrupted as he stared in disbelief at Symone.

Alex smiled. "You know you might be right. I never thought about it like that. I just don't know. My babygirl just wants things a certain way, or she believes you need to get on the highway." Alex laughed, inhaled deeply and scratched her hair. "So far this morning, Purity is doing just fine."

"I know, Alex," Symone said. "I was just joking with you about Purity. I agree. I don't know where Purity got such a strong, bossy personality from, and she's so young. Maybe she's blessed with an edge because her strength shows, even at her age. She'll grow into it. It might be because she has spent many nights with her Auntie Nanette and with her Tante Symone. You know I got the bitch program copyrighted for my own personal use."

"Symone you are sooo crazy, girl. Pecola told me yall had a great ride. She did say you got on her nerves a little bit, though. You made her mad, too. Between her and Pauletta, it was a comedy club with the kitchen crowd."

"Pauletta's here?" Symone asked with surprise.

"Yep."

"Is Hannibal with her?" Marlon inquired quickly.

"Nope. She said she just decided to come by herself and got the children ready last night. She told Hannibal good-bye. She was outta there and headed home to North Carolina to see her Mama, Daddy, Auntie Hattie Mae, and her sister."

"You're kidding," Symone exclaimed.

"I'm not. Pauletta simply started driving to Greensboro. She said that she arrived at her parent's farm in the middle of the night. It was around one o'clock. When they woke up around seven this morning, her mother made them a smokin' big breakfast, as usual. You know that's standard with Mama Oseola."

Marlon and Symone nodded their heads. Everyone was aware of how hospitable Mama Oseola and Poppaw Rufus Dudley were to everyone who stepped through the entryway of their farm's friendly doors.

"As soon as they ate, Pauletta said that she told the kids that they were on their way to Auntie Alex's house."

"She'll be here for the weekend?" Symone asked Alex.

"No, girl. Pauletta said that she'll be here for the entire week."

"Get out of here."

"No. I'm serious. In all the years that she worked at the bank, she said that she had never taken time off like this—without letting the higher ups know she was going beforehand. But she plans to call on Monday morning and say there was an emergency in North Carolina."

"That doesn't sound like Pauletta at all."

"I know. I know. I'm praying for— Well, nothing. Anyway, she brought a huge case of Parks Sausage for the children's breakfasts for the next two weeks."

"Get out of here, girl. I hadn't had Parks Sausage in years. Remember those commercials?" Alex quickly nodded her head. "That was the only sausage my ex-husband ate. I never really heard of them until I met Billy. How the hell did Pauletta get a case all the way in Augusta?"

"One of her clients knows the salesman who works from the home office in Maryland, but his mother lives in Augusta."

"That's some serious networking," Marlon said with a smile. "Symone was just talking about that."

"I know, but it worked. We had some this morning. Along with Mama Oseola's fresh eggs, some grits, pear preserves and milk gravy, everything was delicious. Cleopatra told me that you told her to hold up on the breakfast. Pauletta got there just as Cleo was starting it up again. Cleopatra hooked it up. Need I say more?" Alex licked her lips. Both Marlon and Symone laughed freely.

"Pauletta said she was heading for the doll room since she wanted to feel like a little girl again. I told her you were in there already and that it was staked out earlier. Pauletta said, 'Heck—'"

Symone casually waved her hand and interrupted Alex. "Knowing Pauletta, she probably said hell and a few other choice words."

"I know, girl. You're right because she sho nuff did. Anyway, she said she was staying in the doll room with you," Alex said with her eyes smiling into Marlon and Symone's.

"That's great, Alex. The damn bed in there is large enough for five people," Symone said. "I don't mind at all. Not one bit."

"That's what Pauletta said you would say, Symone. Pauletta told everybody that the two of you could hang out and talk during the night. You know like a private pajama party. Of course, Pauletta's not even worried about her children. They came in, gave all their aunties a quick kiss, a fast hug, and that was it. When the week is over, Pauletta said that she would find them around here some place and take them back home to Augusta."

Alex chuckled to herself as she once more thought about the wild conversations Pauletta constantly shared with them.

"What's funny?"

"I was thinking about some of the crazy things Pauletta said about men, married life and being in her forties."

"I bet she was her usual funny acting self. I'm sure it was hysterical, girl."

"I know that's right," Marlon inserted. As he took another swig of beer, he remembered how a drunk Pauletta jumped in the pool at Pecola's surprise birthday party in May.

"Funny isn't an appropriate word for Pauletta. It was still a nice surprise for Pecola. You know how crazy Pecola is by herself. Well, she's even worse since Pauletta is here. Pecola had all the women in the kitchen cracking up like crazy about the conversation yall had when yall went riding this morning. Symone, she mimicked you and Rozelle to a T."

"I know. I'm sure she did. Miss Gift for Gab is excellent at gossiping. You know she's like a damn tape recorder when she wants to be. All I did was talk about sororities, fraternities, and those clubs she loves so desperately. She damn near had a conniption. You know that's a sore subject for her."

"I know it's a sore subject for *you*, but one day you'll understand, Sy. I could tell you got her aggravated a little bit." Alex laughed loudly. "Last night, I called Trinidad and spoke to all three of my cutie pie godchildren."

"You're kidding. You call them as much as I do. I called them yesterday, too."

"They told me."

"You know they're having a ball. My baby girls haven't even broken their glasses, yet. Can you believe that?"

"I know. Mum Poussaint and Tante Tutts told me that they were handling themselves fine like little ladies, Sy."

"I know they were glad to hear from their godmother."

"They were. Kyle and Sylvia blew such sweet kisses through the line, but you know how Jared is."

"I do."

"He acted very formal and straight. We got to help him to change a little bit and to soften up some. What do you think about that, Marlon?"

"Baby, that boy is fine. He's just eight," Marlon said easily with a large smile. "Jared's got enough men around him to make him be all that he can be. We're like the army. Trust me. Yall know how it is to deal with younger sisters. You simply feel that you got to be the stronger one because they get on your damn nerves all the time. You really don't appreciate sisters and brothers until you're older. He'll get over it, so chill."

Alex smiled at Marlon. "Nanette said it's time for Solomon to be breast-fed. As the dutiful, doting auntie that I am, that's the real reason I came out. I'm here to pick him up."

"I *thought* it was time for his feeding, Alex. He took a short nap. We all did. About ten minutes ago, he began acting jittery and irritable."

"He'll be fine. Come to Auntie Alex," Alex cooed and reached to grab her curled up nephew off Marlon's shoulders.

"That's ok. I'll take him to Nanette. I need to be going back up to the house now."

"You're sure, Marlon?" she asked worriedly.

"Yeah, I'm sure. I enjoy watching her breast-feed our babies. It makes me want to lay down and suck on her titties," he said with a lazy laugh.

"I bet so." Alex said loudly, and Symone burst out laughing.

"Hell, I did just that one time. The truth is this. Breast milk sho as hell doesn't taste like the milk from the grocery store. You can believe that. It's more like watered-down skim milk. So, I'll take him," Marlon said, still laughing along with Alex and Symone.

"You're sure you don't want to continue relaxing out here in the shade?" Alex inquired and gazed at Symone's face for indications of how she thought Marlon's knees were doing. Symone merely smiled, shook her head slightly, and subtly shrugged her shoulders.

"Yes, I'm sure," he repeated in a firm voice. "I'm fine, Alex. Really I am."

"Do you want me to hold him while you get up?"

"That's the kind of help I need, Alex. Once I get up, I can carry my boy to the house, baby." Marlon handed his fretful son to her.

"I'm going to go up to the house with yall to see Pauletta," Symone announced.

"Pauletta was dressed in tennis whites when she got here. When I was heading out here, she and Jodria were finally heading toward the tennis courts," Alex said as she quickly bounced Solomon up and down on her shoulders to keep him from crying louder. Her worried gaze fell on Marlon.

Slowly, Marlon tried to stand. He sat back down and took a deep breath. It was excruciatingly difficult. His legs were in such unbearable pain. He tried it again; however, it was hopeless and had to resort to Symone using her body to help him get to his feet. While he held the tree for support, Symone handed him the two crutches that were lying on the grass beside the chaise lounge. Marlon took them from her and carefully propped them under each armpit. Very slowly, he hobbled up to the house with Alex at his side carrying the baby. The son he said that he wanted to carry up to the house all by himself.

Symone watched the normally strong and athletic Marlon use the crutches as he walked into the sun. It hurt her to see him like that. Her heart swelled for him, and she felt heavy with sadness. Suddenly, she took a deep breath and quickly glanced away from the heartbreaking scene. After she drank the rest of Marlon's beer, she stretched out on the chaise lounge and took another restful nap.

Chapter Fifty-Two

"...Hey, Miss Hampton," Romallus declared as he softly rubbed Symone's shoulder to awaken her. "It's time for you to get up, baby."

Symone shaded her eyes with her hands. Since she had fallen asleep, the sun had moved to another spot, and it was blinding her. She put her sunglasses back on.

"How the hell are you, Romallus?"

"I'm just fine, baby. I saw you coming up the hill, and I said to myself, 'Uh oh. The queen of conflict. The lightning rod of controversy finally made it up to paradise."

"Thanks for waking me up with such words of praise. Where are the other guys? I thought yall were playing basketball," she questioned as she looked up into Romallus' good-looking, cocoa face. She noticed it looked like his full beard had a little more gray in it this month.

"We were, but we're going to go for a quick, cool swim. It looks like it's going to rain, and we wanted to get a fast dip in the pool before it comes. We kicked Carlos, Scott, Rico, and that crew's ass big time."

"You're kidding," she said since she was partial to the older guys winning all the basketball games.

"Well, you know how it is. Winning is no fun if there are no losers. My brother and his buddies were the losers today."

Symone stood and stretched lazily. She noticed that the other guys were already diving into the pool. Along with several children, a couple of the men were sliding down the blue, curvy sliding board and making a big splash into the water. Once Symone stopped stretching, she and Romallus embraced. SJ, Scott's oldest son, walked up behind them.

"Hey, Tante Symone," SJ greeted with a wide grin on his handsome, dark-skinned face.

"Umph. When someone as tall as you call me Tante, I feel old as the hills, SJ. How are things going with you?"

"Well, you know. It's all good."

"It's all good?" Symone asked with a funny look on her face.

"You know. Everything is cool. Just chillin'. Knowhatimsayin'? Takin' life easy. How's it with you?" he asked as he reached down to hug her.

"I'm just fine."

"Where's GJ?"

"He's playing tennis with a certified cute, little honey named Athena. He scoped her at poolside. Oh, mannn. My brother flipped over her."

Symone nodded her head with understanding. "She certainly is gorgeous."

"That she is." SJ quickly bobbed his head in agreement.

"More importantly, she's very smart," Symone added as she pointed an index finger at his face.

"I heard," SJ said.

"Thanks for *The Science of Rap*," Symone said. "KRS-One's book was excellent, SJ. We gave it to two boys who really needed it. They both loved it and prepared a written report on it, SJ."

"I know," SJ said laughing as he wiped his face with the white towel around his neck. "Tante Pecola told me, too."

"I'm glad she did. We told Scott to thank you, but we weren't sure if he gave you the message or not."

"You know, Pop. He didn't give us the message, but that was ok. We got yall thank you cards back in July. All Pop thinks about now is flying them planes, Miss Charmaine, and his investments. All in that order exactly," he confessed and winked at his uncle.

"I know," Symone agreed. "The stock market is seductive and is known to reward people long term. Your father has been very lucky in that area."

Romallus nodded his head in understanding. "I know that, too. Lately, he has earned his big brother here a few dollars. Without a doubt, the market has made Scott a millionaire. When I was in the investment banking game years ago, I used to drop a lot of stock leads on him and his buddies. Just the other day, I told my pop that Scott continues to work at Northworld Airlines because he simply loves to fly. That's still his first love."

"I agree with you, Rommie. As far as Charmaine, what can you say about that?" Symone asked, turning to look at SJ. "Your father is in love. It must be in the air or something around all my friends."

"That love air hasn't hit me yet, Tante Symone," SJ mumbled.

"You got plenty of time, baby." She stared into SJ's eyes.

"Thanks for reminding me."

"It'll happen soon enough. Trust me. I always heard there's somebody for everybody," Symone said. A smiling SJ carefully eyed his uncle. "Those two young men we got the books for are supposed to be here this afternoon. If you can talk to them and give them an autograph, that'll really motivate them."

"No problem," SJ answered. "My brother and I told Tante Alex that we would be here to work with the children until Tuesday evening. Anything she needs us to do, we're committed to doing that. So yeah. Just let us know who they are. Knowhatimsayin'? I'll be happy to check them out and take care of it."

"We certainly do appreciate it, SJ. Any other books you think would be good to help them understand rap music better, just let me know. Pecola and I will order them from you like pronto. Alex will too especially since she has several children here who are interested in a rap career."

"That's great. My pop told me to bring extra copies of the book. So I brought about fifty copies with us. I'm going to surprise Tante Alex with them tomorrow."

"I can tell you are your father's son, SJ. Scott is considerate as hell, too."

SJ shrugged his shoulders, chuckled lightly, and jabbed his uncle's left arm.

"Are you getting Jared ready for Morehouse, Tante Symone?" SJ asked politely with a sly grin on his face already knowing the answer.

"Hell no!" Symone exclaimed. "You know where I want him to go. Hampton University. Period."

"It's nothing like a Morehouse Man. It'll be good for the young brother."

"Ain't nothing like a Grambling State Tigers man, baby," Romallus quickly inserted.

"That might be true. Since his father is a Hampton alumnus, and I'm one too, it's like we already have a place reserved for him there. If he doesn't go to HU, my next choice for my son *would* be Morehouse. Of course, Grambling would be my next choice."

"Listen to Miss Diplomatic. Now ya talking, Tante Symone," SJ said. "Way to go. When I see Jared at Thanksgiving, I might put a bug in his ear."

"Watch your mouth," Symone said and playfully punched SJ on his arm.

"Did you notice we're dressed alike again, Symone? It's a royal blue and white thang, girl," Romallus joked.

"You know why I'm dressed this way, Rommie baby?" Symone asked.

"No, I don't. Talk to me again in a sweet way and tell me, Sy."

Symone rolled her eyes playfully and laughed frivolously at the romance covering Romallus' voice.

"I know those are your frat colors, Mr. Sigma Man. But I'm wearing my alma mater's colors. It's Hampton University, sugar pie honey bun," she explained and shook a raised fist in the air. "Hampton Pirates, rah rah rah! The best in the world. Nothing more and nothing less."

Romallus began laughing and flexed his branded muscled right shoulder for her to see.

"Ummm-hmmm," Symone moaned. She gingerly touched the dark, taut skin and idly traced the branded letters of GOMAB with her index finger.

"Wooo! Every time I see those brands on guys, they amaze me. Billy has the same thing on both his shoulders, too. Fraternity madness is still unbelievably strong even with your old ass, Romallus. Back in the day, yall must have been wild as hell to have some nigger burn your skin with blazing red-hot steel. Umph Umph Umph."

"That's me, too. A little crazy but still totally committed to our colors and to the mission. I'm a Sigma man all the way. Nothing more. Nothing less. That's why I got GOMAB branded for the entire world to see. We're the most powerful fraternity out. Group Of Men about Business. Yessiree. That's us, baby."

"Whoa, Uncle Rommie. You know the Ques are the bomb," SJ blurted out and flexed his branded arm and chest for Symone to see. Through all the hair on SJ's chest, she tried to notice it. But his hair was slightly blurring her vision. She sighed deeply and quietly. SJ was such a muscular, young fine thing. Cleopatra was right when she talked about Scott's sons this morning. SJ had the hairy chest and all. The two could probably pass for twins. Symone smiled inwardly and tried to regain her focus.

"I really hope yall fraternities *are* about business. That's exactly what we talked about earlier. Yall both should have been with us out on the horse trail. We had a major discussion about fraternities and sororities. Better yet, go speak with Rozelle. He's like a damn tape recorder anyway and can tell you what we talked about. I'm sure he'll give you an excellent recap," Symone said in a tough voice as she still continued to admire Romallus' nicely muscular arm out the corner of her sunglassed eyes.

While Symone made other comments and continued to chuckle lightly, she was thinking *umph umph umph umph umph* about the two generations of fine Alexander men who stood before her. SJ and Romallus started walking toward the swimming pool, and Symone sauntered along between them. Once there, she told them that she wasn't ready to swim yet, but she waved and smiled happily at everyone at poolside. Symone had to agree with Pecola. The lifeguards *were* cute. Both were dark-skinned, buff men. Even though they looked a little too short for her blood, she eyed them up and down a good five minutes behind the privacy of her sunglasses. Today, they were certainly on the job. They were sitting in their high chairs and watching the frenzied activity of both adults and children splashing in the gigantic swimming pool. Symone chatted pleasantly with Carlos' parents, Scott, Rozelle, and Darilyn. Then, she headed for the house.

Alex escorted Marlon into the music room and spoke quietly to him. She was trying to get him to smile and enjoy himself, but he was uncharacteristically quiet. Brooding. She decided to play the piano with the hopes the beautiful melodies would spark his morale. If he was depressed, Alex knew he always enjoyed her doing that for him.

When Pecola heard the piano music float out the room, she was heading upstairs to go to bed. Since she came into the house from horseback riding with Symone and Rozelle, she had been trying her best to get upstairs to her bedroom for some necessary peace and quiet. But Pecola ended up hanging out in the kitchen with her sister, and the other zany bunch of women. Cleopatra was frying chicken and making old-fashioned mashed potatoes with brown gravy. Pecola ate two pieces of crispy fried chicken and whatever else she could find amongst all the food that had been prepared by Alex, Nanette, Jodria, and Darilyn. Pecola still hadn't taken the time to get the additional sleep needed for her to be in perfect form for the afternoon, opening services.

Pecola especially loved hearing Alex play the piano and equally enjoyed listening to her sing in her lovely soprano voice. Most times, Pecola even sang along with her. As Pecola rested her head against the music room's entryway, she gazed somberly at Marlon. Looking as if he was sound asleep, Marlon relaxed quietly with closed eyes. While he sat on the couch that was directly in front of the piano, Alex sang to him a soulful version of *Summertime*.

Summertime an' the livin' is easy,
Fish are jump-in, an' the cotton is high,
Oh, yo' daddy's rich,
An yo' ma is good lookin,
So hush, little baby, don' you cry.

One of these mornin's
You goin' to rise up singin

Then you'll spread yo' wings
An' you'll take the sky
But till that mornin'
There's a nothing can harm you
With Daddy an' Mammy standin' by.

Very quickly, Pecola rubbed the sting of tears from her eyes. She knew the song from the *Porgy and Bess* musical was Marlon's favorite one, and that summertime was Marlon's most special time of year. Now, he couldn't even enjoy the season the way he wanted. The way he had done all his life. That was by playing basketball with his friends and by being active. While Pecola felt the tears fall from her eyes, she realized that she was not just crying for Marlon's suffering. His tears became her own. As she wiped the tears away from her eyes, she swiftly turned to go upstairs and go to bed.

Chapter Fifty-Three

After the furious thunderstorm with crackling lightning bolts and rolling, growling thunder, the Saturday afternoon unfolded into a sapphire clear day with the temperature in the high seventies. Alex was glad to see the sudden change in temperature. She prayed that the high ninety-degree broiling weather would swiftly go away so the over two hundred and thirty guests would not be uncomfortable during the four hour opening celebration speeches and songs. The evening was going to take place under a lovely, huge clear tent decorated with colorful flowers in every available spot and corner. At least there would be a slight breeze blowing through every now and then, and the tent's air condition generators wouldn't have to work as hard.

Alex inhaled deeply and glanced at her watch. It was four-thirty. DJ Cool Breeze softly played the background music of Sly and The Family Stone *It's a Family Affair*. The invited guests were milling throughout the tent trying to find the best seats behind the roped off section. The formal, elegantly engraved invitations describing the opening afternoon announced that the opening ceremony would be like a Sunday evening African village affair. Alex didn't want guests to come in casual clothes, and she was glad to see the attendees listened to those polite instructions. Many were dressed in the traditional and colorful African attire. For the others who chose to forego the African clothes, the men were dressed in pinstriped, dark business suits. The women wore complementing summer dresses, suits, and hats.

Cleopatra walked up to Alex, hugged her waist, and leaned her head on her right shoulder. "Are you ok, Alex?" she inquired tenderly.

"You know me. I'm a little jittery, nervous, excited, and anxious. Gosh, girl, I don't know," Alex exclaimed with wide eyes.

"Alex, everything is fine. You've done a great job as usual. It'll be a wonderful afternoon just like it was last month."

"I couldn't have done it without all my friends—without you, Cleopatra." Alex spoke nervously and looked around at all the decorations. The fresh white and red roses were sitting majestically in every corner. The transparent tent was lined with little lights edging the outline of the ceiling. In the second adjoining tent near the dining area, a large fountain was placed in the center of the hardwood floor and released a waterfall of pink tropical flavored punch. Alex was still anxious.

"Excuse me, Mrs. Devereaux," interrupted Aaron Hurdle who was the executive chef and lead caterer for the afternoon. He was a tall, caramel complexioned man with a quick smile. Dressed in a crisp, white chef jacket, he was known to be a quintessential manager of elegant afternoon affairs such as the one planned for the opening ceremonies. This was his first time catering for the Devereauxs, and he wanted to make sure Alex and Cleopatra were pleased with his company's service. "Mrs. Devereaux, may I speak with you a moment?"

"Yes, of course." Alex turned toward him and smiled warmly. He noticed a crease in her pretty brow.

"Mrs. Devereaux, we've taken care of everything in the dining area that you and Ms. Barrow asked that we handle. Did the crew clean up the house and grounds to your liking?"

"Mr. Hurdle, your staff is doing a fantastic job. After last night, everything inside and outside looks sparkly clean again today. They move around like they're not even here. I have to thank Darilyn again for recommending you, too."

"My pleasure, ma'am." Mr. Hurdle grinned at Cleopatra who looked him in the eyes and quickly smiled back. "Ms. Barrows here informed me that you always use Miss Bessie Mae Atkins as your caterer."

"Yes, that's right I do most times. There are occasions when Miss Bessie says that she simply would rather be a guest. Today was that day. She had two weddings scheduled for today, and she decided that she wanted to leave those jobs and come here to enjoy the evening along with everyone else. She's like an old-fashioned mother to all of us, but she's our resident caterer, too," Alex explained with a huge grin. "Miss Bessie is a mess. She even tells us when she is and isn't going to cater our affairs."

"That's for sure," Cleopatra said.

"If we've an engagement we want her to handle, she might turn it down," Alex went on. "One thing about her, she always recommends someone else who's just as reliable as she is."

"I know. I understand, Mrs. Devereaux. Miss Bessie told me. She's a wonderful woman, an excellent cook, and a friend of my father who started this business over twenty-six years ago. If I can help either one of you ladies further, just let me know. In the meantime, I'll be right here in the dining area waiting for your scheduled intermission." Mr. Hurdle bowed slightly and turned to walk away. Cleopatra watched him leave.

"Gosh, he's formal. Isn't he, Alex?" Cleopatra asked.

"Yes, he is. It's just because he doesn't know us. That's all." Alex inhaled furtively. "Why am I so nervous? I know what it is. Any little thing can go wrong. You have to check everything. There are fifteen little things—"

"Alex, girl," Cleopatra interrupted her.

"I know. Maybe I'm getting a little hyper. Ok, I'll calm down. Hold me down, girl. Keep me calm."

"Any time."

Alex took deep breaths, said a tiny prayer, and let her eyes drink in the beauty of the day. The sweet aroma of the flowers floated through the air. Alex finally smiled as she looked forward to the Black voices that would also float through the sweet smelling air.

After Pecola spoke with DJ Cool Breeze about the appropriate music Rozelle wanted to have ready for the afternoon program, Pecola was now walking toward Alex and Cleopatra. Pecola was stepping chic as usual in a purple evening power suit. The flowing jacket was adorned with one large hand-painted gold cowrie button and was lapelled and cuffed with ruffles. With matching ankle wrap and buckle high heel patent sandals gracing her feet, Pecola pranced up to reassure and calm Alex. Fifteen minutes earlier, Pecola realized that Alex appeared more nervous than usual, and she wanted to help settle Alex nerves once more.

"That dress got my name written all over it, honeychile," Pecola said as she admired Alex's stylish purple African dress and head gear which made her look like the wife of an African royal king. "It's time for you to take it off, and let me put it on."

"Thanks, girl." Alex glanced lovingly at Pecola. She smiled, shook her head, and hugged Pecola's shoulders tightly.

"After last month's opening ceremony, I knew what I wanted to wear. So when I visited with Brenda Brunson-Bey in New York in July..."

"In July?" Pecola asked, interrupting her.

"Yes. It was right after closing ceremonies last month. You remember when Madison and I took his parents to New York for their weekend anniversary trip to see Smokey Joe's Café and go sightseeing?"

Pecola still was puzzled. "Lawd, chile," she finally exclaimed. "Yeah, I do. Whew! I tell you. It's getting dusty in my brain."

"You're a mess, Pecola."

Cleopatra was watching and listening intently. She always enjoyed Pecola's animated sense of humor.

"It took you long enough, Pecola. Well, I told Brenda then that this month I wanted something African and just as formal as the other one she designed for me last month."

"I can tell, chile."

Alex laughed quickly. "Ameenah and I went on our usual shopping trip in Brooklyn. We visited Brenda's showroom. Then we went to 4W Circle on Fulton Street. That's always like Black designers' heaven for me with so much talent in that entire building. I ordered all kinds of things for Christmas and found four beautiful Black rag dolls."

"I saw those dolls," Pecola raved. "Absolutely adorable."

"I know. So I bought clothes, artwork, jewelry, and accessories like you wouldn't believe for me and all my friends, girl."

"Uh oh, Santa Claus is in the house, and I know you got something for me, chile."

"You're my friend, aren't you?"

"That's the lie you try to tell me."

"Oh, Pecola. I sho did! I bought you some nice surprises for the holidays."

"Tell me what they are."

"You know I ain't telling you that. Before the limo took me back to the city to meet Madison and his parents for dinner, Ameenah and I had a stone ball shopping all day."

"I won't start shopping for Christmas gifts until October. I've such gift anxiety about what to give people. I believe if I wait until Christmas is closer, I'll make excellent, expensive choices," Pecola explained with a wide grin and a wink at Cleopatra. "Yall just shopped in Brooklyn, Alex?"

"That day we did. Ameenah believes that Brooklyn is what's happening, girl." Alex stopped and gazed suspiciously into Pecola's eyes. "Why are you asking me all of this? Why *am* I repeating all of this? As soon as I got back, I know I told you about my trip over lunch."

"You sho nuff did, chile. I was just trying to get you to relax and lighten up a bit. You look tight as hell. Real tight. All I can say is that my girl Brenda hooked you up, chile. I thought your light fuchsia colored African dress you wore last month was hot. You looked good. Better than me, and you know that's a hard job. Most times, I look better than everybody else in the place."

"You're crazy," Cleopatra said as laughter fell out of both Cleopatra and Alex at Pecola's humor that sounded a bit too much like the truth.

"Yall like my outfit? How come yall hadn't said anything about how good I look?" Pecola asked anxiously and proceeded to twirl around with her arms above her head. "Hell, I don't know why I'm even asking. I know yall love it."

"It's cutting edge," Cleopatra said and nudged Alex.

"Thank you, Cleo. I saw you hunch Alex. What's up with that?"

Cleopatra shook her head and grinned. "You're too much, Pecola."

"I know, chile. That's what my huzzband tells me all the time. I gots to do something to stay sane. This is the outfit Symone gave me for my birthday. Yall know?" Cleopatra and Alex nodded their heads yes. "The real pricey one from Wilbourne Exclusives out of Atlanta. Yall know how it is. If a Black designer is located under a rock somewhere, girlfriend will find them out and go buy whatever they have to sell her. The whole showroom if they let her." Pecola examined her perfectly shaped fingernails.

"Absolutely," Alex said.

"What did I tell yall in the kitchen this morning?"

"That yall argued," Alex answered.

"Yes, we did have a somewhat heated discussion on the horse trail, but I gots to give it to my buddy. In certain areas, she *does* practice what she preaches."

"True," Cleopatra agreed, and Alex nodded. They both understood.

"But yall know clothes like this are my tastes, honeychile. Symone said that these people are couture designers sho nuff. When they're not designing their asses off in Atlanta and Jackson, Tennessee, she told me that they hang out in Paris. That's me all the way live. Wooo, chile! *Paris?"* Pecola exclaimed as she deftly smoothed her ruffled cuff and batted her eyes.

"I know," Cleopatra agreed as she amusingly watched Pecola busy herself with smoothing her flawless suit. "Symone told me about your dress this morning."

"Since Alex told everyone the color theme was going to be purple six months ago, Symone began planning what she wanted to wear—right along with my girlfriend, Alex, over here."

Alex's smiling expression immediately changed to a slight frown, and Pecola quickly noticed Alex's creased forehead as well.

"Alex, don't worry. The cake is baked, and the opening program is the icing. You know we got that together," Pecola assured her as she glanced around the softly lit dining area.

On each of the tables was an arrangement of lilies, roses, and white masterpieces with Queen Anne Lace draped over scalloped red, silk tablecloths. In the center of each one were candles flickering in crystal vases.

"I wanted a look that was beautiful but not too fussy," Alex said. "Tables should shimmer, girl."

"They do, especially with your Delta and WSSU's colors. Pauletta and I walked through the tent earlier. We laughed about how you always say how you love to set a pretty table and go all out with linens, crystals, and flowers. Alex, everything is breathtaking. Go ahead and get your seat in the front row. Relax and let your friends do the rest, honeychile. Take ten deep breaths because everything is beautiful," Pecola said as she once more glanced around the tent for a last look at the elegant decor.

Rozelle checked his watch. It was four fifty-five, and he knew the Devereauxs believed in being absolutely prompt with programs. Attired in a flowing African print gown his wife ordered for him, Rozelle appeared quite distinguished. To complete his outfit, Rozelle selected a Fez, a Moroccan formal headdress for his headpiece. Every time Rozelle moved about, the dark purple tassels scattered about his head. To signal it was time to start the opening ceremonies, he walked to the podium and busied himself with reviewing the program. The buzz of conversations throughout the tent slowly died down, and the two hundred and thirty guests directed their attention to the center stage that was surrounded by tall pedestal vases of red, yellow, and white bouquets of roses. A huge red and white wide banner, which contained the African proverb *It takes a whole village to raise a child*, was stretched across the tent wall behind the stage for all to see.

"Good afternoon, ladies, gentlemen, children, and babies. My name is Rozelle Bellisarion. Once again, I'll be your master of ceremonies for this spectacular afternoon program. It gives me great pleasure to welcome you to Devereaux Country, the home of Dr. and Mrs. Madison Devereaux," he said with pride. "Right now, I would like for you all to stand as we welcome in the honorees for the afternoon."

Outside the tent, the twenty-eight children ages twelve to sixteen were lined up in order according to age. Alex, Nanette, Jodria, Symone, and Cleopatra calmed the children's nerves and made sure the children's corsages and boutonnieres were in place. The children stood tall and straight as they awaited their signal from Pecola to enter the tent. The young boys were dressed in linen suits, white shirts, and bow ties. Kente cloth was draped over the jackets, and their black shoes were spit shiny polished. The girls were dressed in Jennifer Preddie lavender and purple floral party dresses, patent leather pumps, and gorgeous hairbows. To have various entities in the surrounding communities become involved with their efforts, Alex tried to get local merchants to donate clothes for the opening services. When that failed, the Devereauxs handled everything themselves. Marlon, Alex, and three other individuals who chose to remain anonymous donors provided the opening evening outfits.

Kristen Dobbins was the soloist selected to sing the first song. Kristen's mother had been one of the Devereauxs' financial advisors for many years. When the Devereauxs' heard the young girl sing for the first time during a Christmas program at the Stevens Center last year, Madison asked Kristen if she would puhleeze consider singing for both opening ceremonies in July and August. As Kristen sang *To Be Young, Gifted, and Black*, the twenty-eight children proudly marched to their front and second row seats and stood in place until the solo was done. When several of the honored children's parents noticed how dignified their children carried themselves, a few of them wiped tears of joy from their eyes. After the children sat down, the six women who made sure the entrance was handled smoothly, slid into their seats as well. During the thunderous applause, Kristen bowed graciously and walked to her place beside her beaming parents.

"Wooo, girl. I'm amazed," Rozelle raved as he continued to stare Kristen's way. "I remember my sweet Nina Simone belting that classic out years ago. But you did a fantastic job. Your voice has the soulful tones of Anita Baker, Toni Braxton, and Whitney Houston all rolled up into one. That was absolutely a marvelous solo, young lady. Grammy Awards of the future here she comes, and a North Carolina native, too. Let's give her another round of applause," he urged the audience.

The assistant pastor of Emmanuel Baptist Church located on Shalimar Drive provided the opening prayer. When he finished, Rozelle announced the next person on program. It was his son, Rozelle, Jr. who looked just like his father—glasses and all. At twelve years old, he was a math wizard like his father. Rozelle, Jr.'s contribution was to lead the audience in singing the Black National Anthem, *Lift Ev'ry Voice and Sing*. With the help of his father, he had also prepared a brief book report about the creator of the anthem. Rozelle, Jr. walked onto the stage tall and proud. Before he spoke, he adjusted his gold rimmed glasses and smiled at his mother.

"My name is Rozelle Bellisarion, Jr." A medley of laughter floated throughout the crowd.

"That's my baby," Jodria said and continued to clap excitedly.

"Thank you, Mama," Rozelle, Jr. acknowledged calmly to Jodria as he showed his comedic side that was also a character trait he adopted from his father's crazy ways.

"James Weldon Johnson was born in 1871, and he died in 1938. He was a poet, novelist, songwriter, musician, and activist. Born in Jacksonville, Florida, Mr. Johnson was one of the leading poets of the Harlem Renaissance during the 1920s. He came just at the end of the Renaissance. In 1916, he was the first executive secretary of the NAACP. What he is mostly remembered for nowadays is the song, *Lift Ev'ry Voice and Sing*, which we now recognize as the Black National Anthem."

"James Weldon Johnson's brother, J. Rosamond Johnson, created music for the words." Rozelle, Jr. paused slightly and pushed his glasses back up on his nose.

"On January 12, 1900, five-hundred school children performed the song in celebration of Abraham Lincoln's birthday."

"Say so, baby," Jodria encouraged her son.

"After that glorious performance by all those beautiful children, the song became an inspirational staple throughout the Black community," he ended proudly as he adjusted his round, gold-rim glasses again. "Now ladies and gentlemen, please stand and turn to page two of your program. At our monthly Ujima Literary Society meetings, we always sing this song. For those of you who don't know the words, Tante Alex had them written down for your convenience."

"You weren't supposed to say that, son," Rozelle admonished quietly while a few people on the front row snickered at his gentle reproach. "Didn't you forget something else about Mr. Johnson?" Rozelle whispered to his son since he knew the report inside and out as well.

Rozelle, Jr. briefly glanced at the typewritten page. "Oh, yeah. That's right. Mr. James Weldon Johnson was the first Black to pass the bar examination in the State of Florida. Is there anything else, Daddy?" the young boy asked Rozelle.

"No, I believe you've covered everything," Rozelle said as he stood proudly behind his son and placed his hands on his shoulders. The audience rose to their feet as well, and the entire tent resounded with the Black National Anthem.

"Thank you, ladies and gentlemen. That was wonderful. Yall know you gots to give my son another healthy, loud round of hand clapping," Rozelle encouraged as he openly hugged and kissed his son before Rozelle, Jr. left the stage to sit down with his other five siblings.

Rozelle took a few minutes to recognize the local dignitaries that included preachers, government, and corporate officials who were friends of the Devereauxs.

"As you know, we're here this evening to honor twenty-eight exceptional young people, ladies. Since this is the year to combine our strengths for our youth, today is a very special day. Today is a day that we all will become a huge family. This afternoon you'll hear words of encouragement and tremendous inspiration. The words of inspiration aren't only intended for them, but they're intended for your ears and mind, too. The messages that we'll hear tonight are also meant for me. They remind us to believe in our hopes and dreams. They are words of laughter and words of wisdom. Believe you me, if it's anything like it was at last's month opening ceremony, you'll never forget the people who speak or forget their words. They'll make you cry, laugh, and think about your place in society. Your place in history. Most importantly, their words will remind you of our theme for the afternoon. It does *take a whole village to raise a child.* Their words will remind us that we all have little things we can do to make a big difference in society and in our children's lives. This evening will kick off for the youth, who are honored this afternoon, their two-week stay in the clear country air of Advance. That's who we're here for. We're all here because of the twenty-eight young people sitting on the front row."

The crowd erupted in vigorous applause, whooping, and mouth whistling.

"Before I follow the program and introduce the next speaker, I want to say a few words about the Devereauxs who happen to be absolutely wonderful, cherished friends of mine. In this world we live, I honestly believe that people are classified in three categories. There are those who make things happen. There are those who watch things happen, and there are those who wonder what happened?" The audience burst out laughing and began clapping again. "Without question, the Devereauxs are the kind of people that make good things happen."

Throughout the crowd, many people vigorously nodded their heads in agreement.

"For those of you who don't know what the children do up here for two weeks, let me tell you what happens each day. After they eat a mouth-watering home cooked country breakfast each morning from nine to nine forty-five, they have quiet time. Alex wanted this to be a part of their schedule because she believes it's an opportunity for the children to be silent, so that they can hear God speak to their hearts. It also gives them an opportunity to write their most innermost, truthful feelings in their private journals. It's a time of self-reflection in an age of TV, video, games, and boom boxes. From ten to two, the youth receive lessons in Black history, leadership, self-esteem, economic development, peer pressures, drugs, AIDS, village thinking, community service, and anything else they want to bring up. Each day they're introduced to two African-Americans who have made a significant impact in the world. Symone Poussaint, will you stand up puhleeze?"

Symone simply watched him with wide eyes and quickly shook her head no, especially since she didn't know why Rozelle wanted her to stand.

"Last year, Symone, or as we like to call her *Black History* Poussaint, researched and put together individual books for each child. Since Symone fervently believes children should learn how to begin collecting books for their personal library by the time they're eight years-old, she surprised everybody with a book that profiles twenty-eight African-Americans. Symone included the ones we don't hear about all the time during Black history month but who have made just as an important contribution to the advancement of Black people. She also notes some of the ones we do hear about often. So while the children are here for two weeks, they also have a chance to learn about or again become familiar with twenty-eight other Black pioneers that they might not have ever known about otherwise."

"This year, we had a mini-battalion working. The battalion consisted of Symone, Lillie, Pecola, Alex, and Booker T. Symone said that this is volume two, and the young people can use these hard-bound books in their personal libraries for the rest of their lives. Marlon bought everyone pecanwood bookshelves to go in their homes, a personal place for them to keep their books. Hopefully, the children will know the value of their private library. You see that's what I like. All of the Devereauxs' friends helping out. Another thing I admire about this affair is that the Devereauxs don't use any type of government funds. The media maintains that Black folks can't and won't do anything for the community or for each other, at least not without some type of government funding." Rozelle paused. "We know better. We know better than to buy into the stereotypes about our own people."

"The Devereauxs' rely on their own funds. They also simply rely on their friends to donate their time, their love, their money, and definitely their mouths to teach what they already know and have learned during their hard life's journey." Rozelle said.

"Ok. After the four hours of learning and self-reflection have been taken care of each morning, the youth are free to do whatever they want to do until it's time for them to go to bed. Swim, play tennis, ride horses, have a picnic out by the lake, and play chess with seasoned adult players," Rozelle explained.

"What else do they do out here?" Rozelle asked himself while looking toward the tent's ceiling. "Sometimes they have fireside chats where they roast marshmallows. There are great pool parties. For those of you who weren't here last night, you missed a mighty fine one. It's truly wonderful out here. During the year, we go on trips together. We've done ski trips and mountain trips. During spring break this April, two busloads of us all went to New York to what Booker T refers to as the annual class trip to Harlem. Alex loves classical music, so she took all of the children to the opera at Carnegie Hall. The children are involved in many beneficial and uplifting activities. During Memorial Day weekend, we have our awards ceremony that commemorates how well the children did in school and salutes the voracious reading they do. Trophies and certificates are handed out then."

"Praise the Lord," an older woman exclaimed with delight.

"Back in June of this year, we took the older ones to the Hampton Jazz Festival. Last year, the Devereauxs did most of the planning for the summer activities. During the year, they even chartered a bus to pick up all fifty-six children each month. On Friday afternoon to Sunday night the first weekend in the month, they had the ones you see here over. The third weekend in the month, they had the younger group up here. During the Devereauxs' weekend program in commemoration of Martin Luther King's birthday, my buddy, Scott Alexander, and me talked to Alex and Madison. We recommended to Madison and Alex that they *still* should pick up the children each month. However, they should also allow their many, many interested friends to help out and adopt a child as their own, too. Like Madison said that evening, people are willing to make a difference and do their part. Sometimes we have to just ask them to get them going."

"So true," a woman said.

"That evening, both Alex and Madison agreed that it was an excellent idea. They decided this was the year to combine our strengths. They just wanted those volunteering individuals to take responsibility for their culture and nation. When the Devereauxs' many friends agree to voluntarily weave their lives within the lives of the wonderful youth you see here, they have to fill out an application. Then Madison and Alex meet with their interested friends. Most times you'll meet with Alex since Madison is awfully busy working at Baptist Hospital."

"The main requirement is the Devereauxs only ask that the friends be totally sincere about their commitments, and they *must* be consistent. The Devereauxs don't play with this. If you say you're gonna do something with the children, then they expect you to do it. Period. The children start looking for you to come and pick them up, so the Devereauxs' want all of their friends to be focused on this commitment. This is the real nitty gritty here. Not only with their time but committed with their love and the sweat equity of involvement. These volunteers must go to the children's school and speak with their parents or guardians on a continuous basis to see how they're getting along at home. Some of the older youngsters you see here are even interns at various companies owned by the Devereauxs' friends. That gives them another inside view of the business world. As a volunteer to help the children, you *must* do these things. You *must* agree to take the children on family vacations and help them achieve so that they can attend college. We *must* give many children the dream that poverty and discrimination steal from them. Through tutoring and consistent mentoring, they keep their grades up. They know we expect that, and we don't accept anything less. Period. Scott, Booker T, and Pecola came up with an incentive program for grades. If the youngsters make two A's, they're rewarded with a personal computer and cash."

All the children began clapping. As a result of the incentive program, many of the children's grades had increased tremendously. Rozelle smiled at their reaction.

"That sounds like bribery," someone yelled out.

"That's what you think, my man. Some folks *do* call it bribery. We don't call it that out here. We simply say it's a jump-start in the right direction. It's a spark to get our children motivated. Jodria Anne, my lovely wife, has done research on this topic and has made her views known. If we influence the initial behavior, that is of rewarding our youth for making good grades, my Jodria believes that this motivational action will take on a life all its own. Jodria was right because it has. Years ago, I wished someone was willing to pay me money to get great grades." The audience laughed at Rozelle. "So yes, what we do here is a big volunteering responsibility that isn't something for the fainthearted or the selfish minded people. It's an emotional investment, and that's certainly demanding and unselfish work."

"Wooo, Rozelle. I can't believe you said that," Pauletta said in a voice loud enough for Rozelle to hear and snapped her fingers three times. "Black folk selfish? Nah, baby. Say it ain't so."

Symone, who was sitting beside Pauletta, smiled at Pauletta's typical sassiness.

"It's the truth, Pauletta," Rozelle shot back. "You know it is, baby. Ladies and gentlemen, that's another thing. Even though Alex tries to keep sweet little programs like this formal and perfect, there's always a smart heckler or two in the audience. Like the one you just heard from whose name is Missy Pauletta. She's doesn't even live in North Carolina anymore, but she still comes all the way from Augusta, Georgia to say a few words and to kick up a little bit of dust. Believe you me, they'll be others just like her throughout the evening shouting out encouraging words. You name it, so get used to it. Ok? Mrs. Pauletta Dudley-Bing. Stand up so everyone can know who you are with your sweet, fine, chocolate self," Rozelle kindly breathed into the mike with a debonair swagger. He began to fan his face with his hands. "Whenever I see her, my little ole heart begins palpitating beyond control." The audience burst out laughing. With a big grin on her face, Pauletta flippantly waved both hands at him several times.

"Good evening, yall," Pauletta said as she stood up.

"Once it's time for them to start applying to college, the Devereauxs have created a committee that will work with each child to determine what assistance if any is necessary to make their college dreams a reality. We tell the children that as long as they qualify for college, our job is to figure out how they'll get there. We haven't had any of the children that we're working with enter college yet. Let me change that. We have three going to college this year. The plans are such that when the ones that are here graduate from high school and go off to college, the senior citizens of the four public housing communities who helped select these children will recommend other children to fill those slots made empty by our college bound kids. It's a pretty comprehensive program for the youth, and I believe it can be an example for other communities of people just like us. All we're doing is working together. We simply are combining our strengths. I want to commend Alex for having the vision and the heart to create a program like this to help our future Black leaders. She said that the idea came down to her from angels who brought it to her in her dreams. This dream has become a reality that should be a prototype for all Black communities.

"Say so, young man," a man exclaimed.

"Alex has just simply gathered a coalition of volunteers who are her friends and a strong group of people who are Madison's friends. There's also a cross section of volunteers who are doctors, lawyers, teachers, factory workers, homemakers, and even single African-American males and females. Just merely a group of like-minded people that they trust. People who they've talked with who personify the essence of friendship. These are people who care about making a difference. At the end of each interview, the Devereauxs told their friends they didn't want their money. They simply wanted their commitment to giving some of their quality time. That's what Alex told me to say, yall," Rozelle poked easily.

The applause for Alex rocked the tent. Madison and Nanette tried to get Alex to stand up, but she refused to do so.

"Whew! I knew this took up some time. This was for those of you who don't know what we do out here. Yall just thought you were just going to have a nice evening of speeches, drinking, dining, and dancing. I hope you clearly understand our reason for celebration this evening." Rozelle flipped to another page.

Chapter Fifty-Four

"It's time to introduce a young lady that I'm very fond of. She graduated from the North Carolina School of the Arts in Winston-Salem. I met her when she was a bright-eyed teen-ager with a voice. Now, she's a twenty-year old actress, dancer, and singer living in New York. An acting student at the Julliard School, she just finished a run on Broadway. I'm proud to introduce Elizabethe Mercedes Reynolds."

Dressed in a cute, formal hot pink, sundress, and strapping high-heeled sandals, Elizabethe made her way to the stage. At five feet six inches tall, her chestnut sandy hair was now cut very short. When she came home for last month's opening ceremonies, her hair stretched to her shoulders and prettily framed her gorgeous, light-skinned face. So naturally, her parents were shocked when Elizabethe returned home this month with such a boyish looking haircut.

"Thank you, Uncle Rozelle," Elizabethe said in a sexy, singer-sounding voice.

Elizabethe removed the microphone from the podium and held it close to her breasts. She walked to the edge of the stage and stared in her parents' faces.

"Before I sing, I want to honor my Mama and Daddy. Mr. and Mrs. Carlos Reynolds, Jr. sitting down front. I love you both very, very much," she said and blew them a lingering kiss. While her daughter was speaking, Pecola was already searching in her slim pocketbook for one of her two clean handkerchiefs.

"I want to salute my Auntie Pauletta. That's my favorite aunt of all time. The same goes to my brothers, CJ and Haneef. To my Granddaddy Carlos and Grandma Mercedes who are here. The same applies to Uncle Rico, Auntie Darilyn, all my cousins, and to all of Mama and Daddy's friends who are just like sisters and brothers to them. I love you all. It was sooo nice growing up and seeing how close yall were to each other." She stopped and gazed out into the audience sea of faces. Her eyes traveled to the twenty-eight children.

"You're truly blessed to be in the company of these great people. Maybe now you don't understand the beauty of what they do. One day it's going to hit you that this was a simply glorious time in your lives. The times you shared with my aunt and uncle here in Advance and especially with their friends. These are memories you'll never ever forget. When I consider the harshness of the business I chose as my profession, my mind often comes back to my home in Winston-Salem. I think pleasant thoughts about North Carolina, and I think about how homey and friendly everyone is here. It's motivating to know that I can always come back home and recharge my battery."

An overly sensitive and emotional young lady, Elizabethe's green eyes were already becoming moist with tears. She quickly blinked them back. With her face directed toward the heavens, she whispered a quiet message to her dead younger sister.

"Last week, my Mama called me in New York and told me she wanted me to sing something different this month. She wanted me to surprise Tante Alex and Uncle Madison with this song. It's one of Tante Alex's favorite ones. You know I didn't hesitate one second to grant my mama's wishes. Growing up, I spent a lot of time with my Tante Alex. I love her, so singing for her is my pleasure."

When Elizabethe paused for a moment, Pauletta leaned over to whisper a few words to Pecola who now was overcome with maternal and proud tears for her daughter.

"...I swear, Pecola. Each time I see my niece, it reminds me of how she looks just like you—as cute as you did when you were twenty, girl."

"I know." Pecola bit her bottom lip and nodded slowly at the compliment.

"It's unbelievable."

"That's what people tell me all the time, honeychile," Pecola whispered back in an agreeable, trembling voice as she wiped her eyes and blew her nose.

"I can believe it."

"Oh," she hissed in Pauletta's ear as Pecola thought about Pauletta's comments. "So you're saying I'm not pretty now?"

"You're crazy as hell. Of course, I think you're still pretty. But I'm suppose to. I'm your sister. You just don't look like that anymore," Pauletta joked in a low voice and pointed to her niece. "You know how it is when you turn forty. Stuff start shifting around. Real bad. Before you know it, your waist is under your breasts. Thigh starts drooping over your knee. Then you get the dowager's hump right at the tip of your neck," Pauletta added with a smirk and patted Pecola on the back part of her neck. Pecola smiled at Pauletta's comments and lovingly pinched her sister on the arm.

Elizabethe was ready to sing. She motioned to DJ Cool Breeze that it was time to turn on the instrumental background music. Elizabethe swallowed, cleared her throat, and briefly glanced at the floor. In a clear, striking and beautiful husky voice, Elizabethe belted out a spectacular, church rendition of *His Eye is on the Sparrow*.

"...Sing it, babygirl," Pecola said as she wiped her wet eyes. "Sing your song, honeychile," she yelled again and waved her hand in the air from side to side.

"O Lordy, praise God!" an older woman gently cried out.

Sitting on the second row, Rico tenderly patted his brother on the shoulders. Carlos turned to his brother, nodded at him, and smiled. He turned back around and continued to proudly watch his daughter. Every time Elizabethe sang, Carlos was fascinated with the beauty of it all. Because Elizabethe's style was quite similar to her mother's, Elizabethe's singing brought up many old memories. Carlos closed his eyes and became lost in the rich sound of his daughter's powerful voice. Without fail, his mind always catapulted back to the first time he saw Pecola. It was when he heard her sing at the Dudley High School assembly all those many years ago. Today wasn't any different.

"...I sing because I'm happy. I sing because I'm freeeeeee! His eyes are on the sparrowww, and I knowwww He watches me. I say I know— Yes, I know. My God knows. I know he watches meeeee...!

"...That's my baby, up there," Pecola exclaimed through her tears to her friends around her.

Throughout the solo, people in the audience cried like they were at a Sunday morning emotional prayer devotion. Ladies and men were standing in front of their seats swaying to the music. Senior citizens were waving their lacy handkerchiefs in the air. Others were waving their hands and hollering out, *You go, girl. Amen. Sing that song, chile. Thank you, Jesus. Sing it, girl. Glory hallelujah. Umph Umph Umph! Oh lawd have mercy, that chile can sing.*

When Elizabethe was through, she stepped off the stage and slowly sauntered over to Alex and Madison who by now were quietly crying too. It seemed as if the entire audience was wrapped in the emotion of that song. Elizabethe wrapped her arms around the Devereauxs and showered them with love-filled kisses. She hugged her parents, her grandparents, uncle, aunt, and all of the other friends on the first and second row.

"Bravo. Bravo," Alex exclaimed while rising to her feet. The crowd erupted into thunderous applause and a standing ovation. Rozelle walked to the podium. He had to wipe the water from his eyes as well. He waited a long time before speaking.

"It ain't nothing wrong with having a little church up in here, is it? Wasn't that spectacular? The spirit moved through her. The program has just begun. I don't know how much talent I can take tonight. I really don't. The song was quite moving and inspirational. Elizabethe, you're sure you aren't related to Pastor Shirley Caesar? C'mon put your hands together, and let's give her another round of love claps," Rozelle instructed as he noticed that Elizabethe now hugged and kissed the twenty-eight children.

"Marvelous young lady. She's simply marvelous. I wish I could say the same thing about her mother," Rozelle joked which made everyone bust out laughing. Even Pecola. Although she wasn't sure if Rozelle was serious or not, she still giggled along with the crowd.

"His Eye is on the Sparrow," Rozelle bellowed into the mike. "That was a down home version, Elizabethe baby. You certainly got the place full of joy. Wasn't that inspirational? You know if God watches the sparrow, then you know He's watching us. If a little itty bitty sparrow is being taken care of everyday, then you know He's going to take care of us, too."

"Say so, young man."

"Alex, I see why you sing that song every day when you wake up. While Elizabethe was singing, my mind drifted back to when I was a little boy sitting on the front pew in my Grandmother Zula's old wooden, church back in Cold Water, Mississippi. Robert's Chapel was the name. It took me straight back. Way back to when they used to sing those old Negro spirituals when my Grandmother Zula made me sing in the young adult choir every summer I visited her." He hesitated momentarily. "Oh, the olden days. Yall hear me? It was when the deaconess'and missionaries in the church were always the biggest women and they were dressed in white dresses and white tams all the time."

"Talk about how it was, man. Talk about back in the day," an audience member said.

Rozelle nodded. "Yall know what I'm talking about? Back in those old-fashioned Black churches, they were always fanning themselves with a Robert Kennedy fan, a Martin Luther

King, Jr. fan, or some local Black funeral home fan with their advertisements on it. After church, those same big women would seek you out and say to you, 'Come on over here, baby. Lemme just look at you.' Then they grabbed your head with both hands and would give you one of those big old, smelly, sloppy wet jaw kisses. It was so sloppy, they left spit all over your face. You had to wipe it off, but in a real sly way though, so your Grandmama wouldn't see you do it. Yall remember those days? Don't you? Umph. I can still smell the spit on my face now." The audience broke out into wild laughter. Rozelle, too.

"Rozelle ain't no good," Pauletta whispered to Pecola.

"I'm telling you." Still laughing, Rozelle began to speak again. "I was swimming in memories, girl. God blessed your voice, Elizabethe. As a Black man, I know all I need to do is hear someone sing a great gospel song, and the music becomes my personal testimony. Kristen, here's another North Carolina wonder heading to future Grammy Awards," Rozelle said slowly with his voice suddenly much softer.

"That's the truth, Mr. Bellisarion," Kristen replied. The weight of the song dropped joy all through the tent, and the night was still young.

"Moving right along, I would like to introduce you to William and Geraldine White. Mr. and Mrs. White operate the predominantly Black Brisbane Academy in Charlotte, North Carolina. It's a math and science preparatory school that Nanette visited when she and Marlon moved to Lake Norman a few years ago. Although their twin boys, Solomon and Fletcher, are only a few months old, the Dinzelles' want to enroll their two baby sons in the school now. When Nanette and Marlon first told everyone down here about the African-American school Nanette's college roommate discovered for her two daughters, we all tried to figure out how we could have our children attend classes all the way down in Charlotte. My wife Jodria even figured out a schedule for everyone, but we realized it would be absolutely crazy. Each child would have to get up at five-thirty and leave at six-thirty to take the ninety minute bus ride to Charlotte to be there in time for classes starting at eight."

"Wooo!" a guest moaned.

"The kids there are smart, too. At Brisbane, some of their four-year-olds read on the third-grade school level, and their other students' grades have improved dramatically from when they attended other schools in Charlotte. Even their California Achievement Test scores are phenomenal. This is Black operated, people. Isn't that great? I don't know about you, but I like the sound of that," he shouted into the mike, and the audience clapped.

"We're trying to get Mr. and Mrs. White to open up Brisbane Academy Number Two up here in Winston-Salem. Even though we can't get to Charlotte, we believe that every Black family in Charlotte that has any sense about their children's education should send their children to Brisbane Academy. It's the school that Dr. Bernard Harris, Jr., the first African-American to walk in space, deemed important enough to visit when he was in Charlotte. To show their gratitude, Brisbane Academy named a math and science lab after Dr. Harris. People, I introduce you to William and Geraldine White. They're innovative, unique African-

American educators." The crowd clapped happily and sat back to hear the enlightening words from the attractive couple.

"Thank you. Thank you so much. Boy, it's great for us to be here again. We were here last month. What Dr. and Mrs. Devereaux are doing out here in Advance is truly wonderful. We're just glad the Devereauxs thought enough of our educational program to invite us up here so that we could share our philosophy about education and the sincere love we have in our hearts for children." The audience broke out into applause. "I want you to know one thing. Don't you know our children know when you think they can't learn? When they think that, they rise to the occasion to prove that you're absolutely right. At Brisbane, we realize that children also know when you think they can learn, and they do it with phenomenal, inspiring, and tremendous results. Our children then develop an overwhelmingly, profound appreciation of education and their academic abilities." William White spoke anxiously. For the next three minutes, he briefly talked about Brisbane Academy. When he was done, he stepped away from the mike to give his wife an opportunity to speak. The audience clapped vigorously.

"Thank you," Geraldine White said. "When Nanette first met me, we spoke for a good two hours in my office that day. She told me, 'Yall have got to meet my sister. You'll just love her. Every day, Alex recites *I Have to Live*. If she knows that's what your students recite here at Brisbane, she'll have a pure divine fit, girl.'"

As Geraldine spoke, Nanette patted Alex's hand and she began to laugh softly.

"Nanette told me that before she goes to bed each night, she talks to her sister. No matter where Nanette is, she and Alex talk about their day. During those times, Alex always asks her, 'Have you read *Acts of Faith* today, girl? Have you recited *I Have to Live* today? I couldn't believe it when Nanette told William and me that. Nanette was also right. When we met Alex, William and I did fall in love with her, too. Alex was glad to see that Brisbane Academy recited the poem that her mother had taught her years ago when she was a little girl," Geraldine explained with a sparkling smile.

"We would like for you to turn to page four of your program right now so that we all can recite that poem, *I Have to Live*. I'm told that this is what the children say each morning while they're here in Advance. This is what they're encouraged to say while they're at home, too," Geraldine continued in a light voice. The audience turned to the appropriate page, and Rozelle gestured for everyone to stand.

"Ok. Is everyone ready? Let's begin with saying the title," William White urged on.

I Have to Live
Author Unknown

I have to live with myself and so;
I want to be fit for myself to know.
I want to be able as days go by;
Always to look myself straight in the eye.

I don't want to stand in the setting sun;
And hate myself for the things I've done.
I want to go out with my head erect;
I want to deserve all man's respect.

But in the struggle for fame and wealth;
I want to be able to like myself.
I don't want to look at myself and know;
That I'm bluster and bluff, and empty show.
I can never hide myself from me;
I see what others may never see;
I know what others may never know;
I can never fool myself and so.

Whatever happens, I want to be,
Self-respecting and conscious free!

"Very good. Very good," William exclaimed as he clapped for the audience. "You feel good just by saying it. Don't you?" William asked into the mike, and the audience nodded yes. "If you say it every day, you'll be committed to making your life fulfilling and meaningful. We knew that the Devereauxs, my wife, and I were on the same wavelength. Each time we come out to Advance and see what's going on, that thought is confirmed. It's truly spectacular what yall are doing with children. I'm honored to be a part of the opening ceremonies again."

"Like the Devereauxs and all their other volunteer workers, we believe that children are powerful, precious gifts from God." William went on. "At Brisbane, we have a morning assembly. It's a daily affirmation for the children as it is for our faculty. We want the children to accept responsibility, not run from it. In every thing they do, we expect and hold them responsible for what they do. When you hold children responsible, a light goes on in their heads which makes them know they're in control of their destiny and their fate. Then, they don't blame anyone for bad choices. I believe that's a belief that the Devereauxs share out here. You're responsible for your choices. We also want our youth to look within themselves and know that they have a soul and a positive consciousness that they can rely on in the discovery of who they are."

"Talk on, baby," exclaimed an older woman.

While clapping arose from the audience, William stepped aside again and allowed his wife to close out their section.

"Alex, Madison, Nanette, and Marlon—" Geraldine White smiled widely and gazed affectionately at the Devereauxs and the Dinzelles. "I thank you for sharing Brisbane Academy with your friends in Winston-Salem. William and I want you to know that when

Solomon and Fletcher are old enough, we'll be honored to have them enroll at the Academy. We thank you for the love you've sent our way today."

"Praise the Lord, baby," said the same older woman.

Geraldine smiled and continued speaking even though she knew it was time for her to sit down. "This is a wonderful assembly of our people together. It's the same way in Charlotte. If it weren't for the fabulously committed teachers at Brisbane, for our students' devoted parents who are concerned for their children's educational future and who volunteer their time and their resources at Brisbane, our school wouldn't have the success it has. It takes devoted, human commitment to make changes. That's the only way we as a people will be able to build a powerful nation of strong-minded and proud Black boys and girls." Geraldine hesitated ever so briefly since she was becoming emotional.

"Long time ago, Albert Einstein was asked a question. He was asked, 'Why are we here?' I'm sure the anxious people who had gathered around him expected an erudite, scientific explanation for our existence. However, his response was quite a basic one. Einstein said, 'We're here to serve others.' That *should* be the epitome of all our lives. This is the epitome of what's going on here today and in other communities around this country. We *must* serve others. Ladies and gentlemen, I thank you, again," Geraldine said in a soft voice laced with sincerity. The thunderous applause traveled through the tent.

Chapter Fifty-Five

While Rozelle headed to the podium, he continued to nod his head. "Give the Whites another round of applause. Now yall see why we were trying to figure out a way to bus our children to school in Charlotte. My reasons are this. I find that this country traditionally has a history of placing our Black children in learning disabled classes. A history of labeling them as being difficult to work with or stereotyping them by saying our Black children can't learn like white children."

"Tell the truth," an audience member spoke out.

"Whether it's documented in confidential reports or whether it's passed on by word of mouth in the teachers' lounge, it's done. Most times, it isn't because our Black children can't learn. It's because the environment that they're learning in squelches their creativity. Their thirst for knowledge. What we believe Brisbane does. No, let me rephrase that. I know what they do. I've visited the school several times, and I was simply impressed by the energy level of those students. What Brisbane does is this. It ignites. It breeds. It resuscitates the beauty and richness of education from within our Black children. That's all children need. They need to know that they can do anything. They need to know that their teachers care for them and believe in their ability to succeed. The children who are fortunate enough to attend their school in Charlotte are certainly blessed." Before Rozelle made the next statement, he paused to collect his thoughts.

"C'mon, man. Bring it on home, my brother," an audience member urged, and Rozelle grinned slightly at the gentleman's comment.

"I know that people say that the best education is in a racially mixed one because going to school is supposed to prepare students for a multi-racial society especially not one that is once race—with just us Black folk. That's fine. However, I believe if children are academically successful in an all-Black setting, then that's ten times better in my book."

"My book too, Rozelle," agreed Symone. He was definitely discussing another one of her favorite topics.

"With the proper foundation from any all-Black institution of education, those same students who other schools said they didn't have it or said couldn't cut the mustard would be able to forge a name in a world that includes white, Chinese, and Jewish people. It could be done with any kind of people and in any kind of other cultural setting that they want to throw at you. But for me and based upon what my education experience has been, those children in an all-Black school setting will also receive a strong sense of identity. The isolation of being the only minority or maybe one of three in your class doesn't exist in Black institutions."

"That's true."

"You know how sometimes we like to tell our friends that our little Johnny, Jr. or Ashanti Miatta are the only Blacks among twenty-three white students. As Black middle income parents, it's our continuous struggle to figure out how to raise our African children in an European-based American culture."

"Absolutely," a woman said.

"As a result, we sometimes believe there's a mystical fairy tale benefit we assume will occur when our children learn math, science, English, and history sitting beside a white child. Integration caused that messed up thinking, and it's ridiculous. Some of us get a real big pleasure saying that our child is the only Black in his class or his club. But it doesn't stop there. The same is said about them being the only one in the boys and girls scout troupe or the dance class or private school. How does little Johnny Jr. or Ashanti Miatta feel when he can't get his hair to look like Elvis Pressley? Or when Ashanti Miatta wonders why her hair doesn't grow like the white girl, Cindy, who sits in front of her at school? Or she wonders why her ponytail doesn't swing the same way? Sometimes our children are searching for acceptance in this world. They're searching for an identity when they're thrust into an environment where they're a tiny minority." Once again, Rozelle paused thoughtfully. He gazed at the smiling faces along the back row. He wanted to be careful how he phrased his next words.

"C'mon, my brother. Run it down," the same man encouraged.

"We know there are about two hundred million white people in the United States, and there are only about forty million Blacks, if that many. So naturally the images you see on television, in the movies, on magazine racks, and when you walk down the street, those images in the majority of the cases are white—are European looking. Our Black children consistently see those white images on television and everywhere they turn. Because they don't look like that, then they believe those images are better than them. We as parents *got to* sho nuff teach our Black children about the beauty of our culture. The beauty of our people. The intelligence of our race. The richness of our history. The history they don't teach in school."

"You're bringing it home like I thought you would, my man," the same gentleman belted out again. Ripples of applause followed.

"And we, as older Black people, need to get real with this educational issue for our children. When our children have been educated in an effective Black educational environment, you know it's different. Sure, you still got your problems there, but the isolation isn't there. You're around your brothers and sisters who look like you and speak like you. Whose hair is like yours? You're around people who understand and support you."

"Say so."

"They struggle with the same issues as you do, and together they'll know who they are as proud Black people in this world. Believe me, I know. I was a student in a racially mixed high school in Memphis that was predominantly white. I went to an all-Black male college like Morehouse then to a lily-white Harvard University. Trust me. Isolation is a part of the deal to get a degree. It ain't pretty. It really isn't. I had the shakes, and I had to get back to my roots." Rozelle began jerkily walking around the stage like he was Dracula, and everyone laughed until they almost cried.

"Rozelle is crazy," Rico said softly as he gave Oscar and Christopher an abrupt Black power handshake.

"I want my children around as many other Black students, Black teachers, and everything else Black I can find. They'll get enough of a white environment once they move into the corporate world. They'll get enough exposure to white culture by simply turning on their television sets. My wife and I limit that, too. Television monitoring begins in the home. That's the first step. In order for children to be molded properly, then the parents and their guardians have to take a responsibility about what their children watch in the home. When thousands and thousands of children see certain lifestyles on television, they think it's ok to do or be what they see. That's why I believe television watching spawns copycat crimes, copycat behavior, and negative lives. It just does."

"You're on the money, my man," another person volunteered.

"Now, I'd like to make an equally important point. I make sure my children are immersed in our culture. That doesn't mean we don't listen to opera, classical music, and support the arts. Their Tante Alex and my wife make sure of that!" he shouted, and the entire first four rows rippled with laughter.

"That's another stereotypical view society has about us. That Black people don't understand or appreciate the cultural things of life," Rozelle said in a proper English voice. "Both my wife and I make sure our six children are exposed to the arts. We also listen to down home soul music and the blues too. We read Black books. Sometimes my wife and I read in bed together. Jodria always buys two of the same books we select at the Ujima Literary Society. That way when we're sitting in bed, we can discuss the book. When we're done, Jodria passes the extra book on, and she places the other one on our home bookshelf." The audience began clapping again.

"That's sweet, man," came from an audience member.

"Of course we attend a Black church. We're a Black family that lives in our Black culture. We have the North Carolina Black Repertory Company here in our backyard, right in Winston-Salem. They've wonderful plays and events that my family and friends consistently attend. The Diggs Gallery at State always has something going on. We've visited the Schomburg in Harlem. We journey to Atlanta often to see historical landmarks. We thank Charmaine all the time because she was the one who told us about the Ballethnic Dance Company of East Point, Georgia. My girl even coordinated a backstage private meeting for the children with the dancers as well as the creators and founders, Nena Gilreath and Waverly Lucas. They're wonderful, too. That dance company does a beautiful, breathtaking story about the animals of Africa called *The Leopard Tale*. All the youngsters enjoyed that one. Me, too."

"I'm looking forward to attending again this year," Nanette said loud enough for people to hear. "It was a fabulous experience."

A couple of guests stretched their necks to see who made the comment, and several others smiled. "If *you* haven't seen it, I recommend you call Atlanta and find out when the next showing is scheduled. Also, the children absolutely loved the Ballethics African Dance Company's portrayal of *The Urban Nutcracker*. I like the way they did it, too. The characters in *The Urban Nutcracker* are a Black family that lives on Auburn Avenue, the King historical district. Long ago, Auburn Avenue was declared by *Forbes* magazine as being the richest

Negro street in not only Atlanta but the world. During that time, Auburn Avenue generated a positive economic influence and had strong Black churches, banks, and insurance companies. It was such a vibrant community that bristled with commercial activity."

"I know the place, my man," a brother yelled out, and several people laughed.

"What was amazing to me is that the Ballethnics African Dance Company do a wonderful African dance thing. The dancers stand on their toes. Those beautiful, fine Black ballerinas are magnificent. The guys aren't bad, either. Can yall imagine that? It's wild. Totally mind-blowing to me. They combined the ballet with our cultural rhythm and dancing. Go see it. Well, let me shut-up. I'm getting carried away, and I just got a nod from Madison to move on. This is a subject that Booker T and Symone will address later anyway, so let me bow out gracefully. These are just some of the discussions we as parents have about our children. What should we do when we want our children to have a clear sense of who they are in the world of middle class America—in middle class Black America. What do we do? For the cause of education, let's give the Whites of Brisbane Academy another round of applause." Rozelle motioned for the couple to stand. They did, and the audience went wild. When the applause was over, Rozelle gazed out into the crowd.

"I was thinking," Rozelle said slowly. "My, my, my. All my running buddies sho do clean up well. From where I'm standing, yall look fine as all get out. Give your ownself some love claps for dressing up this Saturday afternoon." They did.

Chapter Fifty-Six

Cleopatra was the first person on program to give an inspirational speech. Looking very fashionable in a Kelly green and white, raw silk Ralph Joseph dress and cute patent leather sling back pumps, she walked daintily to the podium. Once there, she placed the pages of her speech on the podium and adjusted the mike for her tall stature.

Although she still is ugly to me, Cleopatra is radiating a sense of well-being and confidence Pecola thought pretentiously while she smiled proudly at her. *I wonder why Alex allowed her to speak first. Cleopatra is a maid. All she does for a living is cook and clean for people. She doesn't own a real business or anything like that.*

Pecola, however, clapped along as the audience gave Cleopatra another round of applause. Pecola suddenly grinned at Symone who had just leaned in front of Pauletta to quietly comment on how nice Cleopatra was dressed today. As a result of Cleopatra's standing two-week beautician appointment at Akao Studios, Cleopatra's sandy red colored hair had grown to her shoulders.

"I want to say good afternoon: ladies, gentlemen, Alex, Madison and my two children, Grandison and Beckett. To all the honored youth and other distinguished guests in the audience, my name is Cleopatra Zee Barrow," she announced with a proud, professional voice. "My business is the glorious art of cooking and cleaning! Isn't that great everybody?" She began clapping for herself. The audience chuckled along and started applauding too.

"About five years ago, I learned that about myself in a truly spectacular way. I learned that I *am* the somebody I knew I was. I *am* the person that was screaming to escape from me. I *am* me. A powerful person with all the rights to receive and live a powerful life." Clapping resounded throughout the tent. "I learned that cleaning and cooking are my fabulous, stupendous gifts. Alex made me appreciate the fact that they were wonderful ones at that. She always told me that if you do something that gives you pleasure and if what you do is being performed as if you were guarding an exquisite glittering jewel that's rare and fulfilling to gaze upon, then that's what you should do. And it should be done proudly. Therefore, I try to be the best cleaner and cook anywhere. The best there is in the whole wide world. So excellence and self-worth aren't defined by the type of work you do but by the way you do it."

"She is dyn-o-mite!" declared Rozelle, trying to sound like Junior, the character Jimmie Walker played on the television show *Good Times*. Once more, the crowd roared with laughter, and Cleopatra merely grinned fondly at Rozelle. Cleopatra went on to briefly discuss her life in Tupelo, Mississippi and how she felt about her now dream-like existence in Winston-Salem.

"…That's why I absolutely, totally eat the books I read. Reading is powerful. Through my life, I've had a lot of curiosity about this world. I wanted to broaden my horizons. That's why

I enjoy reading just as much as I love cooking and cleaning. Everything that I used to read about, I'm doing now. I'm traveling, being with friends, loving my family, my friends, enjoying life, and living in my own home that's lovely and warm. I'm doing exactly that. I'm doing that with people who I love, and who I *know* love me," she explained reflectively and paused to collect herself. "As a person who has made a career of cleaning, I turned it into an art form. I do it well and have achieved financial stability. I've captured my dreams. I *am* respected because I'm good—no, I'm excellent at what I do."

"That's wonderful," Pauletta said to Pecola.

"Just read. If you develop a love for reading, you'll discover that reading a book is your most ultimate, five-star meal in one of the world's best restaurant. It'll become an essential part of your life that'll expand your mind. The human mind is awesome. It's like a rubberband. The more you stretch it, the more it absorbs, and the more you grow. My dear friend Pecola Reynolds told me that."

"Talk your stuff, Cleopatra," exclaimed Symone. While Cleopatra blushed, she paused briefly. Pecola blinked several times in disbelief. She was moved and surprised by the recognition.

"In addition to reading, I also recommend that you always pray. My Mama and Daddy prayed every night and every morning. I grew up praying. To the twenty-eight children and everyone else here, pray about your problems. Seek the Lord's face when life's trials keep you from smiling. When you're not making the grades you want in school, just be quiet. Pray and get to studying. When I met Alex years ago, I had prayed the prayer I had been praying for six straight months. I said, 'Lord, you know it's not working here with me in Winston-Salem. It's time for me to go back to Tupelo. I'm being mean to my children. I'm tired, Lord. I'm frustrated as a parent and need for *You* to help me. If you want me to stay here, show me.' He did show me. Six months later, I met Alex. The door of opportunity was flung open. I had enough determination to walk through it and make a wonderful life for my children."

Pauletta's eyes became wet with tears. She sniffed them back and started clapping about Cleopatra's simple but heartwarming words. Pauletta's response made the others in the audience clap as well.

"Thank you so much. When I go home to Mississippi now, my Mama grabs my hand and prays for me. She can't believe my good fortune in Winston-Salem. Yet, she knew prayer worked and always told me to 'pray and keep the faith in God's ability to work miracles in your lives.' When I met Alex, she took my mother's philosophy to another level. Alex told me not only should I pray about everything, but I should also pray for everybody and everything. Pray before I begin any endeavor and before I begin my day. That I should always do everything with the utmost of courage and love because that's what God honors. It's a daily spiritual thing for me. Praying, reading, and writing in my journal. I learned that spirituality is not a thing you practice on Wednesday night and on Sunday morning, but it's done everyday with every person you meet and know."

Once again, Alex marveled at the maturity and growth of Cleopatra since they first met on the streets of Winston-Salem. With an overwhelming sense of love for the confident woman Alex now saw speaking at the podium, her eyes welled up with tears and slowly tumbled down her face.

"As I end my speech," Cleopatra continued, "I want all my honorees and my other children to remember this. Always remember that when obstacles come your way, embrace them as an opportunity to grow and learn. Always remember that life is like a hem of a dress. Sometimes it's in there real tight. Other times the hem is hanging out. Before I met the Devereauxs, my hem was hanging down by my knees. Now, it has been sewn in place, and I'm doing just fine. I had the tools within myself to sew. I'm living a life just like the one I read in books and what I dreamed about when I wrote in my diary. I say to you, your dreams *do* come true, young people. I thank you, Madison and Alex. I thank all of you. All the friends who've made me feel sooo special. I want all twenty-eight honorees to remember that."

"Say so, young lady."

"As long as you work hard, everyone in here will be behind you each step of the way. I know. That's what they did for me. I'll never, ever forget it. Today, I feel so proud about who I am. I even love myself. I thank all of yall for believing in me and giving me a chance to prove that I could make your toilet bowl shine like a diamond," Cleopatra said with a tiny wink of one eye.

The audience clapped and whistled furiously. Nanette banged the tambourine several times. Alex stood, and the crowd rose to their seat as well to give Cleopatra a standing ovation. Cleopatra smiled and stepped daintily to her front row, first seat beside Madison. Rozelle walked to the podium with a wide grin on his face.

"Cleopatra is wonderful, and she's right. We all do love her. She's so giving and concerned about our well-being. Without a doubt, she really does do the job of cooking and cleaning with the utmost of integrity and dedication." Rozelle paused briefly. "I admire her for that."

"Ladies and gentlemen, we have Lillie Anne Dupri. Lillie and Alex used to briefly work together at D. Britt and Cox law firm as well as being members of the North Carolina Black Lawyers Association. That is until Alex kissed her attorney days good-bye for good. For all of you gentlemen out there who are looking for a high-powered corporate woman, Lillie is the one. Lillie's a corporate litigator you wouldn't want to face or go up against in court. She's single and gorgeous. No, let me stop. I know she's going to get me for saying that. Lillie attended Philander Smith College in Little Rock, Arkansas. She and Alex met when she came all the way up here to North Cackle Lackey to attend law school at Wake Forest University. Please put your hands together for a beautiful sister. She's the one and only Ms. Lillie Dupri."

While the audience clapped, Lillie made her way to the stage. She shared her childhood ambitions and spoke inspirationally about growing up in rural Arkansas the baby in a family of fifteen brothers and sisters whose parents were domestics. All of her siblings were professionals as either doctors, lawyers, and college professors.

"...As Rozelle stated, Alex and I have known each other since law school days. I knew she was always involved with a wide variety of worthwhile activities. Even back then, her weekly planner was filled with our law-school assignments, but she still eeked out time for other worthwhile projects. A few years ago, she told me what she and her husband were doing for children. Just last year I asked her if I could be a part of it. Initially, I was a little concerned because I'm not married. I assumed the Devereauxs were looking for help from married couples only. Yall know how folk are? Of course, I'm speaking to the single ladies in the audience," she exclaimed with a huge smile and turned to her next page of notes.

"I know, girl," Symone agreed. The audience broke out into a round of laughing and clapping.

"However, I was wrong with my assumption. Alex said, 'Giiiirrrrl, what's wrong with you? We need our friends. Whoever we can get to help. Folks who are single, married, old, and young. It doesn't matter. All we ask is that the adults commit to being there and spending the necessary time with the children.'" She said that they needed dedicated people who are willing to give our children mentoring, consistency, and stability. Ladies and gentlemen, let me tell you this. When I looked inside my heart, I realized that I *am* qualified to fulfill that goal. It was something I needed to do. Something inside of me told me I just needed to help out." The audience broke out in excited, booming applause once more.

'You go, girl," was heard by everyone.

"What I like about the Devereauxs' program is that I don't have to be a leader or an organizer. I only make suggestions. On Mondays through Fridays and even sometimes on Saturdays and Sundays, I'm to the grind working like a dog at D. Britt and Cox. I thoroughly explained to Madison and Alex that I'm very busy, and I just need to be where I say I'm going to be. Tell me where to go. That's all. I just wanted to make my small contribution and do my part. Since last summer's opening ceremonies, that's exactly what I've done. However, my small part has since grown to a bigger part. Once you get involved, you can't help but help out more than you planned. It's infectious."

"That's for sure," Darilyn agreed, nodding to her husband, Rico.

"I've volunteered to help the Devereauxs with the children. They sought volunteers for scheduled field trips, other social gatherings, ski outings, and bus trips. For those of you who for some reason decided not to or weren't able to help and support this program, just think about it for the next time. It doesn't take a lot of money to do this work. There are a lot of things that are free that the children can enjoy doing. The museums, the library, and the park to name a few. The children enjoyed taking a quiet walk along Carolina Beach picking up seashells. If you can't think of a place to take the children, you can even bring them out here. It's just like a national park anyway," Lillie explained with a short laugh. "When I first visited the Devereauxs farm years ago, I was stunned by the beauty of the small town of Advance even then. Particularly, the quiet and tranquillity of these three-hundred and fifty acres known as the Devereauxs' Shangri-La. Well, it hadn't changed. It has gotten more beautiful through the years. Now, I'm thoroughly enchanted by the loveliness of the Devereauxs' place. It's like they created this place right out from the pages of a fairy tale for all the children to enjoy."

"You're telling the truth," an audience member said.

Lillie smiled. "For years, I've traveled with the Devereauxs and their friends to different places in the world. Without a doubt, Madison and Alex's home is one of the most gorgeous, breathtaking places on earth."

"I agree wholeheartedly with you, baby," Rozelle interjected boisterously, and Lillie smiled affectionately at him.

"My short message to you is this. If you're looking to do worthwhile community work, and you don't want to coordinate everything yourself, the Devereauxs' program is key. Just think about giving your time. You'll notice it more as this evening unfolds that giving a little quality time is all they truly want from you. Nothing more and nothing less. During last year's opening ceremonies in July, I actually got goose bumps all over my body when I heard the speeches. Between the crying, the listening, the emotions, and the knowledge imparted here, everything was simply overwhelming. If more of us step up to help, whose knows what we can do next summer. Instead of honoring twenty-eight children, we might be able to honor seventy-five children. The summer after that, it can be one-hundred. Just give of yourself. If we can do some good in this world, do it. Just give. My Grandmother Niecey Lou often said that God could only multiply what you give. That's true here, too. You don't need a whole lot of money to work with us. Just a whole lot of heart. That's what it takes to make a difference. Everybody can do that. When you do, you'll feel good about it. But in order for village thinking to prosper, we need you!" Lillie yelled *you* out extremely loud and pointed a finger into the audience.

"You go, girl." Symone said, and Pecola stared at her friend. Pecola's view about Lillie was on the reserve mode. She wasn't sure about her. A suspicious Pecola told Pauletta that Lillie reminded her of one of those, typical womanizers in a corporate suit. There was applause and support for the truth of what Lillie said.

"As a result of the Devereauxs' work, I'm much more aware of what goes on and goes wrong with children. This wonderful opportunity to work with children changes you. Your antennas are up whenever children's issues are discussed on television and on the news. Wherever. Sometimes, I just don't know. It's time for our society to realize what we're doing that's right, and what we're doing that's wrong with our children. Once we do that, we need to stop and figure out what needs to be done to fix it."

"Tell the truth, sister girl," an enthusiastic audience member shouted.

"All of these children are winners already, but everybody who participates in fixing what needs to be done in our society is a winner, too. Madison and Alex, I thank you for my time with you guys, and of course, with the children. Not only do I thank the children for the time and giving me my opportunity to be a part of their lives, but I also thank the Devereauxs for their passionate stand for children. Madison and Alex, I honor you, and I salute you. To all my other co-volunteers, I laude you too. Yall have made me feel sooo welcome. It's like I'm a part of another large, loud, throw down, partying, and rowdy family right here in North Carolina. Just like the one I left back in Arkansas. I feel right at home with all of yall. I do. It's just a great feeling of camaraderie. Now, I'm ready for another year of fun and excitement with the children." Lillie spoke her ending words quietly into the mike. She smiled at the children and the Devereauxs. After gathering up her papers, she exited the stage.

"Thank you, Lillie. Let's give her another round of applause," Rozelle requested heartily. "Last night while Lillie and I were doing the The Bump all over the place, I told Lillie she had ten minutes to speak." Pockets of laughter arose from the audience. "Without question, thank you for letting folks know that Alex does most of the grunt work. That's the mark of a leader. Someone who takes care of the hard stuff. Her friends merely show up and act like we know what's going on." The crowd laughed again. As a wonderful exuberance of excitement rippled through the tent, it appeared as if the whole audience was smiling.

Chapter Fifty-Seven

"Moving right along, I've Rico Reynolds representing CR Construction Group this month. Last month, his brother spoke. Yall know him. His name is Carlos Reynolds. I like the way those pretty Reynolds boys work together," Rozelle said. "I only say pretty cause when my newly divorced forty-five year old sister was here for the Reynolds' July 4th barbecue jam this year, that was how she described my two buddies. I said, 'Down, girl. Down, girl. They're both married, baby. They certainly ain't going nowhere either because their wives are their world. My girls, Darilyn and Pecola, are two intelligent, successful beautiful Black women who stand proudly at Rico and Carlos' sides."

Delightful snickers arose from the audience. Rico was looking fine as usual. Unlike Carlos, Rico was graying at the temples, and his wavy black hair gloriously accented his light honey-colored face. He appeared sleek and cool in an Ozwald Boateng tapered navy blue suit. Along with a white cotton button down shirt, solid gold and onyx cuff links, the tie bar held down a striped silk tie. Several available and unavailable women nodded their heads in agreement with Rozelle's pretty boy assessment of Rico.

Rico glided to the podium and briefly rubbed his thin black mustache. After he acknowledged his wife, three children, and his parents, he began a speech filled with humor.

"...For those of you who don't know, Carlos Reynolds *is* my big brother just like Rozelle said. As yall can see, it's obvious whose the smartest brother, the better looking one, and the one with the best business sense. Now we're battling for the title of physical brute strength, too. Yall know what I'm saying? The finer things of life." Rico pointed an index finger at Carlos, and the audience laughed exuberantly. For the next several minutes, Rico spoke about how his father started CR Construction Company over forty-two years ago.

"Umph. Umph. Umph. Umph. Umph," a very interested lady softly whispered and slowly shook her head about Rico's good looks, too. She then nudged her girlfriend sitting right beside her who smiled back in agreement. All during Rico's speech, the two women continued to be in awe of the beauty of a Black man that exuded so much strength and intelligence.

"...My father emphasized education first, and I truly admired that. Before we could work in the CR Construction Group offices, we had to maintain a certain grade average. I don't think my father realized how that kept us focused on our strong desire to work in the family business so that we could be near him. He kept us sharply tuned to our dreams. Without question, I want yall to pursue your dreams. But I want yall to also take it to another level when your dream involves sports. I've learned that there's more in life to do than to pursue sports. That's what happened to me. I pursued a career in basketball, but it didn't happen. Can you imagine the frustration and the letdown? I started to question my abilities. Let me tell you something. When you try hard to reach your goal, the hardest thing to do is to raise your head once it has been pitifully bowed in defeat. When I realized I wouldn't make it in pro ball, I realized I had to fall back on plan two. My family business," Rico joked easily with a debonair grin.

"You were lucky, man," Rozelle exclaimed while he threw his hands palm up in a casual manner.

"You're right, man. I *was* lucky, Rozelle. A lot of people don't have a family business to fall back on when their initial dream doesn't work out. That's why I tell young people to be versatile. I want all our children to understand that it's wonderful to pursue a career in professional sports. But look at the other areas of sports. Let me ask yall a question. Does anyone know who Arthur Cannon Muller is? Have you ever heard his name before?" Rico waited for a response. At the same time and to quiet the older youth that knew the answer, Rico placed his left index finger over his lips. When no one answered, he resumed talking.

"Arthur Cannon Muller is a big time name in sports. He's known worldwide for his smooth abilities, but guess what? Arthur Cannon Muller doesn't run a football. He doesn't crack a bat, never dribbles a basketball, or punches out a heavyweight champion. Arthur never gets dirty or sweats hard on a court or field unless he's playing a casual game with his family and friends. Listen to me, young people. Mr. Cannon works very effectively and smartly behind the scenes. He allows his mind to wield just as much power in beautifully paneled board rooms as do some of the athletes you see on all the famous cereal commercials, telephone commercials, fast food restaurant commercials and whatever else they can market commercials. Arthur Muller makes his millions in another way. As a top sports agent, he's one of the largest names behind some of the greatest names in sports. Arthur Muller is a mega star sports agent who makes a sixth of what each pro-ball player he represents earns. In other words, he manages the careers of others. He has fun the old-fashioned way. It's by utilizing his mind and by being a shrewd businessman. There's a lesson here. Are you getting it?"

"Tell it, Rico."

"As an agent, you figure you represent a bunch of athletes. Some of them *might* be the top-notch athletes in the world. You ain't got to run another ball, never blow out a knee, never break a leg, or never worry about getting paralyzed on a freak play. Just use the power of your mind, the power of business, the power of contacts, and the power of getting what you want for your players. As a sports agent, I guarantee you'll earn just as much as the athletes you represent, sometimes even more. Look at the numbers. If you're a sports agent who negotiates a twenty-five million-dollar per year deal for your client, think of it like this. Follow what I'm saying and imagine that you're the one who closes the deal. You! I'm talking to the children in this room who aspire to be agents," Rico pointed to different sections of the tent where the older children were sitting. "That's right. I'm talking to you! I pray that one day you'll work as an agent and will earn a *sixth* of that multi-million dollar deal." He paused again. "Sooo, if you make a twenty-five million dollar deal for your client, how much does your agent earn? Don't everyone yell it out at the same time." There were a few moments of silence.

"About one and half million dollars, Uncle Rico," young Miles answered loudly.

"You're right, Miles. Over one and a half million dollars with one player. Sure, the sports agent has a staff to pay and business expenses to handle. But so do the athletes. They got their entourage they have to keep up. Their business endeavors. Their wives. Their families. And they got all the hanger-ons that never go away," Rico added in a joking voice. "But guess what? It doesn't stop there. An agent represents and manages other players who earn millions as well. That's the going rate for salaries these days. Multi-million dollar contracts. Then, Mr. Arthur Cannon negotiates sweet commercial deals for them. In all levels of sports, he's considered the athlete's right hand man. In some cases, they probably love him better than they do their own natural born Mamas." The audience laughed.

"A sports agent does it all. Let's just figure if his cut is six percent. Say he has a minimum of about twenty pro players entering his stable a year, and we're guesstimating here. That means he's making big bucks. Let's think low. Ok? Let's say he earns a cool million from each player he represents. For one year's work of managing, the man pulls in a whopping twenty million dollars a year. He ain't bounced a ball yet. It's all earned by intellect. The intellectual game of managing pro athletes. In other words, Mr. Cannon is paid to be smart, to think with his brains, and to teach his athletes to think with their brains. Well, hopefully he does that, too."

"I hope they do!" Booker T echoed.

"It's an art to know the dealmakers who can make it happen, baby. Pushing papers, wine-ing, and dine-ing the right folk. Even if the athlete's career lasts three years, the agent still earns his cut. That's not a bad job, baby. You must think like that! I want the young Black boys and girls I work with to consider the sports agent career as an entree' into professional sports. Talk to BJ. He spoke last month and will be speaking again to yall on Tuesday."

"I can't wait to hear him," Miles said to his buddy sitting beside him.

"BJ will outline the responsibilities of a sports agent and answer all your questions letting you see that a sports agent career is a viable option that *you* can make work. *You* can make it happen. I want the natural abilities you exhibit in sports to also be balanced out with the churning of the greatest thinking minds at work. Have fun using your intellect. My father always told me that once you get over the fear of doing something new, then you go about doing the good work you know you can do!"

"Lay it out," a male audience member said.

"You go, Rico," Marlon boosted.

"But we don't. For some reason, the sports agent field is an area that many Black people don't even consider going into. Then when they finally do penetrate that glass ceiling of sports agentdom, the majority of the Black athletes don't patronize them. They don't even give them a chance. But if all the top notch Black athletes would allow a high-level Black agent to negotiate their deals, then he would be in the same league with an Arthur Cannon Muller. The up and coming brothers signing major million dollar contracts would see that they could receive just as good a deal with him as they did with an Arthur Muller. Everyone needs a chance. Sure, athletes are going to select the agent that can garner the most lucrative contract. That's good business sense, and that's a sho nuff major business move. But our athletes need to give Black agents a chance."

"We certainly do, baby."

"Arthur Muller had to start somewhere. An athlete and an owner had to open the door for him. Plus, if you're a good, well sort after athlete, you're going places. An Arthur Muller type agent is already negotiating with your blue chip stock capabilities anyway. You've already proven yourself on television, in the newspapers, and in the record books. You've already been featured on ESPN, CNN, Fox Sports, in *Sports Illustrated,* and in *USA Today.* You were given publicity at your college. If you didn't, they wouldn't be after you in the first place." Rico shook his head and briefly massaged his chin. "I only hope I live to see the day when all the first round Black pro athletes will shock the world and work with only Black agents."

"Say so, man," BJ encouraged Rico.

"Give those Black agents a chance the same way someone gave those athletes a chance to prove themselves in their chosen field of sports. If it hadn't been for that coach that opened that first door for them, where would they be? Marlon and his buddies can tell yall about how it feels when someone gives you a chance with that coveted spot on the team. Someone gave *me* a chance down at Fayetteville State University. I knew I was good, but I had to prove it to them. So the same way these athletes are given their first opportunity, I believe they should use their moral and spiritual consciousness every now and then with an agent. Commit to a Black professional to manage your career. If you know you're smart, and you're Black, then you *gots* to know they got some other smart Black brothers and sisters out there who are just as smart as you. That means they can move the right deal through for you in the boardroom. Yet, we don't do that. We think other Blacks are smart, and there's always a big *but* on the end of it, too. And I ain't talking bout a human butt either."

"You go, boy," someone interjected. Rico grinned to himself as he realized how the audience was responding in the tradition of the Black call-response just like they were in church listening to their Sunday morning preacher.

"In certain areas, Black people believe that only a white person can handle their business deals. We forget so easily. I've never seen a white professional athlete with a Black agent. Maybe I'm wrong, but has anybody else in here seen that happen lately?"

"I don't think sooo!" Pauletta responded, and the whole first row of children and adults laughed at her.

"Thanks, girl. As usual, you gave out the one million dollar right answer." Rico smiled at her. "Like Rozelle says about things all the time, we got to get real with issues like this. Marlon, BJ, Christopher Perry, and their other buddies can tell you. Booker T and BJ can tell you the stories about who truly run professional sports. It sure isn't the guys running the ball on the field or down the courts. The only way the complexion of the management is going to change is if we change it. In case you didn't notice, brothers dominate the team rosters. Who those brothers hire can make a big difference in the economic complexion of pro sports. Someone in the audience might be asking why I chose to talk about a subject like this for the youth's opening evening. The reason is simple as apple pie."

"Run it down, my man."

"Without question, a lot of our Black boys and girls have been semi-programmed to believe that the only thing they're capable of doing is to play professional ball. They've been programmed to know that sports is the only means to their achieving the outrageous wealth the athletes make. I, on the other hand, want to let our youth here know that there is another component of sports where they can earn just as much money. Their career will last for an even longer period of time. I want them to look at the management side of sports and the longevity side. Consider the sports agents' side. The ownership side. If I can have these young people thinking that way at this age, as teen-agers and young future dealmakers, my talking will not be in vain. In the event they don't make it in sports, they'll know they got other options that are just as powerful and lucrative. Life is about options and goals."

"Wooo, Rico. Share the truth," Symone said, nodding her head in agreement as she encouraged Rico on. She loved this kind of talk.

"I do hope all the young boys and girls in this room go all the way to the top in their professional field of sports. I want you to be that National Basketball League star or be that National Football Association standout. Be that hockey star or golf pro. That famous star in Europe. A stellar track person who zooms through the one-hundred-yard dash in world record time. That gifted person who can break Hank Aaron's home run record. But don't go all the way with just sports on your mind. Keep academics foremost in your mind, too. So just in case when you *do* make it, it can be said: 'Yeah, my man plays pro ball, but he also is a doctor. He plays pro ball, but he also is an engineer. She plays pro basketball, but she also is an attorney.' Be a professional athlete with a twist. He plays ball, but he's also part owner of the Los Angeles football team.'"

"Go, Rico!" Pauletta blurted and began clapping.

"At the same time strive to become an engineer, attorney or a doctor. Stay in school and work hard. Listen to your parents. At Fayetteville State, my coach taught us to always be hungry, but always be humble. He told us to dream big time, but he reminded us that a dream is nothing but a dream until you write it down. Then, it becomes a goal. Write all your goals down each and every day. I had a great coach at Fayetteville State. He taught us to be the hunter and not the hunted. The two years I played pro ball, I did just that. But I couldn't hold on to that goal because I eventually got cut. I can speculate what went wrong in my career. I could blame it on management. I can say they didn't like me. But the one thing I learned the two years I played was that I wasn't in control of *my* career. I wasn't in control of how long I stayed in the league. The owners were. The general managers were. The coaches were. If they didn't let me play, it was their choice. When they did let me play, I only played for a couple of minutes. Those coaches couldn't possibly see my abilities that I believed they needed to see."

Share the vision, my brother, thought Carlos. As his younger brother spoke, Carlos continued to bob his head. Rico had continually spoke like this about pro sports and Black folk with anyone who cared to listen.

"In closing, I must admit I'm a little traditional. I'm serious about what I said and a little old-fashioned. Believe it or not, I like to get a little funky every now and then, so I'm not *always* talking about business. The kids here know that. They all are like my children, and I'll definitely chastise them. But they also know that their Uncle Rico is going to love them with just as much tenacity. To my young future champions of life, I thank you for allowing me to know you, too. Just don't do athletics at the expense of your academics. It's a total package program. Remember that." Rico smiled quickly and gathered his papers.

Rozelle jumped up and jogged the few steps to the podium. "He does like to get out and have fun. I won't divulge the time we got real "funky," as Rico would say, at the North Sea Jazz Festival." Rozelle spoke about the friend's time in Europe at the festival a couple of years ago. Rico shrugged his shoulders with a loud laugh as he stepped lightly off stage. With everyone shaking Rico's hand, he finally made his way to his seat where Darilyn gently kissed him on the cheek and whispered that she was proud of him.

"My man, Ricardo Alfonso Reynolds. Mr. Check. Only his friends call him Check. That's for the days he was smooth with checking opponents on the basketball court. Darilyn, you know the deal about your husband. We call him the master keeper of the funk. He's right after Madison and Pecola. Those three are still caught up in those Parliament P Funk days. That's the key. Enjoying your life, teaching our children, working hard, and enjoying life some more. We want the children here to know that."

"Absolutely," an audience member said.

"All jokes aside, both Rico and Carlos are traditional, family men. Just like Mr. Carlos Reynolds Senior sitting there." Rozelle affectionately acknowledged the patriarch of the Reynolds family. The tall, well-dressed, distinguished, light-skinned older man stood up and quickly waved to the crowd.

"Thank you, Mr. Reynolds. Of course, right beside him is Mrs. Mercedes Reynolds. His lovely bride is what he still calls her. Back in April, they celebrated fifty years of marriage together. Isn't that wonderful, everybody?" The crowd broke into thunderous applause. "I only asked Mr. Reynolds to stand because I appreciated what he taught his sons while they were growing up. That is to know that a strong man, not just any man, but a strong man's first priority is his family." The audience began clapping again.

"Thank you," Rozelle went on. "The Reynolds are a family that epitomizes the old proverb that a family that works together *do* stay together. Carlos and Rico work with many other children than the ones who are being honored tonight. They have the CR Construction Group Golf Pros. That's a bunch of young boys and girls who are interested in learning and studying the game of golf. Each year, CR Construction hosts a youth golf tournament in Winston-Salem at the East Winston Lake Golf Course and in Greensboro at the Gillespie Golf Course. When I first met Carlos and Rico, I wanted them to teach me the game. Guess what? They said that I was too old to be taught anything. Man, I was surprised!" Several people laughed and others smiled. After Rozelle joked a few more minutes, he introduced his wife, Jodria Anne.

When Rozelle and Jodria lived in California, she worked in private practice as a psychologist who specialized in adolescent counseling. Dressed in a free flowing Nigerian Fabric and Fashions traditional African gown of authentic kente cloth, Jodria appeared quite adorable with headdress and all. Just before her name was announced, she had just told Symone that the outfit felt a little loose around her stomach. Maybe all the dancing last night helped her to drop a few more pounds.

Jodria was still convinced she was thirty pounds overweight, and she told her friends she had lost ten pounds for last month's opening ceremony. However, she said that she gained it back just seven days later. She went on another fast and lost the ten pounds for this month. With the elaborate outfit rather snug around her legs, she carefully walked to the stage. Once there, Rozelle graciously helped his wife up the stage steps and escorted her to the podium.

Not one known to have a bubbly personality, Jodria began her speech in her always quiet yet soothing voice.

"Good afternoon, everyone—especially to the lovely young people being honored and taught many wonderful things this afternoon. Today, I'll speak about self-esteem and what can happen when our children don't have it. Self-esteem isn't something you can inject into your children when they're teenagers, it has to be taught from the time a child is born. As a child psychologist and from many hours of counseling and research, studies have shown and I know this to be true that girls lose a lot of self-esteem by the age of twelve. Boys lose it around the age of thirteen, sometimes earlier. As a result of this, we create a culture of insecure people. Whether they be Black or white, they're insecure. Then, children make poor choices. Sixty percent of all teenage girls have sex because their boyfriends influence them. When they have low self-esteem, they yield to the pressure and say yes. Some girls feel that the only way to share a common kinship with young Black boys is to make love to them without any glint of commitment. It's simply because they feel pressured to have sex against their will. The boys talk to the girls, and the girls talk back with their bodies."

"Very true," someone said.

"Young people, please avoid negative self talk. Comments like 'I'm not worth it' or 'I need to have sex because I need to keep him.' Things like 'I'm a nothing without him.' We got to teach our children to have a complete paradigm shift and to speak positively to themselves. Self-esteem is the foundation. The lack of such a trait is the root of many desperate situations in our society. You would be surprised how children getting into dangerous situations relate to self-esteem. If children have high self-esteem, they are less likely to fall victim to peer pressure or to human predators that lurk in our neighborhoods. Self-esteem should be taught and inbred at the moment a child can understand." Waves of clapping arose from the audience, and Jodria smiled.

"Run it down, sistah," a lady commented, and Jodria smiled again.

"During the early ages and up to the older teen years, children are abducted. Children of all ages fall victim to sophisticated ploys of such abductors because the temptations of today are very high tech. Nowadays, if a kidnapper wants your child, he uses sophisticated lures to get him or her. Child abductors have become very bold in the last decade and use such disguises as modeling opportunities, video games, computer toys, and an opportunity for you to make anywhere from fifty to five hundred quick dollars," Jodria revealed softly and briefly gazed around the listening crowd. Although several parents believed she was telling the truth, the information was startling.

"Tell it."

"We got to teach our children that when certain people approach them in such a way, they must know to not be so hungry for self-esteem that they fall prey to these ploys. We've got to teach them this. It's absolutely imperative. When you share all this information with them, you must ask yourself these questions. How can I teach my children such lessons without making them scared? How can I make that possible without making them totally paranoid about life? The key is to make them aware and to make them smart—street smart. Scared children get kidnapped. Smart children hopefully have responded to what they've been taught and are able to not allow themselves to be placed in such situations. That's why I recommend our children wear identification bracelets. In the event they're snatched, those bracelets can be dropped from their wrists, and the police will then have a beginning point to locate them."

While Jodria spoke, the tent was very quiet as uninformed parents listened to the frightening topic with open mouths and wide bright eyes.

"Typically, all children are at risk to be kidnapped. That's possible for your toddler, your second grader, and even your junior high school student. These are all according to statistics," she said and paused briefly and flipped to a particular page in her notes. "I'm a believer of statistics when it concerns children because each number is a young soul whose life has been damaged. It's a young life they're flashing up there with the numbers."

"Preach on."

"Er, thank you. Fifty percent of the children kidnapped are twelve years and older. So what that tells you is that our older children also fall prey to these vicious people. The even staggering statistic that's even quite mind-blowing is that seventy-five to eighty percent of the children are victimized and/or kidnapped by a person who isn't a total stranger. It's done by people they know, who are often friends of the family."

"Wooo! Oh me," one lady moaned out loud and many others shook their heads heavily from hearing the type of information they had only received from television shows. Jodria glanced up and nodded her head slowly.

"I know. It's quite shocking, but it's better to live, listen, and learn. So we say a kidnapper is a person that isn't a total stranger," she repeated in a sobering voice. "Then you have to ask yourself, who would you classify as strangers? If you're like Alex, me, and several of our other friends, we speak to strangers all the time. That pleasant behavior can confuse our children. When they see us speaking to strangers, they might think it's ok to do the same thing. What we got to do is not teach our children about strangers per se, but teach our children about dangerous situations. They must learn to identify strangers by their actions and not by their appearance. For instance, if a car drives by, that's ok. If that same car stops, and the driver asks that the child get in, that's a dangerous situation with a stranger. For the parents and guardians here, that's what needs to be repeatedly explained to your children. In most abduction cases, a child is transported in a car. These are merely life saving tips for your child. Teach them. Talk to them. Once you do that, your child hopefully can clearly understand the unfathomable atrocities that can happen when they're kidnapped and get into the clutches of ruthless, human vultures." There was a low rumble from the crowd as they responded to Jodria's comments.

"Ump, umph, umph, umph. This is amazing," moaned another older woman.

"I often have discussions with other concerned parents. I ask them this question all the time. What are *we* doing? We got such strange requirements for inanimate objects such as cars, houses, and other luxury items. To drive a car, you must do certain things. To own a house, you must have qualifications. But we don't have the same requirements with our living and breathing most precious commodity. Our children. Listen to this, people. According to statistics, one in four boys is sexually abused by the time he's eighteen. One-hundred and fifty thousand children are solicited for abductions every year. Those are merely the ones who have reported such to the proper officials. Isn't that amazing? What are we doing to insure our children against such dangers? *What?* Our society says it's all right to insure a car or house, but it's not all right to insure our most important, greatest natural resource—our children," Jodria said and the crowd clapped loudly.

"Bring it to the light!"

"Don't get me wrong. We're not trying to scare anyone here this afternoon. We're concerned parents, too. During our monthly Ujima Literary Society meeting, we discuss effective ways to educate our children and ourselves. This education isn't only with our Black history and our values, but it's also with our moral street sense. We cover *all* subjects. I know what some of you are saying. 'I don't want to talk about certain things like sex, AIDS, and drugs. Horrible subjects as someone kidnapping my child, or even discussing my daughter's menstrual cycle with my daughter, let alone with my son or somebody else's child are conversations I'd like to avoid! Believe this much is true. If you don't talk to them, who do you think will? Will it be their peers or a dishonest older person? Who will teach them the true beauty of lovemaking? Is it going to be a sex offender? Maybe it might be a relative or an unscrupulous uncle, aunt, or cousin. It possibly could be your child's boyfriend or girlfriend." Jodria stopped for a moment. "Oh no! That's not the way it should be, but who will do it? You will, and you should. That's who. We believe that's our very important role in this group of friends around here. We want to facilitate an environment where all the children can speak honestly to us and not feel embarrassed by sensitive subjects—by any subject," Jodria shared in her quiet way. The crowd clapped and several people whistled.

"I love it, girl."

"I too believe in sharing information about the treatment of our children. It's bad to say, but every person a child meets isn't always a person who is interested in his or her well-being. Of course, we want all the children here to be loving, friendly, and intelligent. We also want them to be street smart. During the next two weeks, we talk about the kinds of people who are out there to do young people harm. I've found books to help us with this issue. Both parents and all the children you see being honored here have read *Missing* and *Street Sense for Parents.*"

"Run it down, baby," Rozelle said softly to encourage his wife.

"These types of books and these discussions are reinforced repeatedly in this group to provide the real deal about living life as a child in this day and age. It's unfortunate, but it's true. You know how it is to be a parent or guardian during this day and time and not have to deal with what our mother and father did when we were younger. As old folks say in Nashville, 'We're living in perilous times,'" Jodria recited in a shaky, old timey voice. Several members of the audience vigorously bobbed their heads. Clapping rose from the crowd. A surprised Jodria smiled demurely.

"If we don't teach our children to have some degree of street sense about the evil side of life, they could very easily move from being children existing in a pleasant home with you to that of being gruesome statistics. One thing about statistics, they're no respect of persons. It's an equal opportunity program. During our literary society meetings, we also discuss how dangerous strangers can pick up our children in the library, at the malls, in parks, and in our tree-lined neighborhoods."

"Unbelievable," Cleopatra moaned.

"Then there's friends of the family who are really predators on the sly as well. Unfortunately, these predators can be your cousins, mothers, uncles, sisters, brothers, and fathers who touch, rape, and spiritually destroy our children. I know this is an uncomfortable, ugly subject, but our main objective here is to educate our children. This is one way this can be done so that they can be aware of it. We tell them the absolute truth out here in Devereaux Land."

"Umph. Umph. Umph. Lawd have mercy."

"Let's look in other areas where we as a people are sometimes falling short. As a society, what are we doing in the school system? Risk of death shouldn't be an issue associated with the education of our children. Kids have access to guns. The communities, the neighborhoods, and the parents aren't doing enough to teach our children to resolve anger in a non-violent manner."

"Based upon what I've said, self-esteem is the catalyst for healthy children. Nowadays, we as parents try to do everything for our children. That has got to stop. Have your children learn responsibility. Have them do household chores. Those simple skills help them with their organizational skills, perseverance, and positive attitude. Through your prodding, help, or simply showing them to clean the bathroom, wash dishes, and vacuum is long lasting. In a small way, it's structuring role models for future life patterns. This is just another way we can teach our children values."

"This is wonderfully powerful information, Jodria," a man yelled out.

"Our children learn by our actions, and you know how we love the national anthem for parents. *'Do as I say and not as I do.'* It doesn't work that way anymore. That's especially so when so many other things are pulling at our children nowadays. Your child judges you by your last worst act. Admit what has happened in your life. Let them know that you were a child once too and that you understand what they're going through. The most powerful thing to say to a child is, 'Yes I did. I made mistakes, too.' Learn how to communicate with your children. Good communication doesn't start when they're high school seniors; it starts when your children are two, three, and four years old. It's never too young to sit down in a private place in your home and have a wonderful discussion with your child."

"So true, sugar," a senior citizen said.

"Continuously compliment them. Praise them. When children are young and you're teaching them to walk, you know what you do. When the child falls after the third or fourth step, you simply praise them for their efforts. The same thing should hold true during their formative years. Their early teenage years in junior high, through high school, and all through your child's life. When your older child acts a certain way and falls short of your expectations, hug him and reassure him anyway. Even though you're disappointed and your parental feelings are hurt, be honest about it. Children need to know someone has faith in them and believe in them. In the memorable words of Joseph Joubert, *Children have more need of models than of critics.* Parents and guardians, please reminder those words."

"Share your knowledge," Pecola interjected. She was absolutely so very proud of Jodria's speech and delivery.

"Parents need to get over being scared about talking about sex. It's about living and dying nowadays, especially with AIDS. I also tell our youth here not to be sexually active if you aren't in a position to care for another human being. Without question, if you're active you'll become pregnant. What pregnancy does is close the door to your childhood and open the door to adulthood. Once that door is closed, you can't go back. You might be a pregnant twelve-year old, but you'll quickly become a twelve-year old with adult responsibilities and problems. A baby adult. You certainly can't go back to your childhood again. Over one million teenagers become pregnant each year. But if you ask them if they had a chance to do it over again, they would say no. An adult's life is too hard. It's too hard on a child."

Jodria briefly surveyed the crowd. "I remember when several members of our literary society were having a problem discussing drugs and sex with their teenaged daughters. Yet, the girls were crying out for guidance. They came to me and asked for my opinion. The young girls continued to ask their mothers private and intimate questions and got no responses. Their mothers asked me to help them to respond to their daughters' questions. These mothers wanted me to help them to look within themselves to answer their daughter as honestly as possible but in a way to not cause their daughters to think their mothers were total hippies."

"That sounds like a doosie," Pauletta whispered to Pecola.

"You know we did," a woman exclaimed.

"If we can have boys and girls talking about their bodies at an early age, I believe they'll be adequately prepared to deal with any pressure that come their way. We must learn how to give information to our children like a prescription in small dosages at a time," Jodria said lightly, and the entire audience broke out in understanding giggles. Jodria grinned too.

"Finding information we all can utilize on the parent journey is the key. Talking it out with other parents is just as important. It helps everyone to merely work together to raise children. Work together in cities and neighborhood all across America like the Devereauxs are doing here. I believe we can have small uprisings of positiveness all across the country where people attempt to make a difference in the lives of our beautiful future leaders. Our children."

"C'mon with it, sister friend."

"Quite frankly, I believe the success of our race will come from the support we give each other. I personally don't care for government funding for all community programs, either. A lot of times, these funds never trickle down to the people who need the most help. That's why we as a people need to rally behind anyone. Rally behind people like the Devereauxs that we know are truly trying to make a difference in the lives of many. I know the Devereauxs are perfect for this. They've contributed significantly in my life and in my family's lives. If Madison and Alex can make a difference in these children's lives the way they made in my family's life since we moved from California, then you can believe they're going to make an impact in the lives of the children who are being honored here this afternoon." The audience politely applauded.

"They didn't pay me to say that," Jodria remarked gleefully while the crowd chuckled. "My assignment is to speak about children's issues, self-esteem, and street dangers. During my family reunion last year in Tennessee, we wore T-shirts that said 'Families are about caring, sharing, and loving.' If there are any doubting Thomases out in the audience, let me tell you this. That's exactly what we're attempting to do with all our children. That's exactly what we're attempting to do with the ones that are being honored here and with whom we have spent the last eighteen months. I thank them, and I thank all of you for coming to see for yourself what's going on out here. Always know that the communication of values and self-esteem is a worthy, jewel of a pursuit for you, me, and our children." There was polite applause again.

"Speak the truth, Jodria," Pauletta shouted.

"In closing, remember to always believe your children are sooo anxious to succeed, too. It's there in them bursting to come out. I always ask my friends this question. Do you settle for what our children say they can or cannot do, or do you raise the expectation baton? Do you raise the expectation level and wait for them to do it?" Jodria took a brief pause and glanced into the crowd. "I've found that our children rise to the occasion and meet whatever goals and expectations we throw at them, we give them, and what we believe in them."

"Wonderful," a man yelled out as the tent resounded with animated hand clapping. Once more, Jodria smiled shyly and waved her right hand to silence the crowd.

"Last but not least, I want you to remember this. If you *ever* think you see a child that looks like a missing child, whether you saw him or her on television or not, call the National Center for Missing and Exploited Children. It might be that child who is desperately trying to figure out how to get home. Thank you."

Although Jodria's subject was highly frightening, the audience roared with applause. They were impressed with the way Jodria frankly shared the sensitive information.

"Bravo, baby. Come on, yall. Isn't my sweetheart an inspiration? I believe you can give my wife a better hand than that," Rozelle yelled into the mike. "Like my baby said, you can talk to kids all day and tell them things. Without a doubt, they watch what you do and how you live. What she recommended you do to your children, my wife does just that with our six. Pecola teases us all the time. She says my family looks just like stair-steps. That's true, but you can believe that my wife has them organized like a little efficient, military school that is laced in an environment of tremendous love and attention. Alex dubbed my wife The Self-Esteem Champion. It's Jodria's goal to help every child that comes into her path to be true to his or herself. Baby, I thank you for doing a great job with our children and especially with me," he said sweetly and blew Jodria an air kiss. She smiled back, and the audience clapped resoundly.

"You know I love to see a man honor his wife," Madison said loudly. Rozelle chuckled lightly, pointed a finger at Madison, and flipped to another page of notes.

Chapter Fifty-Eight

"Ladies, gentlemen, and honored guests, we have another wonderful story. I present to you our next speaker. Listen, all you young girls in the audience. He's a young man who has pulled his life together, and now he wants to become a doctor. I proudly present to you someone who is like a son to me. I introduce Carlos Reynolds, Third." As the crowd clapped, CJ confidently strolled to the podium.

"My name is Carlos Reynolds the Third. My story is different from the others, but yet it is the same," CJ explained in calm voice as he glared into the faces of the crowd.

Carlos was a nice looking young man who at the age of twenty-three spoke with the utmost maturity and appeared much older than his years. A handsome guy, he looked like a younger clone of his father. Tall, with a full goatee and silky wavy black hair, Carlos Junior was a dark cocoa complexioned young man who possessed the green sparkling eyes of his mother. Without a doubt, his green eyes enthralled the ladies because it was a unique and startling contrast to his dark-skinned face.

"...I was very smart as a young boy. This is all according to my Dad. When he and my Moms were courting', my Grandmother Oseola used to always tell her friends that she had some 'smart assed chilluns.' My Grandmother used to say things like that long, long way before she became more involved in church." CJ spoke proudly of his grandmother, and Pauletta nodded her head rapidly in agreement.

"That's my sweet Mama for you," Pauletta declared just as proudly regarding the comment about her mother whom she adored immensely and knew was true. As Pecola heard her son fondly discuss his grandmother, she suddenly became stoic and quiet.

"Thanks, Auntie Pauletta. You know my grandmother was right. I *was* a smart chillun, but I often hid that from others. I used to hide the fact that I was in the gifted and talented class. Since I wanted to hide it sooo much, I thought it would be a good idea for me to learn how to act tough. It was me. I hung out with my partner, Ossiris Abdul Hopkins, Jr. Me and another partner of mine, who I'll introduce to you later on in my speech were tight, tight buddies. We were tighter than white on rice, and you know how that's tight."

"Yes we do, young man."

"Ossiris Abdul. My Mama always said that his first and second names had a kingly ring to it. Now, he was kingly all right. My friend was a charismatic guy. He was just like me. He laughed easily, and we were good friends. We were young, and we believed we were invincible. But a bullet shattered Ossiris' life, and he died in my arms. I'll never forget that as long as I live. The two bullets whizzed past me and tore up *his* insides. Before he died, I looked him in the eyes, and I asked him to don't die on me."

"Lawd Jesus," someone moaned.

"When my friend died like that, his death was like a splash of icy cold water in my face. I just knew that I was in a dream. I said to myself, 'Man, this can't be happening.' It *was* real. Blood was everywhere, and it wasn't a movie either. Last year, I spoke at the July opening ceremonies for the younger children. This year, I asked my Uncle Madison if I could speak to the older group. The August group. Yall know what I'm saying. The August group is at an age where they think they know it all." CJ glared in the children's faces.

"Say so, young, man."

"After my speech last year, my eight-year-old little cousin asked me an interesting question. The opening ceremonies were over, and we were all sitting down having dinner. When my little cousin heard me say that Ossiris was killed again, he thought I was joking. He said. '...Oh, he got shot just like they do in the movies, Cousin CJ? I said 'No, Rico, Jr. It's not like it is in the movies. Ossiris won't be back. When people are killed in the movies, they get up.' Real life isn't a rehearsal, young people. You just don't get second chances. It ain't no more takes at trying to have a better life." The audience broke out in a round of unabashed, enthusiastic clapping.

"Speak the truth, young man."

"Like my parents, Ossiris' parents had thought they had done all the right things parents should do. They provided him with a lovely home, wonderful tasting southern food, his own room, a nice allowance, and the freedom to explore his dreams. He came from a Black family steeped in the tradition of Black colleges and church. Ossiris' parents did nothing but display hardworking ethics. They were both professional people. They were just like my parents. His father was a dentist. His mother was a history teacher at Reynolds High School. Who his parents were didn't matter. It was *who* Ossiris *was*. It was who *I* was, and it was the *choices* we made. It wasn't until later that I realized that. It finally hit me. With the help of strong Black men in my life, I understood that Ossiris and me had made a lot of bad decisions. Some seriously bad decisions. The type of decisions that cost my friend his life. The street coupled with fate had finally caught up with us. It's as simple as that. Our succumbing to peer pressure culminated in the death of a person. It was the death of Ossiris. My best buddy. What do parents do short of tying their children up and keeping them as prisoners? What do you do?" As Carlos Junior spoke, many parents nodded their heads with understanding.

"Tell the truth."

"Right now, the ushers are passing around a piece of paper that I would like for you to look at very closely." CJ paused while the ushers busied themselves to make sure each person in the tent received a copy.

"What you have before you are copies of my seventh and eight grade report cards. Before I dropped out of school two weeks into my eighth grade, those were my grades. Take a good look at them. Does anyone know what a resume is?" CJ asked the question and waited for an answer.

"A resume is an account of one's career or of one's qualifications. It's prepared by someone in quest of a specific position or job," Marsha Elon hollered out the correct response. A B-honor student who lived in Cleveland Avenue Homes, she was one of the young girls being honored.

"That's right, Marsha. You're absolutely right. That's exactly what my report card was. My resume. According to my report card, you'll see that it looks like I didn't learn anything while I was in school. Look at it closely. It's obvious I did poorly in most of my seventh grade classes, and I failed every one of my eighth grade classes." As CJ uttered each word, the audience was captivated with his charismatic way of discussing what happened to him.

"Listen to me, young people. It's a very thin line between success and failure. I had a bunch of posters on my wall. Yall know the type. Sports posters and my favorite singing group. But it doesn't matter how many posters I had on the wall if I didn't have a diploma up there."

"Tell the truth, young man," a guest yelled out and began to clap.

"You gots to realize that the first eight years that you attend school, that you pursue education are very important. That's your foundation. You're building the foundation of your mental, intellectual house. When you don't do well in school, you could be— No, not could be. Let me rephrase that. You're hurting yourself. When you took math in the seventh grade, you needed to understand what you learned in the sixth grade. Each year, your education builds. Each year, it builds until you reach the twelfth grade and eventually graduate."

"Absolutely."

"Check this out. One of these days, you're going to package your educational knowledge. That's your report card. You're going to send it off to someone for admission into college where they carefully review everything you've done from the ninth to the twelfth grades. A guy like my father's golfing buddy, Dr. Eric Rhett Ward, who is Director of Admissions at North Carolina A&T State University, will be waiting on you. Dr. Ward is sitting in the audience today." CJ directed his gaze to Dr. Ward, and the older gentleman waved his hand to let the people know where he was.

"Someone like Dr. Ward is going to open your admissions package. The package that includes your report card, your college application, and your low SAT scores. What do you think he's going to do? Dr. Ward will send you a nice little letter. In thirty words or less, he'll inform you that you're not coming to A&T. That's exactly what he's going to tell you." As the crowd nodded their heads, they began to clap vigorously. Some even laughed.

"Your not being accepted into the college of your choice will not be anybody's fault but your own. Believe it or not, colleges are in the business to make money. Sure, they educate people. That's their product. But they're in the business of educating people who are willing to learn, not dead beats. Certainly not the person I was over ten years ago. So you see the only person's name that's on the report card that you get after each semester, and that's on your resume, is you. The only person's name on the report card is yours. Remember that. Not your mama's and not your daddy's. Not your grandmother, grandfather, aunt, or uncle. It's *your* name. You're the only person that'll benefit directly or indirectly from your qualifications and your work habits listed on your report card. Sure, your parents or guardians are the ones that care about your grades, but you're the only one that can earn them." Once more, the audience broke out into a hearty round of applause.

"When I acted up and when other children act terrible, it evokes an emotional response from our parents. It's a sad spirit and a response of disappointment. They feel let down. We all know that disappointment isn't an easy emotion to display. Now, I know it was very difficult for my parents to do it with me, with my sisters, and with my brother. It was especially so when we did something wrong, were acting crazy, and had slid off the page of adolescent life. So the message from the ones we love, like our parents, confuses us when those geysers of emotions come out in the form of anger. It made our parents say and do things to us—their children—as a result of their anger and disappointment in our behavior."

"Preach, young man," a man hollered out.

"The people who are around us such as our parents, our guardians, our uncles, our aunts, and their friends. You know the ones I'm talking about. All those adults that get on our nerves when we're growing up. The ones who try to pull us to the side and give us a good word or two. They've been there. Believe it or not, they've been our ages before and were confronted with obstacles and pressures relative to their time. These same older people who are trying to get *you* and *me* to do the right thing have been twelve, thirteen, fourteen, fifteen, and sixteen years old a long time ago," CJ joked easily, and the younger crowd laughed.

"I like the way Uncle Rommie says it. He calls it the TOE Group. That stands for the *Time on Earth* folks. They're also known as adults." The audience laughed again. "Adults have been around this earth a lot longer than we have. They know just a tad more about life than we do. They can see your future, especially if you're making bad choices. I *can* see it. We see it because we can look into our past. We've been there. Although I'm not much older than a lot of you sitting out there, I've been there. I've been around, and I feel much older than my years. I know it's hard being young nowadays. I just made life a lot even harder on myself by getting caught up with the wrong crowd. I was always trying to be Mister Big. I was hanging out at the malls, drinking MD2020 and wine coolers. I used to sip forty ounces like they were cool water on a hot summer day. Snorting. Sniffing. Smoking reefer. I was having unprotected sex like I couldn't die from it."

"Tell it like it is, babyboy," Pauletta yelled out, and CJ smiled at his auntie.

"Some of yall think that older people aren't wiser than you are. You think they're just older. That they don't know. It's ironic I'm saying these things to you. Haven't yall heard this before?" The parents in the audience bobbed their heads like lapping dogs.

"My Uncle Rommie and Uncle Madison used to tell me this. They said, 'CJ, one day you'll have children. It—will—happen. We one-hundred percent guarantee you of that. It's all a part of life, and we hope you don't go through what you have put your parents through.' Lawd, I hate to see how Carlos Reynolds the Fourth will be." CJ laughed loudly as did the entire audience. "You know before Ossiris was killed, we both had our plans. We had dreams, too. We were going to play football on the same college team and do everything together. Our lives were laid out for us. I had the perfect world. As a thirteen, fourteen, and fifteen year old, I came in the house whenever I felt like it. I was out of control, and it was as if I couldn't do a thing to stop it. Even though I was out of control, I wasn't dumb. I wasn't dumb enough to get wrapped up in all the things my friends wanted to do. I didn't believe in mugging people or snatching cars. I even had some limits back then. During those times, I often heard the sweet country, voice of my Grandma Oseola quietly speaking to me, and I couldn't do certain things. I just couldn't do it. I always had a caring heart, and I always had a love for my family."

"That's for sure," Pauletta nodded.

"Through those trying periods, my grandmother was a wonderful beam of light for me. Many times I would go visit her and stay with her. She hugged me to her bosom and sang to me like I was a small, tender baby who simply had an unrelenting, tortured mind. My grandmother has a wonderful voice. Years ago, she even performed at The Top Hat Club in Atlanta. It's a beautiful voice just like my mother and my sister. During those down years, my grandmother helped me through so very, very, very much. She always wanted me to look at each angle of things from an old-fashioned perspective," CJ said in a soft voice. "But I also possessed some sense. Not only did I look at folks in an old-fashioned perspective like Grandma Oseola wanted me to, I also had the gift of looking at people and analyzing them. When I did that with my friends, it was amazing sometimes. All the stuff that my friends and I talked about was a pipe dream. Nothing more. Because without a good education and some sense, we couldn't do dittly squat."

CJ took a deep breath and paused before he continued speaking. He stared into his parents' faces. In the meantime, Pecola's mind was screaming, *Don't say it, CJ. Please don't mention it today, baby. Your Mama can't bear to hear the name today, son.* CJ took another deep breath and cleared his throat.

"When my little sister was killed nine years ago, that pushed me to another frightening level. Ossiris hadn't even been shot yet. But her death was another excuse for me to act a fool. My sister, little Marva, was extra special to me. Yet, I used my baby sister's dying as another reason why I should act even worse with my parents and to even torture myself some more."

At the mention of her dead daughter's name, Pecola allowed the tears to quietly fall down her cheeks. With her back straight and her head held high, she continued to listen to her son. Pauletta patted her sister's thigh with understanding. Alex fervently prayed that Pecola would remain calm. The friends knew that sometimes if Pecola's youngest, dead child's name was mentioned, no matter where Pecola was, she broke down into an uncontrollable spell of non-stop sobbing and melancholy.

CJ took another deep breath. "After many months of counseling, mentoring, and self-reflection, one day I decided it was time to change. Time to get my life together. I couldn't blame my life on my baby sister, Marva. I couldn't even blame it on Ossiris' death. It was all about *me.* I realized that I had to get my life in order so I could go to college and make something out of myself. That's what Uncle Madison and Rommie said to me. They knew if they got me to think differently about myself, I would eventually think I could be successful somewhere, somehow. They were wonderful mentors to me."

"That's wonderful."

"Romallus Alexander and Madison Devereaux. To this day, I believe I owe those two men my life. I was their personal pet project. It's ironic I'm speaking to you today and saying the same things they said to me. Even though my two uncles said some of the same things my parents preached to me, it made more sense to me the way my uncles said it. I could accept it from them better. It just sounded a little different than when your parents were nagging you with all the time." The children in the audience laughed and began to clap with large smiles upon their faces.

"Uncle Madison and Uncle Rommie told me that your junior and high school friends were great people. But when you graduate from high school, nine times out of ten you'll never see them again. Sometimes you kept up with them, and sometimes you didn't. Unless you attend a twenty-year class reunion or stay in the same town or something, you drifted apart. They told me that your true friends are the ones you have yet to meet. You meet them in college. The friends you meet in college will be the people you will keep for life. Your college roommate will be your best man at your wedding or your maid of honor. Your frat brother or your soror."

"Amen to that," Rozelle declared, and the audience began to clap again.

"If your parents care for you like I know that they do and like the way mine cared for me, they hope that you don't fall through the system. Won't slip in the cracks. Along with your parents and your guardians, that's what the Devereauxs' and their friends are trying to do. They want to make sure young people see the possibilities and opportunities their future holds. Look around you. All of the Devereauxs' friends are working toward *your* success. Boy, do they have a lot of friends."

"They certainly do," a lady who knew the Devereauxs from a distance whispered to the man who invited her to this function.

"So, I'm speaking to you as a high school drop-out who made it up to this point. On Tuesday afternoon, we'll do a different kind of assignment. My assignment. The one that Uncle Rommie and Uncle Madison made me do over and over and over again. We'll write down where we expect to be in ten years. Just think about it. If you do nothing, the ten years are going to roll right on by. If you're going to do something, they're gonna roll right on by, too," CJ explained with a comedic flair. "When you look in the mirror in ten years and if you've followed all your goals, that's admirable. It would be all good. But if you've failed at whatever you strive to be or do in the next ten years, you can blame no one but yourself. That's what I like about the man in the mirror thing. When you look in the mirror, you have to stare only at your face." A hearty round of clapping erupted once more.

"I'm only twenty-three years old, but I feel older than that. During my roaming years, I got real old real fast. When I missed going to school, I realized education was wonderful, yet I realized there were many ways to get an education. Education is more than being in school. One must become educated about life, and that education comes from being in life. It's from experience. It's what you see or do. School is recall and remembering. In spite of my street education, I can still look back and say I thank God I made it through. I *did* beat the odds. But life is like that sometimes. You wonder if you'll win at it. Sometimes, you *do* win, and sometimes you *do* lose. You may not like it. It might be bitter. Life might not always taste good to you. It may not even be fair. It wasn't fair to Marva or Ossiris. It wasn't fair to sooo many others who were cut short and never had a chance to blossom into powerful human beings."

"Tell the truth, young man," another man yelled out.

"If you can imagine the end of the rainbow, you'll be glad you applied yourself in your neighborhood, in your schools, and in your college classes. If you do the work now and if you lay that strong foundation now, you'll be able to take it easy later on in life. You'll be a great doctor. A fantastic lawyer. A fabulous teacher. A wonderful singer. A noted actor, or that super entrepreneur. You can be whatever you want to be."

"Say so, baby boy," Pauletta encouraged.

"One time Uncle Rommie told me that life is like a long hallway that's full of doors." CJ gazed heavenward and smiled to himself. "You come in one end of the hallway, and you go out the other. As you make choices and decisions, those doors will close behind you. Once you close them, very rarely can you open them up ever again. You'll never know how it could have been. As usual, Uncle Rommie was right. I never knew what it was like to walk across the stage at my high school graduation. That was a closed door because I wasn't there. Remember that I was a high school dropout. I never knew what it was like to attend my high school prom, to appear in the yearbook, or to have my fellow students sign it with their congratulatory words. Those doors of potential memories are shut tight because of the choices I had made long ago," CJ spoke quietly and stopped to inhale deeply. "I only tell my story to let you see what happened in my life. All of that has changed. It didn't happen over night, but it came slowly. It took a few years. I know my parents were thankful to God I finally saw the light. I'd like to quote the Chinese Proverb my Auntie Pauletta says all the time. She said that she learned it from my Grandma Oseola. *Patience is power; with time and patience the mulberry leaf becomes silk.*" CJ's father listened to the mature, enlightening words of his son. With closed eyes, Carlos nodded his head slowly.

"Remember that! With patience, a lot of hard work, supportive parents, and strong Black male mentors, I finally made it out. Now, I have a goal in mind. That's the key to a prosperous life—having goals. You have a mark. You put it on the wall, and you shoot for it. To all the young people here, listen! These next few years in your life are important. Whatever you do in life, remember this. There's only one person sitting in this tent to make it happen, and that *is* you. As a young Black person in this country, you and I don't fit the norm. Don't give it to them. When they say you're a Black kid with an attitude, prove them wrong."

"Say so, CJ."

"Sometimes instead of stepping up, you need to step back. I know yall heard this before, but learn how to turn your stumbling blocks into stepping-stones. Don't use excuses all the time. Don't say I failed because of where I live or what I don't have. Don't say it's because I'm different. I'm Black. We're poor. I can't do any better. Those white so and so won't give me a job. Yeah, I know there's racism out there. It's not as overt as it was when our parents and grandparents were growing up, but it's still there. Tante Symone calls it modern-day racism. She say that's the worst type because it's real subtle. It's the kind you can barely detect if you're lulled into thinking that everything is equal and fair. In spite of all of that, there's a great world out there. I want yall to understand that you too can enjoy the wonders of it all."

"Wonderful words, young man!" someone shouted.

"Now, I'm a junior at Alabama State University in Montgomery, Alabama. I'm following in my Uncle's Ezunial's tradition. He went to that school, and now he's a very successful architect out in California. My dad thought it would be better for me to go out of state to get a new experience. My Dad was right, and so I'm maintaining the family tradition in Alabama. Quite honestly, I think my father wanted an excuse. An excellent reason to attend those good ole classic games in Montgomery. My Dad and Uncle Rico will go anywhere for a Black College sports outing. They always attend homecoming and the Magic City Classic." Both Rico and Carlos laughed at the comments. "I'll graduate on time next spring. When I do, I plan to enroll in medical school at Duke University—just like my Uncle Madison did. Who would've ever thought it?"

"Wonderful, young man. Wonderful," an older woman suddenly erupted.

Before CJ continued speaking, he hesitated and looked into his friend's eyes. "John Philander, please let them know who you are."

"It was great, man," exclaimed a smiling John. Sitting in a wheelchair in the aisle of the second row, John quickly waved.

"John is my good, good friend. This is the other friend I mentioned earlier. We've been tight for years. Like Ossiris, John was tragically injured by a random gunshot one night. John got shot one year before Ossiris. The legacy of his injury and the knowledge that such violence was out there waiting on us didn't mean anything to Ossiris and me. We still believed it could and would never ever happen to us. To see John go down like that wasn't even the wake-up call me and Ossiris needed to change. If we had learned from it, maybe Ossiris would've still been alive today. The difference between my two friends is simple. John survived the bullet, and Ossiris didn't. John is a gunshot victim who lives to share his story with other young people, too. But now he's paralyzed from the waist down. It's John's goal to walk by the time he's thirty. It's my goal to become a surgeon within the field of spinal cord injuries to make that happen for him. See, I know now that I'm capable of doing great things."

"Bravo," Alex said.

"I just wanted yall to meet him today. Last month, he spoke to the young people at opening ceremonies. Young people need to know this is *real life*. Bullets don't play. In an instant, a life can be snuffed out or tragically altered. This isn't a video or an urban western happening. It's a real live civil war going on in some communities, and we need to address it. Thanks, John."

"You bet, CJ," John answered, waved his hand, and CJ resumed his speech.

"Truly, it has been an honor speaking to the older group this time around. I'm glad Uncle Madison gave me this beautiful first time opportunity. Young people!" CJ excitedly yelled the two words. "Remember, getting even is succeeding against the odds. It's your responsibility whether you're successful or not; no one else's. Young people! Remain persistent in all your endeavors, and you'll see how your self-discipline will pay off. Young people! Remember that the choices you make decide *your* fate. Nobody else's. Thank you," CJ said quietly and sauntered off the stage.

When CJ finished, he received a resounding round of applause. Several of the parents and guardians stood to also honor him with a standing ovation.

"Carlos Reynolds the Third, you spoke some powerful words today, my brother. Carlos and Pecola, yall should be proud of this young man. I'm proud of him. I saw where he came from. I know the journey he took to get here." The audience clapped again. "One of the things he said stood out, and we tell this to the children all the time. You *gots* to believe in yourself. No matter how bad things look, believe you can achieve it. Also, write it down just like Rico said that his college coach always told him. Until you write it down, it's nothing but a dream. When you write it down, it somehow becomes more concrete. Let's give that young man another round of applause."

Rozelle introduced Jack Drummond and Cosby Upshaw, two young Black males who were excellent violinists. Both graduated from West Forsyth High School in Clemmons, and their parents were members of the Ujima Literary Society. In the fall, Drummond was heading to Simmons University Bible College in Louisville, Kentucky. Cosby was heading to Virginia Seminary & College in Lynchburg, Virginia. As a treat for the children being honored as well as for Madison and Alex, Cleopatra requested that the duo perform *Forever Young* and *You are My Friend*. Those were two of the Devereauxs' very favorite songs. When they were done, Rozelle made his way to the podium clapping and talking as he walked to his place on stage.

"Don't we have a lot of talent? Put your hands together again for these young men. That was great Jack and Cosby. My wife plays the violin, too. Before we go to bed at night, she sometimes plays the violin to relax me after my stressful days at work," Rozelle explained. The audience broke out into applause once more.

"That's wonderful," a guy announced loudly.

"I know, man. I know," Rozelle said and checked his notes.

Chapter Fifty-Nine

"I would like to introduce you to one half of a young rap duo that's making great strides in the rap world. Yall know them as SJ, which stands for Scott Junior. GJ stands for Granville Junior. He was named after Scott's brother. I know they're going to get me for saying that. They like to keep that part of their name a secret, especially since they're a popular rap group. As you can see from all the juniors and the Thirds around here, you can tell we believe in the tradition of not being able to think of new and different names." A few people snickered. "What I like about the Alexander rap guys is these three things. First of all, they graduated from Morehouse. Second, they're Ques. Didn't their father train them well?" Laughter rose from pockets of people throughout the audience. Rozelle held his hands up.

"Let me finish. The third thing I like about these boys is that they sing positive Black rap, and their mouth isn't full of gold teeth. Gold link chains aren't stacked around their necks like huge rolls of spaghetti. Like GJ said, they're not the norm. They're businessmen who happen to be rappers. I'm glad to see they ain't into that gangsta rap where they tell you to shoot this one, that one, and cuss every other word," Rozelle added with a smile. "Ladies and gentlemen, I present to you the oldest brother of the duo. Please put your hands together for Scott Broadus Alexander, Jr. We know him as SJ."

Looking tall, sleek and handsomely attired in a Mecca USA, nautical, preppy outfit, SJ sauntered slowly to the stage and waited for the thunderous applause to end. Like everyone else who spoke before him, he briefly acknowledged both family and friends.

"...Before I go any further," SJ spoke seriously. "I want to let you know that all rap isn't out to destroy your children's mind or to turn their brains into mush. Ok? Rap is a culture. It's not a contrived industry to make your children be disrespectful or to make them curse. That's not what rap is about. That's not what me and my brother rap about. When we make sounds in concerts, we share the truth. We give a little history lesson. We let our fans know that rap is a cultural phenomenon with roots all the way back to the African griot. It certainly embraces the oral tradition of the slaves. During our concerts, we always want to take the time to get into the history of rap and to educate our fans. We also want to let both the youth and the adults this afternoon know that the rap culture is more than meets the eye. It's tradition. It's roots. It's a rich legacy that needs to be recognized as a magnificent contribution to the way we think, move, grove, advertise, and exist."

"You go, go boy."

"Rap music is a way of culture and racial harmony. When I look at television, I see contradictory things about my profession. The political and the supposedly, socially moral critics ridicule the genre of rap music. Yet, I noticed that from Europe to America, the big corporate people use our hip-hop beat to sell malt liquor, beer, telephone services, homes, cars, and designer clothes. Rappers thumping out a smooth beat now sell everything under the sun. I see white kids bobbing their heads to our jams just as quickly as Black kids. In the rap industry, we're aware that our music's rhythm is embraced all over the world, yet they continually squeal that the rap industry is a menace to society." To think, he stopped for a moment.

"But what the critics are saying is yes, it's a menace to society. But business people say it's also an economic boom to society, too. Rap has passed the billion-dollar mark, and now others think it might not be so negative. People are starting to realize that maybe it's an art form, and a lot of money can be earned from it. Closely watch your commercials and see which corporations are using our rap lyrics to pump up the volume of their company sales."

"...Music in general is a healer," SJ was saying five minutes later. "No question about it. Rap is no different. It's an international language that transcends borders. Transcends everything. We have to always remember that music was always a form of expression available to people in bondage. Our Black people, African people—from birth to death. Our music *has* always been a part of Black folks' rhythm of life. Rap is no different. By the same token, we all have to acknowledge the positive force hip-hop has made in the world. Even though white folks and some Black folk, too, act like rap is poison, they damn the industry and act like hip-hop isn't this and hip-hop ain't that. But they still play our sounds from New York to England, in preppy private schools in Boston and Connecticut. Many of their children espouse to be like us—like rap stars. In the suburbs of Arkansas, to the streets of Brooklyn, New York, all cultures are patting their feet to the sweet rap beat."

"Tell the truth, young man." SJ smiled at the older woman's comment.

"In the beginning, the powers that be thought rap was a fluke. A misfit sound. The early critics believed it wouldn't get far. We've proven them wrong. Hip-hop is now a billion dollar industry, in large part to our sisters and brothers throughout urban America and the young people who live in the hood who believed the messages that they projected. Now, I believe it's time for hip-hop artists to work on stopping the violence. There has been a massive campaign to educate our brothers in the community. If this doesn't change—" SJ stated firmly and pointed to his head. "If the mental capacity of a man doesn't change, then no matter what rap stars sing about, no matter what anyone says, young people will continue to remain mentally immersed in what they believe is all that they know. We have to provide alternatives."

"Absolutely," a man yelled out.

"Since the youth of America listens to us, we as Black rap artists need to become advocates for peace and do kudos to promote brotherhood, education, and Black love. That's why me, my brother, and other rap stars out there try to influence our fans to vote. If we can sell two million CDs, that's two million votes especially if those people who buy the CDs are old enough to vote. One-hundred-thousand votes in a state can influence the outcome of an election. It's a rare thing to have a Black senator in this country. If you vote, you can make it happen. We can be a force to sway elections. I say these things in concerts, and I hope young brothers and sisters get the message. But we as rap artists need to be consistent. When we go out on tour, get out there on stage and say MF this and MF that, that's not the message we want to spread. We must speak to each other with respect," SJ said finishing up his speech.

"Run it down, my man."

"I understand what Uncle Rozelle said about the gangsta rap. I really do. Not all rap music is bad. Just like not all rappers are bad, but older people gots to realize that a lot of brothers rap about what they know. Just as artists begin painting on a blank canvas and hope to project what they see. Just as writers create what they know and teachers teach what they've been taught, rappers do the same thing. They rap about the pimping, the shootings, the fast women, the gangs, the thug life, numbers running, doping, and the street life. That's what they know. It's a reflection of their reality that takes place in the streets every day. To them, there's a war going on out there. Sure parents, teachers, and politicians want to hear the positive and good news across the airwaves, but that's not what's going down on certain streets in America. I don't think it's any different from all the negative propaganda the six o'clock news blasts across the screen night after night after night. Instead of the newscasters rapping it out to a beat, they simply share the gory happenings in business suits, silk ties, Johnny Bull shoes, and polished voices. What's the difference? It's no different from what the rap stars shout about on their tracks."

"Tell the truth, SJ," exclaimed Booker T.

"Just stop it. Don't downgrade our young people's language and their expressions. Our young Blacks speak their own language. The way we rap *is* in their language. Our grooving and moving is nothing but a language in itself. The same way a man from North Carolina struggles to understand a Spanish-speaking person who just arrived in Winston-Salem from Puerto Rico, why not make an effort to understand the language and culture of a lot of the young Black people? If they're understood better, maybe that would be the beginning blocks to building a bond of understanding with our parents, teachers, older people in this country, and around the world. I think adults gots to have more respect for young people. I believe they need to take time to learn about them, too. If older people do that, they'll learn that a lot of our young people are mature and very determined to do the right thing." SJ smiled before he continued.

"C'mon with it, my man."

Before SJ resumed his talk, he grinned and slowly rubbed his chin. "You know when my Pop initially asked me and my brother to help out, we said sure. But my brother and I wanted to see how this program was going to go down. Last summer when we came to do our part, we didn't speak. We didn't want to. We decided we wanted to check everything out first. Remember, man?" SJ asked his brother, who quickly nodded yes. "So we kept our eyes and ears open to see how the Devereauxs and their friends would deal with young people. Keep in mind we knew they were all good people. Our father made sure that we've been around them a lot, but we still wanted to make sure. We got a reputation to uphold. You know what I'm saying?" The audience laughed.

"The Devereauxs are real. They're all the way live real. Everyone else that's affiliated with them appeared truly concerned and committed to do a little something to make an impact. My brother and I decided this would be one of the projects around the country that we would step up to help with. Last month, GJ spoke. This month, it was my turn." Clapping erupted throughout the tent. "All I'm saying to the adults today is to puhleeze learn about our youth. There's a lot of pressure out there. The kind of pressures that can cause a child to make bad decisions that can cost him his life."

"Tell the truth, young man," a woman exclaimed, and SJ smiled quickly.

"There's a method to the madness of rap. It's a glorious tradition of song and words that has been ingrained in us since our days in Africa. Remember that. So the next time you're dancing around at a party, and you hear a familiar rap beat blasting out of the box, remember rap is deep. Rap is rich. Rap is you. Rap is your children and their way of emptying their souls. It's giving them a voice—even if you don't want to hear what they're saying." Once more, there was thunderous applause.

"To my parents who are my nurturers, I certainly do thank you. They taught me how to be a man and gave me my wings to fly." SJ stared into his father's face. Scott returned the look while Charmaine patted his thigh. "On behalf of my brother and myself, we want to let you know we love ya, Pop. I tell my Pop that I love him because I do. He was very influential with the direction we took with music. My brother and I were raised on the vibrant sounds of music. Every time we turned around, our Pop was always playing the piano for us. My father turned me and my brother onto everything from Billie Holiday to Socrates. He also told me, 'I don't care what you want to do, son. *You'll* get your education.' My pop ain't changing regarding that issue." A smattering of clapping began again. "What's going on out here is real. Peace and love." SJ spoke softly, blew a kiss between two fingers, and exited the stage. The audience clapped vigorously. Some of the young people whistled and gave SJ a standing ovation. Rozelle walked up to the podium.

"Don't you love the intelligence of that young man? He certainly squashes the stereotypical view about rap singers. This young man and his brother certainly are focused about their family, careers, and their desire to do worthwhile work with children. I like the way he acknowledged how his mother and father were always there guiding them to make the right choices. They always pushed them to achieve their dreams but didn't squelch their creativity. Even though their parents thought their dreams of a rap career were a little too big and wild, they didn't suffocate them with their own ambitions for their lives. They allowed those boys to be who they wanted to be. Didn't he give yall a different view of rappers?" It seemed as if the entire audience nodded their heads yes. "Good! That's why you cannot believe everything you hear in the news. There are a lot of family-oriented and business-minded people in the rap world. The media never showcases those individuals, though. They concentrate on the negative in the business," Rozelle exclaimed to SJ as he shrugged casually.

"Like my Grandma Zula used to always say, "There are three versions to every story you hear. That applies to whether it's on the news or if you hear it from a friend. There's your version. The other person's version. And, the truth." The crowd laughed to acknowledge what he said was true. "You're a bright, intelligent young man whose success is unlimited, SJ."

"Say it well, Rozelle," Romallus said as he clapped along with everyone else.

"Investigate your musical heritage. You *ought* to tap into other than what's playing on the popular radio stations. Try swing, jazz, or classical music. Even try to understand rap. Stretch your musical horizons." Clapping erupted again.

"Ladies and gentlemen, we've another sports celebrity in our midst at this time. His name is Christopher Perry. Knowing the Devereauxs gives me a chance to mingle with people other folks only see on television. That's a nice friendly, fringe benefit, if I must say so myself," Rozelle said with a half smile as the audience broke out into laughter. "Ladies, gentlemen and all our young people here, let's show love to Mr. Perry. He's a professional in every sense of the word and especially in the National Basketball League."

"Thank you, Rozelle," Christopher exclaimed as he gave Rozelle the Black power handshake, a quick hug, and a fast pat on the back. Rozelle relinquished the podium to Christopher and went back to his seat on stage.

"Last year when Marlon asked me if I was interested in coming to speak, I said I didn't know what my schedule looked like. After coming last year when I wasn't a speaker and after seeing the children at the Devereauxs' throughout the year, there was no way I was going to miss these opening ceremonies this summer. I was here last month, and here I am again. Believe me. The camaraderie and love here are contagious." There was another round of applause.

"After my mother died from a diabetic coma when I was seven, I was raised by my father and grandmother who lived with us. My father was killed when I was eleven, and my grandmother who inspired me and told me to dream and never lose sight of my goals raised me. We didn't have a lot of money either, and we lived in a small shack in the poor Black community, which was considered the wrong side of the tracks in Beaufort, North Carolina. Because my grandmother raised me with love, discipline, and determination, I never knew we were on the wrong side—didn't know we lived in the wrong neighborhood. Our so-called "shack" was a warm and loving home. Even though she didn't have much, she always believed that Blacks were simply wonderful people who were just as intelligent and equal to anyone else. I didn't realize I lived on the wrong side of the tracks until I was in junior high school. Then I became ashamed of who I was and where I lived. But my Granny told me to remember who I am and to remember my dreams." With these words, Christopher pounded his chest.

"My granny told me that I was a Black man who inherited his strength from my family and our history. She told me not to let anybody tell me what I could not do. If they did, I was to work harder and longer to prove them wrong. Even though we were poor in terms of having money, my granny had wisdom and joy. She raised me from an early age to be a man."

"You're on it, man," an older gentleman said.

"Some of us have lived in poor sections and still live in the projects. Because of the color of our skin and the rough life we survive from day to day, we've been told not to dream. A lot of times, poverty doesn't let you dream. How are you going to dream about seeing the Mona Lisa at the Louvre in Paris if you don't know it's there or if you haven't been taught its significance?" Christopher paused to give room to the applause that followed words that touched everyone.

"Preach, young man."

"But remember this." His voice was even, deliberate, sincere, and strong. "No matter who you are or where you live, share your dreams with other people."

"Say so!"

"From the time I was a young boy, I told my Granny and everyone else I was going to play in the NBL. It actually happened. By talking about your dream, it gets out of your head. It comes into fruition. Also realize that any dream takes planning, too. You gots to devise a plan of little steps to make it happen. With hard work, dedication, and a little luck, you can make it a reality."

"Beautiful words, young man."

"When I go back home to Beaufort, I visit the old neighborhood. I tell the young people the same thing. Like my Granny, Alex always told me to go back. Always remember your start. Your roots." His hand went to his heart as he paused to let his point sink in. "Too many of us try hard to forget our roots. Some of us hate ourselves so much that we change our skin color. We bleach it white. To lose your roots is a death of the true self."

"I'll never forget the time we were floating on the tranquil waters of Wakaya in a huge yacht we chartered for two weeks. It was nothing but a whole bunch of successful, wealthy, Black folks having a good time. On several occasions during that trip, I had to look around and pinch myself to make me realize I was there in the midst of it, too. Me. Christopher Perry from little Beaufort, North Carolina, was sailing in the South Pacific. It was right after I met Marlon, and it was the first trip with my wife. This absolutely breathtaking and glorious rainbow suddenly mesmerized all of us on the yacht. The beauty closed everybody's mouth out of respect for nature's magnificent beauty."

"It did."

"While the yacht was gliding along afterwards, Alex spoke to me. She said that if I'm fortunate enough and blessed enough to visit places such as this, it's only right and good to go back to visit the places that still whisper childhood memories. Only then can you truly appreciate where you've come from, to know why, to know how you were able to experience so much of God's big world. The many things people only dream of."

"Wonderful. Absolutely wonderful."

"When I step into the old neighborhood, I remember my past. The good times, the fun, the love and the struggles. It's a good grounding point for me. It's reminds me of what I had to do to get to where I am today. I tell those kids in the neighborhood that every day they must learn to overcome obstacles. It's a daily routine. Each day you get out of bed, the day begins with obstacles that you gots to work on overcoming. For the people who are here today, you know that you're smart enough to see the obstacles that are in your life. You know what you need to do to work on going around them and jumping over them."

When Christopher spoke those words, Symone's thoughts were poignantly bittersweet as she remembered her childhood.

"Speak on, young man," someone said.

"Be a master planner. Mentally know that you're the pilot of your whole existence in life. I believe there are two definite in the world. The day you're born and the date you're gonna die. Those are the only two definites that I believe in. What you do in between those two times in your life is totally up to you. Only *you* can determine which doors you're going to open or close in your life."

"When you plan, be selective about who you choose as friends, young people. It's not how many friends you make. It's how many friends you keep. When you're approached with peer pressure, ask yourself what's more important? If all my friends like me *or* if I like myself? Don't follow the crowd and do things you don't want to do. Always listen to your quiet voice. Your conscience as my granny called it. I still rely on those words even now as a player in the NBL where temptation is an everyday thing. Each and every time you need to make a decision, just stop. Be still and listen to what your quiet voice says."

Christopher spoke for approximately two more minutes. As he was closing his speech, he decided he wanted to say a few words about Marlon. His inspiration. A concerned Christopher knew Marlon's knees were hurting him. He wanted his words to embrace him and make Marlon forget about the pain, if only for a moment.

"...I've had the opportunity to walk with my other hero, Marlon Dinzelle. Without a doubt, I'm sooo honored to know him. He has the unique and rare combination of ferocious drive, humility, and awesome love for family and friends. To have that kind of humility is unusual. That's very rare, especially when you're a highly talented and taunted superstar. I've never publicly heard Marlon brag about his ball playing abilities, but he does have a mean tongue around his friends about what he can physically do to you."

"He does," Booker T agreed.

"For me, Marlon Dinzelle was the standard by which basketball excellence was measured. He was the standard for being genuine with his family and being kind to his fans. He was my role model and dear friend. Each day I'm with him and he runs into adoring people, it's remarkable how much he still appreciates his fans. He graciously signs autographs all the time. It's obvious his fans realize it too because they still show him tremendous love. I believe it's because he signs their autographs without fail and acts as if he never tired of signing them or gets tired of their admiration of him."

As Christopher spoke the kind words about Marlon, Nanette gently massaged her husband's right thigh. Marlon's eyes filled up with water and sparkled bright with humility and pride.

"Marlon always speaks with the mind of a champion. He still has the goal and spirit of a champion. As my mentor, I hope I can only poise myself to join you as well as the other legends in pro basketball," Christopher said the last few words, and his eyes locked on Cleopatra's face. With legs crossed at the knees and sitting absolutely erect, Cleopatra assumed he was looking at someone behind her. She grinned easily at his words anyway. Along with the rest of the crowd, she was thoroughly absorbed with his speech.

Christopher gave the peace sign to the audience and spoke softly. "When you have goals, continue to do what people tell you that you can't do. To the twenty-eight young people being honored this afternoon, I want you to give your dreams everything you have and never believe you cannot achieve them. Your success lies in your determination. I thank you for this opportunity." The crowd clapped wildly and gave Christopher a standing ovation.

Rozelle came to the podium with a smile on his face. "Thanks, Christopher. I'm telling you. This opening ceremony is just getting better and better." Joyous affirmations were heard from the crowd.

"Next on the scheduled list of speakers is my man, Scott Alexander."

"That's fine, man."

"Scott takes his pilot work at Northworld Airlines very seriously. But he doesn't take himself seriously even though he tries to act like he does. His friends know that it's a front because everyone knows. I mean *everybody* realizes that Scott believes in standing by his friends. He's the type of person that has your back, your front, and your side. He's just there whenever you need him," Rozelle introduced his close friend with a flair. "Ladies and gentlemen, I gladly introduce my good buddy for over twenty years. At the "House," we shared the same dorm together. We even went on line together. I clear the way for the one and only Scott Broadus Alexander. He's Mr. Cool. Mr. Collected. Like Jerry Butler, one of his favorite crooners, he's a debonair man. He's the Iceman himself. My man doesn't sing as smooth as Mr. Jerry Butler, but he sure as heck plays the piano just as nice."

"Good afternoon, everyone," Scott said once he was settled in front of the podium. Dressed in a conservative Shaka King black suit with a white Nehru shirt and gold cuff links, Scott was handsome and fearless. Like the other speakers, Scott spoke glowingly about his family, sons, and friends. Of course, he gave Charmaine a special acknowledgment. She beamed at the glittering words of praise for her.

"It's certainly an honor to speak before you about goals, family, and tradition. I'm proud to discuss my accomplishments, my antidote for success. My exceedingly strong ties to family and friends. The reasons why my family, the Alexander family, has succeeded and why you have to do what you believe in."

"Run it down, Scott," Romallus instructed his brother.

"I had a wonderful childhood. A great childhood. It was almost idyllic. But as I got older, I realized that everyone didn't have parents like mine. My parents talked to me and instilled a strong, work ethnic in my three brothers and me. My Pop always told us to never tell a lie but to always do your best at every task set before you. There were certain responsibilities we were required to fulfill. We had to make our beds every morning before we left to go to school, and we had to do all the chores around the house. I learned responsibilities and how to organize my life so that I can enjoy my life. My mother only had a sixth grade education, but she always checked our homework as if she had graduated with a Ph.D. Her philosophy was that whatever task you have before you, just do it with all your heart and soul. Take the next step and repeat the process all over again." Romallus nodded with understanding.

"My mother as well as my father taught us all to love family and to be there for family. Early on, my father often used to share slave stories with me and my brothers that had been shared with him. Pop said that history was an excellent map for living, especially the history of slavery. He explained that many times, slaves were told by their owners that they were going to put them in their pockets. What they meant is that if they continued to act the way that the white slave owners didn't like, they would be sold, and the money would be placed in the white owner's pockets.

"Lawd have mercy," moaned a young church going woman.

"When we were forced to be slaves and when the slave man had a child, the master sold the father to another plantation to break up the bonds of attachment. It was a specific Willie Lynch philosophy implemented to destroy the family and to sever the bonding ties. The slaveowner wanted walking Mandingos who had no attachments and no thinking abilities. But you cannot stop a mother's love for her child, a man's love for his woman, or the love of friends." He paused to look at Charmaine. "The master couldn't drain the love out of our hearts or the strength out of our souls. The slaveowners simply wanted broken men and women. Read the Black Arcade Liberation Library's piece entitled *Let's Make a Slave*. It'll make you drop your head with grief about the stinking, rotten truth of slavery. What your ancestors endured so that you can sit in midst of beauty and be at the home of wealthy blacks who parade before you other successful blacks."

"Lawd have mercy," moaned one of the senior citizens.

"You'll understand what I'm saying. Because of the poison of slavery, many Black men never had a chance to raise their children since this detachment thinking was transmitted from generation to generation. My job with the children is to show them the beauty of parental nurturing and of fatherly nurturing. I love to see men cuddle and hug their children. Watching Black men love and nurture their children is like watching a flower bloom in the dead of winter. It's a wonderful sight. Many men think that it's unmanly to show love. Several of the children here have told us that they've never, ever had their father visit them for their birthday, for Christmas, for Thanksgiving, or for any time at all. Some have even told us they don't know who their parents are."

"Umph, umph, umph," an older woman moaned.

"We, therefore, believe it's the mission of the men who work within the Devereauxs' program to show our young boys and girls that we're real. We want to let them know we love them, and we're here for them. That we're proud of them and want to be that missing father, mother, aunt, or uncle."

"Share the truth, my brother," Booker T encouraged.

"For over three hundred years, Black people were owned as slaves in this country. Because slaves' families were constantly disrupted, many negative parental habits have flourished from those years of bondage. We know unequivocally that all Black men aren't that way. Many Black men have been taught to respect family and children above all others. We've been taught to do our part as diligent fathers. True, I was lucky. My father often spoke to us in such simple ways. He wanted to give us an understanding of the struggle our race has had in this country. During slavery, the Black family was destroyed, separated, and sold like live-stock. We lost ties regarding family, and we lost ties regarding our ancestors' powerful history. Booker T and Symone always say, 'Slavery was the Black folk's holocaust. Our holocaust was ten times worst than the European holocaust could ever be. But we don't hear about *that* holocaust. But the Jewish holocaust is what everyone reads and continues to make movies about.'"

"Say so, young man," a woman exclaimed.

"And the financial, economical, and racial destruction that Black folks continue to inflict upon ourselves is the continuation of our holocaust's mutilation of ties, faithfulness, honesty, and success toward each other." The audience exploded in agreeing applause. Scott paused briefly and turned another page.

"I know a lot of you are saying that slavery is in the past. That it was sooo long ago. That it's not relevant anymore. But it is. It's an education about *your* history. Learn it, and think for yourselves. Recognize that slavery was like an oil spill in the ocean. When the oil spill happens, the proper authorities will try their best to save the affected environment. Most times they do, and the ocean waves can once again explode upon the shore without a trace of oil. Yet, the damage has already been done with the wildlife that's even below the surface."

"Say so."

"Although the sea creatures, seals, and fish swim below the surface and survive the violation of their environment, deep down inside they really haven't. We've seen cases where the oil company clean up crew attempts to towel off the oil-covered fish and birds. But it's not enough. Many of these creatures have been injured and have long range effects. The wildlife has already inhaled the filthy oil. Those creatures might die a few months later and eventually wash upon the sandy shore. Their bodies bobbing upon the sea with lifeless eyes. The truth of the matter is the oil was still in their system. I equate slavery to that."

"Umph. Umph. Umph."

"The Thirteenth Amendment supposedly freed the slaves decades ago. However, the pollution of slavery continues to rear its ugly head in a very subtle, far reaching way. It's in ways we as a people can't even begin to fathom. I'm not making excuses for our people when I say Willie Lynch thinking is prevalent in our world today. It's a reality. When we as a people begin to recognize these tendencies, I believe hope begins. My greatest hope is that we'll see the resiliency of Black folk and change some of these pitiful attitudes."

"Speak the truth."

"If Black folks endorse the teachings of Dr. Claud Anderson's *Powernomics* and if we follow the strategies he outlined in his book, we as a people will bond more in the next few years. We'll bond economically and financially to make changes in our communities throughout this country."

"Tell it."

"We'll realize that we're a strong race of people capable of achieving all goals—in our homes and in communities. If we make changes in the communities that need it, we can make positive changes in the world. We can make economic changes and make investment changes." Many heads nodded positively to his words.

"Today, the Devereauxs and their friends have joined hands to fight the human war of disparity and hopelessness. The war of our troubled youth. There's a brutal war going on out there on the streets of urban America, ladies and gentlemen. There's a battle out there where young Black children are killing other children. Pent up anger and frustrations are destroying them. The Devereauxs and their friends have waged a war to save our young people. It's time out for playing. Time out for looking at the evening news shaking our heads at our troubled Black children like they're lost causes or an embarrassment. We need to arm ourselves and prepare for this tough battle so that we in later years won't have to look back and admit to ourselves that we did nothing. '*I* was one of the ones who let the next generation, our youth, down. *I* saw the despair, yet *I* did nothing to change or help one child.' Who wants to move to old age with anguished thoughts like that?"

"Tell the truth," a woman yelled out and began clapping which precipitated a hearty round of applause from the crowd.

"From the time I was a small boy, my Mama and my Pop said that a Black man has to work twice as hard to get half the recognition that he deserves. I stashed that information inside my soul. I never forgot it. I always used it. My parents were right. *Absolutely right.* As a pilot for Northworld Airlines, some folks say I've made it. But check this out. Even with my bars on my shoulders, people still mistake me for a skycap. They constantly ask me to check their bags and carry their dog bins. Can yall believe that? And I could be the one to fly the plane they're riding in. Their lives are in my big, Black hands."

"Tell the truth, young man."

"As a pilot at Northworld Airlines, there are approximately forty-five hundred other pilots. Guess how many are Black?" The crowd was quiet and waiting on his answer.

"Two hundred," a woman responded.

"Madam, you're not that far off because it's right around ten percent. Less than four hundred and fifty pilots in an organization that sends off thousands of flights a day. I'm one of the lucky ones. Why? It's certainly not because Black men aren't qualified to become pilots. It's the lack of opportunity, people. It's not going to get any better. They just voted out affirmative action." The crowd mumbled in agreement. "Sometimes, it's difficult for us to break through subtle barriers for opportunities, and we don't receive those jobs that we're capable of receiving. White folks aren't letting Blacks in certain circles of corporate America. We need to know this is a fact of life. This is nothing new, yet the way we deal with it must be changed. We can't wait on corporate America to give us our just due. That's not going to happen."

"So true," Pauletta nodded.

"We can't continue to act like victims regarding our jobs, our communities, and our families. It's time for us to peer within ourselves to broaden the economic base of communities and to make them strong and powerful. We must ensure that our children, the future of our race, are directed onto a path that's prosperous and effective. We must work to ensure that our families are loving, concerned, and educated. This can only be done if we walk upon the battleground for our youth. Fight for them. Fight for better schools, for a better way of living, for a better life, and for better families. We must make our young people know that the only way they can receive their just due in this society is through excelling in academics and through our controlling our own economic bases throughout the country. Economic power. Green power. Spending power. Investment power. So if we're waiting around for a savior, we must let them know that *we* have the power to save ourselves, our communities, and our families."

"Amen," Pauletta declared. Immediately, she turned to Pecola and commented once more how she thought Scott was not only smart, but he was fine as all get out.

"I admire all the young people we work with. I certainly do. Sometimes, yall have come up to me and told me that it's hard being young. When I ask you why, you always say it's because some older person is always telling you what to do. Guess what? It doesn't change when you get older. People will always be telling you what to do whether you're in school, in college, at work, or even if you're an entrepreneur. I'm forty-two years old, and I'm still being told what to do by my managers at Northworld Airlines. It applies to everybody. Even the president of these said United States is being told what to do."

"So true, young man," an older man said, clapping all by himself.

"Don't ever take shortcuts. Take the harder less traveled road and do it with determination, tremendous energy, and spirit. Like Marva Collins, the founder of Westside Preparatory School in Chicago, said one time, 'Your I will is more important than your IQ.' In other words, your determination is your key to success and change. When you have a dream, go for it. Tell yourself these words: 'This is my heart, and this is my dream. Nothing else on earth will keep me from achieving success. I *will* allow no one to steal it. No one. Nothing at all.'"

"Absolutely," the same older man said. This time, the crowd clapped.

"If you continue to think that way, you'll protect your mind from anything that's not powerful to your advancement of the goal. You'll only develop positive mental images. Always visualize yourself as a community activist, a doctor, a judge, a lawyer, a millionaire, an entrepreneur, or a professional athlete. Cut out magazine pictures of your chosen careers and paste it in a book. Write your dreams down. Let that be your goal book. Look at it every day. Visualize yourself in the life you want to have, then go do it." The crowd clapped with excitement.

"As adults, yall know how it is. We're constantly searching for meaning, freedom, and love. We're hoping that the children will find that by working with the Devereauxs' program, they'll find a little piece of that, too. It has been a joy for me to work with all the honorees tonight. To travel with them and to take them places. I'll always remember these days. When I lived in Houston, I was involved with a variety of organizations that worked with young people. However, working with the Devereauxs has given me the opportunity to be in on the planning sessions to discuss what I believe is needed by our youth today. Another good thing about this program is this. In addition to adults being on the various committees, youngsters from the four public housing communities are on them, too. There is selflessness about the Devereauxs, which translates to an unabashed commitment to help others. Out here, their home is such a magical place to visit. Madison and Alex, I thank you for the privilege of even being here in the midst. To my twenty-eight buddies, remember these words my father burned into my mind: 'Never, never, never, never, never, never give up," Scott ended in a firm voice that wrapped around the crowd, and he headed toward his seat.

The audience broke out in a jubilant roar of applause, and Rozelle went to the podium in smiles. "I'm honored to call Scott my friend. You know what they say about us House men. 'You can always tell a Morehouse Man, but you just can't tell him much!'"

Scott sat back down beside Charmaine and waved a hand at his friend. Since Charmaine was so proud of Scott's eloquent speech, she quickly hugged his neck then tenderly kissed him on the lips.

It was time for Rozelle to introduce Marlon, and Rozelle wanted to be careful with his words. Alex had told him he was having a hard time dealing with his injury today. She believed that as a result of the rain, Marlon's knees were hurting, and he was feeling quite despondent. At one point, he even told Alex he didn't feel like speaking. After she spoke with him, she convinced him to change his mind. When the clapping died down from the funny joke Rozelle shared, he walked back to the podium.

"Ladies, gentlemen, honored guests, and children, I would like to introduce a man who has been a powerful force in the game of basketball. Christopher Perry hinted about his greatness. Many who know the game said that he was the best player that has ever lived, and his accolades are destined to find a resting place in the Hall of Fame. With a Michelangelo body fashioned just like mine," Rozelle joked as he flexed his arm muscles to the left and to the right. The audience snickered. "Marlon has done it all. The Olympics, NBL championships, all-star games, most valuable player, and lucrative endorsements. He was a man who defied gravity every time he stepped on the court. Aw, man. I could go on and on. Before he retired, he had the highest career scoring average in the history of basketball. He was an awesome, formidable opponent whenever he stepped out on the court for whoever guarded him."

"You know it," Booker T exclaimed.

"He's a truly giving man who takes his friends on the best vacations." Rozelle hesitated momentarily. With closed hands in front of his face, he acted as if he was praying while he glared into the heavens. "And I'm so happy Marlon considers me his friend." The crowd roared with laughter and began to clap.

"All jokes aside. Marlon is my buddy and a dear, dear friend whom I love." Rozelle paused, wanting to be careful how he phrased his words. "Marlon knows adversity, and he knows how to transcend it, too. He knows. He exemplifies strength. Ladies and gentlemen, I can go and on, but I'm not. Without any further adieu, I'm proud to introduce a mega superstar. A talented Black man who was blessed by God to share his talent with the world. He's my friend. My brother, and my inspiration. Mr. Marlon Dinzel-l-l-l-l-le! I proudly bring to you, "MAD DOG!""

"Woo! Woo!" BJ whistled and pumped his hands in the air. The crowd erupted into a volcanic burst of applause. Because of his notoriety in the world of sports, they honored Marlon with a thunderous standing ovation. Marlon stood slowly, carefully and was praying he could walk to the podium without limping. Nanette told Marlon he needed to rest. That he needed to cancel his speech this month, especially since he did his part last month. But Marlon couldn't and wouldn't do that. He made a commitment. The children were expecting him to speak. That's exactly what he was going to do since giving up easily wasn't a part of his nature.

From the damp, hot humid air and all the dancing he did last night, Marlon's knees were throbbing like crazy once more. When they hurt in such a way, it was sometimes even difficult for him to walk with the aid of crutches. Marlon hated he had to use the crutches earlier, but this afternoon was different. He was determined to not use them in front of the opening crowd.

"We love you, Marlon," were the words different people in the crowd gave to Marlon as they saw him walk slowly up to the podium. Nanette wiped the beginning of tears from the corner of her eyes. Alex held her sister's hand tightly.

Marlon smiled at the remarks that seemed to lessen the pain that was shooting through his legs. The words gave him a surge of inner strength. Very slowly, he made it to the podium. Several people began snapping pictures like crazy, and lightning rods of camera bulb flashes lit up the tent. The clapping ended five minutes after he stood before them. When the moving, standing ovation ceased, after the whistling sounds and the shouting voices were silent, everyone sat down. The audience then slipped into a revered quietness and waited anxiously to hear every word one of the greatest basketball players of all time had to say.

"Thank you. Thank you," Marlon said in an appreciative voice. "Thank you so very much," he repeated softly. Marlon was inspired yet also saddened by the audience's display of love for him. In the back of his mind, he believed they felt sorry about his injury and noticed how he limped to the podium. He took a deep breath and began to speak. Very quickly, he acknowledged Nanette, their twins, the Devereauxs, his other family members and friends in attendance. He recognized his mother. The beautiful and young-looking Larryetta Pamela Dinzelle of Greensboro was the way Marlon always described his mother, too. For the next three minutes or so, he discussed his life as a young AAU player up until the time he went off to North Carolina University.

"...I always believed that playing basketball was about life." He paused briefly. "You know why? Because at sometime or another, you were always behind in various goals you set for yourself. Years ago, when I started playing high school ball, AAU ball, and even college ball, we weren't always rated number one. Many times our team would go somewhere, and we were behind already even before we got there. We were the considered the underdogs. In college, we were always trying to defeat teams that were rated nationally higher than we were. So you learn early on how to motivate each other when you're down."

"Absolutely," Booker T said. Marlon laughed and glanced back down at his notes.

"That why I often say life is like a basketball game. You have to catch up one play at a time. Live life one day at a time. Each *play* makes a difference. Each *day* makes a difference. That's why many teams aren't successful. They can't think mentally or can't function under pressure. That's the same reason why kids mess up in life. They don't think for themselves, either. They follow the crowd and get in trouble. Sports make you think all the time. Your mind is always clicking. That's why I tell the young people I speak with that you learn a lot about life through playing basketball and through sports in general. Consider this—"

"Run it down, Marlon," a proud Booker T encouraged.

"Basketball is a team sport. It's the type of sport that teaches you about dealing with people and with the way they think about politics, attitudes, and egos. It helps instill in you a competitive factor. Life is competitive, and competing in sports will give you a little edge. That's why I encourage young people to get involved in all levels of sports. But we like to always remind the kids around here one thing. Even though your goal is to be a professional player, always keep your academic goals foremost in mind." Another healthy round of boisterous applause erupted.

"We love you, Marlon," said a lady. Her voice was filled with emotion.

"Love you, man," a male voice said matter-of-factly.

"In college, I majored in business administration and psychology. Booker T made me consider those two majors. My uncle literally twisted my arm to lean toward the business classes, but I was interested in psychology. I wanted to understand the minds of people. The ones I had to deal with and how I was supposed to deal with them. Not only on the basketball courts but throughout day to day life in general."

"My Uncle Booker T was one of the best guards in the world. The best the pros ever drafted." Marlon spoke with genuine affection. "True, I learned a lot from my coaches. But from the very beginning, I learned the most from a Black man—my uncle. Booker T was there. That's who raised me with a level head. Who taught me with the basics? I learned the game of life and basketball from my uncle. Booker T taught me how to always know where everybody was on the court. So all during my younger days, my goal was to beat my uncle who was bigger and more experienced than me. He "used and abused" me on the basketball court. I hated to check him and hated to play him cause I knew he would beat me and embarrass me with his finesse in the process."

"Tell the truth, son," Booker T said.

"Guess what? My motivation was to believe in my talent and in my ability to beat him. It taught me a lot about myself. It taught me to never allow someone to keep messing and messing and messing with your game and not learn from it. When that happens and if you're not careful, you allow people to win two games. The head game and the game you play on the court. Well, the same applies with life. Don't let people try to get inside your head and program you for failure. Learn, watch, work like hell, practice, learn some more, and grow. My natural born talent and my determination eventually made me better. I got better than my uncle, a whole lot better," Marlon bragged with a wide smile.

Booker T openly shook his head no for everyone to see. His smile was one of pride for his nephew. Marlon's mother glanced around at a grinning Booker T. Larryetta winked at Booker T, who smiled and winked back at his sister-in-law.

"My uncle was always there motivating me. He did that all through my career. He had such a high standard of excellence for my cousins and for me. He would always say, 'I love you, Marlon man. That's why I'm telling you the truth.' His words weren't always that pretty. That's what he always said to his children, to me, my sister, and my brothers. He always instilled in me to be the hunter and not the hunted in the game of sports."

"I realized that I was a role model for some of you and for other children and adults around the world. Whether I wanted the responsibility or not, that's what I was. And that's what I still am," Marlon continued quietly as he swiftly reflected on the freak accident that always persecuted his mind. It always haunted him.

"Tell the truth, man." There was another small round of clapping.

"Role models. That's another issue that gets a lot of press and deservedly so. But people and children need to be more selective about who they choose as a role model. It's a precarious position to be in. When so many expect you to be a certain way," he continued and thought *you need to be picky with me, too*. However, he spoke calmly and from his heart.

"After my accident, I have another aspect of Marlon Dinzelle to offer as a role model. I now have another perspective about life and sports. I want to be known for my intelligence and my work with children. My father was five years older than I was when he died. He was dead at the age of thirty-seven from too much work, too much pain, and a lot of disappointment. Just five years older than me," Marlon said sadly and paused for a minute.

What is Marlon getting at? Nanette thought with concern. *He seems to be rambling now. This isn't like my husband. He didn't do this in last month's speech.*

"After the accident, I learned a lot about myself. Without question, surviving the accident gave me a new challenge. That challenge seemed to be too big for me. I felt like I'd rather not even deal with it. When you're a professional athlete, you think you're invincible, and your career will last forever. You read about life-altering things happening to people but not to anyone that you know. I had never thought about ever being without my three college buddies for any period of time. It's hard, man. It was a gut check of unparalleled proportions." As the audience listened to Marlon, there was a stunned silence throughout the tent.

"When you're on top of your career one day and down on your back the next, it's brutal. This isn't something that time can ever heal or ever remove from your soul. I know that part of being a champion is dealing with all the failures and the successes that comes along. Words that I know can't describe this type of struggle. It can only be described through tears," he explained hesitantly as water fell from his eyes and slowly rolled down his face.

The audience was in shock. There was silence and confusion. The guests became very sympathetic and were immediately swept up in his sadness. Marlon pulled out his handkerchief and wiped his eyes. Larryetta began praying for her son. Several people throughout the crowd were crying, too. The others remained totally stunned by the display of open emotions from the former superstar ball player.

"I had always heard that a part of success is always worrying if it's going to end. I never thought about success like that. Yet, I've learned other lessons. It was unfortunate how I had to learn what I've learned. It was through a personal tragedy that changed my life and changed who I thought I was. I realized that this was a country that would try to tear down heroes as fast as they could build them up with the false lies in the newspaper and on the television," Marlon said quietly and wondered why he was revealing his pain to the audience. Why was he, Marlon Dinzelle, being emotional in front of all these people? Normally, he tried to be stoic about the accident—other than in the privacy of friends. Now he felt naked. Exposed. He hoped the tears wouldn't overshadow the impact of the words he had planned to say.

This isn't like my husband, Nanette thought again. Wondering what to do, she began to nervously glance at Alex and Madison.

"The media tried to blame the car accident on something other than what it was. But I'm here to tell you that it was nothing more than a freak accident. I've stood my ground. I'm standing strong. As long as I have breath in my body, the press will not tarnish the memories of my three friends. Steve, Alfonso, and Lawrence were my teammates, my brothers, and like my blood." Marlon moved his fist to his heart.

"Share your love, Marlon baby," Larryetta encouraged her son, and Marlon tried to grin at his mother.

"With renewed determination, I plan to work hard to keep their vision to help youth in the urban communities around this country a reality. Their dedication a burning light. Their vision of love is a continuation of how they showered their all and all on The SLAM Foundation," he continued in an unmistakably clear and stronger voice. "Young people, remember to always have light in your life and in your mind. Know that everyone who walks upon this earth has a purpose. Sometimes their purposes might be short-lived, but they fulfilled their destiny. Hold hard to your purposes, to your dreams, and don't release them until those purposes are fulfilled."

"We still love you, Marlon," an unidentified young man yelled out. Marlon acknowledged the statement with a slight nod.

"When I left the game of basketball, I believed that I was one of the best that ever played the game. That hasn't changed. Now I hope my life, my career, and my accident will give you the determination to know that you can be the best you want to be. Even with the type of tragedy I've had to experience in life, you can still survive and even triumph. Don't worry. I'm not bitter about the past. I'm just a little wiser. Learn from your past and keep pushing. Like Booker T's favorite man Curtis Mayfield used to say, *We're Moving on Up.*

"Tell it, Marlon," Alex said.

"Young people, I want you to enjoy your two weeks out here in Advance, baby. I know I will with you. Thank you."

When Marlon completed his speech, a quiet Rozelle walked to the stand and remain silent as he acknowledged the heartfelt standing ovation the crowd presented to Marlon. There was a great deal of emotion traveling throughout the tent, and Rozelle wanted everyone to bask in it for a few moments. Larryetta was softly crying for her son.

"I know. There's nothing I can add to that," Rozelle said softly. "That's why he remains an icon, not only in basketball, but in the entire world." The clapping continued.

Once the audience was done with their recognition of Marlon, Rozelle introduced Charmaine. She was originally scheduled to provide a speech on African dancing as well as a dance routine just as she did for last month's opening ceremonies for the younger children. At the barbecue last night, she asked Alex and Madison if she could instead dance for the crowd and eliminate the speech. The Devereauxs said that the change was fine with them.

In the background, DJ Cool Breeze played the sounds of Bette Midler singing *Wind Beneath My Wings* that faded into John Lennon singing *Imagine.* The audience became captivated with the beauty of the flowing movements of the dancers. Charmaine, Tiffany, and one of Charmaine's top dancing students glided effortlessly around the stage as they performed a beautiful interpretative dance to the two poignant and meaningful songs. Dressed in rose colored leotards, chiffon skirts and pointe shoes, the three dancers hypnotized the crowd with their billowing, butterfly ballet movements and their ability to delicately pirouette on their toes. At the end of the performance, Scott stood up and clapped with unabashed enthusiasm. His exuberance made the entire audience also graciously rise to their feet to provide the three dancers with an overwhelming standing ovation as well. Rozelle walked to the podium as his eyes followed the three dancers off the stage.

"Wasn't that beautiful? Poetry in motion. Nothing but soulful African rhythms." Rozelle flipped to another page of notes. "When you can successfully make a difference in a child's life, you can become the wind beneath their wings. Umph. Umph. Umph. *Wind Beneath My Wings.* That was totally fantastic. That's what you are to me, Jodria. All these years we've been married, I want you to know that." Rozelle spoke tenderly with ultimate sincerity toward his wife who blushed and smiled as she ate the pretty words of praise. When Symone heard

Rozelle's comments, she winked at him and gave Jodria, who was sitting beside her, a tight, affectionate hug.

Chapter Sixty

"Ladies and gentlemen, I bring Mrs. Pecola Marva Reynolds to the stage. Last night, I told Alex that we really didn't need to have Pecola speak because her son, CJ, spoke. Her daughter, Elizabethe, sang. Rico, her brother-in-law, gave his two cents worth. I was convinced we didn't need to hear from Pecola Reynolds. Since I'm the master of ceremonies, I thought I could make those kinds of decisions. Anyone that knows Pecola knows that she loves to talk. The Devereauxs' put their foot down. They said if Pecola couldn't speak, the program would be canceled." Several friends laughed and Rozelle voice turned serious.

"Ladies, gentlemen, and honored guests, she's a titan in the business world. Her inner-circle of friends know her as being one third of our local Winston-Salem Blue Belles group. The other two controversial members of the Blue Belles will be speaking later. Pecola is always telling people that she absolutely loved growing up in North Carolina."

"Me too, man!"

"Well, I'm glad to hear that, sir," Rozelle replied to the mysterious voice. "Pecola said that it's the vastness of this beautiful state, and the land in the so-called "country" made her think that she could have anything she dreamed about. Everybody that knows her particularly loves her seriously deep, southern twang that drips with every word. The accent is so thick, I'm surprised a truckload of mint julep isn't following right behind her. In spite of all her crazy ways, my girl knows I believe she's a smart, successful Black businesswoman."

When Rozelle completed his introduction of Pecola, she strolled regally to the podium. She smiled at the well-dressed guests throughout the audience and quickly honored her family, friends, and the Devereauxs.

Pecola's speech began in a different way than last month. "...I don't want this to sound ingratiating, but I must say it. I've never known two people who had such an unlimited wealth of human compassion. Never. That's why the Devereauxs do what they do. I've known them twenty years, and Alex and Madison haven't changed. They have a dripping, sweet affection for family, friends, children, and even animals. Not only do we honor the twenty-eight children, but we honor those two people today as well." Everybody clapped. Satisfied, Pecola began her speech.

"...Let's begin with this premise. All of us sitting here have the distinct opportunity to make an impact on the lives of each other and with the children. Young people, not only are we honored to have you with us, I hope that our lives, our actions, our sincerity, and the love that are exhibited here will help people to realize we're serious about our commitment to children. Many people might say this is a drip in the bucket of societal problems. I say it's a quiet start, and I'm proud to be a part of that drip."

"You're right, girl."

"I tell the youth we work with that there's only one line of demarcation that separates any two extremes. It's neither here nor there, up or down, backwards and forwards. But it's attitude. It's the big A word. That's why all through my life, I've been inspired by a very, very famous boxer. Muhammad Ali inspired Pecola Reynolds. I know you say a boxer inspired you, Pecola? A sweet delicate woman like yourself?" Several guests laughed freely. "That's right. He sho nuff did. Muhammad Ali declared to one and all, 'I'm the greatest.' He believed that. He ate it. He slept it. As a result of such thinking, he was a champ for many years. He convinced himself of that fact, and he obviously convinced his opponents of the same. But he armed himself for success. He armed his mind to overcome. I used to tell myself that if I wanted to see the world from the top, then I needed to arm myself to make the climb. I needed to receive an education and change. I read voraciously. I read the old book, *Laws of Success*. It was a gift from my Aunt Hattie Mae, and I read it over and over and over again."

"You talk your stuff, chile," Pauletta encouraged her sister.

"Even though I had to be a mother to four children and a wife to my husband, I was determined to earn my BS and Master's degrees. *You* all can do the same thing. We as a Black race can do anything we want to do. You know why? Because you're a chosen people. That's one of the most powerful pieces of information that Symone shared with me. After I met her, she told me that she was a chosen child from a chosen people. Now keep in mind I had always heard that the Jewish people were *the* chosen people. That was grounded into me. It's in the *Bible!* As a woman who was raised in the church, I accepted that the Jews were God's chosen people. Symone gave me her explanation. It was a beautiful one that she inherited from her family."

"During my long, personal journey, I learned more about our people. I learned more about our past history and our present, political state of our people. As a child, I was taught that Black people didn't have a language. We didn't have any way to communicate with each other until we came to America. I learned that all Africans used to say to each other was *unger unger*. That's all I knew. My parents didn't know any better, either. So you can imagine that this destroyed my sense of pride and self-worth as a young, Black girl living in the rural south. I believed that Black people came from apes and were ignorant people. But I found out that Darwin was right, people did come from apes—but it was the white people who came from those animals, not Black people."

"Talk your stuff, girl."

"Consequently, and as a result of that belief about me, my forefathers, and my parents, Pecola Marva Dudley didn't like who she was. I was ashamed of my Blackness, but lawd have mercy. I found out that there was sooo much more to my people and to me, too," she added.

"Yes, it's true. We do work with children that live in public housing, but get this. The president of this country lives in public housing. For four years, he and his entire family never pay one red penny to live in that huge old White House. But not only is he getting free housing, they got a whole lot of people we've voted for doing the same thing. They're taking advantage of public housing. They are governors, some mayors, diplomats, and ambassadors from other countries. The list is endless."

"Umph, umph, umph."

"The United States foots the housing bills for politicians, unnecessary diplomats, and rich folk to have public housing all the time. So I tell these young people, don't feel bad about where you live. When you're poor, they want you to think it's a deep, ugly scarlet brand. I know it's hard, but that'll make you just strive to do your best. Believe you're special and don't let people who are dream stealers get to you. Let your dreams fuel your determination to be successful. Then, go back and help your neighbors. If everyone is in there struggling together, nobody can help each other. If one crawls out, the key is to stretch your hand to help another one to do the same. I know what I'm talking about."

The audience was quiet as Pecola spoke. She loved it when a crowd responded to her in this way. Loved to be the center of attention. She knew she had the audience in her hands.

"It's not where you start the race of life, it's how you finish it. It's just not where you come from, it's where you end up. Black people and adults, *we* are the chosen people. When *you* realize that you come from a land of kings, queens, scholars, artisans, and inventors, your children realize it, too. Then their children will realize it. You'll embrace your African heritage and be proud of who you are. Being known as African-Americans doesn't take anything away from you being an American. A lot of people get all aggravated with the title, African-American. Africa was here on what is called America. Since they developed this country and named it America, that's how I look at the title. Plus, the sweat of many Black people's backs built this land."

"Speak your mind, young lady," a woman said loudly.

"So I'm proud to be an African-American. We all should be proud of who we are. We're a proud and regal people who deserve to love, marry, and worship each other. Marry each other to share the wealth with one another. When you embrace your heritage, only then will you understand that you're a chosen people, set apart, special, and powerful."

"So true," a man said.

"I had to understand this thinking as an older person. Sometimes, we go through a lot in life. We believe that everybody else is better than who we are. But with the children we work with out here, we want them to learn that they are somebody right now. Not when they're adults and a whole lot of learned behavior is pressure packed into their consciousness. Pride and self love will and should be learned while yall are young and still impressionable."

"Say it right."

"Study the glorious legacy of our people. Black people must know you're a chosen people. No matter what your complexion may be. You may be dark-skinned, light-skinned, and caramel complexions. It's any one of our beautiful shades of color. Repeat that within yourself. Repeat it, now. Say I *am* a prince of the chosen people," Pecola said proudly.

"I *am* a prince of the chosen people!" several people in the audience yelled out.

"I *am* a princess of the chosen people!" Pecola said with a wide grin.

"I *am* a princess of the chosen people!" members of the audience responded.

"I *am* proud. My skin is beautiful, and my legacy is glorious," Pecola added. The audience repeated her words. "The messages we receive as children help shape the adults we become. As I've grown in the knowledge of my heritage, my youngest son, Haneef, became an advocate for Black folks' issues. He began hanging out at Black bookstores and hanging on to his Tante Symone's knees." CJ patted Haneef on his thigh. "He soaked himself in the history of who we are as a people because he had a burning desire to know. Now, he's my teacher. Black mothers and fathers can raise our Black sons with a love for their Black women. We can raise our Black daughters with a love for their Black men, and we can instill such pride in our children." Pecola briefly smiled at the heavens and tried to phrase her next words with care.

"Go on, baby," Mercedes, Carlos' mother, encouraged her daughter-in-law.

"I leave you with this very appropriate poem entitled *What Matters*. A writer who chooses to remain anonymous left it for us. When I was pregnant with my fourth child, my dear sister read this poem to me over the phone. Pauletta was away attending Kentucky State University in Frankfurt. When Pauletta hung up the phone, she had a copy framed. My sister mailed it to me the next day. On this day, I want yall to listen to the words."

What Matters
One hundred years from now,
It will not matter what kind of car I drove,
What kind of house I lived in
How much I had in my bank account,
Nor what my clothes looked like
But the world may be a little better
Because I was important in the life of a child.

As Pecola recited the poem in a semi-lilting, yet singing voice without the aid of notes, the audience was awed with the delivery. When Pecola was done, she smiled in the direction of the front row.

"If you knew what I was going through at that time in my life when I was pregnant, you would understand why my sister blessed me with this poem. Young people, all these speeches given today in your honor and in honor of the Devereauxs are similar to beautiful poems. Yes, the speeches are a little longer than a poem, but they're still a style of poetry to inspire our youth and adults in attendance today." Pecola smiled and nodded her head with satisfaction.

"Go on, baby," Mercedes cheered her daughter-in-law on again.

"The Devereauxs have garnered a remarkable display of unity and adult volunteers who truly care for yall's well-being. We simply want yall to emerge from the shells of young girls and boys to become magnificent men and women. Think like Muhammad Ali. Think that you *are* the greatest! We want yall to know that a whole, wide beautiful world full of opportunity and joy is just waiting on you. We want yall to know this within your soul because that's where it sticks. Remember the words of Oliver Wendell Holmes. '...Man's mind, stretched to a new idea, never goes back to its original dimensions.'"

"You're right, ma'am," an unidentified man said.

"Young people, I hope I've said something that will lodge in your brain and remind you that you must have pride, that you must love yourself, and that you must love each other. If we don't learn how to do that, who will? To the honored guests, you know I love yall. I'm behind you one-hundred percent. Thank you." The audience clapped as she stepped off the podium.

"Bravo. Bravo," yelled Cleopatra, Alex, Symone, and Pauletta. "Bravo, girl." They stood in front of their seats, which precipitated others in the audience to do the same. Pecola was surprised and moved when she saw that the entire audience eventually rose to its feet to give her a standing ovation.

"Wonderful, girl," Rozelle said as he claimed the podium again. "I hope every person within the sound of your voice was fed by our words." The crowd clapped excitedly.

"You did a great job, baby," Carlos whispered in Pecola's ear, and she squeezed his hand in thankful reply.

"Our next speaker is one of the young girls being honored this evening," Rozelle informed. "Her name is Miss Denethria Beatty."

Denethria Beatty attended the two-week session last year as a twelve-year-old, and this year she was bumped up to the older group. Last night, she pleaded with Alex non-stop to let her talk about how the Devereauxs' had helped her and changed her life. Even though she wasn't on program, Alex asked Rozelle to insert her in an appropriate place. Since Alex believed the opening ceremony was a special time of sharing and encouragement for the children, she didn't want them to feel they had to speak and say words she believed other people wouldn't understand or would assume they were asked to say only positive comments on behalf of the Devereauxs. During the two weeks the children were in Advance, they were consistently given many opportunities to give personal testimonies in the privacy of their peers and the volunteer speakers.

When Rozelle announced Denethria's name and since now she was feeling quite nervous, she walked carefully up to the podium and took a deep breath.

"My name is Denethria Alicia Beatty, and I live in Happy Hills Gardens. The projects. Alex, Madison, and Cleopatra told me to learn how to be proud about whom I am and where I live. Tante Pecola said it today. She told me that it's not where you live that counts, it's who you are. All of Madison and Alex's friends told me the same thing. I understand what they're saying, too. Finally. Now I believe that if I want to make it out, I can. No matter if the odds against me are stacked high, I can do it. Cleopatra even told me that she used to live in the projects, but now her life is a dream of happiness."

"Last year, I couldn't even admit to anyone that I lived in the projects. I was ashamed. But Alex told me that shame is something that's taught. It's acquired. It's not a characteristic. It's not one of our five senses. It's not something we're born with. The point is, it's something that can be changed," Denethria said with clarity and sounded wise beyond her years.

"Lawd have mercy. The chile is sho nuff telling the truth," moaned one of the senior citizens.

"But I do know coming to the Devereauxs' home has saved my life. Before I met them, I was ready to drop out of school. I used to curse my mother out every day. I mean every day, too. My mama is here. She'll confirm what I'm saying is true. I hated where I lived and who I was. Every time my mother told me to not do something, I did it anyway just simply because she told me not to. My anger was deep and destructive. I felt I had no hope and would end up pregnant or using drugs like so many of my friends. I believe the teachers at school disrespected me because of where I lived, so I disrespected them back. I was sooo angry at the world and at myself, too." She inhaled quickly.

"Take your time, baby."

"When I was selected last year to come to the Devereauxs' house, I said ok. Here's an opportunity to go to the country once a month. Spend two weeks in the country during the summer, and it's free, too. Yeah, that's me all right," she said as she rolled her eyes to the sky and sucked her teeth to show her "bad girl" attitude. A few snickers arose from the audience.

"It *was* me. Then I got here and met people who acted like they cared. They were some of the same people that spoke today, and I had a phat time. You know what I'm saying? I met Marlon Dinzelle, the superstar basketball player. Before then, I had never seen a famous person up close. Not close enough where I could touch them. But Marlon actually talked to me. He looked me in the eyes one day and told me that he cared about how my life was going. He said those words to Denethria Beatty. Sometimes, Marlon hugged me when he talked, too. It was phat and all of that," she said as she looked knowingly at the other children sitting in their special places on the front row. They quickly nodded their heads in agreement.

"Then I realized the experience of coming to the Devereauxs every month and meeting so many nice people *was* quite overwhelming. You know I learned the word overwhelming from Alex. That's a word she uses all the time. It's either overwhelming or abominable to Alex. It's either inappropriate or appropriate." The audience laughed quickly, and Denethria waited until they were finished.

"But she's right. It was so overwhelming that I could meet so many people who were so kind and understanding and caring to me. They acted like they loved me even though I wasn't their baby. I ain't never experience nothing like that before. I wanted to write a letter to Madison and Alex, and I did. It's a private letter that only they could read. I gave it to them last night during the fish fry and pool party," she said with a smile. "But I told Alex I wanted to tell you all today how I felt. They *are* real. They really are. Every month—sometimes two and three times a month, they would come and pick me up. You know I really thought that after I left from being here for two weeks last summer that they probably would forget about me, but they didn't. They came back for me. They always, always, always came back for me," she continued poignantly and paused to regain her composure. Denethria felt her eyes fill up with tears and felt their warmth as they gently tumbled down her face.

"My father left my Mama years ago. He never ever came back. Never sent a birthday card or a Christmas gift. He never even called to see how I was doing. I thought the Devereauxs was lying when they told me they would see me again. Even though I had been coming every month since January, I don't know what happened. But I got scared. I thought after my summer with them, they would suddenly change their minds and not come back to get me."

As Denethria's mother listened to the words of her daughter, she dabbed at her eyes with pink tissue and tried to smile valiantly. "I thought they would do the same thing like my daddy. But they didn't. They came back for me and took me to art shows, took me to Winston-Salem State University's football games and to North Carolina's A&T's Homecoming. I had never been there before—never left Winston-Salem. We all went to New York to visit the Shomburg. Uncle Booker T took us there. Then we went to see a Broadway play. Ms. Charmaine took a whole bunch of us to Charlotte to see the African-American Dance Ensemble. It was the bomb," she said with the memories of her good times reappearing vividly.

"We've done it all. You name it, we've done it. Even though we went to see the original *Nutcracker* at the Steven's Center, Uncle Rozelle is right. I know for a fact that I enjoyed *The Urban Nutcracker* when we were in Atlanta. I could relate to that story better than I could the one here. I had never seen a Black ballerina before. Never. It made me believe I could dance like that, too. When Ms. Charmaine took us backstage, we kept asking the dancers, 'How do yall stand up on your toes like that?' Let me see. What else did we do?" Denethria stopped and glanced at Alex who smiled back at her.

"The Devereauxs took me fishing. They took me to the library. We all have our little piece of land out here with our name on it, and we can plant whatever we want. I planted tulips and a rose bush. I like pretty flowers just like my Mama and Alex. Yall will never guess what Miles Valley planted? He's always planting some vegetables. This year he planted collard greens, squash, string beans, and tomatoes in his section. He said he was going to sell it in the community," Denethria said with a big grin, and the audience began laughing, too.

"When he wasn't working, Uncle Scottie would read bedtime stories to us at night. So did Uncle Marlon, Uncle Rozelle, Uncle Carlos, and my Uncle Rico."

"Just wonderful, chile."

"That's right. Alex and Madison read to us, too. Then before we went to bed, they kissed us. We all prayed together down on our knees right beside our beds. The way they do in books. They invited me to formal, dress up parties at their house. They even let me play with their two children and their friend's children. I never felt like I was a project kid when I was with them. I felt like I *was* somebody when I was with them. I felt like I *was* an important part of their family as well as their friends' family. They always came back for me." She stopped momentarily and shook her head slowly with closed eyes.

"That's what always stood out in my mind about the Devereauxs. In the beginning, my neighbors used to laugh at me and say, 'Girl you better get real. Those rich Black people definitely don't care nothing' about you, girl. They won't be back no more.' That's what my neighbors told me all the time. Each month they would say that to me. They used to tell me that people like me—the ones who lived in The Gardens—were just a passing fancy for successful Black folk and white folks, too. They said it made them feel good to give us old clothes, old books, a little bit of their time, and just as little interest," she continued with maturity.

By now Alex was crying visibly. Nanette who was sitting in the chair right beside her sister tightly hugged Alex's shoulders and handed her a frilly white handkerchief to wipe her eyes.

"They were wrong about Alex and Madison Devereaux. Not only did they come back for me, they came back for a lot of us, and they always gave us their best," she said softly as she leaned into the microphone and considered the pretty dress she was wearing today. Once again, the other children quickly nodded their heads in agreement, too.

"We slept in their beautiful bedrooms. One time I even peed in the bed. It was in one of the guestrooms with the pretty, painted ceilings. I peed all over Neema, too," Denethria said with a little embarrassment as she watched her friend, Neema Davis. Neema was thirteen and lived in Piedmont Park Public Housing in Winston. Before last summer, the two girls had never met each other. Last year, they became fast friends.

"You know what? Alex and Madison didn't beat me up or nothin'. They didn't even yell or holler. Neema did, though. She told me off big time, but that was because I peed all over her. Madison even helped me change the sheets. He joked with me the whole time, and I washed down the rubber padding myself. Alex said that she put the padding on the bed anyway when the children came over because sometimes things like that happen, especially when children don't sleep in their own beds. Then Cleopatra went and got some more sheets and pillow cases that were just as pretty as the one I had just peed on," Denethria said with amazement, and the audience roared with laughter as they began to clap.

"Take your time, babygirl," a senior citizen told her.

"That's why I wanted to tell you how the Devereauxs have made an impact on my life. I want to let them know that coming here was certainly a turning point for me. They made me realize that there's more out there in the world. That there are other choices that I can make to change my life around if I really wanted to. If I worked hard and was given a little opportunity, a helping hand, it could be done. That's what Alex and Madison gave me. A helping hand. I now believe that I could even go to college. Tante Symone said she would pay my way, especially if I attended Hampton University. Tante Symone wants everyone to go there for college," Denethria added with a proud grin. Even though Symone specifically told Denethria that the college promise was supposed to be a secret, Denethria said it anyway.

"So many of the Devereauxs' friends made me believe in myself and made me believe I could be somebody that could make a difference, too. I believe I always had it in me. Alex and Madison were just the ones able to bring it out of me. My mother tried, and I didn't listen to her. Sometimes the voice of your parents isn't the one to make you change. Sometimes you just need someone else to punch you dead hard in the face. That's exactly what you need. Alex and Madison, I thank yall for punching me in the face. I love you both." Denethria paused briefly.

"Beautiful," a woman moaned.

"Mama, I love you with everything in my body. I thank you for being my role model. My mama has always been behind me with my schoolwork, with doing her best to buy me things, and making sure I turn out ok. I love her very much." She laughed quickly. "I mean that from my heart. Alex told us that it's abominable. I told you she loves that word." Several people snickered. "It's abominable to have anybody but your parents as your first role model— especially if they've tried their best to give you a good life. And whenever you're asked the question of who's your role model, the answer should always be your parents." Many people in the crowd applauded and shouted *Amen* about that positive statement.

"Madison, Alex, and Auntie Jodria always reminded us to acknowledge our mothers and fathers. The elders in our community. The ones in the projects. No matter where we are or who we're with. Alex and Auntie Jodria said that to always be respectful and tell your parents you love them. Mama, I love you," she said once more with tenderness as Denethria noticed her mother dab at her eyes again.

"That's another thing I like. They hug a lot up here in Advance. They say I love you a lot up here in Advance. They say it all the time. Don't they?" she asked the other children who bobbed their heads vigorously with silent yes's. "They say those three words all the time. They smile a lot, too. I'm sure adults have their own problems. We know that although they might have a little bit of money, their lives aren't perfect by no means. They haven't always lived like this." She hesitated slightly as she waved her hand in the air at the elaborate surroundings of the Devereauxs' country place. "But when they're with us, all of the older people make us smile because they always smile at us."

"Wonderful," a man said in the crowd.

"Last summer, all the friends of the Devereauxs told us to call them Uncle and Tante because we would all now be one big family. I like that. My mother was the only baby in her family, and I'm the only baby for her. Now, I feel like I've aunts. Well, I mean tantes now," she informed quickly. She glared tenderly at Symone who smiled back at her while she continued to reassuringly pat Pauletta's thigh as she cried quietly.

"Now I have uncles and a whole lot of new first and second cousins. Do you know what all our Tantes and Uncles did last year? They gave our parents a copy of *Black Pearls for Parents*. The book has comments for each day of the year. My Mama took Auntie Jodria's advice and read certain days to me. Mama loves that book. I do, too. The Devereauxs and their friends told us that since they believed all Black children were Black Pearls, they thought it would be a great idea for us to share the books with our parents." The entire audience broke out into wild applause.

"Every month, me and the other Black Pearls have some serious family reunions when we meet for the book club readings." The other children nodded their heads again, and Denethria paused briefly once more as the crowd began clapping again. "It was the bomb. We really threw down. They really showed me love up here in Advance. They really show love," she repeated and stopped speaking and rubbed her eyes quickly. "When I graduate from college, I plan to do the same thing. Being with the Devereauxs and their friends has made me want to give back to *my* community. I want to work in homeless shelters and to do and be all that I can be. Everyone has been such a huge inspiration to me."

Denethria thought she wanted to say something else. However, she believed she was going to cry for sure now, and she didn't want to do it in front of all those people. Instead, as the crowd clapped thunderously to her words, she slowly walked to her seat.

Mesmerized by her speech, Rozelle was speechless. While he listened to the crowd clap and whistle, he was thoroughly moved. He encouraged the crowd to give Denethria and all the other twenty-seven children a standing ovation, which they did. Rozelle noticed the reaction of the video cam operators. The two muscular looking men Alex hired to film the evening seemed to have moist, sparkling eyes. Soon the clapping died down, and Rozelle was able to resume with the program.

"...You said you had a few words to say, Denethria girl. Thank God you didn't have to prepare a speech. You spoke eloquently. I declare. I'm such a sucker for this stuff. How can you follow that up with any words that could express what Denethria's speech did to me, for me, and probably for you? I'm proud to be a part of what the Devereauxs are trying to do. It's good to hear how Denethria changed her life based on what she discovered about her life's abilities. She knows that there's power in making choices—in knowing a person can take a stand and make a change. Denethria—" Rozelle said as he watched her, "I know you spoke for yourself. If the other teenagers had an opportunity to speak tonight, I hope that they would say the same things. Your presentation was a wonderful display of love, courage, and emotion. I commend you for it, young lady." The audience clapped again, and Rozelle continued speaking.

"Bravo. Bravo," shouted several members of the audience.

"I also liked what Denethria said about Marlon. He and his buddies have always been committed to spending time with young people, especially with Marlon's SLAM Foundation that he now funds almost single-handedly. These are the professional athletes you don't read about that are here today. They're not so big that they can't come and spend time with the children for free. Oscar Oaklay, Donald Kemper, Christopher Perry, Jesse Birth, and Curtis Shawn Johnson took time out of their hectic schedules to be here last month. They're doing the same thing again this month. We need to celebrate those athletes who try so hard to help out when they can. Many of these individuals are just like you and me." Rozelle paused briefly.

"They're great guys who give their time, their energy, and their money year round to worthy Black causes. However, you don't hear about them or that as much in the media. You often hear about the ones that get involved in drugs, who get caught with the wrong women, who end up in jail, who get drunk, have accidents, and those guys who beat up on the referees. We thank you, guys. We really do," Rozelle said seriously and waved for the professional athletes to stand. The audience recognized them again with loud applause that echoed much love for the guys.

"Now, it's time to hear some rap music. They're straight from the West Coast. The city of Los Angeles located right there in Cal-lee-fornia," Rozelle announced. "You heard one half of the duo speak tonight. Last year, they toured as an opening act with L. L. Cool J. This year they blazed a name for themselves when they toured with KRS-One! I present to you the one and only GJ and SJ. The Alexander Brothers as they do their thing."

All of the children in the front row jumped up and down. They began to holler *woof, woof, woof, woof, woof* with raised fists moving in circular motions throughout the air. They were acting like they were all guests on the old *Arsenio Hall* Show. Even King, Queen, and Dreams adorned in their special occasion red and white pretty neck bows began to bark loudly. Along with the other children that were scattered throughout the audience, the entire tent went crazy with excitement. Last night everyone who was hanging out at the opening fish fry got a taste of the Alexander Brothers. They tore up the place at poolside with their rap. The entire audience had heard about it and was ready for some more.

When the Alexander brothers stopped rapping, it seemed like it took a whole nother ten minutes to get the audience calmed down. They wanted an encore, but Madison pointed to his watch and quietly mouthed to Rozelle that it had to wait until later.

Chapter Sixty-One

"I tell you one thing. This evening has been like one of those Black awards show on BET or like an evening of those political speeches you hear at the Democratic Convention." Many people in the audience rapidly nodded their heads. "Ohhhh, my. What a night in the Devereauxs' Shangri-La village."

"That's for sure," a lady agreed.

"Well, moving right along. The next three people we have on program don't play. I know you just got a healthy dose from the RDs. The rapping dons. Now, we're getting ready to have our toes and feet mashed in. I call the next three people, the RD group. That stands for the *Real Deal* crew. We call them the real deal because they discuss issues that may make you feel very, very uncomfortable."

"So true," Cleopatra said.

"If you think my wife's topic was thought-provoking, wait until you hear this next group. They're going to motivate us regarding the truth about drugs, economic development, and Black history. People, I present to you the first one in the Real Deal crew. Years ago, he was one of the best linebackers at Grambling. From there, he went on to become a top-notch investment banker. That's not where his story ends. Romallus tells us his life has just begun. Ladies and gentlemen, I very proudly introduce you to Mr. Romallus Alexanderrrrr!" Rozelle exclaimed as the crowd erupted in anxious applause.

"...It's good to see yall again," Romallus said with a huge grin, and the children waved wildly at him once again. All last night, they couldn't stop hugging him. At closing ceremonies last summer, Romallus and Booker T were selected the camp's best male counselors. The children awarded both men with a trophy they paid for with their own money. Even though Romallus didn't live in North Carolina, he frequently telephoned and religiously wrote letters to each child.

"Didn't we have a great time last night?" he asked everyone.

Even though they all weren't there, the entire audience excitedly yelled, *Yeah!* The young people knew one thing about Romallus. He spoke tough, and he loved them. The children knew he consistently said things to them that needed to be said.

"For those of you who don't know me, my name is Romallus Arna Bontemps Alexander. I'm just blessed to be alive!" he exclaimed as he raised his fist in salute, and the audience broke into applause. "My parents named me after my mother's brother, Romallus. The Arna W. Bontemps part is from a famous educator and author who wrote during and after the Harlem Renaissance. My father and mother had such high hopes for me, so they named me after him, too. Unfortunately, a drug habit destroyed it," he explained quietly while gazing into shocked faces. "Like a bolt of lightning, drugs destroyed those hopes. Don't look sooo surprised, ladies and gentlemen. That's right. You got a drug addict talking to you now. The power of drugs robbed me of everything: my friends, my cars, and my job. I lost more than my livelihood. I lost my life. Now, I'm a recovering drug addict. A recovering junkie and I'm here to tell you my story. So listen and learn."

The audience slipped into shocked silence. "My problem was drugs in every form. I was stoned on crack cocaine, angel dust, alcohol, and whatever else I got my hands on. When I was strung out on heroin my last year out there, I was existing in a living hell, and I finally got tired of being miserable. I was dirty and stinking. I didn't have any appetite, so I was skin and bones. It got to a point that even all the drugs I was using didn't make me high. They couldn't make me happy or satisfied, but the drugs were all I had. My whole world became dark, and I lived in that darkness."

"Run down the truth, man."

"Let me tell you about my sweet, baby love Cocaine. Now *that* was the one. Cocaine was my lover, pure and simple. The drug was my wife. It sexed me up and down better than the best woman in the world, but it also was a poison that almost killed me. As a user, cocaine took me to another realm. I was inconsiderate. Because I wasn't thinking rationally, I stole from my father, myself, my brother, Scott, and from whoever was in my path. When you snort and shoot up, you don't even think anymore. When you do crack, one is not enough and a thousand is too many."

"Lawd have mercy," an older woman moaned.

"For drugs, you'll sell your body, your clothes, and even your Mama and Daddy. When you're on crack, some people don't have a pot to piss in, let alone a cup to catch it. Crack cocaine is rough. You don't even have a life that you can claim as your own. The scary part about all of this is I don't believe the drugs are the problem. Don't get me wrong. It's the motivation within each drug addict to use the drugs, and those reasons are different for each person. Everyone has a motivation to do it and to use it as an escape. If you ask people why do they do it or did it, they got a lot of answers for the motivation and for the reasons. Folks are trying to fill emptiness. That's one motivation." Romallus said and paused briefly as he gathered his thoughts to phrase the next sentence.

"Umph, umph, umph," Scott moaned, remembering those days with his brother.

"My addiction for crack cocaine and whatever else I could get my hands on went on for years. During that time, I was sooo tired. But one day, I finally was motivated to live. Keep in mind, this was after many, many trips to rehab. But one day I said to myself, 'Romallus enough is enough.' Then, I thought and prayed out to God. I said, 'Lord, if you just hear me this one more time, I'll change. If I could just get a call through to my Daddy, I'll be ok. If I can reach my brother, I know he would help me.' As Scott had done so many times in the past, he did come through for me once again," Romallus shared in a poignant way. Just as swiftly, he smiled broadly at Scott.

"Although I'm forty-three years old, I consider myself to be six and a half years old. That's because I haven't gotten high on drugs in six and half years. That's a long time for me to be clean, so I consider that my new birthday," he said solemnly. "Six and a half years ago, I walked out of a rehab center. But it wasn't before I had been there for five long months and had been through extensive therapy. They had to build my body back up. Potassium three times a day. All kinds of things. I know you're saying, *"But* he doesn't look like your typical drug addict. I'm wearing a suit. I'm tall, am not bad looking, and am kinda handsome. I know I look a lot better than my brother. The cool, calm, and collected Scott. He's Mr. Iceman himself," he teased lightly with tremendous love for his younger brother. Everyone who knew the Alexander siblings burst out laughing, and several of Scott's friends chuckled at the comment.

"I look like I'm all business and very professional," he said and pulled on the lapels of his single-breasted, Shaka King blue suit and strutted around the podium for a few moments. The teenagers laughed. He stopped strutting and began speaking seriously again.

"When I was an investment banker on Wall Street, I really was kicking it straight for several years. Then, it slowly became a facade. I was all of that and a great big ole bag of chips. I was everybody's picture of a successful Black man. My picture, too. You couldn't tell me one thing. I walked with my head held high. I had *The Wall Street Journal, Black Enterprise, Emerge, Barrons, The New York Times, and Investor's Business Daily* under one arm. My soft kid lambskin suede attaché case was in the other. I—was—tough. I wore Italian tailored suits, Italian shoes, and RABA monograms on my French cuffed, custom shirts."

"Tell the truth, Rommie," Rico said.

"Anything foreign made, that was me. The more European, the better. I wore it. I was a well-educated man and a highly successful New York stockbroker. You name it. I had it. A nice crib on Manhattan's Central Park West. A sleek gorgeous red convertible Corvette and a Black Rolls Royce sedan. I had women by the barrel loads. I spent weekends in East Hampton. I lived in the fast lane and thought I was all of that. I was clean as ten tacks."

"I was fooling the world because my life was controlled by drugs. Success was sweet, and I made my weekend sampling of drugs a full-blown addiction. I became a consummate liar. I became so used to lying to others, that lying to myself was easy." He stopped briefly and gazed at the clear sky through the transparent tent.

"But now what you see is me. The real Romallus who has been set free. I'm sober, clean, and have been given a second chance at living. It's such a privilege to be alive. Now, I have the opportunity to love my family. I say things to my friends and family that I needed and wanted to say. You know why? Here's why. I liken drug addiction and then the recovery from it as being similar to someone who has tried to commit suicide. The suicide attempt failed, but the person has a new lease on life. That's me. No longer do I live my life in a drug haze. This is the real Romallus Alexander you see. My mission is to share my story with whoever listens—especially the children." The audience broke out into wild applause.

"I want to let the children know that I had it all as a child. I'm not one of those Black men that's a part of the statistics the media loves to flash across the television screen every day to explain why they believe Black men are such supposed failures. I wasn't born in poverty or in an abusive home. I didn't live in a bad neighborhood. My parents loved and cherished me. My parents weren't on drugs, and they certainly weren't abusive. There was a whole lot of love and hugging in my house. My father was around. I believe I had the two strongest parents in all of New Orleans, Louisiana. My three brothers and I were all taught to be, to know, and to excel as leaders. Where did I go wrong? I had an excellent family life. I never went hungry. I wasn't poor. I had the intelligence to achieve honor roll status every time I opened by book bag, pulled out my pen, and took a test in school." The crowd was engrossed in his story, for Romallus spoke with such naked passion.

"I was *real* smart. I got great grades in high school and even in college. I even excelled in sports. Where did I go wrong? Good question. With all of the positives in my life, I *still* fell into the drug game in spite of my good family, my intelligence, and my common sense! For the next two weeks, I'm here to tell you again that my mission in life is to tell people about the destruction drugs can cause. I'm here to tell you that drugs are an equal opportunity thing with no respect of person, economic standings, or color. The epidemic of drugs can rape you and destroy your lives if you're not careful or not smart. You must be on guard against them."

Romallus went on to explain about his upbringing in the Alexander household in New Orleans, his successful career as a stockbroker, and his demise as a result of drugs. Suddenly, Romallus rolled up his starched, white shirtsleeves to show the audience the needle tracks on his arms and to explain how he used his body as a human pincushion to chase the high.

"You see these tracks on my arm? These scars are a painful reminder to keep me straight. For every scar that's on me, that's how many people *I* knew who overdosed out there in the streets. They did it in Fifth Avenue penthouses, in shady places, and in swank hotel rooms. Why didn't it happen to me? I was there with them. I was doing the same stuff. Why did I survive? I don't know. As my Mama used to say when I was child, 'Somebody is praying for you, baby boy. When I'm not able to pray, somebody else is doing it for me. Saints all over are praying for my four big baby boys and for my family.' That's what my Mama, Thony Mae Alexander, used to say all the time. And I never forgot it even as high as I used to be."

"Umph, umph, umph," a senior citizen groaned as she shook her head from side to side.

"I used to see people turn their noses up at me—*me*—an educated and intelligent homeless, drug addict on the street. I was a man who had received an MBA degree with high distinction. Now, I was living in the gutter, tasting the dirt and the slime from the feet of passersby. The filth and grime of the many New York streets kissed my lips daily. During those times, I never ever forgot my Mama's words, though." Scott bobbed his head sympathetically as he considered the always-religious encouraging advice of his mother.

"...According to statistics, two million people use cocaine at least once a week, people. Isn't that amazing? They're not even giving us the number of people who use drugs every day. It's probably too overwhelming to consider. Believe me, baby. Drugs are poison, but you couldn't tell me that. That is until it was too late. I took it like people drank their morning coffee. I know that drugs are a terrible scourge on our society that's a disease that surpasses alcoholism. Cocaine was my sweetheart, my woman, my job, my food, and my sex."

"Young people, understand there's another side to drugs. Drugs *do* take away the bad feelings, at least temporarily. But drugs certainly don't take away the problems. They push them away momentarily. When the high is over, the problems are still there. In the beginning, it made me feel real good. I mean *great* good. It made me feel happier, and I loved the way it made me feel," he raved with a huge grin, and the audience giggled tentatively. "But while it was making me feel good, it was literally destroying me. We used to have a running joke in my East Hampton circle. 'I hate cocaine. I just like the way it smells.'" Several people in the audience laughed.

"Unbelievable," a man exclaimed.

"Like my girl Roberta Flack used to sing all the time back in the day, it was literally *Killing Me Softly with His Song.* The drug song. The drug life. The drug game was killing me very softly and slowly, and it's doing the same thing nowadays to so many people.

"Tell it like it is, my man," another guy encouraged.

"But until it *really* came from my head to my heart to do it, I couldn't have made a decision to become sober and stop the madness. The biggest decision is to get off drugs, decide it, and mean it. I realized I had to change. I just chose life instead of death on earth. I said to myself that I never am gonna treat my body, this gift from God, that badly ever again."

"The day I decided to get off drugs, I changed my position in life. I realized I couldn't fix what I did yesterday, but I could at least change what I could do for tomorrow. You can do the same thing with any problem in your life. You can either decide to be the bird, or you can decide to be the statue. I decided that I wanted to soar. Now I believe that anything is possible, and I see the world from a beautiful vantage point." Romallus spoke softly as the crowd erupted in wild applause. "I thank you for this opportunity. Truly I do. Reach for your zenith!" he proclaimed loudly over the clapping noise and walked to his seat.

"You go, boy. You go," Rozelle exclaimed as he shook his head from side to side. "It was truly inspiring and totally powerful."

"It certainly was," a lady exclaimed loudly.

"Ladies and gentlemen, we're going to take a short thirty-five minute intermission. Afterwards, we'll come back and wrap up the second half of the program. Everyone needs to be sitting in his or her place in thirty minutes. It's a prompt thirty minutes around here. For those of you who want to stretch your legs and smoke a cigarette, that's fine. We only ask that you step outdoors. Ok?"

"Ok," several people said.

Rozelle paused and smiled to himself. He was pleased. The first half of the program had gone quite well. "The ushers will direct everyone to the bathrooms. If you want to munch on the luscious refreshments prepared by Hurdle Food Service, just simply go to the adjacent tent and help yourself. Ok, ladies, gentlemen, and young people, I'll see you right back here in thirty minutes."

The audience rose to their feet. Milling about and chitchatting amongst themselves, the excited crowd strolled into the adjacent tent. The Charles Greene Group, dressed in white tuxedos, was already in place and playing old favorite, jazzy tunes. Before Rozelle left to take the break, he swiftly reviewed his notes for the second half of the program. Then he quickly hopped off the stage to go join his friends.

Chapter Sixty-Two

"...Did yall enjoy the intermission? The music. The food." The majority of the people in the audience nodded their heads, and a few guests were still heading back to their seats. "Me too. I know it was a dash to try to eat everything. Wasn't those sweet little pretty shrimp and crabcake hors d'oeuvres just delicious?" Many guests bobbed their heads yes again.

"Just wonderful," one man said.

"The stuffed mushrooms were exquisite, too," Rozelle added.

"I think we need to thank Cleopatra for preparing such wonderful food, man," Christopher bellowed, teasing. Cleopatra turned around and gazed in his face. He winked at her, and she blushed slightly.

"You know Cleopatra didn't prepare the food this time. We all know she's good. Cleopatra is the administrator for this here affair, so she can't be the cook, too," Rozelle explained playfully and everyone broke out into laughter. "Since we've been refreshed, it's time to listen to the next singing duo. They're the oldest ones we got on program this evening. Mr. Scott Alexander and the vivacious Mrs. Pecola Reynolds. They're going to bring you their powerful rendition of *The Greatest Love of All*. If you close your eyes, you'll find that Scott has a voice that's similar to George Benson, ladies."

"Holding up the other side of the duo is Miss Motown herself. We know her as Pecola. Yall heard her talk earlier. Well, she's back again. She's everywhere." Pecola stopped patting her perfect hair and stared at Rozelle with wide eyes.

"Since Pecola and I have known each for years, I know what Pecola is thinking right about now. She's imagining that this large tent is Madison Square Garden, and my girl is visualizing she's in front of thousands instead of over two hundred folks in the small town of Advance, North Carolina. She's probably thinking that she's Miss Patti LaBelle reincarnate in Winston-Salem and of Greensboro. Put your hands together for my two great friends. They're Scott Broadus Alexander and Pecola Marva Reynolds." The audience broke out into wild clapping and free laughter.

Once on stage, Pecola and Scott bowed slightly to acknowledge the crowd. Scott briefly talked about what the song meant to him in regards to young people. He suddenly became silent as he prepared to sing. Pecola and Scott waited for DJ Cool Breeze to strike up the instrumentals, and the two friends began their duet. As Scott held Pecola's waist, they smiled into each other's face. The crowd was delighted by both their rich voices and was amazed that Scott *did* actually sound like George Benson. It was obvious to them that Pecola and Scott were good friends and had often sung together in the past. Charmaine moved uncomfortably in her seat as she watched Scott sing while tenderly smiling down into Pecola's happy face. When Scott and Pecola were finished, the audience rose to their feet yelling, *Bravo, Bravo.*

Rozelle went back to the podium. "Wasn't that an appropriate song? *The Greatest Love of All*. That's the key, everybody. Learning to love the person you see in the mirror every day—yourself. Let's give them another round of applause." The audience did happily.

"Fabulous. Simply, fabulous," Charmaine said out loud.

"Ladies and gentlemen, our next speaker is Booker Taliaferro Dinzelle. I'm telling yall right now, he's going to step all over your toes and even mash your corns real hard, too. He's a heavy brother whom I truly enjoy talking with about any number of subjects. My man always has an answer, no matter what the question. He's an inspiration to young people all over Greensboro, Winston-Salem, and this entire country. If there's an audience, he has something to say." The crowd was attentive to every word Rozelle said.

"Go, Booker T," a young kid yelled out.

"Without a doubt, he cherishes words, and he cherishes reading," Rozelle continued. "A very introspective man, Booker T thinks a lot. His mind is constantly at work. He convinced the Devereauxs to add chess lessons to the summer program because he believes the game of chess forces young people to think things through. He's right. Chess does that for the children. So when they win, it's because they've *thought* their way to a victory. People get ready for an educational blast into your consciousness. I proudly introduce Booker Taliaferro Dinzelle. He's also known as Uncle Booker T around these parts."

The crowd provided Booker T with a polite round of applause. As always, Booker T was looking chic in a tapered, khaki suit, white Nehru shirt with gold cuff links, baby alligator shoes, and matching skullcap. A smiling Booker T looked quite fashionable and dashing as he walked to the stage.

"Rozelle is right. I talk about things Black and white people like to push under the carpet. Things we like to forget about. I talk about things like AIDS and prison. On Sunday morning, look around you," Booker T said into the microphone. "A lot of our Black women are at prison visiting their sons, daughters, husbands, cousins, uncles, brothers, friends, and sisters. They're more folks visiting prisons on Sunday morning than there are sitting on the pews of our churches. I talk about Black history and race relations. The raw, ugly, beautiful truth. So, I hope you receive my presentation in the loving spirit I give it. I—love—my—people. All of us. The weak. The strong. The lost. The enlightened."

"C'mon with it, my man."

"When the Devereauxs decided how they wanted to work with the children on a organized basis, they invited me over for lunch. It was about thirty of us sitting around their dining room table that day. Then Madison and Alex shared their vision with us. They told me they wanted the children to receive teachings that would be honest and thought-provoking."

As Booker T recalled the Sunday luncheon date the Christmas before last, Madison and Alex nudged each other and smiled. They knew what Booker T was going to say next. He delivered a similar speech last month. Not one to stand still at a podium, he removed the mike and spoke while he walked around the stage with his diamond pinkie ring flashing on his finger in a soulful Black man way.

"I'm a realist, and I know how the game is played in this world. I had to learn it for me and for others. I've been working with the youth of Greensboro, with my three children, nieces, nephews, and as a basketball coach for years. For as long as I can remember, I've been talking about what Black people need to do to make the best of their lives here in America. The greatest power you have young people is your mind. The man who believes in his mind he can do something is probably right and so is the man who believes he can't is probably right, too." The applause resounded through the tent.

"One of the traits that I work to build in children is character. And in order to build character, you must have discipline. Absolutely! Categorically! This is what I tell them. You got to have D-I-S-C-I-P-L-I-N-E!" Booker T spelled the word dramatically, taking the time to carefully articulate each letter. "Discipline wrapped up with enthusiasm."

"You go, young man," an elderly man said.

"Did you know that enthusiasm is Greek in origin? It means 'the spirit within' and means 'God within us.' That why the CED Course is popular around here. CED stands for Character. Enthusiasm. Discipline." Both men and women in the audience yelled a few *Amen, brotha* as they laughed.

"...Today, my voice hasn't changed, and I'm still strict. My job is to still let you and the young folks know that. Over the years, a lot of people have gotten mad with me. Why? Well, they don't agree with my thinking because I'm not soft with kids. I don't cuddle them with nonsense when they do wrong. They tell me I'm too tough on their kids. Whimping up to my face like they're weak and accept and tolerate weakness."

"Uh oh," Pecola moaned to Pauletta. "Booker T's is getting ready to go there."

"Even during recreational programs I host at the Windsor Community Center in Greensboro, I've listened to the disparaging words of some parents. There have been times when well-meaning parents wanted to take their children out of my programs, but listen to this. The children didn't want to go. Can yall believe that? Throughout the years, I haven't changed either. This is how I feel. If your kids can't go by my rules out here in Advance and with the ones I work with in Greensboro, we don't want them involved with us. Period. They must learn that children are children. They need guidance, and they must learn to follow rules."

"Tell it like it is, Booker T," Pauletta interjected quickly.

"I expect them to dress respectably around me, too. That's why I respect the Nation of Islam. One thing about them, they've always been well-groomed and strikingly well-dressed. Whether we agree or disagree with their principles, they make a statement about the seriousness of their lives. I've certain requirements for the way young people dress around me. I don't like to see kids with their shoelaces untied. I don't like to see the youth I work with wearing their hair like Buckwheat."

"Tell it."

"Fifty rubber-bands and braids sticking out all over the place like you done been in a scary movie. Don't get me wrong," Booker T said holding one hand up. "I'm totally down with the best of them for our youth having individuality, but give me a break. Those rappers who wear their hair that way, that's their business. They're entertainers. They don't live down in the deep, deep hood. They sing about it, but they are hanging out on Fifth Avenue, in the Hamptons, and wherever other stars are. They aren't trying to find a job to support a family. They're not trying to make an impression on anybody. They got it already. Do yall know what I'm saying?"

"You're right, my man," exclaimed a concerned parent.

"They *are* legends all right. Legends in their own mind. According to societal standards, the brothers have arrived. They're getting paid millions to entertain you not only with their hip-hop sounds but also with their dress and with their hairstyle. It's a business pure and simple. When I see my young brothers emulating such ridiculous Buckwheat hairstyles on the street, I drop my head and shake it with pain—serious pain. Why? Have they not looked in the mirror lately? Understand me. I'm down with ethnicity. Cornrows. Afros. Dreds. Braids. And even weaves are great to see. But some of us have taken hair creativity to another level."

"Tell the truth," a man said, and several people in the audience began laughing boisterously and clapping wildly.

"I'm serious. It makes me sad, man. I don't like to see the kids I work with wearing earrings in their ears, either. You know how they used to tag the slaves. They used to tag them with earrings, and that's why I refuse to allow my young people to wear them. It's a symbol of slavery."

"Uh oh," Scott moaned jokingly to Charmaine.

"Learn the history behind fads and fashion, and you won't do certain things. And I definitely better not catch my young men wearing scarves tied around their head like Aunt Jemima, and there's a baseball cap on top of that. I don't want to see the big boots and oversized shirts with white undershirts hanging below them. I definitely won't allow our young people to wear their pants pulled halfway down their behinds so you can see their drawers. I refuse to tolerate that at all! This style came from prisoners. If you were a sissy in the prison, you were told to wear your pants low so the other men could see your colored underwear. Showing your underwear in prison determined your status. It divided all male prisoners in two categories. The men and the women. So you know I cannot accept this style."

"Say so."

"That's why we have rules young folk must abide by. If you can't abide by the simple rules out here, you certainly won't make the ones that life throws at you. That's why we've such an epidemic of uninspired Black youth. Many times, the smothering mothering types of sistahs these days don't think no other females are good enough for their boys. They believe that no one else should chastise them. Then there are the doting fathers. Brothers who don't believe that anybody can say anything to their children. In an acceptable era of weak parents, it makes me want to throw up. It's an ugly epidemic out there in the Black community, especially with unruly children. It has got to change! The only way that it can be done is for parents and guardians to demand respect and require discipline from our young people."

The crowd erupted into applause as they began to get into the message and rhythm of his speech.

"That's how you create proud Black citizens who come back to you five, ten, and fifteen years later. These same young people come back looking for you. When they find you, they look you in the eyes and they let you know what a powerful, life-changing impact you had on their lives. As a coach in South Carolina and Greensboro, it happened to me. When those troubled youth returned to town, they looked up my name and number in the phone book. It happened whenever they came back. They do it so that you can just shake their hand, look in their eyes, and know now that they're successful as adults even though they had serious problems growing up. Without question, it has made me cry a number of times," Booker T admitted honestly and glared into Marlon's face.

"Wonderful," an older woman said.

"I realize it's hard these days. I remember growing up trying to figure out what to do with my life, but it was a little different for me than it is for a lot of kids growing up today. I had my father around. My father represented a strong Black tradition all right. He represented a hellatious potion of discipline, respect, and a strong dose of a can of whip ass, too."

"Tell the truth," one guy said. It seemed as if all the men in the crowd bust out laughing and began to clap relentlessly.

"That was my consequence when I didn't do what I was supposed to do. I believe children have the right to be angry, sad, happy, and experience a whole lot of other emotions that's human. However, they don't have a right to act any way they want to around me. They can't do anything they want to, especially if it's unacceptable behavior. I'll not tolerate it in any shape, form, or fashion. You cannot love children too much, but you can give them too much power."

"Tell the truth," a woman said, spellbound with Booker T.

"Nowadays, kids make decisions because they don't think they'll face any consequences. They don't believe they'll be punished. Sure, most people know the difference between right and wrong. Common sense helps them with that. But common sense is also learned from within their home, their exterior environment, and also from basic instincts of hearing. When children have someone in the home that makes them responsible for unacceptable behavior, many times they realize certain consequences will follow blatantly bad decisions. If there isn't a consequence, children, adults, and everyone goes berserk. That's why I make it clear to the honored guests and to all the other children that grace my path. If you do bad things, there are consequences. Period. *I'm* going to get you." Everyone, including the children knew he was serious and a hush fell over the crowd. Everybody's brain was turning.

"My other goal is to keep our young Black men strong and honorable. Once again, it requires discipline on their part, too. I believe there are seven ways our fertile Black male minds are being destroyed and being weakened. Number One: Black young men are actually killing each other. It's unfortunate, but it's true. The people who control the economy and dictate the media are one in the same. Those people like us at each other's neck and killing each other. It looks great on the evening news, and it makes it easier for them to control us."

"Run it down, Booker T," Symone rooted him on.

"Number Two: Homosexuality. I don't have to explain the irrationality and sinfulness of this. Number Three: Black cats are dating outside their race and then are *actually* marrying these white women and women of other races. It not only weakens our strong seed, but our Black women must feel hurt and ignored. Integration validated the white woman, and the media perpetuates them to be perfect, and now it's gotten totally out of hand. Number Four: Black males are going to jail like people go to the mall. It's always crowded in the mall, too. Isn't it? Number five: Drugs have killed us and weakened us. It's an abomination. Number Six: The lack of education brings about the lack of employment, and this brings about a propensity for violence. What happened to us? When they enslaved us, all we wanted to do was get free, have land, and get an education. We were hard workers striving toward a better life. Some of us still pursue those goals, but a lot of us do not. What happened?"

"Good question, man."

"Somewhere down through the years, our priorities got totally messed up. Last but least, my seventh downfall of the Black man is racial profiling. Because you're Black and driving along, you're pulled over without good cause. You're harassed. You're arrested. In some cases, our Black men are assaulted and even killed. The blue wall of silence covers those so-called justified murders. That means cops are keeping quiet. They're keeping their reckless behavior a secret under the pretense that they're doing their job and wouldn't do anything to hurt a Black man driving his bought and paid for car."

"He's speaking the truth," Cleopatra said to Alex.

"But racial profiling is out there, and Black men are experiencing it daily. It *even* happened to Marlon. When they realized who he was, their negative attitude changed. Those same cops who actually wanted to know why he was driving a brand new Ferrari changed their tune and wanted his autograph once they realized who he was. This actually happened in North Carolina. They didn't kick him, punch him, or hit him with their billy club. If they did, you can believe we would've owned North Carolina. Right, BJ?"

"Right, Pop," BJ replied and the audience began laughing.

"But all jokes aside, it's serious these days. Those are the seven downfalls of the Black man. And if I have anything to do with it, the young brothers I work with will not fall in *any* of those categories I mentioned."

Booker T received sporadic claps for his frankness. He did not apologize for either one of them. When he started with number one, the audience listened intently. After he got pass number four, a few people felt uncomfortable and believed Booker T was a racist. However, Booker T plowed forward with the truth according to him.

"...We as a people allow so much to go on where we live," Booker T was saying five minutes later. "You've never seen a liquor store in a Jewish community. I know I haven't. Why? It's because Jewish people know how to rally together and protect their communities. They also have a lot of economic power, and they absolutely put their foot down on issues that will affect the growth of their children or the future of Jewish generations. We've got to do the same thing. Band together. We need to know that they only make forty-ounce containers of beer for Black people. Don't yall know they did a study on us and determined that was the law of the land for beer drinkers in our Black communities? It can be a chilled forty-ounce of whatever. Most white people don't buy those large bottles. The beer company trucks that bring beer into our communities are sooo long. Just check them out the next time. They are constantly appealing to the junk we think we need to survive. A get high attitude."

"You go, Booker T," Pauletta shouted to him, and Booker T turned to the next page of notes.

"In Carlos Reynolds' speech last month, he shared how he read somewhere that in one of the Black areas in New York, a study showed that there was a total of 230 billboards in that small, Black community. One-hundred-ninety-three of them advertised alcohol. Thirty-seven of them advertised tobacco products. In another instance, Carlos told us that in a different area of New York, they found one-hundred and forty-two advertisements on billboards, corner stores, and bar windows in the low-income areas. However, when a comparative analysis was performed in a nearby, white affluent community, they only found that six such advertisements were displayed."

"Wow," another woman groaned.

"I know this surprises you. It shouldn't, but it does. There are reasons so many of our people are suffering." Booker T had to pause for the applause. "I wonder how that happened? Why that was allowed? The next time you're outside, check out the advertisement on billboards and in windows that bombard the landscape of your neighborhoods. Check out the advertisements that are in East Winston, in poor communities in Greensboro, and throughout this country. Take time to notice these things. Without a doubt, you'll be surprised at what you'll see. Many of us never noticed the way these malt liquor companies, beer companies, cigarette companies, liquor companies fuse our habits and believe these kinds of advertisements are appropriate for our buying truckloads of their products. And we do."

Several people moaned *umph, umph, umph, umph.*

"You go, boy," Nanette exclaimed.

"Let me give you some statistics that Jodria compiled for me," Booker T said and turned to his specific page. "I want you to listen carefully. Did you know that one in three Blacks between the ages of twenty and twenty-nine are in prison or are on probation? Twenty-five percent of all Black youth are in prison. Eighty percent of the people in our prison systems are a product of either an abusive home or a foster home. Twenty-three hundred children are reported missing each day that we live. It takes less than a minute to abduct a child and snatch him off the streets and take them away. Every five hours a child dies from abuse or neglect. One in five children are born into poverty. The average age of homeless children is six years old. Can you believe that? Four out of five children that are born in this country are born to single parents. One point three million runaways are roaming the streets of America. Every day, fifteen children are killed violently with guns. That includes murder, suicide, or whatever. It's happening, people. Eight and nine year old children run around with more lethal guns than the police do. Two hundred and seventy thousand young people carry guns to school every day. Can you believe that? I repeat two hundred and seventy thousand kids do that."

"Lawd have mercy," sighed a senior citizen.

"Stay with me now," Booker T said to the audience as he tried to catch as many eyes as he could. "Everyone here will receive a copy of each speaker's speech, but I still want yall to carefully listen to these numbers."

"We're with you," said a concerned father.

"There have been more Americans killed in the past two years with hand guns than in the entire Vietnam War. Violent crimes committed by young people have risen sixty-eight percent in the last five years. Three thousand teens are arrested on murder charges each year. AIDS is the number one cause of death in America for people under the age of forty-five. One million children worldwide is afflicted with AIDS or HIV, and three million children have already died of this disease. Fifty-three percent of all African American men don't have a job. Then, the ones that do have a job and work everyday don't even earn enough to make it without a struggle. Two thirds of all Black men earn less than twenty thousand a year. Unemployment among Black men is twice as high among white men. So, do you wonder where Black folk's frustration and a sense of powerlessness come from?"

"Umph, umph, umph," several people moaned.

"We have many of our strong Black men working every day and still not making it. I could go on and on with statistical information; however I won't. Jodria reminds us all the time that we need to understand all those statistics. Those pretty numbers we hear about represent human beings—possibly a person you know. When you equate the numbers to human lives, there's a massive toll on our race. True, people might say statistics could prove anything. But if you know of one person who qualifies in the areas I mentioned, that's staggering."

The crowd listened to him with intense interest and was amazed at his intelligence, commitment, and the way he rattled off the statistics he shared with them.

"Break it on down for us, Booker T," yelled a buddy of Booker T.

"Think about these other disturbing statistics. There are one-hundred-thousand traffic deaths per year caused by alcohol. Billion of dollars are spent to help with alcohol-related injuries and problems. Even though the government and the public are diligently after the cigarette industry, the liquor industry has taken a reach out and touch everyone attitude toward our Black youth and adults. We need to get real with this, people. Alcohol isn't a cakewalk, either. Are they doing anything about it?"

"No," answered an audience member.

"Smoking has been banned almost everywhere, but you know what's amazing. How we are allowing folk to drink alcohol everywhere. I was on a plane to Kansas City, and the stewardesses were slinging vodka, rum, gin, and beer all over the plane. But could you smoke a cigarette? Nope. What's the difference? The bad habit of drinking is just as bad as smoking. In my opinion, it's even worse. You know why?"

"No."

Booker T smiled. He wasn't expecting an answer. "It might be socially acceptable, but check out its damage. Drunk drivers kill one-hundred-thousand people on our highways each year. One million more are injured. Our congressional and senate people aren't going to change laws in that arena. You know why? Because they do more than take an occasional drink during those wonderful Washington cocktail hours. The same applies for our state officials. That's why they're lax on alcohol. Everybody's doing it. Drinking it. Loving it. Accepting it. Lushing it up. But folks are dying from that, too. So what are our legislature folk going to do about that? Not a thing."

"C'mon with it, my brother."

"It doesn't stop with alcohol. Smoking is another serious plague on young people, too. Cigarettes are like a loaded gun in my opinion. The numbers of young people developing this habit are staggering. Just today alone, three thousand high school students will begin smoking. Multiply those three thousand students' times three hundred and sixty-five days a year. What does that tell you? You might as well throw arsenic down your throat because eventually you'll not be able to make it through life with a habit like that."

I can't believe he said that about cigarettes especially with the way he smokes reefer. Blunts are more like it, Pecola thought as she continued to gaze at Booker T with a big smile on her face.

"Another killer in the Black community and in the schools is guns. Poverty, crime, and drugs already ravaged many of our communities. Now we got to deal with guns. We're killing each other like we're the enemy. Each day our population is condemned to death. Each day young people are still dying at the hands of other young Blacks who have become their executioners. A buddy of mine in DC said that the Metro Section of the *Washington Post* reports that an average of three young Blacks are killed every day as a result of shootings, fights, and cops' bullets. That's just in DC alone. We cannot continue to kill each other. We're losing lawyers, doctors, congressmen, and future presidents. Why? Where is all the firepower coming from? I have never seen a gun factory in the Black community. But we literally are trying to blow each other off the face of the earth with the guns that are coming from somewhere. Poverty, discrimination, and rage can twist a community. It can warp it and make it turn on itself. That's so senseless."

"Speak the truth, my brother."

"I believe that *one* person who loses his life to guns is one too many. Then there are guns in school? Our school system is the poster child institution of America for confusion, discord, and economic decline within families. Schools should be a place for learning, not a place where you fear for your life. But today, children are scared to learn. Teachers are scared to teach and are intimidated by the students. What is going on? The children and I have talked about this. They tell us that they've seen a lot of guns in the school, as well as on their neighborhood streets. Contrary to popular belief that they're hardened youth, seeing guns all the time actually scares the hell out of them." Booker T's voice was full of passion as thunderous applause resounded through the tent. "We should do what they do in Canada. Every gun should be registered, and everyone should take a test before they get one. Yes, it would be expensive, but sooo many lives would be saved. A life is priceless. Compare Canada's crime statistics to our country, and you'll know that their gun control system is obviously working!"

"Tell it, brother," a spellbound man said as he clapped.

"Each day our population is condemned to death. Each day they're still dying at the hands of other young Blacks who have become their executioners. Whether they are in gangs or whether they're shooting people for no good reason, it's African-American genocide at the hands of other African-Americans. I use gang as an acronym. Around here, GANG means this. **G**reat **A**ttitude is **N**ecessary **G**roundwork to success and a long, happy life."

"Share the truth," another man encouraged. Once more, the clapping of hands roared throughout the tent. The clapping died down. The audience became silent and listened.

"...None of us is safe from AIDS unless we save our own life. We always think that we won't get AIDS. I won't get pregnant. We're such consummate rationalizers who never think bad things will happen to us. Since there is no cure for AIDS, prevention is the best method to get this disease under control. We need to educate our youth in this area, so that we can decrease the number of new young and old people that become infected with AIDS."

"Say so, young man."

"Most importantly, we gots to talk to each other about it. Children need to know that drug abuse and sex are the two most common ways AIDS is spreading across this country and around the world. Jodria introduced me to a thought-provoking video entitled, *In our own Words: Teens and Aids.* I require that the young people I work with see the video at least three times a year. Then write me a report on it and tell me what you think. Like Rufus and Chaka Kahn used to sing, *Tell me Something Good.* For me, just put it in writing."

"Preach, young man," a senior citizen exclaimed loudly as she nodded her head in agreement.

"We got a mental war going on out here. Don't yall realize that yet? The evidence is all around us. We also gots to fight against the negative images on television. When our women have a boy child, the media informs our women that they're giving birth to an endangered species. It's like the rote method. If you keep hearing the timetables over and over and over again, you'll finally get it. That's what happening in communities around this country. Our Black people believe the hype. Many children believe that they're not going to live past the age of twenty-one cause it's expected that they will kill each other off. And they fall into this trap."

"Speak the truth."

"It's a perception which then becomes racial propaganda by the media. True, the white man isn't pulling the gun trigger in the urban areas where killing is an hourly occurrence, but I believe the sins of the blighted history of this country, and the media are pulling an even worse trigger. The electronic trigger on the propaganda about our people. We're dealing with the mind here," he said as he pointed an index finger to his left temple.

As smattering of clapping arose, Booker T thoughtfully studied the crowd. "I'm like William and Geraldine White. I believe in pushing our Black youth to excel. I believe in their standing tall. When Uncle Booker T comes around, he expects book reports! Doesn't he?" Booker T asked the twenty-eight children.

They all nodded yes. That is except the two teen-aged boys, Armstrong Harris and Brian Agnew, who were both fourteen years old. The boys knew they were in trouble with Booker T. They were supposed to turn in book reports on James Baldwin's *Native Son* by Friday when they arrived to Advance or no later than seven o'clock that same evening. However theirs weren't ready, so they missed the important, written in stone deadline. Late Friday night, Booker T looked both boys straight in the eyes and told them that he wanted the perfectly handwritten reports by no later than nine-thirty Monday morning. He didn't care what Alex, Madison, Cleopatra, and Jodria had planned for them to do.

"We read a lot of books around here, don't we?" Booker T bellowed out to the audience.

"Yeahhhh!" yelled the youth who were the honorees and also the people who were in the audience whose parents were members of the Ujima Literary Society.

"Uncle Booker T's motto about books is what?"

"Reading books should be as important as eating! As breathing! As talking! As downright living!" The twenty-eight young people, the other children in the roped off section, plus pockets of other youngsters scattered throughout the tent yelled out in unison.

The audience began laughing and applauded loudly. Nanette and Jodria banged their tambourines.

"How many books does Uncle Booker T want yall to read by the time you're twenty-five?" he shouted into the microphone.

"At least two-hundred and fifty books that teach us about our proud Black people, about our beautiful race, and about our glorious inventions known the world over!" yelled all the children who were aware of the teachings of Booker T.

"Why do I want yall to read these books?"

"Because Uncle Booker T believes that all Black folk who are our most prolific readers will eventually become are our most effective leaders!"

"Way to go, baby," Booker T replied with a huge smile. "Aren't they smart? The reason they're that way is because they're being taught to excel. That's why. Their characters are being molded as proud Black young people in this country. We're not going to have these children thinking like second class citizens and neither will they be easily intimidated. We instill in our children that they should be confident. That they can mentally wheel and deal with the best in the world no matter where they're from or who they come up against. We tell them to always stand tall. Stand still and look people in the eyes when they talk. We teach them that when they speak, don't look down, don't look up, and don't look to the side. Look the person you're speaking to straight dead smack in the eyes."

"Preach, brother," an unidentified woman hollered out from the next to last row.

"Yes, I'm preaching. But more than that, our role here is to teach. There's too much preaching going on in pulpits now and not enough teaching," Booker T told her bluntly.

"My mission is to fight ignorance and to teach children to cherish words and reading. That's what Alex and Madison wanted me to do, and that's what I'm doing. I'm teaching them what I was taught back in the day by my father and his brothers when I was a young kid growing up on Winston Street in Greensboro. Strong men taught me. I had a real strong father and strong uncles who took time with me, my brother, and my sister. My father and my uncles gave me advice about life. I got good advice from good, strong Black men, and I'm teaching the same."

"Say so," a woman said.

"We want them to learn everything that they possibly can. We even have the eight to eleven years old group reading some intellectually challenging books." Booker T gazed at Alex and Jodria.

"The eight to eleven year olds books are monitored by Alex, Jodria, and Cleopatra." Booker T laughed. "Those three ladies just about had a fit when I said I wanted the small children to read Wright's *Native Son*. They thought the subject was advanced. I don't know it all, and sometimes I have to step back and hear another view. I understand their view. But hey, I was going to go with it until those three vicious wardens stopped me. Those three women working together for the sake of children are a stone trip. You got a whole armor of steel around when they're in the area. Believe you me." The audience began laughing.

"In May, all twenty-eight of the older children had the assignment to read Haki R. Madhubuti's work *Black Men: Obsolete, Single, Dangerous?* The Devereauxs and their friends purchase all the books that the children read. For the young people that have jobs, we expect them to contribute in the purchase of their books. We don't want them to think everything is free. So once they explain their expenses to us, we figure out what they have left to contribute toward purchasing a book to add to their personal library."

"That's fantastic, man."

"We read a lot around here," Booker T said, flipping pages to find the books he listed. "So far we've read Chinua Achebe, *Things Fall Apart*. Dr. Ben Carson's, *Think Big*. The Claude Brown classic, *Manchild in the Promise Land*. Gordon Park's, *The Learning Tree*. Eldridge Cleaver's, *Soul on Ice*, *Life without Father*, and *Black Pioneers of Science and Invention*. Let's me see. They also read Alex Haley's *The Autobiography of Malcolm X*. Dr. Mary Frances Berry's, *The Politics of Parenthood*. That was deep. Wasn't it?"

"Yes," answered some of the children.

"We've read Mumia Abu-Jamal's piece, *Live From Death Row*. Another one is *Faith of our Fathers: African American Men Reflect on Fatherhood*. Help me out here," Booker T said with his voice trailing off.

"*There is a River*, *Black Labor White Wealth*, and the *Stolen Legacy*," Miles Valley shouted out along with his friend, Harden Franchot, a thirteen year old that lived in Cleveland Avenue Homes. Since Franchot wanted to be like Booker T, he wore a skullcap today.

"You're right, man. *The Stolen Legacy* by George James, *Black Labor White Wealth* by Claud Anderson, and Vincent Harding's *There is a River*. Those three books are part of a collection that Symone calls required reading. Also, we read books out loud around here. When the young ones aren't sure how to say words, we teach them to sound them out. They'll learn. If they're having problems in school, we get tutors for them. What they don't get in school, we try to help them. Carlos and Rico Reynolds personally purchased subscriptions to *The Black Collegian* and *Black College Today* magazines for all fifty-eight children. We want them to think college, college, college, and more college."

"Me too," a retired teacher said.

"In spite of what several of them have been told by incompetent teachers, we believe every last one of *our* kids are college material. Copies of the college magazines and other worthwhile magazines are delivered straight to their home. They also have their personal copies of *Acts of Faith*. Twice a year, we all sit down and watch *Eye on the Prize*. Whenever I see that piece, it brings tears to my eyes. I'm reminded of our struggles as a culture to just be recognized. To be restored to the powerful people we once were before they took our land from our ancestors and called the stolen land the United States of America."

"Tell the truth," Symone exclaimed.

"After viewing *Eye on the Prize*, everyone writes a report that's read at our literary society meetings. That goes for adults and children alike. My point is if the children don't get anything else from working with us and any of these adult volunteers, they'll be armed until death with knowledge. Most importantly, they'll have the true knowledge about their history and culture. If they know the glory and richness of their past, they can march toward the future with pride. If they read, they'll keep getting stronger and stronger, opening up their world."

"Wonderful."

"Just little over a hundred years ago, laws on most of the United States books stated that slaves couldn't even be educated. It was against the law for Black folks to learn to read or write. The way some of us act today, we think the law is still in place. We got to learn, baby. Learn all there is and then some."

"Say so," an older woman exclaimed.

"When I was growing up, smart niggers died or were killed when they had powerful head knowledge." Booker T said with fervency.

I can't believe he said the word nigger in here, thought several people in the audience.

"That's right. I said *nigger.* Let me get another thing straight before I go any further. Years ago and not too many years ago, either, I had a great uncle and a cousin that were lynched. It happened years ago, but I haven't forgotten it. I'm like the Jews in that respect. Jews might forgive, but they have never forgotten. They'll never forget the Holocaust. They keep talking about it and keep referring to it. They forgive, but they never forget how Hitler and his soldiers tried to get rid of an entire race."

"So true," Symone nodded.

"I haven't forgotten either. That's how it should be with Black folk. We may forgive the atrocities that have occurred with our over one-hundred million Black brothers and sisters, but we should never forget our holocaust, either. Between the Europeans exterminating thousands of our people when they stepped upon this soil known now as America and as a result of slavery, more Blacks died during those times than *ever* was fathomed during the Jewish holocaust of World War II. We don't hear about that! Our slave holocaust was twenty-five times worst than the European holocaust. Twenty-five—times—worse, people. Do yall hear me? We gots to understand that."

"Lawd have mercy," an older woman exclaimed. Several people were sadly nodding their heads too. Others were weeping from the sadness of the old hurt of Black folk's history.

"But have we gotten reparation?" Booker T asked. "No. Have the Jews and other people received reparation from this country for being killed, mistreated, and abused? Yes they have!"

"Tell it like it is, Booker T, man," Rozelle shouted out.

"Never ever should we allow the gruesomeness of what we as people have suffered through and continue to experience slip from our remembrance. So when you hear my name Booker T, don't confuse me with Booker T. Washington, the infamous one. I am not your Sambo. Learn your history. If you know your history, you'll know that Booker T Washington believed that Blacks should primarily be concerned with agriculture and being good laborers. Booker T Washington believed Black folk should wait patiently on white people to change their ways and to not do anything to anger them. That if we just make ourselves indispensable to them, they'll accept us in time." Booker T's tone was very sarcastic.

"Uh oh," moaned Symone. She often got on Booker T for criticizing one of Hampton's most famous graduates.

"Booker T was quite conciliatory and stroked the whites. In other words, he was a white man's nigger. A house nigger. Just because my name is Booker T, I am not about any of that. I am not the Booker T you know about. Sure he did some good, but a lot of stuff he supported that I read about hurt me to my soul. He's one of those heroes that white folk have designated for us."

"The white historians have written down and extensively documented their white heroes. In many cases, they've written down nothing about the thousands of Black folk who have played an important role in the history of this country and of this world. It was necessary for them to remove an entire people from the world. African history—our history is the missing story, folks."

"Speak the truth, man," a guy yelled.

"But guess what? That's where we come in, ladies and gentlemen. We have to fill in those wide gaps. Learn your history, my brothers and sisters. Marinate in it. Stop accepting the heroes they've chosen for us to know about. Read about Nat Turner. Do the same about David Walker, who was born right in Wilmington, North Carolina. He was a boldly, militant brother. He wrote a piece called *Walker's Appeal* long, long time ago. If a Black person was caught reading *Walker's Appeal* or even if a Black person had it in his possession back then, it was a crime punishable by death. David Walker said, '...killed or be killed.' It was way before Malcolm said 'By any means necessary.' Back then, David Walker wanted the slaves to secure their freedom by any means necessary. Learn your history, children and adults."

"Tell the truth, young man."

"My goal is to build strong, Black young men and women who realize the power within themselves. We're working on the inside. The mind," Booker T said and pointed to his right temple. "Until the image of the Black man and Black woman is changed within themselves, nothing will change for our culture."

"Rap on, my brother," Rozelle exclaimed and saluted Booker T with a Black Power fist.

"Back to why I said nigger earlier. I know the roots of the word "nigger" are in slavery, but I still use it. Some of you do, too. Maybe you don't do it in public, but you certainly do say it when you get ready. All of a sudden, Black folks have gotten so proper and all. When I came along, if I called you *brother* or *sister that* was what it was about. You were my brother or sister for the cause, for unity, and for being Black. Just like nigger. It was a word of affection and camaraderie with your other Black brothers."

"Absolutely."

"We embraced that horrible term and turned it into something beautiful. The word is never going to disappear cause white folks still are calling us niggers behind our backs—even if you can't hear it. I embrace the term. Whether or not you want to use the word 'nigger,' that's your choice. Just don't bash me for using it. Don't scold me about it like you're scolding a white man cause I say it with love and respect wrapped all around it."

"Speak the truth," Marlon said with a nod.

"Nowadays, we got the freedom to read and to attain almost any dream we have. But many of us don't take advantage of the free opportunity of learning because we don't read. Old folks had a saying that said the easiest way for information to be hidden away from our culture, from all Black people, is for it to be written in a book. Why? Traditionally, it has been said that Black folk don't read. But guess what? They're lying. For four hundred years, we weren't legally allowed to read and write. They didn't want us to know we were here first and that they were on our land. Blacks folk's land. Not Native Americans."

"What is he talking about?" a man whispered to his wife. "Indians were here first, and Christopher Columbus discovered America."

"...We *were* reading," Booker T was saying. "That never stopped a slave. We bucked the law and reading fueled our hunger to be free. So we certainly can eat up the knowledge that's found in books today!"

"Wonderful words," a woman exclaimed.

"Out here in Devereaux Land, we want to start nurturing a strong bunch of readers and a strong bunch of bold, educated Black young men and women. Reading to them will become second nature as breathing. It's said that forty million Americans can't read. One in four African-Americans can't read and understand the story of their glorious history of being the first people on earth. If there's approximately forty million of us here, that means about ten million of us can't read. That's unacceptable. We don't want these children here to be a part of such statistics. We have a tradition of reading. We want reading books to be a part of their daily lives so that they can see the whole beautiful world even if they do live in the projects. Reading fuels self-esteem and forces you to be proud of whom they are. That's why I want them to read. That's the only way they'll know their possibilities."

"Tell the truth. Tell the truth," a woman yelled out. She wondered if the dapper Booker T was single and available.

"In other words, academics are very important out here. We tell the children we mentor that academics should be more important than sports, fun, and your friends. As a young person, your first priority of business in school is your academics. We tell them to be careful whom they choose as friends. They need to know that their friends should be academically inclined, too. If you know this, check out your friend's attitude. If you follow someone with an ugly attitude home, you can believe someone with an ugly attitude is bound to open the door."

"Say so," someone yelled out. The audience began an exuberant round of laughing and clapping.

"I want you to know that my discussion wasn't delivered to petrify anyone or cause you to have your pretentious attitude get worse, or to make you feel good about coming out here this Saturday afternoon. That's not me. You got the wrong brother. The Devereauxs wanted me to provide you with a capsule view of the teachings I provide to the children. We do have a lot of fun here, but we're serious about the assignment to teach, teach, and teach some more about all aspects of life."

"Wonderful," the same man shouted.

"Well, I ask that you dig out the good in my speech if it was too strong for you." Booker T inhaled deeply and gazed into the obviously uncomfortable faces of some people in the crowd. He hesitated for a moment. "Now for all you doomsayers out there in the audience who say this won't work long and that the Devereauxs' are doing this for show, that's exactly where you belong. Out there in the audience. I know that you're smiling in the Devereauxs' face. Everybody here today isn't happy about what they're doing. You know who you are. You're harboring jealousy in your heart, and you're praying for failure."

"I knew Booker T was going to rock our world today," Pauletta whispered to Pecola.

"Don't feel bad. You're not alone in this world. There are busloads of pitifully pessimistic people stepping out of factories and living dead, dark basement lives everyday. So join the club. Everyone that sits around and smiles in your face isn't smiling for your good. They don't bask in your success with a pure mind. People who don't do their human homework about what needs to be done in our world to make a difference always rise against the ones who are trying to do their all and all," he said quietly in a firm voice. *"What are you doing?* Look in your mirror. Ask yourself what have I done to make a positive influence in my community, in my family, and in my whatever. Look in the mirror. It never lies back."

"Tell the truth, young man."

"Because what we're doing here is nothing special. This should be a way of life for people all across this neighborhood, this city, this state, and this nation. That's why we say we need committed, unselfish people who are willing to make an emotional investment. We're serious about this. We're serious about our children's lives. We only want people who care about the future of our people. That's the whole picture we need to see. That you need to see. Sure, the Devereauxs are the leading architects for this. The masterminds for providing an exciting country outlet for our children. But all that the Devereauxs are doing and all their friends that work with them are doing is simple. We all are developing a need to understand, to love our young people, to be patient with them and to help them to learn. We all are simply trying to figure out what in the world to do to not only save our children but to save a few of somebody's else's." The audience erupted into wild clapping and a round of woof, woof, and woofing.

"Talk your stuff, brother," exclaimed the same unidentified man from the back row.

"Some might say, 'But you're not those children's parents, Booker T.' You know what, ladies and gentlemen? This work has nothing to do with blood. Yet, we know we're related to these young people being honored this afternoon by caring. We're not their parents. Yet, we can be that uncle, that aunt, or that mentor who can make a difference. We can be that voice they need to hear every so often which can give them the energy, guidance, and inspiration they need to make it in school."

"That's right."

"We can be a firm father figure and mother figure, too. For them to have the knowledge that as the bond of association grows between all of us, they'll know that someone else loves them as their own. Discipline is there, too. When I need to be the enforcer, I am. Consequences follow bad decisions." A lot of the children bobbed their heads with understanding from prior incidents. They knew Booker T was telling the absolute truth. The parents in the audience broke out in a round of boisterous laughing, and Booker T continued to speak.

"All the children we work with aren't going to listen to what we say when they leave us. Unfortunately, some still aren't going to work hard to be successful. If the children I work with in Greensboro, out here in Devereaux Land, and with over the country don't make it, I'll be upset. They're not making it won't be because they felt they had no one who cared for them or no one to turn to. It'll be because of the wrong choices they decided to make in their lives." Once more wild applause followed Booker T's words.

"Tell it, my man."

"All we want to do for these children is give them all that's most important to them. Some children want to just simply go to the mall, go to the beach, or spend time in the country at a place like this. They want to go to the mountains and to summer camp. Children want simple things, but children also want discipline, love, and understanding. They want to talk to us about what's going on in their heads. They want unconditional love and a sense of cohesiveness in a family-spirited way. These are such basic needs for children——for a man and a woman for that matter. I'm looking for a good woman to love me tight and right about now," Booker T quipped and laughed right along with the audience.

"I'm available," a woman yelled out, and Booker T smiled. Several people turned around and gazed into the direction they believed the voice came from. Booker T didn't know where the woman was either, wasn't going to look, and resumed his speech.

Booker T lowered his voice. "That's why you must go to school and do well in school, children. But don't stop there. Go to college. Educate your mind. Your most powerful weapon is your mind. It's your greatest asset, not a gun. Graduate from college. Get a good job. Work. But we as Black people also have to develop innovative ways to survive. Therefore, it's incumbent upon you to design your life. Identify your bliss. See the needs in society, then create your reality. Create your business from that need. Instead of looking for a job, simply create one. Cultivate your natural God given talents into a career of your choice. Please, children, see your possibilities."

"Not only are our children seeking their possibilities, they're also seeking a mushroom of love from us, they're looking for an opportunity to explore the world and to allow their brains to be stimulated. They want exposure to learning. The children are also looking for unconditional love laced with principles, character, and morals. Nothing more and nothing less. These are basic human needs."

"Lawd have mercy. You're telling the truth," one of the senior citizens said with heartfelt emotions.

"Without question, the young people sitting here are the catalysts for change in their communities. And in order to have change in the neighborhoods in which you live, those changes must come from within those communities' boundaries. It must come from within the hearts and minds of the residents. We're just sharing. We know that everybody just needs to do something. That's all we're doing because we know one day all the children we deal with will do the same thing. We're teaching them to think about future generations and not only about themselves."

"Wonderful."

"Symone once told me that she read somewhere that our ancestors always considered five generations when making decisions. For instance, if they had an opportunity to achieve stellar success and wealth, they thought about it long and hard. If our ancestors believed it would affect the third generation in any shape or form—whether it was profitable or not, our ancestors refused to take part in it. Now, that's some powerful planning on the part of an entire culture. Black folks of today need to do the same."

"Amen, my man."

"We want our children to know that they're our future but they're our present as well. Still, they're future generations beyond them that they need to think about. When our children here are older and get in a position to help someone, they too should reach out and give a child a helping hand. Eventually, they too will share hope, dignity, dedication, and love. They'll teach respect and help other youth to develop character. It just helps when young people learn how to give back, so they too can grow more passionate about giving. We're just recycling.

Like my Pop used to say to me, 'If your intentions are good, then your results will be pure, son.'"

"These are powerful words, brother," another man yelled out.

"You may not liked some of the things I've said this afternoon, and that's ok. I always tell my critics, it's not what I say that matters. Let me be judged by the work I've done. Let me be judged by the long list of young people I've worked with who went on to become successful adults. Not only in the monetary sense, but strong and powerful within their minds. That where it counts the most. We're on a journey here, ladies and gentlemen. It's a journey for the future of our people, and that journey must begin with our taking the first step. Every deed that's done always begins with one person. That's all. It's real simple to understand." Booker T paused and smiled.

"You're right, Booker T."

"In closing, I leave you with the words of Paul Robeson: '...We realize that our future lies chiefly in our own hands. We know that neither institution nor friends can make a race stand unless it has strength in its own foundation; that race, like individuals, must stand or fall by their own merit; that to fully succeed they must practice the virtues of self-reliance, self-respect, industry, perseverance, and economy.' People, I thank you for this moment. To the twenty-eight young people who are being honored this afternoon and to the audience, I love you. Stay strong and keep striving. Peace," Booker T ended solemnly with a peace sign and tried to exit the stage.

"This is for you, Booker T!" yelled the young Harden Franchot with his skullcap on and all. Harden stood and encouraged the other twenty-seven honorees to stand and give Booker T a standing ovation too. Everyone else followed suit.

"You got it, baby," Booker T said as he pointed both index fingers at the youngsters. His eyes became moist, and he finally exited the stage.

Once in his chair, Booker T pounded fists with Christopher and Oscar who were sitting in seats beside him on the second row. His children, who were sitting behind him, rubbed his shoulders. The tent rumbled with claps of praise. Whistle blowing, shouts of *Amen, Amen,* and the banging of the tambourines filled the evening air.

"Wasn't he spectacular? Didn't he tell it like it is? Booker T is known for giving a fearless and penetrating discussion of America's problems, and problems are never pretty."

"Absolutely."

"They say if you want something done, ask a busy person to do it. The more they do, the more they can do. As long as I've known Booker T, he has been busy working with youth, athletes, and with sharing his heavy philosophy about life," Rozelle divulged affectionately. "He's all about sharing the truth. Just like his nephew, Marlon Dinzelle, he was also a great athlete. About a year ago, me and my buddy, Rico, had just beaten everybody on the golf course."

"Don't tell that story again this month, man," Rico moaned with pleasure.

"Let me say it. I gotta say it, man. While we were shooting the breeze on the green grass of Club View Court. It's a little community off Holden Road in Greensboro," Rozelle said as if he were sharing a secret. "Marlon surprised his uncle with a lovely home there about four years ago. Booker T can fall out of bed and play golf twenty-four seven."

"Just wonderful," an older woman said.

"Booker T had a rude awakening himself that day. Jack Goldsberry is a young professional basketball star. He's a twenty-five-year-old player who's still wet behind the ears. He's not here today, so I can talk about him. Anyway, Marlon was introducing Goldsberry to the game of golf. Goldsberry couldn't believe that Booker T played three years with the Carolina team of the American Basketball League. He didn't know Booker T had broken all kinds of records before he was injured. Goldsberry just knew Booker T as Marlon's uncle, and he had heard Marlon say that Booker T had coached at Benedict College. Sure, Booker T laughed it off. But he turned to the other older guys and said, 'I know I'm getting old, man. These young brothers don't even remember I played basketball. They only remember me as a college coach in South Carolina,'" Rozelle ended in a joking tone, mimicking Booker T's voice.

"Break it on down, man."

"Learn about people like Tommie Smith, John Carlos, Curt Flood, and Spencer Haywood. Read and learn about *their* bravery. Research how Haywood's strong stance helped the basket-ball players of today. I only mentioned four people, but there are many, many, many others. Just learn about them. Read their story. And when you realize what they did, thank them. Write a letter. E-mail them. Whatever, yall. Just thank them. Honor them and respect them for their bravery. They don't want you to worship them. They simply want you to remember and appreciate their sacrifices that they made for the future."

"Absolutely," Madison nodded.

"I only tell this to get a point across. Learn your history, but learn it in all aspects of life. If you're a pro ball player, learn about the guys who went before you and who paved the way. They made it possible for you to have an opportunity today. Whether it was in the American Baseball League, the National Football Association, the National Basketball League, baseball, track, tennis, or golf, just learn about all the Black brothers and sisters who was there seventy-five, fifty, thirty, twenty, and even ten years ago. It hasn't always been a sweet deal for Black athletes. Just because you've made it now, don't think you just need to only know the juice about the guys you currently play with."

"You're on the money, Rozelle," Carlos ventured to belt out to the surprise of everyone sitting beside him. Although Carlos had been quiet all evening, he fervently believed that what Rozelle was saying was absolutely right. He too often said athletes these days didn't know dittly about the patriarchs of their respective games who paved the way in opportunity and in salary.

Chapter Sixty-Three

"Moving right along cause it's enough preaching for me. The beauty of friendship is the opportunity to learn all you can from each other. Well, there's more to come. The next speaker is Symone Angela Poussaint. I know she's going to get upset with me, but I'm going to say it anyway. We all know about her being an excellent, tough businesswoman in Winston-Salem, and she's the devoted mother of three children. More importantly, she's also a fabulous friend. Born in Santa Cruz, Trinidad, you couldn't tell that by the way she speaks now. She's a bona fide North Carolinian and loves to say "ain't." She said she likes the way it rolls off her tongue," Rozelle revealed with a comic flair.

"When she's mad, that West Indian accent may escape from her subconscious, and she'll sing you a melodious West Indian tune that you won't forget. Symone immigrated to the United States when she was ten, and she moved and grooved in a very privileged level of society. Her life is truly the ultimate American success story." There was a smattering of applause.

"For those of you who don't really know her like I do, let me share another secret with you. Yes, she's brutally honest, straightforward, and never hesitates to call it like it is on any subject. I call her my little modernistic friend who has a traditionalist bent to her personality. Still, underneath all that exterior toughness, let me tell yall this. Symone is one of the most generous, sensitive, caring, and softest people I know. She really wears her heart on her silk blouse sleeves and really oozes with family, friends, and love," Rozelle said glancing down at the notes his wife helped him prepare about Symone.

"Ladies and gentlemen, she's a courageous warrior for Black folks knowing their history, culture, and recognizing our strength as a proud people through the use of collective economics. Without any further adieu, I proudly present Ms. Poussaint."

As Symone walked to the podium she smiled at Rozelle and slowly shook her head. Pauletta kept telling her she really looked absolutely dazzling this evening, and she did. Even though Symone believed she was twenty pounds overweight, she still appeared slender in an Anne Marie Emmanuel sleeveless purple sheath made of glittery fabric. Symone was delighted to know that Anne Marie was a native Trinidadian whom she discovered on her many trips to the Kilgour & Sweet designer salon in Millburn, New Jersey. Symone had the dress accentuated with a chiffon scarf draped around her neck. Her stocking legs were accentuated with see-through slingbacks. Today, she decided to wear the huge diamond earrings, the pear shaped, cluster diamond ring, and tennis bracelet she received from her Uncle Samuel when she graduated from Hampton. Her friends affectionately called the jewelry, the Eisner Rocks. The flawless jewelry now glistened under the tent's bright lighting. Several people in the audience who didn't know her closely knew beyond a shadow of a doubt that she certainly had to be wearing cubic zirconium. They were convinced that nothing that large could actually be *real* diamonds. Symone poised herself in front of the podium and took a deep breath. When the clapping throughout the audience died down, she spoke firmly with a twist of humor.

"My Mummy always said that if you don't have anything nice to say, don't say anything at all. However, I just wasn't an excellent student in that school of philosophy," she said with a flurry of hand movement and an inward smile. "Still, I'm not going to say what I want about Mr. Rozelle here, but I do want yall to give our illustrious MC for the evening a round of an applause. He's doing a fantastic job. Isn't he?"

"Yesss," the audience responded to her request and began a boisterous round of clapping and shouting.

Symone directed her thoughts to the speech she had labored on most of Friday morning and had planned to deliver in a business like manner. Very briefly, she described mere glimmers of her tumultuous childhood in Trinidad and her dreamlike years in New York; she began speaking to the children about knowing the importance of family.

"...Children and family are at the center of my life," Symone said in a soft voice as she recalled her childhood. "Sure, I have my businesses, and I have my other successful trappings. But the most important thing to me is my family and my children. I feel like I'm a protector of sorts for my family. So, I often let them know that I love them, and let them know I care with my hugs, my kisses, all my letters, and my words. Although I grew up in a family where women routinely participated in business discussions, I also grew up in a family where the well-being of the children was paramount. That's why I admire the stay-at-home mother. To me, that's one of the most important jobs on earth. The stay-at-home mother. It's an exhaustive job that requires lots of discipline, a lot of strength, a lot of love, and certainly sacrifice of time.

The stay-at-home mothers in the audience clapped vigorously with that response. Jodria banged the tambourine, and Symone smiled at her friend.

"My younger sister tried the corporate world for a while. Ameenah quickly left it to stay home with her children. After getting a Master's Degree in African Studies from Temple University, she walked away from it all to raise a family. I admire people like her, Alex, Jodria, and so many others that I know as friends that have decided to make that commitment."

"Because I've chosen to work and still have also chosen to have my family be paramount in my life as well, I hope that the stay-at-home mothers don't think my commitment as a working single mother is any different from theirs," Symone said firmly and flipped to the next page.

There were many nods from the crowd.

"As I tell Ameenah, child care is defined as a woman's only responsibility today. I don't agree with that. I believe a mother's part in her children's lives is a bond like any other, but shared parenting is equally important. Having a family network of family and friends who constantly treat children as their own is family."

"When I say shared parenting, I mean what we do around here within this group of friends. We're friends who care for each other's children. The men get involved with our children's lives. Take my children, for example. They're being raised by me and Miss Jessica, a woman who's like a grandmother to them. Since we live quite far away from my blood family in New York and Trinidad, I value the bonding process my friendship with these people in North Carolina has provided for my children. So, it was never difficult for me to see the scope of the Devereauxs' vision. I see the logic behind their concern. The passion in their eyes, and I understand. As their close friend, I noticed they had been practicing this philosophy with me and my children for years."

"My son and my twin daughters have been a recipient of the unconditional love of the Devereauxs for a very long time. The Devereauxs love you for who you are. They only see you and your desires. They see your soul—not your hang-ups, or your bad side. If they did see that side, they would have left me alone as a friend a long time ago." Symone chuckled lightly as did the audience.

"That's for sure," Rozelle piped in.

"They just *see* you. That's the type of friends I need around me," Symone stated with vast affection as she gazed in Alex and Madison's faces. Before continuing, Symone inhaled deeply and prayed she spoke in a strong voice.

"Before you can get to solutions, you have to look at the problems in their harsh realities. To excel in the future, you must face the realities. One of those realities is this: Our generation takes the many small and large strides Black people have made in this country and around the world for granted. We believe that the rights we have as Black citizens have always been a given. We've become such a complacent generation of Black people. A generation that has an extremely, very short memory."

"Ain't that the truth," an older woman said.

"I'll be forty years old in January, but I still recall the vicious daggers of racism when I was a child taking vacation trips down to the sweltering south. White people want to forget our history, and Black people don't know their history. It's a sin against an entire race of people to deny your roots, to deny your heritage, to deny your identity, and to try to blend in when we're not white. When Black people do that, I wonder whom they think they're fooling? Being or acting white isn't our salvation. We're our own salvation."

"Say so."

"We don't know who we are as Black people. We do things and date other races because it's fashionable to do so or to justify or validate who we are. Some blacks do it to lighten the race. All that will change. It'll change once you know your history, understand the beauty of your culture, and when you see your African complexion and features as beautiful. The most effective way to plant the experience of history in our hearts is by making it part of our memory. We must become absorbed in our culture. The best way to do that is to teach our young and old people to read fervently every day and to go to places where various events took place." There was a rumble of affirmation from the crowd.

"You should've seen the reactions of the children when we took them to The Schomburg Center for Research in Black Culture. The reaction was the same when we took them to the Guggenheim Museum to see the African History display. They saw the evidence that their ancestors were kings, queens, artisans, and common workers in a thriving intelligent society. They saw artifacts and artful messages from the past to substantiate our past. During the entire trip to New York, all our children's eyes were wide open with shock as they learned about the rich and beautiful past of Black people. They don't learn these things in public schools. A mere glimpse is exposed but not much. At the Schomburg, they saw the richness of their culture. It made each and every last one of them feel absolutely proud of their heritage. Such positive feelings are crucial for children. Jodria could tell you horror stories about what some of the children you see sitting before you today have said to her and what many of our children feel. It's unbelievable what our children think about themselves. Jodria could shock you, and make you literally weep with shame if she really told you what these and other Black children think about themselves.

"Lawd have mercy," moaned an older woman as she shook her head from side to side.

"A strong foundation for learning, loving, and succeeding is built around our Black children being proud of who they are as individuals as well as who they are in the beautiful canvas art of Black life. Then when they go through the rites of passage program that Alex and Jodria put together, it's amazing how their internal outlooks and self-esteem soar. They begin to have the kind of pride that changes their outlook and demeanor. That's why everyone who is here today and is involved with working with our children believes it's essential to visit excellent institutions of knowledge and learning about African-Americans. It's all about Black pride. That is what inspired Arthur A. Schomburg to become the legend historian that he was. It was his destiny. His contribution to the world was that his collected works would teach many, many, many people about his heritage. Our African heritage. To achieve success, we're sometimes inspired by ugly words and cruel actions. It was a negative comment that pierced Arthur A. Schomburg's heart and made him dedicate his life to preserving our heritage. A teacher once told him that the Negro people had no history. Those words inspired Arthur A. Schomburg to prove that teacher wrong. He dedicated his life to discovering the truth about his people. He collected five thousand books, three thousand manuscripts, two thousand etchings, and several thousand pamphlets that were the core of the Schomburg Center for Research in Harlem. Read Schomburg's essay, *The Negro Digs up His Past*. Whenever a person told Mr. Schomburg that he wanted to learn about Black folk's history. Schomburg always told them to first '...study the history of your oppressor. That's where the history got lost.'"

"Umph. Umph. Umph," moaned Cleopatra as she shook her head. She was always fascinated by their trips to the Schomburg and by Symone's knowledge of Black history. Symone inhaled deeply and continued her speech.

"I know I've mentioned a lot, but I have a lot more to say," Symone was saying a few minutes later. "For your convenience, a copy of each speech given this afternoon has been prepared for you. I wanted to stick that in so you wouldn't think you had to memorize everything I just said."

"Whew," Rozelle moaned. "Thank God."

"In November of 1898, right here in Wilmington, North Carolina a white mob murdered eleven Black people. Since Black people were here first, they controlled Wilmington. It was during a riot to remove the then powerful Black political structure that was legally operating at that time. If such an uprising had occurred anywhere else in the world as it did in Wilmington, it would have been a coup d'etat. It's considered the nation's only coup by historians. Read

Dr. H. Leon Prather, Sr.'s book, *We Have Taken A City, The Wilmington Racial Massacre and Coup of 1898.* What a glorious story. I would love to see one of our famous Black Hollywood directors bring that story to the big screen."

"Read and learn that George Washington Carver was Tuskegee's most famous scientist of agriculture who developed more than three hundred products. Did you know that a Black man, Jean Pointe Batpist DuSable, founded the city of Chicago, Illinois? It's shameful that the city of Chicago doesn't even have one street named after him." The crowd was amazed.

"I believe if you know your history, these are just a few of powerful things you should know. When you know your history, you'll cry when you hear the words of *We Will Overcome* because then you know what the civil rights struggle was talking about. You'll understand the struggles of our ancestors as they sang the song in their quest for equal opportunities. You would understand the sweat, the grief, the pain, the sadness of fighting for rights that should have been ours in the first place—that had been stolen from us."

"Preach, young lady," yelled out the same robust, older man. Reminded of her people's struggle, tears were falling down Symone's cheeks. Rozelle handed her a handkerchief, and she thanked him. She wiped her eyes, took a long, deep breath, and began speaking.

"When I remind myself of what my ancestors endured and when I think about the struggles they encountered, I'm moved. When I think about the towering strength, about the armor of integrity that carried Black people over the dark, vast sea of frustration, I'm overwhelmed. I'm sooo fortunate that I didn't live during that time. Like Booker T often says, there are certain things you see and words you read that simply bring tears to your eye."

"Say so, young lady."

"...Yes, I've been extremely blessed," Symone was saying. "Many of the civil rights heroes you read and talk about that are known as our civil rights heroes actually ate and slept in my uncles' homes in Harlem. I've met many of these people. As a child, my uncles took their children, my sisters, and my brother to the Schomburg all the time. It was a requirement, and we learned."

"Wonderful."

"Start studying and reading about who you are. The deeper you get into it, the more distant you get from the masses of Black people that think Blacks are doing ok, or that we've done nothing significant. Culturally, Black people control this country. Economically, we're consistently losing. Yet, the powers at be make us think they're more intelligent than we are. When you think about it, Africans were the inventors of many of the gadgets used to make your life livable from the time you get up, till the time you get to the office, and till the time you come home." Symone inhaled heavily and flipped to another page.

"African-Americans have been taught to hate the images of our dark skin, light skin, caramel skin, and mahogany skinned faces we see in the mirror. These are many images of our Black collage of beauty. As a result of the idealization of European ways and pedestal-putting-position society has placed on human beings other than people of color, we've developed a vast self-hatred for who we are. That's a double punch. Not only do we hate ourselves, our looks and who we are, we're also considered the most hated culture of all time."

"Tell the truth."

"White folk's standards are different, and yet we've taken them up. They place white, porcelain skin, long, billowing blonde hair, and the flat behind that ain't nothing like our butts as the pinnacle of beauty," she declared with a smirk, and the audience broke out in a roar of laughter. "Those media standards have destroyed Black people's sense of self-worth, and this has caused us to despise the Negroid features that reflect our beautiful African ancestry.

"Say it, girl."

"I do not allow my children to watch certain shows. I'm almost to the point that I'm seriously thinking about removing all the televisions from my home. You know why? I have three very dark-skinned, cocoa complexioned children, and those aren't the images that explode from the television on a daily basis. They don't even explode from the stations that supposedly say they cater specifically to Black people. You rarely see dark-skinned Black people on television anymore. My children can't watch their TV and see images of themselves as beautiful, intelligent, and powerful people. That's even so in the commercials."

"You're right."

"We need to let those corporate people know that if you're interested in our business and our Black dollars, then you'd better use Black folks in your commercials. It's very important to make a collective stand. Sometimes, I believe that we don't even notice that we're not in the commercials that go after our dollars. We don't notice that we're not depicted accurately. It's almost as if we've been brainwashed."

"Speak the truth, Sy," Pauletta exclaimed.

"Now lately, it's like a fad. All the talk shows, movies, and soap operas try to do is to make interracial this and that seem quite fashionable. It's as if Black folk can't have a healthy, loving, and romantic relationship, especially if it's with a Black partner. It's as if Black men can't have pure, honest, successful, and rewarding relationships unless of course they're loving a white woman or any other woman other than a Black one. I simply can't stand that popular philosophy because that's not indicative of what I see of my friends or indicative of what I know about myself." The crowd murmured their support of what she was saying.

Uh oh, girl, Pauletta thought to herself, enjoying the speech. *You're stepping on some more toes, now.*

"What can you expect? According to research done by Jodria, only two point six percent of the television and movie industry writers are Black. I repeat two point six percent. That's a pathetic number. So the other 97.4% of the writers who are white and are other nationalities have no idea how we as Black people live. They think they do. That's why you see such junk on television. They don't know. They don't know anything about our college homecomings, our family reunions, our loving each other, and our nurturing our children with glistening moments such as this. They don't know about our beautiful gathering of Black folk at jazz festivals, those Classic football games at Black colleges across the country, or the serious throw-down times we have at the Summit with the National Black Brotherhood of Skiers. They probably don't know that Black folks even ski. Simply put, they just don't know us. So since they don't know, I'm convinced they make things up and the big wheels at the studios believe it as truth."

"Tell the truth, sister."

"One way you can have direct, effective, and impressive access to people is through their television sets. Why is a TV so effective? It's because people believe what they see on the tube. That's why all of what we see that's continually contrived or negative is all created by the corporate people such as the producers and the studio heads who control the media. Naturally, they say the world of Hollywood indisputably has a certain nervousness about interracial romance, but you could've fooled me. Just a month ago, I went to the movies with the girls. Now, I wanted to see the movie because the two main characters were Black men whom I happen to enjoy watching on television. Well, guess what?"

"What?" a person asked and several people laughed.

"In the movies, the Black model was shot and killed off early on. Of course, these two Black Mandingo warrior brothers had to do what most Black Mandingo warriors have always been known to do throughout history and in the movies. They had to protect the all-American white woman who was distressed, scared, and running for her life. I couldn't believe it. I couldn't believe they killed off the Black sister. Why? Why not kill the white girl off, and let the two brothers protect the sister? It didn't make sense to me, but I understood the economics of the situation."

"Run it down, young lady."

"There are forty million Black people in this country, and two hundred million white folk. Who do you think Hollywood is going to cater to? They're certainly not going for the forty million especially if we don't speak up and demand better movies and television shows that honestly depict our lives and our culture, especially if we don't change the way we spend our money at the box office. Remember, white people think they know what we want to watch anyway. They think they know how we live. They even think they know our dreams. But children, you'd better form your own dreams."

I remember that movie too, Jodria thought with a small grin as she listened to her dear friend speak. *Symone was certainly ready to leave the theater, and she made sure she let it be known.*

"Once again, it's those subtle messages from powerful people who control what goes over our airwaves. The media and Hollywood, especially out in Los Angeles, nowadays perpetuate interracial pairing as fashionable. Everybody's doing it. Quite frankly, everybody isn't doing it. I'm not. It isn't every Black person's dream to have a white woman or have a white man."

Oh my! She's just as much a racist as that Booker T guy who spoke before her. I can't believe this is how they want these children to think, thought a few people in the audience. Symone continued speaking in a very calm manner.

"I don't think this way because I'm a racist, either. We always like to pin that racism title on Black folk if they speak honestly or speak with pride. If a Black person speaks the truth, that person is labeled angry. Alex's friend, Dr. Patricia Bonner, sums it up excellently. She's an English college professor who conducted a wonderful session with the children last year. Dr. Bonner told them that, 'Black pride doesn't equal white hatred. It's about empowering your Black self, so that you can deal with the injustices still buried in the fabric of American life."

"You go, girl."

"Maybe yall don't see what's going on. Maybe you've been in a dark basement all your life. I don't know what it is about us. We cannot see what's right before us. Ever since I was ten and a half years old, I was raised in a multicultural setting where I was exposed to the best there was in the world. I mingled freely with liberal, sympathetic white people, Jewish people, and very proud Black people. But one of the things my Uncle Samuel, Uncle Cecil, and Uncle Willie required was that I know *my* culture. They didn't expect me to know about all these other cultures first. They insisted that I learn my culture as a Trinidadian American and as a Black woman. I'm proud to say that I did, and I'm still learning. As a child, I had private tutors to come in. After my Mummy and my uncles, my private teachers were my consummate role models. These teachers sat me, my sisters, brother, and cousins down. They taught us about our rich, powerful legacy as Negro children living in America. We learned as if they were teaching us a foreign language. My Black history teachers were diligent, fiery, and truthful with the knowledge that they shared with me until I left home to attend Hampton Institute.

"Speak the truth." Symone smiled in the direction of those words.

"So if you think I'm a racist, you're wrong. If you think I'm proud of who I am, you're sooo right. If you think I teach the children here to practice racism, you're wrong. I don't teach the children racism. I teach them their history, and they can make informed choices from that moment on. I teach them to become immersed in their culture. I teach them to be proud of who they are which is a legacy this world would like to deny them. Learning of our struggles as a people provide us with a wonderful, yet sad window into our past."

"Talk your stuff, girl."

"I teach the children that Black babies are born with the best advance motor skills in the world. Do yall hear me? It's not the second best or the third best, but *our Black children* are born with the best. How many of you know that? So what happens after birth? What happens with the conditioning this country and other countries inflict upon us through the pitifulness of poverty, through prison, and through it's effective subtle messages that make our Black daughters and sons think otherwise—and think so little of their heritage? I'm not an Aunt Jemima or Steppin' Fetchin' type Black woman. I'm not a Black woman who's a member of the shuffling and grinning club. I certainly will not bite my tongue about what I feel about the garbage on television that depicts our Black lives as nothing more than drug dealers, criminals, crack addicts, welfare cheats, womanizers, ignoramuses, abusive men, and absentee fathers. Just the overall impression that we're an irresponsible people. Then they blast across the television and movie screen that the only way we can have positive, acceptable, and healthy relationships is to have them with other cultures. I will not remain mum about such. I repeat. I—will—not." Several people stood up as sporadic clapping swirled around the tent.

"Black people love their children. Contrary to popular belief, many Black folks have gone to colleges. Contrary to popular belief, many of our Black men *do* take care of their children, are wonderful fathers, and are excellent husbands. They drive their children to school, and romance their women in a downright absolutely exquisite way."

"Preach, sistah," a woman exclaimed.

"But the television screens and the movie theaters are quiet about our lives. The evening news, the bookshelves in libraries, and the bookstores don't portray this truth. There are many

Black folk living their lives in an upstanding way and who are maintaining their commitment to family and community. There are Black folks who are breathing wonderful lives. Their integrity is impeachable, their concern is enormous, and their love is paramount. Those are the types of people I know. This is what I teach to the twenty-eight children who are being honored here this afternoon and all other children that cross my path."

"I see positive examples of Black life when I visit Hampton and tune into WGBS, Genesis TV7. That station is one of a few around the country that airs the fact that there are many, many, many positive examples of African-Americans exemplifying powerful lives in their communities. They specialize in it. I refuse to accept those supposedly stupid reasons that these other cultures supposedly can appropriately handle our Black people's successes or are the ones to deal with the riches once our best and brightest achieve world-class prominence and status in the world of business, sports, or Hollywood. I refused to be a part of this contrived mental stupidity that we've convinced ourselves because we've been totally warped by the media. We've been warped by Eurocentric thinking, warped by some Black mothers and fathers who don't choose to share the truth of our history with their children, and we've been warped by cases of ultimate first class delusion that we as a Black people tend to embrace wholeheartedly."

"Tell the truth, Sy," Pauletta exclaimed proudly and clapped her hands. Symone offered her a quick smile and waited while the audience began applauding, too.

"My strongest ally is the rich cultural heritage of my people. That's one pillar of strength in my life. That's something that the American media cannot destroy with its racial propaganda. When you know you're the ancestors of queens, kings and an intelligent society—when you know your ancestors ruled ancient Egypt, ruled the Africa of the West that was right here on this land—American soil—then you can't even imagine embracing another race when so many of your own are still suffering. I liken my beautiful Black culture to a much more powerful version of European royalty that was contrived after our Black royalty was brutally battered. Read *The Stolen Legacy*. Learn the truth about who you are. Read that book and learn that Black people are the father of medicine and science. Not anyone else."

"Say so, baby," a senior citizen said.

"Black people are innate, consummate, and gifted thinkers. Read Lerone Bennett, Jr.'s. *Before the Mayflower.* We're a royal people with regal roots. We traded uprightly with people in the Orient as proud people. We were proud. That's what the Boston tea party was about. Not white folks. It was about white people destroying our ships, killing our people and stealing our goods. They fixed history the way they wanted it to be. But there's people always telling how it was. There's always somebody out there that has written how it was *supposed* to be. With the Internet, you can find out the truth of many facts I'm mentioning this afternoon because the Internet is the knowledge of the planet."

"Tell it, young lady."

"Just like there ain't no way the queen or king of England, the monarch, is going to allow their royal heirs to marry commoners or a person or another race, Black people must begin to show some kind of loyalty to each other. The *Bible* says that if you don't take care of your own...you're like an imbecile. And I believe that applies to the way we as Black people chose to treat each other in this day and time." More sporadic claps could be heard, but other people were feeling uncomfortable about the tone of Symone's racist speech.

"I believe many mothers and fathers are guilty of this atrocity too because they're too afraid to tell their children the truth. They don't want to share the past in order for our youth to forge proudly and positively toward the future. So no, I'm not a racist. I'm a realist. We as a family of people have to ground our children in their own culture very early in life. If you love yourself, your culture, and who you are as an African, that doesn't mean you hate other people." There was a smattering of clapping from the audience.

"So many of our young and old people are thoroughly mixed up. They're trying to be white. We're not white people, and Black people cannot be white. You can't be a square if you're a circle. It's just that simple. You may act like it, but that's as far as it can go. How can we be anything that we're not. Even more, why would we want to be something we're not? I refused to. How can I be or act any way else when all my blood and my body yell out that I *am* a Black woman?"

"We need to understand this down in our souls. No matter how much money we have, the color of our skin still is a determining factor in America. That's what most folk see. Marlon Dinzelle can confirm that to all of you here. He can verify to you that it's not a money issue. I'm assuming you all read about Marlon's incident. It was another example of blatant American racism and another glimpse of American racial debauchery was featured in *Sports Highlights*, so I'm not sharing information that isn't public knowledge."

"Run it down, girl."

"Five years ago, Marlon was reminded that no matter how much money he had, the color of his skin still drew racial snubs. He was refused membership in a prestigious country club located right here in North Carolina. Regardless of Marlon's notoriety and superstar status, he was denied admission to the elite club simply because he was a Black man. All his millions couldn't change his skin color. Marlon would've had a better chance of being nominated and voted president of this said United States of America than of being accepted into a lily-white country club here in our very illustrious state."

Although Symone spoke solemnly as she looked into Marlon's eyes, several snickers arose from the crowd. Marlon and Symone had talked about this subject earlier, and Marlon had said that he didn't mind her speaking freely about it because it did actually happen. It *was* public knowledge, plus it *was* the truth. Now Marlon winked at her with a half smile.

"Blatant examples of prejudice is what I'm talking about. Because of the United States' gruesome past not only regarding my Black ancestors who ruled *this* land we know as America, but with other minorities too, race and racism will always be an issue in this country. Violence will be an issue. Violence and race problems headline the six o'clock news every day. Why is the country shocked? Why are we surprised about the influx of guns in our communities? It's merely civil wars that have erupted in the urban areas of our country. Why are *we* shocked? We must remember this is a country that was taken from the Washitaw people by the use of guns. The Washitaw people didn't own any guns. For hundreds of years, nothing has changed. We in America are learning that violence has throughout the generations begot violence. Learn the history of America's turbulent and violent past, and you'll know that this country was made prosperous on the backs of a gentle people and nurtured by a breeding ongoing air of anger."

"Tell your stuff, babygirl," Booker T said.

"We as a Black race still don't get it. As a result, we always will try to compromise and do whatever we can to be accepted by the white ruling majority. We *need* to get it. It *doesn't* matter what we do. It doesn't matter how much money we have. We—are—Black. Then, when we realize we're Black and powerless, we really develop anguish. It's not about education. Lots of us are educated and still haven't received the pinnacles of our success. Why? You cannot make up four hundred years of mental subjugation overnight. It takes time to purge the hopelessness and negativeness that was fed to us on a daily basis. The negative info we as a people feel about who we are."

"Speak the truth," a man exploded and stood up. A few prominent friends of the Devereauxs became even more uncomfortable and began to shift nervously in their seats. They had heard that Symone was a very outspoken person on racial and social issues.

"The negativity we feel about our Black ancestry is staggering. It runs deep, very deep. The hatred we have for ourselves as a people constantly astounds me. Yet, when you're financially poor, it runs even deeper. As you heard Denethria say, you feel shame. The people in control of our world economy want you to feel shame. This is why I try to instill pride in all young people. As a result of my strong foundation of who I am as a Black woman, I really don't understand the hatred that exists within so many of *our* people. Yet, I can see how it can be easily perpetuated to fester from generation to generation. When our most famous entertainer has the genes of a Black man—whether he wants to admit it or not. This musical icon is adored by many Black children the world over. He drains the color from his body to make himself appear as a pale, unnaturally white Barbie doll. The self-hatred we have is evident and unbelievable.

"Tell the truth, sister," a man yelled out. "Tell the truth, girl." Symone hesitated and waited for the clapping to cease.

"Last year, we journeyed to the Greensboro Historical Museum to see the exhibit, *Before Freedom Came.* True, many of you said it was difficult to look at the photos of Black folk's struggles. Just like what we learn at the Schomburg, I believe it's an excellent way for our young people to see human, violent behavior in action. Although we didn't come over here in ships like they want us to believe we did, we still need to see *Roots* each and every time it comes on television. We need to remember the horror of what was done to our people in slavery. *Roots* remind us of the awful, brutality of men toward one another. *That's* why we should never forget it. Some of our people don't like such movies because they remind people of the ugliness that has blighted a country and a race of people. The circumstances are different now, but race relations are still a sad topic—even today. The freedom and opportunities that we cherish nowadays in this world didn't come without much suffering, struggle and sacrifice."

A group of about ten people stood up to clap, and the clapping was contagious. It spread through the tent like wildfire.

"It's up to us. For sooo many years, Black people have been overlooked, understated, and we continue to seek respect. However, no other group of people is going to give us respect until we learn how to respect ourselves and learn how to speak with our pocketbooks. Then they'll listen to us. We aren't going to ever be able to impact the political side of our economy until we can control or be an integral part of the economic sector of this country. We need to become a part of corporate America. Those are the entities that run this country. These organizations with the big bucks who can pay the piper to blow. I'm talking about the Fortune Five Hundred corporations, automobile companies, the food companies, the banks, the brokerage houses, and the insurance companies. These corporate entities run this country with their political puppets that pander to specific special interest groups who are managed by their strong lobbyists. This equates to who has the most money." The crowd was silent and listening.

"We've got to become a part of the economic structure of this country in order to have any political influence in what's going on. Economic power brings about stellar changes. Black people must begin to buy from each other in all aspects of our day to day lives. We must have a better awareness regarding business development and target our buying power toward Black businesses and toward service businesses that encompass doing business with the likes of Black doctors, dentists, plumbers, electricians, and lawyers. We must seek them out. In order to change the reality of the world's financial and political dynamics, we must vote for political candidates who represent our best interests. We must move our billions of dollars from white establishments to Black owned businesses and banks." The audience erupted in polite, agreeable applause and Symone paused briefly.

"As a people who spend well over four hundred billion a year, the earning and buying power we control is larger than the gross national products of most mid-size countries. We can control the destiny of our communities if we practice collective economics and use these funds properly. But we got to prepare strategic plans. Things won't change for us overnight. Things definitely won't change until we get a stronghold on the political and economic structure of the United States. Economic power brings about change. You must say that to yourself day after day and practice it too. Yet, while we're making rational and focused choices with our dollars, we need to strive toward fulfilling the strategic plan of a very dear friend of my brother Quentin, who suggests a very simple strategy. Quentin's friend, Dr. Robert Jeffrey of Seattle, Washington wrote a wonderful book that I encouraged everyone to read. The title is *Beyond the Den of Thieves*. Read it. His philosophy is quite simple. Twenty million Black people should become stakeholders in our future and donate $200 a year to a National Endowment Fund set up specifically for the betterment of our communities. This endowment is controlled by representatives from the community and not by one person. We as a people would gain a power that can help to direct and control our destinies. Almost everyone has $200 dollars. Look at the expensive tennis shoes that grace our children's feet. People on welfare and millionaires alike could become equal stakeholders for the advancement of our communities which will ensure the advancement of our race." Some people in the audience marveled at the simplicity of the endowment fund and began clapping again.

"Almost a hundred years ago, Jewish people did the same thing by creating the National Jewish Fund. When Jewish individuals immigrated to the United States, other Jewish people provided them with loans to create businesses as soon as they stepped off the boat. When those loans were paid off, they were provided with other loans. That's why even though the Jewish population is a small percentage of this country's population, they control approximately eighty to ninety percent of the wealth in America. They control just as much worldwide. Why? Because early on, they practiced collective economics as a people and they control the Federal Reserve System, a privately held company for your information. Believe you me, they certainly still do it today. I know that to be true. As a people, they know that's the key."

"We as a Black people must understand that the movement of money creates wealth. Period. The banks understand that. That's why they move trillions why we're sleeping at night. While we're playing tennis, bouncing basketball, hitting baseballs, and catching footballs, the banks are moving their money to create more trillions. The insurance companies understand that. The brokerage companies understand that. It's time that we as a Black people understand that, too. That's what we need to do. That's how I was raised. Ever since I came to this country, I was taught to think about collective economics for my culture and to collectively work with other Black people, so that we could make financial decisions that have an impact on our communities. The success of our businesses, will of course eventually impact many families."

"Amen, sister," someone hollered out.

"Even though we've been on this land since the beginning and toiled on this land for centuries in bondage, Black folks never had the same level playing field as other immigrants coming to America. Therefore, we couldn't get ahead as quickly. We were never considered men and women, but mere chattel that deserved to be housed in slums. We didn't have any rights to vote or rights to even to exist. We worked hard for nothing. Slave labor was free to white folks, but it cost us tremendously. Yet we never received one penny of reparation from the companies and massive homes that were built upon our backs."

"Amen," the same person hollered out.

"Pecola's Aunt Hattie Mae often said that back in the day when she was coming up, the Black women was considered the mule of the world. In my opinion," Symone said, pausing briefly. "The Black man was the cart. But it's time for us to get to stepping, to get involved in business, and to change our own lives."

"Talk your stuff, young lady," encouraged an older man.

"We as a people have influence, but we don't have power or control. Sure, we have influence in the world of dancing, sports, the record industry, television, and rap. But do we traditionally control and own those companies? No, we don't. We all know how rap has taken the world by storm and is a billion-dollar industry. Whether we like it or not, that's just a fact of life. However, the power scenario in the rap industry is typical. Sure Black rap stars have considerable influences. We see them on the videos, at the awards shows enjoying life, and in some cases acting totally crazy. We see them on the nightly news. We see them rapping on commercials to sell everything imaginable produced by major corporations, but these rappers don't have control in an industry created by urban blacks. In the end, white men are crunching out the numbers and making all the powerful decisions. That's who control the wealth. Even though Black boys rap, white people control the power of hip-hop. Once white folks discovered it was a multi-million dollar business heading toward a multi billion dollar industry that could alter and influence a person's behavior, it was open season for the profiteers. Isn't that amazing?"

"Yes it is."

"Learn how to buy clothes designed by Black people. I look for that when I see our Black rappers, our talk show hosts, movie stars, and other celebrities parading around. Whoever is continually under the camera's eye, I look to see what they have on. Yet, I notice they still haven't gotten it, either. They continue to promote those white designers. We give those powerhouse white designers organizations free advertisement that reach millions of other Black people. Do we not realize that? The rap stars sing about white designers that they wear all the time. Sometimes, I believe certain rap stars only sing about what they eat, what they wear, and where they shop. Seek out the Black designers. They can use the exposure, too. Give them notoriety. Now, I know rap stars can make rhymes with Black designer names. A rapper can make anything rhyme. I can, too. You know how they say 'romance without finance is a nuisance. But I got a new rap to send out, 'Black folk need to realize that 'without our controlling our *finance,* there is no healthy *chance* for us to make a powerful economic *stance.*'"

The crowd was silent and waiting to hear more. Symone paused and patted her dress to straighten a crease. She felt the power of the speech settling over the people in the audience, and she faced them standing tall like a dark, regal princess.

"I believe we're basically the only race of people where we allow other cultures to produce our make-up, our hair products, our foods, our media, and anything else for us. We continue to accept it and to buy it. Why? I told my three uncles this one time. A Black woman could never create a make-up that caters specifically to Jewish women. Even my uncles had to admit I was right. The Jewish people wouldn't allow it. Well, they would allow it, but they wouldn't buy it. A Black person couldn't create an industry which was specifically for the care of a Greek person's hair. They wouldn't allow it. Once again, it may be allowed. But the Greeks wouldn't buy the products. But we do. It's as if we have no loyalties. We don't investigate who owns what. A Black person couldn't create a company that catered specifically to the Italian culture or even the oriental culture. Why? Who would buy it? Certainly not the people it was created for, especially after they find out that it's a company that was created by a Black man or a Black woman to cater specifically to them. It just doesn't work like that. Those cultures are taught to create the things they need themselves."

"Speak the truth, chile."

"If you look throughout our communities, you'll find that the Chinese, the Koreans, Iranian and many other cultures have found out that there is so much money in our communities. There's so much money there. Collectively, I'm talking billions of dollars. Stratospheric levels of money. So naturally when Black tee shirts with Black messages came out, other races began to sell them. Why? They're still doing quite well in that market. But you know what? The Asians will sell anything to us, but most of them won't sell Black literature. If they sold Black literature, they would slowly put themselves out of business. You know why? Contrary to popular belief, a lot of Black people *do* read. Therefore, if we start reading those powerful books I mentioned and other books that are out there, we'll begin to feel better about whom we are. Our self-esteem rises, and we would realize that we could sell tee shirts and hair care products, too. We can have a beauty supply store. If my brother down the street has a beauty supply store, then I'll patronize his store more so than another one. Start to see yourself, a friend, or a relative as business owners. Your mindset changes, and our potential for growth explodes."

"You go, girl." Now there was a healthy round of applause again.

"Believe me, you can find a lot of books in white bookstores, but they'll not sell certain books because some of them *do* know the real deal about our history. Therefore, they try to hide the fact that Black people are inventors and stellar contributors to the entire world. The fewer people who know about it, the better off things are. Because if more of us know who *we* truly are, then that mentally places us on the same level with all people, scientifically and spiritually. And, you know—" Symone paused to get the audience's attention, "Black people are the most spiritual and soulful group of people in the world. We're some deeply spiritual and religious people who have been singing and praying to the creator for a long time." A few amens erupted from the crowd and everyone was clapping

"Amen, sister—"

"Without question, some of us are very successful, are powerful in our own right and in our corner of the world. I see it when I read the top businesses in *Black Enterprise, Ebony,* and *Emerge.* I see it when I reminisce about my family in New York and even in Trinidad. I thank God I'm successful. I'm fortunate, but I'm not alone. Many in the audience have "made it." I see it when I hear about the astounding salaries received by our athletes, actors, actresses, singers, and successful business people. When we see ourselves in such a privileged position, we must look around and ask ourselves, what can I do for the advancement of our people? What can I do to make a difference? It shouldn't be left to just the Urban League, just the NAACP, or other agencies to make changes. There are approximately forty million Black folk living in this country. All of them aren't living in poverty. If just twenty million of us give $200 a year, look at the mathematics involved. It's staggering, and it's overwhelming." Symone paused, smiled politely, and continued speaking.

"There are so many worthwhile things we teach the children here. We want to also teach them the power of their votes. Even the eight-years olds that we work with know that Black people died to make our right to vote a reality. They gladly laid down their lives to make it possible. Body parts still haven't been found—for the ones who made the ultimate sacrifice. Yet, we take it all so lightly. It's because we have such short memories. So I get very angry when I hear Black people say their votes don't count. If you don't vote, you have blood on your hands. It's the blood of the slaughtered Blacks and sympathetic whites that died to provide us with our unquestionable right, our coveted right as citizens of this said country. The many sidewalks and ground are red with their blood. The freedom and opportunities that we gained back and cherish as a people nowadays in this country didn't come freely. Some Black people know that, and others refuse to remember it. That too is sad. To know your past is to have insight on your future. Voting is another form of power."

"I want to remind everyone of this other fact. A lot of us here graduated from predominantly Black colleges. They were created during a time when Blacks weren't allowed to attend white universities and colleges. Those campuses were places where a lot of us met our husbands and wives. It's where we developed friendships that have lasted for a lifetime. I appreciate my Black college and believe in the work it's doing. Not only do I believe in it, I support it with my dollars. Learn that giving is food for the soul. I take my children to the events at my alma mater because that's where I want my children to go to school. I want them to go to Hampton. I went to a predominantly Black college, and I'm a competent, well-educated Black woman with the knowledge of my history."

"Say so, sister."

"I don't know. Sometimes Black people think that even though we did ok, we want our children to go to *those* other schools. I don't understand it. I guess we believe that we've finally arrived and deserved something better. It's like all the other Black colleges across the country are suddenly not good enough to educate our children—even though they were acceptable for us. I love Hampton. I have a connection there. No matter whatever accomplishments I've achieved since my undergraduate years, nothing can compare to those four years. Those glorious, reckless days of freedom in Hampton, Virginia. Hampton has that feeling of history and family with their reunions as well as their sporting events. I've even witnessed how ninety-year old graduates come back to celebrate various events and to give their money."

"You're telling the truth."

"I've just stopped crying when I step onto Hampton's campus. When I go and visit the Emancipation Oak, that huge old tree just touches me deeply. It's the place where the Blacks who were slaves in the area were set free. Emancipation Oak is what we call it at Hampton. Under the tree that day, the Emancipation Proclamation was read to them. Can you imagine what must have been going through our ancestors' minds? Not only there but throughout the country. Freedom. I love to hear the word, and I'm sure the slaves were aware of its horrible cost. Can you imagine their nervousness? Their fears of the expected and unexpected?"

"Umph, umph. Umph," moaned several older people.

"You *do* receive a wonderful foundation in historically Black schools—a foundation that'll enable you to go into the world and handle all kinds of situations in the corporate area. I encourage our young Black children to attend a Black college. There, they can learn without being victims of prejudice. They can get grounded in their roots and develop their identity as African-Americans. Then, if you want the white educational experience, go to a predominantly white school for your master's degree—for graduate work. It's a wonderful combination. It absolutely is."

"I agree with you one thousand percent, Symone," Rozelle interjected quickly, and several people nodded knowingly.

"Remember the words of Desmond Tutu who said, 'The only way we're going to survive is to survive together.' I believe that's the only way Black people can absolutely achieve ultimate success in this said country. We must work together as one. We must do this economically, politically, and within our communities. This afternoon, I ask that you search your heart and ask yourself if you are doing all that you can do for the future of our culture, ladies and gentlemen. Are you letting your children, your neighbors' children, your friends, and your loved ones know in some small way that you are someone that cares and someone who's willing to make a difference? Sometimes we look around at community programs and say, 'I can't tell a difference in what they're doing over there. I don't think they're doing it right. They're not helping the community in *any* big way.' Sometimes when we don't detect a difference in our communities and in our lives, maybe it's because we're not making a difference ourselves. Think about it."

"So true, sistah girl. So true," Darilyn exclaimed and began to clap.

"To the twenty-eight children who are honored today, I want you and all the other young souls in here to be creative and true to yourselves. *Always.* Some of you have seen a lot for young eyes. You've told me you have. You've heard and have had much to happen in your young lives. Quite frankly, too much. That's so unfortunate. A person's childhood should be a blissful experience, but they're not always that way. I always beseech you. If something wrong is going on in your life, please tell me. Tell your Tante Symone or your Tante Jodria. She's trained in handling delicate adolescent issues. Tell the other adults. Tell someone. Whatever it is, just speak about it. Don't ever. I say *never ever* allow your spirit to be broken by anyone. I mean no one," Symone said in an almost whisper into the mike, and the children nodded as if they understood.

Since Symone's friends knew that she was speaking about the tragedy in her childhood in Trinidad, some were quiet and a little worried while they listened to her heartfelt words.

"I've always been concerned about children in that respect. Real concerned about the secrets they keep. As a world-class veteran in that area, I want you to know I speak from experience. Never carry such tremendous, heavy burdens of secrets around in your head and in your heart. Just don't because that's not what our hearts are for. Our hearts aren't in our chests to harbor pain and hurt. If someone is loving you and it hurts, it's not love. It's not love," she repeated with conviction and a heavy sigh.

Symone didn't say any of this in her speech last month, Pecola thought with a twinge of sadness for her friend. *I wonder what's up?*

"When I first came to this country, my Uncle Samuel glanced at the beaten down posture of my family, my mother, my brother, my two sisters, and me. We were frightened to be in America. We were also just scared about life in general. As we stood clustered together in the airport hanger that winter day almost thirty years ago, my Uncle Samuel spoke first. One of the first things he said to me was what I see to be words of poetry to a young girl who had no inkling of self-esteem whatsoever. I had no hope and felt I wanted to die. As my Uncle Samuel lifted my chin with his right hand, I'll never forget those words as long as I live. He spoke to me in a clear voice and said, '...Look at my little Trinidadian Princess. Hold your head up high, my beautiful niece. Always hold it up high like a graceful, soaring eagle who can fly high in the sky and view all things...' When he called me this morning, he told me the exact same thing. My uncle seems to always know when I need to hear those words." To collect herself and to calm her propelling emotions, Symone hesitated a moment. Cleopatra bobbed her head with understanding and flicked a tear from the bridge of her nose.

"Those words are scorched in my mind, and I never forgot them. As I end my speech, I say the same to you. Hold your head up my little Black princes and princesses. No matter what people say about who you are and say about where you live, hold your head up and know that you can soar. Know that you can fly like an eagle through life." Symone inhaled deeply.

"Wonderful words."

"Alex and Madison, you know I love yall. What a privilege for me to have you both as friends. I pay tribute to you without one ounce or one millimeter of hesitation. I honor you both. Alex, girl—we've been amazing, inseparable friends for a long time. It's been you, me, and Pecola—for such a long time." Pecola smiled and wiped her eyes. "My dear Alex. You've come inside my heart and walked all around inside me."

As Symone watched Alex's serene and compassionate face, Symone considered her branding secret about the incestuous relationship with her father that she had only shared with one other person in the world, Alex. Alex was the only person that Symone felt truly safe to share such a secret with. Symone blew her dear good friend a lingering kiss. With tears in her eyes, Alex returned the tender gesture.

"Alex, you always said that we need to respect, honor, and recognize our favorite people before they leave this world. We should recognize them with our verbal flower of salute and to laude them with peace and serenity. I honor you and Madison. I admire your dedication. The two of you realized there are a lot of dreams and aspirations in this world. A lot of people want peace and serenity. As I stand here, I can feel those emotions floating up from the children. All you and Madison desire is that for each and every one of those dreams, aspirations and spirit of peace be achieved. That's why it's a tremendous pleasure to work with you both in such a magnificent way. I thank you for your invitation to help. The goals you both had for our youth are admirable. That was enough for me," Symone said quickly, trying to smile. She gathered her papers and went to sit down. Before she could sit down, Pecola and Pauletta strongly embraced her. While all three friends tightly hugged one another, they rocked quietly from side to side.

Once again, the tent was lost in an awed silence. Finally, a few ripples of claps arose. It became louder and grew to a thunderous pitch. Slowly, a solemn Rozelle walked to the podium. He was quiet as he inhaled her message and the strength of the applause. Knowing that Symone was normally tight lipped with her emotions and always had a brick wall up, especially if she wasn't around her inner circle of friends, Rozelle chose to remain mum until the clapping ceased.

Looking into the sea of faces, Rozelle finally spoke. "This speech was quite compelling. Her words were inspiring, truthful, and honest. You see what I'm saying about being around such intelligent, gifted, and warm people. You can see why the circle of friendship we have is quite amazing. Without question, we have our arguments and fights. We're all just like brothers and sisters in that respect," Rozelle said as he considered the heated discussion along the horse trail earlier that day. "I can say one thing about my relationship with these people in North Carolina. When all the dust settles, we still remain very close friends and business associates." The audience released another round of heartfelt applause.

Chapter Six-Four

Rozelle took a deep breath. "Ladies, gentlemen, honored guests, and children, it's time to move on. Athena Davis is a young lady who'll be an entering freshman at Cheyney State in the fall. She was selected to speak on behalf of the success stories that go on in public housing. They are the ones that people didn't hear about as often. Let's give a wide round of applause for Miss Athena Davis," Rozelle encouraged.

Athena smiled graciously at the audience and began speaking. "Thank you. I'm glad Madison asked me to talk to you about the success stories that live in public housing. Let me say this first because it gets on my nerves. When a crime goes on in my neighborhood, all three local network news shows are there to stick the camera in everyone's face. It seems like they crawl out of the woodwork for stories like that. Then, there are times we can't drag the media into our community for them to do a story that showcases the positive actions other people are taking to make our community a safe environment for the residents. Now that's what burns me up. The murders and drug busts are always blasted on the front page. Any exciting, positive things we do in Piedmont Park don't even make it into the newspaper nine times out of ten. When positive stories are featured in the newspapers, it's on the same page as the obituary," she muttered in disbelief, and a few guests clapped. "Ok, I can move on. My sister is Neema Davis. She's the one who Denethria peed on," Athena said lightly, and the audience broke out in giggles.

"Like Denethria, I was ashamed to tell people where I lived. To be honest, even sometimes now I still am ashamed. But it's not as bad as it was before. I don't think anyone actually said it to my face, but I got the feeling that society, as a whole doesn't expect much of poor people who live in public housing. According to statistics, we have a higher rate for failure. Then, there are those that think poor children can't learn like rich children can because we live in public housing. However, my Tante Pecola helped me out with that little situation." Remembering Pecola's speech, several people smiled.

"Eighteen months ago, I found out my sister had been selected to come to the Devereauxs' country estate. I was happy for her, but I was jealous at the same time. I had just turned seventeen, so I missed the cut-off point of sixteen years of age. Neema came back and told me all the things she did in Advance. She said that these people would be coming to get her every month, and I decided I was going to figure out a way to get involved, too. I wanted to be like her Siamese twin or something." The crowd hummed with laughter once more. "It worked. They came to pick up Neema three months straight. When that fourth month rolled around, I finagled my way on the bus, too. So here I am, and I've been here ever since!" she exclaimed and waved her hands in the air from side to side.

"Me, my sister, and my brother were raised by my father. We grew up really poor. I know that sounds stereotypical for the projects, but it's the truth. Booker T says that society has failed poor people. People are poor because they've no other options and because the country let them be poor. They can't find work. In some cases, they've been dealt unfortunate life blows. That *was* my family. Poor people. The Davis Klan. I must admit that my father had everything else going for us. Everything that is, except money." Athena spoke in a clear voice, and she tried to smile.

"We weren't deprived, and we always had the desire and determination to improve ourselves. My father taught me to be content with the little that I have but never be satisfied with it. And I wasn't. Believe you me, it really was rough living in Piedmont Park. Not because of where it was, but because of what I dreamed of doing. Since Piedmont Park is the projects, people often called *it* and classified *it* as the ghettos. There's no other way to say it. So, I guess that's where I live. I live in the ghetto. But I'm convinced ghetto thinking is a mental thing. Uncle Carlos told me that you can live in a million dollar home but have a ghetto mind."

"Tell it like it tis, young lady." Athena smiled at the encouragement.

"My family and I were lucky, though. I believe it's a wonderful blessing for me to be here with all the different tragedies I saw throughout my community. I live in the projects. I can't help but see. That's what happens when you put hundreds of people together with a lot of pent up emotions, deferred dreams, and empty lives in a small square mile radius. You can believe there's going to be anger, frustration, and violence on a continuous basis. Every day. We're living on top of each other. A lot of my neighbors believed all their hope was gone and found drugs to be a sweet relief. A lot of them believed they wanted to cling to hope. I was one of those people who knew I could change my situation, and I clung to hope. Why shouldn't I?" Polite applause arose from the audience.

"My sister, my brother, and I still were lucky because we had people who actually cared about us were placed all around us as neighbors in Piedmont Park. Now, my brother is an engineering major at the University of Maryland at Eastern Shore. He's sitting over there," Athena pointed out and began clapping for him, as did the entire audience. Her father was absent since he couldn't get the day off from work. "And I'll be entering Cheyney University in the fall. I also received a musical scholarship to Elizabeth City State University." Before she could finish, the crowd issued another round of applause. "But I decided to go to Pennsylvania instead. They offered me a full musical scholarship as well."

"Go ahead with your smart self," GJ yelled out. It was obvious Scott's son had a slight crush on her. So that he could sit beside Athena, he refused the opportunity to sit with his father on the second row.

"I don't think anyone actually said it to my face when I was growing up, but I got the feeling that the people of Winston-Salem didn't expect much of people who live in the projects. Then there are those people that think poor children can't learn like rich children can. Well, I'm here to squelch that view," she declared with a wide grin, and the audience began laughing, too. "I'm very smart, and I'm going to college. When I told Alex and Madison that I got musical scholarships to both schools, they were excited for me. When Madison asked me which one was I going to select, I told him I probably would be going to Elizabeth City State

University because it was closer to home. I admitted to him that it would've been nice for me to see what it was like to go to school out of state. Quite frankly, I couldn't afford the extra expenses involved with an out-of state school. I told him that I thought it would be easier for me to get a ride home to Winston-Salem from Elizabeth City than it would be for me to get one from Cheyney, Pennsylvania."

"Let me tell you how the Lord blessed my family again! Alex and Madison told me that anonymous individuals informed them that they would take care of all my traveling expenses back and forth to Cheyney as long as I maintained a B average. Madison also said that they would even handle any spending money I needed, so I wouldn't have to work at a Wendy's like I do now. Once more, I said, 'Thank you, Jesus.' I accepted the scholarship from Cheyney State. It's such a wonderful feeling to know that I can attend college and not have to worry about anything except maintaining my grades. Since I worked at Wendy's while I was a junior and senior in high school, I was always tired. When you don't have as much as you would like to have, you feel like it's your place to help your family out any way you can. You work a part-time job after school. You do whatever you can to help the family survive. There's nothing 'project' about that."

"Say so, young lady," a woman said.

Athena spoke in an unabashed, lilting voice. Haneef Reynolds nudged his older brother, CJ. CJ smiled back at him and knowingly nodded his head as he gazed at the pretty, honey-complexioned Athena. CJ was wondering which approach he should use to get with her. He would wait and see what happened between her and GJ. If it didn't work out, he would approach her. CJ didn't want anything to come between his friendship with Granville, Jr.

Pecola turned around to send a doting glance to her two handsome sons just as they were smiling and nodding their heads toward Athena. A worried Pecola wondered what they were thinking about the charismatic young girl speaking and only hoped it wasn't anything romantic.

Athena is from the projects, Pecola thought with a raised eyebrow. *She can't possibly be my sons' type.*

"You know that's nothing unusual for the Davis family. All through our lives, we've received help. Even the drug dealers in the projects have helped me out. For years, the dealers have paid for my piano and singing lessons just like I was their kin or something. These were drug dealers who did that. I'm not embarrassed to say they helped me, either. If it hadn't been for them, my brother never would've gone to summer science camps. I never would've progressed in the musical field the way that I did. My father simply didn't have the money for the extra lessons."

"We were fortunate. We did have people around us who cared. They may not have been what you considered successful or upstanding folk in the city, but they had love in their hearts for me. They felt the same about some of the other kids they saw in the neighborhood who were really trying to make something out of their lives. For that, I'll forever be grateful to them. When Madison heard the story about the drug dealers and my family's success story, he told me he wanted me to talk about that side of the projects you never hear about. It *would* be difficult to have something like that in the newspapers. I can see it now on the front page of the *Winston-Salem Chronicle. Drug Dealer Pays for Girl's Piano and Singing Lessons.* First of all, no drug dealer is going to admit that they're drug dealers, so the media can forget about ever getting that front page article," Athena exclaimed as the audience resounded with laughter about the truth of the comment.

"When Madison found out who my benefactors were, he told me that it wasn't his place to judge people. True, I believe those drug dealers have their dark sides. Their dark basement situations, but they were also thinking about doing good for the children who lived in their village, too," she said happily. "I'm one of those project village children that they helped, and I'll never forget them. Don't get me wrong. I'm not glorifying drug dealers, but you don't know what has driven them to do what they do. Poverty and lack of education make your scope of choices seem small." The crowd applauded. "I thank you for my place to speak here today. I'm definitely honored by it. Now, I ask that you pray for me as I head to Pennsylvania next week. I plan to major in pre-law as well. I guess I'll be known as the singing attorney. Uncle Rozelle said that if I mix together a lot of studying with a little bit of partying, I'll be just fine," she ended with a brilliant, pretty smile.

As the audience rocked the tent with boisterous applause and laughter, Athena walked to her seat and sat down. The people around Athena patted her on her shoulders, and her brother promptly hugged her neck tightly.

"Wasn't that another wonderful testimony? Absolutely marvelous," Rozelle barked into the mike. "Madison always said that if we could change the boys around, they would change the girls around. Then the children could turn the parents around. We never considered the sisters," Rozelle joked as he gazed in Athena's eyes. "Ladies and gentlemen, I salute the parents of all these children. They've instilled such amazing values in their children, and it shows."

"It sure does," someone said, and sporadic clapping occurred this time.

"I love it, folks. I simply love it." Rozelle checked his watch; he knew how Alex was about adhering to the prompt schedule. "The program is scheduled to end in thirty minutes. Right now, we're about ten minutes behind schedule. Do yall care?" he asked the crowd.

"Nooo!" the audience said loudly.

"Great," Rozelle responded quickly. "I didn't think yall did. When I heard such motivating speeches from the young people and from my friends, the main thing I pulled from their words is that they believed all things were possible. As I stand here, I think about the story of the bumblebee. When Cleopatra spoke last month, she told us she had read about this in one of her many books. Cleopatra said that the bumblebee's body is so heavy and his wings are so small that the bumblebee shouldn't be able to fly. The only problem is the bumblebee doesn't know that. In spite of his heavy body, the bumble bee flies all over the yard and has a good time stinging people," Rozelle revealed as he released a boisterous laughter. The audience did the same thing and clapped for several minutes. Rozelle threw Cleopatra a fast wink. She blushed and beamed proudly back at him.

"At this time, ladies and gentlemen, I'm ready to introduce the next to the last speaker. It's my man, Madison Devereaux. He's the Morehouse Textbook study for a Black man with leadership qualities." Rozelle spoke with a huge smile. "Even though he didn't attend that college, I did. So, I can tell what it takes." Many people laughed at the way Rozelle was keeping the long program lively with cute remarks here and there.

"He's the quiet support behind Alex. If she didn't have a receptive husband, she certainly couldn't do all of the things she wanted to do with the children or with the many people she enjoys working with. Madison often shares a southern expression that his doctor grandfather used to say to him and his two brothers. That is 'You're not a man until your daddy tells you you're one, and you can't be a man until you see examples of one.'"

"Say so."

"But Madison also says you have to know that you're a man your ownself. I certainly commend him. He's a frat brother who's about really making a difference. He has showed his hard-nosed buddies what manly, Black love is all about. What respecting your wife is all about," he said with a sheepish grin.

"Wonderful," a senior citizen said and began to clap.

"Madison has shown us what devotion is about and what friendship is about. I love him. I speak not only for myself but also for all the brothers we hang with. Every man needs a friend of amazing character, and Madison is that kind of man for all of us. When I first met him and his wife, he and Alex were the only people I had ever met who graduated from the University of Beautiful Love. I later found out that it was a school that Madison created. Both Devereauxs received a master's degree in the marriage of Madison and Alex with a dissertation that explains how to enjoy being a King, a Queen, and living your Dreams in a marriage."

"Woof, woof," barked one of the Devereauxs' dogs and settled into a quiet growl.

"Madison keeps his framed degree at his office at the hospital. Alex keeps her degree in their home office on the second floor. I present to you the most humble, brilliant, and bravest man I know after me, of course," Rozelle joked easily as the crowd laughed again. "Dr. Madison Nehemiah Devereaux, Jr."

The audience gave Madison a rousing standing ovation. Always the emotional one, Madison's eyes became moist before he even said a word. Once in front of the podium, he laid his papers down. A calm Madison became quiet as he gazed into the smiling faces of the crowd. Before he spoke, he was silent for at least fifteen seconds.

"Thanks for the glowing introduction, Rozelle. I couldn't ask for a better endorsement. You read it the exact way I wrote it. Good work, man," Madison joked and smiled. The audience broke out into laughter.

"Thanks, Dr. D," Rozelle said.

"It's an honor for me to stand before you, ladies, gentlemen, and our children. To Alex, my heart's twin, thanks for sticking with me, baby. After all these years, I still am very much in love with you." He paused to stare in her eyes, and everyone witnessed the love flowing between them.

"Alex is the greatest gift of love a man could ever have. She's my motivator. My wife. My rock. She's the mother of my two beautiful children, Trey and Purity, whom I love and adore as well. I heard a lot tonight about how my wife has motivated many people. But she's there for me with every breath she takes." Madison paused briefly. "This evening, we're here to inspire and speak words of motivation, encouragement, and excitement about the wonderful opportunity to work with the twenty-eight children who are being honored tonight. It has been an absolute joy to have the children spend time with us in Advance. I believe I get more rewards than I give."

"Me too," Marlon said quietly to his wife.

"Keep in mind. It's not your responsibility to do anything. When you lay down at night and you ask yourself, 'how did I achieve the success that I have?' What do you say? When you think about it, you'll realize you didn't do it on your own. How are you successful now? Was it a promotion or a loan from the bank? How did you do it? Who gave you opportunities and chances to improve your life? If you can honestly say *you* did it all by yourself with no help from no one else, then it isn't your responsibility."

"For a lot of Black people, including myself, I got a lot of help along the way. I got encouraging words from teachers who cared, from my parents, my cousins, my professors at Winston-Salem State University, and at Duke University. I got a lot of help from so many, many people. I've been very fortunate. There have been great people around me. I did the work. But I had others beside me, in front of me, behind me, and around me that you never see when you see this Madison person before you. That's why there's no limit to how far a man can rise as long as he doesn't mind who gets the credit. I got help. I realized that, and that's what we're doing here today. Once Black people have made it, we often relegate ourselves to another race of people. They're called the haves and those other Black people who are struggling as the have nots."

"We as Black folk practice discriminatory practices more than white folk. We've just as much lip service regarding racial equality as they do. We care if our children go to school with poor or inappropriate behaving Blacks. We blame the children for their situations. We teach our children to act like we have more than they do and act like they're better than they are. It's sad, man. We as Black folks got to figure out a way to deal with the class system we've implemented in our society, too. We got a lot work ahead of us. Sometimes, I look at various situations and listen to the conversations of my upper, middle-class Black friends in California, in New York, in Atlanta, and Boca Raton, Florida. All over for that matter. I say to myself, we act worse than white people do when we talk about class and integration. The class structure is amazing. We intentionally insulate ourselves in the hope of keeping poorer, uneducated Blacks away from us. You know the ones I'm talking about? The ones we consider to be bad influences upon our children and upon ourselves."

"Tell the truth, baby," Alex said quietly.

"Some Black people have run from the tragedy of our people. They simply don't care. As long as they take care of themselves and their children, that's all they're concerned with. Before integration, Black people weren't acting like that. Everyone helped each other out. The purpose of the civil rights movement was for blacks to obtain equality, equal education, get better books, supplies, and appropriate learning places."

"Say so, Dr. Devereaux."

"As a young boy years ago, I went to the same church as my teachers. My parents knew my teachers, and my teachers knew my parents. They watched out for me, and I respected my teachers. Both my wife and I believe that there is a coldness in this society nowadays, and it hurts me whenever I see it. Black people need to start touching again and start holding hands again. We used to do it before. We need to start nodding at each other, waving at each other, and speaking to each other."

"Absolutely."

"We must connect and bond because we got such a distance between each other now. We can be in the same room with other Blacks. For whatever reason, we won't speak or nod our heads. I don't understand it. It's so sad. We'd rather buy a Mercedes than lend a helping hand to those less fortunate. I however was taught to understand that money and success are nothing if you forget who you are or if you save it for a rainy day. If you keep a tight fist around your money, God can't bless you. God can only multiply what you give. If you don't take the time to care, God knows that. You do, too. Just do something to help. Purchase a dress sometimes. A book. A suit. Donate it anonymously, or give it to your friends so you can see huge smiles cover their faces."

"Let's take networking. You got to respect other cultures for that. They take care of their own. Sometimes, we expect white people to take care of us. We expect them to be our saviors, and they aren't. Most times they don't consider us as being a part of the whole picture. We need to wake up. They practice the old boy's network to a tee. They network with friends, whether it's helping their friends with a bank loan, a job, real estate, or connections in any form. They do it. That's one of the things they're known for and other cultures are known for, too. I used to get mad because I didn't think it was fair."

"I understand," a voice said from the middle of the audience.

"Now I understand why they move in such a manner. Their philosophy galvanized me and made me realize I needed to do the same thing. When you're in a position of authority and can call the shots, make sure everyone that's capable has a chance to improve. If you read Carter G. Woodson's, *Miseducation of the Negro*, it sounds like he wrote it today even though the powerful brother penned it back in the 1930s. But the discussions are on the money, man. When we as Black people become educated from prominent white schools, we sometimes turn our backs on our brothers and sisters who haven't gone to school or who aren't where we are. We don't even try to catapult them through the system. Once we have made it, many of us don't do anything but think of how we can distance ourselves from those less fortunate than us. It's not right. Remember, you'll reap what you sow."

"You're right, Madison," Pecola declared loudly.

"Our children can't vote, and their voices aren't respected. That's where the adults should come in because children trust us. A lot of them do want to help themselves. They just want someone there to say that they can do it. Children trust us, and they deserve to be honored with high expectations from their parents, their guardians, and their mentors. If we as parents and mentors can't do that, our children won't have high expectations for themselves. We then help them fulfill the negative view that's running rampant in this country. Every two hours, we lose a child in America. Alex, our friends, and I don't know the root of all our youth's problems. We just feel that if maybe, just maybe, if we can get to know the children, they can tell us the causes of their discontent. Their sadness. Their needs." There was a hearty round of applause.

"African-Americans have the resources to make changes and to help people who are in need. Even our churches are powerful entities. There was a study done several years ago that revealed that if every church in this country does *one* thing, that would make a huge impact. Do yall hear me? Let me tell you what it is. If *every* church would be responsible for the clothing, feeding, and housing of five needy families, that action would totally wipe out poverty and homelessness. Is your church helping five families? Are they helping even one? When you attend church on Sunday, remember to find that out."

"I will," a lady said with a quick nod.

"Tell that to your preacher, your deacons, and whoever is in the power of authority to make it a collective effort. *You* can start the group in your church yourself. *You* can take control of the situation. That's what churches are supposed to be for anyway. *You* take that stand and be the catalyst for making that happen where you attend church. Five is the magic number. Such a simple plan is an easy way to wipe out homelessness and hopelessness. Ladies and gentlemen, I leave you with these questions." Madison gazed heavenward and paused a moment. "What's your mission in life? If you have a worthwhile mission, you'll certainly leave a powerful legacy. What's your mission with children? What's your mission with family and friends? What's your mission with yourself?" As the audience considered the questions, they began clapping.

"Preach, brother."

"Before I end my speech, I'd like to honor my family and a few other people that are in attendance today. To Trey and Purity, yall know that I love you. Being your father validates my life. To the twenty-eight honorees that are my other children, know that I love you. Know that I care, and know that I'll always be here for you.

"Amen, Madison."

"This is to my buddy, Dr. Zachary Richard. I know a lot of yall know about him. For those who don't, I wanted yall to know we've been friends since our freshman year at Winston-Salem State University. He came to the school all the way from Bainbridge, Georgia. He's a prominent ophthalmologist in Brentwood, California. Now, whenever I have an important event going on in my life, Zachary comes. So does his gorgeous wife, Marietta, and their four children. They all take the time to come be with me. Having him come to Winston is wonderful. We're just like brothers, and I love him." Madison stopped briefly and gazed upward.

"Like so many others I could rattle off, he has always been there for me. That was especially so during my senior year at State when I was struggling to handle the serious love Jones I had for my future wife to be," Madison teased as he winked at Alex again. The audience laughed. "Thank you Zachary for being my friend for all these years, man."

"You're welcome," Zachary said simply by nodding his head with a smile. The crowd gave Dr. Richard and his family a big hand salute.

"My parents are here. Puhleeze stand," Madison instructed the older distinguished looking couple. "Dr. and Mrs. Madison Nehemiah Devereaux, Sr. I love you Mama and Daddy. My father just retired from private practice. He was a wonderful pediatrician in this city for almost fifty years, but I guess my father decided it was time to move on. My brother Marquis is here. Stand up, man. For those of you who don't know him, he operates Devereaux

Funeral Home off Highway fifty-two. I guess it's in our blood to work with the human body. Marquis just decided he wanted to work it from that end." The audience broke out in ripples of laughter.

"What happened to Marquis' wife and two children, girl? I thought you said that they were here last month? How come they're not here today?" Pauletta whispered the questions to Pecola.

"They're legally separated, chile," Pecola whispered back just as feverishly.

"Get the hell out of here, girl!" Pauletta continued to speak with her eyes toward Madison.

"I swear to Jesus. It shocked the hell out of everyone, too. Alex said that his wife came home late on a Sunday night about three weeks ago. Girlfriend told Marquis that she wanted to live, and she sure as hell couldn't do it with him because he was just as dead as the people he embalmed for funerals were. It's pitiful, chile. He's taking it pretty bad, too," Pecola continued to say out the corner of her mouth.

"Umph. Umph. Umph," moaned Pauletta as she shook her head slowly. "That's so sad, girl. So sad."

"...And last but not least. My youngest brother Keith is an orthodontist in Columbia, South Carolina. He's the only licensed and trained African-American in the state. Keith went to Allen University. That's why he doesn't live here anymore. After graduating from Howard University College of Dentistry, he shocked my parents and decided to make Columbia his home. That's his beautiful wife, Sarah. She's a homemaker. My three cute nieces are here, too. Go ahead, yall. Please stand up." Madison requested as he noticed his family was trying to sit down even though he wasn't finished. He stared tenderly at his family. "I thank you for being patient with me. I know we're running behind schedule, but I just wanted yall to recognize my family. I love all of them, and I thank yall for coming to be with us again, today."

"You take as much time as you want," Pauletta said. "When it comes to family, I don't blame you."

"Thanks, Pauletta," Madison acknowledged. "When we all are finished with our life's journey, when we can no longer drive the Mercedes, the Blazer, the Jaguar, or the Corvette, what will happen to you? When we can't live in our beautiful homes or walk along the shore in front of our beach houses, think about this. What will we most be remembered for? What will all your children remember and the children of others you have helped remember? They'll remember your action. Your actions are the legacy you leave."

"Tell the truth."

"It's a dastardly shame that we're the richest country in the entire world, yet we have such insensitive policies and practices regarding our children and our old people. These two sectors of our society include some of our nation's most vulnerable and weakest citizens. We must stop it. We must change it. I pray that we—my family, and my friends can be the beginning seeds for a change. One of our missions out here is that we can inspire our youth, so they can know that they have a responsibility to lead the next generation into the unknown future." Madison paused for a moment. "Puhleeze, just do the right thing. When you look inside yourself, just listen. Your intuition will tell you and only you exactly what the right thing is. I thank you for my space this evening."

Madison said a few more words, and he finally ended his speech. During the rousing applause and standing ovation, Rozelle walked to the podium and began speaking. The crowd clapped vigorously. Rozelle shared more jokes, and the audience laughed freely. During this part of the ceremony, Athena Davis was selected to sing a solo. DJ Cool Breeze played the appropriate instrumental, and Athena sang a glorious, soul stirring version of *I Surrender All.* This was the song Alex's mother often sang as the lead soloist in church. While Athena belted out the words, Alex and Nanette cried quietly on the inside as they remembered their parents. Just like the earlier solo with Elizabethe, people stood and waved their hands in the air. Once more comments such as *Sing, chile, Thank you, Yes ma'am, yes ma'am, Lord, and Umph umph umph* resounded through the tent. At the end of the solo, the audience exploded into applause. Athena bowed graciously and headed to her seat beside her brother.

Still clapping as he walked to the podium, Rozelle yelled into the mike. "After listening to all these talented young people this evening, I'm convinced I'm in the wrong business. I should be listening to the advice of Rico and become an agent for some of this talent. You know I could earn boocoo bucks," he wisecracked swiftly. A lot of folks in the audience smiled and nodded their heads in agreement. "I thought for sure that one time Athena was CeCe Winans up here. Several times I had to blink my eyes to make sure."

Chapter Sixty-Five

"Well, we've heard the speeches about the lives, and the changes that each of these individuals has made to succeed against all odds to reach for the mountaintop. Now, I'm at the most exciting point in the evening. I'm at the point where I can introduce Alex, the real mastermind of our success here."

"That's ri-ight," a woman yelled out.

Rozelle stopped talking for a moment. "Alex does it all. She can goof around and throw down with the best of them, yet she's a meticulous and fastidious woman when it comes to business. She also plans one of those fantastic Devereaux parties just like the one she has planned for all of us this evening. She has never forgotten where she came from and always reminds people it all started for her on Cameron Avenue in East Winston known as the Black section of Winston-Salem." Rozelle took a deep breath and continued speaking.

"Wonderful."

"Her impressive record of volunteer service that takes place around Winston-Salem would leave even the most resilient out of breath and very tired. But not her. I remember when I first met her years ago. She, Madison, and Symone had just returned from taking twenty children up to the mountains on a weekend ski trip. Scott brought me here that Sunday night. As we spoke, she told me then that 'Either you sit back and say and do nothing, or you can reach out and do something. Everyone should positively touch one or two people.' Ladies and gentlemen, it gives me great, great, great pleasure to present to you a person who lives her life inspired by humanity. I present to you, Mrs. Alexandria Phylicia Johnson-Devereaux."

The entire audience rose to its feet, clapped zealously, and refused to sit down. As Alex walked toward the podium, she knew she wouldn't make it without shedding a tear. Instead, she waited patiently during the standing ovation. As tears glistened in her eyes, she watched the smiling faces of the huge crowd. She thought about her mother and her father and suddenly became calm and strong. Tears refused to fall from her eyes.

"Thank you. Thank you sooo much. Your outpouring of emotions moves me. I'm humbled by it all. I really, really am. This evening is beyond anything I ever imagined it could be, and I'm gratified beyond words. Each opening ceremony seems to get better and better. The adult speakers say they work hard to prepare an inspirational speech for the children, but I'm convinced that the speeches we heard tonight are also vital reaffirmation of life for the adults in ways I'm sure they never ever knew possible. All of the speeches were all quite touching, quite real, and quite educational. I graciously thank you for your words of praise and support." Clapping bellowed throughout the tent once more. "Before I go any further, I first want to acknowledge and thank everyone here. Of course, Madison. My husband is my soul mate, my life's partner, and my heart's twin. I love you, baby. I'm sooo in love with you. We always do this." Madison saw the sparkle in her eyes and blushed like a young boy in love for the first time.

"Beautiful," a man moaned.

"I honor my husband, yall. He's the bedrock of my life, and I want everyone to know that. To my children, my sister, her husband, Marlon, please let my love shower you. To all my wonderful friends and to this impressive audience, I thank you. I commend you. Parents, we thank you for allowing your children to share in our lives, too. I thank you all for making this happen." Alex hesitated slightly as the audience clapped lustily.

"You know everyone wants to see beauty when they look in the mirror, but what I strive for and work toward when I work with children is that they see their inner beauty. What's inside is most powerful for their lives. There are two houses in this world. Your inner one and your outer one. We want the children we work with to see inside their mind—their innerhouse—and to know about the wonderfully beautiful gifts that our God has blessed each and everyone with." The audience clapped again. "All this wouldn't be possible if it weren't for gifts that we all have shared today. We all have gifts. When we as proud Black people are able to join our talents together to help, to care, and to love, that gift can make a tremendous difference."

"Say it loud, sugar."

"Our talents together can create a tremendous, overwhelming successful spirit in our young people. It's the words of the African proverb that keeps me most hopeful. Those words are, *It takes a whole village to raise a child.* Every time Madison and I journeyed to Africa, I noticed how children were always with their mothers. Whether they were on their backs, hanging onto their legs, or holding their hands in a line as they followed their mothers and the other women around, there were always several women around the children. They all were constantly taking care of them, kissing them, chastising them, and loving them. We all were in Africa just this year. All of us talked about that during the flight coming back home," she said reflectively. Many members of the literary society who took the African learning trip nodded their heads in agreement.

"I thank Scott and Rozelle for suggesting to me and Madison a new way to work with the children. My two brothers convinced Madison and me that we couldn't do all we wanted to do for the children, so he told us we needed to gather our friends to do what's valuable in life. Maybe I was selfish," Alex explained with a sheepish grin. "I enjoyed having the children all around me, but it won't change. We will still have them over once a month, too. Now, their presence will be around our other friends and family members who are just as committed to the cause of children as Madison and I are." The audience clapped vigorously.

"One of the main things a parent must do and practice without fail is participation in your children's lives. I know that can be hard with the crazy schedules we have nowadays, but we must set aside the time. Remember back in the old days? Everybody's family ate breakfast and dinner together? Children were outside playing along the sidewalks in the evenings, but the children stopped playing right at the same time because all the children was inside eating dinner."

"That's ri-ight, baby," someone exclaimed.

"Don't allow your children to drift into their rooms, prop themselves in front of the television, and eat a frozen pizza or the take out order from the restaurant down the street. If you can't sit down together and eat every day, make up a schedule. Make sure you enjoy each other sitting at the kitchen or dining room table at least three times a week, especially on Sundays. When I was little, I always loved my Sunday afternoon dinners after church with my family. You know the tasty, crispy fried chicken, collard greens, potato salad, good old sweet lemonade, and my favorite—a sweet potato pie." The crowd murmured at the old memories.

"I fondly remember the days when friends, family, church members, and even the preacher came over to relax on the front porch or chitchat in the living room. I loved that. Madison was raised the same way. That's why we always try to maintain that same ambiance out here. We always try to have a big ole Sunday dinner and hope that our friends stop by and eat, too. Black people must do whatever is necessary to develop those strong family ties of old."

"Absolutely," a man said.

"As usual, Pauletta had us laughing this morning. She said that back when she was a child growing up, the adults were always right. The children were always wrong, and you prayed the neighbors didn't tell your parents about you when you did something wrong." The audience laughed and clapped with understanding.

"You *must* participate in what your children are doing. Whatever they're involved in, support them. Have lunch with them at school. If you're not a homemaker like me and you work outside the home, plan to volunteer in their classrooms—even if it's only a small amount of time."

"Every day on the television and at the major malls across the country, children are bombarded with the values and morals of today's society. It's time for us to come together as professional Black people and interject *our* values. The same ones we grew up with. Those old values caused us to be who we are. We were such an obedient generation. That's because our parents didn't spare the rod, either. We got serious whippings back then, not spankings. That's what they call them now, but they were pure divine whippings. The punishment of *time out* was only something they said as they got ready to whip us." The crowd laughed. "My Mama was the main disciplinarian. Daddy never hit me. The only time I heard my mother say *time out* was when she said, 'It's *time out* now for talking, baby. You go get me a switch, Alexandria. It better not be a little one either!' That's the only time I heard *time out*," Alex exclaimed. Rippling of clapping sounded throughout the audience too along with the laughter.

"Without question, discipline is teaching, and discipline strengthens children. I too agree that we can deal with our children rationally. We don't have to discipline them by slapping them around or by yelling degrading comments to them. But in the Devereauxs' household, Trey and Purity are spanked whenever it's necessary to do so. It's not an every day occurrence. It's not even an every month situation, but our children know that there are certain boundaries that they cannot cross. I agree spanking shouldn't be the first thing a parent does to a child, but I don't believe it's possible to raise children without them having some consequences for their behavior. True, parents have to be compassionate, but we must discipline them. If we don't, they'll run all over us and ruin their own lives."

"When I was a young girl, we went to church each and every Sunday. It wasn't one Sunday out of the month. I'm talking *every* Sunday. It was a big thing. We *had* to go. We had no choice in the matter. Sometimes, we'd have to go on Wednesdays and Saturdays, too. Those church folks prayed for us, and everybody else around town. I enjoyed reading *Reviving the Spirit* by Beverly Hall Laurence that tells about Black people going home to church."

"Black folks have gotten away from praying, too. Nowadays, it's against the law to even pray in schools, and they wonder why children are out of control? The answer is sooo obvious. Religion isn't alive in homes anymore, and it's definitely dead in the school system. Coldness reigns supreme. Anything and everything goes in the movies and on television. It's because morality, goodness, and family are a thing of the past in today's society. That's why fifty percent of all marriages end in divorce. Divorce is entirely too easy in America. Working on a marriage is the hard job."

"Tell the truth, young lady." After a few silent moments, Alex began speaking again.

"You know several people asked me and Madison why is the opening ceremony evening program four hours long with just one little intermission? 'The children will become bored, they told us. *Four hours?* That's too long. That's crazy, Alex.' You know what I told them? I said that it might be too long, but if our children are able to sit and watch television non-stop from morning to evening, surely they can sit through an opening celebration program such as this. They should want to be a part of a celebratory evening that talks about African-Americans in all their glory. Acknowledging the tragedy and the beauty in our lives." Everyone clapped and stood up.

"According to the statistics, the average child spends twenty-seven hours a week in front of the television. By the time they reach eighth grade, they see one-hundred-thousand acts of television violence and eight thousand murders. So four hours for an opening ceremony that includes an evening program of motivation, education, information, celebration, spirituality, singing, and love isn't too long. It's not too long for children, you, me, or the animals you see strutting around here," Alex ended with a smile, and everyone clapped boisterously in agreement. A few people stood up.

Suddenly, Alex noticed that two of the Devereauxs' sweet little female pigs were prancing along the back left sidewall of the tent. A slight commotion erupted as several children tried to pet them, and they quickly scurried away. Until the pigs found a place they were comfortable with, the two animals would continue to sniff around. Knowing how rambunctious they were, Alex realized that if she took the time to bring any attention to them over the microphone, the whole program would turn into a spectacle with both children and adults chasing the pigs around the tent. As she flipped a page, she smiled to herself. If she knew they were coming, she would have tied a red and white ribbon around their necks, too. She chuckled to herself again and continued speaking.

"Remember our society tends to measure people by their athletic abilities, by their economic stature in life, and by their intelligence. Those are the ones they like to uplift as heroes. But I have another compass where I determine measurement. I call it the love compass that is calibrated by unity. Promoting love is as great as any aspect. It's as fantastic as any quality of life anyone can give or have for another human being. Some people believe it's Pollyanna acting. I don't. I believe it's quite natural. When you have love in your heart, your life will make a difference because people respond to love." The crowd applauded boisterously.

"Although Black people have suffered through a lot in this country, we're not a sad people. We've had the capacity to enjoy life despite the poverty in our lives. We laugh and can laugh. Laughter is therapeutic. Always laugh. Crying is cleansing, but laughing is absolutely uplifting. It defuses tension and reduces stress. A lot of people think they're sick, but they're not ill one bit. They're simply miserable with their lives, their jobs, their existence, and their marriages. They say people who don't laugh, smile, and remain angry all the time are seven times as likely to die by the age of fifty. Let it go and laugh. That's why we love old crazy Rozelle so much. If nothing else, he always keeps everyone laughing."

"That's for sure," Madison said.

"I believe God laughs when He's pleased with us, and I know God is happy with our work with children. You know why? These children are happy. They tell us this with their smiles, their hugs of love, their improved grades, and their changes in behavior at home. God *is* happy." The raucous crowd broke out in a roaring applause and whistles.

"Preach, young lady."

Alex smiled. "What I would like to leave you with is this. Always pray. Meditate on your life, and your dreams. I'm proud to say that I *still* write my hopes and dreams down in my journal each and every day. I take time to reflect, meditate, and write my innermost thoughts. Every morning when I pray over Imani, my prayer box, my creative visualizations cause me to think of this perfectly wonderful world where adults, children, and everyone are living in total bliss."

"That's true, baby."

"Always remember the words of Joseph Joubert. 'You will find poetry nowhere unless you bring some with you.' The words of William James, '...The great use of life is to spend it for something that outlasts it.' You may not agree with everything we do out here. You may not even agree with everything that was said this evening. I want you to know that each and every one of these speakers gave you what was inside their hearts, and they're truly committed to being there for *our* children. What we're doing with the children isn't heroic. It shouldn't even be inspirational. It should all be so truly, truly natural and so effortless. However, if what we try to do with the youth inspires you, then I'm glad." Alex talked with moist eyes.

"In closing, I thank my family and my friends. I thank yall so very much, and I love yall. We reached out to yall for help, and yall responded in a magnificent, glorious way. From the bottom of my heart, I thank you," Alex ended with a broad grin.

Alex slowly gathered her typed pages together and attempted to head back to her seat. However, Rozelle quickly grabbed her left arm and raised her hand victoriously in the air. Eventually, Alex hugged him and went to sit down. For five minutes, the crowd gave her a thunderous standing ovation. Finally, Rozelle noticed Madison was making quick hand signals to him. Rozelle covered the mike with his hand and leaned over to better hear what Madison was quietly saying. Rozelle nodded with understanding.

"I need to bring Alex back on stage again. Ladies and Gentlemen, I present Alex to you one more timeee!"

Alex walked on stage and spoke quickly. "Thank you, Rozelle. This won't take up too much time. When Madison, Rozelle, Cleopatra, and I reviewed the program yesterday afternoon, we said that we would recognize the following people during my part in the program. Although Rozelle recognized the dignitaries and others in the audience at the beginning of the program, I saved a special place for five other special people. Well, I neglected to do that, so here I am again."

"Take your time, baby," Pauletta shouted.

Alex glanced up from reviewing her notes. "Thank you, Pauletta. At this time, I would like to recognize the four senior citizens that have volunteered their time to help us select the twenty-eight children we're honoring tonight and the twenty-eight children that were honored last month. Since we don't live in public housing, these older women are our eyes and ears in the four public housing communities of Winston-Salem. Every so often, I would get a call from one of them. They would say, *Alex baby, I got another one for you. They say he's having problems in school. Other than that, he's a good, sweet boy. They say this one talks back to her mother, but she's worthy and needs help, Alex. This other one we found is a good boy. They said that he could be a scientist; he's sooo smart with numbers. Tell Madison about him. I bet he could help him out at the hospital. Alex, this one got something they say is ADD. It's attention deficit disorganization or something. Sugar, we don't know what that means, but he's a good boy, Alex. The baby just needs a little help..."*

The crowd began laughing and clapping again as they listen to Alex mimic the older women's voices. "These four women continuously scoured the neighborhood. As I call their names, I would like for them to stand. Before they rise to their feet, go ahead and honor them with your love applause." The audience clapped freely. Alex turned to look into the direction of the four older women.

"We have Mrs. Ivy Peoples. She's from Cleveland Avenue Homes." A light-skinned older lady stood and waved. Mrs. Peoples went to sit back down.

"Mrs. Peoples, please remain standing. We have Mrs. Jessie Drooner. She's from Happy Hills Garden. Mrs. Vanessa Safeguard is from Kimberly Park, and Mrs. Willie Mae Simmons is from Piedmont Park."

All four women were dressed in flowery Sunday dresses and wore their hats proudly propped on their pepper gray-wigged heads.

"Like everyone else here, these wonderful matriarchs have volunteered their time and energy. We love you. We thank you for your involvement and for sharing your wisdom," Alex continued fondly.

"Baby, don't forget about the homemade cakes, pies, and potato salad," Madison reminded casually.

"Thanks, baby. As always, your cakes and pies are out of this world, too. The potato salad with paprika sprinkled all over it was magnificent. We thank you. We certainly do." The tent roared with thunderous applause. The older ladies sat down, and Alex continued speaking.

"I have profound respect for the very old and the very young. I've found that I've learned tremendously from these two groups of people. For this reason, I would next like to recognize my Aunt Susie Mae Devereaux." Alex laughed freely. "Aunt Susie Mae married my husband's great uncle's youngest brother on his father's side. I know yall said, 'Say whaaat?

Say that again, Alex.' Anyway, my Aunt Susie Mae is sooo wonderful to me. After I met Madison, I told the Devereaux family that I had to claim her as an aunt for Nanette and me. After my parents died, I claimed her as my aunt, mother, and grandmother, too. Aunt Susie Mae, can you please stand?" Susie Mae Devereaux sat beside Madison's father. When she heard the request, the elderly woman stood fragilely and leaned heavily on a metal circular waist cane. The audience clapped.

"My Aunt Susie Mae. Doesn't she look good? She's eighty-nine years old, and she turns ninety in October. She always tells me that if she doesn't look that old, it's because she has enjoyed the pleasure of what she has done in life. Before Aunt Susie Mae retired, she was a schoolteacher for almost forty-seven years. Aunt Susie Mae loves telling people her age and letting them know she still dips her snuff whenever she gets ready. She told me that the doctor put her on it," Alex informed jokingly and everyone laughed.

"I love going over to her house because I feel like a little girl when I'm there. She always has that hard candy with the very soft fruit center. It's always right there in a crystal bowl that is sitting on her living room's shiny dark wood coffee table. Yall know the kind of candy I'm talking about?" Several people nodded their heads. "I believe I gots to eat at least five pieces before I leave. All the children we work with just love her, too. She'll be speaking to them on Thursday afternoon and I can't begin to tell you how spellbound everyone is when she speaks. She has such wonders to share."

"When I first met her, she truly reminded me of my Mama. She used to say to me, and I'm paraphrasing as best I can. 'Chile, listen to the words of old folk cause they got jewels of information to share. Since you look like you got an old soul and know that to be true, learn how to become a jewel snatcher. Snatching diamonds, rubies, sapphires, pearls, and dazzling crystals from the conversations you hear.'"

"Wonderful advice," a man said.

"'Everything I might say to you may not make a lot of sense to you, sugar. But for the every forty-eight comments I share with you, there might be thirty of them with profound knowledge dancing all around them words. Learn how to snatch those thirty jewels from the conversations. Those pearls. Cause if you know how to snatch them, then you'll certainly learn how to pass them jewels of information on to other folk, chile,'" Alex said with just as much tenacity. One would think Aunt Susie Mae had given the information to Alex just yesterday instead of over twenty years ago. The older woman smiled proudly.

"My Aunt Susie Mae is very courageous and a strong-willed woman. I absolutely love and adore her. Everybody that knows her says the same thing. She has buried all of her three children, and her husband. Yet in spite of all of life's tragedy and adversity, she always has a smile on her face. She received a college degree when it was hard for blacks to do so. She still talks about when Winston-Salem State University was known as Slater Industrial Academy. For years, she has been a member of Links, Inc. She doesn't hesitate to let folk know that Links is the world's most prestigious African-American woman's service organization. Aunt Susie Mae has done it all. At our reception later on, you'll see her dance a sweet little two-step, especially if the band plays the jazzy sounds of Harry Mills and the Mills Brothers like she asked me to." While Alex spoke, the modest, silver gray-haired Susie Mae smiled contentedly. "Aunt Susie Mae, do you want to say something?"

"No, chile. I clare you done said enough for the both of us, sugar," the older woman responded in a spry voice. With the help of Madison's father, Aunt Susie Mae proceeded to sit down. The crowd broke out into another round of hand clapping. Alex thanked everyone and sat down.

The crowd gave Alex another standing ovation. Rozelle instructed the audience to turn to the *Oath of Commitment to our Children*. It was a covenant, which reminded each volunteer of their earnest commitment to spend quality time with the child they selected. The *Oath* was typed on the next to the last page of the beige colored calligraphy designed program. The adult volunteers who indicated they were truly committed to helping the children stood in front of their seats, and the oath was animatedly recited loudly for all to hear. Afterwards, DJ Cool Breeze played Black Men United singing *U Will Know*. During the song, Rozelle instructed everyone to hug four people they didn't know and give kisses to the ones they did know.

"...To all the speakers, it was great. I thought it was fantastic last month. This month was just as marvelous and overwhelming to me," Rozelle added. "We thank all the speakers for sharing your accomplishments, your dreams, and what was truly inside your hearts today."

The crowd broke out with a wild spree of clapping. When the applause ended, another round of presentations began. Cleopatra and Charmaine walked to the stage. They presented the twenty-eight honorees as well as their parents or guardians with their own gorgeously wrapped personal copies of *African American Voices of Triumph: Perseverance* and *The African-Americans*. On the inside flap of each book were calligraphy written words that said, *You give but little when you give of your possessions. It is when you give of your heart that you truly give. It is with our hearts that we love you.* The two books were signed by Alex, Madison, Symone, Pecola, Carlos, Scott, Cleopatra, Jodria, Rozelle, Booker T, Marlon, and all the other volunteers that would make the youngsters' two week stay in Advance both memorable and enjoyable.

Chapter Sixty-Six

"Ladies and gentlemen, this is what we all have been waiting for. We've been waiting to see who will be matched with whom. We'll now see who will have a new member added to their family. Are you ready? DJ Cool Breeze, puhleeze give me a drum roll."

Athena held the rose basket with all the children's names in it. A smiling CJ held the rose basket with all the volunteer adults in it. Pecola noticed how her son continued to makes eyes at Athena and she at him. Once more, Pecola became concerned. When the drum roll sounded, everyone in the audience became quiet, but Pecola's mind was distracted. Rozelle reached into the children's basket and pulled out a name.

"...Ladies and gentlemen, I have Octavia Shante Hatton. She's fourteen years old and lives in Cleveland Avenues Homes."

The audience broke out into a whole lot of hollering and yelling. During the wild display of support, Nanette crazily banged the tambourine while the dogs barked and ran around in circles.

"I'm going to ask yall this today. It's the same question they ask when people get baptized in those old-fashioned, back in the wood, red dirt country road, Black churches in Nashville, Tennessee. Who came to be with Octavia today as she meets her second family?" Rozelle asked.

The entire audience stood up, and Rozelle laughed as he noticed different people throughout the crowd giving each other high fives for standing for Octavia. Many of the people who were familiar with last month's electrifying ceremony felt compelled to stand this time.

"We're all off to a good start here. DJ Cool Breeze, puhleeze hit me with another drum roll, "Rozelle said and reached into the adult rose basket to pull out a name.

"Ladies and gentlemen, the family to willingly share their lives with our wonderful, beautiful Octavia is Dr. and Mrs. Ewing Barr of Summerfield, North Carolina. They're the parents of two boys, five and eight." Rozelle smiled broadly. "People, this is wonderful."

"And Mrs. Barr. Excuse me. It's Dr. Sherry Barr. Alex just informed me the sister is a doctor, too. Now, we don't want to leave off the right title. Some of my Black folks get excited if you don't address them with the correct title and don't accurately recall all their accomplishments," Rozelle joked lightly and gave Sherry Barr a vigorous Black power fist. Sherry laughed good-naturedly at Rozelle and casually waved her hand in the air at him. The audience laughed again.

"Dr. Sherry Barr teaches computer science at UNC-Greensboro, and Ewing is a chiropractor in Greensboro. Go hug your new family members, Octaviaaaaa!"

The Barr family rushed up and hugged Octavia. The audience smiled contentedly at the display of affection between the adults and their two young boys. Some members of the audience began to cry.

"Here we go again! This is fabulous, ladies and gentlemen," Rozelle exclaimed as he reached into the rose bag and pulled out another name. "This time we have another special person. It's another girl. That's ok, guys. We ain't going nowhere until every name is pulled," he quickly informed as he gazed at Miles who looked like he had a worried expression on his face.

"The young girl we pulled this time is Kitty Green Hayes. She's twelve years old and lives in Kimberly Park."

The wild yelling and screaming from the audience began once more. The video operators didn't know which section to film first. Glorious displays of emotions were erupting rampantly throughout the entire well-dressed crowd. Finally, the audience settled down, and Rozelle began speaking once more.

"I ask you. Who came to be with Kitty Green Hayes today as she meets her second family!" Rozelle bellowed for the young girl's supporters. Once again, the whole audience stood up, and he burst out laughing into the mike. Rozelle reached into the adult rose basket. Once the audience calmed down, Rozelle tried to get a few words in.

"The second family we have for the wonderful, adorable, sweet Miss Kitty Green Hayes is Clark and Adelaide Cade of Tobaccoville, North Carolina. Both Adelaide and Clark work at MUB Industries at Plant #640. Their son and daughter are grown and away at college during the year. They said that they wanted to have a young voice in their home again. It didn't matter whether it was a boy or girl. Uh oh. That sounds like Kitty might get a little spoiled hanging out with the Cades. Go hug your new second family members, girl!"

Clark and Adelaide raced over to hug Kitty Green Hayes. The clapping and yelling began once more. The audience exhibited such an overwhelming display of euphoria.

"This is wonderful. Working with children as we do has shown us it's all about love. That's the ultimate contribution to society. We think it's toys and things, which sometimes we try to equate to time. But I believe it's a combination of open hearts ready to love, and a conscientious sharing of my time and your time. I salute the Cades and the Barrs for giving of themselves. They're sharing the most precious commodity they can ever have. Their time. Bravo to you," Rozelle exclaimed as he clapped.

"Baby, this is absolutely beautiful all over again," Darilyn whispered to Rico.

"I know, baby. I know," Rico replied smiling at his wife while he tightly hugged his wife's shoulders and smiled back at her. Darilyn and Rico told the Devereauxs they wanted to mentor three older children to go with their three younger ones, ages six, eight, and nine. It didn't matter if they were matched with boys or girls. Now, Rico and Darilyn were too anxiously waiting to see which three children would be selected to share their lives.

"I'm going to try my best to not get emotional anymore." Rozelle sighed and inhaled quickly. "I don't know why? I was naive enough to think that once again this part of the opening ceremony wouldn't be overly powerful and sensitive. I went through this same thing last month. I was wrong. This is what I meant earlier," he explained wistfully. "In the end, it's hard to see whose lives are enriched most. The Devereauxs, or our lives. Their many friends who took the oath to care, or the twenty-eight children we are honoring tonight."

Rozelle had twenty-six more children to go. Some of the other people in the audience who didn't volunteer to help with their free time now wished they had stepped up to do their part, too.

"...Ah sookie sookie, now," Rozelle hollered. "Here we go. I know we got twenty-six more names to go. But before we go any further, I wanted to tell yall to enjoy your two weeks in Advance, young people. I know you will! DJ Cool Breeze, hit me with a little James Brown. You know the number one soul brother. Hit me with a little, *Say It Loud, I'm Black and I'm Proud*," Rozelle hollered and began gliding around the stage doing the mash potatoes dance like a James Brown prodigy at the Apollo on opening night.

When DJ Cool Breeze inserted the classic James Brown's song, the audience began crazily singing the words, too. Many of them began dancing around in front of their seats. After the singing ended, Rozelle began pulling names once more. As an excited child's name was called out, each one was given a red rose. When all of the children were matched with the appropriate family, Rozelle said a few more motivating words. He reminded everyone the closing ceremonies would be two weeks from Sunday, but for right now, it was time to go eat and party.

The Devereauxs' pastor prayed, and the portion of the evening where dining on the lavishly catered meal unfolded quickly. As DJ Cool Breeze played Bob Marley's well-known reggae song, *One Love*, everyone hugged each other, cried, laughed, and headed to their appropriate, numbered tables.

After dinner, the Devereauxs' planned to have another evening float away in the huge transparent tent which was prepped with a large hardwood floor for non-stop dancing to the jazzy sounds of the Charles Greene Group as well as classic soul jams played by DJ Cool Breeze. Without question, it was going to be another glorious night of throw down electric sliding, carousel riding, talking, and fun under the starry, moonlit yet dark Advance night.

Chapter Sixty-Seven

"...I'm serious. I *really* can't go with yall to the mountains, girl. Labor Day Weekend is coming up, and you know how it is. If you're a Trinidadian whose from New York or from any Caribbean country for that matter, it's tradition to be on Eastern Parkway in Brooklyn on that Monday. Having a good time leading up to the day of the parade," Symone explained once more to Pecola, "is one great joy in my life."

Pecola was finally convinced that Symone wouldn't be going with all the other friends to the mountains. After the twenty-eight older children left the Devereauxs, the adult volunteers had the past week to recuperate. It was now their turn to hang out. Naturally, they were ready to bask in moments of rest and relaxation for themselves.

"So does this mean you're not going, Sy?"

"Exactly."

"Ok. I finally believe you. We're getting ready to pull out, honeychile," Pecola exclaimed through the telephone wires. "You should see the two buses that Marlon got for us, girl. They're nothing but motorized mansions."

"Marlon told me, Pecola."

"The one I'm riding in is complete with a bed in the back, satellite, and television. It's like a living room on wheels, chile. It's sooo huge, it's unbelievable. They furnished us with drivers and everything. You sure you don't want to go to the mountains with us?"

Symone took an impatient breath. "I'm telling you. Not this time. Yall just have a good time. I'm heading to New York. I need to finish up the children's back-to-school shopping since I got to do my part for the eleven billion dollar industry of getting children back into the groove of school, girl."

"You're too crazy, Sy."

"Plus, Hazele has tickets to the Boys Choir of Harlem's concert for tomorrow night. Mummy and all the children are due in on Friday afternoon. So me, Hazele, Quentin, and Ameenah are going to hang out together to savor those free moments until our children get back."

"That sounds like a fun family affair, chile."

"I'm still not over the fact yall aren't going to Brooklyn to play mas with me for Labor Day, Pecola. You know The West Indian American Day Carnival Association does put on a great show. It'll be five days of Caribbean culture."

"Honeychile, I know. We go all the time. Don't act like that this time. We're all tired from working in the trenches for two weeks with all those children. Seventeen straight days is more like it. I'm pooped."

"Pooped? Hell, you didn't work that much. You only volunteered for five evenings and two days, Pecola." As Symone spoke, she casually flipped through the pages of Meetings Odyssey's recent copy of *Black Meetings and Tourism* magazine.

"I'm still pooped. I had to leave the office, rush home to change clothes, and go over there. That took a lot out of me." Just thinking about the action-packed two weeks with all the children made Pecola inhale deeply. "Plus, the guys said they wanted to go to the Aggie-Eagle Labor Day Classic this week-end. They got frat brothers coming in from everywhere. Gorgeous frat guys, honeychile. Your type. You need to be here for that good time because you never know who you'll meet."

"I'll pass, Pecola."

"Come on, now. You know we were all in New York with you last year and missed the game. That's one of the biggest rivalries out, honeychile. This year Carlos, Madison, Rico, and the boys said that they were going to be right there in their season seats on the fifty-yard line rooting for the Aggies. You know how they are. The Aggie gold rush is on, chile."

"It always is this time of year."

"Marlon plans to keep the bus for at least another week. DC is coming down from Atlanta in his house on wheels. You know he brought that huge thing to drive to games."

"Get out of here."

"Seriously. Carlos said that Rico and Darilyn have already placed an order with Parker Brothers for at least two tons of fried chicken. They're getting chitlins from Cafe Bessie and who knows what else. Our men folks plan to do just a teeny bit of tailgating at the classic."

Symone shook her head helplessly. "That sounds typical, girl. Most times, I don't know why we even go to games anymore. Folks are profiling, trying to look their best, and checking everybody else out. Nobody knows the score or who made the last play. It's a trip."

Pecola shook her head and smiled. "I know, honeychile. That's the Black College game experience. All the men do is bullshit about stuff. The women, too. It's just a gathering of sorts. You know you enjoy it as well, so stop sounding like a spoilsport. You're just jealous you're not going to be here to enjoy all the fun. Anyway, enough about football. Guess whose going with us to the mountains, Symone?" Pecola lowered her voice to a conspiratory whisper.

"Who?"

"Lillie Dupri."

"So? That's nothing new. She's gone a whole lot of other places with us before."

"Well, I know *that.* Are you listening to me? I hear pages turning." Symone rested the magazine on her desk and gave Pecola her undivided attention.

"Now I am."

"Most times Lillie has had a date with her, chile. She doesn't have a date this time. This is a couple's thing, Symone. She's a single lady, you know."

"No kidding. So is Cleopatra, and she's going."

"That's different, Symone. You know *exactly* what I mean. Cleopatra acts like everyone's mama. Everybody knows she's harmless." Pecola took a deep breath and frowned as she pondered how to phrase her next words. "I hope Lillie doesn't try to take anybody's stuff while she's up there."

"Pecola, girl puhleeze. A woman can't take nobody's stuff unless they're ready to go. Now I get nothing but good vibes from her. What made Lillie decide to go?" While Symone spoke, she stared out her office window at the startling blue sky.

"Alex. You know Alex *told* her. She discussed it with her during the time the children were here. Then while we were trying to act dignified at the Bostic Evening of Extraordinaire on Saturday night, Alex told her again."

"Trying? Speak for yourself."

Pecola laughed. "But can you believe that? With all that mingling that was going on at the Bostics, Alex had nothing else to do but invite a single woman to go to the mountains with a whole bunch of married people."

"You're a mess, girl. I'm single, too. So what you're saying?"

"You're different. Everybody *really* knows you. The most you will do with our husbands is curse them out as you tell them off."

"Alex and Lillie have known each other for a long time too, Pecola."

Pecola let out a big exasperated sigh. She realized it was helpless making Symone see her point. "You know who asked for you on Saturday night?"

"Who?"

"Dr. Cletus Ingram. Madison's surgeon friend who has that huge practice down in Chapel Hill. You know he's single now."

"You know he's still too short now, Pecola. He's only five seven or something. Why did he ask for me?"

"He's legally separated, honeychile. Are you listening?" Pecola spoke impatiently. "Mr. Doctor is fresh out the blocks and ready to roll with dating again. Said he wanted to take you out for a nice candlelight French dinner, not in Winston-Salem but along the French Riviera. Can you believe that?"

"I'm still not impressed. I've been to the French Riviera a number of times. That was a regular family vacation for us. He needs to try that dead rap on somebody else. Like I said, he's too short."

Pecola smiled. "I know you've been to every corner of the world. It was a good try on Cletus' part, though. I think you need to lower your standards to include shorter men. You would have dates all the time."

"I don't want dates all the time. Sometimes, I want to be left alone. There are times I want a man's warm body and hard dick to go with it."

"Umph. Umph. Umph. Cletus wants an opportunity with you. It was funny watching him look for you. Madison said that he got there like thirty minutes after you left, but he was hoping you were still around."

"I already see he's not an excellent prospect. If he didn't listen to Madison, he doesn't follow instructions well. Give me a break, girl. On Saturday night, I was out of there with the quickness. Remember?"

"I know, chile. Everybody kept asking me, Alex, Madison, and Scott where you were."

"I wish people would stay out of my damn business."

"I believed the women kept asking Madison and Scott because they wanted to grin up in their faces."

"You're right, girl. They both looked quite dapper and handsome in their tuxedos."

"Weren't our men folk looking fine on Saturday? Carlos, too."

"Yep. That's why I know those folk looking for me really didn't care where I was. They were just being nosy. They should've known where I was. Always asking my friends for me. You and Alex would've been proud of me, though. I left in polite fashion right after the private VIP reception. I *told* the Bostics it was a wonderful evening, and I said the same thing to the officials of the College Foundation."

"Well, you missed them recognizing you as a Bostic Contributor, honeychile. Of course, I clapped very delicately for you when they mentioned your name." Symone laughed loudly at Pecola.

"How many Bostic Contributors were recognized?"

"I can't remember. Along with you, the Devereauxs, the Dinzelles, me and Carlos, and a few other names I didn't recognize, about six other people gave five thousand. Of course, you know there were several corporations that gave ten thousand dollars, too."

"Humph. Ten thousand dollars? They *should* give that much. They could at least have given one-hundred-thousand or more, especially with all the products Black folks all over the country buy from those corporations."

"I believe Marlon said somebody did."

"Did what?"

"Gave one-hundred-thousand dollars. It was a surprise donation."

"Well, that's downright wonderful. I'm glad."

"Now, chile."

"I just get upset about my people's giving practices. If they were selling a Rolls Royce that night for ten thousand dollars, Black folks would pull out their checkbooks in a heartbeat. You know it's true."

"They *would* pull out their checkbooks a lot faster for that car, chile."

"This isn't different, Pecola. This is the Rolls Royce for our Black children's minds and for them to receive their education. I'm telling you what I know. A lot of folk got seriously tight rubber bands around their checkbooks, girl. You know it's a damn—"

"Some Black people have just lost sight with things like that, of the vision of giving," Pecola interrupted her. "That's all."

"*That's all?* You said that's all. That's enough. You had the nerve to say they lost sight. Some of them never had sight, Pecola. You can never lose sight of something you never had, girl. If anything, Black people need to develop sight. We need to understand the vision that we *do* have a responsibility to those coming behind us the same way it was made possible for us to move forward by those who were in front of us."

"It's a wonderful day, girl. The sun's shining along the horizon and it was a beautiful evening on Saturday. Thank God you weren't there yelling that out to the other guests. If people knew what you said about them being cheap and things and how they don't do this and don't do that, we wouldn't get invited to nothing in this town, chile."

"Yes, we would."

"How you know that?"

"Because we're known for giving in Winston-Salem. That's why. If you're known for giving fat checks to charitable causes, that's your silver ticket. It doesn't matter whether people like you or not. Humph. If they hate your guts, they'll still invite you to all kinds of benefits. Treat you like royalty with silk kid gloves when you get there just so you can give other hefty checks to their causes and smile for the newspapers. As usual, you might not want to admit it, but you know I'm telling the God's heaven truth."

Pecola grimaced pleasantly and gazed at the master bathroom's Louis XVI geranium-print fabric love seat.

"You know what, Sy?" She was amused at Symone's typical attitude.

"What?"

"You got a serious case of sermonitis where you're always preaching about shit. You sure you're in the right profession? Instead of getting your MBA, you should've gotten a Divinity Degree from the Jarvis Christian College."

"The what?"

"The one in Hawkins, Texas. That's where Pauletta's nephew on Hannibal's side goes. Kerry is his name. You know the one whose studying to be a missionary."

"Yeah right," Symone answered quickly even though she had no idea that Pecola was talking about. "But you know it's true, Pecola. Hell, I know it is. I got a letter just this morning for me to host a museum benefit in Charlotte, and another long letter asking me to host some charity function in Linwood." Symone closed her eyes and leaned back in her chair.

"What's wrong, Sy?"

"Got a lot on my mind."

"Maybe at the Charlotte benefit you'll see Arman."

"Thanks for reminding me about that stupid ass man. Now I know for sure I'm going to write back and tell those people I am not hosting anything, at least in Charlotte. You're right. I might run into Arman down there. The thought of that is thoroughly frightening to me, girl. Thoroughly."

Pecola inhaled deeply again as Symone cracked up at her own words. It was obvious Symone was in an awfully good mood, and Pecola was glad to see it for a change.

Madison checked his watch and glanced around at everyone socializing in his circular driveway. "It's time for us to pull out. Is everyone readddy?"

"As long as my fried chicken is warm, I'm ready," Marlon joked and patted his wife on the behind. "C'mon, baby. Let's get the best seats on our bus."

"Can yall believe Marlon's ready to eat?" Nanette said, talking to her sister. "We haven't left Advance yet, and he's wants a chicken sandwich with hot sauce all over it."

"It's something about taking a road trip that makes you want to eat from point go," Alex said. She noticed Rico and Darilyn stepping into the bus, too.

"Has anyone seen my wife?" Carlos asked, looking around. "I ain't going nowhere without my baby."

"If I were you, I would leave her ass with the quickness," Rozelle shouted and Jodria nudged her husband.

"Where's Pecola?" Carlos asked again.

"Hell, you can never tell with Pecola, man," Scott said. He took Charmaine's hand and they headed toward their chosen bus.

Chapter Sixty-Eight

"...But I must say, Sy," Pecola continued, relaxing on Alex's bed. "There's only one you, chile. I am not even going to try to have a major discussion with you today about charity and what Black people should be doing subjects. Ain't nothing I can add to that. I got my other problems right now I need to focus on. But really, you should have stayed longer Saturday night and hobnobbed with everyone."

"Why? I was ready to leave. You know how I get when I'm dateless. Paranoid. So leave my girl Lillie alone." The two friends chuckled together at that comment. "I just wanted to relax. There was a jasmine scented aromatherapy bubble bath at home with my name on it. I decided to go home and luxuriate in it. While I took my bath, I listened to Miss Jessica's Lena Horne CDs. Girl, you can believe I played *Stormy Weather* over and over and over again."

"I bet you did," Pecola inserted amusingly. "I believe it."

"Then I ate popcorn and watched a movie."

"In your bathroom?"

"No, girl."

"Well hell, I didn't know. Since you put that built-in television set up in your bathroom, I just didn't know where. Forgive me for living, chile."

"You're right. It's just another way for me to watch the news or the AMC channel while I take my addictive hits of bubble baths and quiet sips of Cristal. That's all. Don't be jealous, girlfriend."

"Oh, me jealous of *you*? Yeah right, chile. Tell me which movies you watched this time?"

"A couple of my favorites. *Daughters of the Dust* and *The Color Purple.*"

"Hmmm. That's an interesting combination."

"You're telling me."

"Every time I see *The Color Purple,* I can't believe how all those talented Black people were ignored at the Oscars and at the various other awards, Sy."

"Some white people were ignored, but I agree, too. That movie is a phenomenal piece of work."

"You realize that award isn't for us, Sy," Pecola said quietly after thinking for a few seconds.

"You're absolutely right. Yet, many of our Black actors desire to have it for validation and acceptance of a job well done."

"Black folks can forget that?" Pecola exclaimed. "They'll give a white girl an Oscar for playing a prostitute and everything else ridiculous, but do you think they would do the same for a movie the caliber of *The Color Purple.* Hell no!"

"It goes back to typical principles. If you create it, you must own it and control it. The movie industry and the folk who select as well as vote on who receive those various awards are mostly white people. Once you understand that basic premise, the outcome should always be crystal clear when we're in a competition like that. We ain't controlling nothing there, baby. Token representation is all there is, sistergurl."

"Enough of this serious stuff. I'm going out of town and want to keep a pleasant mind."

"Fine with me. You brought it up."

"I'm dropping it."

"Good! As young folks say, I just wanted to chill last night. So I watched videos all night, Pecola."

"Not me, honeychile. You know me and Carlos were one of the last people to leave the Bostics."

"Knowing your behind, you probably forced Carlos to stay longer than he wanted. I should've known."

"What can I say? It's terrible how money and power attract some people."

"Whaaat? Some people?"

"I know. You're right. It's so unfortunate I'm one of *those* people," Pecola admitted.

"You're crazy as hell."

"I know, chile. So you really don't think I need to worry about Lillie?"

"Nope. Like I said, she has been a number of places with us."

"I know, but she should at least come along with a date. One time Jodria told me that she heard Lillie say that she thought Carlos was down right old-fashioned handsome."

"No Carlos ain't handsome. His ass is fiinnne. You know that. His blue eyes are what throws women off. I can give you a long list of women who look like they're seriously eyeing your stuff. Uh oh. Is that a little jealousy I hear creeping up?"

"No. Not really." Pecola spoke slowly. She couldn't disguise the worry in her voice. "I'm just wondering why a single girl would want to go on a mountain trip with couples?"

"Because she feels like it. That's why. Anyway, she always has fun when she hangs out with us. Marlon told me that three of his pro football buddies are going to meet yall up there. If I'm not mistaken, I think one of them is Morocco Grissett. You know the one who is challenging Walter Payton's seventeen thousand career rushing record."

"Well, he can forget that. To be exact, Walter Payton's record is sixteen thousand seven hundred and twenty-six yards. He might as well give up on ever getting close to Mr. Payton."

"No, Morocco is pretty good, Pecola."

"Good where? I don't hear Carlos talking about him much."

"Hell, girl. Carlos doesn't know everything. Your husband loves Walter Payton's accomplishments as much as he loves his brother, Rico. So anybody chasing Payton's record isn't high up on Carlos' discussion mode. The main thing I'm trying to let you know is that Marlon says Grissett is going on the trip."

"How's that supposed to make me feel better?"

"Whose knows what might happen? Older woman. Young pro ball player. Lillie is tough now, mentally and body wise."

"I declare I wish Elizabethe was interested in Marlon's buddies. Morocco makes a gazillion dollars a year. Every time I suggest one of those guys to her, she says she's not interested. Marlon told me that a few of them are dying to meet her and take her out, too. Whenever they see her, they always ask Marlon to set them up. Elizabethe could care less about Marlon's rich friends. My daughter leans more toward the artsy, actor type. Poor niggers."

"She'll be fine, girl. Money isn't everything to everybody. It's amazing she turned out like that especially with a mercenary mother like you," Symone teased easily.

"Watch the jabs, chile. I'm in a good mood, too. Let's not push it."

Symone grinned inwardly. "Elizabethe probably acts more like her Tante Alex."

"Yeah, you're right, chile. While growing up, it seemed like she spent enough time with Alex. So that's highly possible. From the time I met Alex in Madison's father office, she's been baby-sitting my children. You know it's down-right awful how she rubs off on people."

"Yeah, I do. Sometimes I have to check myself. I don't want to get a reputation of being *too* nice," Symone exclaimed as she leaned back in her chair again. "Have you gotten over Athena and CJ dancing all over the place at the children's opening night?"

"Why do you keep asking me that? You asked me that on Saturday night." Pecola breathed deeply and batted her eyes. "Well, to be honest, I'm kind of over it. CJ told me he's not interested in her, at least not in a serious relationship way right now. I was happy to hear that since she doesn't seem like his type, Symone."

"As a mother of a handsome, young man like CJ, no woman is going to be his type or be perfect for him as far as you're concerned, Pecola. You're just acting in a typical smothering mothering kind of way, girl. Booker T's favorite two words, smothering mothering. That's all."

"Ok, I got it. I know what you're trying to do. You're trying to make me get my mind off Lillie going with us to the mountains."

"Gimme a break."

"I still might try and drown her when we go white water rafting, though."

"Get in line, girl. That's the second woman who's going to get drowned in the mountains. According to Rozelle, Christopher Perry talked about drowning his wife."

"Get out of here!" Pecola laughed jubilantly for a few seconds. "Those pro players are a stone strip."

"Men are a stone trip. They're just worse when they got a little money and world-class notoriety under their belt. Then they really act a fool. That's for damn sure. No question about it."

"Maybe if Christopher drowns his wife, he might want to deal with Lillie next. Then I won't have to drown her," Pecola persisted.

"You're awful, Pecola. Let it go. I'm telling you. Lillie's cool. She and Alex have been hanging out for years, girl. You know that. Nobody wants your stuff, Pecola. As long as you're treating your husband right, why worry? That's what I tell you all the time. After twenty-three years of marriage, you and Carlos better figure out ways to keep the home fire burning. That way neither one of you ain't got to worry about competition, girl."

"Humph. That's what you say, honeychile." Symone could hear Pecola's preoccupation with Lillie behind her pleasant tone. "Alex told me she tried to get in touch with you all day yesterday. What's up with you and these disappearing acts? Hold on just a moment. Someone's coming into the master bedroom. I'm hiding out in Madison and Alex's huge ass bathroom, chile."

"Pecola, we're waiting on you. The bus was ready to pull out until Carlos yelled out that his wife was missing. He couldn't find his baby. I can't believe you're on the phone," Alex exclaimed in a soft voice. "Tell Symone I said hello."

"How do you know I'm talking to Symone?" Pecola began walking toward the bed where she sat down and carefully crossed her legs.

"I know you. As soon as I saw your supposedly subtle surprised reaction to Lillie, I knew you would disappear soon. You looked just like you thought an intruder drove up in my front yard. Your phone call to Symone was inevitable."

"Alex knows you, girl," Symone teased heartily. "Put her on the line, Pecola."

"Why?"

"Just put her on the line, Pecola." Pecola smiled sweetly and handed Alex the phone.

"Hey, girl," Alex said.

"Hi, Alex. You read Miss Thang like a book. She didn't even ask me how the Monday staff meeting went this morning. She was so interested in telling me about Lillie or the intruder, as you called her." The two friends burst out laughing. Pecola walked over to the bedroom bar and grabbed a bottle of Fiji water from the refrigerator. Pecola took a few sips. Out the corners of her eyes, she quietly watched Alex speak with Symone.

"We gots to go, Symone. I hate you're missing the trip. Tell everyone in New York that we said hello. Tell Mum Poussaint I got the card, and it was lovely. Remember to bring Madison, Nanette, and Scott their jars of pepper sauce."

"I will, girl. Mummy's bringing it straight from Trinidad. Get some rest, Alex. You run all the damn time, and you need to relax a little. I'll call yall from New York. Pecola gave me the number to the chalet. Take care, and I hope yall have a great time. I know that'll be hard cause I won't be there."

"You know we will. Nanette said that the chalet Marlon reserved is beautiful. A lovely castle in the mountains. Doesn't that sound romantic, Symone?"

"If you say so, girl. It's amazing how you believe any trip is romantic. You and Madison aren't going by yourself. That would be more romantic to me. You're going with a bunch of crazy and sho nuff wild Black folks."

"Don't matter to me, chile. My toes are twinkling just thinking about the invigorating fresh mountain air. The evening fireside chats—"

"Stop it, puhleeze," Symone interrupted Alex's fantasy. "If you get too descriptive, I might just cancel my plane reservation to New York." Symone paused briefly. "Just kidding!"

"I knew you were, girl. In the meantime, I'll do my best to make sure our buddy over here doesn't get into any trouble." Pecola rolled her eyes heavenward and shrugged her shoulders several times.

"That might be a difficult assignment."

"I know, Symone. Well, we got to be going. If I talk to you any longer, they'll send the posse looking for me."

"You're right."

"Love ya, girl."

"Love ya too, Alex. Tell Pecola the same."

"I will, Sy."

Thirty minutes after Symone hung up the phone, Gloria buzzed through on the intercom and announced that her sister was on line three. Symone pressed down the blinking button. Hazele's energetic, thick West Indian accent burst through the wires.

"Hello, Seamone! Oh God nah, gurl. Did yuh change yuh flight far tanight?"

"Yes I did." Symone spoke calmly and smiled.

"Ah'll have dey limo ta pick yuh up. Wat time will yuh reach here?"

"I'm taking the last flight out; I don't have my ticket in front of me. So I wouldn't lose them, Elisha is holding them until I leave. I think it gets into LaGuardia at nine-thirty or so."

"Dat's fine, gurl. Wen ah does meet yuh, weh must cum back ta mey restaurant. Ok? Far a little old calypso and food mey chef prepared especially far yuh. Ameenah said she made homemade butter bread far yuh."

"Hmmm, yummy. That's fine."

"She say she buy dey currant roll frum Allan Bakery in Brooklyn."

Since Symone knew the answer, she smiled quietly. "What about your chef?"

"Ameenah say Allan Bakery's currant roll is better den dey one mey chef does cook," Hazele said, laughing, and Symone giggled as well. "Ah hate yuh weren't here last night, Seamone. Gurl, meh and Brutus went ta dey Calypso and Soca Monarch Finals at Brooklyn College. Dey were battling far dey title dere, and it was bacchanal time last night. Yuh would have luv it too too bad, gurl."

"I hate I missed it, too, Hazele."

"Seamone, hold on a minute. Mey tellyphone is beeping." Hazele clicked over. Symone began reviewing the two reports Ted prepared for the Zawadi Corporation. A few minutes later, Hazele came back on the line.

"It was Ameenah, gurl. Ah told she ta hang up and ah would call she back. Hold on again, Seamone. Dat way weh all can speak at dey same time, gurl." There were a few moments of silence on the telephone.

"Seamone! Seamone! Oh Goooddd, gurl. Yuh such a hard person ta catch. Ah does try and try and try ta call yuh last night. Did yuh get mey message?" Ameenah blurted out. Symone could just about visualize how Ameenah's bright wide eyes illuminated her dark moon face. Symone believed her twin daughters resembled Ameenah even more than they resembled her.

Symone was always amazed at how her two sisters never lost their West Indian accent. Most times, both Symone and Quentin spoke like Americans. But not those two. One would think they had just stepped off the plane from Santa Cruz. After speaking with her sisters, oftentimes Symone allowed herself to slip into her native Trinidadian dialect as well.

"I went out with a friend to straighten some tings out," Symone explained as she considered how she finally had an opportunity to apologize face to face with Orlando.

After Orlando completed his Sunday evening service pastor duties, he came straight to Clemmons. Orlando made love to Symone in such a beautiful, sweet, and tender way. From nine o'clock to seven in the morning, Symone and Orlando were involved in a medley of comforting activities. They talked, made love, ate, danced, slept for a few hours, talked some more, and stayed in each other's arms. They did all the romantic things the two normally did when they were together. As a result of Orlando's thoroughly satisfying visit, Symone felt sexually fulfilled and somewhat content. With Orlando twisting her every which way but loose like a Gumby doll, her thigh joints were sore as if she had just began exercising on Nautilus for the first time.

"Seamone, yuh dere, gurl? Did yuh hear meh?" Hazele bellowed and continued to speak. "Yuh sure yuh cumin' tanight and not Wednesday night as yuh does first planned, gurl?"

"Wat did ah say, nah? Ah'll be dere tanight. Yuh got mey costume, Hazele?"

"Yeah, gurl. Ah got it ordered. Weh can pick it up wen yuh cum. Ay. Ay. Ameenah, listen ta dey Trini accent cumming out she mouth, gurl."

"Seamone ah does hear yuh talkin' diffrent, like a Trini. But let meh tell yuh dis ting. Dey costumes are too, too hot, gurl," Ameenah added with enthusiasm.

"Brutus say dis is a hot section of dey Hawks International Band, Seamone," Hazele added in a proud voice. She believed her husband was familiar with everyone and everything about the Brooklyn Labor Day West Indian Parade.

"Weh not playin' wit Borokeete USA dis year?" Symone asked surprised.

"No, gurl. Weh playing wit dey Hawks," Hazele said. "Let's give dem a play. Yuh know how dey Hawks does have a big name and ting in Brooklyn. Last year, dey were band of dey year. Plus, Brutus does know wich band is dey hot ting."

"Dat's wat yuh said last year," Symone mumbled. "Last year, Cousin Della said that dey Sesame Flyers is dey best."

"No, she didn't," Ameenah exclaimed. "Blackfoot was dey bad band. Ah know."

"Listen ta mey. Yuh know ah know dey better band, and it's dey Hawks. Mey husband does say he knows dis section leader well from his days from home, and Brutus sez everyone wants ta play wit dem. Ah tellin' yuh, dat is a bad section. Wen yuh does see dey costumes, yuh will agree wit meh. Won't she, Ameenah?"

"She right about dat ting," Ameenah said.

"Yuh certainly don't need ta have dey extra twenty pounds on yuh body far dis one. Dey costume is too too bad, gurl."

"Wat color are dey costumes, Hazele?" Symone asked.

"A fiery red, gurl," Hazele replied.

"Red? Dat's good, Hazele," Symone answered. "Red will look great on our dark complexion. Meh can see it nah. Yuh know dey color stands far passion, sex, and energy. Dey men better watch out far meh because dat's exactly how ah feel, nah. Ah feelin' wassy. Ah feelin' good. Ah feelin' ta wine mey bumcie on dere big, fat toe-tees." The three sisters laughed crazily for a good minute.

"Seamone and Ameenah, listen ta meh. Ah told Brutus dat ah don't want ta play mas wit a bunch of ugly woomen and tings. Mey friends frum dey restaurant are going ta video meh on dey Parkway, gurl. Ah can't have dat. Brutus said it was no problem cause dey woomen in dey new section were very pretty."

"Yuh too too crazy, Hazele. So yuh know far a fact it's a good section?" Symone questioned further. While she talked, she gazed lovingly at the red, white, and black flag of Trinidad and Tobago. It was strategically placed on Symone's office wall within an ornate gold frame. "Wat's dey section leader's name?"

"Matthew," Hazele said. "Matthew Cox, gurl. Dey section bad."

"Hazele's right, Seamone," Ameenah said. "Even dey chillren's costumes are beauteeful. Kiddies Carnival will be a lovely sight ta see. Ah does get dey costumes far Jared and dey gurls already like yuh ask meh ta. Ah just hope weh chillren didn't grow too much over dey summer. Ah added a few more inches on dey measurements."

"Tank yuh. Ah ready ta wine. Ah ready ta cum home ta Brooklyn!" Symone sang loudly in a bad lilting voice.

"Lemme tell yuh dis awful ting, Seamone," Hazele said quietly. "Yuh know dey girl dat does wine down ta dey ground last Labor Day? Every time yuh does turn around, she was wine-ing up on some other wooman's man bumcie?"

"Wich one is dat?" Symone asked. "Everybody was doing it."

"Yuh know dey one day weh visited Borokeete's mas camp last year ta pick up our costumes," Hazele added. "Weh were dere just a minute. Yuh know weh had just cum frum Uncle Willie. Ah does ask dey driver ta go by dey place where Brutus was lime-ing and ting. She was dey woman who had ben wine-ing all over dey place in front of dey mas camp."

"Remind she about Cousin Della," Ameenah said.

"Dat a good point, Ameenah," Hazele said and spoke slowly.

"Wat happened ta Uncle Willie's daughter?" Symone asked, nervous.

"Not a ting. Weh trying ta get yuh ta place dey wooman," Hazele said quickly. "Ok. Remember wen Cousin Della got mad wit dey wooman far touching she huzzband up so. Ameenah convinced Cousin Della ta get back in dey limo. Remember? Brutus said dey woman's name was Bradlina Vibrant."

"Oh yes," Symone nodded. "Now ah does remember."

"She dead now," Hazele said.

"Dead?" Symone asked.

"Dey does find she body in downtown Brooklyn by Prospect Park."

"Get out of here, Hazele!"

"Tis true. She was all cut up. Dead."

"Umph. Umph. Umph. Dat's unbelievable," Symone said softly. "People are so mean."

"Ah know. Dat's wat Quentin does say wen he heard dey news, too," Hazele informed quietly.

"Seamone," Ameenah cut in. "Uncle Samuel say he does try ta call yuh last night frum dey plane."

"Where was he going?"

"He was leaving Burbank Airport. Ah does speak wit he right after he does try and call yuh. Now he and Auntie Gerda decided ta fly ta Trinidad and spend a few days dere wit Uncle Willie and Cecil. Hazele, didn't yuh tell she?"

Hazele was contentedly listening to the words of the old Mighty Striker's tune, *Don't Blame the P.N.M.* She didn't answer Ameenah's question.

"Dey whole family will be flying back on Uncle Samuel's jet on Thursday afternoon," Ameenah went on.

"Get out of here, Ameenah," Symone exclaimed, surprised. "Ah tought dey had other plans. Mummy was cumin in on Friday. Ah need ta play mey messages ta see whom all called meh yesterday. Ah sorry ah missed dat call. Yuh sure?"

"Yes, it tis true," Ameenah said. "Yuh know dey chillren prefer dat. Yuh know how Uncle Samuel is about dem. He didn't want Mummy and dey uncles ta travel wit all dey grandchillren on a crowded commercial flight. Of course, Mummy told him it wasn't necessary. Yuh know Mummy does always reserve seats on BWIA. It's dey only airline far Trinidadian travel far she, and she always want ta give dem a play."

"Dat's our Mummy," Hazele piped in. "Anyting Trinidadian, Mummy wants ta patronize it. Yuh know weh does get such tinking like dat frum she, Seamone."

"Hazele, let meh finish, nah," Ameenah exclaimed. "So Uncle Samuel was either going ta send one of dey corporate jets or go meet dem heself. But Auntie Gerda was able ta talk him inta taking a short vacation, instead."

"Ah bet she did. Uncle Samuel's works all dey time," Symone said. "Just like Uncle Willie and Cecil. Ah don't tink dey'll ever retire. Sumtimes ah tink dey work too too hard. Did Mummy convince Tante Tutts ta cum ta Brooklyn far Labor Day?"

"She try. But yuh know our Tante, gurl," Ameenah responded quickly. "Tante Tutts does say dey Trinidad carnival is enough far she. Nati wants she ta visit him in Miami far dere jump up in October. So, she might visit she son far dat."

"She going, Ameenah?" Symone asked in a surprised voice.

"Meh don't know," Ameenah said. "She talk so."

"Seamone, do yuh want ta go wit meh and Brutus ta dey Baltimore Carnival?" Hazele asked. "It's dey Saturday after Labor Day."

"Ah can't go, gurl. Let meh tink about it," Symone said. "Ah might meet yuh dere on Saturday. How's dat?"

"She not cumin, Hazele," Ameenah said. "Ah can tell in she voice."

"Cousin Della just came back from dey Notting Hill carnival," Hazele informed.

"How was it in England?" Symone asked.

"Cousin Della said she had a fabulous time. Dey weather was great. Cousin Abraham went wit she dis time," Hazele replied.

"Uncle Samuel's son is turning inta a lazy lima bean like Cousin Della," Ameenah laughed.

"Ah see dat," Symone said, giggling too.

"Ah sorry ah didn't go ta England wit dem," Hazele went on. "Dey wanted meh ta. Ah can't go ta all dey carnivals. Ah never be here ta work."

"Meh neither," Ameenah piped in. "Cousin Della said dat she will let meh see dey video dis weekend wen weh meet at Uncle Samuel far dey familee gathering."

"Good. How are yuh and Brutus doing, Hazele?" Symone inquired.

"Yuh does know everyting is fine, gurl." Hazele swallowed hard and lied quickly to her big sister. "Just fine wit us. Mey husband sent meh beauteeful flowers just dey other day, gurl."

Suddenly, Elisha stepped into Symone's office. Along with another hot cup of vanilla cappuccino she exchanged for the cold one Symone had ignored all morning, Elisha slipped a note in front of Symone. Reuben Jakes of the Zawadi Corporation was holding on line three. Two other lights were blinking on Symone's block of phone lines. Elisha explained to Symone that she and Gloria would handle those other calls, but Elisha motioned that Reuben said it was urgent that he speak with her.

"Ah got ta go, mey sisters," Symone said softly as she sat straight up in her chair. Hazele breathed a sigh of relief. She would speak with Symone about Brutus when Ameenah wasn't around.

"Remember ta be on time far yuh flight," Ameenah reminded.

"Ah will. Kisses kisses ta both of yuh," Symone said. "Ah'll see yuh tonight. Hazele and Ameenah, ah ready to partee. Ah ready ta jam big time in a big time way, mon. Ah mean it."

"No problem. Weh does know. Weh ready far yuh," Ameenah exclaimed in her always gay voice. "See yuh tonight, Seamone. Yuh know weh have a wonderful nine days planned far yuh. On Thursday night weh going ta dey Caribbean Brass Festival ta see Traffic, Massive Chandelier, and dey Roy Cape All Stars."

"Oh God, nah," Symone shouted. "Ah does luv dose bands, gurl."

"Ah does know. Meh too," Ameenah said quickly. "Ah not finish. Weh got tickets ta dey Hawks' boat ride on Saturday, too. Quentin says he going ta dey Steel Band Panorama Competition instead at dey Brooklyn Museum. But on Friday, weh goin' ta see dey Mighty Sparrow, Lord Kitchener, and Singing Sandra witout he. Quentin said he got tings planned dat night wit he wife and he chillren. He'll meet us dere."

Hazele chuckled freely. "Ah forced she ta get dem, Seamone. Ameenah and Quentin wanted ta go see Superblue, Viking Tundah, and Black Stalin. Ah told her she and weh brother was outvoted because she does know dat Mummy, meh, and yuh does love dey old calypsonians best, gurl."

"Tis true, Hazele. Yuh know meh," Symone agreed quickly as she vigorously nodded her head.

"Ah tellin yuh. Ah does know such about yuh, too," Ameenah said. "But Mummy say befar weh does go anywhere, weh must do dey family ting."

"Dose kinds of tings always cum first wit Mummy." Symone nodded with understanding.

"Ah know," Hazele agreed. "Before weh go ta dey Dimanche Gras Show on Sunday, Mummy sez dey family is scheduled ta have dinner at Uncle Samuel's place in dey city. It's far someting dat's already planned by Auntie Gerda since she knew dat dey entire family would be in New York far dey Labor Day festivities."

"Just hurry up and cum, Seamone," Ameenah said. "Ah luv yuh, Seamone."

"Ah luv yuh too, Ameenah." Symone's voice was brimming with affection. "Luv yuh, Hazele."

"Ah know yuh does luv meh. Yuh know ah does luv yuh too, meh big seester. Bye-bye," Hazele replied in a soft, slow voice. She laced it with a small laugh that for some reason always reminded Symone of Lennious when her sister spoke in such a tender way. A remnant of a small smile lingered on Symone's face as she finally clicked over to speak with Reuben Jakes, who by now had gotten quite impatient.

Chapter Sixty-Nine

The second weekend after Symone and the children returned from playing mas in New York, Symone took Kyle and Sylvia to spend the weekend with Alex. The Winston-Salem Children's Theater was showcasing Joyce Grear's play entitled *Phillis Wheatley.* Wheatley was the second African-American poetess who was kidnapped and sold into slavery when she was eight-years-old. Alex and Jodria reserved tickets for the Saturday evening show. Alex and the other adult volunteers were also going to treat thirty of the other children to a dress up dinner at the Tanglewood Park Manor House. Kyle and Sylvia were extremely excited about the day and looked forward to the time with Tante Alex and all the other children.

In order to get an early start, Symone shook the girls from their Saturday morning sleep at eight to ensure they arrived at Alex's house by ten. As she did every Saturday morning without fail and at least three times a week when she was in town, she read a book to her children. This morning, the twins selected the Pinkneys' *Dear Benjamin Banneker.* While the girls snuggled under each of Symone's arms, she read the book in a highly animated voice.

When they were done, Kyle and Sylvia got dressed and ate a bowl of Miss Jessica's hot cinnamon oatmeal. Symone took a quick shower during which she gave herself the usual monthly breast examination. A few years ago, Jodria informed all the ladies of the literary group that African-American women got breast cancer at an alarming rate. It was thirteen percent higher than the national average. And that in the United States alone, five thousand African-American women die each year from the disease. Since Symone had heard the startling information from Jodria, she had made it a point to give herself a breast examination every month. Lately, it seemed like she did one every time she stepped into the shower.

When Symone was through showering, she threw on a pair of exercise shorts, tank top, and baseball cap. According to what Pecola indicated older people in the South say all the time, Jared was "smelling his own musk" and decided to stay at home and play Nintendo in his room. He was also angry with his mother because she refused to allow him to go play Putt Putt in Winston-Salem with three boys she didn't know and whose parents she had never met. Miss Jessica recommended that Symone allow him to stew by himself. Maybe then he would realize how his stubbornness made him miss a delightful afternoon with his Tante Alex and Uncle Madison.

Symone drove the Towncar halfway to the end of the Devereauxs' driveway around the side of the house beside the garage. Kyle and Sylvia spotted Trey and Purity leaving the large gingerbread playhouse to jump on the wooden swing set in the backyard. Without closing the car door, Kyle and Sylvia raced to join them. The sun shone brightly through several scattered clouds, and the excited barks of King, Queen, and Dreams rang throughout the still hot September air. When Symone got out the car, the three dogs pounced all over her, and she took the time to pet each one.

Symone walked over to embrace Trey and Purity. She told them that they looked adorable as usual, and both children proceeded to give her big, affectionate hugs. Purity's chubby hands held Symone's arm tightly for a few moments, then she tried to skip away. Symone smiled. Each time she saw Purity, she was always amazed that she looked like a little replica porcelain doll of Alex with thick, black hair already down her back. Trey was just like his father, friendly, yet serious. The young boy often appeared as if he were always thinking about something way past his years.

Appearing outdoorsy in blue jeans and khaki shirt soaked with sweat circles under the armpits and wet spots on his back, Madison worked diligently in the picture-perfect flowerbed beside the house. While he offered Symone a huge grin and his typical good-natured greetings, he wiped his forehead with a dirt-splattered arm. He embraced Symone tightly, kissed her gently on the lips and right cheek, and told her that Alex was upstairs in the master bedroom.

"Knock, Knock," Symone said as she tapped on the door a couple of times. Alex was on the floor unpacking a box. She looked up, startled. Symone kneeled down to give her two kisses and a tight hug.

"Mmmm. It's *sooo* great to see you, Symone," Alex said while hugging her neck firmly. "I missed you so much."

"I just saw your ass on Wednesday, girl."

"It doesn't matter when I saw you last. I still have missed you, period," she replied softly but emphatically. "I didn't hear you drive up. Where are the children?"

"They're outside playing."

"My goodness. They didn't even come upstairs to give me a sweet, wet sugar."

"When they saw your children playing, they jumped out the car. I even had to close the door, girl. I'm just glad they at least waited until I stopped the car."

"How ya doing, Sy?" Alex spoke to Symone with a twinge of concern in her voice.

"As usual, I'm tired." Symone took a deep breath. "You know what I need. A good damn dose of vitamin freaky sex to straighten out that fatigue, to take some of the kinks out of me." Symone smiled slyly at her friend. Alex rolled her eyes and looked amused.

Symone dropped her pocketbook on the couch. She kicked off her sandals and stretched her body across the dual king size Nikolina bed to watch Alex. As usual, beautiful background opera music was playing on the stereo.

"Trey and Purity looked cute as can be," Symone said as she thought how she and Alex were so alike in that way. They both believed in dressing their children up for pre-school or playtime.

"Thanks, girl. Those are the clothes I got from that company out of Walkertown, North Carolina. You know the one I told you about—MaShona Kids?" Symone appeared puzzled. "I know *your* behind knows. Remember I gave you three outfits for Jared and your girls?"

"Oh, yesss! The one with the animals? I recall it now. Those were cute sets. Plus, Sylvia and Kyle loved them. That's the main thing, or it would be a fight for them to put the clothes on," Symone continued while smiling widely.

"Well, you know me. Since I've been buying MaShona Kids ever since Trey was little, I've become friends with the company president, Forbee Wettiford."

"Knowing you, it figures. Hmmm, Forbee. Nice name."

Alex smiled. "When Forbee told me the concept for the clothing, I immediately said to myself that this is a person I need to know."

"You say that about everybody you meet."

"No I don't, Symone. I know yall think I do. The sistah is tough, and she's knowledgeable about our heritage. You would love talking to her." Alex spoke in a soothing voice. Symone shrugged her shoulders as if it didn't matter either way.

"Forbee said she created the company because she wanted children of all nationalities, especially our Black children, to understand there's a lot more in our culture than just slavery. We must instill pride and teach them that we're originally from a rich, noble, and educated nation that contributed natural resources, knowledge, and beauty to the world."

"Like I said, she sounds like my kind of person."

"Forbee also explained, which I told her I agreed with wholeheartedly, that the educational system focuses on European royalty. You know the King David and Queen Elizabeth types. But we don't learn about the royalty of our African ancestors, the royalty that existed in *our* history. We've been told sooo long to believe we're only jungle bunnies and only became civilized through the teaching of white people who brought us to this country. It's such a stupid lie. I can't believe Black and white folks have bought into it, Symone."

"Me neither. Especially when the truth is they took *this* land from us."

"Forbee *is* right in the fact that a lot of Black and white people out there believe it as law. She believes that all nationalities should be taught the truth and is just like you. She's a very interesting lady," Alex ended excitedly to know she found another friend to share thought-provoking conversations with.

"You're right. She does sound like someone I need to know. I'd like to meet her. I know you'll have her up here talking with all fifty-eight children before it's over with," laughed Symone while she stretched her legs toward the ceiling.

Alex smiled. "Well to be honest, I did tell her about what we do with the children and asked her to consider coming up to speak to them during one of their weekends with us. She would be another excellent role model to introduce them to, Symone. You know how I feel about television role models. They don't see those people."

"Here, here," Symone exclaimed as she wrapped her arms around her knees.

"I tell Marlon this all the time. Movie stars and celebrities never come to Winston-Salem. Maybe I shouldn't say they never come because Marlon brings a lot of them this way. When they do visit, they're unable for a variety of reasons, to walk through those certain communities and speak to the children. So Forbee is touchable like all the other people we work with.

She's someone we could call up and have visit us from time to time. She owns a business and is totally for Black pride. Each time I speak to her, I think about you, girl," Alex said with a small giggle as she continued to dig in a huge corrugated, brown box.

Symone thought for a moment. She stretched her legs out in front of her and grabbed them at the knees. "Just the other day for instance," Symone said lazily. "I had a discussion with Jared about what they teach him in school. During his first week in school, they had a discussion about who discovered America. The entire class went on and on about Christopher Columbus. Of course, Jared piped in and said that wasn't true since you couldn't discover a country that was already inhabited by Black people."

"Go, Jared boo. He was right to say that, girl. I'm proud of him."

"Me too, Alex. He's something else when he wants to be. Well, it doesn't stop there. Some kid then told him that even though the Black people were already living here, the white people who discovered America were the only ones who knew what to do with it."

"Get out of here," Alex wailed in a surprised voice.

"No, I'm telling you. It totally blew my mind, girl. So, I got through that discussion with him, and everything was fine. The next day he brought home his history book, and I noticed that it discussed nothing but a bunch of untruths about American history and African-American history. After I reviewed it, I tried to once again explain the real history to Jared. You know I've been doing this since he was a little thing."

"I know, Sy."

"Still, I believe this is still kinda confusing to him, Alex. I'm saying one thing, and he's reading another thing at school. His schoolbooks reflect something else. To make a long story short, I scheduled an appointment with the teacher. On Thursday, I went to the school and talked with his new history teacher, which I don't mind doing at the drop of a hat. Sometimes I wonder why I pay all this money to send him to a private school."

"Pecola told me about parts of it. She had me laughing all over the place about you. But go ahead, girl."

While Symone talked to her about the school issue, Alex stopped everything because this topic was a favorite one of hers. She wanted to give her undivided attention and gazed at Symone with a penetrating stare.

"...The teacher's name is Georgee Washington. She explained to me that she received a master's degree in American history from NCU."

"Marlon's alma mater?"

"Yep. And it was blah, blah blah, and rah rah rah. I told her that was wonderful. Truly, I was impressed with her educational accomplishments, but I also explained to Miss Washington that the truth of history isn't being taught in this school, and I'll not allow it."

"What she say?"

"I asked her how could she teach Jared what *you* say is true history. *And,* you have a master's degree, and you're teaching my child a lie?" Symone asked Alex with a perplexed expression on her face as she opened both hands.

"No you didn't, girl."

"I damn sure did. You know the history books don't show the contributions Black people have made. Nowadays, they're getting a little better. Still, it's nothing but negative stuff or passive information. Thank God Jared happens to have a parent who knows the real deal. What about the many other Black folks who don't know how powerful Black people were on this land or on other lands throughout the world? I just told Miss Washington that my son's papers will reflect *what I know* about American history, which is also Black History."

"I understand."

"We were here first, then they took the land from us. They used *us* to build this country, so that it could be the superpower it is. Millions of *us* died in the process. Jared's papers will reflect how powerful Black people are as inventors, doctors, lawyers, theologians, motivators, and how rich our history has always been."

"What did she say, girl?"

"Of course, she looked at me like I was crazy, but I told her that Jared's research assignments will show this. I mean it, and I expect her to grade his papers accordingly. If she needed substantial proof about anything he wrote about, I would be happy to give her a book list."

"I'm sure."

"I told her that she could even come to my personal library at the house and check them out. I don't care what she does," Symone rattled on non-stop, exasperated. She shook her head for a long time. "She just better do right by Jared. I did give her copies of J.A. Rogers' *100 Amazing Facts about the Negro, What They Never Taught You in History Class* and *Dirty Little Secrets about Black History, It's Heroes and Other Trouble Makers.*"

"*Dirty Little Secrets* is by Claud Anderson? Right?"

"Yeah."

"He's an excellent speaker. I saw him at a workshop in Wyoming on my last visit there in February. I've since contacted his office to see if he would come and speak to the children."

"Good move. Anyway, you know how I always keep extra copies of those books around the house."

"Girl, I know," Alex said laughing as she patted her thigh. "Pecola had me cracking up all over the place when she told me *that* part. I figured Jared had gotten a new teacher. Jared's other teachers know exactly how you are."

"That's true. I guess they didn't warn her about me. That pesky Poussaint woman who's always coming up to school to volunteer or to find out what's going on with her son's class."

"That's the only way we can keep involved with our children's education. I told Nanette that's what I truly admire about you. Even though you're busy as heck, you still try to schedule visiting time with your son's school. I always thought that was wonderful, Symone."

"Lawd, I'm drowning. You know I can't handle all this praise so early in the day." Both friends laughed. "Private school or no private school, I'm seriously thinking about having him chauffeured down to Brisbane every day, Alex."

"You can't do that, Sy. That would be too hard on his little body to travel to Charlotte each morning. Just be patient. God will provide another avenue, girl. He always does."

"That's what we need here. A Black private school that provides an excellent, well-rounded education."

"I know we do, Sy."

"Jodria talks about opening one all the time. I told her I would definitely help her with financing if she decided to do it."

"She told me. Yet, she's afraid that such an endeavor would take up too much time away from her six children, sacrifice time from the fifty-eight children we're committed to working with now, and the senior citizens mentoring program she established at her church. You know how Jodria feels about those commitments."

"I know, Alex. I understand Jodria's reluctance to lead the way with another major project like a school."

"Remember my words. God will provide a way, Sy. It's already been done in heaven. It's just not been done here on earth."

"You're right, girl." Symone briefly reflected on Alex's religious nature. Alex winked at her. "That's one of the main things I like about Charmaine's dance school. History is even laced throughout the classes. She teaches the children about the influences and contributions of Blacks in the dance world. Don't get me started on this subject on this pretty morning," Symone ended with a big round of chuckling. Alex vigorously nodded her head with understanding and dug into the large box again.

"Are you and Pecola still going shopping?"

"Oh my gosh. I forgot. She told me to call and wake her up," Symone said as she turned over and reached for the phone.

For the third time this morning, Pecola slipped deeper under her bed covers when she heard the whirring of the vacuum cleaner outside her bedroom door. Although Cleopatra made Pecola and Carlos an early morning breakfast, Pecola jumped right back in bed not long after she finished eating. Pecola peeped out from under the blankets and stared at the clock. She couldn't believe it was almost eleven o'clock. She had been sleeping this time for two straight hours. It was time to get up and get dressed. Once she figured out what fabulous looking outfit she wanted to wear for the day, she decided to take a long, hot bath. While brushing her teeth afterwards, Pecola heard Cleopatra yell out for her.

"I'm in the bathroom," Pecola tried to shout with a bunch of baking soda in her mouth.

"Hey, girl," Cleopatra said, smiling, standing in the bathroom doorway. "You finally decided to get up, huh?"

"Yep. Sure did. Is Carlos helping you clean like he normally does?"

A happy laugh fell out of Cleopatra's mouth. "Surprisingly, no. Right after you went to sleep, he said he needed to go by the office. He didn't tell you?"

"Damn sure didn't."

"Hmmm. He said he was. Maybe you didn't hear him."

"I hear everything my huzzband says to me, Missy Cleopatra," Pecola snapped and began to gargle with warm water and salt.

"Ok." Cleopatra smiled again, intently studying Pecola. "Want me to get you a glass of grape juice, Pecola? *Anything?*"

"No. That's ok. Look, Cleo—" Pecola held up her hand. "I'm sorry for being short with you."

"No problem atall."

"I *told* Carlos I needed to speak with him." She took a deep breath. "I'm just surprised he left without saying one damn word. Enough of this. Let me see if Symone is still going shopping with me."

"She called earlier, but I told her you were sleep. You didn't hear the phone?"

"Hell no! Damn, Cleopatra! What in the living hell did you put in them biscuits, grits, and sausages this morning? A bulldozer of a tranquilizer?"

"You're just tired, Pecola. Sometimes you gots to stop and rest your body, or your body will stop for you." Cleopatra gently patted Pecola's right arm. "I told Symone you would be ready after one or so."

"Thanks, girl."

"I've done everything you wanted me. After I change your sheets, clean, and dust in your bedroom, I gots to head out. Ok?" She nodded and glanced at her wristwatch. "I told Carlos that I couldn't iron everything today, but I'll do the rest on Monday morning. Is that ok, Pecola?"

"Fine, fine, fine. Whatever."

"You know Alex made plans for some of the children this weekend."

"Yeah, yeah, yeah. I know. Dealing with all those excited kids today would definitely drive me crazy and give me a migraine. Whew! How do yall do it, girl?" Scratching her head while she walked back to her bed, Pecola turned to stare into Cleopatra's kind eyes. "Lawd have mercy, what would I do without you?"

"Iron, clean, and cook all that processed food for you and your husband, Mrs. Can Queen."

"Look! Don't get smart with me today, Cleo. Don't you know I'm already feeling grouchy. I'm ready to fight somebody, anybody," Pecola mumbled, and they both giggled.

"What are you looking for, girl?" Symone asked as she inhaled deeply, still trying to catch her breath from the round of laughing at the funny joke Cleopatra said that Carlos showed her in some magazine. By the time Symone hung up the phone, Alex was digging further down into the huge box in front of her. "What are you doing?"

"Unpacking some old pictures." Alex frowned and spoke softly. "After my parents died, for years I wondered what happened to these pictures. I tore my house apart several times. Back then, I remembered looking everywhere. Then, Nanette found this box. Can you believe that? Nanette had them and didn't realize it until she cleaned out her attic this week."

"How's Nanette doing? I haven't spoken to her or Marlon since I've been back from New York. Have they been out of town?" Symone asked in a preoccupied voice as she considered their conversation about Black pride and history.

"Oh, yeah. That's right. You don't know. She and Marlon left for Grand Cayman last week. Although Nanette is trying to discourage him, Marlon wants to buy a house there."

"Probably somewhere smacked dead in the middle of Seven Mile Beach."

"You're absolutely right. And this week—well really for the next two weeks, they'll be there looking for a home."

"Grand Cayman is a great place to have a home."

"I know, girl. Marlon will probably find the largest one he can get. I told Marlon that small and cozy aren't words he cherishes too much when it comes to homes."

"You can talk, Alex. This place ain't a one room shack either."

"I know, but this is our main house, girl. If we never go anywhere in life, Madison, me and our friends can vacation year round right here in Advance."

"True."

"But Marlon wants vacation homes all over the place."

"My kind of man."

"Nanette is content to just have one. She loves living right here in North Carolina year round. So other than that, Nanette is doing just fine. Even though Fletcher and Solomon are five-months-old, Nanette declares the cesarean incision is still sensitive as heck." Alex carefully unwrapped two broken gold frames as she began peacefully humming to the opera sounds playing in the background.

"Is she still enjoying her leave of absence from her job at the hospital?"

"Yeah. I'm hoping that she decides to stay home full-time with the twins, Sy. Marlon wants her to stay home, too. I don't know why she feels she can only stay home a year. Well, you know, Nanette."

"That I do. She definitely is her own woman."

"She doesn't need the money, Sy. It'll be great for Fletcher and Solomon, at least until they're six-years old or are in kindergarten or pre-school."

"It's not about money, Alex. You know that. Everyone doesn't want to be a stay-at-home mother even though they can afford it. Believe me. I love my children more than anything, but there's something in me to work the daily grind within the business world. It's no different with Nanette being a nurse. She merely loves her career and enjoys doing it."

"I know. I know. I do understand," Alex replied softly with a faraway expression on her face.

Although Alex listened to all kinds of music, her most favorite remained gospel and opera. Because of Alex's influence, Symone also enjoyed listening to certain opera singers as well. For some reason, she couldn't figure out whom this particular singer was belting out the beautiful words in the background. To Symone, most opera singers sounded alike. She turned over on her back, placed her hands under her head, and watched the ceiling fan spin around.

"Which opera singer is that, Alex?"

"Symone, I *know* you recognize her. I certainly have played her enough, girl. It's Helen Battle, of course."

Symone smiled. "You're right. I should've recognized that voice. None other than Ms. Battle. Please forgive me for that little error."

Symone chuckled to herself. The last time Alex prepared the annual summer garden lunch, Helen Battle was right there in the background. When she surprised Cleopatra with the limousine ride just for the joy of it last month, she gave the chauffeur a Helen Battle CD to play. Alex *was* right. By now, Symone should immediately be able to recognize Ms. Thang's opera singing.

"Symone! Look at these pictures of my mother and her sister. Aren't they absolutely wonderful? I wonder what they were thinking when their photos were taken?"

Symone didn't respond to the question. She was too busy enjoying the firm, softness of the Devereauxs' bed.

This bed is so damnnn comfortable. It just sucks you in, Symone thought. *Makes you want to cuddle up and go to sleep right here. I can understand why the children love relaxing in my bed.*

"Girl, look at my mother!" Alex exclaimed with delight.

Symone slowly turned over on her stomach and studied the photograph handed to her. Alex did look just like her mother, and the resemblance was uncanny.

"Wooo! When was this photo taken, girl? You look just like your mother," Symone said quietly. She carefully eyed her friend then the picture again.

Alex examined the picture and found a date inscribed in the corner on the back.

"This was taken over twenty-five years ago. I always heard that if you want to find out how you'll look when you get older, just look at your mother or father. Since I can't do that, these pictures are wonderful for me. I look just like Mama," she said while eyeing the photo with longing. A melancholy mood enveloped the bedroom, and Symone noticed Alex's sudden dark expression. "I knew I would look like her one day. I just knew it."

Since Alex's parents were killed in a car crash years ago, just looking at the photos made her recall a variety of memorable times she shared with them. Almost immediately, her mind zoomed to her childhood days. Just as quickly, she closed her eyes and mentally heard the echoes of her parents' voices. The voices were warmly reassuring, as they often were when she was a little girl.

"Are you ok, Alex?"

"Yes. When I was younger, people always said I looked like her, Sy. I couldn't see it then. Now that I'm older, I see that it's sooo true. I'm so honored." She spoke tenderly as she caressed the photos.

"I'm sure you are."

"Look, Symone," Alex exclaimed with a wide-eyed expression on her face. "Here's a picture of my Grandmother Carmen and Granddaddy Larry. My, Godddd! These photos go so far back—for years."

The pictures were obviously discolored from age, and the edges were tattered. Symone knew that the next time she saw the photographs, they wouldn't be recognizable in their present state. Alex would definitely have each and every one restored to their original perfection and placed on display in ornate frames throughout her house. She looked at Symone with tears in her eyes.

"After your parents die, you do a lot of soul searching. You love them. After you've spent your life loving them, I simply can't explain the emptiness. I miss them so much, Sy." Alex wiped the tears from the corners of her eyes and took a deep, reflective breath.

"I'm sure you do."

"You know I'm convinced that nobody becomes a real adult until both their parents are dead."

"That's a powerful statement, Alex. Very powerful."

"And, it's true, too. I look at the pictures of my relatives from fifty and sixty years ago and feel such a loss. When they were alive here with me, it seemed like such a lifetime ago. Thinking about them like that is like another world to me, Sy. I guess it really was a lifetime ago. Another chapter in my life."

Just before Alex's mother died, her mother was diagnosed with breast cancer. Alex's mother's two sisters were diagnosed with the ravaging disease as well, one with lung cancer and the other with cervical cancer. Both Alex's aunts died within five years of Alex's parents' car accident. In January of last year, Alex's father's only brother died from a stroke. Death seemed to hover around her family like a thick fog.

"Since my family was so small, these pictures are great. Such a wonderful legacy. It's just Nanette and me now. At least I can rely on the pictures that were left for us. They left them for a reason. It's for me and my children to know—" she explained sadly. Alex paused and waited for Symone to comment. Since Symone didn't know what to say, she remained quiet and listened.

"I look at my family's smiling faces and realized they had dreams and visions when they took those pictures—just like us, girl. They were young then and so full of life. The clothes they wore were in style back then. When they smiled for the photographer, they had no idea how much longer they would live or anything. The years flew by. They had children. They got older, and they died. I often think about life, Sy. Years don't wait for anyone. If we live or die, they keep right on going. In ten years, we'll look at the pictures we took with the children at the opening last month. We'll probably say, 'Look at me when—"

Just then, Madison walked into the bedroom and pretended to act like a waiter working in a high-class restaurant. With a pale yellow, linen napkin draped over one arm, he balanced a sterling silver tray with the other and served them cappuccino in pretty, delicate Limoge china cups and saucers.

"I thought you ladies could use this right about now," he explained gallantly.

"Madam, this is for you." Madison bowed to serve Alex first, and he spoke with a very stately, British accent. Alex thanked him and gave him a wet kiss. Then, he did the same for Symone, who laughed loudly at the service.

"Look, I'm not going to kiss you like your wife did." Symone winked at him instead and Madison leaned over to kiss her on each cheek. "Thanks, Madison. This is very thoughtful of you."

Madison smiled and danced out of the room.

It's a shame all his brothers are married. Well, almost. Since his brother's wife left him, he no longer qualifies in that area, Symone reflected with a sheepish grin. *When they made Madison, the mold was shattered. And, he's a damn doctor to boot. It would be Mummy's dream if I had someone like that. It would be my dream, too.*

"When you get tired of Madison, please let me know," Symone joked while taking a sip of the hot cappuccino. "They just don't make men like him anymore. He's a great father and a damn doctor, too. He's a sensitive man, a church-going man, a crier, and a romantic all rolled into one. You know I haven't found one like that cause I can at least recognize a good man." Symone considered Orlando. When she really thought about it, Orlando had the same wonderful personality traits as Madison. He was just simply too young.

"Ummm-hmmm."

"What I meant to say is I haven't met anyone like that that I want to marry. I was just thinking. If I did find someone like Madison, my mother would do a backflip and somersault over to the senior citizen's center she visits in the summer to announce the news," she bellowed with a laugh.

"You're crazy, Sy." Alex exclaimed as her thick eyebrows, which matched her thick black hair, crinkled together. "There are other good men out there."

"Where?"

"I know I'm blessed. Like I tell you all the time, Madison and I have to really work at it each and every day."

"I know. I know."

"Keep that in mind. A good marriage takes work, hard work. If I only saw Madison as a lover, our marriage would've been over years ago. We're friends first, Sy. He's my *main* man, the father of my children, and we support each other. Madison's love inspires me—makes me sooo much stronger. The good thing is that he says my love encourages him, too," Alex said with an expression of wonder.

"You sound like a greeting card for marriage, girl."

Alex stared Symone straight into her eyes and laughed. She sipped more cappuccino.

"I do feel quite comfortable with my love for him, Sy. I truly do. That's crucial, too. I keep telling you, Lillie, and all of Nanette's single friends the same thing. Whoever you find and whenever you find him, just always communicate and talk to each another. That's the key. At least it is for Madison and me," Alex explained wistfully.

"Obviously, it's working."

"Make sure they attend college classes at the University of Beautiful Love. You know Madison will be happy to sign your lucky guy up for classes," she added with her tremendous throaty hallmark laugh.

"You can believe that any man I can find will definitely take classes at the university," Symone said with a huge grin. "I told Madison to keep a seat for me at all times. You just never know. I might surprise yall one day and find the perfect man that God made just for me."

"Just remember, perfection ain't out there, Sy. Every man and woman has faults. You just have to determine if they have faults you want to live with, girl."

"Whaaat! The Devereauxs have faults? I can't believe that. I thought you two were as perfect as two peas in a pod can be and had the most absolutely perfect marriage," Symone bellowed with a big grin. Alex smiled warmly.

Symone loved Madison and Alex's philosophy regarding the institution they created called the University of Beautiful Love. It was popular among all the friends. The Love College was created many years ago by Madison while he was in medical school. Back then and since he was always studying and relished the precious moments he spent with Alex, he came up with the idea. Now all of the Devereauxs' friends who were married or in a serious relationship were either Queen or King converts. As soon as each interested individual fulfilled certain relationship requirements, they even received framed degrees Alex designed especially for University of Beautiful Love graduates.

Alex always said that people focus more attention on jobs and education than they do with their marriage and relationships. The same due diligence brought to a company or a business on a daily basis should be given with just as much intensity to respecting, loving and devotion to a wife or husband. "A marriage takes a lot of work each and every day" was both Alex and Madison's national anthem.

Chapter Seventy

"Where are you now, man?" Rozelle asked Carlos.

"Where did you call?"

"I hit you on your cell this time. How come you didn't show up for my frat brother's bachelor party last night? Conrad wanted to know what happened to you."

"On Friday night, I needed to chill with my wife, RB," Carlos said as he continued to type a special e-mail to a special friend. "Remember, I'm married, Dog."

"So am I."

"Act the hell like it," Carlos laughed.

"I do when I'm around my wife and kids."

"You ain't nothing, man. I called you on Thursday night to tell you I couldn't make it. I left a message on your cell phone. Where were you?"

"Hanging out."

"All night?"

"Most of it. We hung out at Unique Upstairs to around one o'clock. It was off the hook, baby. Sweet Dreams was in the house, and Bertha was kicking up a storm, man."

"I heard."

"Later on, we rolled to my favorite strip club. Where else could I go?"

"A whole lot of other places, man."

"My frat brother's uncle wanted to check out big titties, hairy pussies, and fat asses. You know RB. I had to oblige the old player, man."

"Your frat's uncle?"

"Yep. The nigger is sixty-two years old. You can't tell it, though. My man said that he'll never get tired of getting pussy, looking at pussy, or eating pussy."

"Umph. That's a tough man."

"Who you telling? He's an old dog from Edward Waters College. You met him at the Black and White Ball last Thanksgiving."

"You mean Conrad's Uncle Smitty? The retired army man who made one of the largest donations to his college. I believe it was a million dollars."

"You know it. One and the same. Strip clubs are the first place the illustrious Uncle Smitty wants to check out when he rolls into our town."

"I know exactly," Carlos mumbled when he read the angry response that was sent back to him on the computer screen. "Uh, Rozelle. Let me check you later, man."

"What's up?"

"Nothing. I just gots to meet a friend about a dog."

"Be careful."

"I always am. Later, man," Carlos said and quickly hung up the phone to place a very important phone call to his very pissed off friend.

Alex and Symone sipped the hot cappuccino and didn't say a word to each other for a few minutes. They just simply listened to the divinely, melodic opera music. Then, as if it were an afterthought, Alex spoke very quietly, as if almost to herself.

"Those pictures are really something. Aren't they, girl?"

"Yeah!"

"They were taken twenty-five years ago. I can't believe I don't even remember what type of car my parents drove back then. Isn't that amazing? I was fifteen-years-old. I lived in the house on Cameron Avenue during that time with my family, yet I can't remember. In twenty years, who'll remember the great conversations we've had? The one that you and I are having right now? You know it's what we do with the time we're given, Sy. Life is what you make it." Alex slowly shook her head from side to side and placed the cup in the saucer.

"You're right, Alex." Symone carefully watched her face. "Sometimes I can't remember the conversations I had last week," she replied as she swallowed more cappuccino and rested the cup back in the saucer on the bed tray. "When you were talking about those pictures, I thought about my high school and college yearbook. I don't even recognize me in them. I know it's me, but I can't believe I've aged. Even though I feel like I look the same, I know there are differences in my life. Those are differences that show on my face as well." Symone exclaimed slowly while curling up on the bed and pulling her knees to her chest.

Alex nodded slowly. Suddenly, she soberly looked at Symone and brushed the thick black hair off her shoulders. "We all change as we get older, Symone. That's life. Some people waste life and hate it. Others enjoy it. I, on the other hand, bask in the wonders and the beautiful splendors of living life. It's truly a gift that's all mine. No one can speak death. They've created all kinds of technology. One thing the scientists will never discover or do is create life. It isn't theirs to do."

"Thank God."

"Sure they can transfer the existing eggs and the living sperm from one dish to another, but they cannot create that which isn't from nothing. Only God can do it. Almighty God is the only one who can allow us to grow old and allow death and our time to enter eternity to meet on the same road," she said forlornly as she held the picture of her mother.

Symone listened intently while Alex was speaking. Sometimes, when Symone considered the truthfulness of what Alex said, the words saddened and depressed her. Alex was always so philosophical, melancholy, and serious, and yet full of bursting, vibrant life. Such a combination was confusing. Symone felt that people should either be satisfied or dissatisfied with life. She knew she was perfectly lodged in the dark basement of dissatisfaction. The combination that Alex possessed was a strange dichotomy. During the two friends' most intimate discussions like this, Symone thought Alex took life way too seriously. She felt that Alex saw too much with the passionate eyes she was given.

"God's gift to us is life," Alex said and grinned at her with a faint look of despair. "What we do with our life is our gift to Him. Our return—"

"Maybe it's me," Symone inhaled furtively, cutting Alex off. "But this subject is really depressing me."

"I'm sorry."

"That's ok. Quite frankly, I really can't handle any depressing shit today," she explained quickly and laughed. "Let's do something else. Would you like to play some music downstairs?" Symone asked cheerfully in the hopes that Alex would agree.

"Well, yes." Alex sighed heavily and put her mother's picture down. "We haven't done that in a long time, Sy."

Alex carefully stacked the other pictures back and placed the box in the closet. She removed a picture of Madison and herself from a pewter frame on the nightstand and placed the newly found one of her mother in its place. With very slow movements, Alex positioned the picture on the elegant antique white dressing table beside the bedroom's French doors. She extended her left hand to help Symone off the bed, and the two friends walked downstairs holding each other's waists.

"So are you doing a lot of traveling in the next few weeks, Sy?"

"No. Not too much. In the next couple of months, we got to handle meetings in Atlanta, California, Chicago, Augusta, and Atlantic City. Other than that, it'll be quiet around Meetings Odyssey. Akao Studios is busy as hell. That's nothing new, though. Pecola even had to hire another masseuse."

"Other than that? Girl, that sounds very, very busy to me."

Symone nodded her head. "On Tuesday morning, Pecola, Ted, Elisha, and three members of our staff are heading to Los Angeles for the National Black MBA Association Conference. Umph, umph, umph. You know I would love to be there for that one. Since the children are just getting back home, I passed on that trip."

"Well, that's good. They're probably glad to have you around at least until they get settled with being back home in North Carolina, girl."

"They are, Alex. I took your advice. I talked to each one of my babies. I told them that I love them enormously, but I explained to them that I love what I do." Remembering the conversation with her children, Symone hesitated briefly. "I told them that my companies are quite fulfilling, and I get paid very well to manage them. Then I told them I wouldn't be traveling out of town on any business trips, that is at least until they've been home for a good month. The children, especially Jared, was pleased with that decision."

"I can imagine."

"I didn't *even* go to see Hampton play Howard last weekend. You know that's not me, girl. Are you happy now, Alex?"

"If you're happy, then you know I am, Sy. Do what you think is right within you. Trust your instincts. Even though you tell me you don't think you know what's right anymore, I know for a fact that you have excellent intuition about things. Mama always said that intuitively, we got all the answers. So follow your mind, Sy. That's what my Mama used to say," Alex answered as she affectionately tightened her grip on Symone's waist and leaned her head on her shoulder.

"You're a mess, Alex." But Symone felt comforted by Alex's tender embrace. "You really, really are."

Alex nodded but didn't say anything for a moment. "Madison and I are looking forward to going to Augusta for the NMA conference in three weeks. That should be a lot of fun. I was glad to see yall got that contract. If yall keep it up, your competitors might think you've a monopoly on the conference and meeting planning market."

"I know. Pecola said the same thing during lunch on Friday with Elisha and Ted. We simply work hard, Alex."

"Plus, a little networking helps too, girl."

"That's always key, Alex. That's for damn sure. We're meticulous with details, and that's why we continue to get repeat business, too. That's the key. Ted always says we can only compete against ourselves. That's our competition. No one else."

"Ted's right. I was just kidding, girl," Alex exclaimed.

"I know."

"You're only getting the business that God wants you to have. That's all." She briefly rested her head on Symone's shoulder again. For some reason, she felt unusually weak and tired today.

"Ok, I got it, Pastor Alex."

"I do know how it is in the corporate world," Alex giggled. "Just because I'm a housewife, don't you think for one minute that I haven't totally forgotten how I always felt I needed to do my best."

"I understand, girl. Do your best? That's an understatement. You were a detail freak. You still are, honeychilllle." Symone spoke the last word with southern emphasis, and Alex laughed loudly.

"I'm telling you. As a Black attorney, I was always over prepared. I had to be. Whenever I stepped into court, I believed that the presumption was, whether it was true or not Symone, I believed that people automatically assumed I didn't know my stuff. It's a club with white folks. The old boys network. The judges, the elite law firms, they're going to law schools together, and families knowing families. You know that unspoken bond that they declare to us isn't real. I believe it's especially true in the legal profession. So the only way I felt I could over compensate for those white folks' birthright advantages was to be over competent. I mean every eeny miney detail was reviewed each and every time I was in court or any time I was in charge of a meeting."

"I think the same way, Alex. No question about it. The only difference is I ain't an attorney."

"It doesn't make any difference. Not in the corporate jungle as Pecola loves to call it," Alex said as they strolled through the entryway of the music room. She inhaled deeply. "Pecola told me that Pauletta is real excited about our coming to Augusta. You know she and Hannibal are going to roll out the red carpet for all of us."

"Ummm-hmmm." Symone moaned the reply as she eyed the peaceful lake in the distance through the music room window.

"Pecola had me laughing, girl. She told me that Rozelle wants to go to Augusta for the conference, too."

"He's not a doctor."

"I know. He told Pecola that he's a math and chemistry major and a Harvard graduate. That should count for something."

"Rozelle is a stone to the bone trip. He'll do anything to take advantage of a good time with his friends."

"Well, here we are," Alex said as she headed toward the piano bench. You're ready to sing, girl?"

"Yes I am, especially if you are."

"Symone, let's think about what we're going to play first." Alex dreamingly gazed out the picture window toward the lake.

In Symone's opinion, one of the loveliest rooms in Alex's house was the music room. Influenced by Alex's love of the small four bedroom cottage home they owned in St. Bart, the huge room was absolutely airy, light, and painted a turquoise blue, the color of a Caribbean ocean. One wall was made up of forty feet of a thirteen-foot tall window paneled glass. The wall stretched from the floor to the ceiling and overlooked a spectacular view of the gardens below and of the lake in the distance. Beautiful turquoise, floral curtains draped the tubular rods in a willowy fashion. Large green palm trees and hand blown bulb jars with colorful flower arrangements within each one were positioned throughout. Lovely gold framed original artwork by Haitian artist, Alix Baptiste, decorated the walls, as well as the colorful abstract expression images of nature paintings by Olivia Gatewood. African-American porcelain figurines and family photographs adorned every available surface of the piano and was on all the other sparkling, shining, and stately furniture.

But the most breathtaking combination that always swept Symone off her feet with thoughts of fantasy and romance was the white grand Steinway piano and the exquisite golden harp. Both instruments were majestically placed smacked dead in the middle of the room for both the Devereauxs and their friend's enjoyment.

Years ago, when Symone moved to the United States, the Poussaint family attended a lavish party at the Eisners' Fifth Avenue apartment. A female harpist was hired for the evening, and she played in the library. Out of all the children there, Symone was totally fascinated by the angelic sounds floating from the woman's fingertips. For a straight hour, Symone sat on the floor at the musician's feet. When Uncle Samuel noticed how his niece refused to move from the coveted spot, he finally pulled up a chair for her. When the evening ended, Uncle Samuel recommended to Uncle Willie that Symone take harp lessons. Two weeks later, the lesson started. All through junior high school, Symone was the harpist for the orchestra. Up until the time she graduated from Hampton, she was one of three harpists for the college orchestra and was considered a rarity.

Oftentimes, when Alex planned evenings at home with close friends, either Alex or Scott played the piano. Rozelle blew notes on his trumpet, and Symone played the harp. During those times, Pecola swore she definitely sang like Patti LaBelle. The friends jokingly said that they should take the group on the road; however, such engagements were kept to intimate settings with their families or with one another. When Alex planned those exquisitely special dinner parties evenings she so loved doing, of course she hired tuxedo-attired jazz or classical musicians. However, when either friend wanted to have a knock down, throw down, get real party, DJ Cool Breeze, a close friend of Rico, was absolutely, categorically booked for those occasions.

All of the friends in their tight inner-circle had a grand piano elegantly displayed in their homes, but it was Alex who also owned the harp. To Symone, that was such a wonderful combination. Harp music sounded so heavenly. It was quite romantic and reminded her of blissful relationships with Black men. It was the perfect sound to accompany a fantasy. Such reactions to romance and fantasy probably stemmed from Symone's teenage mind's need to soak up fairy tales to escape from her past. Whatever the reason, her mind definitely journeyed to the dreaming stratosphere when she played the harp.

Symone was infatuated with Wynton Marsalis' trumpet playing abilities as well as his full, luscious curvy lips. She always imagined Wynton playing the trumpet beside her. Pecola often swore that whoever Symone thought about when she played the harp, it must have been someone pretty special. Sometimes it took an actual soft pinch by one of the friends to awaken Symone from her self-induced harp playing daze. Always listening to the harp sounds and feeling the strings under her fingers were amazing and wondrously relaxing. When Symone played, she never thought about her problems, men, or even her past. It simply took her back to another era of total relaxation.

Many times, Symone thought about buying a harp, but she never got around to it. The Poussaint Family owned one. However, since it was a gift that had been in the family for years, it remained in the Brooklyn's brownstone formal living room. The harp was given to the family six months after Symone started taking lessons. One day Uncle Samuel drove up and surprised Keturah and her four children with the ancient instrument. Now, Keturah enjoyed watching it and adored Symone's playing during her visits home. Recently, Ameenah began taking harp lessons and several times serenaded the family at family gatherings, too.

However, Symone frequently told Alex that if she had a harp at home, it would be different. It would be like having another piece of exercise equipment around. In the beginning, Symone probably would be excited to have it. She would serenade the hell out of her family each and every day. Then eventually it would become like a piece of art that she appreciated every now and then. With Alex having a harp, it was different. It was a fresh observation each and every time that Symone visited the Devereauxs' home. And, anytime Symone was moved to the need for romanticism and escape, she had an open invitation to play the harp at Alex's house.

Romanticism and escape. That was where Symone's mind was today. Fantasyland—or at least that was where it traveled during the discussion with Alex about her dead family members. Since Symone had been dealing with an unexplained bout of depression for the past three days, talking about death, old pictures, and reaching the senior citizens' age just weren't favorite topics of hers this bright, Saturday morning.

Once Alex and Symone decided what they were going to play, Symone convinced Alex to play the piano for about an hour. Alex explained that they couldn't play for any longer than that because she did not want to infringe on the special time she had planned for Trey, Purity, Kyle, and Sylvia before it was time for them to leave. In addition, Alex explained that

Cleopatra, Jodria, Rozelle, Scott, Charmaine, Rico, Darilyn and Lillie would arrive in three hours with at least thirty other children in tow to take them out for the afternoon play and dinner.

After those guidelines were settled with Symone, Alex played and sang gospel favorite tunes in her beautiful soprano voice. Symone, who could not carry a tune to the garbage dumpster, quietly played complementing background harp music. All through the session, Alex reminded Symone that there was a voice inside of everybody. Symone just had to simply find hers. The two friends laughed and talked so much that eventually when Madison ushered the children into the kitchen for something to drink, the lyrical sounds drew them to the music room. They too sat on the floor to enjoy the music as well. In the end, Alex and Symone graciously bowed when they received a standing ovation from the small, sweaty audience, along with the three barking dogs.

Chapter Seventy-One

Once Pecola realized that she had indeed left the leather pouch at home with all four pairs of her shoes in it, she slammed her Gucci overnight bag against the wall. She was still reeling from the brief yet angry argument she and Carlos had over breakfast this morning. She checked her watch. It was still early—eleven in the afternoon. She had at least five hours before the limo arrived to whisk her away to catch her flight to Augusta. In the meantime, she would simply have to send Gloria to the house to pick up the bag of shoes.

When Pecola was a young girl, she always dreamed about traveling the world, singing at this club and that hot spot. She had to admit that she certainly traveled a lot. But it wasn't for the Motown singing career she dreamt about. It was for the corporate paper chase routine. Today, she was tired of it. Lately, it seemed she was either in the air on some turbulent flight or always checking into some swank hotel with rubber tasting room service food. Pecola pressed the intercom button and politely asked Gloria to come into the office. She needed her to run a fast errand.

Later on that afternoon, Pecola heard two taps on her open office door. She looked up and noticed Captain Scott with a huge grin on his face. Dressed in a white short sleeve shirt with stripes on his shoulders, his loose tie revealed the chest hairs pushing through his shirt collar. He walked toward her with his arms outstretched. Pecola stood up and met him halfway, and the two friends embraced affectionately. A small flowery shopping bag Scott held in his hand kept flapping her on the back. Scott didn't say what was in it, and Pecola refused to ask. She sat back down, took off her glasses and gazed at him. Scott positioned himself on the edge of Pecola's desk; he rested the bag on the floor beside his leg and returned Pecola's empty, tired stare.

"Look at my babycake's face," Scott said good-naturedly. "Are you ok, Pecola?" As he spoke, he played with the pewter paperweight on her desk.

"Chile, yeah. I'm fine, Scott. Just the rigors of meetings and the endless paper chase," she explained wearily.

Pecola put her glasses back on and pointed to the desk. Scott noticed eight neat stacks of folders placed in strategic spots all over the entire desk's surface. Pecola realized that the earlier, heated conversation with Carlos didn't help her stress compass one bit.

"What is it really, baby?" He inquired in his typical brotherly fashion.

Pecola glanced away from him and gazed at the new bronze bust of herself. Alex persuaded Pecola to pose for the bust, and Alex got it one of Pecola's fortieth birthday gifts. Oftentimes, Pecola's friends always teased her about placing the bust on a pedestal in her office. But during stressful workdays, Pecola believed it was always comforting for her to peer at her likeness and consider life. Somehow or another, it made her realize how vulnerable she was about life's problems. Everyone walked around in their corporate power costumes always trying to be people they truly weren't—including her. In reality, they were nothing but human statues that moved about within the world as other human statues do. They were in the dark and terribly unhappy. Pecola inhaled slowly, frowned deeply and finally confessed to Scott.

"All I wanted was very simple. I wanted Carlos to go out of town with me, Scott. That's all. Carlos said that he couldn't make this business trip. We argued about it this morning." She shook her head in disgust. "After the way we both acted and some of the things we said, I'm not going to ask him anymore. That was my fifth damn request, Scott."

"Carlos is just as busy as you are, baby. You know that. Yall are running a high-power two-career household, Pecola."

"Don't remind me, Scott."

Scott moved from off Pecola's desk and went to plop his body on the hand-made leather couch. While he continued to gaze affectionately at Pecola, he dug his hands into his pockets and stretched his legs out in front of him.

"Is that it?" He studied Pecola's face for any other clues.

"That's all I want to talk about right now," she grumbled with slow deliberation.

"Ok. Whenever you want to talk, you know I'm here to listen." He continued to smile at her. "It's one-hundred and fifty thousand degrees out there, baby. It's so hot outside for October. Wooo! I came straight here from the airport, but I started to take my black ass home."

"I haven't been out since I arrived this morning at eight. But that's the exact same thing Alex told me. She was here for her monthly Akao Ultra Package—a condensed version that is."

Scott's eyes sparkled to know Alex was in the building. "Is she still here?"

Pecola checked her watch. "Hell no. You probably missed her by fifteen minutes. She stopped in my office just very briefly real early this morning to bring flowers, of course." Pecola pointed to the pastel profusion of flowers sitting majestically in a silver trumpet vase atop the walnut cellarette.

"Those are pretty, baby. You got any of that apple shine in that thing there? Rozelle told me he gave you and Carlos two gallons of the stuff."

Pecola shook her head quickly.

"No, baby. It's more refined liquor in my little cellarette there. You know that. Even if there was some white liquor in there, I'm not drinking that hard liquor right now with you. I got to catch a plane and don't need to smell like a first-class drunk in my first class seat. I'll save my drinking for the flight."

"You go with your bad self." Scott clapped several times and began to laugh.

"Would you like Gloria to bring you a soda and some fruit? If you want something major to eat, I'll have to call the dining room. What do you want? Just name it," she said wearily as she checked files and wrote notes as she spoke. Immediately, she turned around and entered important numbers into her computer.

"Yeah, soda. That'll be great. Tell her to also spike it with a little Hennessy on the side," he added laughing. Pecola slowly whirled around to face him. She pressed the button for the intercom and asked Gloria to bring in three bottles of Coke, a bucket of ice, and a bowl of macadamia nuts.

"I declare, Scott. Something tells me that I need to speak to Tierra. Our receptionist didn't even announce you were in the Akao Building. That's interesting," she joked and watched him out the corner of her eyes. She resumed writing notes on four yellow post-it papers and placed each on various stacks.

"Don't even try it. I get the new security code every quarter. Just like Alex," he exclaimed while reaching for the *Emerge* magazine on the table beside the couch and quickly flipped through the pages.

Five minutes later, Gloria walked in. She smiled professionally at Scott and placed the silver tray on the antique table beside him. Gloria loved serving her employers when he visited. She didn't know where Pecola and Symone found such handsome friends or even the good-looking clients they paraded around the building. But every time Gloria turned around, they had the nicest looking men visiting the office.

If I were those two women and had as much money as they do, my bedroom door would be a revolving one twenty-four hours a day. Seven days a week, Gloria thought with an inward grin.

With a careful, subtle stare, Gloria eyed Scott from head to toes again. He certainly was one fine Black, sexy man. She told Elisha the same on several occasions. Gloria believed Scott should be in the centerfold of *Blackgirl* magazine. Without question, she definitely would buy it that month. Scott noticed the young girl was nervous and was being extremely careful to pour his soda perfectly. He wanted to put her at ease. When Gloria glanced away, he winked at Pecola.

"Congratulations, Gloria," he said smiling as he crossed his legs.

The young woman quickly glanced at him with a surprised expression.

"Pecola and Symone told me you just finished your sophomore year at A&T," he said genuinely pleased with her accomplishments. To take advantage of the tuition reimbursement plan offered by MO, Gloria was working on an undergraduate degree in business administration and attended classes in Greensboro three nights a week.

"Well, uh. I certainly thank you, Mr. Alexander," she replied softly, clearly flustered.

"Call me Scott, please," he requested while intently watching her face.

"Thank you, Scott," Gloria said now avoiding his piercing black eyes. He placed the magazine back on the table. Gloria turned to face a smiling Pecola.

"Will there be anything else you need, Pecola?"

"That'll be all. Thanks, girl."

"You sure you don't want anything to drink or snack on while you work, Pecola?" Now, Gloria avoided Pecola's eyes.

"Not really. Thanks a lot, Gloria. I'm fine. Thanks again for running out to my house."

"No problem, Pecola. I was glad to do it."

Gloria meant it. She truly was delighted that she was trusted in such a way. She even knew the security code to the Reynolds' home alarm system. She had to admit it did take her about ten minutes longer than necessary to return to the office from the errand. As usual, it took Gloria that long to admire the Reynolds' beautifully decorated, antique and Black art filled home. Gloria wasn't jealous of her employers' wealth. If anything, Pecola and Symone's success motivated her to desire to be a force in the business world as well. Since they were both fair people with their employees, Gloria truly believed what Elisha frequently told her was absolutely true. When Gloria was business ready and was educationally qualified, Pecola and Symone wouldn't hesitate to promote her into the position she often told the owners she dreamt about having with Meetings Odyssey. Gloria swiftly smiled at Pecola and turned to leave.

"Gloria, please shut the door for me on your way out," Pecola asked in a business-like tone.

Still not gazing at either one of them, Gloria quickly nodded her head and walked out and closed the door. With an amused expression on her face, Pecola watched Scott drink the cold soda for a few moments.

"You had to go over there and get her flustered? Didn't you?" she asked laughing with affection. She waved a frosty pink polished square index finger at him in a naughty way. He raised his left eyebrow in classic Scott Alexander fashion.

"What?"

"I believe Gloria has a slight crush on you, sugar. You just talking to her probably pushed her goo goo buttons to the top." They both smiled at each other. "Hell, she's young. When you're that age, you've got a crush on just about everybody who's dressed up and packaged like you."

Scott continued to swig down the soda. He immediately burst out laughing, which made him choke a bit. Pecola continued in a nonchalant voice.

"I got to give it to Gloria. She has good taste because you know you're fine. Then, you walk up here in that pilot monkey suit. You know Black women love a man in nice clothes, but a uniform definitely sends them reeling," Pecola ended, laughing half-heartedly.

"I like her, Pecola. Was just trying to put her at ease. That's all."

"We love her around here, too. She's an excellent worker. Very devoted and quite trustworthy. Elisha told us that we better keep her happy."

"Told you?"

"Yeah. You know Elisha and Ted are the ones that really run things around here. Symone and I are just a front for the finances," Pecola explained, laughing.

"I do remember Alex telling me something to that effect." Scott grinned, too.

"Elisha told us that when she retires in a few years, she wants Gloria to take her place as our executive assistant."

"So what yall think about that?"

"She would be great in the job. No question about it. She's a little green around the ears, especially when someone like you is sitting in the office. Most times you can't tell she's frazzled. That's why I know she got it bad for you."

"C'mon, Pecola."

"It's real, baby. I can tell those things. I've seen Gloria in action, and she's normally cool, calm, and collected. Gloria travels with us sometimes. She was with me on the West Coast and did a fantastic job with all those impressive looking MBAs who were running all over the place. We're just bringing her along slowly. You know Symone loves her to death, especially since Gloria knows Black history like you wouldn't believe and to be so young. Elisha calls Symone and Gloria the Meetings Odyssey resident militant sisters."

"Well, good. I'm glad to hear that she's in line for a position like that here. Symone does talk about her a lot. When people believe they have a chance to advance in a company, they tend to do better. Their morale is better, too."

"Well, you know us. We try. Symone always reminds me about how we must provide incentives for our employees, nah," she ended in a West Indian accent. "You know how she is?"

"That I certainly damn do." Scott spoke slowly.

Pecola glanced at her watch. It was three o'clock. She picked up the weekly calendar, reviewed the schedule for tomorrow, took off her glasses, and rubbed her eyes. Scott sensed the tension and wondered if her mood were a result of something more than the argument with Carlos that was causing Pecola to brood.

"Are you ok, Pecola?" he asked with concerned and took a big gulp of soda.

"Chile, I'm just exhausted. I told you. Carlos and me argued. I got a whole lot of other bullshit on my mind," she said tiredly as she leaned back in her chair and thought about Carlos again.

"Well, I got something to brighten up your day." Scott stood up and walked over to pick up the bag. Just as quickly, he decided against it for right now and began to soothingly massage Pecola's shoulders for a few minutes. Pecola closed her eyes and thought about her husband. As Scott pressed the muscles at the base of Pecola's neck, he realized how tight she was.

"You *are* tense, baby," he said with authority and continued massaging her neck for ten more minutes. Pecola slowly opened her eyes as she realized he was winding down. When he stopped, he kissed her tenderly on the forehead and hugged her shoulders.

"Relax, baby. Ok?"

She nodded her head but didn't answer and twisted her neck slowly from side to side.

"Thanks, Scott. I needed that. I should walk myself downstairs and tell whoever's on the massage tables to get off and lay my own damn self on it." Tiredness was all over her voice. There was an uneasy quiet.

"Where's Symone? I stopped in her office. The lights were off, the desk was clean, and the lamp was on." He grabbed the flowery bag and plopped back down on the sofa.

"I'm trying to tell you. Are you not listening or what? She's in Augusta with Ted and six other staff people. You know we organized a huge conference down there for the National Medical Association."

"Please forgive me. I didn't know," he said with a smirk. "I thought yall were heading to Los Angeles."

"Nah, baby. I was in Los Angeles three weeks ago for the Black MBA Conference."

"Nobody told me. I know you were out west somewhere. You told me you were going. I thought you said San Francisco. As much as you talk, how did I miss it? How come you didn't tell me exactly where you were going, baby? Trying to hide something from your older brother?"

"Honeychile, we ain't got to tell you everything we do, Mr. Scott Alexander," she said sweetly with a half grin.

"Earlier, I heard you say something about Augusta. I got it now. You women are rolling. The lobby was full downstairs. Yall are flying all over the place and putting deals together. I'm proud of you two."

"We aim to please, chile." As Pecola spoke, she rubbed her temples.

"How come you're not the one in Augusta, and Pauletta lives there?"

"Me and Symone do split up every now and then, honeychile. Symone worked more with the NMA officials than I did. I think she was trying to find a tall, Black doctor—just like Madison," Pecola added smiling. Both she and Scott laughed freely at the truth of the statement.

"Symone promised her children she wouldn't go out of town until after they had been home at least a whole month. I think she's trying to catch up on the corporate meeting brouhaha down in Augusta."

"Leave my girl alone, Pecola. Like everyone else, you and me included, she wants to find that special someone to love."

"You're right." Pecola rubbed her temples again. "You know I'm tired, Scott. Yesterday, I returned from wrapping up a deal with Delaware State College in Dover and got in late last night," she explained as she opened and closed manila folders. She scribbled notes in each one. "I'm leaving this afternoon on a five-thirty flight to Augusta. I sure feel like rescheduling my flight for tomorrow morning, though." She mumbled as if thinking out aloud.

"Why, baby?"

"Well for starters, I left my shoe pouch at home. Gloria went to the house to get it. If I had gone home to pick it up, I probably would've ended up in bed. Nobody would see me for awhile, let alone in Augusta."

"Sounds like you're having a great day. Perk up, baby. It can't be that bad."

"It's that bad to me." She frowned again. "We won't be back from Augusta until Monday afternoon. That's why I tried to convince Carlos to go. He and Hannibal could golf together, but my darling huzzband has construction sites he said that he needs to monitor. Plus, his long lost cousin is coming to visit us."

"Now you know that even though Carlos is president of the company, he still likes to get out there in the field every now and then with the hard hat and all."

"You're the typical man. I see you're taking up for him as usual."

"C'mon, Pecola. Don't dog what I'm saying. I was your friend first. Ain't nothing going to change that tight bond we share, but my man works hard. You know it."

Pecola ignored Scott's reasonable explanation. "Well, after Carlos told me he had to monitor those sites, I asked him what in the hell happened to project managers? The bottom line is he's not going with me. Why don't you come and go with us, Scott? You know Alex and Madison will be there. We all are taking the flight together this afternoon. You can always leave in the morning. I'll pay for it."

"I know you would. Can't do it, baby. I'm just getting back in town today, myself. I promised Charmaine I'd spend time with her when I returned from this trip. Next week, she's going to Europe for ten days. So we're trying to squeeze in as much loving as possible." He drank soda and gazed at the oak trees through the picture window.

"Wasn't she just in Europe?" Pecola asked suspiciously.

"Yes she was, and she's going back again. Is that ok with you, Sherlock Holmes?"

"As long as you don't mind, Scott baby."

"I don't mind. While she's gone, I'm going to New Orleans. Rose Bobbie needs to see me. That's unusual for my ex-wife to call and say she wants to talk."

"Uh oh. Maybe yall might get back together."

"Nah, baby. That definitely isn't happening. We're just good friends. You know where my heart is."

"Don't remind me. Charmaine, Charmaine, Charmaine. I hope she knows you're definitely a catch. If she doesn't, you let your loving and faithfully devoted Sister Pecola know. I got fifty sorors who are waiting in line for an opportunity to show you the AKA way. Since you're no longer are on the highly eligible availability block, don't you know there's a nation of women in mourning? Well, more like the women of the city of Winston-Salem."

"Girl, you too crazy."

"I'm serious, Scott baby."

"Listen to me," he said trying to change the subject. "While Charmaine is gone, I'll be checking SJ and GJ out." Scott hesitated for a moment. "You know now that I think about it, I remember Alex telling me she was going to Augusta. Madison, his father, and brother were attending some meeting," he said as he munched on a couple of nuts. "Crazy Marshall Fudge and his wife are supposed to be there. Yall should have some fun."

"Maybe they will, but we'll be working like a motha making sure all activities are according to contract specifications," she advised dejectedly.

Just then, someone knocked on the door, and Pecola told the person to come in. With a professional business air enveloping her, Elisha stepped in with Pecola's airline tickets, itinerary, and several files that created a ninth stack on Pecola's desk. Elisha spoke briefly with Scott, reviewed the schedule with Pecola, walked out, and closed the door. After she left, Pecola gently placed the ticket and additional information on one of the paper stacks. As if she was saying a silent prayer, she folded her hands together and stared straight at him.

"While you're working hard in Augusta, squeeze in a cocktail hour every now and then," Scott said.

"It'll be hard work. We're dealing with a bunch of doctors. Like you were saying, it's one in the same meeting the Devereauxs were telling you about. The NMA is a medical association that's mostly comprised of African-American physicians," she said quietly and rubbed her temples and took off her glasses for the third time. Scott continued to watch her intently.

"Uh huh. I see."

"You know it's been a killer week so far. Its times like this that make me understand why Alex chucked the paper chase, rat race, endless meetings, boardroom shit, wheeling and mega-dealing, flying here, and staying there. I see why she resigned from this fast-paced business world to have a life and spend time with her family to enjoy the roses. Today, I feel like walking away myself," she said as she rocked in her chair and put her glasses back on.

"Wooo! You feel better now?" he asked gently.

"Yes," she nodded and smiled affectionately.

"Well, I got a surprise for you." He finally handed the flowery bag to her. She dug inside and found a Whispers CD.

"Thanks, Scott," she said grinning and blew him an air kiss. He smiled broadly.

"I went into the record store on Liberty Street. I said 'What you got that's serious, man? New or old, give it to me. I need something bad as it wanna be.' Anyway, the brother recommended the Whispers."

"I adore them."

"I thought about you, Pecola," he explained good-naturedly. "So I brought you a CD. It's soulful music, and it's good for the soul. Smooth R&B that fit into the grooves of your heart." Very quickly, Scott drained his glass. When he poured more soda in the glass, it almost fizzled over.

"I'm sure the Whispers can give me the soothing I need."

"You think your parents would want this CD?"

"Scott, puhleeze. These songs are a little young for Mama and Daddy," she said as she reviewed the cuts on the back. "They're into gospel. But if you get them Billie Holiday, Ethel Waters, some Count Basie, Lionel Hampton, and a little Duke Ellington, that's still right down their alley."

"Girl, I was just joking," he said with a huge grin. For the next long moments, Pecola focused her attention on the work she had to get out.

Between flipping pages in the book he was reading, Scott watched her shuffle the paperwork for thirty more minutes. He decided it was time to leave, and Pecola glanced up just as he was placing *In the Spirit* back on the table. She noticed that he straightened up his shoulders as if it was a signal that he was ready to go.

"Thanks for stopping by. You brightened up my day. I especially appreciate the CD." Pecola smiled warmly.

Pecola stood up and walked to the door with him then decided to continue onto the first floor. Scott placed his right arm around Pecola's shoulders. While the two friends chitchatted, they strolled to the second floor reception area. As Scott held Pecola's right hand with his left hand, they walked past Gloria's desk. After Scott said good-bye to Gloria, she quickly used her hands to fan herself as soon as they turned the corner.

When they made it to the downstairs front lobby, Tierra was writing reminders to herself. She glanced up and smiled at the two friends. By then, Scott had placed his black cap back on his head. Three attractive Black women were reading magazines and books in the reception area. However, all stopped flipping pages and hungrily eyed Scott. The women straightened their shoulders as he strolled by. Scott, always the polite one, casually greeted each lady with a small grin. Once outside, Pecola laughed merrily about the joke he told her, and they again kissed each other good-bye. He eased into the car, closed the door, and rolled down the window. Before he drove off, she leaned against the window and repeated what she said in the office.

"You know Black women love a man in damn nice clothes, but a hellatious uniform definitely makes them work harder," she declared and burst out laughing.

Scott laughed hard. "You're a mess, baby. Hey, remember I love you, Pecola."

"Hell, I know that. You tell me that shit enough."

He smiled again and hoped his voice would coax her. "Well, I'm telling it to you once more. Tell Pauletta, Hannibal, and the children I said hello. Get some rest in Augusta. Send Carlos a dozen yellow roses, baby. Knowing you like I do, you probably let him have it something awful. I bet you cut my nigger up with the quickness."

"I ain't saying."

"That means you did, baby. Be sweet. Ok? I mean it. Let Symone handle the heavy shit and you enjoy a little rest and relaxation with Pauletta," he instructed firmly in his always brotherly fashion.

"I might."

"I'll call Carlos and see what he's doing this weekend. You want me to take care of Carlos, baby?" he asked jokingly. Pecola continued to stare at him with a blank expression on her face. "Rozelle and I are going to the Vantage Championships at Tanglewood Park on Saturday. Our man, Calvin Peete is supposed to be there. He's due to tee-off at ten Saturday morning. Carlos and his cousin might want to check him out, too."

Pecola was studying Scott strangely. "Uh huh. Ummm-hmmm. I got it now. Wait until I speak with my huzzband. That's probably the real reason why he's not going with me. Golf. And a Black legend is in town, too. My ass should've known."

"C'mon, Pecola. He didn't mention a thing to me about it. Knowing how Carlos loves golf, he would've brought it up. I had forgotten, too. Rozelle reminded me about the tournament. Don't make assumptions, baby."

"Don't worry. I'm fine with it now that I know the real reasons."

"Look at your face." Scott lowered his voice. "Are you sure?"

"I'm sure." She stared at him with wide, sad eyes. Then she gave him a small shrug as if to say, what the hell? Nothing mattered.

"Ok. Be sweet, baby." He sighed with relief.

"Don't worry. I'm really fine, big brother. Let me go back inside and talk to these ladies. I know they want to know who you are."

Scott grinned freely and bared his perfect, white teeth. Pecola smiled back into his handsome face and finally waved him off. She turned and headed toward the building. Pecola chuckled inwardly at Scott's nonchalant attitude about his sexy good looks and walked inside to speak with the three women who were waiting to enter Akao Studios. Pecola was right. All three were also wondering who was the attractive man that Pecola was hugging like a long, lost brother.

Chapter Seventy-Two

Billy's explanation wasn't making any sense. The more Symone spoke with him, the angrier she was at herself for staying on the telephone line so long. The hell with him. For the last fifteen minutes, he had been rambling on about how busy he was and speaking endlessly about his new clients in South Africa. Symone thought this was a fine damn way to start the week. It was Monday evening. This afternoon, Symone, Pecola, Ted, and six of their staff people returned from a grueling five days in Augusta with the National Medical Association Conference. Symone was still exhausted.

Symone arrived home from the office less than half an hour ago and had just removed her black bra, panties, and garters. As soon as she slipped into a pair of emerald silk crested pajamas, Miss Jessica announced that Billy was on the line. Before she picked up the master bedroom telephone, Symone glanced at her watch. It was eight o'clock. Now, it was eight fifteen, and she was ready to tell Billy to kiss her ass. Period.

"...Billy, you can't walk away from your entire past, and your children, return weeks later, and think they're business as usual," she said in a frustrated voice. Since the children were back from spending their three month summer vacation in Trinidad, he hadn't made many attempts to see them and only stopped by the house for a brief hour last week.

"I'm not walking away from my past, Symone," he responded icily. "I'm just simply giving you my schedule. And it does not include the children right now because I'll be out of the country for the next month."

"That's ridiculous, Billy. I'm so sick of your total disregard for visitation with them. You should be more intimately involved with our children—your children's development, especially Jared."

"What do you mean about Jared? I love my three children, Sy. Hell, you know that."

Symone breathed deeply. "It's not a question if you love them, Billy. They *need* to see you. When you have kids, you need to see them and be a daily part of their lives, regardless of how you feel about me. Kids know who love them."

"My kids *know* I love them. They don't question my love. Why should you?"

"I question it cause I'm older and see shit like it really is. I can smell the stench from it. I'm looking at the situation with old, experienced eyes."

"Like hell you are."

"Tell me why, Billy. Since Jared has been home, why haven't you attended one of his soccer games? You haven't been to just one, Billy. Not even a damn practice. Don't you think he notices that? Don't you think it hurts when he looks up in the stands and doesn't see you rooting him on like the other fathers are rooting for their sons? Kids aren't dumb. Your absence can send him the other way."

"What other way?"

"The wrong damn way. You know what I'm talking about. He'll be out trying to get the attention you won't give him anyway he can. Any damn way possible cause his father is too busy. Then jail becomes a real possibility in his life."

"My son ain't going to jail. He's made from good stock. We're good at academics, business, and sports. Our minds—"

"Your minds?"

"That's right. The Butlers' mind doesn't know anything about prison. If Jared doesn't do fine, he knows I'll kill him."

"He's acting out now. He must not fear doing the wrong thing that much."

"Let me tell you something. My son, William Jared Butler the Third, isn't a bad kid."

"I'm not saying he's a bad kid. Jared *is* very good, Billy. At eight years old, he's smart and all those things we expect him to be. He needs you, Billy. He needs the love and attention that only you as his father can give him. That's why I believe he's always sooo angry."

"*Angry?* What do you mean angry? I get so sick of you saying that. He has everything he wants or that he even thinks about having. He's angry?" he asked in disbelief.

"Yes. That's right. He's angry about our divorce. He's angry with you and the whole world it seems like—especially me. His anger rears its ugly head when you don't come get him and spend time with him. Sure, I have male friends who give him pep talks along with a pat on his back. It's still not the same as—"

"I bet you do have men patting his back. Probably rubbing up on your ass, too," Billy said in a voice etched with spite, interrupting her. In spite of the way he mistreated her during their marriage, Billy actually believed he still loved her.

Symone ignored the statements and his tone. "Jared probably would prefer to get a pat on his back from you, his father. I didn't have a father—"

"Your father was a damn idiot, and you can't *even* compare me to him," he muttered and poured himself another glass of Chardonnay.

"Don't talk about my father, Billy. This conversation isn't about him, Billy. It's about *you* being a better father. Maybe you should look up the meaning of the word in the dictionary cause it's obvious you sure as hell don't understand what I'm saying."

"Look! Don't fuck with me this evening, Sy. I'm not in no damn mood for your senseless nagging. I'm too busy for that."

"I ain't in no damn mood for you avoiding your children, either."

"You see what I'm saying? There you go again. Always trying to start some shit and stir up some controversy. If it's ain't one thing with you, it's another, Sy. You come with a whole bag of chips and a two-liter bottle of Pepsi. All that old baggage shit you be dealing with is probably fucking with you again."

"*Old baggage shit?* What has *my* old baggage shit got to do with our children, Billy? It's obvious you sure don't want to talk about the reality of things. Let alone have a common sense conversation."

"Hell! Let's not go there about reality, Symone. As a matter of fact, I gotta run anyway. I got a late dinner meeting scheduled with some NOMA buddies." He checked his platinum Swiss watch and gulped more Chardonnay. "My time is too valuable for this. As usual, you ain't making much damn sense."

"You'll see, Billy. You'll see. I saw a classic example last night on TV about what I'm saying. This Black guy became a famous baseball player. All of sudden, his father came from out of nowhere and finally decided it was time to notice his son. It was too late then. All during his years growing up, his father never was a part of his life. Now that the young man is famous, guess who was stepping up in his face? His long lost father."

"Sheee-it, Sy. You must be high as hell. Drunk or something. That guilt trip isn't working on me. I'm just a businessman with a tight schedule. I spend time with my children, and I ain't no damn long lost father, either. Save that sob story bullshit for somebody else, baby."

"How come you didn't pick them up this weekend, Billy? You said you would. You told me you weren't leaving until Wednesday. That's a whole day after tomorrow. You could've done it then. I shouldn't have to ask you when they could see you. These are your children, too. Jared's at an age where he needs attention from you. You need to get it. Understand what I'm saying. What would you do if you had custody of them? Just like me?"

"I would do what you do and have someone else. A hired gun like Miss Jessica to raise them all the fucking time the same way you are," Billy snapped with just as much vigor.

Symone's eyes stared hate. "You low down, son-of-a-bitch. How dare you."

"How dare I what?"

Symone was so mad; her eyes began to turn red. "I resent you saying I'm having someone else raise my children. *I* have quiet time with them. *I* sit down and read to them. When I'm in town, *I* have dinner with them at least four evenings a week. We eat breakfast together. *I* help with their homework. *I* visit the school, and *I'm* the one who takes them shopping."

"Yeah, right."

"How you let that foul shit come out of your mouth to the mother of your children? You ain't shit, and I'm glad to be rid of the foulness you spread."

"Oh, puhleeze. Spare me with your melodrama, Sy. You probably do take them shopping and everything else especially with all the damn money I have to pay you monthly. Your ass probably could buy the department store. You know you don't need it, Sy!" he grumbled disgustingly.

You're right. I don't need your money. That's why every month your payments are deposited in a trust account for the children, Symone thought with a vengeance.

"If it wasn't mandatory for you to pay, you probably wouldn't give them a penny. You barely see them, Billy."

"That's a damn lie."

"You know what, Billy? If I had all the money in the world, you wouldn't want to contribute to your children. That's sad," she said shaking her head and paused for added dramatic affect. "When you get older, you're going to wish you spent more time with your children."

As usual, Billy was just as quick with his fiery, mean responses as well. "I spend time with them when I can. Jared understands, and so do the girls. As they get older, I'll explain my responsibilities. The children will know that I work like a motha. I work earnestly like a dog to pay you alimony, child support, and to ensure they have a better life than I did." Bill hesitated briefly. "You say the dumbest things, girl. If I didn't know any better, I'd think you got your MBA from a Cracker Jack box instead of from Wharton."

"What?" Symone was so enraged she believed she would actually try to fight him if he was nearby. She realized Billy was thinking of another degrading insult and she decided she was going to win the war tonight. *Just hang up on his ass*, she thought.

"You know what I just recognized about you, Billy Butler?" She hollered each word with loud sarcasm.

"No. What? Tell me? I can't guess. Since you know every damn thing and have all the answers. Puhleeze tell my Black ass cause I know you got the damn corner on the prescription drug called know it all!" he replied crisply.

Symone grew angrier, but she persevered with winning.

"I realize that I'm just as stupid as you are because I'm stooping to your hamster brain level with this conversation. As of right now, it's over with me trying to ever speak sensibly with you. Have a damn good life." Symone exploded and slammed the phone down.

Two second after his parents' conversation ended, Jared quietly replaced the telephone receiver on the hook in the downstairs library. Clad in his favorite blue dinosaur pajamas, Jared angrily kicked the Persian rug several times and turned to walk in the kitchen to get a shiny red apple out of the refrigerator.

Close to tears, Symone really hated herself for thinking that she and Billy could ever have an amicable relationship. It was amazing how she used to love Billy. Now she didn't know what she felt. It wasn't hate, just nothingness toward her ex-husband. Symone covered her face with her hands and shook her head heavily.

For as long as Symone could remember, the Eisners ensured all monetary and real estate wealth accumulated by the Poussaint family was quietly moved into and handled by blind trusts. When Symone and Pecola started Akao Studios and Meetings Odyssey years ago, those entities were transferred into trusts controlled by the two women. During the lengthy, legal haggling with Billy over joint assets, the legal separation, and the eventual divorce, Symone therefore told her darling husband she didn't own anything. And the supposedly expert, private investigators Billy's attorneys hired couldn't locate one penny of Symone's money either. During those traumatic days, Symone thanked God for Uncle Willie's timely advice many years ago.

On the day of Symone's wedding to Billy, Uncle Willie quietly repeated what he said to Symone when the Poussaint Family of New York announced her engagement to the young, handsome and hard-working North Carolinian.

Uncle Willie's eyes were dark and serious. "...Seamone, always remember ta keep dey secrecy of dey family trusts separate frum yuh luv. Ah want yuh ta luv, cherish, and respect Billy because he will be yuh partner in life and dey father of yuh chillren. Dey father of Poussaint heirs. However, yuh husband isn't bloodline, Seamone. And, if dey luv dies, wich ah hope it doesn't, dey divorce war is not pretty."

While Uncle Willie spoke, he held her chin in his hand. His grim expression demanded that Symone stare directly in his eyes and her mind and eyes were riveted to his face.

"Yuh huzzband, Seamone. Dey one yuh believe yuh luv so desperately. Dey one yuh said God-giving vows ta will turn on yuh, and he will becum yuh enemy. Den dey financial battle of divorce gets very nasty and bloody, mey niece. Nevah farget wat ah does say ta yuh. Nevah farget dat dey trusts set up far yuh since yuh were a child along wit all dey assets yuh accumulated as an adult, must be preserved. It should be preserved far yuh chillren, dere chillren, and all dey other many Poussaint generations ta cum. Always remember dat, Seamone," Uncle Willie ended adamantly. Then he added with a huge grin. "Congratulations, mey niece. May yuh be married far many years, and may yuh and Billy have a wonderfully prosperous life."

Afterwards, Uncle Willie kissed her several times on each cheek. Uncle Cecil, who was quietly listening to his brother speak with his fingers curled under his chin as in deep thought, kissed and hugged her tightly as well. Both uncles handed Symone two huge checks for her white satin pouch. Two minutes after Uncle Willie completed his trust lecture, Uncle Samuel walked up and asked the Poussaint brothers if they once again told Symone what she needed to know about the secrecy of the family trust. Both nodded yes and smiled again. As Uncle Samuel gazed into Symone's happy face, he laughed loudly. With much tenderness, he affectionately hugged Symone and gave her an envelope from him and Auntie Gerda.

To this day, Symone profusely thanked God once more that her uncles reminded her about the wisdom of trust and asset management on her wedding day. Her three uncles probably knew that she was absolutely giddy with love for Billy, and she certainly was just that. Back then, Symone worshipped Billy. She was totally fascinated with his intellect, his lovemaking, and what she presumed was his utmost devotion to her.

When Symone first laid eyes on Billy during her sophomore year at Hampton and his third year there, she knew she was ready to fall in love. That year, she was elected vice president of the student government association. When William Jared Butler, Jr. casually strolled into the SGA meeting being held in the Old Gym, Symone's mind immediately began fantasizing about getting with him. Just from her initial three-second review of him, Symone assumed two things about Billy: He was smart, and he certainly could dress well.

Billy wore an open collar starched white linen shirt with cuff links, khaki pants and absolutely shiny brown penny loafers without socks. Before he sat down, Symone flipped. He was a dark-skinned man with full luscious lips. A rugged looking young collegian with a deep penetrating stare, Billy was categorically her type. And more importantly, he actually reminded her of the pretty, mahogany dark-skinned, Black men of Trinidad. Out of the corner of Symone's eyes, she quickly glanced at him from head to toe then back to the bulge between his legs and thought to herself, *Damn! Who in the hell is that? And, how did I miss him my freshman year?*

Billy exuded a dark skin man's beauty and charm, and he was talll! Since Symone was five ten, she was a height bigot and refused to speak to a man if he wasn't over six feet. Billy was six one; he barely made it. But it didn't matter. At Hampton, Symone normally pursued the basketball player types, but they didn't matter either, not with this one because this man was extremely smart, and she realized that from the first conversation with him. He knew what he wanted to do with his life and had already mapped out his plans to create one of the largest architectural firms in North Carolina. More than anything else in the beginning,

Symone was impressed with Billy's intelligence. He was totally dedicated to his studies and focused his attention on the benefits of education.

Oftentimes, Billy took Symone on dates to observe exhibits of Frank Lloyd Wright's drawings at the Chrysler Museum in Norfolk or to an AIA Chapter lecture in Richmond. He was consumed with being an architect and just as passionate about being successful. If Symone needed to talk to him, she always found him studying. If he wasn't in his room at Harkness Hall, most times she located him in the departmental studio. There she found him working meticulously to design his projects and to perfect his drawing or drafting techniques. Almost every night he was there. So devoted was Billy to his goal that sometimes he didn't shave or shower for a few days when he needed to complete a project.

Subtly cocky but obviously smart and confident, Billy won all kinds of awards in college, a truly astounding number of honors at Hampton, and he was considered a prize to be had by the other girls on campus. He was on the dean's list, a Phi Beta Sigma man, and on the Who's Who List. During his fourth year and because he had the best design average, Billy received the Bonnie and Anthony Johns Award as well as an Alpha Rho Chai Scholar his fifth year. His all-around pleasant attitude and his leadership qualities snagged that honor. The year he won, he was also the president of the AIA Student Chapter and a recipient of the Henry Adams AIA Medal his fifth year, too. He was elected the student representative of NOMA, the National Organization of Minority Architects. The list of accomplishments was endless.

Symone was a dean's list student her four years at Hampton too, but she couldn't keep track of all the national honor societies into which Billy was inducted. Such honors were bestowed as a result of his consummate dedication to his major. When Billy completed his five- year curriculum at Hampton, he was judged the top in his class and was bestowed the Award for the Best Thesis in the Department of Architecture. It didn't stop there. He even received The Presidential Award, an award that was given to the highest ranking graduating student at Hampton for that year. To know that Billy had earned such an illustrious award along with all the others impressed the hell out of the Poussaint Family.

After graduation, Billy could have garnered a plumb, high paying job anywhere he chose. And he consequently received numerous offers from the powerhouse architectural firms throughout the country, from New York to California, but he turned them all down. He had other plans on his mind, and that was to receive his MBA degree. Billy knew the business degree would provide him the additional, powerful corporate ammunition necessary to operate his own firm in North Carolina, so he decided to attend Wharton. That was the business school of his dreams. Since Symone was accepted at Harvard, Dartmouth, and the University of Pennsylvania's business schools, her three uncles wanted her to attend Harvard. And, initially she was going to. But when Billy chose Wharton, Symone changed her mind about heading to Harvard and chose to attend school with him.

Before Billy and Symone graduated from Hampton and after they met in Old Gym that first day, they dated for six months. During that time, Billy romanced her like a blue-blooded Romeo champion. Very artistically inclined, Billy loved inviting Symone to art shows, to the opera, and to plays during his spare time. Oftentimes, while they strolled around on Hampton's sprawling and lovely historical campus, he would grab her hand and walk her down to the waterfront. With the oak and maple tree leaves crunching underneath their shoes and the Hampton River or the Chesapeake Bay waves crashing upon the shores, he quietly shared his dreams with her. His need to make good back in his native North Carolina was deeply rooted. His ultimate desire to not only make his poor, hard-working parents proud, but his sincere passion to also be immortalized in his small town of Tarboro made him driven, even at a young age.

Symone always listened intently to his aspirations although she told him very little about herself as well. She shared with him her marketing career visions and a fake flowery version of her past days in Trinidad. She never mentioned the Poussaint's Family wealth or her affiliation with the famous Eisners. Always sensitive about her family's wealth, that was nothing new. No one on campus was aware of it either. She refused even to tell her roommate or the other girls who lived in Twitchell Hall. Symone simply wanted her college friends to merely like her for her intelligence and her sharp wit. Many times, Uncle Samuel took Symone to school in his private jet. If Uncle Samuel was busy when Symone was home for break and if he wanted to spend a special day with her, the two would take a slow limousine ride to Hampton from New York. During those times, Symone politely asked him to take her as far as Yorktown, Virginia, a small town fifteen miles from the college. From there she would take a Greyhound bus to Hampton. She was very careful about people knowing how much money she actually possessed, and she didn't want her wealth to be the common denominator for her meeting and having friends.

When Symone finally decided to go to bed with Billy in the seventh month of their friendship, Billy's lovemaking simply changed her world. For the first time in her life, making love was an absolutely overwhelming and powerfully awesome experience. Period. And that was the only way Symone could even describe the sexual relationship in her many intimate letters to Hazele. Billy could make fulfilling love, and Symone climaxed each and every time they were together. Just to even think about Billy or mention his name, Symone would wet her panties. With Billy, climaxing was Symone's ultimate birthright. It was a given. Oral sex, straight up and down sex, and the missionary position. Every which way he twisted her, it didn't matter. She climaxed religiously. It happened over and over again.

First, Symone was shocked. Then she fell crazily in love. While at Hampton, she blew through at least twenty-five fine Black men searching for Mister Right. Symone ran into only one potential good lover named Briscoe Jones, who was considered one of the most popular basketball players on campus. But Billy was a hundred times better than Briscoe. Billy was a Black man born to make good Black love to women. Those other men Symone dealt with were deadbeat college studs who still hadn't figured out that making love was more than bumping back and forth on a woman's stomach. However, William Jared Butler, Jr. won her mind and her heart. He was her Black Crown Jewel, and Symone decided she wanted him and only him as a husband.

No doubt, both Uncle Willie and Uncle Cecil saw the lovestruck expression all over Symone's face. And on the day of her wedding, they merely told Symone what any good trustee concerned about family assets should share with a young heir. Even though Symone was taught to not discuss the secrecy of the trust with outsiders, the uncles noticed their niece's utter vulnerability with this young man. Who knew what family financial secrets Symone eventually would have divulged to Billy? Willie and Cecil knew she was in love.

When she brought him home to New York, there was no question about how much Symone adored Billy. Although Symone was known to be one of the most levelheaded young ladies in the Poussaint family, the uncles also understood how she quietly sought the approval of husbandly love, of a good man. They knew she wanted someone she could love and call her own, and that she was silently screaming out to be loved and accepted for herself, especially after the abusive childhood love she received from Honeyboy.

While Symone's siblings and cousins searched for appropriate suitors, she continually heard her uncles amusingly say that love made people do unusual and unpredictable things. Those crazy decisions especially occurred during those sexually, passionate moments when they could possibly lose their mind and reveal the Poussaint family's long-cherished financial and trust secrets. Or as Scott often called his personal secrets, his Achilles Heel. That wouldn't be the case with Symone. On Symone's wedding day for some reason, the verbal charge from Uncle Willie became branded like a lightning rod in the abyss of Symone's soul.

Years later when Symone's marriage to Billy began to falter, it was then she truly appreciated the magnitude of Uncle Willie's advice for trust and asset secrecy. It definitely was her savior during their bitter divorce battle. When Billy and his attorneys attempted to investigate Symone's financial portfolio, they continued to bang up against steel lined, double laid brick walls. On the other hand and since Symone's power attorneys hired top notched private detectives, her legal team secured explicit video footage and still photographs which graphically described Billy's adulterous ways with several other women. The judge awarded Symone the house in Clemmons. To top it off, Billy was required to dole over hefty alimony and child support payments.

A heartbroken Symone still was considerate. As Billy's wife and since he wasn't educated on how to successfully hide his burgeoning assets, she was eligible to attach almost fifty percent of Billy's multi-million dollar and highly profitable architectural company, The Butler Group. Yet during the legal haggling, Symone was still nice that day in the attorney's office. She decided to relinquish the fifty percent ownership for herself. Symone stipulated that all of her ownership claims be passed to her three children. To protect the profit interest of her children and to ensure they would not be cheated of their just fifty percent share, she demanded that independent audits often be prepared on The Butler Group in the event Billy attempted to filter profits elsewhere. And in Symone's opinion, Billy still hadn't recovered from the smoothly maneuvered financial ass whipping.

Still fuming over the conversation with Billy, Symone glanced at the clock. It was eight forty-five, and the children had been in bed for fifteen minutes. Symone knew her three babies were waiting for her. It was time to read Sylvia and Kyle a short bedtime story and tuck them into bed. Then she needed to go talk and read to Jared, spend a little quality time with him before he went to bed. Symone stood and stretched her hands above her head several times. Her body felt stiff and tired from the angry words she slung at Billy. Why couldn't her ex-husband see her point about spending time with the children?

Symone sat back down on the bed and studied the old photograph of Lennious for a brief eternity. When she was angry, sometimes just watching her twin brother's young, cheerful, and innocent face calmed her spiraling shattering emotions. As Symone frustratingly rubbed her eyes and temple, she considered calling Alex. She suddenly realized the entire Devereaux family was enjoying an evening listening to the Winston-Salem Symphony at the Stevens Center. Pecola and Carlos was busy entertaining Carlos' cousin visiting from Arizona. Scott was out of town with Charmaine and wasn't due in until later. So was Rozelle. Just like always. She wondered where the hell were her friends when she absolutely needed to talk to them.

Symone sat on her bed for no more than five minutes when the phone rang again. Grudgingly, she picked it up on the first ring and answered hello in an extremely perturbed voice.

"...And, another thing. Don't call my ass no damn more if your men don't take care of your shit, *Ms. Freak,*" Billy furiously yelled the pet name he often called her when they were married.

"You low down dirty ass. That was the last time I'll call you for sex, Billy. You can believe that, *Mr. Freak,*" she hissed her pet name for him back.

"Yeah, I bet. You'll never find a man to fuck you the way I do, Symone. That's why your ass is so damn miserable now. You ain't getting the right kind of dick."

"That's not it, Billy. The man I wanted wasn't available. He was out of town. You can believe you were my gutter choice of last and final resorts."

"Sy, I may have been your last resort, but you sucked my dick off like I was a first choice big beef damn hot-dog," he said sarcastically with a loud laugh. "I'll take that kind of final resort treatment any day. You can't find another nigger no way like me. I know what it takes to please your sex-crazed ass. I know what it takes, baby. I could always rock your damn world. Ain't nothing changed. Ain't no new rules. You'll call me again."

"Hell no I won't either."

"I know you. I know what you want better than you know your damn self. You'll call," he added with cocky, sneering confidence.

"I won't."

"Yes you will, and I'll give it to you like I always do," he said smugly.

"I know me too, Billy. You're dreaming."

"You're just like a boomerang, baby. Pure and simple. Constantly groveling on your knees to your ex-husband for sex. The man you always tell everyone that you supposedly love to hate. You'll call me again, baby. I'll stake my damn life and my company on that, and I won't be risking shit either. I know your freaky ass. You'll call me."

"No hell, I won't. You just wait and see, Billy Butler. You just wait and damn fucking see!" Symone repeated angrily as she hung up the phone on him.

Chapter Seventy-Three

Pecola and Carlos' cousin had been back in her private office from lunch for about an hour. Just chitchatting and reminiscing about how things had changed in Greensboro since he had left the city as a young man over twenty years ago, the two laughed constantly. Bradley Kelly Reynolds was Carlos' second cousin on his father's side and now lived in Arizona. Twenty-one years ago, his parents moved to Phoenix. Although his parents visited North Carolina for family reunions and other gatherings, Bradley hadn't been back as often since they left the state. It seemed as if Bradley, Carlos, and Pecola were always missing each other. When Bradley was in North Carolina, Carlos and Pecola were always out of town or vice versa.

"...Pecola, this has been real. I'm telling you. It's great to see your building. Your furniture. Everything is laid out. Man, this is top drawer," he exclaimed as he continued to gaze around Pecola's lavishly furnished office. She had just taken him on a tour of the entire building, and he was thoroughly mesmerized with the apparent efficient operation of both companies. The building reeked of success.

"Thanks a lot, honeychile. Well, with my furniture, you know how I just love mixing antique items from various centuries, chile."

Pecola spoke proudly and delicately sipped coffee from a fine bone china cup edged in twenty-four carat gold. To show off further for Bradley, Pecola asked the dining room staff to specifically serve them with her favorite Victorian pattern. She carefully placed the cup in the saucer and again amusingly watched Bradley's amazed expression. Of course, Pecola knew he was impressed. Everyone that stepped into her office was enchanted with the museum quality of her interior decorating. That wasn't anything unusual. More than anyone else that she knew, she was aware she personified elegance and good taste. She knew she simply had an exquisite eye when it came to selecting decorative items for her home and for her office. So in Pecola's typical confident almost cocky manner, she expected people to have a drop mouth reaction to the timeless elegance of it all. How could they not? It was obvious the furnishings were breathtaking and classily stylish, expensive, and beautiful. The way visitors reacted to the lush fabrics, her beautiful antiques, and other personal items she had collected over the years which were strategically scattered throughout the office on the different furniture surfaces continued to gratify her ego, too.

Pecola delighted in how Bradley's eyes slowly moved around the softly colored creme walls and how he quietly admired the original artwork. Tastefully placed around the spacious, very light, very airy corner office was her great collection of works by artists Dwayne Crockett, Ed Halessie, Leo Rucker, Paul Goodnight, and Paul Roseboro. Atop each table on either side of the couch were Marbro swirled crystal lamps, pictures of family, and porcelain objets d'art. When she met with clients, Pecola sat majestically behind a lovely antique Italian square desk and graciously negotiated business deals. Five Venetian chairs upholstered in damask like salmon silk encircled the small conference table by the window. Bradley's gaze suddenly fell upon the bronze statue in the corner. As was the reaction with everyone who observed it, Bradley smiled when he saw the bronze bust of Pecola. He shook his head and began laughing. Before he spoke, Bradley checked his gold Audemars Piguet watch.

"I got to be sliding out of here soon, baby. Need to stop in Greensboro first for an important pow-wow. After that, I might head over to Danville, Virginia to check some buddies out and buy a lottery ticket."

"Good luck."

"Thanks, baby. I mean to tell you. You got the corporate thang going on like a pot of neck bones. You're a tough lady," Bradley said as he rubbed the side of his thighs with both hands and leaned forward to stare into her face.

Hell, I know that. Tell me something I don't know, Pecola thought with bright eyes and a wide grin.

"Come on now, Bradley. You're trying to give me the big head or something?" she asked as she batted her eyes in a modest manner. A rarity for her. She politely sipped more coffee. "You know how twenty years ago I used to help Carlos and his family design and decorate homes and office buildings. I guess it's still in my system."

"I ain't lyin'. It sure is, cuz. I mean big time, too." Bradley slapped his thighs and laughed loudly. "That's right. I keep forgetting you got your degree in architectural engineering from A&T. An MBA from A&T, too. Umph. Umph. Umph. Bad, bad girl."

"Sure did, honeychile." Pecola proudly pointed to her framed BS and Master's degrees hanging on the wall. "I want them around me all the time to remind me of the blood, sweat, tears, and pure divine suffering I went through to get those d-grees. Especially with four children to take care of, it was hard as hell."

"Well, I know your parents are proud of all their children. Ezunial, Pauletta, and you girl. Wow! I *know* they're proud of you. When you and Carlos were dating back in high school, I used to love to come to your house with him. Girl, your mama cooked the best damn collard greens and finger lickin' Sunday after church barbecue chicken. You *know* Miss Oseola sho did. Remember her candy yammms? You know how I loved her sweet potato pies. Wooo! It was screaming, baby. The chitlins. Wooo! They were always cutting up."

"Uh, yes I do remember," Pecola answered snobbishly with a raised head and a very patrician expression.

"Hell, you know *I* know *you* know. I told you how Carlos, Rico, and me glided by your parents' farm the same day I slid into town. At first, Mr. Rufus didn't remember who I was. When I reminded him I was Big Bubba Slim, he looked at me for a long while. My nickname came back to him, and Mr. Rufus hugged my neck like I was his son. Aw man, your parents are sweet, old-fashioned people, girl."

"I know."

"I told Miss Oseola that I ain't never been able to find a woman like her who could cook that good, ole, home-made bread and those yellow cakes from scratch. Those cakes were moist like velvet, baby. I ain't never known your mama, Miss Oseola, to ever cook nothing that came out of a can, girl." He paused briefly and gazed quickly around the office again. "You've come a long way, Pecola. Got it going on like popcorn, too. I knew you when you didn't have..." As Bradley spoke anxiously with pride, Pecola smiled sweetly.

Pecola quickly glanced away from him and hoped he didn't attempt to rehash that *I knew you when* conversation again. She stared at her half-opened office door. Just never knew who would be listening. Since Bradley had been visiting with her and Carlos, that's all he talked about. Twenty-five year old shit. Pecola was tired of hearing it. This wasn't twenty-five years ago. It was now. She wanted to focus on the present. Not the past. Pecola wanted to focus on how *she* was now thoroughly entrenched in the world of the socially eminent and the socially prosperous. She wanted to focus on the Pecola she had created.

"...Hell, I thought I enjoyed hanging out with Carlos and Rico at their offices. When Rico took me to Robinson's in downtown Greensboro, and I had hog brains with scrambled eggs for breakfast on Monday morning, I knew I was back in North Carolina, baby. But your place here in Winston-Salem is it." He pulled on his monogrammed shirt cuffs and absentmindedly twirled one of his fourteen-karat gold African Adinkra symbol cuff links for a moment.

"Oh, Bradley."

"If I didn't have a job I love, I damn guarantee you I could work with you here forever. The mood is right. A little Stanley Turrentine on the CD. I still can't believe how you remembered he was my favorite jazzman, girl. This building is awesome, and the CR Group built it? My man, Carlos? And Rico? What can I say?" He shrugged and held up both hands.

The light conversation continued through the playing of an entire Marion Meadows CD. Ivenue, from the dining room, stepped in to see if everything was ok. Pecola politely said everything was fine. But Bradley did request she bring another soda. His fifth one. Pecola believed he had talked so much that his mouth was probably dry as hell.

When Symone returned from meeting with Alex and Scott in Greensboro, she walked toward Pecola's office and saw that the door was slightly ajar. The three chairs in front of Pecola's desk were empty, and Symone assumed she was in there by herself. She didn't notice the man sitting on the couch. With a huge smile gracing her face, Symone strolled in to share the funny jokes Alex had everyone laughing about over lunch.

"...Excuse me. I couldn't tell you had a client," Symone said, genuinely surprised and looked at Pecola for some indication of who the gentleman was. Bradley stood up. Symone dropped her leather valise, folders, and the many pink telephone forms received from the receptionist on Pecola's desk and extended her hand into his large outstretched one.

"Symone Poussaint, I'd like for you to meet Bradley Kelly Reynolds." Pecola spoke with a huge, smug smile on her face. "Bradley, this is my business partner and my friend. You know the other one I told you so much about and said that you had to meet since—"

"Yes, I know. I remember what you said," he answered quietly, interrupting Pecola as he subtly and carefully devoured Symone's entire body with his penetrating stare. He was thoroughly overwhelmed and enormously fascinated with her beautiful face. Carlos and Rico were quite accurate about their vivid description of her. Pecola continued speaking in an animated voice.

"Last night, Symone," Pecola laughed quickly as she looked at her prettily polished nails. "Scott even joked you were the last, missing other Blue Belle. You met Alex last night, Bradley. She's the second Blue Belle. Since I'm the lead singer and all," Pecola laughed pretentiously again and batted her eyes. "You know that's why they told you I'm the first one. The lead singer just like Patti..."

Damn! thought Symone. *This brother is fine as hell.*

While Pecola was babbling on in an unusually strange voice about trivial stuff, Symone and Bradley shook hands for several long seconds. Symone made sure she gripped his hand real tight and quite firm. Bradley gazed into Symone's eyes and began to slowly nod his head with a knowing expression.

"It's *indeed* my pleasure to meet you. I've heard nothing but absolutely wonderful, wonderful things about you, Symone," he said sexily with a smatter of professionalism. "Great handshake, too."

"Pleasure to meet you, Bradley."

Damn! You got a great handshake your own self. Nice smile and large hands which according to my past experiences equates to a big dick, Symone thought with a straight face. Interrupting the silent eye language between the two, Pecola cleared her throat and spoke in a quiet voice.

"Remember, Symone? I *told* you. This is Carlos' cousin from Phoenix, Arizona."

"Yes. You did tell me he would be in this week. I had completely forgotten he was coming here today." Symone's tone was businesslike. She stared at Bradley again who boldly stared back.

"Symone, I was looking forward to finally meeting you last night," Bradley said looking down into Symone's face. He continued to nod his head slowly.

Last night? Symone thought rapidly for a moment. "Uh huh, yes. That's right. On Tuesday night. I'm sorry I couldn't make it. We had just gotten back in town from Augusta on Monday. I was pooped and needed to be Mummy again."

"Last night at dinner," Bradley said. "Everyone there said that I shouldn't leave Winston until I met you."

"Really? Who said that?" Symone asked in a pleasant, suspicious voice.

"Chile, you know? The regulars. Alex, Scott, Madison, Darilyn, Rozelle, and Cleopatra said it. That's who, chile. You know how your play brothers Carlos and Rico adore you to death, Symone. Those two had been giving Bradley the total four-one-one about you all week long. I think the only thing they left out the description was your shoe size." Pecola explained excitedly through proper sips of coffee.

"They were right," Bradley added with a handsome grin on his face as he clasped his hands in front of him. "Totally, right. I shouldn't have left until I had a chance to meet you."

"Want some coffee, Symone?" Pecola asked in a somewhat high-pitched, shrill voice. Symone turned around to glance briefly at Pecola who was sitting behind her ornate desk watching the scene with a strange, overly dignified expression on her face. Symone shook her head no.

"What about some of my soda, Symone?" Bradley asked good-naturedly and pointed to the three bottles of RC Cola chilling in the silver bucket.

"Thanks a lot. But no," Symone mumbled quickly and gazed away from him.

What was going on here? Symone thought. Why was she acting like a dumbstruck high school girl? Symone normally wasn't the one to react this way, especially when a good-looking Black man was staring dead in her face. She took great pride in not being weak to a soulfully seductive Black man. But, it was something quite interesting about this one, though. Symone moved her head slightly again and couldn't keep her eyes from sneaking a glance at him. He looked like he was about forty to forty-three years old and stood about six four. That's what was doing it to her—his height, his creamy brown skin, and pearly brown eyes.

Bradley had a closely cropped fade haircut, juicy lips, chiseled cheekbones, and dark brown eyes. Symone noticed how muscles softly protruded through his fashionable clothes. He wore a black European suit with a white Nehru cuff link shirt, black Italian soft leather shoes, and black silk socks. She could tell that his shoes were definitely Italian. When it came to men, she was an expert on things like that. As she gave Bradley an intense five-second review, she noticed gold. The thick identification bracelet on his left wrist and the gold wedding band on the third finger. How the hell did Pecola neglect to tell her he was married? How did she miss it? He was too finnne—couldn't see everything at once.

Damn, damn, damn! Oh well. This brother is already taken. Since I don't deal with married guys, move right along, Symone thought with a blank expression.

"I'll talk to you later, Pecola. Ok? Let me go, girl. I got to plow through this work," she explained quickly in a good-humored voice as she gathered up her things and pointed to her valise. "Since I'll be out of town tomorrow, you know I got a lot to do, girl."

Symone turned to Bradley who was scrutinizing her with inviting eyes. She refused to return the invitational gaze. Instead, she spoke firmly and graciously.

"Nice meeting you, Bradley," Symone added and whirled abruptly to go into her office.

When Bradley left about ninety minutes later, it was six forty-five. Pecola came into Symone's office and plopped her tired body on the couch. Trying to impress folks took a lot of strength out of her, and she was ready to take an entire bottle of multi-vitamins to rejuvenate her energy level for the work that needed completing before she left to go home. The soft calming sounds of the Neville Brothers were floating out of Symone's office CD player. During Symone's meeting in Greensboro, Scott gave the CD to her. He told her to pay special attention to the vocals of Aaron Neville on the first five tracks. Since she was feeling her usual stressed out self, he believed it would definitely help her to relax.

"Chile, chile, chile, this has been a day in more ways than one," Pecola said tiredly and patted her perfect hair bun in place.

Symone nodded intelligently as if she were thoroughly interested in the conversation. Pecola raised her eyebrows and gazed at Symone, who appeared disinterested. Pecola proceeded to select a mint out of the candy dish.

"Carlos' cousin, I should say your cousin too, is fine, but—" Symone studied the various notes from Elisha.

"You're right. It's a big damn but. Chile, he's married," Pecola finished with a laugh.

"I know. I noticed the anchor of gold around his finger. But I can still look at him." She spoke in a matter of fact tone as she opened a sealed envelope.

"Bradley was definitely smitten with you, though." Pecola watched her closely.

"Most men are," Symone said jokingly as she scanned the various confidential notes from Ted that she removed from the envelope. "No. I was just kidding, girl. I could tell. He gave me enough eye messages in those few seconds. I could've sent a damn telegram to Europe. I sure thought he was fine as hell until I saw the wedding band."

Pecola laughed and kicked her shoes off. She folded her legs underneath her.

"I know, chile. He's not leaving until Friday night. I tried to get him to stay until Sunday or come back next week."

"Next week?"

"Yeah. He's leaving here on Friday and heading to Memphis. From there to DC, back to Charlotte to order some suits and shirts from Checkmate International, then back to Phoenix." She hesitated slightly and glanced at her watch. "After he left Charlotte, I figured he could come back here. We all could hang out, especially since Haneef is coming home. He hasn't seen my youngest son since he was a baby."

"Ok. I see why you said he should come back next week. Makes sense."

"Bradley can't do it. Said he had to get back home to his woman."

"Which one?"

"His wife, of course. Now honeychile, aren't you a bad girl? Saying things like that about someone you don't know. But then, Bradley is bad too." Pecola breathed in deeply. "You know what he asked me?"

"What?"

"He wanted to know that if he invited you to dinner tonight, did I think you would go out with him?" She watched Symone. "Chile, I told him hell no. That you categorically didn't deal with married men."

"Told him right, girl," Symone replied hastily as she remembered her ex-husband's disrespectful behavior to her while they were married.

When Symone considered putting another sister through what she had been through with Billy, she vowed to herself she would never deal with a married man. To stay away from them. Period. Behind every married man was a sister. All too often, Symone believed women never put a face on those women, the married men's wives. If they did, maybe the other women would act better and tell those philandering men to go straight to hell. Symone shook her head and began scribbling notes.

"Pecola, It seems lately that all the men who proposition me for dates are married men," Symone mumbled. "If they want to date, they should've never gotten married. They need to get divorced or something."

"You know the old saying. Men want it all. The cow and the milk. That applies to women nowadays, too. I'm convinced it's an epidemic that's spreading like cancer nowadays. Scott said that he's been approached by more married women than ever before. Carlos, too. Sometimes while I'm standing right beside him, chile."

Symone breathed deeply and thought about what Pecola said. She started to say something. Then she paused, as if something profound was coming out of her mouth.

"You know Pecola, when you told me Carlos' cousin was coming from Arizona, I was expecting him to be light-skinned like Carlos. I was shocked to see he was a pretty dark man. He's sooo chocolate like a good old Hershey Kisses Candy."

"He's nice to look at. Isn't he? And he's dark too, chile." Pecola selected another piece of candy. "The last time we saw Bradley, it was every bit twenty years ago."

"Damn, girl! Why so long?"

"We never could hook up. You know how people lose touch. He left North Carolina to go to Langston University in Oklahoma on a basketball scholarship. Only college to give him one, too. From there, he went to business school at Krannert."

Symone stopped moving papers around her desk for a moment. "In West Lafayette, Indiana, right? That's Purdue University's business school."

"You go, girl. You know your business schools."

Symone shrugged casually. "I only know about it because that's where my Uncle Willie's daughter thought about going. Cousin Della wanted to attend school on the other side of the United States, that is in perspective to New York so she wouldn't be so close to the family."

"Hell, I still hadn't heard of it until Bradley. After graduate school, Bradley worked in Hawaii for five years, divorced his wife, and headed back to Arizona to be near his parents. He's been there ever since working in advertising. He's a corporate senior vice president or something. Without question, he's big time now and got serious bank. You know he actually bought him a candy red Corvette while he was here."

"Great car for an older guy."

"Hmmm. It's a wonderful car for any woman."

"Exactly."

"I hope he doesn't think he's gonna leave it parked at my house." Pecola stopped speaking and used her finger to pry out the glob of candy that was stuck to her teeth. "He and Carlos hadn't hooked up in years. I mean many years, chile. But while he was here, they hit it off like old friends. They were always real tight in high school." Pecola dug deeper in her mouth. "So you're think he's fine, huh?"

"Yeah he is. Fine as hell, girl. He kinda reminded me of Scott and is a bonafide Hershey's candy bar. The way he dressed and his whole appearance thang was striking."

Pecola began to bob her head in agreement. "Now that you mentioned it, there are some similarities. You know what? That's right, chile. Come to think about it, Cleopatra said the same thing last night."

"I don't doubt it."

"He's just as smooth as Scott. Boy, he treated Cleopatra like a queen, bragging about her cooking and hugging her. He doesn't even know her. The way he carried on, you would've thought Cleopatra was the hostess for my dinner instead of the cook. It blew my mind, chile." Symone smiled to herself and continued writing informational notes to three staff people.

"Ummm-hmmm." Symone moaned to simply let Pecola know she was at least listening.

"You're crazy, chile. A Hershey Kisses bar." Pecola chuckled at the comparison. "I done told you. Carlos' family has two shades. Light-skinned people like us and dark-skinned ones like Bradley. There are no in-betweens. Because they all look alike, it's the most amazing thing to see the difference in complexions."

"That's what surprised me, too." Symone turned to look out of the office window for a moment.

"Another thing, Sy. You wouldn't want him after you *really* met him," Pecola informed with much drama in her voice.

"I wouldn't want him anyway," she said suddenly, turning away from the window to look at Pecola. "He's married. Just like you told him, I don't deal with married men. Bradley was indeed good to look at, but that's where it stops for me. What else has he done, though?" Symone asked as she shuffled notes and files on her desk.

"Well, Bradley's married to a sister. It's his second marriage, chile. But he acts as if he sees stars in blonde, blue eyed faces," Pecola said disgustedly.

"Get out of here! *White girls?*" Symone asked coolly in disbelief. Pecola nodded. "Lord, that would be such a waste for a fine brother like that. You're right. Just thinking about it makes me sick. Let me erase him from my computer bank of fine assed chocolate men." Symone made all kinds of hand movements and beep bleep computer sounds around her head.

"How innovative, girl. My life should be so easy to erase."

"Ok. He's been deleted," laughed Symone freely and Pecola smiled at her.

"I'm just glad you didn't go out to lunch with us. The man definitely would've turned your stomach. I let him know how I felt about it. Most Black men and women in America would've been proud of me. You too, girl! That's what kinda scared me. I sounded just like a cross between you and Booker T."

"What did you say, Pecola?" Symone asked with a small grin.

There was a very long pause as Pecola thought about the conversation she had with Bradley over lunch. She breathed deeply.

"Hell, the question is what didn't I say. I don't even know where to begin, chile."
Pecola went on to tell her what Bradley did at lunch and what she told him.

"...As we were talking, Bradley's eyes continually left me and followed white girls as they walked by. I don't believe I felt jealousy. If I weren't married to someone like Carlos and Bradley was my main man and this happened while I was talking to him, then my attitude would've been serious to deal with."

"I can dig that, girl."

Pecola smiled. "Get this, Symone. I told him that as a sister, sometimes we don't have a lot nowadays. If we have a man that loves all women no matter what color, it's worse. It's like someone being bi-sexual. I used Bradley's behavior as an opportunity to find out about him, how he had changed since I last saw him, and I guess to find out a little bit about me, too. Now you know Carlos doesn't deal with white women."

"No kidding?" Symone asked jokingly with a smirk. "I didn't know that about your husband."

"Let me finish, girl. I'm trying to build a scene here. Anyway, I asked Bradley if he was attracted to white women. Of course, he said no. You know how our Black men always deny it—that blunt question to their Black women faces sometimes. Yet, they are sliding around all over town with them. Guess what he *did* say, Symone? That's what blew my mind."

"What he say?" Symone just wanted her to get to the point, and Pecola always tried to share stories with such drama.

"He told me that with the way a lot of the sisters are and the way they act sometimes, he doesn't blame the brothers for leaving Black women alone. Keep in mind, he told me his friends talked that shit. Maybe he was ashamed to tell me the real deal, especially when he saw me break it on down like I didn't want to hear that from him. So, I was shocked from his comments. I couldn't believe he was saying what he said. But it didn't stop there. Bradley said that he believes Black women are always dictatorial, loud, obnoxious, and that they always want Black men to be sexually powerful. The way they portray them in the media. And that white women got their act together. They're calmer and don't expect a whole lot from them."

"Oh no. Puhleeze don't tell me he said that, girl." Symone was more disappointed than angry.

"I'm telling you. Wait. I'm not finished, honeychile. I got sooo fucking mad, but I took a deep breath. That's when I believe you jumped into my body. I went off on him and took him back through history. I asked Bradley did white women have to keep living after their babies were ripped from their arms at birth? Then, they were given another baby to breast-feed after having to watch their child being taken away to be sold under another slave master—never to be seen again?"

"I know, girl."

"Or was this same white woman ever taken away during her wedding night to be raped by the white slave owner before she was ever touched by the Black man she loved? Feeling so dirty that she never felt good enough for the man she loved and for the man who loved her? I told him that rape is a deep thing. Although it happens in a quick moment, the memory of it soils you for a lifetime."

Symone stopped working and gazed into Pecola's face. "You go, girl."

Pecola nodded. "I told Bradley now supposed her Black man tried to fight back in an attempt to defend his woman's honor, his family, his integrity, his manhood, and his mere sanity. And this same Black woman watched her man be brutally taken away from the family. He was viciously buried alive with his head above the ground as they poured honey over his face next to an anthill. Has this same white woman ever seen her daughter's stomach sliced open and watched her grandchild's lifeless body drop to the dusty ground? Not atall. After I broke it down to Bradley like that, his mouth was wide open, honeychile."

"I bet it was."

"So I explained to Bradley that he's got to look beyond the stereotypes of what he heard about sisters and ask himself some honest questions. It's those same questions a lot of Black women ask their man and themselves. Why are we frustrated when our man leaves at night? It's hard out there for the Black man, Symone. You know it. The policemen are out there.

Then there's crime, joblessness, drugs, and pressure. You know the deal. Even though Carlos and I look prosperous, he still gets stopped all the damn time when he's driving my BMW. That's a common occurrence for well-to-do Black men."

"Bradley knows it, too. But he sounds like he's someone that can't see problems in other places cause he has made it big."

"I told him that it's a huge myth about Black women being hard. We're women who are hard and soft but just bursting with love."

"Absolutely."

"Our strength is being misinterpreted. So you do get the stereotype that Black women are too cold. That we're too hard. But hell, we've had to develop a muscle of nonchalantness. Nourish our backbone to survive throughout the generations. Through hundred of years, we had to learn to live with pain, squelch the tears, then cry alone in the dark night. It's perceived that we don't care or we're too hard on a brother because we ask them to spend time with us. Spend time with the kids. Don't stay out late. Don't get high. Pay the bills. Puhleeze don't fight me, Black man. Make love to us. Just hold me. Without question, being responsible and loving is an aphrodisiac."

"While you were saying all of this, what did he say, Pecola?"

"Nothing, chile. He just kept staring me in my face. I definitely had his undivided attention. It was a different Pecola for him to see. I told Bradley that it was a known and documented damn fact that brothers weren't allowed to be a man in front of his family. He had to turn the other cheek and allow his wife to be raped. He had to watch his wife be touched by another man, by the white man. Then watch his Black woman bring this same white's man seed into the world. He had to watch this child that he wasn't the father of become a part of his household."

"Umph. I know."

"Then the villainous origin of the child was always there to remind him—to slap him dead in the face again." Pecola took a deep breath and sadly shook her head. "Symone, sometimes I do see why you say people don't want to know our history. It does hurt. Just remembering what I said to Bradley makes me feel extremely sad. I couldn't have lived back then."

"It's easy to say that now."

"There's no way, Sy. I told Mr. Bradley that the Black sisters remind many brothers about the pain of their reality of being Black, of his own blackness, of the anguish, and of the reality of the Black woman's strength."

"I'm proud of you, Pecola." Symone leaned back in her chair and began chewing on the tip of her pen.

"So, when our Black man makes it, I told him that he now believes the prize is the white woman. That's his ultimate trophy. The sign that he's not Black anymore. But try as he might, white America is still gonna see his color. That's why I told Bradley I try to listen to Booker T's advice when he tells the young people to check out the Muslims. Notice the way they carry themselves in the streets. You know I don't endorse everything Muslims do. Quite frankly, I think it's a chauvinistic religion."

"Me too, girl. At least what I've read about their practices."

"But I do appreciate the dedication of the Fruit of Islam. You know if they don't do anything else, they definitely show discipline in the streets. Here in Winston-Salem and all over the United States, they don't have a problem with telling an almost naked sister the truth. If a woman is wearing practically nothing, looking like a pure divine slut, they'll set her straight by telling her, 'Sister you need to put some clothes on. You look like you could be a beautiful Black queen, but I couldn't tell with the little bit of clothes you got on, my sister.'" Symone began laughing. So did Pecola.

"You're right, girl. They do that now," Symone nodded. "Still, I need to do more research on them. Read some of their books, especially the ones Booker T keeps pushing on me."

"When a sister walks by those Muslim brothers on the street, he has one thing on his mind, and that is maintaining a respectful posture for Allah. Their goal is to sell their wares, their newspapers, preach their religion, and try to get new converts. Remember how Booker T told us how those Africans act who were from some part of West Africa and have vendor businesses on the streets of New York? When women try to flirt to get them to lower their prices, they ignore them. All those brothers want to know is this. 'My sister, are you going to buy or what?'"

"What was Bradley saying throughout all of this?"

"I'm telling you, Symone. He was just quiet with wide eyes. I told Bradley that this dedicated and focused behavior didn't apply to all West Africans and Muslims. What I was trying to get him to see was there are some focused, strong Black men out there that are well tuned. They're thinking they got to bring their other family members to the United States so that they can get opportunities. They're on a mission. They have a vision. In other words, they're letting folks know they haven't got time for games, chile. I told him that they're into business. And, they certainly don't deal with white women, at least in public. They know the deal."

"Giiiirrrrl, what did he say?"

"He asked me if I believe a Black woman could love a white man?"

"And what did you say?"

"I told him I thought it was slightly possible. But a sistah is no different from a brother, mind you. She would definitely have to work hard at it, chile. It wouldn't be natural in the beginning. If she closed her eyes to the realities of what or how her life would change as the result of the relationship with this person, it could be done, tentatively at first. Like every other thing one does in life, I guess it can become a habit, a norm, and after awhile a pattern. I told Bradley it certainly wasn't my cup of tea."

"What he say after that?"

Pecola began to laugh again. Symone sounded like a prosecuting attorney in a courtroom. "I'm telling you, girl. He didn't have much to say. I asked him if a white woman knows what it's like to walk beside a Black man who steps into an elevator, and the white women clutch their pocketbooks and stare the Black man up and down as if they're going to get mugged."

"Absolutely. I've been with a few and have seen it happen."

"Or does she know what it's like to walk down the street and hear car door locks clank shut cause a Black person passes by. Does she know the emotions wrapped up in that moment? Or does she know what's it like to be harassed by the police just because she's

Black? Or does she know how to take care of a Black baby's hair? It's the collective experiences of a whole race of people that a Black man and woman can share together. That is, if they know who they are."

"You said all of that to your long lost cousin?"

"Damn right. I just took this opportunity to school him on a lot of stuff."

"Giiirrrl, you were seriously out there, weren't you? You were definitely being a staunch advocate for the sanctity of the race. What did he say, P?"

"Yeah, I was out there further than normal, honeychile. Must've been the liquor I was drinking."

Symone laughed. "No what it is, is this. And, I've said it over and over again. The more you read, the more you learn. The wider your eyes are opened to the truth of who you are and who your ancestors are, you grow into the knowledge of what Black folks go through every day. Then when things rest in your spirit, you just gots to get it out. You know how I am. I'm not good at holding many things in. I got that bad habit of whatever comes up must come out."

"Hell, I know that, honeychile."

"So what did he say when you asked him about white women taking care of Black kids' hair?"

"I'm telling you," Pecola said and suddenly jumped up. "The brother was speechless through my little dissertation. Let me tell you the rest after I use the little girl's room. My stomach is bubbling." While holding her stomach, Pecola hurried into Symone's private bathroom.

"Make sure you close the door. Don't stink it up, either," Symone yelled and resumed reviewing various reports.

"...So you got a chance to meet her?" Carlos asked Bradley about Symone.

"Wooo is all I can say," Bradley moaned. "Umph, umph, umph, umph, umph."

"I know, man. It's as much about what's between her ears as it is what's below the neck."

"She's a sharp girl."

"I've seen her in action a number of times, and she makes the smartest man act dumb."

"Noooo doubt." Bradley licked his lips.

"Trust me on this. You can forget about hitting that one."

"Are you her pussy protector or what?"

"Quite the contrary, I'm her good friend. I just know she don't roll with married men, dog."

"C'mon, man," Bradley said from his car phone. "Put in a good word for me. You know how I like an excellent challenge."

"It ain't happening, Big Bubba Slim," Carlos said, packing papers into his briefcase.

"Ok. Ok. Ok. Forget about Symone for now," Bradley said quickly.

"Finally." Carlos laughed.

"Your secretary told me that you were working in the Greensboro office this afternoon. That's good, man. I'm rolling your way as we speak. I'm about ten miles from you. Gots me an important meeting with two executives. Two fiiinnne females. It's a big deal."

"Good luck, man."

"It ain't about luck, dog," Bradley laughed and changed gears in his new Corvette. "It's about me making thangs happen."

"Yeah, right." Carlos yawned.

"Wanna meet me at the Hilton and have a couple of drinks with them?"

"That's not possible."

"What you say?" Bradley said, suddenly turning down the volume on The Braxton Brothers CD. "I *thought* you said you couldn't make it. I had to shut the music off, man."

"You heard right, Big Bubba Slim. Maybe we can work things out next time."

"Wooo, man. You're getting old."

"That ain't got shit to do with it."

"C'mon, Carlos. These two ladies are familiar with your reputation in this neck of the woods. They even told me that they met you before at some First Friday shit and were impressed like hell with your reputation. Come on and meet me, man. I promise I'll give you one of the ladies as my welcome back home gift."

Carlos laughed again. "Nope. Can't do it. I'm heading home to cook a nice dinner for my wife, man."

"You been married too long, Blue."

"You ain't been married long enough. Just page me tonight when you're done," Carlos said, smiling. "I'll be home. Right now, I'm heading out of here."

"Where's Rico?"

"In his office."

"What about him?"

"He's worse than me, Bubba. He's going home to Darilyn and their kids." Carlos took a deep breath. "Hey, I got to call Pecola. Talk to you later, man."

"I'll page you, but it'll be late. Reaalll late. Bye, my man."

Carlos hung up the telephone, closed his briefcase, and glanced around his office. He thought about making another important phone call, but he decided against it. If he did, he might find himself staying out late again this evening and that definitely was out. Tonight, he decided he wasn't going to attend no meetings. He was taking his tired behind home. For the past four weeks, all he seemed to do was work, work, work, and he could tell Pecola was getting tired of it. He was getting tired of it, too.

Before Carlos left, he grabbed a fat cigar from his humidor to enjoy during the drive to Winston-Salem. He still considered making that last call. *Forget it, man. Leave the shit alone,* he thought wearily. *Call your wife.* Carlos reached for the phone to call Pecola, wondering if she was still in her office. Shaking his head no, Carlos decided he would call his wife when he got in his car.

"Whew," Pecola moaned after plopping back down on Symone's couch. "I don't know what that was about."

"Me neither," Symone mumbled. "Your ass is getting old, though. That's what happens when you turn forty. I just hope you didn't funk up my bathroom."

"My shit don't stink, chile."

"Ri-ight. Maybe not to Carlos. By the way, your husband called. He's going home. But he wanted to let you know he's cooking for you—mainly leftovers from yall's dinner last night."

"Isn't that sweet of my huzzband?"

"I thought so. Finish up the story with Bradley. I got things to do here before I head out myself."

"Well—" Pecola leaned back and crossed her legs. "I just told him to not give up on our Black women, Symone. With Black women, he could have a wide spectrum to chose from. From the dark, black midnight colored women, and—"

"I know, chile," Symone interrupted her. "Humph. Black midnight. You're talking about me, aren't you?"

"Honey chile, puhleeze. To the lightest light-skinned to the darkest of dark, we come in all colors. You don't have that choice with white women. They have the same grades of hair. It just comes in different colors with a variation of colored eyes. Other than that, they all have the same complexion. I told him that everything a white woman has, Black women have one-hundredfold and then some."

"You got that right. That's the biggest mystery of the universe. Where did the Black woman come from? They know we're the first people. In order for any human to be here, that person came through a Black woman."

"I didn't mention *all* that. I did tell him that with Black women, our eyes go from brown to green to hazel. There's light-light skin and all kinds of complexions to chose from. We have long hair. Short hair. No hair. Blonde hair. Black hair. Coarse hair. Nappy hair. Wavy, good hair." Pecola inhaled slowly. "I told Bradley that Black men and women didn't have to leave our race to control the complexion. You know that lie people tell about going outside the race cause they want children a certain color."

"*You* said that?" Pecola nodded victoriously. "Get out of here, girl."

"I'm serious, chile. Because of our diversity, I told him that planning the right complexion for our children can be controlled within the race."

"Pecola, this is too funny."

"I know. After Bradley finally shut his mouth, he picked his jaw up off the table and asked me if we have any white employees."

"What does that have to do with anything?"

"Who the hell knows, honeychile? I told him we did, and I left it at that. I said a few more things, and he leaned back in the booth and thought real hard for a moment. Then he told me I was full of it."

"Whaaat?"

Pecola was laughing now. "He sho nuff did. He said that Carlos and I had sooo much money that we wouldn't know what Black was our own damn self. He had the nerve to say that we're totally removed from the Black experience of what really goes on with Black folk who don't live in the lap of luxury. And that a whole lot of bull I was pushing his way sounded real good in theory—"

"Touché' for Bradley. That was a skillful comeback, girl. A punch below the belt for real."

"Yes, it was. Here I was running the deal down as I saw it. I guess he said to himself if I was going to break on him in such a way, then he would do the same thing. He would come out fighting."

"So what did you say after that?

"By then, I was tired of talking and was ready to eat. Since the waitress had just delivered our lunch, I munched on that for awhile. I just glared in his face and rolled my eyes."

"I guess that worked." Symone laughed quickly. "It normally gets folks' attention."

"Whew. After I rolled my eyes at him, broke it down as best as I could, Bradley was quiet for a few minutes while he ate his steak. Then he had another nerve to tell me I was being insensitive to the white women of America because some white women preferred Black men, and some Black men preferred white women. It was time for Black men to have their way with white ladies since traditionally it had been denied to them throughout the years. And that white women simply wanted an opportunity to love who they wanted and create businesses," Pecola explained as she reached into the fruit bowl and grabbed a bunch of seedless green grapes.

Symone jerked her eyes away from all the papers surrounding her desk and stared at Pecola with a shocked expression on her face.

"Create businesses? What has that got to do with dating outside your race? Insensitive? Well, he had some damn nerve. I should've been there to talk to him about the reality behind that insensitive crap he's talking. What does he think about how Black women have been treated insensitively like ever since they took over our land? So no one is supposed to hurt white women's feeling by being honest and expressing what they believe? He sounds like an Oreo Cookie sho nuff. Insensitive?" she repeated the word again with disgust. When she mumbled the word once more, she briefly shut her eyes, shook her head, and glanced out the window again.

"I know, chile." Pecola was munching on a grape and listening closely.

"Insensitive? How insensitive was this country to us when they said white women were a minority? I bet they didn't think that was insensitive when it came to business. Especially when they were allowed to take the place of real minorities who deserved those bidding opportunities. I can't believe that white women are classified as a minority business."

"You and me both."

"Most time, white women are married to white men. So by allowing them to be minorities, their white husbands, fathers, and boyfriends just simply boosted them up to be the presidents and owners of the companies so that the same white people could still qualify as a minority-owned business. *Insensitive?* That's so hypercritical and racist, it's ridiculous. This country traditionally protects white people, especially women. Don't get me going this afternoon about being insensitive to white people, girl."

Pecola nodded her head with understanding. "But it totally blew my mind how Bradley acted with me sitting there. The brothers we hang with don't act or think like him. You know how Scott, Rozelle, Carlos, and even Madison are. They don't do that. They're stone to the bone for Black women. I was totally shocked by the flagrant way he ignored me." Pecola spoke slowly, biting another grape.

"Oh, now I got it. Since Bradley was looking at those other women, he ignored you. That started the whole thing." While scanning other files, Symone began to laugh.

"All jokes aside. That's not what the issue is, Symone. We all grew up in Greensboro together. We go way, way back in Greensboro. I just definitely was surprised to see how his eyes glided their way." She hesitated briefly and thought about Bradley.

"It happens."

"I guess folks change," she mumbled after a long silence.

"Did he think you had changed much?"

"Hell no." Pecola spoke quickly. "Are you kidding? He said I was the same ole skinny Pecola he remembered from back in the day."

"Well, you know he was lying, especially if he said you were skinny."

"Tsk. Tsk. Tsk. Now you know that wasn't nice, chile. I do believe he's changed a lot, though. Bradley didn't deal with any white girls in high school. That's a sho nuff change in my book."

"Get real. The brother went to school in Oklahoma."

"Langston *is* a Black school."

"But the majority of the population in Oklahoma is white."

"True."

"So it's the Cinderella complex. They love to shower those women, especially after they make it. I'm telling you. I'm convinced a lot of successful Black men think that the only thing Black women were created for was to be kitchen help, to be a nanny and mammy for their children, and to clean their homes. It's like our successful Black men think Black women weren't created to be adored and pampered like they want to worship white women. You know what I'm saying?"

"Hell yeah. You *know* I do."

"My man Bradley probably ain't used to seeing sisters in Arizona. That's why. But still—" Symone shook her head slowly.

"Maybe so. Like I say, I thought I acted just like you a little bit. Can you believe that? Then sometimes I believe you act just like Alex. What's going on and going wrong with us?" Pecola laughed and clapped her hands.

"I know what it is, Pecola." Symone had a glint in her eyes. "We've been friends too long, and our personalities are merging together. That's exactly what the hell it is."

"Great explanation, chile. That'll work for me."

"You're totally right. I'm glad I wasn't there. When I speak out now, I get in enough trouble with you and all of my old friends, let alone causing a new person to have a stone fit about my conversation. As I get older, my patience is not as long. My tolerance for ignorant Black men or women just screws with me. In any event, it sounds like you gave him a little bit of history, which is what Bradley needed to be reminded of."

Symone shook her head, stacked her papers and stood up.

"I'm heading home right now." Symone was reaching for her linen bolero jacket. "It's review night with the children, and I wanted to first talk with Miss Jessica."

"How is Alex and Scott?" Pecola inquired in a suspicious manner. She still couldn't understand why Symone met with their two closest friends without her. That indeed was a rarity.

"They were fine, girl," Symone replied without looking at her.

Symone remembered Alex and Scott's intense warnings to not tell Pecola anything about the surprise birthday gift. She was shocked that Scott didn't chokehold her neck when he issued the threat. *I don't know why they believe I have diarrhea of the mouth,* thought Symone. *That honor is reserved for Pecola. If someone was planning a surprise of any kind, it always slipped out of her, not me.*

Even though Pecola turned forty in May, Alex thought it would be a grand idea to surprise her again by putting together a *This is Your Life* evening at the Devereauxs' home. But not only would it be for Pecola's birthday, it would also be in honor of Carlos and Pecola's twenty-fourth wedding anniversary. Since Carlos was unaware of the real intention of the affair, he scheduled a confidential luncheon meeting at CR Construction Group's Greensboro office. With his help, Alex, Symone, and Scott were able to compile a lot of information about Carlos and Pecola's family tree and about their lives together. Symone gathered the other important papers together that were scattered on her desk and placed them in her briefcase.

"Gotta go, Pecola. Alex said to call her tonight after nine."

"Ok. Is everything all right with her?" Pecola inquired in a concerned voice.

"Yeah. Sure, she's fine." Symone spoke quickly to calm her; she knew how easily Pecola became hysterical over things. "Alex merely said that *you* called her. When she returned your call, you were in a meeting."

"That's right. I got *that* message. I was meeting with Bradley." Pecola finished the grapes and tossed the remnants in the brass wastebasket. She stood up and put on her shoes. "Have you heard from Billy anymore since yall argued?"

Symone sucked her teeth, gazed at the ceiling, and flashed a weary smile. "You know he called me on my private line today about ten minutes after I left you and Bradley. When I heard his voice, I gave him a serious clickum. I slammed the phone down so hard, I actually hoped it broke his eardrum. I'm seriously thinking about changing the number of that line. That's how disgusted I am with Billy."

"I can dig that. That's a nigger for you, honeychile. Trying to signify on you after what he said to you and about you. And the way he's always parading around Winston-Salem with other women. Some men are a stone trip, girl. If you ever went back with him for anything, I mean anything, I would kick your Black ass myself."

"Lord Pecola, don't remind me about Billy. My mind is already on overload. Anyway, give me a hug. I'll see you. Talk to you tonight, but it'll be late though."

"Remember we have the fourth Zawadi Corporation presentation Friday morning. It's at eleven in Greensboro," Pecola reminded in a motherly fashion. "The top brass is doing the talking this time. This is the one, girl. So you can't be late, chile."

"How can I forget? We've been working on this project for almost seven months. Just don't worry yourself, Pecola. I'll be on time for the signing. As a matter fact, I plan to be here by eight-thirty on Friday. We can ride over together. It's a done deal. Just chalk them up as our new client."

"I know. You're right, honeychile."

"How long will you be here?"

"For at least another couple of hours. Meeting with Bradley threw off my to-do-list for today. Since Carlos told you he isn't going to be working late in Greensboro, I'm not going to stay here any longer than that. I'm looking forward to Cleopatra's leftovers. Anyway, I'll talk to you later."

"Fine."

"Oh, yeah—" Suddenly, Pecola remembered what Elisha advised earlier.

"What?"

"Gloria has your airline ticket for your trip to Atlanta tomorrow," Pecola said throwing her a guilty, sideways glance. "I told Gloria to leave it out on her desk."

"Ah hell, why on her desk?" Symone asked, without smiling at her. "And you're just telling me, girl?"

"Honeychile, I forgot. I tell you my day is off a tad," she replied with a slight yawn and a long stretch of hands above her head. "Just remember to get it before you leave the building."

"Next time, don't tell Gloria to do that, Pecola," Symone said, and Pecola knew that she was aggravated. "I don't ask for much, but you know how I am. I always tell Elisha to put my crap on my desk. She knows that, too. Not on nobody else's desk but on my desk," she repeated with emphasis as she began to point an index finger at her desk. "If I'm in the office, then I specifically ask her to stick it in my briefcase, right in my top flap. My briefcase is always with me."

"Sheese. Excuse me for living," Pecola exclaimed with wide eyes. "I thought you would be back earlier than you were. She was merely putting it on her desk to give to you since she wanted to go over everything with you when you returned to the office."

"Then how come she didn't?"

"Sy, come on now, girl. You didn't get back until a little after five. Gloria goes to school tonight."

Symone wasn't satisfied with the explanation. "Then what about Elisha? Where was she? How come she didn't review my schedule with me? She doesn't leave until late most nights. Like us."

"She had to leave at three today." There was a stunned, long pause on the part of Pecola as she stared in Symone's angry face. "Wooo, chile. What's wrong with you all of a sudden? I mean really, Sy. You know you got to do better anyway, girl. It's hard for me to understand how a smart, businesswoman like you often forgets and loses your airline tickets. How in the hell do you do that?"

"Easy. It's not hard for me to see how that can happen. I got a whole lot of other crap on my mind, and I don't feel like thinking sometimes. Those are small details I shouldn't have to worry about or have to think about. I don't want to be concerned with the trivial stuff. That's why we hired a secretary, Pecola."

"Well. I'm sure Elisha and Gloria will always remind you from this point on—"

Symone cut her off. "I don't need to be reminded, Pecola. I need my tickets and my itinerary placed in my face. That's what I need. Just like today. I've already told them this. When I tell them what I want, don't tell them anything differently. Puhleeze? Ok? Then they'll think that you probably spoke to me, and that it's ok that I've changed my mind. Now, if you hadn't remembered to tell me, I would've walked out of here without my airline tickets and would have had to stand in line at the airport tomorrow to get another one. I don't like standing in line for anything. You know that. If it was placed on my desk like I asked, at least I would know to stick it in my briefcase."

"Ok already." Pecola spoke dryly. She took a deep breath and eyed Symone carefully. "Ted has everything else yall need for your meeting with Brounner Brothers tomorrow. The limo will pick him up at six and get to you around six-twenty in the morning to get yall to the airport in time. I believe your flight leaves at seven forty-five. You know how you are."

"And what does *that* mean?"

"It means that I know how you are about being on time. You're always running late. That's what the hell I mean. You know it, too."

"No problem. I must admit, you got that right. But I'm doing better, girl. Scott even complimented me today. I was on time." Symone's tone softened. She knew her temper had risen for no apparent major life or death reason. *But over some tickets?* She pulled on the end of her jacket sleeves and smiled as she glanced at her watch. As she closed her briefcase, she checked around her office to see if she had gotten everything and headed toward the door.

"Do you know if they got the car service Ted and I like in Atlanta? The last time we were there, I told Gloria that new limo service was lousy."

"Yep. Gloria reserved yall's favorite ones coming and going."

"Great."

"Just call me when you get to Atlanta. Puhleeze don't do it from the car on the way to the airport in the morning, girl. That'll be too early for my blood."

"I understand. I'll call from Hotlanta."

"Talk to you then, Sy. Love ya, girl."

"No. I'll talk to you tonight after I'm done spending time with the children. Love you, too."

They hugged each other, and Symone rushed out. As Pecola watched Symone walk hurriedly down the hall, she shook her head from side to side. Many times, Symone's mood was like a roller coaster, and the girl didn't even suffer from PMS. If Symone had PMS like Pecola, she definitely would be a trip to handle if she had to deal with that hormonal tornado during her period each month. Pecola smiled to herself and quickly turned to head toward her office to crunch more paperwork.

Chapter Seventy-Four

Symone was very tired by the time she arrived at the Triad Airport from Atlanta. As a result of the fierce storm, the five o'clock flight from Atlanta turned into an afternoon Northworld plane trip from hell. It was one rocky ride during which Symone repeatedly promised a smiling Ted that she would never fly again in life. Three times during the flight, she believed that if the plane took another dip, the rum and coke she ordered would be all over Ted, along with the insides of her stomach. But thank God, she made it. It wasn't her time to die yet, which meant she would probably fly again whenever necessary.

Symone was stressed beyond belief and simply wanted to go home, hug her children and go straight to bed. Symone glanced over at Ted. Always the energetic one, he was still gently bobbing his head to the jazz music playing on the limo's stereo speaker. Before they stopped talking so she could take a quick nap, she and Ted were drinking sodas and casually discussing the successful Atlanta meeting to the jazzy piano compositions of Don Pullen. Ted was a consummate, gifted lover of jazz and carefully tried to explain to Symone that she needed go past the surface sounds of jazz and escape into every sound. He wanted her to appreciate the essence of each track. Based upon his tuned ears, he even knew that Tony Williams was on the drums and Gary Peacock was playing the bass. How Ted knew that information was beyond her. When Symone considered Ted's crash course on listening to jazz notes, she chuckled to herself.

"You're up now, Sy?" Ted asked with a smile when he noticed her eyes were opened.

"I'm trying to get there," she mumbled and turned to gaze outside.

"You're up just in time cause I'm outta here. See you tomorrow."

"Have I been sleeping that long?"

"You sure have." As the limo rolled to a stop in front of Ted's condo, he smiled and firmly shook her hand. "And yeah, remember what I told you about jazz."

"It was sooo exciting, how can I forget."

"Great." Still smiling, Ted winked at her and jumped out the car.

When the limo driver slammed the door shut, the abrupt clanging noise quickly jolted Symone's mind into reality. A tired frown graced her face when she realized that her long day was just beginning all over again. As the limo glided away from Ted's house with Symone's head plastered to the back seat, she suddenly remembered that tonight was the second evening this week the children would have their articles ready for her to review.

Whenever Symone was in town or whether she was traveling, the schedule was prepared and had to be honored. At least twice a week, the children were required to read assignments for her. It could be an article from any of the African-American publications and books Symone kept around the house or in the library. Or it could be from the children's personal collection of books selected from their bedroom bookshelves. If necessary, either Symone or Miss Jessica assisted the children with making copies of their articles and helping them to understand what they were reading. Jared, Sylvia, and Kyle each gave Symone a copy, which she quickly reviewed before she met with them. During the dinner review sessions, the children were expected to tell their mother who wrote the article, what the article covered, and what it meant to them.

Since Symone's children were beneficiaries of the trusts, heirs to any companies she created, plus real estate property in Trinidad and Manhattan, Symone wanted her children to learn about money. Since land couldn't be produced, it was essential the children were aware that land and real estate were paramount to having money in the bank. Each month, Symone and the children gathered in her home office to handle the disbursement of household expenses. Operating as a four-man accounting team, they calculated the check amounts for the mortgage payments, electricity bill, telephone, charge accounts, ballet, piano lessons, and any other household items. This gave the children another view about money and how it was budgeted and allocated. Symone even required little Kyle and Sylvia to attempt to read the bills out loud to their big brother even though they were only in pre-school. Jared was responsible for writing the checks, and Symone signed each one. Since Symone continually reminded the children to save money they received as gifts, the children journeyed to Mechanics and Farmers Bank in Winston-Salem to make deposits into their personal savings account every two weeks.

Before Symone came to America, her trust fund assets were managed by New York attorneys and accountants selected by Uncle Samuel's family. As she got older, that arrangement was never changed. However, all of Symone's other business expenses in North Carolina were handled by Norvella Eldridge, the certified public accountant she and Pecola chose eight years ago. Not only was Norvella in the Deltas with Alex, which was a big plus, she came highly recommended by a lot of other African-American business owners in Winston-Salem. Norvella was simply an intellectually sophisticated accountant sistah who understood the dynamics of what tax shelters, loopholes, and financial family planning really signified.

Norvella charted financial progress and prepared checks for Akao Studios and Meetings Odyssey, but Pecola and Symone were the ones who signed all of the paperwork. Not one check was mailed out if the partners did not review it first. If appropriate back up documents were not clearly attached to each disbursement so Pecola and Symone could understand what the accounts payable were about, those items weren't released for payment until an explanation was given. Pecola had read somewhere that Bill Cosby said that one never gets so big he can't sign his own checks. And from those words of wisdom, the partners developed the check signing policy for both companies.

That was so different to Symone. When she was small, all of her needs were handled by outside people. Yet, while growing up, Uncle Willie did always advise that the fiscal integrity of an organization was crucial. Without question, he knew the movement of money created wealth. He believed that effective business people always accounted for every single quarter flowing in their organizations and especially accounted for the ones that flowed out.

Symone certainly believed Norvella could very easily handle the household bills for her as well, but Symone wanted her children to learn the value of money. She wanted them to be aware of the money she had to sensibly disburse in order for them to live in their home and to enjoy their pleasant lifestyle. The children needed to realize that in order for them to bask in the activities they were blessed and allowed to do, it costs money. For Symone, it was absolutely necessary that her children were aware they did not reside in their lovely home simply because they just did.

Oftentimes, Pecola confessed that she wished she had done the same with her children. Now that her brood was all older, she was convinced the Reynolds' children actually believed that their mama and daddy had their own money tree. Carlos, Jr., Haneef, and Elizabethe expected to receive money whenever they called and asked their parents for it. As a result of the way Symone dealt with money with her three children, her family, friends and Ujima Literary Society members now performed the same monthly financial lesson with their offsprings. Like Rozelle said many times, it was simply another way they all continued to learn from each other.

Symone developed the monthly practice because she did not have such teachings as a young child. Without question, the Eisners and her uncles were the impetus for trust knowledge and her every need was always provided for. When she looked back now, she never knew how much money her mother needed to live in their Brooklyn brownstone. The Eisner and Poussaints patriarchs certainly instilled the fervent allegiance within Symone to protect and be proud of her Trinidadian and African-American culture. That she was proud of. But it was Yolanda Francis Young, a college roommate, who told her that the same financial family practice was required of her six brothers and sisters. The daughter of an investment banker, Yolanda explained that the monthly practice was law in the Young's household. When Yolanda talked about it with Symone in their dorm room that day, Symone was fascinated by the idea. She vowed that if she ever had any children, each month they would be required to do the same thing.

Even when Honeyboy died and since Keturah didn't handle the plantation finances, Symone remembered the struggles her mother encountered trying to determine what to do. Keturah had to frequently rely totally on the suggestions of Cecil and Willie when making any financial decisions. Before Honeyboy's death, finances were never discussed in the Melieneux home. Symone as well as her sisters and brothers took everything for granted and believed angels, maybe a fairy godmother or even an apparition handled financial matters. They just didn't know. Nobody knew but Honeyboy. Symone made a promise to herself that she would always do certain things with the children she was blessed with. She would tell them she loved them every day and hug them, too. Enlighten them regarding finances, business, and as much as she could share about life. But Symone was also fervent about educating the children about the beauty of their Trinidadian culture.

Uncle Willie often told Symone that according to Biblical teachings, the Jewish people were said to be God's chosen people. However, he said that those were mere words if individuals did not believe such family tradition to have the knowledge instilled in their hearts. Uncle Willie taught that as far as he was concerned, such a philosophy didn't stop there. He reinforced that powerful thinking was taught to strong cultures. Uncle Willie believed that if every race, if the next generation, if the children are taught to be leaders and are indoctrinated regarding the uniqueness of their culture at an early age, then they too are grounded in the knowledge for themselves that they are God's chosen people.

When Symone formed Ujima Literary Society many, many years ago, she explained why she believed this kind of group was absolutely essential. Since Symone was required to read ever since she stepped on American soil, she had been an avid reader. Yet, her required business reading began when Uncle Willie gave Symone a copy of D. Parke Gibson's *Forty Billion Dollar Negro* as a sweet thirteenth birthday gift. This book present was a drastic change to her uncles' customary shopping trip to stores of her choice, to an envelope full of money, or to expensive toys. Her uncles believed it was time for Symone to begin learning about the corporate world and Black folks' tremendous contribution to it. After her birthday party, Symone was allotted a certain time frame to finish reading Gibson's book and was expected to discuss with both uncles its entire contents with a high-degree of understanding.

As the limo glided down the interstate to Clemmons, Symone gazed out the black tinted window and once again considered her early years in New York. Since she was required to read from such an early age, reading was a natural part of her life. Even though Symone was extremely busy, she still tried to read two and three books a week. Those books about African-American culture and lifestyle, she especially absorbed their content like a dry sponge. Now, whenever a new member is welcomed into the Ujima Literary Society's fold, Symone began the tradition of passing on the teachings of her uncles.

Just like the committed group of people that worked with the Devereauxs' children, each member of the literary society is committed and is educated to understand that African-American children are the keys for the future. As Scott said his mother told them all the time, *reading books are essential vitamins for the mind.* That's why all of the friends always enjoyed the Devereauxs' affairs. If possible, each affair included their children. Whenever Alex scheduled dinner parties or other get-togethers, the children were always right there in attendance, dressed in their finest duds and ready to socialize along with everyone else until it was time for them to go to bed. Then of course, Alex always hired a competent individual to take care of their needs. Without question, Rozelle was right. Everyone's children truly enjoyed going to the Devereauxs' house for fun-filled activities. If Symone were honest, she would have to admit that the other friends tried to emulate the parties Alex organized. The same community spirit among the friends spread to the Ujima Literary Society as well. Many times, the friendship she had with Alex, Madison, Pecola, Carlos, Rozelle and Scott often reminded Symone of the unique one Keturah shared with her friends in Trinidad, especially the one with Tante Tutts. It also reminded her of the way people took care of each other years ago in Brooklyn and in Trinidad.

As Symone thought about Trinidad again, she noticed the limo had just turned off at the Clemmons exit. *Oh, Trinidad,* Symone thought. Symone closed her eyes and thought some more. She was always homesick for her country. After all these years, she still felt such emotions. It had been years since she first came to the United States. But it did not matter. She missed her home. She wondered why? During restless, dark velvet nights, she longed for the talk, the food, and just the presence of the country earth of Santa Cruz, Trinidad. Just to simply sit on the land and talk to her cousins and neighbors who nourished the Poussaint family, especially during the times Honeyboy would be drunk and chase them from the estate.

A few of those elders still lived in Santa Cruz, and Symone clearly remembered their smiling dark cocoa faces. When Symone was a child, she enjoyed their comforting presence. Now that she was approaching middle age, she cherished their protective spirit for her family. Maybe it was because she was thirty-nine and approaching forty. She did not know the reason. Whatever it was, that was why at every opportunity Symone went home to visit the relatives who remained there. As Alex often said, "don't forget where you came from." Go home to hear the whispers of your childhood to try to find peace with her country and herself.

Symone remembered Carnival in Trinidad as happy euphoric times. Nowadays, Carnival was celebrated all over the United States—in Miami, Baltimore, and Brooklyn. Even in Toronto, Canada. But a person absolutely couldn't truly know Carnival until it was experienced in Port of Spain, Trinidad, West Indies. There, they could smell the dirt, eat a fresh mango, and enjoy a good pot of peas and rice and drink coconut. They could jump up in a section and enjoy the flavor of the people. Bacchanal time during carnival time is the ting to do.

Symone was thankful for the opportunity and education experienced in the United States and was now even a United States citizen. The stellar education received at Hampton and Wharton were without a doubt unforgettable experiences. On paper, her legal standing reflected the status as an American. But in her heart, Symone would always be Trinidadian. She wished she could cure all of the ills that were going on there. The problems of drugs and crime. Keturah often exclaimed that crime had really gotten out of hand. Unemployment and desperation were a part of Trinidadian life as was similar in other Caribbean countries. It simply was a mirror of what ailed the United States, but just on a smaller scale. As a result of the ailing economy, everything was very expensive. Each time Symone turned around, Hazele told her how Keturah continued to send barrel upon barrels of expensive items to relatives at home. Since Symone, her sisters and brother did not travel home as often as Keturah, Uncle Willie, and Uncle Cecil, they kept up with news from other relatives. Symone subscribed to the Trinidadian newspapers, *The Guardian* and *The Express,* and those publications were delivered to her in North Carolina.

Thinking about Trinidad was always an adrenaline rush for Symone. But not today. Still feeling pensive and tired during the limo ride home, Symone prayed for the necessary strength to deal with her three children. Whenever she returned from a trip, they acted as if Miss Jessica had fed them a constant flow of candy two hours before her arrival. They were always ultra keyed up.

Chapter Seventy-Five

Miss Jessica glanced at the clock. "Jared, your mother will be home at seven-thirty. Shouldn't you have your assignments waiting for her, sugar?" Miss Jessica prodded gently.

The children were in the den watching the *Blank Man* videotape. Jared looked up frustrated.

"We will in a minute, Miss Jessica," he answered without moving. "We're with you. Don't sweat it, ok?"

While listening to him, Miss Jessica breathed deeply. "Jared, Sylvia, and Kyle, yall know better. You know your mother doesn't like you watching television or videos on a school night, baby. Who cut the television on?" With hands on hips, Miss Jessica spoke to all three children.

Miss Jessica had just finished washing the dinner dishes five minutes ago. While she cleaned the kitchen, she made sure the children took their evening bath and were in their pajamas. Now she wanted to make sure their assignments would be ready to present when Symone arrived home.

"Who cut the television on?" She repeated the question. No one responded for a few seconds.

"He cut it on, Mith Jessica," Kyle admitted and quickly pointing an accusing finger to Jared.

"Weh told him not to," Sylvia chimed in with a scared voice as she pointed her finger at her big brother. Jared immediately knocked Sylvia's hand out of his way. "But he wouldn't listen. Ah told him ah was going ta tell on him."

"Jared, don't hit your little sister," Miss Jessica scolded and glared firmly in his eyes. Jared gazed down guiltily. "You should try and be patient with them. Love your sisters, baby."

"They were looking at it, too, Miss Jessica," Jared explained in a hateful voice with a sulky expression. "They make me sick. Always telling on me." He began pouting and his eyes were full of anger.

"Sylvia and Kyle, now yall know it's not nice to point, baby," Miss Jessica quietly chastised with grandmotherly reserve. "Neither one of you didn't even give your brother a chance to tell me he cut it on. Did you, baby?"

Kyle turned away from Miss Jessica's stern looking face. Sylvia slowly shook her head, watching her, and then spoke up.

"No. Uh, Jared took too long ta talk," she said. She stuck her left thumb in her mouth and began idly twisting her long, braided hair with her right index finger. Miss Jessica gazed at her three charges with an inward grin.

"Jared baby, it's time to turn it off. You know watching television and videos aren't allowed on weeknights. Go on. Do what I say." Still with a slight pout on his face, Jared very dutifully stood up and turned off the television. Miss Jessica smiled. "Now c'mon, baby. Give your Miss Jessica a big hug."

Miss Jessica looked into Jared's eyes sympathetically. The love she felt for him and his sisters was evident as always in her eyes. More than anything else, Jared knew that about her. He slowly walked over to her and tightly placed his arms around her soft waist. Miss Jessica always smelled fresh and clean to him, like the pretty, colorfully fresh flowers in his Tante Alex's rose garden. Even though he stood almost as tall as her shoulders, he leaned his head against her breasts, and she gently squeezed him back. When Kyle and Sylvia noticed the affection Miss Jessica was showering on their brother, they jumped up and began hugging her waist, too. She gave the twins a healthy dose of love and devotion hugs as well.

"Let's go on into the library to get ready." She checked her watch. It was seven-thirty. "Your mother should be here any minute, and I want all my three babies to be prepared."

Trailed by the three children, Miss Jessica headed down the hallway to the walnut paneled library. Kyle and Sylvia sat on the leather sofa, and Jared positioned himself at his mother's reading desk. He had selected an article from *Black Diaspora* magazine, and the girls wanted to talk about the book, *Brown Baby*. Miss Jessica had read it to them this afternoon during their snack time. Once Miss Jessica began asking each child the appropriate questions again, the telephone rang. She told Jared she would answer it.

"...Good night, the Poussaint residence," she responded in the way Symone preferred the telephone be answered in the evening.

"Miss Jessica, how you doing? This is Pecola."

"Hey, baby. I know it's you. I'm fine. How you be doing?"

"I'm fine, ma'am."

"I have Alex on the line. We were wondering if Symone was back in town yet?"

"Hello, Miss Jessica," Alex greeted quietly.

"Hey, baby. You be doing all-right?"

"Yes ma'am. Just fine." As did Pecola, Alex always found herself replying to Miss Jessica the same way she was taught to answer all older people when she was a child. *Yes ma'am* this and *No ma'am* that.

"How's my Maddy, Alex?" she inquired fondly. Miss Jessica and Miss Bessie were the only ones who called Madison "Maddy," and he just loved hearing it. Pecola wondered why she didn't ask about Carlos.

"He's fine, ma'am. He's reading to the children."

"Tell him I said hello." Miss Jessica laughed quickly. "Well that's exactly what I'm doing, sugar. Helping my babies get ready for their mother. She called from the car and told me she would be here at seven-thirty." Miss Jessica checked the time again. It was seven forty-five. "I expect her any second. It's getting late. I don't want my babies staying up too late. It'll be hard for them to get up in the morning."

As Alex considered the tender and motherly disposition of Miss Jessica, she smiled into the phone.

"She'll probably will have a short review time with them tonight, Miss Jessica, especially if she's too pooped," Alex said softly.

"You know, she did sound so very tired, sugar. I believed she said something about her flight being bad. Real bad, baby. That's why your Miss Jessica don't want to go up in the air on no plane to go nowhere. You want me to tell her to call you, baby?"

"If you can, puhleeze," Pecola said suddenly and impatiently. Miss Jessica still hadn't asked about Carlos. "I was calling to remind her about our Zawadi Corporation meeting in the morning."

"I understand, baby. I'm sure she knows about it. But I'll tell her for you." As Miss Jessica thought about something else to say, she smiled soundlessly. "How's my Carlos, Pecola baby?"

"Fine, Miss Jessica," she answered happily.

"Pecola, sugar. You know what my Carlos did today?"

"No ma'am?" Pecola replied cautiously. Alex laughed quietly. Rozelle and Scott had already called and told what Carlos did.

"This morning on his way to Charlotte, he brought me some apple white liquor. Pure divine shine to give to Leroy Lee. Can yall believe that?"

"Wellll—" Pecola replied softly to the question.

"When my family was here for your July fourth barbecue, Carlos gave him some then and told him he knew where to get him some more from that tasted just like it. You know my Carlos ought to be ashamed of hisself," she teased as she thought about it.

"He sho should," Pecola said.

"My sister's gonna git your husband, sugar," Miss Jessica explained in a heavy southern accent. Pecola and Alex burst out laughing.

"So what you gonna do with it, Miss Jessica?" Pecola asked with an amused expression and a wide grin.

"Well, sugar. I'm gonna have to give it to Leroy Lee like Carlos asked me to. That's what I'm gonna do. Is he there now?"

"Uh. No, ma'am. He's not back from Charlotte yet, Miss Jessica."

Kyle and Sylvia suddenly jumped off the couch. They saw the headlights of the limo coming down the long driveway.

"...Mummy's home! Mummy's back! Mith Jessica! Mey Mummy's here, Mith Jessica," the twins exclaimed excitedly and began jumping up and down. The two pink pajama-clad girls raced out of the library, down the hallway, and headed straight for the foyer.

"Oh, Lawd have mercy. The children are hollering and carrying on so. I believe Symone's here. Pecola and Alex, yall want to hold on?"

"I don't mind holding for a little while anyway, Miss Jessica," Alex said as her eyes rested upon her husband.

Madison had just finished reading to Trey and Purity. He prayed with them, kissed them good night, and tucked them into their beds. While walking through the master bedroom entryway, Alex saw him slowly loosen his necktie. Earlier that day, Madison had performed a difficult, microscopic five-hour surgery, and the six-year old child ended up dying on the operating table. Mentally, he was thoroughly exhausted. Before Pecola called Alex, she had prepared steaming hot water in the Jacuzzi for him, and she wanted to be there to wash his weariness away. Alex gazed worriedly into Madison's sensitive, pained eyes, and he gently clutched her hand.

"Miss Jessica, I'm gonna go. Tell Symone that I'll talk to her later tonight, ok? If not, I'll talk to her in the morning. I always speak with her first thing in the morning." Madison kissed Alex lightly on her forehead and headed toward the bathroom.

"I know, baby. Ok Alex, sugar. Pecola, you hold on, baby. I'll get her for you."

The limousine glided around the circular driveway and stopped in front of the house. The driver jumped out and opened the door for Symone. She took a deep breath, stepped out, and thanked him for his excellent service. He grabbed her bulky briefcase and carried it to the front door. Before Symone could stick her key in the lock, Jared opened the mammoth oak door.

"...Jared boo, baby. How you doing, boy?" Symone inquired quickly with a huge smile on her face. She opened her arms to embrace her son. With bright dancing eyes and a smile gracing his entire face, he hugged his mother back.

"Fine, Mummy. And you?" With his face against her warm body, his words were muffled. Symone released him and poured her smile all over her children.

"I'm tired, baby. Mommy's real tired."

"Does that mean we don't have to review tonight?"

"No it doesn't, boy." Symone offered him a weary grin and a fast rub on his neatly barbered head. "That's not what it means, son."

"...Mummy. Mummy. We're so happy ta see yuh again, Mummy," the twins jumped up and down and grabbed her waist tightly. Almost pulling her down from their weight, she kissed and hugged them both. When Symone left this morning, they all were still in bed. Even though she kissed each one of her children on their sleeping foreheads, she always liked to speak to them face to face before she left to go out of town.

Tison Handel, the new limo driver, swiftly eyed the massive and elegantly decorated foyer. He whistled silently under his breath and placed Symone's briefcase on the marble floor. She turned to face him.

"Thank you so much, Tison."

Dressed in her pearly white, starched uniform that never seemed to ever get soiled, Miss Jessica rushed into the foyer. "Symone sugar."

"Uh, yes-s-s, Miss Jessica."

"Pecola's on the phone, baby." She saw that Symone was speaking with the chauffeur. "Sorry, baby. Didn't mean to interrupt you. Are you ok?"

"I'm fine, Miss Jessica." Symone smiled kindly at her and turned to face Tison. "Thank you, Tison."

"You're welcome, ma'am."

"Ted and I thought you were great," she acknowledged again and handed him a generous tip.

"This is for you."

Without looking at the bills, Tison grinned broadly. He had heard about her generosity from his friend, the regular chauffeur that normally worked with Meetings Odyssey.

"Thank you, ma'am. It was *my* pleasure, Ms. Poussaint."

"Mummy. Come on, Mummy. Ah have mey book ready far yuh," Kyle shouted as she continued to frantically tug on Symone's suit. It was a Constance Saunders signature classic power suit, and the children were treating it like it was Silly Putty.

"Baby, don't pull on Mummy's clothes like that. I'm coming, little girl. Miss Jessica, puhleeze tell Pecola that I'll call her later." Symone shook her head, checked her watch, and exhaled deeply. Almost under her breath, she spoke. "Lawd help me." She closed her eyes for an instant, then she yelled to Miss Jessica. "Tell her I know about Zawadi in the morning, and I'll meet her at the office at eight-thirty like we said. Tison here will be picking me up and taking us to Greensboro. After that flight, I don't think I can drive for at least a good two days. It was totally, totally draining."

"Ok, sugar. I'll tell her," she replied with a worried look on her face. Symone looked fatigued. Instead of going all the way back down to the library, Miss Jessica headed toward the living room to get the phone and give Pecola the message.

Tison nodded his head, bowed slightly, and touched his hat with two fingers. "Eight did you say, Ms. Poussaint?"

"Yes. Yes, I did. Pick me up here at eight tomorrow morning, but we need you for the entire day."

"No problem," Tison answered immediately. Symone tiredly extended her hand. Surprised she did that, he shook it firmly and quickly left through the front door.

Symone headed toward the library. Kyle and Sylvia were gibbering happily and still pulling and stretching her designer suit. Jared was carrying his mother's briefcase and visualizing himself as an architectural executive in his father's firm.

Still dressed in her business suit, Symone relaxed barefoot in the library while she questioned and listened to the children review their books and article. All three smelled fresh and clean. This evening, Miss Jessica dressed them in their animal print pajamas and their scrubbed shiny, contented faces were a joy for Symone to see. As Symone listened to their words, she smiled. Her children were blessed. When she was Kyle, Sylvia and Jared's ages, there was so much violent turmoil within the walls of her home in Trinidad. No child should ever have to grow up in such a horrible and life altering environment. It was her silent, mental tragedy, being with her Papa. It was a mentally, bitter, pus-filled nightmare that Symone knew changed the course of her life—the way she thought and how she looked at herself. Through it all, Symone was thankful to God. She was glad, truly glad that her three babies would never experience the agony of an abusive and violent home the same way she did.

As Jared was finishing up his very mature review of his article, Symone beamed proudly. With large smiles on their faces, Kyle and Sylvia were each sitting quite comfortably on their mother's lap. When Jared ended his review by saying "...Thank you very much for your attention this evening," the twins began clapping happily for their brother. Earlier, he had done the same for them. Miss Jessica always listened to the children as if she were sitting in church listening to a fiery Sunday morning sermon. Her eyes were always closed. Hands clasped in her lap. And as she patted her feet, she continually bobbed her head slowly up and down.

"...That's was great, Jared boo." Symone winked at him. "Wasn't it, everyone? Isn't he a wonderful speaker?" They all nodded yes. The twins began clapping again. Symone glanced at her watch. It was nine-fifteen. Symone and Miss Jessica preferred that the children be in bed at least by eight-thirty every night. When she was in town, it allowed her time to settle down before she went to bed. From the looks of things, they were already forty-five minutes past schedule.

"Miss Jessica, I know we're running late with bedtime, but I just want to go over a few other things this evening."

"Don't worry, baby. While you're talking to them, I'll go on upstairs and turn their bed covers back. Just don't talk to the children all night, baby. In a few more minutes, it'll be an hour past their bedtime." Miss Jessica admonished Symone in a motherly manner. "You know how Jared is when he doesn't get his sleep. It's not so bad with the girls. If they're too tired tomorrow morning, I can just keep them out of pre-school."

"I understand, Miss Jessica. I do."

"...Like I always tell you, I want the best for you, Jared, for you, Sylvia, and for you, Kyle. That's why Mummy wants you to always think about your choices," Symone said quietly. They were all sitting on the floor in a little circle.

"Ah tink about mey choices all—dey—time—, Mummy," Kyle said slowly with wide eyes as she pushed her round gold-framed glasses back up on her nose. "Wen Mith Jessica asked meh wat ah want far breakfast, ah tink about it first. Den ah chose wat ah like ta eat dey bestest."

Jared rolled his eyes at his sister's stupid answer and shook his head slowly. Sylvia stuck her left thumb in her mouth and began idly twisting her braided, coarse black hair again. Since Sylvia was the quieter twin, this was her favorite thing to do when she was either being chastised or when she was attempting to listen intently to grown-up conversations.

Symone eyed her daughter for a moment and smiled. "That's true, Kyle. That's one way you can think about choices, little girl. Mummy wants you to always think quietly. Listen to yourself. Think first. Ok?" Symone wasn't sure if they comprehended what she was saying. "When you're around your friends and don't want to do something, don't do it. Never follow the crowd."

"Ah don't like crowds, Mummy." Sylvia confessed softly as she gazed in Symone's face. "Wen ah was with Grandmum at Kiddies Carnival parade, all dey people in dey crowd stepped on mey toes."

"I understand, baby." Symone stared into Sylvia's timid eyes and smiled again at her overly sensitive daughter. "Always try to be the leader in the group. It's nothing wrong with being a leader. Leaders are individuals who are presidents of companies, ambassadors for countries, missionaries, volunteers, and business owners. People like our Uncle Willie, Uncle Cecil, Uncle Samuel, and Uncle Quentin. Your Tante Hazele, Tante Alex, and Tante Pecola. So many other people that you know."

"What about Daddy?" Jared asked quickly. "Isn't he a leader, too?"

Symone studied his face carefully. "Yes, son. Your daddy is a leader. Not only because he's your daddy, but because of many things he's done. He's well-known. As an architect, he's very much respected throughout the country." Symone paused for a moment as she considered her words and life with her own father. "Sometimes, children have daddies, and they aren't leaders. Don't worry. That's not the case with your daddy, Jared."

When Jared heard those words, his whole face became one big smile.

"Mummy would rather you respect your teachers and other people around you more so than the athletes and celebrities you see on television. Do you understand?"

All three children shook their heads yes.

"What about Uncle Marlon, Mummy?" Jared asked. "He's an athlete. I see him on TV a lot. I see his friends, too."

"That's true, Jared." Symone laughed quickly. "I almost forgot about him, boy. That's a good question. Yall are blessed in that respect. Your Uncle Marlon is an athlete in the family that is respected by millions of people around the world. He's a role model to so many others and is considered an African-American hero. The only difference is that you can see him whenever you want. He knows you, and you know him. Lots of other children who worship and keep Uncle Marlon as a role model and as their hero never ever get to see him in person. Even though Uncle Marlon tries to visit as many children as he can, he just can't reach everyone. That's why you're fortunate to have such a leader, such a legend as Uncle Marlon around you."

"Mummy, I know it is, too. When I tell my friends about Uncle Marlon at school, they don't believe me."

"Jared, I understand, baby."

"They don't really think I know him." Jared became silent. "Do you think he'll come to my class for show and tell?"

Symone laughed suddenly. "He just might, baby. Just call him up and ask him. Knowing him like I do, he probably will do that for you, Jared."

Symone hesitated slightly. She wanted to be careful. In her opinion, a lot of celebrities and athletes sold out and did everything to try to immerse themselves in the white world that took care of them. From the white house with the white picket fence to the white women, they wanted to operate in the world void of all cultural connections to Black folks. Always saying ridiculous, dumb things like they were not Black but simply universal, not only with their color, but also with their thinking. Symone was embarrassed to hear it or know such words were ever uttered from their born and bred Black mouths. She didn't want to share such information about those celebrities or athletes with her children, but she also didn't want them to worship those so-called, pre-fabricated celebrities and athletes, either. Before Symone spoke again, she gazed into each one of her children's anxious faces.

"Like other athletes you know, I want yall to respect their athletic abilities. Let that be a role model for you. Their abilities. As far as their lifestyle and who they are—you don't know them well. I don't, either. When we watch television, the media only shows us their God-given talent to play a specific sport. They show us what they want us to see."

So that she could speak, Sylvia took her thumb out of her mouth. "Mummy, is Mith Jessica a leader?"

"Yes, baby. She certainly is. So are your teachers at school."

"Is leader dere first name?" Kyle asked as she slid closer to her mother and snuggled into her arms. Symone kissed her forehead, smiled, and chuckled lightly.

"It can be, girl. I just never knew anyone with that name. But I guess you could have a name like that. Mummy has just always heard people described as leaders."

"Well, that's how I want people to know me and to describe me." Jared spoke with his chest poked out. "I want to be a leader. I want to be just like my daddy."

Symone was startled by Jared's words and watched her son's determined face. It was amazing. Jared barely saw his father, but he still yearned to be like him. Totally amazing.

"At the rate you're going in school, you'll be just like him, Jared. You know your father was always very smart, too. Just like you."

Kyle's face became serious. "Mummy, you know Imani in my class? She doesn't tink our teacher is a leader."

"Why do you say that, little girl?"

"Cause Imani screamed at Mith Edwards yesterday, den she went ta dey office," Kyle continued. "Wen Mith Jessica picked meh up frum school, ah told on her. Ah looked Mith Jessica in dey eye, and ah told dey truth just like yuh told meh ta do."

"Is that right, girl?"

"Uh huh. Imani didn't treat dey teacher like a leader. Right?"

"You're right. If I ever hear anything about yall disrespecting your teachers and not treating them like leaders, you certainly will be in big trouble."

As Sylvia considered what her mother had just told her, she opened her eyes widely. She began sucking her thumb and twirling her hair. Although she glared with frightened eyes at her mother, she said nothing.

"...Just remember our main topic for tonight. Ok?" Symone said a few moments later. "Mummy wants you to be a leader and to be different. You know why? Tell me why, Jared?"

Jared took a deep breath and repeated what he was expected to say.

"When you're a leader, you'll walk tall and hold your head high. You'll be proud of who you are. You'll think for yourself and not follow the crowd." He seemed to hesitate near the end of his summation.

"And?" Symone edged him on.

"When you're different and when you think different, it's better. Because when everybody thinks the same, nobody thinks," Jared finished proudly.

"Very good, boy. Very good." Symone grinned contentedly and nodded her head in approval. She was satisfied that at least Jared understood what she was talking about this evening. Once more, she began another round of clapping.

Ten minutes later, they were finished with their review discussion. Symone walked the children upstairs. Jared was holding his mother's left hand. Kyle and Sylvia were tightly clasping the right one. While walking up the steps, Symone shared bits and pieces of her trip to Atlanta and talked about what fun activities she had planned for them on the weekend. Symone got all three of them to calm down and put them to bed. Afterwards, Symone went into Miss Jessica's bedroom to speak with her. Miss Jessica had a light fruit snack all ready for Symone there and while she ate it, the two women talked about their day and the children.

At ten forty-five that night, Symone was finally within the peacefulness of her own bedroom. As the mellow jazzy sounds of Miles Davis splashing notes out the CD player enveloped her, she savored her time alone and was getting ready for bed. The way she felt this evening, she decided to slip into a silk georgette nightshirt with layers of ruffles along the buttons and cuffs. It was frilly feminine and quite an appropriate contrast to her tense mood. Without question, Symone loved the feel of silk, satin, and velour against her skin. Yet, there were many times where she simply slept in an old, over-sized cotton T-shirt. There were also those stressed-filled moments where she needed nothing but silk and satin to caress her skin. And tonight was that kind of night.

Relaxing on her bed sipping wine and flipping through the pages of *Smithsonian* magazine, Symone first dialed Alex's number. Since Alex was busy with Madison, they spoke for only a few minutes. Next, she called Pecola, and she quickly told her about the flight then briefly rehashed the successful meeting with the Brounner Brothers. While they were talking, Scott telephoned Pecola, and Pecola immediately said that she had to go. Before Pecola hung up, Symone reminded her that the limo would be picking her up tomorrow morning, too.

Now listening to the jazzy, sultry sounds of Dianne Reeves, Symone carefully reviewed the notes for The Zawadi Corporation morning meeting. She scribbled short letters to three cousins in Trinidad; she would try and remember to mail them out first thing in the morning. After writing four brutally honest pages in her journal about herself, she prayed to God that no one would ever read or ever discover it. Finally, after drinking her third glass of red wine, Symone believed she was relaxed enough to go to sleep. She strolled into the bathroom to wash her face and to floss and brush her teeth. Back in bed, when she took a long deep breath and reached to turn off the bedside lamp, it was two o'clock in the morning. Symone sighed heavily once more, pulled the sweet smelling luxury bed linen over her head, and closed her eyes to peaceful, tired rest.

Chapter Seventy-Six

Since The Zawadi Corporation contract was signed before one in the afternoon, Symone, Pecola, Ted, and Elisha screamed and hugged each other with laughter filling up the limousine. They still became excited when they closed a huge deal. Then they went to lunch at Salt Marsh Willie in Greensboro, had a few drinks, and called it a day.

When Pecola stepped out the limo at her house, she breathed a sigh of relief. She was tired and decided to take a long, hot bubble bath as soon as she made it up to her bedroom. After her African-peach scented bath, she remained naked as she puttered around her bedroom. She wanted to straighten up a few things while she listened to the mellow sounds of Maze, with silk soul Frankie Beverly singing *Joy and Pain.*

Cleopatra cleaned yesterday. Once again, Pecola noticed that Cleopatra moved various object d'art to different places in her bedroom. Singing loudly and snapping her fingers to the music, Pecola moved the items back to their proper places. Every now and then, she did the down home blues stroll with an invisible partner. She laughed to herself. She noticed that her stiff, old, young, fortyish legs were sleepy nowadays. The fluid dance movements that used to come so swift and effortlessly before were slowing down somewhat.

After she finished dancing, Pecola laid down on the bed and thought about how wonderful the day went in Greensboro. *This was great,* thought Pecola. It was just three-thirty in the afternoon, and she was at home enjoying the fruits of being a successful businesswoman, an entrepreneur. Startled by a distant noise she heard come from downstairs, Pecola quickly raised her head. At that moment, Pecola thought she heard the garage door churn open. She turned down the music and listened intently. Now she realized someone had slammed a door and was slowly walking up the steps. She searched frantically for her pepper spray.

Damn! It was Carlos, she thought with relief as she heard the familiar whistling. *Scared me half to death!*

As if nothing were unusual about either one of them being home that early, Carlos strolled into the master bedroom with a large smile on his face.

"Hey, baby. I guess we were thinking the same way. Short day!" he exclaimed as he looked at her closely. He bowed down and kissed her with an overly wet mouth. "What's wrong, baby?"

"Carlos honey, you scared me half to death. I forgot to turn on the alarm. When I heard the noise, I panicked like you wouldn't believe."

"Whose gonna step into our house this time of day other than me, baby?"

"Hell, I don't know. Crime doesn't have any time of day. I didn't know you were coming home early." She looked at him with frustration. Carlos looked around the room as if to figure out what to say, then he let his eyes enjoy his wife's nakedness.

"I didn't know you would be home, either. Hmmm. I guess you didn't expect me, but it looks like you were waiting for someone to tighten your bootie up. So here I am, Pecola," he said playfully.

"You're crazy." Pecola laughed like a teenager.

"How did it go today?" As Carlos spoke, he began taking off his jacket and danced into his closet. Snapping his fingers, bobbing his head, and singing, he sleekly swayed his body to Maze and Frankie Beverly's funky tune, *Before I Let Go.*

"We did it, baby. We finally closed the deal and signed one of the largest businesses in the country. It's number forty-four on the Fortune 500 list. The Zawadi Corporation, located right here in Greensboro, North Cackle Lackey, baby. Can you imagine that?" There was a geyser of excitement in Pecola's voice.

"Yes I can." Still singing and dancing, Carlos sashayed back out the closet.

"Look at you, Carlos. Sing your song. I'm checking you out, baby. Your moves. Your delightful moves, baby. You're dancing like a fine young thang."

Pecola encouraged him with a huge smile on her face. She always believed Carlos was a smooth dancer. Once more, he noticed how she was standing naked, happy, and gorgeous before him. That turned him on. While he provocatively rolled his belly in and out, he held his arms out to receive her. Pecola walked over and hugged his neck tightly, and together they wildly danced to *I Can't Get Over You.*

"I may be forty-two, but I still got it going on, Sweet Pea. Age ain't nothing but a number." Pecola broke out into a loud laugh. Carlos did too, as he twirled her around several times.

"Whew, chile," Pecola exclaimed out of breath as the song ended. "Don't remind me. Whew. After that, I need to rest big time."

"Your signing the deal with Zawadi is fantastic news. Really great, baby. Now tell me how they found out about MO again?"

Carlos removed his onyx cuff links, the diamond tie pin, and placed it in his cherry desk box along with his money clip. He loosened the tie and pulled it over his head. Pecola went to the bed and folded the covers back. She fluffed up the pillows, sat down on the edge, and began polishing her toenails.

"It was DC, baby. You know crazy DC? Rozelle and Scott's frat buddy?"

"Of course, I know DC, baby."

"Carlos, let me tell the story my way, puhleeze. I got to take you from the beginning. DC and Scott were golfing in a celebrity tournament in Atlanta. This guy, some big time executive who happened to be the vice-chairman of the company, was on DC's team. They became tight as sho nuff soul brothers. You know how crazy DC is? I can imagine what happened. By the time DC got through with him, the vice-chairman probably thought the two of them were childhood buddies from the hood in Washington."

"You're right, baby. DC never meets a stranger."

"Well, the vice-chairman casually mentioned that his organization was putting this major fiftieth year anniversary celebration together in a few years." Pecola sucked in a deep breath, took a sip of iced tea, and resumed speaking.

"My man, DC—"

"Keep in mind The Zawadi Corporation has a worldwide sales force twenty-thousand strong. Anyway, DC told the vice-chairman about us. The vice-chairman called us. DC called him. We called them, and so on and so on. Long story short, we got the deal. It's the usual I-know-someone-that-knows-someone-stuff. Anyway, it worked. Plus, our client list is so extensive that Zawadi was simply impressed with our track record. We worked our asses off, too, especially with the way we handled the four presentations to woo them," she said as she leaned back and surveyed how pretty the red polish looked on her left big toe.

"Let me do that, honey." Carlos took the bottle out of her hands. While he listened, he began slowly polishing Pecola's toes.

"Carlos, this is so sweet of you, baby."

"I love my Sweet Pea. What can I say?"

Pecola affectionately rubbed his wavy, black hair and gently pinched his ear. He quickly glanced at her and softly kissed the sole of her feet several times.

"Oooh! That feels nice, Carlos." Her voice was now softer and sexier as she continued her story. "We have to handle the entire celebration agenda, everything from coordinating hotels, to travel, selecting the facilitators, and on and on and on. So we hooked up a deal with that Black owned travel agency, Platinumm Travel. They'll handle that portion. You remember the agency that handled the Ujima Literary Society's trip to Africa in January? We met with the owners, Desiree Shepperd, Majeeda Sabree, and Atiya Sabree."

"Are they sisters?"

"Yep. They're three sharp, together, Black women. It's amazing. Before that trip to Africa, no one we knew was aware that there was a Black owned travel agency in Winston." She spoke excitedly with a huge grin on her face.

"That's great, baby."

"Carlos, they're very, very nice ladies. They were extremely happy we chose to do business with them on such a large scale, especially since they told us that most of their business is from out of town and that Black folks in Winston-Salem don't think their Northworld, USAir, American and Delta Airlines planes fly the same places the white boy agencies do." Pecola laughed. "Symone told them that she and I could tell them a few stories about support from our Black brothers and sisters in the city. You know about problems with patronizing anything Black." She sucked her teeth in disgust.

Carlos could tell she was unusually excited about MO clinching this contract. At the rate she was going, Pecola would talk about the Zawadi deal non-stop. But right now, he had other, erotic thoughts on his mind.

"That's fantastic, baby. I'm really glad to hear the good news." He kissed her knees.

"Carlos sugar dumpling, whenever we coordinate other meetings that require extensive travel, we'll contract with their company. Platinumm Travel makes money. Meetings Odyssey makes money, and everyone is happy."

She paused for a moment. She reflected on the meeting and how well it went last week. Those three women had a lot to share about the positives and negatives of being a Black-owned business in cliquish Winston-Salem."

"When Ujima booked the trip to Africa, Symone and Alex helped me." Carlos laughed quietly as he remembered how Symone and Alex tried to boss him around incessantly.

Every two years, the Ujima Literary Society's families plan an education vacation, and Africa was the unanimous choice of the members for the last trip they took in January. As president of the society, Carlos was responsible for handling payments from each member along with his two trusty helpers, Symone and Alex. Symone was the treasurer, and Alex was the financial secretary. To this day, Carlos, Symone, and Alex laugh about how crazy it was to keep up with payments for the adults, children and anybody else the members dragged in off the street to take the trip to Africa.

"When I visited the office to pay for the tickets and meet with their manager, even then I was impressed with the entire operation. I was shocked when they told me that they had been in business for five years, and I had never heard of them," Carlos added in disbelief. "You know they must have boocoo business in this town with the way Black people travel all the time. And their company *is* the only African-American owned agency. That's the best kept secret in Winston-Salem, baby."

Pecola nodded her head knowingly. "Dumpling, we're just happy to know they're here. You know Symone believes that whatever Black folk needs are, there are Black-owned businesses somewhere who can handle it."

"My Trini girl is absolutely right. That's how Rico and I think too with the subcontractors we use."

"The older I get, I gots to agree. It's amazing the talent we can find within our own people."

"Exactly, baby."

"You remember how Symone and I often talked about opening our own travel agency? We believed it would be a good idea for us to create a travel division as part of MO." Pecola smiled at the ambitious memory. "Humph. I told Symone that the main reason she wanted an in-house agency was so that she and her family could travel back and forth to Trinidad for little or nothing."

"I don't believe that's the reason. Not with the way the Eisners have them traveling all over the world, they don't pay a thing anyway. Plus, they have access to those private jets."

"I know, baby. Like everybody, there are still ways you try to economize no matter how much you have. So Symone doesn't mind pinching her pennies every now and then, either."

"You mean pinching her millions every now and then," Carlos said quickly and began laughing. He paused briefly and interrupted her. "Baby, all this sounds fantastic. It really does, but can we change the subject, sweetheart?"

"Carlos! I'm trying to tell you something."

"Ok, baby," he said, smiling. Hunger for sex was making him impatient.

"It was an excellent day."

"Great. As far as you and I are concerned, we need to figure out how to celebrate yall signing the deal. Maybe we can have a celebratory dinner with Platinumm Travel or simply with Meetings Odyssey staff. Hell, I don't care right now. All I want to do is relax with my baby." Carlos uttered each word very slowly and gazed sexily into Pecola's bright, green eyes. Carlos sat on the bed and started to massage Pecola's feet.

"Carlos, you're going to mess up my nails," she wailed. He watched her hungrily.

"Who cares if I mess them up? I'll just do them again," he whispered as he pulled her closer and rubbed her breasts against his chest. Pecola didn't mind if he smeared her toes or not, not right now. Very slowly, her mind surely forgot about the Zawadi meetings. His hands moved methodically up her legs, and he started fingering her moist pubic hairs. He pulled his fingers from between her legs and smelled them.

"Hmmm. You smell so fresh down there, Sweet Pea. Now, explain to me again what happened today," he said softly in a joking voice. Carlos continued to place his fingers up in her, pulled them out, and licked them one by one. He did that several times, and Pecola closed her eyes.

"Well, uh, that's about all that happened today, baby," Pecola murmured lazily and very sensually.

"Let's take a hot Jacuzzi bath, darling."

"I've already had one, but I can take another one if you want me to, Carlos." Her words came out in a sexy whisper. Carlos' lips found the spot behind her ears, and little quivers shot all through her as he kissed and licked it. She nibbled, sucked his neck, and rubbed his crotch with one hand while the other hand rapidly rubbed his hair back and forth. He too shuddered as sensations raced all over his body.

Carlos stood up and began to slowly unbutton his shirt. As if she were viewing a private strip tease, Pecola leaned on her elbows to watch his every movement. She motioned him to come to her, and she opened his belt and unzipped his pants. Carlos stepped out of them. Once he straightened up, Pecola took his hard, long, and fat penis into her mouth. She began sucking tenderly, softly and making loud slurping sounds. Carlos definitely smelled good to her even though it wasn't a squeaky clean odor. He had worked half a day. It was a combination scent of a little sweat and cologne, but not offensive to her at all. He was her man, and right now, his smell was intoxicating. The bath Carlos suggested could wait. Pecola continued to vigorously suck him, and his knees buckled.

"...Woooo! Aah, baby. Oooh! That feels good, Sweet Pea. Not now, baby. I'm not ready to have it happen like that. Not right now. Not like that. Come on, baby." With glazed eyes, he spoke the words with a soft urgency. He gently pried her hot mouth away from his penis and backed away.

Carlos pulled off his socks and lay in the bed beside her. With her lips looking sultry, wet and inviting, he kissed her mouth and each side of her neck. Pecola played with his balls, softly rubbing them together as if they were round, silver Chinese exercise balls. When he slid his tongue down her body, he spread her legs and buried his mouth between them. From the pure ecstasy of it all, Pecola's breath got caught in her throat.

"You know, I've been breathing you and tasting you all day, baby. I wanted to come home to do just this. To get myself ready to suck your pussy real good when you got here tonight." While quickly licking Pecola's tip of tips or as Carlos called the clitoris, the little man in the boat, Pecola writhed from the delightful, pleasurable emotions his warm sucking sprayed all over her body.

"Your pussy is sooo good and sweet."

"Oooh, Carlos. I love it when you talk dirty to me," she said quietly as she stretched her arms luxuriously above her head for a moment.

Pecola smiled and opened her legs wider as Carlos made her bend her knees slightly and hold them close to her body. Carlos used his thumbs to open her up as wide as possible, and he began to rhythmically suck her clitoris gently. He came up to kiss her breasts and went back down for more. Pecola stretched her legs out and tried to push his head through her body as pleasure ravished her weary body. Carlos didn't stop either. He knew his wife enjoyed oral sex, and he knew he was an expert at it. He had been kissing her all over for over twenty-five years.

Carlos began to feel Pecola's body stiffen and tremble in his mouth. He knew she was reaching the peak, which made him nibble and suck even harder. Finally, she screamed his name repeatedly. He loved the way she moaned his name when they made love. It made him know that he still had it going on with her. All these years later, she still hollered for him, and he was more determined than ever to please her. Carlos continued to pull until he felt the juices fill his mouth. He raised his body and sucked each breast. Then, he moved his ass around until he found the opening where he forcefully entered her.

"Oh, Carlos baby. Hmmm. This is absolutely, wonderful and fantastic, baby. Damn, you feel great in me." As she bit her bottom lip and licked her mouth, she breathed the compliments to him in tones of satisfaction.

Carlos pulled her head back by the hair, and the two kissed each other hard on the mouth. Pecola groaned with awesome delight as she squeezed his behind and grabbed his body. She wrapped her arms around the back of his shoulder. The movements started slowly then became fast until both climaxed together in one heap. To catch their breath, they laid together silently for a few moments. While they remained in the braid-like embrace, their hands continued stroking each other, and they talked quietly and kissed tenderly. A few minutes later, Pecola stopped talking. Eventually, she fell asleep and started snoring. She was out cold.

Chapter Seventy-Seven

Carlos cracked his knuckles and gave the sleeping Pecola a kiss. He stood up and went to get a cigar out the humidor. He clipped the edges and lit it. After being with Bradley for five straight days, Carlos was now on a jazz kick. He had been playing jazz sounds at the CR Group's Winston-Salem office as well as in his car. Carlos walked over to the stereo system and stuck in the Terence Blanchard CD that Scott presented to all the male volunteers during the children's closing ceremonies at the Devereauxs' back in August.

Once Carlos was back in bed beside Pecola, he took a deep, long drag from the cigar. He watched the trail of cigar smoke journey and disappear into the bedroom air. As he basked in the zone of satisfaction, he smiled. He puffed slowly again and blew smoke rings at the bedroom chandelier. *Yep. I know I'm an expert at sucking pussy. I should be. The best trained me,* Carlos thought to himself with a small grin on his face as he watched a knocked-out Pecola.

Carlos had been engaging in oral sex for twenty-eight years, ever since old lady Morehead led him into her house when he was just fourteen years old. That was the summer the CR Construction Group was installing a new roof on her brick home on Benbow Road, the house she inherited from her parents. Miss Jeanette Donna Morehead was a thirty-three-year-old divorcee who was a friend of his mother. She offered Carlos a glass of icy cold, cranberry juice that hot day, and while he gulped down the juice, she brushed her large breasts up against him. As a young boy on the Dudley High basketball team, the guys talked about what an older woman could do, but Carlos had never experienced being with one. Miss Morehead invited him to visit with her later on that evening. Carlos was scared, but he was ready. For what, he didn't know. He was still a virgin, but he still promised Miss Morehead that he would return later that night.

Because Carlos didn't know the first thing to do with a woman's body, Miss Morehead taught him all the special places he needed to massage and lick so that women would come back begging for more. Everything that he needed to know for a female's enjoyment and what pleasure he was supposed to receive as a man, he learned from Miss Jeannette Donna Morehead.

Just three months after Carlos began having sex with her, she explained to him why she selected him. An Ethel Waters album was playing softly on the old, brownwood RCA phonograph in her bedroom. As Miss Jeannette spoke, her body swayed slightly to the left and right to the sweet beat of the music.

"Since you and your brother were a little thing, I've been watching you."

"Watching us, Miss Jeannette?"

"That's what I said, baby boy."

To Carlos, Miss Jeannette was one of the most beautiful women he had ever seen in Greensboro. A tall, medium sized, light-skinned, high yellow woman with jet-black balls for eyes, she had long coarse rope black hair that stretched to her waist. While they were having this discussion, Carlos was brushing her hair as she sat on the vanity stool in front of her dressing table. The two of them had just finished making love. It was on a Saturday night, and Carlos had told his parents that he was going to the movies with some of his basketball buddies.

"Watching us?" He repeated the question. "Why, Miss Jeannette?" Even though she asked him not to call her Miss Jeannette, he continued to do it out of habit. She still was one of his mother's best friends.

"*Why?* You should ask me why."

"Yes, ma'am. Why?"

"Well, you and Rico are two pretty red young niggers. One day, I said to myself, 'They need your help, Jeannette. You don't want them to become a RAM, Jeannette. You know that. So help them Reynolds boys out.'"

"*A RAM?*" Carlos asked, suddenly curious.

"Yes, baby boy. It isn't about *ramming* your big dick in a woman either. It's Red Ass Men. Those initials spell RAM. That's what a RAM stands for in my book, especially red ass men who can't fuck. I done run into a lot of them in my day. They're sooo pretty that all women want to do is look at them and admire their honey-colored, light-skinned faces, and their pretty hair. Women want to take care of them and buy them gifts. Those men get so ruined just cause they're pretty. They never learn how to take care of a woman cause they don't have to. That's cause women been doing it sexually for them a long time. Women are sho nuff color-struck by them. Those men ain't had to give much of anything. They just lay down in bed and receive—just live off all the attention heaped on them. So yeah, baby. Those RAMs are all into themselves and their prettiness. Can't even fuck a woman right let alone handle a helluva woman like myself. You understand what I'm saying, baby boy?"

"Yes, ma'am." Carlos really didn't. *If a red ass man is a RAM, then a Black ass man must be a BAM,* Carlos thought. However he said nothing. Carlos laid Miss Jeannette's lovely hair against his open palm and brushed it with long, tender strokes.

"I don't want you to be a RAM, so that's why I picked you, baby. You'll know what to do and how to do it. Everything. Your Mama done told me how smart you and your brother is. When I get through teaching you, you'll be one well-rounded little red nigger," she said with an immense smile. As usual, her manner was direct, but her voice was soft. Whenever she talked to Carlos, he always listened to her intently.

"Now I don't teach just anybody else what I know. Married men? Humph, I stay away from them two-timing kind of niggers. Just dark-skinned single men, young boys mostly, and sons of my friends. Just the light-skinned, quiet ones, especially if I get a liking to them and can tell, can feel the vibes that they need my help. Like you did, Carlos."

"Er, uh, Miss Jeannette. Mr. Morehead, your husband, was light-skinned like you. He was a red nigger like us, and you married him." She had shown Carlos old photographs of her ex-husband. Carlos stopped brushing her hair and gazed into her eyes. She blew him a kiss. When she did that, his penis stiffened again and bounced around on her back.

"I know that, baby boy. That's why he ain't living here no mo'. He couldn't do shit for me. That's why I put him out seven years ago. He ain't never loved me right. I knew something was missing deep down in me, that is until I met McLean Andre Harrison, Jr."

"McLean Andre Harrison?"

"Yeah, baby boy. I done shown your Mama plenty pictures of him. She met him twice. Just briefly, though. Big, jet black pretty man. Smooth-chocolate, handsome man. After he made love to me, he made me feel like I was God's gift to the human race. He gave me substance. Opened up my legs and changed my whole world. Made me feel special like I had a song in me all the time. That's how he talked to me and loved me. After McLean, I hadn't been right since." She stopped speaking for a moment and recalled a few glorious memories about McLean. "Happiness can't last always. I done found that out real fast. God fixed mine. God put an end to my happiness, baby boy. Three years ago, my McLean got killed over a card game in a liquor house in Winston-Salem. Another Black man shot him through the heart. Killed him dead. When he died, my heart died with him. It sho did. You know why?"

"No, I don't, ma'am." Immediately, Carlos felt sorry for her. From the melancholy on her face, he could tell that McLean meant a whole lot to her.

"Cause he opened my heart up to be loved the right way, then he left me all alone. That's why, baby. It was real simple. McLean changed me, Carlos. Damn sho did. After him, I don't deal with no red niggers atall. Now the only thing a red nigger can do for me is show me where all the chocolate black ones be hanging out." To recover from the sadness of thinking and talking about Mclean, Miss Jeannette began a throaty, soulful round of laughing. Carlos broke out into laughter, too.

"I declare, Miss Jeannette."

"I ain't lying. Put me in a room full of light-skinned men and white people on a Friday morning and tell me I had to stay there for the whole weekend. Umph, umph, umph. You can believe that when the folks came back on Monday morning to open the door, I would be in the same position, baby boy. Your Miss Jeannette would be beating the door down asking them when it's time for me to get the hell out. Is it time for me to leave?"

"That's funny, Miss Jeannette. So are you. You always make me laugh."

"I know I do, my sweet red man."

"Making love with you is fun, Miss Jeannette."

"I know, baby boy. Making love *is* fun, but being in love is wholes lot better, Carlos. You'll learn that as you get older," she said tenderly as she thought about McLean again. "Just always remember that. Men need to be loved just like a woman needs it. Sometimes more so, specially with the pain and anguish of being a Black man always hanging around their necks like a five-hundred pound steel wedding band that they received from the world." She spoke almost in a whisper and breathed deeply. "But hell, every woman needs to be caressed. After you screw them Carlos, don't just get up and go. Hold them tight, baby boy. Kiss them. Whisper sweet words in their ears. Talk to them like they're the most important, most beautiful Black woman in this whole wide world."

"Like I talk to you? Like I talk to you about everything?"

"Yeah, just like you talk to me, baby boy. If you do those things, a woman will never forget you. You'll always be a wonderful memory to her. That way if you leave a nice trail behind you with every woman you be with, she won't ever forget you. I guarantee you that you'll be able to go back to her, be a part of her, and be her friend. You'll always be a fleeting smile and a beautiful memory to her. You know why, sweetie?"

"No, ma'am. Why?"

"Cause there's a part of a woman that any man can touch. Did you know that? You know what it is, Carlos?"

"No, ma'am. I don't."

"It's her heart, baby boy. The key to a woman is through her heart. Treat her nice. Love her right. Talk to her all the time. Walk with her. Surprise her with a blossoming flower from side the road. If you do those things, you can win her heart. That's what McLean did for me. One day, when you leave me alone, you'll learn that."

"I don't want to ever leave you alone, Miss Jeannette."

"I know. You s'pose to say that. I done opened up the doorway to your manhood, baby. You lost your virginity with me, and I understand. I done showed you how a man can feel once he embraces a woman the right way, but I got a whole lot more to show you, baby. Then, you'll leave. Our time will be over. You'll know when it's time to move on and get a girlfriend your own age. You'll get you a nice little high school sweetheart you can take to the movies, to the prom, and to park down a red dirt country road with and make love to."

"But I don't want nobody else. I clare I know I don't want to ever leave you," he said with his eyebrows suddenly serious.

Miss Jeannette turned away from the mirror and smiled into Carlos fourteen-year old, loyal blue eyes. She spoke tenderly. "I'm not the one to be with you for your whole life, baby. I'm just here for a season, Carlos. That's all, baby boy. No more than that. Just a season."

Carlos vigorously shook his head no. "It don't matter, ma'am."

She smiled at his innocence again. "You know how you were when we first started seeing one another, baby boy?" Carlos grinned widely. "I figured you remembered. This here older woman had to calm your ass down. Every time you jumped on my bones, you acted like you were running to the races. Now I must admit, you got a nice, long dick on you. It's good and fat, shaped in a perfect pretty way most women like a dick to be."

"You think so?"

"Humph. I know so. Your lovemaking was still damn good for a fourteen-year-old boy, but you just needed to let it flow. Don't be so fast. You acted like you were always getting your last piece. Like you were having a heart attack or worried that I might be dead tomorrow or something and you couldn't visit me no more. But baby boy, you done calm down a whole lot. Now you're learning that it's mind over matter. Let it happen. Let it build."

"I know, Miss Jeannette. I know." As she spoke to him, Carlos closed his eyes tightly for a few seconds. He carefully placed the brush on the vanity table and marveled at her beautiful reflection in the mirror. He wanted to have sex with her again.

For the moment, she ignored his starving, penetrating stare. "Remember. Don't jump into bed with everyone you meet who wants to jump in bed with you, Carlos. You don't want no easy woman either. I never liked an easy man. A man I could get just by asking. Men are the same way. They don't like no easy woman, either. I think of it like this." She thought for a minute. Then she spoke in a low husky voice. "Cause when you lay with someone, you release a little part of your spirit in them. That happens whether they have babies for you or not, Carlos. When you allow your juices to go up in her soul, when your sperm goes inside her body, a little more of your strength is released, too. At that moment, yall become one soul, body, mind, and spirit. So the woman you make love to should be special. Real special. That's why I believe you should always have a woman at your side whom believes in God. Your lovin' you're learning about from me, what I'm teaching you shouldn't be just for anybody, baby boy."

"Miss Jeanette—" Carlos interrupted her.

"I know, sweet red. You want to fuck some more? Sho thing. I feel like it, too. I done talked up another horny spell. You ready for me?"

Carlos nodded slowly but said nothing. His eyes said it all. She took his large, rough hands in hers and led him to her canopy bed. She laid down and open her legs real wide and Carlos immediately began sucking her breasts. Very softly, she massaged his head.

"Carlos, baby. It's time for me to teach you something else."

Carlos listened, but he didn't stop making moaning sounds as he continued to devour her breasts with his mouth. Miss Jeannette gently began pushing his head down to her navel. His tender, young, inquisitive lips found the edges of her pubic hairs. Finally, she directed him to the heartbeat of her vagina. She moved his face to her clitoris. Scared, Carlos jerked his head away. When he stared at Miss Jeannette between her legs, he had a confused expression on his face.

"What is it, baby boy?"

"Miss Jeannette, I can't do that. I can't put my mouth down there. Don't you pee from down there?" He shook his head and sat up on the bed to look in disbelief at her. "I just can't do it, ma'am."

"And why not?" she asked very patiently as she ran her right hand over his wavy, black hair. She kindly held his chin in her hand so that she could look in his face.

"Well, er, uh, I always overheard my Mama say that it was nasty. The guys on my basketball team say the same thing, ma'am. Don't ever put your mouth between a woman's legs. That's what I've always heard." He explained his honest reasons with wide eyes and a scared nervousness. He looked down. "I just can't do it, ma'am."

"Carlos, puhleeze lock your pretty blue eyes on mine, baby. You have nothing to *ever* be ashamed of, to be timid about. Speak your mind. Say the truth as you know it. Don't ever be shame with me, baby. Puhleeze hold your head up." Carlos slowly raised his face to stare in her eyes. He didn't want to ever disappoint her, but he just couldn't do it.

"Why do you think it's dirty, Carlos? Is it because of what your Mama and what your other friends told you about it, or do you know it's true for yourself?"

"Uh," he moaned and glanced away. She took his hand and gently placed it on her vagina where she instructed him to rub her. He did, and she became moist again.

"Does my pussy feel dirty to you now?"

"No, ma'am." He inhaled deeply. Now his breathing became rapid once more. "It feels nice and hot. Like I need to be up in it—"

"I know what you mean, baby. I bet it don't feel nasty to you now." As he continued to softly rub her vagina, she threw her head back and began to moan guttural noises from deep down in her stomach. The sounds turned Carlos on even more.

"Can I stick it in right now, Miss Jeannette?"

"In a moment, baby. Carlos baby, do you eat pickled pig feet? Oh, yeahhhh. What about raw oysters? Do you love to eat all those kinds of foods, baby?"

"Yes, ma'am." His response was almost instantaneous. "You know that. You done served me some when I visited you. I ate raw oysters and clams for the first time with you, Miss Jeannette."

"Ummm-hmmm." Her voice was smooth and soft under the magic of his fingers. "What about pickled eggs?"

"You know I love them too, Miss Jeannette."

"You still eat collard greens dripping in greasy ham hocks? Don't you?"

"Yes, ma'am. You know my Mama always fix collard greens on each and every Sunday."

"Ok, I see." Miss Jeannette nodded her head slowly. "What about chitlins with hot sauce? You still eating them hog guts like they vanilla ice cream or something?"

A wide grin graced his young face, and his blue eyes sparkled. "Oh yes, ma'am. I sho nuff do, Miss Jeannette. You know my Mama fixes chitlins at least twice a month. Mama would cook it more if it didn't smell so bad. It's hard to get the odor out our new house. You done ate some at my house, and you know how my Daddy loves them though." Carlos spoke excitedly. He continued to massage her between her legs, and she offered him a satisfied smile. His penis was about to explode.

"Well, if you can eat pickled damn pig feet, raw oysters, pickled eggs, collard greens, and chitlins with hot sauce, pure damn hog guts, no less, then you can eat my pussy. Get on down there. Put your mouth all over it, and do what I tell you do to, baby boy. Savor the flavor."

Carlos stared at Miss Jeannette and thought about what she said for a brief moment. He laughed lightly. She did, too. Before he knew it, he kissed down to her stomach until he reach her curly pubic hairs where he took a long, deep breath to think some more about what he was getting ready to do. Very nervously, he began sucking on Miss Jeannette's clitoris the way she quietly instructed him to do. He discovered it wasn't dirty, and that it tasted all right. But the power it gave him blew his mind. He also eventually learned that if he did it right, he could make a woman scream loud and just as passionately than him just sticking his penis in her.

So began Carlos' odyssey of eating pussy at the age of fourteen, and he had been eating it ever since. Miss Jeannette explained everything to him about oral sex. She taught him that it was spiritually uplifting for both a man and a woman to receive the joys of mouth loving. Made him learn how to pace himself when he made love to a woman and to control his climax until the woman was satisfied. She taught him how to do other things. Take his penis out of a woman before he felt it coming. Do other things. Control. Control. He learned that if he paced himself, he would last a long time. He would climax and climax again and still be able to go some more.

Every week for two and a half years, he went back for sex and life lessons. She was an Encyclopedia of Lovemaking, and he was her avid student doing research. With her, Carlos performed the required homework necessary to become an excellent lover for life and to the woman he chose to share the magnificent lessons with.

Even back then Carlos was always amused with the way Miss Jeannette spoke to him about life. She was a zealous listener of Moms Mabley, and she often played the famous Black comedienne's albums for him to hear. As Carlos got older and continued to think about her, he could see the influence humor played in her life. She was always so funny as she explained sexual things to him. Good laughter, and good loving. Many days, he thought he would explode from the happiness those visits with Miss Jeannette gave him.

Carlos never shared the secret, lovemaking visits with anyone, that is other than Rico. But then Rico became Miss Jeannette's sexual apprentice for fifteen months, too. During the summer between his junior and senior year in high school, Miss Jeannette said that it wasn't too late for Rico to learn. He still had time to know what he needed to not become a RAM. Their rendezvous happened a whole year before Rico left to attend college at Fayetteville State University, and Rico understood early on how to keep the liaisons quiet as well.

Many times, Carlos wished there were some way he could introduce all his children to a person like Jeannette Donna Morehead. She was a sex connoisseur. As an older woman, she could dispel the myth that the human body was dirty, and let her protégé know that the body is an awesome miracle to understand. To appreciate the fact that every fiber of the body is beautiful and making love, licking, sucking, and kissing the body is a part of life that when done properly could bring a man and a woman to the peak of ecstasy and total fulfillment. Carlos spoke with his children about sex. So did Pecola, but experience was the best teacher. For him when he was younger, older was better. Miss Jeannette Morehead was the ultimate.

When Carlos finally got Pecola to simply open her legs so that he could merely finger fuck her three months after he had met her, his sexual prowess won her over. She was totally infatuated with his handsome good looks and impressed with his tremendous foreplay skills. Although he never had intercourse with her, from that point on he ate her pussy on a continuous basis for four straight months. Almost every day after high school. Whenever they were together, he did it. It drove her crazy. Pecola was a virgin. Carlos appreciated her honesty when she told him this, and he remembered how gentle Miss Jeannette had been with him. Pecola told him that she wanted to sing and become a Motown recording star. That was her number one dream. Music was her first love before anything or anybody else. That was all she had ever imagined doing with her life. Yet, when Pecola finally agreed to make love with Carlos, she became pregnant the very first time they had sex. She couldn't believe it. She had just turned sixteen, and he was eighteen. Six months later, they were married.

Although Carlos had stopped seeing Miss Jeannette when he was sixteen, he never forgot her and often visited with her just to talk about his life and what he should do in his marriage. When Carlos was twenty-years-old, Miss Jeannette found her another smooth chocolate, handsome man that she couldn't help but fall in love with. This new man could finally take the place of McLean Andre Harrison, Jr. Eventually, she married him, and the newlyweds moved to Portland, Oregon where Miss Jeannette ended up having three children with her newfound love. After a few more years passed by, slowly but surely, Miss Jeannette and his mother eventually lost touch with one another. Carlos never knew what happened to her after that.

A pensive Carlos squished the cigar out in the ashtray. Thinking about Miss Jeannette made him consider listening to some old school soul. He got up and went to the stereo. There was only one song on his mind. *Tonight is the Night* by Betty Wright. It took him ten long minutes, but he finally found it in Pecola's collection of oldies but goldies CDs. He reviewed the various tracks and smiled to himself. It was time for him to go down memory lane in a big way. After he inserted the CD into the system and placed *Tonight is the Night* on the repeat mode, he went back to bed. Carlos tightly wrapped his arms around his wife and kissed her hair again. And with the voice of Betty Wright lullabying him, he fell asleep holding Pecola very close to him.

It was seven o'clock in the evening when Carlos woke up. Pecola was still curled up in a ball in front of him with her arms in his arms protectively wrapped around her stomach. He pushed her hair back, kissed her neck, and watched her sleep peacefully for a few moments. Almost to remind himself, he said quietly, "I love you, Pecola baby."

She smiled slightly, stretched a little, but refused to wake up. Carlos lovingly rubbed her hair and thought how pretty and sexy she still was after all these years. Yet, there were times he knew he didn't appreciate his wife enough and realized he took her for granted. Several nights a week, Carlos came home to relax, watch sports on the big-screen television, listen to music, and to just simply unwind. Those were the instances he really didn't care about small talk, making love with Pecola, or anyone else for that matter. However, today wasn't one of those evenings. He took a deep breath and decided it was finally time to wash off the dried spots of lovemaking that were like tight patches on his body.

To not awaken her, Carlos eased out the bed and took a long, hot shower. He stepped out of the bathroom and toweled off. Trying to figure out what he could eat, he threw on navy blue pajama bottoms. Since he hadn't eaten a meal since lunch, he was starving and went downstairs to prepare whatever he could find in the kitchen. While looking in the cupboard, he decided he wanted to throw down. Carlos decided to cook cheese omelets, bake crescent rolls, buttery grits, and bacon. When he was done, he retrieved a silk, red rose out of the dining room. He placed the flower in a crystal vase, the food on a large, wooden serving tray, and popped a bottle of champagne.

Before he finished cooking, he raced upstairs to the bedroom and kissed Pecola until she woke up. Then, he put the finishing touches together. He took one tray upstairs then went back down to get his tray and to turn off all the downstairs lights. When Carlos returned to the bedroom, Pecola was sitting up in bed wearing a white satin charmeuse gown with black lace around her breasts. Carlos placed his tray on the bed and lifted the champagne glass.

"Congratulations baby on signing the Zawadi account and for forging new business relationships in Winston-Salem. I wish you and Symone continued success. Most importantly, I love you. Cheers," he said with a huge grin.

They toasted. The crystal glasses clinked together, and Pecola motioned for him to bend over so she could give him a lingering kiss on the lips.

"You're so sweet to me, baby."

"I know. I try. Let's eat before our food gets cold," Carlos instructed, as he looked at his wife again who was looking quite lovely in the lacy nightgown. "You see. There you go tempting me with that damn sheer nightgown, Sweet Pea."

Pecola eyed him through bites of food. "Aren't you a raging bull tonight?" she exclaimed while she munched on eggs. "What vitamins are you taking behind my back, Mr. Reynolds? The older you get, the more you act like a sex animal. Don't you know that's only supposed to happen with women? You see we're the ones that are supposed to mellow with age, not men." She nibbled on a warm, buttered, crescent roll.

"Well, you know what they say about wine, baby. It gets better with age. I'm just taking you higher and higher," Carlos said with a tease as he swallowed more champagne. He leaned over to quickly kiss her ear and neck as if he wanted to make love again.

"Oh, Carlos honey—"

Pecola didn't have the strength to perform another round of nothing. Not tonight. She was barely sitting up. What Carlos did earlier could last at least four days. If nothing else, one thing she could always say about her husband was that he had always been an excellent lover. Period.

"Let's look at some Bill Cosby videos, baby," he suggested brightly.

"That's fine, Carlos. Like I said earlier, we still got to talk."

"I know, baby. I know. We have the appointment for next Thursday at Cafe Bessie for one o'clock in the afternoon. Believe this. It's written in stone, baby. I got it on my calendar, and I told Vesta to write it down and place red marks all around it. So it's final. Once my executive secretary has it down, it's law, baby. You know that."

"You're sure?" She stared into his eyes with a questioning gaze.

"I'm sure, baby. You know it's a damn shame. We live in the same house, and we got to make appointments to have a meeting with each other."

"I agree, baby. You're going out of town, and I'll be here for a minute. So what can I do, Carlos?"

"You can go with me, and we can talk then. I can take you shopping in beautiful Beverly Hills, baby."

"You know I can't do that. I'm going to Boston the days you'll be away."

"Sweet Pea, I know. I was just joking."

"It's time, Carlos. Really it is. It's past time. I want to get it out of the way before Haneef comes home next week."

"Ok, baby. I got it. In the meantime, let's not talk about serious issues tonight. I want to simply enjoy you and take pleasure in our being with each other. Let's just look at the videos, baby. We've already decided how we're going to handle that hot topic next week. Ok?"

"Ok, Carlos."

For the rest of the evening, that's exactly what Pecola and Carlos did. They drank champagne and watched old videos of *The Cosby Show*. Carlos was Bill Cosby's number one fan and had a library devoted to his work. From *I Spy* to *The Cosby Show* to all his comedy albums and movies, if anybody wanted to review anything about Mr. Cosby, all their friends knew not to call the library, just simply ask Carlos.

The four-hour tape was inserted in the VCR. Pecola and Carlos both watched it until they fell asleep about two hours later; then the TV watched them. Pecola was awakened in the middle of the night by the loud staticky noise of the TV. Finally, she turned off both the television and VCR and crawled back into bed.

Chapter Seventy-Eight

While Pecola waited patiently for Carlos to arrive for their one o'clock appointment at Cafe Bessie, she browsed through the pages of *The Atlanta Tribune*. She checked her watch again. It was one fifteen and Carlos still wasn't there. And he hadn't called either. Pecola took another deep breath and angrily flipped the page.

Cafe Bessie was bubbling with the early afternoon downtown crowd. Business people and Winston-Salem State University students were racing in to eat the southern style homemade lunches that only a North Carolina mother could prepare. Fried chicken, smothered pork chops, turnip greens, lima beans, candied yams, fried cornbread, stewed tomatoes, fried catfish, yeast rolls, and hot, soft homemade biscuits were just a few items that were always offered on the mouthwatering menu. Located right in the heart of East Winston, the Black section of Winston-Salem, Bessie Mae Atkins opened her restaurant doors at her new location over eleven years ago.

Back then, Pecola read about the restaurant's opening in the *Winston-Salem Chronicle*. The *Chronicle* had featured the ribbon cutting ceremony of the Akao Building in its business section. Although Pecola read the Akao article at least twenty times, she wanted to read it again. Once more, she felt compelled to critique the photograph of her smiling and proud face as well as the wide grins of Symone and the staff of both companies at the time. After Pecola read the article for which she promised herself was certainly the last time, her eyes drifted over to the next page where she read the announcement about a soul food restaurant opening up on Martin Luther King, Jr. Drive. The operation had been a small take out diner on 14th Street for many years, and now it was moving into a new building. Pecola had never heard of the place. Once Pecola discovered Cafe Bessie that day and loved the food, it quickly became a regular hangout for all of the friends.

The owner of Cafe Bessie was Miss Bessie Mae Atkins. She was a plump, robust Black woman that kind of reminded Pecola of the woman on the Aunt Jemima Pancake Box. Black as charcoal with jet-black short hair she always kept completely covered in a hair net, Miss Bessie always had a bright smile on her face with showed her pearly white teeth. Her silky, smooth chocolate cheeks were so round that Pecola often thought she looked like she had a small, round black ball propped up on either side of her face. Always constantly adorned in a clean, white, starched apron, she always changed it at least six times a day. When Miss Bessie spoke, her hands were glued to the sides of her plump, wide waistline.

Pecola enjoyed going there to eat every chance she got. Cafe Bessie reminded Pecola of both her Mama's and her Aunt Hattie Mae's cooking, her mother's sister who had lived in California for thirty years but who still sounded as if she stepped out the back woods of North

Carolina like yesterday. Since Cafe Bessie's second opening twelve years ago, the restaurant expanded. Miss Bessie now had a dessertery in another building right beside the cafe. There she made homemade chocolate cakes, pound cakes, white icing coconut layer cakes, red velvet cakes, Italian cream cakes, sweet potato pies, peach cobbler, custards, sour cream pound cakes with confectionery sugar icing, and whatever types of southern sweets one could imagine. These dessert delicacies could be enjoyed over a cup of coffee or cappuccino. If necessary, special cakes could be ordered by her faithful and loyal customers any day of the week other than Sunday, the only day Cafe Bessie was closed.

When Pecola first met Miss Bessie twelve years ago, the older woman told her that she had worked very hard at cooking all kinds of foods for other people all her natural born life. For fifteen years, Miss Bessie worked at S&J Cafeteria, a chain of cafeterias located in North and South Carolina. There as the head pastry maker, she baked the rolls, the cakes, and pies all day long, day after day and year after year. In the beginning, she worked on the vegetable and meat lines and was famous for recommending recipes and providing certain dishes with an unusual southern flavor to it. Eighteen years ago, Miss Bessie told Pecola that she simply looked up one day and looked around the huge S&J commercial kitchen and said enough was enough. It was then that she decided it was time for her to do something else. That something else was going to be cooking for herself and for the people, who would grow to love her sweet, southern service. Six years after that, she mustered up the courage to quit S&J.

Each time Pecola came into the restaurant, she brought many of her other friends along with her and made sure she very proudly introduced them to Miss Bessie. After Pecola had been visiting with Miss Bessie at the cafe, eating and ordering food for the Reynolds' family on the weekends and ordering other southern dishes and cakes for special occasions, the two women became close buddies. Several months after they met, Bessie Mae Atkins sat Pecola down one Friday afternoon and told her what made her open Cafe Bessie.

"...As Ise looked around the S&J big ole kitchen that day, Peckola, Ise said 'umph, umph, umph.' Ise said to myself, 'Bessie Mae, look around in here, baby. All the kitchen help is Black folk.' The manager who was bossing us Black kitchen help was white. The customers were white. Some of them were Black folk too, chile. The bottom line was this, Peckola. The folks who was cooking everything was Black."

"I understand." Pecola smiled and nodded her head at the charming woman.

"Then Ise says this to myself. All us Blacks can cook good enough in the kitchen and the white folks believe it's good enough for them to be ordering and eating it. Ise says to myself, 'Bessie Mae, youse need to be out front in your own kitchen, chile. If youse can certainly cooks good enough to makes money for other folks, then youse can makes a little money for yerself." Miss Bessie laughed her soulful, vital laugh. Pecola smiled again, too.

"That's understandable, Miss Bessie. I've always wanted to have my own money and make my own money. That's why I'm so proud of my two businesses. It's something I can call my own."

"Everybody needs that, chile. Well, so far Ise making a little duckies with this new place. A lots more than Ise expected, Peckola."

"Good."

"But Ise don't know why. Ise believes if Ise turned in my 14th Street plastic forks for pretty shiny silverware, it would work. Ise just wanted my place to go beyond the oily big cooking pans and haves a nice place for folks to eat food in southern comfort and sho nuff southern style."

"It's an awfully nice place you have here."

Pecola gazed around the sunshiny bright, flower filled cafe. The three waiters were scurrying around helping the hungry customers. Sitting at a table by the middle picture window, Pecola had an excellent view of the outside street traffic as well as a view of the entire floor of the restaurant. Everything was a sparkling, glistening clean down to the beige linoleum floor to the polished cake display where little children pressed their noses up against the glass to get as close to the delicious looking pastries as they could.

"Miss Bessie, I love your starched rose linen tablecloths. The fresh flowers in the center of each table make it so nice in here. You know how Carlos, my children, Alex, Madison, Symone, and Billy go on and on about your place."

"Well chile, Ise sho nuff do. Whenever they step in the door, they always make their Miss Bessie feel real good. Real special, baby. Ise just want people to comes in, sits down, and eats like they was eating at home in they own kitchen, chile. That be all Ise ever wanted. When Ise was down on 14th Street, the place were named Bessie's Kitchen. Ise changed when we moved."

The waiter walked up to fill Pecola's empty coffee cup. "Thank you, John," Pecola said politely as she nodded her head that the half-filled cup was enough for right now.

John smiled at her and pranced away. John Hart Essence was twenty-one years old. He was Miss Bessie's nephew by her older sister, Cula Mae, who lived in Walcut Cove, North Carolina. It was suspected that both John and his younger brother, Carlton Sparks Essence, were gay. However, no one could prove those suspicions were true, other than the fact that they swished all over the restaurant and continually batted their eyes at the male customers. Other than those observations, they were consummate waiters and treated their Aunt Bessie Mae like she was their mother. They hovered diligently over Cafe Bessie and conducted themselves as if the place would be theirs one day. Miss Bessie's three children didn't want anything to do with the cafe. Her daughter was a nurse instructor at Clark-Atlanta University and lived in Decatur, Georgia. Her two sons were career military men and were both stationed out west somewhere.

Miss Bessie fixed her wide, dazzling smile on Pecola and continued speaking. "After Ise decided Ise was going to go on my own, Ise went and tooks a bookkeeping class at Forsyth Technical Community College. All the S&J bakers used to laughs at me while Ise studies my books during the break. Ise didn't care. Ise learned what Ise needs to know. Made a C, too," she exclaimed proudly and clasped her hand together around her large stomach in a satisfied manner.

"That's amazing, Miss Bessie," Pecola said with much admiration in her voice. She loved to talk to this wise, self-made woman.

"No it ain't, chile. It weren't amazing. It were the beginning. Cause Ise believe it were God speaking quietly to me. Ise just knows it were. Ise had no money to speak of, and my Jupiter—"

"Excuse me?"

"That's my husband, chile," she said when she noticed the questioning gaze on Pecola's face. "His full name be Jupiter Moses Atkins. Most folk react that way when Ise say his first name. Some even laugh when Ise says the second one. According to what my husband done told me, he was named after Jupiter Hammon, a slave poet and writer. My Jupiter swears that the slave Jupiter he was named for was one of the first slaves to write poetry. Humph. Ise doesn't know if that be true or not. Ise ain't seen none of his work. All Ise do is cooks for a living. Ain't got much time to reads a lot. So Ise doesn't know if it be something my Jupiter done made up to explains his funny name away."

Pecola burst out laughing. "I don't know either, but I'll ask Symone. She'll know if it's true or not, Miss Bessie. If it's true, she might even have some of his work in her personal library for you to read."

"Won't be necessary. Ise will just shows it to my Jupiter, though. It'll make him quite happy." She took a deep breath. "Let me finish what Ise were sayin', chile. When Ise told Jupiter what Ise were gonna do, he got scared for me. He were tryin' to figure out how them white owners of S&J Cafeteria in Winston-Salem mights act. Ise don't blame Jupiter for being scared. But Ise were thinking that them owners should be scared, too. Ise knew that if Ise opened my kitchen, Ise would take some of their business away, especially some of the customers who always yelled into the kitchen and asked me what I had cookin' good. Then Ise told them, and they orders it exactly the way Ise said. Now that be what those white folks should be scared about, Peckola. Me taking their customers. No question about it."

"Hmmm." As Pecola's face reflected a wide grin, she shook her head and bit her bottom lip. "Hmmm. That's something."

"Ise know it tis, but that be business, Peckola. Well, now yer know. From yer eating my food and all, that were a good decision on my part. Don't yer think?"

"Yes, ma'am. It certainly was, Miss Bessie. It certainly was."

Miss Bessie laughed for a few moments in agreement. "Yessirree. Ise always known Ise was a good cook. My mama was a good cook. Her mama was, too. Ise gots a lot of pictures showing the big kitchens they done cooked in. Yer knows my mama and grandmama had dreams of owning a place like this one day, Peckola. A place where they could cooks their best. But chile, it didn't happen. Sometimes when our mamas and grandmamas die, we still try to fulfills those dreams they talked about for themselves any old way we can. Even though they ain't here to see nothin, it do give us a good feelin'. Gives us some other pleasant things to talk to them about when we goes to the cemetery to visit their gravesite. We can let them know we did it somehow or another. So Ise guess, Peckola, Cafe Bessie are for my mama, my grandmama, for all my family, and anybody else that says it can't be done."

"Oh my." Pecola wiped tears from her eyes. "Miss Bessie, that's such a wonderful story. It really is."

"Thank yer, Peckola. Thank yer. It sho nuff is. Ise can only thanks God from whom all blessings flow," she said confidently with that big, ball cheek smile. "Ise done had my cafe open up here at the new place for thirteen months now. Everything is fine with it. Ise mights not ever get rich like some other folks, and that be ok, Peckola. It ain't about that. As long as

Ise do right by my customers, everything be fine. As long as Ise keeps my place clean and the food good, Ise be all-right."

"Miss Bessie, southern food can't get no better than what you serve here. Now, my Mama." Pecola spoke hesitantly and quietly. "I believe my mama is the best cook in all of North Carolina."

"Yer suppose to say that, chile. That yer Mama. Ain't supposes to be nobody do nothing better than yer Mama, especially if she done treat yer right and done right by yer all yer life." Pecola remained silent. After the two women finished talking, Miss Bessie still wanted Pecola to stay.

"Why doesn't yer wait a little longer. Just so yer can taste a warm piece of my famous pound cake. Get yerself another hot cup of coffee."

"Well, I just might do that." Pecola spoke slowly. "My mama is taking care of my three oldest children in Greensboro for the week-end."

"Where little Marva be?"

Pecola's smile was huge. "Carlos is taking her out for their monthly afternoon date. You know it's Marva's special Friday with her daddy."

"Carlos just dote on that small baby so. Marva's just as cute as she can be with them big, pretty green eyes. Ise clare, she be the spitting image of yer, Peckola."

"I know. That's what everyone says, Miss Bessie." She hesitated briefly. "I believe I'll stay since my family is taken care of."

"Fine, honeychile. Let me go get cake and coffee for yer."

When Miss Bessie had been opened at her new location for four years, she mentioned to Pecola that she wanted to expand her business to efficiently handle more of her burgeoning catering clientele. She also wanted to buy the old building next door to open a dessertery, a place where her customers could just come, sit down, and enjoy all the pie and cake they wanted along with a cup of coffee, cappuccino, or espresso. Unfortunately, a shocked Miss Bessie sadly explained to Pecola that several banks had already turned her down. However, when Pecola asked her how much she needed, Miss Bessie said that it was a whole heap of money, a total of thirty-five thousand dollars. Two weeks later, Pecola walked into Cafe Bessie and handed Miss Bessie an envelope. Inside was a lovely congratulatory greeting card and a check for the full amount Miss Bessie needed. And Pecola added an extra five-thousand for unexpected incidentals that might arise.

"...Miss Bessie, I'm giving this money to you under one condition." Now Miss Bessie was using her white starched apron to wipe the waterfall of tears that wouldn't stop cascading from her eyes. Since Pecola walked in an hour after the restaurant closed, it was empty of customers and employees. John and Carlton had already left to go home.

Miss Bessie took a deep breath. "What be that condition, Peckola? Lawd chile, Ise can't believes yer willing to do something like this for me. Umph. Umph. Umph."

"The one condition is that you don't tell anyone. Don't tell a soul I gave you this money. Ok?" Pecola spoke very quietly and firmly.

"Can Ise tell my Jupiter?"

Pecola laughed quickly. "Yes, ma'am. Of course, tell your husband. I just don't want no one else to know. That's all, Miss Bessie. Nothing more than that."

"Ise understand," she said as she continued to stare in disbelief at the check. "Ise understand, chile. Ise sho nuff do. Might haves a whole heap of other folk expecting yer to loans them money, too. Ise sho do understand."

Pecola and Miss Bessie shook hands on it, and Miss Bessie hugged Pecola tightly. She embraced her as if she were her long lost daughter. They never signed an official promissory agreement, and Miss Bessie often told Pecola that the private loan reminded her of the way Black folk did business a long time ago. They shook hands on it, and their word became their bond. Five years later, the loan was repaid in full to Pecola, and Miss Bessie never forgot her generosity. Oftentimes, when Pecola or her friends came into Cafe Bessie, Miss Bessie tried to cater to their every eating whim. When they were through dining, Miss Bessie refused to allow them to pay. However, Pecola had to finally and patiently explain that her loaning the money wasn't about getting free service. It was about trusting her business sense and talent. It was about making a worthy person's dream come true. Pecola had the extra money. Miss Bessie needed it, and the debt was settled. Pecola wanted to pay for food she ate and for anything else she ordered from her. It wasn't necessary for Miss Bessie to allow Pecola or her friends to eat for free.

Alex and Symone also noticed Miss Bessie's overly protective spirit regarding Pecola, and they too wondered what was going on. A year after she loaned the money to Miss Bessie, a record for keeping information a secret for Pecola, she finally confessed to her two closest friends what she had done. Symone was surprised but happy she had done it. Alex cried. Through her tears, she told Pecola that it was a wonderfully moving and giving gesture. "You did it because you saw beauty in Miss Bessie. You saw her need not only as a business concern, but God had simply showed you the integrity, the love, and the sincerity of Miss Bessie's heart," Alex said ecstatically.

Throughout the years, the dessertery became the talk of Winston-Salem. If desserts were needed for any reason, people knew to call Miss Bessie. Miss Bessie's catering business continued to be quite successful, and she ended up hiring other cooks she worked with at S&J. However, Pecola noticed that in the last year or so, Miss Bessie didn't accept as many catering jobs. She said she was getting tired and getting old. She simply wanted to rest and leave all that running around to Carlton since he truly loved serving their clients and managing the cafe's day to day operations. Three years ago, John died from AIDS. Although John told the many concerned Cafe Bessie customers he had cancer, Carlton secretly told Alex it was the dreaded AIDS virus that killed his brother.

Even Symone loved sitting down and talking to Miss Bessie. She was old-fashioned with a real live southern drawl. But Symone also believed she had such spunk and was a bonafide businesswoman. Miss Bessie often said that any Negro could be a powerful person. They could be whatever they wanted to be in spite of their jet-black skin and their Negroid features that was just like hers. One day she had Symone laughing about banks in Winston-Salem.

"Them white banks couldn't lends me no money when Ise needs it. Then they doesn't need to be holding my moneys for me when Ise needs to save it, either. So Ise took all my money out their banks."

"I don't blame you. I understand, Miss Bessie," Symone said with a slight smile. She couldn't say much more; she had a mouth full of moist coconut cake.

"Ise asks my Peckola which bank she banked at. She tolds me, too. Ise says to myself, 'that where Ise need to be.' Ise tolds Jupiter the same thing. Jupiter will do anything Ise tolds him that Missy Peckola be recommending. My Jupiter believe yer Peckola friend is an angel sent from God."

Symone began laughing again and almost choked on her cake. "Now Miss Bessie, I ain't never heard no one refer to Pecola like that, but you tell Mr. Jupiter that I believe it's a wonderful way to describe her. She can be an angel when she wants to be." Symone offered Miss Bessie a mischievous expression and a quick wink. "And a little devil when she feels like it, too."

"Lawd chile, hush yer mouth," she exclaimed and stared at Symone with stern eyes. Miss Bessie tried her best not to laugh at her wicked humor.

"It's the truth."

"Just like my Peckola did, one of my church members tolds me about Mechanics & Farmers Bank. It be right here in town, and Ise been there ever since. Ain't hads no problems, either. My other friend, Josie Lou, do hair down on 14th Street. Her parlor ain't far away from where Ise uses to be. She tolds me, 'Now Bessie Mae, Ise done tolds yer, girl. Yer knows how that Black bank are down the street. They causes yer to have problems. They make mistakes with yer money.'"

"You're kidding, Miss Bessie. Is that what Josie Lou said?" Symone had no idea who Josie Lou was. But her comments sounded typical.

Miss Bessie vigorously bobbed her head yes and wrapped her hands around her plump waist as if to confirmed to Symone that she was telling the absolute truth.

"Ise hopes to die, Symone chile. Ise declares that be what she said. Ise believes that be white folks talking through her justs so us Black folks won't use the Black bank. It be just another way to confuse us, baby. That ain't the real Josie Lou. She don't know to say those things out right like that."

Symone sipped cappuccino and wiped the sides of her mouth with the linen napkin. "It's a shame though, Miss Bessie. A lot of Black people feel that way about a Black owned anything. So you know they must be truly scared when it comes to putting their money in Black banks. That's ridiculous. Hmmm. Nothing surprises me anymore."

Miss Bessie stared at Symone a moment. "Ise told Josie Lou this. Ise said 'Chile, yer gots a lot of growing up to do in this here business world since she be taught that white folk only one who can do thangs right. Humph. The white banks makes mistakes, too. So what be the difference? Anyway, Ise be at Mechanics and Farmers ever since Pecola worked with me, chile."

"I'm glad to hear that." Symone sipped more cappuccino. She pulled off another piece of the moist, velvet coconut cake before her and stuck it in her mouth. "If just all the people in the Black community decided to use a Black bank when they needed to save, have a checking account, or buy a home, we would definitely have a lot more Black banks around this country. They would qualify to be on high levels like those other major banks."

"Humph. Say so. Ise goes straight to the manager. She know me real well. Sometimes Ise even take her a couple of pies and cakes for her family. For the tellers, too, chile."

"That's probably how you get what you want, Miss Bessie. You know a little bribery helps."

"Oh, lawd have mercy, chile. Whatever is Ise going to do with yer, Symone? Yer just love to say such devilish things." Miss Bessie quickly waved both hands backwards and forth at Symone. Then, she began a round of her throaty, vital laughter.

"That's what they say," and Symone laughed, too.

"Weese, chile. Oh, me. Now yer knows that definitely ain't what it is. Ise go to the manager. They sees how good my kitchen be doing. If Ise needs something, the manager gets it for me. That be why Ise try to do the same thing to all my friends who works cooking food, too. Help them out when Ise can, chile."

With a smirk on her face, Symone nodded that she understood. It was common knowledge that if Miss Bessie turned down a job for some of her high-brow customers who doted on her as if she were their mama, she still always networked with other Black caterers. Miss Bessie recommended that they also receive an opportunity with her chilluns, which was how she often referred to her customers. Even when Symone's family came to town, they enjoyed going to Cafe Bessie for meals. Before Symone moved south, her mother had never tasted much southern cuisine. However, no matter what Miss Bessie prepared for Keturah to taste when she came to Winston-Salem, Keturah still was especially fond of the mouth watering yeast rolls that often appeared as if Miss Bessie had popped them out of the oven with explicit instructions to melt in a person's mouth.

Pecola put *The Atlanta Tribune* magazine down and glanced at her watch again. It was one forty-five, and Carlos still hadn't shown up at Cafe Bessie. She was getting nervous. Maybe something happened to him, and he wasn't able to call. She waited until one thirty-five before she ordered her lunch, and Carlton just delivered her a steaming hot bowl of chicken and dumplings. When Pecola looked up, she noticed that Carlos was quickly stepping in the front door. She quietly sucked her teeth in aggravation several times and continued eating.

"Baby, I'm sooo sorry. I've been trying to call you and so has Vesta," he said as he leaned over. He caressed her shoulders and kissed her on the lips and cheek. "Where's your cell phone, baby?"

"Right here in my damn pocketbook, and it didn't ring one fucking time, Carlos," Pecola said through clenched teeth. Although her angry response surprised Carlos, he smiled good-naturedly at her anyway.

"Well, hell, I don't know why it didn't ring. I done called you twice. Vesta called you at least three times. Listen to your voice mail. You might want to check and see if it's on, baby. Ok?"

Pecola rolled her eyes and continued eating. However, the little steely voice in her mind told her to check her mobile phone. When Pecola pulled the phone out, she noticed it was off. She watched Carlos out of the corner of her eyes. He had an all-knowing expression on his face.

"Is it on, baby?" He spoke quietly, tenderly, and patiently.

"Uh, no." Pecola tried to smile and spoke humbly. "I, er, don't know what happened, Carlos. I thought I cut it on before I got out of my car. The battery must be weak. I'm sorry."

"Apology accepted, baby."

"I just wanted to talk to you so badly today. You know that." Her voice trailed off.

While she was talking, Carlton walked up to their table. He only waited on a certain, select group of people. When he saw the dapper Carlos step through the front door, Carlton quickly put his starched white apron back on. He knew he would be taking Carlos' order and would take his lunch break later. Carlos turned to face a smiling Carlton.

"Whassup, man?" Carlos asked Carlton with a big grin on his face along with a strong, quick Black power handshake. The handshake was so forceful, Carlton groaned under his breath. It slightly hurt his wrist.

"Everything's fine. Just working my ass off. You know the usual and with you, Carlos?" *With your damn fine, handsome ass self,* Carlton thought with a straight face.

"Same thing for me, my man."

I wish I were your man, Carlton thought.

"What you got good today, Carlton?"

Me, thought Carlton. But he loudly answered the question differently and handed Carlos the menu. "Here, Carlos. Check out the Thursday specials."

Carlos closed the menu and handed it back to him. "Ain't got time, man. I'm on the run. You put something kicking' together for me. I gotta eat it in the car."

"I'll be happy to do that for you, Carlos," Carlton answered sweetly in a very business-like manner. He loved the way Carlos' Spanish name rolled off his tongue. Carlton turned and walked away to fulfill Carlos' request.

Pecola's head shot up from her chicken and dumplings, and she had a surprised expression on her face. There was silence for a moment as Pecola considered what she just heard her husband say.

"Carlos, you mean to tell me—"

"I'm sorry, baby," he interrupted her. "We just had a major accident on a construction site in Walkertown. Five men went down. Some are injured. That's why we've been trying to call you to let you know what happened, and why I couldn't come. When I wasn't able to get you, I told Vesta I had to get my ass over to Cafe Bessie. I started to send her, but I thought you could deal better with me giving you the news, especially since we planned this special lunch date last week."

Pecola slowly sipped ice tea through a straw. She rattled the ice cubes in the glass and thought for a brief moment.

"I can't believe this. You're the president of one of the largest damn construction companies in North Carolina, yet every time something happens, you feel you got to be there gawking at it. Where the hell are your project managers? Estimators? Engineers and those fifty thousand other people that work for you, Carlos?"

"Baby, this is different. It's a serious accident." His voice was calm.

"So we can't have our talk, Carlos?"

"Not right now, baby." He quickly rubbed his eyes and glanced at his watch. "Rico's coming. He's driving over to Walkertown from Greensboro. This is a serious one, baby. As soon as Carlton brings my food, I'm outta here. Let's hook up tonight. I should be home by eight, at least no later than nine. How's that, baby?"

Before she answered, she closed her eyes and shook her head slowly. "What difference does it make?"

"It makes a lot of difference to me cause I love you. Baby, this accident is out of my control." She still refused to say anything. Carlos reached across the table to touch her chin, and he smiled. "C'mon, Sweet Pea. We'll discuss whatever you want tonight. Ok, baby?"

"Carlos, I'm not playing. I want to discuss this before Haneef gets here on Saturday, baby. I don't think you're taking me very seriously."

"I always take you seriously, Pecola. You know that? It's just that I can't deal with any major discussion right now. Understand me, baby. You know what happens when an accident occurs on a job site. The red tape and shit."

Pecola ignored his reasons. Carlton walked up with two large brown paper bags full of food, and Carlos stood up. Immediately, Carlton noticed Carlos' gloriously shiny clean black calfskin tassel loafers. Carlton could always tell something about a man who wore nice shoes. They were excellent, meticulous, and passionate lovers. Exquisite just like their shoes.

"Man, what you got in there? The damn restaurant?" Carlos asked and thrust his right hand into his suit pants pocket for some bills.

No. But I wish I could squeeze my damn self in there for you, honey, Carlton thought with a big grin on his face and began laughing.

"Oh, Carlos, you know me. Just a little fried chicken, candied yams, collard greens, melting macaroni and cheese, fried cornbread, sweet tea, banana pudding, and sweet potato pie. That's all," Carlton explained as he batted his eyes with an excessive flair.

"Aw man, that's sound great. Like a damn family reunion summer meal. Baby, I'm outta here." He gave Carlton more than enough money for both his and Pecola's lunch, and he bent down to kiss a pouting Pecola on the lips. "I'll see you tonight, baby. Ok?" Carlos spoke in an understanding voice.

If she won't see you tonight, I damn sho nuff would be willing, Carlton thought slyly.

Pecola stared at Carlos and attempted to smile. When she slowly nodded her head yes, Carlos winked at her and turned to walk out the door.

Chapter Seventy-Nine

Alex sprinkled extra black pepper on the thyme-roasted Cornish hens simmering in Vidalia onions. When she first tasted a piece hot out of the oven, it tasted somewhat bland. She believed the freshly ground black pepper would give the entree the extra spiciness it needed. Madison had made a delightful salad earlier that evening, and he had already taken it upstairs and placed it in the bar refrigerator. While working in the kitchen, Alex was humming along to the Daryl Coley CD. She turned the volume up a tad and began loudly singing the words to *Give and It Shall Come Back* as she prepared the final touches for the weekly, romantic Friday evening with Madison. Between Alex's fierce concentration on preparing the perfect meal and singing happily along to the music, she didn't hear Madison creep up behind her. He gently tugged on her hair, and Alex swiftly turned around.

"Baby, you scared me half to death."

"Sorry, sweet thang." He wrapped her thick hair around his fist and kissed it several times. "You know I wouldn't do nothing to scare my woman. Just wanted to let you know Symone is a calling, baby. With Coley blasting all over the kitchen, I can see why you didn't hear the phone."

"Did you tell her I was busy, baby?"

"Nope. Sure didn't. You can tell her, Alex," he replied with a quick grin.

Madison knew how Alex felt about receiving phone calls and being interrupted for anything or any reason on their Friday nights together. Yet, Madison thought Symone sounded unusually desperate and stressed about a problem. Alex wiped her hands on her fuchsia ruffled apron and took the portable phone receiver out of Madison's hand. Madison quickly licked her cheek, smiled at her, and headed toward the wine cellar to find an appropriate bottle of wine for dinner.

"I won't be long, Madison darling. The bubbly bubbly is on chill, and the do not disturb neon sign is flashing all through my mind, baby."

"I'm waiting on you, girl."

Alex pressed the red talk button. "Hello—"

"Hey, Alex. How ya doing?" Symone spoke in a bright, cheerful voice.

"Now *you* know, Sy."

"Alex, just listen for a sec. What I have to say will take no more than five minutes."

"You know how I am about my Friday evenings, Sy. Call me in the morning. Ok?"

"But, girl—"

"No. I'm serious, Sy. I'm surprised you even dialed my number tonight. You *know* how I feel about my time with my husband."

"Damn! You could at least—"

"No. I couldn't at least do nothing. Just call me in the morning, and it'll be our special time."

"I'm not going to call your ass in the morning. *You* just call me when *you* have *free* time."

Alex refused to get swept up into Symone's guilt trip for her. She simply wasn't taking on anybody's problem tonight.

"That's fine. Ok. I will, girl. Take care, and *know* that I love you, Sy."

"Yeah right. Uh huh. Me, too," she mumbled grudgingly. "Bye!"

Alex clicked off and bobbed her head for a moment. She was really surprised that Symone called her on a Friday night. Maybe Alex should have listened to her. Maybe it *was* an emergency and was something important. Alex quickly shook her head to stop the guilty, rushing river of thoughts about Symone from overpowering her. She took a deep breath and busied herself in the kitchen. Everyone was aware that to call the Devereauxs on a Friday night at all, especially after eight p.m., was an absolute no no.

Alex and Madison's Friday evening celebration started for them eight years after they were married, right after Madison's tempting visit with Destiny Densonlo. When Madison returned from the homecoming rendezvous with Destiny, he knew he was tempted to commit adultery with his old college girlfriend. Talking intimately and laughing easily with Destiny about the good old days in her Marriott hotel room one too long and merry night was a reality check that struck an open nerve in Madison's heart. He realized he never wanted to put himself or his marriage in jeopardy like that ever again.

Two weeks after the Marriott incident, Madison came up with the idea that he and Alex should celebrate each other, celebrate their love. One day a week would be a private joy that they could look forward to for the rest of their lives. Everybody knows that it takes dedicated work to keep a marriage vibrant—this is work they welcomed. Alex and Madison decided their Friday evenings together would be a magnificent way to continually acknowledge each other and to slow down life and steal constant joy from being together. They reaffirmed their commitment to their marriage and their utmost devotion to each other.

Almost every Friday night, the romantic evening for Alex and Madison began at nine p.m. If Madison was on call at the hospital and was called out, then the romantic rendezvous took place on the next day. A week didn't go by when they didn't celebrate each other on a special day.

Since they now had Trey and Purity and when the two toddlers weren't spending the night out, they took care of the children's needs first. They played with them and allowed the children to do whatever they wanted to do. Then they gave them their baths. Madison washed one child, and Alex washed the other. The family gathered in the master bedroom, and they read to Trey and Purity. They also prayed together as a family. Immediately afterwards, the children were tucked into their beds, and the evening unfolded for Alex and Madison. Yet lately, and since everyone knew the sanctity of their evenings, Madison's parents and even their friends began taking care of Trey and Purity on Friday nights.

Every Friday evening, Madison and Alex cooked a meal and ate it in their bedroom with their bedroom dining table positioned by the French doors. The table was decorated with silk table cloth and napkins, sparkly, sterling silverware, bone china, crystal glasses, fresh flowers and three-prong candelabras with tall, scented vanilla candles completing the setting. It seemed as if their bedroom terrace was transformed into a five-star restaurant one would discover along the Mediterranean. Alex and Madison ate their dinner with the lighted lake out in the distance as a magnificent, romantic backdrop.

After Madison and Alex finished eating, they sat in the large bay window and discussed the past week. Alex always laid on Madison's stomach. With his arms tightly clasped around her, she held his hands close to her breasts. In the pillowed comfort of the bay window, the two devoted lovers talked about everything they wanted to discuss about their week. The children. Alex's days at home. His work at the hospital. Their friends. Problems. Whatever happened to them. They kissed. They listened to each other. And they laughed. Even though they always spoke lovingly to one another each and every day, it didn't matter. During those intimate moments in the master bedroom's long bay window, they shared tidbits of their weekly lives all over again.

They selected special music, and they danced to it before they had dinner. Sometimes they ate in the nude. Alex thoroughly loved eating that way. During those times, they each massaged the other's nude body in fragrant warm oils and slowly slithered their bodies in a quiet dance during silent moments of *Prayer Hugging*. That was the name Madison gave this unusual portion of the evening when they asked God to allow His protective spirit to watch over them, their cherished love for one another, their family, and their many friends. While they glided to the sounds of contemporary gospel instrumental music, Alex and Madison prayed softly into each other's ears.

A Friday wasn't complete until each one found a card or wrote a letter that vividly described the love they shared for one another. Those letters and cards were kept in a large book and became the Devereauxs' private album entitled *Love Dedications throughout the Ages*. The reading of those intimate notes was especially poignant. Madison declared that they were required to look into the other's eyes, and they couldn't cheat. They couldn't look down or look up. They could only look into each other's eyes and listen to the words as the other was speaking them. If Alex read her letter or card first, then Madison would always anxiously say with a jumbo grin on his face, "Ok, it's my turn now, baby. Radiate your ears on this..."

After the dinner and the talk, Alex and Madison bathed in the Jacuzzi together, each one washing and soaping the other down. Sometimes they bathed in the Jacuzzi two and three times on a Friday night. Once they toweled off, the second song was selected and they danced naked to it, too. Alex knew she experienced the most wonderful, heavenly, fairy tale Friday evenings with Madison. And for the past ten years, their Friday evenings had become a religious, sexual and enlightening ritual for them both. Unless Alex had her period, they made love on the floor, in the bed, on the kitchen table and counter, in the swimming pool, in the guesthouses, in the theater, on the double sink vanity counter top in the bathroom, on the terrace—wherever they wanted to throughout their spacious home and grounds. They discovered and rediscovered their sexual needs. They explored new sexual positions and experienced extraordinarily, brilliant sexual climaxes.

Alex remembered their first Friday night celebration as if it were yesterday. That first evening they drank Cristal champagne all night long. Madison had the special date catered by a delightful French chef who had two tuxedo waiters fulfilling their every request. Madison selected Jerry Butler's *For Your Precious Love* and Percy Sledge's *When a Man Loves a Woman* and Alex picked Nat King Cole's *When I Fall in Love* and *Unforgettable*. Since they made love well into the night, the first Friday evening celebration ended for them around three o'clock in the morning.

Even though their planned Friday evening ritual was basically the same, it was different, too. Madison always said that spontaneity ruled supreme. Alex never knew which romantic songs to choose, and she didn't know which two songs Madison would pick, either. They weren't aware what the cards would say, or if Madison was going to write a letter to her. Without question, they both tried to select the most perfect cards and write the absolutely most intimate letter. They actually spent time selecting the most ideal and enchanting songs for the other's listening and dancing enjoyment.

Twice a month, they had to surprise each other with a prettily wrapped gift. Even though they weren't supposed to spend more than seventy-five dollars on it, Madison was often the one who cheated and exceeded the spending limit. He often brought his wife lavish jewelry and frilly, delicate costly gifts. Those two Fridays were a pleasant surprise because once again, Alex didn't know when Madison was going to give her a gift, and Madison didn't know when he was going to receive one. So there was always an element of vast excitement and surprise around their weekly Friday evening celebrations.

On these intimate Friday nights during the summer, Alex and Madison often walked naked and barefoot around their picturesque grounds. There they listened to the orchestra of the crickets and frogs' natural music. While walking hand in hand, they watched in awe the city of stars above their heads in the black, velvet sky. Sometimes when they were lucky and there was a full moon glaring down upon them, they made love on the lush carpet of green grass under the blazing moonlight. Alex often exclaimed to Madison that their Friday evenings were absolutely what she lived for. They were just unforgettable, incredible lifetime experiences that visited her in her dreams.

This was why their Friday moments were thoroughly sacred to the Devereauxs, and Symone knew that. As Alex considered why Symone would call her on a Friday evening, she shook her head heavily. Maybe it was something wrong with the children. She reached for the portable phone on the kitchen counter to call Symone. No, not tonight. Whatever it was, it could wait. If it were a dire emergency, Pecola or Scott would have called her by now. Alex would definitely speak to Symone bright and early on Saturday morning.

Suddenly, Alex heard Madison yelled to her through the kitchen's intercom speaker that it was time for her to come upstairs to take their bath. She took a deep breath, tried to erase the flashing worried thoughts about Symone, and went upstairs to get ready. This evening, she and Madison agreed to dress in black tie. Madison planned to wear his tuxedo, and he wanted Alex to wear the shimmering, sexy, sleeveless A. Rene ivory gown he surprised her with just three Fridays ago.

"...Did you radiate your ears on my letter, Pookie Bear?" Madison asked tenderly as he stared fiercely into Alex's eyes. They finished dinner thirty minutes ago, and Madison was placing the letter he just read to her back into the cologne scented envelope. She sipped more champagne.

"I did, baby." She stared back in his eyes and sensuously licked her top and bottom lips.

"I'm trying to make up for the last two Fridays we missed." Alex had a confused expression. "You know when we were in Augusta? Then I couldn't get away from the hospital last weekend, and you and your friends went to the new Danny Glover movie?"

"You *know* I remember, Madison. I was just thinking about something else, baby." Alex suddenly nodded and chuckled lightly. "I could tell you were acting nicer than normal tonight for some reason. This is sooo special."

Madison raised his champagne glass and touched it to hers. "You make me feel like I could turn the world over."

"Did you enjoy my letter to you, Madison?"

"I love anything you do or say to me, Alex. You know that, baby. Did you get my message?"

"Which one?"

He laughed. "My message is that women have a need to be loved, and they deserve it. That's what I want you to understand, baby."

"I do, Madison."

Madison reached across the table for her left hand. With a contented expression enveloping his face, he watched the lines of Alex's brown, pretty slender fingers. He kissed her large, marquise-shaped diamond wedding ring several times and smiled. She smiled back.

"You look gorgeous, baby. Absolutely breathtaking in that dress."

"Thank you. You look totally handsome in your tux." Alex began blushing again and paused briefly. Madison continued to stare in her eyes.

"Girl, you are sooo fine to me. I want you to know that, Alex baby. You know what? I'm ready to rip it right off of you, though. Umph."

Alex winked at him. "Good. I'm glad you like my dress. This pushy, strange man gave it to me right out of the blue three weeks ago. I thought it fit a little snug around my behind, but the strange man told me my husband would love it. At first, I didn't believe him."

"Believe him, baby. No question. He's on the money."

"How did you meet this man? The man who you said gave you the dress, a fine woman like yourself. You need to be careful when strange men give you gifts." Alex slid her right foot out of her ivory t-strapped satin pump and allowed her stocking foot to slowly travel up and down Madison's legs.

"I met him in college when I was a sophomore at Winston-Salem State University."

"Hmmm. You mean the one and only WSSU. I know a lot of outstanding alumni from that school, too. Nice place to meet a man," Madison moaned as he swallowed a little champagne and eyed her over the rim of the glass.

"It was. The only place. Most definitely. That strange man said it was love at first sight for him."

"I can understand why. How was it for you?"

"It was more like love at tenth sight for me." Alex and Madison's delightful and contented laughter floated throughout the master bedroom. "But he was very persistent. You know the type. Very handsome and a pre-med major, too. When I finally settled my tail down and gave him a chance, I stared deep in his eyes one day. I knew he would be the one for me. Knew in my bones he would be my all and all. I finally gave in."

"That was a good move. Definitely. Where is this man now?"

"Well, he's around here somewhere. I visit with him at least once a week. It can only be done on Friday evenings, though. I can't handle being with him any more than that. Just being near him snatches my breath away."

"Oh! I see. I understand. Is he married?"

"Yes, he is. To some frumpy, nagging ole woman he met when he was a senior in college. They live in Advance."

"Advance? Never heard of the place."

"Most people haven't, but that's where they live. They live on a three-hundred and fifty acre farm in the little town of Advance, North Carolina."

"That must be nice. All that room—"

"He talked like it was. He told me that he absolutely loved his home, even his nagging wife and children. He's a pediatric neurosurgeon."

"Must make good money."

"He does. A whole lot," she answered quickly. Alex and Madison began a medley of laughing again.

"A married man gave you an expensive, low-cut dress like that? A dress to show those nice titties of yours? Hmmm. Looks like they may be a full 36B cup. Am I right?"

Alex giggled for a good minute. "You're right. That's my size. I guess it must have been a weak moment for him."

"I understand." Madison licked his full lips. "Just looking at you right now, I'm getting as weak as I wanna be. You know *I* know exactly how the brother must've felt when he stared into your beautiful face."

As Madison spoke, he slowly stood up and reached for Alex's hand and pulled her close to him. They began tongue kissing. They danced again to Bobby Womack's strong voice sprinkling its throaty, soulful sounds in the background. When the song ended, Madison pulled out the chair so Alex could sit back down.

"Baby, I need to get my gift for you," he said as he checked his watch. "It's downstairs. I'll be right back. Ok?"

Alex nodded but said nothing. Madison raised her hands to his lips and kissed them. While Alex waited for Madison to return, she sipped more champagne and thought about Symone. Maybe she *was* too harsh on her. Symone was always so vastly troubled. Alex simply wished there were a way she could slash the spirit of unhappiness out of her. Symone's sad moods disturbed Alex. Made her worry. Alex always wanted the best for her family and friends. Right now, everyone appeared to be doing ok. That is, except Symone. Alex checked her watch. Madison had been downstairs for almost thirty minutes. That was unusual. What was going on down there? She smiled to herself. Knowing her husband, he was probably wrapping a last minute gift for her.

  After Alex finished her champagne, she placed the glass on the table. Alex sighed deeply again and continued to gaze at the full moon's mirrored reflection out on the black glass of lake.

Chapter Eighty

"Wooo! I'm sorry it took so long, baby," Madison explained walking into the dimly lit bedroom.

"That was ok, baby. I was just sitting here thinking."

"C'mon with me. I left your gift downstairs."

Madison held his bent arm out for her, and Alex grabbed it around the elbow. Laughing, talking, and stepping lightly as they walked down the curving mahogany staircase, Madison became more excited than she did about the gift waiting for her. He carefully guided her into their huge living room, and Alex's breath caught in her throat. Since Madison thought she was going to fall backwards, he firmly grabbed her waist.

"Oh, Madison baby. Madisonnnnn." Alex couldn't believe it. A tuxedo attired jazz band with a saxophonist, pianist, drummer, trumpet, flutist, violinist, bass, and a harpist was before her. Standing with the band was a beautifully gowned female singer and a handsomely tuxedoed male singer. It was as if a mini-orchestra was set up against the far wall of their living room. As an added inviting backdrop, a toasty, warm fire sparkled flames and crackled wood in the fireplace. A small antique table by the fireplace was covered in lace. Along with lighted candles, a bottle of champagne was chilling in the sterling silver ice bucket.

"You like it, Alex?"

"Oh Madison, baby," Alex repeated and began to cry. "This is sooo beautiful, baby."

"C'mon, baby. Don't cry now." He spoke softly to calm her and quickly glanced at the bandleader who wore a wide grin. "Remember when we were all at Symone's house for swing jazz night?"

"Yes."

"You loved this band so much, I wanted to do this for you. You know why?"

"No." Alex shook her head no and wiped tears from the corner of her eyes.

"It's been ten years. Ten years since we started our Friday night celebrations. It's our anniversary, baby love. A decade of doing this."

"Thank you, Madison." With a huge smile on her face, she hugged his neck and kissed him deeply on the mouth. "You're so precious to me. So very precious—"

"I know. That's why you better stick with that pushy strange man who has the hots for you. The one who bought you that gorgeous dress, baby. You ain't gonna ever find nobody else like him." They laughed freely.

As the band members patiently watched for instructions from the Devereauxs, Madison nodded to the bandleader to start the music. The bassist walked to the microphone and began speaking in a low, mellow voice.

"Mrs. Devereaux."

Alex squinted her eyes and pointed her index finger several times toward the band as if scolding them.

"You know who you look like, don't you?" she asked the bandleader with an ear to ear smile on her face.

"I know, Mrs. Devereaux. I know. Charles Mingus, the famous jazz bassist. You said the same thing to me several times that night at Ms. Poussaint's house." The entire band and the Devereauxs began laughing.

"Now we got that out of the way, baby," Madison said happily. "Why don't you try it again, man."

"Sure thing, Dr. Devereaux. Mrs. Devereaux, tonight we present your man's dedication to you. His musical affirmation of love and renewed faithfulness is your husband's gift this evening. He loves you, Mrs. Devereaux. We'll serenade you with the sounds of Nat King Cole. We understand that Nat King Cole songs were the ones you selected on your first Friday evening celebration that began ten years ago."

"Oh, Madison," Alex moaned. "You remembered, baby."

"I forget nothing, not even the smallest, minute details when it comes to you, Pookie Bear," Madison breathed gently in her upswept hair.

"Your husband wanted to let you know that he absolutely adores you, Mrs. Devereaux. He loves you more than life itself," the jazz bassist said softly as he read from his notes. He was definitely moved by this particular first-class gig. This was the first time his band had ever performed for just two people, and the fact that they were wealthy Black people in love was a memorable event. His whole band wanted to play their hearts out. "We'll begin with the classics, *When I Fall in Love, Inseparable,* and *Stardust."*

Madison grabbed Alex's waist tighter and spoke quietly. "You ready to dance?"

"You know I am, Madison. I love you, baby."

"I know, Alex. I love you, too—with every breath in my being." He winked at her. "But then you know that, baby."

"Mrs. Devereaux, we dedicate these songs to you. Enjoy," the bandleader said as he took his place. The band began playing, and the male vocalist began singing, *When I Fall In Love.*

As Madison pulled his wife into his arms, he began to gently glide her around the candlelit living room to the silky voice of Nat King Cole sounds. Madison continually told Alex in soft whispers how much he loved her. He needed her. He couldn't live without her. She whispered the same to him. The band played all of the Cole classics. Later on in the evening and while Madison kissed Alex's shoulders, the female singer belted out some of their favorite ones of Natalie Cole, too. *Our Love, This Will Be, I Got Love On My Mind,* and *Inseparable.* The band could tell the distinguished, attractive couple was very much in love. Throughout their playing and singing of the romance the music left behind, the Devereauxs never stopped smiling, kissing, or gazing into each other's eyes. As Madison laughed freely about the sexual treats Alex promised she had waiting for him just as soon as the band left their home, they slow danced gracefully around the huge living room.

"You know I called Alex tonight, and she had the—," Symone said.

"*Tonight?*" Pecola asked incredulously.

"Hell, yeah. That's what I said. Tonight." Symone's' voice was nonchalant as she rapidly flipped through the pages of *Bovanti* magazine. She rested the magazine on her lap and took a big gulp of her second full glass of straight Hines cognac.

"Humph. Then I know you done lost your damn mind. Your children are with Rico and Darilyn. You should be kicking your feet up with some man and enjoying yourself too, chile. Why call her, Sy?"

"Well, I had something to tell her. Something I needed to share with her."

"For what, Sy? Why? Chile, puhleeze. You better get a grip. It could've waited till tomorrow morning."

"It's important to me now, Pecola. Not tomorrow morning."

"Then tell *me* what it is."

For the next couple of minutes, Symone stuttered about what she wanted to tell Alex.

"...I don't blame Alex, chile," Pecola said impatiently as she listened to Symone's explanation about what happened when she tried to speak to Alex. "You know the deal about Madison and Alex's Friday nights, Symone. You know better."

"I wanted to tell her something else, too." Symone sipped more liquor.

"Tell her what?"

"Something. That's all."

"What? More crap about Billy?"

"Well, uh, yeah. How you know?"

"Damn, chile. It was easy to guess the right answer. Everybody knows. How many times are you going to tell her about you and Billy, Symone? Ain't nothing changed about that ongoing problem."

"Well, she could have at least taken five minutes to listen, P."

"She *does* listen each and every other time we need her to listen." Pecola inhaled deeply. "It ain't right, chile. Don't do that again."

"Do what?"

"You know exactly what."

"No I don't," Symone replied stubbornly as she swallowed more liquor. She quickly emptied the glass and walked to the bar to refill her glass to the brim the third time. Very carefully, Symone went to sit back on her bed.

"Symone? Are you there?"

"No, I'm in Trinidad. Where the hell do you think I am? You're talking to me, aren't you? Now what is it that you don't want me to do again?"

"Lawd have mercy." Pecola shook her head and closed her eyes. *Symone must be high,* she thought.

"I'm listening."

"Don't ever call Alex on Friday evenings. That's what. Don't cause Alex to worry about you. You know how she is. Now, she's going to probably be worried about you, wondering if you're ok. That's not right, Sy. Alex is always there for you, me, and anybody else on any day of the week. Even on Friday mornings and Friday afternoons. *But Friday nights?* That's off limits over there. Don't do that."

"Damn, Pecola! You make it seem as if I've robbed a bank or something."

"Nah. You ain't robbed no bank." Pecola laughed quickly. "If you called Alex and caused her to worry about you, you've robbed her of totally enjoying the evening with Madison. That's what you're robbing her of." The guilt Symone should've owned settled over her.

"Sheee-iiiit." Symone's speech was a little slurred. "What kind of bull talking is that?"

"Anyway, I ain't got time to stay on this phone and make you try to see things reasonably. It's obvious you ain't functioning on full capacity. Are you drinking again?"

"Why?"

"You're either drinking or smoking reefer. It's some kind of substance that's affecting your rationality. I can see you're in your usual fucked up mood, and you want to take it out on everybody else."

"Humph." Symone sucked her teeth long, hard, and loud. "I don't smoke reefer anymore. You know that."

"Then you must be drinking."

"That's what you think. You don't know everything, either."

"Maybe I don't, but I do know you."

"Humph. You think you know me. How can you know me? You're not inside my body or my head. I'm the only one who *really* knows me. The real Symone."

"Ok. Fine. I don't know you then. What the hell ever. Alex always tells us how we make appointments to get our nails done, get our hair done, and to make dinner and luncheon appointments with our girlfriends and sorors. Folks should make regular dates with their huzzbands, wives, and friends. That's all I'm saying."

Symone laughed cynically. "There you go again trying to be Dr. Brenda Wade. You of all people."

"What do you mean by that?"

"It means I know you, too. Humph. You know?"

"No I don't, chile. Refresh my memory." Pecola spoke with a small impatient edge.

For the past fifteen minutes, Carlos had patiently sat on the bedroom couch by the fireplace and quietly listened to the trumpet sounds of Don Cherry. As he meditatively puffed on a Cuban cigar, he calmly waited while Pecola spoke with Symone. Now Carlos suddenly made irritating hand motions to Pecola that he was ready for her to get off the telephone. And he meant right now. Cleopatra had just come upstairs and told him she was finishing things up in the kitchen. She and her two sons were getting ready to leave to head to Greensboro for the children's pajama party at Rico and Darilyn's. Carlos left the bedroom to go back downstairs with her.

"Pecola, I'm listening—"

"Refresh your memory?" Pecola laughed quickly again. "You know what, chile?"

"Nope. I don't have no earthly idea."

"I ain't even going to get angry with you tonight over empty, meaningless words. I feel good right now, carefree."

"That's a first."

"This is unreal. You know what? I'm not going to do it." Pecola said the words quietly almost as if talking to herself. "Why should I exert my positive energies to get angry at you? I'm not going to do it this time, girl. Then while I'm thoroughly frustrated over here, you'll be gliding around over there acting like you ain't done nothing wrong."

"What are you talking about?"

"That's right. That's what I said. You know how you are. After you mess everybody up, you roll over and go to sleep like a baby. You act like nothing ever happened, and you dream about angels and pure bliss. It's not going to be that way tonight, baby girl. I'm going to bed with a clear conscience myself, and I'm not going to worry about you. I won't be the one suffering from insomnia when I rest my heavy head on my soft pillows tonight. I feel nothing but good vibes floating all around me, Sy. You're not going mess that up."

"I ain't trying to make you change a damn thing, Pecola. You can believe that much is true."

"On that pleasant note, I'm getting off the phone. When you called, I was in the middle of having a talking date with *my* huzzband."

"Whaaat? Say what? A talking date with your husband?"

"That's what I said, chile. I'm getting off the phone. Carlos and I were having a heavy conversation that you broke up on false pretenses, acting like you were having a heart attack or something."

"Hell! I don't care what you do. Sheee-iiit. Where the hell are my supposedly good friends when I need them? That's what I'd like to know. I can't find my brother or my sisters. Scott is working. Rozelle's somewhere. It's like damn, what the hell is going on with Black folks?"

"Look! I'm hanging up, chile. I might buzz you back later tonight."

"For what? You can't talk to me now?"

"Honeychile, puhleeze. You need to get a serious grip. Everybody ain't supposed to stop and drop everything they're doing just because you picked up the phone to call them. We all got a life to live too you know."

"Don't remind me."

"You're just jealous, Sy."

"Jealous? Me?"

"That's what I said."

"That definitely ain't it, Pecola."

"Admit it. It's all according to the facts, which is your enemy."

"Whaaat!"

"I know it, and you know it, too. Let me say it again. You're just jealous of Alex's evening with Madison. Jealous you don't have anyone like that to spend time with. Jealous! Jealous! Jealous!"

"Now I know you must be totally fucking crazy, girl." Symone interrupted her.

"It's the truth."

"Don't worry about hanging up. Bye!" Symone yelled angrily and hung the phone up on Pecola. Clickum.

For a few long minutes, Pecola watched the phone with an expression of wide-eyed disbelief covering her face. First of all, she couldn't believe Symone actually hung up on her. Secondly, she couldn't believe she even entertained her conversation as long as she did. Pecola slowly shook her head and tried to laugh it off. Still shaking her head and moaning umph, umph, umph, she finally went downstairs to find Carlos and to again check on the food that Cleopatra cooked especially for her son, Haneef. After graduating in May of this year from Lemoyne-Owen College in Memphis, Haneef was now a first-year law school student at Emory University in Atlanta. He was coming home to visit his parents and was bringing a close buddy with him. Pecola wanted to make sure Cleopatra had set the dining room table with the right Italian fine china for their planned Saturday afternoon lunch.

Chapter Eighty-One

Symone woke up with a slight hang over on Saturday morning. Once again, she prayed she wasn't becoming an alcoholic like her father. After Miss Jessica prepared and served her in bed a wonderful breakfast of steaming hot grits, fried fish, molasses, and homemade biscuits with several large hot cups of black coffee, she felt a little better. Since Symone didn't have to pick the children up until later in the evening, she decided that on this Saturday she was simply going to relax around the house, lay in bed, read, write a letter to Tante Tutts, and watch television. The way she felt, it would probably be the Saturday morning cartoons.

After Symone's usual relaxing bubble bath, she slipped into an oversized velour teal sleep shirt and wrote in her journal. She made up her bed and fluffed all the pillows back in place. Since the deafening quiet was driving her crazy, she turned the television on mute and stuck an Angela Winbush CD in the player. She curled up on the bed and began reading, Rayford W. Logan's *The Betrayal of the Negro,* the Ujima Literary Society selection for October. Symone had about fifty more pages to go in the book before the literary meeting next week. She read fifteen pages, if that many, and fell fast asleep.

When Symone awakened three hours later, it was already two o'clock in the afternoon. She decided to call Hazele just to see how things were going with her and Brutus. On Wednesday when she spoke to Hazele, her sister told her that her husband had just left on a morning flight to visit a distant cousin in Negril, Jamaica for ten days. That didn't make a helluva lot of sense to Symone. The brother was from Trinidad. So was his entire family of fifteen people. Not Jamaica. Symone wondered what Brutus was really doing going to Jamaica? When Symone reached for the phone to dial Hazele's number, she didn't hear a dial tone.

"Hello—" Symone spoke tentatively.

"Chile! Chile! Chiiillle!"

"Pecola?"

"Yes, it's me."

"Did the phone ring, Pecola?"

"I don't know. I don't think so."

Symone took a deep breath. "I was getting ready to call Hazele."

"Well, you can't do that because I'm on the phone."

"Look, I don't want to hear no lecture about last night. Ok?"

"Chile, puhleeze. Hell, I'm over that. Last night, I figured you were the one who had the serious problem, not me. I wasn't going to take ownership of your messed up attitude. That's for damn sure. Lemme tell you this first, though."

"Tell me what?" Symone's tone was flat.

"Giiiirrrrl! You'll never believe this. You know the friend I told you Haneef was bringing home from school? Well, they just got here, and get this. The guy is white." Pecola said in a furious whisper. Madam Hysteria aka Pecola was at it again and whispering real low. Symone had to strain to hear.

"Get out of here. You're kidding, Pecola." Since Pecola was whispering, it made Symone do the same.

"Chile, no I'm not." Pecola spoke softly and turned around to see if anyone were watching her.

"Where are you now?" Symone whispered back.

"I'm at home. Where the hell do you think I am?"

"I know you're at home. Where are you in the house? Hell, why am I whispering?" Symone asked loudly. It was driving her crazy.

"I'm upstairs in my bedroom. Everyone else is downstairs in the library drinking Cleopatra's infamous lemonade."

"Haneef didn't tell you the young man was white?"

"No, girl. He just told me what I *told* you. That he was bringing a college buddy home whose a good friend of his from Emory. You'll never guess where he received his undergraduate degree."

"Where?"

"Mississippi Industrial College in Holly Springs, Mississippi."

"That's a historically Black school, girl!"

"Who you telling."

"Hmmm." Symone became silent. "That's interesting."

"So when Haneef said that he was bringing this friend home and after he told me a little about him, I assumed he was Black. All his other friends are, chile." Pecola paused briefly and laughed. "What am I supposed to do? Get an ethnic application from my children when they say they're bringing someone home?" Her voice trailed off.

"Hey, I understand how you feel, Pecola. God forbid he told you he was bringing home his girlfriend and brought home a white girl. That would've been *Guess Who's Coming to Dinner* in reverse. The Black version."

"If he had done that, I would've fainted in my marbled foyer, chile. You can believe that. You know how I feel about that."

"Yeah, I do because you know how I feel about that, too. I feel the same way you do."

"The amazing thing is I can't believe I'm acting like this. We deal with white people all the time. Each and every day. They're our clients! Damn!"

"I know what you're saying, girl. What do you mean we deal with them all the time? We have six white employees, and you know we don't even deal with them every day. We *do* associate with them for staff meetings and when we see them in the hallways, but they don't come to our homes. That's for sure. Even so, look how you're having a fit about Haneef bringing home a white friend. If it were Jared, I would've been shocked, too. It just shows you're just human, Pecola."

"Thank God I'm human," she said sarcastically. "I didn't know what my classification was."

"No, listen to me. What I'm saying is that deep down inside, I think white people think we do things differently with our family, and we feel the same about them. We're just distinctively different cultures. Uncle Samuel always said that people are people with the same blood and guts, but cultural habits aren't similar. That's a major difference. So bringing home people from another culture is always a shock to the family that they're brought home to, especially if they weren't expecting them. It's different doing business with white people than when you have them over for dinner."

"No kidding." They both began laughing.

"Look! I'm trying to help you out here. Back in New York, people were always shocked when Uncle Samuel introduced Uncle Willie and Uncle Cecil as his brothers. It's just different."

Symone hesitated a moment to let her words sink in. Pecola couldn't think of a response to all of this. Quite frankly, she still was in total shock about the unexpected guest.

"Ok, chile. I believe I got a grip now."

"You know what I'm saying? We do business with white people. They may be an employee or a co-worker, but we aren't moved to the point where we invite them over for Sunday brunch or our garden tea. Not yet or maybe not in the South. At least, I'm not. We entertain white people at the office like a big dog and woo them as clients, but when I come home, it's different. In New York, it seems as if I'm always around white people when I visit Uncle Samuel, but it's different down here. Quite refreshing—"

"What are you rambling on about, Sy? Are you still drinking?"

"Hell no, I ain't drinking. I'm trying to explain why you're tripping. Shit, I don't know. That's what happens when you move in two worlds nowadays. The business world and your world. One white and the other totally Black. When I'm at home in North Carolina, I prefer to mingle with my inner-circle of friends. People like you, Alex, Scott, Rozelle, and Marlon. Black folks. That certainly doesn't include a bunch of white people in my face. Maybe sometimes I might have them to my parties because there are a lot of other people they can mingle with. Girl, I don't know. Young people don't think about things like that."

"Yeah right. Sy, let me go. Cleopatra cooked all of Haneef's favorite meals for this afternoon. You know she did a spectacular job as always. The dining room table is beautifully set with candles and china. The whole thang. Giiirrrl, you would think it was Easter, Thanksgiving, or even Christmas around here."

"I thought Cleo was in Greensboro at Rico and Darilyn's."

"She was, but my girl came back this morning and left an hour ago. If I knew some rich white boy was coming, I would've asked her to stay." Pecola thought for a moment. She wondered if she could get in contact with Cleopatra now and ask her to come back over with the quickness.

"Ask her to stay for what reason? That white boy isn't any different than nobody else. Treat him the same way you do when your children bring home their Black friends."

"I will."

"You know how you act bilingual, Pecola? The way you talk one way with white folks and another way with Black people."

"Chile, puhleeze. You do, too."

"Hell no, I don't. I'm a bitch with everybody."

"You like saying that? You like having that title, don't you?"

"Sho nuff do. Folks don't bother you." Symone laughed freely. "Just don't put on all your crazy airs either, girl."

"You know I don't *even* put on airs. Do me a favor, chile?"

"It depends. I certainly am not coming over there to be sociable. You can forget that."

"Hell, that ain't it. I don't want your company, either."

"And don't be rambling on unnecessarily about Marlon and everybody else you know that's supposedly considered rich and famous."

Pecola began a round of throaty laughing. "Stop giving instructions. I'm a big girl. I can handle it. All I want you to do is just ask Miss Jessica to don her formal black and white Hazel outfit and come on over here and serve us," Pecola said with a short giggle and quickly shook her head.

"Whaaat? You see what I'm saying?"

"Chile, just joking. You know that. Anyway, I got to go. Really I do. They're waiting. I know how we can get long-winded once we get going."

"Where's the guy from?"

"Missouri. His parents own half the small town there."

"That's the deep west kind of south, girl. Ain't many Black folks in the state of Missouri, I don't imagine."

Pecola burst out laughing. "How the hell do you know?"

Symone smiled. "Well, at least you're sounding more relaxed. Good. Yeah. Just entertain the white boy well, so he'll know that all Black people aren't the way the media portrays us." Symone's voice was serious. "Your regular lifestyle will show him differently. He can get a free and enjoyable education."

"Absolutely."

"You know how white people think we are. We know what we think about them. It's just that their marketing and public relations are better than ours are. Because they own the television stations and major newspapers, they got the edge on how we appear in the media."

Pecola sensed Symone was heading for her Malcolm X soapbox. However, Pecola needed to end the conversation immediately because her family was waiting downstairs. Now, she envisioned Carlos racing up the steps any moment to look for her.

"You're absolutely right, chile. I need to really go. I must."

"You *need* to go. I was sitting here minding my damn business when you called me. Now you want to rush off the phone."

"Exactly."

"Hmmm. I know. I understand." Symone spoke slowly. "Did CJ come home, too?"

"No he didn't," Pecola said hurriedly.

"What about Elizabethe?"

"Honeychile, no she didn't come, either. Sy, is there anyone else you need to know about? Maybe the UPS man?" Pecola asked with a light, impatient laugh. She thought she heard Carlos, and she quickly turned around to glance at the bedroom door.

"No. That's all I need to know about for right now."

"I'll talk to you. I'll call you late tonight. Ok?"

"Make it *real* late, Pecola. Later on, I'm going over to Rico and Darilyn's to get the children. I might hang out in Greensboro for a little while."

"That's wonderful. I'm just glad you aren't acting mean and ornery the way you were last night. Wooo, chile. After you hung up on me, I was ready to get in my car and drive to Clemmons to kick your crazy Black ass all up and down your staircase."

"Listen to how you sound this Saturday afternoon, Pecola girl. You're cursing, threatening me and thangs. That's mighty awful."

"Just don't try that stupidness again."

"Oh lawdy, I'm sooo scared." Symone laughed and Pecola joined in with her.

"I told Scott about you this morning."

"What he say? I spoke to my dear brother Scott bright and early this morning, too. I didn't feel like mentioning a thing about last night to him."

"I know. I spoke to him after he had spoken to you. He thought it was funny as hell, and he told me that's how close sisters and brothers do each other."

"My man, Scott. He always got my back."

"You're right. He can't see a thing you, Alex, or me do wrong. Rozelle was on the line. It was a three way. Rozelle said that you should have beeped him. He would've cleaned your pipes for you."

"Puhleeze."

"Mr. Rozelle was ready to give you a quick lube tune up job to take care of your sexual frustration with the quickness. I heard Jodria yell at him to stop acting bad sooo early in the morning. They still were in bed."

"Rozelle can forget it." Symone burst out laughing. "Yall are crazy."

"No, we're not. You're the one. We just love your miserable old behind. I don't know why. Bye now, girl."

"I love you, too, Pecola. Sorry about last night. Really I am. Bye now."

"No problem, honeychile. I'm used to it. Oh yeah, I forgot to tell you one last thing, Sy. Haneef's white friend has dreadlocks."

"Whattt, girl?"

"Bye, chile," Pecola ended quickly and hung up the phone.

Chapter Eighty-Two

Quite frankly, Symone would have been surprised if Pecola had said CJ and Elizabethe were home, especially Elizabethe. Whenever she came home, she always stopped by to talk with Symone about problems or whatever about her career in New York. Elizabethe shared some of those intimate discussions with Pecola too, and there were other secrets she didn't share with her mother. Symone noticed Jared was the same way with her. He discussed a wide variety of subjects with Alex, Pecola, and Scott. Most times, Jared was tentative with his mother. Symone wanted her son to talk with her more. She guessed he did when he felt like it, but Symone was simply glad Jared was willing to talk to people she trusted.

In many ways, Symone knew she was from the old school. She always called her mother's friends by their last names. Nowadays, she noticed more and more that people didn't do that. Sometimes, when small children called Symone by her first name, she had to look around to see whom they were speaking to. She believed that was quite disrespectful and that children should be taught manners and respect for adults.

Symone believed that old and young parents weren't teaching them properly, but when children were around her, she made sure she did. Symone always politely told the children to address her as Ms. Poussaint or Tante Symone. Naturally, she was continuously surprised by the adult responses. Many parents would say, "Girl, that's ok. You don't have to be so formal with little Jamal or Barbara."

Hell! Let them be formal. Call me Ms. Symone, Ms. Poussaint, Tante or something. But please don't have your eight and ten-year old child calling me by my first name, Symone thought as she shook her head.

Because Alex practiced the same old-fashioned principles with her children, Alex agreed wholeheartedly with this philosophy. When Alex was growing up in Winston-Salem, she said that calling older people Miss or Mister was a time honored tradition in the Black community. How dare a person refer to an older person by his or her first name? Alex told Symone that if a child didn't properly address an adult or put a handle to a person's name as Alex's mother referred to it, that was a cause for a back hand slap. Period.

When Symone met people she knew and her three children were with her, she always asked their last name because that was how she wanted her children to recognize them. What really aggravated Symone was when those same people told her, "...Girrrl, that's ok. Your children can call me Patty or Jeffrey or Jane."

Pecola told Symone that she didn't know why she allowed simple forgotten old-fashioned habits like that to bother her. When Symone reflected on it, it wasn't simple. Symone could never imagine calling her mother's friends by their first names. Symone's mother's friends were thirty and forty years older than Symone. Symone could hear herself now. "Hello, Judith. How are you today?" and Mrs. Judith Francis is seventy-five years old.

How in hell could I do that? It would be disrespectful, thought Symone. She just couldn't even imagine twisting her mouth to speak without saying Mr. or Miss. It didn't matter that Symone was almost a forty-year old woman herself. Those older women were her mother's friends. It was a matter of respecting those senior matriarchs and patriarchs of the race. That's exactly how Keturah raised her. Symone understood she couldn't raise her children across the board exactly the same way she was brought up, but she definitely adhered to some old-fashioned customs. Symone may not have old-fashioned principles with her lovers, but she certainly wanted to instill them in her children. Then Jared, Kyle, and Sylvia could blossom from the basics learned at home.

Suddenly, Symone laughed to herself when she thought about the white guy with dreadlocks. It flipped Pecola and Carlos out that Haneef told them he was growing dreads, yet Haneef looked good wearing them. A real light-skinned boy with green eyes like Pecola, the natural hairstyle made Haneef look more ethnic. Symone remembered how Keturah almost did a major cartwheel across Manhattan when Hazele announced she was going el natural with locks in her hair. But a white person with dreadlocks? How in the hell do they do that? It was totally unbelievable. White people swore that Blacks want to look and be like them. The way the world was going, a lot of times, it seemed the other way around. Black women have big lips. White women now go have injections of collagen placed in their lips to make them large, too. They call them French lips. Call them what they are. They're Black folk lips. No doubt about it. Nothing but pure, traditional African lips.

Black women have large asses. Symone imagined white people asking the question, "How can we make ours asses a tad bigger? I know what we'll call them. Let's call them European Voluptuous Posteriors."

I'm surprised they haven't developed a formula shot to make their asses larger, too, Symone thought shaking her head.

Symone smiled again. And the biggest attraction or myth is white people think all Black men have big, long dicks. That's probably the number one reason white women can't stay away from them. Some Black guys really do have some nice long ones. Symone laughed at that thought. Yet, she believed she should introduce the world to the Black men she had met during her lifetime with pencil thin ones. Maybe the scientists of the world could develop a procedure to assist those men and every other man that needed a little more thickness and length.

While Symone entertained herself with these amusing thoughts, her bedside telephone rang. It was Alex. She said that she had called Pecola. Of course, Pecola told her she was too busy entertaining and would get back with her later.

"...You know Haneef told Pecola that he was bringing a guest home. Well, the guest is white."

Alex started laughing. "Why was that a shock to her, Sy?"

"She was expecting somebody Black. That's why." Then, Symone told Alex about the things that she was thinking after she talked with Pecola.

"Some of the things you thought about are true, Sy. I don't know why you get all worked up by race issues like that."

"I do it because I want to. That's why. Someone needs to. If enough of us don't say anything, then Black boys and girls will grow up thinking that the white woman or man is better than they are."

"I'm not talking about that, Sy. Haneef isn't bringing home a white woman to marry. We're talking about cosmetic surgery, about white people changing this and changing that to make their stuff look fuller."

"Ok. You're right, but race still applies. They say we're darkies, this and that. Yet, white people are always out there trying to get a damn tan. They're the ones dying of skin cancer trying to get dark like us. The only time Black people tan is to enhance whatever black color their skin is."

"There's only one of you, and I thank God for that. Your friends and I wouldn't know what to do with two folks like you cut out of the same mold running around us."

"Lawd have mercy. The sugar is dripping with you this morning, too. Enough is enough."

"What do you mean?"

"I know what it is. You're talking about last night. Pecola was on the same soapbox when I spoke to her."

"No I'm not. I worried about you a little bit. Eventually, I figured if there was anything serious, Scott or Pecola would call me with the grim news."

"Is that right?"

"Yup. So how are you doing this morning? *And,* what was sooo important?"

Symone began laughing. "Billy called me. We argued. You know. The same shit. That's all. It just hurts me the way he does the children. When children don't have their father around often, what they're missing cannot be replaced. I know, Alex."

"I know you know, girl. I worry about you, Sy. I really do. Stop letting him get to you like that."

"Don't worry about me, Alex. I can handle it. I just needed to vent and to hear a comforting word."

"Sometimes I think you can, but I'm gonna be honest. Lately, I don't know. I care and love you so much. I desperately only want love to radiate from you and your life."

"Love is in me and all around me. Yall need to accept the fact that I'm an interesting dichotomy. I'm an Aquarian, and I got thirty personalities to deal with. That's what my darling baby sister, Ameenah, told me long time ago."

"Sounds accurate to me."

Symone grinned silently. "I'm a complex person one minute and easy to understand the next. I don't have an in between like most people. Just up or down, hot or cold, girl. Lukewarm isn't in my vocabulary."

"I don't care. You're my friend and I love you. Up, down, low, or high, I'm here for you. That is except on Friday nights," Alex said, laughing, and Symone joined in.

"Ummm-hmmm. Now I got it. I know why you're saying these things to me. You wanted to throw me off guard, so I could change the cosmetic surgery subject?" She hesitated a moment and laughed. "Right?"

"Girl, no. I must admit I was worried, but I quickly tried to adopt Madison's philosophy. He told me, 'Baby, don't take on nobody else's problem, especially when we're trying to have our sweet evening thang together on Fridays.'"

"Hmmm. Tell Madison that Pecola said the exact same thing. Yall must be visiting the same therapist behind my back," Symone added with a laugh.

"No. We *love* you. I *adore* you the way you are. You know that's why everyone calls you Miss Malcolm X. It's because of your attitude and your controversial views. You're fiery, determined, and full of spirit, girl. That's all." They both were giggling at this point.

"I done heard that Rozelle was the one that penned that new pet name for me."

"I embrace your butt the way you are. You have so much energy regarding what you believe. That's all. I agree with a lot of things you say. I really do. What you say makes sense. It's what a lot of people might think and have thought about but is afraid to say publicly. You don't care. Don't ever change who you are."

"Don't worry. I've been this way too long to change. That's my problem. My personality is cemented in stone."

"No it's not. It's refreshing to me, even when we disagree. I believe we're the same way. We're just speaking from a different platform. Just say I'm like you with a Christian bent," Alex said with an amusing lilt in her voice.

"Enough already. Too much poop on Saturday morning. I need to go get toilet paper. How did your Friday evening go, girl?"

"It was absolutely, absolutely wonderful, Symone. Madison surprised me with a jazz band. Can you believe that? Right smack in our living room. The piano was in there. The harp, too. He had it planned to a T. While we were upstairs, Wellington was quietly setting things up. I called Wellington this morning to thank him."

"You did?"

"Yeah."

"I told him that I always knew he was an excellent yardman cause he keeps our lawn sho nuff beautiful, but I had not one inkling about his event planning skills."

"I know. I helped Madison hook it up for you and was glad to do it."

"That's what he said. He told me that last night. Thanks a lot, Symone. It was such a pleasure. I felt like I was a classic dancer in an old-fashioned musical movie or was Judith Jamison being glided and waltzed around a romantic Caribbean beach."

"Hmmm. That sounds great."

"You better watch out. Since you helped Madison surprise me in such a way, you know I'm gonna be gunning for you."

"Yall done tried to surprise me in the past. It hasn't ever worked, especially if you tell my girl, Pecola. Somehow or another, it always slips out of her refrigerator mouth."

"You're right. Maybe next time we just won't tell her a thing."

"I don't. When Madison told me what he wanted to do for you, I didn't breathe a word of it to Pecola. She still doesn't know."

"I know we'll have a chance to talk and laugh about all of this when we have our FOFAE dinner next weekend. It's Rehema's turn to plan it. I can see Pecola shocked expression when she finds out. She'll be mad that you didn't tell her."

"Our FOFAE dinner next weekend? What dinner? Has it been a month already?"

"I'm telling you it has, girl. Time flies, Symone."

FOFAE stood for Friends Out for an Evening and was pronounced foe-fay. Initially, the all-women group started out with Alex, Symone, and Pecola. Afterwards, Alex suggested they open the FOFAE outings to include her sister, Nanette. After Nanette graduated from college, she eventually invited two close college friends to become members. They both were thirty years old. The same age as Nanette.

Rehema was a single mother of two toddler boys who worked as a fashion buyer with Dillard's Department Store at Hanes Mall. A six-foot tall, real light-skinned honey complexion, statuesque, and absolutely stunning full-figured woman, Rehema constantly experienced financial troubles and batted a disappointing zero only with the men she wanted to have as companions. For five years, she lived with a professional basketball player friend of Marlon named Sheldon Summer. When Sheldon was cut from the league after just four years, Rehema already had one child by him and another one was on the way.

Since Sheldon stopped playing ball, he drifted across the country trying to get a big league break again. Eventually, he ended up working in a factory in Florida. Trying to get child support from him was like winning a forty million-dollar New York lottery ticket, but Rehema was smart. While she was living with Sheldon, she spent a lot but she saved some, too. Rehema was able to stash some money away that was always accessible when Sheldon played ball. After they broke up, she bought a large split foyer home with the money scraped together from their years together. Located off Waterworks Road in Lake Park, a Black sub-division in Winston-Salem, Rehema tried to remain optimistic. Once Rehema purchased the house, she laughingly often said that now the key for her was keeping it. Since she was a devoutly proud woman and a hard worker, she staunchly refused any financially helpful handouts from her wealthy friends.

On the other hand, Adele Tysinger was Nanette's other close friend who lived in Charlotte. Adele was a registered nurse who worked with Nanette at Presbyterian Hospital. She was married to Tacuma Tysinger, the loud football coach of East Mecklenburg High School. Although his family owned eight Wendy's restaurants throughout South Carolina, Tacuma didn't work in the family business. He preferred to pursue his first love—teaching physical education and basketball to high school students.

Adele was a dark brown caramel complexioned lady, very quiet, and quite demure, which was a stark comparison to the boisterous Tacuma who always had something to say. Everyone said that Tacuma was the blossoming prodigy of Rozelle. Although Adele and Tacuma had been married for six years, they remained childless after four years of trying and now were considering visiting a fertility clinic to see what was physically wrong. Alex nicknamed Nanette and her two college buddies *The Three Musketeers*. They did everything together, with or without the women of FOFAE.

Years ago when Rozelle first met Alex, Symone, and Pecola, he asked if Jodria could join FOFAE. At the time, Alex told him that they would be glad to have her. Not only did these ladies go out monthly, but once a year they took anywhere from a seven to fourteen day vacation without *any* children in tow. So far FOFAE had visited places like the Bahamas, Disneyworld, Alaska, and had skied on the mountainous slopes of Europe and Mountain

Village, Colorado. Presently, there were seven active women who enjoyed a monthly night out on the town, which gave them all wonderful moments to laugh about jokes, cry openly, share personal problems, and to celebrate one another.

Occasionally, Charmaine and Norvella, the AKAO certified public accountant, and Rico's wife, Darilyn, attended the monthly outings as well. When those three women went along, that brought the group's number up to ten. Basically, there were just the seven active women who journeyed together on a continuous basis. When Alex suggested inviting Lillie into the group and when Nanette mentioned inviting another Bennett Belle to the FOFAE fold, Symone finally said that enough was enough, at least for her. Symone believed that if FOFAE exceeded ten women, they would look like a bunch of wolves traveling in a pack, and she would refuse to go with them anywhere. Subsequently, Pecola and Alex also agreed ten women should be the FOFAE limit.

Chapter Eighty-Three

"What date is FOFAE scheduled for this time?" Symone asked Alex and didn't give her a chance to answer. "I tell you what. Alex, hold on a second. Let me get my date book. I don't remember seeing that in it."

"Can't you wait till I hang up? Just write it down on a piece of paper. You can put it in the book when we get off the phone."

"No, I need to get it now. It'll just take a minute. My briefcase is down in the library. Hold on."

Symone is a mess, thought Alex. Five minutes later, she was on the line again.

"Ok, I'm back." Now she was out of breath. "I'm telling you, Alex. The next house I get will be all on one level. All thirty-thousand square feet of it. Between the steps and my titties, I didn't know which one would knock me out first," she exclaimed loudly.

"You know I was just thinking you were crazy, then you get back on the phone and say something like that. What I've been saying all along is true." Alex spoke with a smile and heard the stirring of pages.

Smiling, Symone shook her head slowly. Her date book was filled to the brim with red, white, and blue appointments as usual. Each color was based upon its importance level. Symone noticed the Saturday evening appointment with FOFAE was highlighted in yellow, no doubt by Elisha as a result of threatening instructions from Pecola.

"Well, is it there, Sy?" Alex finally asked after waiting several long seconds.

"It is. Damn! I went through all of that, and it's in the book. Are we still going to see the new Tim Reid movie and then have dinner at Staley's Steakhouse?"

"That's what Rehema said she was still planning to do. Then we're going back to her house afterwards for girl talk. Nanette's going to prepare her serious pina coladas again. Do you have next month's date written down, too?"

"Let me see."

"That's my month, girl!" Alex exclaimed excitedly as she heard Symone's rustling of pages again. Symone noticed that Elisha had once again highlighted the November date for FOFAE in bright yellow.

"Yeah, I have that down, too. Where are we going, Alex?" Symone asked with a short giggle, realizing how Alex felt about coordinating the FOFAE monthly outing. The way Alex planned an afternoon outing with her friends, one would think it was New Year's eve in New York with the glittering, silver ball dropping from the sky at midnight.

"The limo is gonna pick everyone up between one and two o'clock on that Saturday. That's also the same Saturday for Pecola's WGH Club tea that starts at two-thirty. So we have to get that out of the way first," she added, laughing knowing how Symone hated to attend those functions.

"It's a shame we couldn't get tickets to the Patti LaBelle show," Symone moaned. "Pecola and I tried again the other day, but they're completely sold out and have been for weeks. We should've jumped on that show the same day they announced she was coming to town. I even tried to sneak and get some, at least two for Pecola and Carlos, especially since Pecola thinks she's a Patti diva anyway."

"I know. I'm sure it was a disappointment for Pecola to not get to see her, especially since she'll be right here in Winston. That's so close. Maybe next time."

"Hmmm. Are you sure Rehema's and your dates are scheduled for those two Fridays?" Symone asked jokingly.

"Girl, don't even try it. I'm positive it isn't on Fridays. Both dates are on Saturdays. You know they are. You just make sure your bootie is ready and on time for both days. Ok?"

"Ok. I'll be ready, Alex. Do you have a baby-sitter for Saturday?"

"Madison is going to watch the children."

"Girl, puhleeze. Just bring them to my house, and then we can ride to Winston together. I don't think Miss Jessica will mind, but I'll ask her anyway. Just offer to give her something. I never want her to think I'm taking advantage of her."

"You know she doesn't *even* think that."

"I know," Symone said, feeling her usual guilty self when it came to asking Miss Jessica to take care of other children. "If you offer her the money, she won't take it, though. I just prefer giving her an opportunity to refuse. Even better Alex, bring them over on Friday night. I ain't got any man plans right now. You know they love to come to their Tante Symone's house."

"That they do. As long as you promise me you won't let them swim in the pool, I'll be fine."

"Puhleeze."

"You need to be careful with your three swimming in the fall of the year. They might catch colds. I know Miss Jessica is upset that you allow this even with that heating system you got in it."

"Have you noticed how hot the weather is? It's almost November, and we're having seventy-eight degree days."

"It has been hot."

"Swimming and water. I guess that's our Trinidadian nature. Tell me what's the big difference between them taking swimming lessons at the YMCA in December, January, and then going out in the cold. Explain that to me."

"Anyway, forget it. I know you don't close your pool until Thanksgiving. Right?"

"Don't be funny, Alex. I close it when it gets cold *to* me. Whenever that is and not before. Now, back to the children. We can have a pizza picnic on Friday night in the playroom. That'll give Madison time for himself on that Saturday. He might want to hang out with the boys even. Who knows? He might need to go see his old girlfriend since he romanced mama the night before."

"My sweet, sweet Symone. What did I tell you? They threw out the mold when they made you. If Madison wants to see his old girlfriend or his new girlfriend for that matter, that's great. As long as he doesn't let me know about it, I'm ok." There was a hint of genuine amusement in Alex's voice.

"Yeah right. Tell me anything."

"The main thing is God knows. Even if Madison doesn't let me find out, God knows. That's the main person to be concerned about."

"All right already. I was just playing. Don't get serious and go to church on me." Symone spoke in an almost somewhat apologetic way. "Madison ain't going nowhere."

"I know," Alex said.

Carlos politely excused himself from his family and went upstairs to use the telephone. Although he needed to be home with his family, his mind was pulling him toward visiting a very important construction site in Greensboro. Sometimes, he believed Pecola didn't understand the pressures of his position as president of the CR Construction Group. Although she declared she did, Pecola exhibited little patience regarding crisis situations that pulled him away from his family. Pecola believed those disruptions were unnecessary. Most times she believed they were frivolous and would hear nothing about it. As she explained to him last night, she was first. Their children were second, and the family business should be a distant third.

"...Yeah, I understand what you're saying," Carlos said several minutes later, trying to reassure the person on the telephone. "But what do you want me to do? Exactly! My son and his friend are here, and I just can't up and leave like that! We're getting ready to sit down and eat. No. No. That's not what I'm saying. Ok. Ok. Fine then!"

"Carlos—" Pecola yelled for him as she walked down the second floor hallway toward their bedroom. "Carlosssss!"

"That's right. I'll be able to check on thangs tonight," Carlos said wearily and hung up the telephone just as Pecola stepped into their bedroom.

"Is everything ok, Lollipop?" Pecola asked when she sensed her husband looking uncomfortable.

"Uh, yeah, baby," he replied quickly and glanced at his watch. "The usual problem at the site in Greensboro. You know the one I was telling you about. But hey, they can handle thangs without me."

"Absolutely. I tell you that all the time."

"That's true, Sweet Pea," Carlos said, walking over to grab Pecola's waist, which made her shower him with a huge smile. "You sure do tell me that. C'mon, baby. Let's head back downstairs."

Dismiss the shit, man. Dismiss it, Carlos' mind yelled at him for at least the twentieth time today as he walked down the stairs hugging his wife's shoulders. *Leave it alone. Let it go the fuck on, man!*

Chapter Eighty-Four

"I called you about one thing," Alex was saying to Symone. "But as usual, we're talking about everything else."

"That's what friends are for," Symone said with a small laugh.

"The reason I called is that you know A&T's homecoming is in November, next month."

"I know. The crazy thing is North Carolina Central is the same weekend."

"That's what Madison told me, Sy," Alex said with her eyebrow suddenly serious. "I couldn't believe that, either. That was poor planning. I have married friends. One who went to Central, and the other to A&T. Those couples have to decide which homecoming to go to. Some are even splitting up and going their separate ways." Alex grinned slightly because she could just about predict what was coming next out of Symone's mouth.

"You see what I'm saying? That's ridiculous," Symone groaned. "Whoever plans this shit should look around and see what's going on across the state at other Black colleges, especially for homecomings. Seems like you would make more money by having them on different weekends. I declare. My Black people. I love them. I do, but my God. Look at the financial economics of the situation when you plan."

"True."

"If the various homecomings are held on different weekends, you know folks are going to flock down to Durham for Central's. Then they're going to flock to Greensboro for A&T's. When they're on the same weekend, that splits things up. It was very poor planning on those coordinators' part. Very poor planning," she repeated as she shook her head in disbelief.

"I know, girl. What can you do? You certainly got to go to one. I know over here in this house, we'll be hanging out with A&T. That's for sure. I'm thinking about having a get-together after the game. Several of Madison's frat brothers are coming over for the weekend."

"Are they single?"

"Nope. You know one in particular, Dr. Luther Turner. He's the endodontist out of Smithfield. You met him a couple of times before."

"Yeah, I know him. He's the one who acts like a churchgoer and devoted husband, but he's neither in my opinion. That is until he's around you and Madison."

Alex burst out laughing. "Giiiirrrrl, you're a stone to the bone trip."

"I'm serious. I know the brother. I remember the name and certainly know the face. Anybody else going to be there because he sho ain't a good reason for me to come."

Alex shook her head with an inward grin. "Yeah. Four other couples. Some more frat brothers, my two sorors, and their husbands. These couples are from Los Angeles, Atlanta, DC, and Louisville, Kentucky. I'm not sure if you've ever met them before. You probably have in passing. They're all very nice people. You know how it is for A&T's homecoming. A lot of people will be dropping by the house. Folks who aren't even Aggies will be coming into town. What do you think, Sy? Are you interested?"

"Well, I'll think about it. Will it be as big as the bash you had at your house for WSSU's homecoming?"

"No, of course not. It won't be that big of a party. That's our alma mater. You know Madison and I *gots* to go all out for the Rams. It still will be a great Aggie get-together. You know Pecola and Carlos always have something on that Saturday night, too. That's Mr. and Mrs. A&T themselves. I'm surprised they've lived in Winston-Salem all these years." Pecola and Symone laughed for a few seconds. "So I don't want to go totally wild with inviting folks we both know to come over here."

"It still sounds like a couple's fest to me. One that I can pass on."

"Come on, Sy. There will be other people here who aren't coupled off. You'll have a ball. Madison is getting out his old school sounds already."

"I don't think he ever puts them back on the shelf from the opening ceremonies. They always stay out."

"You're right, girl. They're always out, and he'll have them out again. You know how he likes it. The Temptations. The Four Tops. Mary Wells. The Shirelles. The Supremes. Mr. Jerry Butler and Mr. Marvin Gaye. His usual. We'll have a great time. All our friends will be here."

"Scott and Rozelle, too?"

"Yeah, why?"

"Well, I thought that crew was going to the ultra-famous purple and gold party on Saturday night at Omega by the Lake. Rozelle invited me."

"I don't know about that. Who knows? Everywhere is going to be jumping during homecoming. There will be celebrations throughout the whole week in Winston, Greensboro, High Point and Burlington. All over, girl. I know they did say they would pop in here." Alex hesitated slightly. "All twenty-eight young people from the older group will be over here that weekend. You won't have to worry about a baby-sitter. We already got older people in place to help."

"I don't worry about a baby-sitter anyway with Miss Jessica."

"I know that. What I mean is you can bring the children. I'll have different fun activities for them to do. Everyone that's coming has children, so yours will have a wonderful time, too. Since we took the younger children to WSSU's homecoming, the older ones get to hang out with the Aggies this year."

"They'll love that."

"I know. The guys are taking a busload of them to the step show on that Friday night. The annual A&T Stompfest, girl."

"Hmmm. I thought I heard they were. That's right. I remember now. I heard Jared and Rozelle, Jr. talking about it on the phone. Girl, I was standing outside his bedroom door being nosey. You know me. It was sooo funny, Alex. It sounded like Rozelle, Jr. said 'Que Psi Phi till I die.' My Jared repeated the words slowly in disbelief first. I guess he thought he had to say it out loudly to think of something to come back with just as strong."

"Get out of here. What did Jared say?"'"

"He said, 'You're talking to the best Sigma man in all the land.'"

"I can tell their fathers are training them in the ways of the brotherhood. I know how you feel about Greek groups. But bar none, that's an excellent tradition for Black folks to pass on to their children, Sy."

"Ummm-hmmm," Symone moaned noncommittally. "So *that's* how I heard about the fellas taking the young folks to the step show, girl."

"Well, if you hadn't resigned from the activity committee, you would've known all the details planned for the young people."

"I just resigned for six months. Had some serious things to take care of. I'll pick up the mantle in January."

"Lillie said that she misses your forceful voice in their meetings."

"She told me, girl." Symone rubbed her left temple. "I'm getting ready to hang up, Alex. Let me think some more about coming to your house for homecoming. You must know that I'm a sucker for all of Madison's old school music anyway. If I come, I'll bring some old Calypso music. That will put a little Caribbean flair to the whole day."

"Whatever you want. That's fine. I just want you to be here. In fact, if you don't come, just tell Miss Jessica to bring the children over Friday afternoon as soon as they get out of school. I found this wonderful woman, Pearl Marsden. You remember the retired teacher that helped with the children this summer?"

"Yeah. She was great, Alex."

"I know. She's never been married. Never had any children. It's such a shame."

"Why say it like that? It's a shame for you or for her? She might be perfectly happy that way. Every woman doesn't have maternal instincts or want to deal with a husband."

"No, girl," Alex responded quickly. "You misunderstand what I'm saying. It's not a shame for me, Symone. It's a shame for her. Miss Marsden *said* those are *her* regrets. In spite of that, she has worked with children all her life. It made me sad to hear her talk about it."

"Ok, I got it now."

"Any occasion I plan in the future, you can believe that Miss Marsden will be the resident caregiver for the children. She loved working with us and all of our fifty-six young people. You think I'm organized? She is too and is absolutely wonderful."

"I know. I saw her in action all summer long and during the big dinner at your house in September."

"A queenly, African grandmother type. She even said that she'd work with the children at our monthly Ujima Literary meetings, too. Have you finished reading *The Betrayal of the Negro*?"

"Not yet, girl. I pulled it out this morning and fell straight to sleep. It's a good book now. Every time I try to read lately, I've been tired."

"You got just a few days, Sy. Me and Miss Marsden planned three days of action packed adventure for the children during A&T's homecoming weekend, so adding yours to the bunch is no problem."

"Alex, it does sound like a great idea and a lot of fun. It really does. The older I get, the more I believe I just want to hang out, party with my close friends, and have no dealings in the corporate rat race. No responsibility. You know what I'm saying? Just the simple pleasures of listening, laughing, reading, and talking."

"Yeah I do. That's exactly what I love."

"Just the other day, I went up into my loft and pulled out my paint brushes. I've considered getting back into painting. I worked in the loft for a few moments. The only thing I did was paint a bright light, almost the color of a burning orange Trinidadian sun," Symone moaned softly. "For an hour, that was the only thing I worked with on that canvas. I'm telling you, relaxation is what I'm yearning about nowadays, Alex."

"That's exactly what I try to do everyday, too. Lillie mentioned that she was going through that phase as well. It's time to take a Creative Escapes retreat, girl. I got my newsletter from Barbara and Sharon in the mail the other day. I'm definitely going to try and make it. Are you?"

"Nope. Can't make it. Pecola and I will be in Tampa the same weekend. Maybe we'll check out the spring retreat."

"I'm trying to get Nanette to go with me. Maybe I'll treat Lillie, Jodria, Adele, and Rehema to it, too."

"Good. That'll be a spectacular little sister girl trip. Those are always nice." Symone paused briefly. "The more I think about A&T's homecoming, I might hang out with yall and slide back and forth between your house and Pecola's. Who knows? Everybody wants me to go where they're going. Darilyn's trying to get me to go with her and Rico on Saturday night. The Kappas are having their party at the Embassy Suites by the Greensboro airport—" Her words trailed off.

"You just gotta make some choices. Since you don't go out much, it might be hard for you," Alex said with a large smile. "Whatever you want to do is fine with me. Just bring the children over here. You and Miss Jessica can be carefree birds that weekend, chile."

Symone smiled too. "Marvin Gaye's *Got to Give It Up* is popping in my eardrums. It's already floating through my mind," Symone said while reminiscing about the classic song. "Lemme take that flashing thought back. Unfortunately, my mind zoomed straight to dead ass Arman. I played that song repeatedly when I left his house back in June, and I haven't seen him since. Don't ever plan to."

"Symone, girl."

"I know. I'm serious. I haven't seen him. Don't want to. Someone once said that Black people tell time by music, and that's true. Whenever you hear or think of a certain song, you remember how old you were, whom you were with, and what you were doing. Right now, I'd like to forget that last weekend with Arman."

"If it was the way you say it was with him, I don't blame you."

"It was worse."

"I'm glad you like my idea for A&T's homecoming, though. After we had that big to-do for Winston-Salem State's homecoming this year, you know I figured I would calm down a bit to catch my breath."

"You should. That was an awesome jam that Saturday night. My feet didn't stop hurting until four days later. Hazele is *still* talking about how glad she was, she, Ameenah, and their husbands came down for that one."

"I aim to puhleeze. So as A&T's homecoming gets closer, I feel very festive again for some reason. Maybe it's because of my Aggie connection and having spent my freshman year there."

"I believe it's just a good reason for you and Madison to hang out with your old college buddies."

"Well, I do love that now. Thoroughly. I guess this is our way to slide our friends into our upcoming CIAA old school party in February. You know what I mean—a get into the spirit sort of thing. Remember we're doing that party different this year. Everyone has to be dressed in back-in-the day outfits with the Afros, bell-bottoms, leisure suits, and go-go boots. You name it. You should see the Afro wigs I found for the ladies of FOFAE," Alex said, laughing.

"You know you need to start a celebration company? You coordinate all this planning so well. My children as well as all the other ones we work with are still talking about the Halloween decorations you have up everywhere. The white ghosts with the black ball eyes hanging in the trees. The jack-o-lanterns and the lighted pumpkins. With the orange lights, it's absolutely beautiful out there in Devereaux Lane, Alex."

"I know, girl. Thanks. I plan to keep them up through homecoming, too. That's what Madison says I should do on a full-time basis, celebration planning. You know me. Just enjoy life and don't sit down and wait for life to happen. I want my friends and family to do the same. Don't worry about the couples. There will be single men here. I guarantee it."

Symone knew she would, too. One thing about Alex, everything she said, she delivered on it. Integrity was her word. Whatever she told you she would do, it was done. Period. She was always very straightforward. If she felt she was unable to deliver on a particular situation, she wouldn't make a commitment to it or to anyone. Simply put, she was the epitome of a fantastic friend. The type that anyone would wish for or would try to adopt since they only read about such friends in fantasy books. As soon as one holiday or occasion was over with, Alex started planning for something else.

If Pecola and I clicked two silver spoons together, Symone thought with a smile, *Alex would figure out a way to celebrate it, convince us to close the Akao Building, tell the staff to not come in, then celebrate it as a legal holiday.*

Symone inhaled sharply. "Well, I gotta go. I've been on the phone so long. First with Scott, then with Pecola, and now with you. It feels like the phone is a part of my ear. My perm around my ear is an Afro now. So take care. I love ya."

"Wait, Symone! Do you want me to pick up your children?"

Symone took another deep breath and smiled. "That would be fabulous."

"I told Rico and Darilyn that I would be over there around five-thirty to pick up Trey and Purity. I got to drive past Clemmons to come back home anyway, so this will save you a trip to Greensboro."

"Thanks a lot, Alex. This is wonderful. I don't have to put a bra on all day long, chile. I love it. I can let my titties flow freely under my velour, girl."

"You're crazy, Sy."

"Of course, I am. The main thing is, I know it. Miss Jessica says that the crazy people you have to worry about are the ones who are crazy and walk around and don't think they're crazy." The two friends burst out laughing. "This gray, blue day has relaxation written all over it. The only thing that's perfect for me on a day like today is to read and rest. So you're picking up the children is ideal for me. I probably won't leave this house until Monday morning."

"What about church? You're not going tomorrow?"

"Nope. Sure ain't. Miss Jessica will take the children with her. I'll be right here, relaxing. I'm tired. As they say in the West Indies, 'Ah luv yuh too too bad far it, Alex. Too too bad, gurl,'" Symone cooed with a Trinidadian accent. "I'm sorry about last night."

"Don't be. It's over with. I love you, girl. That's the most important thing. It was delicious talking with you. See you later, Sy."

Chapter Eighty-Five

On the first Saturday morning in November, Scott and Charmaine were relaxing on his private patio enjoying the fresh autumn air, the birds' melody, the crickets' singing, and John Coltrane lyrics floating sultry notes in the background. Since Charmaine had planned to take a much needed day off from her dance studio, Scott told her he felt like hibernating for the weekend. And he wanted a gorgeous female grizzly like Charmaine to spend the time with him listening to some melodic blues, tantalizing jazz, spiced with a little bit of reading and a whole lot of lovemaking.

Last night, Scott returned from a three-day trip, and the descent into Greensboro was extremely turbulent. As the two of them enjoyed gazing at the kaleidoscope of foliage, Scott was reliving the anxiety of those final minutes before he safely landed the plane on the runway. Earlier, he and Charmaine discussed whether or not to order pizza, and that decision still hadn't been made. While basking in the hot fall sun, they watched the autumn leaves of the towering oak and maple trees throughout Scott's backyard display the full colors of orange, rust, yellow, and brown.

A large two-story brick contemporary house nestled on three wooded acres in Winston-Salem, Scott's home was located on Willow Ridge Lane and was one of only six homes located in the exclusive and private development. Partial to Louisiana artists, the walls of Scott's home were decorated with artwork by such distinguished names as Dennis Paul Williams, Don Cincone, Clifton Webb, Richard C. Thomas and primitive artist, Clementine Hunter. A light and airy place decorated in neutral soft beige and whites, sculptured pieces by John Scott were scattered throughout the spacious four-bedroom home.

Built five years ago, Alex assisted Scott with selecting the stylishly carefree decorations and told him that even though he was a bachelor, he didn't have to furnish the entire two floors in dark, brown woods as he had planned. She told him that he should focus on comfort and function but definitely have free open windows to receive the magnificent sunlight to match the light leather furniture downstairs in the formal rooms. Although he kept dark woods in his office library and master bedroom, Scott followed her advice everywhere else. His home definitely became a warm and inviting showplace where his tight inner circle of friends often came over to hang out to shoot pool in the basement game room, play chess, smoke cigars, or to just simply chill while watching a major sporting event on the big screen television.

While Charmaine and Scott listened to the chirping birds' melody as they gazed at and discussed the peacefulness of the thick forest of trees in the secluded backyard, they took a short nap. Charmaine awoke first. She turned and noticed that Scott's eyes were still closed.

With both hands dug in his sweat pants, she could tell he was once more holding his penis and gently moving it around while pulling on his genital hairs.

"Scott, baby. Are you up?" Charmaine asked while leaning across the small table that separated their chaise lounges. He turned to face her.

"Now I am."

"Why, baby?"

"Why what?"

"Can you tell me why you're playing with your dick like that?"

Before responding, Scott looked down at his hands as if he didn't realize what he was doing. He eyed her for a brief moment.

"Wooo! That was a good shut eye." He smiled quickly at Charmaine and leaned over to lock his eyes on her. "It makes me feel comfortable, baby. I guess that's the reason I play with my dick. Hell, I don't know why. Maybe it's a comfort zone. I never really thought about it."

"A comfort zone?"

"Yeah. There are so many women going around cutting dicks off nowadays, it's comfortable knowing mine is still here," he said in an amusing tone.

"I see. Now, I understand," she said while laughing and shaking her head.

"I'm serious. What's the name of that first lady that cut her husband's dick off?"

"I can't remember." She shrugged her shoulders and twirled the empty, crystal champagne glass.

Scott burst out laughing. "Baby, the other night I was listening to the news, and they talked about another woman doing the damn same thing. They've even given it a title now. The newscaster referred to it as *The Method*," a shocked Scott said as he sipped the now warm champagne that remained in his glass.

"I remember the woman and the incident, but I still can't think of her name."

"Don't worry about it. I can see her now, though. It probably went like this." Scott changed his voice to mimic a woman's. "'Oh! So you're fucking someone else without my permission? Let me just take care of that piece of meat. Snip, snip, snip.'" His index finger and thumb became slow moving scissors and traveled to Charmaine's nose where he pinched it affectionately.

"Ooooh, Scott baby."

"'You won't be screwing nobody else because the dick will be all mine.' Baby, can you believe that? It's wild what people will do." Scott shook his head and burst out laughing. She rolled her eyes at him and munched a couple of nuts.

"Just remember that, Scott. If you mess with me, I'll go snip snip on your dick, too." Charmaine teased. Now, she opened and closed two fingers together like scissors. Scott pulled his knees up to his chest and turned his body toward the brick wall.

"You're a wild woman. Stay away. Stay away!"

Laughing and still making clicking scissors sounds with her teeth, Charmaine jumped up and sat on Scott's lap. She gave him a wet, tongue kiss, squeezed his crotch several times, and then returned to her chaise lounge.

"You don't have a damn thing to worry about, baby," Charmaine said, smiling. "Ain't no way I'm gonna cut off my stuff. My wondrous, fulfilling supply of Vitamin Sex. I need your dick. Plus it's too pretty, black, nice, and long to destroy. If anything, I should place it in a museum and charge other women a high fee just so they can look at it inside a heavily guarded glass case."

Scott turned to look at her with a smile. "Well, I'm glad to hear that, baby. I feel safer now."

They exchanged more smiles and quiet sensual looks. Scott realized that their glasses were empty again, so he got up and went into the kitchen to get another bottle of champagne. He filled both glasses to the brim, propped the bottle in the ice bucket, and then went to change the music. This time he felt like a little B. B. King and Bobby Blue Bland, and played the *I Like to Live the Love* cut from the CD Alex gave him. Before sitting back down, Scott gave Charmaine several wet kisses on the neck and lips. She touched his chin, pulled his face back to meet hers, and rubbed her nose against his.

"I love you, Scott. I always have." Her tone dripped with a well of admiring emotion.

"I love you too, baby," he said tenderly with just as much sincerity and sat back down.

Charmaine breathed in lazily and watched him for a moment. Scott glanced at his watch.

"Damn, baby. See what you done made me do. I forgot to call Rozelle. I was supposed to call him at two with stock information. It's three already. He has information from New Africa Advisors he wants me to check out."

"I'm not familiar with them, baby."

Scott shook his head and smiled. "I ain't either, but Carlos and Rico are. That's who told us about it. It's an entity that only invests in African-owned companies. Today, Rozelle wants to talk numbers about it. Then Romallus hooked us up with Capital Management. You know that Black-owned investment firm in Chicago?" He winked at her and waited for an answer. Charmaine was aware of the firm. When she was living in Chicago, she didn't have doodling squat to invest anywhere. Her ass was trying to get away from Richard.

"I'm slightly familiar with the organization, baby." She took another sip of champagne.

"Berve Stallworth is our broker there," Scott said looking at her like she should know him, too. Charmaine had no idea who the man was let alone be concerned about extra money for investments. "The brother called with some serious annuity shit that me and Rozelle will probably jump on. I was supposed to call my partner—" Scott's voice trailed off, and he breathed deeply.

"The day is still young, baby."

"You see what happens when I'm with you? Time just flies. I don't even know who I am sometimes." Charmaine smiled contentedly about his typical words of praise.

"By the way, how is Rozelle? I haven't heard you talk about him much lately. Haven't even seen him either."

"His ass is in big trouble. He's in the dog house, so he's staying close to home," Scott explained laughing. "Supposedly, Jodria's friends came to visit from California. Rozelle got excited because the husband said that he was a Que. Rozelle took him under his wings and wanted to show him a taste of the night life in Winston. They went to the house of a lady friend of Rozelle where they were supposedly snorting cocaine, smoking reefer and doing all kinds of crazy wild, shit." Scott shook his head.

"According to Jodria, the condo was packed with women. Rozelle thought that would keep the California brother occupied, so Rozelle and this other woman went into a back bedroom and got busy."

"Get out of here."

"So said Jodria, baby. Then, Rozelle, the other ladies, and the friend from California went dancing at Unique Upstairs and stayed out half the night. When the couple returned to California, the brother must have taken a truth serum or lost his mind because he told his wife about the entire evening."

"No—he—didn't—Scott."

"It's real, baby. The California brother had a chronic case of diarrhea of the mouth. He told his wife every little damn detail. She in turn called North Carolina and gave Jodria the full 411. You know what happened then?"

Chairmaine shook her head. She could only imagine. Jodria was quite sweet and naive, but she wasn't totally fooled about her husband philandering. She couldn't be. Charmaine even heard about the exploits of Rozelle, and she had only been back in Winston-Salem for a few years.

"Rozelle is trying to dig himself out of that. He's denying anything ever happened. Rozelle's philosophy is, 'I might go to hell, but I certainly ain't going to tell.'" Scott paused and laughed quickly.

"When you think about it, you know he's right on the money. That is if he wants to keep his family intact because I would've kicked his ass out long ago."

Scott glanced at her sharply. "I gotta admit, I agree with him too. Some things you just don't share with *anybody*. It should be private because the people you tell don't govern you. Yet, if they see you do something right, wrong, or indifferent, you put yourself in a very vulnerable situation if they become disloyal. Then, they *can* govern you."

"I'm glad to hear you say that," Charmaine confessed sarcastically.

"Nah, baby. C'mon and listen to what I'm saying. It applies to you, too. You've only told me what you wanted me to know about you. Whether it's good or bad info, that's how far you've decided to go with the confessions. Period. I'm the same way, too. That's how you learned about me and how I learned about you. That's the only way people learn about who you are, about your strengths, and your weaknesses. They learn it from what you tell them."

"Ok."

"I'm only saying that certain secrets you share are your Achilles Heel. It's powerful, private information that should be kept inside here," Scott said and pointed to his head. "That's how a person's Achilles Heel gets discovered. You tell them. You spill your guts in a weak moment. Do you see what I'm saying, Charmaine?"

She nodded her head. This explanation made more sense to her now. Most things Scott said to her made wonderful common sense. She was always enthralled and fascinated by his common sense approach to life.

"In other words, you're saying the only way others find out about you, about your Achilles Heel, is from your own lips. There are private things that are better left unsaid and should be taken to the grave in some cases," Charmaine added slowly as she considered half the drama she never discussed with Scott about her ex-husband, Richard.

"Yeah, that's it, baby. If you do talk too much, anyone can use that information to destroy you. Remember Samson and Delilah. Samson told Delilah about his hair. She set the brotha up and had them cut his hair off. He woke up weak as a motha."

"Oh, Scott," Charmaine said, giggling

"It's the same situation, baby. It might sound elementary, but Samson destroyed himself by divulging his Achilles Heel. I rest my case." Scott hesitated before going on. "Hell, I ain't even got to go that far back, baby. If what Jodria said to me is true, look at even more recent times. Check out my man, Rozelle."

"But you said the guy was a frat brother. I thought there was a code of silence. Without a doubt, it's supposed to be one if you're Greek. I would never mention anything about another Zeta sister. You know that as a rule. When you cross over, that's it. They're your life. Brothers and sisters don't talk, shouldn't talk. I truly don't understand."

"*You* don't understand it. Well, you know Rozelle is baffled as hell. I told him the guy had to be an Que impostor." Scott laughed quickly "Had to be, baby. Shit like that doesn't happen with a bona fide Que. It just doesn't. Jodria told me she's fed up with Rozelle's and isn't taking this incident too well."

"Jodria?"

"Yeah, that his wife's name, too."

"Oh, that's pretty." Charmaine looked confused. "I thought her name was Anne. The times I've gone out with your friends on our FOFAE days, they always call her JABria or JAB."

"It is Jodria. Jodria Anne. Rozelle calls her J. Anne sometimes. That's what you're thinking about. He introduces her to everyone that way. At the opening ceremonies, he constantly called her Jodria. I guess it's whatever he wants to say."

"I noticed that. Now, I'm totally confused because I've been calling her JABria."

"Don't be. Most times you heard me call her sis. Sometimes, I'll say Jodria. I always thought that was a pretty name. Ever since we were in college, I've called her Sis Jodria. Initially, she was pledging Delta; then Jodria changed her mind and pledged Sigma Gamma Rho. As we got older, I dropped the sis part. You never asked the other ladies why they sometimes call her JAB?" he asked quietly.

"I never did. I simply called her Anne. She answers to that as well," Charmaine explained matter-of-factly.

"Check this out. The reason they named her JAB is that several years ago we all went to Hawaii. Of course, we attended a serious Luau there. You know Rozelle."

"That I do."

"He lost his mind drooling. I mean sho nuff drooling over the Hawaiian women with all their long hair and twisting their waists. Aw, man, I'm here to tell you. Jodria punched the hell out of him. She gave him several hard left jabs. From that, Pecola told everyone she was Muhammad Ali in disguise and to call her JAB which stood for Jodria Anne Belisarion."

"Ummm-hmmm." Charmaine smiled into his face and her excited eyes locked on his. "That's an interesting reason."

Charmaine rose to her feet and straddled Scott's lap. She moved around a little to make sure her vagina was positioned in the ideal spot over his penis.

"I know, baby. But hey, that's life."

"You wouldn't do that to me, baby. Would you stare at those Hawaiian women?" she seductively asked.

"Not remotely. You're right," Scott assured and gave her a long, hot tongue kiss. "Nah, baby. That ain't even possible, especially when I got a fine sister like you on my arm."

Charmaine smiled, and his mouth traveled down her neck. The rapture of her perfumed body made him sensually intoxicated by it. He unbuttoned her blouse and pulled the tight bra up over her breasts. As he adoringly watched her breasts briefly, he traced the brown nipples with his right index finger and felt them become hard under his passionate touch.

"Your titties are so firm and gorgeous, baby," he whispered as he gazed at them as if he had never ever seen them before.

"It's from the dancing I do all the time. You always say that, Scott," Charmaine murmured, still staring at his handsome face.

"I always mean it, too," he said huskily and gazed at them, then back to her face. A contented Scott squeezed both of her breasts together. He tongued and sucked the nipple tips, slowly, one at a time, repeatedly. In anticipation of the ecstasy he could make her feel, Charmaine closed her eyes and clutched and massaged his head. The ringing telephone interrupted what could have been the beginning of total fulfillment for both of them.

"Don't answer it, Scott," she pleaded in a little girl whine.

"I'm sorry, baby. This won't take long. It's probably Rozelle. After this call, I'll let the answering machine catch the rest." It was Symone. "Hey, babygirl. Whassup with you? Everything ok?"

"Everything is just fine and dandy, Scott," she replied just as brightly. She was amazed he was always in a pleasant mood. He was about like Alex. "And you?"

"Well, you know it. Better than good and better than most. Just chilling."

"Now you sound like your sons."

Scott laughed loudly. "I know, baby. Let me interpret that for you. Everything is just fine over this away. Charmaine and I were on the patio talking, kissing, and shit. You know what I mean?" he added with a smile as he tightly squeezed Charmaine's waist. She grudgingly stood up and went to sit back down in the other chaise lounge.

"Oh, ok. That's great," Symone said laughing lightly, genuinely sorry for disturbing him. "Tell her I said hello. I apologize for the interruption, but this won't take long."

Scott covered the mouthpiece. "Symone said hello, and that she's sorry for interrupting us, baby."

Charmaine threw her hand up to wave and mouthed a silent hello. She pulled her bra back in place and started picking invisible lint off her blue ivory print sarong pants.

"Oh yeah, Scott. Ask Charmaine if she plans to go out with FOFAE this month to the Winston-Salem, Greensboro, and High Point Club tea? If she is, Pecola needs to know so that she can get her ticket." Scott placed his hand over the mouthpiece again and repeated the question.

"Well—" Charmaine shrugged her shoulders and acted like she didn't know yet.

"Yeah, baby. She's going to make it," he said and grinned at Charmaine's surprised expression and shaking head, indicating her answer was really a no.

"This won't take long, Scott. You know Carlos planned to take Pecola to The Greenbriar in White Sulphur Springs, West Virginia. To celebrate their twenty-fourth wedding anniversary, it's his gift. You know where you guys stayed during yall's five day golf tournament last year?"

"Yeah, baby. I remember."

"Carlos told me that he reserved a block of rooms. Alex and I are trying to coordinate the dates and itinerary to see if her closest, dearest friends would take the trip. First of all, would you be interested?"

"That's a dumb ass question, Sy. You know I am."

"Ok. That's good. I got that part covered. It'll probably be the weekend after Thanksgiving. Everybody will be home then."

"You'll be here too, Sy?"

"Yeah. This is my year to stay in North Carolina for Thanksgiving. Remember last year I was in New Jack City."

"Slipped my memory, baby."

"If it wasn't for Alex's annual Thanksgiving hoopla meal, I would be going home to get some family love like you wouldn't believe. But I promised Alex, so it's an every other year thang for me, too."

"Hey, we got just as much of that kind of family love down here in the Carolinas, girl."

"I know," she said with a laugh.

"My girl Alex got me doing the same thing. I'm missing the Bayou Classic this year, baby. That's unheard of for me. You know it."

"I do."

"So I understand, baby."

"We got to try and schedule this Virginia trip around the *This is Your Life* plans for them. Remember? We scheduled it for that weekend."

"Damn! That's right. Carlos still doesn't know a thing about it? That we're recognizing him as well?"

"No, he doesn't. Rico's been watching for him to slip and say anything."

"Hmmm. I can see why Carlos planned thangs for the same weekend."

"I know, but I'll keep you posted. If we have to shuffle that around, we can work on it." Symone paused a moment to take a sip of sweet ice tea Miss Jessica prepared, and Scott heard the ice rattling in the glass. "How's that with you?"

"I need to check, baby. My flying schedules are blocked a month at a time. I need specific dates to check and see if they'll be a conflict. But go ahead and put Charmaine down as my guest. Scott winked at Charmaine, and she winked back. She got up and smoothed her clothes. While she kissed him on the neck, she squeezed his firmly packed crotch and slowly walked inside to the den.

Chapter Eighty-Six

Charmaine didn't know why Symone perturbed her. Quite frankly, all three of them did. Alex, Pecola, and Symone simply aggravated the pure divine shit out of Charmaine whenever she was around them, but she was especially suspicious of Symone. She just was. True, Symone introduced Scott to Charmaine. Symone was extremely cordial, talkative, and always made Charmaine feel welcomed whenever there was a get-together with all the friends. Still, it was something Charmaine couldn't put her finger on about Symone.

Whenever Symone saw Charmaine, she was full of questions about her dancing escapades in England, Germany, and other places. Symone always volunteered to help at the studio when she had free time. Ultimately, Symone did start volunteering more often since Kyle and Sylvia appeared more serious about ballet and began taking ballet and modern dance classes twice a week on Wednesdays and Saturdays instead of just their Saturday afternoon class. Symone remained fascinated with Charmaine's professional dance career, and she didn't mind her knowing that. Oftentimes, Symone listened to Charmaine's dance war stories as if she were a child sitting on Santa Claus' lap and who was totally enraptured by each and every word uttered. Even though Charmaine always felt a tad more comfortable around Alex and Pecola, she still couldn't get good vibes for Symone. It was true that Charmaine also believed that Pecola was somewhat standoffish about her, almost overly protective of Alex, Symone, and Scott. On a couple of occasions, Charmaine even caught Pecola giving her the evil eye. But to Charmaine, Symone still was a different kind of question mark.

"...You're right," Scott said, laughing.

"Are you going to do it, Sy?"

"Yeah!"

"How many tickets can you get me for the Phoenix's black and white ball the Wednesday before Thanksgiving?"

"How many you need?"

"Well, the girls decided to hang out that night. Rehema's heading that charge."

"Oh, damn!"

"I know. Can you get me eight?"

"No problem. If you need more, let me know."

"I clare it helps to know someone who knows everybody in this here illustrious city."

"That's me. What about the Phoenix's New Year's eve dance?"

"You know I won't be here but get a few for that one as well because Rehema might need them."

"It's done, baby." Scott ended the call with Symone and walked in the kitchen while Charmaine was pouring another glass of pineapple juice. Immediately, he noticed her creased brow and the confused expression on her face.

"What's wrong now, baby?"

"Nothing," Charmaine replied quickly and breathed heavily. "I was just thinking. That's all."

"Well hell, that means it's something then."

"Scott, I don't know. I think Symone is nice. I really do. To be honest—" Charmaine paused before continuing, "I sometimes don't get a good feel for her. I'm not sure if she accepts me being with you or not."

"Baby, are *you* kidding?" Because they had this discussion a couple of times before, again Scott was surprised.

"No, I'm not kidding."

"C'mon, Charmaine baby. Symone loves you, especially the dance travels you experienced throughout your career. One thing about her, either she likes you or she doesn't. If she doesn't like you, you would know." Scott paused for a moment and laughed lightly.

"Well, I don't know. It's just that—" Charmaine turned away from him and went to lean her back on the Birds-eye maple cabinet.

Scott reached into the refrigerator and grabbed a kiwi fruit. He offered one to Charmaine; she shook her head no.

"I'll be the first person to say Symone *is* a hard person to get to know. Now, I would agree with you if you said that. Hell, it took her a long time to *even* trust me—a very long time to know that I cared for her, Alex, and Pecola like I would blood sisters. Other than that, she's wonderful once you get to learn her ways. Alex says that Symone isn't anything but a major hardball shell with a lot of fluff on the inside. That's what I've always seen. Yet, she's very intelligent and extremely opinionated."

"I can tell *that,* Scott." Charmaine crossed her arms and carefully watched his face. She thought he was bragging about her.

"Don't get me wrong. She isn't one to back down easily over no shit. You can't manipulate her and never underestimate her. When folks try to do that, that's when they definitely fuck up with her big time. It's very hard for them to get back in her good graces after that," Scott said as he considered Symone's ex-husband and a few memorable incidents with other people.

"I kinda understand."

"And puhleeze don't cross her *or* any of her close friends because then it's really hard to get redemption in that category. Pecola, Alex, and Symone are the types of people who once they latch on to you, it's a lifetime thang. They're devoted to you for life."

"Uh huh," Charmaine spoke with a forced smile.

"Symone is a loyal, loyal, friend. So if you do wrong to her friends, that's when she'll absolutely turn on you with a vicious quickness. No question about it."

"I know."

"But all three of those ladies are that way." He laughed to himself as he even considered Alex's quiet wrath in certain situations. "Other than that, Symone is a good girl. What you see is what you get. Well, you know her. You've been around a lot of the heated discussions. The arguments we've had over a variety of social issues, baby."

Charmaine hesitated before speaking. "I just believe—I just think that you're real close, especially close to her."

Startled by the suspicious comments again, Scott looked at her out of the corners of his eyes. As he carefully analyzed Charmaine's words, he smiled and frowned at the same time. He was determined to make the relationship he had with Alex, Pecola, and Symone crystal clear to Charmaine this time. Scott nodded slowly, and his eyes locked on hers.

"You're right, baby. I *am* real close to her just like I am with Alex and Pecola. Those women are like sisters to me. Period." Although his voice was firm, his tone was pleasant and even. Charmaine noticed there wasn't a hint of anger about discussing this topic once more. Before speaking again, he paused. "Oh, I see now. Just because Symone is the single one in the bunch and happens to be fine as hell, you think there's something going on between us."

"Uh, well—" She smiled and glanced at the floor.

Charmaine didn't say the words and refused to look at him. What Scott said was the absolute truth. That was exactly what she thought and had always believed about him and Symone. Charmaine didn't only have uncomfortable, leery feelings about Symone, there were also times when she was quite suspicious of Pecola and Alex screwing him, too. Charmaine closed her eyes and shook her head. Scott stood up slowly, walked over to her, and took her face in his hands.

"Listen, baby. Let me tell you this one more time, and I hope you get what I'm saying." Scott kissed her nose. "Pecola, Symone, Alex, and I have been friends for many years." He nibbled her left ear. "Nothing ever happened with either one of them." He kissed her soft, wet lips. "We're friends, baby. Period. You got that?" he asked staring at her.

"I do." She smiled and nodded her head.

"Good. I'm glad you understand," he said moving away. "It's hard for people to realize that a man and a woman can have a fulfilling, platonic relationship called true friendship. I know it's difficult to believe, but it does happen in this world. Nowadays, it's so much backstabbing going on. Folks don't believe true friendship occurs. It's happening with those three crazy Black women and me. I'm hear to tell you."

"Thank you for saying that, Scott. I understand. I have male friends, but I've never ever seen a relationship or bond like the one you have with Symone, Alex, and Pecola. Sometimes it's hard for me to understand, and I guess difficult to really accept. If yall were biological sisters and brothers, that would be different."

"We're sisters and brothers—maybe not bloodwise, but that's the only difference."

"Then there are moments—"

Their eyes met briefly, and she glanced away. As Charmaine spoke, Scott continued to stare in her eyes. He loved looking in peoples' eyes when they spoke to him. His father taught the Alexander boys that was the only fair and decent way to talk to people. With Scott's forceful, penetrating stare, he often forced people to either look away or stare back for short moments at a time.

"I'm listening, baby," he said tenderly. Charmaine gazed down, and he raised her chin again so she could look in his concerned face.

"Yall *aren't* brothers and sisters, yet you act like it. So yes, I do get jealous sometimes. I'm only human. There's no need for me to lie and say I'm not." To indicate she had been caught again, Charmaine held both hands up in mock display. Scott pulled her to him.

"You don't have anything to be jealous about with those three or to worry about with me either. I love you, baby. I do. Trust me when I say that. Now, if I were talking about a few other women in town, that would be another issue to deal with." Charmaine rolled her eyes at him and playfully punched him in the chest.

"Hey, just kidding. I'm kidding!" Scott laughed as he quickly grabbed her arms and pulled her back against his stomach. Then he kissed her neck several times.

"You better be kidding."

"Are you ready to eat pizza now, baby?" he asked with a twinkle in his eyes.

"Baby, I don't know about the pizza, but I'm ready to get a piece—of—you." Charmaine began grinding her behind against his crotch. "What about you, sweetie?"

"Let me show you what I really want to eat a piece of," he groaned in a deep husky slur.

"Humph. I've always heard that action speaks louder than words, Scott baby."

Scott lightly sucked on her neck and gave her a small, faint passion mark. Slowly, his hands moved to unbutton her blouse, and they traveled down her back to unhook her bra. Both garments fell to the floor. He easily picked Charmaine up and carried her upstairs to the bedroom where he gently placed her in the middle of the bed. Charmaine sighed. She laid back while he pulled off her sarong pants and lacy thong panties.

Scott was a Phi Beta Kappa and a 4.0 Ph.D. graduate of Super Freaky Deak University. With him, Charmaine felt like a freshman at the same school. He knew all the sensitive, blistering, sexual buttons on her body, and he knew when she wanted them pressed. Without question, he always worked her whimpering body like a professor of bodyology. A consummate lover, he made sure to touch the vital spots with just the right roughness and tenderness. His adeptly wizard tongue moved all over her, searching, while flicking like a limber, leather whip. Finally, his head rested between her enthusiastic, opened legs. With the index finger and thumb of his right hand, Scott gently spread the pubic hairs back and opened up the full lips of Charmaine's vagina. Then, he took the index finger of his left hand and vigorously massaged her clitoris so that his tongue could simultaneously penetrate and lick and suck the clitoris with delightful ease.

"Open your legs real wide for me, baby," he instructed with a growling, low voice.

Charmaine quietly obeyed his instructions and stretched them as wide as she could. It was a perfect split of such magnitude that Mrs. Huntley, her third grade ballet teacher, would be proud. Charmaine held her breath for a moment, smiled, and made all kinds of faces from the pure ecstasy of Scott's sucking her vagina. The wondrous pleasure rising throughout her body was excruciatingly enjoyable. She moved her stomach in and out to the beat of an imaginary slow dance, with his mouth sucking and gliding right along as the perfect partner.

"Hmmm. Mmmm. Oh, Scottfeld. Oh Goddd, baby," Charmaine moaned in soft good-feeling agony.

The delicious sensual explosion took a long time but a short time. It started in Charmaine's toes and traveled up her body until it burst forth in Scott's mouth. While gripping his head, Charmaine screamed his name and shuddered uncontrollably. Yet he wouldn't stop. Scott's mouth was cemented to her throbbing clitoris, and he refused to allow release until she quietly and slowly released the juices he wanted to taste. Then, he licked her up and down like a dripping wet cherry lollipop, making sure to not miss a drop of the essence of pleasure juices flowing out from her. After he kissed her between the legs several times, he surfaced with a satisfied smile on his face. Charmaine pulled him to her and hugged his neck very tightly.

"How was that, baby?" he asked drunk with the pleasure of satisfying his woman.

"Oooh, Scottfeld. That was sooo wonderful. Umph. Umph. Umph. Umph. Umph," she groaned lazily and snuggled up to him. When they made love, she often called him by his whole first name. They stared into each other eyes and smiled. "Oh, damn. I love the way you love my body, baby. Damn! And I love you."

"No, *I* love *you*," he confessed easily as he kissed her nose. "That was wonderful for me, baby." Scott repeatedly licked his thick, black mustache.

"For you? Wooo, baby. I don't know how much more of you I can take. I haven't ever had my pussy sucked and massaged at the same time the way you do it. You make my clit stand straight up at attention. Damn, baby! You're trying to make me forget my mama's name or what?"

A happy Scott burst out laughing. "Just enjoy the ride, sweet thang."

"Trust me. I am."

"Just love me and need me. That's all I desire from you, baby. Nothing more," he said quietly while fiercely gazing into her warm eyes.

"That's wonderful, Scott."

"Mmmm." As he licked his lips and moustache again, he spoke with a laugh. "Damn, girl! As usual, you taste just as good as you smell. I don't think I'll wash my face the rest of the day. I want to remember my gourmet Black pussy I ate for lunch."

"You're one crazy man."

"Nah, I ain't. Just crazy in love with you, baby. Are you ready to have pizza or what? That call is up to you cause I ain't hungry no more," he murmured while tenderly kissing her breasts. "I done had my Black caviar for the day."

Chapter Eighty-Seven

Instead of having pizza, Scott and Charmaine decided to drive to Cafe Bessie and pick up an order of chitlins, candied yams, collard greens, yeast rolls, and sweet potato pie. Pork chitlins were a favorite delicacy of Scott. He could eat them year round, and it wouldn't matter. He was just overjoyed a place like Cafe Bessie prepared them daily, and he knew they were cleaned to the one-hundredth degree.

Later that evening, Scott placed scented candles around the edges of his master bath's humongous Jacuzzi tub that Charmaine thought was actually large enough for at least six other people to relax in with them. With the lyrics of Joe Williams and Danny Barker CDs showering forth from the bathroom speakers, they sipped champagne and talked quietly. The Jacuzzi high-powered jets massaged their bodies. The two laughed happily, affectionately caressed hands, and fiercely stared into each other's eyes.

Scott wore nothing but handsome silk pajamas or long, silk robes when he entertained her, and he always provided personalized monogrammed robes for Charmaine. After the fragrant bath, he slipped a new silk burgundy one around her. As Scott carefully kneeled down to gently tie the belt around Charmaine's waist, she proudly rubbed the monogrammed initials, CVG.

Charmaine and Scott had been going out for about three months when he told her to say her full name, dress, breasts, and panty sizes in her sexiest voice. At the time, they were enjoying a quiet champagne dinner at Fabian's on Reynolda Road while Chris Murrell was serenading the evening crowd with sweet jazz in the background. Charmaine garnered up all the memories of those classic Millie Jackson songs. Then she licked her lips and spoke softly. "My name is Charmaine Violette Gumbel. I wear a 34C bra, size eight dress, and size seven panties." When she was done, she blew him an air kiss, and they both laughed for a good five minutes.

Two weeks later, three beautifully gift-wrapped boxes and a lovely greeting card were placed on the white Wurlitzer grand piano in Scott's living room. It was a silk bathrobe, a Bonnie Brownfield wool and rayon fuchsia shirtwaist dress, and a black lace underwear set with garters. They weren't celebrating her birthday, Christmas, or any particular anniversary. Charmaine later discovered that Pecola, Alex, and Symone helped Scott select everything but the underwear. Scott told Charmaine that he bought the gifts because he wanted to, and there shouldn't have to be a designated holiday to receive major surprises.

Scott and Charmaine had been dating for one year now, and this was the seventh bathrobe she received as a gift from him. Charmaine always felt honored and special when Scott surprised her with unexpected gifts, and he did that quite often. He was an unusual man who had such a generous heart with giving, and Charmaine was totally shocked she had found a Black man who freely pampered her in such a way. Whenever they traveled out of town on a short pleasure trip by themselves or with his close friends in tow, if they were shopping at Hanes Mall or anywhere for that matter, if Charmaine so much as even glanced at an item in a store, Scott asked her if she wanted it. Sometimes Charmaine said yes, and a lot of times she said no. Charmaine's divorced older sister, Maryetta Mae-I, told her that she should say yes every damn time he asked because Scott wouldn't ask her if he didn't long to buy it for her.

Charmaine didn't know how much money Northworld Airline pilots earned. He never discussed his salary. However, this was the third pilot she had been with. The other two she dated briefly certainly weren't as loving, tender, or giving as Scott. Charmaine assumed nothing about his life, but she also realized that his annual income was out there in the stratosphere because Scott definitely believed in living a glamorous, carefree life. He owned a large, absolutely gorgeously decorated home in Winston and another Tudor style one at Lake Norman. He drove a sleek black Porsche and a top-of-the line ruby-red Chevrolet Envoy. He believed in vacationing in exquisite renowned spots throughout the world. A flawless dresser and a staunch stone to-the-bone romantic, Scott's voice resonated with his excitement about life, and he was taking the willing and excited Charmaine along for the pleasure ride.

Charmaine often told Maryetta Mae-I that if her relationship with Scott ended in a day, she would be hurt but satisfied. Why? Charmaine had received more attention, love, and gifts from Scott than she ever did from Richard—the man who was her husband of many years and the father of her two sons. Most men Charmaine dated were just like Richard. Everything revolved around them and their selfish needs. If Charmaine went shopping with those guys, they bought the whole mall and used her to help carry the shopping bags to the car.

But not Mr. Scottfeld Broadus Alexander! If Scott went shopping and Charmaine was there, he took her into that one of kind boutique and insisted they find something. Anything. A designer suit. A flashy, going to church Sunday hat. Whatever. It didn't matter. He bought her things from jewelry to electronics equipment. Price was never an issue with him. If Scott caught a glimpse of something he thought would look stunning on her or would be great for her condo, Scott would buy it and surprise her with it later.

About seven months after they had known each other, Scott eventually admitted to Charmaine that he hadn't always been that way. It wasn't until he became a friend with Pecola, Alex, and Symone that he began to reform his ways. After listening to their conversations and instructions of how Black men should be, Scott transformed his thinking about buying for just himself all the time and became more considerate of others. He instead learned how to focus on people other than just his close family members. With much regret gracing his face, Scott honestly shared with Charmaine how for a very long time, he was a very selfish man with women. And in many cases, he still had to remind himself that life simply was about sharing, caring, and loving. Now Scott's philosophy was to buy what he desired for himself, but he also wanted to lavish gifts on the special woman he enjoyed spending time with as well as for his special friends.

Before the transformation, Scott concentrated on stocks, annuities, fast deals and real estate. Now, he still focused on these typical, profitable investments, but the investment of sharing love, as Alex called it, was a top priority for him. It was times like this that Charmaine felt awfully guilty about being suspicious of Symone, Pecola, Alex, or anyone else for that matter. He gave those three women loads of credit about how they made him a much better, sensitive man for that special person in his life. Charmaine had no idea how Scott was before. She could only imagine, especially since he was so good-looking, and women were always trying to slip him their telephone numbers or business cards. Even when they went out on dates nowadays, she noticed how overly aggressive women still flocked around Scott to get his attention even with Charmaine at his side, hanging on and tightly embracing his arm for dear life.

Charmaine certainly thanked God she *now* was considered Scott's lady, which was how he introduced her to his friends. And he really did treat her unbelievably marvelously, and she did the same for him. However, the budget Charmaine allocated for gift giving wasn't nearly as extensive as Scott's budget. Yet, whenever she gave him a greeting card, a tie, a CD, or even a simple set of white monogrammed, linen handkerchiefs, he acted as if she purchased the most expensive, rare diamond in all of America. Charmaine never found another woman's clothes in his closets or dresser drawers located throughout his home. She certainly did an intricate, Sherlock Holmes search for such evidence. So if Scott provided personalized silk robes for everyone he made love to, Charmaine was the *only* one whose clothes he allowed to stay in his home. The other women had to pack theirs back in a suitcase when they came to visit.

In the back of Charmaine's mind and in spite of all that he continued to do for her, she had this gnawing, tormenting suspicion that she cared for Scott more than he cared for her. After the abusive marriage with Richard, that was considered an absolute no no—a universally learned and memorized lesson she should have understood as a teen-ager taking Love 101 classes from her eternally agonized and heartbroken mother. During those moments when Charmaine considered Scott in such a suspicious way, the angry words of her mother constantly reverberated through her mind. *Chile, don't you ever, never care for no man more than he cares for you. Do you hear me, Charmaine? And don't you ever forget it, neither.* While growing up in Lexington, North Carolina, her mama drilled those words into her brain.

So, Charmaine also believed Scott had other women on the side. Scott told her that he would never lie to her, and most times she believed him. She considered him to be one of the most forthright and sincere men she had ever met. Simply put, he just didn't answer a lot of jealous questions. He honestly admitted that he had women friends other than Pecola, Alex, and Symone, but none he had sex with. Scott said that once he was able to tell her that he loved her just eight months after they started dating, he knew it was over with him and other women. Since Charmaine was only the third woman he had said those three words to, Scott said that he realized he had finally found the right one.

Yet, to Charmaine, those other women she thought he still was dating were still there, lurking like the fleeting, dark night. In the morning, they were gone because she never caught him with anyone. Charmaine desperately wanted to thoroughly trust him, but she was scared and didn't know how. She was frightened by his sexy, good looks and his easy, friendly demeanor he projected with everyone he met. Even though he lavished her magnificently with love, attention, and gifts, she was still starving for so much more from him. Things she couldn't explain. Charmaine believed within her soul that Scott was a tamed, wild Black man with many layers yet to be exposed. Oftentimes, when they were alone together, she watched his handsome dark face and wondered if she could be the woman to truly decipher the password that penetrated through those layers he allowed no one to see.

Later on Saturday evening, Charmaine gave Scott a full body massage, and they made adoring, passion-filled love. This time, Charmaine took the lead and tenderly kissed and sucked him from head to toe. Afterwards, Scott read Wanda McIntyre poems to her. While Charmaine was stretched out on the living room couch like a thoroughly satisfied Siamese cat, he happily serenaded her on the piano with old rhythm and blues songs from way back when. Charmaine wasn't a huge fan of the blues genre, at least not as much as Scott. On the other hand, Scott was a self-proclaimed blues worshipper that he declared was a given birthright for anyone born and raised in New Orleans.

Scott certainly didn't mind letting the world know those musical facts, either. He often educated his friends and Charmaine about Blues legends with names like Koko Taylor, T-Bone Walker, Big Joe Turner, Howlin' Wolf, Memphis Minnie McCoy, Brownie McGhee, Buddy Guy, and Sonny Terry. As a result of his fervency and since he was a knowledgeable historian of his state's favorable cultures, he continually played rhythm and blues music from the Louisiana legends such as Marion "Little Walter" Jacobs, Clarence "Gatemouth" Brown, Huddie "Leadbelly" Ledbetter, and Clifton Chenier, the king of Zydeco music.

While singing to Charmaine on this late Saturday evening, she laughed merrily as Scott's facial expressions imitated the hard life blues he sang about.

Over Sunday morning breakfast, Scott decided to attend New Smith Grove Church in Lexington. It was Charmaine's home church. Even though he had promised twelve-year-old Rozelle, Jr. he would go to church with him and the entire Bellisarion family, Charmaine pleaded like a spoiled little girl for Scott to go with her to the eleven a.m. service. She was expecting Da'Juan, a close cousin from Atlanta to show up for the day. Da'Juan aspired to be a pilot and was taking flying lessons in Atlanta. Charmaine wanted Scott to meet him for inspirational reasons. Eventually, Scott gave in and called Rozelle, Jr. to tell him he would definitely attend church with him for Men's Day on the next Sunday.

Later that evening, Scott was scheduled to meet with Pecola, Alex and Symone for their once a month outing. He called it their time for just the four of them. When they met years ago, Scott quietly asked Alex to continue to arrange luncheons because he didn't believe Symone or Pecola were conducive to such an idea of having him close by. He just wanted to be around the delightful three women in any way he could. However, from that first successful outing years ago at a Black-owned piano bar in Greensboro, they had been doing it ever since. Going out with Pecola, Alex, and Symone of course gave Scott a chance to discover women from another perspective—as friends and not as the conquest. The three ladies also received an opportunity to understand why, as Symone said that men made certain foolish, crazy ass decisions.

The foursome sometimes attended plays, movies, or went shopping. In the beginning, when he used to invite them to his home for an afternoon outing, Scott cooked a fabulous New Orleans dinner of jambalaya, smothered okra, and delicious gumbo. Afterwards, he serenaded the trio. Scott ended up reading works by Lucille Clifton, Ephriam David Tyler, Amiri Baraka, and any other influential African-American author he felt like sharing from the shelves of his office library. Before he began dating Charmaine seriously, Pecola, Alex, and Symone always teased that Scott was either trying to spoil them, or he was testing out new musical material for some fortunate woman in his life. From those intimate engagements with Scott, they excitedly told their other interested female friends all about him. If anyone was looking for a little soulful singing with a little piano playing, then Scott was the man for the job.

Nine times out of ten on Sunday afternoons, Scott believed a good old-fashioned country meal was definitely in order. Most times, he ate at Charmaine, Alex, Pecola, Symone, or even at Rozelle's house on Sundays. As was a typical custom in the south, Pecola and Alex always prepared a huge after-church meal on each and every Sunday.

Since Pecola, Alex, and Symone were scheduled to go out with Scott, they took this Sunday off and left light meals for their families. Their favorite place, Cafe Bessie, was closed. The four friends opted to try Pearl's Fish House instead. Pecola was the only one who initially objected to the foursome's choice for a restaurant. She told them that the last time she and Carlos dined there, they came out smelling like they cooked the fish instead of ordering it. Pecola added that it may have been a new cook in the house and maybe he was burning fish in the kitchen.

"...I'm telling you, honeychile. The acceptable standards are going back to the fifties and sixties where the light-skinned Black person made the decision-makers feel comfortable," Pecola was saying through bites of fish through the watchful stares of Scott, Alex, and Symone.

"You're absolutely right, girl. I thought I noticed it more because I'm dark-skinned. If you feel the same way, well then you go, Pecola girl," Symone said, laughing. She paused and looked around at everyone. Pecola nodded her head and put her wineglass down.

"Ummm-hmmm," Alex moaned since her mouth was full of food.

"Seriously. All jokes aside. I'm curious to know where all the dark people are on televisions, in music videos, and magazines are these days. It's like if you're considered multi-racial or light-skinned with curly hair, that ensures your getting a role on TV, in videos, in commercials, in the corporate world, and in entertainment." Symone talked as she munched on a piece of lettuce and began laughing. "Where in the hell did all this long hair come from? Whether it's real or weave city, I've never seen sooo many Black women with hair down to their asses. Silky hair, too—like it came straight off the horse's tail."

"I agree with you there, chile," Pecola exclaimed and gave her a high five. "I'm not blaming the people who fit that description because I'm light-skinned, too."

"We hadn't notice that, Pecola," Alex inserted with a wide grin.

Pecola couldn't help smiling back at her friend's funny remark. She slowly rolled her eyes and said tsk, tsk, anyway. Pecola took a bite of baked flounder, swallowed it, and wiped her mouth with the linen napkin.

"As I was saying before I was rudely cut off," Pecola said amusingly, eyeing Alex out the corner of her eyes and hesitating for a moment, "there really isn't anyone to blame because it isn't about that. Wooo! I just changed my mind. I should say the people who do the casting are to blame. Like Alex says, God made us all the way we are. I just also believe that we as Black people endorse such thinking. If two children were standing beside one another, and there was a light-skinned child who they said had curly black hair and a little dark-skinned child with kinky hair, can't yall hear the comments they would make about those children?"

"I can," Symone added quickly.

"The reaction is always the same, chile. The light-skinned one is sooo pretty and look at all the *good* hair. They say this about the little dark child. 'Lawd have mercy. Ain't she got some of the world's nappiest hair? We got to do something with it, chile! Grease it. Slap it. Straighten it, or braid it. Wooo! Do something so it won't look *that* nappy!' Yall see what I'm saying?" Pecola said with a slight bit of humor before she drank a little more wine. Alex and Scott laughed with her.

"That only makes a child not feel loved or appreciated. It makes him definitely conscious of his differences. I felt that way as a child," Symone said slowly. "Always out of the loop somehow. It always disturbs me now when I see those comparisons happening anywhere. It's a pitiful indictment of where we are as a people with regard to what we accept as pretty and acceptable."

"That's what I'm saying." Pecola daintily wiped her mouth. "Black people perpetuate the thinking as well. I see that all the time in Carlos' family. My family, too. Pauletta's children are dark-skinned like her and Hannibal. Whenever we go shopping together, people are always surprised I'm those little dark-skinned children's aunt."

"As high yellow as you are, I can see why, girl," Symone said loudly with a laugh. "If I blink too fast, you could pass for a white girl."

"Lawd, now there you go. Listen to my ace boon coon over here calling me high yellow. You know that isn't nice. Yall see what I gotta deal with on a daily basis," Pecola said and Alex, Scott, and Symone began laughing. "I *know* Carlos and my family are a case study for this discussion. Their family shades are either very dark or very light. It's real noticeable at family reunions and get-togethers where they actually do compare the children. Yall remember Bradley? I *know* you do. Don't you, Symone?"

"Yeah." Symone had just stuck a buttered scallop in her mouth and nodded her head to indicate she did. Symone pushed the food to one side of her mouth. "Ain't nothing changed. So what he's stupid. The Negro is still fine as all hell, girl."

"You're right, Pecola. I've heard it enough, too. It's really sad to see," Alex inserted with a serious brow. As she reached for a yeast roll, the others turned their attention to her. Because she first wanted to make a point, she didn't bite into the roll and simply placed it on the bread plate. While she gathered her thoughts, she smoothed one square packet of butter around the top of the roll.

"We're listening, girl," Symone said eagerly.

"I've seen that happen over and over again," Alex said and took a quick sip of orange soda. "It's done that way because white people feel more comfortable dealing with a light-skinned person. Maybe because that complexion is closer to theirs. My mama and my Grandmother Carmen worked, cooked, and cleaned for white people all their lives. She always said that she thought they were a little nervous too because there are a lot of Black people who look white. You know that must be unsettling for them, wondering if some of that blackness is in them."

"Wooo, chile," Pecola murmured.

Alex smiled at Pecola and continued. "There was a lot of that when I worked in the corporate world. Whenever we interviewed people to work at D. Britt & Cox, they all were light-skinned people. Those were the ones they recruited, or those were the people who at least made it to my office for the second round review. I truly believe this—"

"What?" Pecola asked, cutting her off.

"If it weren't for my parents working with their white family for years, my MBA and JD degrees, and graduating number fifteen in my class—"

"Damn, girl! You had a lot going on," Symone exclaimed.

"I know, chile," Alex said with a dripping southern accent. "I'm serious. If that prestigious law firm could've found someone a little lighter than me, I probably never would've been an attorney or a junior partner in that company. All of the other Black attorneys are real light-skinned."

"Nah, I ain't agreeing with that, chile," Pecola quickly inserted. "I believe you would have anyway. Mama Adriola would've made sure of that. The whole time Mama Adriola was taking care of those rich white children and cleaning their kitchen, she was talking about her smart daughter."

"I done heard the story," Symone said.

"She did. Mama Adriola was telling folks how Alex was a genius in elementary school, in junior high school, in high school, and in college. She was a genius in law school the same time she was in business school. I remembered how Mama Adriola always said to me that she knew you would work with her employers' firm one day, chile. She started talking up your coveted spot in that company right after you were born, girl."

"You're right, Pecola," Alex replied wistfully and paused briefly. "You're right. Mama always said that she knew I would be an attorney one day."

"Whenever I hear that about your mother, I believe it's absolutely wonderful, Alex. The role and mission of a good parent is to inspire and motivate their children," Symone said. "I love to hear beautiful stories about devoted parents."

"I know, girl," Alex said quickly. She wanted to change the subject from off her dead mother. "This is no new issue we're discussing here. We all know that America espouses facial features closer to their European looks. That's why we need to teach our children who we are as a powerful, influential race. It's you and Booker T's number one topic, Sy."

"Hear, hear," Symone nodded, laughing.

"I tell Trey and Purity all the time that they're my beautiful Nubian prince and princess, ancestors of Kings and Queens—"

"A few laborers, too," Pecola said to Alex with a grin.

"Absolutely. If we don't tell them this, they'll believe their dark-skinned complexion is inferior." Alex sliced a piece of the fried catfish and used the knife to move it to another section of the plate.

"Mmmm hmmm," Symone moaned. Her mouth was full of shrimps, so she vigorously nodded her head yes in full agreement.

"I know what it was like when I was little," Alex went on. "I'm telling you. I tried to scrub the dark off my skin. Of course, that didn't work. Then, I tried bleaching it to a lighter color with all kinds of cream. Even with my long hair, I was obsessed with and wanted white, blonde hair."

"I can see you now with blonde hair over that dark-skinned face, girl," Symone said. She burst out laughing, along with Pecola.

"I know. Hey watch it, girl," Alex said. "It's not too far-fetched. Maybe back then when I was growing up it was considered unusual, but a lot of our light *and* dark-skinned sistahs are going blonde these days."

"You're damn straight, chile," Pecola agreed.

Alex continued as she gazed at the quiet Scott. "Look at who wins the beauty pageants these days and who are the most successful models. Check out who's in music videos and on television. Observe which models are featured in *Ebony* and are Fashion Fair Models nowadays. It's not only those two forums. Check out all the major Black publications, especially the white ones. Girrrrl, light-skinned is in again." Alex took a bite of the neatly cut catfish and dabbed the corner of her mouth several times with the napkin.

"Hell! When did it go out?" Symone inquired with a laugh. "Don't yall realize they're trying to whiten America up? If you observe the trend, you'll see I'm not talking crazy, either. The lighter you are, the better your chances are in getting places in this world. Check the shit out. If you're mixed, you got it made too. I don't understand that mixed thang too well, either. Yall know I'm mixed. I'm bi-racial, too."

"Puhleeze! Your black ass ain't bi-racial in no shape form nor fashion," Pecola said in a loud, shocked voice.

"Yes I am," Symone replied. "My grandfather somewhere down the line was a white Frenchman. I already told yall that. Quite frankly, I hate to even admit it."

"They're just trying to create a distinct mulatto class," Alex said.

"That's what I don't understand. They're trying to have another classification of people called bi-racial," Symone added. "A person is supposedly bi-racial when their mother is white, their father is Black, or vice versus. Bi-racial isn't accurate. As far as that go, every last one of the Black folks in this country is bi-racial. I got a whole lot of other kinds of bi-racial blood spinning around in my system. The world is a trip."

"You're crazy," Alex said and Symone grinned at her.

"You know it's true," Symone continued slowly. "They just want to figure out another classification to confuse some already stone confused folks even more. None of us sitting around this table are pure, blooded jet Black Africans. So we all got bi-racial or multi-racial blood in us. It's unfortunate, but it's true. Our mixed cultures come from all that dipping and dabbling throughout the generations."

"Absolutely," Alex nodded.

"Even the illustrious president of this said country has our precious black blood in him somewhere, so give me a break. I don't know anyone who isn't bi-racial or multi-racial," Symone added. "Europeans. Washitaws and Africans. Create a new classification for people? Ok. You have to think where does this come from? Puhleeze!"

"Hmmm. That's an interesting view, chile," Pecola agreed.

"Black people need to be careful about this racial propaganda going on," Symone said as she waved her index finger. "They're trying to get all Black folks to be a neutral acceptable color. Remember when the acceptable face and color was on the cover of *Newtimes* magazine a few weeks ago. That's the look they're striving for."

"They who, chile?" Pecola asked.

"Whoever espouses that view, Pecola," Symone replied with shining eyes. "That's who. Folks who make sure it happens. You know there are people who plan to mate with a woman or a man to have their children come out a certain color. That's why I say "they" all the damn time. Give me the blackest, tallest, big-lipped and finest man out. That's what I want. A Mandingo warrior. Grrrrr. A rugged looking Shabba type. Then my offspring will remain dark and black like me, which is absolutely beautiful anyway. Wouldn't yall say so yourself?"

"You don't have one lick of sense, Sy," Alex giggled.

Symone laughed, too. "I know, but I mean every word I said, Alex."

Scott sat between them all, amused at what the discussion was about today. With these three ladies, they could talk about anything, even about him. They wouldn't care if he were sitting right there listening, either. Thus far, Scott hadn't made any comments. He quietly chewed on the broiled red snapper and baked potato dripping in butter and sour cream. He wanted to make sure he thought before he spoke. His three women friends would pounce on him in a heartbeat if his response weren't an educational, insightful, and honest one that supposedly was a representative of all Black men in all of America.

The perky white, brunette waitress stopped by to refill their water glasses and noticed they needed more yeast rolls. Pecola was impressed that she didn't allow one drop of icy water to fall out the pitcher onto the linen tablecloth. She always noticed things like that.

"I agree with what everyone has said so far," Scott said slowly. "I personally think there ain't nothing more beautiful than a Black woman, no matter what color they are. I just enjoy looking at them. My personal preference leans toward the caramel, pecan-tan, and to the dark-skinned Black woman."

"Yippee! That's a vote for Alex and me. We're not caramel, but we sho nuff are dark and chocolate. Why the caramel and dark-skinned woman? What about Pecola?" Symone asked in mock anger as she reached over to pinch his arm.

There's no winning here, Scott thought.

"I was just thinking there's no answer I can give that'll please everyone," Scott added.

"Nigger, puhleeze. You know you can say whatever you want to. Just make sure it's earth shattering comments we like to hear," Pecola laughed as she toyed with the stem of her wineglass. "You should know that by now. Isn't that right, ladies?"

"Yes," Alex said. A smiling Symone quickly nodded her heads toward Scott.

"That's the only reason why we allow you to hang with us," Pecola went on and watched him with mischievous amusement in her eyes.

"Let him finish, P," Alex said. "Tell us why the dark-skinned woman, Scott?"

"Hell, I don't know. Maybe because I'm dark. Maybe it's because my mother was dark. I've gone out with both light-skinned, dark-skinned women and a few white women in my day, too," he said honestly while placing a fork full of baked potato in his mouth.

"Honeychilllle! Did yall hear that? You said what? A few who? Kick his tall, Black butt with the quickness. Beat him up! Hold him down, Alex and Symone," Pecola said, acting as if she was going to stand up and pound Scott's head with her bread plate.

"I'm with you, Pecola," Symone exclaimed. "I just can't even imagine a Morehouse man with a white woman. What the fuck could you be thinking, Scott? I don't understand. That totally confuses me. I could see if you had gone to a predominantly white college, but Morehouse? Do you think those prominent white boys from Duke, Harvard, Brown, Dartmout, and Yale do that?"

"Some of them do, Sy," Scott replied.

"Nooo, they don't. If they do it, it's extremely rare, Scott. You can believe that. So I certainly can't see the brothers from da House with anybody else other than a Black woman. That school is the epitome of Black manhood and talent. Anybody that graduates from there should be primed to the pump for Black women."

"Hey, I had to see what it was like and get it out of my system. Now, I know," he admitted sincerely. "What yall want me to say? You want me to lie? I should be able to say whatever I want to."

"He's right," Alex said slowly, still somewhat shocked.

The waitress walked up with a fresh basket of hot yeast rolls, and Pecola softly requested another glass of wine. *Girlfriend was certainly attentive today with this waitress thing. She's on the job like white on rice. I'll make sure I convince the others to leave her a great tip,* thought Pecola.

"Scott, I'm still ready to beat your ass," Pecola finally replied, staring at Symone.

"May I puhleeze finish? Yes, I've gone out with other races, and they weren't just white girls. As a seasoned, mature Black man, I now just love looking at the brown, chocolate naked body."

"Oh, Scottie. I'm blushing. You've been redeemed," Alex said slowly chewing catfish. With the last bite, she almost swallowed a small bone and wanted to be careful.

"It's a myth that says light-skinned women are stuck up," Scott continued. "Some are. But I've run into my share of dark women who are just as pretty and very conceited. The dark-skinned women happen to be my preference, but Charmaine isn't considered dark. She's more a honey caramel color, and she's a wonderful lady. No matter what her complexion is though, she's a Black woman. I love a Black woman."

"That's why I know she ain't right for you," Pecola blurted out. "She ain't dark enough for your taste."

"Pecola, girl," Symone and Alex exclaimed in mock anger at the same time.

"Thanks, ladies. Somebody needs to muzzle her. She gets out of hand sometimes," Scott joked, and Pecola glared at the ceiling. "I'm trying to prove a point here, Pecola baby."

"*And* I'm trying to get you to see the truth about Charmaine," Pecola added.

"A woman is a woman, baby," Scott ignored her and went on. "A Black woman is a Black woman, no matter how yellow she is unless she chooses to identify with whites. This ugly history here in America has left some of our blackest sisters with the blackest hearts with light, near white skin. No matter what—how many videos they make or how many light-skinned near white-looking Black folks are thrown all over TV, they're still perceived as Black."

The waitress walked up and asked if they wanted to see the dessert menu. Everyone briskly shook his or her heads no.

"You say that to say what?" Symone asked.

"All I'm saying is that we all have different tastes and are different people. So people chose according to their preferences. As far as I'm concerned, it ain't nothing more beautiful than an intelligent, caring, kind, loving Black woman with plump, beautiful, breastsusus," he said with a chuckle, and they all laughed.

"That makes sense," Symone said. "We *are* diversed. We have a rainbow of complexions in our race that men and women can chose from. Just choose to date and marry someone within your race. That's all, and I'm fine with it."

"Me too, Symone," Pecola exclaimed. "I agree with the Muslims on that call. You haven't found a Muslim yet who has married a white person. It's just not done."

"You're right, girl," Symone said while dabbing her mouth with the napkin and placing it back in her lap. "If I didn't learn nothing else from the Eisners growing up, and that was you gots to protect your culture and stick with your own."

"We know that's another long damn subject," Pecola laughed and eyed the others who smiled at her with mutual understanding. "What you learned from the high and mighty Eisners."

The waitress came with the bill. Scott reached into his suit jacket pocket and pulled out his black leather wallet. He flipped through the plastic, selected a gold card, and handed it to her.

"I believe it's sooo in to be Black nowadays," Alex said. "There's Black gangsta rap, African-American clothing, movies, and the whole shebang is in. Marketing people are going after our dollars like crazy." While Symone covered her mouth to conceal several successive belches, Symone vigorously nodded her head in agreement again.

"Don't forget the fact that they're creating all these white boy groups, girl groups as well as white vocalists." Symone spoke slowly. "The interesting thing about it, is those white groups are one-hundred percent taught by Black creative people. Too many white kids were buying all these Black groups CDs. Something had to be done, so another think tank was put together—"

"There she goes with that think tank reason," Scott moaned.

"It's the truth. Check out the scenery," Symone went on. "All those white groups—whether they're solo acts or whatever are backed up by Black folks in some way or nother. Black choreographers are showing those white groups and singers how to move in a Black, sexy way. They're showing them how to dress Black and act Black. I'm telling you. Boyz to Men don't even have a chance right now in these days and times, chile. It's a mighty serious thang."

"Whaaat?" Alex said.

"I'm serious, yall," Symone added. "Just look at what's going on in the entertainment world. Too many dollars were being spent on Black groups. It was time to develop a strategy to move dollars back into white pop culture, so they had to create a white equivalent to get leverage."

"Here, here, chile," Pecola nodded.

"Good point, but let's get back to what I was saying," Alex said.

"Go right ahead, gurl," Symone nodded and glanced at a smiling Scott.

"Ok. We know a lot of us are prosperous. Of course, there are also a large number of Black folks who are still struggling," Alex continued with a deep sigh which signified she too was full. "But we as Black people need to appreciate our Blackness. Learn how to be devoted to our culture. I truly agree with Symone on that call. If you don't know who you are, you certainly have a hard time figuring out who you want to be."

"Spoken like a true advocate for the race, girl," Symone said and began a polite round of clapping.

"Everyone wants to be us," Alex said.

"That's what I meant about those singing groups," Symone shot in.

"Absolutely. We just need to know how really wonderful it is to be us, too. Wooo," Alex groaned suddenly. As a signal she had eaten all her stomach could hold then a few more forkfuls past that, Alex placed the linen napkin beside her plate. Pecola stopped eating minutes ago. While she listened, her eyes proudly admired her large emerald cut diamond ring and her bar designed diamond, tennis bracelet.

"Have yall noticed the television shows?" Symone asked. "They don't even know what an African-American family looks like. The children don't match the parents at all. I know Black people have a variety of complexions, but the matching up with the family should correspond closer to the complexions of the actors. Who the hell is casting those people in the first place? Dark, dark brown, parents with a supposedly multi-racial child as the daughter. Explain that to me."

Pecola, Alex, and Scott were all extremely full now. One by one, they each slumped back in their seats and stared at Symone.

"The way yall are looking at me," Symone went on. "I know I ain't the only one who notices things like that or what?"

"Chile, I'm full as a tic. That's why I'm looking this way. Hell yeah, I noticed it, too," Pecola exclaimed as she searched in her pocket for a much needed antacid tablet. "I don't know if I agree with the other statement you made, Sy. Look at me and my Mama. She's darker than you, but *I'm* her daughter."

"What do you mean darker than me?" Symone asked in amusement.

"You know, chile," Pecola replied. "Pauletta is a cocoa, chocolate brown. My sister is as dark-skinned, maybe darker than you are, Symone. She has green eyes, and she's my biological sister. Ezunial is light-skinned like me with green eyes."

"True," Alex said, bobbing her head.

"My son, CJ, is dark-skinned with green-eyes, and he came right out of this here belly. So puhleeze, honeychile! Who knows how these fidgety genes be jumping around?" Pecola added as she located two dirty Rolaid tablets in the recesses of her leather pocketbook. She quickly popped them in her mouth.

"I'm telling, yall. Like Scott alluded to earlier, all this mixing started back when they stole our land—this land from our ancestors and put us in slavery. With the rape of Black women slaves by white masters, that's how a lot of this happened," Symone said with her usual aggravation. "Nowadays, it has gone downhill ever since."

Scott glanced at his watch and stood up quickly to stretch. Earlier, they agreed to go to the seven o'clock Vanessa Bell Calloway new movie, and it was now six-thirty. Alex and Pecola gathered their pocketbooks and quickly slid out from their inside seats of the circular pleather booth. Before standing up, Alex shook the excess breadcrumbs from her dress. Without the assistance of a mirror, she deftly smoothed on red lipstick. Symone eyed their actions carefully.

"Oh, so whassup with this? Is this my signal to stop talking and to let me know we're leaving?" Symone laughed for a brief moment. "Ain't yall nothing?"

"My, my, my. Tsk, tsk," Pecola moaned. "I tell you, honeychile. If I didn't know any better, I would never know you were born in another country. The older you get, the more you try to sound like a true North Carolinian. Yall listen to the cultured southern street coming out of Ms. Thang."

"I noticed that. Rozelle tells her the same thing all the time, Pecola," Scott said with a shrug of his shoulder. "She's just trying to fit in and is trying to act like she's from the south."

"I know, chile," Pecola nodded. "She's using ain't, yall, and whassup. She certainly ain't the Miss formal Poussaint of Santa Cruz, Trinidad who long time ago refused to use a double negative. Her entire conversation is peppered with such wonderful phrases."

"Doesn't she just fit in just perfectly, girl?" Alex asked laughing.

"Wait until I speak with Mum Poussaint," Pecola continued while she patted her hair to make sure each strand was in place. They all referred to Symone's mother in an affectionate way.

Scott decided to walk to the front of the restaurant to find out what was taking the waitress so long to return for his signature. He had given her the charge card at least ten minutes ago.

"I won't forget this," Symone remarked jokingly.

"Girl, puhleeze. Let's go. Once you get going on your cultural discussion, we won't make it to the movies in time," Alex gently admonished with a wink. She extended an outstretched hand because Symone appeared as if she was still too full to move from the booth and needed assistance.

"I *ain't* going to *forgit* it," Symone said with a little girl pout.

"Just put a paper clip in the place where we left off. You know you'll make sure we pick up this conversation on another day," Alex said. Scott nodded in agreement as he helped Pecola ease into her light overcoat.

Chapter Eighty-Eight

For the past ten years, Pecola had been a proud, boasting member of the Winston-Salem, Greensboro and High Point Group, also known as the WGH Club. It was an African-American women's philanthropic social club whose husbands were the most influential and powerful Black executives, educators, doctors, and entrepreneurs of Winston-Salem, Greensboro, and High Point, North Carolina. The three cities also known as the Triad. Membership was accessible only by recommendation of current members. For eight consecutive years, Pecola invited Symone and Alex to join the group, yet both women declined. Alex politely refused the club's invitation with no explanations given. Symone, on the other hand, hated this group more so than she disliked the sororities her friends were so crazy about. In her opinion, women in such organizations appeared fake, pampered, overdressed, self-centered, and too hoity toity.

According to Symone, the group's real name should have been WGH Club aka Peyton Place. Rumors were widespread within the organization. At one time, the group was accused of swapping spouses knowingly and unknowingly. Without question, the club had a complexion rainbow patent that boasted a variety of high yellow, chocolate brown, pecan-tan, dark-dark, coffee black, almost white women wannabees, gonna bees, and young up and coming bees. However Symone even had to admit to the well-known facts, and that was the group did constructive things in the community.

Once the members plowed through the dumb shit, the group worked diligently each year to support worthwhile programs, to fund college scholarships for low-income children, and every now and then provided homeless families with new houses. Oftentimes, Symone told Pecola that the WGH Club reminded her of an African-American Junior League with a whole lot of soul. It certainly was a cliquish club. The husbands golfed at the country clubs in the Triad, made deals with the help of each other, worked hard, and played even harder. Symone believed they probably chased pussy as a group, too. The women were just as tight. They played bridge with each other, shopped together, attended the theater, played tennis, and appeared miserable collectively.

The club was founded twenty years ago by Johnetta Lou Pettiford, a chic, fifty-somethingish judge's wife who had the aggravating habit of watching people through half glasses that were propped right on the tip of her nostrils. An AKA like Pecola, she was also treasurer of Tennessee State University's alumni association in Winston-Salem. Whatever was considered the right group to be a part of in Winston, Johnetta was an official member in some capacity or another. The annual tea was especially significant for Johnetta this year because she was elected president again for three years. Equally monumentous for the group was that they were celebrating two decades of community activism. The most influential business people in the Triad were in attendance at this annual tea to hear the lauding speeches and be a part of the pre-planned, surprise award presentations.

This year, the annual tea was held at the Benton Convention Center in Winston-Salem. To make sure no one sat with Pecola and her friends. Pecola reserved and paid for a strategically located table of twelve near the front. The location was brilliant. When Pecola spotted certain people entering the reception hall, she gave Symone a graphic, biographical narrative of each one.

Most times, Symone enjoyed attending the tea. It was during those occasions, Pecola's gossip sounded like melodious music, and she discussed with pride everything she knew about anybody there. Since Alex frowned upon the gossip during the banquet, or anywhere for that matter, they chose to sit four seats away from her. Now Alex wouldn't be in hearing distance of the blood and guts gossip taking place at the other end of the table. Finally, the dais' introductions were completed, and Pecola recapped for Symone's ears only what the individuals on the dais *truly* were about.

"...That guy was a judge in Fayetteville, honeychile. Now, he's a high-level executive vice president at MUB Industries," Pecola whispered as she slid her chair closer to Symone's, so they wouldn't have to talk as loudly.

Symone watched him a moment and was impressed with the medium built, powerful looking Black guy with salt pepper gray hair, beard, and impeccable attire. She leaned toward Pecola and spoke quietly in a conversational whisper.

"He's fine, girl," she agreed softly. "Is he married?"

"Yeah. His wife is over there," Pecola said and tried to disguise her pointing toward another front table.

"He's still fine, Pecola."

"He is. Isn't he, Sy? You know the talk here is that he thinks he's such big shit. They claimed he done screwed everything in Winston-Salem," Pecola said confidently.

"Not quite. He hadn't screwed me, Pecola. Although I don't live in Winston-Salem, our business is here. I guess I'm still eligible, especially if he's smart," Symone added, laughing. "But for him to screw every woman here, that's impossible. I never believed rumors like that. It just ain't that much dick on one person."

"Honeychile, puhleeze. There are three hundred and sixty five days in a year. You need to multiply that times twenty years. That's how long he's been living here. Trust me, Sy. He's close to making a dent in the mark."

"Pecola, you're too crazy."

"It's true. Ssssh! Ssssh! Let me see what they're saying now." While the waiter served their table the garden salad, Pecola listened intently for about ten minutes. That was as long as she could be quiet. Without hesitating, she began to gossip with Symone again.

"You see the guy walking over there, Sy?" Pecola didn't want to point, so she made quick head motions in the man's direction.

"Yeah, what about him?"

"He dates my soror sister, and she's also a WGH member."

"The tall, tanned *white* guy over there?" Symone asked shocked with wide eyes.

"Yeah, chile. He's one of the most rich, powerful men in the city. He owns car dealerships, real estate, and my man is screwing a Black woman on the side."

"Get out of here! Is he married?" Symone whispered furiously.

"Chile, yeah. Of course *he's* married. Got six children too, but he takes care of his little Black girlfriend in every way you can imagine. She drives a Mercedes, and he bought it."

"Is that right?"

"Her car is almost like yours, but it's a four-door sedan type, girl. Plus, he brought her a condo on Lake Norman."

Symone picked at her salad. "Lake damn Norman? Get out of here. Dirt there is truly, very expensive, Pecola. Just ask Scott and Marlon. I hope her name is on the deed of trust. Tell her to place those papers in a safe deposit box with her John Hancock on it," she informed wisely.

"Last I heard, they went to St. Lucia this September. He surprised her with a five-carat diamond-studded tennis bracelet. If she comes by the table, I'll kick you twice. Then you look at her left wrist. All girlfriend has to do is think about something, and that pussy-whipped white boy will read her mind and get it for her. This affair has lasted for five years."

"You're kidding, Pecola."

"I'm not. He told her that he just loves the ground Black women walk on—is absolutely addicted to them."

"It figures. For five damn years, they've been doing this? He's a married man, too. Aaargh! That's disgusting for anyone to go with a married man. A low down dirty shame—"

"It's done every day, chile. There are a whole lot of problem marriages, and folks just stray. I'm just glad Carlos and I learned how to talk and nurture ours."

"Whaaat?"

"You heard me."

"Ok. Whatever." Symone smiled, glanced sideways at Pecola, and sprinkled more pepper on her salad.

"It's true."

"But a white married man is even worse," Symone exclaimed softly as she ate several pieces of cucumber. "You know what? In a way, I don't blame her, Pecola."

"Why?"

"If I'm going to bed a white guy, he's going to have some serious bank. My white man has to be a billionaire. That's for sure. I can find a poor Black man to give my distinctive pussy to any day," Symone said laughing while trying to keep her voice low at the same time. She didn't want the other ladies at their table to hear the conversation.

"You know it, chile."

"If most white girls can marry our men for money and status, I can do a little someumph, someumph."

"That'll be the day."

"That's how the white girls do it. They're groomed for the cash."

"Whooo, chile. You know it."

"I'm convinced they got a wealth gauge on their foreheads as early as junior high school and on into college that says, 'He looks like a promising prospect. Nice Mandingo warrior type. Money. Movie star. Professional athlete. Chiseled Black looks and a big dick. What Black women *wouldn't* want him? But lately, the white girls are winning every time."

"Not every time, Sy. Just most of the time."

"You're right. But those women will sacrifice their families and their culture in a heartbeat for a fine assed nigger."

Pecola laughed out loudly and covered her mouth in embarrassment. Alex, who was seated between Norvella and Nanette on the other side of the table, glanced up at them sharply. Yet, her motherly non-verbal expression she flashed did nothing to diffuse Pecola and Symone's animated gossip. Pecola instead winked at Alex and threw a slow, frilly wave.

"The sistah who goes with the white guy. What does she do?" Symone asked quickly.

Pecola sipped a glass of sweetened tea. "She's an executive secretary to the senior vice president of marketing at MUB Industries."

"An executive secretary? You see what I mean? She's depending on him to give her the kind of life she wants since she probably can't afford to buy the things he's getting her."

"Well, you know she can't, girl. You don't need to be a rocket scientist to figure that out."

"She's on the wrong road and needs to get off," she said smugly.

"Damn, chile! That's easy for you to say. Maybe she wants the finer things of life and figures she definitely isn't going to get it at all by typing her fingers to the bone as an executive secretary. Her part-time job is to get it by lying on her back. Hell, you can screw anybody for free, Symone. That's what most women do every day anyway."

"Yeah, I still think it's amazing."

The waiter walked up to the table, and Symone requested a straw. Pecola glanced up and caught Charmaine watching her out the corner of her eyes. Pecola offered her a large, friendly smile across the table. She really felt like asking her, *What the hell are you looking at me for, Charmaine?* Pecola slowly shook her head and turned back to resume the conversation with Symone.

"There are several women in the group going with rich white guys, honeychile."

"I know you told me this before, but where do they find them?" Symone asked thoroughly shocked again.

"I've told you this fifty-thousand times, Sy. The Triad, especially Winston-Salem and High Point, are known for their millionaires, girl."

Symone sipped tea and breathed heavily. "To get a sistah in bed is a fantasy for a white man, too. I always knew that. When I'm in New York, I get approached enough—down here. They just want to wallow in Black love," she mumbled under her breath as she sliced a piece of tomato and placed it in her mouth.

"Right, chile. So you can understand why girlfriend is just living in a dream, and she's still getting bills paid. The white boy is fulfilling his private fantasy too, so both of them are happy."

"Check out the major difference between Black and white men. White men tend to do their thing behind closed doors. Now you got some rare cases where the white boys step out of the closet and say the hell with everybody. But Black men. Humph. Black men buy into that dream that the white girl is supreme, and their ignorant asses marry them."

"That they do."

"One of these days, our people will learn our race is the chosen people, too, and there's nothing more beautiful than to select a Black man or woman as a mate," she explained with flashing eyes.

Pecola patted her hand in a patronizing, understanding way. A chocolate dark-skinned, heavy-set, tall man, who weighed about three hundred and fifty pounds, stopped by the table to speak with Pecola. He was a new friend of Pecola whom she had met at a recent AKA dinner. His name was Braimbridge Murphy. He wanted to meet Symone, and he asked Pecola to introduce him to her. Pecola did. While speaking to Symone, Braimbridge licked his lips four times in slow motion as if he was trying to get lint out of his mustache or was attempting to show Symone the dexterity of his limber tongue.

"Umph. I can't believe Braimbridge did that," Pecola said after he left. She ate a forkful of salad and dabbed her mouth with the sky blue linen napkin. The waiter attempted to hand Symone a straw with a napkin wrapped around it, and she requested he place it in the tea. She thanked him.

"Girl, I thought he was crazy myself."

"Braimbridge is smart as a whip," Pecola whispered feverishly. "He's a Bowie State Man, a Kappa, and has two Master's Degrees in engineering from Harvard."

"I don't care if the degrees are from Wal-Mart. The nigger is crazy to come up to me and do that? He doesn't know me from Adam's house cat, girl. A Harvard graduate? He's another Rozelle," she murmured and glanced at Jodria. She was sitting between Rehema and Norvella and appeared to be paying close attention to the mistress of ceremonies who was recognizing the various dignitaries in the audience. Symone hoped that Jodria didn't hear the negative comments she spoke about her husband.

"He's only been living here six months and just relocated from California."

"I betcha he and Rozelle probably are good friends. What did I tell you? High level politician, CEOs, doctors, lawyers, and scientists are freaky deaks that way. The more wealthy and educated the person, the freakier they are. I don't know why. What Braimbridge did just validates my unofficial research," Symone said while daintily picking a piece of lettuce off the napkin in her lap.

"I still don't believe that's totally true, chile. I got too many friends who have gone the gambit with men who don't fit in those categories, and they're just as big a freak."

In an all-knowing voice, Symone continued. "Pecola, listen to me. They're freaks, girl. Those smart ones are the types that want orgies and a golden shower from three women simultaneously. And another thing, he's a fat ass, big blob butterball of a man. His dick is probably flat from being squished underneath that huge stomach he got. Nobody wants a man that large," Symone said as she politely sipped tea through the straw.

"Are you kidding? That's his woman over there. I heard Braimbridge has boocoo bucks, chile."

"It figures," Symone said distastefully. "The way he threw his body around, he acted like he had money. Nothing worse than a rich, fat, unattractive man whose on an ego trip. Where's his girlfriend?" Symone asked while stretching her neck to gaze around. Pecola made several quick head nods to her left.

"The light-skinned girl in the black, slinky dress. The pretty one with the long hair standing up over there," Pecola informed calmly.

"Whaaat?" Symone's mouth fell open, and she quickly closed it, but her eyes stretched wider.

"That's right. I know. I was shocked the first time I found out," Pecola continued, amused at Symone's reaction. "Honeychile, I guess if you got a little dick, then you certainly better have a limber tongue. Obviously, my brotherman got something going for him other than his brains," Pecola added slyly, and she and Symone laughed together leaning on each other as they covered their mouth to squelch the volume.

"Girl, the inside info you give is worth attending this luncheon."

"I know. That's why it's good to have a friend like me who knows *all* the juicy dirt. If you look at Braimbridge wrong, his girlfriend will kick your arse as she says. I think she's from England somewhere," Pecola added, still trying to muffle her laughter.

Just then, a very stunning, shapely caramel complexion woman stopped by to briefly speak to Pecola. She appeared to be about five feet seven. With short black hair framing her perfectly round face, she was dressed in a black timeless Patrick Robinson suit. Symone took several sips of tea through the straw, eyed the woman briefly, and was definitely impressed with her impeccable attire and smooth air.

"Who—was—she?" Symone asked slowly when the woman left.

"That's Rosalind Neal, chile. Three years ago, she relocated here from Chicago with her husband and four children. She's a former Ebony Fashion Fair model. I think Johnetta said that she was Miss Black Chicago fifteen years ago. She's a Talladega College girl and a Zeta like Charmaine."

"Hmmm. That's interesting. I never met her before."

"I know, chile. That's because you don't go anywhere. Her husband is Michael Maceo Neal, the high-powered, mega deal maker sports attorney. I mean he's a sho nuff tall, old-fashioned handsome Black man, too, girl. Umph. Umph. Umph."

"Definitely my type."

"Yeah. If he weren't married, he *certainly* would be an excellent catch for you, Sy. Michael represents some of the biggest names in basketball, football, baseball, and everything else," Pecola said knowingly under her breath and out the corner of her mouth as she casually waved to another smartly dressed woman two tables over. As the Chicago sister walked gracefully back to her seat, Symone observed her intently.

"She certainly is very, very beautiful," Symone said slowly while she strained her neck to see who was sitting with Mrs. Neal.

"Everyone thinks so."

Symone noticed that Johnetta and ten other equally, super pampered, snooty looking women comprised the twelve for their table. "Michael Neal. I've heard that name before. That's right. When we were at the children's opening ceremonies this summer, Marlon told me what he knew about him."

"Oh yeah, I forgot to tell you that Johnetta recommended Rosalind to WGH."

"That's probably why they're sitting together," Symone said, preoccupied. She continued to study the presidential table curiously and wondered why she kept her eyes on them. "Girl, how come I didn't notice these people last year?"

"All you do is go home and slip into silk, satin, velour or old tee-shirts, chile."

Symone nodded her head and smiled. "True. True—"

"If you socialize a little more often, you would know and meet these people. You act like a recluse most of the time."

"C'mon, Pecola, not all of the time. Not when I'm with my friends."

"It's more to life than that. Everybody always wants to meet you at social events around town. They hear me talk about my partner. You're like invisible to them because they never see you out at important functions."

"That's quite boring and is a waste of my time."

"Then when I try to get you to go, you're always either too tired, depressed, or in a foul mood. So when they do see you hanging out with me, they break their neck to come over here and talk. I get tired of asking you to go places with me, Symone. It ain't anything wrong with a little bit of network and socializing. It's good for your ego," she exclaimed and gazed at her prettily polished pink nails and diamonds shining on both her wrists and fingers.

"Girl, you know I socialize. Just not unnecessarily. All this excess nonsense is boring to me."

"I know it is to you because you don't *have* to socialize."

"Hell, Pecola. You don't either. Don't even try it."

"I know. But I love the glitzy and glamour of the privileged folks during a North Carolina night, chile."

Symone just shook her head at Pecola's remarks. "I bet Carlos would rather stay home most times. Plus, I have three small children I need to raise. Still, how come I didn't see these people last year?"

"Well, you know what they say," Pecola said smiling sweetly and carefully wiped each corner of her mouth with the napkin. "Another year introduces a new look and different faces."

"Sssh. Sssh, puhleeze, " Alex reprimanded as she cleared her throat. Both women stopped talking for a few moments. Symone smiled back at Alex and waved an index finger to her in a naughty, naughty fashion.

During the meal, Symone and Pecola finally settled down and didn't speak as often. Yet the talking didn't altogether cease because Alex continued to watch them. Every now and then, she threw them disapproving glances each time they attempted to rev up the gossip mode to a loud level. However, when the lunch dishes were removed, and the dessert plus coffee were served, the crowd settled back to hear the keynote speaker. Pecola and Symone leaned back to relax and to quietly begin chitchatting again.

Chapter Eighty-Nine

While walking to the black super-stretch Towncar, Alex considered the evening she planned for FOFAE. Wrapped in their wool capes, stylish hats, and still speaking non-stop with Rehema, Pecola and Symone strutted to the limousine waiting out in front of the convention center on Fifth Street. After the tea luncheon ended, Pecola thought that Alex was aggravated by the way she and Symone talked constantly throughout the program. However, Alex wasn't upset with them. As a matter of fact, she was amused by their gossiping antics. No matter what anyone said, Pecola and Symone's personalities were branded in cement. They weren't going to change because they were as crazy as can be. Yet, they were definitely two of the most wonderful women to have as friends.

I know this evening definitely will be a surprise. Oooh! I just love surprises! Alex thought with a smile.

Whenever Alex scheduled the monthly FOFAE, she always hired Kukaribisha Limousine Service to pick up each member. This was the same company Meetings Odyssey used for business travel, too. As a result of Alex using limos during their outings, Pecola, Nanette, and Jodria did the same for their months. Symone grew up riding in limousines, so it wasn't a big deal for her, and she decided she would follow suit and pick up the tabs for the other months as well. Since there were only seven active members, the other women gave Alex permission to plan five outings a year. That was after Alex had talked and talked and twisted their arms. Jodria said that they simply got tired of hearing Alex's continuous pleadings and relented to the simple request.

Since FOFAE had to attend the WGH tea, ten ladies were traveling with the group this month. Once settled in the lush comfort of the limousine, the women recapped the good points about the luncheon tea, who was with whom, and how different women were dressed. All of the other women laughed at Pecola and Symone's gossipy behavior, which didn't seem to bother the two one bit. While the limousine glided through the streets of Winston-Salem, Alex served Evian, soft drinks, macadamia nuts, and petite sandwiches. She wanted to save the Cristal champagne for the special surprise she had planned later for her friends.

"...Honeychile, you don't have nothing harder than this?" Pecola asked smiling while eyeing Symone. With her arms folded and shoes off, Symone was nestled in the left back seat corner with a miserable expression on her face.

"Girl, that's all I'm serving," Alex replied and batted her eyes the way Pecola normally would.

"Turn off that damn music, puhleeze," Symone said dryly.

Of course, they ignored the request. As soon as they entered the limo, Jodria handed a Patti LaBelle greatest hits CD to Togo Laymar King. He was the fine, short, and happily married Black chauffeur they requested each month. Since they couldn't get tickets to the Patti LaBelle show, the singing was depressing Symone, not that she needed any help or an excuse to be that way in the first place.

"I can't believe this! Ms. Patti, my favorite singing diva, is in town, and *we* couldn't get tickets," Jodria said with a huge frown on her chubby face.

"Can you believe that?" Rehema asked.

"What about *our* connections? Even Rozelle said he couldn't get any, girl," she added in disbelief and watched Symone.

I don't know why Jodria thinks that two-timing husband of hers is God and can move mountains, Symone thought as she glared outside the black tinted windows.

Symone slowly shook her head and turned to watch the naive-acting Jodria snap her fingers and gyrate to Patti LaBelle singing *The Right Kinda Lover.* Nanette, Rehema, and Adele were now leaning from side to side on each other, snapping their fingers and singing happily along to the words. Trying to do the Georgia bounce to the song, Pecola and Darilyn were hunching their shoulders up and down as if they were riding a galloping horse. As Symone stared at the happy faces of her close friends, she almost immediately felt bad for thinking such awful thoughts about Jodria. However, she was in a foul mood. *And shit happens when you're that way,* she thought.

Alex merely listened to the discussion. It was rare for the women to meet up with their husbands on a FOFAE outing, but tonight they were. This one was special, not only because Pecola threatened them about attending the WGH Club tea, but unbeknownst to the others, Alex had purchased front row tickets to the show of the year. Patti LaBelle and Steve Harvey were appearing at the Stevens Center in Winston-Salem. Since Marlon was friends with the concert promoter for this special show, Alex also received backstage passes.

The WGH tea ended at five, and the show didn't begin until eight. While the women relaxed in the limousine, they decided to go shopping at Hanes Mall since Alex told them that the dinner reservations at Noble's Grille weren't until seven-thirty. People always stared when they saw so many Black women spilling out of the limousine. Then the curious passersby would ask the same question in their thickest southern accent, "What do yall do?" Jodria always answered the inquiring onlookers with the same unpretentious statement. "Oh, I'm simply a housewife in Winston-Salem," she would say matter of factly. Those remarks always left curious people standing with their mouths and eyes wide open.

Alex smiled to herself as she considered her friends' shocked expressions, especially Pecola's. Patti LaBelle was her all time, favorite performer. She had seen her perform live in concert only once before almost ten years ago in Atlanta. Pecola was a Patti LaBelle fan from the old school days and swore she became pregnant with her firstborn child while making love in the back seat of Carlos' car listening to The Blue Belles sing *I Sold my Heart to the Junkman.* The Blue Belles were her most favorite Motown group. A younger Pecola always envisioned she would sign a major singing contract with Motown and one day tour the world.

Madison and the other men were in another limousine. Alex had planned for all of them to meet up together in front of the Stevens Center for the show. Afterwards, they would all hang out at Unique Upstairs listening to the sounds of Knights of Soul with Jackie D. Alex hadn't really made dinner plans at Noble's Grille. The dinner date was just an excellent ploy to get the women's mind focused on eating a luscious prime rib supper at the elegant restaurant.

As the limo glided down I-40 West toward Hanes Mall, Jodria pulled out her legendary family pictures again. The animated discussion quickly changed to other comical topics as the women laughed at the family photos Jodria shared of her spending time in the park with her six children. In addition, she showed other snapshots of the birthday party Rozelle's parents gave in Nashville for the youngest child even though Jodria hosted a huge one in Winston-Salem. The ladies laughed hysterically at the formal family portrait with Rozelle, of all people, trying to look proper and staid.

The limousine pulled up in front of Hanes Mall, and Alex opted to stay in the car. She felt tired. While resting her head against the plush, black leather seats, she thought back to the first time she had ever rode in a limousine. It was over fifteen years ago. Before then, Alex only noticed such sleekly long impressive black cars when she attended relatives' funerals or when she went to work with her parents in Advance. She often saw the wealthy McIntyres stepping out of them when they returned home to their private estate in the country. In rare cases, friends Alex knew rented the cars for their weddings.

One evening after Alex's mother experienced a particularly rough chemo treatment, she summoned Alex to her bedroom. Adriola told her daughter that it was very important that she talked to her. It was a cold, bleak day in December, and Alex had just finished mid-term law exams. Alex remembered that she kept watching the sky as she drove to her parents' neat brick home that frigid evening. As she turned left onto Cameron Avenue from New Walkertown Road, she noticed how the full moon appeared as a white basketball against the black sheet canvas of endless sky. At the time, Alex thought the eerie-looking heavens reminded her of an Alfred Hitchcock movie.

When Alex arrived home and walked inside, Adriola was sitting propped up on pillows in the four-poster maple bed. Dressed in her favorite blue silk charmeuse gown and robe, she was reviewing old photo albums. Realizing her mother only wore such luxurious nightwear during special occasions or when she was in the hospital, Alex wondered why her mother had the special pajama set on.

The lamps were dimly lit in the quaintly decorated bedroom, and Alex savored the flowery clean jasmine aroma that was always present in the home. As Alex smiled, she glanced with amusement at the always starched, white linen embroidered sheets that adorned her parents' queen-size bed.

On that night, Adriola showed her daughter pictures of Adriola's comfortable childhood in Winston-Salem. She unveiled old photographs of her now deceased parents. It was Alex's Granddaddy, Larry Love Wonder, Jr. along with his pretty, always smiling wife, Grandma Carmen Spirit. There were also photos of Adriola's two sisters, great aunts, uncles, and grade school photos of Alex and Nanette. Included were pictures of Adriola's older brother, Larry

Love Wonder, III, who died of leukemia when he was only sixteen years old. There was one lone picture of Adriola's younger brother, Jackson Love. Jackson was killed with two of his high school buddies when they speed raced with a locomotive train on senior prom night and lost the dare devil challenge. Included were lovely browntone snapshots of Alex's parents, pictures of Adriola and Roger as a young married couple. There were so many photos that reflected all the years of their family up to the present time with Alex and Nanette.

Alex cherished each and every sentimental photograph and was moved to tears as she watched her mother turn the pages, slowly, one by one, reminiscing and commenting on the occasion of each photo. With a Marian Anderson album softly peppering operatic gospel sounds throughout the bedroom, Alex cried softly as she listened to her mother's sad voice relive her life. Since Marian Anderson was Adriola's favorite singer, Alex knew this was a reflective spell for her mother. Adriola always listened to the singer during her most quiet, meditative moments.

To view the night darkness, Alex slowly walked over to the picture window and pulled the curtains opened then returned to sit on the bed. As her mother began talking about her life again, Alex listened without comment as Adriola recapped the days of her youth, to her present age of fifty-two, with each year being experienced in the small, southern town of Winston-Salem.

Finally, Adriola stopped talking for several minutes. What she had to say wasn't easy for her. She reached under her embroidered linen sheet to get something, and the older woman turned to her daughter and observed her for a moment. Then Adriola handed Alex a large, tightly tied brown envelope with several folder sections. Each section had different items in it. There was a United National Bank savings account bankbook, a conveyed whole-life insurance policy with North Carolina Mutual Life Insurance Company, and another bankbook was from Mechanics and Farmers Savings. When Alex calculated the amounts for both bankbook balances, she was shocked.

For over thirty years, Alex's parents had worked as a housekeeper and butler for the wealthy McIntyre family, heirs to MUB Industries of Winston-Salem and JCM Securities out of Charlotte, North Carolina. From what Alex could see, it appeared that her parents managed to save almost nine hundred and eighty thousand dollars. In addition, Adriola handed Alex official documents that reflected at the time almost five hundred thousand shares of MUB restricted company stock and legal certificates detailing a huge insurance policy with Nationwide Insurance that the McIntyres had purchased for the loyal couple.

The McIntyres called Adriola's mother the dedicated Aunt Carmen. Carmen Spirit had worked in the large homes of the prominent family ever since she was a teenager. Recommended to the McIntyres by Larry Love, Sr. who did the yard work and other menial jobs for the family, Carmen was hired as the wet nurse at the age of fifteen. She raised all the McIntyre's children from the time they were born into privilege in a secluded mansion along the beautifully, tree-lined community of the Buena Vista section of Winston-Salem. Carmen passed this coveted position on to Adriola and had taught Adriola that her *only* calling in life was to follow in her footsteps and work for the white family to help raise the next generation of precious McIntyre babies.

Throughout the years, the McIntyre holdings from all family businesses were privately held under several corporate umbrellas. However, seventy-five years after the first company was founded, they decided to combine all the companies under one name and call it McIntyre United Businesses or MUB Industries for short, then sell a piece of the company to the general public.

The second oldest son of the patriarch, Joshua Cox McIntyre, or known simply as "JCM" to everyone in town, was Chipper Cox McIntyre. Unbeknownst to Adriola and Roger, Chipper wanted to award the Black couple for their family's generational faithfulness all the way back to the dependable Larry Love, Sr. To his son, Larry Love, Jr. And, to Chipper's now dead Aunt Carmen who was like a mother to him more so than his real mother ever was or could be because of her alcoholism. Chipper McIntyre loaned MUB Industries money in Adriola and Roger Johnson's name. When MUB Industries went public, Chipper and his younger brother retained seventy-percent ownership of the voting stock for the family, and the other thirty-percent was offered to the public. In appreciation, Chipper and his older brother gave the Johnson's five-hundred-thousand shares of unrestricted stock in exchange for the MUB loan placed in the Johnson's name. Initially, the value of MUB Industries was publicly traded at a paltry ten dollars. With shrewd marketing along with the media excitement on the street about the Winston-Salem based company, the price zoomed to forty-nine dollars a share within three weeks. The stock went back down to thirty dollars. Eventually, it settled at a comfortable sixty dollars a share, to the rate of one-hundred and fourteen dollars a share that it currently sold for today. When Alex's mother shared the stock information with Alex that night, the original five-hundred-thousand shares of stock the Johnsons received had split a total of seven times. On that wintry day back in December those many years ago, Alex held in her hands the generous gift by Chipper that essentially gave the Johnson family a teeny chunk of MUB Industries.

Although Adriola and Roger had lived quite modestly their entire life, they had a warm home that was always filled with pretty fresh smelling flowers, friends, happy guests, and children. Roger and Adriola didn't smoke or drink and believed that to do so was an absolute sin against God. Yet, everyone who lived on Cameron Avenue in Winston-Salem back then knew they could sit on the front porch with the Johnsons and have a wonderful time just laughing, talking and sipping chilled, freshly made, sweet lemonade.

Adriola invited Alex over that frigid December evening because she wanted to assure Alex that in case something happened to her, there was plenty enough money to bury her and her father. Adriola also wanted to let Alex know that neither she nor her sister would ever need to worry themselves about paying for their college education or to concern themselves with having enough money to make a down payment on a home. Nanette was only fifteen at the time, but after her mother was diagnosed with cancer, she was determined to become a registered nurse so that she could help her Mama and other people combat the awful disease.

A week didn't go by and it seemed that at least almost every day of Alex's life, she recalled the poignantly gripping conversation with her mother.

"...I done told my Chipper many times he needed to explain all that MUB stock mumbo jumbo to you, Alex. I don't know much about it. Me or Roger never could understand confusing things like stocks splitting and the dividends jibberish that Chipper spoke about all the time. So you talk to Chipper. My boy will tell it to you straight. Other than that, you and Nanette got right much change coming to you when I die, baby."

"But Mama, all—this—money. You never traveled anywhere," Alex said sadly as tears welled in her eyes. She rested her head on her mother's lap, and Adriola gently stroked Alex's thick, black hair as she continued speaking in a muffled voice.

"Baby, don't worry yourself, now."

"Mama, you never left Winston-Salem. Oh lawd have mercy, Mama. You and Daddy never went anywhere to enjoy *this* money," Alex repeated softly as she again quickly glanced at the large accumulation of money she held in her hands.

Alex realized that her mother had worked thirty-four straight years cooking, cleaning, and taking care of children for the McIntyres. She even went to work sick all the time. Now, Alex recognized the inevitable. Her mother was dying from cancer.

"...Mama, you and Daddy only drove as far as Hilton Head. You only went there because the McIntyres needed yall to be there to serve their guests," she exclaimed grief-stricken.

Alex's mother turned and gazed out of the picture window. She noticed that a misty cloud floated by in the sky and briefly blocked the light of the moon. Alex paused for a moment and gently asked her mother more questions.

"Why, Mama? *Why?* I would've much rather you see the world than save this kind of money for Nanette and me. Oh, Mama. I wish you and Daddy could go to New York, even to Europe, traveled somewhere, Mama." Sincerely heartbroken, Alex's words came out in long drawn out wails.

"Alexandria, puhleeze!" Adriola always pronounced her oldest daughter's first name perfectly. She wanted to silence her. Now her tone softened. "Baby, don't worry about me. I'm fine. Your daddy wanted it this way. Every week we went to the bank and made our deposits. He just enjoyed looking at the dollar amount increase every week." Adriola paused a moment and closed her eyes.

"But Mama, all this money?"

"I know. I know. As the McIntyres gave us more and more gifts of money, we took it to the bank, baby. At Christmas, Easter, birthdays, and holidays, we ran straight to the bank whenever they gave it to us. Alexandria, it became a routine, and your daddy didn't want either one of us to touch one penny of it," she said tightly. "He said it was for when we retired."

"When you retired, Mama?"

With a faraway expression, Adriola casually waved her hand and spoke softly in a bare whisper. "Isn't that funny, baby? Cause I had to retire cause I'm sick. Your Daddy liked looking at it grow, Alexandria. And, and, I—, uh, I became the same way."

Quietly, Adriola began to cry. With fast tears rolling down her cheeks, she slowly nodded her head and bit her bottom lip in disbelief. Alex quickly snatched several sheets of tissue from the brass decanter and tenderly wiped her mother's face.

"Mama, don't cry, puhleeze. It's gonna be all right."

Adriola smiled slightly. "Baby, it was only after I became sick that I wondered if we did the right thing. "Because I—," she sobbed as she blew her nose and wiped her eyes, "I realized I hadn't been anywhere in life, Alexandria. Then I became very sad. All I could visualize on my real sick days like this one today is places I've been to in Winston-Salem," she murmured almost inaudibly. Just as quickly, she became composed and stared Alex in the eyes and held her chin.

"Mama, it's ok."

"Baby, I don't want you to live a life like mine. You hear me, chile? You're goin' be a fine, outstanding attorney. I always knew that, Alexandria. You know why, my little girl?" she asked tenderly.

Alex simply gazed into her mother's eyes, speechless. The words *my little girl* catapulted her mind to quickly recall years of childhood memories of her mother talking to her about enjoying life, traveling, and being an attorney.

"Because you said you would. That's why. I made sure of that. I sho nuff did. The same way my Mama talked to me about working with the McIntyres, I wanted to talk to you. My sweet child." Adriola held Alex's quivering chin. "I wanted to talk to my sweet baby girl about becoming an attorney, so you could work for the McIntyres in another kind of way, baby," she exclaimed proudly.

"Lawd, Mama."

"Right now, we'll stop this legacy of maid and butler. That was my mother's gift to me in a world that beat up Black people some way or another every day. And my mama made a good decision for me, but you're destined to go further, girl. You done married an outstanding man from a mighty fine family. A doctor, chile! Madison's gonna be a doctor one day, baby! And lawd knows I believe Madison truly loves you. I can only dream about the life you two will live together."

"Mama, puhleeze. You'll be here to enjoy my life," Alex blurted quickly, reassuringly.

"Maybe I will. Maybe I won't." Adriola answered stubbornly and studied Alex's face a moment. "If I'm not, this I do want you to do, Alexandria. Love the lord, baby. Love your husband, but make sure you always have a mind of your own, baby. Always, always think for yourself," she said firmly as she pointed an overly straight index finger at Alex's face. Quickly, Adriola smiled. "And travel, baby. See the *whole* world. Enjoy *all* of it. Every bit. Take in God's wonderful creation." She stopped speaking and glanced outside as she allowed her mind to inventory the many regrets about her life. With a wistful and loving smile, she soaked in every inch of Alex's pretty and concerned face.

"Every chance you get, you go. Live every day as if it was your last, Alexandria. You hear me, baby?"

"Yes, Mama," Alex whispered as if she were in a daze.

"Always write it down in a pretty little book, baby. Sorta like a diary or something like the one you grew up with. The days just fly by, and it's just so hard to remember what happens throughout the years. I'm just in my fifties, baby. But even at my age, everything is so jumbled up now."

"Oh, Goddd!" Alex's chin dropped to her chest. She started crying wildly and embraced Adriola's waist tightly. This was the wise advice Adriola had always given her and Nanette.

Now, I know why, Alex thought.

From the time Alex was ten years old, Adriola shared such words of wisdom with her oldest daughter. Right after Nanette was born, she purchased a world globe for Alex. Many nights Adriola and Alex played a game where they twirled the globe as fast it would go. Then Alex stopped it with an index finger, and both she and her mother attempted to pronounce the city or country Alex's finger pointed to. Adriola instructed Alex to write each selection in her flowery pink spiral notebooks so she could visit those faraway places when she was older.

Now, I know why you shared such insight with me and Nanette, Mama, thought Alex. *Now, I know.* Alex began a pitiful round of sobbing and moaning again.

"Alexandria, don't cry," Adriola pleaded sternly. She suddenly remembered to share something else with her. "Another thing, baby. Always remember that friends are for a lifetime. Love and cherish your sister and your family. And, if you find other true friends like Pecola, adore them, baby. Don't live a life like mine. Saving money for what? There's nothing I can dream about resting here on my bed of affliction."

"O lordy, Mama—"

Now Adriola smiled to herself. "You know what Rine use to say?" she asked tenderly as she gently patted Alex's shoulder. Alex sadly shook her head no.

Adriola's friend, Eresterine, died suddenly last year from a massive heart attack when she was just fifty-one. The two women had been friends since they were both thirteen years old. Up until the time of her death, Eresterine always dressed flashily, even when she attended church. Eresterine constantly dated several men simultaneously and traveled to Chicago, New York, Las Vegas and wherever else she felt like going on vacation.

"What did Eresterine say, Mama?"

Adriola laughed freely. "Eresterine often would say to me, 'Adriola, you need to buy yourself some new clothes, honeychile! Adriola, come with me to the big city of Chicago next year or New York this summer. Adriola, money was printed to be spent. Why you and Roger saving all that damn money for them two gurls to enjoy after you're dead and gone? That's why they produce new money every day in that big city of Washington, DC, sugar! Cause folk like me like to spend it! I ain't leaving a dime for nobody to have a good time cause I'm gonna have my great days while I'm living. What good is money if you don't spend it?'" Adriola mimicked Eresterine's voice and began laughing as she recalled the many conversations with her dear, best friend.

Now, I know why you spoke to me in such a way, Mama, Alex's mind silently screamed again.

"I truly miss Eresterine's spunkiness, baby. I declare she was so much fun for me, Alexandria. Such an absolutely, marvelous breath of fresh air. She was a wonderful, true, and devoted friend. I miss her bad, baby," she said in an almost whisper and continued to speak with resignation.

"I know you do. I miss my Auntie Eresterine, too."

"You know what? She was right, baby girl. Eresterine spoke the truth to me, and I refused to see it then. She told me that—" Adriola stopped.

"Yes, mama."

"She told me that me and Roger were hoarders, and we were hoarding money like squirrels do in the summertime. For what? What could cause this kind of sickness? I guess poverty, heartache, and plain old hard times makes you save that away." She paused to reflect on her words. "It was because we didn't want our children to go through the kind of struggle we had."

"A sickness?"

"Yes, baby. It was a pure divine sin." Again, Adriola stopped speaking momentarily. "Eresterine called it a sickness where you save, save and save for a rainy day or for when me and Roger thought we would retire. Saving for what, Alexandria? Roger and I always said we would use it later."

Adriola slowly flipped to another page in the photo album. She glanced fondly at the faces of dead family members and at the smiling face of her best friend, Eresterine. The picture was taken six years ago at Adriola's birthday dinner. Alex continued to cry quietly. Her mother gazed her way briefly, smiled slightly with understanding, and continued speaking.

"I was forty-six at the time, Alex. Baby, you know I was always sooo afraid about turning forty-six because you know my Mama died from cancer at forty-five," she explained again sadly. Alex already knew this.

"I remember Grandma Carmen. I know, Mama."

"I'll never ever forget what Eresterine said that day, baby. We were having a private little celebration, just us girls," she recalled with a loud, throaty laugh.

"You loved her like a sister."

"I sho did." Adriola nodded and hesitated slightly. "Eresterine was crying for me that day—actually shedding crocodile tears. She cried to make her friend see the truth. Eresterine said, 'Adriola, you're saving all that money for later, chile. Girl, sometimes later never comes for us. Later is now, chile. Each day that we wake up and can breath, laugh, and talk, that's later, chile. So come on and go with me to Miami next week, Adriola. Las Vegas in the summer. You're forty-six now. You made it. You can do it, chile.' She was sooo right, Alexandria," she repeated weakly with her voice trailing off. "Later never does come sometimes, baby. It never does."

"Oh, mama."

"Now listen." As Adriola fought back tears, she held Alex's chin in her hand. "And you listen to me good now, baby. I want you to understand that money is nothing, absolutely nothing, baby. Just a piece of paper we give some value. And you know what? It can destroy us, especially if we're consumed by it and not take advantage of the pleasure it can bring to us and to the others close to us by having and sharing it."

Alex vigorously shook her head no. "Mama, I don't want *this* money. None of it. What good is it now? If I can't enjoy it with you and daddy together, what good is it?" Alex cried helplessly. "I wish there was some way I could take all that money and pay to make you well again, Mama." As she wrapped her arms around her mother's petite waist once more, she spoke loudly. "I don't want one penny of it."

"Now wouldn't that be something else if life was like that, baby? To just fix everything with money?" Adriola laughed freely at the understandable, but naive comment.

"Yes."

"Alexandria, money can't buy good health, baby. Nothing can do that. But you know what? I'm calm, baby. My God gave me plenty of that," she mumbled as she slowly glided her hand over Alex's stiff back.

"Oh lawd, Mama."

"If nothing else, remember what I always used to tell you ever since you were a little thing. Every day, get on your bended knees and ask God for inner serenity and peace. You hear me, Alexandria?"

"Yes, Mama."

"You ask your God every day for a beautiful, airy calm breeze of serenity to overtake you each day that you live. A sense of peace within yourself is worth more than all the money in the whole wide world, Alexandria. Hear me good, now. I always had inner peace, baby. I just never knew how to combine it with the money me and your daddy saved up." Adriola leaned her head slightly to the right and grinned swiftly. "Now if I had mixed the two together, that would've been absolutely wonderful, baby girl," she revealed as she laughed loudly. Alex smiled slightly, too. She hugged her mother even tighter and lightly rested her head on her mother's breasts.

"Oh, Mama. My precious, precious Mama."

"Alexandria, it's nothing wrong with being wealthy. Money just magnifies who you are, baby. It just gives you the freedom to make the choices you want. All this money will do is make you, Nanette, your daddy, and my sisters have an opportunity to enjoy life a little more. Just a little better than I did, baby. Enjoy it. Do it better than your Grandma Carmen, Granddaddy Larry, and your great Granddaddy Larry Love, too. Talk to your daddy, Alexandria. Let him know he should travel and see the world when I'm gone, baby."

"Mama, stop talking like that. You're not going anywhere. I'm going to talk to Dr. Payton. Me, you, Daddy, Nanette, and Madison are all going to travel to Hawaii and to Las Vegas. You always said you wanted to go there. I'm going to plan trips for us to leave as soon as we can."

Adriola ignored Alexandria's comments. She barely had strength to go to the bathroom on some days let alone go on a vacation to Hawaii or Las Vegas. Alex knew that too, but she wanted to plan and pray that it was possible anyway.

Adriola laughed, almost to herself. "You know the McIntyres always kept *real* expensive insurance for me and your Daddy. Look at the policy, baby. It's a mighty, mighty good one, too. They were rich people, and they were sooo good to us, baby," Adriola raved on about the wealthy family who treated them unusually well. She often bragged that the McIntyres were unlike some of the other white people Adriola and Roger's friends worked for. These people were the topics of continuous discussions by their domestic help who lived on Cameron Avenue and on other surrounding streets in the Black community.

"During Biblical times, there were many rich people who enjoyed God's blessings even back then, Alexandria." She inhaled heavily. "In the *Bible*, Lazarus, the beggar man, didn't go to heaven because he was poor, baby. He went there because he had a good heart. The rich man was the selfish one. That's why he went to hell. He had all that money, and he was selfish with it. Just wouldn't share nothing with nobody," she said with her voice trailing off. She paused swiftly and her eyes watered again.

"You're not selfish, Mama."

"I know, baby. Thank you for saying that to me. I know that. I never thought your Daddy and I were selfish with our lives," she explained in an almost whisper. "I really don't, Alexandria. We did tithe every Sunday, and we always sent money to people in our church."

"And, and you always cooked for the neighborhood children and always brought children home from church with you and Daddy, Mama," Alex added quickly.

"True, baby. I just always wanted you and Nanette to have company around. It was just the two of yall, and yall were sooo far apart in age. I wanted a lot of happy, laughing faces around my two little precious baby girls. You know the children loved coming so. Didn't they, baby?"

"They sho did, Mama. Nanette loved it, too. Me, too."

"And I loved having them, baby. Wasn't that fun? The barbecues and the fish fries out in the backyard?" Adriola laughed freely again. "Whooo, chile. We had a ball. What about our Thanksgivings and the Christmases?"

"Always beautiful around here, Mama. It was always pretty like the fairy tales you read to me and Nanette."

"I know. I learned that from the McIntyres and being with Mama working with them. Whenever my Mama took me up there to Advance to help during the holidays as a young girl, I thought I was in heaven, chile. Sho did. I wanted the same for my babies and decided I was going to do it, too. I used to tell my Mama that, chile."

"I know."

"My mama would just laugh her laugh. It bout sounds like mine, Alexandria. When I think about it now, we sound just alike." Adriola hesitated slightly. "Mama would say with a huge, pretty, bright smile on her colored face, 'Is that so, Adriola Mae?' Then Alexandria, I would say very respectfully, 'Well, yes ma'am. Mama, it is so.'"

"I loved my childhood with you and Daddy, Mama. I did."

Adriola cried silent tears for a moment. Then she laughed. "My sisters were something, too. Your Auntie Harrietta Mae still says today she ain't never knowed nobody to not know about the real Santa Claus until they were almost over fifteen years old. O, Lordy. Like you did, Alexandria." Adriola smiled as she considered how her sisters constantly told Adriola she was always overly protective of her two daughters.

"I know, Mama. I hated when I found out, too. I sho did."

"Well, I sho wasn't gonna to tell you even though Roger said it was past time. I loved looking at your happy face when you saw all your pretty presents under the fir tree on Christmas Day. All the mighty fine fancy boxes were wrapped just sooo pretty and special, honey. Your face would light up. I enjoyed seeing that as much as I did Nanette's sweet little face, and she was a tiny thing, too. But you never told your sister, neither. It took her a long time to find out."

"It sho did," Alex moaned with a small smile, still tightly hugging her mother's waist.

"Roger and I didn't do too bad by yall." She rubbed Alex's full hair. "We always sent money to people in our church, Alex. You didn't know that did you, baby?"

"No, Mama. I didn't."

"Many times, the folks never knew where it came from. I guess we still hoarded money, too. You know where that came from, baby?" She didn't wait for a response. "Your father grew up poor. I had a little more than he did, but he always knew what it was like to struggle. He hated it, and I hated it. We didn't want to ever struggle again, baby. We didn't, so we saved. But we should've done more. Lawd have mercy, we should've done more," she groaned and began to weep softly. Alex wiped her eyes. Suddenly, Adriola was fine again.

"If something happens to you, I don't want to live in this world anymore. I don't. I want to just lay down and die cause I know I'll go insane wild with sadness, pain, and emptiness."

Adriola grinned. "Listen at my little girl. Lawd knows, don't say that."

"I mean it, Mama."

They both quietly listened to the lullabying notes of Mirian Anderson for a few minutes. Very contentedly, Alex's head was resting against her mother's breasts, and she heard the continuous thumping sounds of Adriola's heart. Alex silently prayed that it was some way she could breathe strength back into it.

"Alexandria, don't ever be a member of the "should have could have club," baby. At the end of your life, it's not a good membership to have. You hear me? It's not a proud place to be, baby. And, sometimes it's too late to change," she said with unparalleled hurt in her tone.

"Oh, puhleeze stop talking like that."

"Your daddy and I—I guess we should've learned how to spend the money, but we should've learned how to also enjoy the money. Traveled a little bit. Stashing all the money away in the bank for what? Alexandria, that wasn't good, either. I just don't think that's a good example for you or Nanette to see, baby," she ended with her voice trailing off.

Alex watched her mother with wide, bloodshot eyes. "Mama, I love you, and I love Daddy. Because of you, your great spirit and wisdom—because of the high standards you and Daddy set for my life, I thank you, Mama. I'm Alexandria, but I'm you and you're me. I'm a part of both of you," she explained lovingly with much maturity.

"Listen at my baby talk."

"You always taught me well," Alex rattled on gently. "It's true everyone always said I acted sooo mature. I'm that way cause you talked righteously to me from the time I came into this world, Mama. That's why I am who I am. You did the best for Nanette and me. The best that yall knew how to do. You did what you could, and I love you for it, Mama. I do. I do. I do!"

Adriola just smiled and cried silently as she listened to the words of her wise, young daughter. From the time Alex was a little girl of five years old, she had the gift to speak soothing, wonderful, glorious words to others. Back then, the folks at church often exclaimed, "...Roger and Adriola, lawd have mercy. That little ole Alexandria, with all that pretty, thick black hair, is precious and special. Whooo! I declare. That baby is much older than her young years, honeychile..."

Adriola's eyes watered with tears again, and she continued to softly rub Alexandria's hair as she listened to her daughter say nothing but loving praises about her parents. Adriola wished Roger were home to hear the baby girl. But knowing Alexandria, she would come back when her Daddy was home and tell him the exact same things. And, like the words had so often done in the past, the beautiful, magnificent praise Alex spoke to her mother sounded like mockingbirds singing on a sunny, bright summer day. The words soothed and caressed Adriola deep down in her soul.

That evening talk with her mother was forever scorched in Alex, and Alex was glad it was. Just four months later in April, Alex's mother and father were killed in a car accident coming from a McIntyre family celebration in Charlotte. Three white boys from blue blooded, old money families were out joyriding and ran a red light at fifty miles-per-hour. All three boys were from three of the wealthiest families in Charlotte. Breham Marshall Dangerfield, IV, the twenty-one year old driver of the Rolls Royce Corniche that killed the Johnsons had already been accused of vehicular homicide when he was sixteen-years-old. However, his family's prestigious attorneys proved that the old Spanish man he hit was intoxicated at the time he walked in front of the Volvo four-door sedan Breham was driving back then. Breham got off scott free with a slight reprimand. His family paid the bereaving Spanish man's family of four surviving children a mere six thousand dollars. It was an amount the Dangerfields normally spent during a one-hour shopping spree on New York's Fifth Avenue.

In the case of Adriola and Roger's death, the powerful McIntyres stepped in. On behalf of Alex and Nanette, they sued the Dangerfields, the Bouchers, and the Dearings, the names of the three drunk boys who were in the car. Old family, blue-blooded North Carolina attorneys were at each other, on opposing sides, a rarity in the corridors of the privilege. Yet, with Chipper at the forefront of the lawsuit issued by D. Britt and Cox, the powerful law firm his grandfather and uncle had founded decades ago in Charlotte, the suit was won in favor of the Johnsons. In a sweeping, unanimous jury decision, Nanette and Alex were awarded a multi-million dollar settlement. At the time, it was one of the largest in the history of the southeast, from North Carolina clear to the state of Mississippi.

The lawsuit money was insignificant to Alex because it couldn't do anything to bring her parents back. For this reason, Madison oftentimes believed Alex thought the money was a blood curse. Alex did all in her power and as much as possible to donate or give away the money she believed she inherited from her precious parents' blood being splattered on the streets of Charlotte, North Carolina.

When Alex's parents were killed, she cried from a deep hurt that seemed not to heal. Madison consoled her as best he could. However, Alex wished she was able to return the stocks, the money, and the enormous insurance policies to simply have the opportunity to speak with her parents once again. A grieving Alex wanted to simply take them on a fabulous vacation to Hawaii or to the Caribbean. She longed to put her arms around them and hug them close to her heart. Since those desires were impossible to fulfill, Alex purchased the finest caskets, tombstones, and paid for the best funeral her parents' money could buy. She even hired stretch limousines for the entire family. While riding to Evergreen Cemetery in Winston-Salem to bury them that day, Alex vowed that when she graduated from law school and was in a position to do so, she would rent limousines for events other than funerals. Just for the heck of it. For friends, for family, and for whatever reason she chose to. She *would* enjoy life to the hilt and live each day as if it was her last. She *would* do what her Mama told her to do. And she would never ever forget those words her mother had shared with her ever since she was a little girl of ten years old. That was exactly what Alex had planned for her family, her friends and had definitely, categorically planned for herself.

Alex's friends were absolutely special people to her. Like her Mama used to say all the time, *Friends are for a lifetime, baby girl. And they deserve it...all the love you care to share with them.* Alex also realized there was nothing like a bunch of crazy acting Black women riding in a limousine, talking, and laughing on a gorgeous Saturday evening.

Chapter Ninety

While Togo spoke briefly with a curious passer-by, he waited patiently by the front of the limo. When he saw the other women exit Hanes Mall, he quickly strolled around to smoothly open the door. The women stepped in. Pecola was the first one inside, and she noticed Alex's eyes were closed. Concerned, she softly touched Alex's right hand.

"Are you ok, Alex?" she asked. Pecola planted a big kiss on Alex's forehead, then smiled broadly at her friend with affectionate eyes.

"Yes, I'm fine, girl. I was simply thinking. That's all," she murmured as she opened her eyes, sat up straight, and glanced at her watch. It was seven. Alex gave Togo the schedule and told him to slowly drive around the city for a few minutes. They were due to arrive in front of the Stevens Center at seven-thirty.

While driving back downtown, the women sipped more bottled water and munched macadamia nuts. Pecola showed Alex the Madilyn Wade's denim fireman jacket, skirt, hat ensemble and two other of the Black designer's sleek suits she purchased in record time.

"Pecola, you're a trip. If nothing else, you certainly put the wow factor into shopping," Alex joked as she admired the three expensive outfits.

While Alex and Pecola spoke, the younger women laughed loudly about another hot situation.

"I'm telling you. Thomasina has a hold on him," Nanette said knowingly as they resumed the discussion they started in the mall about one of the ladies they recognized at the WGH tea.

"Is it spelled h-o-l-d or h-o-l-e?" Adele asked with a huge grin.

"It's a little bit of both, girl. Thomasina got a *hold*, and her *hole* got him puntang whipped," Rehema exclaimed as she finished sipping mineral water and stared mischievously at Nanette. Alex just smiled and slowly shook her head at the young ladies' conversation.

"Can yall believe that? I think his income is up in the high six figures," Adele informed the others.

"Get out of here, girl! Are you sure?" Rehema asked with sudden interest. She had heard that the guy was a founding partner of some sports marketing company in Jackson Creek, North Carolina.

"Thomasina sounds like a gold-digger," Pecola exclaimed. "I hate those types."

"Humph," Rehema moaned. "If she's a gold-digger, then the brother must be the goldmine Thomasina is looking for."

All the women broke out into delightful laughter.

"Yall need to remember what my Auntie Hattie Mae says about—," Pecola added.

"Oh, Gawddd," Nanette exclaimed.

"My Auntie Hattie Mae says you don't marry for money. You simply hang around the rich and you marry for love."

"Good advice," Rehema shouted, and the women started giggling again. "But that's typical Auntie Hattie Mae."

"Yall know that Thomasina has a good job, but she always checks out the credentials first. According to her sister, girlfriend pulled a fast Dun & Bradstreet on the brotha's company. Somebody that knew somebody else pulled his D&B and his TRW credit report," Adele said with wide eyes.

"Girrrl! Get out of here!" exclaimed Nanette. "People are a trip nowadays and can find out anything they want to know about you. Trust me."

"Is the high six figure income net income or gross income?" Norvella inquired with her always certified public accountant's thinking mind.

"Why?" Rehema asked.

"Because you know gross income is so deceiving, girls," Norvella emphasized with a boisterous chuckle. Everyone laughed along with her.

"Knowing Thomasina, she probably has the dibs on his net income. She won't even think about touching a Black man, hell, any man for that matter unless of course he's making some serious dollars. She's very selective and totally stuck-up big time," Rehema declared knowingly. "I ain't never seen two more stuck up people in my life than those two Black women. And my homegirl found out they were both raised by their grandmother in McDougal Terrace projects in Durham. I mean, get real."

"That's probably why they act that way now. They're trying to forget how it all began for them," Adele inserted. "Don't want no reminders of the early struggle, girl."

"That's terrible," Pecola exclaimed with wide eyes.

"I think the whole group of women at the tea were too hoity toity for my blood," Symone inserted in a miserable tone and offered a slight shrug as if to say, *What the hell? I know I'm right.*

"Excuse me?" Pecola asked.

"How many times have I told yall that?" Symone questioned the group.

"Too many, so it's no need to repeat it, gerlie gerl," Adele mumbled.

"And I'm surprised my good buddy and business partner is a part of that stuck-up group," Symone added with a grin and rolled her eyes at Pecola who stopped munching nuts and looked at her in disbelief.

"Look! Don't start no damn shit up in here, Symone," Pecola said. "Not today. I'm in an excellent mood."

"Uh oh. I'm scared of that," Darilyn said with a short laugh. "Pecola's scratching claws are out. You go, sister-in-law."

"You know what? I don't know why yall curse so much," Jodria said calmly as she nibbled on a small roast beef sandwich. "You know that all that cursing yall do is simply a sign of stress. When I used to curse like that before, I was so stressed out with my career and family. I did it so much that I didn't know I was doing it. My sister brought it to my attention, then I read it somewhere—" Jodria explained softly as her voice trailed off when she noticed how the others were smiling and staring intently at her.

As Pecola quickly considered Jodria's remarks, there was a brief moment of silence.

"Sheee-it! You don't say, Jodria Anne. Honeychile, puhleeze. I ain't got time to hear no psychological bullshit," Pecola said as she watched her best friend's chubby, yet serious face. Nanette, Adele, and Rehema began laughing and falling all over each other. Pecola turned to Symone. "Now what was *that* dumb shit you were saying, Symone?"

Symone was giggling now, too. "I *said* I think the nicest people most times are the ones with money although sometimes they can act like someone stuck a corn cob up their asses," Symone said with a grin.

"Whaaat?" Pecola groaned.

"I guess it goes back to what Alex says. If you know who you are, you don't worry about trying to impress people. You just live life and enjoy. Isn't that right, girl?" Symone added with a grin and winked at Alex who winked back.

"If you truly believe it and know it deep down within your soul, it'll work for yall," Alex said calmly. "If you love yourself and know who you are, everything else falls in place. It's just like clockwork."

"Honeychile, puhleeze. All of yall are a stone trip," Pecola insisted with a frown, wanting to prove the worthiness of the organization. As she took a sip of mineral water, she went on to explain all the different projects WGH worked on each year.

"...It's still an *image* thing, Pecola," Symone persevered with her philosophy about rich, stuck-up people. "Image stands for the following. *I* stands for Idiots, *M* stands for Making, *A* stands for A, *G* stands for Great, and *E* stands for Example of what hypocrisy and wannabees are about."

"Sy, you go," Rehema blurted and leaned over to give Symone a high five. "I like that one, girl. Let me keep that in mind so I can rock someone's world when I say it."

"In other words, fake people, plastic smiles, hanging with the right folk, buying the right clothes, and socializing in the right places is what *I'm* talking about. They want to protect their damn *image*. It makes me sick," Symone continued as she gazed absentmindedly out the window. "People are the same no matter who they are."

"Damn tooting," Rehema agreed.

"The only difference between me and other people is that I got a few more dollars, and my shoes are a little bit more expensive," Symone said as she moved to LaBelle belting out *Lady Marmalade.*

"I was with you up until there, Sy," Rehema added quickly. "Hey to me, that's a big damn difference. If my ass had more money, believe you me I know I would be much happier. I was happiest when Sheldon and I were together, girl. When he played pro ball, money was flowing every damn where. I shopped till I dropped. They had to drag me out the clothing stores on Rodeo Drive, Fifth Avenue, and from any boutique I could find. Right, Nae?"

"Sho did," Nanette replied.

"Money matters, sistergirl," Rehema continued. "There's no question about that."

"I can dig that," Pecola said with understanding. "Cause I know it matters a whole heap for me."

"People with money always say it doesn't make a helluva difference. That's a social consciousness lie they like because it sho as hell does. When you don't have as much money, you can really see what a big difference it makes. I done been there and back. Believe you me." Rehema repeated emphatically as she thought about her financial woes and the bank representative who called this morning and asked for the late mortgage payment that was due two weeks ago.

"Humph. I'm still there, and I certainly don't want to move," Pecola said which made Adele and Norvella giggle.

"You need to wake up, Sy," Rehema went on. "You need to get a real live, fat reality check about your close-minded thinking in certain areas. It sounds good in theory, but in reality? Girl, puhleeze."

"Go 'head, Rehema," Nanette encouraged her college buddy. "Ain't my girl bad as hell?"

Symone loved Rehema's personality. Twenty-four seven, she always acted feisty about all topics. "I understand what you're saying, Rehema. Not totally, but I believe I do—especially when it comes to my days in Trinidad. When I was growing up, we bartered vegetables along side the road in Santa Cruz. Still, you have to understand that my family got lucky. That's the difference. Either you were born with it, which is what Uncle Samuel calls the lucky sperm club—"

"Well, then, my children are definitely part of the lucky sperm club, honeychile. They ain't got to worry about a thing," Pecola said, interrupting Symone. Although Symone stared at her for a long moment, Pecola slowly twisted her body to the music of *You Are My Friend*.

"Can I finish, Pecola?" Symone asked.

"Hell yeah! You can finish, Sy. This *is* an open discussion. Isn't it?" Pecola exclaimed and gazed into Norvella's amused expression. "Are you the only one that got it copyrighted for the day in this here car?" Several of the women burst out laughing.

"Like I was saying—" Symone said each word distinctly clear. "You either made your own money the old-fashioned way, or you struggled and worked hard and you earned it. I believe those people got real lucky, too. They made some right moves. Somebody gave them an opportunity. They worked hard. They came out with an uniquely different project, Internet company, or book, or idea for a show, and they earned wealth like that."

"Damn, girl. It don't matter. Whichever way it came, it came," Rehema said as she now sipped a cold Cheerwine soda and bit into a tiny cold-cut turkey on rye sandwich that Alex passed to her. Alex offered a sandwich to Pecola.

"No, I don't want anything heavy to eat, chile. I done told you that, girl. It might spoil my appetite. I clare you're just like them Italian mothers I see on television. Eat-a, eat-a—always trying to push food on folks."

"Hell no! She ain't like none of them E-talian people. That ain't even a good comparison for my sister. She's just like those old-fashioned Black mothers I was raised around, girl," Nanette corrected. "My Mama was the exact same way. Hell, your mother is, too, Pecola."

"The Poussaints were fortunate," Symone continued, trying to get her point in. "They got lucky, then they worked like hell once they got the opportunity."

"La dee da," Pecola mumbled. "I done heard that story enough."

"They never forgot where they came from. I haven't either," Symone said and glared at Pecola. "Black folks with money need to learn how to have wealth and be down to earth with it. I don't like high fallutin people. Don't walk around with your nose stuck up in the air because I *heard* the slide down is much quicker than the climb up, girl."

Pecola ignored Rehema's earlier comments and zoomed in on Symone's words that she believed were aimed toward her.

"Now wait a damn minute," Pecola said trying to laugh at her friend's slant on the WGH Club. She hoped they didn't think she was stuck-up too even though she knew she was overly concerned about her image.

"Don't even worry yourself, Pecola. As long as you enjoy what you're doing and as long as you love being with all those stuck-up, conceited women," Nanette inserted quickly. "You're ok with me."

"Thanks, girl. Whaaat? Aw hell, Nanette. That's not even true. I'm not like that, Sy," Pecola admitted while chewing a piece of her sandwich and looked at the other women's faces for support and confirmation. They all remained quiet and simply smiled knowingly at Pecola.

"Well lately, you ain't far from it," Symone teased with a loud laugh. Pecola frowned and gave her the middle finger. "Just joking. Just joking, girl."

During the whole time Symone spoke, the other women, except Pecola of course, laughed and snickered at the explanation. The women of FOFAE were good with creating acronyms for everything. BAN stood for Black Ass Nigger. PAN stood for Pretty Ass Nigger. PAM meant Pretty Ass Man or Pretty And Married and so on and so forth. That's how the women of FOFAE sometimes talked about people. If a lady in the group wanted to talk about people when they were out at a social gathering, they scribbled notes on pieces of paper. A few seconds later, they all ended up cackling all over the place.

Alex suddenly glanced at her watch again. To get the conversation moving in another direction, she told the other ladies it was time for them to get their monthly gifts of adoration from her. Pecola was glad the conversation shifted off her beloved group.

"Aw, Mama. A gift? Damn!" Rehema whined. "Not another present this month. I know Christmas is around the corner. Don't get me too excited. Didn't you just surprise us with something last weekend at A&T's homecoming?"

"Girl, puhleeze. You're sooo crazy," Alex said as she began digging in the flowery shopping bag Togo took out of the trunk while the others were inside Hanes Mall.

"By the way let's whoop it up for A&T," Rehema demanded. "They kicked butt at homecoming big time. Didn't they?"

"They sho did, Rehema," Nanette agreed quickly as she idly swayed to *If You Ask Me To.* "They spanked that team's bootie sho nuff. Sho nuff. I even felt sorry for them, girl."

"Can yall believe how crowded it was at homecoming?" Rehema continued, giggling. "Umph. Umph. Umph. It was nothing but wall to wall niggers. They were looking good, too. I'm here to tell you. I was ready to drop my date by the wayside. You're right, Sy. When homecoming and other jams like that rolls around, you need to go to them by yourself."

"Next time you'll listen to me," Symone nodded. "Without a date, I was carefree as a bird, girl."

"Remember how I tried to push my date back into the limo on Saturday night, Sy," Rehema went on. "I was trying to get you to convince the limo driver to take him back to Alex's house. When I pushed him back into the limo, I told him I tripped on a crack in the ground. Didn't I dog him that night? Remember, Sy?"

"I do," Symone agreed. "That was damn funny. You're sooo bad. The brotha thought you were crazy too, Rehema. Whew. I kind of think he knew you were trying to get rid of him cause you were busy eyeing other new stuff, girl. It was crowded everywhere. At the game, at the parties, and at Alex and Pecola's houses."

"I know," Pecola said. "It *was* packed like sardines at the game. I think if all those Black folks had sat down in the stadium, there wouldn't have been enough seats for everybody. I got hoarse from damn screaming at all my sorors and at all the other people I hadn't seen in a few years, honeychile. It was just good to see those faces that I hadn't seen in awhile. I declare I didn't get my voice back until Wednesday night, but I enjoyed the hell out of everything."

"Lawd, I did, too," Alex added quickly. "It was great, Pecola. Powerful. I love seeing such an assemblage of Black people for events such as that."

"Me too, chile," Pecola yelled. "Hey, yall know the deal. A&T is all of that and a big ole bag of chips. Like Carlos says, the MEAC rules around here."

"Lawd knows, let's not talk about colleges," Darilyn said with a wide grin. "That talking battle for the best one can take all night. Everybody in here went to a different one. Before I go any further, I still gots to throw props in for Fayetteville State. That's for me and Rico, ladies."

"Oooh! This song is sooo beautiful. Ummm," moaned Jodria as she sang along softly to the romantic sounds of Patti LaBelle and the Blue Belles harmonizing *Unchained Melody.*

"Humph. Maybe so. I still say, where would we be without A&T? Need I say more?" Pecola threw both palms up and shrugged her shoulders. Everybody laughed.

"Let me see." Alex quietly checked the name card on the first gift.

"Alex, don't listen to Rehema," Pecola blurted out. "I love gifts any time you want to give them to me, chile. Hand mine to me first."

"Here's yours, darling," Alex said speaking to Pecola, and she began passing the others a box too. "Everybody, don't open it until everyone gets one. Ok?"

When Alex gave them each a box, she waited to see their delighted expressions. In each beautifully wrapped red and white ribbon box was a book, a black silk charmeuse chemise and a velvet kimono trimmed in rhinestones from designer, Greta Wallace.

"Giiiirrrrls!" Rehema hollered. "This is absolutely beautiful."

"I *knew* you would love it, Rehema." Alex was thrilled. "When I was in New York last month, I stopped by The Brownstone in Harlem and found a lot of things for all my friends. I was just glad that Greta had yall sizes."

"If I wasn't sooo tall, I would stand up, get bucked naked in here and model this thing in front of yall right now. You know who I can wear this for, don't you?" Rehema slyly asked Nanette and Adele. They both nodded yes and smiled. "Love ya, Alex. Thanks. Thanks."

"*Himpressions:* by Valerie Shaw? What the hell is this about, Alex?" Pecola asked with a confused expression. *"The Black Woman's Guide to Pampering the Black Man"* Pecola quietly read the words off the cover of the book in a questioning way.

Symone, Charmaine, Norvella, and Jodria dug deeper into their boxes and found copies of the book, too. Slowly, they began removing the red tissue paper from around their copy. After Jodria read Alex's personal notation written on the inside flap cover of hers, Jodria smiled at Alex. She whispered a silent *thank you. I needed to hear that.* Alex winked at Jodria, and she smiled back.

"It's a good thing to have, girls," Alex said. "Madison found it last week at Special Occasions. He said he liked the way the title sounded, so he bought a copy for me. When I started reading through it, I knew my homegirls of FOFAE would enjoy a copy. Since the books for Ujima have been selected for the next three months, I didn't want to wait that long for yall to read it—"

"Giiiirrrrl! I thank you," Rehema cut off Alex's little speech. "I need all the help I can get to snag the right man. I got a hot, new date next week. I'm going with this nice Sigma brother to see A&T and the Grambling Tigers play at Aggie Stadium. The brother is a physicist."

"Uh oh. A smart Black man," Symone said slowly while snapping her fingers and gently swaying to Patti belting out *Somebody Loves You.* "Watch out, Rehema. He's probably a stone freaky deaky kind of guy."

"Yep! I hope so. Exactly. He's beautifully buff, too. Looks like a damn tall, chunky chocolate candy bar. So any help I can get is highly appreciated," Rehema explained and gave Nanette a high five.

"How many games are you going to that day, Rehema?" Norvella asked.

"Norvella, the main question you should ask her is how many men folks does she really have?" Adele quipped amusingly.

"Rehema, you were supposed to go with us to see WSSU play. Remember?" Norvella asked, surprised. "Afterwards, we were going to head out to my house to listen to some jazz."

"Ooops! Sorry," Rehema said. "Maybe next time. He's an Alumni of A&T. This is a hot prospect. Reaallll hot, Norvella. I gots to go where he invites me."

"Thanks, Alex," Symone suddenly mumbled. She carefully placed the book and the other items back in the box. Then she quickly turned to gaze broodingly out the window at passing cars.

"Well, honeychile," Pecola said in a perky voice. "Now I believe I *do* know how to truly pamper Carlos."

"Whaaat? Not you again," Symone said as she nudged Nanette, and they began laughing.

"But any more important information I can receive is on the money. As yall know, I'll be celebrating my twenty-fourth wedding anniversary this month," Pecola shared proudly. She bowed her head, and everyone clapped loudly for her. "Thank you. Thank you. I love all yall's Black asses, too."

The warm, laughter-filled conversation in the limousine turned to the Patti LaBelle show once more. In a serious voice, Alex reminded them again how unfortunate it was that they couldn't get the prized tickets. Rehema pretended she was crying crocodile tears that made the women chuckle loudly again.

"You know," Pecola mumbled. "I really didn't want to see Ms. Patti anyway, especially since the Blue Belles weren't with her, honeychile."

"Girl, puhleeze. Have you lost your mind? Get out of the Motown time zone. When last were the Blue Belles with her?" Norvella replied as she snapped her fingers to *New Attitude*.

"Norvella, I'm telling you. Pauletta went to some show in Atlanta and saw them. She said the house rocked," Pecola remarked casually and leaned back. She paused long enough to catch her breath and admire her perfectly squared, red manicured fingernails.

"Well, that must have been some fake group, Pecola," Symone said quietly.

"Or the concert was held twenty-five years ago," Jodria added softly.

"Jodria, as I sit here and listen to your CD spinning, I'm reminded that the girl is good," Rehema declared. "I don't think there's another singer like her who can pull out the notes the way she can."

"I'm pretty close, chile," Pecola said seriously and waited for unanimous confirmation from her friends.

"As I was saying," Rehema continued slowly, giving Pecola a sideways glance. "The girl is baaad as hell. Them other singers can sing."

"Like me," Pecola inserted. "I know, chile."

"Yeah, but they ain't got it like Patti," Symone said quietly. "What I like about her is that with all the glitz, glamour, and money she has, she seems like real people to me."

"She got some chops on her and can blow. I know that much," Darilyn added. "I'm with yall. Nobody can beat Ms. Patti. She has such an attitude on her face and in her voice that when she sings, it gets to you. It can either makes you jump up and holler, *Sing it, chile*, or sit down and cry all night long. And I get all of that through the television set. You know that's powerful." Darilyn gave Symone a high five.

"Precisely. That's why I'm heartbroken we couldn't get tickets," Norvella pointed out. "The more yall talk about her, the more depressed I'm getting."

"I'm telling, yall. When yall describe Patti, yall are describing me to a tee," Pecola explained. "Listen to me good. Yall have heard me blow. She's just like me. I'm trying to tell yall. Every time folks hear me sing, they come up to me afterwards. They say, 'Pecola girl, do you know who you sound like?' And I wait *very* patiently for them to tell me cause I already know the answer. Guess who they say each and every damn time? Guess now?" Pecola asked as she glanced around at all her friends' smirking faces.

"Milli Vanilli," Jodria replied lightly, and everyone began a round of stomach hurting hearty giggling.

"You ain't no good, girl. No damn good." Pecola shook her head. "Don't be mean like that, Jodria. You know good and damn well they say I sound like Patti LaBelle. You've been standing beside me a couple of times when they've said it."

"I sure have," Jodria said. "That's how come I know."

"I owe your ass a big damn payback for that smart answer," Pecola said trying not to laugh as she pointed a straight finger at Jodria. Pecola leaned back and took a deep breath. "Whooo, chile."

"Milli Vanilli. That was a classic, Jodria," Adele exclaimed, still smiling and idly swaying her shoulders to *If Only You Knew*. "That was right on time, girl."

"I figured yall would like to hear the whole truth," Jodria said, "And nothing but the truth."

"I *thought* you said we were going to Noble's Grille for dinner. Where are we going to eat again now, Alex?" Pecola asked suspiciously as she sat up and glanced out the window. By then, the limousine was traveling slowly along Broad Street through downtown and just turned right onto Fourth Street. Two minutes after Pecola asked the question, the Towncar stopped in front of the Stevens Center.

"...Girrrlll—no—you—didn't!" Pecola screamed, shocked with wild, wide eyes. "No you didn't get tickets to the show, chile." Everyone else burst out laughing and gave each other dainty high fives. Pecola lifted her glass of Evian in a toast to Alex.

"Hello-o! Hell-o!" Charmaine shouted as she snapped her fingers. Now she was ecstatic that Scott convinced her to attend the tea with his friends.

"Giiiirrrrl, touché. You did it again, Alex," Pecola yelled as she continued smiling and gave her three snaps in the zee formation. Pecola put the glass down and reached over to kiss and hug her dear, oldest friend.

"Diss is it! High five yourselves ladies again. Right now," Rehema instructed as she smacked palms again with the others.

"Honeychile, this is too much for me to take," Charmaine hollered while staring into Jodria's face.

Pecola quickly glared at her out the corners of her eyes and wondered who in the hell gave Charmaine permission to say *honeychile.* Girlfriend lived in Chicago for years. Pecola believed that she and only she had the lock on those two words, especially within the FOFAE circle. Pecola closed her eyes long and slow at Charmaine and turned to face a thrilled Alex.

"As I was saying, you had me fooled. I tend to figure out your surprises most times," Pecola said excitedly with a jumbo smile.

"This is unbelievable, girl," Darilyn said softly to Jodria.

"Yall gots to work with me on this one, honeychile." Pecola said eagerly. "Wooo. Help me get calm. When I see Patti, I believe I'm going to start crying. I just know it."

"Would someone puhleeze muzzle her," Symone commanded.

"Kiss my pretty ass, Sy. Now let me ask yall a little someumph someumph? Since I know yall love me, I know yall will tell me to do the right thing. Tell it to me stra-eight." Pecola hesitated slightly. "I was thinking. Since I sound just like Patti and all, do yall think I should just stand up in the audience and start singing loudly along with her so she can hear how I sound just like her? Tell me the truth now?"

"Giiiirrrrl! Hell damn no!" Rehema yelled at the top of her lungs, and the happy laughter fell out of everyone's throat once more.

"Humph. That's what you say, Rehema," Pecola said. "What the hell do you know? I'll just call it by ear once I'm sitting in there. Whooo, chile! I'm getting hot flashes. Maybe I'm PMSing or something. Yall know I suffer real bad from that."

"Oh, lawd," Nanette moaned. "How many times have we heard about her little menstrual problem?"

"Anybody got any clean, lacy handkerchiefs?" Pecola asked. "You know I can only use those pretty, frilly kind, not those plain white ones. They're so tacky. Let me check and see if I have my extra mascara. Lawd, chile. You should've told me, Alex. I would've been better prepared and better dressed." Pecola began to quickly fan her face with both hands.

"Pecola, you're crazy," Alex said with fondness.

"Lawd, I know," Pecola agreed as she pretended to cry, and Nanette threw a pink, lacy handkerchief at her. "That's the least of my worries."

"You're sick, girl." Rehema said as she shook her head. "Pure divine sick."

The other women were now quiet and speechless, even Symone. That alone was truly a rare occurrence. The women expected Togo to come around and open the door, so they waited patiently inside. Therefore, they were doubly shocked when Madison with a huge grin on his face opened the limo door to help them out. When the women's eyes darted pass Madison's shoulders, there stood Scott, Carlos, Rozelle, Rico, Tacuma, Marlon, and Norvella's husband, Houston.

"Lawd have mercy. Umph. Umph. Umph. I declare. Look at all this luscious beauty in one place! Ain't all yall Black women just as fine as hell?" Rozelle shouted after he took his cigar out his mouth.

"We know that," Pecola snapped. "Just help us out."

"Ain't they gorgeous, man?" Rozelle asked the other guys who all quickly nodded yes.

"*Friends Out For an Evening*. Well, tonight it includes the men, ladies," Scott bellowed while puffing a fat, long cigar. He glanced happily at the women.

"Don't get any ideas for other evenings, guys. Tonight *is* definitely a special and rare occasion," Nanette said jokingly while she contentedly watched Alex who was still receiving tight hugs and affectionate kisses from the other women.

The show was spectacular. Everyone had an opportunity to go backstage to meet Patti LaBelle, Steve Harvey, and some other R&B group whose name nobody could remember. Everybody including Togo and his wife, Fritzi, as Alex purchased show tickets for the young couple, too. Alex laughed loudly throughout the entire evening, especially during the backstage introductions as the entourage of twenty acted as if they were excited teenagers and didn't have any sense. Marlon was surprised that Patti LaBelle and Steve Harvey were just as thrilled to have a chance to meet him. They even got *his* autograph.

Pecola kept saying that she was going to flat out dead faint. Although she didn't, Carlos held his wife's waist the entire time they were backstage, just in case. Everyone was still glad Pecola decided to not stand up and start singing during Patti's performance. After the show, they walked right across the street to Unique Upstairs where they danced the night away to the sounds of the Knights of Soul with Jackie belting out the blues the only way they should be sung. When Togo dropped Alex and Madison off in Advance, it was three-thirty in the morning. Both of them wondered out loud if they would have the energy to make it to Sunday school.

Chapter Ninety-One

Alex kicked off the holiday season by hosting the Devereauxs' annual Thanksgiving sit-down dinner. The Devereauxs Christmas dinner was a gloriously awaited event to be a part of too and since most of her friends stayed in town for Thanksgiving, Alex made this holiday a spectacular event. Alex and Madison's spacious home swarmed with guests, and Alex made sure she rounded up all her friends and family for this traditional feast. Alex took this formal dinner very seriously. With the children dressed in holiday velvet and the men and women dressed in tuxes and fancy dresses, Scott teased that they all appeared as if they were shooting a holiday scene for a Black soap opera. Alex often told Cleopatra that figuring out the final setting for the calligraphy place cards of who was going to sit where at each table was nothing less than social choreography at its best. Each year, the expansive and large mahogany dining room table was prepared for the adults. Other side tables were prepared for the young people and children.

The Devereauxs' enormous dining room and living room appeared as one long continuous room with an ornate arched entryway and beveled French doors dividing the two rooms. Once the French doors were opened, Rozelle always joked that he felt like he was eating in the middle of a football field. Fireplaces in both rooms were lit and packed with eucalyptus logs. Burning fragrances sprayed the home with a lovely, outdoorsy, foliage scent. The orange red flames cast ripples of colorful light to sprinkle upon the crystal glasses set upon the tables and the children ponderously walked around to ooh at the shining table settings. Since the children enjoyed looking at the cozy fireplace flames as well, Alex sometimes allowed them to roast a few marshmallows before dinner—under supervision, of course. She didn't want them to spoil their appetites or dirty up their clothes, but she thought the roasting would calm them down a little. Marlon said that the marshmallow's sugar in their system didn't do nothing but make them act even more hyper.

The children's tables were decorated identically to the adults with Queen Anne lace linen, fresh flowers, sterling silver candelabras, crystal, and fine bone china sparkling everywhere. They were always anxious to know who would be selected to sit with the grown folks. To keep the selection process fair, Alex always had a brass basket drawing that held each child's name to determine which two children sat at the table with the adults. This year, Rozelle, Jr., and Beckett, Cleopatra's youngest son, won those coveted honors. Although a slight argument erupted between the young girls over why two boys were selected this year, Madison told the disgruntled children that the decision was final.

Alex's individualized, calligraphy designed menus included familiar Southern entrees of candied yams, roast beef, stuffing, ham-hocked filled collard greens, cranberry sauce, corn bread, yeast rolls, golden fried chicken, and melting in the mouth macaroni and cheese. The list didn't stop there. The various entrees went on and on and on. Typical southern fare is what Alex called it. Alex wanted the traditional dining to take place in a romantic, fancy setting with old-fashioned, Winston-Salem genteel charm. Sweet potato pies, coconut and chocolate cakes, a variety of pies, other pastries and certain choice entrees were ordered from Cafe Bessie. The infamous chitlins were an absolute requirement, and Miss Bessie handled that expected huge gourmet order with ease. Carlos and Rico always prepared mouth-watering, hand-churned, homemade eggnog ice cream that was supposedly a secret recipe they learned from their father.

Alex, Nanette, and Cleopatra worked relentlessly cooking the traditional turkeys with stuffing, baking glazed hams, and washing collards, decorating, planning and anything else that was needed the entire week before Thanksgiving. However on Thanksgiving Day, when the grandfather clock chimed five o'clock and everyone sat down to dinner, Alex hired a staff of tuxedo-wearing waiters, waitresses, and a chef to serve the meal and to clean up afterwards. She didn't want any of her friends, her family, or even Cleopatra to have to jump up and down to serve this and to do that for anyone. Many of her friends sacrificed not spending the annual holiday with their families but opted to stay in North Carolina to be with the Devereauxs, and Alex wanted them to simply relax and enjoy the festivity of the day. The friends didn't mind, especially since Alex and Nanette's family was so small. They realized that it gave Alex another excuse to bask in friendship, savor family, and give surprise gifts to everyone. All this grandeur definitely spiraled their moods toward Christmas and Kwanzaa.

An hour or so after dinner, there always was a champagne toast by the living room's mantled fireplace during which Aunt Susie Mae was recognized for being the oldest, living Devereaux. Madison always rested his right hand on the mantle and spoke in a long drawn out way, so said Pecola. The children were there in the midst; however, they drank seltzer water out of their tulip-shaped crystal champagne glasses and were quite happy because the seltzer water looked like the real thing. No one told them any differently, and Alex made sure that they were served from champagne bottles as well. Professional photographs were taken. Afterwards, everyone filed into various rooms in the house.

The Devereauxs' home was beautiful in any season. But now the lovely twenty-seven room red brick Georgian Mansion was already glisteningly decorated with Alex's legendary Christmas themes around Black angels, painted terra-cotta nativity figurines, miniature teddy bears, dolls, white tiny lights, gold tear-drop ornaments, gold roping, wreaths, and garland. Any telling ornament Alex believed was necessary to provide the perfect Christmas scenes throughout different rooms in the Devereauxs' home was used.

It was a known fact that Alex started decorating for Christmas right after Halloween ended. A holiday design firm handled the trees and larger, intricate decorating responsibilities throughout the yard and home. Other than that, Alex did the rest. From the time visitors turned down the Devereauxs' Rose Garden Lane from Highway #801, they knew they were in a sparkling winter-like wonderland. It was a holiday topiary menagerie of splendid proportions that always had the visiting children's breath catch in their throats from the wonder of it all. Topiary rabbits, reindeers, sleighs, and other statues of Christmas symbols stood guard all along the brick cobblestone path leading up to the house. Tiny white, colorful bulbs twinkled in the trees and on the pasture's three rail fence all along the two-mile stretch of driveway heading to the Devereauxs' front door.

A harpist was always hired for the afternoon and arrived around four to play a medley of holiday songs for the guests while they ate. Later on in the evening, sometimes, Alex, Pecola, and Scott sang while Alex played the piano. When Alex grew tired of playing, Scott took over. These were unforgettable moments that Alex kept in her heart. Thanksgiving and Christmas were emotional times for her, and she frequently cried openly when she considered that her mother and father never saw her home. They never shared in her quaint life with Madison and the children—with Nanette, Marlon, and their sons. They never saw her live in such a magnificent way with so many of her loved ones nearby.

Alex's holiday spirit didn't stop at just her house. Every year she visited her friends on a certain date and personally decorated their homes with the appropriate Kwanzaa table setting. From the Mazao to the Kinara that held one black, three reds, and three green candles, every recommended symbol of the holiday was prepared in the right spot chosen by her friends. At each house, she hosted a small ceremony and explained the significance of Kwanzaa, ending with a discussion on the purpose of the seven candles. The black candle symbolizes the face of Black people because Black people came first. The red represents the blood Black people shed and is a symbol of the continuous struggle. And, the green symbolizes hope and the color of the motherland, Africa—in addition to the hopes and dreams for the future the Black youth represents. It was tradition for Alex to do this, and Alex's decorating holiday season wasn't complete until she made those rounds to all of her friends. After doing it for nine years straight, even they looked forward to it more than she ever imagined.

On the Saturday morning after Thanksgiving, Marlon surprised everyone with a private jet ride to The Greenbriar in West Virginia. There the friends celebrated Carlos and Pecola's twenty-fourth wedding anniversary that evening over a rack of lamb dinner. Pecola had flown on the Eisners corporate jet with Symone several times to Trinidad, to their home in France, and other family vacations where Pecola was pampered magnificently. She was given a cashmere blanket to warm her chilled arms, satin mule slippers for her tired feet, and the best liquor poured into etched crystal glasses with 24-karat rims. She dined exquisitely and was served royally by the private flight crew. Pecola remained fascinated at traveling in such a luxurious way.

Alex knew that Marlon was toying about buying a jet, but Nanette was against it. She was afraid and preferred he travel the commercial airliner way. She reasoned that the larger the plane, the better and safer the travel. There were many times Marlon preferred traveling in such a private way himself and was often provided complimentary use of corporate jets to go wherever he needed to around the world. So when Alex asked Marlon if he could charter a private jet for Pecola and Carlos' anniversary trip with his hook-ups with people who owned private jets, he said that sure he could handle the assignment. It was no problem.

On Sunday afternoon, Carlos and Pecola were both caught off guard again when their friends hosted the *This Is Your Life* program. The program celebrated and recaptured Pecola and Carlos' life from the time they were fourteen years old. When Pecola heard Rozelle say the words, "...Pecola Marva Dudley-Reynolds, this is your life, baybee!" she cried and whimpered like a newborn baby. A shocked Pecola quickly gazed around at the warm faces of Scott, Symone, and Alex sitting with their families at tables behind her. Scott immediately pointed an index finger at Pecola and smiled widely.

With the help of Rico guiding the way, Alex, Symone, and Scott had done an excellent job with securing old photographs, period songs, and footages of eight-millimeter family silent movies. They also found the right people to give their tender testimonies. Pecola's parents, Aunt Susie Mae, and several other elderly people who were invited to West Virginia were afraid to step on an airplane. Scott made sure a chartered bus was reserved to bring them to West Virginia for the dinner and their Sunday night stay at The Greenbriar. Rozelle was the master of ceremonies. Since he knew how to keep the action moving, he announced each surprise person with his own brand of humor.

When Pecola heard her mother say over the microphone, "...Whooo, honeychile! Ise knew Ise had some smart ass chilluns," she was shocked because she didn't expect to see or hear her parents in West Virginia. But out stepped the pleasant Oseola and Rufus from the adjoining room where the other mystery guests were kept hidden. They gave a definitely flabbergasted Pecola, a smiling Carlos, and everyone else there such warm, tight hugs.

Pauletta, Ezunial, and their entire families attended the celebration. The only person the friends couldn't get to show up was Carlos' sister, Magdalia. She still refused to return to North Carolina from Puerto Rico for this occasion or any other special family affair for that matter. When the old-fashioned, throaty voice Baptist preacher who married Pecola and Carlos said a few words, Carlos finally broke down and cried. The on-going bittersweet testimonials from people Carlos hadn't heard from or hadn't seen in years struck a major, sentimental nerve in his heart. He thought about Miss Jeannette. His youth. How much his life had drastically changed for him from the time he was a fourteen-year old boy. That was twenty-eight years ago. The minutes, the hours, the days, the weeks, the months, and the years just flew by. It was crystal clear to Carlos that time waited for no one—not even him. It made Carlos think about how he was living his life right now.

The friends returned home from West Virginia on Monday night. By Thursday morning, the blissful holiday spirit of everyone took a sad twist. Aunt Susie Mae died in her sleep. She had just turned ninety in October and remained spry as ever. But like Madison's father said, her body simply got tired. Alex had the keys to the older woman's home and always checked on her different days of the week. When Alex went to see her during one of her weekly visits, she discovered Aunt Susie Mae resting peacefully in bed with the bright rays of the morning sunlight shining on her face. The closer Alex got to the bed, she realized that Aunt Susie Mae wasn't breathing or moving. Screaming hysterically, Alex called 911. She called Madison next.

The holidays were already a joyous yet difficult time for Alex. With the death of Aunt Susie Mae, her grief for the special loved ones she lost ballooned even more. As soon as Madison's father heard that the tender hearted Alex was the one to find Aunt Susie Mae, he drove to Advance to talk to her. He and his wife had just rushed back to Winston-Salem from Nashville, North Carolina, where they were visiting old friends. When he arrived, Madison told his father that Alex was upstairs resting in bed. The older man, who Alex absolutely believed looked just like a cookie-cut older version of Madison, came to her bedside. He tried to calm her and assure her that Aunt Susie Mae was at peace. That she had gone to a better place.

"..Aunt Susie Mae is with God, Alex. You know that, baby," he said quietly. Alex was still in bed. He pulled up a chair beside the bed to talk softly to her. Alex nodded her head and began crying again. He noticed that her puffy bloodshot eyes had a distant, faraway look in them. "You see what I'm saying?"

"I know, Daddy Devereaux. I know."

"You know what she told me, Alex? After the last opening ceremonies in August, she said that she was sooo proud of you. Proud of what you and Madison were doing with the children. Very proud. When she heard the song, *His Eye is on the Sparrow*, she couldn't remove the song from her mind."

"She told me the same thing." Alex voice broke, and she abruptly wiped the tears from her eyes.

"When we came back from West Virginia this week, I took her home Tuesday morning. The bus dropped us off, but it was too late to drive to her house. I convinced her to spend the night with us. Aunt Susie Mae was very particular about always wanting to sleep in her own bed and always said she wanted to stay in the home that her husband built."

"He built the whole thing with his own hands. Their place on Lincoln Avenue. That's what she always said to me."

"Aunt Susie Mae asked me to visit in the living room with her for just a little while. She put on the James Cleveland album you and Madison got her."

"She loved it, Daddy Devereaux. When I told her I would buy her a CD player, she said she didn't want no contraption like that. Just wanted me to keep finding good old gospel albums for her. So I would always scour Goodwill, the Salvation Army, and those nostalgia period stores looking for them for her." Alex spoke with a slight smile.

Dr. Devereaux grinned, too. "I asked Aunt Susie Mae if I could help her do anything, and she said no. The whole time I was there she played *Walk Around Heaven All Day*. As she listened to the words, she hummed along a little bit, then tapped her feet, and nodded her head. Clapped a couple of times. She did love to praise God."

"I know."

"We just sat there and listened, baby. All of a sudden, she stared me straight in the eyes. She said 'Nehemiah.' You know she always called me by my middle name and refused to call me anything else even when I was a little boy. Sitting on the couch that day, she called me

'Nehemiah' in a clear, strong voice, Alex. She said, 'I'm tired, Nehemiah. It's time for me to go on to be with Marcellus.' That day she called out her husband's name, Alex."

The tears rolled down Alex's face, and she quickly caught them and wiped them before they made it to her mouth.

"When I read to her on those mornings these last few weeks, on our special days when I was with her, she kept saying she was tired, just reaallll tired, Daddy Devereaux. Uh, I just don't know. I guess deep down inside I was hoping she would make it through the holidays— at least through Christmas. Lawd knows I prayed hard for that."

"You see, Alex. It was time, baby. Try not to be so hard on yourself. That's one of the saddest parts of life. Death. Whichever way and whenever it comes, we're never ready to die." He paused again. "Yet, death also lets us know how wondrously precious life is, Alex. I often told that to my patients. It's a reminder and a wake up call for those of us who are living. We have to grab hold of a vibrant new beginning, the spirit, and the goodness of being alive, baby."

"She was like my Mama to me, Daddy Devereaux. It's like I lost Mama all over again."

"I know, baby." He spoke in almost a whisper. "I know. But know that God doesn't make mistakes, Alex. Aunt Susie Mae knew that."

"As a little girl, I remember my Mama humming and moaning to those Clay Evans songs and to all of the other gospel singers she used to love to hear." Alex attempted to smile. "Mama said it always confused the devil when she did that cause the devil didn't know what she was moaning and humming about. Only God knew. Aunt Susie Mae was the same way."

"Remember the good, Alex. She had so much of that to share."

"I do, Daddy Devereaux." Alex began crying again, and she tasted the saltiness from the rush of tears falling down her face. "It's hard. Sometimes I need help to understand the things I can't change. I do. I can't change the fact that Mama, Daddy, my aunts, and my uncles aren't here with me any longer. Now *my* Aunt Susie Mae is gone. I'm just praying and asking God for wisdom in that area."

"But she's in a better place, Alex. A much better place, baby," he said as he reached out to embrace her.

"I know, Daddy Devereaux. I know, but my heart is sore. My heart hurts sooo bad," Alex said as she hugged him back and tried her best to choke him with the love she felt inside her body.

Aunt Susie Mae's funeral was scheduled for the following Tuesday, and Madison's father asked Alex to sing, *Great is Thy Faithfulness* and *Walk Around Heaven*. Alex said that she would try. Since she didn't think she could do it by herself, she asked Pecola to puhleeze sing with her. While holding Alex's waist to support her, Pecola sang the two songs along with Alex. When the emotionally heartbreaking duet ended, there wasn't a dry eye in the church.

Chapter Ninety-Two

Elisha stepped into Symone's office on the Wednesday morning after Aunt Susie Mae's funeral to tell Symone that Billy was holding on line one. With a concerned expression on her face, Elisha said that Billy emphasized it was very urgent and needed to speak with Symone as soon as possible. Now Symone wondered what was wrong. Knowing Billy, he probably was calling to say he couldn't pick up the children this weekend because he was heading to South Africa again. He had so many damn excuses when it came to visiting and spending time with his children. Symone pressed the blinking button and held her breath. This time she was going to be calm and refuse to argue with him.

For once in a very long time, an argument between the two wasn't necessary. Billy was calling to tell Symone that his mother had just died. His brother Regynald called from Tarboro with the distressing news. Visiting home from New York for a week to check on his parents, Regynald was at her hospital bedside when she stopped breathing. She had finally lost her two-year battle with lung cancer. The funeral would be on Sunday afternoon in Tarboro, and Billy wanted his three children to be there with him. Symone hung up the phone and rocked slowly back in her chair. *What was going on?* she thought sadly. Death must be in the December air or something. First, Aunt Susie Mae. Now, Mrs. Butler. Since Symone heard that death comes in threes, she wondered who would be next.

When Symone returned from Tarboro on Sunday night, she decided to call her mother in Brooklyn. Keturah only returned to the United States to celebrate Thanksgiving and Christmas with her family. Right after New Year's, she would head straight back to Santa Cruz. Even though she had been coming back and forth to United States for many years, she still couldn't get used to the cold, frigid winter weather. All of the fur coats couldn't help her with the chill she constantly felt during that season. Symone dialed the number, and the phone barely rang a full ring before Keturah picked it up.

"Good night, Mummy. How are you?"

"Ah does be doing all right. *Seamone?*" Keturah asked quickly. She always posed the question like she wasn't sure which daughter she was speaking to.

"I'm surprised you picked the phone up on the first ring. That's not like you," Symone said laughing.

Keturah had this practice. Never answer the phone on the first ring. Always wait until it rang three times. It wasn't good to let people know anybody was just waiting for them to call. Many times Keturah was standing beside the phone when it rang, but she patiently waited for that third ring.

"Ummm-hmmm," Keturah moaned harmoniously, which she always did when speaking. "Ah know. Ah was on dey tellyphone talking ta mey gurlfriend," she said matter-of-factly. Keturah was sixty-four years old, and Symone was always amazed she still referred to her friends as *gurlfriends.*

"I see."

Keturah continued. "Ummm-hmmm. She huzzband died and dey were shipping he body ta Brooklyn. Now, dey plans have changed. So ah didn't have ta go ta dey wake tonight, and ah wanted ta see how she doing. Ah tried calling yuh home yesterday afternoon." Keturah spoke in a concerned, inquisitive tone. "Seamone, hold on. Let meh get off dey other line." There was a short click at the other end. "Ok. Now wat did yuh say?"

"I said that I went to Billy's mother's funeral today in Tarboro, Mummy. I left yesterday. Miss Jessica, me, and the children drove down."

While Symone juggled the phone between her ear and shoulder, she tightened the belt of her burgundy, soft cotton terry velour robe around her waist. Since the fire was crackling in the bedroom fireplace, Symone had been walking around earlier with just a satin nightshirt on. She was feeling a little cold now for some reason.

"Ah was in Tarboro."

"Ah know. Yuh said yuh were going. Ah tought dat's why ah missed yuh. How is Miss Jessica and mey grandbaybees doing?"

"Just fine, Mummy. I spoke with Uncle Willie yesterday morning for a long time."

"Ummm-hmmm. He does tell meh. Willie and Cecil took meh and dere wives ta see *A Raisin in the Sun* on Broadway last night again."

"Oh, that's wonderful. The Lorraine Hansberry's classic play."

"Ummm-hmmm. Yuh know ah does luv dey Broadway shows and tings. Since mey bruddas knows so, dey does always try ta take meh ta a diffrent one each week dat ah am here in dey States. Later weh does go ta dinner. Dey conversation was warm and carefree. So lovely ta be with mey bruddas and dey wives. It was quite late in dey night wen dey limo does drop meh back home in Brooklyn. Ah didn't tink ah would be able ta get up ta make it ta mass at nine."

"I'm sure." Symone smiled.

"How's Bully's father doing, Seamone?"

"He's doing alright." Symone spoke slowly. "As well as can be expected. Yuh know they were married over fifty-two years."

"Oh, God nah. Is dat right? Far so long ta be tagether? Hmmm. Sooo sad." Keturah took a long sigh. "Ah need ta call he. Ah have not spoken ta he in a few months, since dey last time ah was in dey States. How's Bully doing?"

"He seemed to be doing ok. It was an emotional funeral with the family crying all over the place although Billy didn't cry much."

"Ummm-hmmm. Ah know. Sometimes it tis so hard, very difficult far a man ta shed tears, Seamone. Ah does know so. Hmmm. Dat is why ah does always get surprised about yuh brudda. Quentin such a sensitive person. He does cry so easeee and ting."

"He brought his girlfriend with him." Symone spoke casually.

"Who? He did wat?" Keturah asked with irritation.

"He brought his girlfriend to the funeral. Dey old one he met before me while we were at Hampton." Symone sat on the edge of her bed and pulled on some cotton footies.

"Oh no, Seamone. Ah can't believe he did dat knowing dat yuh were going ta be dere wit dey chillren. It should have ben common courtesy far him ta not bring she. He should've left she home."

"Well, I guess he didn't think about it like that. Yuh know men. But Mummy, it's ok."

"Dey bum. Bringing another wooman, ah can't believe Bully."

"The only thing that bothered me is he that she is the same woman he was seeing when I was pregnant with the twins. I just had flashbacks about that."

Symone wondered if she should proceed with this discussion. Just thinking about it was making her a little pissed. Keturah didn't know the whole story about Billy and her break-up. She only knew bits and pieces. That was all that Symone felt she could handle at the time she announced they were finally getting a divorce.

"Well, Mummy—" Symone cleared her throat and glanced quickly around her bedroom. "Ah listenin'."

Hell! Why not tell her, thought Symone. *She's gone through a lot in her life, too. Papa was crazy. Abusive. Even now, Mummy refuses to discuss her life with Papa. She even said that half the things Papa did to her, she wanted to take them to her grave.*

"Oh God, Seamone. Ah listenin', now." Keturah was becoming impatient at the silence.

"Uh. Like ah said, ah had flashbacks about him going out wit her while ah was pregnant wit dey twins," Symone said, feeling herself slipping in to her West Indian dialect. "Ah don't mind him seeing other woomen. Ah pass dat, Mummy. It's just dat wen ah was pregnant, ah was so vulnerable and tired of trying ta hold dey marriage tagether. He took advantage of it, and ah allowed it. Dere were many nights ah held onta Billy's ankles pleading wit him ta stay home wit meh and Jared."

"Oh God, nah, gurl. How cum? Wat did he do, Seamone?" She persevered with the questioning.

"Mummy, it's wat ah did. Ah found out he took dis same wooman ta a concert, and he stayed out until tree in dey morning. At tree-ten, ah put Jared in dey car, pajamas and all. Ah drove straight ta she house in Charlotte," she answered nervously.

"Waaat? Yuh did wat? Ah know yuh does not do such a ting, gurl."

"Dat's right. Ah telling yuh. Ah rang she doorbell in dey middle of dey night. Wen she peeked through dey door, ah asked she was Billy dere? She said he had just left."

"How did yuh know were she does live in dis Charleslotte, did yuh say? How did yuh get dere?" The questions just tumbled out of Keturah. She held the receiver closer to her ear and carefully listened to every word her daughter said.

"Dey police, Mummy—," Symone said easily and Keturah interrupted her.

"Wat do yuh mean dey police? Oh God, nah. Did yuh fight she? Wat did dey have ta do wit it?" she asked in a shrilled voice.

"Oh no, Mummy. It was nut-ting like dat. Dey police simply gave meh directions ta she house. Ah knew dey street she lived on. Ah just didn't know how ta get dere, so ah called dey Charlotte police and found out."

One would think the whole mess between her and Billy was going on now, especially with the way her mother was getting all excited about it. Symone thought that maybe she should just forget about it. She didn't want her mother to worry about old shit. But she had gone too far, so she decided to continue. If she stopped now, Keturah would then worry about what she didn't say.

"As ah was driving down I-40 West ta Charlotte, ah knew dat ah shouldn't be going dere. But ah absolutely couldn't stop meyself. All during mey pregnancy, Billy took her out, and ah knew about it. Dat was dey bad part. Mey pride was out of dey picture, and ah just acted out of impulse."

"Dey bum. He a bum too too bad," she repeated in an even thicker West Indian accent.

"Yuh said dat befar, Mummy."

"And ah saying dat agin. He's a bum's bum. Dey nerve of he. But don't yuh worry about it. Just go on. Look at yuh now. Yuh have made a lot more sense out of yuh life since yuh two have divorced. At least dat should make yuh feel strong, feel freer, and good."

Symone couldn't think of an appropriate response to Keturah's remarks. Even though the statement made some sense, right now Symone thought it was the perfect moment for her to really change the subject.

"How's bridge going, Mummy?"

No matter how many times Keturah explained the card game to Symone, it went right over her head. When Keturah was in the United States, which was about four months out of the year, if that long, she played bridge at least three times a week. Symone smiled to herself. For as long as she could remember, Keturah told her two brothers and Samuel Eisner that she wanted her four children to receive an education in America. But during the summer months and for carnival in Port of Spain, she insisted that she and her children would return to live in Trinidad for those occasions.

"Did yuh hear meh, Seamone?"

"Ah'm sorry. No. Wat did yuh say?"

"Ah said mey bridge is going just fine. Ah play wit Gerda, Rosa, and Odetta sometimes. Den dere are times ah don't feel so about going inta dey city. Gerda does say she would send dey limo far meh. But wit dey distance, it's so tiring sometimes. So ah does stay here and play." Symone laughed, and Keturah smiled. "Ameenah does find a senior citizen's center here in Brooklyn far meh wit more white people."

"Really? Hmmm. Do dey still have separate senior citizens centers far white and Black people? Dat's ridiculous. Unbelievable."

"No, no. Seamone, gurl," she replied in a patronizing way. The way Keturah said the words made Symone feel as if she was ten years old.

"It's just dat ah does prefer ta be around Trinidadians wen ah does cum back ta dey States! But where Ameenah does find are more whites people dere den Trinidadians that does play. Ah doesn't like dey small private clubs Odetta and Rosa told meh about here. Ah does prefer ta be around a lot of people. Dis is why ah does luv dey centers. Dey people dere are quite friendly ta meh wen ah cum, no matter wen ah does cum back. In any event, ah'll be going ta play dere while ah here."

"Dat's great. So bridge is becoming a big part of yuh life?"

"Ummm-hmmm. Yes, it tis. Only wen ah does cum ta New York. Yuh know ah does have ta spend time wit mey grandchillren, take dem ta plays, museums, and tings. But bridge does give meh someting else ta do ta pass dey time until ah does go back home ta Santa Cruz. Ah does truly enjoy playing it. Ah still trying ta show dey game ta Tutts and Myrtle. Ah does luv it so."

"Dat's what Hazele and Ameenah told me."

"Yuh seesters does know dey right ting. Now, Seamone, tell meh. How is yuh weight?"

"It's dey same, Mummy."

"Are yuh as big as yuh were wen yuh came home ta Brooklyn far Labor Day?"

Symone laughed slightly. "No, Mummy. Ah lost a few pounds since then. Not much, though. All dey Christmas festivities around Winston-Salem aren't helping me atall. I'm seriously tinking about getting a trainer like Hazele."

"If dat would help yuh wit yuh weight, yuh should. Yuh got dat big exercise room downstairs in yuh house wit all dey diffrent tings and so in it. How cum yuh don't use dem?"

"Ah don't know. Ah just don't."

"Well, yuh should. Maybe dat is why Hazele has stayed dey same nice size since she was a teen-ager. She trainer is always running and ting with she. Yuh don't want ta get too too large, Seamone. Yuh understand meh?"

"Yes, Mummy."

"Well, let meh go. Ah does need ta call Tutts befar it does get too late, befar she does go ta bed." Keturah checked her watch. It was nine. "Remember Seamone, mey birthday is on Tuesday." Symone had completely forgotten it.

"Dat's right. Ah remember," she lied quickly and tried to figure out what to select as a gift. With the death of Aunt Susie Mae and Mrs. Butler, the date had completely slipped Symone's mind.

"Ah will be sixty-five years old. In five years, ah'll be seventy."

"Do yuh feel it, Mummy?"

"No ah doesn't feel a ting, not too too bad," she said laughing her lilting way. "Ah cannot believe how dey time does fly. It does go by one day at a time. So gradual, but so fast. One dey yuh does look up and say ta yuhself. So much time does pass. Now look at yuh face. Yuh spots of gray hair. Yuh does not notice it as much as yuh live life each day. But wen yuh does see people yuh hadn't seen in five or ten years, den yuh does know dey aging is dere."

"Ah can imagine."

"Dey does look older ta yuh wen yuh does stare upon dey face, and yuh realize dat yuh must have aged, too." Keturah slowly shook her head and paused for a moment. "On tamorrow night, Quentin is taking meh and Ameenah ta eat at Hazele's restaurant. Yuh dey only one who won't be here far dat. Ah does feel sorry sometimes wen ah here wit yuh brudda, seesters, nieces, and nephews. Yuh are in North Caroline-a all by yuhself wit just yuh three baybees and no huzzband."

"Ah know, Mummy. Ah know yuh always does say dat, but don't be. It's no need. Ah ok. Really ah am. Ah have such great friends down here in North Carolina. Dey watch over meh like mey blood bruddas and seesters would do."

"Ah does know so. Ah does feel it wen ah cum ta visit wit yuh. So yuh does enjoy yuhself wit Alex and yuh other friends on Thanksgiving and in West Virgenenia?"

"It was absolutely wonderful, Mummy. Beautiful. Yuh know, Alex. She goes all out far dey holidays."

"Ummm-hmmm. Ah does know she. Yuh right." Keturah smiled as she recalled the always-warm reception by Alex when she traveled south to visit Symone.

"Pecola and Carlos were thoroughly surprised, too."

"Ah know so. Ameenah does tell meh a teeny piece about it. Dat was such a nice ting far yuh and yuh other friends ta do far Peecola and she huzzband." Keturah took a deep breath and thought for a moment. "Well, yuh know weh were all up in dey city with Samuel and Gerda far Thanksgiving. Dey whole family was dere, and it was such a lovely time. Dey only one missing was yuh."

"Ah know. Ah'll be dere next year, Mummy."

"Seamone, call yuh sister and tell she ah told yuh she needs ta stop working so hard in she restaurant. Ah does notice she does look sooo tired around she eyes and ting."

"Ah will. Ah will," Symone responded but knew she wouldn't tell Hazele such a thing. Keturah had probably already taken care of that, yet she hoped everything was fine with Hazele and Brutus.

Symone wished her mother could live to be one-hundred-years-old with good health. There were so many things Symone wanted to do with her and for her. Symone did a lot for her now. So did Quentin, Hazele, and Ameenah. Keturah could afford to do anything she wanted, but her four children always felt it was necessary to shower her relentlessly. Symone considered Aunt Susie Mae and Mrs. Butler. With life, one never knew what tomorrow brought with loved ones, and no one wanted a parent to die. Symone considered Billy, then thought that maybe she should send him another greeting card.

Symone inhaled deeply. "Let meh get off dey phone, Mummy."

"Fine, Seamone. Yuh does sound tired. Are yuh getting rest? Yuh need ta write letters and stop calling all yuh cousins so much in Trinidad. Dat does take a lot out of yuh. Yuh Tante Elaine sez yuh does call Trinidad last week and spoke ta she, she brudda and dey six grandchillren far over an hour."

"Ah did."

"Den Tutts sez yuh does call she and talk longer den dat wit she and Myrtle. Dat's too long ta be talking on dey tellyphone. Yuh need ta get some rest. Yuh not taking care of yuhself." Keturah suddenly caught herself and remembered that Symone was a grown woman. "Anyway, ah know yuh does tink ah going on and on about yuh."

Again, Symone smiled. "Ah luv yuh soooo much, Mummy."

"And ah does luv yuh too, gurl. Well, tis time far meh ta go. Oh God, nah! Seamone ah does almost fargot. How's Alex doing about she tante passing?"

"Not well, Mummy. Not well. She goes all out for dey holidays and doesn't believe dere are enough days in December ta enjoy all dey festivities she loves ta plan. Dis is still such a hard time of year far her. Aunt Susie Mae's death didn't help one bit, either. She's taking it pretty hard. Meh and Pecola have ta go ta Chicago dis week, so we're trying ta get her ta take dey trip wit us."

"She does need ta go ta take she mind off she auntie. Ah'll write she a nice letter, and ah'll call she after ah does speak wit Tutts."

"Yuh right. Madison said dey same ting. She'll love hearing frum yuh, Mummy. Remember, ah'll be home far Christmas in ten days."

"Ah know. Yuh does tell meh dis befar, and ah does have it written down in mey appointment book. Ameenah already planning dey dinner and tings far dey whole family, Seamone. Ameenah's house is beautiful wit all dey Christmas lights and tings. Dere's about four large fir trees throughout dey whole place. It's a sight ta see such. She five chillren's eyes have not closed frum all dey looking dey does be doing at dey glittering of everyting—"

"Ah know. Hazele told me. Ah told Alex dat she and Ameenah are alike in dat area."

"Yuh know so. Kiss mey grandchillren in dey morning far meh before dey does go ta school. Tell dem dat dere grandmum does luv and miss dem a lot."

"Ah will, Mummy. Yuh know dey are in bed. Ah'll have dem call yuh tamorrow night."

Symone often felt that Keturah's life only revolved around her surviving children, all her grandchildren, and spending, relaxed-filled days in Santa Cruz. After Honeyboy died, Symone never knew of her mother to be with another man, which always made Symone, her sisters, and brother wonder out loud if Keturah was lonely and wanted more out of life.

"Wat did yuh say, Mummy?"

"Oh God nah, gurl. Wat yuh doing? Are yuh not listening ta meh? Ah *said* dat will be fine. Ah does desire ta speak wit dey chillren. Dat is tall. Ah does receive a sweet letter, a card, and ting from Jared far mey birthday. Dat is why ah call yesterday, but ah remembered about Bully's father. Seamone, ah does getting off dey tellyphone far real. Good night."

Symone hung up the phone and watched it for a moment. Her mind began to race as she realized she needed to do something for her mother's birthday. In spite of Jared's unruly behavior at school and at home, if nothing else, Symone realized that her son was quite businesslike for his age. He kept up with all his cousins, tantes, uncles, his Butler grandparents, and his precious Grandmum Keturah's birthdays in a special appointment notebook. With the help of Miss Jessica, he was the first one to mail a card or short letter to them when the appropriate dates came around.

I'll order flowers for her birthday. Mummy loves to have fresh flowers on the dining room table, everywhere in the house for that matter, Symone thought with a fast nod of her head.

Symone called 1-800 Flowers and placed an order for four dozen red long stem roses to be delivered to her mother at the family's Brooklyn brownstone. Since orchids stood for wisdom, Symone ordered two dozen of those, too. She requested that the flowers be delivered to Keturah bright and early Tuesday afternoon. When Symone arrived at the office tomorrow morning, she would definitely call Tiffany's and have them put a glittering present together for Keturah. Maybe a diamond brooch would be nice. A messenger could deliver it. No, Symone wouldn't use Tiffany's messenger service. Keturah didn't care for that. She would ask Ameenah to handle it from there. And Symone knew her baby sister wouldn't mind going into the city to pick up the birthday gift, either.

Chapter Ninety-Three

"C'mon, Alex. You need to go with us, honeychile," Pecola coaxed in a soft voice through the telephone wires. "I'll treat you. How's that?"

Alex smiled. "Uh, I don't know, P. I'm just a little tired. That's all. Plus, Christmas is right around the corner, and I don't know if I want to leave Trey and Purity. They're so excited about Santa Claus coming. Hmmm. Leave town when it's so close around the holidays; I don't normally do that."

"Chile, puhleeze. What difference does it make? You've been through with Christmas shopping months ago. So c'mon, girl."

"I got to finish coordinating everything for the children's hay ride. We're going to arrange to have all fifty-eight children to come for the same night out here with the Ujima Literary members' children. Wooo! We'll have a bunch of young folks to cart around. Lillie said that she was able to reserve those Percheron Draft Horses for the hayride this year. That should be marvelous, Pecola."

"You see. Lillie can handle the rest. C'mon, girl."

"And we're taking them to the Walt Disney's World on Ice Christmas show on Saturday night. I just don't know. If I go with yall, I wouldn't be here for that nice, weekend family outing with all our young people."

"Hell, I know that, girl. Darilyn told me yall got about twenty adults to help with that so far. You don't have to be there, Alex. It can go on without you." Pecola stopped briefly. "No more excuses, girl. C'mon, now. We fly into Chicago on Thursday morning. Have cocktails Thursday evening. Our meeting begins on Friday morning at nine and should go to about three. After that, we're free."

"Uh huh."

"We had planned to stay for the weekend, to hang out, and to do a little Christmas shopping, anyway. You know I finally convinced Symone to go to the *Oprah* Show on Monday. I sho am hoping that my girl Oprah has someone who is famous and glamorous on. You see what I'm saying? I don't want to hear about nobody else's problems or no other depressing worldly shit. I got enough in my own life to deal with, chile."

"Pecola, girl."

"Humph I'm serious. On Tuesday morning, we'll be flying back. Girl, you should go. It's our last trip for the year."

"If I do that, I'll miss my Friday evening with Madison. You know how I feel about that."

"Yes, I damn sho do," Pecola interrupted her. "I know how Madison feels."

"You do?"

"Yes. He told me, quite confidentially, by the way," Pecola lowered her voice to a passionate whisper, "that it was a secret between me and him that he wouldn't mind. Madison said that it would be an excellent idea for you to go with us to Chicago. Now don't tell him I told you. Ok, girl?"

Alex grinned weakly. Scott and Symone were right. Pecola definitely had a refrigerator mouth. She, too, was beginning to realize it more each and every day about her dear best friend.

"Oh. It was a secret was it, Pecola?"

"Yeah, chile," Pecola replied quickly. "But I don't think Madison really wanted me to keep it as a secret."

"Well, he hadn't mentioned anything to me about our foregoing our Friday celebration for me to go to Chicago."

"Ooops. You know me. Just act like you don't know he said anything about it."

"Hmmm. Let me think about it, Pecola. I hadn't been to Chicago in over twenty years. That's where my Daddy was from you know."

"I remember. You just let me know if you want to go. I did ask Marlon to get in touch with Michael Jordan. We planned to go by his spot on Sunday night, and I wanted to be treated *real* special when I got there. Marlon said no problem. He would take care of it for me."

"Pecola, you're a mess."

"No, I'm not. I just didn't want to wait in line or wait around for a good table like a *regular* tourist has to. I told Symone to call her Uncle Samuel, so that he can use his influence to get excellent seats on the *Oprah* Show. When the show airs, I want to make sure everyone sees us on the front row back here in Winston-Salem. *And,* I want to have an intimate, private meeting with Oprah. Of course, an exclusive tour of Harpo Studios."

"Whaaat?"

"That's right. I sho do. I sho did ask Symone that. Symone said that she wasn't going to do no such a thing." Pecola paused and thought for a moment. "Whooo, chile! She said that if she was going to go on *Oprah,* she wanted to be a part of the audience like everyone else. She didn't want no special privileges."

"That makes sense, Pecola."

"Humph! Not to me it does. If I were Symone, I would bust up in there and tell Oprah about my whole life story. Starting with my life in Trinidad and all the way up to Fifth Avenue. I'd tell them about how the Eisners helped Uncle Cecil and Uncle Willie after they saved Uncle Samuel's life. Hell, I would be on the show before it was over with."

"Pecola—" Alex took a long, patient breath. "Everybody doesn't want the world to know their business. There are a lot of wealthy people in this world that you never ever hear about. I'm like that too, and so is your husband. You know that. I've met so many others through the McIntyres who are the same way. You never ever see them on your favorite show. These people aren't on the *Lifestyles of the Rich and Famous.*"

"That's because it's off the air."

"Even before then, everyone didn't jump on that show. Those same unobtrusive, wealthy people are never on television. They simply live their lives very unassumingly and do what they want with their family and friends without all the glitz and glamour for the whole world to see or know about their balance sheet. That outside validation for them isn't necessary."

"Maybe so. To a lot of other rich people, outside validation definitely is a requirement. That's real life. Lawd, I didn't expect a damn lecture, Alex. I hate I said anything. Sometimes you and Symone are sooo serious about money. Now if you think folks don't think it's something wealthy acting about the way you live out there in all that splendor in that big house of yours in Advance, then you got another thought coming. I mean, really. What are you hiding, Alex?"

"I'm not hiding anything, Pecola. I'm just saying that people can speculate all they want to about how Madison and I live out here. I'm just not going to be the one to discuss my business on the streets of Winston-Salem. Doing things like that can be an onus. A curse. You just never know. Brag about what? I know what I have."

Pecola shook her head with total frustration. "Damn! I can't believe you're lecturing me about this. You do it, too. Humph. You used your contacts to get backstage passes to meet Patti."

"Yes I did, and I'll do it again. But I made a conscious decision to do that for you and my other girlfriends in the privacy of a backstage meeting, not on national television. I didn't spill my guts to her about my life, either. We met Patti and Steve Harvey, then we left."

"I still don't see how it's so damn different. Humph. All I called you about was to see if you wanted to go to Chicago on my dime. Not a lecture."

"I love you for wanting to treat me special, and I know you don't want a lecture. I don't want to give you one. I'm just speaking my mind and telling you the truth. You know how Symone is. She's intensely private."

"She's not the only one. I am, too."

"Symone fervently wants to be accepted the way she is, not for what she has. Other than her close friends, you know she's very conservative with everyone else around here in Winston-Salem. She closed mouth about her affiliation with the Eisners. I'm assuming that those outside folks around town who know her slightly are *only* assuming she makes most of her money from Akao Studios and Meetings Odyssey, not from all her trust funds."

"We *do* make a lot of money there, too. Loads of it. Since we opened the Akao Building's front doors, we've made a major profit each and every year," Pecola inserted proudly.

"I know, girl. I'm glad. Now I just really hope you don't get refrigerator mouth in the area of Symone's personal life and start telling what you shouldn't. Nothing bothers Symone more than that. You know that'll really piss Symone off big time. Plus, it's not even necessary."

"Refrigerator mouth?" Pecola gasped. "Chile, puhleeze. I'm tired of yall putting that label on me. What about me getting pissed off at her? At the shit she does and says to me and everybody else we know."

"I understand that happens a lot, and I've never hesitated to tell Symone the truth about what bothers you and pisses you off. I tell her what bothers me and any of our other friends. Haven't I tried to do that since we all have been friends, girl? Haven't we all been brutally honest with each other as friends about everything? And I do mean, brutally."

"Uh huh! Sometimes," Pecola said softly. She thought again and spoke honestly. "Well, yeah. Most times you do, Alex. We all do. Damn! Now you know I ain't talking about

Symone's relationship with the Eisners, girl. I never have. Even I got some sense about certain shit. True, I do talk a lot about everybody else I know. One thing my friends should know about me is that when I do talk about them, I talk about them *only* with the other friends in our circle. Only with each other and not with outside folks. I'm a selective gossiper. I'm loyal to my friends. Yall should at least know that. I ain't *that* crazy."

"I know you're very loyal. I love that about you, Pecola. I do. And you definitely ain't crazy," Alex said and laughed again.

Pecola grinned with satisfaction. "Humph. Yall are different from me. I just don't think it's that big of a deal if people know what you can and cannot afford sometimes or who you know and don't know in this world. That's all. Pure divine social networking is all I call it. Name dropping." Pecola inhaled deeply. "Hold on a minute, my telephone is beeping." Pecola clicked over.

"Hello," Pecola said quickly with relief. Quite frankly, she was glad for the interruption.

"Pecola girl, I just came from the bathroom, and you'll never guess what I discovered."

"Whooo, chile!" Pecola cut Symone off. "I'm glad it's you. I need the back up troops real bad. I got Alex on the phone, and I'm trying to get her to go with us to Chicago just like Madison encouraged us to do, girl."

"That's good. You didn't tell her that did you? For whatever reason, Madison asked us to keep it strictly confidential."

"Well uh, I was—"

"Yeah, damn right you did. Umph, umph, umph, umph, umph. I declare you can't keep shit in that refrigerator mouth of yours, Pecola. Loose lips sink ships; you're a sinking woman. Now you know what Madison asked us to do that day in our office?"

"Chile, puhleeze. What's this with yall and this refrigerator mouth thang? Is it in the Clemmons and Advance water or what? Look!" Pecola exclaimed with her free hand in the air and stiff. "The hell with you and the horse you rode in on."

"Thanks for the beautiful word of encouragement, girl. Remember? Jodria said that it's really stress talking when you curse. Try not to do it so much. It's so unbecoming. As pretty as you are, you know you shouldn't be cursing at me on a Sunday."

"Shiiiit! You got nerve to talk. I at least go to church each and every Sunday. You don't know dittly about that."

"I went today."

"Yeah—only because your ass had to go to a funeral. Look, girl. We can deal with this later. For right now, let's try to convince Alex to go to Chicago. She's in her lecturing mode, but she still doesn't sound too good and strong to me. It isn't like our normal Alex. Hang up, and I'll call you back. Ok?"

"Right."

Pecola clicked back over to Alex. "Whew, Alex. Sorry about that, girl. That was Symone. Let me put you on hold one more time, so I can get her on the line."

"That's fine, Pecola."

In a few seconds, the three-way connection was made.

"Ok, Alex?"

"I'm here."

"Symone?"

"Me too. How ya doing, Alex girl?" Symone screamed at the top of her lungs.

"Fine? Sheese. What's up with you?" Alex asked.

"Ok. Let me just cut to the chase, Alex. We're leaving on Thursday. Pecola and I will be over there after we leave the office to help you pack on Wednesday night. I'll spend the night with you if you want me to. The limo will pick us up bright and early Thursday morning, take us to the Greensboro airport, and we'll be on our way to Chicago. How's that?" Symone took a deep breath.

"That's fine, Sy. I believe I'll go."

"Damn, chile!" Pecola exclaimed. "Is that all it took? If I had known that, I would've been direct about trying to get you to go."

Alex laughed lightly. "Your talking to me *did* help me decide, Pecola."

"I just got through speaking with my mother, Alex," Symone said. "She said that she was going to call you, too."

"Is that what Mum Poussaint said? Oh my. I look forward to hearing her comforting voice."

"I just can't believe how easy it was for you, chile," Pecola inserted.

"Hell, Pecola. Leave it alone. It worked," Symone said. "I just took your direct, take charge approach, Alex. The same way you do me when I'm down in the dumps. That was all. Plus, I had something else to share with yall. Before I called Pecola, I went to use the bathroom. You'll never guess what I found."

"What, chile?" wondered Pecola.

"I can't guess, Symone," Alex said

"I ain't *even* forty yet, and I found three gray hairs down there," Symone said.

"Down where, chile?" Pecola asked.

"I found three gray hairs down on my cootie cat," Symone insisted.

"Your cootie cat?" Alex repeated.

"That's right." Symone smiled. "Don't even act like yall don't know. That's the southern term for it, isn't it? Or at least it's Rehema's favorite name for her vagina. Cootie cat."

"Sy, you're crazy. We all are getting older, so it's expected," Alex said calmly. "It's a sign of maturity."

"Not me," Symone shot back. "It's not expected for me. I want my hair to stay a pretty, curly jet black down there just like the hair on my head."

"It's not a good sign of maturity for me either, chile. So what are you going to do with the *three hairs?*" Pecola pronounced the last two words in a long drawl.

"I'm plucking them out at the roots with the quickness. That's what. I try to keep my cootie cat closely cropped anyway in a vee-shaped kind of way. I don't want anybody—not one of my dear men friends having a hard time trying to dig for the Poussaint jewels." Symone announced. Alex and Pecola's laughter filled the telephone wires.

"Symone, girl," Alex moaned and slowly shook her head.

"You need to try it, old Alex girl," Symone suggested. "You can shape your cootie cat the same way you've seen guys with designs in their head. Shock the hell out of Madison one night and be a little different."

"I've already done that vee shaped thang a number of times, girl," Alex said. "Thank you just the same. And yes, Madison does enjoy looking at it and fondling it, too."

"Woooo," Pecola exclaimed. "You go, Alex."

"Glad to know you and Madison just ain't having straight up and down sex over there in Advance," Symone said swiftly, and their laughter was friendly music. "I like to keep down there cut real low. I always heard hair holds scent, and I want my cootie coo to always smell good and sweet."

"Now it's your cootie coo. Is that what you had to call me about?" Pecola asked, giggling. "Was that what was so earth shattering, Sy?"

"No. I tried calling Alex first to ask her a question," Symone replied. "When I couldn't get through, I called you, Pecola."

"Oh, so I'm second choice?" Pecola wondered.

"Hell, yeah," Symone replied.

"What's the question, Sy?" Alex asked quietly.

"Jared lost another tooth. I want to know what you recommend the tooth fairy should be bringing him this time," Symone said. "What's the going rate? The tooth fairy is like the stock market. It goes up and down, so I keep getting confused."

"Lawd, chile," Pecola moaned. "When I was little, we got a piece of candy, a penny, or a nickel. If it was a good tooth fairy, we might get a dime. Maybe—"

"That was fifty years ago," Alex said. "I recommend at least a dollar, Sy. That's seems like what Jodria told me the going rate was. Yall hold on a moment. My line is beeping," Alex explained and she clicked over.

"...I don't think so," Pecola was saying to Symone when Alex clicked back over.

"I'm on," Alex said a few moments later. "That was Marlon's mother. I told Larryetta that I would call her back as soon as I was through talking to yall. She told me to tell yall hey. Pecola, Larryetta said for you to definitely call her tonight before you go to bed."

"Plan to," Pecola answered. "As I was saying, chile—"

"Pecola, Larryetta said that you, Pauletta, and her are supposed to hook up a three way this evening," Alex continued. "Something bout a Greensboro sisterhood thang with yall hanging out during the Christmas holidays when Pauletta comes home. She wasn't sure if you remembered. Pauletta called Larryetta. They tried your number, but your line was busy."

"I guess damn so. I'm on here with you and Symone. Whew." Pecola inhaled quickly. "As I was saying, chile—"

"Uh oh. Hold on again, yall. I'm sorry. My phone is beeping," Alex interrupted once more and clicked over again. "I'm back, yall. That's Mum Poussaint, so I gotta go this time. Seniority rules. I'll talk to yall later. Ok? I love you, Pecola. I love you, Sy."

"I love you too, chile," Pecola answered.

"Me too, girl," Symone said and slowly bobbed her head.

"*Me too,* Sy? You hear her, Pecola. Now you know that don't work with us," Alex said with a small smile. "Look, I gotta go."

"I love you too, Alex. Is that better?" Symone asked.

"It sure is," Alex answered. "You know that."

"Tell Mummy I said hello again." Symone stood and stretched. "So it looks like we're on our way to Chicago, girls?"

"Damn straight," Pccola exclaimed. "I love you, Sy."

"And, I love you too, chile. Bye, yall."

Chapter Ninety-Four

On Thursday afternoon, Pecola, Alex, and Symone arrived into bustling Chicago around eleven in the morning. Both Alex and Pecola raved excitedly about the icy, biting Chicago air. The colder the better explained Alex. Since they were in the city that was known for its freezing, snowy December weather, Alex and Pecola said that was exactly what they wanted to experience during their five-night visit. From the time Symone walked outside of O'Hare Airport to simply step into the waiting limousine, she complained that she was already cold all the way down to her bones. The crisp temperature was in the middle twenties, but the wind chill factor pushed the frigid breeze into the low single digits. Even though Symone's full length chinchilla coat and matching hat covered her body, she maintained that she still continued to shiver and told her two friends she was definitely ready to head straight back to a warmer North Carolina.

After Pecola, Alex, and Symone checked into the presidential suite at The Drake Hotel, they quickly unpacked their suitcases and hopped back into the limousine. Pecola wanted to do a little sightseeing and a whole lot of shopping on the section of Michigan Avenue that was known as the Magnificent Mile, according to the Chicago informational packet they received from Platinumm Travel. They had plenty of time. Pecola and Symone were scheduled to meet briefly with Jefferson Dickey at eight for cocktails, and nothing else had been scheduled before then.

One third partner of Dickey, Mahon, and Dickey, Jefferson insisted on having this evening's cocktail meeting that he told Pecola and Symone would only last for about an hour. Ninety minutes at the most. For the past few months, Pecola and Symone had gotten to know the three partners by speaking over the telephone, through letters, faxes, and e-mail. Jefferson believed it would now be an excellent idea to meet face to face before Symone and Pecola's all day review of his company on Friday.

"I don't know about this one, Symone," Pecola said as she pulled off her full-length ranch mink coat and laid it across the living room couch. She removed the matching hat, patted her hair, kicked off her shoes, plopped down, and stretched her long legs along the couch.

"I know, girl," Symone said from the foyer as she hung her coat up in the hall closet. She came back into the living room, got Pecola's coat off the couch, and hung it up. "It was a trip. I just can't put my finger on it," Symone said softly. In the living room, her voice appeared muffled to the other two women who were listening.

"I can't hear you, girl," Pecola said as she twisted her neck to glance around. Symone walked back into the living room.

"I don't know. Jefferson seems to have a somewhat cold and calculating demeanor. Yet it's kind of laced with a sweet face. It's a tough call to make." Symone folded her arms against her chest and began to think for a moment.

"Girl, what happened?" Alex asked with wide eyes from the other couch and laid the book she was reading down.

While Symone and Pecola went out for their cocktail meeting, Alex stayed in the suite where she silently gazed at the beautiful, sweeping view of night lights along Lake Michigan, Lake Shore Drive, and Oak Street Beach. When she grew tired of staring out into the distance at the colorful black brilliance, she took a long, hot almond-scented bath. After she massaged her body in shea butter, she slipped into an ice green full-length velvet nightgown and robe.

Since sad thoughts about Aunt Susie Mae were tearing through her mind, Alex called Madison and the children, then Marlon and Nanette. Each one said that everything was fine. They teasingly told her that nothing had changed with them since she spoke with them before she had left earlier that day, since she spoke to them from the airplane, and after she had checked into the hotel. Feeling warm, comfortable, and contented, Alex listened to classical music. She quietly read several pages in the book, *The Rose of Jericho,* by Vanessa Davis Griggs, one of her all-time favorite authors.

"Will somebody answer me? What happened?" Alex asked.

"It's our potential partners in crime, girl," Symone exclaimed. "The ones that Rozelle said were good people."

"I don't mean to sound callous about this," Pecola said.

"Hell, don't worry. Go ahead and sound callous, Pecola. This is about *our* business," Symone said quickly as she unbuckled her high-heel ankle strap pumps. She kicked them off in the direction of the fireplace and walked straight to the wet bar.

"Chile, I've always said business and friends don't mix," Pecola continued. "Symone and I are different. I mean dealing with anybody else outside of MO that's our friends. Yall know what I'm saying? Those friends who try to get us to give them things all the time and want us to give our services away for free just simply because they know us."

"Get to the point, Pecola," Symone yelled in a teasing voice from the bar. "Yall want anything to drink?" Both Alex and Pecola shook their heads no. Symone fixed herself a large glass of Remy Martin on the rocks and went to sit back down on the couch beside Alex.

"I know we have to network. I'm the biggest proponent of those kinds of business dealings and social networking kind of things. Aren't I, Alex dear?" Pecola asked and winked at her two friends. Alex smiled back.

"And?" Symone edged her on.

"We don't know this firm well enough, Symone," Pecola said. "We know them on paper. That's only via the net and with speaking with them on the telephone."

"How did yall find out about them?" Alex asked, looking from face to face.

"Rozelle. He hooked us up with them. Pecola and I had heard of them. The conference and meeting planning industry is lucrative, small, and cliquish. So you kind of know about the other folks in the business. We weren't familiar with their operation. We're too busy doing our own thing." Symone spoke slowly as she took a thoughtful swallow of liquor.

"I see," Alex said following the story.

"Dickey, Mahon, and Dickey is the number one or two African-American full service meeting management company in the country," Symone explained. "The project we're considering working on together is huge. I think everyone in the conference planning industry got a whiff of this coming down. It's an opportunity to handle this mega, mega, mega, and sho nuff mega conference for the Department of Defense and the Pentagon. I mean we're talking thousands upon thousands of people attending, Alex. So we considered developing a consortium with a colleague in the industry to join forces, so to speak, to go through the red tape of the bidding process. You know? Have an agreement between Meetings Odyssey and Dickey, Mahon, and Dickey to pursue this government business."

"That sounds like a great opportunity," Alex said. "A good plan to develop a mini coalition of sorts."

"It is, Alex," Pecola answered. "There definitely is a mutuality of interest here, honeychile. But we don't like what we're hearing so far or what we're seeing."

"That's why Pecola and I agreed to come to Chicago, Alex," Symone said. "We know what our agenda is about. Our operation is run tight and is fair. We wanted to see how Dickey, Mahon, and Dickey manage their operations and to see if we would jive as potential partners. Just because you have a big time operation, that doesn't mean it's run properly or that we would want to work with them."

"Here, here, chile," Pecola said quickly.

"I like to see the inner workings of a company," Symone continued as she took sips of Remy. "Meet the people, walk around, and get a sense of things the same way we do when people visit us in Winston-Salem. If we're going to put our heads together with another company, it's going to cost us some money in the long run. We know that's a given. When money comes out of MO's budget, Pecola and I need to be sure."

"I understand," Alex said, listening intently.

"We have to consider our excellent reputation when we consider developing a partnership," Symone said. "When Pecola and I even think about rolling around the possibility of Meetings Odyssey going to bed with another company with our name being thrust out there, we want to make damn stra-eight the other guy's reputation is just as impeccable as ours in the full service meeting management industry."

"That's right, chile," Pecola said. "Not only with the spreadsheet because that's easy for an excellent CPA to make look good. Hell, we know Norvella could work magic with our numbers if she had to. We want any affiliations for us to be bulletproof inside out. If we unite with another company to pursue this lucrative government or corporate business, you know the deal? Our reputation is on the line, and we don't want that blemished."

"That's for sure," Symone nodded.

"If anything goes wrong, we're up the creek without a paddle," Pecola said. "You put together a huge government conference like that and have problems, you can forget it, girl. Word gets around real fast like wild fire in a dry forest. That's why we opted to come to

Chicago. It was worth the investment to see if we could work together to see if our goals and objectives meshed well."

"Hmmm," Alex said and shook her head with understanding.

"They got the contract ready for us to sign, too. Don't they, Sy?" Pecola asked and Symone nodded her head yes. "If we like what we see, we'll sign on the dotted line. That is after our legal people back in Winston review it first. Both our companies can make more money. If we don't like what we see, we go back to North Carolina and still continue to make money. We *know* we're one of the best in the country at what we do. We worked too hard to build this company up to what it is today to not check everything out. We do it all the time. Hell, either way, we can still always shop the time away."

"You're crazy, Pecola," Symone said as she swallowed the last of her Remy and got up to pour another towering glass full.

"You got an iron-walled stomach, chile," Pecola said as she glanced at Symone.

"Tank yuh, gurl. Ah does know so," Symone said with a West Indian accent as she swiftly considered her alcoholic father. "Dis ting is in mey blood too too bad, gurl."

"Yall have done a great job," Alex said. "I'm proud of everything yall do."

"Thanks. I know we have," Pecola said quickly and gazed at her soft pink polished, perfect nails. "You know another thing I noticed, Sy?"

"What?" Symone asked.

"Jefferson blinked too much. When I was working on my MBA at A&T, I took a class with— Hmmm. I can't think of the teacher's name, but the class was marketing or something or nother. I know I've told you about this, Sy."

"Tell me," Alex inserted quickly and grinned, ready to listen. She pulled her knees up on the couch and flapped the velvet bathrobe around her legs.

Pecola slapped her thigh. "I got it! His name was Professor Prey. Anyway Professor Prey said you got to watch out for people with that eye-blinking habit, especially during fierce negotiations and important meetings. Professor Prey said that you notice these kinds of things as a shrewd business man or woman."

"How interesting," Alex said.

"You must constantly watch people's eyes when clients are presenting their views or sales pitch," Pecola went on. "If their eyes blink too much, there's a problem. It might be a lack of confidence. Whatever. They might even be lying. It means there's uncertainty lurking around. I find that all three of those brothers blink too much, and I don't trust that. Did you notice that too, Sy?"

"Yes I did. I thought they were trying to look at me and were near-sighted," she teased and sat back down to quickly sip the cool, soothing liquor. Alex and Pecola burst out laughing. "Just joking, girls. I just find that eyes can be a distractive sensory problem especially if someone's damn good-looking. No. I'm just kidding again. Let me be serious. I tend to listen better with closed eyes. That's why sometimes when I'm in meetings, I close my eyes and listen intently. I trust my ears more than my eyes."

"I agree with you there. That's just like blind people. All they can go on is what they hear. Since they're forced to develop their sense of hearing, they're much more perceptive people, too," Alex insisted.

"Did you notice how Jefferson is arrogant, chile?" Pecola asked. "Yet, he's kind of sweet and nonchalant. He acts a little complacent. Wooo, chile! It's hard to fathom those three guys."

"Well, I don't mind the arrogance, Pecola." Symone said. "I get that way sometimes. I didn't get complacency from him. But arrogance and complacency are twin devils that you certainly don't want dancing on your doorstep when you're in business. That's for sure."

"I'm adding up too many negatives, Sy," Pecola said, almost under her breath. "You know what you said that your Uncle Samuel says. I feel the same way. When you feel too many negatives in your gut, bail the hell out of the deal. Carlos always told me this. 'Trust your instincts, Sweet Pea. That's all you got that won't lie to you.'"

"Good advice," Alex mumbled.

"Those three guys blink their eyes too damn much. Plus, there was too much intellectual rambling for my blood. The blinking causes it. Jefferson's two other partners act like they're too scared to say one word, either. Damn wimps if you ask me, Alex."

"Where yall go?" Alex inquired.

"A place called the Pump Room at the Omni Ambassador's East," Pecola answered. "Nice place, chile. We had a small conference three years ago, and a lot of the meetings were held there. Sy didn't make that conference. Didn't you like the Pump Room, Sy?"

"I did," Symone replied. "That is after I stopped feeling cold and took my coat off. Whew, girl. It's just too cold for me. The limo driver said this was nothing. I'm just stepping from car to buildings. God forbid I was walking anywhere. Can yall believe that? The temperature has dropped. The wind chill factor is now below zero. Girl, I'm ready to go. Since I can't, I'm going to get into velour like my girl Alex here. And I'm going to bed."

Pecola stood up. "Me, too. Let's not sleep in the other two bedrooms, honeychile. Let's all gang up in the master bedroom. That king-size bed is a monster. This suite is big as my house."

"Ain't nothing as big as that Beverly Hillbillies' house," Symone blurted out. "This is the only way I travel, Pecola."

"I know, Missy Symone." Pecola smiled. "Hell, you know it is for me as well, chile."

"And the only way for me. Madison adores quaintly romantic places such as this," Alex said quietly as she glanced around at the suite's lovely living room again. "I told him today that we should come and stay here for a week. My baby said if I liked it that much, to go ahead and make a reservation for sometime in the spring."

"My man, Madison," Symone said. "He probably knows it's too cold now for his blood."

"Honeychile," Pecola exclaimed. "Since we all can fit in there on that king-sized bed, what yall think?"

"Oooh, Pecola," Alex gushed. "Now you know ain't nothing I like more than a forty and over pajama party."

"Watch it, girl! I won't be forty till next month. Yall are the ones who are forty," Symone inserted rapidly and stood up. "It does sounds good. Anything to put that firecracker brightness back into your eyes, Alex. After we get out of our meeting tomorrow, I'm taking yall both on a shopping spree. Anything you want. It's on me."

"Thanks, mama. I'm ready. I declare," Pecola exclaimed, propping her hands on her hips. "You're trying to copy off of me or what? Remember when I took yall shopping when we were in Africa this year. Remember? We had a ball. It was Jodria, Rehema, Nanette, and Darilyn. All the girls of FOFAE."

"Girl, puhleeze. That ain't got a thing to do with this," Symone replied, interrupting Pecola's speech. She swallowed the rest of her Remy and placed the empty glass on the table. "I simply feel like doing it. From Saturday through Tuesday, you're on your own."

Alex smiled. "Thanks for convincing me to come. I don't even mind missing my Friday night with my husband as much. When I spoke to Madison, Marlon, and Nanette, I told them the same thing too."

"We love you with your pushy Black self. That's all," Symone said and reached out to hug Alex. Pecola joined the embrace, and the three friends rocked backwards and forth for several seconds.

"Now don't make me cry, yall," Alex pleaded softly as her eyes welled with easy tears.

"This ain't the place for tears, honeychile," Pecola said gently as they began walking, while hugging each other as they headed to the master bedroom.

"I know," Alex said. "I'm getting better with the tears, P."

To raise Alex's spirit, Pecola began yelling and stopped walking. "Yippee! Tante Symone is taking us shopping tomorrow. You know I love to shop my ass off. I hadn't been here in what three years? Not since our last conference we put on here. It's been awhile for Symone. Alex hadn't been here in what, twenty years? So ladies, we need to enjoy big time. Tomorrow evening, we gonna get a chance to shop till we drop."

"You're right, girl," Symone said as they stood in the hallway near the master bedroom. "You sho can shop, Pecola. No limit."

"Are you sure you didn't get enough today when we were out, Pecola?" Alex asked.

"Nope. I was just starting, chile. Because of the cocktail meeting, I felt rushed. When we're done tomorrow, we ain't got to go nowhere. I love the bigness of everything here, girl."

"I love all the stores here myself. They're fabulous. Marvelous," Symone gushed with flashing bright eyes. "Wooo! It's still cold as hell. I know I done said that fifty times. I might bring the children back here in the spring. Maybe I'll come when you come, Alex. I definitely won't be taking them on an educational trip to Chicago in the dead of winter."

"I didn't ask you to come," Alex teased. "Madison and I are coming on a private trip."

"Hmmm. You go, gurly gurl. Claim your space with your huzzband," Symone rattled on with an amusing southern twang. "Last time I was here was for that college conference we coordinated about eight years ago. It was kind of cold then, and it was the end of March. That's why when we lose bids for a winter conference in Chicago or those other places, I don't *even* get too excited."

"Isn't that ridiculous?" Pecola said.

"That might be bad business thinking, but hear what I'm telling you," Symone demanded. "My Trinidadian blood can't handle the frigid cold too too much. Barring the weather, I do think I still like the city, girls. It has vibrancy and excitement and is bout like New York."

"I know," Pecola quickly added, leaned her back against the wall and glanced up at the ceiling.

"If it's ok with you," Symone said, staring into Pecola's face. "Tomorrow morning, I'm gonna tell the finnne limo driver—"

"He's fine now," Alex agreed in an airy whisper when they began walking again. Since Alex was sandwiched between Pecola and Symone, they both stopped moving and glanced sideways to stare in her face.

Shocked, Pecola blinked her eyes. "Excuse me?"

"What yall looking at me like that for?" Alex asked. "I ain't dead. I'm just in love with my sweet baby love, Madison. By the way, I gots to get him a wonderful gift before I leave Chicago."

"You go, girl. Ain't you the spunky one tonight?" Symone asked and gently leaned her head against Alex's head. Alex's loving grip around Pecola and Symone's waists tightened as did theirs. Pecola smiled contentedly and basked in the thick aura of friendship she was sharing with her two best girlfriends.

"Alex." Symone's voice was soft. "His name is Edolphus Lightfoot."

"Hmmm. Nice name," Alex drawled smoothly. "I knew you would get his name before the day was over, Sy."

Symone chuckled. "You're right. I don't like calling them just *driver. Uh, driver, can you tell us this? Driver, can you take us there? Driver. Driver. Driver?* Up close and personal is my philosophy."

"Don't remind us, chile," Pecola mumbled. "Try not to jump his bones."

"Watch it, girl," Symone giggled. "I'm going to tell the fine brother to keep it idling in front of Dickey, Mahon, and Dickey's office building on Congress Avenue. That's for sure. If our vibes don't get any better, we'll be out of there with the quickness, girl."

Pecola nodded her head in agreement, and Alex grinned inwardly and said *oh lawd* under her breath.

Chapter Ninety-Five

As Alex ate lunch room service, she thumbed through the packets of Chicago tourist information that Madison had obtained for her. Since she didn't want to do any major sightseeing by herself, she wondered what she would do for the remainder of the day while she waited for Pecola and Symone. Maybe she should visit the museums. Edolphus informed them yesterday that they were quite wonderful and were very close by. The Eaddys were in Europe skiing; therefore, Alex's hopes of visiting her soror were dashed. So that Alex wouldn't be stuck at the hotel without the limo, Pecola requested that Edolphus go back to The Drake and see if Alex wanted to go anywhere.

Alex ate a light breakfast around eight-thirty. Afterwards, she got dressed in an elegant black cashmere pants suit. She set it off with a yellow paisley silk scarf and Italian suede pumps with gold metal horsebit trim. Then she went for a picturesque ride around town. Even though it was eighteen degrees outside, it was bright, sunny, and windy. The briskness of the arctic-like wind was invigorating to Alex, and she decided not to wear the hat that went with her full-length, Russian sable coat. She wanted to deeply breathe in to savor the energizing air and to allow her long black, thick hair to blow in the slashing, frigid wind.

When the limo rolled by Buckingham Fountain, Edolphus explained in a professional, pleasant voice to Alex that the fountain was closed down for the winter. But he confidently told her that it was a gorgeous sight to see in the spring and summer when the fountain sprayed colorful splashes of water. Historic Old Town was about a mile away from The Drake, and he glided her through there to look at the quaint buildings. Edolphus told Alex that Chicago was a very old city with historic areas all over the place and now the gray stone and limestone landmark buildings constructed in the 1800s were being protected for historical reasons.

When Alex commented passionately on the old-fashioned architecture of many of the Chicago buildings, he asked her if she collected antiques. Once more she replied with an enthusiastic yes. Edolphus then glided her through the River North Area then to the Belmont Area. He drove by the River Mart, a huge building filled with nothing but antiques from top to bottom. After Edolphus wheeled her on a slow tour through Lincoln Park and Hyde Park areas, he showed her the house that used to be owned by Muhammad Ali. On the way back, Edolphus recommended that Alex also have lunch in one of the John Hancock Building's many delightful restaurants; however, Alex quietly told him she preferred going back to the hotel and ordering room service. Edolphus dropped Alex off in front of the hotel around one o'clock, and he headed back to Congress Avenue to wait out front for Pecola and Symone.

Pecola eyed Symone. It was time. After they finished the catered lunch, they went into the bathroom to wash their hands. It was there that Pecola and Symone decided to communicate with their eyes when they finally decided they had had enough. Symone eyed her back, and her perturbed look said that she was definitely ready to go, too. Pecola rose to her feet and spoke to Symone.

"I think we better be heading back, Symone." Symone quickly got up.

"Excuse me, Mrs. Reynolds. Er, Miss Poussaint. I was— I'm not finished with this meeting. What about our contract that's on the table?" Jefferson asked, shocked, with a slight lisp.

"It's a piece of paper we never signed." Symone shrugged. "Tear it up."

"Miss Poussaint and Mrs. Reynolds, I beg your pardon," Jefferson said. "You can't just walk out of *my* office like this."

A heavy silence hung over the room while Jefferson, his two partners, Pecola, and Symone considered Jefferson's statement. Pecola eyed Symone in disbelief, and Symone eyed her back. Symone nodded at Pecola as if to say, *I am not even in the mood to go over there. You need to handle this one. Woof! Grrrr! Woof! Get him the way I know you can, girlfriend!*

"We're not done," Jefferson said. "You can't walk away now."

"Oh, yes I can walk out of here," Pecola said as she calmly gathered up papers, charts, and whatever else she could collect off the conference room table that belonged to MO and placed them in her now open briefcase. She stopped long enough to throw Jefferson a stony, calculating stare.

"We came to Chicago in good faith to work with another African-American owned conference planning firm. We wanted to develop a unique partnership and put together one of the most major government conferences in the last ten years. But from nine—," Pecola checked her watch, "to one thirty, all I've heard you say is *I* this, and *I* that. *I* can. *I* will. *I, I, I,* and nigger this. Nigger that, and niggers ain't shit."

Jefferson gasped. "Mrs. Reynolds, will you puhleeze?"

"What about us hearing that all day? What about your colleagues sitting here? Your employees?" Both men looked down at their notes scribbled on yellow legal-sized sheets and began to shift uncomfortably in their burgundy executive chairs.

"You men supposedly have a three-way partnership. At least that's the name that's on the double wooded front door leading into this place. It's on all the correspondence we've ever received from you. That's what *you* told us. You couldn't tell it by the way you speak, Jefferson. That's another thing. As a matter of fact, you're the only one that has been speaking ever since we got here. It's as if Colin Dickey, your own brother, is invisible. The way you talk, Clinton Mahon doesn't even exist up in here. It's all only about you and only you handling everything."

"Mrs. Reynolds! Enough!"

"No, it's not enough because I'm not finished yet, Jefferson," Pecola said in a clear, strong business voice. "When we decided to come to Chicago, we came. We invested our money. Most importantly, we invested our valuable time because we thought it would give my business partner and me an opportunity to work with that gentleman." Pecola pointed to Colin. "And that gentleman." She then pointed to Clinton. "Not just you, Jefferson. And this is how you do business? What we've seen today is unbelievable. If this is how you do business and host your meetings, I can't believe it. Colin and Clinton are sitting here actually allowing it? That's unbelievable."

The room was extremely quiet. The only sound that was distinctly noticeable was the whirring of the heating system blowing air through the vents. Jefferson's lips were twitching uncontrollably now.

"Mrs. Reynolds, I refuse to sit here and listen to you insult me and *my* organization. I demand that you sit down at once."

"Insult you?" Pecola laughed for a moment. "I'm not insulting you. Not yet. I'm just telling you that *I,* and that other *I* over there." She looked and pointed at Symone who was standing, smirking, and taking in all three men's shocked reactions. "We aren't going to do business with your organization. You got that? You aren't a team player, Jefferson. You have the *I* syndrome, and I hate that."

"Whaaat? What do you mean?" Jefferson finally choked out.

"I don't care how much money you have. I don't care how successful this organization is. I don't even care how many deals you have put together for Dickey, Mahon, and Dickey. You have two partners sitting over there. If you have the nerve to say *I* the way you do, then that to me is insulting. *I* is like a curse when you have business partners that are working hard, shuffling, wheeling, and turning deals just like you are. It's like you're acting as if you're the only one who's doing anything effective around here."

"I've never in all my days of doing business sat and listened to such rambling claims that are absolutely unsubstantiated, Mrs. Reynolds," Jefferson stammered as his caramel-complexioned face became hard with an icy, calculating stare. It was if he were mentally counting to ten to not allow himself to become overly angry with his remarks.

"That's because folks were probably too scared of your ass. Humph! That's probably why. It looks like somebody up in here should've said something to you a long damn time ago—at least before now. That's for sure."

Symone tried her best to not break out in a loud, rowdy laugh at Pecola's comments.

"Mrs. Reynolds, I've been running *my* business in Chicago for over twenty-five years, and *I* don't recall ever—"

"There you go again with another *I.* To me, *I* is a curse, Jefferson," Pecola said tiredly as she leaned slightly over the table in Jefferson's direction. "When you say *I* the way you do all the time, it's like calling everyone else in here mothafucker. It's like they don't even exist."

Now Jefferson's eyes almost bulged out of his face. Colin and Clinton's breath caught in their throats. Symone was amazed they weren't responding any more to Pecola's brutally honest words.

"Whoop dee do! That's right I said it. *Mothafucker.* What difference does it makes, especially with the way you sling the word *nigger* around here at all your employees. You wouldn't say MF in a meeting, so don't say niggers. So don't say *I,* either. Do *you* think only you made this company what it is today? You, you, and you," Pecola illustrated calmly as she pointed to all three men now.

"This is outrageous," Jefferson blurted.

"All of yall told us that yall came up with the idea of this firm, and that was a wonderful initial step. But the wheels couldn't churn, wouldn't turn without you three and those fifty or more other people out there on your office floor that you introduced us to today who are chasing papers, coordinating meetings, selling your name, answering the phones, and greeting clients. It can't work with just one person. Sure, very often the owners of a business get all the credit that our employees normally help make possible. I know that. When we came here this morning, we came to meet with three people. Three partners."

Jefferson rose to his feet. Now his face had a chilled, dark mean-looking expression all over it...the one that Pecola and Symone thought they had noticed slightly over cocktails last night.

"I've sat here and patiently listened to you speak on in an appalling manner, Mrs. Reynolds. It was very unprofessional of you and very uncalled for. I have a magnificent opportunity to make big dollars with your organization, and all you can do is ramble on speculatively," Jefferson growled with a slight lisp.

"Big money? Huh. It doesn't matter. Keep it. Find another conference planning company to work with on this project. We damn sure are. When Symone and I realize it's a deal we don't want to shake rock and roll with, it can be the King of England's private banker's, even Trump himself. But we won't go in a tainted corporate bed for any damn money. *Money?* Humph," Pecola said the words in disbelief.

"This has totally gotten out of hand," Jefferson grunted with genuine distaste.

"No it has not. Not yet, it hasn't," Pecola said crisply. "We make enough money every day. You can believe that. Even when we're not working and when we're vacationing, we earn money. That's only because we have people that work hard with us at Meetings Odyssey. It's ain't always about money, Jefferson. Yet, it *is* about money. In order to earn money the right way, it's about principle, integrity, and fairness. It's a *we* thang for us back home in the good ole south. That's how *we* do business in Winston-Salem, North Carolina. It's about working together for a common good. It's called making a big profit with integrity. Then you brag about how we should consider overcharging those perspective clients by padding at least thirty percent over our normal fees because it's a government agency? Hell damn no."

"Uh, Mrs. Reynolds," Colin Mahon mumbled for the first time. He appeared as if he had to glance tentatively over at Jefferson to get approval to speak. "What you're saying—"

"Colin, put a lid on it right now, man," Jefferson huffingly interrupted him and turned to face Pecola. "Mrs. Reynolds, I demand that you sit down and handle yourself like the business-woman I thought you were."

Pecola laughed hysterically for a few seconds. "That's another thing. Don't you *ever* tell me to sit down again or tell me what I can and cannot do. You're talking to the wrong businesswoman." Now Pecola eyes were aloof and steely looking. "Because you know why? In case you have forgotten, Mr. *I* of Chicago, I work for my own self, too. *I* own my business. I thought I would leave you with that. I don't have to dance to your corporate tune shit. We don't want to do business with you. We don't have to do business with you. Since we own our business, we won't do business with you. Don't you forget it, either," she continued while pointing an utterly straight index finger at him.

With those last words, Pecola and Symone grabbed their fur coats and hats from the conference room closet. Both women shook each man's hand very quickly and quite firmly.

"And another thing, Jefferson," Pecola said as she stood at the opened conference room door. "I quite frankly think your last name is spelled with too many letters. You should've changed it by removing the last *e* and *y*. I find that would be more appropriate." She paused for a few seconds.

"How dare you?" Jefferson gasped.

"Gentlemen, do puhleeze have a marvelous day in the windy city," Pecola added sweetly as she and Symone smiled professionally and turned to strut out.

Before Pecola and Symone exited, they made one last, important stop in the bathroom within the Dickey, Mahon, and Dickey's office. Then they left the building. Once down in the silent comfort of the limo, Pecola and Symone burst out laughing. Symone couldn't believe the whole day and continued to slowly shake her head as the review of how ludicrous it all was continued to flash in her mind. Edolphus asked them if they wanted him to drive around for awhile. They told him no. Pecola and Symone wanted to go straight back to the hotel to pick up Alex so that they all could go do a whole lot of shopping.

As the shiny black stretch limo glided through the downtown streets of Chicago, Pecola began comically mimicking what she had said to the three stuffed shirts again. Laughing and falling all over each other, Pecola and Symone laughed until they cried. Edolphus gazed with amusement at them through the rearview mirror. He wondered what was so funny.

Chapter Ninety-Six

"It's the most ignorant thing I've ever seen," Pecola complained as she stormed into the suite's foyer.

"No, yall didn't leave before three," Alex said as she checked her watch. It was a little after two o'clock. She had just finished lunch and walked into the foyer to get the concierge's business card out of her coat pocket.

"Hell, we stayed too damn long if you ask me, chile," Pecola said with an expression of total despair.

"You wouldn't believe how that organization is operated, Alex. Totally unbelievable," Symone explained while throwing her coat on the couch and jerking her hat off. "I don't know what the bottom line is. Why do their employees even stay around? To think his operation is one of best and largest in the country."

"Oh, Lawd. What happened?" Alex wailed and nervously studied them both.

"The question is what didn't happen, chile," Pecola answered. "That Jefferson man is like God to them. It's a slave mentality over there, pure and simple."

"Unbelievable. Wait till I tell Rozelle about this," Symone said as she walked over to the wet bar. "Who would've ever thunk it?"

"I'll tell you in a minute, Alex. Just need to catch my breath first, chile." Pecola swiftly fanned her face with both hands.

"Let Pecola give you all the details," Symone said. "You know how good she is at recapping things. Wanna drink?"

"Yes, chile. One-hundred-twenty proof Vodka. Make mine straight. No ice," Pecola said lazily as she slumped down on the couch. Alex was right beside her, waiting patiently to hear.

"Alex, girl. Let me tell you. First, we had a small meeting with the three partners. That was strange, but Symone and I said we could deal with it. Of course, they told us that their sales and staff meeting was scheduled every Friday at eleven. Naturally, Symone and I wanted to go just to get a feel for the employees, different things like that." Symone walked up and handed the drink to Pecola. "Thanks, chile."

"After that, Alex," Symone said, "everything when downhill."

"Symone's right. We went to the meeting, and get this, Alex. You're not going to believe it. Jefferson called the Black people who work with him niggers the whole time. Just like that," Pecola said as she snapped her fingers several times.

"*Niggers?* Girl, no. Does he only have all Black employees?" Alex asked with wide eyes.

"Hell no! They don't! As a matter of fact, it's about sixty employees there. They got about twenty-three Blacks, if that many, which shocked the hell out of Symone. Me, too."

"It sho damn did. You know how Black folks love that reverse plantation philosophy when they go into business. The more whites working for them, they believe the better the organization. Well, he's a perfect Harvard case study for that," Symone said with mild disgust as she sipped cognac and sank deeper into the couch.

"Jefferson strutted around in the front like a damn peacock," Pecola went on. "Clean as ten tacks, too. They meet in this big planning room every Friday. You should've heard him. Now keep in mind this is the same brother who had all this intellectual rambling going on last night over cocktails. I told yall. It was the eye blinking thang."

"I believe you, Pecola," Symone interjected as she sipped Courvoisier VSOP. Alex was listening to them both with intense interest.

"Today my man broke it way down—way down deep into the hood, Alex," Pecola said. "He strutted around up there in the front of the conference room. Talking a mile a minute, he was supposedly motivating his staff. Then he began talking about how 'niggers steal from me.' He said, 'You, Black people. That's right. You Black people steal from me. Yall come to work at eight-forty-five, and yall suppose to be here at eight-thirty.'"

"Whaaat," Alex cried out.

"I was there," Symone said. "That's exactly what he said."

"'Yall punch in, but what do yall do? Yall go straight to the bathroom, comb your hair, drink coffee for a long time, talk to each other, eat your sausage and biscuit breakfast, and *you* might finally get to work around nine-thirty or so. Now the white people that work here what do they do? They get here on time each and every day. When they get here, they get busy right away. You niggers in here be stealing from me.'"

"No he didn't say those things, giiiirrrl," Alex exclaimed.

"It gets better, Alex," Symone insisted and gulped a huge mouthful of cognac.

"That's what the brother said, but let me finish. He said, 'That's what all yall niggers do.' Keep in mind, he was speaking specifically to all the Black people, Alex. 'Niggers stealing from me. You Black folks go to your churches all the time. What yall niggers do all that shouting and whooping for? The preacher ain't shouting. He ain't doing nothing but collecting the money. I'm about making money.'" Pecola took a swig of vodka.

"So what did his partners say?" Alex inquired with a frown. She was horrified.

Pecola shook her head from side to side. "Umph, umph, umph, umph."

"Nothing. Not a damn thing." Symone spoke slowly. "They're nothing but stone to the bone Black corporate wimps. That's all, girl. I've seen a lot of them in my day. But those two brothers? Humph. By far, they are the worst case scenario of weak, spineless, corporate yes men."

"That's awful," Alex mumbled.

"I know," Symone agreed quickly. "I guess as long as they're making money, they figure they'll go along with the successful program. Why change things? I always said that in order for Black folks to be successful in white corporate America, you literally have to sell your soul to the devil. You got to compromise and accept so much garbage to just belong. The same applies over there at Dickey, Mahon, and Dickey. It's just in reverse. Umph, umph, umph, umph, umph."

"My girl is right," Pecola added. "Colin Mahon had the nerve to come to me and Symone. Here was Symone now ready to storm up to the front of the conference room and raise holy hell. Of course, I calmed her down. You know a little pat on the knee every now and then."

"That's good," Alex moaned.

"Still, a dumb Colin comes over and has the damn nerve to tell us that Jefferson doesn't mean no harm. He talks like that to make the Black workers strong and to get them to be good workers."

"Whaaat?" Alex exclaimed.

"You think I'm lying?" Pecola said and began to laugh.

"I asked Colin in what area can that kind of talk make a Black person strong and to puhleeze let me know specifically," Symone said.

"Sy was polite about it," Pecola went on. "He was *actually* calling Black folks niggers in front of all those white people, Alex."

Alex was speechless. The more she listened, her face became grim.

"Damn sho did, Alex," Symone nodded.

"Colin told us to not worry about Jefferson because he's a wonderful person once you get to know him." Pecola laughed in disbelief. "He's a savvy businessman and a millionaire. I think they all are. Colin *actually* said that to us. Jefferson sho nuff—sho nuff praised those white folks the whole time. It's obvious he loves the ground they walk on up in there, chile."

"I can't believe this," Alex said.

"All the white folks up there in that conference room were sitting in their chairs acting mighty high, tall, and feeling real great about themselves cause this dumb Black man who owns the company is just giving them power and preference," Pecola said, still disgusted. "Jefferson never talked down to the white people. Not one time, Alex. But he talked to the Black folks like damn dogs."

"That's when I told Pecola that if he says *nigger* one more time up in here, I'm out of here. I walked out and went to the bathroom. Ten minutes later, we went to lunch. That's why I think he's a bastard born from hell. Excuse my French, Alex," Symone purred sincerely. "This planned partnership would've been the worst mistake we ever could've made. You never see shit like this until you do site visits. Sometimes, discontent in a company isn't even obvious during on-site visits."

"Totally unbelievable. If I didn't know, I would almost say you were making it up," Alex confessed reasonably.

"I know, Alex. It *should* be made up," Symone said. "I bet the white people think he's a stupid ass, too. You can imagine how we felt actually sitting through that. I can just about take anything, but someone calling me a nigger like that to my face in front of a group of white people? Oh no, girl. If I was one of his Black employees, it would be time to rumble."

"For me, too," Pecola said, twisting her neck in signature fashion.

"Jefferson was strutting around saying 'Yall niggers this, and yall niggers that. Yall niggers are just stealing from my company. That's the way all Black people are. Like bananas, bunches of niggers together ain't nothing.' Those were his actual words." Symone stopped a moment and shook her head incredulously.

"I'm listening, girl," Alex urged her on.

"Wooo! I got to hand it to him," Symone said after she closed her eyes momentarily. "He's a bold motha. Most people would've changed their presentation around. Not him. He's a stone trip. If he did it today, and we were visiting from another organization, then the brother definitely believes in consistency. He evidently trusts that what he's saying is ok. That's how cocky he is. Maybe he thought we would approve of that garbage since we were from North Carolina and all. Hell! I don't know, girl."

"Get—out—of—here." Alex didn't know what else to say.

"We're telling you the truth, Alex. Would we lie to you?" Symone drawled and took another swig. "You know their employees must be miserable. What do they do? They need jobs. He hired them. They stay and suffer through it. I mean really. You know it must be an enormous amount of sadness behind those office doors. This is a successful Black man talking like this, Alex. That's what hurt me to my heart. I told Pecola to hell with the contract. I'm out of here. This was one time Pecola was ready to leave before me. Then the brother can barely talk worth shit, either. Jefferson has some sort of lisp or whatever."

Suddenly Symone's lilting, loud laughter filled the living room. Alex and Pecola began laughing as well.

"You can tell that he's worked real hard on his speech, Symone," Pecola explained. "It only comes out every now and then, girl. Don't be mean. That's probably why he pontificates a lot, honeychile. Therefore, you won't notice it as well."

"True. It's still there, girl," Symone pointed out. "I certainly heard the word *nigger* clearly and enough to last me a lifetime. Every time I see him at another meeting and planning conference, you can believe I'm going to turn my head and walk the other way. I don't want to hear three syllables he has to say."

"When he sees you again, he probably *won't* be able to say three syllables," Pecola joked and Symone cackled loudly once more while Alex just shook her head slowly at her friend's wit.

"Yall two are very bad." Alex couldn't help from smiling. "Ain't no good atall. Yall know that, don't you?"

"It doesn't stop there, Alex," Pecola said, still giggling. "The stone, super bitch is his wife. She's seems to be a worse bitch than Symone."

"Thank you, girl." Symone smiled and nodded. "I thought so too."

"*His wife?* She's worse than Sy, and she works up there with them?" Alex asked and winked at Pecola.

"Thank you for the compliment, Alex," Symone said with a wink. "Thanks much."

"Wooo!" Alex groaned. "That's deep. What's his wife doing there?"

"She's over marketing or something." Pecola got up and walked out into the foyer for her briefcase. She strolled back into the living room reading the woman's business card. "According to this, she's the senior vice-president of quality control."

"She's got the *quality* going on up in the camp for real," Symone said. "That's why Clinton and Colin are *controlled.* Maybe they're just figureheads or something because sergeant sister girl rules around that office with a George Foreman iron left fist. You can believe that. You can't get supplies or nothing unless she gives them to you. She told us that. She was proud to say that they don't have corporate pilferage in any form around there. Probably not. The employees think they're already in prison. Why steal and have to go to another one? When we spoke to her, her nose was so high in the air, I'm still surprised she didn't choke on her own spit."

"You're right, Sy," Pecola agreed. "When we first got there, she slyly looked at my coat. I know my coordination was kicking. Then she looked at Symone's coat, and I was like 'Whassup with all this surveying? We're here to do business.'"

"It's kind of flashy looking," Alex teased lightly.

"Thank you. Thank you. We aim to puhleeze," Symone said with a southern accent.

"Hmmm. Jefferson must think he's white," Alex sighed suddenly. "What color is he?"

"Well, he's not as Black as Symone," Pecola said. "He certainly ain't as light-skinned as me. He's a more of a dark caramel complexion—a brown-skinned colored man. More brown than you, Alex."

Symone chuckled at Pecola's description. "He's a smooth one now. Impeccable dresser and tall," Symone outlined. "I would never expect this. You would think he was a strong Black man selling himself and the attributes of his company. He's nothing more than a smooth salesman if you ask me. That's all, and I never liked smooth salesmen, either. I just think people like him give Black-owned businesses a bad name."

"Not necessarily, Sy. How would other people know about it? Yall thought it was a good opportunity," Alex said sensibly.

"True. Good point," Symone agreed quietly.

"Jefferson brags a lot, Alex. It was I, I, I, all day long. His two partners just sat there very quietly. You know I'm sure Chicago has a lot of Black organizations that need help. Since he talked about his philanthropic deeds so damn much, I asked which ones he supported. Not one Black one, girl. Not one. He said his fifteen and twenty thousand dollar donations go to organizations in his community. The brother lives in a white affluent community in Chicago, so you can see why a Black organization wouldn't get a dime from him. What about all the Black organizations in Chicago that need help."

"He told you this?" Alex asked.

"No. He didn't say that exactly, Alex," Symone said and paused briefly.

"Don't jump to conclusions," Alex reminded her.

"I'm not. He did brag about how he lives in this mostly white community with all these white athletes who play pro basketball and football for Chicago. And he did share the names of the organizations he gives money to. They certainly didn't sound Black to me. I know you can't go by that. I wrote them down. When I get back home, I'm gonna go on-line and research all of them just to see. Maybe I'll do that even before I leave. It's a disgrace how some Black people act. It was all I could take without throwing up in his face."

"Wooo, girl," Alex moaned. "I'm surprised you and Pecola took it as long as you did."

"The brother must have lost his mind, Alex," Symone continued. "As we were leaving, he had the nerve to try and stop us in the reception area. There we were minding our own business, trying to leave that godforsaken place. We had just left the bathroom. Quite frankly,

I think he was a little perturbed about what Pecola said about his last name, which was certainly an appropriate observation to me."

"Thank you. Thank you, chile," Pecola gushed. "I thought so, too."

"By then, I was ready to let him have it with all I had." Symone carefully placed her empty glass on the coffee table.

Alex was smiling as she asked, "What did you say, girl?"

"Believe me. I was chilling but nice. Through clenched teeth, I quietly told Jefferson eyeball to eyeball that he better be glad I don't like icy, cold weather. Because if I did, I would move my nigger self to Chicago. Buy the damn office building. Evict his ass the next damn day. Open up the same business. *And* hire all of his employees to show them what it's like to work for Black folks whom are sensible and practical. I'd show them how an employer definitely would appreciate their Monday through Friday due diligence. I sho would, Alex."

"That's what she told him," Pecola continued. "Jefferson started to argue, that is until he saw the heartlessly mean expression on Symone's face. Some of his inquisitive employees were walking through the reception lobby. I guess he wanted to act like him and Symone were talking about pleasant business. By then I think they had gotten a whiff of something going on up in that place with the two North Carolina visitors."

"I *would* hire every last one of those people. Humph! I still might do it anyway," Symone said and reflectively leaned back on the couch.

"What type of employees would stay in such a place as that? So sad," Alex said thoughtfully with concerned eyes.

"Check this out, Alex," Pecola said. "During our lunch, I frankly asked him about his employees, too. I was specifically referring to the small number of Black folks working with him. At that time, Symone and I knew we weren't going to do dittly with them. We were just figuring out when we were going to make our grand exit. First, he looked at me for a long time, swallowed a piece of his filet mignon, then he spoke with that damn lisp. It wasn't too covered up then. Maybe because he was eating and food was sticking in his false teeth. I don't know. Anyway, he was sounding a bit more like Buckwheat's eldest baby boy to me."

"Giiiirrrrl! You're too crazy," Symone laughed at Pecola and swallowed cognac.

"Wooo, chile! I'm serious now," Pecola went on, laughing. "He said, 'Well, I think that's a touchy situation, Mrs. Reynolds.' He was still going there with that lisp thing, yall. 'I looked at my company's needs, and some of my Black people didn't fit it, Mrs. Reynolds. They weren't capable or weren't the right person for the job. They weren't qualified in computer skills or were the high-level type quality person I needed. So when we have openings, I don't look specifically for Black people.'"

"I bet not," Alex said loudly.

"That's what I said. You mean to tell me you can't find more qualified Black people in Chicago?" Symone asked as she sat straight up again. "Give me a break. You aren't looking for any. If we can find exceptional Black folks in Winston-Salem and all over North Carolina, I sure know that they can be found in a big city like Chicago that has all these Black folks. A bunch of intelligent ones, too. Puhleeze."

"Let me finish, chile," Pecola said. "Jefferson said, 'Now qualified people are the key for me, Mrs. Reynolds. Whether that person tends to be Black or white, it doesn't matter. Whoever can do the job. I only go to those qualified people. The ones who can do the job.'"

"The nigger should run for president," Symone muttered. "He would fit right in the political and tactical structure of things. Politicians are known for selling the glitz. Lawd only knows what in the hell goes on behind the scenes. We would probably cry if we saw the real deal in the back room offices of Washington."

Alex shook her head hopelessly. "You see there. Uh huh. There you go saying *that* word, Sy."

Symone shrugged indifferently. "I know I said nigger, Alex. I'm just saying it around you two. Just like I do around my friends back home in North Carolina. You ain't never ever seen me bust up in any place and say it in public."

"Me neither, chile," Pecola added.

"Things like that confuse some people," Alex went on. "Mama never used the word. Nanette and I would get a tight, twisting pinch on our mouths even if we did slip and say it for any reason."

"Nanette must've forgotten about all those mouth twists because she sho nuff says it now," Symone shot back.

"Alex, puhleeze," Pecola pleaded. "When *we* say it, *we* know what *we* mean."

"Still, Pecola. After today, yall should be careful how you use it—even amongst friends. That's for sure," Alex instructed carefully.

"We absolutely can't say it around my mummy," Symone said. "She'll not tolerate the word *nigger* coming out our mouth in any form."

"Yall see what I'm saying," Alex pointed out.

"Enough of this," Pecola sighed. "We done wasted too much time already on those stupid ass people."

"You're right, girl," Symone said. "In spite of all of that, I still love this city. I do. To deal with the cold, I gots to think about myself parasailing on the calm waters of Bora Bora. I sho do. It's just too damn cold, girls." All three began a medley of animated laughter. "I'm definitely going to bring the children back here sometime in April for their spring educational trip. They would love it. I know Jared would adore the science museums."

"Fine, fine, fine. Enough talking. I'm ready to go shopping," Pecola exclaimed cheerfully. "It's time to shop till we drop."

"I agree. Edolphus took me by the different antique shopping areas today. He says there's a whole lot more out there," Alex informed them. "I figure we could go do regular shopping this afternoon. Tonight, we'll tell Edolphus to take us to a nice soul food restaurant. Then tomorrow, let's throw on some dungarees and spend all day antique shopping, girls."

"That's fine with me, Alex. Whatever we find, we can simply have it shipped back to North Carolina," Symone said softly as she began unbuttoning her long-sleeve blouse.

"Wooo, chile. I just love it. Just love it!" Pecola exclaimed. She suddenly jumped off the couch and began comically cabbage patching around the living room just like a Rozelle prodigy. She was feeling ecstatic about the high expectations of the shopping delights she would later discover along Chicago's Magnificent Mile.

Chapter Ninety-Seven

When Pecola, Alex and Symone returned from Chicago, they had their private Christmas dinner with Scott at the Zevely House Restaurant in Old Salem. Shortly after, Symone left for New York with her children. The other friends left town to spend the Christmas holidays in their respective cities with family. The remainder of December zoomed by, and before Pecola knew it, another New Year blew in just as quickly. After shopping without a care for cost for Christmas for both her family and friends, the after affects of the holiday season gone by were always a depressing letdown for Pecola. Since it was January and now very cold outside, Pecola resorted to her favorite pastimes: reading, working, and eating meals in the comfort of her bedroom.

An hour after Pecola finished eating an early dinner on a clear, chilly second Tuesday in January, she went upstairs to her bedroom and built a toasty, warm fire. Her last meeting this afternoon at Meetings Odyssey ended at two. When the meeting was adjourned, Pecola simply told Symone that she was heading home. On Monday evening, Pecola, Symone, and Ted had taken a late flight back from a one-day trip to visit with Knoxville College representatives in Knoxville, Tennessee. Pecola was tired and wanted to get some needed rest

Once in the confines of her house, Pecola slipped into a black, stretch velvet unitard and slippers while she listened to the harmonizing old school sounds of The Drifters, The Platters, and The Coasters. As Pecola stared absentmindedly outside in the yard past the covered swimming pool and into the distance, Alex called her. Pecola was glad. She needed the jolt. Her thoughts had lassoed her and were quickly hurdling her toward depression. Pecola had a delightfully animated conversation with Alex, who was now faring considerably better about Aunt Susie Mae's death.

Even though the three friends had been back from Chicago several weeks now, Alex continued to rave about the wonderful five nights she spent there with Pecola and Symone. By the time they left Chicago on Tuesday morning, all three of them had discovered antique pieces and other quaint finds on their shopping sprees and had them shipped back to North Carolina.

About thirty minutes after Pecola finished speaking with Alex, the shrilling ring of the telephone startled her. This time, she was so totally engrossed in the book that she was reading that the normal, piercing ring made her jump with fear.

"Hello." Pecola's voice was flat.

"Hi, Mama," her daughter, Elizabethe, said cheerfully.

"Hey, baby chile!" Pecola answered suddenly, just as enthusiastically. While Pecola spoke, she continued to slowly read the last paragraph of chapter eight in *History Laid Bare*, Ujima's selection for January.

"I just called to say Birtha and I got a *big* part in *The Umoja Tree*. It's the new Black musical opening on Broadway. It's due to open toward the end of this year, and rehearsals start in a month, Mama," Elizabethe gushed, obviously excited.

Elizabethe and her friend, Birtha Ann Lowery, now lived together in a two-bedroom apartment on Manhattan's Upper Westside. Birtha's parents, Dr. and Mrs. Lowery, had purchased one of the ten-acre lots Carlos sold to their Black friends years ago when he first discovered the one-hundred and fifty acres for his family. Friends since sixth grade, Elizabethe and Birtha were both struggling actresses. The two continually auditioned together for roles in plays, movies, and whatever cattle calls they found out about in the trade newspapers.

"Can you believe that, Mama?" Elizabethe went on. "I *finally* got a good role."

"That's great, Elizabethe."

"Fatima Robinson is the lead choreographer."

"Oh really." Pecola wasn't familiar with the name.

"She's famous, Mama."

"Good. I'm sooo glad to hear about your new part, baby. I always knew you could do it," Pecola said proudly as she smiled to herself.

Pecola didn't ask for details about the part. The last time Elizabethe told them she received a *big* role in a play, FOFAE and their dates traveled to New York for opening night. Pecola needed a pair of super sonic binoculars just to find her daughter who appeared in the chorus line for a hot sixty seconds, if that long.

"Mama, let me speak to Daddy. I want to tell him, too." Elizabethe talked with such a musically, vibrant spark in her voice. As if reading her mother's mind, she thought of something else and spoke quickly. "This time I received fourth billing, Mama."

"Chile, that's absolutely great." Pecola paused a moment and placed the book face down in her lap. "Your father is in Washington, DC. He and your Uncle Rico are working on a deal with the federal government and will be back on Thursday night."

"When you speak to him tonight, tell Daddy my good news. Ok?"

After twenty-four years of marriage, Elizabethe knew that whenever her parents were out of town, they still called each other every single evening to say their good nights and I love yous.

"When he calls later, I'll definitely tell him the good news, baby."

"Anyway, we're going to Atlantic City to celebrate. Wish us luck, Mama," Elizabethe said breathlessly. She was glad to have finally celebrated her twenty-first birthday two weeks ago, and now she was itching to live in the adult world and do things that had been denied her so long.

"I wish you all the luck in the world, baby. Take out ten bucks and play the dollar machine for me. If I win, you make sure you give me my money," Pecola said teasingly with a short laugh.

"Ok I will," Elizabethe replied, giggling.

"Go to Trump Plaza, baby. Whenever we're in Atlantic City, that's where we play our slot machines every time. Remember? That's where I won a thousand dollars last year."

Elizabethe smiled. "Ok, Mama. Tell Tantes Alex, Symone, and everybody else hello. Don't forget my Uncle Scott. I spoke to CJ and Haneef right after they called home on Saturday. As usual, they're doing fine."

Pecola was glad that her three children continued to be extremely close even though they lived in separate cities and basically saw one another during the holidays or during other special family occasions.

"Who's this Athena girl that CJ mentioned?" Elizabethe asked, and Pecola sat straight up. "Is that the same girl he met at the children's opening ceremony last summer?"

"Uh, I think so. It's nothing. Just a passing fancy."

"Well, I don't know. CJ sounded pretty serious about her to me, Mama. That's all he talked about."

"Hazele told me that you and your friends came to her restaurant for dinner a couple of times last week," Pecola said, changing the subject.

"Yeah. It was me, Birtha, and two of my other girlfriends. Tante Hazele served us so much Trinidadian curry chicken, roti, and rice and peas. Wooo! And everything else I can't remember the names of. Then she gave us a huge doggie bag to take home, Mama. I like her so much. It's amazing how she looks just like my Tante Symone, just a little shorter, though."

"I know, baby. I'm just glad you have her looking after you up there. People just act so cold in New York, baby. It's so different from down here."

"Not everybody, Mama. Don't worry. Birtha and I are fine."

"Symone wants to know if you'll be home for her fortieth birthday dinner at our house? I told her I would ask you. She'll probably call you. You know how she is. Just remember to tell her you can't make it for that evening and come the following week for the party. Ok?"

"Don't worry. When she calls, I'll play along. I definitely will be there for her surprise party in two weeks. Tante Hazele said Birtha and I could probably fly down with their family. Once we start rehearsing in a month, I won't be able to get away as often."

"I understand, baby. It takes time and energy to put those Broadway shows together. Just come when you can."

"You know I will," Elizabethe sighed and motioned to Birtha she was getting off the phone. "I got to go now, Mama. Remember that I love you. Bye."

"Baby, I love you, too. Tell Birtha hello for me. Remember to be careful and stay safe," Pecola said tenderly and marveled at the good times Elizabethe must be having.

Pecola gently put the phone down. She glanced at the crackling fireplace and thought about Elizabethe as she walked idly toward the French doors. There she gazed out at the barren trees in the backyard, chewed on her bottom lip, and held back tears. Pecola was excited for her daughter. If she were honest with herself, she would admit that she was also a little jealous of the life Elizabethe now enjoyed. By the time Pecola was Elizabethe's age, she had three babies and her own dreams didn't have space to live. The entertainment career Pecola so desperately wanted was definitely placed on the back burner of simply living, fighting, and scrambling through life. Pecola realized that Elizabethe was living the life that Pecola had constantly dreamed about for herself—singing and dancing in the Broadway theaters of New York.

Pecola laughed quietly and slowly glanced around her luxuriously decorated massive master bedroom. She tried hard not to cry, to not shed tears about the dreams she fantasized about as a young girl singing at Dudley High School in Greensboro. Her coveted Motown dreams, one of many dreams that had escaped her—had been stolen from her. As Pecola grew older, she began to discover the truth about life. She knew that she could never ever retrieve those dreams, either. It was time for Pecola to take a break from the memories that seemed to choke her. They were trying to lasso her thoughts again. She walked back to the bed, picked up the book, and began reading once more.

Trump Plaza was bubbling with excitement, and people were crawling everywhere. The gamblers were dressed in a variety of colorful outfits that matched the vast room's assortment of white, red, and yellow lights flashing. The continuous clanging sounds of bells and whistles from the different winning jackpot machines made you think that this was your lucky night. Elizabethe paused to take in the scene of rows and rows of tuxedo outfitted dealers, slot machines, players, and scantily clad waitresses prancing around serving what Elizabethe assumed were watered-down cocktails.

Elizabethe had the five-hundred dollars she received as a birthday gift from her Tante Alex. Now, she wanted to use a part of that money to try beginner's luck at the blackjack table. It was the game her father had taught CJ, Haneef, and Elizabethe when she was twelve years old. Elizabethe was certainly glad that she had finally turned twenty-one and could gamble. But first, she wanted to browse a moment and get vibes for the right, lucky table her father told her to always be on the lookout for.

For about ten minutes, Elizabethe and Birtha strolled casually around, looking here and there for just the perfect seat. The two young girls took time to stand behind current players to see how the dealers were working the cards. In the movies, Elizabethe saw how beautiful women stood behind their men while they gambled, and she was surprised to see the same thing actually occurring in full living color in Atlantic City. Elizabethe continued to wait for the special feeling that her father told her would hit and guide her feet to the exact winning spot. So far, Elizabethe hadn't noticed any tingling vibes rippling through her bones, and she decided to settle for the blackjack table she spotted on the other side of the floor.

Suddenly, Elizabethe stopped walking and stared across the huge room. Birtha's eyes were focused in the same direction, but she couldn't see a thing clearly since she had just purchased a pair of inexpensive contacts to make her eyes an amber color. Half the time, Birtha couldn't see straight with them in. Elizabethe immediately became nauseous, and she realized that she needed to urgently vomit somewhere—anywhere as the awful bile was quickly rising in her throat. With her hands over her mouth, Elizabethe turned abruptly and went running, bumping into people searching for a lady's room.

"What is it? What's wrong, girl?" Birtha yelled trying to keep up with her.

When Elizabethe finally stumbled into the bathroom, all of the stalls were occupied. She couldn't hold the vomit in any longer and immediately threw up in one of the sparkling clean sinks. Several women looked at her in disgust and assumed the young Black woman was drunk.

"What is it, Elizabethe? Are you ok?" Birtha asked nervously as she gently rubbed her right hand up and down her friend's stiff back. Birtha snatched several white paper towels from the dispenser and wiped her friend's clammy forehead. Elizabeth was so weak now that Birtha had to help her walk over to lean on a stool in the corner.

"Elizabethe!" Birtha cried as she held Elizabethe's face in one hand. With the other hand, Birtha quickly wiped under Elizabethe's chin and her spotted silk blouse. Vomit had splattered everywhere and had stained Elizabethe's new and favorite Tracey Reese black cashmere jacket that her Tante Symone had given her as a birthday gift.

"What's going on in here?" an old, white woman asked loudly.

Dressed in a black and gray uniform with white stripes, there was a Trump nametag above her left breast. She carried a bucket filled with plastic bottles of pink-looking disinfectant. After she carefully surveyed the vomit in the sink and on the floor, she coldly glared at the two young Black women standing in the corner.

"My friend got sick all of sudden, ma'am," Birtha replied in a voice full of fear. "We might need to call an ambulance—"

"You people! You people just expect to come here and make it dirty like—" the woman snarled while looking at Elizabethe and Birtha with a disgusted expression.

Birtha twirled around to face her. "Ex—cuse—me! What did you just say?" *Miss Senior Citizen, you don't want me to read you here this day!* Birtha thought angrily.

The older woman briefly observed Birtha for a moment and noticed that anger was flashing in her funny colored eyes. She decided to keep any negative words she had about Black people to herself because the woman believed that Birtha looked like she wouldn't stand for insulting comments from Jesus Christ himself. Two ladies with teased platinum blonde hair heard the older woman's words and stood to the side to see what would happen next.

"Uh, the bathroom—" the woman mumbled.

"I don't think you *even* want to go there," Birtha warned. Since Birtha's parents taught her to honor elderly people, no matter who they were, Birtha used a tone that was stern but not too disrespectful.

"We can't allow this sort—" the older woman said, looking around, not sure if she should finish the sentence.

"If you work here, I expect you do need to do your job and not interfere in affairs you don't know anything about, ma'am." Birtha's voice was hard as steel. "My best friend is very sick. You can believe that I have no problem in reporting to *my* father's golfing buddy and *my* godfather, my Uncle Donald, how you've treated me in his place of business."

"Humph," the old woman moaned under her breath. She quickly turned around and left mumbling other words to herself.

As the blondes loudly snapped their peppermint chewing gum, they congratulated Birtha on the way she handled the incident. They then asked her to puhleeze say hello to her uncle the next time they were together. Birtha just looked at the two blonde women in disbelief. *Crazy ass bimbos,* thought Birtha and swiftly turned her attention back to Elizabethe who had been quietly crying the whole time.

"What's wrong, girl?" Birtha asked again looking at her friend. She raised Elizabethe's chin so she could stare her in the eyes.

"I can't believe it," Elizabethe murmured longing to run away. She took a long labored sigh.

"Believe what, girl?" Birtha asked with all the patience she could muster. She took her hand from Elizabethe's face and placed it along with the other one on her shoulders. At this point, Birtha was ready to shake what was wrong out of her.

"Damn, Elizabethe! What's wrong? You look like you've seen a ghost or something or worse."

"It was worse, Birtha," she whispered through her crying. Her eyes wandered a moment. "I saw—I believe I saw a woman hugging my father's neck at the blackjack table."

Now, it was time for Birtha's hands to frantically cover her mouth.

"Your father? What the hell would he be doing here? I thought you said that he was in DC. Girl, this is deep! Are you sure that was your father?" she gushed with wide eyes. *Mr. Reynolds with another woman! Oh my God!* Birtha thought in total shock.

"Birtha, I know my Daddy anywhere. I believe that was him. I'm one-hundred percent sure of it." Elizabethe spoke sadly and slowly wiped her eyes with the back of her hands. "But I want to go and look again to be positive. Maybe it was my Uncle Rico. They do look a lot alike you know, like twins."

"You're right, Elizabethe. They do. Check again. That would be a good idea, girl."

Elizabethe stood up and carefully washed her face. By then, the older woman had returned and was quietly cleaning the sink, walls, and floor. Birtha and Elizabethe left the bathroom and returned to the blackjack tables area. In the event it was her father, Elizabethe told Birtha that she wanted to be very careful not to be spotted by him.

I guess any child would find it uncomfortable to confront the reality of a parent's sexual life. And I'm no different, Elizabethe thought pensively.

Elizabethe suddenly saw visions of her father making love with that real dark woman. The mental picture reminded her of the pornographic videos she watched one day after she found them carefully hidden in her parents' bedroom closet. Since Elizabethe was still a virgin, she could only draw on those visions of pornographic movies and on what she heard from Birtha and her other friends. The mental picture of her father and that other woman moaning and grunting almost made her nauseously sick again. Right now, one of the worst things in the world would be to find out that either one of her parents was running around with somebody else.

Elizabethe took another deep, labored breath. Now, she and Birtha watchfully moved four rows over and gingerly walked up to an aisle to get a better view of the blackjack gamblers. As Elizabethe carefully peered between the slot machines, she spotted the man and woman again. She was shocked! It *was* her father! Elizabethe couldn't believe her eyes. As Elizabethe and Birtha discreetly watched from behind the safety of the slot machines, Elizabethe clearly saw her father's face. After winning a big blackjack hand, Carlos laughed proudly and slowly nodded his head in triumph. Then Carlos quickly turned to kiss a very tall, beautifully dark-skinned woman that stood quite regally behind him.

Chapter Ninety-Eight

On the drive back to New York, Birtha and Elizabethe were extremely quiet in the car. To still the conflicting thoughts about her father, Elizabethe finally steered her apple red BMW convertible off the interstate over to a rest stop. The BMW was the car her parents had gotten for her twenty-first birthday, and now she was feeling mixed up about the gift she thought had been given to her by parents she thought was absolutely devoted to one another. A brilliant variety of thousands of thoughts were zooming through her mind—thoughts about family, gifts, birthdays, death, love, and life. Elizabethe needed to think. It was necessary for her to relax her head, which at this point felt like it was about to explode. She didn't know what to do, but Elizabethe knew that if she told her mother what she saw, it would destroy their family.

Then Elizabethe thought that maybe she should tell her Tante Symone. Yet, she was quite afraid to discuss it with her as well. They were all like family, Tante Symone, Tante Alex, Uncle Scott, and her mother. Elizabethe laughed wryly to herself. Now she knew that Symone would probably want to kick her father's ass, then go find that dark Black woman and do the same thing to her. Not only would Symone do that, but if her mother ever found out about her father, she would be in danger of going to prison. The two of them were feisty by themselves, but when they were together, their controversial air was definitely overpowering. On the other hand, Elizabethe assumed her Tante Alex would verbally beat them up. By the time she finished talking to her daddy, he would plead with her to just go ahead and flog him with a whip.

Elizabethe smiled to herself as she considered her mother's very protective friends. Finally, she realized what she had to do. She decided to keep what she saw in Atlantic City to herself. Since Elizabethe was a little girl, she had practiced keeping quiet about certain things that happened in her life. And she consequently carried a major burden through childhood to adolescent and now into womanhood. Seeing her father with that woman jolted Elizabethe's mind to the awful tragedy that occurred in her family when she was just a little girl. And that burden was still awfully heavy for her to carry. But she did it.

It *was* Elizabethe who convinced her baby sister, Marva, to ride their bikes together. Even though Marva pouted and said that she didn't feel like it at the time, Elizabethe pressed forward. Marva was nine and shared love with others as if she were nineteen. She was quietly reading and writing stories in her bedroom, which was a Saturday morning ritual for the precocious child. After Marva listened intently to Elizabethe's persuasive reasons why they should go bike riding, Marva smiled widely at her older sister and agreed to go outside for just a little while. Then she carefully checked her new Mickey Mouse watch. With Marva's green eyes flashing in her chocolate brown round face, she firmly told her sister that she would play with her for only one whole hour. She could only do it for that long because she needed to come back and finish the mockingbird love story she was writing about her mama and daddy, and she needed more time to finish the tale so that her parents could read it when they got home. Elizabethe gently hugged her little sister and said that would be just fine with her. The memory of the idyllic love that she and her sister believed her parents shared stung like burning fire under her skin.

All of Pecola and Carlos' children were smart, but Marva was the creative genius of the family. Only nine years old, Marva had received all kinds of academic certificates and awards confirming the intelligence of the Reynolds' fourth and youngest child. Since she constantly heard her parents talk about their alma mater, Marva often told her mother and father that she wanted to go to college at A&T, just like them. And she wanted to be an astronaut. With Marva's perfect high A grades in math and science, her schoolteachers proudly told Carlos and Pecola that those dreams were quite realistic for the gifted little girl.

Elizabethe and Marva had been riding their bikes all Saturday morning and were heading back home to have lunch. The Reynolds' regular housekeeper was out of town for a week, and their Grandma Mercedes agreed to take care of them since Pecola was at A&T completing the last exam to receive her master's degree. Carlos was out reviewing a twenty-five story office building construction site in Monroe, North Carolina that had gone past a major, costly deadline. Since their Grandma Mercedes was preparing the children's favorite meal of chicken and dumplings, she told them to be careful and stay near the house, so they would hear her when she yelled *Yooo-hooo!*

Elizabethe was riding on one side of the quiet, maple and oak lined street; Marva was on the other when they both heard their grandmother yelling that it was time to come in for lunch. As Elizabethe was taught to do by her parents, she stopped peddling her bike and checked the street both ways and made sure there were no cars coming. Then she maturely motioned to Marva to hurriedly cross over. The instant Marva steered her pink bike toward Elizabethe, a car swerved down the black paved road out of control and hit Marva with a vicious force. Elizabethe screamed and watched in horror as her baby sister and bike were thrown in the air, and Marva landed in a bloody heap up the street in front of her. The driver of the late model blue Chrysler then revved the engine, quickly backed up, and immediately left the scene.

The emergency room surgeon told Carlos and Pecola that little Pecola Marva didn't suffer. Death was quick. The car plunged into Marva at a speed of fifty miles per hour and threw her small body sixty feet in the air. She landed on her skull. From the forceful impact of landing against the pavement, her skull was crushed, both legs were broken, and she had massive internal injuries. Two days later, the female driver was apprehended while driving casually through downtown Winston-Salem, and Marva's dry blood was still obvious on the front fender of the car. The woman had no insurance, no license, and no money. She had smartly gone through the judicial system before where she had been arrested for driving under the influence a number of times. Because of both North Carolina and America's very lenient drunk driving laws, she continued to brazenly slip through court unscathed. She never served any time.

The woman had been caught driving drunk in Maryland, Delaware, South Carolina and Florida, but the legacy of agony, pain, and destruction she had reeked on other lives didn't stop with those convictions. It finally stopped abruptly in Winston-Salem. As a result of the key affluence of CR Construction Company in North Carolina, the dedicated workers of Mothers Against Drunk Driving, the unbelievable public outcry, and massive media publicity bombarding the airwaves about the tragic accident, the woman was eventually sent to jail without any opportunity to secure bond. A few months later, she was convicted of vehicular manslaughter and sentenced to serve the maximum prison term.

That didn't matter to the Reynolds family or to Elizabethe. All the child psychologists in the world couldn't remove the heavy burden Elizabethe carried about little Marva. Elizabethe was the one who asked Marva to go outside that day, and Elizabethe never forgave herself. For years, the salty tears, the profound sadness, the grisly nightmares, and Elizabethe's horrific screams continued from that day on. Even sometimes now, Elizabethe awakened during the night in a cold sweat from the guilt of the first family death that Elizabethe believed she caused.

Back then, Elizabethe knew that it was difficult for her mother, and Pecola never truly recovered from her fourth child's death. Pecola was grief-stricken beyond help and cried non-stop about Marva each and every day from the time she was killed to it seemed to three years later. It was as if silk strands of pain were tightly wrapped around Pecola's body, and she couldn't release them, didn't know how to step out of the death-like pain. It sucked her soul, her heart, and her spirit away. Pecola closed herself off from the inside out. Comfort couldn't be found. Pecola couldn't be calmed or soothed, not by her husband or her children. Nor by her close friends or anyone else in the family.

For these many reasons, the Reynolds' friends and children believed that Pecola was going to eventually lose her mind from the overwhelming, drowning river of sadness. Pecola's three other children always quietly suspected Marva was Pecola's favorite child. Marva was Pecola's namesake, and her sparkling personality brought so much joy to the Reynolds' household. So Pecola handling Marva's death in such a traumatic way was understandable to her children, her family, and her friends, yet heartbreaking still. When Marva died, it took Pecola at least a year to even smile again, longer to even leave the house by herself.

Marva's death zoomed like a ripple effect throughout the family. CJ was especially close to his baby sister and always protected her like a hovering eagle. When Marva was killed, the tortured CJ dropped out of school again. He began doing drugs and hanging out with the wrong crowd. Eighteen months later, Ossiris Hopkins, Jr., his best friend was gunned down during a drive-by shooting. As Ossiris' precious blood poured out of his body, CJ held him close to his chest. He pleaded with him, encouraged him, and told him that he could not die.

"...Don't you die on me, man. Puhleeze don't leave me the same way Marva did," CJ pleaded with his friend. But Ossiris died in CJ's arms anyway. His death brutally traumatized CJ, and for the second time in less than two years, he became completely disenchanted with living. Because of the insurmountable, agonizing bitterness CJ held inside, he repeatedly threatened to kill himself, and he often threatened to do it in front of the family. Said that he wanted to splatter his brains right on the kitchen floor while his family watched in horror during their nightly sit-down dinners.

After Pecola met Scott, he was moved by the pitifully sad story of Marva's death and CJ's overwhelming grief. Scott tried to figure out how he could help the Reynolds' family attempt to close the deeply gashing, open wounds of tragedy. At the urgent suggestions of Scott, and then Madison, Carlos invited Romallus to Winston-Salem to visit with the Reynolds family in their sprawling new house. When Romallus came, it was only then that hope began to unsuspectingly unfold for the family. Only then did CJ consider journeying along the path to receive healing from the two staggering deaths. Romallus walked with CJ, talked with him, cried with him, and did whatever was necessary to bring the young man out of his gripping, suicidal abyss of despair.

Uncle Romie, the name Romallus was affectionately called by Elizabethe, Haneef, and CJ, ended up staying in the Reynolds' home for eight months. Romallus was an inspirational blessing not only for CJ but for the entire Reynolds family as well. A straightforward man, Romallus openly shared his own heartbreaking life story about the untimely death of his mother and his two brothers. Because Romallus discussed his slide into drug addiction and homelessness, he was the crucial genesis for helping the entire Reynolds family accept that inexplicable tragedy happens to ordinary and good people.

Just thinking about what her family had been through after Marva's death caused Elizabethe to shiver all over. She suddenly breathed deeply and nervously rubbed her slightly wrinkled brow. After seeing her father with that other woman, her headache was still pounding inside her skull. Now Elizabethe believed that if she told her mother or anyone else for that matter what she just discovered about her father, she would instigate the spiraling effects of another heartbreaking tragedy in the family. That would be the death of the marriage between her parents. To Elizabethe, having that type of an albatross hanging over her head was much heavier then the burden of a kept secret. *No. I can't do it. I can't tell my Mama,* she thought. Elizabethe knew she would have to deal with this herself. She turned to face a worried looking Birtha.

"Are you ok, Elizabethe?" Birtha asked with concern.

Elizabethe laughed nervously. "No, I'm not, girl. I was just thinking about what we saw back there."

"So what ya gonna do?"

"I really don't know, Birtha. I can't say."

"I think you should tell your mother," Birtha coaxed in a very matter of fact tone.

"I could never do that, Birtha. I just can't!" Elizabethe wailed the words in a high-pitched voice and began crying again.

"Somebody needs to tell her," Birtha murmured knowingly. "Shoot! Do you want me to tell her?"

With hands over her ears, Elizabeth looked at her friend and began screaming hysterically at the top of her lungs for a few tense moments.

"All right! All right. I'm sorry, Elizabethe. Lawd, this is deep."

"Don't you *ever* play with me like that, Birtha. Don't *even* think about doing such a thing. . I don't want my mother to *ever* find out. Do you hear me?" she pleaded with Birtha and started crying again.

From all of the talking, crying, and the January cold outside air, the car windows began to fog slightly. Without question, Elizabethe was hurt and disappointed. She was her father's little girl still for he told her that so often. He even said those words to her the last time she spoke with him when he called her on Saturday night. Elizabethe loved him tremendously, and now she wouldn't stop loving him. But to see her father with another woman severely bruised her heart. Before Elizabethe spoke again, there was a long pause as she swiftly blew her nose on dirty tissue Birtha found in her pocketbook.

"Uh, Birtha—" She hesitated. "You know there's a piece in me that wants to hate my father. That does hate him. But it's piled on top of all the love I've had for him for years. Lawd, I'm confused."

"I know, girl. Me too."

"How in the hell could my Daddy do that to my mother?"

"Who knows?" Birtha was quiet for a moment. "I wish I had better answers for you, Elizabethe."

"Are all men like that? I wonder if Uncle Scott, Uncle Rico, Uncle Madison, and all the other men I know are like that—are like my father. Are they men who look like they care for their women, but in the meantime they're screwing other women behind their back?"

"I don't know, Elizabethe."

"Is what my father's doing—is that what all Black men do? Is it what my husband will possibly do when I get married?"

"I clare. I can't say, Elizabethe. I'm the same age as you, and I ain't got any answers. Check with me in ten years, girl." Birtha wanted Elizabethe to smile. She closed her eyes for a moment. "Don't you think your Mama needs to know?"

"No, I don't."

"You remember that time I caught your boyfriend with Lisa. Remember? I told you about Ray Ray back then. Then you saw Kindall at Carver's basketball game all hugged up with that Clementine girl I thought he was messing with, and you told me about his two-timing behind. We always said that we would tell each other if we saw either one of our boyfriends messing with another girl."

"Yeah, we did tell each other that. But that's different—"

"Well, don't you think Mrs. Reynolds needs to know, girl?"

"No, I don't," Elizabethe whispered. "Not right now, Birtha. Uh, I don't know. Puhleeze don't say Mama needs to know again, Birtha. Puhleeze. If it's to be, my mother will find out—although I hope she never does. But I don't want her to find out from me *or* from you. Puhleeze. What you and me saw today, we must keep it a secret until we die."

"Until—we—die?" Birtha repeated slowly. "C'mon, girl. You're getting too carried away. Just chill a little. Ok?" Birtha coaxed as she now tried to fight back tears.

Elizabethe stared at her friend with hurt eyes for a moment. They had been adoring confidantes for so many years.

"I would do the same for you, Birtha—and—and for Dr. Lowery and Mrs. Lowery. You know that would be a secret I would keep in my heart for you. You know I would! It would hurt, but I would," she said in a pitiful, but defiant little girl whiney voice as tears rolled down her face.

Birtha started crying too as she visualized how she would feel if she had seen her father with another woman.

"I don't know what to say."

"We just can't talk about it, Birtha. We can't."

"Ok. Ok. I was just joking, girl," Birtha exclaimed quickly as she wiped her eyes with her hands. "I wouldn't tell Mrs. Reynolds anything. I clare I won't."

Steam engulfed the car windows, and now they couldn't see outside. Birtha took another dirty handkerchief and wiped a circle on the passenger window and peered out. Then she faced a crying Elizabethe and gazed into her eyes for a long moment.

"I promise I won't tell a soul, Elizabethe. On my sister's head, I vow I won't tell," she said apologetically with moist eyes.

Elizabethe glanced away a few seconds and quickly turned to look at her. "Birtha, puhleeze. You don't *even* have a sister!"

"I know. I just wanted you to stop crying," she said calmly with a wide smile as she reached out to hug Elizabethe. The two friends tightly embraced each other. "That's what I'm talking about, Elizabethe. We need to share the love about this thang, girl. That's all. Now you know there ain't nobody, no nothing can't ever come between us, girl. Not even this. You know that, don't you?"

"I do," Elizabethe whispered back fervently. "I sho do know that."

"And another thing, girl—"

"Oh, lawd. Yesss, Birtha."

"Your dried vomit smells like pure divine shit up in here, girl. We need to do something about that. I'm trying to be real and down with this thang, but I'm bout ready to start throwing up on you," Birtha exclaimed laughing.

"I know, girl. I know."

With her nerves a little calmer five minutes later, Elizabethe steered the car back onto the New Jersey Turnpike. However, she still experienced conflicting emotions and felt a combination of anger, fear, and confusion. Birtha squeezed her right hand and gave her a reassuring smile. Elizabethe's eyes quickly darted to the left side view mirror to make sure the merging lane was clear to zoom over, and she returned Birtha's affectionate gaze. Once again, Elizabethe's mind raced at a hundred miles per hour.

Later on tonight, I know what I'll do. I'll call my Auntie Pauletta, Elizabethe thought. Suddenly, Elizabethe shook her head furiously. *Nope, I won't tell her either, but you know who I should tell? Yeah. That's the one. When I go home for Tante Symone's birthday party, that's exactly who I'll tell.*

Chapter Ninety-Nine

When Carlos and Venus Mae Mayfield-French decided to go back upstairs to the presidential suite he reserved at Trump Plaza for their three-day rendezvous, he was ready to make love. But he first wanted to check in with Pecola to tell her that he loved her and to whisper his daily *good night* in her ears. Carlos initially was a little concerned about what Pecola told him, but he quickly dismissed it. Running into Elizabethe in Atlantic City would be like winning the New York lottery. It would be almost impossible. Like pulling the million-dollar jackpot on the slot machines. A one in a ten million sort of chance.

Although Carlos and Venus enjoyed passionate sex before they went downstairs to play blackjack, he was horny for her again. Carlos popped the cork of Dom Perignon. He poured two heaping champagne tulip-shaped glasses full, and he continued to wait. Venus decided that she wanted to slide into something satiny sexy, and Carlos was ready for her. Other than for a red bathrobe that was wide open showcasing his hairy chest and body, he was sitting on the couch naked, legs straddled wide, smoking a Macanudo torpedo cigar while waiting hungrily for her to reappear from the adjoining bedroom.

That was one of the things Carlos loved about Venus. Each time they got together, she always had something extraordinarily exciting concocted to dazzle him. Even though coming to New Jersey was Carlos' surprise birthday present for her, Venus promised him a sexy private strip tease show plus some other wild, freaky deak stuff to show her appreciation. The trip to Atlantic City was a double whammy celebration. It was Venus' birthday, and they were celebrating their one-year anniversary together as lovers. As Carlos sang bass along with the romantic, classic sounds of the O'Jays' *You Got Your Hooks in Me,* he waited for Venus to make her sensual, electrifying grand entrance.

What the hell is she doing in there? he thought as he sipped more champagne.

Whatever it was, Carlos knew it would be worth the wait. He shook his head slowly and smiled widely from anticipation. As Carlos thought about kissing her dark thighs, kissing between her legs, and sucking those cute ten toes again, he licked his wet lips. Carlos believed that Venus possessed one of the baddest bodies he had ever seen on a Black woman in years. And that was the main thing that stood out when Venus introduced herself to him last year at the North Carolina A&T's Alumni Association Homecoming dance held at the Sheraton Four Seasons in Greensboro.

As usual on that particular Friday night, Carlos was minding his business, jiving with the other brothers who had also attended the dance solo. Earlier that day, Pecola had gotten sick with cramps and PMS. Carlos wasn't sure what it was, but Pecola told him that she wasn't interested in going out and thought a restful evening in bed would give her the energy she needed to attend the football game on Saturday afternoon. Carlos had just finished talking to an Alpha frat brother, Sidney Little, and Carlos walked over to the cash bar for another drink. As soon as the bartender handed him a vodka and orange juice, he heard a sexy, husky female voice say a few words over his shoulder.

"Excuse me for a moment. I'd like to just ask you a simple something—"

Slowly, Carlos turned around and confronted one of the world's most spectacular-looking Black women.

"Er, yes ma'am—" he answered politely.

Damn, he thought immediately. *Who in the hell is this? She's blacker than the ace of spade. Jet black. Purple black. A blue-black damn woman. But absolutely take-your-breath-away stunning with a statuesque body that's lean, curvy, and long.*

"How can I help you?"

"Aren't you Carlos? *The* Carlos Kenzie Reynolds, Jr.?" Venus questioned with a wide smile on her silky smooth, charcoal face.

Before Carlos answered and since he didn't want to let her know that her beauty mesmerized him, he offered her a pleasant, nonchalant grin as he looked down at her. Without budging from her spot directly in front of him, Venus gazed boldly up at him and waited for a reply.

"Well, are you him?"

"Uh, yes I am. Who wants to know?" Carlos asked with an even wider grin. He casually took several swallows of the vodka and orange juice, then carefully eyed her over the rim of the glass. She immediately noticed the simple gold wedding band around the third finger on his left hand.

"*I* want to know. That's who. I thought that was you. My name is Venus Mayfield-French," she answered quickly as she confidently extended her right hand. They shook like they had known each other for years.

"It's a pleasure to meet you, *Miss* French." Carlos figured it was safer to act and speak like the consummate businessman that he was known to be.

"I know it is, Mr. Reynolds. I was one of those serious basketball cheerleaders during your senior year at A&T who used to yell, shake, rock and roll you guys from one victory to another. I came on the cheerleading squad your last year, and bam, you were gone." She talked with a huge, charming smile on her face.

Carlos noticed the gleaming white teeth against the ultra dark, smooth jet-black skin. She was absolutely ravishing, and Carlos continued to look away from the piercing gaze she was directing his way because he felt like he was totally and helplessly sinking deeper into her dark brown eyes...right along with his dick.

"Do you remember all the cheerleaders from your senior year?"

"No I don't, and I certainly don't recall you. I'm sorry," he stammered professionally as he took another sip of liquor and looked around the dance floor in an effort to avoid her penetrating stare.

Venus laughed briefly and smiled up at him as she flashed pretty dark brown eyes with long lashes. "That's ok. You were always very focused. That's why you don't remember me.

From what I remember about you, you played basketball, studied, and you went home," she said teasingly.

"You're right," Carlos agreed with a chuckle.

Responsible for a young wife and small babies, Carlos only thought about four things. That was making it into the National Basketball League, playing basketball, hitting the books, and graduating from A&T. All in that order. Seeing other girls was the furthest thing from his mind.

"Well, anyway, it was good to see you, Carlos. By the way, your Kente cloth and tux combo looks great on you. Enjoy homecoming and you take care," she said sweetly and walked off.

Out the corner of Carlos' eyes, he watched Venus constantly the remainder of the evening. While Carlos and Sidney joked with the other fellas, he knew exactly where she was in the room each and every time he glanced up. Carlos thought Venus stood about five eight, and he noticed that she had the biggest, firmest looking titties he had seen in a long time. Along with a large juicy ass, her big legs rounded off to a small waist that completed the Nubian perfection. Carlos noticed the way she glided around the dance as she was being friendly and talking with the other excited alumni. With tar black, well-groomed dreadlocks that were swept up into a French twist bun wrapped in black shimmering pearls, that night Venus was dressed in an above the knee, opened shoulder onyx sequined evening dress that provided a body molding idea of what was underneath. However, from Carlos' brief, two-minute conversation, he was already fantasizing about screwing her.

After the alumni dance was over, Carlos, Sidney, Rico, and Darilyn went to the Shriners Club in Greensboro. Venus was there, too. Carlos ended up dancing with her to the sounds of The Staple Singers, The Ohio Players, and Kool and the Gang. Not all at once, though. He didn't want Rico's wife, Darilyn, to get suspicious of any promiscuous activities on his part with one particular woman, so he broke the dances up. Eventually, Venus and Carlos quietly exchanged telephone numbers. He called her. She called him back. They scheduled a lunch date. Then dinner. Then breakfast. And two months after meeting at homecoming, the two made love and had been secret lovers ever since.

Eventually, Carlos found out that Venus had overheard a few other guys say that they and Carlos would be heading to the Shriners Club after the homecoming dance. Once Venus discovered where Carlos would be hanging out next, she convinced her husband and the other friends they were partying with to stop by the Shriners Club as well. Venus wanted another opportunity to check Carlos out along with finding out how to get in contact with him. As Carlos and Venus' talk-filled weeks went by, they got to know each other intimately. During those passionately mellow moments, Venus also shared that she had always had a serious crush on him when she was an Aggie cheerleader. Never in all her wildest dreams did she ever expect to see him again. Venus emphatically added that she never really thought much about him after he graduated from A&T. Of course, she moved on with her life, too. That's why she was thoroughly shocked when she spotted him at the alumni dance. After they were lovers for one month, Venus laughingly confessed that it took her at least an hour to get herself together before she mustered up the nerve to even speak to him on homecoming night. But she did it.

And when she looked in his eyes, she realized he hadn't changed a helluva lot either. His steely blue eyes were bluer than she remembered, and he was just as fine and pretty as ever.

When Venus met Carlos at the dance, she and her husband had just relocated to Greensboro from Princeton, New Jersey, just ten months prior. Thomas Brooks French, Venus' husband, was an executive in MUB Industries' international department. A chemistry major at A&T, Venus had worked as a chemist at Vibunzi Laboratories in Princeton. However, when Thomas accepted the lucrative job transfer and promotion with MUB, she decided to finally turn in the white research chemist smock. Venus then became a full-time housewife and mother for their two children, Albertina and Thomas Junior, ages five and eight.

A smart and well-traveled woman, Venus dabbled in learning several languages as a hobby, and her most favorite language was French. When Thomas received a four-year assignment in France for MUB, Venus went along and became fluent in French. Although she studied the language in college, it was only when she lived in Europe that she became a proficient conversationalist. After they returned to North Carolina to live in Greensboro, Venus tutored high-school students. Once more, she tired of that stint as well.

Venus noticed that as she got older, she got bored very easily. Now at her age, she was committed to creating nothing but absolutely breathtaking adventure in her life. Brothella Mae, Venus' married and holier-than-thou-church-going sister, often declared it was a late thirties and a forties restless thing women went through just before they entered menopause. Venus totally disagreed with Brothella Mae and told her sister that she believed it was because she was more in touch with herself than ever before. She realized what she wanted out of life and simply wanted to satisfy all of those fantasies and desires before she closed her eyes to die. Like she told Brothella Mae, "...in case you hadn't heard, my dear sistah, this life ain't no damn dress rehearsal."

However, Venus' search for enlightenment changed when she met Carlos. Carlos ran the gamut of what Venus needed in another person. She knew that from the first time he made the most wondrously satisfying love to her. The relationship with him was thoroughly exciting, a dream come true. It certainly provided the extra umph to Venus' life and to her marriage. Carlos possessed a unique flair for having fantastic fun, and he definitely was a consummate lover, the best Venus had ever experienced. Just like Venus, Carlos possessed a strong, super freaky deak, insatiable sexual appetite. Once Carlos made soulfully passionate, hard love to her, Venus was able to return home and be the perfect, doting mother to her two children and the darling, devoted corporate executive wife to Thomas.

Venus was thirty-eight and had been married for twelve long years that felt as if it was a prison sentence. Carlos was her third affair in the past four years, yet Venus believed that she would have never gotten involved with other men if her husband were a different person. For years, Venus worked diligently as a chemist and did all of the motherly and wifely things for her husband and children. She attended the PTA meetings and entertained Thomas' dull ass corporate friends. And she never considered running around on her husband. But over the years, Thomas became quite boring and lax in the way he made love to her. If nothing else, Venus knew that Thomas was a great provider and father. Of course, he allowed her to freely spend his executive salary on her and the children. He even willingly gave her time to be with the girls. In spite of that, she wasn't happy with him and wanted more than just his name, title, and the security that he provided.

There were only two real reasons why Venus married Thomas in the first place. Thomas was an ambitious corporate man climbing the ladder to success. Most importantly, he also possessed the appropriate coloring for fathering Venus' babies. Thomas was a light-skinned Black man. Her children would never have to experience what she did growing up with a glistening, jet-black complexion. She was called tar baby and often heard remarks such as *black as soot* with your *nappy nippy hair.* No, she had decided that her children would be lighter than she was and have good hair. Venus would make sure of it. So before Venus even considered having a relationship with a man, he had to be the right complexion. That was light, even almost white. She only dealt with high yellow niggers, and although Thomas looked like a light-skinned, half-white man like Carlos, he wasn't as fine or as tall as Carlos. Another thing about Thomas that irked her nerves was that he focused more on pleasing MUB management then he did satisfying Venus and their children.

That's what Venus loved about Carlos. He wasn't like Thomas at all. When they were together, Carlos' number one priority was to treat Venus like a reigning queen. And just like a dry, neglected kitchen sponge that Venus was, she soaked up all the well-deserved attention Carlos lavished upon her and her body. Ever since Venus' cheerleading days at A&T, she was always extremely conscientious about maintaining her physique. Once she and Thomas moved back to North Carolina, she signed on to teach aerobics classes five mornings a week at the local sports club in Kernersville, a small town about fifteen miles from Greensboro. It didn't stopped there. Venus worked out on Nautilus three times a week and jogged four miles a day, except on Sundays. In other words, Venus didn't have an ounce of fat on her healthy frame, and she was proud of it. It was nothing but lean muscle, and Carlos enjoyed licking and kissing every inch of her body every chance he got.

Carlos and Venus supposedly also knew the rules of the affair game. From the very beginning, they agreed to move very cautiously and to not take the relationship too seriously. Both of them were married, which ultimately made the dynamics of their steamy liaison even more interesting. Carlos and Venus wholeheartedly admitted that they would get out of their romantic affair if it was necessary and if it affected the well-being of either one's family. Since Venus and Carlos had been involved with extra-marital flings before, they believed that they knew how and when to end them delicately without any hard feelings.

Yet, just before Pecola's fortieth birthday party in May, Carlos suddenly realized that this relationship was a little different from all the other frivolous affairs he had been involved with. He had fallen desperately in love with Venus. The more he thought about it, the more he realized that he needed to see her more. He desired to make freaky love to her twenty-four seven. Carlos calmly tried to ignore those stark facts. He constantly told himself, *Dismiss it, man. Dismiss the shit!* But it didn't work. Carlos was hopelessly in love with her. Venus was a totally different kind of woman from any he had been involved with, including Pecola. She was sensual, loving, and carefree—unlike any woman he had ever met before. A collector of slavery memorabilia and historical manuscripts, Venus was an awesome, unusual, and intelligent lady he couldn't get enough of in the bedroom.

Oftentimes, when Venus and Carlos made love, she spoke to Carlos in whispering, lilting French. That was another thing that made him weak for her. Nowadays, whenever Carlos thought about Venus' beautifully jet-black body intertwined like a human pretzel with his lighter complexioned one, his penis got hard as a wooden board. It didn't matter where Carlos was when it happened, either. Whether Carlos was at work, in bed with Pecola, or even on the golf course for that matter, it made no difference. When Carlos thought about Venus' ultimate loving, inevitably his penis responded with longing for her ebony charms.

Chapter One-Hundred

As the limo glided Pecola and Alex toward Fixed Based Operations at Piedmont Aviation in Greensboro, Pecola was chatting to Alex about the excitement she was feeling. It was about time she was excited about something. For the past two weeks, she had been sinking into depression. But after spending thousands of dollars on shopping sprees at her favorite boutiques around the Triad, she finally was beginning to feel a little better.

Tomorrow was Symone's surprise fortieth birthday party, and Pecola and Alex were heading to the corporate hanger at Greensboro Airport to meet her family. Samuel Eisner, Cecil, Willie, Keturah, and many more family and friends were due in Greensboro in just thirty minutes. Leading a procession of eight super stretch black limousines, Pecola felt as if she were meeting the president of the United States and his whole crew of Air Force One returning from an international meeting over in Europe.

Staying in Winston-Salem for just three nights, Samuel Eisner's executive assistant secretly coordinated all the itinerary arrangements with Pecola and Alex for the Eisner and Poussaint families' surprise appearance. For the overnight accommodations, Samuel Eisner's people reserved the beautiful mansion located on the grounds of the Gralyn International Conference Center property. The mansion alone had thirty-five sleeping rooms, but that wasn't enough. To ensure utmost seclusion for his family that weekend, the entire fifty-five acre estate that encompassed Gralyn was also reserved for his family's private use.

As Alex told Samuel Eisner's assistant, Connor, the Gralyn International Conference Center was the second largest private residence in North Carolina after the Biltmore House in Asheville. Donated to Wake Forest University by Bowman Gray, Jr. and located on Reynolda Road in the Buena Vista section of Winston-Salem, Alex and Pecola felt Gralyn would be an absolutely perfect place for the Eisners and the Poussaints to stay, especially since the entourage that traveled to Winston-Salem for the party would be a large one and since they expected to be able to roam freely in a bucolic, discreet setting.

Since Pecola and Symone always hosted their employees' quarterly three-day retreats at Gralyn, Alex and Pecola also knew that the serenity of the sprawling mansion would definitely be an excellent, almost gothically romantic location for Symone's party. Nestled among large, sweeping umbrella old oak, maple and other trees of splendor, Pecola and Alex believed that once Symone's family came through the large steel gates, Gralyn would provide the Eisners and the Poussaints with the grandeur they expected and the ultimate, southern charm they would receive at any five-star, five-diamond hotel anywhere in the world. This delectable charm would be enjoyed in the confines of the city of Winston-Salem with absolute, utter privacy.

Built during the early 1900s, the Gralyn mansion was the home of Mr. and Mrs. Bowman Gray, Sr. and their two sons. The architectural style of the mansion was Norman Revival Architecture. As Alex told Connor, history documented that the mansion was originally copied after the large estates in Normandy. Its rooms were massive, ornate, and lovely. Even though the residence had been changed to a conference center, some of the original antiques and drapes that were first brought over from Europe still remained inside the estate.

When Pecola considered again how Samuel Eisner's people had *actually* paid for and reserved the entire Gralyn Estate, it literally took her breath away. She had to momentarily stop talking to Alex to imagine the scope and breadth of such affluent actions. Suddenly, Pecola rested her head against the limo seat. Thinking about the fact that she would be seeing the Eisner patriarch in a matter of minutes, she began to take slow deep breaths once more. Pecola always became excited when she had an opportunity to stand near Samuel Eisner. He was a real live billionaire, a man worth over twenty-two billion dollars. A member of an exclusive club—The Ninth Zero Club. Pecola wondered what that must feel like to have so much money that a person could receive the title of one of the wealthiest people in the world. It was mind-blowing to know that all your money was more than even ten thousand or two million, regular working-class individuals could even imagine spending or ever conceive of having together in many lifetimes.

Pecola inhaled deeply and thanked God Alex was nearby. She was the soothing, gentle force Pecola needed right now, or Pecola believed she would pass out from the excitement of meeting the Eisners. Alex had to continually remind Pecola to puhleeze calm down. She told her that Samuel Eisner was a man like everyone else who used the bathroom and needed to use toilet paper to wipe himself. Samuel Eisner just happened to be a human being who possessed tremendous wealth, nothing more in Alex's eyes. Although the toilet paper example was an unusual, clear, and an interesting point to Pecola that was well taken, she couldn't see the relevancy of it with what she was experiencing at the present time.

Even though Pecola had been in Samuel Eisner's presence a number of other occasions before with Symone, she was still overwhelmed by his great wealth and power. Yet, he smiled and acted like he was familiar with her, that he knew her. Somehow, he made her know that she too was close to him as any of his other family members. Samuel Eisner knew Pecola's name. Each and every time she met him in person, he even asked her about Carlos and the children. Alex was right. He was just regular people. And today, Pecola was determined to not allow the Poussaints and the Eisners' notice her excitement because she was just in their midst. She was so happy for Elizabethe and Birtha. The two young girls would be traveling from New York to Greensboro on the Eisner's main corporate jet. Looking as huge as a 747 in Pecola's opinion, Pecola told Symone that the Eisner plane reminded her of an exquisitely decorated living room in the sky.

Symone continually said that it was the suspicious reactions of other people while she was growing up in New York that made her decide early on she would keep her relationships with the Eisner family private. Because she wore loud, colorful clothes to after school outings, it was difficult for Symone to make friends. She was continuously the butt of jokes in the all-girl and elite school in Manhattan. Yet, when a quietly shy, thirteen year-old Symone told a classmate who her uncle was, the classmate immediately decided that she wanted to become

Symone's best friend. That surprised Symone. In the past, this particular girl was the ringleader of meanness at the school and had ridiculed Symone incessantly about her Caribbean accent, colorful clothes, and her unusually quiet, standoffish behavior. That new friend in turn told all the other girls in the school who Symone's uncle was, and suddenly they all wanted to become her buddies.

When Symone and Pecola became friends, Pecola had no thoughts about the Eisners, either. Of course, she had seen the man on television once or twice, but that was it. She didn't think about the Kennedy family even though she saw them on TV, too. From the initial meetings with the young, married Billy and Symone Butler, Pecola just assumed that they were a highly successful, corporate couple designing a mega home in Clemmons. They simply wanted the Black-owned CR Construction Group to build it. And, Pecola was merely there to assist with decorating it. Even when the two women became fast friends, Symone still refused to share her Eisner ties with Pecola. It wasn't until they decided to go into business together and to build the Akao office building that Pecola actually found out about a small slice of Symone's spicy past and discovered a smattering of the magnitude of her wealth.

Pecola and Symone had finally selected the Stratford Road pricey land for their building and quickly decided on the design of the high-tech building they wanted to construct. Pecola had money too, but a lot of her money was tied up with Carlos. But she told Symone that she wanted to do these two businesses on her own. She didn't want to go to Carlos to ask for a dime on this project. She loved him, and he loved her, but she wanted these companies to be something she could call her own. Symone said that it was fine, and that she understood. Once Pecola and Symone were given the seven-figure final cost for their three-story state-of-the-art building, Symone told her that she would handle a portion of the financing by using some money from her trust fund. Pecola was shocked to learn about Symone's trust fund and only believed that white people were that fortunate.

Bank note negotiations were handled for the Akao Building. A payment contract was signed between Pecola and Symone for Pecola's share of the building costs. A fifty-percent partnership agreement was inked between the two women. The Stratford Road property was purchased, and CR Construction broke ground for the Akao building. Back then, Symone firmly explained to Pecola that any assets ever obtained by a Poussaint were required to be placed in trust. Not long after that conversation, the assets of both Meetings Odyssey and Akao Studios were quickly moved into blind business trusts controlled by Pecola and Symone. And, to make sure all of the North Carolina legal paperwork was being handled properly and yet needing to keep the interests of the family trust foremost and sacred above all, Eisner family attorneys came to Winston-Salem to properly handle those complex transactions. It was still another two years after the Akao Building was completed that Symone eventually decided to open up to Pecola about most of her past. It was only then that Symone felt totally secure in their friendship and finally told Alex and Pecola the sad, private story about the Poussaint family days in Trinidad and their journey to New York.

"…Alex, what a pleasure to see you again," Samuel Eisner said in a stately voice. He had just finished greeting Alex with a warm embrace and several minutes of face to face, quiet conversation. "And, my dear Pecola. It's good to see you as well. How's Carlos and your two sons?"

Just before Samuel walked over to Pecola, Elizabethe, and Birtha breathlessly greeted Pecola and raved about how exciting and wonderful the flight was. Although Elizabethe was steel reeling emotionally from seeing her father in Atlantic City, she was all smiles when she saw her mother. She was mainly concerned with how she would react when she met her father. For right now, she didn't want anything to diffuse everyone's excited, party mood. When Elizabethe and Birtha were through talking to Pecola, the two excited young girls were already sitting down in all their reigning splendor, chatting non-stop in one of the waiting limousines.

"So your family is doing ok, Pecola?" Samuel Eisner asked.

"Just fine— Er, Mr. Eisner, uh, Uncle Samuel," she stammered as he quickly shook her hand and gently hugged her shoulders as if he had known her all her natural born life.

Six years ago when all of Symone's friends vacationed in Mustique with the Eisners and Poussaints, Symone asked Alex and Pecola to call him uncle. She told them that he would definitely enjoy that since he knew Symone considered her two girlfriends to be more like blood sisters. Symone told them that her Uncle Samuel was a "simple man regarding family and friends. But like all-powerful, affluent and great men, he's always surrounded by a lot of people. That's the only difference with my Uncle Samuel," Symone explained, "and this is why he would enjoy my dearest friends acknowledging him in such a manner."

"Symone told me that your son is a first-year law student at Emory, and your other son plans to go to Duke next year," Samuel Eisner continued.

"Yes, that's right. Haneef is doing well there in law school, too. Uh, yes. My oldest, CJ, declares that er, uh, he wants to become a doctor— I mean a surgeon." Pecola grinned nervously and quickly as she thought about Alex's eloquent reference to super wealthy people and toilet paper. She became a little calmer as she stared into Samuel Eisner's astute, dark, and piercing eyes.

"Both are excellent professions, Pecola. Excellent."

"Uh, thank you." Pecola believed no one had ever spoken her name with such richness the way Samuel Eisner did.

"And both you and Alex are extremely sure my niece knows nothing of this surprise party, eh? Symone tends to be very, very perceptive about things," Samuel Eisner said, smiling at Pecola and Alex.

"We know, Uncle Samuel," Alex said quietly as she began moving toward the others. "We're hoping we haven't had any leaks in the camp, either," she added and winked at Pecola.

Samuel chuckled lightly, cut his eyes at Pecola, and Pecola wondered nervously if anyone had told him about her reputation for having a refrigerator mouth. *Damn Alex, girl!* thought Pecola. Now she was stressed again.

"How's business, Pecola?" With one hand casually placed in his suit pants pocket, his whole face was covered in a genuine, interested smile.

"Uh. Mr. Ei—, er, just fantastic, Uncle Samuel. The last quarter— Uh, last year was our best one yet."

"Symone told me. Glad to hear it. If you need anything, call me," he said with the utmost sincerity as his wife walked up to speak with him.

Pecola wanted to scream, *Can I puhleeze have your autograph? Why don't you give me one of your billions? I don't think you'll miss it too much.* But instead she smiled pleasantly at the elegantly attired Gerda and at everyone else. The whole crowd of Eisners and Poussaints was quite distinguished looking to Pecola. *Even the mannered, well-groomed, and happy children running about look good,* thought Pecola as she tactfully eyed their carefree spirit.

Samuel Eisner was about six-two with a full-head of streaked peppered gray and black hair. Tastefully dressed in what Pecola assumed was the finest black pure cashmere coat she had ever seen, a dark pin-striped suit, a starched white shirt and striped tie, he appeared tall and strong for his years. With a finely sculptured face that contained a pointed, elegant nose, dark piercing eyes and strong cleft jaw, Samuel Eisner looked good for the approaching age of sixty-nine.

Along with Samuel Eisner were his three sons, whom Pecola thought were absolutely drop dead handsome white boys. The oldest one, who handled the entertainment subsidiary created twenty-five years ago, was just as tall as Samuel Eisner. With a tanned face cut from his father's likeness, he had jet-black hair that he wore in a sleek, long ponytail. His two younger brothers were just as attractive but more traditional looking. They appeared as conservatively dressed Wall Street banker twins with the typical, corporate white boy haircuts with the part down the side of their heads. On the arms of Samuel's three sons were their friendly, gorgeous, sable coated and well-taken care of Jewish wives. And, behind them skipping and jumping about the place were their appropriately attired and well-behaved children. Pecola just marveled at the air of power and wealth encircling the entire entourage that was milling about in front of her fascinated and attentive eyes.

Just think, thought Pecola. *If it hadn't been for Willie and Cecil saving Samuel Eisner's life over forty-one years ago, none of these people basking in all this wealth would be here right now. Umph, umph, umph. Like CJ said, that's amazing how some doors of life are opened to you. When it opens, you need to walk the hell right through it.*

While their many pieces of luggage were unloaded off the plane and placed into the limos by the chauffeurs, Pecola and Alex continued to talk to the Eisners and the Poussaints. Keturah Ciesta Poussaint Mellineux was an exquisite older-looking woman with caramel smooth skin wrapped around high-cheek bones and faint lines of wrinkles around the eyes. With just a tad of gray streaks of strands shining in her hair, Pecola could see how much Symone resembled her mother. But then Keturah's other two daughters favored her in their own way, too. So did Quentin whom Symone said truly favored their father more than anyone else. Just like Symone, they all had dark chocolate brown complexions and licorice, shiny jet-black hair. Ameenah was almost as tall as Symone, but had a softer edge to her disposition and a friendly smile on her round, pretty, high-cheek boned face.

Hazele, the non-stop talker of the group, wasn't as tall as Ameenah yet was stunningly lean, polished, and affectionate. *She looks real rich in her bad assed sable coat, too,* thought Pecola with a blank expression as she discreetly eyed the expensive clothes on everybody's backs. Pecola's eyes darted to Quentin, who was strolling about with his four children in tow. Pecola had always told Symone that if she weren't already married, she would definitely jump on her brother's bones. A strikingly handsome man with full thick lips and dark, sexy, brooding brown eyes, when Quentin laughed, all Pecola could see was his gleaming white teeth smile and hear his deep bass voice. Symone's sisters, brother, and cousins were there with their husbands, wives and all their children.

When Pecola first saw everyone get off the plane, she didn't think the long line of people exiting the plane would ever end. Including children, nannies, security and Samuel Eisner's business entourage of assistants, it looked like over seventy people had journeyed down from New York to participate in Symone's surprise fortieth birthday party.

"Peecola, yuh does be doing all right, gurl?" Keturah asked Pecola after she finished talking to Alex. Pecola just finished hugging all of Symone's nieces and nephews and was glad the older talkative ones remembered to greet her as their *Tante Peecola.*

"I'm doing fine, Mum Poussaint," Pecola said happily and reached out to hug the attractive older woman. Dressed in a full-length sable coat and hat, Keturah tightly wrapped her arms around Pecola's neck. She was adequately dressed for the biting Greensboro temperature of twenty degrees, but Keturah said that she didn't feel as chilled as she normally did when she was in Brooklyn. Pecola told them that twenty degrees in New York and twenty degrees in North Carolina are two different things.

"Ah does feel good about being back in North Caroline-a. Ah tank yuh far meeting us at dey airport. Were yuh waiting a long time, Peecola?"

"No, Mum Poussaint. Yall arrived like twenty-five minutes after we got here."

"Ah didn't know so. Dey plane had ta circle dey airport twice, and ah was quite concerned. Ah does tell Samuel ah was ready ta parachute meyself down," she teased with a lilting laugh.

"I know. Sometimes, I feel the same way on certain flights."

"Peecola, where's mey grandchillren? Symone's baybees? Ah was looking far dem ta be here as well."

"Miss Jessica is going to bring them over to Gralyn after she picks Jared up from school." Pecola checked her watch. It was three o'clock. "She'll probably be there when we get there. Then they're going to spend the night with Jodria because after they see yall, there ain't no way in this here world the party will be a big secret anymore."

"Ummm-hmmm, yuh right. As long as ah does get ta see mey grandchillren. Do yuh tink dey might want ta change dey mind and stay wit meh at dey hotel? It will give dem a chance ta play wit all dere cousins."

"I hadn't even thought about that. They probably will, Mum Poussaint. After they see yall, we just want to try to keep them as far away from their mother as possible."

"Peecola, yuh sure mey seester does know nut-ting about she par-tee on tamorrow," Hazele asked as she firmly hugged Pecola's neck again for the second time. Ameenah strolled up and did the same with just as much vigor. While hugging one another's waists, Ameenah and Alex walked off toward Gerda, Odetta, and Rosa who were speaking to their many grandchildren skipping and playing around with invisible butterflies in the air.

"Yuh sure she knows nut-ting?" Hazele inquired.

"Not a thing, Hazele," Pecola replied. "Girl, you look damn good."

"Ah tank yuh. Ah still working out strong wit mey trainer ta keep mey weight so. Seamone does tell meh yuh have a trainer now. Dat's dey best ting a person can have."

As Hazele spoke, Pecola noticed out the corner of her eyes how Hazele's husband slithered quietly into a limo with their two children. Barrington, Ameenah's handsome assed husband, was carrying his two youngest kids in his arms. The other three were running beside him as they made an amusing game out of deciding which limo to select for the ride over to Gralyn.

"So do yuh have a trainer, yet, Pecola?"

"Yes, we do have a trainer, girl. Symone didn't tell you, Hazele?" Pecola asked. "That's was one of her Christmas gifts to the women of FOFAE. She hired a private trainer for everybody, girl!"

"Ummm-hmmm," Hazele nodded. "She does mention it, but it slipped mey mind."

"What about Cleopatra?"

Hazele grinned widely. "Yes, ah does know dat, too. She does give Cleopatra a cleaning lady far Christmas. Someone dat does cum in twice a week ah tink she say. Seamone has always ben so toughtful, even wen weh were chillren in Trinidad. True, she does cry often wen weh were back home in Santa Cruz, but she does try ta read ta us and give us dey flowers she pulled up from dey garden far Mummy, Lennious, meh, and dey others. Papa told her ta not pull dem up so often, but she does do it anyway ta try ta make us happy. She doesn't change she way she does be wen weh came ta dey States. She always dey one who gave so much ta everyone. Dat was a nice gift far Cleopatra. Such a sweet ting ta do."

"Yeah," Pecola said. "It was quite interesting. It surprised everyone, even Cleopatra. But knowing Cleopatra, she'll clean up after the woman whenever she leaves her house."

"Ah hear so," Hazele murmured.

"So I'm going to see how my trainer helps me, Hazele. So far she said I've lost two inches and three pounds. It's great having one. I need to just stop eating everything else when she's not around. I should've hired one long time ago. She comes to the house and almost drags me outdoors. That's exactly what I need because I sure wasn't getting out there myself trying to get rid of these extra twenty pounds. It doesn't make sense. Carlos has a state of the art gym right in our house."

"Humph. Ah does know it tis hard, but yuh does look good, gurl. Keep up dey good work."

"How was dey flight, Hazele chile?" Pecola asked with a slight West Indian accent mixed in with her southern twang.

After hearing so much of the Poussaint family dialect, Pecola was ready to speak as if she stepped off the boat from Trinidad, too. Just then, Willie and Cecil came up to talk to Pecola. They were handsome, aristocratic older Black men who displayed an aura of confidence and success. As they puffed on long, fat cigars, Willie and Cecil introduced Pecola to their sons and daughters for the twentieth time. Dressed in fine tailored dark suits, black pure cashmere overcoats, matching scarves and fedoras, Pecola thought Willie and Cecil could easily model in the senior citizen's edition of *Ebony Male*.

"And dey flight, chile?" Pecola inquired once more to Hazele.

"Yuh know it was wonderful, gurl. Ah was tired, so meh slept most of dey time. It still was quite pleasant and ting. Since dey chillren watched a movie, it was quiet and dey weren't running around so. Dere were no bumps atall atall in dey air."

"It's time to go, Hazele. Uncle Samuel is ready," Quentin interrupted in a pleasant voice without a trace of a Trinidadian accent. He was gently clutching his young son's hand. "I'll see you back at Gralyn, Pecola. It's good seeing you again."

"It's good seeing *you*, Quentin. I clare you smell lucious. When you hugged me to your nice hard chest earlier, I said, 'Damn! What's the name of his cologne? Don't let me go, baby.'" Hazele burst out laughing and pinched Quentin's arm. "I definitely need to get some of it for my huzzband."

Quentin smiled and winked at Pecola. "Thanks. I'll check it out for you, and you can get some for Carlos. My wife picked it up somewhere," Quentin said as he suddenly bent down to hear what his son was saying. Immediately, Quentin patted the pockets of his single-breasted navy cashmere overcoat. He handed his son a board toy.

"Thank you, Papa," the young boy said in a soft, polite voice.

"You're welcome son," Quentin answered him and turned to face Pecola. "On the ride over to Gralyn, I'll find out the name. Ok?"

"Sho you're right, chile. Anything you say," Pecola moaned, looking all up into Quentin's handsome face. "Carlos would love the cologne."

"Well, c'mon. Let's head out, Hazele," Quentin encouraged his sister. He looked around and realized that they were the only ones left who hadn't gotten in a car. "Pecola, we can talk later. Like I said, it's good seeing you again."

Chapter One-Hundred-One

As soon as Pecola got home, Carlos called her to say that he wouldn't be home until nine-thirty, which facilitated Pecola's decision to go to bed early. When they finally reached Gralyn, the entire entourage enjoyed a light meal that was prepared and ready when they arrived. Not long after, Alex and Pecola informed everyone that it was time for them to leave. For the party tomorrow night, they needed to check on a few last minor details. Since Symone wasn't due in from Hampton, Virginia, until later in the evening, Pecola and Alex weren't concerned with her family bumping into her if they decided to venture out in Winston-Salem.

Alex invited Ameenah and Hazele to stay in Advance, but even Symone's two sisters were aware of the Devereauxs' Friday night tradition and opted to spend the night at Gralyn as arranged. Because Pecola preferred to be alone and was suddenly fighting off depression and other indescribable emotions, she was glad they decided to pass on her warm and gracious invitation to spend the night at her house, too. Keeping the party a secret was giving Pecola a serious headache, and she was simply exhausted.

Pecola had to admit that Hazele was wonderful to be around, but she talked incessantly. Non-stop. The whole time they were in the car heading to Gralyn, Hazele talked each minute of the short trip to Winston-Salem. *Even more than I do,* Pecola thought. Right now, Pecola definitely preferred not to deal with another fast-talking mouth this evening. Like she told Scott and Alex over their early morning breakfast, it *was* extremely difficult for her to keep a secret. There it was. She admitted it. It was finally out in the open. Pecola confessed that she kind of understood why her friends called her refrigerator mouth even though in public she appeared annoyed with the title.

Since Symone turned forty last Friday night, it made Pecola realize that once again her life was quickly hurdling away from her. *It must be something about the forty decade which is considered to be like that ten-year slide toward senior citizen status,* Pecola thought. All of her girlfriends were either in their forties or just turning forty. Nanette and her two cohorts were just thirty, and it was always interesting to Pecola to see the way they handled life's problems, which always seemed to include men, especially Rehema. *When those three women turn forty, they will be in for a rude awakening about a whole lot of other things,* Pecola thought with a tired smile. In particular, if they didn't take care of their bodies, they were going to have some problems fitting into clothes. *That's horrendous when there's so much shopping to be done,* Pecola thought.

Pecola was fortunate though to be blessed with the type of figure she had. Definitely shaped like an hourglass, she still had about seventeen extra pounds here or there since her trainer said that she lost three pounds in time for Symone's birthday party. Other than that,

Pecola knew that she looked damn good for forty. She couldn't say that about some other people. Once several of Pecola's friends reached middle age, it was common knowledge that those ladies' waists shifted and now were up by their breasts—like one long trunk. Even their feet grew larger, increasing sometimes by two and three sizes. *Lord, don't even talk about cellulite and breasts,* Pecola thought with amusement.

When Pecola considered the surprise birthday party planned for Symone, she laughed softly. Girlfriend was definitely going to be shocked. So far, Pecola was proud that she hadn't allowed any inkling of hints to slip out of her mouth.

Since last Friday was Symone's birthday, Carlos and Pecola hosted a small surprise dinner in their home on Saturday evening to fool Symone and throw her off the scent of the real celebration. And that she was, especially because of the way everyone was giving Symone gifts, cards, and congratulatory comments about turning the big four o. Jokes and laughter filled the room. Symone even cried. Pecola could just see it now. When the limo pulled up to the Gralyn Center on tomorrow night, Symone was going to probably faint from pure shock when she walked into the mansion and saw her family. The friends invited Symone out for a formal evening. It was under the guise of attending a black-tie literary reception honoring poets that was put on by the North Carolina Black Repertory Theater. Supposedly, the Black Repertory Theater was honoring poets, with Dr. Maya Angelou being one. Naturally, Symone was eager to oblige Pecola, Alex, and Scott's invitation that they said they received by pulling a lot of strings to make it happen.

That was why Pecola was convinced that Symone had no earthly idea. If Symone did know about the party, she definitely would have mentioned something to Alex. Up until now, Symone revealed absolutely nothing to Alex other than the fact she was honored to celebrate the big fortieth dinner with such great friends because she damn sure didn't have a great man to speak of in her life right now.

Pecola lazily walked upstairs to the master bedroom and began to slowly undress. Once there, she decided to play the Marvelettes CD she borrowed from the Devereauxs. Pecola hadn't heard the Marvelettes in years and had been playing the CD all week. At Symone's birthday dinner, Madison formed a classic Soul Train line with *Please Mr. Postman* blasting away in the background. When he did that, Pecola snapped her fingers and screamed, "Ok. This is it, honeychile. Honeychile, honeychile. Ah sookie sookie, now." The lyrics zoomed her mind straight to her younger days when she was hanging out in Greensboro. Pecola laughed out loud as she thought about the fun they had last week at the dinner.

Now naked, Pecola strutted in front of the Chippendale full-length gilt mirror she discovered in an antique store in Chicago. For above five minutes, Pecola watched her body closely to reassure herself she still was an attractive woman whom men still wanted. She held her stomach in, straightened up her shoulders, and noticed that she really needed to improve her posture. One thing Pecola could say about Symone was that Symone always walked extremely upright. Symone said that it was an early lesson from her mother that became a habit when she was a little girl in Trinidad. For as long as Symone could remember, while her

Papa was brutally beating her and her siblings and destroying their spirits, Keturah constantly reminded her five children to stand straight, keep their shoulders back, and never slouch. Every time Pecola thought about drooping shoulders, she heard Mum Poussaint's instructions.

Pecola turned around a couple of times to observe her body in the mirror from different angles. She scrutinized her breasts, thighs, and other bodily spots as if she were a jeweler examining a precious, rare gem. Pecola definitely believed that she was a rare diamond; however, she simply had a few gray spots of seventeen pounds to deal with. Pecola smiled. Still looking at herself, she noticed just a small midriff bulge problem. There was a petite pooch below the navel area, tiny flab above the elbow, and a slight sag in her breasts. That did it! After noticing all her body negatives, Pecola became depressed for the second time of the day. When it was all said and done, the truthful bottom line was that she absolutely realized she was getting older. She wasn't eighteen. Her body was only looking like a forty-year old woman's body. No longer was Pecola the landlord of the young-girl figure, nor was she any longer the proprietor of firm, upturned breasts that automatically stayed pointed even without bra support. When Pecola carefully eyed her daughter's body, she remembered how petite and firm everything used to be on her. Pecola sighed deeply as she came to the conclusion that she still didn't look as bad as some people. The only thing was her body didn't appear as youthful and supple anymore.

Totally frustrated with the honest assessment of her body, Pecola traipsed to the bathroom to take a shower. When she couldn't find the bath cap, she wrapped a towel around her head sarong style and took a long, hot steaming shower. While soaping down, Pecola felt very sensual and allowed the hot, smooth water to glide between her thighs. Now, she was horny.

That's another thing about being in my forties, she thought. *You have so many damn moods. And, my ass somehow or another was selected to be the million-dollar lottery winner for PMS. Maybe I'm going through the change of life. At night, I get hot as hell. I can't handle the comforter in the winter. Yet, I want it in the summer. What I really like to know is where in the hell did the years go? Just yesterday, I was twenty, then thirty, and now I'm forty. I don't remember all those 365 days of those twenty years. What happened to me? Lord, I'm aging and I'm changing. I don't want to! But I'm an adult. Get a grip! I know that being in my forties isn't the end of the world, but sometimes I think it sure is the beginning of the end.*

What happened to the time? As I tell Alex, Scott, and Symone all of the time, life is a trip! These thoughts are making me depressed again. Maybe it's because I'm thinking about my mortality—facing that I'm getting older. That's just depressing. Period. I remember when I used to have a shape like those women on music videos, but not anymore, chile! Humph. Well, thank God. I feel sexy and horny. Boy, do I have something for Carlos when he gets here tonight.

As Pecola talked to herself, the motley of wild thoughts made her laugh. Then she couldn't stop for a good five minutes. If she didn't know herself any better, she would really think that she was actually going crazy. Instead, she stepped out of the shower and dried off. Trying to work up an aura of fragrant sensuality, she powdered herself down with talc and sprayed her body with Zahra perfume. She did the same to other places in her room—even on the Bischoff comforter and sheets. After she found a good book to read, Pecola remained naked and slipped into bed. It was time for her to patiently wait for Carlos to come home. She desperately wanted to make passionate love with her husband, and she wanted him to tell her that she was the most beautiful woman in all of God's land. To softly breathe those comforting words to her even though she was now forty and would be forty-one in May. Maybe that would somehow soothe her ravaging thoughts.

Carlos didn't turn the key in the kitchen door until eleven-thirty that night. That was two hours past the scheduled time he gave to Pecola, and that was rare for him. By the time Carlos reached home, Pecola was watching *Nightline,* and he noticed how his wife eyed him quite seductively by batting her eyes and slowly licking her wet lips. When Pecola gave him that long and hard welcome home tongue kiss, Carlos realized that his ass was in serious trouble.

Venus had just finished screwing Carlos' brains out less than forty-five minutes earlier. She handcuffed him to the bed, sprayed whip cream all around his penis, and slowly licked it off. Carlos was an uncontrollably loud screamer when he was with Venus. Afterwards, he couldn't believe the way he hollered and screamed so much to the point that he was ashamed to leave their Marriott Hotel room, but he did. Quietly opening the hotel room door, Carlos carefully scanned the long hallway to the left and to the right several times before he quickly made his exit down the back stairwell. Venus opted to spend the night. She pleaded with him to stay with her, but Carlos knew that was impossible. One thing Carlos didn't do and that was to stay out all night. While growing up, Carlos repeatedly heard his father say that adulterous behavior was quite disrespectful and uncalled for, and strong men didn't behave like a dog in heat, especially when they had a wife and family at home.

It took all the strength Carlos could muster to break away from Venus' voluptuous body then drive home from the Greensboro Marriott to Winston-Salem. As Carlos gazed into his wife's face, he knew he was in trouble. Pecola was pleasantly watching him like a female Cheshire Cat with an *I'm ready to make love* expression covering her pretty face. *How much sexual torture can a man take?* Carlos thought tiredly. After Carlos gave Pecola his logical apologies for coming home so late, he reluctantly began to undress. He quickly walked into the bathroom and took a long, hot shower. While drying off, he considered how he could handle the second round with Pecola because right not he truly felt unusually weak and drained. All he wanted to do was get some rest.

While I'm in here thinking, maybe she'll drift off to sleep, Carlos thought with hope.

After a rough time with Venus, Carlos could sometimes wait it out in the safety of the bathroom. By the time he stepped out, Pecola would be fast asleep. Carlos poked his head out of the door to see if that happened this time. Pecola glanced up from her journal writing, smiled at him, and blew him a lingering air kiss.

"Sheee-it!" Carlos whispered and quickly twisted his head in mild disgust.

In an effort to see if there were any signs of life in his dick, Carlos tenderly fondled it a moment to determine if there was the slightest potential for his penis to get hard. It wasn't. His dick hung long and limp between his legs.

Come on, Johnson. Wake up, baby. Daddy's got to deliver one more time tonight. Damn! I don't even think a bulldozer can lift him tonight, Carlos thought. The double duty routine with two women was wearing Carlos out. In order to pull off second shift tonight with Pecola, he needed to rely on some true to life fantasizing and work like hell to get it up. Carlos placed his hands on his temple, squeezed his eyes shut, and began to meditate about the sexual love fest session he just finished with Venus.

There are always things in a man's life that you go back and pull on to make you go forward. Thoughts that get your dick hard enough to do what you gotta do, Carlos thought calmly.

The earlier, all day sexual rendezvous with Venus was the stimulus he used to satisfy his wife. Later on when Carlos plunged his partially hard dick into Pecola, his mind was totally lost in fantasizing memories of his lover. In order to have sex with his wife, he visualized the tantalizing jet-black Venus, and he visualized only her.

Chapter One-Hundred-Two

The next day, the super stretch limousine pulled up into Symone's circular driveway at eight o'clock sharp. Togo held the door open for Symone and the tuxedoed Madison, Carlos, and Scott jumped out and flanked her as she walked to the car. Once inside, Pecola, Alex, and Charmaine were inside relaxing, sipping champagne. They were dressed in their finest formal eveningwear. Dressed in a shimmering, sleeveless, beaded white Kilgour and Sweet gown and dripping in the Eisner jewels, Symone felt beautiful this evening. Since she had been with her trainer, she had lost twelve pounds and could really see a difference.

"...To die for. That's what you look like, Symone," Pecola joked and leaned forward to give her a soft kiss and a tight hug.

"Thank you, girl. I told you I clean up pretty well," Symone said as she let her fur coat slide backwards. Sparkling in her ears were the Eisner jewels she received as a gift from Samuel Eisner when she graduated from Hampton. They were three-carat diamond stud earrings that each suspended into a four-carat pear shape drop. Each earring's color was delicately mix matched with one being a canary yellow, and the other a rare blue white. On her right wrist was the large diamond tennis bracelet, and gently wrapping her neck was a diamond necklace. Similar diamond exquisiteness graced each third finger on Symone's hands.

"Damn, girl!" Carlos bellowed as he leaned over to kiss Symone on the forehead and lips. "You look like Black royalty."

"Tank yuh. Tank yuh," she said with a smile as bright as the diamonds that adorned her. "Alex suggested that I wear them."

"You look good, baby. Real good," Scott said and kissed Symone lightly on the left cheek and lips.

"Most people will probably think it's cubic zirconium. So you sure don't have anything to worry about, Symone," Charmaine said with sour humor and a large dose of jealousy.

"Humph. Hell no, they won't, Symone. What made you say a thing like that, chile?" Pecola said defensively and cut her eyes at Charmaine with a weak attempt at concealing her distaste for her and her comment. Carlos slightly nudge his wife to calm her down. He knew how Pecola felt about Charmaine. As Charmaine leaned closer to Scott, he hugged her shoulders tightly in support.

"You look absolutely gorgeous, Sy," Alex added with loving admiration.

"Umph, umph, umph," Madison moaned. "That's all I can say. You're stunning, girl. Just absolutely stunning." As Madison embraced Symone tightly, he kissed her lips and each cheek.

Symone stopped smiling and thought for a moment. "Ok. What's up with all these compliments?"

"Not a ting, gurl," Pecola teased in a West Indian accent.

"Now yall have seen me get sharp before. A few pounds less, a few diamonds, and yall are ooohing and aaahing over me like I'm done something amazing. C'mon, now. What's up with all of this?" Symone asked in a light-hearted, dubious tone.

"You look good tonight, girl," Alex said sincerely. "Like you're off the emotional roller coaster you've been on."

"So let us tell you how beautiful you are," Madison said softly.

"And, uh," Alex added. "I told them that you said you were a little depressed earlier and was seriously thinking about not going anywhere tonight."

Symone carefully eyed Alex as she spoke. "Oh. Ok. That makes sense. I was beginning to get nervous about all this sugary sweetness." Symone laughed. She accepted a full glass of champagne from Pecola and smiled from way deep down inside. Everyone raised his or her champagne glass to a toast.

"To loyal, devoted, lifetime friendship that is rooted in our love for each other. Forever and always," Alex said her eyes smiling into Symone's. Alex turned to stare face to face with Pecola, Scott, Carlos, Madison, and Charmaine.

"Here. Here," Scott added, and they all clinked glasses. They were now fifteen minutes away from the Gralyn International Conference Center.

With the entire Ujima Literary society, friends, business associates and children that would be in attendance, Pecola and Alex were expecting over three-hundred people to be waiting at Symone's surprise party. The Gralyn mansion was lit in its entire splendor. To accommodate the large crowd, a clear, full-blown tent was connected to doors leading out back and to the rear terrace area. Therefore people could float through the various rooms of the mansion but could also stroll outside where there was a large hardwood floor set up under the tent for all-night dancing.

Although Gralyn could provide music, Alex and Pecola wanted their resident DJ Cool Breeze to spin the top forty hits, classic old school jams, and Symone's favorite old calypsonians that Hazele brought along with her. The Plunky and Oneness Band of Richmond, Virginia, was positioned in a strategic place in the mansion to handle the live entertainment. Several beef carving stations, seafood, hot buffet stations, shrimp cocktail, dessert, and coffee stations were there for the guests to feast on. Hosted bars and servers moved around taking care of the guests until an unsuspecting Symone was due to arrive at eight-thirty. While they waited for Symone, Tonya of Plunky & Oneness sprinkled the festive air with a little bit of Ella Fitzgerald's mellow sounding sounds. At exactly eight twenty-five, the lights in the tent and the back of the house were supposed to be dimmed slightly.

Now Togo was gliding down Reynolda Road. It was eight-twenty. Symone and her friends were three minutes away from Gralyn.

At eight twenty-four, Togo pulled up in front of the mansion. He stopped the car and quickly jumped out to open the door for Carlos, Pecola, Alex, Madison, Scott, Charmaine, and Symone. Laughing as they walked in, the seven friends said that Pecola wanted to be fashionably late. It was just her typical ploy. She emphasized she wanted all the noted poets and other people to see her walk inside with her bad-ass, embroidered, strapless, black ball gown of organza peau de soie. Madison said that he didn't know what the heck that meant, and with a dress sounding like an hors d'oeuvre, he didn't know if he should eat it or look at it. Everybody laughed.

Then Scott reminded everybody about the CIAA Basketball Tournament that was taking place in Winston-Salem toward the end of February. The point he made was that he had gotten his tickets last year and would be sitting just eight rows back from the center tip-off line. He didn't know where the hell his friends would be, and he frankly didn't care either. Alex held Symone's right hand as they stepped inside the mansion. Symone commented that she always loved coming to Gralyn and got just as big a kick out of the Akao quarterly retreat as did their employees.

Once they stepped on to the back terrace, the lights were abruptly turned on, and Symone was greeted by a deafening chant from over three hundred people.

"Surprise! Surprise, Symone! Happy fortieth birthday!" the guests roared, and the whole tent began singing *Happy Birthday* to her.

Both of Symone's hands flew to her mouth, and her eyes slowly traveled around the room. She soaked in the faces of the ones who were there and thought that she was going to faint from the shock of it all. *My God. When did they all get here? How?* Symone thought.

Symone saw her Mummy, her sisters, brother, Uncle Samuel, Uncle Willie, and Uncle Cecil. All of her aunts, cousins, friends, nieces, and nephews were there. Included in the bunch were the women of FOFAE and employees from both Akao Studios and Meetings Odyssey. The tent was crawling with friends, family, and business associates. Even her three children were there with large smiles on their little faces. Jared was dressed in his favorite black tuxedo, looking like a younger version of Billy. There was Sylvia and Kyle attired in their cute floor length velvet pink party dresses and tightly holding onto Miss Jessica's firm hands. When Symone saw the huge, bright pink hair bows in her daughters' full head of hair, her mind hurdled her to the past. She thought about a young Teresa Shannon growing up in long ago Harlem with Uncle Willie and Uncle Cecil. And, Symone became overwhelmed with a mixture of sadness and happiness.

Symone stepped back, and Carlos and Madison carefully caught her waist. With a surprised and frantic look upon her face, Symone stared into the tender, moist eyes of Alex, Madison, Pecola, Carlos, and Scott.

"...Didn't I tell you I was gunning to surprise you, girl?" Alex said softly. "You got me for my fortieth surprise party at the Sawtooth last February and jazz at my house. I knew I was going to get you and get you good, too."

"But, uh, how?" Symone moaned as tears welled in her eyes, and she immediately blinked them back.

"You surprised the hell out of me for my fortieth birthday," Pecola said. "West Virginia messed me up real bad, too. I said that I'm gonna get her if it's the last thing I do. You say I got such a refrigerator mouth? See how my refrigerator mouth was cutting up for this!"

"You worked with me every day, Pecola. You never mentioned one thing," Symone mumbled. "I can't believe it!"

"Humph, chile. I fooled you," Pecola said, winking her eye at Symone with a smile.

DJ Cool Breeze increased the volume on the old Calypsonian Lord Pretender singing *Que Sera Sera* and Symone's mind catapulted to visions of Lennious dancing for her in Trinidad. Her twin adored that song. It had been sooo many, many years since she had heard that old favorite tune of Keturah, who was presently standing solemnly and teary eyed before her too. Symone allowed the tears to fall slowly down her face. The room of people was silent and still as they gazed affectionately at Symone's startled reactions.

After they finished singing *Happy Birthday*, Symone's review of the crowd took thirty seconds at the most. Yet, Symone felt as if she were frozen in her spot for a small eternity.

"C'mon now, honeychile. Don't cry. Not a hard ass like you," Pecola whispered with teardrops in her eyes. She wiped Symone's eyes with one of her frilly, lacy handkerchiefs. Madison was comforting Alex, who was whimpering quietly.

"I'm shocked," Symone shocked.

"Go ahead and speak to everyone, chile," Pecola coaxed. "They're waiting for you. I love you, girl."

"I love *you*, Pecola. I love all of yall too too bad," Symone said softly as she soaked in the faces of her five closest friends standing beside her.

"I know, chile," Pecola sighed. "I know."

Quickly, Symone affectionately embraced Pecola, Alex, Scott, Madison, Carlos, and Charmaine. Then, Symone left the terrace to hug and speak with her children, family, and friends.

At eleven thirty, Alex, and Pecola told Symone that it was time for her to make a speech. Everybody's children were hanging out. If Symone made her speech now, the nannies and baby-sitters could take their charges upstairs or outside to the appropriate rooms on the estate. The children would be put to bed before it got too much later. Symone walked to the front of the crowd and stood on the terrace podium that was prepared for her. Through all the hoopla of the clapping and the whistling, Symone heard background comments like *You go, girl* from Rozelle in his crazy ass Martin Lawrence voice. And *Lordy, Lordy, Symone is forty. You look good, girl.*

Symone took about five minutes to honor her mother. She did the same for her three uncles, aunts, sisters, brother, nieces, nephews, and Uncle Samuel's three sons, whom she said she was raised with and were just like brothers to her as well.

"...To my children, Jared, Sylvia, and Kyle. You're my three precious gifts from God. Mummy loves you with all there is in me to do so. When it is all said and done, I don't want my success to be measured by all my business accomplishments or personal notoriety. I want my success to be measured by the children that I raise. I want them to have the confidence to go off into the world and be happy. That's what my Mummy used to always say to us. That it was her mission in life to have my two sisters, my brother, and I be happy and free as we were growing up in Brooklyn and Trinidad. I want to be measured that way. And I sincerely believe that was my Mummy's calling. She did a wonderful job. I try to live my life according to those standards that she raised me with."

"Me, too," Hazele whispered to Ameenah.

"When we moved to Brooklyn, New York, a lot changed for us. But my Mummy didn't want us to change. My Mummy required that we give away at least twenty cents out of every dollar of our allowance to a worthy cause. Yall remember those days?" Symone asked her brother and sisters with a laugh.

"Ah do," Hazele said softly looking at Symone. Her sister and brother nodded and smiled briefly.

"So many other wonderful lessons Mummy shared with us. I'm a good mother because of her." She paused then continued. "Miss Jessica, I love you. Thank you for helping me with the awesome job of raising my children. You're a glorious part of our family, and we love you."

As Quentin hugged Keturah's shoulders, she cried softly. The birthday crowd broke out into a thunderous round of applause.

"I wholeheartedly agree with Susan Taylor who said that it is a special privilege to have been born Black and female. When I first read that in *Essence,* I smiled to myself. But I must add that it's a special privilege to have true, sincere, friends like I have in North Carolina. My Uncle Samuel taught me that friendship and lifetime bonds of commitment can bring the ultimate joy."

"These friends I have here exemplify that in every sense of the word." The crowd clapped again. "Alex, Madison, Pecola, Carlos, Scott, and so many others that are here that I love, yall really pulled this off. You fooled me big time. This was great. Ladies and gentlemen, those people standing over there are my dear best friends. Puhleeze give them a standing ovation." Symone led the round of clapping and she blew a kiss at the smiling group of friends.

"Thank you so much for coming. Enjoy the wonderful food and make sure you dance the night away. I only have this left to say. For the ladies in the audience, I'm letting you know that I had to shake and shimmy to get into this tight dress. I'm here to tell you a little secret. If I eat another hors d'oeuvre, I believe this dress will be on the floor. Have a great time, everybody!"

The crowd began laughing, clapping, and whistling. DJ Cool Breeze stuck in Sister Sledge's, *We are Family,* and Rozelle tried to form an electric slide line with both adults and children. People weren't sure which foot to start with so there were several versions of the dance going on. For the rest of the evening, everybody talked and danced to a wide range of music under the colorfully lighted tent. They did the hustle, the mash potatoes, and the LaLa dance because Romallus was back in town from New Orleans. Even the Poussaints had the guests trying to twist to the left and to the right as several conga lines were sashaying around the tent. There even was a little bit of sweet wine-ing by Ameenah and Barrington, as well as Quentin and his wife, Condoleeza. When the old calypsonian tunes floated throughout the late night air, Keturah had such a contented expression on her face as a tall and smiling Quentin whirled his mother around the dance floor. The party lasted until four in the morning. From there, many of the guests were either going to head to their rooms or simply over to Carlos and Pecola's house where Carlos was having a lavish, southern style breakfast catered in Symone's honor.

Chapter One-Hundred-Three

"...We're ready to go now, Sy. Puhleeze don't stay in there too long," Pecola admonished gently.

"Give me a break," Symone grumbled. "I'm just going to the bathroom. Is the limo out front now?"

"Yes, honeychile. It's *been* out front." Pecola took a deep breath and spoke impatiently. "Alex, Madison, Scott, and Charmaine are already in there waiting for us. Carlos left in Rozelle, Jodria, Darilyn, and Rico's limo to make sure someone would be at our house. All the other people have gone on and are probably waiting there."

"All right already," Symone replied flippantly.

The surprise party was over, and everyone was anxious to go enjoy breakfast at Pecola's house. Pecola shook her head and checked her watch. It was four-thirty in the morning, and Symone was obviously quite tipsy.

"I'm serious, chile. We gots to go, Sy."

Symone was heading to the bathroom when she noticed Casnoff Miller walking toward her. He was a former professional football player that Marlon introduced her to a few years ago while he played ball for Pittsburgh. Casnoff had since retired from the league and opened up a car dealership in Reidsville, North Carolina. Symone was surprised that she had missed seeing him all night.

Who in the hell invited him, Symone thought drunkenly. *It probably was Madam Diplomat also known as Miss Pecola.*

Symone remembered that Casnoff had a little, pencil dick. She really didn't want to deal with him or think about it right now. Since Symone had drunk at least twenty glasses of champagne and everything else she could pour down her throat, she just prayed fervently that she could keep a straight face while speaking to Casnoff. It would be rude to cackle in his face, but just visualizing Casnoff's pinkie dick trying to get hard like it did the first and only time they were in bed together was already causing her to almost choke.

"Hey, Symone. Happy birthday, baby. This was a bad assed party, girl. I was trying to get to you all evening. Every time I was close by, there were so many people around."

Symone bit her lip to keep from laughing. Casnoff gave her a wet sloppy kiss, which reeked of what Symone believed was Martell.

"How's every *little* thing going on these days, Casnoff?" Symone asked as she kissed him back.

That is, if you know what I mean, she thought amusingly. Symone held back the rowdy laugh that was rising like a volcano in her throat. She couldn't restrain it any longer and pretended she was choking on something. She started coughing and patting her chest.

"You're ok?"

"Oh, God. Puhleeze forgive me. Something went down the wrong way," she explained with a sincere face.

"That's ok, baby. Every *little* thing is just fine, Symone. You know what? You're just as black and gorgeous as ever. That dress is you all the way live, baby. Umph, umph."

"Thank you, Casnoff."

"You're welcome." He clasped his hands in front of him and leaned his head back to gaze at her for a long moment. "When can I see you again, baby?"

I know he didn't go there and ask that damn question, she thought with a blank expression. *That proves he doesn't know his dick is little. How in the hell can he not know that?*

"Talk to me, baby. Give me a day, a night, or what the hell ever."

"You mean to tell me you don't know? No one told you the news tonight?"

"Told me what?" he asked with flashing eyes. "All I know is that I want to see you again, baby. Look, here's my card."

"Wonderful."

"My home number has changed, so let me write the new one down." He patted his jacket pockets to locate a pen. "Damn! Do you have a pen or a pencil?"

"No, I don't. Don't *you* have a pencil?"

"Hell no. Why would you think I had one? I just asked you for one."

"Well, uh. Since you own a car dealership, and you're a car salesman and all, I just thought you did. A pen or pencil? Hmmm. Let me see, Casnoff."

Symone looked through her sequin evening bag and pulled out a sterling silver Omas Mandela pen. Casnoff wrote his number down and handed Symone her pen back. Symone smiled for a moment. That was it. She lost all sense of reserve and burst out laughing all over the place. Casnoff started laughing, too. The two of them leaned on each other for support and cackled for a good few minutes.

Isn't this a trip? thought Symone. *He's laughing because I'm laughing, and I'm laughing at his pencil penis.*

"You ain't no good, girl."

"I know. I tell you. I'm as high as a kite, Casnoff." Symone had laughed so much that tears were rolling down her face.

"Me too, baby. Me too."

"Uh, what—what I was trying to tell you, Casnoff—" As Symone lied, she attempted to muffle the laughing. "I wanted to know if you knew I was getting married in a month and was going off to Trinidad to do it. Can you believe that?"

"Get out of here, Symone! You mean I can't see you no more, baby?"

No, you get the hell out of here, Symone thought. *What I should've done is told you the truth. Because your dick is so little, it reminds me of a worm. I don't want to ever see you again. We can never, ever, never get together in this lifetime. Adios, amigos.*

Instead, Symone was nice. It was the night of her surprise birthday, and she didn't have to hurt his feelings to make him see that she didn't want to date him.

"Symone!" Pecola yelled impatiently from the front door of the mansion. Symone turned around, and Pecola vigorously motioned with one hand for her to come on.

"Casnoff, you take care. I told Alex and Pecola I would be right back, and they're ready to go."

"When can I see you again, baby?" he asked with a swagger. "I'm heading over to Carlos. Maybe we can check each other out there."

Nigger, puhleeze. Get a life, Symone thought as she shrugged her shoulders in answer to the question. She smiled at him and walked off to use the bathroom.

Pecola was standing by the front door when Symone finally came out of the ladies room. An aggravated Pecola impatiently glanced at her watch. Once again, Symone burst out laughing as she walked toward her.

"Chile, what's wrong with you?" Pecola asked exasperated. "You're crazy as hell when you're sober. Now you're drunk, and you're a stone trip. What is it, Sy?"

"Remember the guy I told you about long time ago? The one with the PP? You know. A pencil penis," Symone said, still laughing.

"Which one? Maybe I should say what about him?"

"That was him?"

"*Casnoff Miller?* Chile, get out of here. You never told me *he* was the one. I invited him because he's single, available, got money, and is good-looking. You know. Your type. Since you had gone out with him for a couple of months before, I thought you might consider him again."

"Hell, that's probably why he's still available," Symone spoke with a slightly drunk smile. "He has a nice, muscular body, and can eat the hell out of some pussy. But that's all there is to him, girl. When Casnoff dropped his Joe Boxers, I dropped all hope. I was sooo pissed off. It was nothing there, Pecola. Nothing atall. I told him no we can't do a thing tonight because all of a sudden I had a serious stomach ache. You know what I mean? Hell, I was nauseous."

"Ummm-hmmm," Pecola nodded slowly and managed a very small crooked smile. She didn't feel like hearing this conversation. People were waiting at her house, and she was ready to go. Symone stopped walking and thought another moment.

"I rushed into the bathroom, girl. We were in this suite at the Omni Hotel in Durham. I acted like I suddenly got sick on the Martell we were drinking. Wooo, chile! I wish you could've seen his little worm of a dick."

"C'mon, Symone girl."

"I'm serious. It was disgusting and a tremendous disappointment, Pecola. I never told anyone who it was. I was too ashamed to mention his name in the same breath with mine. I know one thing. I was shocked as hell to see him at my party."

Shaking her head from side to side, Pecola made another face. "You know what they say. It's not how big it is that counts. It's what they can do with it, Sy."

"Bull! I heard that before, and it's a lie. Believe you me, the size makes a whole lot of difference. I want to feel some muscle when it goes in. Make me say *oooh, umph* or something. What would you do if Carlos had a skinny dick like that? Like a small finger like this?" Symone asked and waved her right pinkie in Pecola's face.

"Sy, puhleeze," she said with mild disgust and even less humor. Pecola clammed up and refused to say anything else on the subject. Instead, Pecola placed Symone's sable on her shoulders, linked her arm with hers, and led her to the limousine.

Once outside, they both stepped into the waiting car. Scott asked what took them so long. Alex wanted to know if Symone was ok. She could tell by the way Symone was acting that she had too much to drink, and she was concerned. Thank God Symone's family was riding in the other car and didn't see her stagger slightly to the limo. Symone's mother, three uncles, and aunts left the party to go to bed at around one-thirty in the morning.

With a deep, labored sigh as if she were thoroughly relieved to be finally sitting down, Symone settled into the back, right corner seat of the limo. The evening's laughter and excitement for her stopped once and for all. With closed eyes, she listened to the music playing in the background. It was the soft, sad sound of Karyn White singing *Can I Stay With You Baby?*

Who the hell chose that song? Symone thought through her drunken state.

As Symone and her friends rode through the streets of Winston-Salem, Symone watched the drivers of other cars cran their necks to see through the tinted windows of the limo. In a matter of minutes, they were at Pecola and Carlos' house, and suddenly a spirit of depression enveloped Symone. Here she was a week after her fortieth birthday on the night of her surprise party. She was attending a catered breakfast in her honor with a bunch of happy friends and family. Yet, she was alone.

When Togo extended his hand to help Symone out the limo, she started to scream at the top of her voice for him to take her back home to Clemmons immediately. Instead, Symone carefully walked inside the black marbled foyer. She was served a huge breakfast that she didn't taste and laughed at old college jokes that weren't funny. Symone even pretended to be ecstatic about turning forty.

Something is definitely wrong with this picture, Symone thought sadly. *Starting tomorrow, somehow, some way, the problems twirling around in my life is going to change. I'm heading to Trinidad on Monday to play mas for carnival. When I come back to North Carolina, I'm making some changes. Forty has gotta be better...Doggone it, I'm gonna see to it!*

The End
But the beginning of Transitions, Book 2
To Be Continued...

About the Author...

Irene Egerton Perry is a graduate of High Point University and the University of New Hampshire at Manchester where she received a master's degree in Economic Development. Ms. Perry had an ephiphany and made a career change in 1995 which was the beginning steps to *Light in the Basement*. An entrepreneur, she is the mother of two children and resides in North Carolina where she has completed Book Two and Three of the three book series, *Light in the Basement*. This is her first novel.

If your book club or organization would like for Irene Egerton Perry to visit your city, please contact Claire Conliff @ C. E. Publishing.

Telephone: 336-998-2679
E-mail address: CEPublishing@aol.com

Also, visit us at our Web site: www.CEPublishing.net

Peace!